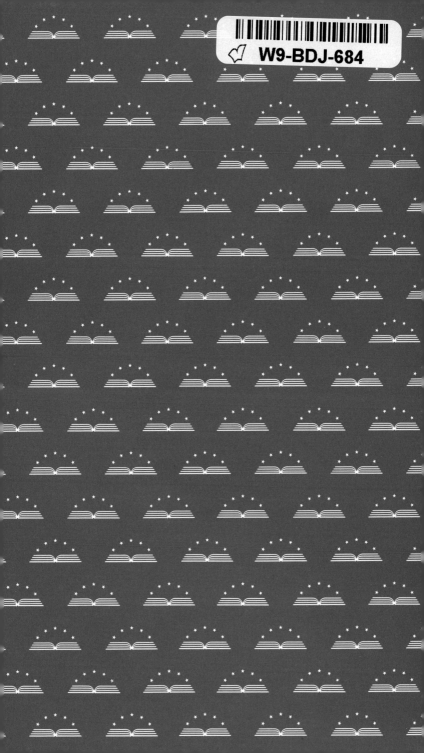

MARK TWAIN

MARK TWAIN

THE GILDED AGE AND LATER NOVELS

The Gilded Age
The American Claimant
Tom Sawyer Abroad
Tom Sawyer, Detective
No. 44, The Mysterious Stranger

THE LIBRARY OF AMERICA

First Printing
The Library of America—130

HAMLIN L. HILL
EDITED THIS VOLUME

Contents

THE GILDED AGE

A TALE OF TO-DAY

by

Mark Twain

and

Charles Dudley Warner

協力力
力山成玉
同心坁變金

PREFACE.

THIS BOOK was not written for private circulation among friends; it was not written to cheer and instruct a diseased relative of the author's; it was not thrown off during intervals of wearing labor to amuse an idle hour. It was not written for any of these reasons, and therefore it is submitted without the usual apologies.

It will be seen that it deals with an entirely ideal state of society; and the chief embarrassment of the writers in this realm of the imagination has been the want of illustrative examples. In a State where there is no fever of speculation, no inflamed desire for sudden wealth, where the poor are all simple-minded and contented, and the rich are all honest and generous, where society is in a condition of primitive purity and politics is the occupation of only the capable and the patriotic, there are necessarily no materials for such a history as we have constructed out of an ideal commonwealth.

No apology is needed for following the learned custom of placing attractive scraps of literature at the heads of our chapters. It has been truly observed by Wagner that such headings, with their vague suggestions of the matter which is to follow them, pleasantly inflame the reader's interest without wholly satisfying his curiosity, and we will hope that it may be found to be so in the present case.

Our quotations are set in a vast number of tongues; this is done for the reason that very few foreign nations among whom the book will circulate can read in any language but their own; whereas we do not write for a particular class or sect or nation, but to take in the whole world.

We do not object to criticism; and we do not expect that the critic will read the book before writing a notice of it. We do not even expect the reviewer of the book will say that he has not read it. No, we have no anticipations of anything unusual in this age of criticism. But if the Jupiter, who passes his opinion on the novel, ever happens to peruse it in some weary moment of his subsequent life, we hope that he will not be the victim of a remorse bitter but too late.

One word more. This is—what it pretends to be—a joint production, in the conception of the story, the exposition of the characters, and in its literal composition. There is scarcely a chapter that does not bear the marks of the two writers of the book.   S. L. C.

                                                                                                          C. D. W.

CONTENTS

Chapter I

Nibiwa win o-dibendan aki.

Eng.   A gallant tract
Of land it is!
   Meercraft.   'Twill yield a pound an acre:
We must let cheap ever at first. But, sir,
This looks too large for you, I see.

JUNE, 18—.   Squire Hawkins sat upon the pyramid of large blocks, called the "stile," in front of his house, contemplating the morning.

The locality was Obedstown, East Tennessee. You would not know that Obedstown stood on the top of a mountain, for there was nothing about the landscape to indicate it—but it did: a mountain that stretched abroad over whole counties, and rose very gradually. The district was called the "Knobs of East Tennessee," and had a reputation like Nazareth, as far as turning out any good thing was concerned.

The Squire's house was a double log cabin, in a state of decay; two or three gaunt hounds lay asleep about the threshold, and lifted their heads sadly whenever Mrs. Hawkins or the children stepped in and out over their bodies. Rubbish was scattered about the grassless yard; a bench stood near the door with a tin wash basin on it and a pail of water and a gourd; a cat had begun to drink from the pail, but the exertion was overtaxing her energies, and she had stopped to rest. There was an ash-hopper by the fence, and an iron pot, for soft-soap-boiling, near it.

This dwelling constituted one-fifteenth of Obedstown; the other fourteen houses were scattered about among the tall pine trees and among the corn-fields in such a way that a man might stand in the midst of the city and not know but that he was in the country if he only depended on his eyes for information.

"Squire" Hawkins got his title from being postmaster of Obedstown—not that the title properly belonged to the office, but because in those regions the chief citizens always must have titles of some sort, and so the usual courtesy had been extended to Hawkins. The mail was monthly, and sometimes amounted to as much as three or four letters at a single delivery. Even a rush like this did not fill up the postmaster's whole month, though, and therefore he "kept store" in the intervals.

The Squire was contemplating the morning. It was balmy and tranquil, the vagrant breezes were laden with the odor of flowers, the murmur of bees was in the air, there was everywhere that suggestion of repose that summer woodlands bring to the senses, and the vague, pleasurable melancholy that such a time and such surroundings inspire.

Presently the United States mail arrived, on horseback. There was but one letter, and it was for the postmaster. The long-legged youth who carried the mail tarried an hour to talk, for there was no hurry; and in a little while the male population of the village had assembled to help. As a general thing, they were dressed in homespun "jeans," blue or yellow—there were no other varieties of it; all wore one suspender and sometimes two—yarn ones knitted at home,— some wore vests, but few wore coats. Such coats and vests as did appear, however, were rather picturesque than otherwise, for they were made of tolerably fanciful patterns of *calico*—a fashion which prevails there to this day among those of the community who have tastes above the common level and are able to afford style. Every individual arrived with his hands in his pockets; a hand came out occasionally for a purpose, but it always went back again after service; and if it was the head that was served, just the cant that the dilapidated straw hat got by being uplifted and rooted under, was retained until the next call altered the inclination; many hats were present, but none were erect and no two were canted just alike. We are speaking impartially of men, youths and boys. And we are also speaking of these three estates when we say that every individual was either chewing natural leaf tobacco prepared on his own premises, or smoking the same in a corn-cob pipe. Few of the men wore whiskers; none wore moustaches; some had a thick jungle of hair under the chin and hiding the throat— the only pattern recognized there as being the correct thing in whiskers; but no part of any individual's face had seen a razor for a week.

These neighbors stood a few moments looking at the mail carrier reflectively while he talked; but fatigue soon began to show itself, and one after another they climbed up and occupied the top rail of the fence, hump-shouldered and grave, like a company of buzzards assembled for supper and listening for the death-rattle. Old Damrell said:

"Tha hain't no news 'bout the jedge, hit ain't likely?"

"Cain't tell for sartin; some thinks he's gwyne to be 'long toreckly, and some thinks 'e hain't. Russ Mosely he tole ole Hanks he mought git to Obeds tomorrer or nex' day he reckoned."

"Well, I wisht I knowed. I got a prime sow and pigs in the cote-house, and I hain't got no place for to put 'em. If the jedge is a gwyne to hold cote, I got to roust 'em out, I reckon. But tomorrer'll do, I 'spect."

The speaker bunched his thick lips together like the stem-end of a tomato and shot a bumble-bee dead that had lit on a weed seven feet away. One after another the several chewers expressed a charge of tobacco juice and delivered it at the deceased with steady aim and faultless accuracy.

"What's a stirrin', down 'bout the Forks?" continued Old Damrell.

"Well, I dunno, skasely. Ole Drake Higgins he's ben down to Shelby las' week. Tuck his crap down; couldn't git shet o' the most uv it; hit warn't no time for to sell, he say, so he fotch it back agin, 'lowin' to wait tell fall. Talks 'bout goin' to Mozouri—lots uv 'ems talkin' that-away down thar, Ole Higgins say. Cain't make a livin' here no mo', sich times as these. Si Higgins he's ben over to Kaintuck n' married a high-toned gal thar, outen the fust families, an' he's come back to the Forks with jist a hell's-mint o' whoop-jamboree notions, folks says. He's tuck an' fixed up the ole house like they does in Kaintuck, he say, an' tha's ben folks come cler from Turpentine for to see it. He's tuck an' gawmed it all over on the inside with plarsterin'."

"What's plarsterin'?"

"*I* dono. Hit's what *he* calls it. Ole Mam Higgins, she tole me. She say she warn't gwyne to hang out in no sich a dern hole like a hog. Says it's mud, or some sich kind o' nastness that sticks on n' kivers up everything. Plarsterin', Si calls it."

This marvel was discussed at considerable length; and almost with animation. But presently there was a dog-fight over in the neighborhood of the blacksmith shop, and the visitors slid off their perch like so many turtles and strode to the battle-field with an interest bordering on eagerness. The Squire remained, and read his letter. Then he sighed, and sat long in meditation. At intervals he said:

"Missouri. Missouri. Well, well, well, everything is so uncertain."

At last he said:

"I believe I'll do it.—A man will just rot, here. My house, my yard, everything around me, in fact, shows that I am becoming one of these cattle—and I used to be thrifty in other times."

He was not more than thirty-five, but he had a worn look that made him seem older. He left the stile, entered that part of his house which was the store, traded a quart of thick molasses for a coonskin and a cake of beeswax to an old dame in linsey-woolsey, put his letter away, and went into the kitchen. His wife was there, constructing some dried apple pies; a slovenly urchin of ten was dreaming over a rude weather-vane of his own contriving; his small sister, close upon four years of age, was sopping corn-bread in some gravy left in the bottom of a frying-pan and trying hard not to sop over a finger-mark that divided the pan through the middle—for the other side belonged to the brother, whose musings made him forget his stomach for the moment; a negro woman was busy cooking, at a vast fire-place. Shiftlessness and poverty reigned in the place.

"Nancy, I've made up my mind. The world is done with me, and perhaps I ought to be done with it. But no matter— I can wait. I am going to Missouri. I won't stay in this dead country and decay with it. I've had it on my mind some time. I'm going to sell out here for whatever I can get, and buy a wagon and team and put you and the children in it and start."

"Anywhere that suits you, suits me, Si. And the children can't be any worse off in Missouri than they are here, I reckon."

Motioning his wife to a private conference in their own room, Hawkins said: "No, they'll be better off. I've looked out for *them*, Nancy," and his face lighted. "Do you see these papers? Well, they are evidence that I have taken up Seventy-five Thousand Acres of Land in this county—think what an enormous fortune it will be some day! Why, Nancy, enormous don't express it—the word's too tame! I tell you, Nancy——"

"For goodness sake, Si——"

"Wait, Nancy, wait—let me finish—I've been secretly boiling and fuming with this grand inspiration for weeks, and I *must* talk or I'll burst! I haven't whispered to a soul—not a word—have had my *countenance* under lock and key, for fear it might drop something that would tell even these animals here how to discern the gold mine that's glaring under their noses. Now all that is necessary to hold this land and keep it in the family is to pay the trifling taxes on it yearly—five or ten dollars—the whole tract would not sell for over a third of a cent an acre now, but some day people will be glad to get it for twenty dollars, fifty dollars, a hundred dollars an acre! What should you say to" [here he dropped his voice to a whisper and looked anxiously around to see that there were no eavesdroppers,] "*a thousand dollars an acre!*

"Well you may open your eyes and stare! But it's so. You and I may not see the day, but *they'll* see it. Mind I tell you, they'll see it. Nancy, you've heard of steamboats, and may be you believed in them—of course you did. You've heard these cattle here scoff at them and call them lies and humbugs,—but they're not lies and humbugs, they're a reality and they're going to be a more wonderful thing some day than they are now. They're going to make a revolution in this world's affairs that will make men dizzy to contemplate. I've been watching—I've been watching while some people slept, and I know what's coming.

"Even you and I will see the day that steamboats will come up that little Turkey river to within twenty miles of this land of ours—and in high water they'll come right *to* it! And this is not all, Nancy—it isn't even half! There's a bigger wonder—the railroad! These worms here have never even heard of it—and when they do they'll not believe in it. But it's another fact. Coaches that fly over the ground twenty miles an hour—heavens and earth, think of that, Nancy! Twenty miles an hour. It makes a man's brain whirl. Some day, when you and I are in our graves, there'll be a railroad stretching hundreds of miles—all the way down from the cities of the Northern States to New Orleans—and it's got to run within thirty miles of this land—may be even touch a corner of it. Well, do you know, they've quit burning wood in some places in the Eastern States? And what do you suppose they burn? Coal!" [He bent over and whispered again:] "*There's whole worlds of it on this land!* You know that black stuff that crops out of the bank of the branch?—well, that's it. You've taken it for rocks; so has every body here; and they've built little dams and such things with it. One man was going to build a chimney out of it. Nancy I expect I turned as white as a sheet! Why, it might have caught fire and told everything. I showed him it was too crumbly. Then he was going to build it of copper ore—splendid yellow forty-per-cent. ore! There's fortunes upon fortunes of copper ore on our land! It scared me to death, the idea of this fool starting a smelting furnace in his house without knowing it, and getting his dull eyes opened. And then he was going to build it of *iron* ore! There's mountains of iron ore here, Nancy—whole mountains of it. I wouldn't take any chances. I just stuck by him—I haunted him—I never let him alone till he built it of mud and sticks like all the rest of the chimneys in this dismal country. Pine forests, wheat land, corn land, iron, copper, coal—wait till the railroads come, and the steamboats! *We'll* never see the day, Nancy—never in the world—never, never, never, child. We've got to drag along, drag along, and eat crusts in toil and poverty, all hopeless and forlorn—but *they'll* ride in coaches, Nancy! They'll live like the princes of the earth; they'll be courted and worshiped; their names will be known from ocean to ocean! Ah, well-a-day! Will they ever come back here, on the railroad and the steamboat, and say 'This one little spot shall not be touched—this hovel shall be sacred—for here our father and our mother suffered for us, thought for us, laid the foundations of our future as solid as the hills!'"

"You are a great, good, noble soul, Si Hawkins, and I am an honored woman to be the wife of such a man"—and the tears stood in her eyes when she said it. "We *will* go to Missouri. You are out of your place, here, among these groping dumb creatures. We will find a higher place, where you can walk with your own kind, and be understood when you speak—not stared at as if you were talking some foreign tongue. I would go anywhere, anywhere in the wide world with you. I would rather my body should starve and die than your mind should hunger and wither away in this lonely land."

"Spoken like yourself, my child! But we'll not starve, Nancy. Far from it. I have a letter from Eschol Sellers—just came this day. A letter that—I'll read you a line from it!"

He flew out of the room. A shadow blurred the sunlight in Nancy's face—there was uneasiness in it, and disappointment. A procession of disturbing thoughts began to troop through her mind. Saying nothing aloud, she sat with her hands in her lap; now and then she clasped them, then unclasped them, then tapped the ends of the fingers together; sighed, nodded, smiled—occasionally paused, shook her head. This pantomime was the elocutionary expression of an unspoken soliloquy which had something of this shape:

"I was afraid of it—was afraid of it. Trying to make our fortune in Virginia, Eschol Sellers nearly ruined us—and we had to settle in Kentucky and start over again. Trying to make our fortune in Kentucky he crippled us again and we had to move here. Trying to make our fortune here, he brought us clear down to the ground, nearly. He's an honest soul, and means the very best in the world, but I'm afraid, I'm afraid he's too flighty. He has splendid ideas, and he'll divide his chances with his friends with a free hand, the good generous soul, but something does seem to always interfere and spoil everything. I never did think he was right well balanced. But I don't blame my husband, for I do think that when that man gets his head full of a new notion, he can out-talk a machine. He'll make anybody believe in that notion that'll listen to him ten minutes—why I do believe he would make a deaf and dumb man believe in it and get beside himself, if you only set him where he could see his eyes talk and watch his hands explain. What a head he has got! When he got up that idea there in Virginia of buying up whole loads of negroes in Delaware and Virginia and Tennessee, very quiet, having papers drawn to have them delivered at a place in Alabama and take them and pay for them, away yonder at a certain time, and then in the meantime get a law made stopping everybody from selling negroes to the south after a certain day—it was somehow that way—mercy how the man would have made money! Negroes would have gone up to four prices. But after he'd spent money and worked hard, and traveled hard, and had heaps of negroes all contracted for, and everything going along just right, he couldn't get the laws passed and down the whole thing tumbled. And there in Kentucky, when he raked up that old numskull that had been inventing away at a perpetual motion machine for twenty-two years, and Eschol Sellers saw at a glance where just one more little cog-wheel would settle the business, why I could see it as plain as day when he came in wild at midnight and hammered us out of bed and told the whole thing in a whisper with the doors bolted and the candle in an empty barrel. Oceans of money in it—anybody could see that. But it did cost a deal to buy the old numskull out—and then when they put the new cog-wheel in they'd overlooked something somewhere and it wasn't any use—the troublesome thing wouldn't go. That notion he got up here did look as handy as anything in the world; and how him and Si did sit up nights working at it with the curtains down and me watching to see if any neighbors were about. The man did honestly believe there was a fortune in that black gummy oil that stews out of the bank Si says is coal; and he refined it himself till it was like water, nearly, and it *did* burn, there's no two ways about that; and I reckon he'd have been all right in Cincinnati with his lamp that he got made, that time he got a house full of rich speculators to see him exhibit only in the middle of his speech it let go and almost blew the heads off the whole crowd. I haven't got over grieving for the money that cost, yet. I am sorry enough Eschol Sellers is in Missouri, now, but I was glad when he went. I wonder what his letter says. But of course it's cheerful; *he's* never down-hearted—never had any trouble in his life—didn't know it if he had. It's always sunrise with that man, and fine and blazing, at that—never gets noon, though—leaves off and rises again. Nobody can help liking the creature, he means so well—but I do dread to come across him again; he's bound to set us all crazy, of course. Well, there goes old widow Hopkins—it always takes her a week to buy a spool of thread and trade a hank of yarn. Maybe Si can come with the letter, now."

And he did:

"Widow Hopkins kept me—I haven't any patience with such tedious people. Now listen, Nancy—just listen at this:

" 'Come right along to Missouri! Don't wait and worry about a good price but sell out for whatever you can get, and come along, or you might be too late. Throw away your traps, if necessary, and come empty-handed. You'll never regret it. It's the grandest country—the loveliest land—the purest atmosphere—I can't describe it; no pen can do it justice. And it's filling up, every day—people coming from everywhere. I've got the biggest scheme on earth—and I'll take you in; I'll take in every friend I've got that's ever stood by me, for there's enough for all, and to spare. Mum's the word—don't whisper—keep yourself to yourself. You'll see! Come!—rush!—hurry!—don't wait for anything!'

"It's the same old boy, Nancy, just the same old boy—ain't he?"

"Yes, I think there's a little of the old sound about his voice yet. I suppose you—you'll still go, Si?"

"Go! Well, I should think so, Nancy. It's all a chance, of course, and chances haven't been kind to us, I'll admit—but whatever comes, old wife, *they*'re provided for. Thank God for that!"

"Amen," came low and earnestly.

And with an activity and a suddenness that bewildered Obedstown and almost took its breath away, the Hawkinses hurried through with their arrangements in four short months and flitted out into the great mysterious blank that lay beyond the Knobs of Tennessee.

Chapter II

መፍትዉ፡ሕዝበ፡ ክርስቲያን ፡እለ ፡ አልቦሙ ፡ ውሉደ ፡
ይሕፀንዎሙ ፡ ለእጓለ ፡ ማውታ ፡ ወራሉት ፡ ወደናግል ፡
ወደረስይዎሙ ፡ ከመ ፡ ውሉደሙ ፡ ወፈደፋ ደ ፡፡

Toward the close of the third day's journey the wayfarers were just beginning to think of camping, when they came upon a log cabin in the woods. Hawkins drew rein and entered the yard. A boy about ten years old was sitting in the cabin door with his face bowed in his hands. Hawkins approached, expecting his footfall to attract attention, but it did not. He halted a moment, and then said:

"Come, come, little chap, you mustn't be going to sleep before sundown."

With a tired expression the small face came up out of the hands,—a face down which tears were flowing.

"Ah, I'm sorry I spoke so, my boy. Tell me—is anything the matter?"

The boy signified with a scarcely perceptible gesture that the trouble was in the house, and made room for Hawkins to pass. Then he put his face in his hands again and rocked himself about as one suffering a grief that is too deep to find help in moan or groan or outcry. Hawkins stepped within. It was a poverty stricken place. Six or eight middle-aged country people of both sexes were grouped about an object in the middle of the room; they were noiselessly busy and they talked in whispers when they spoke. Hawkins uncovered and approached. A coffin stood upon two backless chairs. These neighbors had just finished disposing the body of a woman in it—a woman with a careworn, gentle face that had more the look of sleep about it than of death. An old lady motioned toward the door and said to Hawkins in a whisper:

"His mother, po' thing. Died of the fever, last night. Tha warn't no sich thing as saving of her. But it's better for her —better for her. Husband and the other two children died in the spring, and she hain't ever hilt up her head sence. She jest went around broken-hearted like, and never took no intrust in anything but Clay—that's the boy thar. She jest worshiped Clay—and Clay he worshiped her. They didn't 'pear to live at all, only when they was together, looking at each other, loving one another. She's ben sick three weeks; and if you believe me that child has worked, and kep' the run of the med'cin, and the times of giving it, and sot up nights and nussed her, and tried to keep up her sperits, the same as a grown-up person. And last night when she kep' a sinking and sinking, and turned away her head and didn't know him no mo', it was fitten to make a body's heart break to see him climb onto the bed and lay his cheek agin hern and call her so pitiful and she not answer. But bymeby she roused up, like, and looked around wild, and then she see him, and she made a great cry and snatched him to her breast and hilt him close and kissed him over and over agin; but it took the last po' strength she had, and so her eyelids begin to close down, and her arms sort o' drooped away and then we see she was gone, po' creetur. And Clay, he—Oh, the po' motherless thing—I cain't talk about it—I cain't bear to talk about it."

Clay had disappeared from the door; but he came in, now, and the neighbors reverently fell apart and made way for him. He leaned upon the open coffin and let his tears course silently. Then he put out his small hand and smoothed the hair and stroked the dead face lovingly. After a bit he brought his other hand up from behind him and laid three or four fresh wild flowers upon the breast, bent over and kissed the unresponsive lips time and time again, and then turned away and went out of the house without looking at any of the company. The old lady said to Hawkins:

"She always loved that kind o' flowers. He fetched 'em for her every morning, and she always kissed him. They was from away north somers—she kep' school when she fust come. Goodness knows what's to become o' that po' boy. No father, no mother, no kin folks of no kind. Nobody to go to, nobody that k'yers for him—and all of us is so put to it for to get along and families so large."

Hawkins understood. All eyes were turned inquiringly upon him. He said:

"Friends, I am not very well provided for, myself, but still

I would not turn my back on a homeless orphan. If he will go with me I will give him a home, and loving regard—I will do for him as I would have another do for a child of my own in misfortune."

One after another the people stepped forward and wrung the stranger's hand with cordial good will, and their eyes looked all that their hands could not express or their lips speak.

"Said like a true man," said one.

"You was a stranger to me a minute ago, but you ain't now," said another.

"It's bread cast upon the waters—it'll return after many days," said the old lady whom we have heard speak before.

"You got to camp in my house as long as you hang out here," said one. "If tha hain't room for you and yourn my tribe'll turn out and camp in the hay loft."

A few minutes afterward, while the preparations for the funeral were being concluded, Mr. Hawkins arrived at his wagon leading his little waif by the hand, and told his wife all that had happened, and asked her if he had done right in giving to her and to himself this new care? She said:

"If you've done wrong, Si Hawkins, it's a wrong that will shine brighter at the judgment day than the rights that many a man has done before you. And there isn't any compliment you can pay me equal to doing a thing like this and finishing it up, just taking it for granted that I'll be willing to it. Willing? Come to me, you poor motherless boy, and let me take your grief and help you carry it."

When the child awoke in the morning, it was as if from a troubled dream. But slowly the confusion in his mind took form, and he remembered his great loss; the beloved form in the coffin; his talk with a generous stranger who offered him a home; the funeral, where the stranger's wife held him by the hand at the grave, and cried with him and comforted him; and he remembered how this new mother tucked him in his bed in the neighboring farm house, and coaxed him to talk about his troubles, and then heard him say his prayers and kissed him good night, and left him with the soreness in his heart almost healed and his bruised spirit at rest.

And now the new mother came again, and helped him to

dress, and combed his hair, and drew his mind away by degrees from the dismal yesterday, by telling him about the wonderful journey he was going to take and the strange things he was going to see. And after breakfast they two went alone to the grave, and his heart went out to his new friend and his untaught eloquence poured the praises of his buried idol into her ears without let or hindrance. Together they planted roses by the headboard and strewed wild flowers upon the grave; and then together they went away, hand in hand, and left the dead to the long sleep that heals all heart-aches and ends all sorrows.

Chapter III

—Babillebalou! (disoit-il) voici pis qu'antan. Fuyons! C'est, par la mort bœuf! Leviathan, descript par le noble prophete Mosis en la vie du sainct home Job. Il nous avallera tous, comme pilules. . . . . Voy le cy. O que tu es horrible et abhominable! . . . . Ho ho! Diable, Satanas, Leviathan! Je ne te peux veoir, tant tu es ideux et detestable.

WHATEVER the lagging dragging journey may have been to the rest of the emigrants, it was a wonder and delight to the children, a world of enchantment; and they believed it to be peopled with the mysterious dwarfs and giants and goblins that figured in the tales the negro slaves were in the habit of telling them nightly by the shuddering light of the kitchen fire.

At the end of nearly a week of travel, the party went into camp near a shabby village which was caving, house by house, into the hungry Mississippi. The river astonished the children beyond measure. Its mile-breadth of water seemed an ocean to them, in the shadowy twilight, and the vague riband of trees on the further shore, the verge of a continent which surely none but they had ever seen before.

"Uncle Dan'l" (colored,) aged 40; his wife, "aunt Jinny," aged 30, "Young Miss" Emily Hawkins, "Young Mars" Washington Hawkins and "Young Mars" Clay, the new member of the family, ranged themselves on a log, after supper, and contemplated the marvelous river and discussed it. The moon rose and sailed aloft through a maze of shredded cloud-wreaths; the sombre river just perceptibly brightened under the veiled light; a deep silence pervaded the air and was emphasized, at intervals, rather than broken, by the hooting of an owl, the baying of a dog, or the muffled crash of a caving bank in the distance.

The little company assembled on the log were all children, (at least in simplicity and broad and comprehensive ignorance,) and the remarks they made about the river were in keeping with the character; and so awed were they by the grandeur and the solemnity of the scene before them, and by their belief that the air was filled with invisible spirits and that the faint zephyrs were caused by their passing wings, that all their talk took to itself a tinge of the supernatural, and their voices were subdued to a low and reverent tone. Suddenly Uncle Dan'l exclaimed:

"Chil'en, dah's sumfin a comin'!"

All crowded close together and every heart beat faster. Uncle Dan'l pointed down the river with his bony finger.

A deep coughing sound troubled the stillness, way toward a wooded cape that jutted into the stream a mile distant. All in an instant a fierce eye of fire shot out from behind the cape and sent a long brilliant pathway quivering athwart the dusky water. The coughing grew louder and louder, the glaring eye grew larger and still larger, glared wilder and still wilder. A huge shape developed itself out of the gloom, and from its tall duplicate horns dense volumes of smoke, starred and spangled with sparks, poured out and went tumbling away into the farther darkness. Nearer and nearer the thing came, till its long sides began to glow with spots of light which mirrored themselves in the river and attended the monster like a torchlight procession.

"What is it! Oh, what *is* it, Uncle Dan'l!"

With deep solemnity the answer came:

"It's de Almighty! Git down on yo' knees!"

It was not necessary to say it twice. They were all kneeling, in a moment. And then while the mysterious coughing rose stronger and stronger and the threatening glare reached farther and wider, the negro's voice lifted up its supplications:

"O Lord, we's ben mighty wicked, an' we knows dat we 'zerve to go to de bad place, but good Lord, deah Lord, we ain't ready yit, we ain't ready—let dese po' chil'en hab one mo' chance, jes' one mo' chance. Take de ole niggah if you's got to hab somebody.—Good Lord, good deah Lord, we don't know whah you's a gwyne to, we don't know who you's got yo' eye on, but we knows by de way you's a comin', we knows by de way you's a tiltin' along in yo' charyot o' fiah dat some po' sinner's a gwyne to ketch it. But good Lord, dese chil'en don't b'long heah, dey's f'm Obedstown whah dey don't know nuffin, an' you knows, yo' own sef, dat dey ain't 'sponsible. An' deah Lord, good Lord, it ain't like yo' mercy, it ain't like yo' pity, it ain't like yo' long-sufferin' lovin'-kindness for to take dis kind o' 'vantage o' sich little chil'en as dese is when dey's so many ornery grown folks chuck full o' cussedness dat wants roastin' down dah. Oh, Lord, spah de little chil'en, don't tar de little chil'en away f'm dey frens, jes' let 'em off jes' dis once, and take it out'n de ole niggah. HEAH I IS, LORD, HEAH I IS! De ole niggah's ready, Lord, de ole——"

The flaming and churning steamer was right abreast the party, and not twenty steps away. The awful thunder of a mud-valve suddenly burst forth, drowning the prayer, and as suddenly Uncle Dan'l snatched a child under each arm and scoured into the woods with the rest of the pack at his heels. And then, ashamed of himself, he halted in the deep darkness and shouted, (but rather feebly:)

"Heah I is, Lord, heah I is!"

There was a moment of throbbing suspense, and then, to the surprise and the comfort of the party, it was plain that the august presence had gone by, for its dreadful noises were receding. Uncle Dan'l headed a cautious reconnoissance in the direction of the log. Sure enough "the Lord" was just turning a point a short distance up the river, and while they looked the lights winked out and the coughing diminished by degrees and presently ceased altogether.

"H'wsh! Well now dey's some folks says dey ain't no 'ficiency in prah. Dis chile would like to know whah we'd a ben *now* if it warn't fo' dat prah? Dat's it. Dat's it!"

"Uncle Dan'l, do you reckon it was the prayer that saved us?" said Clay.

"Does I *reckon*? Don't I *know* it! Whah was yo' eyes? Warn't de Lord jes' a comin' *chow! chow!* CHOW! an' a goin' on turrible—an' do de Lord carry on dat way 'dout dey's sumfin don't suit him? An' warn't he a lookin' right at dis gang heah, an' warn't he jes' a reachin' for 'em? An' d'you spec' he gwyne to let 'em off 'dout somebody ast him to do it? No indeedy!"

"Do you reckon he saw us, Uncle Dan'l?"

"De law sakes, chile, didn't I see him a lookin' at us?"

"Did you feel scared, Uncle Dan'l?"

"*No* sah! When a man is 'gaged in prah, he ain't fraid o' nuffin—dey can't nuffin tetch him."

"Well what did you run for?"

"Well, I—I—mars Clay, when a man is under de influence ob de sperit, he do-no what he's 'bout—no sah; dat man do-no what he's 'bout. You mout take an' tah de head off'n dat man an' he wouldn't scasely fine it out. Dah's de Hebrew chil'en dat went frough de fiah; dey was burnt considable—ob *coase* dey was; but *dey* didn't know nuffin 'bout it—heal right up agin; if dey'd ben gals dey'd missed dey long haah, (hair,) maybe, but dey wouldn't felt de burn."

"*I* don't know but what they *were* girls. I think they were."

"Now mars Clay, you knows bettern dat. Sometimes a body can't tell whedder you's a sayin' what you means or whedder you's a sayin' what you don't mean, 'case you says 'em bofe de same way."

"But how should *I* know whether they were boys or girls?"

"Goodness sakes, mars Clay, don't de Good Book say? 'Sides, don't it call 'em de *he*-brew chil'en? If dey was gals wouldn't dey be de she-brew chil'en? Some people dat kin read don't 'pear to take no notice when dey *do* read."

"Well, Uncle Dan'l, I think that—— My! here comes another one up the river! There can't be *two*!"

"We gone dis time—we done gone dis time, sho'! Dey ain't two, mars Clay—dat's de same one. De Lord kin 'pear ebery-whah in a second. Goodness, how de fiah and de smoke do belch up! Dat mean business, honey. He comin' now like he fo'got sumfin. Come 'long, chil'en, time you's gwyne to roos'. Go 'long wid you—ole Uncle Daniel gwyne out in de woods to rastle in prah—de ole nigger gwyne to do what he kin to sabe you agin."

He did go to the woods and pray; but he went so far that he doubted, himself, if the Lord heard him when He went by.

Chapter IV

—Seventhly, Before his Voyage, He should make his peace
with God, satisfie his Creditors if he be in debt; Pray earnestly
to God to prosper him in his Voyage, and to keep him from
danger, and, if he be *sui juris*, he should make his last will, and
wisely order all his affairs, since many that go far abroad, return
not home. (This good and Christian Counsel is given by
Martinus Zeilerus in his Apodemical Canons before his Itin-
erary of Spain and Portugal.)

ARLY in the morning Squire Hawkins took passage in a
small steamboat, with his family and his two slaves, and
presently the bell rang, the stage-plank was hauled in, and the
vessel proceeded up the river. The children and the slaves
were not much more at ease after finding out that this monster was a creature of human contrivance than they were the
night before when they thought it the Lord of heaven and
earth. They started, in fright, every time the gauge-cocks sent
out an angry hiss, and they quaked from head to foot when
the mud-valves thundered. The shivering of the boat under
the beating of the wheels was sheer misery to them.

But of course familiarity with these things soon took away
their terrors, and then the voyage at once become a glorious
adventure, a royal progress through the very heart and home
of romance, a realization of their rosiest wonder-dreams.
They sat by the hour in the shade of the pilot house on the
hurricane deck and looked out over the curving expanses of
the river sparkling in the sunlight. Sometimes the boat fought
the mid-stream current, with a verdant world on either hand,
and remote from both; sometimes she closed in under a
point, where the dead water and the helping eddies were, and
shaved the bank so closely that the decks were swept by the
jungle of over-hanging willows and littered with a spoil of
leaves; departing from these "points" she regularly crossed
the river every five miles, avoiding the "bight" of the great
bends and thus escaping the strong current; sometimes she
went out and skirted a high "bluff" sand-bar in the middle of
the stream, and occasionally followed it up a little too far and

touched upon the shoal water at its head—and then the intelligent craft refused to run herself aground, but "smelt" the
bar, and straightway the foamy streak that streamed away
from her bows vanished, a great foamless wave rolled forward
and passed her under way, and in this instant she leaned far
over on her side, shied from the bar and fled square away
from the danger like a frightened thing—and the pilot was
lucky if he managed to "straighten her up" before she drove
her nose into the opposite bank; sometimes she approached a
solid wall of tall trees as if she meant to break through it, but
all of a sudden a little crack would open just enough to admit
her, and away she would go plowing through the "chute"
with just barely room enough between the island on one side
and the main land on the other; in this sluggish water she
seemed to go like a racehorse; now and then small log cabins
appeared in little clearings, with the never-failing frowsy
women and girls in soiled and faded linsey-woolsey leaning in
the doors or against wood-piles and rail fences, gazing sleepily at the passing show; sometimes she found shoal water,
going out at the head of those "chutes" or crossing the river,
and then a deck-hand stood on the bow and hove the lead,
while the boat slowed down and moved cautiously; sometimes she stopped a moment at a landing and took on some
freight or a passenger while a crowd of slouchy white men
and negroes stood on the bank and looked sleepily on with
their hands in their pantaloons pockets,—of course—for they
never took them out except to stretch, and when they did this
they squirmed about and reached their fists up into the air
and lifted themselves on tip-toe in an ecstasy of enjoyment.

When the sun went down it turned all the broad river to a
national banner laid in gleaming bars of gold and purple and
crimson; and in time these glories faded out in the twilight
and left the fairy archipelagoes reflecting their fringing foliage
in the steely mirror of the stream.

At night the boat forged on through the deep solitudes of
the river, hardly ever discovering a light to testify to a human
presence—mile after mile and league after league the vast
bends were guarded by unbroken walls of forest that had
never been disturbed by the voice or the foot-fall of a man or
felt the edge of his sacrilegious axe.

An hour after supper the moon came up, and Clay and Washington ascended to the hurricane deck to revel again in their new realm of enchantment. They ran races up and down the deck; climbed about the bell; made friends with the passenger-dogs chained under the life-boat; tried to make friends with a passenger-bear fastened to the verge-staff but were not encouraged; "skinned the cat" on the hog-chains; in a word, exhausted the amusement-possibilities of the deck. Then they looked wistfully up at the pilot house, and finally, little by little, Clay ventured up there, followed diffidently by Washington. The pilot turned presently to "get his stern-marks," saw the lads and invited them in. Now their happiness was complete. This cosy little house, built entirely of glass and commanding a marvelous prospect in every direction was a magician's throne to them and their enjoyment of the place was simply boundless.

They sat them down on a high bench and looked miles ahead and saw the wooded capes fold back and reveal the bends beyond; and they looked miles to the rear and saw the silvery highway diminish its breadth by degrees and close itself together in the distance. Presently the pilot said:

"By George, yonder comes the Amaranth!"

A spark appeared, close to the water, several miles down the river. The pilot took his glass and looked at it steadily for a moment, and said, chiefly to himself:

"It can't be the Blue Wing. She couldn't pick us up this way. It's the Amaranth, sure."

He bent over a speaking-tube and said:

"Who's on watch down there?"

A hollow, unhuman voice rumbled up through the tube in answer:

"*I* am. Second engineer."

"Good! You want to stir your stumps, now, Harry—the Amaranth's just turned the point—and she's just a-humping herself, too!"

The pilot took hold of a rope that stretched out forward, jerked it twice, and two mellow strokes of the big bell responded. A voice out on the deck shouted:

"Stand by, down there, with that labboard lead!"

"No, I don't want the lead," said the pilot, "I want *you*. Roust out the old man—tell him the Amaranth's coming. And go and call Jim—tell *him*."

"Aye-aye, sir!"

The "old man" was the captain—he is always called so, on steamboats and ships; "Jim" was the other pilot. Within two minutes both of these men were flying up the pilot-house stairway, three steps at a jump. Jim was in his shirt-sleeves, with his coat and vest on his arm. He said:

"I was just turning in. Where's the glass?"

He took it and looked:

"Don't appear to be any night-hawk on the jack-staff—it's the Amaranth, dead sure!"

The captain took a good long look, and only said:

"Damnation!"

George Davis, the pilot on watch, shouted to the night-watchman on deck:

"How's she loaded?"

"Two inches by the head, sir."

"'T ain't enough!"

The captain shouted, now:

"Call the mate. Tell him to call all hands and get a lot of that sugar forrard—put her ten inches by the head. Lively, now!"

"Aye-aye, sir!"

A riot of shouting and trampling floated up from below, presently, and the uneasy steering of the boat soon showed that she was getting "down by the head."

The three men in the pilot house began to talk in short, sharp sentences, low and earnestly. As their excitement rose, their voices went down. As fast as one of them put down the spy-glass another took it up—but always with a studied air of calmness. Each time the verdict was:

"She's a gaining!"

The captain spoke through the tube:

"What steam are you carrying?"

"A hundred and forty-two, sir! But she's getting hotter and hotter all the time."

The boat was straining and groaning and quivering like a monster in pain. Both pilots were at work now, one on each side of the wheel, with their coats and vests off, their bosoms and collars wide open and the perspiration flowing down their faces. They were holding the boat so close to the shore that the willows swept the guards almost from stem to stern.

"Stand by!" whispered George.

"All ready!" said Jim, under his breath.

"Let her come!"

The boat sprang away from the bank like a deer, and darted in a long diagonal toward the other shore. She closed in again and thrashed her fierce way along the willows as before. The captain put down the glass:

"Lord how she walks up on us! I do hate to be beat!"

"Jim," said George, looking straight ahead, watching the slightest yawing of the boat and promptly meeting it with the wheel, "how'll it do to try Murderer's Chute?"

"Well, it's—it's taking chances. How was the cotton-wood stump on the false point below Boardman's Island this morning?"

"Water just touching the roots."

"Well it's pretty close work. That gives six feet scant in the head of Murderer's Chute. We can just barely rub through if we hit it exactly right. But it's worth trying. *She* don't dare tackle it!"—meaning the Amaranth.

In another instant the Boreas plunged into what seemed a crooked creek, and the Amaranth's approaching lights were shut out in a moment. Not a whisper was uttered, now, but the three men stared ahead into the shadows and two of them spun the wheel back and forth with anxious watchfulness while the steamer tore along. The chute seemed to come to an end every fifty yards, but always opened out in time. Now the head of it was at hand. George tapped the big bell three times, two leadsmen sprang to their posts, and in a moment their weird cries rose on the night air and were caught up and repeated by two men on the upper deck:

"No-o bottom!"

"De-e-p four!"

"Half three!"

"Quarter three!"

"Mark under wa-a-ter three!"

"Half twain!"

"Quarter twain!——"

Davis pulled a couple of ropes—there was a jingling of small bells far below, the boat's speed slackened, and the pent steam began to whistle and the gauge-cocks to scream:

"By the mark twain!"

"Quar-ter-*her*-er-*less* twain!"

"Eight *and* a half!"

"Eight feet!"

"Seven-ana-half!——"

Another jingling of little bells and the wheels ceased turning altogether. The whistling of the steam was something frightful, now—it almost drowned all other noises.

"Stand by to meet her!"

George had the wheel hard down and was standing on a spoke.

"All ready!"

The boat hesitated—seemed to hold her breath, as did the captain and pilots—and then she began to fall away to starboard and every eye lighted:

"*Now* then!—meet her! meet her! Snatch her!"

The wheel flew to port so fast that the spokes blended into a spider-web—the swing of the boat subsided—she steadied herself——

"Seven feet!"

"Sev—six and a *half!*"

"*Six* feet! Six f——"

Bang! She hit the bottom! George shouted through the tube:

"Spread her wide open! *Whale it at her!*"

Pow—wow—chow! The escape-pipes belched snowy pillars of steam aloft, the boat ground and surged and trembled—and slid over into——

"M-a-r-k twain!"

"Quarter-*her*——"

"Tap! tap! tap!" (to signify "Lay in the leads.")

And away she went, flying up the willow shore, with the whole silver sea of the Mississippi stretching abroad on every hand.

No Amaranth in sight!

"Ha-ha, boys, we took a couple of tricks that time!" said the captain.

And just at that moment a red glare appeared in the head of the chute and the Amaranth came springing after them!

"Well, I swear!"

"Jim, what *is* the meaning of that?"

"I'll tell you what's the meaning of it. That hail we had at Napoleon was Wash Hastings, wanting to come to Cairo—and we didn't stop. He's in that pilot house, now, showing those mud turtles how to hunt for easy water."

"That's it! I thought it wasn't any slouch that was running that middle bar in Hog-eye Bend. If it's Wash Hastings—well, what he don't know about the river ain't worth knowing—a regular gold-leaf, kid-glove, diamond-breastpin pilot Wash Hastings is. We won't take any tricks off of *him*, old man!"

"I wish I'd a stopped for him, that's all."

The Amaranth was within three hundred yards of the Boreas, and still gaining. The "old man" spoke through the tube:

"What is she carrying now?"

"A hundred and sixty-five, sir!"

"How's your wood?"

"Pine all out—cypress half gone—eating up cotton-wood like pie!"

"Break into that rosin on the main deck—pile it in, the boat can pay for it!"

Soon the boat was plunging and quivering and screaming more madly than ever. But the Amaranth's head was almost abreast the Boreas's stern:

"How's your steam, now, Harry?"

"Hundred and eighty-two, sir!"

"Break up the casks of bacon in the forrard hold! Pile it in! Levy on that turpentine in the fantail—drench every stick of wood with it!"

The boat was a moving earthquake by this time:

"How is she now?"

"A hundred and ninety-six and still a-swelling!—water below the middle gauge-cocks!—carrying every pound she can stand!—nigger roosting on the safety-valve!"

"Good! How's your draft?"

"Bully! Every time a nigger heaves a stick of wood into the furnace he goes out the chimney with it!"

The Amaranth drew steadily up till her jack-staff breasted the Boreas's wheel-house—climbed along inch by inch till her chimneys breasted it—crept along, further and further till the boats were wheel to wheel—and then they closed up with a heavy jolt and locked together tight and fast in the middle of the big river under the flooding moonlight! A roar and a hurrah went up from the crowded decks of both steamers—all hands rushed to the guards to look and shout and gesticulate—the weight careened the vessels over toward each other—officers flew hither and thither cursing and storming, trying to drive the people amidships—both captains were leaning over their railings shaking their fists, swearing and threatening—black volumes of smoke rolled up and canopied the scene, delivering a rain of sparks upon the vessels—two pistol shots rang out, and both captains dodged unhurt and the packed masses of passengers surged back and fell apart while the shrieks of women and children soared above the intolerable din——

And then there was a booming roar, a thundering crash, and the riddled Amaranth dropped loose from her hold and drifted helplessly away!

Instantly the fire-doors of the Boreas were thrown open and the men began dashing buckets of water into the furnaces—for it would have been death and destruction to stop the engines with such a head of steam on.

As soon as possible the Boreas dropped down to the floating wreck and took off the dead, the wounded and the unhurt—at least all that could be got at, for the whole forward half of the boat was a shapeless ruin, with the great chimneys lying crossed on top of it, and underneath were a dozen victims imprisoned alive and wailing for help. While men with axes worked with might and main to free these poor fellows, the Boreas's boats went about, picking up stragglers from the river.

And now a new horror presented itself. The wreck took fire from the dismantled furnaces! Never did men work with a heartier will than did those stalwart braves with the axes. But it was of no use. The fire ate its way steadily, despising the bucket brigade that fought it. It scorched the clothes, it singed the hair of the axemen—it drove them back, foot by foot—inch by inch—they wavered, struck a final blow in the teeth of the enemy, and surrendered. And as they fell back they heard prisoned voices saying:

"Don't leave us! Don't desert us! Don't, don't do it!"

And one poor fellow said:

"I am Henry Worley, striker of the Amaranth! My mother lives in St. Louis. Tell her a lie for a poor devil's sake, please. Say I was killed in an instant and never knew what hurt me—though God knows I've neither scratch nor bruise this moment! It's hard to burn up in a coop like this with the whole wide world so near. Good-bye boys—we've all got to come to it at last, anyway!"

The Boreas stood away out of danger, and the ruined steamer went drifting down the stream an island of wreathing and climbing flame that vomited clouds of smoke from time to time, and glared more fiercely and sent its luminous tongues higher and higher after each emission. A shriek at intervals told of a captive that had met his doom. The wreck lodged upon a sandbar, and when the Boreas turned the next point on her upward journey it was still burning with scarcely abated fury.

When the boys came down into the main saloon of the Boreas, they saw a pitiful sight and heard a world of pitiful sounds. Eleven poor creatures lay dead and forty more lay moaning, or pleading or screaming, while a score of Good Samaritans moved among them doing what they could to relieve their sufferings; bathing their skinless faces and bodies with linseed oil and lime water and covering the places with bulging masses of raw cotton that gave to every face and form a dreadful and unhuman aspect.

A little wee French midshipman of fourteen lay fearfully injured, but never uttered a sound till a physician of Memphis was about to dress his hurts. Then he said:

"Can I get well? You need not be afraid to tell me."

"No—I—I am afraid you can not."

"Then do not waste your time with me—help those that can get well."

"But——"

"Help those that can get well! It is not for me to be a girl. I carry the blood of eleven generations of soldiers in my veins!"

The physician—himself a man who had seen service in the navy in his time—touched his hat to this little hero, and passed on.

The head engineer of the Amaranth, a grand specimen of physical manhood, struggled to his feet a ghastly spectacle and strode toward his brother, the second engineer, who was unhurt. He said:

"You were on watch. You were boss. You would not listen to me when I begged you to reduce your steam. Take that!—take it to my wife and tell her it comes from me by the hand of my murderer! Take it—and take my curse with it to blister your heart a hundred years—and may you live so long!"

And he tore a ring from his finger, stripping flesh and skin with it, threw it down and fell dead!

But these things must not be dwelt upon. The Boreas landed her dreadful cargo at the next large town and delivered it over to a multitude of eager hands and warm southern hearts—a cargo amounting by this time to 39 wounded persons and 22 dead bodies. And with these she delivered a list of 96 missing persons that had drowned or otherwise perished at the scene of the disaster.

A jury of inquest was impaneled, and after due deliberation and inquiry they returned the inevitable American verdict which has been so familiar to our ears all the days of our lives—"NOBODY TO BLAME."*

*The incidents of the explosion are not invented. They happened just as they are told.—THE AUTHORS.

Chapter V

دِهِمَّزِيَ كِهِي أُتِهَارِي بَشْهَن جِي كِهَرِ رِقَارِي بَاتِزِهِيْنَدَا هُسِّ

Il veut faire sécher de la neige au four et la vendre pour du sel blanc.

WHEN the Boreas backed away from the land to continue her voyage up the river, the Hawkinses were richer by twenty-four hours of experience in the contemplation of human suffering and in learning through honest hard work how to relieve it. And they were richer in another way also. In the early turmoil an hour after the explosion, a little black-eyed girl of five years, frightened and crying bitterly, was struggling through the throng in the Boreas' saloon calling her mother and father, but no one answered.—Something in the face of Mr. Hawkins attracted her and she came and looked up at him; was satisfied, and took refuge with him. He petted her, listened to her troubles, and said he would find her friends for her. Then he put her in a state-room with his children and told them to be kind to her (the adults of his party were all busy with the wounded) and straightway began his search.

It was fruitless. But all day he and his wife made inquiries, and hoped against hope. All that they could learn was that the child and her parents came on board at New Orleans, where they had just arrived in a vessel from Cuba; that they looked like people from the Atlantic States; that the family name was Van Brunt and the child's name Laura. This was all. The parents had not been seen since the explosion. The child's manners were those of a little lady, and her clothes were daintier and finer than any Mrs. Hawkins had ever seen before.

As the hours dragged on the child lost heart, and cried so piteously for her mother that it seemed to the Hawkinses that the moanings and the wailings of the mutilated men and women in the saloon did not so strain at their heart-strings as the sufferings of this little desolate creature. They tried hard to comfort her; and in trying, learned to love her; they could not help it, seeing how she clung to them and put her arms about their necks and found no solace but in their kind eyes and comforting words. There was a question in both their hearts—a question that rose up and asserted itself with more and more pertinacity as the hours wore on—but both hesitated to give it voice—both kept silence and waited. But a time came at last when the matter would bear delay no longer. The boat had landed, and the dead and the wounded were being conveyed to the shore. The tired child was asleep in the arms of Mrs. Hawkins. Mr. Hawkins came into their presence and stood without speaking. His eyes met his wife's; then both looked at the child—and as they looked it stirred in its sleep and nestled closer; an expression of contentment and peace settled upon its face that touched the mother-heart; and when the eyes of husband and wife met again, the question was asked and answered.

When the Boreas had journeyed some four hundred miles from the time the Hawkinses joined her, a long rank of steamboats was sighted, packed side by side at a wharf like sardines in a box, and above and beyond them rose the domes and steeples and general architectural confusion of a city—a city with an imposing umbrella of black smoke spread over it. This was St. Louis. The children of the Hawkins family were playing about the hurricane deck, and the father and mother were sitting in the lee of the pilot house essaying to keep order and not greatly grieved that they were not succeeding.

"They're worth all the trouble they are, Nancy."

"Yes, and more, Si."

"I believe you! You wouldn't sell one of them at a good round figure?"

"Not for all the money in the bank, Si."

"My own sentiments every time. It is true we are not rich—but still you are not sorry—you haven't any misgivings about the additions?"

"No. God will provide."

"Amen. And so you wouldn't even part with Clay? Or Laura!"

"Not for anything in the world. I love them just the same as I love my own. They pet me and spoil me even more than the others do, I think. I reckon we'll get along, Si."

"Oh yes, it will all come out right, old mother. I wouldn't be afraid to adopt a thousand children if I wanted to, for there's that Tennessee Land, you know—enough to make an army of them rich. A whole army, Nancy! You and I will never see the day, but these little chaps will. Indeed they will. One of these days it will be 'the rich Miss Emily Hawkins—and the wealthy Miss Laura Van Brunt Hawkins—and the Hon. George Washington Hawkins, millionaire—and Gov. Henry Clay Hawkins, millionaire!' That is the way the world will word it! Don't let's ever fret about the children, Nancy—never in the world. They're all right. Nancy, there's oceans and oceans of money in that land—mark my words!"

The children had stopped playing, for the moment, and drawn near to listen. Hawkins said:

"Washington, my boy, what will you do when you get to be one of the richest men in the world?"

"I don't know, father. Sometimes I think I'll have a balloon and go up in the air; and sometimes I think I'll have ever so many books; and sometimes I think I'll have ever so many weather-cocks and water-wheels; or have a machine like that one you and Colonel Sellers bought; and sometimes I think I'll have—well, somehow I don't know—somehow I ain't certain; maybe I'll get a steamboat first."

"The same old chap!—always just a little bit divided about things.—And what will *you* do when you get to be one of the richest men in the world, Clay?"

"I don't know, sir. My mother—my other mother that's gone away—she always told me to work along and not be much expecting to get rich, and then I wouldn't be disappointed if I didn't get rich. And so I reckon it's better for me to wait till I get rich, and then by that time maybe I'll know what I'll want—but I don't now, sir."

"Careful old head!—Governor Henry Clay Hawkins!—that's what you'll be, Clay, one of these days. Wise old head! weighty old head! Go on, now, and play—all of you. It's a prime lot, Nancy, as the Obedstown folk say about their hogs."

A smaller steamboat received the Hawkinses and their fortunes, and bore them a hundred and thirty miles still higher up the Mississippi, and landed them at a little tumble-down village on the Missouri shore in the twilight of a mellow October day.

The next morning they harnessed up their team and for two days they wended slowly into the interior through almost roadless and uninhabited forest solitudes. And when for the last time they pitched their tents, metaphorically speaking, it was at the goal of their hopes, their new home.

By the muddy roadside stood a new log cabin, one story high—the store; clustered in the neighborhood were ten or twelve more cabins, some new, some old.

In the sad light of the departing day the place looked homeless enough. Two or three coatless young men sat in front of the store on a dry-goods box, and whittled it with their knives, kicked it with their vast boots, and shot tobacco-juice at various marks. Several ragged negroes leaned comfortably against the posts of the awning and contemplated the arrival of the wayfarers with lazy curiosity. All these people presently managed to drag themselves to the vicinity of the Hawkins' wagon, and there they took up permanent positions, hands in pockets and resting on one leg; and thus anchored they proceeded to look and enjoy. Vagrant dogs came wagging around and making inquiries of Hawkins's dog, which were not satisfactory and they made war on him in concert. This would have interested the citizens but it was too many on one to amount to anything as a fight, and so they commanded the peace and the foreign dog furled his tail and took sanctuary under the wagon. Slatternly negro girls and women slouched along with pails deftly balanced on their heads, and joined the group and stared. Little half dressed white boys, and little negro boys with nothing whatever on but tow-linen shirts with a fine southern exposure, came from various directions and stood with their hands locked together behind them and aided in the inspection. The rest of the population were laying down their employments and getting ready to come, when a man burst through the assemblage and seized the new-comers by the hands in a frenzy of welcome, and exclaimed—indeed almost shouted:

"Well who *could* have believed it! Now is it you sure enough—turn around! hold up your heads! I want to look at you good! Well, well, well, it does seem most too good to be true, I declare! Lord, I'm so glad to see you! Does a body's whole soul good to look at you! Shake hands again! Keep *on* shaking hands! Goodness gracious alive. What *will* my wife say?—Oh yes indeed, it's so!—married only last week—lovely, perfectly lovely creature, the noblest woman that ever—you'll like her, Nancy! Like her? Lord bless me you'll love her—you'll dote on her—you'll be twins! Well, well, well, let me look at you again! Same old—why bless my life it was only just this very morning that my wife says, 'Colonel'—she will call me Colonel spite of everything I can do—she says 'Colonel, something tells me somebody's coming!' and sure enough here you are, the last people on earth a body could have expected. Why she'll think she's a prophetess—and hanged if I don't think so too—and you know there ain't any country but what a prophet's an honor to, as the proverb says. Lord bless me—and here's the children, too! Washington, Emily, don't you know me? Come, give us a kiss. Won't I fix *you*, though!—ponies, cows, dogs, everything you can think of that'll delight a child's heart—and——. Why how's this? Little strangers? Well you won't be any strangers here, I can tell you. Bless your souls we'll make you think you never was at home before—'deed and 'deed we will, *I* can tell you! Come, now, bundle right along with me. You can't glorify any hearth stone but mine in *this* camp, you know—can't eat anybody's bread but mine—can't do *any*thing but just make yourselves perfectly at home and comfortable, and spread yourselves out and *rest*! You hear *me*! Here—Jim, Tom, Pete, Jake, fly around! Take that team to my place—put the wagon in my lot—put the horses under the shed, and get out hay and oats and fill them up! Ain't any hay and oats? Well *get* some—have it charged to me—come, spin around, now! Now, Hawkins, the procession's ready; mark time, by the left flank, *for*ward—march!"

And the Colonel took the lead, with Laura astride his neck, and the newly-inspired and very grateful immigrants picked up their tired limbs with quite a spring in them and dropped into his wake.

Presently they were ranged about an old-time fire-place whose blazing logs sent out rather an unnecessary amount of heat, but that was no matter—supper was needed, and to have it, it had to be cooked. This apartment was the family bed-room, parlor, library and kitchen, all in one. The matronly little wife of the Colonel moved hither and thither and in and out with her pots and pans in her hands, happiness in her heart and a world of admiration of her husband in her eyes. And when at least she had spread the cloth and loaded it with hot corn bread, fried chickens, bacon, buttermilk, coffee, and all manner of country luxuries, Col. Sellers modified his harangue and for a moment throttled it down to the orthodox pitch for a blessing, and then instantly burst forth again as from a parenthesis and clattered on with might and main till every stomach in the party was laden with all it could carry. And when the new-comers ascended the ladder to their comfortable feather beds on the second floor—to wit, the garret—Mrs. Hawkins was obliged to say:

"Hang the fellow, I do believe he has gone wilder than ever, but still a body can't help liking him if they would—and what is more, they don't ever want to try when they see his eyes and hear him talk."

Within a week or two the Hawkinses were comfortably domiciled in a new log house, and were beginning to feel at home. The children were put to school, at least it was what passed for a school in those days: a place where tender young humanity devoted itself for eight or ten hours a day to learning incomprehensible rubbish by heart out of books and reciting it by rote, like parrots; so that a finished education consisted simply of a permanent headache and the ability to read without stopping to spell the words or take breath. Hawkins bought out the village store for a song and proceeded to reap the profits, which amounted to but little more than another song.

The wonderful speculation hinted at by Col. Sellers in his letter turned out to be the raising of mules for the Southern market; and really it promised very well. The young stock cost but a trifle, the rearing but another trifle, and so Hawkins was easily persuaded to embark his slender means in the enterprise and turn over the keep and care of the animals to Sellers and Uncle Dan'l.

All went well. Business prospered little by little. Hawkins even built a new house, made it two full stories high and put

a lightning rod on it. People came two or three miles to look
at it. But they knew that the rod attracted the lightning, and
so they gave the place a wide berth in a storm, for they were
familiar with marksmanship and doubted if the lightning
could hit that small stick at a distance of a mile and a half oftener than once in a hundred and fifty times. Hawkins fitted
out his house with "store" furniture from St. Louis, and the
fame of its magnificence went abroad in the land. Even the
parlor carpet was from St. Louis—though the other rooms
were clothed in the "rag" carpeting of the country. Hawkins
put up the first "paling" fence that had ever adorned the village; and he did not stop there, but whitewashed it. His oil-
cloth window-curtains had noble pictures on them of castles
such as had never been seen anywhere in the world but on
window-curtains. Hawkins enjoyed the admiration these
prodigies compelled, but he always smiled to think how poor
and cheap they were, compared to what the Hawkins mansion would display in a future day after the Tennessee Land
should have borne its minted fruit. Even Washington observed, once, that when the Tennessee Land was sold he
would have a "store" carpet in his and Clay's room like the
one in the parlor. This pleased Hawkins, but it troubled his
wife. It did not seem wise, to her, to put one's entire earthly
trust in the Tennessee Land and never think of doing any
work.

Hawkins took a weekly Philadelphia newspaper and a semi-
weekly St. Louis journal—almost the only papers that came to
the village, though Godey's Lady's Book found a good market there and was regarded as the perfection of polite literature by some of the ablest critics in the place. Perhaps it is
only fair to explain that we are writing of a by gone age—
some twenty or thirty years ago. In the two newspapers referred to lay the secret of Hawkins's growing prosperity. They
kept him informed of the condition of the crops south and
east, and thus he knew which articles were likely to be in demand and which articles were likely to be unsalable, weeks
and even months in advance of the simple folk about him. As
the months went by he came to be regarded as a wonderfully
lucky man. It did not occur to the citizens that brains were at
the bottom of his luck.

His title of "Squire" came into vogue again, but only for a season; for, as his wealth and popularity augmented, that title, by imperceptible stages, grew up into "Judge;" indeed it bade fair to swell into "General" bye and bye. All strangers of consequence who visited the village gravitated to the Hawkins Mansion and became guests of the "Judge."

Hawkins had learned to like the people of his section very much. They were uncouth and not cultivated, and not particularly industrious; but they were honest and straightforward, and their virtuous ways commanded respect. Their patriotism was strong, their pride in the flag was of the old-fashioned pattern, their love of country amounted to idolatry. Whoever dragged the national honor in the dirt won their deathless hatred. They still cursed Benedict Arnold as if he were a personal friend who had broken faith but a week gone by.

Chapter VI

十 年 前 事 幾 翻 新

Mesu eu azheīâshet
Washkebemâtizitaking,
Nâwuj beshegandâguzé
Manwâbegonig edush wen.

WE SKIP ten years and this history finds certain changes to record.

Judge Hawkins and Col. Sellers have made and lost two or three moderate fortunes in the meantime and are now pinched by poverty. Sellers has two pairs of twins and four extras. In Hawkins's family are six children of his own and two adopted ones. From time to time, as fortune smiled, the elder children got the benefit of it, spending the lucky seasons at excellent schools in St. Louis and the unlucky ones at home in the chafing discomfort of straightened circumstances.

Neither the Hawkins children nor the world that knew them ever supposed that one of the girls was of alien blood and parentage. Such difference as existed between Laura and Emily is not uncommon in a family. The girls had grown up as sisters, and they were both too young at the time of the fearful accident on the Mississippi to know that it was that which had thrown their lives together.

And yet any one who had known the secret of Laura's birth and had seen her during these passing years, say at the happy age of twelve or thirteen, would have fancied that he knew the reason why she was more winsome than her school companion.

Philosophers dispute whether it is the promise of what she will be in the careless school-girl, that makes her attractive, the undeveloped maidenhood, or the mere natural, careless sweetness of childhood. If Laura at twelve was beginning to be a beauty, the thought of it had never entered her head. No, indeed. Her mind was filled with more important thoughts. To her simple school-girl dress she was beginning to add those mysterious little adornments of ribbon-knots and ear-rings, which were the subject of earnest consultations with her grown friends.

When she tripped down the street on a summer's day with her dainty hands propped into the ribbon-broidered pockets of her apron, and elbows consequently more or less akimbo with her wide Leghorn hat flapping down and hiding her face one moment and blowing straight up against her forehead the next and making its revealment of fresh young beauty; with all her pretty girlish airs and graces in full play, and that sweet ignorance of care and that atmosphere of innocence and purity all about her that belong to her gracious time of life, indeed she was a vision to warm the coldest heart and bless and cheer the saddest.

Willful, generous, forgiving, imperious, affectionate, improvident, bewitching, in short—was Laura at this period. Could she have remained there, this history would not need to be written. But Laura had grown to be almost a woman in these few years, to the end of which we have now come—years which had seen Judge Hawkins pass through so many trials.

When the judge's first bankruptcy came upon him, a homely human angel intruded upon him with an offer of $1,500 for the Tennessee Land. Mrs. Hawkins said take it. It was a grievous temptation, but the judge withstood it. He said the land was for the children—he could not rob them of their future millions for so paltry a sum. When the second blight fell upon him, another angel appeared and offered $3,000 for the land. He was in such deep distress that he allowed his wife to persuade him to let the papers be drawn; but when his children came into his presence in their poor apparel, he felt like a traitor and refused to sign.

But now he was down again, and deeper in the mire than ever. He paced the floor all day, he scarcely slept at night. He blushed even to acknowledge it to himself, but treason was in his mind—he was meditating, at last, the sale of the land. Mrs. Hawkins stepped into the room. He had not spoken a word, but he felt as guilty as if she had caught him in some shameful act. She said:

"Si, I do not know what we are going to do. The children are not fit to be seen, their clothes are in such a state. But there's something more serious still.—There is scarcely a bite in the house to eat."

"Why, Nancy, go to Johnson——."

"Johnson indeed! You took that man's part when he hadn't a friend in the world, and you built him up and made him rich. And here's the result of it: He lives in our fine house, and we live in his miserable log cabin. He has hinted to our children that he would rather they wouldn't come about his yard to play with his children,—which I can bear, and bear easy enough, for they're not a sort we want to associate with much—but what I *can't* bear with any quietness at all, is his telling Franky our bill was running pretty high this morning when I sent him for some meal—and that was all he said, too—didn't give him the meal—turned off and went to talking with the Hargrave girls about some stuff they wanted to cheapen."

"Nancy, this is astounding!"

"And so it is, I warrant you. I've kept still, Si, as long as ever I could. Things have been getting worse and worse, and worse and worse, every single day; I don't go out of the house, I feel so down; but you had trouble enough, and I wouldn't say a word—and I wouldn't say a word now, only things have got so bad that I don't know what to do, nor where to turn." And she gave way and put her face in her hands and cried.

"Poor child, don't grieve so. I never thought that of Johnson. I am clear at my wit's end. I don't know what in the world to do. *Now* if somebody would come along and offer $3,000—Oh, if somebody only *would* come along and offer $3,000 for that Tennessee Land——"

"You'd sell it, Si?" said Mrs. Hawkins excitedly.

"Try me!"

Mrs. Hawkins was out of the room in a moment. Within a minute she was back again with a business-looking stranger, whom she seated, and then she took her leave again. Hawkins said to himself, "How can a man ever lose faith? When the blackest hour comes, Providence always comes with it—ah, this is the very timeliest help that ever poor harried devil had; if this blessed man offers but a thousand I'll embrace him like a brother!"

The stranger said:

"I am aware that you own 75,000 acres of land in East Tennessee, and without sacrificing your time, I will come to the point at once. I am agent of an iron manufacturing company, and they empower me to offer you ten thousand dollars for that land."

Hawkins's heart bounded within him. His whole frame was racked and wrenched with fettered hurrahs. His first impulse was to shout—"Done! and God bless the iron company, too!"

But a something flitted through his mind, and his opened lips uttered nothing. The enthusiasm faded away from his eyes, and the look of a man who is thinking took its place. Presently, in a hesitating, undecided way, he said:

"Well, I—it don't seem quite enough. That—that is a very valuable property—very valuable. It's brim full of iron ore, sir—brim full of it! And copper, coal,—everything—everything you can think of! Now, I'll tell you what I'll do. I'll reserve everything except the iron, and I'll sell them the iron property for $15,000 cash, I to go in with them and own an undivided interest of one-half the concern,—or the stock, as you may say. I'm out of business, and I'd just as soon help run the thing as not. Now how does that strike you?"

"Well, I am only an agent of these people, who are friends of mine, and I am not even paid for my services. To tell you the truth, I have tried to persuade them not to go into the thing; and I have come square out with their offer, without throwing out any feelers—and I did it in the hope that you would refuse. A man pretty much always refuses another man's first offer, no matter what it is. But I have performed my duty, and will take pleasure in telling them what you say."

He was about to rise. Hawkins said,

"Wait a bit."

Hawkins thought again. And the substance of his thought was: "This is a deep man; this is a very deep man; I don't like his candor; your ostentatiously candid business man's a deep fox—always a deep fox; this man's that iron company himself—that's what *he* is; he wants that property, too; I am not so blind but I can see that; *he* don't want the company to go into this thing—O, that's very good; yes, that's very good indeed—stuff! he'll be back here to-morrow, sure, and take my offer; take it? I'll risk anything he is suffering to take it now; here—I must mind what I'm about. What has started this sudden excitement about iron? I wonder what *is* in the wind? just as sure as I'm alive this moment, there's something tremendous stirring in iron speculation" [here Hawkins got up and began to pace the floor with excited eyes and with gesturing hands]—"something enormous going on in iron, without the shadow of a doubt, and here I sit mousing in the dark and never knowing anything about it; great heaven, what an escape I've made! this underhanded mercenary creature might have taken me up—and ruined me! but I *have* escaped, and I warrant me I'll not put my foot into—

He stopped and turned toward the stranger, saying:

"I have made you a proposition,—you have not accepted it, and I desire that you will consider that I have made none. At the same time my conscience will not allow me to—. Please alter the figures I named to thirty thousand dollars, if you will, and let the proposition go to the company—I will stick to it if it breaks my heart!"

The stranger looked amused, and there was a pretty well defined touch of surprise in his expression, too, but Hawkins never noticed it. Indeed he scarcely noticed anything or knew what he was about. The man left; Hawkins flung himself into a chair; thought a few moments, then glanced around, looked frightened, sprang to the door——

"Too late—too late! He's gone! Fool that I am!—always a fool! Thirty thousand—ass that I am! Oh, *why* didn't I say fifty thousand!"

He plunged his hands into his hair and leaned his elbows on his knees, and fell to rocking himself back and forth in anguish. Mrs. Hawkins sprang in, beaming:

"Well, Si?"

"Oh, con-found the con-founded—con-*found* it, Nancy. I've gone and done it, now!"

"Done what, Si, for mercy's sake!"

"Done everything! *Ruined* everything!"

"Tell me, tell me, *tell* me! Don't keep a body in such suspense. Didn't he buy, after all? Didn't he make an offer?"

"Offer? He offered $10,000 for our land, and——"

"Thank the good providence from the very bottom of my heart of hearts! What sort of ruin do you call that, Si!"

"Nancy, do you suppose I listened to such a preposterous proposition? No! Thank fortune I'm not a simpleton! I saw through the pretty scheme in a second. It's a vast iron speculation!—millions upon millions in it! But fool as I am I told him he could have half the iron property for thirty thousand—and if I only had him back here he couldn't touch it for a cent less than a quarter of a million!"

Mrs. Hawkins looked up white and despairing:

"You threw away this chance, you let this man go, and we in this awful trouble? You don't mean it, you *can't* mean it!"

"Throw it away? Catch me at it! Why woman, do you suppose that man don't know what he is about? Bless you, he'll be back fast enough to-morrow."

"Never, never, never. He never will come back. I don't know what is to become of us. I don't know what in the world is to become of us."

A shade of uneasiness came into Hawkins's face. He said:

"Why, Nancy, you—you can't believe what you are saying."

"Believe it, indeed? I *know* it, Si. And I know that we haven't a cent in the world, and we've sent ten thousand dollars a-begging."

"Nancy, you frighten me. Now could that man—is it possible that I—hanged if I don't believe I *have* missed a chance! Don't grieve, Nancy, don't grieve. I'll go right after him. I'll take—I'll take—what a fool I am!—I'll take anything he'll give!"

The next instant he left the house on a run. But the man was no longer in the town. Nobody knew where he belonged or whither he had gone. Hawkins came slowly back, watching wistfully but hopelessly for the stranger, and lowering his price steadily with his sinking heart. And when his foot finally pressed his own threshold, the value he held the entire Tennessee property at was five hundred dollars—two hundred down and the rest in three equal annual payments, without interest.

There was a sad gathering at the Hawkins fireside the next night. All the children were present but Clay. Mr. Hawkins said:

"Washington, we seem to be hopelessly fallen, hopelessly involved. I am ready to give up. I do not know where to turn—I never have been down so low before, I never have seen things so dismal. There are many mouths to feed; Clay is at work; we must lose you, also, for a little while, my boy. But it will not be long—the Tennessee land——"

He stopped, and was conscious of a blush. There was silence for a moment, and then Washington—now a lank, dreamy-eyed stripling between twenty-two and twenty-three years of age—said:

"If Col. Sellers would come for me, I would go and stay with him a while, till the Tennessee land is sold. He has often wanted me to come, ever since he moved to Hawkeye."

"I'm afraid he can't well come for you, Washington. From what I can hear—not from *him* of course, but from others— he is not far from as bad off as we are—and his family is as large, too. He might find something for you to do, maybe, but you'd better try to get to him yourself, Washington—it's only thirty miles."

"But how can I, father? There's no stage or anything."

"And if there were, stages require money. A stage goes from Swansea, five miles from here. But it would be cheaper to walk."

"Father, they must know you there, and no doubt they would credit you in a moment, for a little stage ride like that. Couldn't you write and ask them?"

"Couldn't *you*, Washington—seeing it's you that wants the ride? And what do you think you'll do, Washington, when you get to Hawkeye? Finish your invention for making window-glass opaque?"

"No, sir, I have given that up. I almost knew I could do it, but it was so tedious and troublesome I quit it."

"I was afraid of it, my boy. Then I suppose you'll finish your plan of coloring hen's eggs by feeding a peculiar diet to the hen?"

"No, sir. I believe I have found out the stuff that will do it, but it kills the hen; so I have dropped that for the present, though I can take it up again some day when I learn how to manage the mixture better."

"Well, what have you got on hand—anything?"

"Yes, sir, three or four things. I think they are all good and can all be done, but they are tiresome, and besides they require money. But as soon as the land is sold——"

"Emily, were you about to say something?" said Hawkins.

"Yes, sir. If you are willing, I will go to St. Louis. That will make another mouth less to feed. Mrs. Buckner has always wanted me to come."

"But the money, child?"

"Why I think she would send it, if you would write her—and I know she would wait for her pay till——"

"Come, Laura, let's hear from you, my girl."

Emily and Laura were about the same age—between seventeen and eighteen. Emily was fair and pretty, girlish and diffident—blue eyes and light hair. Laura had a proud bearing and a somewhat mature look; she had fine, clean-cut features, her complexion was pure white and contrasted vividly with her black hair and eyes; she was not what one calls pretty—she was beautiful. She said:

"I will go to St. Louis, too, sir. I will find a way to get there. I will *make* a way. And I will find a way to help myself along, and do what I can to help the rest, too."

She spoke it like a princess. Mrs. Hawkins smiled proudly and kissed her, saying in a tone of fond reproof:

"So one of my girls is going to turn out and work for her living! It's like your pluck and spirit, child, but we will hope that we haven't got quite down to that, yet."

The girl's eyes beamed affection under her mother's caress. Then she straightened up, folded her white hands in her lap and became a splendid ice-berg. Clay's dog put up his brown nose for a little attention, and got it. He retired under the table with an apologetic yelp, which did not affect the iceberg.

Judge Hawkins had written and asked Clay to return home and consult with him upon family affairs. He arrived the evening after this conversation, and the whole household gave him a rapturous welcome. He brought sadly needed help with him, consisting of the savings of a year and a half of work—nearly two hundred dollars in money.

It was a ray of sunshine which (to this easy household) was the earnest of a clearing sky.

Bright and early in the morning the family were astir, and all were busy preparing Washington for his journey—at least all but Washington himself, who sat apart, steeped in a reverie. When the time for his departure came, it was easy to see how fondly all loved him and how hard it was to let him go, notwithstanding they had often seen him go before, in his St. Louis schooling days. In the most matter-of-course way they had borne the burden of getting him ready for his trip, never seeming to think of *his* helping in the matter; in the same matter-of-course way Clay had hired a horse and cart; and now that the good-byes were ended he bundled Washington's baggage in and drove away with the exile.

At Swansea Clay paid his stage fare, stowed him away in the vehicle, and saw him off. Then he returned home and reported progress, like a committee of the whole.

Clay remained at home several days. He held many consultations with his mother upon the financial condition of the family, and talked once with his father upon the same subject, but only once. He found a change in that quarter which was distressing; years of fluctuating fortune had done their work; each reverse had weakened the father's spirit and impaired his energies; his last misfortune seemed to have left hope and ambition dead within him; he had no projects, formed no plans—evidently he was a vanquished man. He looked worn and tired. He inquired into Clay's affairs and prospects, and when he found that Clay was doing pretty well and was likely to do still better, it was plain that he resigned himself with easy facility to look to the son for a support; and he said, "Keep yourself informed of poor Washington's condition and movements, and help him along all you can, Clay."

The younger children, also, seemed relieved of all fears and distresses, and very ready and willing to look to Clay for a livelihood. Within three days a general tranquility and satisfaction reigned in the household. Clay's hundred and eighty or ninety dollars had worked a wonder. The family were as contented, now, and as free from care as they could have been with a fortune. It was well that Mrs. Hawkins held the purse—otherwise the treasure would have lasted but a very little while.

It took but a trifle to pay Hawkins's outstanding obligations, for he had always had a horror of debt.

When Clay bade his home good-bye and set out to return to the field of his labors, he was conscious that henceforth he was to have his father's family on his hands as pensioners; but he did not allow himself to chafe at the thought, for he reasoned that his father had dealt by him with a free hand and a loving one all his life, and now that hard fortune had broken his spirit it ought to be a pleasure, not a pain, to work for him. The younger children were born and educated dependents. They had never been taught to do anything for themselves, and it did not seem to occur to them to make an attempt now.

The girls would not have been permitted to work for a living under any circumstances whatever. It was a southern family, and of good blood; and for any person except Laura, either within or without the household to have suggested such an idea would have brought upon the suggester the suspicion of being a lunatic.

Chapter VII

Via, Pecunia! when she's run and gone
And fled, and dead, then will I fetch her again
With aqua vitæ, out of an old hogshead!
While there are lees of wine, or dregs of beer,
I'll never want her! Coin her out of cobwebs,
Dust, but I'll have her! raise wool upon egg-shells,
Sir, and make grass grow out of marrow-bones,
To make her come!

B. Jonson.

BEARING Washington Hawkins and his fortunes, the stage-coach tore out of Swansea at a fearful gait, with horn tooting gaily and half the town admiring from doors and windows. But it did not tear any more after it got to the outskirts; it dragged along stupidly enough, then—till it came in sight of the next hamlet; and then the bugle tooted gaily again and again the vehicle went tearing by the houses. This sort of conduct marked every entry to a station and every exit from it; and so in those days children grew up with the idea that stage-coaches always tore and always tooted; but they also grew up with the idea that pirates went into action in their Sunday clothes, carrying the black flag in one hand and pistolling people with the other, merely because they were so represented in the pictures—but these illusions vanished when later years brought their disenchanting wisdom. They learned then that the stage-coach is but a poor, plodding, vulgar thing in the solitudes of the highway; and that the pirate is only a seedy, unfantastic "rough," when he is out of the pictures.

Toward evening, the stage-coach came thundering into Hawkeye with a perfectly triumphant ostentation—which was natural and proper, for Hawkeye was a pretty large town for interior Missouri. Washington, very stiff and tired and hungry, climbed out, and wondered how he was to proceed now. But his difficulty was quickly solved. Col. Sellers came down the street on a run and arrived panting for breath. He said:

"Lord bless you—I'm glad to see you, Washington—perfectly delighted to see you, my boy! I got your message. Been on the look-out for you. Heard the stage horn, but had a party I couldn't shake off—man that's got an enormous thing on hand—wants me to put some capital into it—and I tell you, my boy, I could do worse, I could do a deal worse. No, now, let that luggage alone; I'll fix that. Here, Jerry, got anything to do? All right—shoulder this plunder and follow me. Come along, Washington. Lord I'm glad to see you! Wife and the children are just perishing to look at you. Bless you, they won't know you, you've grown so. Folks all well, I suppose? That's good—glad to hear that. We're always going to run down and see them, but I'm into so many operations, and they're not things a man feels like trusting to other people, and so somehow we keep putting it off. Fortunes in them! Good gracious, it's the country to pile up wealth in! Here we are—here's where the Sellers dynasty hangs out. Dump it on the door-step, Jerry—the blackest niggro in the State, Washington, but got a good heart—mighty likely boy, is Jerry. And now I suppose you've got to have ten cents, Jerry. That's all right—when a man works for me—when a man—in the other pocket, I reckon—when a man—why, where the mischief *is* that port-monnaie!—when a—well now that's odd—Oh, now I remember, must have left it at the bank; and b'George I've left my check-book, too—Polly says I ought to have a nurse—well, no matter. Let me have a dime, Washington, if you've got—ah, thanks. Now clear out, Jerry, your complexion has brought on the twilight half an hour ahead of time. Pretty fair joke—pretty fair. Here he is, Polly! Washington's come, children!—come now, don't eat him up—finish him in the house. Welcome, my boy, to a mansion that is proud to shelter the son of the best man that walks on the ground. Si Hawkins has been a good friend to me, and I believe I can say that whenever I've had a chance to put him into a good thing I've done it, and done it pretty cheerfully, too. I put him into that sugar speculation—what a grand thing that was, if we hadn't held on too long!"

True enough; but holding on too long had utterly ruined both of them; and the saddest part of it was, that they never had had so much money to lose before, for Sellers's sale of their mule crop that year in New Orleans had been a great financial success. If he had kept out of sugar and gone back home content to stick to mules it would have been a happy wisdom. As it was, he managed to kill two birds with one stone—that is to say, he killed the sugar speculation by holding for high rates till he had to sell at the bottom figure, and that calamity killed the mule that laid the golden egg—which is but a figurative expression and will be so understood. Sellers had returned home cheerful but empty-handed, and the mule business lapsed into other hands. The sale of the Hawkins property by the Sheriff had followed, and the Hawkins hearts been torn to see Uncle Dan'l and his wife pass from the auction-block into the hands of a negro trader and depart for the remote South to be seen no more by the family. It had seemed like seeing their own flesh and blood sold into banishment.

Washington was greatly pleased with the Sellers mansion. It was a two-story-and-a-half brick, and much more stylish than any of its neighbors. He was borne to the family sitting room in triumph by the swarm of little Sellerses, the parents following with their arms about each other's waists.

The whole family were poorly and cheaply dressed; and the clothing, although neat and clean, showed many evidences of having seen long service. The Colonel's "stovepipe" hat was napless and shiny with much polishing, but nevertheless it had an almost convincing expression about it of having been just purchased new. The rest of his clothing was napless and shiny, too, but it had the air of being entirely satisfied with itself and blandly sorry for other people's clothes. It was growing rather dark in the house, and the evening air was chilly, too. Sellers said:

"Lay off your overcoat, Washington, and draw up to the stove and make yourself at home—just consider yourself under your own shingles my boy—I'll have a fire going, in a jiffy. Light the lamp, Polly, dear, and let's have things cheerful—just as glad to see you, Washington, as if you'd been lost a century and we'd found you again!"

By this time the Colonel was conveying a lighted match into a poor little stove. Then he propped the stove door to its place by leaning the poker against it, for the hinges had retired from business. This door framed a small square of isinglass, which now warmed up with a faint glow. Mrs. Sellers lit a cheap, showy lamp, which dissipated a good deal of the gloom, and then everybody gathered into the light and took the stove into close companionship.

The children climbed all over Sellers, fondled him, petted him, and were lavishly petted in return. Out from this tugging, laughing, chattering disguise of legs and arms and little faces, the Colonel's voice worked its way and his tireless tongue ran blithely on without interruption; and the purring little wife, diligent with her knitting, sat near at hand and looked happy and proud and grateful; and she listened as one who listens to oracles and gospels and whose grateful soul is being refreshed with the bread of life. Bye and bye the children quieted down to listen; clustered about their father, and resting their elbows on his legs, they hung upon his words as if he were uttering the music of the spheres.

A dreary old hair-cloth sofa against the wall; a few damaged chairs; the small table the lamp stood on; the crippled stove—these things constituted the furniture of the room. There was no carpet on the floor; on the wall were occasional square-shaped interruptions of the general tint of the plaster which betrayed that there used to be pictures in the house—but there were none now. There were no mantel ornaments, unless one might bring himself to regard as an ornament a clock which never came within fifteen strokes of striking the right time, and whose hands always hitched together at twenty-two minutes past anything and traveled in company the rest of the way home.

"Remarkable clock!" said Sellers, and got up and wound it. "I've been offered—well, I wouldn't expect you to believe what I've been offered for that clock. Old Gov. Hager never sees me but he says, 'Come, now, Colonel, name your price—I *must* have that clock!' But my goodness I'd as soon think of selling my wife. As I was saying to——silence in the court, now, she's begun to strike! You can't talk against her—you have to just be patient and hold up till she's said her say. Ah—well, as I was saying, when—she's beginning again! Nineteen, twenty, twenty-one, twenty-two, twen——ah, that's all.—Yes, as I was saying to old Judge——go it, old girl, don't mind me.—Now how is that?—isn't that a good, spirited tone? She can wake the dead! Sleep? Why you might as well try to sleep in a thunder-factory. Now just listen at that. She'll strike a hundred and fifty, now, without stopping,—you'll see. There ain't another clock like that in Christendom."

Washington hoped that this might be true, for the din was distracting—though the family, one and all, seemed filled with joy; and the more the clock "buckled down to her work" as the Colonel expressed it, and the more insupportable the clatter became, the more enchanted they all appeared to be. When there was silence, Mrs Sellers lifted upon Washington a face that beamed with a childlike pride, and said:

"It belonged to his grandmother."

The look and the tone were a plain call for admiring surprise, and therefore Washington said—(it was the only thing that offered itself at the moment:)

"Indeed!"

"Yes, it did, didn't it father!" exclaimed one of the twins. "She was my great-grandmother—and George's too; wasn't she, father! *You* never saw her, but Sis has seen her, when Sis was a baby—didn't you, Sis! Sis has seen her most a hundred times. She was awful deef—she's dead, now. Ain't she, father!"

All the children chimed in, now, with one general Babel of information about deceased—nobody offering to read the riot act or seeming to discountenance the insurrection or disapprove of it in any way—but the head twin drowned all the turmoil and held his own against the field:

"It's our clock, now—and it's got wheels inside of it, and a thing that flutters every time she strikes—don't it, father! Great-grandmother died before hardly any of us was born— she was an Old-School Baptist and had warts all over her— you ask father if she didn't. She had an uncle once that was bald-headed and used to have fits; he wasn't *our* uncle, I don't know what he was to us—some kin or another I reckon—father's seen him a thousand times—hain't you, father! We used to have a calf that et apples and just chawed up dishrags like nothing, and if you stay here you'll see lots of funerals—won't he, Sis! Did you ever see a house afire? *I* have! Once me and Jim Terry——"

But Sellers began to speak now, and the storm ceased. He began to tell about an enormous speculation he was thinking of embarking some capital in—a speculation which some London bankers had been over to consult with him about—and soon he was building glittering pyramids of coin, and Washington was presently growing opulent under the magic of his eloquence. But at the same time Washington was not able to ignore the cold entirely. He was nearly as close to the stove as he could get, and yet he could not persuade himself that he felt the slightest heat, notwithstanding the isinglass door was still gently and serenely glowing. He tried to get a trifle closer to the stove, and the consequence was, he tripped the supporting poker and the stove-door tumbled to the floor. And then there was a revelation—there was nothing in the stove but a lighted tallow-candle!

The poor youth blushed and felt as if he must die with shame. But the Colonel was only disconcerted for a moment—he straightway found his voice again:

"A little idea of my own, Washington—one of the greatest things in the world! You must write and tell your father about it—don't forget that, now. I have been reading up some European Scientific reports—friend of mine, Count Fugier, sent them to me—sends me all sorts of things from Paris—he thinks the world of me, Fugier does. Well, I saw that the Academy of France had been testing the properties of heat, and they came to the conclusion that it was a non-conductor or something like that, and of course its influence must necessarily be deadly in nervous organizations with excitable temperaments, especially where there is any tendency toward rheumatic affections. Bless you I saw in a moment what was the matter with us, and says I, out goes your fires!—no more slow torture and certain death for me, sir. What you want is the *appearance* of heat, not the heat itself—that's the idea. Well how to do it was the next thing. I just put my head to work, pegged away a couple of days, and here you are! Rheumatism? Why a man can't any more start a case of rheumatism in this house than he can shake an opinion out of a mummy! Stove with a candle in it and a transparent door—that's it—it has been the salvation of this family. Don't you fail to write your father about it, Washington. And tell him the idea is mine—I'm no more conceited than most people, I reckon, but you know it is human nature for a man to want credit for a thing like that."

Washington said with his blue lips that he would, but he said in his secret heart that he would promote no such iniquity. He tried to believe in the healthfulness of the invention, and succeeded tolerably well; but after all he could not feel that good health in a frozen body was any real improvement on the rheumatism.

Chapter VIII

—Whan þe borde is thynne, as of seruyse,
    Nought replenesshed with grete diuersite
Of mete & drinke, good chere may then suffise
    With honest talkyng——
                        The Book of Curtesye.

Mammon.   Come on, sir. Now, you set your foot on shore
In *Novo Orbe*; here's the rich Peru:
And there within, sir, are the golden mines,
Great Solomon's Ophir!——   *B. Jonson.*

THE SUPPER at Col. Sellers's was not sumptuous, in the beginning, but it improved on acquaintance. That is to say, that what Washington regarded at first sight as mere lowly potatoes, presently became awe-inspiring agricultural productions that had been reared in some ducal garden beyond the sea, under the sacred eye of the duke himself, who had sent them to Sellers; the bread was from corn which could be grown in only one favored locality in the earth and only a favored few could get it; the Rio coffee, which at first seemed execrable to the taste, took to itself an improved flavor when Washington was told to drink it slowly and not hurry what should be a lingering luxury in order to be fully appreciated— it was from the private stores of a Brazilian nobleman with an unrememberable name. The Colonel's tongue was a magician's wand that turned dried apples into figs and water into wine as easily as it could change a hovel into a palace and present poverty into imminent future riches.

Washington slept in a cold bed in a carpetless room and woke up in a palace in the morning; at least the palace lingered during the moment that he was rubbing his eyes and getting his bearings—and then it disappeared and he recognized that the Colonel's inspiring talk had been influencing his dreams. Fatigue had made him sleep late; when he entered the sitting room he noticed that the old hair-cloth sofa was absent; when he sat down to breakfast the Colonel tossed six or seven dollars in bills on the table, counted them over, said

he was a little short and must call upon his banker; then returned the bills to his wallet with the indifferent air of a man
who is used to money. The breakfast was not an improvement
upon the supper, but the Colonel talked it up and transformed it into an oriental feast. Bye and bye, he said:

"I intend to look out for you, Washington, my boy. I hunted
up a place for you yesterday, but I am not referring to that,
now—that is a mere livelihood—mere bread and butter; but
when I say I mean to look out for you I mean something very
different. I mean to put things in your way that will make a
mere livelihood a trifling thing. I'll put you in a way to make
more money than you'll ever know what to do with. You'll be
right here where I can put my hand on you when anything
turns up. I've got some prodigious operations on foot; but I'm
keeping quiet; mum's the word; your old hand don't go
around pow-wowing and letting everybody see his k'yards and
find out his little game. But all in good time, Washington, all
in good time. You'll see. Now there's an operation in corn that
looks well. Some New York men are trying to get me to go
into it—buy up all the growing crops and just boss the market
when they mature—ah I tell you it's a great thing. And it only
costs a trifle; two millions or two and a half will do it. I haven't
exactly promised yet—there's no hurry—the more indifferent
I seem, you know, the more anxious those fellows will get. And
then there is the hog speculation—that's bigger still. We've got
quiet men at work," [he was very impressive here,] "mousing
around, to get propositions out of all the farmers in the whole
west and northwest for the hog crop, and other agents quietly
getting propositions and terms out of all the manufactories—
and don't you see, if we can get all the hogs and all the slaugh-
ter houses into our hands on the dead quiet—whew! it would
take three ships to carry the money.—I've looked into the
thing—calculated all the chances for and all the chances
against, and though I shake my head and hesitate and keep on
thinking, apparently, I've got my mind made up that if the
thing can be done on a capital of six millions, that's the horse
to put up money on! Why Washington—but what's the use of
talking about it—any man can see that there's whole Atlantic
oceans of cash in it, gulfs and bays thrown in. But there's a bigger thing than that, yet—a bigger——"

"Why Colonel, you can't want anything bigger!" said Washington, his eyes blazing. "Oh, I wish I could go into either of those speculations—I only wish I had money—I wish I wasn't cramped and kept down and fettered with poverty, and such prodigious chances lying right here in sight! Oh, it is a fearful thing to be poor. But don't throw away those things—they are so splendid and I can see how sure they are. Don't throw them away for something still better and maybe fail in it! I wouldn't, Colonel. I would stick to these. I wish father were here and were his old self again—Oh, he never in his life had such chances as these are. Colonel, you *can't* improve on these—no man can improve on them!"

A sweet, compassionate smile played about the Colonel's features, and he leaned over the table with the air of a man who is "going to show you" and do it without the least trouble:

"Why Washington, my boy, these things are nothing. They *look* large—of course they look large to a novice, but to a man who has been all his life accustomed to large operations—shaw! They're well enough to while away an idle hour with, or furnish a bit of employment that will give a trifle of idle capital a chance to earn its bread while it is waiting for something to *do*, but—now just listen a moment—just let me give you an idea of what we old veterans of commerce call 'business.' Here's the Rothschild's proposition—this is between you and me, you understand——"

Washington nodded three or four times impatiently, and his glowing eyes said, "Yes, yes—hurry—I understand——"

——"for I wouldn't have it get out for a fortune. They want me to go in with them on the sly—agent was here two weeks ago about it—go in on the sly"[voice down to an impressive whisper, now,] "and buy up a hundred and thirteen wild cat banks in Ohio, Indiana, Kentucky, Illinois and Missouri—notes of these banks are at all sorts of discount now—average discount of the hundred and thirteen is forty-four per cent—buy them all up, you see, and then all of a sudden let the cat out of the bag! Whiz! the stock of every one of those wildcats would spin up to a tremendous premium before you could turn a handspring—profit on the speculation not a dollar less than forty millions!" [An eloquent pause, while the marvelous vision settled into W.'s focus.] "Where's your hogs now! Why my dear innocent boy, we would just sit down on the front door-steps and peddle banks like lucifer matches!"

Washington finally got his breath and said:

"Oh, it is perfectly wonderful! Why couldn't these things have happened in father's day? And I—it's of no use—they simply lie before my face and mock me. There is nothing for me but to stand helpless and see other people reap the astonishing harvest."

"Never mind, Washington, don't you worry. I'll fix you. There's plenty of chances. How much money have you got?"

In the presence of so many millions, Washington could not keep from blushing when he had to confess that he had but eighteen dollars in the world.

"Well, all right—don't despair. Other people have been obliged to begin with less. I have a small idea that may develop into something for us both, all in good time. Keep your money close and add to it. I'll make it breed. I've been experimenting (to pass away the time,) on a little preparation for curing sore eyes—a kind of decoction nine-tenths water and the other tenth drugs that don't cost more than a dollar a barrel; I'm still experimenting; there's one ingredient wanted yet to perfect the thing, and somehow I can't just manage to hit upon the thing that's necessary, and I don't dare talk with a chemist, of course. But I'm progressing, and before many weeks I wager the country will ring with the fame of Eschol Sellers' Infallible Imperial Oriental Optic Liniment and Salvation for Sore Eyes—the Medical Wonder of the Age! Small bottles fifty cents, large ones a dollar. Average cost, five and seven cents for the two sizes. The first year sell, say, ten thousand bottles in Missouri, seven thousand in Iowa, three thousand in Arkansas, four thousand in Kentucky, six thousand in Illinois, and say twenty-five thousand in the rest of the country. Total, fifty-five thousand bottles; profit clear of all expenses, twenty thousand dollars at the very lowest calculation. All the capital needed is to manufacture the first two thousand bottles—say a hundred and fifty dollars—then the money would begin to flow in. The second year, sales would reach 200,000 bottles—clear profit, say, $75,000—and in the meantime the great factory would be building in St. Louis, to cost, say, $100,000. The third year we could easily sell 1,000,000 bottles in the United States and——"

"O, splendid!" said Washington. "Let's commence right away—let's——"

"——1,000,000 bottles in the United States—profit at least $350,000—and *then* it would begin to be time to turn our attention toward the *real* idea of the business."

"The *real* idea of it! Ain't $350,000 a year a pretty real——"

"Stuff! Why what an infant you are, Washington—what a guileless, short-sighted, easily-contented innocent you are, my poor little country-bred know-nothing! Would I go to all that trouble and bother for the poor crumbs a body might pick up in *this* country? Now do I look like a man who—does my history suggest that I am a man who deals in trifles, contents himself with the narrow horizon that hems in the common herd, sees no further than the end of his nose? Now *you* know that that is not me—couldn't *be* me. *You* ought to know that if I throw my time and abilities into a patent medicine, it's a patent medicine whose field of operations is the solid earth! its clients the swarming nations that inhabit it! Why what is the republic of America for an eye-water country? Lord bless you, it is nothing but a barren highway that you've got to cross to get *to* the true eye-water market! Why, Washington, in the Oriental countries people swarm like the sands of the desert; every square mile of ground upholds its thousands upon thousands of struggling human creatures—and every separate and individual devil of them's got the ophthalmia! It's as natural to them as noses are—and sin. It's born with them, it stays with them, it's all that some of them have left when they die. Three years of introductory trade in the orient and what will be the result? Why, our headquarters would be in Constantinople and our hindquarters in Further India! Factories and warehouses in Cairo, Ispahan, Bagdad, Damascus, Jerusalem, Yedo, Peking, Bangkok, Delhi, Bombay and Calcutta! Annual income—well, God only knows how many millions and millions apiece!"

Washington was so dazed, so bewildered—his heart and his eyes had wandered so far away among the strange lands beyond the seas, and such avalanches of coin and currency had fluttered and jingled confusedly down before him, that he was now as one who has been whirling round and round for a time, and, stopping all at once, finds his surroundings still whirling and all objects a dancing chaos. However, little by little the Sellers family cooled down and crystalized into shape, and the poor room lost its glitter and resumed its poverty. Then the youth found his voice and begged Sellers to drop everything and hurry up the eye-water; and he got his eighteen dollars and tried to force it upon the Colonel— pleaded with him to take it—implored him to do it. But the Colonel would not; said he would not need the capital (in his native magnificent way he called that eighteen dollars Capital) till the eye-water was an accomplished fact. He made Washington easy in his mind, though, by promising that he would call for it just as soon as the invention was finished, and he added the glad tidings that nobody but just they two should be admitted to a share in the speculation.

When Washington left the breakfast table he could have worshiped that man. Washington was one of that kind of people whose hopes are in the very clouds one day and in the gutter the next. He walked on air, now. The Colonel was ready to take him around and introduce him to the employment he had found for him, but Washington begged for a few moments in which to write home; with his kind of people, to ride to-day's new interest to death and put off yesterday's till another time, is nature itself. He ran up stairs and wrote glowingly, enthusiastically, to his mother about the hogs and the corn, the banks and the eye-water—and added a few inconsequential millions to each project. And he said that people little dreamed what a man Col. Sellers was, and that the world would open its eyes when it found out. And he closed his letter thus:

> "So make yourself perfectly easy, mother—in a little while you shall have everything you want, and more. I am not likely to stint *you* in anything, I fancy. This money will not be for me, alone, but for all of us. I want all to share alike; and there is going to be far more for each than one person can spend. Break it to father cautiously—you understand the need of that—break it to him cautiously, for he has had such cruel hard fortune, and is so stricken by it that great good news might prostrate him more surely than even bad, for he is used to

the bad but is grown sadly unaccustomed to the other. Tell Laura—tell all the children. And write to Clay about it if he is not with you yet. You may tell Clay that whatever I get he can freely share in—freely. He knows that that is true—there will be no need that I should swear to that to make him believe it. Good-bye—and mind what I say: Rest perfectly easy, one and all of you, for our troubles are nearly at an end."

Poor lad, he could not know that his mother would cry some loving, compassionate tears over his letter and put off the family with a synopsis of its contents which conveyed a deal of love to them but not much idea of his prospects or projects. And he never dreamed that such a joyful letter could sadden her and fill her night with sighs, and troubled thoughts, and bodings of the future, instead of filling it with peace and blessing it with restful sleep.

When the letter was done, Washington and the Colonel sallied forth, and as they walked along Washington learned what he was to be. He was to be a clerk in a real estate office. Instantly the fickle youth's dreams forsook the magic eye-water and flew back to the Tennessee Land. And the gorgeous possibilities of that great domain straightway began to occupy his imagination to such a degree that he could scarcely manage to keep even enough of his attention upon the Colonel's talk to retain the general run of what he was saying. He was glad it was a real estate office—he was a made man now, sure.

The Colonel said that General Boswell was a rich man and had a good and growing business; and that Washington's work would be light and he would get forty dollars a month and be boarded and lodged in the General's family—which was as good as ten dollars more; and even better, for he could not live as well even at the "City Hotel" as he would there, and yet the hotel charged fifteen dollars a month where a man had a good room.

General Boswell was in his office; a comfortable looking place, with plenty of outline maps hanging about the walls and in the windows, and a spectacled man was marking out another one on a long table. The office was in the principal street. The General received Washington with a kindly but reserved politeness. Washington rather liked his looks. He was about fifty years old, dignified, well preserved and well dressed. After the Colonel took his leave, the General talked a while with Washington—his talk consisting chiefly of instructions about the clerical duties of the place. He seemed satisfied as to Washington's ability to take care of the books, he was evidently a pretty fair theoretical book-keeper, and experience would soon harden theory into practice. By and by dinner-time came, and the two walked to the General's house; and now Washington noticed an instinct in himself that moved him to keep not in the General's rear, exactly, but yet not at his side—somehow the old gentleman's dignity and reserve did not inspire familiarity.

Chapter IX

Quando ti veddi per la prima volta,
Parse che mi s'aprisse il paradiso,
E veniss no gli angioli a un per volta
Tutti ad apporsi sopra al tuo bel viso,
Tutti ad apporsi sopra il tuo bel volto,
M'incatenasti, e non mi so'anco sciolto—

Yɪmohmi hoka, himak a̱ yakni ilɪppɪt immi ha chi̱ ho̱—

—Tajma kittôrnaminut innèiziungnærame, isikkæne sinikbingmun
illièj, annerningærdlunilo siurdliminut piok.   *Mos. Agl. Siurdl.* 49.32.

WASHINGTON dreamed his way along the street, his
fancy flitting from grain to hogs, from hogs to banks,
from banks to eye-water, from eye-water to Tennessee Land,
and lingering but a feverish moment upon each of these fascinations. He was conscious of but one outward thing, to wit,
the General, and he was really not vividly conscious of him.

Arrived at the finest dwelling in the town, they entered it
and were at home. Washington was introduced to Mrs.
Boswell, and his imagination was on the point of flitting into
the vapory realms of speculation again, when a lovely girl of
sixteen or seventeen came in. This vision swept Washington's
mind clear of its chaos of glittering rubbish in an instant.
Beauty had fascinated him before; many times he had been in
love—even for weeks at a time with the same object—but his
heart had never suffered so sudden and so fierce an assault as
this, within his recollection.

Louise Boswell occupied his mind and drifted among his
multiplication tables all the afternoon. He was constantly catching himself in a reverie—reveries made up of recalling how she
looked when she first burst upon him; how her voice thrilled
him when she first spoke; how charmed the very air seemed by
her presence. Blissful as the afternoon was, delivered up to
such a revel as this, it seemed an eternity, so impatient was he
to see the girl again. Other afternoons like it followed. Washington plunged into this love affair as he plunged into everything else—upon impulse and without reflection. As the days

went by it seemed plain that he was growing in favor with Louise,—not sweepingly so, but yet perceptibly, he fancied. His attentions to her troubled her father and mother a little, and they warned Louise, without stating particulars or making allusions to any special person, that a girl was sure to make a mistake who allowed herself to marry anybody but a man who could support her well.

Some instinct taught Washington that his present lack of money would be an obstruction, though possibly not a bar, to his hopes, and straightway his poverty became a torture to him which cast all his former sufferings under that head into the shade. He longed for riches now as he had never longed for them before.

He had been once or twice to dine with Col. Sellers, and had been discouraged to note that the Colonel's bill of fare was falling off both in quantity and quality—a sign, he feared, that the lacking ingredient in the eye-water still remained undiscovered—though Sellers always explained that these changes in the family diet had been ordered by the doctor, or suggested by some new scientific work the Colonel had stumbled upon. But it always turned out that the lacking ingredient *was* still lacking—though it always appeared, at the same time, that the Colonel was right on its heels.

Every time the Colonel came into the real estate office Washington's heart bounded and his eyes lighted with hope, but it always turned out that the Colonel was merely on the scent of some vast, undefined landed speculation—although he was customarily able to say that he was nearer to the all-necessary ingredient than ever, and could almost name the hour when success would dawn. And then Washington's heart would sink again and a sigh would tell when it touched bottom.

About this time a letter came, saying that Judge Hawkins had been ailing for a fortnight, and was now considered to be seriously ill. It was thought best that Washington should come home. The news filled him with grief, for he loved and honored his father; the Boswells were touched by the youth's sorrow, and even the General unbent and said encouraging things to him.—There was balm in this; but when Louise bade him good-bye, and shook his hand and said, "Don't be cast down—it will all come out right—I *know* it will all come out right," it seemed a blessed thing to be in misfortune, and the tears that welled up to his eyes were the messengers of an adoring and a grateful heart; and when the girl saw them and answering tears came into her own eyes, Washington could hardly contain the excess of happiness that poured into the cavities of his breast that were so lately stored to the roof with grief.

All the way home he nursed his woe and exalted it. He pictured himself as *she* must be picturing him: a noble, struggling young spirit persecuted by misfortune, but bravely and patiently waiting in the shadow of a dread calamity and preparing to meet the blow as became one who was all too used to hard fortune and the pitiless buffetings of fate. These thoughts made him weep, and weep more broken-heartedly than ever; and he wished that she could see his sufferings *now*.

There was nothing significant in the fact that Louise, dreamy and distraught, stood at her bedroom bureau that night, scribbling "Washington" here and there over a sheet of paper. But there was something significant in the fact that she scratched the word out every time she wrote it; examined the erasure critically to see if anybody could guess at what the word had been; then buried it under a maze of obliterating lines; and finally, as if still unsatisfied, burned the paper.

When Washington reached home, he recognized at once how serious his father's case was. The darkened room, the labored breathing and occasional moanings of the patient, the tip-toeing of the attendants and their whispered consultations, were full of sad meaning. For three or four nights Mrs. Hawkins and Laura had been watching by the bedside; Clay had arrived, preceding Washington by one day, and he was now added to the corps of watchers. Mr. Hawkins would have none but these three, though neighborly assistance was offered by old friends. From this time forth three-hour watches were instituted, and day and night the watchers kept their vigils. By degrees Laura and her mother began to show wear, but neither of them would yield a minute of their tasks to Clay.— He ventured once to let the midnight hour pass without calling Laura, but he ventured no more; there was that about her rebuke when he tried to explain, that taught him that to let

one who is done with life and has no further interest in its joys and sorrows, its hopes or its ambitions. Clay buried his face in the coverlet of the bed; when the other children and the mother realized that death was indeed come at last, they threw themselves into each others' arms and gave way to a frenzy of grief.

Chapter X

—Okarbigàlo: "Kia pannigátit? Assarsara! uamnut nevsoïngoarna"—
Mo. Agleg. Siurdl. 24. 23.

Nœotah nuttaunes, natwontash
Kukkeihtash, wonk yeuyeu
Wannanum kummissinninnumog
Kak Kœosh week pannuppu.

—La Giannetta rispose: Madama, voi dalla povertà di mio
padre togliendomi, come figliuola cresciuta m'avete, e per
questo agni vostro piacer far dovrei—
Boccacio, Decam. Giom. 2, Nov. 6.

ONLY two or three days had elapsed since the funeral, when something happened which was to change the drift of Laura's life somewhat, and influence in a greater or lesser degree the formation of her character.

Major Lackland had once been a man of note in the State—a man of extraordinary natural ability and as extraordinary learning. He had been universally trusted and honored in his day, but had finally fallen into misfortune; while serving his third term in Congress, and while upon the point of being elevated to the Senate—which was considered the summit of earthly aggrandizement in those days—he had yielded to temptation, when in distress for money wherewith to save his estate, and sold his vote. His crime was discovered, and his fall followed instantly. Nothing could reinstate him in the confidence of the people, his ruin was irretrievable—his disgrace complete. All doors were closed against him, all men avoided him. After years of skulking retirement and dissipation, death had relieved him of his troubles at last, and his funeral followed close upon that of Mr. Hawkins. He died as he had latterly lived—wholly alone and friendless. He had no relatives—or if he had they did not acknowledge him. The coroner's jury found certain memoranda upon his body and about the premises which revealed a fact not suspected by the villagers before—viz., that Laura was not the child of Mr. and Mrs. Hawkins.

The gossips were soon at work. They were but little hampered by the fact that the memoranda referred to betrayed nothing but the bare circumstance that Laura's real parents were unknown, and stopped there. So far from being hampered by this, the gossips seemed to gain all the more freedom from it. They supplied all the missing information themselves, they filled up all the blanks. The town soon teemed with histories of Laura's origin and secret history, no two versions precisely alike, but all elaborate, exhaustive, mysterious and interesting, and all agreeing in one vital particular—to wit, that there was a suspicious cloud about her birth, not to say a disreputable one.

Laura began to encounter cold looks, averted eyes and peculiar nods and gestures which perplexed her beyond measure; but presently the pervading gossip found its way to her, and she understood them then. Her pride was stung. She was astonished, and at first incredulous. She was about to ask her mother if there was any truth in these reports, but upon second thought held her peace. She soon gathered that Major Lackland's memoranda seemed to refer to letters which had passed between himself and Judge Hawkins. She shaped her course without difficulty the day that that hint reached her.

That night she sat in her room till all was still, and then she stole into the garret and began a search. She rummaged long among boxes of musty papers relating to business matters of no interest to her, but at last she found several bundles of letters. One bundle was marked "private," and in that she found what she wanted. She selected six or eight letters from the package and began to devour their contents, heedless of the cold.

By the dates, these letters were from five to seven years old. They were all from Major Lackland to Mr. Hawkins. The substance of them was, that some one in the east had been inquiring of Major Lackland about a lost child and its parents, and that it was conjectured that the child might be Laura.

Evidently some of the letters were missing, for the name of the inquirer was not mentioned; there was a casual reference to "this handsome-featured aristocratic gentleman," as if the reader and the writer were accustomed to speak of him and knew who was meant.

In one letter the Major said he agreed with Mr. Hawkins that the inquirer seemed not altogether on the wrong track; but he also agreed that it would be best to keep quiet until more convincing developments were forthcoming.

Another letter said that "the poor soul broke completely down when he saw Laura's picture, and declared it must be she."

Still another said,

"He seems entirely alone in the world, and his heart is so wrapped up in this thing that I believe that if it proved a false hope, it would kill him; I have persuaded him to wait a little while and go west when I go."

Another letter had this paragraph in it:

"He is better one day and worse the next, and is out of his mind a good deal of the time. Lately his case has developed a something which is a wonder to the hired nurses, but which will not be much of a marvel to you if you have read medical philosophy much. It is this: his lost memory returns to him when he is delirious, and goes away again when he is himself—just as old Canada Joe used to talk the French *patois* of his boyhood in the delirium of typhus fever, though he could not do it when his mind was clear. Now this poor gentleman's memory has always broken down before he reached the explosion of the steamer; he could only remember starting up the river with his wife and child, and he had an idea that there was a race, but he was not certain; he could not name the boat he was on; there was a dead blank of a month or more that supplied not an item to his recollection. It was not for me to assist him, of course. But now in his delirium *it all comes out*: the names of the boats, every incident of the explosion, and likewise the details of his astonishing escape—that is, up to where, just as a yawl-boat was approaching him (he was clinging to the starboard wheel of the burning wreck at the time), a falling timber struck him on the head. But I will write out his wonderful escape in full to-morrow or next day. Of course the physicians will not

let me tell him now that our Laura is indeed his child—
that must come later, when his health is thoroughly restored. His case is not considered dangerous at all; he
will recover presently, the doctors say. But they insist
that he must travel a little when he gets well—they recommend a short sea voyage, and they say he can be persuaded to try it if we continue to keep him in ignorance
and promise to let him see L. as soon as he returns."

The letter that bore the latest date of all, contained this
clause:

"It is the most unaccountable thing in the world; the
mystery remains as impenetrable as ever; I have hunted
high and low for him, and inquired of everybody, but in
vain; all trace of him ends at that hotel in New York; I
never have seen or heard of him since, up to this day; he
could hardly have sailed, for his name does not appear
upon the books of any shipping office in New York or
Boston or Baltimore. How fortunate it seems, now, that
we kept this thing to ourselves; Laura still has a father in
you, and it is better for her that we drop this subject
here forever."

That was all. Random remarks here and there, being pieced
together gave Laura a vague impression of a man of fine presence, about forty-three or forty-five years of age, with dark
hair and eyes, and a slight limp in his walk—it was not stated
which leg was defective. And this indistinct shadow represented her father. She made an exhaustive search for the missing letters, but found none. They had probably been burned;
and she doubted not that the ones she had ferreted out would
have shared the same fate if Mr. Hawkins had not been a
dreamer, void of method, whose mind was perhaps in a state
of conflagration over some bright new speculation when he
received them.

She sat long, with the letters in her lap, thinking—and unconsciously freezing. She felt like a lost person who has traveled down a long lane in good hope of escape, and, just as the
night descends finds his progress barred by a bridgeless river
whose further shore, if it has one, is lost in the darkness. If

she could only have found these letters a month sooner! That was her thought. But now the dead had carried their secrets with them. A dreary melancholy settled down upon her. An undefined sense of injury crept into her heart. She grew very miserable.

She had just reached the romantic age—the age when there is a sad sweetness, a dismal comfort to a girl to find out that there is a mystery connected with her birth, which no other piece of good luck can afford. She had more than her rightful share of practical good sense, but still she was human; and to be human is to have one's little modicum of romance secreted away in one's composition. One never ceases to make a hero of one's self, (in private,) during life, but only alters the style of his heroism from time to time as the drifting years belittle certain gods of his admiration and raise up others in their stead that seem greater.

The recent wearing days and nights of watching, and the wasting grief that had possessed her, combined with the profound depression that naturally came with the reaction of idleness, made Laura peculiarly susceptible at this time to romantic impressions. She was a heroine, now, with a mysterious father somewhere. She could not really tell whether she wanted to find him and spoil it all or not; but still all the traditions of romance pointed to the making the attempt as the usual and necessary course to follow; therefore she would some day begin the search when opportunity should offer.

Now a former thought struck her—she would speak to Mrs. Hawkins. And naturally enough Mrs. Hawkins appeared on the stage at that moment.

She said she knew all—she knew that Laura had discovered the secret that Mr. Hawkins, the elder children, Col. Sellers and herself had kept so long and so faithfully; and she cried and said that now that troubles had begun they would never end; her daughter's love would wean itself away from her and her heart would break. Her grief so wrought upon Laura that the girl almost forgot her own troubles for the moment in her compassion for her mother's distress. Finally Mrs. Hawkins said:

"Speak to me, child—do not forsake me. Forget all this miserable talk. Say I am your mother!—I have loved you so long, and there is no other. I *am* your mother, in the sight of God, and nothing shall ever take you from me!"

All barriers fell, before this appeal. Laura put her arms about her mother's neck and said:

"You *are* my mother, and always shall be. We will be as we have always been; and neither this foolish talk nor any other thing shall part us or make us less to each other than we are this hour."

There was no longer any sense of separation or estrangement between them. Indeed their love seemed more perfect now than it had ever been before. By and by they went down stairs and sat by the fire and talked long and earnestly about Laura's history and the letters. But it transpired that Mrs. Hawkins had never known of this correspondence between her husband and Major Lackland. With his usual consideration for his wife, Mr. Hawkins had shielded her from the worry the matter would have caused her.

Laura went to bed at last with a mind that had gained largely in tranquility and had lost correspondingly in morbid romantic exaltation. She was pensive, the next day, and subdued; but that was not matter for remark, for she did not differ from the mournful friends about her in that respect. Clay and Washington were the same loving and admiring brothers now that they had always been. The great secret was new to some of the younger children, but their love suffered no change under the wonderful revelation.

It is barely possible that things might have presently settled down into their old rut and the mystery have lost the bulk of its romantic sublimity in Laura's eyes, if the village gossips could have quieted down. But they could not quiet down and they did not. Day after day they called at the house, ostensibly upon visits of condolence, and they pumped away at the mother and the children without seeming to know that their questionings were in bad taste. They meant no harm—they only wanted to know. Villagers always want to know.

The family fought shy of the questionings, and of course that was high testimony—"if the Duchess was respectably born, why didn't they come out and prove it?—why did they stick to that poor thin story about picking her up out of a steamboat explosion?"

Under this ceaseless persecution, Laura's morbid self-communing was renewed. At night the day's contribution of detraction, innuendo and malicious conjecture would be canvassed in her mind, and then she would drift into a course of thinking. As her thoughts ran on, the indignant tears would spring to her eyes, and she would spit out fierce little ejaculations at intervals. But finally she would grow calmer and say some comforting disdainful thing—something like this:

"But who are they?—Animals! What are their opinions to me? Let them talk—I will not stoop to be affected by it. I could hate——. Nonsense—nobody I care for or in any way respect is changed toward me, I fancy."

She may have supposed she was thinking of many individuals, but it was not so—she was thinking of only one. And her heart warmed somewhat, too, the while. One day a friend overheard a conversation like this:—and naturally came and told her all about it:

"Ned, they say you don't go there any more. How is that?"

"Well, I don't; but I tell you it's not because I don't want to and it's not because *I* think it is any matter who her father was or who he wasn't, either; it's only on account of this talk, talk, talk. I think she is a fine girl every way, and so would you if you knew her as well as I do; but you know how it is when a girl once gets talked about—it's all up with her—the world won't ever let her alone, after that."

The only comment Laura made upon this revelation, was:

"Then it appears that if this trouble had not occurred I could have had the happiness of Mr. Ned Thurston's serious attentions. He is well favored in person, and well liked, too, I believe, and comes of one of the first families of the village. He is prosperous, too, I hear; has been a doctor a year, now, and has had two patients—no, three, I think; yes, it *was* three. I attended their funerals. Well, other people have hoped and been disappointed; I am not alone in that. I wish you could stay to dinner, Maria—we are going to have sausages; and besides, I wanted to talk to you about Hawkeye and make you promise to come and see us when we are settled there."

But Maria could not stay. She had come to mingle romantic tears with Laura's over the lover's defection and had found

herself dealing with a heart that could not rise to an appreciation of affliction because its interest was all centred in
sausages.

But as soon as Maria was gone, Laura stamped her expressive foot and said:

"The coward! Are all books lies? I thought he would fly to
the front, and be brave and noble, and stand up for me
against all the world, and defy my enemies, and wither these
gossips with his scorn! Poor crawling thing, let him go. I *do*
begin to despise this world!"

She lapsed into thought. Presently she said:

"If the time ever comes, and I get a chance, Oh, I'll——"

She could not find a word that was strong enough, perhaps. By and by she said:

"Well, I am glad of it—I'm glad of it. I never cared anything for him anyway!"

And then, with small consistency, she cried a little, and patted her foot more indignantly than ever.

Chapter XI

ずら たぞあ もど へら く

TWO MONTHS had gone by and the Hawkins family were domiciled in Hawkeye. Washington was at work in the real estate office again, and was alternately in paradise or the other place just as it happened that Louise was gracious to him or seemingly indifferent—because indifference or preoccupation could mean nothing else than that she was thinking of some other young person. Col. Sellers had asked him several times, to dine with him, when he first returned to Hawkeye, but Washington, for no particular reason, had not accepted. No particular reason except one which he preferred to keep to himself—viz. that he could not bear to be away from Louise. It occurred to him, now, that the Colonel had not invited him lately—could he be offended? He resolved to go that very day, and give the Colonel a pleasant surprise. It was a good idea; especially as Louise had absented herself from breakfast that morning, and torn his heart; he would tear hers, now, and let her see how it felt.

The Sellers family were just starting to dinner when Washington burst upon them with his surprise. For an instant the Colonel looked nonplussed, and just a bit uncomfortable; and Mrs. Sellers looked actually distressed; but the next moment the head of the house was himself again, and exclaimed:

"All right, my boy, all right—always glad to see you—always glad to hear your voice and take you by the hand. Don't wait for special invitations—that's all nonsense among friends. Just come whenever you can, and come as often as you can—the oftener the better. You can't please us any better than that, Washington; the little woman will tell you so herself. We don't pretend to style. Plain folks, you know—plain folks. Just a plain family dinner, but such as it is, our friends are *always* welcome, I reckon you know that yourself, Washington.

Run along, children, run along; Lafayette,* stand off the cat's
tail, child, can't you see what you're doing?—Come, come,
come, Roderick Dhu, it isn't nice for little boys to hang onto
young gentlemen's coat tails—but never mind him, Washington, he's full of spirits and don't mean any harm. Children
will be children, you know. Take the chair next to Mrs. Sellers, Washington—tut, tut, Marie Antoinette, let your brother
have the fork if he wants it, you are bigger than he is."

Washington contemplated the banquet, and wondered if he
were in his right mind. Was this the plain family dinner? And
was it all present? It was soon apparent that this was indeed the
dinner: it was all on the table: it consisted of abundance of
clear, fresh water, and a basin of raw turnips—nothing more.

Washington stole a glance at Mrs. Sellers's face, and would
have given the world, the next moment, if he could have
spared her that. The poor woman's face was crimson, and the
tears stood in her eyes. Washington did not know what to do.
He wished he had never come there and spied out this cruel
poverty and brought pain to that poor little lady's heart and
shame to her cheek; but he was there, and there was no escape. Col. Sellers hitched back his coat sleeves airily from his
wrists as who should say "*Now* for solid enjoyment!" seized a
fork, flourished it and began to harpoon turnips and deposit
them in the plates before him:

"Let me help you, Washington—Lafayette pass this plate to
Washington—ah, well, well, my boy, things are looking pretty
bright, now, *I* tell you. Speculation—my! the whole atmosphere's full of money. I wouldn't take three fortunes for one
little operation I've got on hand now—have anything from
the casters? No? Well, you're right, you're right. Some people
like mustard with turnips, but—now there was Baron Poniatowski—Lord, but that man did know how to live!—true

---

*In those old days the average man called his children after his most
revered literary and historical idols; consequently there was hardly a family, at
least in the West, but had a Washington in it—and also a Lafayette, a
Franklin, and six or eight sounding names from Byron, Scott, and the Bible,
if the offspring held out. To visit such a family, was to find one's self confronted by a congress made up of representatives of the imperial myths and
the majestic dead of all the ages. There was something thrilling about it, to a
stranger, not to say awe inspiring.

Russian you know, Russian to the back bone; I say to my wife, give me a Russian every time, for a table comrade. The Baron used to say, 'Take mustard, Sellers, try the mustard,—a man *can't* know what turnips are in perfection without mustard,' but I always said, 'No, Baron, I'm a plain man, and I want my food plain—none of your embellishments for Eschol Sellers— no made dishes for me! And it's the best way—high living kills more than it cures in this world, you can rest assured of that.—Yes indeed, Washington, I've got one little operation on hand that—take some more water—help yourself, won't you?—help yourself, there's plenty of it.—You'll find it pretty good, I guess. How does that fruit strike you?"

Washington said he did not know that he had ever tasted better. He did not add that he detested turnips even when they were cooked—loathed them in their natural state. No, he kept this to himself, and praised the turnips to the peril of his soul.

"I thought you'd like them. Examine them—examine them—they'll bear it. See how perfectly firm and juicy they are—they can't start any like them in this part of the country, I can tell you. These are from New Jersey—I imported them myself. They cost like sin, too; but lord bless me, I go in for having the best of a thing, even if it does cost a little more— it's the best economy, in the long run. These are the Early Malcolm—it's a turnip that can't be produced except in just one orchard, and the supply never is up to the demand. Take some more water, Washington—you can't drink too much water with fruit—all the doctors say that. The plague can't come where this article is, my boy!"

"Plague? What plague?"

"What plague, indeed? Why the Asiatic plague that nearly depopulated London a couple of centuries ago."

"But how does that concern us? There is no plague here, I reckon."

"Sh! I've let it out! Well, never mind—just keep it to your-self. Perhaps I oughtn't said anything, but its *bound* to come out sooner or later, so what is the odds? Old McDowells wouldn't like me to—to—bother it all, I'll just tell the whole thing and let it go. You see, I've been down to St. Louis, and I happened to run across old Dr. McDowells—thinks the world of me, does the doctor. He's a man that keeps himself to himself, and well he may, for he knows that he's got a reputation that covers the whole earth—he won't condescend to open himself out to many people, but lord bless you, he and I are just like brothers; he won't let me go to a hotel when I'm in the city—says I'm the only man that's company to him, and I don't know but there's some truth in it, too, because although I never like to glorify myself and make a great to-do over what I am or what I can do or what I know, I don't mind saying here among friends that I *am* better read up in most sciences, maybe, than the general run of professional men in these days. Well, the other day he let me into a little secret, strictly on the quiet, about this matter of the plague.

"You see it's booming right along in our direction—follows the Gulf Stream, you know, just as all those epidemics do,—and within three months it will be just waltzing through this land like a whirlwind! And whoever it touches can make his will and contract for the funeral. Well you can't *cure* it, you know, but you can prevent it. How? Turnips! that's it! Turnips and water! Nothing like it in the world, old McDowells says, just fill yourself up two or three times a day, and you can snap your fingers at the plague. Sh!—keep mum, but just you confine yourself to that diet and you're all right. I wouldn't have old McDowells know that I told about it for anything—he never would speak to me again. Take some more water, Washington—the more water you drink, the better. Here, let me give you some more of the turnips. No, no, no, now, I insist. There, now. Absorb those. They're mighty sustaining—brim full of nutriment—all the medical books say so. Just eat from four to seven good-sized turnips at a meal, and drink from a pint and a half to a quart of water, and then just sit around a couple of hours and let them ferment. You'll feel like a fighting cock next day."

Fifteen or twenty minutes later the Colonel's tongue was still chattering away—he had piled up several future fortunes out of several incipient "operations" which he had blundered into within the past week, and was now soaring along through some brilliant expectations born of late promising experiments upon the lacking ingredient of the eye-water.

And at such a time Washington ought to have been a rapt and enthusiastic listener, but he was not, for two matters disturbed his mind and distracted his attention. One was, that he discovered, to his confusion and shame, that in allowing himself to be helped a second time to the turnips, he had robbed those hungry children. He had not needed the dreadful "fruit," and had not wanted it; and when he saw the pathetic sorrow in their faces when they asked for more and there was no more to give them, he hated himself for his stupidity and pitied the famishing young things with all his heart. The other matter that disturbed him was the dire inflation that had begun in his stomach. It grew and grew, it became more and more insupportable. Evidently the turnips were "fermenting." He forced himself to sit still as long as he could, but his anguish conquered him at last.

He rose in the midst of the Colonel's talk and excused himself on the plea of a previous engagement. The Colonel followed him to the door, promising over and over again that he would use his influence to get some of the Early Malcolms for him, and insisting that he should not be such a stranger but come and take pot-luck with him every chance he got. Washington was glad enough to get away and feel free again. He immediately bent his steps toward home.

In bed he passed an hour that threatened to turn his hair gray, and then a blessed calm settled down upon him that filled his heart with gratitude. Weak and languid, he made shift to turn himself about and seek rest and sleep; and as his soul hovered upon the brink of unconsciousness, he heaved a long, deep sigh, and said to himself that in his heart he had cursed the Colonel's preventive of rheumatism, before, and now *let* the plague come if it must—he was done with preventives; if ever any man beguiled him with turnips and water again, let him die the death.

If he dreamed at all that night, no gossiping spirit disturbed his visions to whisper in his ear of certain matters just then in bud in the East, more than a thousand miles away that after the lapse of a few years would develop influences which would profoundly affect the fate and fortunes of the Hawkins family.

Chapter XII

Todtenb. 141. 17, 4.

"O H, it's easy enough to make a fortune," Henry said.
     "It seems to be easier than it is, I begin to think,"
replied Philip.

"Well, why don't you go into something? You'll never dig
it out of the Astor Library."

If there be any place and time in the world where and when
it seems easy to "go into something" it is in Broadway on a
spring morning, when one is walking city-ward, and has before him the long lines of palace-shops with an occasional
spire seen through the soft haze that lies over the lower town,
and hears the roar and hum of its multitudinous traffic.

To the young American, here or elsewhere, the paths to
fortune are innumerable and all open; there is invitation in
the air and success in all his wide horizon. He is embarrassed
which to choose, and is not unlikely to waste years in dallying
with his chances, before giving himself to the serious tug and
strain of a single object. He has no traditions to bind him or
guide him, and his impulse is to break away from the occupation his father has followed, and make a new way for himself.

Philip Sterling used to say that if he should seriously set
himself for ten years to any one of the dozen projects that
were in his brain, he felt that he could be a rich man. He
wanted to be rich, he had a sincere desire for a fortune, but
for some unaccountable reason he hesitated about addressing
himself to the narrow work of getting it. He never walked
Broadway, a part of its tide of abundant shifting life, without
feeling something of the flush of wealth, and unconsciously
taking the elastic step of one well-to-do in this prosperous
world.

Especially at night in the crowded theatre—Philip was too
young to remember the old Chambers' Street box, where the

serious Burton led his hilarious and pagan crew—in the intervals of the screaming comedy, when the orchestra scraped and grunted and tooted its dissolute tunes, the world seemed full of opportunities to Philip, and his heart exulted with a conscious ability to take any of its prizes he chose to pluck.

Perhaps it was the swimming ease of the acting on the stage, where virtue had its reward in three easy acts, perhaps it was the excessive light of the house, or the music, or the buzz of the excited talk between acts, perhaps it was youth which believed everything, but for some reason while Philip was at the theatre he had the utmost confidence in life and his ready victory in it.

Delightful illusion of paint and tinsel and silk attire; of cheap sentiment and high and mighty dialogue! Will there not always be rosin enough for the squeaking fiddle-bow? Do we not all like the maudlin hero, who is sneaking round the right entrance, in wait to steal the pretty wife of his rich and tyrannical neighbor from the paste-board cottage at the left entrance? and when he advances down to the foot-lights and defiantly informs the audience that, "he who lays his hand on a woman except in the way of kindness," do we not all applaud so as to drown the rest of the sentence?

Philip never was fortunate enough to hear what would become of a man who should lay his hand on a woman with the exception named; but he learned afterwards that the woman who lays her hand on a man, without any exception whatsoever, is always acquitted by the jury.

The fact was, though Philip Sterling did not know it, that he wanted several other things quite as much as he wanted wealth. The modest fellow would have liked fame thrust upon him for some worthy achievement; it might be for a book, or for the skillful management of some great newspaper, or for some daring expedition like that of Lt. Strain or Dr. Kane. He was unable to decide exactly what it should be. Sometimes he thought he would like to stand in a conspicuous pulpit and humbly preach the gospel of repentance; and it even crossed his mind that it would be noble to give himself to a missionary life to some benighted region, where the date-palm grows, and the nightingale's voice is in tune, and the bulbul sings on the off nights. If he were good enough he would attach himself to that company of young men in the Theological Seminary, who were seeing New York life in preparation for the ministry.

Philip was a New England boy and had graduated at Yale; he had not carried off with him all the learning of that venerable institution, but he knew some things that were not in the regular course of study. A very good use of the English language and considerable knowledge of its literature was one of them; he could sing a song very well, not in time to be sure, but with enthusiasm; he could make a magnetic speech at a moment's notice in the class room, the debating society, or upon any fence or dry-goods box that was convenient; he could lift himself by one arm, and do the giant swing in the gymnasium; he could strike out from his left shoulder; he could handle an oar like a professional and pull stroke in a winning race. Philip had a good appetite, a sunny temper, and a clear hearty laugh. He had brown hair, hazel eyes set wide apart, a broad but not high forehead, and a fresh winning face. He was six feet high, with broad shoulders, long legs and a swinging gait; one of those loose-jointed, capable fellows, who saunter into the world with a free air and usually make a stir in whatever company they enter.

After he left college Philip took the advice of friends and read law. Law seemed to him well enough as a science, but he never could discover a practical case where it appeared to him worth while to go to law, and all the clients who stopped with this new clerk in the ante-room of the law office where he was writing, Philip invariably advised to settle—no matter how, but settle—greatly to the disgust of his employer, who knew that justice between man and man could only be attained by the recognized processes, with the attendant fees. Besides Philip hated the copying of pleadings, and he was certain that a life of "whereases" and "aforesaids" and whipping the devil round the stump, would be intolerable.

His pen therefore, and whereas, and not as aforesaid, strayed off into other scribbling. In an unfortunate hour, he had two or three papers accepted by first-class magazines, at three dollars the printed page, and, behold, his vocation was open to him. He would make his mark in literature. Life has no moment so sweet as that in which a young man believes himself called into the immortal ranks of the masters of literature. It is such a noble ambition, that it is a pity it has usually such a shallow foundation.

At the time of this history, Philip had gone to New York for a career. With his talent he thought he should have little difficulty in getting an editorial position upon a metropolitan newspaper; not that he knew anything about newspaper work, or had the least idea of journalism; he knew he was not fitted for the technicalities of the subordinate departments, but he could write leaders with perfect ease, he was sure. The drudgery of the newspaper office was too distasteful, and besides it would be beneath the dignity of a graduate and a successful magazine writer. He wanted to begin at the top of the ladder.

To his surprise he found that every situation in the editorial department of the journals was full, always had been full, was always likely to be full. It seemed to him that the newspaper managers didn't want genius, but mere plodding and grubbing. Philip therefore read diligently in the Astor library, planned literary works that should compel attention, and nursed his genius. He had no friend wise enough to tell him to step into the Dorking Convention, then in session, make a sketch of the men and women on the platform, and take it to the editor of the *Daily Grapevine*, and see what he could get a line for it.

One day he had an offer from some country friends, who believed in him, to take charge of a provincial daily newspaper, and he went to consult Mr. Gringo—Gringo who years ago managed the *Atlas*—about taking the situation.

"Take it of course," says Gringo, take anything that offers, why not?"

"But they want me to make it an opposition paper."

"Well, make it that. That party is going to succeed, it's going to elect the next president."

"I don't believe it," said Philip, stoutly, "it's wrong in principle, and it ought not to succeed, but I don't see how I can go for a thing I don't believe in."

"O, very well," said Gringo, turning away with a shade of contempt, "you'll find if you are going into literature and newspaper work that you can't afford a conscience like that."

But Philip did afford it, and he wrote, thanking his friends, and declining because he said the political scheme would fail, and ought to fail. And he went back to his books and to his waiting for an opening large enough for his dignified entrance into the literary world.

It was in this time of rather impatient waiting that Philip was one morning walking down Broadway with Henry Brierly. He frequently accompanied Henry part way down town to what the latter called his office in Broad Street, to which he went, or pretended to go, with regularity every day. It was evident to the most casual acquaintance that he was a man of affairs, and that his time was engrossed in the largest sort of operations, about which there was a mysterious air. His liability to be suddenly summoned to Washington, or Boston or Montreal or even to Liverpool was always imminent. He never was so summoned, but none of his acquaintances would have been surprised to hear any day that he had gone to Panama or Peoria, or to hear from him that he had bought the Bank of Commerce.

The two were intimate at that time,—they had been class-mates—and saw a great deal of each other. Indeed, they lived together in Ninth Street, in a boarding-house there, which had the honor of lodging and partially feeding several other young fellows of like kidney, who have since gone their several ways into fame or into obscurity.

It was during the morning walk to which reference has been made that Henry Brierly suddenly said, "Philip, how would you like to go to St. Jo?"

"I think I should like it of all things," replied Philip, with some hesitation, "but what for."

"Oh, it's a big operation. We are going, a lot of us, railroad men, engineers, contractors. You know my uncle is a great railroad man. I've no doubt I can get you a chance to go if you'll go."

"But in what capacity would I go?"

"Well, I'm going as an engineer. You can go as one."

"I don't know an engine from a coal cart."

"Field engineer, civil engineer. You can begin by carrying a rod, and putting down the figures. It's easy enough. I'll show you about that. We'll get Trautwine and some of those books."

"Yes, but what is it for, what is it all about?"

"Why don't you see? We lay out a line, spot the good land, enter it up, know where the stations are to be, spot them, buy lots; there's heaps of money in it. We wouldn't engineer long."

"When do you go?" was Philip's next question, after some moments of silence.

"To-morrow. Is that too soon?"

"No, it's not too soon. I've been ready to go anywhere for six months. The fact is, Henry, that I'm about tired of trying to force myself into things, and am quite willing to try floating with the stream for a while, and see where I will land. This seems like a providential call; it's sudden enough."

The two young men who were by this time full of the adventure, went down to the Wall street office of Henry's uncle and had a talk with that wily operator. The uncle knew Philip very well, and was pleased with his frank enthusiasm, and willing enough to give him a trial in the western venture. It was settled therefore, in the prompt way in which things are settled in New York, that they would start with the rest of the company next morning for the west.

On the way up town these adventurers bought books on engineering, and suits of India-rubber, which they supposed they would need in a new and probably damp country, and many other things which nobody ever needed anywhere.

The night was spent in packing up and writing letters, for Philip would not take such an important step without informing his friends. If they disapprove, thought he, I've done my duty by letting them know. Happy youth, that is ready to pack its valise, and start for Cathay on an hour's notice.

"By the way," calls out Philip from his bed-room, to Henry, "where is St. Jo.?"

"Why, it's in Missouri somewhere, on the frontier I think. We'll get a map."

"Never mind the map. We will find the place itself. I was afraid it was nearer home."

Philip wrote a long letter, first of all, to his mother, full of love and glowing anticipations of his new opening. He wouldn't bother her with business details, but he hoped that the day was not far off when she would see him return, with a moderate fortune, and something to add to the comfort of her advancing years.

To his uncle he said that he had made an arrangement with some New York capitalists to go to Missouri, in a land and railroad operation, which would at least give him a knowledge of the world and not unlikely offer him a business opening. He knew his uncle would be glad to hear that he had at last turned his thoughts to a practical matter.

It was to Ruth Bolton that Philip wrote last. He might never see her again; he went to seek his fortune. He well knew the perils of the frontier, the savage state of society, the lurking Indians and the dangers of fever. But there was no real danger to a person who took care of himself. Might he write to her often and tell her of his life. If he returned with a fortune, perhaps and perhaps. If he was unsuccessful, or if he never returned—perhaps it would be as well. No time or distance, however, would ever lessen his interest in her. He would say good-night, but not good-bye.

In the soft beginning of a Spring morning, long before New York had breakfasted, while yet the air of expectation hung about the wharves of the metropolis, our young adventurers made their way to the Jersey City railway station of the Erie road, to begin the long, swinging, crooked journey, over what a writer of a former day called a causeway of cracked rails and cows, to the West.

Chapter XIII

What ever to say he toke in his entente,
his langage was so fayer & pertynante,
yt semeth vnto manys herying
not only the worde, but veryly the thyng.
Caxton's Book of Curtesye.

I N the party of which our travelers found themselves members, was Duff Brown, the great railroad contractor, and
subsequently a well-known member of congress; a bluff, jovial
Bost'n man, thick-set, close shaven, with a heavy jaw and a
low forehead—a very pleasant man if you were not in his way.
He had government contracts also, custom houses and dry
docks, from Portland to New Orleans, and managed to get
out of congress, in appropriations, about weight for weight of
gold for the stone furnished.

Associated with him, and also of this party, was Rodney
Schaick, a sleek New York broker, a man as prominent in the
church as in the stock exchange, dainty in his dress, smooth
of speech, the necessary complement of Duff Brown in any
enterprise that needed assurance and adroitness.

It would be difficult to find a pleasanter traveling party, one
that shook off more readily the artificial restraints of Puritanic
strictness, and took the world with good-natured allowance.
Money was plenty for every attainable luxury, and there
seemed to be no doubt that its supply would continue, and
that fortunes were about to be made without a great deal of
toil. Even Philip soon caught the prevailing spirit; Harry did
not need any inoculation, he always talked in six figures. It
was as natural for the dear boy to be rich as it is for most
people to be poor.

The elders of the party were not long in discovering the
fact, which almost all travelers to the west soon find out, that
the water was poor. It must have been by a lucky premonition
of this that they all had brandy flasks with which to qualify the
water of the country; and it was no doubt from an uneasy
feeling of the danger of being poisoned that they kept experimenting, mixing a little of the dangerous and changing fluid,

as they passed along, with the contents of the flasks, thus saving their lives hour by hour. Philip learned afterwards that temperance and the strict observance of Sunday and a certain gravity of deportment are geographical habits, which people do not usually carry with them away from home.

Our travelers stopped in Chicago long enough to see that they could make their fortunes there in two week's time, but it did not seem worth while; the west was more attractive; the further one went the wider the opportunities opened. They took railroad to Alton and the steamboat from there to St. Louis, for the change and to have a glimpse of the river.

"Isn't this jolly?" cried Henry, dancing out of the barber's room, and coming down the deck with a one, two, three step, shaven, curled and perfumed after his usual exquisite fashion.

"What's jolly?" asked Philip, looking out upon the dreary and monotonous waste through which the shaking steamboat was coughing its way.

"Why, the whole thing; it's immense I can tell you. I wouldn't give *that* to be guaranteed a hundred thousand cold cash in a year's time."

"Where's Mr. Brown?"

"He is in the saloon, playing poker with Schaick, and that long haired party with the striped trousers, who scrambled aboard when the stage plank was half hauled in, and the big Delegate to Congress from out west."

"That's a fine looking fellow, that delegate, with his glossy black whiskers; looks like a Washington man; I shouldn't think he'd be at poker."

"Oh, its only five cent ante, just to make it interesting, the Delegate said."

"But I shouldn't think a representative in Congress would play poker any way in a public steamboat."

"Nonsense, you've got to pass the time. I tried a hand myself, but those old fellows are too many for me. The Delegate knows all the points. I'd bet a hundred dollars he will ante his way right into the United States Senate when his territory comes in. He's got the cheek for it."

"He has the grave and thoughtful manner of expectoration of a public man, for one thing," added Philip.

"Harry," said Philip, after a pause, "what have you got on those big boots for; do you expect to wade ashore?"

"I'm breaking 'em in."

The fact was Harry had got himself up in what he thought a proper costume for a new country, and was in appearance a sort of compromise between a dandy of Broadway and a backwoodsman. Harry, with blue eyes, fresh complexion, silken whiskers and curly chestnut hair, was as handsome as a fashion plate. He wore this morning a soft hat, a short cut-away coat, an open vest displaying immaculate linen, a leathern belt round his waist, and top-boots of soft leather, well polished, that came above his knees and required a string attached to his belt to keep them up. The light hearted fellow gloried in these shining encasements of his well shaped legs, and told Philip that they were a perfect protection against prairie rattle-snakes, which never strike above the knee.

The landscape still wore an almost wintry appearance when our travelers left Chicago. It was a genial spring day when they landed at St. Louis; the birds were singing, the blossoms of peach trees in city garden plots, made the air sweet, and in the roar and tumult on the long river levee they found an excitement that accorded with their own hopeful anticipations.

The party went to the Southern Hotel, where the great Duff Brown was very well known, and indeed was a man of so much importance that even the office clerk was respectful to him. He might have respected in him also a certain vulgar swagger and insolence of money, which the clerk greatly admired.

The young fellows liked the house and liked the city; it seemed to them a mighty free and hospitable town. Coming from the East they were struck with many peculiarities. Everybody smoked in the streets, for one thing, they noticed; everybody "took a drink" in an open manner whenever he wished to do so or was asked, as if the habit needed no concealment or apology. In the evening when they walked about they found people sitting on the door-steps of their dwellings, in a manner not usual in a northern city; in front of some of the hotels and saloons the side walks were filled with chairs and benches—Paris fashion, said Harry—upon which people lounged in these warm spring evenings, smoking, always smoking; and the clink of glasses and of billiard balls was in the air. It was delightful.

Harry at once found on landing that his back-woods custom would not be needed in St. Louis, and that, in fact, he had need of all the resources of his wardrobe to keep even with the young swells of the town. But this did not much matter, for Harry was always superior to his clothes. As they were likely to be detained some time in the city, Harry told Philip that he was going to improve his time. And he did. It was an encouragement to any industrious man to see this young fellow rise, carefully dress himself, eat his breakfast deliberately, smoke his cigar tranquilly, and then repair to his room, to what he called his work, with a grave and occupied manner, but with perfect cheerfulness.

Harry would take off his coat, remove his cravat, roll up his shirt-sleeves, give his curly hair the right touch before the glass, get out his book on engineering, his boxes of instruments, his drawing-paper, his profile paper, open the book of logarithms, mix his India ink, sharpen his pencils, light a cigar, and sit down at the table to "lay out a line," with the most grave notion that he was mastering the details of engineering. He would spend half a day in these preparations without ever working out a problem or having the faintest conception of the use of lines or logarithms. And when he had finished, he had the most cheerful confidence that he had done a good day's work.

It made no difference, however, whether Harry was in his room in a hotel or in a tent, Philip soon found, he was just the same. In camp he would get himself up in the most elaborate toilet at his command, polish his long boots to the top, lay out his work before him, and spend an hour or longer, if anybody was looking at him, humming airs, knitting his brows, and "working" at engineering; and if a crowd of gaping rustics were looking on all the while it was perfectly satisfactory to him.

"You see," he says to Philip one morning at the hotel when he was thus engaged, "I want to get the theory of this thing, so that I can have a check on the engineers."

"I thought you were going to be an engineer yourself," queried Philip.

"Not many times, if the court knows herself. There's better game. Brown and Schaick have, or will have, the control for the whole line of the Salt Lick Pacific Extension, forty thousand dollars a mile over the prairie, with extra for hard-pan— and it'll be pretty much all hard-pan I can tell you; besides every alternate section of land on this line. There's millions in the job. I'm to have the sub-contract for the first fifty miles, and you can bet it's a soft thing."

"I'll tell you what you do, Philip," continued Harry, in a burst of generosity, "if I don't get you into my contract, you'll be with the engineers, and you just stick a stake at the first ground marked for a dêpot, buy the land of the farmer before he knows where the dêpot will be, and we'll turn a hundred or so on that. I'll advance the money for the payments, and you can sell the lots. Schaick is going to let me have ten thousand just for a flyer in such operations."

"But that's a good deal of money."

"Wait till you are used to handling money. I didn't come out here for a bagatelle. My uncle wanted me to stay East and go in on the Mobile custom house, work up the Washington end of it; he said there was a fortune in it for a smart young fellow, but I preferred to take the chances out here. Did I tell you I had an offer from Bobbett and Fanshaw to go into their office as confidential clerk on a salary of ten thousand?"

"Why didn't you take it?" asked Philip, to whom a salary of two thousand would have seemed wealth, before he started on this journey.

"Take it? I'd rather operate on my own hook," said Harry, in his most airy manner.

A few evenings after their arrival at the Southern, Philip and Harry made the acquaintance of a very agreeable gentleman, whom they had frequently seen before about the hotel corridors, and passed a casual word with. He had the air of a man of business, and was evidently a person of importance.

The precipitating of this casual intercourse into the more substantial form of an acquaintanceship was the work of the gentleman himself, and occurred in this wise. Meeting the two friends in the lobby one evening, he asked them to give him the time, and added:

"Excuse me, gentlemen—strangers in St. Louis? Ah, yes—yes. From the East, perhaps? Ah, just so, just so. Eastern born myself—Virginia. Sellers is my name—Eschol Sellers. Ah—by the way—New York, did you say? That reminds me; just met some gentlemen from your State a week or two ago—very prominent gentlemen—in public life they are; you must know them, without doubt. Let me see—let me see. Curious those names have escaped me. I know they were from your State, because I remember afterward my old friend Governor Shackleby said to me—fine man, is the Governor—one of the finest men our country has produced—said he, 'Colonel, how did you like those New York gentlemen?—not many such men in the world, Colonel Sellers,' said the Governor—yes, it was New York he said—I remember it distinctly. I *can't* recall those names, somehow. But no matter. Stopping here, gentlemen—stopping at the Southern?"

In shaping their reply in their minds, the title "Mr." had a place in it; but when their turn had arrived to speak, the title "Colonel" came from their lips instead.

They said yes, they were abiding at the Southern, and thought it a very good house.

"Yes, yes, the Southern is fair. I myself go to the Planter's, old, aristocratic house. We Southern gentlemen don't change our ways, you know. I always make it my home there when I run down from Hawkeye—my plantation is in Hawkeye, a little up in the country. You should know the Planter's."

Philip and Harry both said they should like to see a hotel that had been so famous in its day—a cheerful hostelrie, Philip said it must have been where duels were fought there across the dining-room table.

"You may believe it, sir, an uncommonly pleasant lodging. Shall we walk?"

And the three strolled along the streets, the Colonel talking all the way in the most liberal and friendly manner, and with a frank open-heartedness that inspired confidence.

"Yes, born East myself, raised all along, know the West—a great country, gentlemen. The place for a young fellow of spirit to pick up a fortune, simply pick it up, it's lying round loose here. Not a day that I don't put aside an opportunity, too busy to look into it. Management of my own property takes my time. First visit? Looking for an opening?"

"Yes, looking around," replied Harry.

"Ah, here we are. You'd rather sit here in front than go to my apartments? So had I. An opening, eh?"

The Colonel's eyes twinkled. "Ah, just so. The whole country is opening up, all we want is capital to develope it. Slap down the rails and bring the land into market. The richest land on God Almighty's footstool is lying right out there. If I had my capital free I could plant it for millions."

"I suppose your capital is largely in your plantation?" asked Philip.

"Well, partly, sir, partly. I'm down here now with reference to a little operation—a little side thing merely. By the way gentlemen, excuse the liberty, but it's about my usual time"—

The Colonel paused, but as no movement of his acquaintances followed this plain remark, he added, in an explanatory manner,

"I'm rather particular about the exact time—have to be in this climate."

Even this open declaration of his hospitable intention not being understood the Colonel politely said,

"Gentlemen, will you take something?"

Col. Sellers led the way to a saloon on Fourth street under the hotel, and the young gentlemen fell into the custom of the country.

"Not that," said the Colonel to the bar-keeper, who shoved along the counter a bottle of apparently corn-whiskey, as if he had done it before on the same order; "not that," with a wave of the hand. "That Otard if you please. Yes. Never take an inferior liquor, gentlemen, not in the evening, in this climate. There. That's the stuff. My respects!"

The hospitable gentleman, having disposed of his liquor, remarking that it was not quite the thing—"when a man has his own cellar to go to, he is apt to get a little fastidious about his liquors"—called for cigars. But the brand offered did not suit him; he motioned the box away, and asked for some particular Havana's, those in separate wrappers.

"I always smoke this sort, gentlemen; they are a little more expensive, but you'll learn, in this climate, that you'd better not economize on poor cigars."

Having imparted this valuable piece of information, the Colonel lighted the fragrant cigar with satisfaction, and then carelessly put his fingers into his right vest pocket. That movement being without result, with a shade of disappointment on his face, he felt in his left vest pocket. Not finding anything there, he looked up with a serious and annoyed air, anxiously slapped his right pantaloon's pocket, and then his left, and exclaimed,

"By George, that's annoying. By George, that's mortifying. Never had anything of that kind happen to me before. I've left my pocket-book. Hold! Here's a bill, after all. No, thunder, it's a receipt."

"Allow me," said Philip, seeing how seriously the Colonel was annoyed, and taking out his purse.

The Colonel protested he couldn't think of it, and muttered something to the bar-keeper about "hanging it up," but the vender of exhilaration made no sign, and Philip had the privilege of paying the costly shot; Col. Sellers profusely apologizing and claiming the right "next time, next time."

As soon as Eschol Sellers had bade his friends good night and seen them depart, he did not retire to apartments in the Planter's, but took his way to his lodgings with a friend in a distant part of the city.

Chapter XIV

Pulchra duos inter sita stat Philadelphia rivos;
    Inter quos duo sunt millia longa viæ.
Delawar his major, Sculkil minor ille vocatur;
    Indis et Suevis notus uterque diu.
Hic plateas mensor spatiis delineat æquis,
    Et domui recto est ordine juncta domus.
T. Makin.

    Vergin era fra lor di già matura
      Verginità, d'alti pensieri e regi,
    D'alta beltà; ma sua beltà non cura,
      O tanta sol, quant' onestà sen fregi.
Tasso.

THE LETTER that Philip Sterling wrote to Ruth Bolton, on the evening of setting out to seek his fortune in the west, found that young lady in her own father's house in Philadelphia. It was one of the pleasantest of the many charming suburban houses in that hospitable city, which is territorially one of the largest cities in the world, and only prevented from becoming the convenient metropolis of the country by the intrusive strip of Camden and Amboy sand which shuts it off from the Atlantic ocean. It is a city of steady thrift, the arms of which might well be the deliberate but delicious terrapin that imparts such a royal flavor to its feasts.

It was a spring morning, and perhaps it was the influence of it that made Ruth a little restless, satisfied neither with the out-doors nor the in-doors. Her sisters had gone to the city to show some country visitors Independence Hall, Girard College and Fairmount Water Works and Park, four objects which Americans cannot die peacefully, even in Naples, without having seen. But Ruth confessed that she was tired of them, and also of the Mint. She was tired of other things. She tried this morning an air or two upon the piano, sang a simple song in a sweet, but slightly metallic voice, and then seating herself by the open window, read Philip's letter.

Was she thinking about Philip, as she gazed across the fresh lawn over the tree tops to the Chelton Hills, or of that world which his entrance into her tradition-bound life had been one of the means of opening to her? Whatever she thought, she was not idly musing, as one might see by the expression of her face. After a time she took up a book; it was a medical work, and to all appearance about as interesting to a girl of eighteen as the statutes at large; but her face was soon aglow over its pages, and she was so absorbed in it that she did not notice the entrance of her mother at the open door.

"Ruth?"

"Well, mother," said the young student, looking up, with a shade of impatience.

"I wanted to talk with thee a little about thy plans."

"Mother, thee knows I couldn't stand it at Westfield; the school stifled me, it's a place to turn young people into dried fruit."

"I know," said Margaret Bolton, with a half anxious smile, "thee chafes against all the ways of Friends, but what will thee do? Why is thee so discontented?"

"If I must say it, mother, I want to go away, and get out of this dead level."

With a look half of pain and half of pity, her mother answered, "I am sure thee is little interfered with; thee dresses as thee will, and goes where thee pleases, to any church thee likes, and thee has music. I had a visit yesterday from the society's committee by way of discipline, because we have a piano in the house, which is against the rules."

"I hope thee told the elders that father and I are responsible for the piano, and that, much as thee loves music, thee is never in the room when it is played. Fortunately father is already out of meeting, so they can't discipline him. I heard father tell cousin Abner that he was whipped so often for whistling when he was a boy that he was determined to have what compensation he could get now."

"Thy ways greatly try me, Ruth, and all thy relations. I desire thy happiness first of all, but thee is starting out on a dangerous path. Is thy father willing thee should go away to a school of the world's people?"

"I have not asked him," Ruth replied with a look that might imply that she was one of those determined little bodies who first made up her own mind and then compelled others to make up theirs in accordance with hers.

"And when thee has got the education thee wants, and lost all relish for the society of thy friends and the ways of thy ancestors, what then?"

Ruth turned square round to her mother, and with an impassive face and not the slightest change of tone, said,

"Mother, I'm going to study medicine?"

Margaret Bolton almost lost for a moment her habitual placidity.

"Thee, study medicine! A slight frail girl like thee, study medicine! Does thee think thee could stand it six months? And the lectures, and the dissecting rooms, has thee thought of the dissecting rooms?"

"Mother," said Ruth calmly, "I have thought it all over. I know I can go through the whole, clinics, dissecting room and all. Does thee think I lack nerve? What is there to fear in a person dead more than in a person living?"

"But thy health and strength, child; thee can never stand the severe application. And, besides, suppose thee does learn medicine?"

"I will practice it."

"Here?"

"Here."

"Where thee and thy family are known?"

"If I can get patients."

"I hope at least, Ruth, thee will let us know when thee opens an office," said her mother, with an approach to sarcasm that she rarely indulged in, as she rose and left the room.

Ruth sat quite still for a time, with face intent and flushed. It was out now. She had begun her open battle.

The sight-seers returned in high spirits from the city. Was there any building in Greece to compare with Girard College, was there ever such a magnificent pile of stone devised for the shelter of poor orphans? Think of the stone shingles of the roof eight inches thick! Ruth asked the enthusiasts if they would like to live in such a sounding mausoleum, with its great halls and echoing rooms, and no comfortable place in it for the accommodation of any body? If they were orphans, would they like to be brought up in a Grecian temple?

And then there was Broad street! Wasn't it the broadest and the longest street in the world? There certainly was no end to it, and even Ruth was Philadelphian enough to believe that a street ought not to have any end, or architectural point upon which the weary eye could rest.

But neither St. Girard, nor Broad street, neither wonders of the Mint nor the glories of the Hall where the ghosts of our fathers sit always signing the Declaration, impressed the visitors so much as the splendors of the Chestnut street windows, and the bargains on Eighth street. The truth is that the country cousins had come to town to attend the Yearly Meeting, and the amount of shopping that preceded that religious event was scarcely exceeded by the preparations for the opera in more worldly circles.

"Is thee going to the Yearly Meeting, Ruth?" asked one of the girls.

"I have nothing to wear," replied that demure person. "If thee wants to see new bonnets, orthodox to a shade and conformed to the letter of the true form, thee must go to the Arch Street Meeting. Any departure from either color or shape would be instantly taken note of. It has occupied mother a long time, to find at the shops the exact shade for her new bonnet. Oh, thee must go by all means. But thee won't see there a sweeter woman than mother."

"And thee won't go?"

"Why should I? I've been again and again. If I go to Meeting at all I like best to sit in the quiet old house in Germantown, where the windows are all open and I can see the trees, and hear the stir of the leaves. It's such a crush at the Yearly Meeting at Arch Street, and then there's the row of sleek-looking young men who line the curbstone and stare at us as we come out. No, I don't feel at home there."

That evening Ruth and her father sat late by the drawing-room fire, as they were quite apt to do at night. It was always a time of confidences.

"Thee has another letter from young Sterling," said Eli Bolton.

"Yes. Philip has gone to the far west."

"How far?"

"He doesn't say, but it's on the frontier, and on the map everything beyond it is marked 'Indians' and 'desert,' and looks as desolate as a Wednesday Meeting."

"Humph. It was time for him to do something. Is he going to start a daily newspaper among the Kick-a-poos?"

"Father, thee's unjust to Philip. He's going into business."

"What sort of business can a young man go into without capital?"

"He doesn't say exactly what it is," said Ruth a little dubiously, "but it's something about land and railroads, and thee knows, father, that fortunes are made nobody knows exactly how, in a new country."

"I should think so, you innocent puss, and in an old one too. But Philip is honest, and he has talent enough, if he will stop scribbling, to make his way. But thee may as well take care of theeself, Ruth, and not go dawdling along with a young man in his adventures, until thy own mind is a little more settled what thee wants."

This excellent advice did not seem to impress Ruth greatly, for she was looking away with that abstraction of vision which often came into her grey eyes, and at length she exclaimed, with a sort of impatience,

"I wish I could go west, or south, or somewhere. What a box women are put into, measured for it, and put in young; if we go anywhere it's in a box, veiled and pinioned and shut in by disabilities. Father, I should like to break things and get loose."

What a sweet-voiced little innocent, it was to be sure.

"Thee will no doubt break things enough when thy time comes, child; women always have; but what does thee want now that thee hasn't?"

"I want to be something, to make myself something, to do something. Why should I rust, and be stupid, and sit in inaction because I am a girl? What would happen to me if thee should lose thy property and die? What one useful thing could I do for a living, for the support of mother and the children? And if I had a fortune, would thee want me to lead a useless life?"

"Has thy mother led a useless life?"

"Somewhat that depends upon whether her children amount to anything," retorted the sharp little disputant. "What's the good, father, of a series of human beings who don't advance any?"

Friend Eli, who had long ago laid aside the Quaker dress, and was out of Meeting, and who in fact after a youth of doubt could not yet define his belief, nevertheless looked with some wonder at this fierce young eagle of his, hatched in a Friend's dove-cote. But he only said,

"Has thee consulted thy mother about a career, I suppose it is a career thee wants?"

Ruth did not reply directly; she complained that her mother didn't understand her. But that wise and placid woman understood the sweet rebel a great deal better than Ruth understood herself. She also had a history, possibly, and had sometime beaten her young wings against the cage of custom, and indulged in dreams of a new social order, and had passed through that fiery period when it seems possible for one mind, which has not yet tried its limits, to break up and re-arrange the world.

Ruth replied to Philip's letter in due time and in the most cordial and unsentimental manner. Philip liked the letter, as he did everything she did; but he had a dim notion that there was more about herself in the letter than about him. He took it with him from the Southern Hotel, when he went to walk, and read it over and again in an unfrequented street as he stumbled along. The rather common-place and unformed hand-writing seemed to him peculiar and characteristic, different from that of any other woman.

Ruth was glad to hear that Philip had made a push into the world, and she was sure that his talent and courage would make a way for him. She should pray for his success at any rate, and especially that the Indians, in St. Louis, would not take his scalp.

Philip looked rather dubious at this sentence, and wished that he had written nothing about Indians.

Chapter XV

—Rationalem quidem puto medicinam esse debere: instrui vero ab evidentibus causis, obscuris omnibus non à cogitatione artificis, sed ab ipsa arte rejectis. Incidere autem vivorum corpora, et crudele, et supervacuum est: mortuorum corpora discentibus necessarium.

Celsus.

E LI BOLTON and his wife talked over Ruth's case, as they had often done before, with no little anxiety. Alone of all their children she was impatient of the restraints and monotony of the Friends' Society, and wholly indisposed to accept the "inner light" as a guide into a life of acceptance and inaction. When Margaret told her husband of Ruth's newest project, he did not exhibit so much surprise as she looked for. In fact he said that he did not see why a woman should not enter the medical profession if she felt a call to it.

"But," said Margaret, "consider her total inexperience of the world, and her frail health. Can such a slight little body endure the ordeal of the preparation for, or the strain of, the practice of the profession?"

"Did thee ever think, Margaret, whether she can endure being thwarted in an object on which she has so set her heart, as she has on this? Thee has trained her thyself at home, in her enfeebled childhood, and thee knows how strong her will is, and what she has been able to accomplish in self-culture by the simple force of her determination. She never will be satisfied until she has tried her own strength."

"I wish," said Margaret, with an inconsequence that is not exclusively feminine, "that she were in the way to fall in love and marry by and by. I think that would cure her of some of her notions. I am not sure but if she went away to some distant school, into an entirely new life, her thoughts would be diverted."

Eli Bolton almost laughed as he regarded his wife, with eyes that never looked at her except fondly, and replied,

"Perhaps thee remembers that thee had notions also, before we were married, and before thee became a member of

Meeting. I think Ruth comes honestly by certain tendencies which thee has hidden under the Friend's dress."

Margaret could not say no to this, and while she paused, it was evident that memory was busy with suggestions to shake her present opinions.

"Why not let Ruth try the study for a time," suggested Eli; "there is a fair beginning of a Woman's Medical College in the city. Quite likely she will soon find that she needs first a more general culture, and fall in with thy wish that she should see more of the world at some large school."

There really seemed to be nothing else to be done, and Margaret consented at length without approving. And it was agreed that Ruth, in order to spare her fatigue, should take lodgings with friends near the college and make a trial in the pursuit of that science to which we all owe our lives, and sometimes as by a miracle of escape.

That day Mr. Bolton brought home a stranger to dinner, Mr. Bigler of the great firm of Pennybacker, Bigler & Small, railroad contractors. He was always bringing home somebody, who had a scheme; to build a road, or open a mine, or plant a swamp with cane to grow paper-stock, or found a hospital, or invest in a patent shad-bone separator, or start a college somewhere on the frontier, contiguous to a land speculation.

The Bolton house was a sort of hotel for this kind of people. They were always coming. Ruth had known them from childhood, and she used to say that her father attracted them as naturally as a sugar hogshead does flies. Ruth had an idea that a large portion of the world lived by getting the rest of the world into schemes. Mr. Bolton never could say "no" to any of them, not even, said Ruth again, to the society for stamping oyster shells with scripture texts before they were sold at retail.

Mr. Bigler's plan this time, about which he talked loudly, with his mouth full, all dinner time, was the building of the Tunkhannock, Rattlesnake and Youngwomanstown railroad, which would not only be a great highway to the west, but would open to market inexhaustible coal-fields and untold millions of lumber. The plan of operations was very simple.

"We'll buy the lands," explained he, "on long time, backed by the notes of good men; and then mortgage them for money enough to get the road well on. Then get the towns on the line to issue their bonds for stock, and sell their bonds for enough to complete the road, and partly stock it, especially if we mortgage each section as we complete it. We can then sell the rest of the stock on the prospect of the business of the road through an improved country, and also sell the lands at a big advance, on the strength of the road. All we want," continued Mr. Bigler in his frank manner, "is a few thousand dollars to start the surveys, and arrange things in the legislature. There is some parties will have to be seen, who might make us trouble."

"It will take a good deal of money to start the enterprise," remarked Mr. Bolton, who knew very well what "seeing" a Pennsylvania Legislature meant, but was too polite to tell Mr. Bigler what he thought of him, while he was his guest; "what security would one have for it?"

Mr. Bigler smiled a hard kind of smile, and said, "You'd be inside, Mr. Bolton, and you'd have the first chance in the deal."

This was rather unintelligible to Ruth, who was nevertheless somewhat amused by the study of a type of character she had seen before. At length she interrupted the conversation by asking,

"You'd sell the stock, I suppose, Mr. Bigler, to anybody who was attracted by the prospectus?"

"O, certainly, serve all alike," said Mr. Bigler, now noticing Ruth for the first time, and a little puzzled by the serene, intelligent face that was turned towards him.

"Well, what would become of the poor people who had been led to put their little money into the speculation, when you got out of it and left it half way?"

It would be no more true to say of Mr. Bigler that he was or could be embarrassed, than to say that a brass counterfeit dollar-piece would change color when refused; the question annoyed him a little, in Mr. Bolton's presence.

"Why, yes, Miss, of course, in a great enterprise for the benefit of the community there will little things occur, which, which—and, of course, the poor ought to be looked to; I tell my wife, that the poor must *be* looked to; if you can tell who are poor—there's so many impostors. And then, there's so many poor in the legislature to be looked after," said the contractor with a sort of a chuckle, "isn't that so, Mr. Bolton?"

Eli Bolton replied that he never had much to do with the legislature.

"Yes," continued this public benefactor, "an uncommon poor lot this year, uncommon. Consequently an expensive lot. The fat is, Mr. Bolton, that the price is raised so high on United States Senator now, that it affects the whole market; you can't get any public improvement through on reasonable terms. Simony is what I call it, Simony," repeated Mr. Bigler, as if he had said a good thing.

Mr. Bigler went on and gave some very interesting details of the intimate connection between railroads and politics, and thoroughly entertained himself all dinner time, and as much disgusted Ruth, who asked no more questions, and her father who replied in monosyllables.

"I wish," said Ruth to her father, after the guest had gone, "that you wouldn't bring home any more such horrid men. Do all men who wear big diamond breast-pins, flourish their knives at table, and use bad grammar, and cheat?"

"O, child, thee mustn't be too observing. Mr. Bigler is one of the most important men in the state; nobody has more influence at Harrisburg. I don't like him any more than thee does, but I'd better lend him a little money than to have his ill will."

"Father, I think thee'd better have his ill-will than his company. Is it true that he gave money to help build the pretty little church of St. James the Less, and that he is one of the vestrymen?"

"Yes. He is not such a bad fellow. One of the men in Third street asked him the other day, whether his was a high church or a low church? Bigler said he didn't know; he'd been in it once, and he could touch the ceiling in the side aisle with his hand."

"I think he's just horrid," was Ruth's final summary of him, after the manner of the swift judgment of women, with no consideration of the extenuating circumstances. Mr. Bigler had no idea that he had not made a good impression on the whole family; he certainly intended to be agreeable. Margaret agreed with her daughter, and though she never said anything to such people, she was grateful to Ruth for sticking at least one pin into him.

Such was the serenity of the Bolton household that a stranger in it would never have suspected there was any opposition to Ruth's going to the Medical School. And she went quietly to take her residence in town, and began her attendance of the lectures, as if it were the most natural thing in the world. She did not heed, if she heard, the busy and wondering gossip of relations and acquaintances, gossip that has no less currency among the Friends than elsewhere because it is whispered slyly and creeps about in an undertone.

Ruth was absorbed, and for the first time in her life thoroughly happy; happy in the freedom of her life, and in the keen enjoyment of the investigation that broadened its field day by day. She was in high spirits when she came home to spend First Days; the house was full of her gaiety and her merry laugh, and the children wished that Ruth would never go away again. But her mother noticed, with a little anxiety, the sometimes flushed face, and the sign of an eager spirit in the kindling eyes, and, as well, the serious air of determination and endurance in her face at unguarded moments.

The college was a small one and it sustained itself not without difficulty in this city, which is so conservative, and is yet the origin of so many radical movements. There were not more than a dozen attendants on the lectures all together, so that the enterprise had the air of an experiment, and the fascination of pioneering for those engaged in it. There was one woman physician driving about town in her carriage, attacking the most violent diseases in all quarters with persistent courage, like a modern Bellona in her war chariot, who was popularly supposed to gather in fees to the amount of ten to twenty thousand dollars a year. Perhaps some of these students looked forward to the near day when they would support such a practice and a husband besides, but it is unknown that any of them ever went further than practice in hospitals and in their own nurseries, and it is feared that some of them were quite as ready as their sisters, in emergencies, to "call a man."

If Ruth had any exaggerated expectations of a professional life, she kept them to herself, and was known to her fellows of the class simply as a cheerful, sincere student, eager in her investigations, and never impatient at anything, except an insinuation that women had not as much mental capacity for science as men.

They really say," said one young Quaker sprig to another youth of his age, "that Ruth Bolton is really going to be a saw-bones, attends lectures, cuts up bodies, and all that. She's cool enough for a surgeon, anyway." He spoke feelingly, for he had very likely been weighed in Ruth's calm eyes sometime, and thoroughly scared by the little laugh that accompanied a puzzling reply to one of his conversational nothings. Such young gentlemen, at this time, did not come very distinctly into Ruth's horizon, except as amusing circumstances.

About the details of her student life, Ruth said very little to her friends, but they had reason to know, afterwards, that it required all her nerve and the almost complete exhaustion of her physical strength, to carry her through. She began her anatomical practice upon detached portions of the human frame, which were brought into the demonstrating room—dissecting the eye, the ear, and a small tangle of muscles and nerves—an occupation which had not much more savor of death in it than the analysis of a portion of a plant out of which the life went when it was plucked up by the roots. Custom inures the most sensitive persons to that which is at first most repellant; and in the late war we saw the most delicate women, who could not at home endure the sight of blood, become so used to scenes of carnage, that they walked the hospitals and the margins of battle-fields, amid the poor remnants of torn humanity, with as perfect self-possession as if they were strolling in a flower garden.

It happened that Ruth was one evening deep in a line of investigation which she could not finish or understand without demonstration, and so eager was she in it, that it seemed as if she could not wait till the next day. She, therefore, persuaded a fellow student, who was reading that evening with her, to go down to the dissecting room of the college, and ascertain what they wanted to know by an hour's work there. Perhaps, also, Ruth wanted to test her own nerve, and to see whether the power of association was stronger in her mind than her own will.

The janitor of the shabby and comfortless old building admitted the girls, not without suspicion, and gave them lighted candles, which they would need, without other remark than "there's a new one, Miss," as the girls went up the broad stairs.

They climbed to the third story, and paused before a door, which they unlocked, and which admitted them into a long apartment, with a row of windows on one side and one at the end. The room was without light, save from the stars and the candles the girls carried, which revealed to them dimly two long and several small tables, a few benches and chairs, a couple of skeletons hanging on the wall, a sink, and cloth-covered heaps of something upon the tables here and there.

The windows were open, and the cool night wind came in strong enough to flutter a white covering now and then, and to shake the loose casements. But all the sweet odors of the night could not take from the room a faint suggestion of mortality.

The young ladies paused a moment. The room itself was familiar enough, but night makes almost any chamber eerie, and especially such a room of detention as this where the mortal parts of the unburied might almost be supposed to be visited, on the sighing night winds, by the wandering spirits of their late tenants.

Opposite and at some distance across the roofs of lower buildings, the girls saw a tall edifice, the long upper story of which seemed to be a dancing hall. The windows of that were also open, and through them they heard the scream of the jiggered and tortured violin, and the pump, pump of the oboe, and saw the moving shapes of men and women in quick transition, and heard the prompter's drawl.

"I wonder," said Ruth, "what the girls dancing there would think if they saw us, or knew that there was such a room as this so near them."

She did not speak very loud, and, perhaps unconsciously, the girls drew near to each other as they approached the long table in the centre of the room. A straight object lay upon it, covered with a sheet. This was doubtless "the new one" of which the janitor spoke. Ruth advanced, and with a not very steady hand lifted the white covering from the upper part of the figure and turned it down. Both the girls started. It was a negro. The black face seemed to defy the pallor of death, and asserted an ugly life-likeness that was frightful. Ruth was as pale as the white sheet, and her comrade whispered, "Come away, Ruth, it is awful."

Perhaps it was the wavering light of the candles, perhaps it was only the agony from a death of pain, but the repulsive black face seemed to wear a scowl that said, "Haven't you yet done with the outcast, persecuted black man, but you must now haul him from his grave, and send even your women to dismember his body?"

Who is this dead man, one of thousands who died yesterday, and will be dust anon, to protest that science shall not turn his worthless carcass to some account?

Ruth could have had no such thought, for with a pity in her sweet face, that for the moment overcame fear and disgust, she reverently replaced the covering, and went away to her own table, as her companion did to hers. And there for an hour they worked at their several problems, without speaking, but not without an awe of the presence there, "the new one," and not without an awful sense of life itself, as they heard the pulsations of the music and the light laughter from the dancing-hall.

When, at length, they went away, and locked the dreadful room behind them, and came out into the street, where people were passing, they, for the first time, realized, in the relief they felt, what a nervous strain they had been under.

Chapter XVI

Todtenb. 117. 1. 3.

WHILE Ruth was thus absorbed in her new occupation, and the spring was wearing away, Philip and his friends were still detained at the Southern Hotel. The great contractors had concluded their business with the state and railroad officials and with the lesser contractors, and departed for the East. But the serious illness of one of the engineers kept Philip and Henry in the city and occupied in alternate watchings.

Philip wrote to Ruth of the new acquaintance they had made, Col. Sellers, an enthusiastic and hospitable gentleman, very much interested in the development of the country, and in their success. They had not had an opportunity to visit at his place "up in the country" yet, but the Colonel often dined with them, and in confidence, confided to them his projects, and seemed to take a great liking to them, especially to his friend Harry. It was true that he never seemed to have ready money, but he was engaged in very large operations.

The correspondence was not very brisk between these two young persons, so differently occupied; for though Philip wrote long letters, he got brief ones in reply, full of sharp little observations however, such as one concerning Col. Sellers, namely, that such men dined at their house every week.

Ruth's proposed occupation astonished Philip immensely, but while he argued it and discussed it, he did not dare hint to her his fear that it would interfere with his most cherished plans. He too sincerely respected Ruth's judgment to make any protest, however, and he would have defended her course against the world.

This enforced waiting at St. Louis was very irksome to Philip. His money was running away, for one thing, and he longed to get into the field, and see for himself what chance there was for a fortune or even an occupation. The contractors had given the young men leave to join the engineer corps as soon as they could, but otherwise had made no provision for them, and in fact had left them with only the most indefinite expectations of something large in the future.

Harry was entirely happy, in his circumstances. He very soon knew everybody, from the governor of the state down to the waiters at the hotel. He had the Wall street slang at his tongue's end; he always talked like a capitalist, and entered with enthusiasm into all the land and railway schemes with which the air was thick.

Col. Sellers and Harry talked together by the hour and by the day. Harry informed his new friend that he was going out with the engineer corps of the Salt Lick Pacific Extension, but that wasn't his real business.

"I'm to have, with another party," said Harry, "a big contract in the road, as soon as it is let; and, meantime, I'm with the engineers to spy out the best land and the dépot sites."

"It's everything," suggested the Colonel, "in knowing where to invest. I've known people throw away their money because they were too consequential to take Sellers' advice. Others, again, have made their pile on taking it. I've looked over the ground, I've been studying it for twenty years. You can't put your finger on a spot in the map of Missouri that I don't know as if I'd made it. When you want to place anything," continued the Colonel, confidently, "just let Eschol Sellers know. That's all."

"Oh, I haven't got much in ready money I can lay my hands on now, but if a fellow could do anything with fifteen or twenty thousand dollars, as a beginning, I shall draw for that when I see the right opening."

"Well, that's something, that's something, fifteen or twenty thousand dollars, say twenty—as an advance," said the Colonel reflectively, as if turning over his mind for a project that could be entered on with such a trifling sum.

"I'll tell you what it is—but only to you Mr. Brierly, only to you, mind; I've got a little project that I've been keeping. It looks small, looks small on paper, but it's got a big future. What should you say, sir, to a city, built up like the rod of Aladdin had touched it, built up in two years, where now you wouldn't expect it any more than you'd expect a light-house on the top of Pilot Knob? and you could own the land! It can be done, sir. It can be done!"

The Colonel hitched up his chair close to Harry, laid his hand on his knee, and, first looking about him, said in a low voice, "The Salt Lick Pacific Extension is going to run through Stone's Landing! The Almighty never laid out a cleaner piece of level prairie for a city; and it's the natural center of all that region of hemp and tobacco."

"What makes you think the road will go there? It's twenty miles, on the map, off the straight line of the road?"

"You can't tell what is the straight line till the engineers have been over it. Between us, I have talked with Jeff Thompson, the division engineer. He understands the wants of Stone's Landing, and the claims of the inhabitants—who are to be there. Jeff says that a railroad is for the accommodation of the people and not for the benefit of gophers; and if he don't run this to Stone's Landing he'll be damned! You ought to know Jeff; he's one of the most enthusiastic engineers in this western country, and one of the best fellows that ever looked through the bottom of a glass."

The recommendation was not undeserved. There was nothing that Jeff wouldn't do, to accommodate a friend, from sharing his last dollar with him, to winging him in a duel. When he understood from Col. Sellers how the land lay at Stone's Landing, he cordially shook hands with that gentleman, asked him to drink, and fairly roared out, "Why, God bless my soul, Colonel, a word from one Virginia gentleman to another is 'nuff ced.' There's Stone's Landing been waiting for a railroad more than four thousand years, and damme if she shan't have it."

Philip had not so much faith as Harry in Stone's Landing, when the latter opened the project to him, but Harry talked about it as if he already owned that incipient city.

Harry thoroughly believed in all his projects and inventions, and lived day by day in their golden atmosphere. Everybody liked the young fellow, for how could they help liking one of such engaging manners and large fortune? The waiters at the hotel would do more for him than for any other guest, and he made a great many acquaintances among the people of

St. Louis, who liked his sensible and liberal views about the development of the western country, and about St. Louis. He said it ought to be the national capital. Harry made partial arrangements with several of the merchants for furnishing supplies for his contract on the Salt Lick Pacific Extension; consulted the maps with the engineers, and went over the profiles with the contractors, figuring out estimates for bids. He was exceedingly busy with those things when he was not at the bedside of his sick acquaintance, or arranging the details of his speculation with Col. Sellers.

Meantime the days went along and the weeks, and the money in Harry's pocket got lower and lower. He was just as liberal with what he had as before, indeed it was his nature to be free with his money or with that of others, and he could lend or spend a dollar with an air that made it seem like ten. At length, at the end of one week, when his hotel bill was presented, Harry found not a cent in his pocket to meet it. He carelessly remarked to the landlord that he was not that day in funds, but he would draw on New York, and he sat down and wrote to the contractors in that city a glowing letter about the prospects of the road, and asked them to advance a hundred or two, until he got at work. No reply came. He wrote again, in an unoffended business like tone, suggesting that he had better draw at three days. A short answer came to this, simply saying that money was very tight in Wall street just then, and that he had better join the engineer corps as soon as he could.

But the bill had to be paid, and Harry took it to Philip, and asked him if he thought he hadn't better draw on his uncle. Philip had not much faith in Harry's power of "drawing," and told him that he would pay the bill himself. Whereupon Harry dismissed the matter then and thereafter from his thoughts, and, like a light-hearted good fellow as he was, gave himself no more trouble about his board-bills. Philip paid them, swollen as they were with a monstrous list of extras; but he seriously counted the diminishing bulk of his own hoard, which was all the money he had in the world. Had he not tacitly agreed to share with Harry to the last in this adventure, and would not the generous fellow divide with him if he, Philip, were in want and Harry had anything?

The fever at length got tired of tormenting the stout young engineer, who lay sick at the hotel, and left him, very thin, a little sallow but an "acclimated" man. Everybody said he was "acclimated" now, and said it cheerfully. What it is to be acclimated to western fevers no two persons exactly agree. Some say it is a sort of vaccination that renders death by some malignant type of fever less probable. Some regard it as a sort of initiation, like that into the Odd Fellows, which renders one liable to his regular dues thereafter. Others consider it merely the acquisition of a habit of taking every morning before breakfast a dose of bitters, composed of whiskey and assafœtida, out of the acclimation jug.

Jeff Thompson afterwards told Philip that he once asked Senator Atchison, then acting Vice-President of the United States, about the possibility of acclimation; he thought the opinion of the second officer of our great government would be valuable on this point. They were sitting together on a bench before a country tavern, in the free converse permitted by our democratic habits.

"I suppose, Senator, that you have become acclimated to this country?"

"Well," said the Vice-President, crossing his legs, pulling his wide-awake down over his forehead, causing a passing chicken to hop quickly one side by the accuracy of his aim, and speaking with senatorial deliberation, "I think I have. I've been here twenty-five years, and dash, dash my dash to dash, if I haven't entertained twenty-five separate and distinct earthquakes, one a year. The niggro is the only person who can stand the fever and ague of this region."

The convalescence of the engineer was the signal for breaking up quarters at St. Louis, and the young fortune-hunters started up the river in good spirits. It was only the second time either of them had been upon a Mississippi steamboat, and nearly everything they saw had the charm of novelty. Col. Sellers was at the landing to bid them good-bye.

"I shall send you up that basket of champagne by the next boat; no, no; no thanks; you'll find it not bad in camp," he cried out as the plank was hauled in. "My respects to Thompson. Tell him to sight for Stone's. Let me know, Mr. Brierly, when you are ready to locate; I'll come over from Hawkeye. Good-bye."

And the last the young fellows saw of the Colonel, he was waving his hat, and beaming prosperity and good luck.

The voyage was delightful, and was not long enough to become monotonous. The travelers scarcely had time indeed to get accustomed to the splendors of the great saloon where the tables were spread for meals, a marvel of paint and gilding, its ceiling hung with fancifully cut tissue-paper of many colors, festooned and arranged in endless patterns. The whole was more beautiful than a barber's shop. The printed bill of fare at dinner was longer and more varied, the proprietors justly boasted, than that of any hotel in New York. It must have been the work of an author of talent and imagination, and it surely was not his fault if the dinner itself was to a certain extent a delusion, and if the guests got something that tasted pretty much the same whatever dish they ordered; nor was it his fault if a general flavor of rose in all the dessert dishes suggested that they had passed through the barber's saloon on their way from the kitchen.

The travelers landed at a little settlement on the left bank, and at once took horses for the camp in the interior, carrying their clothes and blankets strapped behind the saddles. Harry was dressed as we have seen him once before, and his long and shining boots attracted not a little the attention of the few persons they met on the road, and especially of the bright faced wenches who lightly stepped along the highway, picturesque in their colored kerchiefs, carrying light baskets, or riding upon mules and balancing before them a heavier load.

Harry sang fragments of operas and talked about their fortune. Philip even was excited by the sense of freedom and adventure, and the beauty of the landscape. The prairie, with its new grass and unending acres of brilliant flowers—chiefly the innumerable varieties of phlox—bore the look of years of cultivation, and the occasional open groves of white oaks gave it a park-like appearance. It was hardly unreasonable to expect to see at any moment, the gables and square windows of an Elizabethan mansion in one of the well kept groves.

Towards sunset of the third day, when the young gentlemen thought they ought to be near the town of Magnolia, near which they had been directed to find the engineers' camp, they descried a log house and drew up before it to enquire the way. Half the building was store, and half was dwelling house. At the door of the latter stood a negress with a bright turban on her head, to whom Philip called,

"Can you tell me, auntie, how far it is to the town of Magnolia?"

"Why, bress you chile," laughed the woman, "you's dere now."

It was true. This log house was the compactly built town, and all creation was its suburbs. The engineers' camp was only two or three miles distant.

"You's boun' to find it," directed auntie, "if you don't keah nuffin 'bout de road, and go fo' de sun-down."

A brisk gallop brought the riders in sight of the twinkling light of the camp, just as the stars came out. It lay in a little hollow, where a small stream ran through a sparse grove of young white oaks. A half dozen tents were pitched under the trees, horses and oxen were corraled at a little distance, and a group of men sat on camp stools or lay on blankets about a bright fire. The twang of a banjo became audible as they drew nearer, and they saw a couple of negroes, from some neighboring plantation, "breaking down" a juba in approved style, amid the "hi, hi's" of the spectators.

Mr. Jeff Thompson, for it was the camp of this redoubtable engineer, gave the travelers a hearty welcome, offered them ground room in his own tent, ordered supper, and set out a small jug, a drop from which he declared necessary on account of the chill of the evening.

"I never saw an Eastern man," said Jeff, "who knew how to drink from a jug with one hand. It's as easy as lying. So." He grasped the handle with the right hand, threw the jug back upon his arm, and applied his lips to the nozzle. It was an act as graceful as it was simple. "Besides," said Mr. Thompson, setting it down, "it puts every man on his honor as to quantity."

Early to turn in was the rule of the camp, and by nine o'clock everybody was under his blanket, except Jeff himself, who worked awhile at his table over his field-book, and then arose, stepped outside the tent door and sang, in a strong and not unmelodious tenor, the Star Spangled Banner from beginning to end. It proved to be his nightly practice to let off the unexpended steam of his conversational powers, in the words of this stirring song.

It was a long time before Philip got to sleep. He saw the fire light, he saw the clear stars through the tree-tops, he heard the gurgle of the stream, the stamp of the horses, the occasional barking of the dog which followed the cook's wagon, the hooting of an owl; and when these failed he saw Jeff, standing on a battlement, mid the rocket's red glare, and heard him sing, "Oh, say, can you see?" It was the first time he had ever slept on the ground.

Chapter XVII

—We have view'd it,
And measur'd it within all, by the scale:
The richest tract of land, love, in the kingdom!
There will be made seventeen or eighteen millions,
Or more, as't may be handled!

The Devil is an Ass.

NOBODY dressed more like an engineer than Mr. Henry Brierly. The completeness of his appointments was the envy of the corps, and the gay fellow himself was the admiration of the camp servants, axemen, teamsters and cooks.

"I reckon you didn't git them boots no wher's this side o' Sent Louis?" queried the tall Missouri youth who acted as commissariy's assistant.

"No, New York."

"Yas, I've heern o' New York," continued the butternut lad, attentively studying each item of Harry's dress, and endeavoring to cover his design with interesting conversation. "'N there's Massachusetts."

"It's not far off."

"I've heern Massachusetts was a —— of a place. Les' see, what state's Massachusetts in?"

"Massachusetts," kindly replied Harry, "is in the state of Boston."

"Abolish'n wan't it? They must a cost right smart," referring to the boots.

Harry shouldered his rod and went to the field, tramped over the prairie by day, and figured up results at night, with the utmost cheerfulness and industry, and plotted the line on the profile paper, without, however, the least idea of engineering practical or theoretical. Perhaps there was not a great deal of scientific knowledge in the entire corps, nor was very much needed. They were making what is called a preliminary survey, and the chief object of a preliminary survey was to get up an excitement about the road, to interest every town in that part of the state in it, under the belief that the road would run through it, and to get the aid of every planter upon the prospect that a station would be on his land.

Mr. Jeff Thompson was the most popular engineer who could be found for this work. He did not bother himself much about details or practicabilities of location, but ran merrily along, sighting from the top of one divide to the top of another, and striking "plumb" every town site and big plantation within twenty or thirty miles of his route. In his own language he "just went booming."

This course gave Harry an opportunity, as he said, to learn the practical details of engineering, and it gave Philip a chance to see the country, and to judge for himself what prospect of a fortune it offered. Both he and Harry got the "refusal" of more than one plantation as they went along, and wrote urgent letters to their eastern correspondents, upon the beauty of the land and the certainty that it would quadruple in value as soon as the road was finally located. It seemed strange to them that capitalists did not flock out there and secure this land.

They had not been in the field over two weeks when Harry wrote to his friend Col. Sellers that he'd better be on the move, for the line was certain to go to Stone's Landing. Any one who looked at the line on the map, as it was laid down from day to day, would have been uncertain which way it was going; but Jeff had declared that in his judgment the only practicable route from the point they then stood on was to follow the divide to Stone's Landing, and it was generally understood that that town would be the next one hit.

"We'll make it, boys," said the chief, "if we have to go in a balloon."

And make it they did. In less than a week, this indomitable engineer had carried his moving caravan over slues and branches, across bottoms and along divides, and pitched his tents in the very heart of the city of Stone's Landing.

"Well, I'll be dashed," was heard the cheery voice of Mr. Thompson, as he stepped outside the tent door at sunrise next morning. "If this don't get me. I say, you, Grayson, get out your sighting iron and see if you can find old Sellers' town. Blame me if we wouldn't have run plumb by it if twilight had held on a little longer. Oh! Sterling, Brierly, get up and see the city. There's a steamboat just coming round the bend." And Jeff roared with laughter. "The mayor'll be round here to breakfast."

The fellows turned out of the tents, rubbing their eyes, and stared about them. They were camped on the second bench of the narrow bottom of a crooked, sluggish stream, that was some five rods wide in the present good stage of water. Before them were a dozen log cabins, with stick and mud chimneys, irregularly disposed on either side of a not very well defined road, which did not seem to know its own mind exactly, and, after straggling through the town, wandered off over the rolling prairie in an uncertain way, as if it had started for nowhere and was quite likely to reach its destination. Just as it left the town, however, it was cheered and assisted by a guide-board, upon which was the legend "10 Mils to Hawk-eye."

The road had never been made except by the travel over it, and at this season—the rainy June—it was a way of ruts cut in the black soil, and of fathomless mud-holes. In the principal street of the city, it had received more attention; for hogs, great and small, rooted about in it and wallowed in it, turning the street into a liquid quagmire which could only be crossed on pieces of plank thrown here and there.

About the chief cabin, which was the store and grocery of this mart of trade, the mud was more liquid than elsewhere, and the rude platform in front of it and the dry-goods boxes mounted thereon were places of refuge for all the loafers of the place. Down by the stream was a dilapidated building which served for a hemp warehouse, and a shaky wharf extended out from it into the water. In fact a flat-boat was there moored by it, its setting poles lying across the gunwales. Above the town the stream was crossed by a crazy wooden bridge, the supports of which leaned all ways in the soggy soil; the absence of a plank here and there in the flooring made the crossing of the bridge faster than a walk an offense not necessary to be prohibited by law.

"This, gentlemen," said Jeff, "is Columbus River, *alias* Goose Run. If it was widened, and deepened, and straightened, and made long enough, it would be one of the finest rivers in the western country."

As the sun rose and sent his level beams along the stream, the thin stratum of mist, or malaria, rose also and dispersed, but the light was not able to enliven the dull water nor give any hint of its apparently fathomless depth. Venerable mud-turtles crawled up and roosted upon the old logs in the stream, their backs glistening in the sun, the first inhabitants of the metropolis to begin the active business of the day.

It was not long, however, before smoke began to issue from the city chimneys; and before the engineers had finished their breakfast they were the object of the curious inspection of six or eight boys and men, who lounged into the camp and gazed about them with languid interest, their hands in their pockets every one.

"Good morning, gentlemen," called out the chief engineer, from the table.

"Good mawning," drawled out the spokesman of the party. "I allow thish-yers the railroad, I heern it was a-comin'."

"Yes, this is the railroad, all but the rails and the iron-horse."

"I reckon you kin git all the rails you want outen my white oak timber over thar," replied the first speaker, who appeared to be a man of property and willing to strike up a trade.

"You'll have to negotiate with the contractors about the rails, sir," said Jeff; "here's Mr. Brierly, I've no doubt would like to buy your rails when the time comes."

"O," said the man, "I thought maybe you'd fetch the whole bilin along with you. But if you want rails, I've got em, haint I Eph."

"Heaps," said Eph, without taking his eyes off the group at the table.

"Well," said Mr. Thompson, rising from his seat and moving towards his tent, "the railroad has come to Stone's Landing, sure; I move we take a drink on it all round."

The proposal met with universal favor. Jeff gave prosperity to Stone's Landing and navigation to Goose Run, and the toast was washed down with gusto, in the simple fluid of corn, and with the return compliment that a rail road was a good thing, and that Jeff Thompson was no slouch.

About ten o'clock a horse and wagon was descried making a slow approach to the camp over the prairie. As it drew near, the wagon was seen to contain a portly gentleman, who hitched impatiently forward on his seat, shook the reins and gently touched up his horse, in the vain attempt to communicate his own energy to that dull beast, and looked eagerly at the tents. When the conveyance at length drew up to Mr. Thompson's door, the gentleman descended with great deliberation, straightened himself up, rubbed his hands, and beaming satisfaction from every part of his radiant frame, advanced to the group that was gathered to welcome him, and which had saluted him by name as soon as he came within hearing.

"Welcome to Napoleon, gentlemen, welcome. I am proud to see you here Mr. Thompson. You are looking well Mr. Sterling. This is the country, sir. Right glad to see you Mr. Brierly. You got that basket of champagne? No? Those blasted river thieves! I'll never send anything more by 'em. The best brand, Roederer. The last I had in my cellar, from a lot sent me by Sir George Gore—took him out on a buffalo hunt, when he visited our country. Is always sending me some trifle. You haven't looked about any yet, gentlemen? It's in the rough yet, in the rough. Those buildings will all have to come down. That's the place for the public square, Court House, hotels, churches, jail—all that sort of thing. About where we stand, the deepo. How does that strike your engineering eye, Mr. Thompson? Down yonder the business streets, running to the wharves. The University up there, on rising ground, sightly place, see the river for miles. That's Columbus river, only forty-nine miles to the Missouri. You see what it is, placid, steady, no current to interfere with navigation, wants widening in places and dredging, dredge out the harbor and raise a levee in front of the town; made by nature on purpose for a mart. Look at all this country, not another building within ten miles, no other navigable stream, lay of the land points right here; hemp, tobacco, corn, must come here. The railroad will do it, Napoleon won't know itself in a year."

"Don't now evidently," said Philip aside to Harry. "Have you breakfasted Colonel?"

"Hastily. Cup of coffee. Can't trust any coffee I don't import myself. But I put up a basket of provisions, wife would put in a few delicacies, women always will, and a half dozen of that Burgundy, I was telling you of Mr. Brierly. By the way, you never got to dine with me." And the Colonel strode away to the wagon and looked under the seat for the basket.

Apparently it was not there. For the Colonel raised up the flap, looked in front and behind, and then exclaimed,

"Confound it. That comes of not doing a thing yourself. I trusted to the women folks to set that basket in the wagon, and it ain't there."

The camp cook speedily prepared a savory breakfast for the Colonel, broiled chicken, eggs, corn-bread, and coffee, to which he did ample justice, and topped off with a drop of Old Bourbon, from Mr. Thompson's private store, a brand which he said he knew well, he should think it came from his own side-board.

While the engineer corps went to the field, to run back a couple of miles and ascertain, approximately, if a road could ever get down to the Landing, and to sight ahead across the Run, and see if it could ever get out again, Col. Sellers and Harry sat down and began to roughly map out the city of Napoleon on a large piece of drawing paper.

"I've got the refusal of a mile square here," said the Colonel, "in our names, for a year, with a quarter interest reserved for the four owners."

They laid out the town liberally, not lacking room, leaving space for the railroad to come in, and for the river as it was to be when improved.

The engineers reported that the railroad could come in, by taking a little sweep and crossing the stream on a high bridge, but the grades would be steep. Col. Sellers said he didn't care so much about the grades, if the road could only be made to reach the elevators on the river. The next day Mr. Thompson made a hasty survey of the stream for a mile or two, so that the Colonel and Harry were enabled to show on their map how nobly that would accommodate the city. Jeff took a little writing from the Colonel and Harry for a prospective share, but Philip declined to join in, saying that he had no money, and didn't want to make engagements he couldn't fulfill.

The next morning the camp moved on, followed till it was out of sight by the listless eyes of the group in front of the store, one of whom remarked that, "he'd be doggoned if he ever expected to see *that* railroad any mo'."

Harry went with the Colonel to Hawkeye to complete their arrangements, a part of which was the preparation of a petition to congress for the improvement of the navigation of Columbus River.

Chapter XVIII

·O|+/‖·:⊙Ǝ⊐⋈+□|
··:++|O:⊙‖⊐···⋛O:

Bedda ag Idda.

—"Eve us lo convintz qals er,
Que voill que m prendats a moiler.
—Qu'en aissi l'a Dieus establida
Per que not pot esser partida."
Roman de Jaufre.

EIGHT YEARS have passed since the death of Mr. Hawkins. Eight years are not many in the life of a nation or the history of a state, but they may be years of destiny that shall fix the current of the century following. Such years were those that followed the little scrimmage on Lexington Common. Such years were those that followed the double-shotted demand for the surrender of Fort Sumter. History is never done with inquiring of these years, and summoning witnesses about them, and trying to understand their significance.

The eight years in America from 1860 to 1868 uprooted institutions that were centuries old, changed the politics of a people, transformed the social life of half the country, and wrought so profoundly upon the entire national character that the influence cannot be measured short of two or three generations.

As we are accustomed to interpret the economy of providence, the life of the individual is as nothing to that of the nation or the race; but who can say, in the broader view and the more intelligent weight of values, that the life of one man is not more than that of a nationality, and that there is not a tribunal where the tragedy of one human soul shall not seem more significant than the overturning of any human institution whatever?

When one thinks of the tremendous forces of the upper and the nether world which play for the mastery of the soul of a woman during the few years in which she passes from plastic girlhood to the ripe maturity of womanhood, he may well stand in awe before the momentous drama.

What capacities she has of purity, tenderness, goodness; what capacities of vileness, bitterness and evil. Nature must needs be lavish with the mother and creator of men, and centre in her all the possibilities of life. And a few critical years can decide whether her life is to be full of sweetness and light, whether she is to be the vestal of a holy temple, or whether she will be the fallen priestess of a desecrated shrine. There are women, it is true, who seem to be capable neither of rising much nor of falling much, and whom a conventional life saves from any special development of character.

But Laura was not one of them. She had the fatal gift of beauty, and that more fatal gift which does not always accompany mere beauty, the power of fascination, a power that may, indeed, exist without beauty. She had will, and pride and courage and ambition, and she was left to be very much her own guide at the age when romance comes to the aid of passion, and when the awakening powers of her vigorous mind had little object on which to discipline themselves.

The tremendous conflict that was fought in this girl's soul none of those about her knew, and very few knew that her life had in it anything unusual or romantic or strange.

Those were troublous days in Hawkeye as well as in most other Missouri towns, days of confusion, when between Unionist and Confederate occupations, sudden maraudings and bush-whackings and raids, individuals escaped observation or comment in actions that would have filled the town with scandal in quiet times.

Fortunately we only need to deal with Laura's life at this period historically, and look back upon such portions of it as will serve to reveal the woman as she was at the time of the arrival of Mr. Harry Brierly in Hawkeye.

The Hawkins family were settled there, and had a hard enough struggle with poverty and the necessity of keeping up appearances in accord with their own family pride and the large expectations they secretly cherished of a fortune in the Knobs of East Tennessee. How pinched they were perhaps no one knew but Clay, to whom they looked for almost their whole support. Washington had been in Hawkeye off and on, attracted away occasionally by some tremendous speculation, from which he invariably returned to Gen. Boswell's office as poor as he went. He was the inventor of no one knew how many useless contrivances, which were not worth patenting, and his years had been passed in dreaming and planning to no purpose; until he was now a man of about thirty, without a profession or a permanent occupation, a tall, brown-haired, dreamy person of the best intentions and the frailest resolution. Probably however the eight years had been happier to him than to any others in his circle, for the time had been mostly spent in a blissful dream of the coming of enormous wealth.

He went out with a company from Hawkeye to the war, and was not wanting in courage, but he would have been a better soldier if he had been less engaged in contrivances for circumventing the enemy by strategy unknown to the books.

It happened to him to be captured in one of his self-appointed expeditions, but the federal colonel released him, after a short examination, satisfied that he could most injure the confederate forces opposed to the Unionists by returning him to his regiment.

Col. Sellers was of course a prominent man during the war. He was captain of the home guards in Hawkeye, and he never left home except upon one occasion, when on the strength of a rumor, he executed a flank movement and fortified Stone's Landing, a place which no one unacquainted with the country would be likely to find.

"Gad," said the Colonel afterwards, "the Landing is the key to upper Missouri, and it is the only place the enemy never captured. If other places had been defended as well as that was, the result would have been different, sir."

The Colonel had his own theories about war as he had in other things. If everybody had stayed at home as he did, he said, the South never would have been conquered. For what would there have been to conquer? Mr. Jeff Davis was constantly writing him to take command of a corps in the confederate army, but Col. Sellers said, no, his duty was at home. And he was by no means idle. He was the inventor of the famous air torpedo, which came very near destroying the Union armies in Missouri, and the city of St. Louis itself.

His plan was to fill a torpedo with Greek fire and poisonous and deadly missiles, attach it to a balloon, and then let it sail away over the hostile camp and explode at the right moment, when the time-fuse burned out. He intended to use this invention in the capture of St. Louis, exploding his torpedoes over the city, and raining destruction upon it until the army of occupation would gladly capitulate. He was unable to procure the Greek fire, but he constructed a vicious torpedo which would have answered the purpose, but the first one prematurely exploded in his wood-house, blowing it clean away, and setting fire to his house. The neighbors helped him put out the conflagration, but they discouraged any more experiments of that sort.

The patriotic old gentleman, however, planted so much powder and so many explosive contrivances in the roads leading into Hawkeye, and then forgot the exact spots of danger, that people were afraid to travel the highways, and used to come to town across the fields. The Colonel's motto was, "Millions for defence but not one cent for tribute."

When Laura came to Hawkeye she might have forgotten the annoyances of the gossips of Murpheysburg and have outlived the bitterness that was growing in her heart, if she had been thrown less upon herself, or if the surroundings of her life had been more congenial and helpful. But she had little society, less and less as she grew older that was congenial to her, and her mind preyed upon itself, and the mystery of her birth at once chagrined her and raised in her the most extravagant expectations.

She was proud and she felt the sting of poverty. She could not but be conscious of her beauty also, and she was vain of that, and came to take a sort of delight in the exercise of her fascinations upon the rather loutish young men who came in her way and whom she despised.

There was another world opened to her—a world of books. But it was not the best world of that sort, for the small libraries she had access to in Hawkeye were decidedly miscellaneous, and largely made up of romances and fictions which fed her imagination with the most exaggerated notions of life, and showed her men and women in a very false sort of heroism. From these stories she learned what a woman of keen intellect and some culture joined to beauty and fascination of manner, might expect to accomplish in society as she read of it; and along with these ideas she imbibed other very crude ones in regard to the emancipation of woman.

There were also other books—histories, biographies of distinguished people, travels in far lands, poems, especially those of Byron, Scott and Shelley and Moore, which she eagerly absorbed, and appropriated therefrom what was to her liking. Nobody in Hawkeye had read so much or, after a fashion, studied so diligently as Laura. She passed for an accomplished girl, and no doubt thought herself one, as she was, judged by any standard near her.

During the war there came to Hawkeye a confederate officer, Col. Selby, who was stationed there for a time, in command of that district. He was a handsome, soldierly man of thirty years, a graduate of the University of Virginia, and of distinguished family, if his story might be believed, and, it was evident, a man of the world and of extensive travel and adventure.

To find in such an out of the way country place a woman like Laura was a piece of good luck upon which Col. Selby congratulated himself. He was studiously polite to her and treated her with a consideration to which she was unaccustomed. She had read of such men, but she had never seen one before, one so high-bred, so noble in sentiment, so entertaining in conversation, so engaging in manner.

It is a long story; unfortunately it is an old story, and it need not be dwelt on. Laura loved him, and believed that his love for her was as pure and deep as her own. She worshipped him and would have counted her life a little thing to give him, if he would only love her and let her feed the hunger of her heart upon him.

The passion possessed her whole being, and lifted her up, till she seemed to walk on air. It was all true, then, the romances she had read, the bliss of love she had dreamed of. Why had she never noticed before how blithesome the world was, how jocund with love; the birds sang it, the trees whispered it to her as she passed, the very flowers beneath her feet strewed the way as for a bridal march.

When the Colonel went away they were engaged to be married, as soon as he could make certain arrangements which he represented to be necessary, and quit the army.

He wrote to her from Harding, a small town in the southwest corner of the state, saying that he should be held in the service longer than he had expected, but that it would not be more than a few months, then he should be at liberty to take her to Chicago where he had property, and should have business, either now or as soon as the war was over, which he thought could not last long. Meantime why should they be separated? He was established in comfortable quarters, and if she could find company and join him, they would be married, and gain so many more months of happiness.

Was woman ever prudent when she loved? Laura went to Harding, the neighbors supposed to nurse Washington who had fallen ill there.

Her engagement was, of course, known in Hawkeye, and was indeed a matter of pride to her family. Mrs. Hawkins would have told the first inquirer that Laura had gone to be married; but Laura had cautioned her; she did not want to be thought of, she said, as going in search of a husband; let the news come back after she was married.

So she traveled to Harding on the pretence we have mentioned, and was married. She was married, but something must have happened on that very day or the next that alarmed her. Washington did not know then or after what it was, but Laura bound him not to send news of her marriage to Hawkeye yet, and to enjoin her mother not to speak of it. Whatever cruel suspicion or nameless dread this was, Laura tried bravely to put it away, and not let it cloud her happiness.

Communication that summer, as may be imagined, was neither regular nor frequent between the remote confederate camp at Harding and Hawkeye, and Laura was in a measure lost sight of—indeed, everyone had troubles enough of his own without borrowing from his neighbors.

Laura had given herself utterly to her husband, and if he had faults, if he was selfish, if he was sometimes coarse, if he was dissipated, she did not or would not see it. It was the passion of her life, the time when her whole nature went to flood tide and swept away all barriers. Was her husband ever cold or indifferent? She shut her eyes to everything but her sense of possession of her idol.

Three months passed. One morning her husband informed her that he had been ordered South, and must go within two hours.

"I can be ready," said Laura, cheerfully.

"But I can't take you. You must go back to Hawkeye."

"Can't—take—me?" Laura asked, with wonder in her eyes. "I can't live without you. You said"—

"O bother what I said"—and the Colonel took up his sword to buckle it on, and then continued coolly, "the fact is Laura, our romance is played out."

Laura heard, but she did not comprehend. She caught his arm and cried, "George, how can you joke so cruelly? I will go any where with you. I will wait any where. I can't go back to Hawkeye."

"Well, go where you like. Perhaps," continued he with a sneer, "you would do as well to wait here, for another colonel."

Laura's brain whirled. She did not yet comprehend. "What does this mean? Where are you going?"

"It means," said the officer, in measured words, "that you haven't anything to show for a legal marriage, and that I am going to New Orleans."

"It's a lie, George, it's a lie. I am your wife. I shall go. I shall follow you to New Orleans."

"Perhaps my wife might not like it!"

Laura raised her head, her eyes flamed with fire, she tried to utter a cry, and fell senseless on the floor.

When she came to herself the Colonel was gone. Washington Hawkins stood at her bedside. Did she come to herself? Was there anything left in her heart but hate and bitterness, a sense of an infamous wrong at the hands of the only man she had ever loved?

She returned to Hawkeye. With the exception of Washington and his mother, no one knew what had happened. The neighbors supposed that the engagement with Col. Selby had fallen through. Laura was ill for a long time, but she recovered; she had that resolution in her that could conquer death almost. And with her health came back her beauty, and an added fascination, a something that might be mistaken for sadness. Is there a beauty in the knowledge of evil, a beauty that shines out in the face of a person whose inward life is transformed by some terrible experience? Is the pathos in the eyes of the Beatrice Cenci from her guilt or her innocence?

Laura was not much changed. The lovely woman had a devil in her heart. That was all.

Chapter XIX

Wie entwickeln sich doch schnelle
Aus der flüchtigsten Empfindung
Leidenschaften ohne Grenzen
Und die zärtlichste Verbindung?

    Täglich wächst zu dieser Dame
Meines Herzens tiefste Neigung,
Und dass ich in sie verliebt sei,
Wird mir fast zür Ueberzeugung.

Heine.

M R. HARRY BRIERLY drew his pay as an engineer while he was living at the City Hotel in Hawkeye. Mr. Thompson had been kind enough to say that it didn't make any difference whether he was with the corps or not; and although Harry protested to the Colonel daily and to Washington Hawkins that he must go back at once to the line and superintend the lay-out with reference to his contract, yet he did not go, but wrote instead long letters to Philip, instructing him to keep his eye out, and to let him know when any difficulty occurred that required his presence.

Meantime Harry blossomed out in the society of Hawkeye, as he did in any society where fortune cast him and he had the slightest opportunity to expand. Indeed the talents of a rich and accomplished young fellow like Harry were not likely to go unappreciated in such a place. A land operator, engaged in vast speculations, a favorite in the select circles of New York, in correspondence with brokers and bankers, intimate with public men at Washington, one who could play the guitar and touch the banjo lightly, and who had an eye for a pretty girl, and knew the language of flattery, was welcome everywhere in Hawkeye. Even Miss Laura Hawkins thought it worth while to use her fascinations upon him, and to endeavor to entangle the volatile fellow in the meshes of her attractions.

"Gad," says Harry to the Colonel, "she's a superb creature, she'd make a stir in New York, money or no money. There are men I know would give her a railroad or an opera house, or whatever she wanted—at least they'd promise."

Harry had a way of looking at women as he looked at anything else in the world he wanted, and he half resolved to appropriate Miss Laura, during his stay in Hawkeye. Perhaps the Colonel divined his thoughts, or was offended at Harry's talk, for he replied,

"No nonsense, Mr. Brierly. Nonsense won't do in Hawkeye, not with my friends. The Hawkins' blood is good blood, all the way from Tennessee. The Hawkinses are under the weather now, but their Tennessee property is millions when it comes into market."

"Of course, Colonel. Not the least offense intended. But you can see she is a fascinating woman. I was only thinking, as to this appropriation, now, what such a woman could do in Washington. All correct, too, all correct. Common thing, I assure you in Washington; the wives of senators, representatives, cabinet officers, all sorts of wives, and some who are not wives, use their influence. You want an appointment? Do you go to Senator X? Not much. You get on the right side of his wife. Is it an appropriation? You'd go straight to the Committee, or to the Interior office, I suppose? You'd learn better than that. It takes a woman to get any thing through the Land Office. I tell you, Miss Laura would fascinate an appropriation right through the Senate and the House of Representatives in one session, if she was in Washington, as your friend, Colonel, of course as your friend."

"Would you have her sign our petition?" asked the Colonel, innocently.

Harry laughed. "Women don't get anything by petitioning Congress; nobody does, that's for form. Petitions are referred somewhere, and that's the last of them; you can't refer a handsome woman so easily, when she is present. They prefer 'em mostly."

The petition however was elaborately drawn up, with a glowing description of Napoleon and the adjacent country, and a statement of the absolute necessity to the prosperity of that region and of one of the stations on the great through route to the Pacific, of the immediate improvement of

Columbus River; to this was appended a map of the city and a survey of the river. It was signed by all the people at Stone's Landing who could write their names, by Col. Eschol Sellers, and the Colonel agreed to have the names headed by all the senators and representatives from the state and by a sprinkling of ex-governors and ex-members of congress. When completed it was a formidable document. Its preparation and that of more minute plots of the new city consumed the valuable time of Sellers and Harry for many weeks, and served to keep them both in the highest spirits.

In the eyes of Washington Hawkins, Harry was a superior being, a man who was able to bring things to pass in a way that excited his enthusiasm. He never tired of listening to his stories of what he had done and of what he was going to do. As for Washington, Harry thought he was a man of ability and comprehension, but "too visionary," he told the Colonel. The Colonel said he might be right, but he had never noticed anything visionary about him.

"He's got his plans, sir. God bless my soul, at his age, I was full of plans. But experience sobers a man, I never touch any thing now that hasn't been weighed in my judgment; and when Eschol Sellers puts his judgment on a thing, there it is."

Whatever might have been Harry's intentions with regard to Laura, he saw more and more of her every day, until he got to be restless and nervous when he was not with her. That consummate artist in passion allowed him to believe that the fascination was mainly on his side, and so worked upon his vanity, while inflaming his ardor, that he scarcely knew what he was about. Her coolness and coyness were even made to appear the simple precautions of a modest timidity, and attracted him even more than the little tendernesses into which she was occasionally surprised. He could never be away from her long, day or evening; and in a short time their intimacy was the town talk. She played with him so adroitly that Harry thought she was absorbed in love for him, and yet he was amazed that he did not get on faster in his conquest.

And when he thought of it, he was piqued as well. A country girl, poor enough, that was evident; living with her family in a cheap and most unattractive frame house, such as carpenters build in America, scantily furnished and unadorned;

without the adventitious aids of dress or jewels or the fine manners of society—Harry couldn't understand it. But she fascinated him, and held him just beyond the line of absolute familiarity at the same time. While he was with her she made him forget that the Hawkins' house was nothing but a wooden tenement, with four small square rooms on the ground floor and a half story; it might have been a palace for aught he knew.

Perhaps Laura was older than Harry. She was, at any rate, at that ripe age when beauty in woman seems more solid than in the budding period of girlhood, and she had come to understand her powers perfectly, and to know exactly how much of the susceptibility and archness of the girl it was profitable to retain. She saw that many women, with the best intentions, make a mistake of carrying too much girlishness into womanhood. Such a woman would have attracted Harry at any time, but only a woman with a cool brain and exquisite art could have made him lose his head in this way; for Harry thought himself a man of the world. The young fellow never dreamed that he was merely being experimented on; he was to her a man of another society and another culture, different from that she had any knowledge of except in books, and she was not unwilling to try on him the fascinations of her mind and person.

For Laura had her dreams. She detested the narrow limits in which her lot was cast, she hated poverty. Much of her reading had been of modern works of fiction, written by her own sex, which had revealed to her something of her own powers and given her indeed, an exaggerated notion of the influence, the wealth, the position a woman may attain who has beauty and talent and ambition and a little culture, and is not too scrupulous in the the use of them. She wanted to be rich, she wanted luxury, she wanted men at her feet, her slaves, and she had not—thanks to some of the novels she had read—the nicest discrimination between notoriety and reputation; perhaps she did not know how fatal notoriety usually is to the bloom of womanhood.

With the other Hawkins children Laura had been brought up in the belief that they had inherited a fortune in the Tennessee Lands. She did not by any means share all the delusion of the family; but her brain was not seldom busy with schemes about it. Washington seemed to her only to dream of it and to be willing to wait for its riches to fall upon him in a golden shower; but she was impatient, and wished she were a man to take hold of the business.

"You men must enjoy your schemes and your activity and liberty to go about the world," she said to Harry one day, when he had been talking of New York and Washington and his incessant engagements.

"Oh, yes," replied that martyr to business, "it's all well enough, if you don't have too much of it, but it only has one object."

"What is that?"

"If a woman doesn't know, it's useless to tell her. What do you suppose I am staying in Hawkeye for, week after week, when I ought to be with my corps?"

"I suppose it's your business with Col. Sellers about Napoleon, you've always told me so," answered Laura, with a look intended to contradict her words.

"And now I tell you that is all arranged, I suppose you'll tell me I ought to go?"

"Harry!" exclaimed Laura, touching his arm and letting her pretty hand rest there a moment. "Why should I want you to go away? The only person in Hawkeye who understands me."

"But you refuse to understand *me*," replied Harry, flattered but still petulent. "You are like an iceberg, when we are alone."

Laura looked up with wonder in her great eyes, and something like a blush suffusing her face, followed by a look of langour that penetrated Harry's heart as if it had been longing. "Did I ever show any want of confidence in you, Harry?" And she gave him her hand, which Harry pressed with effusion—something in her manner told him that he must be content with that favor.

It was always so. She excited his hopes and denied him, inflamed his passion and restrained it, and wound him in her toils day by day. To what purpose? It was keen delight to Laura to prove that she had power over men.

Laura liked to hear about life at the east, and especially about the luxurious society in which Mr. Brierly moved when he was at home. It pleased her imagination to fancy herself a queen in it.

"You should be a winter in Washington," Harry said.

"But I have no acquaintances there."

"Don't know any of the families of the congressmen? They like to have a pretty woman staying with them."

"Not one."

"Suppose Col. Sellers should have business there; say, about this Columbus River appropriation?"

"Sellers!" and Laura laughed.

"You needn't laugh. Queerer things have happened. Sellers knows everybody from Missouri, and from the West, too, for that matter. He'd introduce you to Washington life quick enough. It doesn't need a crowbar to break your way into society there as it does in Philadelphia. It's democratic, Washington is. Money or beauty will open any door. If I were a handsome woman, I shouldn't want any better place than the capital to pick up a prince or a fortune."

"Thank you," replied Laura. "But I prefer the quiet of home, and the love of those I know;" and her face wore a look of sweet contentment and unworldliness that finished Mr. Harry Brierly for the day.

Nevertheless, the hint that Harry had dropped fell upon good ground, and bore fruit an hundred fold; it worked in her mind until she had built up a plan on it, and almost a career for herself. Why not, she said, why shouldn't I do as other women have done? She took the first opportunity to see Col. Sellers, and to sound him about the Washington visit. How was he getting on with his navigation scheme, would it be likely to take him from home to Jefferson City; or to Washington, perhaps?

"Well, maybe. If the people of Napoleon want me to go to Washington, and look after that matter, I might tear myself from my home. It's been suggested to me, but—not a word of it to Mrs. Sellers and the children. Maybe they wouldn't like to think of their father in Washington. But Dilworthy, Senator Dilworthy, says to me, 'Colonel, you are the man, you could influence more votes than any one else on such a measure, an old settler, a man of the people, you know the wants of Missouri; you've a respect for religion too, says he, and know how the cause of the gospel goes with improvements.' Which is true enough, Miss Laura, and hasn't been enough thought of in connection with Napoleon. He's an able man, Dilworthy, and a good man. A man has got to be good to succeed as he has. He's only been in Congress a few years, and he must be worth a million. First thing in the morning when he stayed with me he asked about family prayers, whether we had 'em before or after breakfast. I hated to disappoint the Senator, but I had to out with it, tell him we didn't have 'em, not steady. He said he understood, business interruptions and all that, some men were well enough without, but as for him he never neglected the ordinances of religion. He doubted if the Columbus River appropriation would succeed if we did not invoke the Divine Blessing on it."

Perhaps it is unnecessary to say to the reader that Senator Dilworthy had not stayed with Col. Sellers while he was in Hawkeye; this visit to his house being only one of the Colonel's hallucinations—one of those instant creations of his fertile fancy, which were always flashing into his brain and out of his mouth in the course of any conversation and without interrupting the flow of it.

During the summer Philip rode across the country and made a short visit in Hawkeye, giving Harry an opportunity to show him the progress that he and the Colonel had made in their operation at Stone's Landing, to introduce him also to Laura, and to borrow a little money when he departed. Harry bragged about his conquest, as was his habit, and took Philip round to see his western prize.

Laura received Mr. Philip with a courtesy and a slight hauteur that rather surprised and not a little interested him. He saw at once that she was older than Harry, and soon made up his mind that she was leading his friend a country dance to which he was unaccustomed. At least he thought he saw that, and half hinted as much to Harry, who flared up at once; but on a second visit Philip was not so sure, the young lady was certainly kind and friendly and almost confiding with Harry, and treated Philip with the greatest consideration. She deferred to his opinions, and listened attentively when he talked, and in time met his frank manner with an equal frankness, so that he was quite convinced that whatever she might feel towards Harry, she was sincere with him. Perhaps his manly way did win her liking. Perhaps in her mind, she compared him with Harry, and recognized in him a man to whom a woman might give her whole soul, recklessly and with little care if she lost it. Philip was not invincible to her beauty nor to the intellectual charm of her presence.

The week seemed very short that he passed in Hawkeye, and when he bade Laura good by, he seemed to have known her a year.

"We shall see you again, Mr. Sterling," she said as she gave him her hand, with just a shade of sadness in her handsome eyes.

And when he turned away she followed him with a look that might have disturbed his serenity, if he had not at the moment had a little square letter in his breast pocket, dated at Philadelphia, and signed "Ruth."

Chapter XX

—ⱱuaⱱall ⰱⱶoⱏⱏⰷloⱔaⰐ ⰷo mⰱuaⱶⱄ ⱏⱶⱏⱏⱅⰐⱏe Ⰳ ⱏuⱔlaⰱⱔa ceⱶlle, Ⰳ coⰙaⱶⱔle, ⰷo ⰐⰐaⱶⱄⱄⱔⱶⰄ ⱅeⱶⱔce ⱶⱏa ⰄⱏeⱶⰐ aⰐⰐaⱔ la ⰷaⰐ aeⱏ aⰐ aⱅ cⱶoⰄ—

THE VISIT of Senator Abner Dilworthy was an event in Hawkeye. When a Senator, whose place is in Washington moving among the Great and guiding the destinies of the nation, condescends to mingle among the people and accept the hospitalities of such a place as Hawkeye, the honor is not considered a light one. All parties are flattered by it and politics are forgotten in the presence of one so distinguished among his fellows.

Senator Dilworthy, who was from a neighboring state, had been a Unionist in the darkest days of his country, and had thriven by it, but was that any reason why Col. Sellers, who had been a confederate and had not thriven by it, should give him the cold shoulder?

The Senator was the guest of his old friend Gen. Boswell, but it almost appeared that he was indebted to Col. Sellers for the unreserved hospitalities of the town. It was the large hearted Colonel who, in a manner, gave him the freedom of the city.

"You are known here, sir," said the Colonel, "and Hawkeye is proud of you. You will find every door open, and a welcome at every hearthstone. I should insist upon your going to my house, if you were not claimed by your older friend Gen. Boswell. But you will mingle with our people, and you will see here developments that will surprise you."

The Colonel was so profuse in his hospitality that he must have made the impression upon himself that he had entertained the Senator at his own mansion during his stay; at any rate, he afterwards always spoke of him as his guest, and not seldom referred to the Senator's relish of certain viands on his table. He did, in fact, press him to dine upon the morning of the day the Senator was going away.

Senator Dilworthy was large and portly, though not tall—a pleasant spoken man, a popular man with the people.

He took a lively interest in the town and all the surrounding country, and made many inquiries as to the progress of agriculture, of education, and of religion, and especially as to the condition of the emancipated race.

"Providence," he said, "has placed them in our hands, and although you and I, General, might have chosen a different destiny for them, under the Constitution, yet Providence knows best."

"You can't do much with 'em," interrupted Col. Sellers. "They are a speculating race, sir, disinclined to work for white folks without security, planning how to live by only working for themselves. Idle, sir, there's my garden just a ruin of weeds. Nothing practical in 'em."

"There is some truth in your observation, Colonel, but you must educate them."

"You educate the niggro and you make him more speculating than he was before. If he won't stick to any industry except for himself now, what will he do then?"

"But, Colonel, the negro when educated will be more able to make his speculations fruitful."

"Never, sir, never. He would only have a wider scope to injure himself. A niggro has no grasp, sir. Now, a white man can conceive great operations, and carry them out; a niggro can't."

"Still," replied the Senator, "granting that he might injure himself in a worldly point of view, his elevation through education would multiply his chances for the hereafter—which is the important thing after all, Colonel. And no matter what the result is, we must fulfill our duty by this being."

"I'd elevate his soul," promptly responded the Colonel; "that's just it; you can't make his soul too immortal, but I wouldn't touch *him*, himself. Yes, sir! make his soul immortal, but don't disturb the niggro as he is."

Of course one of the entertainments offered the Senator was a public reception, held in the court house, at which he made a speech to his fellow citizens. Col. Sellers was master of ceremonies. He escorted the band from the city hotel to Gen. Boswell's; he marshalled the procession of Masons, of Odd Fellows, and of Firemen, the Good Templars, the Sons of Temperance, the Cadets of Temperance, the Daughters of

Rebecca, the Sunday School children, and citizens generally, which followed the Senator to the court house; he bustled about the room long after every one else was seated, and loudly cried "Order!" in the dead silence which preceded the introduction of the Senator by Gen. Boswell. The occasion was one to call out his finest powers of personal appearance, and one he long dwelt on with pleasure.

This not being an edition of the *Congressional Globe* it is impossible to give Senator Dilworthy's speech in full. He began somewhat as follows:—

"Fellow citizens: It gives me great pleasure to thus meet and mingle with you, to lay aside for a moment the heavy duties of an official and burdensome station, and confer in familiar converse with my friends in your great state. The good opinion of my fellow citizens of all sections is the sweetest solace in all my anxieties. I look forward with longing to the time when I can lay aside the cares of office—" ["dam sight," shouted a tipsy fellow near the door. Cries of "put him out."]

"My friends, do not remove him. Let the misguided man stay. I see that he is a victim of that evil which is swallowing up public virtue and sapping the foundation of society. As I was saying, when I can lay down the cares of office and retire to the sweets of private life in some such sweet, peaceful, intelligent, wide-awake and patriotic place as Hawkeye (applause). I have traveled much, I have seen all parts of our glorious union, but I have never seen a lovelier village than yours, or one that has more signs of commercial and industrial and religious prosperity—(more applause)."

The Senator then launched into a sketch of our great country, and dwelt for an hour or more upon its prosperity and the dangers which threatened it.

He then touched reverently upon the institutions of religion, and upon the necessity of private purity, if we were to have any public morality. "I trust," he said, "that there are children within the sound of my voice," and after some remarks to them, the Senator closed with an apostrophe to "the genius of American Liberty, walking with the Sunday School in one hand and Temperance in the other up the glorified steps of the National Capitol."

Col. Sellers did not of course lose the opportunity to impress upon so influential a person as the Senator the desirability of improving the navigation of Columbus river. He and Mr. Brierly took the Senator over to Napoleon and opened to him their plan. It was a plan that the Senator could understand without a great deal of explanation, for he seemed to be familiar with the like improvements elsewhere. When, however, they reached Stone's Landing the Senator looked about him and inquired,

"Is this Napoleon?"

"This is the nucleus, the nucleus," said the Colonel, unrolling his map. "Here is the deepo, the church, the City Hall and so on."

"Ah, I see. How far from here is Columbus River? Does that stream empty—"

"That, why, that's Goose Run. Thar ain't no Columbus, thout'n it's over to Hawkeye," interrupted one of the citizens, who had come out to stare at the strangers. "A railroad come here last summer, but it haint been here no mo'."

"Yes, sir," the Colonel hastened to explain, "in the old records Columbus River is called Goose Run. You see how it sweeps round the town—forty-nine miles to the Missouri; sloop navigation all the way pretty much, drains this whole country; when it's improved steamboats will run right up here. It's got to be enlarged, deepened. You see by the map, Columbus River. This country must have water communication!"

"You'll want a considerable appropriation, Col. Sellers.

"I should say a million; is that your figure Mr. Brierly."

"According to our surveys," said Harry, "a million would do it; a million spent on the river would make Napoleon worth two millions at least."

"I see," nodded the Senator. "But you'd better begin by asking only for two or three hundred thousand, the usual way. You can begin to sell town lots on that appropriation you know."

The Senator, himself, to do him justice, was not very much interested in the country or the stream, but he favored the appropriation, and he gave the Colonel and Mr. Brierly to understand that he would endeavor to get it through. Harry, who thought he was shrewd and understood Washington, suggested an interest.

But he saw that the Senator was wounded by the suggestion.

"You will offend me by repeating such an observation," he said. "Whatever I do will be for the public interest. It will require a portion of the appropriation for necessary expenses, and I am sorry to say that there are members who will have to be seen. But you can reckon upon my humble services."

This aspect of the subject was not again alluded to. The Senator possessed himself of the facts, not from his observation of the ground, but from the lips of Col. Sellers, and laid the appropriation scheme away among his other plans for benefiting the public.

It was on this visit also that the Senator made the acquaintance of Mr. Washington Hawkins, and was greatly taken with his innocence, his guileless manner and perhaps with his ready adaptability to enter upon any plan proposed.

Col. Sellers was pleased to see this interest that Washington had awakened, especially since it was likely to further his expectations with regard to the Tennessee lands; the Senator having remarked to the Colonel, that he delighted to help any deserving young man, when the promotion of a private advantage could at the same time be made to contribute to the general good. And he did not doubt that this was an opportunity of that kind.

The result of several conferences with Washington was that the Senator proposed that he should go to Washington with him and become his private secretary and the secretary of his committee; a proposal which was eagerly accepted.

The Senator spent Sunday in Hawkeye and attended church. He cheered the heart of the worthy and zealous minister by an expression of his sympathy in his labors, and by many inquiries in regard to the religious state of the region. It was not a very promising state, and the good man felt how much lighter his task would be, if he had the aid of such a man as Senator Dilworthy.

"I am glad to see, my dear sir," said the Senator, "that you give them the doctrines. It is owing to a neglect of the doctrines, that there is such a fearful falling away in the country.

I wish that we might have you in Washington—as chaplain, now, in the senate."

The good man could not but be a little flattered, and if sometimes, thereafter, in his discouraging work, he allowed the thought that he might perhaps be called to Washington as chaplain of the Senate, to cheer him, who can wonder. The Senator's commendation at least did one service for him, it elevated him in the opinion of Hawkeye.

Laura was at church alone that day, and Mr. Brierly walked home with her. A part of their way lay with that of General Boswell and Senator Dilworthy, and introductions were made. Laura had her own reasons for wishing to know the Senator, and the Senator was not a man who could be called indifferent to charms such as hers. That meek young lady so commended herself to him in the short walk, that he announced his intentions of paying his respects to her the next day, an intention which Harry received glumly; and when the Senator was out of hearing he called him "an old fool."

"Fie," said Laura, "I do believe you are jealous, Harry. He is a very pleasant man. He said you were a young man of great promise."

The Senator did call next day, and the result of his visit was that he was confirmed in his impression that there was something about him very attractive to ladies. He saw Laura again and again during his stay, and felt more and more the subtle influence of her feminine beauty, which every man felt who came near her.

Harry was beside himself with rage while the Senator remained in town; he declared that women were always ready to drop any man for higher game; and he attributed his own ill-luck to the Senator's appearance. The fellow was in fact crazy about her beauty and ready to beat his brains out in chagrin. Perhaps Laura enjoyed his torment, but she soothed him with blandishments that increased his ardor, and she smiled to herself to think that he had, with all his protestations of love, never spoken of marriage. Probably the vivacious fellow never had thought of it. At any rate when he at length went away from Hawkeye he was no nearer it. But there was no telling to what desperate lengths his passion might not carry him.

Laura bade him good bye with tender regret, which, however, did not disturb her peace or interfere with her plans. The visit of Senator Dilworthy had become of more importance to her, and it by and by bore the fruit she longed for, in an invitation to visit his family in the National Capital during the winter session of Congress.

Chapter XXI

Unusquisque sua noverit ire via.—
Propert. Eleg. 25.

O lift your natures up:
Embrace our aims: work out your freedom. Girls,
Knowledge is now no more a fountain sealed;
Drink deep until the habits of the slave,
The sins of emptiness, gossip and spite
And slander, die.

The Princess.

WHETHER medicine is a science, or only an empirical method of getting a living out of the ignorance of the human race, Ruth found before her first term was over at the medical school that there were other things she needed to know quite as much as that which is taught in medical books, and that she could never satisfy her aspirations without more general culture.

"Does your doctor know any thing—I don't mean about medicine, but about things in general, is he a man of information and good sense?" once asked an old practitioner. "If he doesn't know any thing but medicine the chance is he doesn't know that."

The close application to her special study was beginning to tell upon Ruth's delicate health also, and the summer brought with it only weariness and indisposition for any mental effort.

In this condition of mind and body the quiet of her home and the unexciting companionship of those about her were more than ever tiresome.

She followed with more interest Philip's sparkling account of his life in the west, and longed for his experiences, and to know some of those people of a world so different from hers, who alternately amused and displeased him. He at least was learning the world, the good and the bad of it, as must happen to every one who accomplishes anything in it.

But what, Ruth wrote, could a woman do, tied up by custom, and cast into particular circumstances out of which it was almost impossible to extricate herself? Philip thought that he would go some day and extricate Ruth, but he did not write that, for he had the instinct to know that this was not the extrication she dreamed of, and that she must find out by her own experience what her heart really wanted.

Philip was not a philosopher, to be sure, but he had the old fashioned notion, that whatever a woman's theories of life might be, she would come round to matrimony, only give her time. He could indeed recall to mind one woman—and he never knew a nobler—whose whole soul was devoted and who believed that her life was consecrated to a certain benevolent project in singleness of life, who yielded to the touch of matrimony, as an icicle yields to a sunbeam.

Neither at home nor elsewhere did Ruth utter any complaint, or admit any weariness or doubt of her ability to pursue the path she had marked out for herself. But her mother saw clearly enough her struggle with infirmity, and was not deceived by either her gaiety or by the cheerful composure which she carried into all the ordinary duties that fell to her. She saw plainly enough that Ruth needed an entire change of scene and of occupation, and perhaps she believed that such a change, with the knowledge of the world it would bring, would divert Ruth from a course for which she felt she was physically entirely unfitted.

It therefore suited the wishes of all concerned, when autumn came, that Ruth should go away to school. She selected a large New England Seminary, of which she had often heard Philip speak, which was attended by both sexes and offered almost collegiate advantages of education. Thither she went in September, and began for the second time in the year a life new to her.

The Seminary was the chief feature of Fallkill, a village of two to three thousand inhabitants. It was a prosperous school, with three hundred students, a large corps of teachers, men and women, and with a venerable rusty row of academic buildings on the shaded square of the town. The students lodged and boarded in private families in the place, and so it came about that while the school did a great deal to support the town, the town gave the students society and the sweet influences of home life. It is at least respectful to say that the influences of home life are sweet.

Ruth's home, by the intervention of Philip, was in a family—one of the rare exceptions in life or in fiction—that had never known better days. The Montagues, it is perhaps well to say, had intended to come over in the Mayflower, but were detained at Delft Haven by the illness of a child. They came over to Massachusetts Bay in another vessel, and thus escaped the onus of that brevet nobility under which the successors of the Mayflower Pilgrims have descended. Having no factitious weight of dignity to carry, the Montagues steadily improved their condition from the day they landed, and they were never more vigorous or prosperous than at the date of this narrative. With character compacted by the rigid Puritan discipline of more than two centuries, they had retained its strength and purity and thrown off its narrowness, and were now blossoming under the generous modern influences. Squire Oliver Montague, a lawyer who had retired from the practice of his profession except in rare cases, dwelt in a square old fashioned New England mansion a quarter of a mile away from the green. It was called a mansion because it stood alone with ample fields about it, and had an avenue of trees leading to it from the road, and on the west commanded a view of a pretty little lake with gentle slopes and nodding groves. But it was just a plain, roomy house, capable of extending to many guests an unpretending hospitality.

The family consisted of the Squire and his wife, a son and a daughter married and not at home, a son in college at Cambridge, another son at the Seminary, and a daughter Alice, who was a year or more older than Ruth. Having only riches enough to be able to gratify reasonable desires, and yet make their gratifications always a novelty and a pleasure, the family occupied that just mean in life which is so rarely attained, and still more rarely enjoyed without discontent.

If Ruth did not find so much luxury in the house as in her own home, there were evidences of culture, of intellectual activity and of a zest in the affairs of all the world, which greatly impressed her. Every room had its book-cases or book-shelves, and was more or less a library; upon every table was liable to be a litter of new books, fresh periodicals and daily newspapers. There were plants in the sunny windows and some choice engravings on the walls, with bits of color in oil or water-colors; the piano was sure to be open and strewn with music; and there were photographs and little souvenirs here and there of foreign travel. An absence of any "what-nots" in the corners with rows of cheerful shells, and Hindoo gods, and Chinese idols, and nests of useless boxes of lac-quered wood, might be taken as denoting a languidness in the family concerning foreign missions, but perhaps unjustly.

At any rate the life of the world flowed freely into this hos-pitable house, and there was always so much talk there of the news of the day, of the new books and of authors, of Boston radicalism and New York civilization, and the virtue of Con-gress, that small gossip stood a very poor chance.

All this was in many ways so new to Ruth that she seemed to have passed into another world, in which she experienced a freedom and a mental exhilaration unknown to her before. Under this influence she entered upon her studies with keen enjoyment, finding for a time all the relaxation she needed, in the charming social life at the Montague house.

It is strange, she wrote to Philip, in one of her occasional letters, that you never told me more about this delightful family, and scarcely mentioned Alice who is the life of it, *just the noblest* girl, unselfish, knows how to do so many things, with lots of talent, with a dry humor, and an odd way of look-ing at things, and yet quiet and even serious often—one of your "capable" New England girls. We shall be great friends. It had never occurred to Philip that there was any thing ex-traordinary about the family that needed mention. He knew dozens of girls like Alice, he thought to himself, but only one like Ruth.

Good friends the two girls were from the beginning. Ruth was a study to Alice, the product of a culture entirely foreign to her experience, so much a child in some things, so much a woman in others; and Ruth in turn, it must be confessed, probing Alice sometimes with her serious grey eyes, won-dered what her object in life was, and whether she had any purpose beyond living as she now saw her. For she could scarcely conceive of a life that should not be devoted to the accomplishment of some definite work, and she had no doubt that in her own case everything else would yield to the pro-fessional career she had marked out.

"So you know Philip Sterling," said Ruth one day as the girls sat at their sewing. Ruth never embroidered, and never sewed when she could avoid it. Bless her.

"Oh yes, we are old friends. Philip used to come to Fallkill often while he was in college. He was once rusticated here for a term."

"Rusticated?"

"Suspended for some College scrape. He was a great favorite here. Father and he were famous friends. Father said that Philip had no end of nonsense in him and was always blundering into something, but he was a royal good fellow and would come out all right."

"Did you think he was fickle?"

"Why, I never thought whether he was or not," replied Alice looking up. "I suppose he was always in love with some girl or another, as college boys are. He used to make me his confidant now and then, and be terribly in the dumps."

"Why did he come to you?" pursued Ruth. "You were younger than he."

"I'm sure I don't know. He was at our house a good deal. Once at a picnic by the lake, at the risk of his own life, he saved sister Millie from drowning, and we all liked to have him here. Perhaps he thought as he had saved one sister, the other ought to help him when he was in trouble. I don't know."

The fact was that Alice was a person who invited confidences, because she never betrayed them, and gave abundant sympathy in return. There are persons, whom we all know, to whom human confidences, troubles and heart-aches flow as naturally as streams to a placid lake.

This is not a history of Fallkill, nor of the Montague family, worthy as both are of that honor, and this narrative cannot be diverted into long loitering with them. If the reader visits the village to-day, he will doubtless be pointed out the Montague dwelling, where Ruth lived, the cross-lots path she traversed to the Seminary, and the venerable chapel with its cracked bell.

In the little society of the place, the Quaker girl was a favorite, and no considerable social gathering or pleasure party was thought complete without her. There was something in this seemingly transparent and yet deep character, in her childlike gaiety and enjoyment of the society about her, and in her not seldom absorption in herself, that would have made her long remembered there if no events had subsequently occurred to recall her to mind.

To the surprise of Alice, Ruth took to the small gaieties of the village with a zest of enjoyment that seemed foreign to one who had devoted her life to a serious profession from the highest motives. Alice liked society well enough, she thought, but there was nothing exciting in that of Fallkill, nor anything novel in the attentions of the well-bred young gentlemen one met in it. It must have worn a different aspect to Ruth, for she entered into its pleasures at first with curiosity, and then with interest and finally with a kind of staid abandon that no one would have deemed possible for her. Parties, picnics, rowing-matches, moonlight strolls, nutting-expeditions in the October woods,—Alice declared that it was a whirl of dissipation. The fondness of Ruth, which was scarcely disguised, for the company of agreeable young fellows, who talked nothings, gave Alice opportunity for no end of banter.

"Do you look upon them as 'subjects,' dear?" she would ask.

And Ruth laughed her merriest laugh, and then looked sober again. Perhaps she was thinking, after all, whether she knew herself.

If you should rear a duck in the heart of the Sahara, no doubt it would swim if you brought it to the Nile.

Surely no one would have predicted when Ruth left Philadelphia that she would become absorbed to this extent, and so happy, in a life so unlike that she thought she desired. But no one can tell how a woman will act under any circumstances. The reason novelists nearly always fail in depicting women when they make them act, is that they let them do what they have observed some woman has done at sometime or another. And that is where they make a mistake; for a woman will never do again what has been done before. It is this uncertainty that causes women, considered as materials for fiction, to be so interesting to themselves and to others.

As the fall went on and the winter, Ruth did not distinguish herself greatly at the Fallkill Seminary as a student, a fact that apparently gave her no anxiety, and did not diminish her enjoyment of a new sort of power which had awakened within her.

Chapter XXII

Wohl giebt es im Leben kein süsseres Glück,
Als der Liebe Geständniss im Liebchen's Blick;
Wohl giebt es im Leben nicht höhere Lust,
Als Freuden der Liebe an liebender Brust.
Dem hat nie das Leben freundlich begegnet,
Den nicht die Weihe der Liebe gesegnet.
       Doch der Liebe Glück, so himmlisch, so schön,
       Kann nie ohne Glauben an Tugend bestehn.
                          Körner.

O ke aloha ka mea i oi aku ka maikai mamua o ka umeki poi a me ka ipukaia.

I N MID-WINTER, an event occurred of unusual interest to the inhabitants of the Montague house, and to the friends of the young ladies who sought their society.

This was the arrival at the Sassacus Hotel of two young gentlemen from the west.

It is the fashion in New England to give Indian names to the public houses, not that the late lamented savage knew how to keep a hotel, but that his warlike name may impress the traveler who humbly craves shelter there, and make him grateful to the noble and gentlemanly clerk if he is allowed to depart with his scalp safe.

The two young gentlemen were neither students for the Fallkill Seminary, nor lecturers on physiology, nor yet life assurance solicitors, three suppositions that almost exhausted the guessing power of the people at the hotel in respect to the names of "Philip Sterling and Henry Brierly, Missouri," on the register. They were handsome enough fellows, that was evident, browned by out-door exposure, and with a free and lordly way about them that almost awed the hotel clerk himself. Indeed, he very soon set down Mr. Brierly as a gentleman of large fortune, with enormous interests on his shoulders. Harry had a way of casually mentioning western investments, through lines, the freighting business, and the route through the Indian territory to Lower California, which was calculated to give an importance to his lightest word.

"You've a pleasant town here, sir, and the most comfortable looking hotel I've seen out of New York," said Harry to the clerk; "we shall stay here a few days if you can give us a roomy suite of apartments."

Harry usually had the best of everything, wherever he went, as such fellows always do have in this accommodating world. Philip would have been quite content with less expensive quarters, but there was no resisting Harry's generosity in such matters.

Railroad surveying and real-estate operations were at a standstill during the winter in Missouri, and the young men had taken advantage of the lull to come east, Philip to see if there was any disposition in his friends, the railway contractors, to give him a share in the Salt Lick Union Pacific Extension, and Harry to open out to his uncle the prospects of the new city at Stone's Landing, and to procure congressional appropriations for the harbor and for making Goose Run navigable. Harry had with him a map of that noble stream and of the harbor, with a perfect net-work of railroads centering in it, pictures of wharves, crowded with steamboats, and of huge grain-elevators on the bank, all of which grew out of the combined imaginations of Col. Sellers and Mr. Brierly. The Colonel had entire confidence in Harry's influence with Wall street, and with congressmen, to bring about the consummation of their scheme, and he waited his return in the empty house at Hawkeye, feeding his pinched family upon the most gorgeous expectations with a reckless prodigality.

"Don't let 'em into the thing more than is necessary," says the Colonel to Harry; "give 'em a small interest; a lot apiece in the suburbs of the Landing ought to do a congressman, but I reckon you'll have to mortgage a part of the city itself to the brokers."

Harry did not find that eagerness to lend money on Stone's Landing in Wall street which Col. Sellers had expected, (it had seen too many such maps as he exhibited), although his uncle and some of the brokers looked with more favor on the appropriation for improving the navigation of Columbus River, and were not disinclined to form a company for that purpose. An appropriation was a tangible thing, if you could get hold of it, and it made little difference what it was appropriated for, so long as you got hold of it.

Pending these weighty negotiations, Philip has persuaded Harry to take a little run up to Fallkill, a not difficult task, for that young man would at any time have turned his back upon all the land in the West at sight of a new and pretty face, and he had, it must be confessed, a facility in love making which made it not at all an interference with the more serious business of life. He could not, to be sure, conceive how Philip could be interested in a young lady who was studying medicine, but he had no objection to going, for he did not doubt that there were other girls in Fallkill who were worth a week's attention.

The young men were received at the house of the Montagues with the hospitality which never failed there.

"We are glad to see you again," exclaimed the Squire heartily; "you are welcome Mr. Brierly, any friend of Phil's is welcome at our house."

"It's more like home to me, than any place except my own home," cried Philip, as he looked about the cheerful house and went through a general hand-shaking.

"It's a long time, though, since you have been here to say so," Alice said, with her father's frankness of manner; and I suspect we owe the visit now to your sudden interest in the Fallkill Seminary."

Philip's color came, as it had an awkward way of doing in his tell-tale face, but before he could stammer a reply, Harry came in with,

"That accounts for Phil's wish to build a Seminary at Stone's Landing, our place in Missouri, when Col. Sellers insisted it should be a University. Phil appears to have a weakness for Seminaries."

"It would have been better for your friend Sellers," retorted Philip, "if he had had a weakness for district schools. Col. Sellers, Miss Alice, is a great friend of Harry's, who is always trying to build a house by beginning at the top."

"I suppose it's as easy to build a University on paper as a Seminary, and it looks better," was Harry's reflection; at which the Squire laughed, and said he quite agreed with him. The old gentleman understood Stone's Landing a good deal better than he would have done after an hour's talk with either of its expectant proprietors.

At this moment, and while Philip was trying to frame a question that he found it exceedingly difficult to put into words, the door opened quietly, and Ruth entered. Taking in the group with a quick glance, her eye lighted up, and with a merry smile she advanced and shook hands with Philip. She was so unconstrained and sincerely cordial, that it made that hero of the west feel somehow young, and very ill at ease.

For months and months he had thought of this meeting and pictured it to himself a hundred times, but he had never imagined it would be like this. He should meet Ruth unexpectedly, as she was walking alone from the school, perhaps, or entering the room where he was waiting for her, and she would cry "Oh! Phil," and then check herself, and perhaps blush, and Philip calm but eager and enthusiastic, would reassure her by his warm manner, and he would take her hand impressively, and she would look up timidly, and after his long absence, perhaps he would be permitted to——. Good heavens, how many times he had come to this point, and wondered if it could happen so. Well, well; he had never supposed that he should be the one embarrassed, and above all by a sincere and cordial welcome.

"We heard you were at the Sassacus House," were Ruth's first words; "and this I suppose is your friend?"

"I beg your pardon," Philip at length blundered out, "this is Mr. Brierly of whom I have written you."

And Ruth welcomed Harry with a friendliness that Philip thought was due to his friend, to be sure, but which seemed to him too level with her reception of himself, but which Harry received as his due from the other sex.

Questions were asked about the journey and about the West, and the conversation became a general one, until Philip at length found himself talking with the Squire in relation to land and railroads and things he couldn't keep his mind on; especially as he heard Ruth and Harry in an animated discourse, and caught the words "New York," and "opera," and "reception," and knew that Harry was giving his imagination full range in the world of fashion.

Harry knew all about the opera, green room and all (at least he said so) and knew a good many of the operas and could make very entertaining stories of their plots, telling how the soprano came in here, and the basso here, humming the beginning of their airs—tum-ti-tum-ti-ti—suggesting the profound dissatisfaction of the basso recitative—down-among-the-dead-men—and touching off the whole with an airy grace quite captivating; though he couldn't have sung a single air through to save himself, and he hadn't an ear to know whether it was sung correctly. All the same he doted on the opera, and kept a box there, into which he lounged occasionally to hear a favorite scene and meet his society friends. If Ruth was ever in the city he should be happy to place his box at the disposal of Ruth and her friends. Needless to say that she was delighted with the offer.

When she told Philip of it, that discreet young fellow only smiled, and said that he hoped she would be fortunate enough to be in New York some evening when Harry had not already given the use of his private box to some other friend.

The Squire pressed the visitors to let him send for their trunks and urged them to stay at his house, and Alice joined in the invitation, but Philip had reasons for declining. They staid to supper, however, and in the evening Philip had a long talk apart with Ruth, a delightful hour to him, in which she spoke freely of herself as of old, of her studies at Philadelphia and of her plans, and she entered into his adventures and prospects in the West with a genuine and almost sisterly interest; an interest, however, which did not exactly satisfy Philip—it was too general and not personal enough to suit him. And with all her freedom in speaking of her own hopes, Philip could not detect any reference to himself in them; whereas he never undertook anything that he did not think of Ruth in connection with it, he never made a plan that had not reference to her, and he never thought of anything as complete if she could not share it. Fortune, reputation—these had no value to him except in Ruth's eyes, and there were times when it seemed to him that if Ruth was not on this earth, he should plunge off into some remote wilderness and live in a purposeless seclusion.

"I hoped," said Philip, "to get a little start in connection with this new railroad, and make a little money, so that I could come east and engage in something more suited to my tastes. I shouldn't like to live in the West. Would you?

"It never occurred to me whether I would or not," was the unembarrassed reply. "One of our graduates went to Chicago, and has a nice practice there. I don't know where I shall go. It would mortify mother dreadfully to have me driving about Philadelphia in a doctor's gig."

Philip laughed at the idea of it. "And does it seem as necessary to you to do it as it did before you came to Fallkill?"

It was a home question, and went deeper than Philip knew, for Ruth at once thought of practicing her profession among the young gentlemen and ladies of her acquaintance in the village; but she was reluctant to admit to herself that her notions of a career had undergone any change.

"Oh, I don't think I should come to Fallkill to practice, but I must do something when I am through school; and why not medicine?"

Philip would like to have explained why not, but the explanation would be of no use if it were not already obvious to Ruth.

Harry was equally in his element whether instructing Squire Montague about the investment of capital in Missouri, the improvement of Columbus River, the project he and some gentlemen in New York had for making a shorter Pacific connection with the Mississippi than the present one; or diverting Mrs. Montague with his experience in cooking in camp; or drawing for Miss Alice an amusing picture of the social contrasts of New England and the border where he had been.

Harry was a very entertaining fellow, having his imagination to help his memory, and telling his stories as if he believed them—as perhaps he did. Alice was greatly amused with Harry and listened so seriously to his romancing that he exceeded his usual limits. Chance allusions to his bachelor establishment in town and the place of his family on the Hudson, could not have been made by a millionaire more naturally.

"I should think," queried Alice, "you would rather stay in New York than to try the rough life at the West you have been speaking of."

"Oh, adventure," says Harry, "I get tired of New York. And besides I got involved in some operations that I had to see through. Parties in New York only last week wanted me to go down into Arizona in a big diamond interest. I told them, no, no speculation for me. I've got my interests in Missouri; and I wouldn't leave Philip, as long as he stays there."

When the young gentlemen were on their way back to the hotel, Mr. Philip, who was not in very good humor, broke out,

"What the deuce, Harry, did you go on in that style to the Montagues for?"

"Go on?" cried Harry. "Why shouldn't I try to make a pleasant evening? And besides, ain't I going to do those things? What difference does it make about the mood and tense of a mere verb? Didn't uncle tell me only last Saturday, that I might as well go down to Arizona and hunt for diamonds? A fellow might as well make a good impression as a poor one."

"Nonsense. You'll get to believing your own romancing by and by."

"Well, you'll see. When Sellers and I get that appropriation, I'll show you an establishment in town and another on the Hudson and a box at the opera."

"Yes, it will be like Col. Sellers' plantation at Hawkeye. Did you ever see that?"

"Now, don't be cross, Phil. She's just superb, that little woman. You never told me."

"Who's just superb?" growled Philip, fancying this turn of the conversation less than the other.

"Well, Mrs. Montague, if you must know." And Harry stopped to light a cigar, and then puffed on in silence.

The little quarrel didn't last over night, for Harry never appeared to cherish any ill-will half a second, and Philip was too sensible to continue a row about nothing; and he had invited Harry to come with him.

The young gentlemen stayed in Fallkill a week, and were every day at the Montagues, and took part in the winter gaieties of the village. There were parties here and there to which the friends of Ruth and the Montagues were of course invited, and Harry in the generosity of his nature, gave in return a little supper at the hotel, very simple indeed, with dancing in the hall, and some refreshments passed round. And Philip found the whole thing in the bill when he came to pay it.

Before the week was over Philip thought he had a new light on the character of Ruth. Her absorption in the small gaieties of the society there surprised him. He had few opportunities for serious conversation with her. There was always some butterfly or another flitting about, and when Philip showed by his manner that he was not pleased, Ruth laughed merrily enough and rallied him on his soberness—she declared he was getting to be grim and unsocial. He talked indeed more with Alice than with Ruth, and scarcely concealed from her the trouble that was in his mind. It needed, in fact, no word from him, for she saw clearly enough what was going forward, and knew her sex well enough to know there was no remedy for it but time.

"Ruth is a dear girl, Philip, and has as much firmness of purpose as ever, but don't you see she has just discovered that she is fond of society? Don't you let her see you are selfish about it, is my advice."

The last evening they were to spend in Fallkill, they were at the Montagues, and Philip hoped that he would find Ruth in a different mood. But she was never more gay, and there was a spice of mischief in her eye and in her laugh. "Confound it," said Philip to himself, "she's in a perfect twitter." He would have liked to quarrel with her, and fling himself out of the house in tragedy style, going perhaps so far as to blindly wander off miles into the country and bathe his throbbing brow in the chilling rain of the stars, as people do in novels; but he had no opportunity. For Ruth was as serenely unconscious of mischief as women can be at times, and fascinated him more than ever with her little demureness and half-confidences. She even said "Thee" to him once in reproach for a cutting speech he began. And the sweet little word made his heart beat like a trip-hammer, for never in all her life had she said "thee" to him before.

Was she fascinated with Harry's careless *bon homie* and gay assurance? Both chatted away in high spirits, and made the evening whirl along in the most mirthful manner. Ruth sang for Harry, and that young gentleman turned the leaves for her at the piano, and put in a bass note now and then where he thought it would tell.

Yes, it was a merry evening, and Philip was heartily glad when it was over, and the long leave-taking with the family was through with.

"Farewell Philip. Good night Mr. Brierly," Ruth's clear voice sounded after them as they went down the walk.

And she spoke Harry's name last, thought Philip.

Chapter XXIII

"O see ye not yon narrow road
　So thick beset wi' thorns and briers?
That is the Path of Righteousness,
　Though after it but few inquires.

"And see ye not yon braid, braid road,
　That lies across the lily leven?
That is the Path of Wickedness,
　Though some call it the road to Heaven."
Thomas the Rhymer.

P HILIP and Harry reached New York in very different states of mind. Harry was buoyant. He found a letter from Col. Sellers urging him to go to Washington and confer with Senator Dilworthy. The petition was in his hands. It had been signed by everybody of any importance in Missouri, and would be presented immediately.

"I should go on myself," wrote the Colonel, "but I am engaged in the invention of a process for lighting such a city as St. Louis by means of water; just attach my machine to the water-pipes anywhere and the decomposition of the fluid begins, and you will have floods of light for the mere cost of the machine. I've nearly got the lighting part, but I want to attach to it a heating, cooking, washing and ironing apparatus. It's going to be the great thing, but we'd better keep this appropriation going while I am perfecting it."

Harry took letters to several congressmen from his uncle and from Mr. Duff Brown, each of whom had an extensive acquaintance in both houses where they were well known as men engaged in large private operations for the public good, and men, besides, who, in the slang of the day, understood the virtues of "addition, division and silence."

Senator Dilworthy introduced the petition into the Senate with the remark that he knew, personally, the signers of it, that they were men interested, it was true, in the improvement of the country, but he believed without any selfish motive, and that so far as he knew the signers were loyal. It pleased him to see upon the roll the names of many colored citizens, and it must rejoice every friend of humanity to know that this lately emancipated race were intelligently taking part in the development of the resources of their native land. He moved the reference of the petition to the proper committee.

Senator Dilworthy introduced his young friend to influential members, as a person who was very well informed about the Salt Lick Extension of the Pacific, and was one of the Engineers who had made a careful survey of Columbus River; and left him to exhibit his maps and plans and to show the connection between the public treasury, the city of Napoleon and legislation for the benefit of the whole country.

Harry was the guest of Senator Dilworthy. There was scarcely any good movement in which the Senator was not interested. His house was open to all the laborers in the field of total abstinence, and much of his time was taken up in attending the meetings of this cause. He had a Bible class in the Sunday school of the church which he attended, and he suggested to Harry that he might take a class during the time he remained in Washington; Mr. Washington Hawkins had a class. Harry asked the Senator if there was a class of young ladies for him to teach, and after that the Senator did not press the subject.

Philip, if the truth must be told, was not well satisfied with his western prospects, nor altogether with the people he had fallen in with. The railroad contractors held out large but rather indefinite promises. Opportunities for a fortune he did not doubt existed in Missouri, but for himself he saw no better means for livelihood than the mastery of the profession he had rather thoughtlessly entered upon. During the summer he had made considerable practical advance in the science of engineering; he had been diligent, and made himself to a certain extent necessary to the work he was engaged on. The contractors called him into their consultations frequently, as to the character of the country he had been over, and the cost of constructing the road, the nature of the work, etc.

Still Philip felt that if he was going to make either reputation or money as an engineer, he had a great deal of hard study before him, and it is to his credit that he did not shrink from it. While Harry was in Washington dancing attendance upon the national legislature and making the acquaintance of the vast lobby that encircled it, Philip devoted himself day and night, with an energy and a concentration he was capable of, to the learning and theory of his profession, and to the science of railroad building. He wrote some papers at this time for the "Plow, the Loom and the Anvil," upon the strength of materials, and especially upon bridge-building, which attracted considerable attention, and were copied into the English "Practical Magazine." They served at any rate to raise Philip in the opinion of his friends the contractors, for practical men have a certain superstitious estimation of ability with the pen, and though they may a little despise the talent, they are quite ready to make use of it.

Philip sent copies of his performances to Ruth's father and to other gentlemen whose good opinion he coveted, but he did not rest upon his laurels. Indeed, so diligently had he applied himself, that when it came time for him to return to the West, he felt himself, at least in theory, competent to take charge of a division in the field.

Chapter XXIV

Cante-teca. Iapi-Waxte otonwe kin he cajeyatapi nawaḣon;
otonwe wijice ḣinca keyape se wacanmi.

Toketu-kaxta. Han, hecetu; takuwicawaye wijicapi ota hen
tipi.

Mahp. Ekta Oicim. ya.

THE CAPITAL of the Great Republic was a new world to
country-bred Washington Hawkins. St. Louis was a
greater city, but its floating population did not hail from great
distances, and so it had the general family aspect of the permanent population; but Washington gathered its people from
the four winds of heaven, and so the manners, the faces and
the fashions there, presented a variety that was infinite. Washington had never been in "society" in St. Louis, and he knew
nothing of the ways of its wealthier citizens and had never in-
spected one of their dwellings. Consequently, everything in
the nature of modern fashion and grandeur was a new and
wonderful revelation to him.

Washington is an interesting city to any of us. It seems to
become more and more interesting the oftener we visit it.
Perhaps the reader has never been there? Very well. You arrive either at night, rather too late to do anything or see
anything until morning, or you arrive so early in the morning that you consider it best to go to your hotel and sleep
an hour or two while the sun bothers along over the Atlantic. You cannot well arrive at a pleasant intermediate
hour, because the railway corporation that keeps the keys of
the only door that leads into the town or out of it take
care of that. You arrive in tolerably good spirits, because it
is only thirty-eight miles from Baltimore to the capital, and
so you have only been insulted three times (provided you
are not in a sleeping car—the average is higher, there):
once when you renewed your ticket after stopping over in
Baltimore, once when you were about to enter the "ladies'
car" without knowing it *was* a lady's car, and once when
you asked the conductor at what hour you would reach
Washington.

You are assailed by a long rank of hackmen who shake their whips in your face as you step out upon the sidewalk; you enter what they regard as a "carriage," in the capital, and you wonder why they do not take it out of service and put it in the museum: we have few enough antiquities, and it is little to our credit that we make scarcely any effort to preserve the few we have. You reach your hotel, presently—and here let us draw the curtain of charity—because of course you have gone to the wrong one. You being a stranger, how could you do otherwise? There are a hundred and eighteen bad hotels, and only one good one. The most renowned and popular hotel of them all is perhaps the worst one known to history.

It is winter, and night. When you arrived, it was snowing. When you reached the hotel, it was sleeting. When you went to bed, it was raining. During the night it froze hard, and the wind blew some chimneys down. When you got up in the morning, it was foggy. When you finished your breakfast at ten o'clock and went out, the sunshine was brilliant, the weather balmy and delicious, and the mud and slush deep and all-pervading. You will like the climate—when you get used to it.

You naturally wish to view the city; so you take an umbrella, an overcoat, and a fan, and go forth. The prominent features you soon locate and get familiar with; first you glimpse the ornamental upper works of a long, snowy palace projecting above a grove of trees, and a tall, graceful white dome with a statue on it surmounting the palace and pleasantly contrasting with the back-ground of blue sky. That building is the capitol; gossips will tell you that by the original estimates it was to cost $12,000,000, and that the government did come within $27,200,000 of building it for that sum.

You stand at the back of the capitol to treat yourself to a view, and it is a very noble one. You understand, the capitol stands upon the verge of a high piece of table land, a fine commanding position, and its front looks out over this noble situation for a city—but it don't see it, for the reason that when the capitol extension was decided upon, the property owners at once advanced their prices to such inhuman figures that the people went down and built the city in the muddy

low marsh *behind* the temple of liberty; so now the lordly
front of the building, with its imposing colonades, its projecting, graceful wings, its picturesque groups of statuary, and its
long terraced ranges of steps, flowing down in white marble
waves to the ground, merely looks out upon a sorrowful little
desert of cheap boarding houses.

So you observe, that you take your view from the back of
the capitol. And yet not from the airy outlooks of the dome,
by the way, because to get there you must pass through the
great rotunda: and to do that, you would have to see the marvelous Historical Paintings that hang there, and the bas-
reliefs—and what have you done that you should suffer thus?
And besides, you might have to pass through the old part of
the building, and you could not help seeing Mr. Lincoln, as
petrified by a young lady artist for $10,000—and you might
take his marble emancipation proclamation, which he holds
out in his hand and contemplates, for a folded napkin; and
you might conceive from his expression and his attitude, that
he is finding fault with the washing. Which is not the case.
Nobody knows what *is* the matter with him; but everybody
feels for him. Well, you ought not to go into the dome any
how, because it would be utterly impossible to go up there
without seeing the frescoes in it—and why should you be interested in the delirium tremens of art?

The capitol is a very noble and a very beautiful building,
both within and without, but you need not examine it now.
Still, if you greatly prefer going into the dome, go. Now your
general glance gives you picturesque stretches of gleaming
water, on your left, with a sail here and there and a lunatic
asylum on shore; over beyond the water, on a distant elevation, you see a squat yellow temple which your eye dwells
upon lovingly through a blur of unmanly moisture, for it re-
calls your lost boyhood and the Parthenons done in molasses
candy which made it blest and beautiful. Still in the distance,
but on this side of the water and close to its edge, the Monument to the Father of his Country towers out of the mud—
sacred soil is the customary term. It has the aspect of a factory
chimney with the top broken off. The skeleton of a decaying
scaffolding lingers about its summit, and tradition says that
the spirit of Washington often comes down and sits on those

rafters to enjoy this tribute of respect which the nation has reared as the symbol of its unappeasable gratitude. The Monument is to be finished, some day, and at that time our Washington will have risen still higher in the nation's veneration, and will be known as the Great-Great-Grandfather of his Country. The memorial Chimney stands in a quiet pastoral locality that is full of reposeful expression. With a glass you can see the cow-sheds about its base, and the contented sheep nimbling pebbles in the desert solitudes that surround it, and the tired pigs dozing in the holy calm of its protecting shadow.

Now you wrench your gaze loose and you look down in front of you and see the broad Pennsylvania Avenue stretching straight ahead for a mile or more till it brings up against the iron fence in front of a pillared granite pile, the Treasury building—an edifice that would command respect in any capital. The stores and hotels that wall in this broad avenue are mean, and cheap, and dingy, and are better left without comment. Beyond the Treasury is a fine large white barn, with wide unhandsome grounds about it. The President lives there. It is ugly enough outside, but that is nothing to what it is inside. Dreariness, flimsiness, bad taste reduced to mathematical completeness is what the inside offers to the eye, if it remains yet what it always has been.

The front and right hand views give you the city at large. It is a wide stretch of cheap little brick houses, with here and there a noble architectural pile lifting itself out of the midst—government buildings, these. If the thaw is still going on when you come down and go about town, you will wonder at the short-sightedness of the city fathers, when you come to inspect the streets, in that they do not dilute the mud a little more and use them for canals.

If you inquire around a little, you will find that there are more boarding houses to the square acre in Washington than there are in any other city in the land, perhaps. If you apply for a home in one of them, it will seem odd to you to have the landlady inspect you with a severe eye and then ask you if you are a member of Congress. Perhaps, just as a pleasantry, you will say yes. And then she will tell you that she is "full." Then you show her her advertisement in the morning paper, and there she stands, convicted and ashamed. She will try to blush, and it will be only polite in you to take the effort for the deed. She shows you her rooms, now, and lets you take one—but she makes you pay in advance for it. That is what you will get for pretending to be a member of Congress. If you had been content to be merely a private citizen, your trunk would have been sufficient security for your board. If you are curious and inquire into this thing, the chances are that your landlady will be ill-natured enough to say that the person and property of a Congressman are exempt from arrest or detention, and that with the tears in her eyes she has seen several of the people's representatives walk off to their several States and Territories carrying her unreceipted board bills in their pockets for keepsakes. And before you have been in Washington many weeks you will be mean enough to believe her, too.

Of course you contrive to see everything and find out everything. And one of the first and most startling things you find out is, that every individual you encounter in the City of Washington almost—and certainly every separate and distinct individual in the public employment, from the highest bureau chief, clear down to the maid who scrubs Department halls, the night watchmen of the public buildings and the darkey boy who purifies the Department spittoons—represents Political Influence. Unless you can get the ear of a Senator, or a Congressman, or a Chief of a Bureau or Department, and persuade him to use his "influence" in your behalf, you cannot get an employment of the most trivial nature in Washington. Mere merit, fitness and capability, are useless baggage to you without "influence." The population of Washington consists pretty much entirely of government employés and the people who board them. There are thousands of these employés, and they have gathered there from every corner of the Union and got their berths through the intercession (command is nearer the word) of the Senators and Representatives of their respective States. It would be an odd circumstance to see a girl get employment at three or four dollars a week in one of the great public cribs without any political grandee to back her, but merely because she was worthy, and competent, and a good citizen of a free country that "treats all persons alike." Washington would be mildly thunderstruck at such a thing as that. If you are a member of Congress, (no offence,) and one of your constituents who doesn't know anything, and does not want to go into the bother of learning something, and has no money, and no employment, and can't earn a living, comes besieging you for help, do you say, "Come, my friend, if your services were valuable you could get employment elsewhere—don't want you here?" Oh, no. You take him to a Department and say, "Here, give this person something to pass away the time at—and a salary"—and the thing is done. You throw him on his country. He is his country's child, let his country support him. There is something good and motherly about Washington, the grand old benevolent National Asylum for the Helpless.

The wages received by this great hive of employés are placed at the liberal figure meet and just for skilled and competent labor. Such of them as are immediately employed about the two Houses of Congress, are not only liberally paid also, but are remembered in the customary Extra Compensation bill which slides neatly through, annually, with the general grab that signalizes the last night of a session, and thus twenty per cent. is added to their wages, for—for fun, no doubt.

Washington Hawkins' new life was an unceasing delight to him. Senator Dilworthy lived sumptuously, and Washington's quarters were charming—gas; running water, hot and cold; bath-room, coal fires, rich carpets, beautiful pictures on the walls; books on religion, temperance, public charities and financial schemes; trim colored servants, dainty food—everything a body could wish for. And as for stationery, there was no end to it; the government furnished it; postage stamps were not needed—the Senator's frank could convey a horse through the mails, if necessary.

And then he saw such dazzling company. Renowned generals and admirals who had seemed but colossal myths when he was in the far west, went in and out before him or sat at the Senator's table, solidified into palpable flesh and blood; famous statesmen crossed his path daily; that once rare and awe-inspiring being, a Congressman, was become a common spectacle—a spectacle so common, indeed, that he could

contemplate it without excitement, even without embarrassment; foreign ministers were visible to the naked eye at happy
intervals; he had looked upon the President himself, and
lived. And more, this world of enchantment teemed with
speculation—the whole atmosphere was thick with it—and
that indeed was Washington Hawkins' native air; none other
refreshed his lungs so gratefully. He had found paradise at
last.

The more he saw of his chief the Senator, the more he honored him, and the more conspicuously the moral grandeur of
his character appeared to stand out. To possess the friendship
and the kindly interest of such a man, Washington said in a
letter to Louise, was a happy fortune for a young man whose
career had been so impeded and so clouded as his.

The weeks drifted by; Harry Brierly flirted, danced, added
lustre to the brilliant Senatorial receptions, and diligently
"buzzed" and "button-holed" Congressmen in the interest of
the Columbus River scheme; meantime Senator Dilworthy labored hard in the same interest—and in others of equal national importance. Harry wrote frequently to Sellers, and
always encouragingly; and from these letters it was easy to see
that Harry was a pet with all Washington, and was likely to
carry the thing through; that the assistance rendered him by
"old Dilworthy" was pretty fair—pretty fair; "and every little
helps, you know," said Harry.

Washington wrote Sellers officially, now and then. In one
of his letters it appeared that whereas no member of the
House committee favored the scheme at first, there was now
needed but one more vote to compass a majority report.
Closing sentence:

"Providence seems to further our efforts."
    (Signed,)   "ABNER DILWORTHY, U. S. S.,
                      per WASHINGTON HAWKINS, P. S."

At the end of a week, Washington was able to send the
happy news,—officially, as usual,—that the needed vote had
been added and the bill favorably reported from the Committee. Other letters recorded its perils in Committee of the
whole, and by and by its victory, by just the skin of its teeth,
on third reading and final passage. Then came letters telling

of Mr. Dilworthy's struggles with a stubborn majority in his own Committee in the Senate; of how these gentlemen succumbed, one by one, till a majority was secured.

Then there was a hiatus. Washington watched every move on the board, and he was in a good position to do this, for he was clerk of this committee, and also one other. He received no salary as private secretary, but these two clerkships, procured by his benefactor, paid him an aggregate of twelve dollars a day, without counting the twenty per cent. extra compensation which would of course be voted to him on the last night of the session.

He saw the bill go into Committee of the whole and struggle for its life again, and finally worry through. In the fullness of time he noted its second reading, and by and by the day arrived when the grand ordeal came, and it was put upon its final passage. Washington listened with bated breath to the "Aye!" "No!" "No!" "Aye!" of the voters, for a few dread minutes, and then could bear the suspense no longer. He ran down from the gallery and hurried home to wait.

At the end of two or three hours the Senator arrived in the bosom of his family, and dinner was waiting. Washington sprang forward, with the eager question on his lips, and the Senator said:

"We may rejoice freely, now, my son—Providence has crowned our efforts with success."

Chapter XXV

𒐕 𒐊𒑖𒐊 𒐊𒑏𒐊 𒐊𒑏𒐊 𒑉𒐖

WASHINGTON sent grand good news to Col. Sellers that night. To Louise he wrote:

"It is beautiful to hear him talk when his heart is full of thankfulness for some manifestation of the Divine favor. You shall know him, some day my Louise, and knowing him you will honor him, as I do."

Harry wrote:

"I pulled it through, Colonel, but it was a tough job, there is no question about that. There was not a friend to the measure in the House committee when I began, and not a friend in the Senate committee except old Dil himself, but they were all fixed for a majority report when I hauled off my forces. Everybody here says you *can't* get a thing like this through Congress without buying committees for straight-out cash on delivery, but I think I've taught them a thing or two—if I could only make them believe it. When I tell the old residenters that this thing went through without buying a vote or making a promise, they say, 'That's rather too thin.' And when I say thin or not thin it's a fact, anyway, they say 'Come, now, but do you really believe that?' and when I say I don't believe anything about it, I *know* it, they smile and say, 'Well, you are pretty innocent, or pretty blind, one or the other—there's no getting around that.' Why they really do believe that votes *have* been bought—they do indeed. But let them keep on thinking so. I have found out that if a man knows how to talk to women, and has a little gift in the way of argument with men, he can afford to play for an appropriation against a money bag and give the money bag odds in the game. We've raked in $200,000 of Uncle Sam's money, say what they will—and there is more where this came from, when we want it, and I rather fancy I am the person that can go in and occupy it, too, if I do say it myself, that shouldn't, perhaps. I'll be with you within a week. Scare up all the men you can, and put them to work at once. When I get there I propose to make things hum."

The great news lifted Sellers into the clouds. He went to work on the instant. He flew hither and thither making contracts, engaging men, and steeping his soul in the ecstasies of business. He was the happiest man in Missouri. And Louise was the happiest woman; for presently came a letter from Washington which said:

"Rejoice with me, for the long agony is over! We have waited patiently and faithfully, all these years, and now at last the reward is at hand. A man is to pay our family $40,000 for the Tennessee Land! It is but a little sum compared to what we could get by waiting, but I do so long to see the day when I can call you my own, that I have said to myself, better take this and enjoy life in a humble way than wear out our best days in this miserable separation. Besides, I can put this money into operations here that will increase it a hundred fold, yes, a thousand fold, in a few months. The air is full of such chances, and I know our family would consent in a moment that I should put in their shares with mine. Without a doubt we shall be worth half a million dollars in a year from this time—I put it at the very lowest figure, because it is always best to be on the safe side—half a million at the very lowest calculation, and then your father will give his consent and we can marry at last. Oh, that will be a glorious day. Tell our friends the good news—I want all to share it."

And she did tell her father and mother, but they said, let it be kept still for the present. The careful father also told her to write Washington and warn him not to speculate with the money, but to wait a little and advise with one or two wise old heads. She did this. And she managed to keep the good news to herself, though it would seem that the most careless observer might have seen by her springing step and her radiant countenance that some fine piece of good fortune had descended upon her.

Harry joined the Colonel at Stone's Landing, and that dead place sprang into sudden life. A swarm of men were hard at work, and the dull air was filled with the cheery music of labor. Harry had been constituted engineer-in-general, and he threw the full strength of his powers into his work. He moved among his hirelings like a king. Authority seemed to invest him with a new splendor. Col. Sellers, as general superintendent of a great public enterprise, was all that a mere human being could be—and more. These two grandees went at their imposing "improvement" with the air of men who had been charged with the work of altering the foundations of the globe.

They turned their first attention to straightening the river just above the Landing, where it made a deep bend, and where the maps and plans showed that the process of straightening would not only shorten distance but increase the "fall." They started a cut-off canal across the peninsula formed by the bend, and such another tearing up of the earth and slopping around in the mud as followed the order to the men, had never been seen in that region before. There was such a panic among the turtles that at the end of six hours there was not one to be found within three miles of Stone's Landing. They took the young and the aged, the decrepit and the sick upon their backs and left for tide-water in disorderly procession, the tadpoles following and the bull-frogs bringing up the rear.

Saturday night came, but the men were obliged to wait, because the appropriation had not come. Harry said he had written to hurry up the money and it would be along presently. So the work continued, on Monday. Stone's Landing was making quite a stir in the vicinity, by this time. Sellers threw a lot or two on the market, "as a feeler," and they sold well. He re-clothed his family, laid in a good stock of provisions, and still had money left. He started a bank account, in a small way—and mentioned the deposit casually to friends; and to strangers, too; to everybody, in fact; but not as a new thing—on the contrary, as a matter of life-long standing. He could not keep from buying trifles every day that were not wholly necessary, it was such a gaudy thing to get out his bank-book and draw a check, instead of using his old customary formula, "Charge it." Harry sold a lot or two, also— and had a dinner party or two at Hawkeye and a general good time with the money. Both men held on pretty strenuously for the coming big prices, however.

At the end of a month things were looking bad. Harry had besieged the New York headquarters of the Columbus River

Slack-water Navigation Company with demands, then commands, and finally appeals, but to no purpose; the appropriation did not come; the letters were not even answered. The
workmen were clamorous, now. The Colonel and Harry retired to consult.

"What's to be done?" said the Colonel.

"Hang'd if I know."

"Company say anything?"

"Not a word."

"You telegraphed yesterday?"

"Yes, and the day before, too."

"No answer?"

"None—confound them!"

Then there was a long pause. Finally both spoke at once:

"I've got it!"

"*I've* got it!"

"What's yours?" said Harry.

"Give the boys thirty-day orders on the Company for the
back pay."

"That's it—that's my own idea to a dot. But then—but
then——"

"Yes, I know," said the Colonel; "I know they can't wait
for the orders to go to New York and be cashed, but what's
the reason they can't get them discounted in Hawkeye?"

"Of course they can. That solves the difficulty. Everybody
knows the appropriation's been made and the Company's
perfectly good."

So the orders were given and the men appeased, though
they grumbled a little at first. The orders went well enough
for groceries and such things at a fair discount, and the
work danced along gaily for a time. Two or three purchasers put up frame houses at the Landing and moved in,
and of course a far-sighted but easy-going journeyman printer
wandered along and started the "Napoleon Weekly Telegraph and Literary Repository"—a paper with a Latin
motto from the Unabridged dictionary, and plenty of "fat"
conversational tales and double-leaded poetry—all for two
dollars a year, strictly in advance. Of course the merchants forwarded the orders at once to New York—and never heard of
them again.

At the end of some weeks Harry's orders were a drug in the market—nobody would take them at any discount whatever. The second month closed with a riot.—Sellers was absent at the time, and Harry began an active absence himself with the mob at his heels. But being on horseback, he had the advantage. He did not tarry in Hawkeye, but went on, thus missing several appointments with creditors. He was far on his flight eastward, and well out of danger when the next morning dawned. He telegraphed the Colonel to go down and quiet the laborers—*he* was bound east for money—everything would be right in a week—tell the men so—tell them to rely on him and not be afraid.

Sellers found the mob quiet enough when he reached the Landing. They had gutted the Navigation office, then piled the beautiful engraved stock-books and things in the middle of the floor and enjoyed the bonfire while it lasted. They had a liking for the Colonel, but still they had some idea of hanging him, as a sort of make-shift that might answer, after a fashion, in place of more satisfactory game.

But they made the mistake of waiting to hear what he had to say first. Within fifteen minutes his tongue had done its work and they were all rich men.—He gave every one of them a lot in the suburbs of the city of Stone's Landing, within a mile and a half of the future post office and railway station, and they promised to resume work as soon as Harry got east and started the money along. Now things were blooming and pleasant again, but the men had no money, and nothing to live on. The Colonel divided with them the money he still had in bank—an act which had nothing surprising about it because he was generally ready to divide whatever he had with anybody that wanted it, and it was owing to this very trait that his family spent their days in poverty and at times were pinched with famine.

When the men's minds had cooled and Sellers was gone, they hated themselves for letting him beguile them with fine speeches, but it was too late, now—they agreed to hang him another time—such time as Providence should appoint.

Chapter XXVI

பணம் எமத்த அரிதாய் இருக்கிறது

RUMORS of Ruth's frivolity and worldliness at Fallkill traveled to Philadelphia in due time, and occasioned no little undertalk among the Bolton relatives.

Hannah Shoecraft told another cousin that, for her part, she never believed that Ruth had so much more "mind" than other people; and Cousin Hulda added that she always thought Ruth was fond of admiration, and that was the reason she was unwilling to wear plain clothes and attend Meeting. The story that Ruth was "engaged" to a young gentleman of fortune in Fallkill came with the other news, and helped to give point to the little satirical remarks that went round about Ruth's desire to be a doctor!

Margaret Bolton was too wise to be either surprised or alarmed by these rumors. They might be true; she knew a woman's nature too well to think them improbable, but she also knew how steadfast Ruth was in her purposes, and that, as a brook breaks into ripples and eddies and dances and sports by the way, and yet keeps on to the sea, it was in Ruth's nature to give back cheerful answer to the solicitations of friendliness and pleasure, to appear idly delaying even, and sporting in the sunshine, while the current of her resolution flowed steadily on.

That Ruth had this delight in the mere surface play of life—that she could, for instance, be interested in that somewhat serious by-play called "flirtation," or take any delight in the exercise of those little arts of pleasing and winning which are none the less genuine and charming because they are not intellectual, Ruth, herself, had never suspected until she went to Fallkill. She had believed it her duty to subdue her gaiety of temperament, and let nothing divert her from what are called serious pursuits. In her limited experience she brought everything to the judgment of her own conscience, and settled the affairs of all the world in her own serene judgment hall. Perhaps her mother saw this, and saw also that there was nothing in the Friends' society to prevent her from growing more and more opinionated.

When Ruth returned to Philadelphia, it must be confessed—though it would not have been by her—that a medical career did seem a little less necessary for her than formerly; and coming back in a glow of triumph, as it were, and in the consciousness of the freedom and life in a lively society and in new and sympathetic friendship, she anticipated pleasure in an attempt to break up the stiffness and levelness of the society at home, and infusing into it something of the motion and sparkle which were so agreeable at Fallkill. She expected visits from her new friends, she would have company, the new books and the periodicals about which all the world was talking, and, in short, she would have life.

For a little while she lived in this atmosphere which she had brought with her. Her mother was delighted with this change in her, with the improvement in her health and the interest she exhibited in home affairs. Her father enjoyed the society of his favorite daughter as he did few things besides; he liked her mirthful and teasing ways, and not less a keen battle over something she had read. He had been a great reader all his life, and a remarkable memory had stored his mind with encyclopædic information. It was one of Ruth's delights to cram herself with some out of the way subject and endeavor to catch her father; but she almost always failed. Mr. Bolton liked company, a house full of it, and the mirth of young people, and he would have willingly entered into any revolutionary plans Ruth might have suggested in relation to Friends' society.

But custom and the fixed order are stronger than the most enthusiastic and rebellious young lady, as Ruth very soon found. In spite of all her brave efforts, her frequent correspondence, and her determined animation, her books and her music, she found herself settling into the clutches of the old monotony, and as she realized the hopelessness of her endeavors, the medical scheme took new hold of her, and seemed to her the only method of escape.

"Mother, thee does not know how different it is in Fallkill, how much more interesting the people are one meets, how much more life there is."

"But thee will find the world, child, pretty much all the same, when thee knows it better. I thought once as thee does now, and had as little thought of being a Friend as thee has. Perhaps when thee has seen more, thee will better appreciate a quiet life."

"Thee married young. I shall not marry young, and perhaps not at all," said Ruth, with a look of vast experience.

"Perhaps thee doesn't know thee own mind; I have known persons of thy age who did not. Did thee see anybody whom thee would like to live with always in Fallkill?"

"Not always," replied Ruth with a little laugh. "Mother, I think I wouldn't say 'always' to any one until I have a profession and am as independent as he is. Then my love would be a free act, and not in any way a necessity."

Margaret Bolton smiled at this new-fangled philosophy. "Thee will find that love, Ruth, is a thing thee won't reason about, when it comes, nor make any bargains about. Thee wrote that Philip Sterling was at Fallkill."

"Yes, and Henry Brierly, a friend of his; a very amusing young fellow and not so serious-minded as Philip, but a bit of a fop maybe."

"And thee preferred the fop to the serious-minded?"

"I didn't prefer anybody, but Henry Brierly was good company, which Philip wasn't always."

"Did thee know thee father had been in correspondence with Philip?"

Ruth looked up surprised and with a plain question in her eyes.

"Oh, it's not about thee."

"What then?" and if there was any shade of disappointment in her tone, probably Ruth herself did not know it.

"It's about some land up in the country. That man Bigler has got father into another speculation."

"That odious man! Why will father have any thing to do with him? Is it that railroad?"

"Yes. Father advanced money and took land as security, and whatever has gone with the money and the bonds, he has on his hands a large tract of wild land."

"And what has Philip to do with that?"

"It has good timber, if it could ever be got out, and father says that there must be coal in it; it's in a coal region. He wants Philip to survey it, and examine it for indications of coal."

"It's another of father's fortunes, I suppose," said Ruth. "He has put away so many fortunes for us that I'm afraid we never shall find them."

Ruth was interested in it nevertheless, and perhaps mainly because Philip was to be connected with the enterprise. Mr. Bigler came to dinner with her father next day, and talked a great deal about Mr. Bolton's magnificent tract of land, extolled the sagacity that led him to secure such a property, and led the talk along to another railroad which would open a northern communication to this very land.

"Pennybacker says it's full of coal, he's no doubt of it, and a railroad to strike the Erie would make it a fortune."

"Suppose you take the land and work the thing up, Mr. Bigler; you may have the tract for three dollars an acre."

"You'd throw it away, then," replied Mr. Bigler, "and I'm not the man to take advantage of a friend. But if you'll put a mortgage on it for the northern road, I wouldn't mind taking an interest, if Pennybacker is willing; but Pennybacker, you know, don't go much on land, he sticks to the legislature." And Mr. Bigler laughed.

When Mr. Bigler had gone, Ruth asked her father about Philip's connection with the land scheme.

"There's nothing definite," said Mr. Bolton. "Philip is showing aptitude for his profession. I hear the best reports of him in New York, though those sharpers don't intend to do anything but use him. I've written and offered him employment in surveying and examining the land. We want to know what it is. And if there is anything in it that his enterprise can dig out, he shall have an interest. I should be glad to give the young fellow a lift."

All his life Eli Bolton had been giving young fellows a lift, and shouldering the losses when things turned out unfortunately. His ledger, take it altogether, would not show a balance on the right side; but perhaps the losses on his books will turn out to be credits in a world where accounts are kept on a different basis. The left hand of the ledger will appear the right, looked at from the other side.

Philip wrote to Ruth rather a comical account of the bursting up of the city of Napoleon and the navigation improvement scheme, of Harry's flight and the Colonel's discomfiture. Harry left in such a hurry that he hadn't even time to bid Miss Laura Hawkins good-bye, but he had no doubt that Harry would console himself with the next pretty face he saw—a remark which was thrown in for Ruth's benefit. Col. Sellers had in all probability, by this time, some other equally brilliant speculation in his brain.

As to the railroad, Philip had made up his mind that it was merely kept on foot for speculative purposes in Wall street, and he was about to quit it. Would Ruth be glad to hear, he wondered, that he was coming East? For he was coming, in spite of a letter from Harry in New York, advising him to hold on until he had made some arrangements in regard to contracts, he to be a little careful about Sellers, who was somewhat visionary, Harry said.

The summer went on without much excitement for Ruth. She kept up a correspondence with Alice, who promised a visit in the fall, she read, she earnestly tried to interest herself in home affairs and such people as came to the house; but she found herself falling more and more into reveries, and growing weary of things as they were. She felt that everybody might become in time like two relatives from a Shaker establishment in Ohio, who visited the Boltons about this time, a father and son, clad exactly alike, and alike in manners. The son, however, who was not of age, was more unworldly and sanctimonious than his father; he always addressed his parent as "Brother Plum," and bore himself altogether in such a superior manner that Ruth longed to put bent pins in his chair. Both father and son wore the long, single breasted collarless coats of their society, without buttons, before or behind, but with a row of hooks and eyes on either side in front. It was Ruth's suggestion that the coats would be improved by a single hook and eye sewed on in the small of the back where the buttons usually are.

Amusing as this Shaker caricature of the Friends was, it oppressed Ruth beyond measure, and increased her feeling of being stifled.

It was a most unreasonable feeling. No home could be pleasanter than Ruth's. The house, a little out of the city, was one of those elegant country residences which so much charm visitors to the suburbs of Philadelphia. A modern dwelling and luxurious in everything that wealth could suggest for comfort, it stood in the midst of exquisitely kept lawns, with groups of trees, parterres of flowers massed in colors, with greenhouse, grapery and garden; and on one side, the garden sloped away in undulations to a shallow brook that ran over a pebbly bottom and sang under forest trees. The country about was the perfection of cultivated landscape, dotted with cottages, and stately mansions of Revolutionary date, and sweet as an English country-side, whether seen in the soft bloom of May or in the mellow ripeness of late October.

It needed only the peace of the mind within, to make it a paradise. One riding by on the Old Germantown road, and seeing a young girl swinging in the hammock on the piazza and intent upon some volume of old poetry or the latest novel, would no doubt have envied a life so idyllic. He could not have imagined that the young girl was reading a volume of reports of clinics and longing to be elsewhere.

Ruth could not have been more discontented if all the wealth about her had been as unsubstantial as a dream. Perhaps she so thought it.

"I feel," she once said to her father, "as if I were living in a house of cards."

"And thee would like to turn it into a hospital?"

"No. But tell me father," continued Ruth, not to be put off, "is thee still going on with that Bigler and those other men who come here and entice thee?"

Mr. Bolton smiled, as men do when they talk with women about "business." "Such men have their uses, Ruth. They keep the world active, and I owe a great many of my best operations to such men. Who knows, Ruth, but this new land purchase, which I confess I yielded a little too much to Bigler in, may not turn out a fortune for thee and the rest of the children?"

"Ah, father, thee sees every thing in a rose-colored light. I do believe thee wouldn't have so readily allowed me to begin the study of medicine, if it hadn't had the novelty of an experiment to thee."

"And is thee satisfied with it?"

"If thee means, if I have had enough of it, no. I just begin to see what I can do in it, and what a noble profession it is for a woman. Would thee have me sit here like a bird on a bough and wait for somebody to come and put me in a cage?"

Mr. Bolton was not sorry to divert the talk from his own affairs, and he did not think it worth while to tell his family of a performance that very day which was entirely characteristic of him.

Ruth might well say that she felt as if she were living in a house of cards, although the Bolton household had no idea of the number of perils that hovered over them, any more than thousands of families in America have of the business risks and contingencies upon which their prosperity and luxury hang.

A sudden call upon Mr. Bolton for a large sum of money, which must be forthcoming at once, had found him in the midst of a dozen ventures, from no one of which a dollar could be realized. It was in vain that he applied to his business acquaintances and friends; it was a period of sudden panic and no money. "A hundred thousand! Mr. Bolton," said Plumly. "Good God, if you should ask me for ten, I shouldn't know where to get it."

And yet that day Mr. Small (Pennybacker, Bigler and Small) came to Mr. Bolton with a piteous story of ruin in a coal operation, if he could not raise ten thousand dollars. Only ten, and he was sure of a fortune. Without it he was a beggar. Mr. Bolton had already Small's notes for a large amount in his safe, labeled "doubtful;" he had helped him again and again, and always with the same result. But Mr. Small spoke with a faltering voice of his family, his daughter in school, his wife ignorant of his calamity, and drew such a picture of their agony, that Mr. Bolton put by his own more pressing necessity, and devoted the day to scraping together, here and there, ten thousand dollars for this brazen beggar, who had never kept a promise to him nor paid a debt.

Beautiful credit! The foundation of modern society. Who shall say that this is not the golden age of mutual trust, of un-

limited reliance upon human promises? That is a peculiar condition of society which enables a whole nation to instantly
recognize point and meaning in the familiar newspaper anecdote, which puts into the mouth of a distinguished speculator
in lands and mines this remark:—"I wasn't worth a cent two
years ago, and now I owe two millions of dollars."

Chapter XXVII

⊘\\ 〰️〰️) 🚶 ⌇×〰️🚶 🎚️

ὡς οὖν τὰ πραχθέντ᾽ ἔβλεπεν, τυφλὸς γεγώς,
οὐ μὴν ὑπέπτηξ᾽ οὐδὲν, ἀλλ᾽ εὐκαρδίως
βάτον τιν᾽ ἄλλην ἤλατ᾽ εἰς ἀκανθίνην,
κἄκ᾽ τοῦδ᾽ ἐγένετ᾽ ἐξαῦθις ἐκ τυφλοῦ βλέπων.

IT WAS a hard blow to poor Sellers to see the work on his darling enterprise stop, and the noise and bustle and confusion that had been such refreshment to his soul, sicken and die out. It was hard to come down to humdrum ordinary life again after being a General Superintendent and the most conspicuous man in the community. It was sad to see his name disappear from the newspapers; sadder still to see it resurrected at intervals, shorn of its aforetime gaudy gear of compliments and clothed on with rhetorical tar and feathers.

But his friends suffered more on his account than he did. He was a cork that could not be kept under the water many moments at a time.

He had to bolster up his wife's spirits every now and then. On one of these occasions he said:

"It's all right, my dear, all right; it will all come right in a little while. There's $200,000 coming, and that will set things booming again. Harry seems to be having some difficulty, but that's to be expected—you can't move these big operations to the tune of Fisher's Hornpipe, you know. But Harry will get it started along presently, and then you'll see! I expect the news every day now."

"But Eschol, you've *been* expecting it every day, all along, haven't you?"

"Well, yes; yes—I don't know but I have. But anyway, the longer it's delayed, the nearer it grows to the time when it will start—same as every day you live brings you nearer to—nearer—"

"The grave?"

"Well, no—not that exactly; but you can't understand these things, Polly dear—women haven't much head for business, you know. You make yourself perfectly comfortable, old lady, and you'll see how we'll trot this right along. Why bless you, *let* the appropriation lag, if it wants to—that's no great matter—there's a bigger thing than that."

"Bigger than $200,000, Eschol?"

"Bigger, child?—why, what's $200,000? Pocket money! Mere pocket money! Look at the railroad! Did you forget the railroad? It ain't many months till spring; it will be coming right along, and the railroad swimming right along behind it. Where'll it be by the middle of summer? Just stop and fancy a moment—just think a little—don't anything suggest itself? Bless your heart, you dear women live right in the present all the time—but a man, why a man lives——"

"In the future, Eschol? But don't we live in the future most too much, Eschol? We do somehow seem to manage to live on next year's crop of corn and potatoes as a general thing while this year is still dragging along, but sometimes it's not a robust diet,—Eschol. But don't look that way, dear—don't mind what I say. I don't mean to fret, I don't mean to worry; and I *don't*, once a month, *do* I, dear? But when I get a little low and feel bad, I get a bit troubled and worrisome, but it don't mean anything in the world. It passes right away. I know you're doing all you can, and I don't want to seem repining and ungrateful—for I'm *not*, Eschol—you know I'm not, don't you?"

"Lord bless you, child, I know you are the very best little woman that ever lived—that ever lived on the whole face of the Earth! And I know that I would be a dog not to work for you and think for you and scheme for you with all my might. And I'll bring things all right yet, honey—cheer up and don't you fear. The railroad——"

"Oh, I *had* forgotten the railroad, dear, but when a body gets blue, a body forgets everything. Yes, the railroad—tell me about the railroad."

"Aha, my girl, don't you see? Things ain't so dark, are they? Now *I* didn't forget the railroad. Now just think for a moment—just figure up a little on the future dead moral certainties. For instance, call this waiter St. Louis.

"And we'll lay this fork (representing the railroad) from St. Louis to this potato, which is Slouchburg:

"Then with this carving knife we'll continue the railroad from Slouchburg to Doodleville, shown by the black pepper:

"Then we run along the—yes—the comb—to the tumbler —that's Brimstone:

"Thence by the pipe to Belshazzar, which is the salt-cellar:

"Thence to, to—that quill—Catfish—hand me the pin-cushion, Marie Antoinette:

"Thence right along these shears to this horse, Babylon:

"Then by the spoon to Bloody Run—thank you, the ink:

"Thence to Hail Columbia—snuffers, Polly, please—move that cup and saucer close up, that's Hail Columbia:

"Then—let me open my knife—to Hark-from-the-Tomb, where we'll put the candle-stick—only a little distance from Hail Columbia to Hark-from-the-Tomb—down-grade all the way.

"And there we strike Columbus River—pass me two or three skeins of thread to stand for the river; the sugar bowl will do for Hawkeye, and the rat trap for Stone's Landing— Napoleon, I mean—and you can see how much better Napoleon is located than Hawkeye. Now here you are with your railroad complete, and showing its continuation to Hal-lelujah and thence to Corruptionville.

"Now then—there you are! It's a beautiful road, beautiful. Jeff Thompson can out-engineer any civil engineer that ever sighted through an aneroid, or a theodolite, or whatever they call it—*he* calls it sometimes one and sometimes the other— just whichever levels off his sentence neatest, I reckon. But ain't it a ripping road, though? I tell you, it'll make a stir when it gets along. Just see what a country it goes through. There's your onions at Slouchburg—noblest onion country that graces God's footstool; and there's your turnip country all around Doodleville—bless my life, what fortunes are going to be made there when they get that contrivance perfected for extracting olive oil out of turnips—if there's any in them; and I reckon there is, because Congress has made an appropria-tion of money to test the thing, and they wouldn't have done that just on conjecture, of course. And now we come to the Brimstone region—cattle raised there till you can't rest—and corn, and all that sort of thing. Then you've got a little stretch along through Belshazzar that don't produce anything now—at least nothing but rocks—but irrigation will fetch it. Then from Catfish to Babylon it's a little swampy, but there's dead loads of peat down under there somewhere. Next is the Bloody Run and Hail Columbia country—tobacco enough can be raised there to support two such railroads. Next is the sassparilla region. I reckon there's enough of that truck along in there on the line of the pocket-knife, from Hail Columbia to Hark-from-the-Tomb to fat up all the consumptives in all the hospitals from Halifax to the Holy Land. It just grows like weeds! I've got a little belt of sassparilla land in there just tucked away unobstrusively waiting for my little Universal Expectorant to get into shape in my head. And I'll fix that, you know. One of these days I'll have all the nations of the earth expecto—"

"But Eschol, dear—"

"Don't interrupt me, Polly—I don't want you to lose the run of the map—well, *take* your toy-horse, James Fitz-James, if you must have it—and run along with you. Here, now—the soap will do for Babylon. Let me see—where was I? Oh yes—now we run down to Stone's Lan—Napoleon—now we run down to Napoleon. Beautiful road. Look at that, now. Perfectly straight line—straight as the way to the grave. And see where it leaves Hawkeye—clear out in the cold, my dear, clear out in the cold. That town's as bound to die as—well if I owned it I'd get its obituary ready, now, and notify the mourners. Polly, mark my words—in three years from this, Hawkeye'll be a howling wilderness. You'll see. And just look at that river—noblest stream that meanders over the thirsty earth!—calmest, gentlest artery that refreshes her weary bosom! Railroad goes all over it and all through it—wades right along on stilts. Seventeen bridges in three miles and a half—forty-nine bridges from Hark-from-the-Tomb to Stone's Landing altogether—forty-nine bridges, and culverts enough to culvert creation itself! Hadn't skeins of thread enough to represent them all—but you get an idea—perfect trestle-work of bridges for seventy-two miles. Jeff Thompson and I fixed all that, you know; he's to get the contracts and I'm to put them through on the divide. Just oceans of money in those bridges. It's the only part of the railroad I'm interested in,—down along the line—and it's all I want, too. It's enough, I should judge. Now here we are at Napoleon. Good enough country—plenty good enough—all it wants is population. That's all right—that will come. And it's no bad country *now* for calmness and solitude, I can tell you—though there's no money in that, of course. No money, but a man wants rest, a man wants peace—a man don't want to rip and tear around *all* the time. And here we go, now, just as straight as a string for Hallelujah—it's a beautiful angle—handsome upgrade all the way—and then away you go to Corruptionville, the gaudiest country for early carrots and cauliflowers that ever—good missionary field, too. There ain't such another missionary field outside the jungles of Central Africa. And patriotic?—why they named it after Congress itself. Oh, I warn you, my dear, there's a good time coming, and it'll be right along before you know what you're about, too. That railroad's fetching it. You see what it is as far as I've got, and if I had enough bottles and soap and boot-jacks and such things to carry it along to where it joins onto the Union Pacific, fourteen hundred miles from here, I should exhibit to you in that little internal improvement a spectacle of inconceivable sublimity. So, don't you see? We've got the railroad to fall back on; and in the meantime, what are we worrying about that $200,000 appropriation for? That's all right. I'd be willing to bet anything that the very next letter that comes from Harry will—"

The eldest boy entered just in the nick of time and brought a letter, warm from the post-office.

"Things *do* look bright, after all, Eschol. I'm sorry I was blue, but it did seem as if everything had been going against us for whole ages. Open the letter—open it quick, and let's know all about it before we stir out of our places. I am all in a fidget to know what it says."

The letter was opened, without any unnecessary delay.

Chapter XXVIII

Hvo der vil kjöbe Pölse af Hunden maa give ham Flesk igjen.

—Mit seinem eignen Verstande wurde Thrasyllus schwerlich durchgekommen seyn. Aber in solchen Fällen finden seines-gleichen für ihr Geld immer einen Spitzbuben, der ihnen seinen Kopf leiht; und dann ist es so viel als ob sie selbst einen hätten.

Wieland. Die Abderiten.

WHATEVER may have been the language of Harry's letter to the Colonel, the information it conveyed was con-densed or expanded, one or the other, from the following episode of his visit to New York:

He called, with official importance in his mien, at No. —, Wall street, where a great gilt sign betokened the presence of the head-quarters of the "Columbus River Slack-Water Navi-gation Company." He entered and gave a dressy porter his card, and was requested to wait a moment in a sort of ante-room. The porter returned in a minute, and asked whom he would like to see?

"The president of the company, of course."

"He is busy with some gentlemen, sir; says he will be done with them directly."

That a copper-plate card with "Engineer-in-Chief" on it should be received with such tranquility as this, annoyed Mr. Brierly not a little. But he had to submit. Indeed his annoy-ance had time to augment a good deal; for he was allowed to cool his heels a full half hour in the ante-room before those gentlemen emerged and he was ushered into the pres-ence. He found a stately dignitary occupying a very official chair behind a long green morocco-covered table, in a room sumptuously carpeted and furnished, and well garnished with pictures.

"Good morning, sir; take a seat—take a seat."

"Thank you sir," said Harry, throwing as much chill into his manner as his ruffled dignity prompted.

"We perceive by your reports and the reports of the Chief Superintendent, that you have been making gratifying progress with the work.—We are all very much pleased."

"Indeed? We did not discover it from your letters—which we have not received; nor by the treatment our drafts have met with—which were not honored; nor by the reception of any part of the appropriation, no part of it having come to hand."

"Why, my dear Mr. Brierly, there must be some mistake. I am sure we wrote you and also Mr. Sellers, recently—when my clerk comes he will show copies—letters informing you of the ten per cent. assessment."

"Oh, certainly, we got *those* letters. But what we wanted was money to carry on the work—money to pay the men."

"Certainly, certainly—true enough—but we credited you both for a large part of your assessments—I am sure that was in our letters."

"Of course that was in—I remember that."

"Ah, very well then. Now we begin to understand each other."

"Well, I don't see that we do. There's two months' wages due the men, and——"

"How? Haven't you paid the men?"

"Paid them! How are we going to pay them when you don't honor our drafts?"

"Why, my *dear* sir, I cannot see how you can find any fault with us. I am sure we have acted in a perfectly straight forward business way. Now let us look at the thing a moment. You subscribed for 100 shares of the capital stock, at $1,000 a share, I believe?"

"Yes, sir, I did."

"And Mr. Sellers took a like amount?"

"Yes, sir."

"Very well. No concern can get along without money. We levied a ten per cent. assessment. It was the original understanding that you and Mr. Sellers were to have the positions you now hold, with salaries of $600 a month each, while in active service. You were duly elected to these places, and you accepted them. Am I right?"

"Certainly."

"Very well. You were given your instructions and put to work. By your reports it appears that you have expended the sum of $9,640 upon the said work. Two months salary to you two officers amounts altogether to $2,400—about one-eighth of your ten per cent. assessment, you see; which leaves you in debt to the company for the other seven-eighths of the assessment—viz, something over $8,000 apiece. Now instead of requiring you to forward this aggregate of $16,000 or $17,000 to New York, the company voted unanimously to let you pay it over to the contractors, laborers from time to time, and give you credit on the books for it. And they did it without a murmur, too, for they were pleased with the progress you had made, and were glad to pay you that little compliment— and a very neat one it was, too, I am sure. The work you did fell short of $10,000, a trifle. Let me see—$9,640 from $20,000—salary $2,400 added—ah yes, the balance due the company from yourself and Mr. Sellers is $7,960, which I will take the responsibility of allowing to stand for the present, unless you prefer to draw a check now, and thus——"

"Confound it, do you mean to say that instead of the company owing us $2,400, we owe the company $7,960?"

"Well, yes."

"And that we owe the men and the contractors nearly ten thousand dollars besides?"

"Owe them! Oh bless my soul, you can't mean that you have not paid these people?"

"But I *do* mean it!"

The president rose and walked the floor like a man in bodily pain. His brows contracted, he put his hand up and clasped his forehead, and kept saying, "Oh, it is too bad, too bad, too bad! Oh, it is bound to be found out—nothing can prevent it—nothing!"

Then he threw himself into his chair and said:

"My dear Mr. Brierson, this is dreadful—perfectly dreadful. It will be found out. It is bound to tarnish the good name of the company; our credit will be seriously, most seriously impaired. How could you be so thoughtless—the men ought to have been paid though it beggared us all!"

"They ought, ought they? Then why the devil—my name is not Bryerson, by the way—why the mischief didn't the compa—why what in the nation ever became of the appropriation? Where *is* that appropriation?—if a stockholder may make so bold as to ask."

"The appropriation?—that paltry $200,000, do you mean?"

"Of course—but I didn't know that $200,000 was so very paltry. Though I grant, of course, that it is not a large sum, strictly speaking. But where is it?"

"My dear sir, you surprise me. You surely cannot have had a large acquaintance with this sort of thing. Otherwise you would not have expected much of a result from a mere *initial* appropriation like that. It was never intended for anything but a mere nest egg for the future and *real* appropriations to cluster around."

"Indeed? Well, was it a myth, or was it a reality? Whatever become of it?"

"Why the matter is simple enough. A Congressional appropriation costs money. Just reflect, for instance. A majority of the House Committee, say $10,000 apiece—$40,000; a majority of the Senate Committee, the same each—say $40,000; a little extra to one or two chairmen of one or two such committees, say $10,000 each—$20,000; and there's $100,000 of the money gone, to begin with. Then, seven male lobbyists, at $3,000 each—$21,000; one female lobbyist, $10,000; a high moral Congressman or Senator here and there—the high moral ones cost more, because they give tone to a measure—say ten of these at $3,000 each, is $30,000; then a lot of small-fry country members who won't vote for anything whatever without pay—say twenty at $500 apiece, is $10,000; a lot of dinners to members—say $10,000 altogether; lot of jimcracks for Congressmen's wives and children—those go a long way—you can't spend too much money in that line—well, those things cost in a lump, say $10,000—along there somewhere;—and then comes your printed documents—your maps, your tinted engravings, your pamphlets, your illuminated show cards, your advertisements in a hundred and fifty papers at ever so much a line—because you've *got* to keep the papers all right or you are gone up, you know. Oh, my dear sir, printing bills are destruction itself. Ours, so far amount to—let me see—10; 52; 22; 13;—and then there's 11; 14; 33—well, never mind the details, the total in clean numbers foots up $118,254.42 thus far!"

"What!"

"Oh, yes indeed. Printing's no bagatelle, I can tell you. And then there's your contributions, as a company, to Chicago fires and Boston fires, and orphan asylums and all that sort of thing—head the list, you see, with the company's full name and a thousand dollars set opposite—great card, sir—one of the finest advertisements in the world—the preachers mention it in the pulpit when it's a religious charity—one of the happiest advertisements in the world is your benevolent donation. Ours have amounted to sixteen thousand dollars and some cents up to this time."

"Good heavens!"

"Oh, yes. Perhaps the biggest thing we've done in the advertising line was to get an officer of the U.S. government, of perfectly Himmalayan official altitude, to write up our little internal improvement for a religious paper of enormous circulation—I tell you that makes our bonds go handsomely among the pious poor. Your religious paper is by far the best vehicle for a thing of this kind, because they'll 'lead' your article and put it right in the midst of the reading matter; and if it's got a few Scripture quotations in it, and some temperance platitudes and a bit of gush here and there about Sunday Schools, and a sentimental snuffle now and then about 'God's precious ones, the honest hard-handed poor,' it works the nation like a charm, my dear sir, and never a man suspects that it is an advertisement; but your secular paper sticks you right into the advertising columns and of course you don't take a trick. Give me a religious paper to advertise in, every time; and if you'll just look at their advertising pages, you'll observe that other people think a good deal as I do—especially people who have got little financial schemes to make everybody rich with. Of course I mean your great big metropolitan religious papers that know how to serve God and make money at the same time—that's your sort, sir, that's your sort—a religious paper that isn't run to make money is no use to *us*, sir, as an advertising medium—no use to anybody in our line of business. I guess our next best dodge was sending a pleasure trip of newspaper reporters out to Napoleon. Never paid them a cent; just filled them up with champagne and the fat of the land, put pen, ink and paper before them while they were red-hot, and bless your soul when you come to read their letters

you'd have supposed they'd been to heaven. And if a sentimental squeamishness held one or two of them back from
taking a less rosy view of Napoleon, our hospitalities tied his
tongue, at least, and he said nothing at all and so did us no
harm. Let me see—have I stated all the expenses I've been at?
No, I was near forgetting one or two items. There's your official salaries—you can't get good men for nothing. Salaries
cost pretty lively. And then there's your big high-sounding
millionaire names stuck into your advertisements as stockholders—another card, that—and they *are* stockholders, too,
but you have to *give* them the stock and non-assessable at
that—so they're an expensive lot. Very, very expensive thing,
take it all around, is a big internal improvement concern—but
you see that yourself, Mr. Bryerman—you see that, yourself,
sir."

"But look here. I think you are a little mistaken about its
ever having cost anything for Congressional votes. I happen
to know something about that. I've let you say your say—
now let me say mine. I don't wish to seem to throw any suspicion on anybody's statements, because we are all liable to be
mistaken. But how would it strike you if I were to say that *I*
was in Washington all the time this bill was pending?—and
what if I added that *I* put the measure through myself? Yes,
sir, I did that little thing. And moreover, I never paid a dollar
for any man's vote and never promised one. There are some
ways of doing a thing that are as good as others which other
people don't happen to think about, or don't have the knack
of succeeding in, if they do happen to think of them. My dear
sir, I am obliged to knock some of your expenses in the
head—for never a cent was paid a Congressman or Senator on
the part of this Navigation Company.

The president smiled blandly, even sweetly, all through this
harangue, and then said:

"Is that so?"

"Every word of it."

"Well it does seem to alter the complexion of things a
little. You are acquainted with the members down there, of
course, else you could not have worked to such advantage?"

"I know them all, sir. I know their wives, their children,
their babies—I even made it a point to be on good terms

with their lackeys. I know every Congressman well—even familiarly."

"Very good. Do you know any of their signatures? Do you know their handwriting?"

"Why I know their handwriting as well as I know my own—have had correspondence enough with them, I should think. And their signatures—why I can tell their initials, even."

The president went to a private safe, unlocked it and got out some letters and certain slips of paper. Then he said:

"Now here, for instance; do you believe that that is a genuine letter? Do you know this signature here?—and this one? Do you know who those initials represent—and are they forgeries?"

Harry was stupefied. There were things there that made his brain swim. Presently, at the bottom of one of the letters he saw a signature that restored his equilibrium; it even brought the sunshine of a smile to his face.

The president said:

"That name amuses you. You never suspected him?"

"Of course I ought to have suspected him, but I don't believe it ever really occurred to me. Well, well, well—how did you ever have the nerve to approach him, of all others?"

"Why my friend, we never think of accomplishing anything without his help. He is our mainstay. But how do those letters strike you?"

"They strike me dumb! What a stone-blind idiot I have been!"

"Well, take it all around, I suppose you had a pleasant time in Washington," said the president, gathering up the letters; "of course you must have had. Very few men could go there and get a money bill through without buying a single—"

"Come, now, Mr. President, that's plenty of that! I take back everything I said on *that* head. I'm a wiser man to-day than I was yesterday, I can tell you."

"I think you are. In fact I am satisfied you are. But now I showed you these things in confidence, you understand. Mention facts as much as you want to, but don't mention *names* to *anybody*. I can depend on you for that, can't I?"

"Oh, of course. I understand the necessity of that. I will not betray the names. But to go back a bit, it begins to look as if you never saw any of that appropriation at all?"

"We saw nearly ten thousand dollars of it—and that was all. Several of us took turns at log-rolling in Washington, and if we had charged anything for that service, none of that $10,000 would ever have reached New York."

"If you hadn't levied the assessment you would have been in a close place I judge?"

"Close? Have you figured up the total of the disbursements I told you of?"

"No, I didn't think of that."

"Well, let's see:

Spent in Washington, say, ...	$191,000
Printing, advertising, etc., say, ...	118,000
Charity, say, ...	16,000
Total, ...	$325,000

"The money to do that with, comes from——

Appropriation, ...	$200,000
Ten per cent. assessment on capital of	
$1,000,000	100,000
Total, ...	$300,000

"Which leaves us in debt some $25,000 at this moment. Salaries of home officers are still going on; also printing and advertising. Next month will show a state of things!"

"And then—burst up, I suppose?"

"By no means. Levy another assessment."

"Oh, I see. That's dismal."

"By no means."

"Why isn't it? What's the road out?"

"Another appropriation, don't you see?"

"Bother the appropriations. They cost more than they come to."

"Not the next one. We'll call for half a million—get it and go for a million the very next month."

"Yes, but the cost of it!"

The president smiled, and patted his secret letters affectionately. He said:

"All these people are in the next Congress. We shan't have to pay them a cent. And what is more, they will work like beavers for us—perhaps it might be to their advantage."

Harry reflected profoundly a while. Then he said:

"We send many missionaries to lift up the benighted races of other lands. How much cheaper and better it would be if those people could only come here and drink of our civilization at its fountain head."

"I perfectly agree with you, Mr. Beverly. Must you go? Well, good morning. Look in, when you are passing; and whenever I can give you any information about our affairs and prospects, I shall be glad to do it."

Harry's letter was not a long one, but it contained at least the calamitous figures that came out in the above conversation. The Colonel found himself in a rather uncomfortable place—no $1,200 salary forthcoming; and himself held responsible for half of the $9,640 due the workmen, to say nothing of being in debt to the company to the extent of nearly $4,000. Polly's heart was nearly broken; the "blues" returned in fearful force, and she had to go out of the room to hide the tears that nothing could keep back now.

There was mourning in another quarter, too, for Louise had a letter. Washington had refused, at the last moment, to take $40,000 for the Tennessee Land, and had demanded $150,000! So the trade fell through, and now Washington was wailing because he had been so foolish. But he wrote that his man might probably return to the city, soon, and then he meant to sell to him, sure, even if he had to take $10,000. Louise had a good cry—several of them, indeed—and the family charitably forebore to make any comments that would increase her grief.

Spring blossomed, summer came, dragged its hot weeks by, and the Colonel's spirits rose, day by day, for the railroad was making good progress. But by and by something happened. Hawkeye had always declined to subscribe anything toward the railway, imagining that her large business would be a sufficient compulsory influence; but now Hawkeye was frightened; and before Col. Sellers knew what he was about, Hawkeye, in a panic, had rushed to the front and subscribed such a sum that Napoleon's attractions suddenly sank into insignificance and the railroad concluded to follow a comparatively straight course instead of going miles out of its way to build up a metropolis in the muddy desert of Stone's Landing.

The thunderbolt fell. After all the Colonel's deep planning; after all his brain work and tongue work in drawing public attention to his pet project and enlisting interest in it; after all his faithful hard toil with his hands, and running hither and thither on his busy feet; after all his high hopes and splendid prophecies, the fates had turned their backs on him at last, and all in a moment his air-castles crumbled to ruins about him. Hawkeye rose from her fright triumphant and rejoicing, and down went Stone's Landing! One by one its meagre parcel of inhabitants packed up and moved away, as the summer waned and fall approached. Town lots were no longer salable, traffic ceased, a deadly lethargy fell upon the place once more, the "Weekly Telegraph" faded into an early grave, the wary tadpole returned from exile, the bullfrog resumed his ancient song, the tranquil turtle sunned his back upon bank and log and drowsed his grateful life away as in the old sweet days of yore.

Chapter XXIX

—Mihma hatak ash osh ilhkolit yakni ya hlopullit tʋmaha
holihta ʋlhpisa ho kʋshkoa untuklo ho hollissochit holisso
afohkit tahli cha.

Chosh. 18. 9.

PHILIP STERLING was on his way to Ilium, in the state of
Pennsylvania. Ilium was the railway station nearest to the
tract of wild land which Mr. Bolton had commissioned him to
examine.

On the last day of the journey as the railway train Philip
was on was leaving a large city, a lady timidly entered the
drawing-room car, and hesitatingly took a chair that was at
the moment unoccupied. Philip saw from the window that a
gentleman had put her upon the car just as it was starting. In
a few moments the conductor entered, and without waiting
an explanation, said roughly to the lady,

"Now *you* can't sit there. That seat's taken. Go into the
other car."

"I did not intend to take the seat," said the lady rising, "I
only sat down a moment till the conductor should come and
give me a seat."

"There aint any. Car's full. You'll have to leave."

"But, sir," said the lady, appealingly, "I thought——"

"Can't help what you thought—you must go into the
other car."

"The train is going very fast, let me stand here till we
stop."

"The lady can have my seat," cried Philip, springing up.

The conductor turned towards Philip, and coolly and deliberately surveyed him from head to foot, with contempt in
every line of his face, turned his back upon him without a
word, and said to the lady,

"Come, I've got no time to talk. You must go *now.*"

The lady, entirely disconcerted by such rudeness, and
frightened, moved towards the door, opened it and stepped

out. The train was swinging along at a rapid rate, jarring from side to side; the step was a long one between the cars and there was no protecting grating. The lady attempted it, but lost her balance, in the wind and the motion of the car, and fell! She would inevitably have gone down under the wheels, if Philip, who had swiftly followed her, had not caught her arm and drawn her up. He then assisted her across, found her a seat, received her bewildered thanks, and returned to his car.

The conductor was still there, taking his tickets, and growling something about imposition. Philip marched up to him, and burst out with,

"You are a brute, an infernal brute, to treat a woman that way."

"Perhaps you'd like to make a fuss about it," sneered the conductor.

Philip's reply was a blow, given so suddenly and planted so squarely in the conductor's face, that it sent him reeling over a fat passenger, who was looking up in mild wonder that any one should dare to dispute with a conductor, and against the side of the car.

He recovered himself, reached the bell rope, "Damn you, I'll learn you," stepped to the door and called a couple of brakemen, and then, as the speed slackened, roared out,

"Get off this train."

"I shall not get off. I have as much right here as you."

"We'll see," said the conductor, advancing with the brakemen. The passengers protested, and some of them said to each other, "That's too bad," as they always do in such cases, but none of them offered to take a hand with Philip. The men seized him, wrenched him from his seat, dragged him along the aisle, tearing his clothes, thrust him from the car, and then flung his carpet-bag, overcoat and umbrella after him. And the train went on.

The conductor, red in the face and puffing from his exertion, swaggered through the car, muttering "Puppy, I'll learn him." The passengers, when he had gone, were loud in their indignation, and talked about signing a protest, but they did nothing more than talk.

The next morning the Hooverville *Patriot and Clarion* had this "item":—

SLIGHTUALLY OVERBOARD.

"We learn that as the down noon express was leaving H—— yesterday a lady! (God save the mark) attempted to force herself into the already full palatial car. Conductor Slum, who is too old a bird to be caught with chaff, courteously informed her that the car was full, and when she insisted on remaining, he persuaded her to go into the car where she belonged. Thereupon a young sprig, from the East, blustered up, like a Shanghai rooster, and began to sass the conductor with his chin music. That gentleman delivered the young aspirant for a muss one of his elegant little left-handers, which so astonished him that he began to feel for his shooter. Whereupon Mr. Slum gentle raised the youth, carried him forth, and set him down just outside the car to cool off. Whether the young blood has yet made his way out of Bascom's swamp, we have not learned. Conductor Slum is one of the most gentlemanly and efficient officers on the road; but he ain't trifled with, not much. We learn that the company have put a new engine on the seven o'clock train, and newly upholstered the drawing-room car throughout. It spares no effort for the comfort of the traveling public."

Philip never had been before in Bascom's swamp, and there was nothing inviting in it to detain him. After the train got out of the way he crawled out of the briars and the mud, and got upon the track. He was somewhat bruised, but he was too angry to mind that. He plodded along over the ties in a very hot condition of mind and body. In the scuffle, his railway check had disappeared, and he grimly wondered, as he noticed the loss, if the company would permit him to walk over their track if they should know he hadn't a ticket.

Philip had to walk some five miles before he reached a little station, where he could wait for a train, and he had ample time for reflection. At first he was full of vengeance on the company. He would sue it. He would make it pay roundly. But then it occurred to him that he did not know the name of a witness he could summon, and that a personal fight against a railway corporation was about the most hopeless in the world. He then thought he would seek out that conductor, lie in wait for him at some station, and thrash him, or get thrashed himself.

But as he got cooler, that did not seem to him a project worthy of a gentleman exactly. Was it possible for a gentleman to get even with such a fellow as that conductor on the latter's own plane? And when he came to this point, he began to ask himself, if he had not acted very much like a fool. He didn't regret striking the fellow—he hoped he had left a mark on him. But, after all, was that the best way? Here was he, Philip Sterling, calling himself a gentleman, in a brawl with a vulgar conductor, about a woman he had never seen before. Why should he have put himself in such a ridiculous position? Wasn't it enough to have offered the lady his seat, to have rescued her from an accident, perhaps from death? Suppose he had simply said to the conductor, "Sir, your conduct is brutal, I shall report you." The passengers, who saw the affair, might have joined in a report against the conductor, and he might really have accomplished something. And, now! Philip looked at his torn clothes, and thought with disgust of his haste in getting into a fight with such an autocrat.

At the little station where Philip waited for the next train, he met a man who turned out to be a justice of the peace in that neighborhood, and told him his adventure. He was a kindly sort of man, and seemed very much interested.

"Dum 'em" said he, when he had heard the story.

"Do you think any thing can be done, sir?"

"Wal, I guess tain't no use. I hain't a mite of doubt of every word you say. But suin's no use. The railroad company owns all these people along here, and the judges on the bench too. Spiled your clothes! wal, "least said's soonest mended." You haint no chance with the company."

When next morning, he read the humorous account in the *Patriot and Clarion*, he saw still more clearly what chance he would have had before the public in a fight with the railroad company.

Still Philip's conscience told him that it was his plain duty to carry the matter into the courts, even with the certainty of defeat. He confessed that neither he nor any citizen had a right to consult his own feelings or conscience in a case where a law of the land had been violated before his own eyes. He confessed that every citizen's first duty in such a case is to put aside his own business and devote his time and his best efforts to seeing that the infraction is promptly punished; and he knew that no country can be well governed unless its citizens as a body keep religiously before their minds that they are the guardians of the law, and that the law officers are only the machinery for its execution, nothing more. As a finality he was obliged to confess that he was a bad citizen, and also that the general laxity of the time, and the absence of a sense of duty toward any part of the community but the individual himself were ingrained in him, and he was no better than the rest of the people.

The result of this little adventure was that Philip did not reach Ilium till daylight the next morning, when he descended, sleepy and sore, from a way train, and looked about him. Ilium was in a narrow mountain gorge, through which a rapid stream ran. It consisted of the plank platform on which he stood, a wooden house, half painted, with a dirty piazza (unroofed) in front, and a sign board hung on a slanting pole bearing the legend, "Hotel. P. Dusenheimer," a sawmill further down the stream, a blacksmith-shop, and a store, and three or four unpainted dwellings of the slab variety.

As Philip approached the hotel he saw what appeared to be a wild beast crouching on the piazza. It did not stir, however, and he soon found that it was only a stuffed skin. This cheerful invitation to the tavern was the remains of a huge panther which had been killed in the region a few weeks before. Philip examined his ugly visage and strong crooked fore-arm, as he was waiting admittance, having pounded upon the door.

"Vait a bit. I'll shoost put on my trowsers," shouted a voice from the window, and the door was soon opened by the yawning landlord.

"Morgen! Didn't hear d' drain oncet. Dem boys geeps me up zo spate. Gom right in."

Philip was shown into a dirty bar-room. It was a small room, with a stove in the middle, set in a long shallow box of sand, for the benefit of the "spitters," a bar across one end—a mere counter with a sliding glass-case behind it containing a few bottles having ambitious labels, and a wash-sink in one corner. On the walls were the bright yellow and black hand-bills of a traveling circus, with pictures of acrobats in human pyramids, horses flying in long leaps through the air, and sylph-like women in a paradisaic costume, balancing themselves upon the tips of their toes on the bare backs of frantic and plunging steeds, and kissing their hands to the spectators meanwhile.

As Philip did not desire a room at that hour, he was invited to wash himself at the nasty sink, a feat somewhat easier than drying his face, for the towel that hung in a roller over the sink was evidently as much a fixture as the sink itself, and belonged, like the suspended brush and comb, to the traveling public. Philip managed to complete his toilet by the use of his pocket-handkerchief, and declining the hospitality of the landlord, implied in the remark, "You won'd dake notin'?" he went into the open air to wait for breakfast.

The country he saw was wild but not picturesque. The mountain before him might be eight hundred feet high, and was only a portion of a long unbroken range, savagely wooded, which followed the stream. Behind the hotel, and across the brawling brook, was another level-topped, wooded range exactly like it. Ilium itself, seen at a glance, was old enough to be dilapidated, and if it had gained anything by being made a wood and water station of the new railroad, it was only a new sort of grime and rawness. P. Dusenheimer, standing in the door of his uninviting groggery, when the trains stopped for water, never received from the traveling public any patronage except facetious remarks upon his personal appearance. Perhaps a thousand times he had heard the remark, "*Ilium fuit,*" followed in most instances by a hail to himself as "Æneas," with the inquiry "Where is old Anchises?" At first he had replied, "Dere ain't no such man;" but irritated by its senseless repetition, he had latterly dropped into the formula of, "You be dam."

Philip was recalled from the contemplation of Ilium by the rolling and growling of the gong within the hotel, the din and clamor increasing till the house was apparently unable to contain it, when it burst out of the front door and informed the world that breakfast was on the table.

The dining room was long, low and narrow, and a narrow table extended its whole length. Upon this was spread a cloth which from appearance might have been as long in use as the towel in the bar-room. Upon the table was the usual service, the heavy, much nicked stone ware, the row of plated and rusty castors, the sugar bowls with the zinc tea-spoons sticking up in them, the piles of yellow biscuits, the discouraged-looking plates of butter. The landlord waited, and Philip was pleased to observe the change in his manner. In the bar-room he was the conciliatory landlord. Standing behind his guests at table, he had an air of peremptory patronage, and the voice in which he shot out the inquiry, as he seized Philip's plate, "Beefsteak or liver?" quite took away Philip's power of choice. He begged for a glass of milk, after trying that green hued compound called coffee, and made his breakfast out of that and some hard crackers which seemed to have been imported into Ilium before the introduction of the iron horse, and to have withstood a ten years siege of regular boarders, Greeks and others.

The land that Philip had come to look at was at least five miles distant from Ilium station. A corner of it touched the railroad, but the rest was pretty much an unbroken wilderness, eight or ten thousand acres of rough country, most of it such a mountain range as he saw at Ilium.

His first step was to hire three woodsmen to accompany him. By their help he built a log hut, and established a camp on the land, and then began his explorations, mapping down his survey as he went along, noting the timber, and the lay of the land, and making superficial observations as to the prospect of coal.

The landlord at Ilium endeavored to persuade Philip to hire the services of a witch-hazel professor of that region, who could walk over the land with his wand and tell him infallibly whether it contained coal, and exactly where the strata ran. But Philip preferred to trust to his own study of the country, and his knowledge of the geological formation. He spent a month in traveling over the land and making calculations; and made up his mind that a fine vein of coal ran through the mountain about a mile from the railroad, and that the place to run in a tunnel was half way towards its summit.

Acting with his usual promptness, Philip, with the consent of Mr. Bolton, broke ground there at once, and, before snow came, had some rude buildings up, and was ready for active operations in the spring. It was true that there were no outcroppings of coal at the place, and the people at Ilium said he "mought as well dig for plug terbaccer there;" but Philip had great faith in the uniformity of nature's operations in ages past, and he had no doubt that he should strike at this spot the rich vein that had made the fortune of the Golden Briar Company.

Chapter XXX

—"Gran pensier volgo; e, se tu lui secondi,
Seguiranno gli effetti alle speranze:
Tessi la tela, ch' io ti mostro ordita,
Di cauto vecchio esecutrice ardita."

"Belle domna vostre socors
    M'agra mestier, s'a vos plagues."

                    B. de Ventador.

ONCE MORE Louise had good news from her Washington—
Senator Dilworthy was going to sell the Tennessee Land
to the government! Louise told Laura in confidence. She had
told her parents, too, and also several bosom friends; but all
of these people had simply looked sad when they heard the
news, except Laura. Laura's face suddenly brightened under
it—only for an instant, it is true, but poor Louise was grateful for even that fleeting ray of encouragement. When next
Laura was alone, she fell into a train of thought something
like this:

"If the Senator has really taken hold of this matter, I may
look for that invitation to his house at any moment. I am
perishing to go! I do long to know whether I am only
simply a large-sized pigmy among these pigmies here, who
tumble over so easily when one strikes them, or whether I am
really—." Her thoughts drifted into other channels, for a season. Then she continued:—"He said I could be useful in the
great cause of philanthropy, and help in the blessed work of
uplifting the poor and the ignorant, if he found it feasible to
take hold of our Land. Well, that is neither here nor there;
what I want, is to go to Washington and find out what I am.
I want money, too; and if one may judge by what she hears,
there are chances there for a—." For a fascinating woman, she
was going to say, perhaps, but she did not.

Along in the fall the invitation came, sure enough. It came
officially through brother Washington, the private Secretary,
who appended a postscript that was brimming with delight
over the prospect of seeing the Duchess again. He said it

would be happiness enough to look upon her face once more—it would be almost too much happiness when to it was added the fact that she would bring messages with her that were fresh from Louise's lips.

In Washington's letter were several important enclosures. For instance, there was the Senator's check for $2,000—"to buy suitable clothing in New York with!" It was a loan to be refunded when the Land was sold. Two thousand—this was fine indeed. Louise's father was called rich, but Laura doubted if Louise had ever had $400 worth of new clothing at one time in her life. With the check came two through tickets—good on the railroad from Hawkeye to Washington via New York—and they were "dead-head" tickets, too, which had been given to Senator Dilworthy by the railway companies. Senators and representatives were paid thousands of dollars by the government for traveling expenses, but they always traveled "dead-head" both ways, and then did as any honorable, high-minded men would naturally do—declined to receive the mileage tendered them by the government. The Senator had plenty of railway passes, and could easily spare two to Laura—one for herself and one for a male escort. Washington suggested that she get some old friend of the family to come with her, and said the Senator would "dead-head" him home again as soon as he had grown tired of the sights of the capital. Laura thought the thing over. At first she was pleased with the idea, but presently she began to feel differently about it. Finally she said, "No, our staid, steady-going Hawkeye friends' notions and mine differ about some things—they respect me, now, and I respect them—better leave it so—I will go alone; I am not afraid to travel by myself." And so communing with herself, she left the house for an afternoon walk.

Almost at the door she met Col. Sellers. She told him about her invitation to Washington.

"Bless me!" said the Colonel. "I have about made up my mind to go there myself. You see we've got to get another appropriation through, and the Company want me to come east and put it through Congress. Harry's there, and he'll do what he can, of course; and Harry's a good fellow and always does the very best he knows how, but then he's young—rather young for some parts of such work, you know—and besides he talks too much, talks a good deal too much; and sometimes he appears to be a little bit visionary, too, I think—the worst thing in the world for a business man. A man like that always exposes his cards, sooner or later. This sort of thing wants an old, quiet, steady hand—wants an old cool head, you know, that knows men, through and through, and is used to large operations. I'm expecting my salary, and also some dividends from the company, and if they get along in time, I'll go along with you Laura—take you under my wing—you mustn't travel alone. Lord I wish I had the money right now.—But there'll be plenty soon—plenty."

Laura reasoned with herself that if the kindly, simple-hearted Colonel was going anyhow, what could she gain by traveling alone and throwing away his company? So she told him she accepted his offer gladly, gratefully. She said it would be the greatest of favors if he would go with her and protect her—not at his own expense as far as railway fares were concerned, of course; she could not expect him to put himself to so much trouble for her and pay his fare besides. But he wouldn't hear of her paying his fare—it would be only a pleasure to him to serve her. Laura insisted on furnishing the tickets; and finally, when argument failed, she said the tickets cost neither her nor any one else a cent—she had two of them—she needed but one—and if he would not take the other she would not go with him. That settled the matter. He took the ticket. Laura was glad that she had the check for new clothing, for she felt very certain of being able to get the Colonel to borrow a little of the money to pay hotel bills with, here and there.

She wrote Washington to look for her and Col. Sellers toward the end of November; and at about the time set the two travelers arrived safe in the capital of the nation, sure enough.

Chapter XXXI

Deh! ben fôra all' incontro ufficio umano,
  E bed n'avresti tu gioja e diletto,
Se la pietosa tua medica mano
Avvicinassi al valoroso petto.

Tasso.

She, gracious lady, yet no paines did spare
To doe him ease, or doe him remedy:
Many restoratives of vertues rare
And costly cordialles she did apply,
To mitigate his stubborne malady.
Spenser's Faerie Queene.

MR. HENRY BRIERLY was exceedingly busy in New York, so he wrote Col. Sellers, but he would drop everything and go to Washington.

The Colonel believed that Harry was the prince of lobbyists, a little too sanguine, may be, and given to speculation, but, then, he knew everybody; the Columbus River navigation scheme was got through almost entirely by his aid. He was needed now to help through another scheme, a benevolent scheme in which Col. Sellers, through the Hawkinses, had a deep interest.

"I don't care, you know," he wrote to Harry, "so much about the niggroes. But if the government will buy this land, it will set up the Hawkins family—make Laura an heiress—and I shouldn't wonder if Eschol Sellers would set up his carriage again. Dilworthy looks at it different, of course. He's all for philanthropy, for benefiting the colored race. There's old Balaam, was in the Interior—used to be the Rev. Orson Balaam of Iowa—he's made the riffle on the Injun; great Injun pacificator and land dealer. Balaam's got the Injun to himself, and I suppose that Senator Dilworthy feels that there is nothing left him but the colored man. I do reckon he is the best friend the colored man has got in Washington."

Though Harry was in a hurry to reach Washington, he stopped in Philadelphia, and prolonged his visit day after day, greatly to the detriment of his business both in New York and

223

Washington. The society at the Bolton's might have been a valid excuse for neglecting business much more important than his. Philip was there; he was a partner with Mr. Bolton now in the new coal venture, concerning which there was much to be arranged in preparation for the Spring work, and Philip lingered week after week in the hospitable house. Alice was making a winter visit. Ruth only went to town twice a week to attend lectures, and the household was quite to Mr. Bolton's taste, for he liked the cheer of company and something going on evenings. Harry was cordially asked to bring his traveling-bag there, and he did not need urging to do so. Not even the thought of seeing Laura at the capital made him restless in the society of the two young ladies; two birds in hand are worth one in the bush certainly.

Philip was at home—he sometimes wished he were not so much so. He felt that too much or not enough was taken for granted. Ruth had met him, when he first came, with a cordial frankness, and her manner continued entirely unrestrained. She neither sought his company nor avoided it, and this perfectly level treatment irritated him more than any other could have done. It was impossible to advance much in love-making with one who offered no obstacles, had no concealments and no embarrassments, and whom any approach to sentimentality would be quite likely to set into a fit of laughter.

"Why, Phil," she would say, "what puts you in the dumps to day? You are as solemn as the upper bench in Meeting. I shall have to call Alice to raise your spirits; my presence seems to depress you."

"It's not your presence, but your absence when you *are* present," began Philip, dolefully, with the idea that he was saying a rather deep thing. "But you won't understand me."

"No, I confess I cannot. If you really are so low as to think I am absent when I am present, it's a frightful case of aberration; I shall ask father to bring out Dr. Jackson. Does Alice appear to be present when she is absent?"

"Alice has some human feeling, anyway. She cares for something besides musty books and dry bones. I think, Ruth, when I die," said Philip, intending to be very grim and sarcastic, "I'll leave you my skeleton. You might like that."

"It might be more cheerful than you are at times," Ruth replied with a laugh. "But you mustn't do it without consulting Alice. She might not like it."

"I don't know why you should bring Alice up on every occasion. Do you think I am in love with her?"

"Bless you, no. It never entered my head. Are you? The thought of Philip Sterling in love is too comical. I thought you were only in love with the Ilium coal mine, which you and father talk about half the time."

This is a specimen of Philip's wooing. Confound the girl, he would say to himself, why does she never tease Harry and that young Shepley who comes here?

How differently Alice treated him. She at least never mocked him, and it was a relief to talk with one who had some sympathy with him. And he did talk to her, by the hour, about Ruth. The blundering fellow poured all his doubts and anxieties into her ear, as if she had been the impassive occupant of one of those little wooden confessionals in the Cathedral on Logan Square. Has a confessor, if she is young and pretty, any feeling? Does it mend the matter by calling her your sister?

Philip called Alice his good sister, and talked to her about love and marriage, meaning Ruth, as if sisters could by no possibility have any personal concern in such things. Did Ruth ever speak of him? Did she think Ruth cared for him? Did Ruth care for anybody at Fallkill? Did she care for anything except her profession? And so on.

Alice was loyal to Ruth, and if she knew anything she did not betray her friend. She did not, at any rate, give Philip too much encouragement. What woman, under the circumstances, would?

"I can tell you one thing, Philip," she said, "if ever Ruth Bolton loves, it will be with her whole soul, in a depth of passion that will sweep everything before it and surprise even herself."

A remark that did not much console Philip, who imagined that only some grand heroism could unlock the sweetness of such a heart; and Philip feared that he wasn't a hero. He did not know out of what materials a woman can construct a hero, when she is in the creative mood.

Harry skipped into this society with his usual lightness and gaiety. His good nature was inexhaustible, and though he liked to relate his own exploits, he had a little tact in adapting himself to the tastes of his hearers. He was not long in finding out that Alice liked to hear about Philip, and Harry launched out into the career of his friend in the West, with a prodigality of invention that would have astonished the chief actor. He was the most generous fellow in the world, and picturesque conversation was the one thing in which he never was bankrupt. With Mr. Bolton he was the serious man of business, enjoying the confidence of many of the monied men in New York, whom Mr. Bolton knew, and engaged with them in railway schemes and government contracts. Philip, who had so long known Harry, never could make up his mind that Harry did not himself believe that he was a chief actor in all these large operations of which he talked so much.

Harry did not neglect to endeavor to make himself agreeable to Mrs. Bolton, by paying great attention to the children, and by professing the warmest interest in the Friends' faith. It always seemed to him the most peaceful religion; he thought it must be much easier to live by an internal light than by a lot of outward rules; he had a dear Quaker aunt in Providence of whom Mrs. Bolton constantly reminded him. He insisted upon going with Mrs. Bolton and the children to the Friends Meeting on First Day, when Ruth and Alice and Philip, "world's people," went to a church in town, and he sat through the hour of silence with his hat on, in most exemplary patience. In short, this amazing actor succeeded so well with Mrs. Bolton, that she said to Philip one day,

"Thy friend, Henry Brierly, appears to be a very worldly-minded young man. Does he believe in anything?"

"Oh, yes," said Philip laughing, "he believes in more things than any other person I ever saw."

To Ruth Harry seemed to be very congenial. He was never moody for one thing, but lent himself with alacrity to whatever her fancy was. He was gay or grave as the need might be. No one apparently could enter more fully into her plans for an independent career.

"My father," said Harry, "was bred a physician, and practiced a little before he went into Wall street. I always had a leaning to the study. There was a skeleton hanging in the closet of my father's study when I was a boy, that I used to dress up in old clothes. Oh, I got quite familiar with the human frame."

"You must have," said Philip. "Was that where you learned to play the bones? He is a master of those musical instruments, Ruth; he plays well enough to go on the stage."

"Philip hates science of any kind, and steady application," retorted Harry. He didn't fancy Philip's banter, and when the latter had gone out, and Ruth asked,

"Why don't you take up medicine, Mr. Brierly?"

Harry said, "I have it in mind. I believe I would begin attending lectures this winter if it weren't for being wanted in Washington. But medicine is particularly women's province."

"Why so?" asked Ruth, rather amused.

"Well, the treatment of disease is a good deal a matter of sympathy. A woman's intuition is better than a man's. Nobody knows anything, really, you know, and a woman can guess a good deal nearer than a man."

"You are very complimentary to my sex."

"But," said Harry frankly, "I should want to choose my doctor; an ugly woman would ruin me, the disease would be sure to strike in and kill me at sight of her. I think a pretty physician, with engaging manners, would coax a fellow to live through almost anything."

"I am afraid you are a scoffer, Mr. Brierly."

"On the contrary, I am quite sincere. Wasn't it old what's his name? that said only the beautiful is useful?"

Whether Ruth was anything more than diverted with Harry's company, Philip could not determine. He scorned at any rate to advance his own interest by any disparaging communications about Harry, both because he could not help liking the fellow himself, and because he may have known that he could not more surely create a sympathy for him in Ruth's mind. That Ruth was in no danger of any serious impression he felt pretty sure, felt certain of it when he reflected upon her severe occupation with her profession. Hang it, he would say to himself, she is nothing but pure intellect anyway. And he only felt uncertain of it when she was in one of her moods of raillery, with mocking mischief in her eyes. At such times she seemed to prefer Harry's society to his. When Philip was miserable about this, he always took refuge with Alice, who was never moody, and who generally laughed him out of his sentimental nonsense. He felt at his ease with Alice, and was never in want of something to talk about; and he could not account for the fact that he was so often dull with Ruth, with whom, of all persons in the world, he wanted to appear at his best.

Harry was entirely satisfied with his own situation. A bird of passage is always at its ease, having no house to build, and no responsibility. He talked freely with Philip about Ruth, an almighty fine girl, he said, but what the deuce she wanted to study medicine for, he couldn't see.

There was a concert one night at the Musical Fund Hall and the four had arranged to go in and return by the Germantown cars. It was Philip's plan, who had engaged the seats, and promised himself an evening with Ruth, walking with her, sitting by her in the hall, and enjoying the feeling of protecting that a man always has of a woman in a public place. He was fond of music, too, in a sympathetic way; at least, he knew that Ruth's delight in it would be enough for him.

Perhaps he meant to take advantage of the occasion to say some very serious things. His love for Ruth was no secret to Mrs. Bolton, and he felt almost sure that he should have no opposition in the family. Mrs. Bolton had been cautious in what she said, but Philip inferred everything from her reply to his own questions, one day, "Has thee ever spoken thy mind to Ruth?"

Why shouldn't he speak his mind, and end his doubts? Ruth had been more tricksy than usual that day, and in a flow of spirits quite inconsistent, it would seem, in a young lady devoted to grave studies.

Had Ruth a premonition of Philip's intention, in his manner? It may be, for when the girls came down stairs, ready to walk to the cars, and met Philip and Harry in the hall, Ruth said, laughing,

"The two tallest must walk together," and before Philip knew how it happened Ruth had taken Harry's arm, and his evening was spoiled. He had too much politeness and good sense and kindness to show in his manner that he was hit. So he said to Harry,

"That's your disadvantage in being short." And he gave Alice no reason to feel during the evening that she would not have been his first choice for the excursion. But he was none the less chagrined, and not a little angry at the turn the affair took.

The Hall was crowded with the fashion of the town.—The concert was one of those fragmentary drearinesses that people endure because they are fashionable; *tours de force* on the piano, and fragments from operas, which have no meaning without the setting, with weary pauses of waiting between; there is the comic basso who is so amusing and on such familiar terms with the audience, and always sings the Barber; the attitudinizing tenor, with his languishing "Oh, Summer Night;" the soprano with her "Batti Batti," who warbles and trills and runs and fetches her breath, and ends with a noble scream that brings down a tempest of applause in the midst of which she backs off the stage smiling and bowing. It was this sort of concert, and Philip was thinking that it was the most stupid one he ever sat through, when just as the soprano was in the midst of that touching ballad, "Comin' thro' the Rye" (the soprano always sings "Comin' thro' the Rye" on an encore—the Black Swan used to make it irresistible, Philip remembered, with her arch, "If a body kiss a body") there was a cry of Fire!

The hall is long and narrow, and there is only one place of egress. Instantly the audience was on its feet, and a rush began for the door. Men shouted, women screamed, and panic seized the swaying mass. A second's thought would have convinced every one that getting out was impossible, and that the only effect of a rush would be to crush people to death. But a second's thought was not given. A few cried "Sit down, sit down," but the mass was turned towards the door. Women were down and trampled on in the aisles, and stout men, utterly lost to self-control, were mounting the benches, as if to run a race over the mass to the entrance.

Philip who had forced the girls to keep their seats saw, in a flash, the new danger, and sprang to avert it. In a second more those infuriated men would be over the benches and crushing Ruth and Alice under their boots. He leaped upon the bench in front of them and struck out before him with all his might, felling one man who was rushing on him, and checking for an instant the movement, or rather parting it, and causing it to flow on either side of him. But it was only for an instant; the pressure behind was too great, and the next Philip was dashed backwards over the seat.

And yet that instant of arrest had probably saved the girls, for as Philip fell, the orchestra struck up "Yankee Doodle" in the liveliest manner. The familiar tune caught the ear of the mass, which paused in wonder, and gave the conductor's voice a chance to be heard—"It's a false alarm!"

The tumult was over in a minute, and the next, laughter was heard, and not a few said, "I knew it wasn't anything." "What fools people are at such a time."

The concert was over, however. A good many people were hurt, some of them seriously, and among them Philip Sterling was found bent across the seat, insensible, with his left arm hanging limp and a bleeding wound on his head.

When he was carried into the air he revived, and said it was nothing. A surgeon was called, and it was thought best to drive at once to the Bolton's, the surgeon supporting Philip, who did not speak the whole way. His arm was set and his head dressed, and the surgeon said he would come round all right in his mind by morning; he was very weak. Alice who was not much frightened while the panic lasted in the hall, was very much unnerved by seeing Philip so pale and bloody. Ruth assisted the surgeon with the utmost coolness and with skillful hands helped to dress Philip's wounds. And there was a certain intentness and fierce energy in what she did that might have revealed something to Philip if he had been in his senses.

But he was not, or he would not have murmured "Let Alice do it, she is not too tall."

It was Ruth's first case.

Chapter XXXII

Lo, swiche sleightes and subtiltees
In women ben; for ay as besy as bees
Ben they us sely men for to deceive,
And from a sothe wol they ever weive.
Chaucer.

WASHINGTON'S delight in his beautiful sister was measureless. He said that she had always been the queenliest creature in the land, but that she was only commonplace before, compared to what she was now, so extraordinary was the improvement wrought by rich fashionable attire.

"But your criticisms are too full of brotherly partiality to be depended on, Washington. Other people will judge differently."

"Indeed they won't. You'll see. There will never be a woman in Washington that can compare with you. You'll be famous within a fortnight, Laura. Everybody will want to know you. You wait—you'll see."

Laura wished in her heart that the prophecy might come true; and privately she even believed it might—for she had brought all the women whom she had seen since she left home under sharp inspection, and the result had not been unsatisfactory to her.

During a week or two Washington drove about the city every day with her and familiarized her with all of its salient features. She was beginning to feel very much at home with the town itself, and she was also fast acquiring ease with the distinguished people she met at the Dilworthy table, and losing what little of country timidity she had brought with her from Hawkeye. She noticed with secret pleasure the little start of admiration that always manifested itself in the faces of the guests when she entered the drawing-room arrayed in evening costume:—she took comforting note of the fact that these guests directed a very liberal share of their conversation toward her; she observed with surprise, that famous statesmen and soldiers did not talk like gods, as a general thing, but said rather commonplace things for the most part; and she was filled with gratification to discover that she, on the contrary, was making a good many shrewd speeches and now and then a really brilliant one, and furthermore, that they were beginning to be repeated in social circles about the town.

Congress began its sittings, and every day or two Washington escorted her to the galleries set apart for lady members of the households of Senators and Representatives. Here was a larger field and a wider competition, but still she saw that many eyes were uplifted toward her face, and that first one person and then another called a neighbor's attention to her; she was not too dull to perceive that the speeches of some of the younger statesmen were delivered about as much and perhaps more at her than to the presiding officer; and she was not sorry to see that the dapper young Senator from Iowa came at once and stood in the open space before the president's desk to exhibit his feet as soon as she entered the gallery, whereas she had early learned from common report that his usual custom was to prop them on his desk and enjoy them himself with a selfish disregard of other people's longings.

Invitations began to flow in upon her and soon she was fairly "in society." "The season" was now in full bloom, and the first select reception was at hand—that is to say, a reception confined to invited guests.

Senator Dilworthy had become well convinced, by this time, that his judgment of the country-bred Missouri girl had not deceived him—it was plain that she was going to be a peerless missionary in the field of labor he designed her for, and therefore it would be perfectly safe and likewise judicious to send her forth well panoplied for her work.—So he had added new and still richer costumes to her wardrobe, and assisted their attractions with costly jewelry—loans on the future land sale.

This first select reception took place at a cabinet minister's—or rather a cabinet secretary's—mansion. When Laura and the Senator arrived, about half past nine or ten in the evening, the place was already pretty well crowded, and the white-gloved negro servant at the door was still receiving streams of guests.—The drawing-rooms were brilliant with gaslight, and as hot as ovens. The host and hostess stood just within the door of entrance; Laura was presented, and then she passed on into the maelstrom of be-jeweled and richly attired low-necked ladies and white-kid-gloved and steel pen-coated gentlemen—and wherever she moved she was followed by a buzz of admiration that was grateful to all her senses—so grateful, indeed, that her white face was tinged and its beauty heightened by a perceptible suffusion of color. She caught such remarks as, "Who is she?" "Superb woman!" "That is the new beauty from the west," etc., etc.

Whenever she halted, she was presently surrounded by Ministers, Generals, Congressmen, and all manner of aristocratic people. Introductions followed, and then the usual original question, "How do you like Washington, Miss Hawkins?" supplemented by that other usual original question, "Is this your first visit?"

These two exciting topics being exhausted, conversation generally drifted into calmer channels, only to be interrupted at frequent intervals by new introductions and new inquiries as to how Laura liked the capital and whether it was her first visit or not. And thus for an hour or more the Duchess moved through the crush in a rapture of happiness, for her doubts were dead and gone, now—she knew she could conquer here. A familiar face appeared in the midst of the multitude and Harry Brierly fought his difficult way to her side, his eyes shouting their gratification, so to speak:

"Oh, this *is* a happiness! Tell me, my dear Miss Hawkins—"

"Sh! I know what you are going to ask. I *do* like Washington—I like it ever so much!"

"No, but I was going to ask—"

"Yes, I am coming to it, coming to it as fast as I can. It *is* my first visit. I think you should know that yourself."

And straightway a wave of the crowd swept her beyond his reach.

"Now what can the girl mean? Of course she likes Washington—I'm not such a dummy as to have to ask her that. And as to its being her first visit, why hang it, she knows that I *knew* it was. Does she think I have turned idiot? Curious girl, anyway. But how they do swarm about her! She is the reigning belle of Washington after this night. She'll know five hundred of the heaviest guns in the town before this night's nonsense is over.

And this isn't even the beginning. Just as I used to say—she'll be a card in the matter of—yes *sir*! She shall turn the men's heads and I'll turn the women's! What a team that will be in politics here. I wouldn't take a quarter of a million for what I can do in this present session—no indeed I wouldn't. Now, here—I don't altogether like this. That insignificant secretary of legation is—why, she's smiling on him as if he—and now on the Admiral! Now she's illuminating that stuffy Congressman from Massachusetts—vulgar ungrammatical shovel-maker—greasy knave of spades. I don't like this sort of thing. She doesn't appear to be much distressed about *me*—she hasn't looked this way once. All right, my bird of Paradise, if it suits you, go on. But I think I know your sex. *I'll* go to smiling around a little, too, and see what effect *that* will have on you."

And he did "smile around a little," and got as near to her as he could to watch the effect, but the scheme was a failure—he could not get her attention. She seemed wholly unconscious of him, and so he could not flirt with any spirit; he could only talk disjointedly; he could not keep his eyes on the charmers he talked to; he grew irritable, jealous, and very unhappy. He gave up his enterprise, leaned his shoulder against a fluted pilaster and pouted while he kept watch upon Laura's every movement. His other shoulder stole the bloom from many a lovely cheek that brushed him in the surging crush, but he noted it not. He was too busy cursing himself inwardly for being an egotistical imbecile. An hour ago he had thought to take this country lass under his protection and show her "life" and enjoy her wonder and delight—and here she was, immersed in the marvel up to her eyes, and just a trifle more at home in it than he was himself. And now his angry comments ran on again:

"Now she's sweetening old Brother Balaam; and he—well he is inviting her to the Congressional prayer-meeting, no doubt—better let old Dilworthy alone to see that she doesn't overlook that. And now it's Splurge, of New York; and now it's Batters of New Hampshire—and now the Vice President! Well I may as well adjourn. I've got enough."

But he hadn't. He got as far as the door—and then struggled back to take one more look, hating himself all the while for his weakness.

Toward midnight, when supper was announced, the crowd thronged to the supper room where a long table was decked out with what seemed a rare repast, but which consisted of things better calculated to feast the eye than the appetite. The ladies were soon seated in files along the wall, and in groups here and there, and the colored waiters filled the plates and glasses and the male guests moved hither and thither conveying them to the privileged sex.

Harry took an ice and stood up by the table with other gentlemen, and listened to the buzz of conversation while he ate.

From these remarks he learned a good deal about Laura that was news to him. For instance, that she was of a distinguished western family; that she was highly educated; that she was very rich and a great landed heiress; that she was not a professor of religion, and yet was a Christian in the truest and best sense of the word, for her whole heart was devoted to the accomplishment of a great and noble enterprise—none other than the sacrificing of her landed estates to the uplifting of the down-trodden negro and the turning of his erring feet into the way of light and righteousness. Harry observed that as soon as one listener had absorbed the story, he turned about and delivered it to his next neighbor and the latter individual straightway passed it on. And thus he saw it travel the round of the gentlemen and overflow rearward among the ladies. He could not trace it backward to its fountain head, and so he could not tell who it was that started it.

One thing annoyed Harry a great deal; and that was the reflection that he might have been in Washington days and days ago and thrown his fascinations about Laura with permanent effect while she was new and strange to the capital, instead of dawdling in Philadelphia to no purpose. He feared he had "missed a trick," as he expressed it.

He only found one little opportunity of speaking again with Laura before the evening's festivities ended, and then, for the first time in years, his airy self-complacency failed him, his tongue's easy confidence forsook it in a great measure, and he was conscious of an unheroic timidity. He was glad to get away and find a place where he could despise himself in private and try to grow his clipped plumes again.

When Laura reached home she was tired but exultant, and Senator Dilworthy was pleased and satisfied. He called Laura "my daughter," next morning, and gave her some "pin money," as he termed it, and she sent a hundred and fifty dollars of it to her mother and loaned a trifle to Col. Sellers. Then the Senator had a long private conference with Laura, and unfolded certain plans of his for the good of the country, and religion, and the poor, and temperance, and showed her how she could assist him in developing these worthy and noble enterprises.

Chapter XXXIII

—Itancan Ihduhomni eciyapi, Itancan Tohanokihi-eca eciyapi, Itancan Iapiwaxte eciyapi, he hunkakewicaye cin etanhan
otonwe kin caxtonpi; nakun Akicita Wicaxta-ceji-skuya, Akicita
Anogite, Akicita Taku-kaxta—

> þe richeste wifmen alle : þat were in londe,
> and þere hehere monnen dohtere. . . . .
> þere wes moni pal hende: on faire þā uolke.
> þar was mochel honde: of manicunnes londe,
> for ech wende to beon: betere þan oþer.
>
> *Layamon.*

LAURA soon discovered that there were three distinct aristocracies in Washington. One of these, (nick-named the
Antiques,) consisted of cultivated, high-bred old families who
looked back with pride upon an ancestry that had been always
great in the nation's councils and its wars from the birth of
the republic downward. Into this select circle it was difficult
to gain admission. No. 2 was the aristocracy of the middle
ground—of which, more anon. No. 3 lay beyond; of it we will
say a word here. We will call it the Aristocracy of the Parvenus—as, indeed, the general public did. Official position,
no matter how obtained, entitled a man to a place in it, and
carried his family with him, no matter whence they sprang.
Great wealth gave a man a still higher and nobler place in it
than did official position. If this wealth had been acquired by
conspicuous ingenuity, with just a pleasant little spice of ille-
gality about it, all the better. This aristocracy was "fast," and
not averse to ostentation. The aristocracy of the Antiques ig-
nored the aristocracy of the Parvenus; the Parvenus laughed
at the Antiques, (and secretly envied them.)

There were certain important "society" customs which one
in Laura's position needed to understand. For instance, when
a lady of any prominence comes to one of our cities and takes
up her residence, all the ladies of her grade favor her in turn
with an initial call, giving their cards to the servant at the
door by way of introduction. They come singly, sometimes;
sometimes in couples;—and always in elaborate full dress.

They talk two minutes and a quarter and then go. If the lady receiving the call desires a further acquaintance, she must return the visit within two weeks; to neglect it beyond that time means "let the matter drop." But if she does return the visit within two weeks, it then becomes the other party's privilege to continue the acquaintance or drop it. She signifies her willingness to continue it by calling again any time within twelve months; after that, if the parties go on calling upon each other once a year, in our large cities, that is sufficient, and the acquaintanceship holds good. The thing goes along smoothly, now. The annual visits are made and returned with peaceful regularity and bland satisfaction, although it is not necessary that the two ladies shall actually *see* each other oftener than once every few years. Their cards preserve the intimacy and keep the acquaintanceship intact.

For instance, Mrs. A. pays her annual visit, sits in her carriage and sends in her card with the lower right hand corner turned down, which signifies that she has "called in person;" Mrs. B. sends down word that she is "engaged" or "wishes to be excused"—or if she is a Parvenu and low-bred, she perhaps sends word that she is "not at home." Very good; Mrs. A. drives on happy and content. If Mrs. A.'s daughter marries, or a child is born to the family, Mrs. B. calls, sends in her card with the upper left hand corner turned down, and then goes along about her affairs—for that inverted corner means "Congratulations." If Mrs. B.'s husband falls down stairs and breaks his neck, Mrs. A. calls, leaves her card with the upper right hand corner turned down, and then takes her departure; this corner means "Condolence." It is very necessary to get the corners right, else one may unintentionally condole with a friend on a wedding or congratulate her upon a funeral. If either lady is about to leave the city, she goes to the other's house and leaves her card with "P.P.C." engraved under the name—which signifies, "Pay Parting Call." But enough of etiquette. Laura was early instructed in the mysteries of society life by a competent mentor, and thus was preserved from troublesome mistakes.

The first fashionable call she received from a member of the ancient nobility, otherwise the Antiques, was of a pattern with all she received from that limb of the aristocracy afterward.

This call was paid by Mrs. Major-General Fulke-Fulkerson and daughter. They drove up at one in the afternoon in a rather antiquated vehicle with a faded coat of arms on the panels, an aged white-wooled negro coachman on the box and a younger darkey beside him—the footman. Both of these servants were dressed in dull brown livery that had seen considerable service.

The ladies entered the drawing-room in full character; that is to say, with Elizabethan stateliness on the part of the dowager, and an easy grace and dignity on the part of the young lady that had a nameless something about it that suggested conscious superiority. The dresses of both ladies were exceedingly rich, as to material, but as notably modest as to color and ornament. All parties having seated themselves, the dowager delivered herself of a remark that was not unusual in its form, and yet it came from her lips with the impressiveness of Scripture:

"The weather has been unpropitious of late, Miss Hawkins."

"It has indeed," said Laura. "The climate seems to be variable."

"It is its nature of old, here," said the daughter—stating it apparently as a fact, only, and by her manner waving aside all personal responsibility on account of it. "Is it not so, mamma?"

"Quite so, my child. Do you like winter, Miss Hawkins?" She said "like" as if she had an idea that its dictionary meaning was "approve of."

"Not as well as summer—though I think all seasons have their charms."

"It is a very just remark. The general held similar views. He considered snow in winter proper; sultriness in summer legitimate; frosts in the autumn the same, and rains in spring not objectionable. He was not an exacting man. And I call to mind now that he always admired thunder. You remember, child, your father always admired thunder?"

"He adored it."

"No doubt it reminded him of battle," said Laura.

"Yes, I think perhaps it did. He had a great respect for Nature. He often said there was something striking about the ocean. You remember his saying that, daughter?"

"Yes, often, mother. I remember it very well."

"And hurricanes. He took a great interest in hurricanes. And animals. Dogs, especially—hunting dogs. Also comets. I think we all have our predilections. I think it is this that gives variety to our tastes." Laura coincided with this view. "Do you find it hard and lonely to be so far from your home and friends, Miss Hawkins?"

"I do find it depressing sometimes, but then there is so much about me here that is novel and interesting that my days are made up more of sunshine than shadow."

"Washington is not a dull city in the season," said the young lady. "We have some very good society indeed, and one need not be at a loss for means to pass the time pleasantly. Are you fond of watering-places, Miss Hawkins?"

"I have really had no experience of them, but I have always felt a strong desire to see something of fashionable watering-place life."

"We of Washington are unfortunately situated in that respect," said the dowager. "It is a tedious distance to Newport. But there is no help for it."

Laura said to herself, "Long Branch and Cape May are nearer than Newport; doubtless these places are low; I'll feel my way a little and see." Then she said aloud:

"Why I thought that Long Branch—"

There was no need to "feel" any further—there was that in both faces before her which made that truth apparent. The dowager said:

"Nobody goes *there*, Miss Hawkins—at least only persons of no position in society. And the President." She added that with tranquility.

"Newport is damp, and cold, and windy and excessively disagreeable," said the daughter, "but it is very select. One cannot be fastidious about minor matters when one has no choice."

The visit had spun out nearly three minutes, now. Both ladies rose with grave dignity, conferred upon Laura a formal invitation to call, and then retired from the conference. Laura remained in the drawing-room and left them to pilot themselves out of the house—an inhospitable thing, it seemed to her, but then she was following her instructions. She stood, steeped in reverie, a while, and then she said:

"I think I could always enjoy icebergs—as scenery—but not as company."

Still, she knew these two people by reputation, and was aware that they were not ice-bergs when they were in their own waters and amid their legitimate surroundings, but on the contrary were people to be respected for their stainless characters and esteemed for their social virtues and their benevolent impulses. She thought it a pity that they had to be such changed and dreary creatures on occasions of state.

The first call Laura received from the other extremity of the Washington aristocracy followed close upon the heels of the one we have just been describing. The callers this time were the Hon. Mrs. Oliver Higgins, the Hon. Mrs. Patrique Oreillé (pronounced O-re*lay*,) Miss Bridget (pronounced Breezhay) Oreillé, Mrs. Peter Gashly, Miss Gashly, and Miss Emmeline Gashly.

The three carriages arrived at the same moment from different directions. They were new and wonderfully shiny, and the brasses on the harness were highly polished and bore complicated monograms. There were showy coats of arms, too, with Latin mottoes. The coachmen and footmen were clad in bright new livery, of striking colors, and they had black rosettes with shaving-brushes projecting above them, on the sides of their stove-pipe hats.

When the visitors swept into the drawing-room they filled the place with a suffocating sweetness procured at the perfumer's. Their costumes, as to architecture, were the latest fashion intensified; they were rainbow-hued; they were hung with jewels—chiefly diamonds. It would have been plain to any eye that it had cost something to upholster these women.

The Hon. Mrs. Oliver Higgins was the wife of a delegate from a distant territory—a gentleman who had kept the principal "saloon," and sold the best whiskey in the principal village in his wilderness, and so, of course, was recognized as the first man of his commonwealth and its fittest representative. He was a man of paramount influence at home, for he was public spirited, he was chief of the fire department, he had an admirable command of profane language, and had killed several "parties." His shirt fronts were always immaculate; his boots daintily polished, and no man could lift a foot and fire

a dead shot at a stray speck of dirt on it with a white handkerchief with a finer grace than he; his watch chain weighed a
pound; the gold in his finger ring was worth forty five dollars;
he wore a diamond cluster-pin and he parted his hair behind.
He had always been regarded as the most elegant gentleman
in his territory, and it was conceded by all that no man there-
abouts was anywhere near his equal in the telling of an ob-
scene story except the venerable white-haired governor
himself. The Hon. Higgins had not come to serve his country in Washington for nothing. The appropriation which he
had engineered through Congress for the maintenance of the
Indians in his Territory would have made all those savages
rich if it had ever got to them.

The Hon. Mrs. Higgins was a picturesque woman, and a
fluent talker, and she held a tolerably high station among the
Parvenus. Her English was fair enough, as a general thing—
though, being of New York origin, she had the fashion peculiar to many natives of that city of pronouncing saw and law
as if they were spelt sawr and lawr.

Petroleum was the agent that had suddenly transformed the
Gashlys from modest hard-working country village folk into
"loud" aristocrats and ornaments of the city.

The Hon. Patrique Oreillé was a wealthy Frenchman from
Cork. Not that he was wealthy when he first came from Cork,
but just the reverse. When he first landed in New York with
his wife, he had only halted at Castle Garden for a few minutes to receive and exhibit papers showing that he had resided
in this country two years—and then he voted the democratic
ticket and went up town to hunt a house. He found one and
then went to work as assistant to an architect and builder, carrying a hod all day and studying politics evenings. Industry
and economy soon enabled him to start a low rum shop in a
foul locality, and this gave him political influence. In our
country it is always our first care to see that our people have
the opportunity of voting for their choice of men to represent
and govern them—we do not permit our great officials to appoint the little officials. We prefer to have so tremendous a
power as that in our own hands. We hold it safest to elect our
judges and everybody else. In our cities, the ward meetings
elect delegates to the nominating conventions and instruct

them whom to nominate. The publicans and their retainers rule the ward meetings (for everybody else hates the worry of politics and stays at home); the delegates from the ward meetings organize as a nominating convention and make up a list of candidates—one convention offering a democratic and another a republican list of—incorruptibles; and then the great meek public come forward at the proper time and make unhampered choice and bless Heaven that they live in a free land where no form of despotism can ever intrude.

Patrick O'Riley (as his name then stood) created friends and influence very fast, for he was always on hand at the police courts to give straw bail for his customers or establish an *alibi* for them in case they had been beating anybody to death on his premises. Consequently he presently became a political leader, and was elected to a petty office under the city government. Out of a meager salary he soon saved money enough to open quite a stylish liquor saloon higher up town, with a faro bank attached and plenty of capital to conduct it with. This gave him fame and great respectability. The position of alderman was forced upon him, and it was just the same as presenting him a gold mine. He had fine horses and carriages, now, and closed up his whiskey mill.

By and by he became a large contractor for city work, and was a bosom friend of the great and good Wm. M. Weed himself, who had stolen $20,000,000 from the city and was a man so envied, so honored, so adored, indeed, that when the sheriff went to his office to arrest him as a felon, that sheriff blushed and apologized, and one of the illustrated papers made a picture of the scene and spoke of the matter in such a way as to show that the editor regretted that the offense of an arrest had been offered to so exalted a personage as Mr. Weed.

Mr. O'Riley furnished shingle nails to the new Court House at three thousand dollars a keg, and eighteen gross of 60-cent thermometers at fifteen hundred dollars a dozen; the controller and the board of audit passed the bills, and a mayor, who was simply ignorant but not criminal, signed them. When they were paid, Mr. O'Riley's admirers gave him a solitaire diamond pin of the size of a filbert, in imitation of the liberality of Mr. Weed's friends, and then Mr. O'Riley retired from active service and amused himself with buying real estate at enormous figures and holding it in other people's names. By and by the newspapers came out with exposures and called Weed and O'Riley "thieves,"—whereupon the people rose as one man (voting repeatedly) and elected the two gentlemen to their proper theatre of action, the New York legislature. The newspapers clamored, and the courts proceeded to try the new legislators for their small irregularities. Our admirable jury system enabled the persecuted ex-officials to secure a jury of nine gentlemen from a neighboring asylum and three graduates from Sing-Sing, and presently they walked forth with characters vindicated. The legislature was called upon to spew them forth—a thing which the legislature declined to do. It was like asking children to repudiate their own father. It was a legislature of the modern pattern.

Being now wealthy and distinguished, Mr. O'Riley, still bearing the legislative "Hon." attached to his name (for titles never die in America, although we *do* take a republican pride in poking fun at such trifles), sailed for Europe with his family. They traveled all about, turning their noses up at every thing, and not finding it a difficult thing to do, either, because nature had originally given those features a cast in that direction; and finally they established themselves in Paris, that Paradise of Americans of their sort.—They staid there two years and learned to speak English with a foreign accent—not that it hadn't always had a foreign accent (which was indeed the case) but now the nature of it was changed. Finally they returned home and became ultra fashionables. They landed here as the Hon. Patrique Oreillé and family, and so are known unto this day.

Laura provided seats for her visitors and they immediately launched forth into a breezy, sparkling conversation with that easy confidence which is to be found only among persons accustomed to high life.

"I've been intending to call sooner, Miss Hawkins," said the Hon. Mrs. Oreillé, but the weather's been *so* horrid.— How do you like Washington?"

Laura liked it very well indeed.

Mrs. Gashly—"Is it your first visit?"

Yes, it was her first.

All—"Indeed?"

Mrs. Oreillé—"I'm afraid you'll despise the weather, Miss Hawkins. It's perfectly awful. It always is. I tell Mr. Oreillé I can't and I won't put up with any such a climate. If we were obliged to do it, I wouldn't mind it; but we are *not* obliged to, and so I don't see the use of it. Sometimes it's real pitiful the way the children pine for Parry—don't look *so* sad, Bridget, *ma chere*—poor child, she can't hear Parry mentioned without getting the blues."

Mrs. Gashly—"Well I should think so, Mrs. Oreille. A body *lives* in Paris, but a body only *stays* here. I dote on Paris; I'd druther scrimp along on ten thousand dollars a year there, than suffer and worry here on a real decent income."

Miss Gashly—"Well then I wish you'd take us back, mother; I'm sure *I* hate this stoopid country enough, even if it *is* our dear native land."

Miss Emmeline Gashly—"What, and leave poor Johnny Peterson behind?" [An airy general laugh applauded this sally].

Miss Gashly—"Sister, I should think you'd be ashamed of yourself!"

Miss Emmeline—"Oh, you needn't ruffle your feathers so. I was only joking. He don't mean anything by coming to the house every evening—only comes to see mother. Of course that's all!" [General laughter].

Miss G. prettily confused—"Emmeline, how *can* you!"

Mrs. G.,—"Let your sister alone, Emmeline.—I never saw such a tease!"

Mrs. Oreillé—"What lovely corals you have, Miss Hawkins! Just look at them, Bridget, dear. I've a great passion for corals—it's a pity they're getting a little common. I have some elegant ones—not as elegant as yours, though—but of course I don't wear them now."

Laura—"I suppose they are rather common, but still I have a great affection for these, because they were given to me by a dear old friend of our family named Murphy. He was a very charming man, but very eccentric. We always supposed he was an Irishman, but after he got rich he went abroad for a year or two, and when he came back you would have been amused to see how interested he was in a potato. He asked what it was! Now you know that when Providence shapes a mouth especially for the accommodation of a potato you can detect that fact at a glance when that mouth is in repose—foreign travel can never remove *that* sign. But he was a very delightful gentleman, and his little foible did not hurt him at all. We all have our shams—I suppose there is a sham somewhere about every individual, if we could manage to ferret it out. I would so like to go to France. I suppose our society here compares very favorably with French society does it not, Mrs. Oreillé?"

Mrs. O.—"Not by any means, Miss Hawkins! French society is much more elegant—much more so."

Laura—"I am sorry to hear that. I suppose ours has deteriorated of late."

Mrs. O.—"Very much indeed. There are people in society here that have really no more money to live on than what some of us pay for servant hire. Still I won't say but what some of them are very good people—and respectable, too."

Laura—"The old families seem to be holding themselves aloof, from what I hear. I suppose you seldom meet in society now, the people you used to be familiar with twelve or fifteen years ago?"

Mrs. O.—"Oh, no—hardly ever."

Mr. O'Riley kept his first rum-mill and protected his customers from the law in those days, and this turn of the conversation was rather uncomfortable to madame than otherwise.

Hon. Mrs. Higgins—"Is François' health good now, Mrs. Oreillé?"

Mrs. O.—(*Thankful for the intervention*)—"Not very. A body couldn't expect it. He was always delicate—especially his lungs—and this odious climate tells on him strong, now, after Parry, which is so mild."

Mrs. H.—"I should think so. Husband says Percy'll die if he don't have a change; and so I'm going to swap round a little and see what can be done. I saw a lady from Florida last week, and she recommended Key West. I told her Percy couldn't abide winds, as he was threatened with a pulmonary affection, and then she said try St. Augustine. It's an awful distance—ten or twelve hundred mile, they say—but then in a case of this kind a body can't stand back for trouble, you know."

Mrs. O.—"No, of course that's so. If François don't get

better soon we've got to look out for some other place, or else Europe. We've thought some of the Hot Springs, but I don't know. It's a great responsibility and a body wants to go cautious. Is Hildebrand about again, Mrs. Gashly?"

Mrs. G.—"Yes, but that's about all. It was indigestion, you know, and it looks as if it was chronic. And you know I do dread dyspepsia. We've all been worried a good deal about him. The doctor recommended baked apple and spoiled meat, and I think it done him good. It's about the only thing that will stay on his stomach now-a-days. We have Dr. Shovel now. Who's your doctor, Mrs. Higgins?"

Mrs. H.—"Well, we had Dr. Spooner a good while, but he runs so much to emetics, which I think are weakening, that we changed off and took Dr. Leathers. We like him very much. He has a fine European reputation, too. The first thing he suggested for Percy was to have him taken out in the back yard for an airing, every afternoon, with nothing at all on."

Mrs. O. and Mrs. G.—"What!"

Mrs. H.—"As true as I'm sitting here. And it actually helped him for two or three days; it did indeed. But after that the doctor said it seemed to be too severe and so he has fell back on hot foot-baths at night and cold showers in the morning. But I don't think there can be any good sound help for him in such a climate as this. I believe we are going to lose him if we don't make a change."

Mrs. O.—"I suppose you heard of the fright we had two weeks ago last Saturday? No? Why that is strange—but come to remember, you've all been away to Richmond. François tumbled from the sky light in the second-story hall clean down to the first floor—"

Everybody—"Mercy!"

Mrs. O.—Yes indeed—and broke two of his ribs—"

Everybody—"What!"

Mrs. O.—"Just as true as you live. First we thought he must be injured internally. It was fifteen minutes past 8 in the evening. Of course we were all distracted in a moment—everybody was flying everywhere, and nobody doing anything *worth* anything. By and by I flung out next door and dragged in Dr. Sprague, President of the Medical University—no time to go for our own doctor of course—and the minute he saw

François he said, 'Send for your own physician, madam'—said it as cross as a bear, too, and turned right on his heel and cleared out without doing a thing!"

Everybody—"The mean, contemptible brute!"

Mrs. O.—"Well you may say it. I was nearly out of my wits by this time. But we hurried off the servants after our own doctor and telegraphed mother—she was in New York and rushed down on the first train; and when the doctor got there, lo and behold you he found François had broke one of his legs, too!"

Everybody—"Goodness!"

Mrs. O.—"Yes. So he set his leg and bandaged it up, and fixed his ribs and gave him a dose of something to quiet down his excitement and put him to sleep—poor thing he was trembling and frightened to death and it was pitiful to see him. We had him in my bed—Mr. Oreillé slept in the guest room and I laid down beside François—but not to sleep—bless you no. Bridget and I set up all night, and the doctor staid till two in the morning, bless his old heart.—When mother got there she was so used up with anxiety that she had to go to bed and have the doctor; but when she found that François was not in immediate danger she rallied, and by night she was able to take a watch herself. Well for three days and nights we three never left that bedside only to take an hour's nap at a time. And then the doctor said François was out of danger and if ever there was a thankful set, in this world, it was us."

Laura's respect for these women had augmented during this conversation, naturally enough; affection and devotion are qualities that are able to adorn and render beautiful a character that is otherwise unattractive, and even repulsive.

Mrs. Gashly—"I do believe I should a died if I had been in your place, Mrs. Oreillé. The time Hildebrand was so low with the pneumonia Emmeline and me were all alone with him most of the time and we never took a minute's sleep for as much as two days and nights. It was at Newport and we wouldn't trust hired nurses. One afternoon he had a fit, and jumped up and run out on the portico of the hotel with nothing in the world on and the wind a blowing like ice and we after him scared to death; and when the ladies and gentlemen saw that he had a fit, every lady scattered for her room and not a gentleman lifted his hand to help, the wretches! Well after that his life hung by a thread for as much as ten days, and the minute he was out of danger Emmeline and me just went to bed sick and worn out. *I* never want to pass through such a time again. Poor dear François—which leg did he break, Mrs. Oreillé?"

Mrs. O.—"It was his right hand hind leg. Jump down, François dear, and show the ladies what a cruel limp you've got yet."

François demurred, but being coaxed and delivered gently upon the floor, he performed very satisfactorily, with his "right hand hind leg" in the air. All were affected—even Laura—but hers was an affection of the stomach. The country-bred girl had not suspected that the little whining ten-ounce black and tan reptile, clad in a red embroidered pigmy blanket and reposing in Mrs. Oreillé's lap all through the visit was the individual whose sufferings had been stirring the dormant generosities of her nature. She said:

"Poor little creature! You might have lost him!"

Mrs. O.—"O pray don't mention it, Miss Hawkins—it gives me such a turn!"

Laura—"And Hildebrand and Percy—are they—are they like this one?"

Mrs. G.—"No, Hilly has considerable Skye blood in him, I believe."

Mrs. H.—"Percy's the same, only he is two months and ten days older and has his ears cropped.—His father, Martin Farquhar Tupper, was sickly, and died young, but he was the sweetest disposition.—His mother had heart disease but was very gentle and resigned, and a wonderful ratter."*

So carried away had the visitors become by their interest attaching to this discussion of family matters, that their stay had been prolonged to a very improper and unfashionable length; but they suddenly recollected themselves now and took their departure.

---

*As impossible and exasperating as this conversation may sound to a person who is not an idiot, it is scarcely in any respect an exaggeration of one which one of us actually listened to in an American drawing room—otherwise we could not venture to put such a chapter into a book which professes to deal with social possibilities.—THE AUTHORS.

Laura's scorn was boundless. The more she thought of these people and their extraordinary talk, the more offensive they seemed to her; and yet she confessed that if one must choose between the two extreme aristocracies it might be best, on the whole, looking at things from a strictly business point of view, to herd with the Parvenus; she was in Washington solely to compass a certain matter and to do it at any cost, and these people might be useful to her, while it was plain that her purposes and her schemes for pushing them would not find favor in the eyes of the Antiques. If it came to choice—and it might come to that, sooner or later—she believed she could come to a decision without much difficulty or many pangs.

But the best aristocracy of the three Washington castes, and really the most powerful, by far, was that of the Middle Ground. It was made up of the families of public men from nearly every state in the Union—men who held positions in both the executive and legislative branches of the government, and whose characters had been for years blemishless, both at home and at the capital. These gentlemen and their households were unostentatious people; they were educated and refined; they troubled themselves but little about the two other orders of nobility, but moved serenely in their wide orbit, confident in their own strength and well aware of the potency of their influence. They had no troublesome appearances to keep up, no rivalries which they cared to distress themselves about, no jealousies to fret over. They could afford to mind their own affairs and leave other combinations to do the same or do otherwise, just as they chose. They were people who were beyond reproach, and that was sufficient.

Senator Dilworthy never came into collision with any of these factions. He labored for them all and with them all. He said that all men were brethren and all were entitled to the honest unselfish help and countenance of a Christian laborer in the public vineyard.

Laura concluded, after reflection, to let circumstances determine the course it might be best for her to pursue as regarded the several aristocracies.

Now it might occur to the reader that perhaps Laura had been somewhat rudely suggestive in her remarks to Mrs. Oreillé when the subject of corals was under discussion, but it did not occur to Laura herself. She was not a person of exaggerated refinement; indeed the society and the influences that had formed her character had not been of a nature calculated to make her so; she thought that "give and take was fair play," and that to parry an offensive thrust with a sarcasm was a neat and legitimate thing to do. She sometimes talked to people in a way which some ladies would consider actually shocking; but Laura rather prided herself upon some of her exploits of that character. We are sorry we cannot make her a faultless heroine; but we cannot, for the reason that she was human.

She considered herself a superior conversationist. Long ago, when the possibility had first been brought before her mind that some day she might move in Washington society, she had recognized the fact that practiced conversational powers would be a necessary weapon in that field; she had also recognized the fact that since her dealings there must be mainly with men, and men whom she supposed to be exceptionally cultivated and able, she would need heavier shot in her magazine than mere brilliant "society" nothings; whereupon she had at once entered upon a tireless and elaborate course of reading, and had never since ceased to devote every unoccupied moment to this sort of preparation. Having now acquired a happy smattering of various information, she used it with good effect—she passed for a singularly well informed woman in Washington. The quality of her literary tastes had necessarily undergone constant improvement under this regimen, and as necessarily, also, the quality of her language had improved, though it cannot be denied that now and then her former condition of life betrayed itself in just perceptible inelegancies of expression and lapses of grammar.

Chapter XXXIV

Eet Jomfru Haar drager stærkere end ti Par Öxen.

WHEN Laura had been in Washington three months, she was still the same person, in one respect, that she was when she first arrived there—that is to say, she still bore the name of Laura Hawkins. Otherwise she was perceptibly changed.—

She had arrived in a state of grievous uncertainty as to what manner of woman she was, physically and intellectually, as compared with eastern women; she was well satisfied, now, that her beauty was confessed, her mind a grade above the average, and her powers of fascination rather extraordinary. So she was at ease upon those points. When she arrived, she was posessed of habits of economy and not possessed of money; now she dressed elaborately, gave but little thought to the cost of things, and was very well fortified financially.—She kept her mother and Washington freely supplied with money, and did the same by Col. Sellers—who always insisted upon giving his note for loans—with interest; he was rigid upon that; she *must* take interest; and one of the Colonel's greatest satisfactions was to go over his accounts and note what a handsome sum this accruing interest amounted to, and what a comfortable though modest support it would yield Laura in case reverses should overtake her. In truth he could not help feeling that he was an efficient shield for her against poverty; and so, if her expensive ways ever troubled him for a brief moment, he presently dismissed the thought and said to himself, "Let her go on—even if she loses everything she is still safe—this interest will always afford her a good easy income."

Laura was on excellent terms with a great many members of Congress, and there was an undercurrent of suspicion in some quarters that she was one of that detested class known as "lobbyists;" but what belle could escape slander in such a city? Fair-minded people declined to condemn her on mere suspicion, and so the injurious talk made no very damaging headway. She was very gay, now, and very celebrated, and she might well expect to be assailed by many kinds of gossip. She was growing used to celebrity, and could already sit calm and seemingly unconscious, under the fire of fifty lorgnettes in a theatre, or even overhear the low voice "That's she!" as she passed along the street without betraying annoyance.

The whole air was full of a vague vast scheme which was to eventuate in filling Laura's pockets with millions of money; some had one idea of the scheme, and some another, but nobody had any exact knowledge upon the subject. All that any one felt sure about, was that Laura's landed estates were princely in value and extent, and that the government was anxious to get hold of them for public purposes, and that Laura was willing to make the sale but not at all anxious about the matter and not at all in a hurry. It was whispered that Senator Dilworthy was a stumbling block in the way of an immediate sale, because he was resolved that the government should not have the lands except with the understanding that they should be devoted to the uplifting of the negro race; Laura did not care what they were devoted to, it was said, (a world of very different gossip to the contrary notwithstanding,) but there were several other heirs and they would be guided entirely by the Senator's wishes; and finally, many people averred that while it would be easy to sell the lands to the government for the benefit of the negro, by resorting to the usual methods of influencing votes, Senator Dilworthy was unwilling to have so noble a charity sullied by any taint of corruption—he was resolved that not a vote should be bought. Nobody could get anything definite from Laura about these matters, and so gossip had to feed itself chiefly upon guesses. But the effect of it all was, that Laura was considered to be very wealthy and likely to be vastly more so in a little while. Consequently she was much courted and as much envied. Her wealth attracted many suitors. Perhaps they came to worship her riches, but they remained to worship her. Some of the noblest men of the time succumbed to her fascinations. She frowned upon no lover when he made his first advances, but by and by when he was hopelessly enthralled, he learned from her own lips that she had formed a resolution never to marry. Then he would go away hating and cursing the whole sex, and she would calmly add his scalp to her string, while she mused upon the bitter day that Col. Selby trampled her love and her pride in the dust. In time it came to be said that her way was paved with broken hearts.

Poor Washington gradually woke up to the fact that he too was an intellectual marvel as well as his gifted sister. He could not conceive how it had come about (it did not occur to him that the gossip about his family's great wealth had anything to do with it). He could not account for it by any process of reasoning, and was simply obliged to accept the fact and give up trying to solve the riddle. He found himself dragged into society and courted, wondered at and envied very much as if he were one of those foreign barbers who flit over here now and then with a self-conferred title of nobility and marry some rich fool's absurd daughter. Sometimes at a dinner party or a reception he would find himself the centre of interest, and feel unutterably uncomfortable in the discovery. Being obliged to say something, he would mine his brain and put in a blast and when the smoke and flying debris had cleared away the result would be what seemed to him but a poor little intellectual clod of dirt or two, and then he would be astonished to see everybody as lost in admiration as if he had brought up a ton or two of virgin gold. Every remark he made delighted his hearers and compelled their applause; he overheard people say he was exceedingly bright—they were chiefly mammas and marriageable young ladies. He found that some of his good things were being repeated about the town. Whenever he heard of an instance of this kind, he would keep that particular remark in mind and analyze it at home in private. At first he could not see that the remark was anything better than a parrot might originate; but by and by he began to feel that perhaps he underrated his powers; and after that he used to analyze his good things with a deal of comfort, and find in them a brilliancy which would have been unapparent to him in earlier days—and then he would make a note of that good thing and say it again the first time he found himself in a new company. Presently he had saved up quite a repertoire of brilliancies; and after that he confined himself to repeating these and ceased to originate any more, lest he might injure his reputation by an unlucky effort.

He was constantly having young ladies thrust upon his notice at receptions, or left upon his hands at parties, and in

time he began to feel that he was being deliberately persecuted in this way; and after that he could not enjoy society
because of his constant dread of these female ambushes and
surprises. He was distressed to find that nearly every time he
showed a young lady a polite attention he was straightway reported to be engaged to her; and as some of these reports got
into the newspapers occasionally, he had to keep writing to
Louise that they were lies and she must believe in him and
not mind them or allow them to grieve her.

Washington was as much in the dark as anybody with regard to the great wealth that was hovering in the air and
seemingly on the point of tumbling into the family pocket.
Laura would give him no satisfaction. All she would say, was:

"Wait. Be patient. You will see."

"But will it be soon, Laura?"

"It will not be very long, I think."

"But what makes you think so?"

"I have reasons—and good ones. Just wait, and be patient."

"But is it going to be as much as people say it is?"

"What do they say it is?"

"Oh, ever so much. Millions!"

"Yes, it will be a great sum."

"But *how* great, Laura? Will it be millions?"

"Yes, you may call it that. Yes, it *will* be millions. There,
now—does that satisfy you?"

"Splendid! I can wait. I can wait patiently—ever so patiently. Once I was near selling the land for twenty thousand
dollars; once for thirty thousand dollars; once after that for
seven thousand dollars; and once for forty thousand dollars—
but something always told me not to do it. What a fool I
would have been to sell it for such a beggarly trifle! It *is* the
land that's to bring the money, isn't it Laura? You can tell me
that much, can't you?"

"Yes, I don't mind saying that much. It *is* the land. But
mind—don't ever hint that you got it from me. Don't mention me in the matter at all, Washington."

"All right—I won't. Millions! Isn't it splendid! I mean to
look around for a building lot; a lot with fine ornamental
shrubbery and all that sort of thing. I will do it to-day. And I
might as well see an architect, too, and get him to go to work

at a plan for a house. I don't intend to spare any expense; I mean to have the noblest house that money can build." Then after a pause—he did not notice Laura's smiles—"Laura, would you lay the main hall in encaustic tiles, or just in fancy patterns of hard wood?"

Laura laughed a good old-fashioned laugh that had more of her former natural self about it than any sound that had issued from her mouth in many weeks. She said:

"*You* don't change, Washington. You still begin to squander a fortune right and left the instant you hear of it in the distance; you never wait till the foremost dollar of it arrives within a hundred miles of you,"—and she kissed her brother good bye and left him weltering in his dreams, so to speak.

He got up and walked the floor feverishly during two hours; and when he sat down he had married Louise, built a house, reared a family, married them off, spent upwards of eight hundred thousand dollars on mere luxuries, and died worth twelve millions.

Chapter XXXV

"Mi-x-in tzakcaamah, x-in tzakcolobch chirech nu zaki caam,
nu zaki colo. . nu chincu, nu galgab, nu zalmet" . . . . .

Rabinal-Achi.

Chascus hom a sas palmas deves se meteys viradas.

LAURA went down stairs, knocked at the study door, and entered, scarcely waiting for the response. Senator Dilworthy was alone—with an open Bible in his hand, upside down.
Laura smiled, and said, forgetting her acquired correctness of
speech,

"It is only me."

"Ah, come in, sit down," and the Senator closed the book
and laid it down. "I wanted to see you. Time to report
progress from the committee of the whole," and the Senator
beamed with his own congressional wit.

"In the committee of the whole things are working very
well. We have made ever so much progress in a week. I believe that you and I together could run this government
beautifully, uncle."

The Senator beamed again. He liked to be called "uncle"
by this beautiful woman.

"Did you see Hopperson last night after the congressional
prayer meeting?"

"Yes. He came. He's a kind of—"

"Eh? he is one of my friends, Laura. He's a fine man, a very
fine man. I don't know any man in congress I'd sooner go to
for help in any Christian work. What did he say?"

"Oh, he beat around a little. He said he should like to help
the negro, his heart went out to the negro, and all that—
plenty of them say that—but he was a little afraid of the Tennessee Land bill; if Senator Dilworthy wasn't in it, he should
suspect there was a fraud on the government."

"He said that, did he?"

"Yes. And he said he felt he couldn't vote for it. He was shy."

"Not shy, child, cautious. He's a very cautious man. I have
been with him a great deal on conference committees. He

wants reasons, good ones. Didn't you show him he was in error about the bill?"

"I did. I went over the whole thing. I had to tell him some of the side arrangements, some of the—"

"You didn't mention me?"

"Oh, no. I told him you were daft about the negro and the philanthropy part of it, as you are."

"Daft is a little strong, Laura. But you know that I wouldn't touch this bill if it were not for the public good, and for the good of the colored race, much as I am interested in the heirs of this property, and would like to have them succeed."

Laura looked a little incredulous, and the Senator proceeded.

"Don't misunderstand *me*, Laura. I don't deny that it is for the interest of all of us that this bill should go through, and it will. I have no concealments from you. But I have one principle in my public life, which I should like you to keep in mind; it has always been my guide. I never push a private interest if it is not justified and ennobled by some larger public good. I doubt if a Christian would be justified in working for his own salvation if it was not to aid in the salvation of his fellow men."

The Senator spoke with feeling, and then added,

"I hope you showed Hopperson that our motives were pure?"

"Yes, and he seemed to have a new light on the measure. I think he will vote for it."

"I hope so; his name will give tone and strength to it. I knew you would only have to show him that it was just and pure, in order to secure his cordial support."

"I think I convinced him. Yes, I am perfectly sure he will vote right now."

"That's good, that's good," said the Senator, smiling, and rubbing his hands. "Is there anything more?"

"You'll find some changes in that I guess," handing the Senator a printed list of names. "Those checked off are all right."

"Ah—'m—'m," running his eye down the list. "That's encouraging. What is the 'C' before some of the names, and the 'B. B.'?"

"Those are my private marks. That 'C' stands for 'convinced,' with argument. The 'B. B.' is a general sign for a relative. You see it stands before three of the Hon. Committee. I expect to see the chairman of the committee to-day, Mr. Buckstone."

"So you must, he ought to be seen without any delay. Buckstone is a worldly sort of a fellow, but he has charitable impulses. If we secure him we shall have a favorable report by the committee, and it will be a great thing to be able to state that fact quietly where it will do good."

"Oh, I saw Senator Balloon."

"He will help us, I suppose? Balloon is a whole-hearted fellow. I can't *help* loving that man, for all his drollery and waggishness. He puts on an air of levity sometimes, but there aint a man in the senate knows the scriptures as he does. He did not make any objections?"

"Not exactly, he said—shall I tell you what he said?" asked Laura glancing furtively at him.

"Certainly."

"He said he had no doubt it was a good thing; if Senator Dilworthy was in it, it would pay to look into it."

The Senator laughed, but rather feebly, and said, "Balloon is always full of his jokes."

"I explained it to him. He said it was all right, he only wanted a word with you," continued Laura. "He is a handsome old gentleman, and he is gallant for an old man."

"My daughter," said the Senator, with a grave look, "I trust there was nothing free in his manner?"

"Free?" repeated Laura, with indignation in her face. "With *me*!"

"There, there, child. I meant nothing, Balloon talks a little freely sometimes, with men. But he is right at heart. His term expires next year and I fear we shall lose him."

"He seemed to be packing the day I was there. His rooms were full of dry goods boxes, into which his servant was crowding all manner of old clothes and stuff. I suppose he will paint 'Pub. Docs' on them and frank them home. That's good economy, isn't it?"

"Yes, yes, but child, all Congressmen do that. It may not be strictly honest, indeed it is not unless he had some public documents mixed in with the clothes."

"It's a funny world. Good-bye, uncle. I'm going to see that chairman."

And humming a cheery opera air, she departed to her room to dress for going out. Before she did that, however, she took out her note book and was soon deep in its contents, marking, dashing, erasing, figuring, and talking to herself.

"Free! I wonder what Dilworthy *does* think of me anyway? One . . . two . . . eight . . . seventeen . . . twenty-one, . . . 'm'm . . . it takes a heap for a majority. Wouldn't Dilworthy open his eyes if he knew some of the things Balloon *did* say to me. There. . . . Hopperson's influence ought to count twenty . . . . the sanctimonious old curmudgeon. Son-in-law . . . . sinecure in the negro institution. . . . . That about gauges *him*. . . . . The three committeemen . . . . sons-in-law. Nothing like a son-in-law here in Washington . . . . or a brother-in-law. . . . And everybody has 'em. . . . . Let's see . . . . sixty-one . . . . with places; . . . . twenty-five . . . persuaded—it is getting on; . . . . we'll have two-thirds of Congress in time. . . . . Dilworthy must surely know I understand him. Uncle Dilworthy . . . . Uncle Balloon! . . . Tells very amusing stories . . . . when ladies are not present. . . . I should think so. . . . 'm . . . 'm. Eighty-five. . . . There. I must find that chairman. Queer . . . . Buckstone acts. . . . . Seemed to be in love. . . . . I was *sure* of it. He promised to come here . . . . and he hasn't. . . . Strange. *Very* strange. . . . I must chance to meet him to-day."

Laura dressed and went out, thinking she was perhaps too early for Mr. Buckstone to come from the house, but as he lodged near the bookstore she would drop in there and keep a look out for him.

While Laura is on her errand to find Mr. Buckstone, it may not be out of the way to remark that she knew quite as much of Washington life as Senator Dilworthy gave her credit for, and more than she thought proper to tell him. She was acquainted by this time with a good many of the young fellows of Newspaper Row, and exchanged gossip with them to their mutual advantage.

They were always talking in the Row, everlastingly gossiping, bantering and sarcastically praising things, and going on in a style which was a curious commingling of earnest and persiflage. Col. Sellers liked this talk amazingly, though he was sometimes a little at sea in it—and perhaps that didn't lessen the relish of the conversation to the correspondents.

It seems that they had got hold of the dry-goods box packing story about Balloon, one day, and were talking it over when the Colonel came in. The Colonel wanted to know all about it, and Hicks told him. And then Hicks went on, with a serious air,

"Colonel, if you register a letter, it means that it is of value, doesn't it? And if you pay fifteen cents for registering it, the government will have to take extra care of it and even pay you back its full value if it is lost. Isn't that so?"

"Yes. I suppose it's so."

"Well Senator Balloon put fifteen cents worth of stamps on each of those seven huge boxes of old clothes, and shipped that ton of second-hand rubbish, old boots and pantaloons and what not through the mails as registered matter! It was an ingenious thing and it had a genuine touch of humor about it, too. I think there is more real talent among our public men of to-day than there was among those of old times— a far more fertile fancy, a much happier ingenuity. Now, Colonel, can you picture Jefferson, or Washington or John Adams franking their wardrobes through the mails and adding the facetious idea of making the government responsible for the cargo for the sum of one dollar and five cents? Statesmen were dull creatures in those days. I have a much greater admiration for Senator Balloon."

"Yes, Balloon is a man of parts, there is no denying it."

"I think so. He is spoken of for the post of Minister to China, or Austria, and I hope will be appointed. What we want abroad is good examples of the national character. John Jay and Benjamin Franklin were well enough in their day, but the nation has made progress since then. Balloon is a man we know and can depend on to be true to—himself."

"Yes, and Balloon has had a good deal of public experience. He is an old friend of mine. He was governor of one of the territories a while, and was very satisfactory."

"Indeed he was. He was ex-officio Indian agent, too. Many a man would have taken the Indian appropriation and devoted the money to feeding and clothing the helpless savages, whose land had been taken from them by the white man in the interests of civilization; but Balloon knew their needs better. He built a government saw-mill on the reservation with the money, and the lumber sold for enormous prices—a relative of his did all the work free of charge—that is to say he charged nothing more than the lumber would bring."

"But the poor Injuns—not that I care much for Injuns—what did he do for them?"

"Gave them the outside slabs to fence in the reservation with. Governor Balloon was nothing less than a father to the poor Indians. But Balloon is not alone, we have many truly noble statesmen in our country's service like Balloon. The Senate is full of them. Don't you think so Colonel?"

"Well, I dunno. I honor my country's public servants as much as any one can. I meet them, Sir, every day, and the more I see of them the more I esteem them and the more grateful I am that our institutions give us the opportunity of securing their services. Few lands are so blest."

"That is true, Colonel. To be sure you can buy now and then a Senator or a Representative; but they do not know it is wrong, and so they are not ashamed of it. They are gentle, and confiding and childlike, and in my opinion these are qualities that ennoble them far more than any amount of sinful sagacity could. I quite agree with you, Col. Sellers."

"Well"—hesitated the Colonel—"I am afraid some of them do buy their seats—yes, I am afraid they do—but as Senator Dilworthy himself said to me, it is sinful,—it is very wrong—it is shameful; Heaven protect *me* from such a charge. That is what Dilworthy said. And yet when you come to look at it you cannot deny that we would have to go without the services of some of our ablest men, sir, if the country were opposed to—to—bribery. It is a harsh term. I do not like to use it."

The Colonel interrupted himself at this point to meet an engagement with the Austrian minister, and took his leave with his usual courtly bow.

Chapter XXXVI

"Bataïnadon nin-masinaiganan, kakina gaie onijishinon."
—"Missawa onijishining kakina o masinaiganan, kawin
gwetch o-wabandansinan."   *Baraga.*

புத்தகங்கள்

I N DUE TIME Laura alighted at the book store, and began to
look at the titles of the handsome array of books on the
counter. A dapper clerk of perhaps nineteen or twenty years,
with hair accurately parted and surprisingly slick, came bus-
tling up and leaned over with a pretty smile and an affable—

"Can I—was there any particular book you wished to see?"

"Have you Taine's England?"

"Beg pardon?"

"Taine's Notes on England."

The young gentleman scratched the side of his nose with a
cedar pencil which he took down from its bracket on the side
of his head, and reflected a moment:

"'Ah—I see," [with a bright smile]—"Train, you mean—
not Taine. George Francis Train. No, ma'm we—"

"I mean *Taine*—if I may take the liberty."

The clerk reflected again—then:

"Taine. . . . Taine. . . . Is it hymns?"

"No, it isn't hymns. It is a volume that is making a deal of
talk just now, and is very widely known—except among parties who sell it."

The clerk glanced at her face to see if a sarcasm might not
lurk somewhere in that obscure speech, but the gentle simplicity of the beautiful eyes that met his, banished that suspicion. He went away and conferred with the proprietor. Both
appeared to be nonplussed. They thought and talked, and
talked and thought by turns. Then both came forward and
the proprietor said:

"Is it an American book, ma'm?"

"No, it is an American reprint of an English translation."

"Oh! Yes—yes—I remember, now. We are expecting it
every day. It isn't out yet."

"I think you must be mistaken, because you advertised it a week ago."

"Why no—can that be so?"

"Yes, I am sure of it. And besides, here is the book itself, on the counter."

She bought it and the proprietor retired from the field. Then she asked the clerk for the Autocrat of the Breakfast Table—and was pained to see the admiration her beauty had inspired in him fade out of his face. He said with cold dignity, that cook books were somewhat out of their line, but he would order it if she desired it. She said, no, never mind. Then she fell to conning the titles again, finding a delight in the inspection of the Hawthornes, the Longfellows, the Tennysons, and other favorites of her idle hours. Meantime the clerk's eyes were busy, and no doubt his admiration was returning again—or may be he was only gauging her probable literary tastes by some sagacious system of admeasurement only known to his guild. Now he began to "assist" her in making a selection; but his efforts met with no success—indeed they only annoyed her and unpleasantly interrupted her meditations. Presently, while she was holding a copy of "Venetian Life" in her hand and running over a familiar passage here and there, the clerk said, briskly, snatching up a paper-covered volume and striking the counter a smart blow with it to dislodge the dust:

"Now here is a work that we've sold a lot of. Everybody that's read it likes it"—and he intruded it under her nose; "it's a book that I can recommend—'The Pirate's Doom, or the Last of the Buccaneers.' I think it's one of the best things that's come out this season."

Laura pushed it gently aside with her hand and went on filching from "Venetian Life."

"I believe I do not want it," she said.

The clerk hunted around awhile, glancing at one title and then another, but apparently not finding what he wanted. However, he succeeded at last. Said he:

"Have you ever read this, ma'm? I am sure you'll like it. It's by the author of 'The Hooligans of Hackensack.' It is full of love troubles and mysteries and all sorts of such things. The heroine strangles her own mother. Just glance at the title

please,—'Gonderil the Vampire, or The Dance of Death.'
And here is 'The Jokist's Own Treasury, or, The Phunny
Phellow's Bosom Phriend.' The funniest thing!—I've read it
four times, ma'm, and I can laugh at the very sight of it yet.
And 'Gonderil,'—I assure you it is the most splendid book I
ever read. I know you will like these books, ma'm, because
I've read them myself and I know what they are."

"Oh, I was perplexed—but I see how it is, now. You must
have thought I asked you to tell me what sort of books I
wanted—for I am apt to say things which I don't really mean,
when I am absent minded. I suppose I did ask you, didn't I?"

"No ma'm,—but I—"

"Yes, I must have done it, else you would not have offered
your services, for fear it might be rude. But don't be troubled—it was all my fault. I ought not to have been so heedless—I ought not to have asked you."

"But you didn't ask me, ma'm. We always help customers
all we can. You see our experience—living right among books
all the time—that sort of thing makes us able to help a customer make a selection, you know."

"Now does it, indeed? It is part of your business, then?"

"Yes'm, we always help."

"How good it is of you. Some people would think it rather
obtrusive, perhaps, but I don't—I think it is real kindness—
even charity. Some people jump to conclusions without any
thought—you have noticed that?"

"O yes," said the clerk, a little perplexed as to whether to
feel comfortable or the reverse; "oh yes, indeed, I've often
noticed that, ma'm."

"Yes, they jump to conclusions with an absurd heedless-
ness. Now some people would think it odd that because you,
with the budding tastes and the innocent enthusiasms natural
to your time of life, enjoyed the Vampires and the volume of
nursery jokes, you should imagine that an older person would
delight in them too—but I do not think it odd at all. I think
it natural—perfectly natural—in you. And kind, too. You look
like a person who not only finds a deep pleasure in any little
thing in the way of literature that strikes you forcibly, but is
willing and glad to share that pleasure with others—and that,
I think, is noble and admirable—very noble and admirable. I

think we ought all to share our pleasures with others, and do what we can to make each other happy, do not you?"

"Oh, yes. Oh, yes, indeed. Yes, you are quite right, ma'm."

But he was getting unmistakably uncomfortable, now, notwithstanding Laura's confiding sociability and almost affectionate tone.

"Yes, indeed. Many people would think that what a bookseller—or perhaps his clerk—knows about literature *as* literature, in contradistinction to its character as merchandise, would hardly be of much assistance to a person—that is, to an adult, of course—in the selection of food for the mind—except of course wrapping paper, or twine, or wafers, or something like that—but I never feel that way. I feel that whatever service you offer me, you offer with a good heart, and I am as grateful for it as if it were the greatest boon to me. And it *is* useful to me—it is bound to be so.—It cannot be otherwise. If you show me a book which you have read—not skimmed over or merely glanced at, but *read*—and you tell me that *you* enjoyed it and that *you* could read it three or four times, then I know what book I want—"

"Thank you!—th—"

—"to avoid. Yes indeed. I think that no information ever comes amiss in this world. Once or twice I have traveled in the cars—and there you know, the peanut boy always measures you with his eye, and hands you out a book of murders if you are fond of theology; or Tupper or a dictionary or T. S. Arthur if you are fond of poetry; or he hands you a volume of distressing jokes or a copy of the American Miscellany if you particularly dislike that sort of literary fatty degeneration of the heart—just for the world like a pleasant-spoken well-meaning gentleman in any bookstore—. But here I am running on as if business men had nothing to do but listen to women talk. You must pardon me, for I was not thinking.— And you must let me thank you again for helping me. I read a good deal, and shall be in nearly every day; and I would be sorry to have you think me a customer who talks too much and buys too little. Might I ask you to give me the time? Ah—two—twenty-two. Thank you very much. I will set mine while I have the opportunity."

But she could not get her watch open, apparently. She

tried, and tried again. Then the clerk, trembling at his own audacity, begged to be allowed to assist. She allowed him. He succeeded, and was radiant under the sweet influences of her pleased face and her seductively worded acknowledgements with gratification. Then he gave her the exact time again, and anxiously watched her turn the hands slowly till they reached the precise spot without accident or loss of life, and then he looked as happy as a man who had helped a fellow being through a momentous undertaking, and was grateful to know that he had not lived in vain. Laura thanked him once more. The words were music to his ear; but what were they compared to the ravishing smile with which she flooded his whole system? When she bowed her adieu and turned away, he was no longer suffering torture in the pillory where she had had him trussed up during so many distressing moments, but he belonged to the list of her conquests and was a flattered and happy thrall, with the dawn-light of love breaking over the eastern elevations of his heart.

It was about the hour, now, for the chairman of the House Committee on Benevolent Appropriations to make his appearance, and Laura stepped to the door to reconnoitre. She glanced up the street, and sure enough—

Chapter XXXVII

𒀹 𒂍𒀹 𒍑 𒐈 𒍢 𒐀 𒐒 𒑖

Usa ogn' arte la donna, onde sia cólto
Nella sua rete alcun novello amante;
Nè con tutti, nè sempre un stesso volto
Serba, ma cangia a tempo atti e sembiante.

Tasso.

THAT Chairman was nowhere in sight. Such disappointments seldom occur in novels, but are always happening in real life.

She was obliged to make a new plan. She sent him a note, and asked him to call in the evening—which he did.

She received the Hon. Mr. Buckstone with a sunny smile, and said:

"I don't know how I ever dared to send you a note, Mr. Buckstone, for you have the reputation of not being very partial to our sex."

"Why I am sure my reputation does me wrong, then, Miss Hawkins. I have been married once—is that nothing in my favor?"

"Oh, yes—that is, it may be and it may not be. If you have known what perfection is in woman, it is fair to argue that inferiority cannot interest you now."

"Even if that were the case it could not affect *you*, Miss Hawkins," said the chairman gallantly. "Fame does not place you in the list of ladies who rank below perfection."

This happy speech delighted Mr. Buckstone as much as it seemed to delight Laura. But it did not confuse him as much as it apparently did her.

"I wish in all sincerity that I could be worthy of such a felicitous compliment as that. But I am a woman, and so I am gratified for it just as it is, and would not have it altered."

"But it is not merely a compliment—that is, an empty compliment—it is the truth. All men will endorse that."

Laura looked pleased, and said:

"It is very kind of you to say it. It is a distinction indeed, for a country-bred girl like me to be so spoken of by people of brains and culture. You are so kind that I know you will pardon my putting you to the trouble to come this evening."

"Indeed it was no trouble. It was a pleasure. I am alone in the world since I lost my wife, and I often long for the society of your sex, Miss Hawkins, notwithstanding what people may say to the contrary."

"It is pleasant to hear you say that. I am sure it must be so. If I feel lonely at times, because of my exile from old friends, although surrounded by new ones who are already very dear to me, how much more lonely must you feel, bereft as you are, and with no wholesome relief from the cares of state that weigh you down. For your own sake, as well as for the sake of others, you ought to go into society oftener. I seldom see you at a reception, and when I do you do not usually give me very much of your attention."

"I never imagined that you wished it or I would have been very glad to make myself happy in that way.—But one seldom gets an opportunity to say more than a sentence to you in a place like that. You are always the centre of a group—a fact which you may have noticed yourself. But if one might come here—"

"Indeed you would always find a hearty welcome, Mr. Buckstone. I have often wished you would come and tell me more about Cairo and the Pyramids, as you once promised me you would."

"Why, do you remember that yet, Miss Hawkins? I thought ladies' memories were more fickle than that."

"Oh, they are not so fickle as gentlemen's promises. And besides, if I had been inclined to forget, I—did you not give me something by way of a remembrancer?"

"Did I?"

"Think."

"It does seem to me that I did; but I have forgotten what it was now."

"Never, never call a lady's memory fickle again! Do you recognize this?"

"A little spray of box! I am beaten—I surrender. But have you kept that all this time?"

Laura's confusion was very pretty. She tried to hide it, but the more she tried the more manifest it became and withal the more captivating to look upon. Presently she threw the spray of box from her with an annoyed air, and said:

"I forgot myself. I have been very foolish. I beg that you will forget this absurd thing."

Mr. Buckstone picked up the spray, and sitting down by Laura's side on the sofa, said:

"Please let me keep it, Miss Hawkins. I set a very high value upon it now."

"Give it to me, Mr. Buckstone, and do not speak so. I have been sufficiently punished for my thoughtlessness. You cannot take pleasure in adding to my distress. Please give it to me."

"Indeed I do not wish to distress you. But do not consider the matter so gravely; you have done yourself no wrong. You probably forgot that you had it; but if you had given it to me I would have kept it—and not forgotten it."

"Do not talk so, Mr. Buckstone. Give it to me, please, and forget the matter."

"It would not be kind to refuse, since it troubles you so, and so I restore it. But if you would give me part of it and keep the rest—"

"So that you might have something to remind you of me when you wished to laugh at my foolishness?"

"Oh, by no means, no! Simply that I might remember that I had once assisted to discomfort you, and be reminded to do so no more."

Laura looked up, and scanned his face a moment. She was about to break the twig, but she hesitated and said:

"If I were sure that you—" She threw the spray away, and continued: "This is silly! We will change the subject. No, do not insist—I must have my way in this."

Then Mr. Buckstone drew off his forces and proceeded to make a wily advance upon the fortress under cover of carefully-contrived artifices and stratagems of war. But he contended with an alert and suspicious enemy; and so at the end of two hours it was manifest to him that he had made but little progress. Still, he had made some; he was sure of that.

Laura sat alone and communed with herself;

"He is fairly hooked, poor thing. I can play him at my

leisure and land him when I choose. He was all ready to be caught, days and days ago—I saw that, very well. He will vote for our bill—no fear about that; and moreover he will work for it, too, before I am done with him. If he had a woman's eyes he would have noticed that the spray of box had grown three inches since he first gave it to me, but a man never sees anything and never suspects. If I had shown him a whole bush he would have thought it was the same. Well, it is a good night's work: the committee is safe. But this is a desperate game I am playing in these days—a wearing, sordid, heartless game. If I lose, I lose everything—even myself. And if I win the game, will it be worth its cost after all? I do not know. Sometimes I doubt. Sometimes I half wish I had not begun. But no matter; I *have* begun, and I will never turn back; never while I live."

Mr. Buckstone indulged in a reverie as he walked homeward:

"She is shrewd and deep, and plays her cards with considerable discretion—but she will lose, for all that. There is no hurry; I shall come out winner, all in good time. She *is* the most beautiful woman in the world; and she surpassed herself to-night. I suppose I must vote for that bill, in the end maybe; but that is not a matter of much consequence—the government can stand it. She is bent on capturing me, that is plain; but she will find by and by that what she took for a sleeping garrison was an ambuscade."

Chapter XXXVIII

Now this surprising news scaus'd her fall in a trance,
Life as she were dead, no limbs she could advance,
Then her dear brother came, her from the ground he took
And she spake up and said, O my poor heart is broke.
The Barnardcastle Tragedy.

DON'T you think he is distinguished looking?"

"What! That gawky looking person, with Miss Hawkins?"

"There. He's just speaking to Mrs. Schoonmaker. Such high-bred negligence and unconsciousness. Nothing studied. See his fine eyes."

"Very. They are moving this way now. Maybe he is coming here. But he looks as helpless as a rag baby. Who is he, Blanche?"

"Who is he? And you've been here a week, Grace, and don't know? He's the catch of the season. That's Washington Hawkins—her brother."

"No, is it?"

"Very old family, old Kentucky family I believe. He's got enormous landed property in Tennessee, I think. The family lost everything, slaves and that sort of thing, you know, in the war. But they have a great deal of land, minerals, mines and all that. Mr. Hawkins and his sister too are very much interested in the amelioration of the condition of the colored race; they have some plan, with Senator Dilworthy, to convert a large part of their property to something another for the freedmen."

"You don't say so? I thought he was some guy from Pennsylvania. But he *is* different from others. Probably he has lived all his life on his plantation."

It was a day reception of Mrs. Representative Schoonmaker, a sweet woman, of simple and sincere manners. Her house was one of the most popular in Washington. There was less ostentation there than in some others, and people liked to go where the atmosphere reminded them of the peace and purity of home. Mrs. Schoonmaker was as natural and unaffected in Washington society as she was in her own New York house, and kept up the spirit of home-life there, with her husband and children. And that was the reason, probably, why people of refinement liked to go there.

Washington is a microcosm, and one can suit himself with any sort of society within a radius of a mile. To a large portion of the people who frequent Washington or dwell there, the ultra fashion, the shoddy, the jobbery are as utterly distasteful as they would be in a refined New England City. Schoonmaker was not exactly a leader in the House, but he was greatly respected for his fine talents and his honesty. No one would have thought of offering to carry National Improvement Directors Relief stock for him.

These day receptions were attended by more women than men, and those interested in the problem might have studied the costumes of the ladies present, in view of this fact, to discover whether women dress more for the eyes of women or for effect upon men. It is a very important problem, and has been a good deal discussed, and its solution would form one fixed, philosophical basis, upon which to estimate woman's character. We are inclined to take a medium ground, and aver that woman dresses to please herself, and in obedience to a law of her own nature.

"They are coming this way," said Blanche. People who made way for them to pass, turned to look at them. Washington began to feel that the eyes of the public were on him also, and his eyes rolled about, now towards the ceiling, now towards the floor, in an effort to look unconscious.

"Good morning, Miss Hawkins. Delighted. Mr. Hawkins. My friend, Miss Medlar."

Mr. Hawkins, who was endeavoring to square himself for a bow, put his foot through the train of Mrs. Senator Poplin, who looked round with a scowl, which turned into a smile as she saw who it was. In extricating himself, Mr. Hawkins, who had the care of his hat as well as the introduction on his mind, shambled against Miss Blanche, who said *pardon*, with the prettiest accent, as if the awkwardness were her own. And Mr. Hawkins righted himself.

"Don't you find it very warm to-day, Mr. Hawkins?" said Blanche, by way of a remark.

"It's awful hot," said Washington.

"It's warm for the season," continued Blanche pleasantly. "But I suppose you are accustomed to it," she added, with a general idea that the thermometer always stands at 90° in all parts of the late slave states. "Washington weather generally cannot be very congenial to you?"

"It's congenial," said Washington brightening up, "when it's not congealed."

"That's very good. Did you hear, Grace, Mr. Hawkins says it's congenial when it's not congealed."

"What is, dear?" said Grace, who was talking with Laura.

The conversation was now finely under way. Washington launched out an observation of his own.

"Did you see those Japs, Miss Leavitt?"

"Oh, yes, aren't they queer. But so high-bred, so picturesque. Do you think that color makes any difference, Mr. Hawkins? I used to be so prejudiced against color."

"Did you? I never was. I used to think my old mammy was handsome."

"How interesting your life must have been! I should like to hear about it."

Washington was about settling himself into his narrative style, when Mrs. Gen. McFingal caught his eye.

"Have you been at the Capitol to-day, Mr. Hawkins?"

Washington had not. "Is anything uncommon going on?"

"They say it was very exciting. The Alabama business you know. Gen. Sutler, of Massachusetts, defied England, and they say he wants war."

"He wants to make himself conspicuous more like," said Laura. "He always, you have noticed, talks with one eye on the gallery, while the other is on the speaker."

"Well, my husband says, its nonsense to talk of war, and wicked. *He* knows what war is. If we *do* have war, I hope it will be for the patriots of Cuba. Don't you think we want Cuba, Mr. Hawkins?"

"I think we want it bad," said Washington. "And Santo Domingo. Senator Dilworthy says, we are bound to extend our religion over the isles of the sea. We've got to round out our territory, and"

Washington's further observations were broken off by Laura, who whisked him off to another part of the room, and reminded him that they must make their adieux.

"How stupid and tiresome these people are," she said. "Let's go."

They were turning to say good-by to the hostess, when Laura's attention was arrested by the sight of a gentleman who was just speaking to Mrs. Schoonmaker. For a second her heart stopped beating. He was a handsome man of forty and perhaps more, with grayish hair and whiskers, and he walked with a cane, as if he were slightly lame. He might be less than forty, for his face was worn into hard lines, and he was pale.

No. It could not be, she said to herself. It is only a resemblance. But as the gentleman turned and she saw his full face, Laura put out her hand and clutched Washington's arm to prevent herself from falling.

Washington, who was not minding anything, as usual looked 'round in wonder. Laura's eyes were blazing fire and hatred; he had never seen her look so before; and her face was livid.

"Why, what is it, sis? Your face is as white as paper."

"It's he, it's he. Come, come," and she dragged him away.

"It's who?" asked Washington, when they had gained the carriage.

"It's nobody, it's nothing. Did I say he? I was faint with the heat. Don't mention it. Don't you speak of it," she added earnestly, grasping his arm.

When she had gained her room she went to the glass and saw a pallid and haggard face.

"My God," she cried, "this will never do. I should have killed him, if I could. The scoundrel still lives, and dares to come here. I ought to kill him. He has no right to live. How I hate him. And yet I loved him. Oh heavens, how I did love that man. And why didn't he kill me? He might better. He did kill all that was good in me. Oh, but he shall not escape. He shall not escape this time. He may have forgotten. He will find that a woman's hate doesn't forget. The law? What would the law do but protect him and make me an outcast?

How all Washington would gather up its virtuous skirts and avoid me, if it knew. I wonder if he hates me as I do him?"

So Laura raved, in tears and in rage by turns, tossed in a tumult of passion, which she gave way to with little effort to control.

A servant came to summon her to dinner. She had a headache. The hour came for the President's reception. She had a raving headache, and the Senator must go without her.

That night of agony was like another night she recalled. How vividly it all came back to her. And at that time she remembered she thought she might be mistaken. He might come back to her. Perhaps he loved her, a little, after all. *Now*, she knew he did not. Now, she knew he was a cold-blooded scoundrel, without pity. Never a word in all these years. She had hoped he was dead. Did his wife live, she wondered. She caught at that, and it gave a new current to her thoughts. Perhaps, after all—she must see him. She could not live without seeing him. Would he smile as in the old days when she loved him so; or would he sneer as when she last saw him? If he looked so, she hated him. If he should call her "Laura, darling," and look *so*! She must find him. She must end her doubts.

Laura kept her room for two days, on one excuse and another—a nervous headache, a cold—to the great anxiety of the Senator's household. Callers, who went away, said she had been too gay—they did not say "fast," though some of them may have thought it. One so conspicuous and successful in society as Laura could not be out of the way two days, without remarks being made, and not all of them complimentary.

When she came down she appeared as usual, a little pale may be, but unchanged in manner. If there were any deepened lines about the eyes they had been concealed. Her course of action was quite determined.

At breakfast she asked if any one had heard any unusual noise during the night? Nobody had. Washington never heard any noise of any kind after his eyes were shut. Some people thought he never did when they were open either.

Senator Dilworthy said he had come in late. He was detained in a little consultation after the Congressional prayer meeting. Perhaps it was his entrance.

No, Laura said. She heard that. It was later. She might have been nervous, but she fancied somebody was trying to get into the house.

Mr. Brierly humorously suggested that it might be, as none of the members were occupied in night session.

The Senator frowned, and said he did not like to hear that kind of newspaper slang. There might be burglars about.

Laura said that very likely it was only her nervousness. But she thought she would feel safer if Washington would let her take one of this pistols. Washington brought her one of his revolvers, and instructed her in the art of loading and firing it.

During the morning Laura drove down to Mrs. Schoon-maker's to pay a friendly call.

"Your receptions are always delightful," she said to that lady, "the pleasant people all seem to come here."

"It's pleasant to hear you say so, Miss Hawkins. I believe my friends like to come here. Though society in Washington is mixed; we have a little of everything."

"I suppose, though, you don't see much of the old rebel element?" said Laura with a smile.

If this seemed to Mrs. Schoonmaker a singular remark for a lady to make, who was meeting "rebels" in society every day, she did not express it in any way, but only said,

"You know we don't say 'rebel' anymore. Before we came to Washington I thought rebels would look unlike other people. I find we are very much alike, and that kindness and good nature wear away prejudice. And then you know there are all sorts of common interests. My husband sometimes says that he doesn't see but confederates are just as eager to get at the treasury as Unionists. You know that Mr. Schoonmaker is on the appropriations."

"Does he know many Southerners?"

"Oh, yes. There were several at my reception the other day. Among others a confederate Colonel—a stranger—handsome man with gray hair, probably you didn't notice him, uses a cane in walking. A very agreeable man. I wondered why he called. When my husband came home and looked over the cards, he said he had a cotton claim. A real southerner. Perhaps you might know him if I could think of his name. Yes, here's his card—Louisiana."

Laura took the card, looked at it intently till she was sure of the address, and then laid it down, with,

"No, he is no friend of ours."

That afternoon, Laura wrote and dispatched the following note. It was in a round hand, unlike her flowing style, and it was directed to a number and street in Georgetown:—

"A Lady at Senator Dilworthy's would like to see Col. George Selby, on business connected with the Cotton Claims. Can he call Wednesday at three o'clock P.M.?"

On Wednesday at 3 P.M. no one of the family was likely to be in the house except Laura.

Chapter XXXIX

—Belhs amics, tornatz,
Per merce, vas me de cors.
Alphonse II.

Ala khambiatü da zure deseiña?
Hitz eman zenereitan,
Ez behin, bai berritan,
    Enia zinela.
—Ohikua nüzü;
Enüzü khambiatü,
Bihotzian beinin hartü,
    Eta zü maithatü.
Maitia, nun zira?

C OL. SELBY had just come to Washington, and taken
lodgings in Georgetown. His business was to get pay for
some cotton that was destroyed during the war. There were
many others in Washington on the same errand, some of
them with claims as difficult to establish as his. A concert of
action was necessary, and he was not, therefore, at all surprised to receive the note from a lady asking him to call at
Senator Dilworthy's.

At a little after three on Wednesday he rang the bell of the
Senator's residence. It was a handsome mansion on the
Square opposite the President's house. The owner must be a
man of great wealth, the Colonel thought; perhaps, who
knows, said he with a smile, he may have got some of my cotton in exchange for salt and quinine after the capture of New
Orleans. As this thought passed through his mind he was
looking at the remarkable figure of the Hero of New Orleans,
holding itself by main strength from sliding off the back of
the rearing bronze horse, and lifting its hat in the manner of
one who acknowledges the playing of that martial air: "See,
the Conquering Hero Comes!" "Gad," said the Colonel to
himself, "Old Hickory ought to get down and give his seat to
Gen. Sutler—but they'd have to tie him on."

Laura was in the drawing room. She heard the bell, she
heard the steps in the hall, and the emphatic thud of the

supporting cane. She had risen from her chair and was leaning against the piano, pressing her left hand against the violent beating of her heart. The door opened and the Colonel entered, standing in the full light of the opposite window. Laura was more in the shadow and stood for an instant, long enough for the Colonel to make the inward observation that she was a magnificent woman. She then advanced a step.

"Col. Selby, is it not?"

The Colonel staggered back, caught himself by a chair, and turned towards her a look of terror.

"Laura? My God!"

"Yes, your wife!"

"Oh, no, it can't be. How came you here? I thought you were—"

"You thought I was dead? You thought you were rid of me? Not so long as you live, Col. Selby, not so long as you live," Laura in her passion was hurried on to say.

No man had ever accused Col. Selby of cowardice. But he was a coward before this woman. May be he was not the man he once was. Where was his coolness? Where was his sneering, imperturbable manner, with which he could have met, and would have met, any woman he had wronged, if he had only been forewarned. He felt now that he must temporize, that he must gain time. There was danger in Laura's tone. There was something frightful in her calmness. Her steady eyes seemed to devour him.

"You have ruined my life," she said; "and I was so young, so ignorant, and loved you so. You betrayed me, and left me, mocking me and trampling me into the dust, a soiled cast-off. You might better have killed me then. Then I should not have hated you."

"Laura," said the Colonel, nerving himself, but still pale, and speaking appealingly, "don't say that. Reproach me. I deserve it. I was a scoundrel. I was everything monstrous. But your beauty made me crazy. You are right. I was a brute in leaving you as I did. But what could I do? I was married, and—"

"And your wife still lives?" asked Laura, bending a little forward in her eagerness.

The Colonel noticed the action, and he almost said "no," but he thought of the folly of attempting concealment.

"Yes. She is here."

What little color had wandered back into Laura's face forsook it again. Her heart stood still, her strength seemed going from her limbs. Her last hope was gone. The room swam before her for a moment, and the Colonel stepped towards her, but she waved him back, as hot anger again coursed through her veins, and said,

"And you dare come with her, *here*, and tell me of it, here and mock me with it! And you think I will have it, George? You think I will let you live with that woman? You think I am as powerless as that day I fell dead at your feet?"

She raged now. She was in a tempest of excitement. And she advanced towards him with a threatening mien. She would kill me if she could, thought the Colonel; but he thought at the same moment, how beautiful she is. He had recovered his head now. She was lovely when he knew her, then a simple country girl. Now she was dazzling, in the fullness of ripe womanhood, a superb creature, with all the fascination that a woman of the world has for such a man as Col. Selby. Nothing of this was lost on him. He stepped quickly to her, grasped both her hands in his, and said,

"Laura, stop! think! Suppose I loved you yet! Suppose I hated my fate! What can I do? I am broken by the war. I have lost everything almost. I had as lief be dead and done with it."

The Colonel spoke with a low remembered voice that thrilled through Laura. He was looking into her eyes as he had looked in those old days, when no birds of all those that sang in the groves where they walked sang a note of warning. He was wounded. He had been punished. Her strength forsook her with her rage, and she sank upon a chair, sobbing,

"Oh! my God, I thought I hated him!"

The Colonel knelt beside her. He took her hand and she let him keep it. She looked down into his face, with a pitiable tenderness, and said in a weak voice.

"And you do love me a little?"

The Colonel vowed and protested. He kissed her hand and her lips. He swore his false soul into perdition.

She wanted love, this woman. Was not her love for George Selby deeper than any other woman's could be? Had she not a right to him? Did he not belong to her by virtue of her overmastering passion? His wife—she was not his wife, except by the law. She could not be. Even with the law she could have no right to stand between two souls that were one. It was an infamous condition in society that George should be tied to *her*.

Laura thought this, believed it, because she desired to believe it. She came to it as an original proposition, founded on the requirements of her own nature. She may have heard, doubtless she had, similar theories that were prevalent at that day, theories of the tyranny of marriage and of the freedom of marriage. She had even heard women lecturers say that marriage should only continue so long as it pleased either party to it—for a year, or a month, or a day. She had not given much heed to this. But she saw its justice now in a flash of revealing desire. It must be right. God would not have permitted her to love George Selby as she did, and him to love her, if it was right for society to raise up a barrier between them. He belonged to her. Had he not confessed it himself?

Not even the religious atmosphere of Senator Dilworthy's house had been sufficient to instill into Laura that deep Christian principle which had been somehow omitted in her training. Indeed in that very house had she not heard women, prominent before the country and besieging Congress, utter sentiments that fully justified the course she was marking out for herself?

They were seated now, side by side, talking with more calmness. Laura was happy, or thought she was. But it was that feverish sort of happiness which is snatched out of the black shadow of falsehood, and is at the moment recognized as fleeting and perilous, and indulged tremblingly. She loved. She was loved. That is happiness certainly. And the black past and the troubled present and the uncertain future could not snatch that from her.

What did they say as they sat there? What nothings do people usually say in such circumstances, even if they are three-score and ten? It was enough for Laura to hear his voice and be near him. It was enough for him to be near her, and avoid committing himself as much as he could. Enough for him was the present also. Had there not always been some way out of such scrapes?

And yet Laura could not be quite content without prying into to-morrow. *How* could the Colonel manage to free himself from his wife? Would it be long? Could he not go into some State where it would not take much time? He could not say exactly. That they must think of. That they must talk over. And so on. Did this seem like a damnable plot to Laura against the life, maybe, of a sister, a woman like herself? Probably not. It was right that this man should be hers, and there were some obstacles in the way. That was all. There are as good reasons for bad actions as for good ones, to those who commit them. When one has broken the tenth commandment, the others are not of much account.

Was it unnatural, therefore, that when George Selby departed, Laura should watch him from the window, with an almost joyful heart as he went down the sunny square? "I shall see him to-morrow," she said, "and the next day, and the next. He is mine now."

"Damn the woman," said the Colonel as he picked his way down the steps. "Or," he added, as his thoughts took a new turn, "I wish my wife was in New Orleans."

Chapter XL

Open your ears; for which of you will stop
The vent of hearing, when loud Rumor speaks?
I, from the orient to the drooping west,
Making the wind my post-horse, still unfold
The acts commenced on this ball of earth:
Upon my tongues continual slanders ride;
The which in every language I pronounce,
Stuffing the ears of men with false reports.
                              King Henry IV.

As MAY be readily believed, Col. Eschol Sellers was by this time one of the best known men in Washington. For the first time in his life his talents had a fair field.

He was now at the centre of the manufacture of gigantic schemes, of speculations of all sorts, of political and social gossip. The atmosphere was full of little and big rumors and of vast, undefined expectations. Everybody was in haste, too, to push on his private plan, and feverish in his haste, as if in constant apprehension that to-morrow would be Judgment Day. Work while Congress is in session, said the uneasy spirit, for in the recess there is no work and no device.

The Colonel enjoyed this bustle and confusion amazingly; he thrived in the air of indefinite expectation. All his own schemes took larger shape and more misty and majestic proportions; and in this congenial air, the Colonel seemed even to himself to expand into something large and mysterious. If he respected himself before, he almost worshipped Eschol Sellers now, as a superior being. If he could have chosen an official position out of the highest, he would have been embarrassed in the selection. The presidency of the republic seemed too limited and cramped in the constitutional restrictions. If he could have been Grand Llama of the United States, that might have come the nearest to his idea of a position. And next to that he would have luxuriated in the irresponsible omniscience of the Special Correspondent.

Col. Sellers knew the President very well, and had access to his presence when officials were kept cooling their heels in the waiting-room. The President liked to hear the Colonel talk, his voluble ease was a refreshment after the decorous dullness of men who only talked business and government, and everlastingly expounded their notions of justice and the distribution of patronage. The Colonel was as much a lover of farming and of horses as Thomas Jefferson was. He talked to the President by the hour about his magnificent stud, and his plantation at Hawkeye, a kind of principality he represented it. He urged the President to pay him a visit during the recess, and see his stock farm.

"The President's table is well enough," he used to say, to the loafers who gathered about him at Willard's, "well enough for a man on a salary, but God bless my soul, I should like him to see a little old-fashioned hospitality—open house, you know. A person seeing me at home might think I paid no attention to what was in the house, just let things flow in and out. He'd be mistaken. What I look to is quality, sir. The President has variety enough, but the quality! Vegetables of course you can't expect here. I'm very particular about mine. Take celery, now—there's only one spot in this country where celery will grow. But I *am* surprised about the wines. I should think they were manufactured in the New York Custom House. I must send the President some from my cellar. I was really mortified the other day at dinner to see Blacque Bey leave his standing in the glasses."

When the Colonel first came to Washington he had thoughts of taking the mission to Constantinople, in order to be on the spot to look after the dissemination of his Eye Water, but as that invention was not yet quite ready, the project shrank a little in the presence of vaster schemes. Besides he felt that he could do the country more good by remaining at home. He was one of the Southerners who were constantly quoted as heartily "accepting the situation."

"I'm whipped," he used to say with a jolly laugh, "the government was too many for me; I'm cleaned out, done for, except my plantation and private mansion. We played for a big thing, and lost it, and I don't whine, for one. I go for putting the old flag on all the vacant lots. I said to the President, says I, 'Grant, why don't you take Santo Domingo, annex the whole thing, and settle the bill afterwards.' That's my way. I'd take the job to manage Congress. The South would come into it. You've got to conciliate the South, consolidate the two debts, pay 'em off in greenbacks, and go ahead. That's my notion. Boutwell's got the right notion about the value of paper, but he lacks courage. I *should* like to run the treasury department about six months. I'd make things plenty, and business look up."

The Colonel had access to the departments. He knew all the senators and representatives, and especially the lobby. He was consequently a great favorite in Newspaper Row, and was often lounging in the offices there, dropping bits of private, official information, which were immediately caught up and telegraphed all over the country. But it used to surprise even the Colonel when he read it, it was embellished to that degree that he hardly recognized it, and the hint was not lost on him. He began to exaggerate his heretofore simple conversation to suit the newspaper demand.

People used to wonder in the winters of 187– and 187–, where the "Specials" got that remarkable information with which they every morning surprised the country, revealing the most secret intentions of the President and his cabinet, the private thoughts of political leaders, the hidden meaning of every movement. This information was furnished by Col. Sellers.

When he was asked, afterwards, about the stolen copy of the Alabama Treaty which got into the "New York Tribune," he only looked mysterious, and said that neither he nor Senator Dilworthy knew anything about it. But those whom he was in the habit of meeting occasionally felt almost certain that he did know.

It must not be supposed that the Colonel in his general patriotic labors neglected his own affairs. The Columbus River Navigation Scheme absorbed only a part of his time, so he was enabled to throw quite a strong reserve force of energy into the Tennessee Land plan, a vast enterprise commensurate with his abilities, and in the prosecution of which he was greatly aided by Mr. Henry Brierly, who was buzzing about the capitol and the hotels day and night, and making capital for it in some mysterious way.

"We must create a public opinion," said Senator Dilworthy. "My only interest in it is a public one, and if the country wants the institution, Congress will have to yield."

It may have been after a conversation between the Colonel and Senator Dilworthy that the following special despatch was sent to a New York newspaper:—

"We understand that a philanthropic plan is on foot in relation to the colored race that will, if successful, revolutionize the whole character of southern industry. An experimental institution is in contemplation in Tennessee which will do for that state what the Industrial School at Zurich did for Switzerland. We learn that approaches have been made to the heirs of the late Hon. Silas Hawkins of Missouri, in reference to a lease of a portion of their valuable property in East Tennessee. Senator Dilworthy, it is understood, is inflexibly opposed to any arrangement that will not give the government absolute control. Private interests must give way to the public good. It is to be hoped that Col. Sellers, who represents the heirs, will be led to see the matter in this light."

When Washington Hawkins read this despatch, he went to the Colonel in some anxiety. He was for a lease, he didn't want to surrender anything. What did he think the government would offer? Two millions?

"May be three, may be four," said the Colonel, "it's worth more than the bank of England."

"If they will not lease," said Washington, "let 'em make it two millions for an undivided half. I'm not going to throw it away, not the whole of it."

Harry told the Colonel that they must drive the thing through, he couldn't be dallying round Washington when Spring opened. Phil wanted him, Phil had a great thing on hand up in Pennsylvania.

"What is that?" inquired the Colonel, always ready to interest himself in anything large.

"A mountain of coal; that's all. He's going to run a tunnel into it in the Spring."

"Does he want any capital?" asked the Colonel, in the tone of a man who is given to calculating carefully before he makes an investment.

"No. Old man Bolton's behind him. He has capital, but I judged that he wanted my experience in starting."

"If he wants me, tell him I'll come, after Congress adjourns. I should like to give him a little lift. He lacks enterprise—now, about that Columbus River. He doesn't see his chances. But he's a good fellow, and you can tell him that Sellers won't go back on him."

"By the way," asked Harry, "who is that rather handsome party that's hanging 'round Laura? I see him with her everywhere, at the Capitol, in the horse cars, and he comes to Dilworthy's. If he weren't lame, I should think he was going to run off with her."

"Oh, that's nothing. Laura knows her business. He has a cotton claim. Used to be at Hawkeye during the war—Selby's his name, was a Colonel. Got a wife and family. Very respectable people, the Selby's."

"Well, that's all right," said Harry, "if it's business. But if a woman looked at me as I've seen her at Selby, I should understand it. And it's talked about, I can tell you."

Jealousy had no doubt sharpened this young gentleman's observation. Laura could not have treated him with more lofty condescension if she had been the Queen of Sheba, on a royal visit to the great republic. And he resented it, and was "huffy" when he was with her, and ran her errands, and brought her gossip, and bragged of his intimacy with the lovely creature among the fellows at Newspaper Row.

Laura's life was rushing on now in the full stream of intrigue and fashionable dissipation. She was conspicuous at the balls of the fastest set, and was suspected of being present at those doubtful suppers that began late and ended early. If Senator Dilworthy remonstrated about appearances, she had a way of silencing him. Perhaps she had some hold on him, perhaps she was necessary to his plan for ameliorating the condition of the colored race.

She saw Col. Selby, when the public knew and when it did not know. She would see him, whatever excuses he made, and however he avoided her. She was urged on by a fever of love and hatred and jealousy, which alternately possessed her. Sometimes she petted him, and coaxed him and tried all her fascinations. And again she threatened him and reproached him. What was he doing? Why had he taken no steps to free himself? Why didn't he send his wife home? She should have *money* soon. They could go to Europe,—anywhere. What did she care for talk?

And he promised, and lied, and invented fresh excuses for delay, like a cowardly gambler and roué as he was, fearing to break with her, and half the time unwilling to give her up.

"That woman doesn't know what fear is," he said to himself, "and she watches me like a hawk."

He told his wife that this woman was a lobbyist, whom he had to tolerate and use in getting through his claims, and that he should pay her and have done with her, when he succeeded.

Chapter XLI.

وَزَادَهُ كَلَفًا فِى الْحُبِّ أَنْ مَنَعَتْ
وَحُبُّ شَيْءٍ اِلَى الاِنْسَانِ مَا مُنِعَا

Táj el-'Aroos.

Egundano yçan daya ni baydienetacoric?
Ny amoriac enu mayte, nic hura ecin gayecxi.
Bern. d'Echeparre.

HENRY BRIERLY was at the Dilworthy's constantly and on such terms of intimacy that he came and went without question. The Senator was not an inhospitable man, he liked to have guests in his house, and Harry's gay humor and rattling way entertained him; for even the most devout men and busy statesmen must have hours of relaxation.

Harry himself believed that he was of great service in the University business, and that the success of the scheme depended upon him to a great degree. He spent many hours in talking it over with the Senator after dinner. He went so far as to consider whether it would be worth his while to take the professorship of civil engineering in the new institution.

But it was not the Senator's society nor his dinners—at which this scapegrace remarked that there was too much grace and too little wine—which attracted him to the house. The fact was the poor fellow hung around there day after day for the chance of seeing Laura for five minutes at a time. For her presence at dinner he would endure the long bore of the Senator's talk afterwards, while Laura was off at some assembly, or excused herself on the plea of fatigue. Now and then he accompanied her to some reception, and rarely, on off nights, he was blessed with her company in the parlor, when he sang, and was chatty and vivacious and performed a hundred little tricks of imitation and ventriloquism, and made himself as entertaining as a man could be.

It puzzled him not a little that all his fascinations seemed to go for so little with Laura; it was beyond his experience with women. Sometimes Laura was exceedingly kind and petted him a little, and took the trouble to exert her powers of pleasing, and to entangle him deeper and deeper. But this, it angered him afterwards to think, was in private; in public she was beyond his reach, and never gave occasion to the suspicion that she had any affair with him. He was never permitted to achieve the dignity of a serious flirtation with her in public.

"Why do you treat me so?" he once said, reproachfully.

"Treat you how?" asked Laura in a sweet voice, lifting her eyebrows.

"You know well enough. You let other fellows monopolize you in society, and you are as indifferent to me as if we were strangers."

"Can I help it if they are attentive, can I be rude? But we are such old friends, Mr. Brierly, that I didn't suppose you would be jealous."

"I think I must be a very old friend, then, by your conduct towards me. By the same rule I should judge that Col. Selby must be very new."

Laura looked up quickly, as if about to return an indignant answer to such impertinence, but she only said, "Well, what of Col. Selby, sauce-box?"

"Nothing, probably, you'll care for. Your being with him so much is the town talk, that's all?"

"What do people say?" asked Laura calmly.

"Oh, they say a good many things. You are offended, though, to have me speak of it?"

"Not in the least. You are my true friend. I feel that I can trust you. You wouldn't deceive me, Harry?" throwing into her eyes a look of trust and tenderness that melted away all his petulance and distrust. "What do they say?"

"Some say that you've lost your head about him; others that you don't care any more for him than you do for a dozen others, but that he is completely fascinated with you and about to desert his wife; and others say it is nonsense to suppose you would entangle yourself with a married man, and that your intimacy only arises from the matter of the cotton claims, for which he wants your influence with Dilworthy. But you know everybody is talked about more or less in Washington. I shouldn't care; but I wish you wouldn't have so much to do with Selby, Laura," continued Harry, fancying that he was now upon such terms that his advice would be heeded.

"And you believed these slanders?"

"I don't believe anything against you, Laura, but Col. Selby does not mean you any good. I know you wouldn't be seen with him if you knew his reputation."

"Do you know him?" Laura asked, as indifferently as she could.

"Only a little. I was at his lodgings in Georgetown a day or two ago, with Col. Sellers. Sellers wanted to talk with him about some patent remedy he has, Eye Water, or something of that sort, which he wants to introduce into Europe. Selby is going abroad very soon."

Laura started, in spite of her self-control.

"And his wife? Does he take his family? Did you see his wife?"

"Yes. A dark little woman, rather worn—must have been pretty once though. Has three or four children, one of them a baby. They'll all go, of course. She said she should be glad enough to get away from Washington. You know Selby has got his claim allowed, and they say he has had a run of luck lately at Morrissey's."

Laura heard all this in a kind of stupor, looking straight at Harry, without seeing him. Is it possible, she was thinking, that this base wretch, after all his promises, will take his wife and children and leave me? Is it possible the town is saying all these things about me? And—a look of bitterness coming into her face—does the fool think he can escape so?

"You are angry with me, Laura," said Harry, not comprehending in the least what was going on in her mind.

"Angry?" she said, forcing herself to come back to his presence. "With you? Oh, no. I'm angry with the cruel world, which pursues an independent woman as it never does a man. I'm grateful to you, Harry; I'm grateful to you for telling me of that odious man."

And she rose from her chair and gave him her pretty hand, which the silly fellow took, and kissed and clung to. And he said many silly things, before she disengaged herself gently, and left him, saying it was time to dress, for dinner.

And Harry went away, excited, and a little hopeful, but

only a little. The happiness was only a gleam, which departed and left him thoroughly miserable She never would love him, and she was going to the devil, besides. He couldn't shut his eyes to what he saw, nor his ears to what he heard of her.

What had come over this trifling young lady-killer? It was a pity to see such a gay butterfly broken on a wheel. Was there something good in him, after all, that had been touched? He was in fact madly in love with this woman. It is not for us to analyze the passion and say whether it was a worthy one. It absorbed his whole nature and made him wretched enough. If he deserved punishment, what more would you have? Perhaps this love was kindling a new heroism in him.

He saw the road on which Laura was going clearly enough, though he did not believe the worst he heard of her. He loved her too passionately to credit that for a moment. And it seemed to him that if he could compel her to recognize her position, and his own devotion, she might love him, and that he could save her. His love was so far ennobled, and become a very different thing from its beginning in Hawkeye. Whether he ever thought that if he could save her from ruin, he could give her up himself, is doubtful. Such a pitch of virtue does not occur often in real life, especially in such natures as Harry's, whose generosity and unselfishness were matters of temperament rather than habits or principles.

He wrote a long letter to Laura, an incoherent, passionate letter, pouring out his love as he could not do in her presence, and warning her as plainly as he dared of the dangers that surrounded her, and the risks she ran of compromising herself in many ways.

Laura read the letter, with a little sigh may be, as she thought of other days, but with contempt also, and she put it into the fire with the thought, "They are all alike."

Harry was in the habit of writing to Philip freely, and boasting also about his doings, as he could not help doing and remain himself. Mixed up with his own exploits, and his daily triumphs as a lobbyist, especially in the matter of the new University, in which Harry was to have something handsome, were amusing sketches of Washington society, hints about Dilworthy, stories about Col. Sellers, who had become a well-known character, and wise remarks upon the machinery of private legislation for the public good, which greatly entertained Philip in his convalescence.

Laura's name occurred very often in these letters, at first in casual mention as the belle of the season, carrying everything before her with her wit and beauty, and then more seriously, as if Harry did not exactly like so much general admiration of her, and was a little nettled by her treatment of him. This was so different from Harry's usual tone about women, that Philip wondered a good deal over it. Could it be possible that he was seriously affected? Then came stories about Laura, town talk, gossip which Harry denied the truth of indignantly; but he was evidently uneasy, and at length wrote in such miserable spirits that Philip asked him squarely what the trouble was; was he in love?

Upon this, Harry made a clean breast of it, and told Philip all he knew about the Selby affair, and Laura's treatment of him, sometimes encouraging him and then throwing him off, and finally his belief that she would go to the bad if something was not done to arouse her from her infatuation. He wished Philip was in Washington. He knew Laura, and she had a great respect for his character, his opinions, his judgment. Perhaps he, as an uninterested person in whom she would have some confidence, and as one of the public, could say something to her that would show her where she stood.

Philip saw the situation clearly enough. Of Laura he knew not much, except that she was a woman of uncommon fascination, and he thought from what he had seen of her in Hawkeye, her conduct towards him and towards Harry, of not too much principle. Of course he knew nothing of her history; he knew nothing seriously against her, and if Harry was desperately enamored of her, why should he not win her if he could. If, however, she had already become what Harry uneasily felt she might become, was it not his duty to go to the rescue of his friend and try to save him from any rash act on account of a woman that might prove to be entirely unworthy of him; for trifler and visionary as he was, Harry deserved a better fate than this.

Philip determined to go to Washington and see for himself. He had other reasons also. He began to know enough of Mr. Bolton's affairs to be uneasy. Pennybacker had been there several times during the winter, and he suspected that he was involving Mr. Bolton in some doubtful scheme. Pennybacker was in Washington, and Philip thought he might perhaps find out something about him, and his plans, that would be of service to Mr. Bolton.

Philip had enjoyed his winter very well, for a man with his arm broken and his head smashed. With two such nurses as Ruth and Alice, illness seemed to him rather a nice holiday, and every moment of his convalescence had been precious and all too fleeting. With a young fellow of the habits of Philip, such injuries cannot be counted on to tarry long, even for the purpose of love-making, and Philip found himself getting strong with even disagreeable rapidity.

During his first weeks of pain and weakness, Ruth was unceasing in her ministrations; she quietly took charge of him, and with a gentle firmness resisted all attempts of Alice or any one else to share to any great extent the burden with her. She was clear, decisive and peremptory in whatever she did; but often when Philip opened his eyes in those first days of suffering and found her standing by his bedside, he saw a look of tenderness in her anxious face that quickened his already feverish pulse, a look that remained in his heart long after he closed his eyes. Sometimes he felt her hand on his forehead, and did not open his eyes for fear she would take it away. He watched for her coming to his chamber; he could distinguish her light footstep from all others. If this is what is meant by women practicing medicine, thought Philip to himself, I like it.

"Ruth," said he one day when he was getting to be quite himself, "I believe in it?"

"Believe in what?"

"Why, in women physicians."

"Then, I'd better call in Mrs. Dr. Longstreet."

"Oh, no. One will do, one at a time. I think I should be well to-morrow, if I thought I should never have any other."

"Thy physician thinks thee mustn't talk, Philip," said Ruth putting her finger on his lips.

"But, Ruth, I want to tell you that I should wish I never had got well if—"

"There, there, thee must *not* talk. Thee is wandering

again," and Ruth closed his lips, with a smile on her own that broadened into a merry laugh as she ran away.

Philip was not weary, however, of making these attempts, he rather enjoyed it. But whenever he inclined to be sentimental, Ruth would cut him off, with some such gravely conceived speech as, "Does thee think that thy physician will take advantage of the condition of a man who is as weak as thee is? I will call Alice, if thee has any dying confessions to make."

As Philip convalesced, Alice more and more took Ruth's place as his entertainer, and read to him by the hour, when he did not want to talk—to talk about Ruth, as he did a good deal of the time. Nor was this altogether unsatisfactory to Philip. He was always happy and contented with Alice. She was the most restful person he knew. Better informed than Ruth and with a much more varied culture, and bright and sympathetic, he was never weary of her company, if he was not greatly excited by it. She had upon his mind that peaceful influence that Mrs. Bolton had when, occasionally, she sat by his bedside with her work. Some people have this influence, which is like an emanation. They bring peace to a house, they diffuse serene content in a room full of mixed company, though they may say very little, and are apparently unconscious of their own power.

Not that Philip did not long for Ruth's presence all the same. Since he was well enough to be about the house, she was busy again with her studies. Now and then her teasing humor came again. She always had a playful shield against his sentiment. Philip used sometimes to declare that she had no sentiment; and then he doubted if he should be pleased with her after all if she were at all sentimental; and he rejoiced that she had, in such matters, what he called the airy grace of sanity. She was the most gay serious person he ever saw.

Perhaps he was not so much at rest or so contented with her as with Alice. But then he loved her. And what have rest and contentment to do with love?

Chapter XLII

Subtle. Would I were hang'd then! I'll conform myself
Dol. Will you, sir? do so then, and quickly: swear.
Sub. What should I swear?
Dol. To leave your faction, sir,
   And labour kindly in the common work.

The Alchemist.

Eku edue mfine, mfine ata eku: miduehe mfine, mfine itaha.

Epik Proverb.

MR. BUCKSTONE'S campaign was brief—much briefer than he supposed it would be. He began it purposing to win Laura without being won himself; but his experience was that of all who had fought on that field before him; he diligently continued his effort to win her, but he presently found that while as yet he could not feel entirely certain of having won her, it was very manifest that she had won him. He had made an able fight, brief as it was, and that at least was to his credit. He was in good company, now; he walked in a leash of conspicuous captives. These unfortunates followed Laura helplessly, for whenever she took a prisoner he remained her slave henceforth. Sometimes they chafed in their bondage; sometimes they tore themselves free and said their serfdom was ended; but sooner or later they always came back penitent and worshiping. Laura pursued her usual course: she encouraged Mr. Buckstone by turns, and by turns she harassed him; she exalted him to the clouds at one time, and at another she dragged him down again. She constituted him chief champion of the Knobs University bill, and he accepted the position, at first reluctantly, but later as a valued means of serving her—he even came to look upon it as a piece of great good fortune, since it brought him into such frequent contact with her.

Through him she learned that the Hon. Mr. Trollop was a bitter enemy of her bill. He urged her not to attempt to influence Mr. Trollop in any way, and explained that whatever she might attempt in that direction would surely be used against her and with damaging effect.

She at first said she knew Mr. Trollop, "and was aware that he had a Blank-Blank;"* but Mr. Buckstone said that while he was not able to conceive what so curious a phrase as Blank-Blank might mean, and had no wish to pry into the matter, since it was probably private, he "would nevertheless venture the blind assertion that *nothing* would answer in this particular case and during this particular session but to be exceedingly wary and keep clear away from Mr. Trollop; any other course would be fatal."

It seemed that nothing could be done. Laura was seriously troubled. Everything was looking well, and yet it was plain that one vigorous and determined enemy might eventually succeed in overthrowing all her plans. A suggestion came into her mind presently and she said:

"Can't you fight against his great Pension bill and bring him to terms?"

"Oh, never; he and I are sworn brothers on that measure; we work in harness and are very loving—I do everything I possibly can for him there. But I work with might and main against his Immigration bill,—as pertinaciously and as vindictively, indeed, as he works against our University. We hate each other through half a conversation and are all affection through the other half. We understand each other. He is an admirable worker outside the capitol; he will do more for the Pension bill than any other man could do; I wish he would make the great speech on it which he wants to make—and then I would make another and we would be safe."

"Well if he wants to make a great speech why doesn't he do it?"

Visitors interrupted the conversation and Mr. Buckstone took his leave. It was not of the least moment to Laura that her question had not been answered, inasmuch as it concerned a thing which did not interest her; and yet, human being like, she thought she would have liked to know. An opportunity occurring presently, she put the same question to another person and got an answer that satisfied her. She pondered a good while, that night, after she had gone to bed, and when she finally turned over to go to sleep, she had thought

---

*Her private figure of speech for Brother—or Son-in-law.

out a new scheme. The next evening at Mrs. Gloverson's party, she said to Mr. Buckstone:

"I want Mr. Trollop to make his great speech on the Pension bill."

"*Do* you! But you remember I was interrupted, and did not explain to you—"

"Never mind, I know. You must make him make that speech. I very particularly desire it."

"Oh, it is easy to say make him do it, but *how* am I to make him?"

"It is perfectly easy; I have thought it all out."

She then went into the details. At length Mr. Buckstone said:

"I see now. I can manage it, I am sure. Indeed I wonder he never thought of it himself—there are no end of precedents. But how is this going to benefit you, after I *have* managed it? There is where the mystery lies."

"But I will take care of that. It will benefit me a great deal."

"I only wish I could see how; it is the oddest freak. You seem to go the furthest around to get at a thing—but you are in earnest, aren't you?"

"Yes, I am, indeed."

"Very well, I will do it—but why not tell me how you imagine it is going to help you?"

"I will, by and by.—Now there is nobody talking to him. Go straight and do it, there's a good fellow."

A moment or two later the two sworn friends of the Pension bill were talking together, earnestly, and seemingly unconscious of the moving throng about them. They talked an hour, and then Mr. Buckstone came back and said:

"He hardly fancied it at first, but he fell in love with it after a bit. And we have made a compact, too. I am to keep his secret and he is to spare me, in future, when he gets ready to denounce the supporters of the University bill—and I can easily believe he will keep his word on this occasion."

A fortnight elapsed, and the University bill had gathered to itself many friends, meantime. Senator Dilworthy began to think the harvest was ripe. He conferred with Laura privately. She was able to tell him exactly how the House would vote. There was a majority—the bill would pass, unless weak members got frightened at the last, and deserted—a thing pretty likely to occur. The Senator said:

"I wish we had one more good strong man. Now Trollop ought to be on our side, for he is a friend of the negro. But he is against us, and is our bitterest opponent. If he would simply vote No, but keep quiet and not molest us, I would feel perfectly cheerful and content. But perhaps there is no use in thinking of that."

"Why I laid a little plan for his benefit two weeks ago. I think he will be tractable, maybe. He is to come here tonight."

"Look out for him, my child! He means mischief, sure. It is said that he claims to know of improper practices having been used in the interest of this bill, and he thinks he sees a chance to make a great sensation when the bill comes up. Be wary. Be very, very careful, my dear. Do your very ablest talking, now. You can convince a man of anything, when you try. You must convince him that if anything improper has been done, you at least are ignorant of it and sorry for it. And if you *could* only persuade him out of his hostility to the bill, too—but don't overdo the thing; don't seem too anxious, dear."

"I won't; I'll be ever so careful. I'll talk as sweetly to him as if he were my own child! You may trust me—indeed you may."

The door-bell rang.

"That is the gentleman now," said Laura. Senator Dilworthy retired to his study.

Laura welcomed Mr. Trollop, a grave, carefully dressed and very respectable looking man, with a bald head, standing collar and old fashioned watch seals.

"Promptness is a virtue, Mr. Trollop, and I perceive that you have it. You are always prompt with me."

"I always meet my engagements, of every kind, Miss Hawkins."

"It is a quality which is rarer in the world than it has been, I believe. I wished to see you on business, Mr. Trollop."

"I judged so. What can I do for you?"

"You know my bill—the Knobs University bill?"

"Ah, I believe it *is* your bill. I had forgotten. Yes, I know the bill."

"Well, would you mind telling me your opinion of it?"

"Indeed, since you seem to ask it without reserve, I am obliged to say that I do not regard it favorably. I have not seen the bill itself, but from what I can hear, it—it—well, it has a bad look about it. It—"

"Speak it out—never fear."

"Well, it—they say it contemplates a fraud upon the government."

"Well?" said Laura tranquilly.

"Well! *I* say 'Well?' too."

"Well, suppose it *were* a fraud—which I feel able to deny—would it be the first one?"

"You take a body's breath away! Would you—did you wish me to vote for it? Was that what you wanted to see me about?"

"Your instinct is correct. I *did* want you—I *do* want you to vote for it."

"Vote for a fr—for a measure which is generally believed to be at least questionable? I am afraid we cannot come to an understanding, Miss Hawkins."

"No, I am afraid not—if you have resumed your principles, Mr. Trollop."

"Did you send for me merely to insult me? It is time for me to take my leave, Miss Hawkins."

"No—wait a moment. Don't be offended at a trifle. Do not be offish and unsociable. The Steamship Subsidy bill was a fraud on the government. You voted for it, Mr. Trollop, though you always opposed the measure until after you had an interview one evening with a certain Mrs. McCarter at her house. She was my agent. She was acting for me. Ah, that is right—sit down again. You can be sociable, easily enough if you have a mind to. Well? I am waiting. Have you nothing to say?"

"Miss Hawkins, I voted for that bill because when I came to examine into it—"

"Ah yes. When you came to examine into it. Well, I only want you to examine into *my* bill. Mr. Trollop, you would not sell your vote on that subsidy bill—which was perfectly right—but you accepted of some of the stock, with the understanding that it was to stand in your brother-in-law's name."

"There is no pr—I mean, this is utterly groundless, Miss Hawkins." But the gentleman seemed somewhat uneasy, nevertheless.

"Well, not entirely so, perhaps. I and a person whom we will call Miss Blank (never mind the real name,) were in a closet at your elbow all the while."

Mr. Trollop winced—then he said with dignity:

"Miss Hawkins is it possible that you were capable of such a thing as that?"

"It was bad; I confess that. It *was* bad. Almost as bad as selling one's vote for—but I forget; you did not sell your vote—you only accepted a little trifle, a small token of esteem, for your brother-in-law. Oh, let us come out and be frank with each other. I know you, Mr. Trollop. I have met you on business three or four times; true, I never offered to corrupt your principles—never hinted such a thing; but always when I had finished sounding you, I manipulated you through an agent. Let us be frank. Wear this comely disguise of virtue before the public—it will count there; but here it is out of place. My dear sir, by and by there is going to be an investigation into that National Internal Improvement Directors' Relief Measure of a few years ago, and you know very well that you will be a crippled man, as likely as not, when it is completed."

"It cannot be shown that a man is a knave merely for owning that stock. I am not distressed about the National Improvement Relief Measure."

"Oh indeed I am not trying to distress you. I only wished to make good my assertion that I knew you. Several of you gentlemen bought of that stock (without paying a penny down) received dividends from it, (think of the happy idea of receiving dividends, and very large ones, too, from stock one hasn't paid for!) and all the while your names never appeared in the transaction; if ever you took the stock at all, you took it in other people's names. Now you see, you had to know one of two things; namely, you either knew that the idea of all this preposterous generosity was to bribe you into future legislative friendship, or you *didn't* know it. That is to say, you had to be either a knave or a—well, a fool—there was no middle ground. *You* are not a fool, Mr. Trollop."

"Miss Hawkins you flatter me. But seriously, you do not forget that some of the best and purest men in Congress took that stock in that way?"

"Did Senator Blank?"

"Well, no—I believe not."

"Of course you believe not. Do you suppose he was ever approached, on the subject?"

"Perhaps not."

"If *you* had approached him, for instance, fortified with the fact that some of the best men in Congress, and the purest, etc., etc., what would have been the result?"

"Well, what *would* have been the result?"

"He would have shown you the door! For Mr. Blank is neither a knave *nor* a fool. There are other men in the Senate and the House whom no one would have been hardy enough to approach with that Relief Stock in that peculiarly generous way, but they are not of the class that *you* regard as the best and purest. No, I say I know you Mr. Trollop. That is to say, one may suggest a thing to Mr.Trollop which it would not do to suggest to Mr. Blank. Mr. Trollop, you are pledged to support the Indigent Congressmen's Retroactive Appropriation which is to come up, either in this or the next session. You do not deny that, even in public. The man that will vote for that bill will break the eighth commandment in any *other* way, sir!"

"But he will not vote for *your* corrupt measure, nevertheless, madam!" exclaimed Mr. Trollop, rising from his seat in a passion.

"Ah, but he will. Sit down again, and let me explain why. Oh, come, don't behave so. It is very unpleasant. Now be good, and you shall have the missing page of your great speech. Here it is!"—and she displayed a sheet of manuscript.

Mr. Trollop turned immediately back from the threshold. It might have been gladness that flashed into his face; it might have been something else; but at any rate there was much astonishment mixed with it.

"Good! Where did you get it? Give it me!"

"Now there is no hurry. Sit down; sit down and let us talk and be friendly."

The gentleman wavered. Then he said:

"No, this is only a subterfuge. I will go. It is not the missing page."

Laura tore off a couple of lines from the bottom of the sheet.

"Now," she said, "you will know whether this is the handwriting or not. You know it *is* the handwriting. Now if you will listen, you will know that this must be the list of statistics which was to be the 'nub' of your great effort, and the accompanying blast the beginning of the burst of eloquence which was continued on the next page—and you will recognize that there was where you broke down."

She read the page. Mr. Trollop said:

"This is perfectly astounding. Still, what is all this to me? It is nothing. It does not concern me. The speech is made, and there an end. I *did* break down for a moment, and in a rather uncomfortable place, since I had led up to those statistics with some grandeur; the hiatus was pleasanter to the House and the galleries than it was to me. But it is no matter now. A week has passed; the jests about it ceased three or four days ago. The whole thing is a matter of indifference to me, Miss Hawkins."

"But you apologized, and promised the statistics for next day. Why didn't you keep your promise?"

"The matter was not of sufficient consequence. The time was gone by to produce an effect with them."

"But I hear that other friends of the Soldiers' Pension Bill desire them very much. I think you ought to let them have them."

"Miss Hawkins, this silly blunder of my copyist evidently has more interest for you than it has for me. I will send my private secretary to you and let him discuss the subject with you at length."

"Did he copy your speech for you?"

"Of course he did. Why all these questions? Tell me—how did you get hold of that page of manuscript? *That* is the only thing that stirs a passing interest in my mind."

"I'm coming to that." Then she said, much as if she were talking to herself: "It does seem like taking a deal of unnecessary pains, for a body to hire another body to construct a great speech for him and then go and get still another body to copy it before it can be read in the House."

"Miss Hawkins, what do you mean by such talk as that?"

"Why I am sure I mean no harm—no harm to anybody in the world. I am certain that I overheard the Hon. Mr. Buckstone either promise to write your great speech for you or else get some other competent person to do it."

"This is perfectly absurd, madam, perfectly absurd!" and Mr. Trollop affected a laugh of derision.

"Why, the thing has occurred before now. I mean that I have heard that Congressmen have sometimes hired literary grubs to build speeches for them. Now didn't I overhear a conversation like that I spoke of?"

"Pshaw! Why of course you may have overheard some such jesting nonsense. But would one be in earnest about so farcical a thing?"

"Well if it was only a joke, why did you make a serious matter of it? Why did you get the speech written for you, and then read it in the House without ever having it copied?"

Mr. Trollop did not laugh, this time; he seemed seriously perplexed. He said:

"Come, play out your jest, Miss Hawkins. I can't understand what you are contriving—but it seems to entertain you—so please go on."

"I will, I assure you; but I hope to make the matter entertaining to you, too. Your private secretary never copied your speech."

"Indeed? Really you seem to know my affairs better than I do myself."

"I believe I do. You can't name your own amanuensis, Mr. Trollop."

"That is sad, indeed. Perhaps Miss Hawkins can?"

"Yes, I *can*. *I* wrote your speech myself, and you read it from my manuscript. There, now!"

Mr. Trollop did not spring to his feet and smite his brow with his hand while a cold sweat broke out all over him and the color forsook his face—no, he only said, "Good God!" and looked greatly astonished.

Laura handed him her commonplace-book and called his attention to the fact that the handwriting there and the handwriting of this speech were the same. He was shortly convinced. He laid the book aside and said, composedly:

"Well, the wonderful tragedy is done, and it transpires that I am indebted to you for my late eloquence. What of it? What was all this for, and what does it amount to, after all? What do you propose to do about it?"

"Oh nothing. It is only a bit of pleasantry. When I overheard that conversation I took an early opportunity to ask Mr. Buckstone if he knew of anybody who might want a speech written—I had a friend, and so forth and so on. *I* was the friend, myself; I thought I might do you a good turn then and depend on you to do me one by and by. I never let Mr. Buckstone have the speech till the last moment, and when you hurried off to the House with it, you did not know there was a missing page, of course, but I did."

"And now perhaps you think that if I refuse to support your bill, you will make a grand exposure?"

"Well I had not thought of that. I only kept back the page for the mere fun of the thing; but since you mention it, I don't know but I might do something if I were angry."

"My dear Miss Hawkins, if you were to give out that you composed my speech, you know very well that people would say it was only your raillery, your fondness for putting a victim in the pillory and amusing the public at his expense. It is too flimsy, Miss Hawkins, for a person of your fine inventive talent—contrive an abler device than that. Come!"

"It is easily done, Mr. Trollop. I will hire a man, and pin this page on his breast, and label it, 'The Missing Fragment of the Hon. Mr. Trollop's Great Speech—which speech was written and composed by Miss Laura Hawkins under a secret understanding for one hundred dollars—and the money has not been paid.' And I will pin round about it notes in my handwriting, which I will procure from prominent friends of mine for the occasion; also your printed speech in the *Globe*, showing the connection between its bracketed hiatus and my Fragment; and I give you my word of honor that I will stand that human bulletin board in the rotunda of the capitol and make him stay there a week! You see you are premature, Mr. Trollop, the wonderful tragedy is not done yet, by any means. Come, now, doesn't it improve?"

Mr. Trollop opened his eyes rather widely at this novel aspect of the case. He got up and walked the floor and gave himself a moment for reflection. Then he stopped and studied Laura's face a while, and ended by saying:

"Well, I am obliged to believe you *would* be reckless enough to do that."

"Then don't put me to the test, Mr. Trollop. But let's drop the matter. I have had my joke and you've borne the infliction becomingly enough. It spoils a jest to harp on it after one has had one's laugh. I would much rather talk about my bill."

"So would I, now, my clandestine amanuensis. Compared with some other subjects, even your bill is a pleasant topic to discuss."

"Very good indeed! I thought I could persuade you. Now I am sure you will be generous to the poor negro and vote for that bill."

"Yes, I feel more tenderly toward the oppressed colored man than I did. Shall we bury the hatchet and be good friends and respect each other's little secrets, on condition that I vote Aye on the measure?"

"With all my heart, Mr. Trollop. I give you my word of that."

"It is a bargain. But isn't there something else you could give me, too?"

Laura looked at him inquiringly a moment, and then she comprehended.

"Oh, yes! You may have it now. I haven't any more use for it." She picked up the page of manuscript, but she reconsidered her intention of handing it to him, and said, "But never mind; I will keep it close; no one shall see it; you shall have it as soon as your vote is recorded."

Mr. Trollop looked disappointed. But presently made his adieux, and had got as far as the hall, when something occurred to Laura. She said to herself, "I don't simply want his vote, under compulsion—he might vote aye, but work against the bill in secret, for revenge; that man is unscrupulous enough to do anything. I must have his hearty co-operation as well as his vote. There is only one way to get that."

She called him back, and said;

"I value your vote, Mr. Trollop, but I value your influence more. You are able to help a measure along in many ways, if you choose.—I want to ask you to work for the bill as well as vote for it."

"It takes so much of one's time, Miss Hawkins—and time is money, you know."

"Yes, I know it is—especially in Congress. Now there is no use in you and I dealing in pretenses and going at matters in round-about ways. We know each other—disguises are nonsense. Let us be plain. I will make it an object to you to work for the bill."

"Don't make it unnecessarily plain, please. There are little proprieties that are best preserved. What do you propose?"

"Well, this." She mentioned the names of several prominent Congressmen. "Now," said she, "these gentlemen are to vote and work for the bill, simply out of love for the negro—and out of pure generosity I have put in a relative of each as a member of the University incorporation. They will handle a million or so of money, officially, but will receive no salaries.—A larger number of statesmen are to vote and work for the bill—also out of love for the negro—gentlemen of but moderate influence, these—and out of pure generosity I am to see that relatives of theirs have positions in the University, *with* salaries, and good ones, too. You will vote and work for the bill, from mere affection for the negro, and I desire to testify my gratitude becomingly. Make free choice. Have you any friend whom you would like to present with a salaried or unsalaried position in our institution?"

"Well, I have a brother-in-law—"

"That same old brother-in-law, you good unselfish provider! I have heard of him often, through my agents. How regularly he does 'turn up,' to be sure. He could deal with those millions virtuously, and withal with ability, too—but of course you would rather he had a salaried position?"

"Oh, no," said the gentleman, facetiously, "we are very humble, very humble in our desires; we want no money; we labor solely for our country and require no reward but the luxury of an applauding conscience. Make him one of those poor hard working unsalaried corporators and let him do every body good with those millions—and go hungry himself! I will try to exert a little influence in favor of the bill."

Arrived at home, Mr. Trollop sat down and thought it all over—something after this fashion: it is about the shape it might have taken if he had spoken it aloud.

"My reputation is getting a little damaged, and I meant to clear it up brilliantly with an exposure of this bill at the supreme moment, and ride back into Congress on the éclat of it; and if I had that bit of manuscript, I would do it yet. It would be more money in my pocket, in the end, than my brother-in-law will get out of that incorporatorship, fat as it is. But that sheet of paper is out of my reach—she will never let that get out of her hands. And what a mountain it is! It blocks up *my* road, completely. She was going to hand it to me, once. Why *didn't* she! Must be a deep woman. Deep devil! That is what she is; a beautiful devil—and perfectly fearless, too. The idea of her pinning that paper on a man and standing him up in the rotunda looks absurd at a first glance. But she would do it! She is capable of doing anything. I went there hoping she would try to bribe me—good solid capital that would be in the exposure. Well, my prayer was answered; she did try to bribe me; and I made the best of a bad bargain and let her. I am check-mated. I must contrive something fresh to get back to Congress on. Very well; a bird in the hand is worth two in the bush; I will work for the bill—the incorporatorship will be a very good thing."

As soon as Mr. Trollop had taken his leave, Laura ran to Senator Dilworthy and began to speak, but he interrupted her and said distressfully, without even turning from his writing to look at her:

"Only half an hour! You gave it up early, child. However, it was best, it was best—I'm sure it was best—and safest."

"Give it up! *I!*"

The Senator sprang up, all aglow:

"My child, you can't mean that you—"

"I've made him promise on honor to think about a compromise to-night and come and tell me his decision in the morning."

"Good! There's hope yet that—"

"Nonsense, uncle. I've made him engage to let the Tennessee Land bill utterly alone!"

"*Impossible!* You—"

"I've made him promise to vote with us!"

"INCREDIBLE! Abso—"

"I've made him swear that he'll *work* for us!"

"PRE---POSTEROUS!—Utterly pre—break a window, child, before I suffocate!"

"No matter, it's true anyway. Now we can march into Congress with drums beating and colors flying!"

"Well—well—well. I'm sadly bewildered, sadly bewildered. I can't understand it at all—the most extraordinary woman that ever—it's a great day, it's a great day. There—there—let me put my hand in benediction on this precious head. Ah, my child, the poor negro will bless—"

"Oh bother the poor negro, uncle! Put it in your speech. Good-night, good-bye—we'll marshal our forces and march with the dawn!"

Laura reflected a while, when she was alone, and then fell to laughing, peacefully.

"Everybody works for me,"—so ran her thought. "It was a good idea to make Buckstone lead Mr. Trollop on to get a great speech written for him; and it was a happy part of the same idea for me to copy the speech after Mr. Buckstone had written it, and then keep back a page. Mr. B. was very complimentary to me when Trollop's break-down in the House showed him the *object* of my mysterious scheme; I think he will say still finer things when I tell him the triumph the sequel to it has gained for us.

"But what a coward the man was, to believe I would have exposed that page in the rotunda, and so exposed myself. However, I don't know—I don't know. I will think a moment. Suppose he voted no; suppose the bill failed; that is to suppose this stupendous game lost forever, that I have played so desperately for; suppose people came around pitying me—odious! And he could have saved me by his single voice. Yes, I *would* have exposed him! What would I care for the talk that that would have made about me when I was gone to Europe with Selby and all the world was busy with my history and my dishonor? It would be almost happiness to spite somebody at such a time.'

Chapter XLIII

"Ikkaké gidiamuttu Wamallitakoanti likissitu anissia ukunnaria
ni rubu kurru naussa abbanu aboahüddunnua namonnua."

THE very next day, sure enough, the campaign opened. In
due course, the Speaker of the House reached that Order
of Business which is termed "Notices of Bills," and then the
Hon. Mr. Buckstone rose in his place and gave notice of a bill
"To Found and Incorporate the Knobs Industrial University,"
and then sat down without saying anything further. The busy
gentlemen in the reporters' gallery jotted a line in their notebooks, ran to the telegraphic desk in a room which commu-
nicated with their own writing-parlor, and then hurried back
to their places in the gallery; and by the time they had resumed their seats, the line which they had delivered to the operator had been read in telegraphic offices in towns and cities
hundreds of miles away. It was distinguished by frankness of
language as well as by brevity:

> "The child is born. Buckstone gives notice of the
> thieving Knobs University job. It is said the noses have
> been counted and enough votes have been bought to
> pass it."

For some time the correspondents had been posting their
several journals upon the alleged disreputable nature of the
bill, and furnishing daily reports of the Washington gossip
concerning it. So the next morning, nearly every newspaper
of character in the land assailed the measure and hurled
broadsides of invective at Mr. Buckstone. The Washington
papers were more respectful, as usual—and conciliatory, also,
as usual. They generally supported measures, when it was
possible; but when they could not they "deprecated" violent
expressions of opinion in other journalistic quarters. They
always deprecated, when there was trouble ahead.

However, *The Washington Daily Love-Feast* hailed the bill
with warm approbation. This was Senator Balaam's paper—or
rather, "Brother" Balaam, as he was popularly called, for he
had been a clergyman, in his day; and he himself and all that

he did still emitted an odor of sanctity now that he had di-
verged into journalism and politics. He was a power in the
Congressional prayer meeting, and in all movements that
looked to the spread of religion and temperance. His paper
supported the new bill with gushing affection; it was a noble
measure; it was a just measure; it was a generous measure; it
was a pure measure, and that surely should recommend it in
these corrupt times; and finally, if the nature of the bill were
not known at all, the *Love-Feast* would support it anyway, and
unhesitatingly, for the fact that Senator Dilworthy was the
originator of the measure was a guaranty that it contemplated
a worthy and righteous work.

Senator Dilworthy was so anxious to know what the New
York papers would say about the bill, that he had arranged to
have synopses of their editorials telegraphed to him; he could
not wait for the papers themselves to crawl along down to
Washington by a mail train which has never run over a cow
since the road was built, for the reason that it has never been
able to overtake one. It carries the usual "cow-catcher" in
front of the locomotive, but this is mere ostentation. It ought
to be attached to the rear car, where it could do some good;
but instead, no provision is made there for the protection of
the traveling public, and hence it is not a matter of surprise
that cows so frequently climb aboard that train and among
the passengers.

The Senator read his dispatches aloud at the breakfast table.
Laura was troubled beyond measure at their tone, and said
that that sort of comment would defeat the bill; but the Senator said:

"Oh, not at all, not at all, my child. It is just what we want.
Persecution is the one thing needful, now—all the other
forces are secured. Give us newspaper persecution enough,
and we are safe. Vigorous persecution will alone carry a bill
sometimes, dear; and when you start with a strong vote in the
first place, persecution comes in with double effect. It scares
off some of the weak supporters, true, but it soon turns
strong ones into stubborn ones. And then, presently, it
changes the tide of public opinion. The great public is weak-
minded; the great public is sentimental; the great public always turns around and weeps for an odious murderer, and

prays for him, and carries flowers to his prison and besieges the governor with appeals to his clemency, as soon as the papers begin to howl for that man's blood.—In a word, the great putty-hearted public loves to 'gush,' and there is no such darling opportunity to gush as a case of persecution affords."

"Well, uncle, dear, if your theory is right, let us go into raptures, for nobody can ask a heartier persecution than these editorials are furnishing."

"I am not so sure of that, my daughter. I don't entirely like the tone of some of these remarks. They lack vim, they lack venom. Here is one calls it a 'questionable measure.' Bah, there is no strength in that. This one is better; it calls it 'highway robbery.' That sounds something like. But now this one seems satisfied to call it an 'iniquitous scheme!'—'Iniquitous' does not exasperate anybody; it is weak—puerile. The ignorant will imagine it to be intended for a compliment. But this other one—the one I read last—has the true ring: 'This vile, dirty effort to rob the public treasury, by the kites and vultures that now infest the filthy den called Congress'—that is admirable, admirable! We must have more of that sort. But it will come—no fear of that; they're not warmed up, yet. A week from now you'll see."

"Uncle, you and Brother Balaam are bosom friends—why don't you get his paper to persecute us, too?"

"It isn't worth while, my daughter. His support doesn't hurt a bill. Nobody reads his editorials but himself. But I wish the New York papers would talk a little plainer. It is annoying to have to wait a week for them to warm up. I expected better things at their hands—and time is precious, now."

At the proper hour, according to his previous notice, Mr. Buckstone duly introduced his bill entitled "An Act to Found and Incorporate the Knobs Industrial University," moved its proper reference, and sat down.

The Speaker of the House rattled off this observation:

"'Fnobjectionbilltakuzhlcourssoreferred!'"

Habitués of the House comprehended that this long, lightning-heeled word signified that if there was no objection, the bill would take the customary course of a measure of its nature, and be referred to the Committee on Benevolent

Appropriations, and that it was accordingly so referred. Strangers merely supposed that the Speaker was taking a gargle for some affection of the throat.

The reporters immediately telegraphed the introduction of the bill.—And they added:

> "The assertion that the bill will pass was premature. It is said that many favorers of it will desert when the storm breaks upon them from the public press."

The storm came, and during ten days it waxed more and more violent day by day. The great "Negro University Swindle" became the one absorbing topic of conversation throughout the Union. Individuals denounced it, journals denounced it, public meetings denounced it, the pictorial papers caricatured its friends, the whole nation seemed to be growing frantic over it. Meantime the Washington correspondents were sending such telegrams as these abroad in the land: Under date of—

> SATURDAY. "Congressmen Jex and Fluke are wavering; it is believed they will desert the execrable bill."
> MONDAY. "Jex and Fluke *have* deserted!"
> THURSDAY. "Tubbs and Huffy left the sinking ship last night."

Later on:

> "Three desertions. The University thieves are getting scared, though they will not own it."

Later:

> "The leaders are growing stubborn—they swear they can carry it, but it is now almost certain that they no longer have a majority!"

After a day or two of reluctant and ambiguous telegrams:

> "Public sentiment seems changing, a trifle, in favor of the bill—but only a trifle."

And still later:

> "It is whispered that the Hon. Mr. Trollop has gone over to the pirates. It is probably a canard. Mr. Trollop

has all along been the bravest and most efficient champion of virtue and the people against the bill, and the report is without doubt a shameless invention."

Next day:

"With characteristic treachery, the truckling and pusillanimous reptile, Crippled-Speech Trollop, has gone over to the enemy. It is contended, now, that *he has been a friend to the bill, in secret, since the day it was introduced,* and has had bankable reasons for being so; but he himself declares that he has gone over because the malignant persecution of the bill by the newspapers caused him to study its provisions with more care than he had previously done, and this close examination revealed the fact that the measure is one in every way worthy of support. (Pretty thin!) It cannot be denied that this desertion has had a damaging effect. Jex and Fluke have returned to their iniquitous allegiance, with six or eight others of lesser calibre, and it is reported and believed that Tubbs and Huffy are ready to go back. It is feared that the University swindle is stronger to-day than it has ever been before."

Later—midnight:

"It is said that the committee will report the bill back to-morrow. Both sides are marshaling their forces, and the fight on this bill is evidently going to be the hottest of the session.—All Washington is boiling.

Chapter XLIV

Capienda rebus in malis præceps via est.—*Seneca.*

Et enim ipse se impellunt, ubi semel à ratione discessum est: ipsaque sibi imbecillitas indulget, in altumque provebitur imprudenter: nec reperet locum consistendi.—*Cicero.*

I T'S easy enough for another fellow to talk," said Harry, despondingly, after he had put Philip in possession of his view of the case. "It's easy enough to say 'give her up,' if you don't care for her. What am I going to do to give her up?"

It seemed to Harry that it was a situation requiring some active measures. He couldn't realize that he had fallen hopelessly in love without some rights accruing to him for the possession of the object of his passion. Quiet resignation under relinquishment of any thing he wanted was not in his line. And when it appeared to him that his surrender of Laura would be the withdrawal of the one barrier that kept her from ruin, it was unreasonable to expect that he could see how to give her up.

Harry had the most buoyant confidence in his own projects always; he saw everything connected with himself in a large way and in rosy hues. This predominance of the imagination over the judgment gave that appearance of exaggeration to his conversation and to his communications with regard to himself, which sometimes conveyed the impression that he was not speaking the truth. His acquaintances had been known to say that they invariably allowed a half for shrinkage in his statements, and held the other half under advisement for confirmation.

Philip in this case could not tell from Harry's story exactly how much encouragement Laura had given him, nor what hopes he might justly have of winning her. He had never seen him desponding before. The "brag" appeared to be all taken out of him, and his airy manner only asserted itself now and then in a comical imitation of its old self.

Philip wanted time to look about him before he decided what to do. He was not familiar with Washington, and it was difficult to adjust his feelings and perceptions to its peculiarities. Coming out of the sweet sanity of the Bolton household, this was by contrast the maddest Vanity Fair one could conceive. It seemed to him a feverish, unhealthy atmosphere in which lunacy would be easily developed. He fancied that everybody attached to himself an exaggerated importance, from the fact of being at the national capital, the center of political influence, the fountain of patronage, preferment, jobs and opportunities.

People were introduced to each other as from this or that state, not from cities or towns, and this gave a largeness to their representative feeling. All the women talked politics as naturally and glibly as they talk fashion or literature elsewhere. There was always some exciting topic at the Capitol, or some huge slander was rising up like a miasmatic exhalation from the Potomac, threatening to settle no one knew exactly where. Every other person was an aspirant for a place, or, if he had one, for a better place, or more pay; almost every other one had some claim or interest or remedy to urge; even the women were all advocates for the advancement of some person, and they violently espoused or denounced this or that measure as it would affect some relative, acquaintance or friend.

Love, travel, even death itself, waited on the chances of the dies daily thrown in the two Houses, and the committee rooms there. If the measure went through, love could afford to ripen into marriage, and longing for foreign travel would have fruition; and it must have been only eternal hope springing in the breast that kept alive numerous old claimants who for years and years had besieged the doors of Congress, and who looked as if they needed not so much an appropriation of money as six feet of ground. And those who stood so long waiting for success to bring them death were usually those who had a just claim.

Representing states and talking of national and even international affairs, as familiarly as neighbors at home talk of poor crops and the extravagance of their ministers, was likely at first to impose upon Philip as to the importance of the people gathered here.

There was a little newspaper editor from Phil's native town, the assistant on a Peddletonian weekly, who made his little annual joke about the "first egg laid on our table," and who was the menial of every tradesman in the village and under bonds to him for frequent "puffs," except the undertaker, about whose employment he was recklessly facetious. In Washington he was an important man, correspondent, and clerk of two house committees, a "worker" in politics, and a confident critic of every woman and every man in Washington. He would be a consul no doubt by and by, at some foreign port, of the language of which he was ignorant—though if ignorance of language were a qualification he might have been a consul at home. His easy familiarity with great men was beautiful to see, and when Philip learned what a tremendous underground influence this little ignoramus had, he no longer wondered at the queer appointments and the queerer legislation.

Philip was not long in discovering that people in Washington did not differ much from other people; they had the same meannesses, generosities, and tastes. A Washington boarding house had the odor of a boarding house the world over.

Col. Sellers was as unchanged as any one Philip saw whom he had known elsewhere. Washington appeared to be the native element of this man. His pretentions were equal to any he encountered there. He saw nothing in its society that equalled that of Hawkeye, he sat down to no table that could not be unfavorably contrasted with his own at home; the most airy scheme inflated in the hot air of the capital only reached in magnitude some of his lesser fancies, the by-play of his constructive imagination.

"The country is getting along very well," he said to Philip, "but our public men are too timid. What we want is more money. I've told Boutwell so. Talk about basing the currency on gold; you might as well base it on pork. Gold is only one product. Base it on everything! You've got to do something for the West. How am I to move my crops? We must have improvements. Grant's got the idea. We want a canal from the James River to the Mississippi. Government ought to build it."

It was difficult to get the Colonel off from these large themes when he was once started, but Philip brought the conversation round to Laura and her reputation in the City.

"No," he said, "I haven't noticed much. We've been so busy about this University. It will make Laura rich with the rest of us, and she has done nearly as much as if she were a man. She has great talent, and will make a big match. I see the foreign ministers and that sort after her. Yes, there is talk, always will be about a pretty woman so much in public as she is. Tough stories come to me, but I put 'em away. 'Taint likely one of Si. Hawkins's children would do that—for she is the same as a child of his. I told her, though, to go slow," added the Colonel, as if that mysterious admonition from him would set everything right.

"Do you know anything about a Col. Selby?"

"Know all about him. Fine fellow. But he's got a wife; and I told him, as a friend, he'd better sheer off from Laura. I reckon he thought better of it and did."

But Philip was not long in learning the truth. Courted as Laura was by a certain class and still admitted into society, that, nevertheless, buzzed with disreputable stories about her, she had lost character with the best people. Her intimacy with Selby was open gossip, and there were winks and thrustings of the tongue in any group of men when she passed by. It was clear enough that Harry's delusion must be broken up, and that no such feeble obstacle as his passion could interpose would turn Laura from her fate. Philip determined to see her, and put himself in possession of the truth, as he suspected it, in order to show Harry his folly.

Laura, after her last conversation with Harry, had a new sense of her position. She had noticed before the signs of a change in manner towards her, a little less respect perhaps from men, and an avoidance by women. She had attributed this latter partly to jealousy of her, for no one is willing to acknowledge a fault in himself when a more agreeable motive can be found for the estrangement of his acquaintances. But, now, if society had turned on her, she would defy it. It was not in her nature to shrink. She knew she had been wronged, and she knew that she had no remedy.

What she heard of Col. Selby's proposed departure alarmed her more than anything else, and she calmly determined that if he was deceiving her the second time it should be the last. Let society finish the tragedy if it liked; she was indifferent what came after. At the first opportunity, she charged Selby with his intention to abandon her. He unblushingly denied it. He had not thought of going to Europe. He had only been amusing himself with Sellers' schemes. He swore that as soon as she succeeded with her bill, he would fly with her to any part of the world.

She did not quite believe him, for she saw that he feared her, and she began to suspect that his were the protestations of a coward to gain time. But she showed him no doubts. She only watched his movements day by day, and always held herself ready to act promptly.

When Philip came into the presence of this attractive woman, he could not realize that she was the subject of all the scandal he had heard. She received him with quite the old Hawkeye openness and cordiality, and fell to talking at once of their little acquaintance there; and it seemed impossible that he could ever say to her what he had come determined to say. Such a man as Philip has only one standard by which to judge women.

Laura recognized that fact no doubt. The better part of her woman's nature saw it. Such a man might, years ago, not now, have changed her nature, and made the issue of her life so different, even after her cruel abandonment. She had a dim feeling of this, and she would like now to stand well with him. The spark of truth and honor that was left in her was elicited by his presence. It was this influence that governed her conduct in this interview.

"I have come," said Philip in his direct manner, "from my friend Mr. Brierly. You are not ignorant of his feeling towards you?"

"Perhaps not."

"But perhaps you do not know, you who have so much admiration, how sincere and overmastering his love is for you?" Philip would not have spoken so plainly, if he had in mind anything except to draw from Laura something that would end Harry's passion.

"And is sincere love so rare, Mr. Sterling?" asked Laura, moving her foot a little, and speaking with a shade of sarcasm.

"Perhaps not in Washington," replied Philip, tempted into a similar tone. "Excuse my bluntness," he continued, "but would the knowledge of his love, would his devotion, make any difference to you in your Washington life?"

"In respect to what?" asked Laura quickly.

"Well, to others. I won't equivocate—to Col. Selby?"

Laura's face flushed with anger, or shame; she looked steadily at Philip and began,

"By what right, sir,—"

"By the right of friendship," interrupted Philip stoutly. "It may matter little to you. It is everything to him. He has a Quixotic notion that you would turn back from what is before you for his sake. You cannot be ignorant of what all the city is talking of." Philip said this determinedly and with some bitterness.

It was a full minute before Laura spoke. Both had risen, Philip as if to go, and Laura in suppressed excitement. When she spoke her voice was very unsteady, and she looked down.

"Yes, I know. I perfectly understand what you mean. Mr. Brierly is nothing—simply nothing. He is a moth singed, that is all—the trifler with women thought he was a wasp. I have no pity for him, not the least. You may tell him not to make a fool of himself, and to keep away. I say this on your account, not his. You are not like him. It is enough for me that you want it so. Mr. Sterling," she continued, looking up, and there were tears in her eyes that contradicted the hardness of her language, "you might not pity him if you knew my history; perhaps you would not wonder at some things you hear. No; it is useless to ask me why it must be so. You can't make a life over—society wouldn't let you if you would—and mine must be lived as it is. There, sir, I'm not offended; but it is useless for you to say anything more."

Philip went away with his heart lightened about Harry, but profoundly saddened by the glimpse of what this woman might have been. He told Harry all that was necessary of the conversation—she was bent on going her own way, he had not the ghost of a chance—he was a fool, she had said, for thinking he had.

And Harry accepted it meekly, and made up his own mind that Philip didn't know much about women.

Chapter XLV

—Nakila cu ch'y cu yao chike, chi ka togobah cu y vach, x-e u chax-cut?—Utz, chi ka ya puvak chyve, x-e cha-cu ri amag.

Popul Vuh.

THE GALLERIES of the House were packed, on the momentous day, not because the reporting of an important bill back by a committee was a thing to be excited about, if the bill were going to take the ordinary course afterward; it would be like getting excited over the empaneling of a coroner's jury in a murder case, instead of saving up one's emotions for the grander occasion of the hanging of the accused, two years later, after all the tedious forms of law had been gone through with.

But suppose you understand that this coroner's jury is going to turn out to be a vigilance committee in disguise, who will hear testimony for an hour and then hang the murderer on the spot? That puts a different aspect upon the matter. Now it was whispered that the legitimate forms of procedure usual in the House, and which keep a bill hanging along for days and even weeks, before it is finally passed upon, were going to be overruled, in this case, and short work made of the measure; and so, what was beginning as a mere inquest might turn out to be something very different.

In the course of the day's business the Order of "Reports of Committees" was finally reached and when the weary crowds heard that glad announcement issue from the Speaker's lips they ceased to fret at the dragging delay, and plucked up spirit. The Chairman of the Committee on Benevolent Appropriations rose and made his report, and just then a blue-uniformed brass-mounted little page put a note into his hand. It was from Senator Dilworthy, who had appeared upon the floor of the House for a moment and flitted away again:

"Everybody expects a grand assault in force; no doubt you believe, as I certainly do, that it is the thing to do; we are strong, and everything is hot for the contest.

Trollop's espousal of our cause has immensely helped us and we grow in power constantly. Ten of the opposition were called away from town about noon (*but*—so it is said—*only for one day*). Six others are sick, but expect to be about again *to-morrow or next day*, a friend tells me. A bold onslaught is worth trying. Go for a suspension of the rules! You will find we can swing a two-thirds vote—I am perfectly satisfied of it. The Lord's truth will prevail.

"DILWORTHY.

Mr. Buckstone had reported the bills from his committee, one by one, leaving *the* bill to the last. When the House had voted upon the acceptance or rejection of the report upon all but it, and the question now being upon *its* disposal—

Mr. Buckstone begged that the House would give its attention to a few remarks which he desired to make. His committee had instructed him to report the bill favorably; he wished to explain the nature of the measure, and thus justify the committee's action; the hostility roused by the press would then disappear, and the bill would shine forth in its true and noble character. He said that its provisions were simple. It incorporated the Knobs Industrial University, locating it in East Tennessee, declaring it open to all persons without distinction of sex, color or religion, and committing its management to a board of perpetual trustees, with power to fill vacancies in their own number. It provided for the erection of certain buildings for the University, dormitories, lecture-halls, museums, libraries, laboratories, work-shops, furnaces, and mills. It provided also for the purchase of sixty-five thousand acres of land, (fully described) for the purposes of the University, in the Knobs of East Tennessee. And it appropriated [blank] dollars for the purchase of the Land, which should be the property of the national trustees in trust for the uses named.

Every effort had been made to secure the refusal of the whole amount of the property of the Hawkins heirs in the Knobs, some seventy-five thousand acres Mr. Buckstone said. But Mr. Washington Hawkins (one of the heirs) objected. He was, indeed, very reluctant to sell any part of the land at any price; and indeed this reluctance was justifiable when one considers how constantly and how greatly the property is rising in value.

What the South needed, continued Mr. Buckstone, was skilled labor. Without that it would be unable to develop its mines, build its roads, work to advantage and without great waste its fruitful land, establish manufactures or enter upon a prosperous industrial career. Its laborers were almost altogether unskilled. Change them into intelligent, trained workmen, and you increased at once the capital, the resources of the entire south, which would enter upon a prosperity hitherto unknown. In five years the increase in local wealth would not only reimburse the government for the outlay in this appropriation, but pour untold wealth into the treasury.

This was the material view, and the least important in the honorable gentleman's opinion. [Here he referred to some notes furnished him by Senator Dilworthy, and then continued.] God had given us the care of these colored millions. What account should we render to Him of our stewardship? We had made them free. Should we leave them ignorant? We had cast them upon their own resources. Should we leave them without tools? We could not tell what the intentions of Providence are in regard to these peculiar people, but our duty was plain. The Knobs Industrial University would be a vast school of modern science and practice, worthy of a great nation. It would combine the advantages of Zurich, Freiburg, Creuzot and the Sheffield Scientific. Providence had apparently reserved and set apart the Knobs of East Tennessee for this purpose. What else were they for? Was it not wonderful that for more than thirty years, over a generation, the choicest portion of them had remained in one family, untouched, as if consecrated for some great use!

It might be asked why the government should buy this land, when it had millions of acres, more than the railroad companies desired, which it might devote to this purpose? He answered, that the government had no such tract of land as this. It had nothing comparable to it for the purposes of the University. This was to be a school of mining, of engineering, of the working of metals, of chemistry, zoology, botany, manufactures, agriculture, in short of all the complicated indus-

tries that make a state great. There was no place for the location of such a school like the Knobs of East Tennessee. The
hills abounded in metals of all sorts, iron in all its combinations, copper, bismuth, gold and silver in small quantities,
platinum he believed, tin, aluminium; it was covered with
forests and strange plants; in the woods were found the coon,
the opossum, the fox, the deer and many other animals who
roamed in the domain of natural history; coal existed in enormous quantity and no doubt oil; it was such a place for the
practice of agricultural experiments that any student who had
been successful there would have an easy task in any other
portion of the country.

No place offered equal facilities for experiments in mining,
metallurgy, engineering. He expected to live to see the day
when the youth of the south would resort to its mines, its
workshops, its laboratories, its furnaces and factories for practical instruction in all the great industrial pursuits.

A noisy and rather ill-natured debate followed, now, and
lasted hour after hour. The friends of the bill were instructed
by the leaders to *make no effort to check this;* it was deemed
better strategy to tire out the opposition; it was decided to
vote down every proposition to adjourn, and so continue the
sitting into the night; opponents might desert, then, one by
one and weaken their party, for they had no personal stake in
the bill.

Sunset came, and still the fight went on; the gas was lit, the
crowd in the galleries began to thin, but the contest continued; the crowd returned, by and by, with hunger and thirst
appeased, and aggravated the hungry and thirsty House by
looking contented and comfortable; but still the wrangle lost
nothing of its bitterness. Recesses were moved plaintively by
the opposition, and invariably voted down by the University
army.

At midnight the House presented a spectacle calculated to
interest a stranger. The great galleries were still thronged—
though only with men, now; the bright colors that had made
them look like hanging gardens were gone, with the ladies.
The reporters' gallery was merely occupied by one or two
watchful sentinels of the quill-driving guild; the main body
cared nothing for a debate that had dwindled to a mere

vaporing of dull speakers and now and then a brief quarrel over a point of order; but there was an unusually large attendance of journalists in the reporters' waiting-room, chatting, smoking, and keeping on the *qui vive* for the general irruption of the Congressional volcano that must come when the time was ripe for it. Senator Dilworthy and Philip were in the Diplomatic Gallery; Washington sat in the public gallery, and Col. Sellers was not far away. The Colonel had been flying about the corridors and button-holing Congressmen all the evening, and believed that he had accomplished a world of valuable service; but fatigue was telling upon him, now, and he was quiet and speechless—for once. Below, a few Senators lounged upon the sofas set apart for visitors, and talked with idle Congressmen. A dreary member was speaking; the presiding officer was nodding; here and there little knots of members stood in the aisles, whispering together; all about the House others sat in all the various attitudes that express weariness; some, tilted back, had one or more legs disposed upon their desks; some sharpened pencils indolently; some scribbled aimlessly; some yawned and stretched; a great many lay upon their breasts upon the desks, sound asleep and gently snoring. The flooding gaslight from the fancifully wrought roof poured down upon the tranquil scene. Hardly a sound disturbed the stillness, save the monotonous eloquence of the gentleman who occupied the floor. Now and then a warrior of the opposition broke down under the pressure, gave it up and went home.

Mr. Buckstone began to think it might be safe, now, to "proceed to business." He consulted with Trollop and one or two others. Senator Dilworthy descended to the floor of the House and they went to meet him. After a brief comparison of notes, the Congressmen sought their seats and sent pages about the House with messages to friends. These latter instantly roused up, yawned, and began to look alert. The moment the floor was unoccupied, Mr. Buckstone rose, with an injured look, and said it was evident that the opponents of the bill were merely talking against time, hoping in this unbecoming way to tire out the friends of the measure and so defeat it. Such conduct might be respectable enough in a village debating society, but it was trivial among statesmen, it was out of place in so august an assemblage as the House of Representatives of the United States. The friends of the bill had been not only willing that its opponents should express their opinions, but had strongly desired it. They courted the fullest and freest discussion; but it seemed to him that this fairness was but illy appreciated, since gentlemen were capable of taking advantage of it for selfish and unworthy ends. This trifling had gone far enough. He called for the question.

The instant Mr. Buckstone sat down, the storm burst forth. A dozen gentlemen sprang to their feet.

"Mr. Speaker!"

"Mr. Speaker!"

"Mr. Speaker!"

"Order! Order! Order! Question! Question!"

The sharp blows of the Speaker's gavel rose above the din.

The "previous question," that hated gag, was moved and carried. All debate came to a sudden end, of course. Triumph No. 1.

Then the vote was taken on the adoption of the report and it carried by a surprising majority.

Mr. Buckstone got the floor again and moved that the rules be suspended and the bill read a first time.

Mr. Trollop—"Second the motion!"

The Speaker—"It is moved and—"

Clamor of Voices. "Move we adjourn! Second the motion! Adjourn! Adjourn! Order! Order!"

The Speaker, (after using his gavel vigorously)—"It is moved and seconded that the House do now adjourn. All those in favor—"

Voices—"Division! Division! Ayes and nays! Ayes and nays!"

It was decided to vote upon the adjournment by ayes and nays. This was war in earnest. The excitement was furious. The galleries were in commotion in an instant, the reporters swarmed to their places, idling members of the House flocked to their seats, nervous gentlemen sprang to their feet, pages flew hither and thither, life and animation were visible everywhere, all the long ranks of faces in the building were kindled.

"This thing decides it!" thought Mr. Buckstone; "but let the fight proceed."

The voting began, and every sound ceased but the calling of the names and the "Aye!" "No!" "No!" "Aye!" of the responses. There was not a movement in the House; the people seemed to hold their breath.

The voting ceased, and then there was an interval of dead silence while the clerk made up his count. There was a two-thirds vote on the University side—and two over!

The Speaker—"The rules are suspended, the motion is carried—first reading of the *bill!*"

By one impulse the galleries broke forth into stormy applause, and even some of the members of the House were not wholly able to restrain their feelings. The Speaker's gavel came to the rescue and his clear voice followed:

"Order, gentlemen! The House will come to order! If spectators offend again, the Sergeant-at-arms will clear the galleries!"

Then he cast his eyes aloft and gazed at some object attentively for a moment. All eyes followed the direction of the Speaker's, and then there was a general titter. The Speaker said:

"Let the Sergeant-at Arms inform the gentleman that his conduct is an infringement of the dignity of the House—and one which is not warranted by the state of the weather."

Poor Sellers was the culprit. He sat in the front seat of the gallery, with his arms and his tired body overflowing the balustrade—sound asleep, dead to all excitements, all disturbances. The fluctuations of the Washington weather had influenced his dreams, perhaps, for during the recent tempest of applause he had hoisted his gingham umbrella and calmly gone on with his slumbers. Washington Hawkins had seen the act, but was not near enough at hand to save his friend, and no one who was near enough desired to spoil the effect. But a neighbor stirred up the Colonel, now that the House had its eye upon him, and the great speculator furled his tent like the Arab. He said:

"Bless my soul, I'm so absent-minded when I get to thinking! I never wear an umbrella in the house—did anybody notice it? What—asleep? Indeed? And did you wake me sir? Thank you—thank you very much indeed. It might have fallen out of my hands and been injured. Admirable article, sir—present from a friend in Hong Kong; one doesn't come across silk like that in this country—it's the real Young Hyson, I'm told."

By this time the incident was forgotten, for the House was at war again. Victory was almost in sight, now, and the friends of the bill threw themselves into their work with enthusiasm. They soon moved and carried its second reading, and after a strong, sharp fight, carried a motion to go into Committee of the whole. The Speaker left his place, of course, and a chairman was appointed.

Now the contest raged hotter than ever—for the authority that compels order when the House sits *as* a House, is greatly diminished when it sits as a Committee. The main fight came upon the filling of the blanks with the sum to be appropriated for the purchase of the land, of course.

Mr. Buckstone—"Mr. Chairman, I move you, sir, that the words *three millions of* be inserted."

Mr. Hadley—"Mr. Chairman, I move that the words *two and a half dollars* be inserted."

Mr. Clawson—"Mr. Chairman, I move the insertion of the words *five and twenty cents*, as representing the true value of this barren and isolated tract of desolation."

The question, according to rule, was taken upon the smallest sum first. It was lost.

Then upon the next smallest sum. Lost, also.

And then upon the three millions. After a vigorous battle that lasted a considerable time, this motion was carried.

Then, clause by clause the bill was read, discussed, and amended in trifling particulars, and now the Committee rose and reported.

The moment the House had resumed its functions and received the report, Mr. Buckstone moved and carried the third reading of the bill.

The same bitter war over the sum to be paid was fought over again, and now that the ayes and nays could be called and placed on record, every man was compelled to vote by name on the three millions, and indeed on every paragraph of the bill from the enacting clause straight through. But as before, the friends of the measure stood firm and voted in a solid body every time, and so did its enemies.

The supreme moment was come, now, but so sure was the result that not even a voice was raised to interpose an adjournment. The enemy were totally demoralized. The bill was put upon its final passage almost without dissent, and the calling of the ayes and nays began. When it was ended the triumph was complete—the two-thirds vote held good, and a veto was impossible, as far as the House was concerned!

Mr. Buckstone resolved that now that the nail was driven home, he would clinch it on the other side and make it stay forever. He moved a reconsideration of the vote by which the bill had passed. The motion was lost, of course, and the great Industrial University act was an accomplished fact as far as it was in the power of the House of Representatives to make it so.

There was no need to move an adjournment. The instant the last motion was decided, the enemies of the University rose and flocked out of the Hall, talking angrily, and its friends flocked after them jubilant and congratulatory. The galleries disgorged their burden, and presently the House was silent and deserted.

When Col. Sellers and Washington stepped out of the building they were surprised to find that the daylight was old and the sun well up. Said the Colonel:

"Give me your hand, my boy! You're all right at last! You're a millionaire! At least you're going to be. The thing is dead sure. Don't you bother about the Senate. Leave me and Dilworthy to take care of that. Run along home, now, and tell Laura. Lord, it's magnificent news—perfectly magnificent! Run, now. I'll telegraph my wife. She must come here and help me build a house. Everything's all right now!"

Washington was so dazed by his good fortune and so bewildered by the gaudy pageant of dreams that was already trailing its long ranks through his brain, that he wandered he knew not where, and so loitered by the way that when at last he reached home he woke to a sudden annoyance in the fact that his news must be old to Laura, now, for of course Senator Dilworthy must have already been home and told her an hour before. He knocked at her door, but there was no answer.

"That is like the Duchess," said he. "Always cool. A body can't excite her—can't keep her excited, anyway. Now she has gone off to sleep again, as comfortably as if she were used to picking up a million dollars every day or two."

Then he went to bed. But he could not sleep; so he got up and wrote a long, rapturous letter to Louise, and another to his mother. And he closed both to much the same effect:

"Laura will be queen of America, now, and she will be applauded, and honored and petted by the whole nation. Her name will be in every one's mouth more than ever, and how they will court her and quote her bright speeches. And mine, too, I suppose; though they do that more already, than they really seem to deserve. Oh, the world is so bright, now, and so cheery; the clouds are all gone, our long struggle is ended, our troubles are all over. Nothing can ever make us unhappy any more. You dear faithful ones will have the reward of your patient waiting now. How father's wisdom is proven at last! And how I repent me, that there have been times when I lost faith and said the blessing he stored up for us a tedious generation ago was but a long-drawn curse, a blight upon us all. But everything is well, now—we are done with poverty, and toil, weariness and heartbreakings; all the world is filled with sunshine."

Chapter XLVI

Forte è l'aceto di vin dolce.

Ne biđ swylc cwénlíc þeaw
idese to efnanne,
þeáh đe hió ænlícu sy,
þætte freođu-webbe
feores onsæce,
æfter lig-torne,
leófne mannan.

Beowulf.

PHILIP left the capitol and walked up Pennsylvania Avenue in company with Senator Dilworthy. It was a bright spring morning, the air was soft and inspiring; in the deepening wayside green, the pink flush of the blossoming peach trees, the soft suffusion on the heights of Arlington, and the breath of the warm south wind was apparent the annual miracle of the resurrection of the earth.

The Senator took off his hat and seemed to open his soul to the sweet influences of the morning. After the heat and noise of the chamber, under its dull gas-illuminated glass canopy, and the all night struggle of passion and feverish excitement there, the open, tranquil world seemed like Heaven. The Senator was not in an exultant mood, but rather in a condition of holy joy, befitting a Christian statesman whose benevolent plans Providence has made its own and stamped with approval. The great battle had been fought, but the measure had still to encounter the scrutiny of the Senate, and Providence sometimes acts differently in the two Houses. Still the Senator was tranquil, for he knew that there is an *esprit de corps* in the Senate which does not exist in the House, the effect of which is to make the members complaisant towards the projects of each other, and to extend a mutual aid which in a more vulgar body would be called "log-rolling."

"It is, under Providence, a good night's work, Mr. Sterling. The government has founded an institution which will remove half the difficulty from the Southern problem. And it is a good thing for the Hawkins heirs, a very good thing. Laura will be almost a millionaire."

"Do you think, Mr. Dilworthy, that the Hawkinses will get much of the money?" asked Philip innocently, remembering the fate of the Columbus River appropriation.

The Senator looked at his companion scrutinizingly for a moment to see if he meant any thing personal, and then replied,

"Undoubtedly, undoubtedly. I have had their interests greatly at heart. There will of course be a few expenses, but the widow and orphans will realize all that Mr. Hawkins dreamed of for them."

The birds were singing as they crossed the Presidential Square, now bright with its green turf and tender foliage. After the two had gained the steps of the Senator's house they stood a moment, looking upon the lovely prospect.

"It is like the peace of God," said the Senator devoutly.

Entering the house, the Senator called a servant and said, "Tell Miss Laura that we are waiting to see her. I ought to have sent a messenger on horseback half an hour ago," he added to Philip, "she will be transported with our victory. You must stop to breakfast, and see the excitement." The servant soon came back, with a wondering look and reported,

"Miss Laura ain't dah, sah. I reckon she hain't been dah all night."

The Senator and Philip both started up. In Laura's room there were the marks of a confused and hasty departure, drawers half open, little articles strewn on the floor. The bed had not been disturbed. Upon inquiry it appeared that Laura had not been at dinner, excusing herself to Mrs. Dilworthy on the plea of a violent headache; that she made a request to the servants that she might not be disturbed.

The Senator was astounded. Philip thought at once of Col. Selby. Could Laura have run away with him? The Senator thought not. In fact it could not be. Gen. Leffenwell, the member from New Orleans, had casually told him at the house last night that Selby and his family went to New York yesterday morning and were to sail for Europe to-day.

Philip had another idea which he did not mention. He seized his hat, and saying that he would go and see what he could learn, ran to the lodgings of Harry, whom he had not seen since yesterday afternoon, when he left him to go to the House.

Harry was not in. He had gone out with a hand-bag before six o'clock yesterday, saying that he had to go to New York, but should return next day. In Harry's room on the table Philip found this note:—

"Dear Mr. Brierly:—Can you meet me at the six o'clock train, and be my escort to New York? I have to go about this University bill, the vote of an absent member we must have here. Senator Dilworthy cannot go.
                    Yours &c.,   L. H."

"Confound it," said Philip, "the noodle has fallen into her trap. And she promised me she would let him alone."

He only stopped to send a note to Senator Dilworthy, telling him what he had found, and that he should go at once to New York, and then hastened to the railway station. He had to wait an hour for a train, and when it did start it seemed to go at a snail's pace.

Philip was devoured with anxiety. Where could they have gone? What was Laura's object in taking Harry? Had the flight anything to do with Selby? Would Harry be such a fool as to be dragged into some public scandal?

It seemed as if the train would never reach Baltimore. Then there was a long delay at Havre de Grace. A hot box had to be cooled at Wilmington. Would it never get on? Only in passing around the city of Philadelphia did the train not seem to go slow. Philip stood upon the platform and watched for the Boltons' house, fancied he could distinguish its roof among the trees, and wondered how Ruth would feel if she knew he was so near her.

Then came Jersey, everlasting Jersey, stupid irritating Jersey, where the passengers are always asking which line they are on, and where they are to come out, and whether they have yet reached Elizabeth. Launched into Jersey, one has a vague notion that he is on many lines and no one in particular, and that he is liable at any moment to come to Elizabeth. He has no notion what Elizabeth is, and always resolves that the next time he goes that way he will look out of the window and see what it is like; but he never does. Or if he does, he probably finds that it is Princeton or something of that sort. He gets annoyed, and never can see the use of having different names for stations in Jersey. By and by there is Newark, three or four Newarks apparently; then marshes, then long rock cuttings devoted to the advertisements of patent medicines and ready-made clothing, and New York tonics for Jersey agues, and— Jersey City is reached.

On the ferry-boat Philip bought an evening paper from a boy crying "'Ere's the *Evening Gram*, all about the murder," and with breathless haste ran his eyes over the following:—

SHOCKING MURDER!!!
TRAGEDY IN HIGH LIFE!!
A BEAUTIFUL WOMAN SHOOTS A DISTINGUISHED
CONFEDERATE SOLDIER AT THE SOUTHERN HOTEL!!!
JEALOUSY THE CAUSE!!!!

This morning occurred another of those shocking murders which have become the almost daily food of the newspapers, the direct re- sult of the socialistic doctrines and woman's rights agitations, which have made every woman the avenger of her own wrongs, and all so- ciety the hunting ground for her victims.

About nine o'clock a lady deliberately shot a man dead in the public parlor of the Southern Hotel, coolly remarking, as she threw down her revolver and permitted herself to be taken into custody, "He brought it on himself." Our reporters were immediately dis- patched to the scene of the tragedy, and gathered the following particulars.

Yesterday afternoon arrived at the hotel from Washington, Col. George Selby and family, who had taken passage and were to sail at noon to-day in the steamer Scotia for England. The Colonel was a handsome man about forty, a gentleman of wealth and high social position, a resident of New Orleans. He served with distinction in the confederate army, and received a wound in the leg from which he has never entirely recovered, being obliged to use a cane in loco- motion.

This morning at about nine o'clock, a lady, accompanied by a gentleman, called at the office of the hotel and asked for Col. Selby. The Colonel was at breakfast. Would the clerk tell him that a lady and gentleman wished to see him for a moment in the parlor? The clerk says that the gentleman asked her, "What do you want to see *him* for?" and that she replied, "He is going to Europe, and I ought to just say good by."

Col. Selby was informed, and the lady and gentleman were shown to the parlor, in which were at the time three or four other persons. Five minutes after two shots were fired in quick succession, and there was a rush to the parlor from which the reports came.

Col. Selby was found lying on the floor, bleeding, but not dead. Two gentlemen, who had just come in, had seized the lady, who made no resistance, and she was at once given in charge of a police officer who arrived. The persons who were in the parlor agree substantially as to what occurred. They had happened to be looking towards the door when the man—Col. Selby—entered with his cane, and they looked at him, because he stopped as if surprised and frightened, and made a backward movement. At the same moment the lady in the bonnet advanced towards him and said something like, "George, will you go with me?" He replied, throwing up his hand and retreating, "My God! I can't, don't fire," and the next instant two shots were heard and he fell. The lady appeared to be beside herself with rage or excitement, and trembled very much when the gentlemen took hold of her; it was to them she said, "He brought it on himself."

Col. Selby was carried at once to his room and Dr. Puffer, the eminent surgeon, was sent for. It was found that he was shot through the breast and through the abdomen. Other aid was summoned, but the wounds were mortal, and Col. Selby expired in an hour, in pain, but his mind was clear to the last, and he made a full deposition. The substance of it was that his murderess is a Miss Laura Hawkins, whom he had known at Washington as a lobbyist, and had had some business with her. She had followed him with her attentions and solicitations, and had endeavored to make him desert his wife and go to Europe with her. When he resisted and avoided her, she had threatened him. Only the day before he left Washington she had declared that he should never go out of the city alive without her.

It seems to have been a deliberate and premeditated murder, the woman following him from Washington on purpose to commit it.

We learn that the murderess, who is a woman of dazzling and transcendent beauty and about twenty-six or seven, is a niece of Senator Dilworthy, at whose house she has been spending the winter. She belongs to a high Southern family, and has the reputation of being an heiress. Like some other great beauties and belles in Washington however there have been whispers that she had something to do with the lobby. If we mistake not we have heard her name mentioned in connection with the sale of the Tennessee

Lands to the Knobs University, the bill for which passed the House last night.

Her companion is Mr. Harry Brierly, a New York dandy, who has been in Washington. His connection with her and with this tragedy is not known, but he was also taken into custody, and will be detained at least as a witness.

P.S. One of the persons present in the parlor says that after Laura Hawkins had fired twice, she turned the pistol towards herself, but that Brierly sprang and caught it from her hand, and that it was he who threw it on the floor.

Further particulars with full biographies of all the parties in our next edition.

Philip hastened at once to the Southern Hotel, where he found still a great state of excitement, and a thousand different and exaggerated stories passing from mouth to mouth. The witnesses of the event had told it over so many times that they had worked it up into a most dramatic scene, and embellished it with whatever could heighten its awfulness. Outsiders had taken up invention also. The Colonel's wife had gone insane, they said. The children had rushed into the parlor and rolled themselves in their father's blood. The hotel clerk said that he noticed there was murder in the woman's eye when he saw her. A person who had met the woman on the stairs felt a creeping sensation. Some thought Brierly was an accomplice, and that he had set the woman on to kill his rival. Some said the woman showed the calmness and indifference of insanity.

Philip learned that Harry and Laura had both been taken to the city prison, and he went there; but he was not admitted. Not being a newspaper reporter, he could not see either of them that night; but the officer questioned him suspiciously and asked him who he was. He might perhaps see Brierly in the morning.

The latest editions of the evening papers had the result of the inquest. It was a plain enough case for the jury, but they sat over it a long time, listening to the wrangling of the physicians. Dr. Puffer insisted that the man died from the effects of the wound in the chest. Dr. Dobb as strongly insisted that the wound in the abdomen caused death. Dr. Golightly suggested that in his opinion death ensued from a complication of the two wounds and perhaps other causes. He examined the table waiter, as to whether Col. Selby ate any breakfast, and what he ate, and if he had any appetite.

The jury finally threw themselves back upon the indisputable fact that Selby was dead, that either wound would have killed him (admitted by the doctors), and rendered a verdict that he died from pistol-shot wounds inflicted by a pistol in the hands of Laura Hawkins.

The morning papers blazed with big type, and overflowed with details of the murder. The accounts in the evening papers were only the premonitory drops to this mighty shower. The scene was dramatically worked up in column after column. There were sketches, biographical and historical. There were long "specials" from Washington, giving a full history of Laura's career there, with the names of men with whom she was said to be intimate, a description of Senator Dilworthy's residence and of his family, and of Laura's room in his house, and a sketch of the Senator's appearance and what he said. There was a great deal about her beauty, her accomplishments and her brilliant position in society, and her doubtful position in society. There was also an interview with Col. Sellers and another with Washington Hawkins, the brother of the murderess. One journal had a long dispatch from Hawkeye, reporting the excitement in that quiet village and the reception of the awful intelligence.

All the parties had been "interviewed." There were reports of conversations with the clerk at the hotel; with the call-boy; with the waiter at table, with all the witnesses, with the policeman, with the landlord (who wanted it understood that nothing of that sort had ever happened in his house before, although it had always been frequented by the best Southern society,) and with Mrs. Col. Selby. There were diagrams illustrating the scene of the shooting, and views of the hotel and street, and portraits of the parties.

There were three minute and different statements from the doctors about the wounds, so technically worded that nobody could understand them. Harry and Laura had also been "interviewed" and there was a statement from Philip himself, which a reporter had knocked him up out of bed at midnight to give, though how he found him, Philip never could conjecture.

What some of the journals lacked in suitable length for the occasion, they made up in encyclopœdic information about other similar murders and shootings.

The statement from Laura was not full, in fact it was fragmentary, and consisted of nine parts of the reporter's valuable observations to one of Laura's, and it was, as the reporter significantly remarked, "incoherent." But it appeared that Laura claimed to be Selby's wife, or to have been his wife, that he had deserted her and betrayed her, and that she was going to follow him to Europe. When the reporter asked:

"What made you shoot him, Miss Hawkins?" Laura's only reply was, very simply,

"Did I shoot him? Do they say I shot him?" And she would say no more.

The news of the murder was made the excitement of the day. Talk of it filled the town. The facts reported were scrutinized, the standing of the parties was discussed, the dozen different theories of the motive, broached in the newspapers, were disputed over.

During the night subtle electricity had carried the tale over all the wires of the continent and under the sea; and in all villages and towns of the Union, from the Atlantic to the territories, and away up and down the Pacific slope, and as far as London and Paris and Berlin, that morning the name of Laura Hawkins was spoken by millions and millions of people, while the owner of it—the sweet child of years ago, the beautiful queen of Washington drawing rooms—sat shivering on her cot-bed in the darkness of a damp cell in the Tombs.

Chapter XLVII

—Mana qo c'u x-opon-vi ri v'oyeualal, ri v'achihilal! ahcarroc cah, ahcarroc uleu! la quitzih varal in camel, in zachel varal chuxmut cah, chuxmut uleu!

Rabinal-Achi.

PHILIP'S first effort was to get Harry out of the Tombs. He gained permission to see him, in the presence of an officer, during the day, and he found that hero very much cast down.

"I never intended to come to such a place as this, old fellow," he said to Philip; "it's no place for a gentleman, they've no idea how to treat a gentleman. Look at that provender," pointing to his uneaten prison ration. "They tell me I am detained as a witness, and I passed the night among a lot of cut-throats and dirty rascals—a pretty witness I'd be in a month spent in such company."

"But what under heavens," asked Philip, "induced you to come to New York with Laura! What was it for?"

"What for? Why, she wanted me to come. I didn't know anything about that cursed Selby. She said it was lobby business for the University. I'd no idea what she was dragging me into that confounded hotel for. I suppose she knew that the Southerners all go there, and thought she'd find her man. Oh! Lord, I wish I'd taken your advice. You might as well murder somebody and have the credit of it, as get into the newspapers the way I have. She's pure devil, that girl. You ought to have seen how sweet she was on me; what an ass I am."

"Well, I'm not going to dispute a poor prisoner. But the first thing is to get you out of this. I've brought the note Laura wrote you, for one thing, and I've seen your uncle, and explained the truth of the case to him. He will be here soon."

Harry's uncle came, with other friends, and in the course of the day made such a showing to the authorities that Harry was released, on giving bonds to appear as a witness when wanted. His spirits rose with their usual elasticity as soon as he was out of Centre Street, and he insisted on giving Philip and his friends a royal supper at Delmonico's, an excess which was perhaps excusable in the rebound of his feelings, and which was committed with his usual reckless generosity. Harry ordered the supper, and it is perhaps needless to say that Philip paid the bill.

Neither of the young men felt like attempting to see Laura that day, and she saw no company except the newspaper reporters, until the arrival of Col. Sellers and Washington Hawkins, who had hastened to New York with all speed.

They found Laura in a cell in the upper tier of the women's department. The cell was somewhat larger than those in the men's department, and might be eight feet by ten square, perhaps a little longer. It was of stone, floor and all, and the roof was oven shaped. A narrow slit in the roof admitted sufficient light, and was the only means of ventilation; when the window was opened there was nothing to prevent the rain coming in. The only means of heating being from the corridor, when the door was ajar, the cell was chilly and at this time damp. It was whitewashed and clean, but it had a slight jail odor; its only furniture was a narrow iron bedstead, with a tick of straw and some blankets, not too clean.

When Col. Sellers was conducted to this cell by the matron and looked in, his emotions quite overcame him, the tears rolled down his cheeks and his voice trembled so that he could hardly speak. Washington was unable to say anything; he looked from Laura to the miserable creatures who were walking in the corridor with unutterable disgust. Laura was alone calm and self-contained, though she was not unmoved by the sight of the grief of her friends.

"Are you comfortable, Laura?" was the first word the Colonel could get out.

"You see," she replied. "I can't say it's exactly comfortable."

"Are you cold?"

"It is pretty chilly. The stone floor is like ice. It chills me through to step on it. I have to sit on the bed."

"Poor thing, poor thing. And can you eat any thing?"

"No, I am not hungry. I don't know that I could eat any thing, I can't eat *that*."

"Oh dear," continued the Colonel, "it's dreadful. But cheer up, dear, cheer up;" and the Colonel broke down entirely.

"But," he went on, "we'll stand by you. We'll do everything for you. I know you couldn't have meant to do it, it must have been insanity, you know, or something of that sort. You never did anything of the sort before."

Laura smiled very faintly and said,

"Yes, it was something of that sort. It's all a whirl. He was a villain; you don't know."

"I'd rather have killed him myself, in a duel you know, all fair. I wish I had. But don't you be down. We'll get you off— the best counsel, the lawyers in New York can do anything; I've read of cases. But you must be comfortable now. We've brought some of your clothes, at the hotel. What else can we get for you?"

Laura suggested that she would like some sheets for her bed, a piece of carpet to step on, and her meals sent in; and some books and writing materials if it was allowed. The Colonel and Washington promised to procure all these things, and then took their sorrowful leave, a great deal more affected than the criminal was, apparently, by her situation.

The Colonel told the matron as he went away that if she would look to Laura's comfort a little it shouldn't be the worse for her; and to the turnkey who let them out he patronizingly said,

"You've got a big establishment here, a credit to the city. I've got a friend in there—I shall see you again, sir."

By the next day something more of Laura's own story began to appear in the newspapers, colored and heightened by reporters' rhetoric. Some of them cast a lurid light upon the Colonel's career, and represented his victim as a beautiful avenger of her murdered innocence; and others pictured her as his willing paramour and pitiless slayer. Her communications to the reporters were stopped by her lawyers as soon as they were retained and visited her, but this fact did not prevent—it may have facilitated—the appearance of casual paragraphs here and there which were likely to beget popular sympathy for the poor girl.

The occasion did not pass without "improvement" by the leading journals; and Philip preserved the editorial comments of three or four of them which pleased him most. These he used to read aloud to his friends afterwards and ask them to guess from which journal each of them had been cut. One began in this simple manner:—

History never repeats itself, but the Kaleidoscopic combinations of the pictured present often seem to be constructed out of the broken fragments of antique legends. Washington is not Corinth, and Lais, the beautiful daughter of Timandra, might not have been the prototype of the ravishing Laura, daughter of the plebeian house of Hawkins; but the orators and statesmen who were the purchasers of the favors of the one, may have been as incorruptible as the Republican statesmen who learned how to love and how to vote from the sweet lips of the Washington lobbyist; and perhaps the modern Lais would never have departed from the national Capital if there had been there even one republican Xenocrates who resisted her blandishments. But here the parallel fails. Lais, wandering away with the youth Hippostratus, is slain by the women who are jealous of her charms. Laura, straying into her Thessaly with the youth Brierly, slays her other lover and becomes the champion of the wrongs of her sex.

Another journal began its editorial with less lyrical beauty, but with equal force. It closed as follows:—

With Laura Hawkins, fair, fascinating and fatal, and with the dissolute Colonel of a lost cause, who has reaped the harvest he sowed, we have nothing to do. But as the curtain rises on this awful tragedy, we catch a glimpse of the society at the capital under this Administration, which we cannot contemplate without alarm for the fate of the Republic.

A third newspaper took up the subject in a different tone. It said:—

Our repeated predictions are verified. The pernicious doctrines which we have announced as prevailing in American society have been again illustrated. The name of the city is becoming a reproach. We may have done something in averting its ruin in our resolute exposure of the Great Frauds; we shall not be deterred from insisting that the outraged laws for the protection of human life shall be vindicated now, so that a person can walk the streets or enter the public houses, at least in the day-time, without the risk of a bullet through his brain.

A fourth journal began its remarks as follows:—

The fullness with which we present our readers this morning the details of the Selby-Hawkins homicide is a miracle of modern journalism. Subsequent investigation can do little to fill out the picture. It is the old story. A beautiful woman shoots her absconding lover in cold-blood; and we shall doubtless learn in due time that if she was not as mad as a hare in this month of March, she was at least laboring under what is termed "momentary insanity."

It would not be too much to say that upon the first publication of the facts of the tragedy, there was an almost universal feeling of rage against the murderess in the Tombs, and that reports of her beauty only heightened the indignation. It was as if she presumed upon that and upon her sex, to defy the law; and there was a fervent hope that the law would take its plain course.

Yet Laura was not without friends, and some of them very influential too. She had in her keeping a great many secrets and a great many reputations, perhaps. Who shall set himself up to judge human motives? Why, indeed, might we not feel pity for a woman whose brilliant career had been so suddenly extinguished in misfortune and crime? Those who had known her so well in Washington might find it impossible to believe that the fascinating woman could have had murder in her heart, and would readily give ear to the current sentimentality about the temporary aberration of mind under the stress of personal calamity.

Senator Dilworthy was greatly shocked, of course, but he was full of charity for the erring.

"We shall all need mercy," he said. "Laura as an inmate of my family was a most exemplary female, amiable, affectionate and truthful, perhaps too fond of gaiety, and neglectful of the externals of religion, but a woman of principle. She may have had experiences of which I am ignorant, but she could not have gone to this extremity if she had been in her own right mind."

To the Senator's credit be it said, he was willing to help Laura and her family in this dreadful trial. She, herself, was not without money, for the Washington lobbyist is not seldom more fortunate than the Washington claimant, and she was able to procure a good many luxuries to mitigate the severity of her prison life. It enabled her also to have her own family near her, and to see some of them daily. The tender solicitude of her mother, her childlike grief, and her firm belief in the real guiltlessness of her daughter, touched even the custodians of the Tombs who are enured to scenes of pathos.

Mrs. Hawkins had hastened to her daughter as soon as she received money for the journey. She had no reproaches, she had only tenderness and pity. She could not shut out the dreadful facts of the case, but it had been enough for her that Laura had said, in their first interview, "mother, I did not know what I was doing." She obtained lodgings near the prison and devoted her life to her daughter, as if she had been really her own child. She would have remained in the prison day and night if it had been permitted. She was aged and feeble, but this great necessity seemed to give her new life.

The pathetic story of the old lady's ministrations, and her simplicity and faith, also got into the newspapers in time, and probably added to the pathos of this wrecked woman's fate, which was beginning to be felt by the public. It was certain that she had champions who thought that her wrongs ought to be placed against her crime, and expressions of this feeling came to her in various ways. Visitors came to see her, and gifts of fruit and flowers were sent, which brought some cheer into her hard and gloomy cell.

Laura had declined to see either Philip or Harry, somewhat to the former's relief, who had a notion that she would necessarily feel humiliated by seeing him after breaking faith with him, but to the discomfiture of Harry, who still felt her fascination, and thought her refusal heartless. He told Philip that of course he had got through with such a woman, but he wanted to see her.

Philip, to keep him from some new foolishness, persuaded him to go with him to Philadelphia, and give his valuable services in the mining operations at Ilium.

The law took its course with Laura. She was indicted for murder in the first degree, and held for trial at the summer term. The two most distinguished criminal lawyers in the city had been retained for her defence, and to that the resolute woman devoted her days, with a courage that rose as she consulted with her counsel and understood the methods of criminal procedure in New York.

She was greatly depressed, however, by the news from Washington. Congress adjourned and her bill had failed to pass the Senate. It must wait for the next session.

Chapter XLVIII

—In our werking, nothing us availle;
For lost is all our labour and travaille,
And all the cost a twenty devil way
Is lost also, which we upon it lay.
Chaucer.

He moonihoawa ka aie.
Hawaiian Proverb.

I T HAD BEEN a bad winter, somehow, for the firm of Pennybacker, Bigler and Small. These celebrated contractors
usually made more money during the session of the legislature at Harrisburg than upon all their summer work, and this
winter had been unfruitful. It was unaccountable to Bigler.

"You see, Mr. Bolton," he said, and Philip was present at
the conversation, "it puts us all out. It looks as if politics was
played out. We'd counted on the year of Simon's re-election.
And, now, he's re-elected, and I've yet to see the first man
who's the better for it."

"You don't mean to say," asked Philip, "that he went in
without paying anything?"

"Not a cent, not a dash cent, as I can hear," repeated Mr.
Bigler, indignantly. "I call it a swindle on the state. How it
was done gets me. I never saw such a tight time for money in
Harrisburg."

"Were there no combinations, no railroad jobs, no mining
schemes put through in connection with the election?"

"Not that I know," said Bigler, shaking his head in disgust.
"In fact it was openly said, that there was no money in the
election. It's perfectly unheard of."

"Perhaps," suggested Philip, "it was effected on what the
insurance companies call the 'endowment,' or the 'paid up'
plan, by which a policy is secured after a certain time without
further payment."

"You think then," said Mr. Bolton smiling, "that a liberal
and sagacious politician might own a legislature after a time,
and not be bothered with keeping up his payments?"

"Whatever it is," interrupted Mr. Bigler, "it's devilish inge-nious, and goes ahead of my calculations; it's cleaned me out, when I thought we had a dead sure thing. I tell you what it is, gentlemen, I shall go in for reform. Things have got pretty mixed when a legislature will give away a United States sena-torship."

It was melancholy, but Mr. Bigler was not a man to be crushed by one misfortune, or to lose his confidence in hu-man nature, on one exhibition of apparent honesty. He was already on his feet again, or would be if Mr. Bolton could tide him over shoal water for ninety days.

"We've got something with money in it," he explained to Mr. Bolton, "got hold of it by good luck. We've got the en-tire contract for Dobson's Patent Pavement for the city of Mobile. See here."

Mr. Bigler made some figures; contract so much, cost of work and materials so much, profits so much. At the end of three months the city would owe the company three hundred and seventy-five thousand dollars—two hundred thousand of that would be profits. The whole job was worth at least a mil-lion to the company—it might be more. There could be no mistake in these figures; here was the contract, Mr. Bolton knew what materials were worth and what the labor would cost.

Mr. Bolton knew perfectly well from sore experience that there was always a mistake in figures when Bigler or Small made them, and he knew that he ought to send the fellow about his business. Instead of that, he let him talk.

They only wanted to raise fifty thousand dollars to carry on the contract—that expended they would have city bonds. Mr. Bolton said he hadn't the money. But Bigler could raise it on his name. Mr. Bolton said he had no right to put his family to that risk. But the entire contract could be assigned to him— the security was ample—it was a fortune to him if it was for-feited. Besides Mr. Bigler had been unfortunate, he didn't know where to look for the necessaries of life for his family. If he could only have one more chance, he was sure he could right himself. He begged for it.

And Mr. Bolton yielded. He could never refuse such ap-peals. If he had befriended a man once and been cheated by him, that man appeared to have a claim upon him forever. He shrank, however, from telling his wife what he had done on this occasion, for he knew that if any person was more odious than Small to his family it was Bigler.

"Philip tells me," Mrs. Bolton said that evening, "that the man Bigler has been with thee again to-day. I hope thee will have nothing more to do with him."

"He has been very unfortunate," replied Mr. Bolton, uneasily.

"He is always unfortunate, and he is always getting thee into trouble. But thee didn't listen to him again?"

"Well, mother, his family is in want, and I lent him my name—but I took ample security. The worst that can happen will be a little inconvenience."

Mrs. Bolton looked grave and anxious, but she did not complain or remonstrate; she knew what a "little inconvenience" meant, but she knew there was no help for it. If Mr. Bolton had been on his way to market to buy a dinner for his family with the only dollar he had in the world in his pocket, he would have given it to a chance beggar who asked him for it. Mrs. Bolton only asked (and the question showed that she was no more provident than her husband where her heart was interested),

"But has thee provided money for Philip to use in opening the coal mine?"

"Yes, I have set apart as much as it ought to cost to open the mine, as much as we can afford to lose if no coal is found. Philip has the control of it, as equal partner in the venture, deducting the capital invested. He has great confidence in his success, and I hope for his sake he won't be disappointed."

Philip could not but feel that he was treated very much like one of the Bolton family—by all except Ruth. His mother, when he went home after his recovery from his accident, had affected to be very jealous of Mrs. Bolton, about whom and Ruth she asked a thousand questions—an affectation of jealousy which no doubt concealed a real heartache, which comes to every mother when her son goes out into the world and forms new ties. And to Mrs. Sterling, a widow, living on a small income in a remote Massachusetts village, Philadelphia was a city of many splendors. All its inhabitants seemed highly

favored, dwelling in ease and surrounded by superior advantages. Some of her neighbors had relations living in Philadelphia, and it seemed to them somehow a guarantee of
respectability to have relations in Philadelphia. Mrs. Sterling
was not sorry to have Philip make his way among such well-
to-do people, and she was sure that no good fortune could be
too good for his deserts.

"So, sir," said Ruth, when Philip came from New York,
"you have been assisting in a pretty tragedy. I saw your name
in the papers. Is this woman a specimen of your western
friends?"

"My only assistance," replied Philip, a little annoyed, "was
in trying to keep Harry out of a bad scrape, and I failed after
all. He walked into her trap, and he has been punished for it.
I'm going to take him up to Ilium to see if he won't work
steadily at one thing, and quit his nonsense."

"Is she as beautiful as the newspapers say she is?"

"I don't know, she has a kind of beauty—she is not like—"

"Not like Alice?"

"Well, she is brilliant; she was called the handsomest
woman in Washington—dashing, you know, and sarcastic and
witty. Ruth, do you believe a woman ever becomes a devil?"

"Men do, and I don't know why women shouldn't. But I
never saw one."

"Well, Laura Hawkins comes very near it. But it is dreadful
to think of her fate."

"Why, do you suppose they will hang a woman? Do you
suppose they will be so barbarous as that?"

"I wasn't thinking of that—it's doubtful if a New York jury
would find a woman guilty of any such crime. But to think of
her life if she is acquitted."

"It is dreadful," said Ruth, thoughtfully, "but the worst of
it is that you men do not want women educated to do anything, to be able to earn an honest living by their own exer-
tions. They are educated as if they were always to be petted
and supported, and there was never to be any such thing as
misfortune. I suppose, now, that you would all choose to have
me stay idly at home, and give up my profession."

"Oh, no," said Philip, earnestly, "I respect your resolution.
But, Ruth, do you think you would be happier or do more

good in following your profession than in having a home of your own?"

"What is to hinder having a home of my own?"

"Nothing, perhaps, only you never would be in it—you would be away day and night, if you had any practice; and what sort of a home would that make for your husband?"

"What sort of a home is it for the wife whose husband is always away riding about in his doctor's gig?"

"Ah, you know that is not fair. The woman makes the home."

Philip and Ruth often had this sort of discussion, to which Philip was always trying to give a personal turn. He was now about to go to Ilium for the season, and he did not like to go without some assurance from Ruth that she might perhaps love him some day, when he was worthy of it, and when he could offer her something better than a partnership in his poverty.

"I should work with a great deal better heart, Ruth," he said the morning he was taking leave, "if I knew you cared for me a little."

Ruth was looking down; the color came faintly to her cheeks, and she hesitated. She needn't be looking down, he thought, for she was ever so much shorter than tall Philip.

"It's not much of a place, Ilium," Philip went on, as if a little geographical remark would fit in here as well as anything else, "and I shall have plenty of time to think over the responsibility I have taken, and—" his observation did not seem to be coming out any where.

But Ruth looked up, and there was a light in her eyes that quickened Phil's pulse. She took his hand, and said with serious sweetness:

"Thee mustn't lose heart, Philip." And then she added, in another mood, "Thee knows I graduate in the summer and shall have my diploma. And if any thing happens—mines explode sometimes—thee can send for me. Farewell."

The opening of the Ilium coal mine was begun with energy, but without many omens of success. Philip was running a tunnel into the breast of the mountain, in faith that the coal stratum ran there as it ought to. How far he must go in he believed he knew, but no one could tell exactly. Some of the miners said that they should probably go through the mountain, and that the hole could be used for a railway tunnel. The mining camp was a busy place at any rate. Quite a settlement of board and log shanties had gone up, with a blacksmith shop, a small machine shop, and a temporary store for supplying the wants of the workmen. Philip and Harry pitched a commodious tent, and lived in the full enjoyment of the free life.

There is no difficulty in digging a hole in the ground, if you have money enough to pay for the digging, but those who try this sort of work are always surprised at the large amount of money necessary to make a small hole. The earth is never willing to yield one product, hidden in her bosom, without an equivalent for it. And when a person asks of her coal, she is quite apt to require gold in exchange.

It was exciting work for all concerned in it. As the tunnel advanced into the rock every day promised to be the golden day. This very blast might disclose the treasure.

The work went on week after week, and at length during the night as well as the daytime. Gangs relieved each other, and the tunnel was every hour, inch by inch and foot by foot, crawling into the mountain. Philip was on the stretch of hope and excitement. Every pay day he saw his funds melting away, and still there was only the faintest show of what the miners call "signs."

The life suited Harry, whose buoyant hopefulness was never disturbed. He made endless calculations, which nobody could understand, of the probable position of the vein. He stood about among the workmen with the busiest air. When he was down at Ilium he called himself the engineer of the works, and he used to spend hours smoking his pipe with the Dutch landlord on the hotel porch, and astonishing the idlers there with the stories of his railroad operations in Missouri. He talked with the landlord, too, about enlarging his hotel, and about buying some village lots, in the prospect of a rise, when the mine was opened. He taught the Dutchman how to mix a great many cooling drinks for the summer time, and had a bill at the hotel, the growing length of which Mr. Dusenheimer contemplated with pleasant anticipations. Mr. Brierly was a very useful and cheering person wherever he went.

Midsummer arrived. Philip could report to Mr. Bolton only progress, and this was not a cheerful message for him to send to Philadelphia in reply to inquiries that he thought became more and more anxious. Philip himself was a prey to the constant fear that the money would give out before the coal was struck.

At this time Harry was summoned to New York, to attend the trial of Laura Hawkins. It was possible that Philip would have to go also, her lawyer wrote, but they hoped for a postponement. There was important evidence that they could not yet obtain, and he hoped the judge would not force them to a trial unprepared. There were many reasons for a delay, reasons which of course are never mentioned, but which it would seem that a New York judge sometimes must understand, when he grants a postponement upon a motion that seems to the public altogether inadequate.

Harry went, but he soon came back. The trial was put off. Every week we can gain, said the learned counsel, Braham, improves our chances. The popular rage never lasts long.

Chapter XLIX

Солнце заблистало, но не надолго: блеснуло и скрылось.

"Mofère ipa eiye nā." "Aki ije *ofère* li obbè."

W E'VE struck it!"
    This was the electric announcement at the tent door
that woke Philip out of a sound sleep at dead of night, and
shook all the sleepiness out of him in a trice.

"What! Where is it? When? Coal? Let me see it. What quality is it?" were some of the rapid questions that Philip poured
out as he hurriedly dressed. "Harry, wake up, my boy. The
coal train is coming. Struck it, eh? Let's see?"

The foreman put down his lantern, and handed Philip a
black lump. There was no mistake about it, it was the hard,
shining anthracite, and its freshly fractured surface, glistened
in the light like polished steel. Diamond never shone with
such lustre in the eyes of Philip.

Harry was exuberant, but Philip's natural caution found expression in his next remark.

"Now, Roberts, you are sure about this?"

"What—sure that it's coal?"

"O, no, sure that it's the main vein."

"Well, yes. We took it to be that."

"Did you from the first?"

"I can't say we did at first. No, we didn't. Most of the indications were there, but not all of them, not all of them. So
we thought we'd prospect a bit."

"Well?"

"It was tolerable thick, and looked as if it might be the
vein—looked as if it *ought* to be the vein. Then we went
down on it a little. Looked better all the time."

"When did you strike it?"

"About ten o'clock."

"Then you've been prospecting about four hours."

"Yes, been sinking on it something over four hours."

"I'm afraid you couldn't go down very far in four hours—
could you?"

"O yes—it's a good deal broke up, nothing but picking and gadding stuff."

"Well, it *does* look encouraging, sure enough—but then the lacking indications—"

"I'd rather we had them, Mr. Sterling, but I've seen more than one good permanent mine struck without 'em in my time."

"Well, *that* is encouraging too."

"Yes, there was the Union, the Alabama and the Black Mohawk—all good, sound mines, you know—all just exactly like this one when we first struck them."

"Well, I begin to feel a good deal more easy. I guess we've really got it. I remember hearing them tell about the Black Mohawk."

"I'm free to say that *I* believe it, and the men all think so too. They are all old hands at this business."

"Come Harry, let's go up and look at it, just for the comfort of it," said Philip. They came back in the course of an hour, satisfied and happy.

There was no more sleep for them that night. They lit their pipes, put a specimen of the coal on the table, and made it a kind of loadstone of thought and conversation.

"Of course," said Harry, "there will have to be a branch track built, and a 'switch-back' up the hill."

"Yes, there will be no trouble about getting the money for that now. We could sell out to-morrow for a handsome sum. That sort of coal doesn't go begging within a mile of a railroad. I wonder if Mr. Bolton would rather sell out or work it?"

"Oh, work it," says Harry, "probably the whole mountain is coal now you've got to it."

"Possibly it might not be much of a vein after all," suggested Philip.

"Possibly it *is*, I'll bet it's forty feet thick. I told you. I knew the sort of thing as soon as I put my eyes on it."

Philip's next thought was to write to his friends and announce their good fortune. To Mr. Bolton he wrote a short, business letter, as calm as he could make it. They had found coal of excellent quality, but they could not yet tell with absolute certainty what the vein was. The prospecting was still going on. Philip also wrote to Ruth; but though this letter may have glowed, it was not with the heat of burning anthracite. He needed no artificial heat to warm his pen and kindle his ardor when he sat down to write to Ruth. But it must be confessed that the words never flowed so easily before, and he ran on for an hour disporting in all the extravagance of his imagination. When Ruth read it, she doubted if the fellow had not gone out of his senses. And it was not until she reached the postscript that she discovered the cause of the exhilaration. "P.S.—We have found coal."

The news couldn't have come to Mr. Bolton in better time. He had never been so sorely pressed. A dozen schemes which he had in hand, any one of which might turn up a fortune, all languished, and each needed just a little more money to save that which had been invested. He hadn't a piece of real estate that was not covered with mortgages, even to the wild tract which Philip was experimenting on, and which had no marketable value above the incumbrance on it.

He had come home that day early, unusually dejected.

"I am afraid," he said to his wife, "that we shall have to give up our house. I don't care for myself, but for thee and the children."

"That will be the least of misfortunes," said Mrs. Bolton, cheerfully, "if thee can clear thyself from debt and anxiety, which is wearing thee out, we can live any where. Thee knows we were never happier than when we were in a much humbler home."

"The truth is, Margaret, that affair of Bigler and Small's has come on me just when I couldn't stand another ounce. They have made another failure of it. I might have known they would; and the sharpers, or fools, I don't know which, have contrived to involve me for three times as much as the first obligation. The security is in my hands, but it is good for nothing to me. I have not the money to do anything with the contract."

Ruth heard this dismal news without great surprise. She had long felt that they were living on a volcano, that might go in to active operation at any hour. Inheriting from her father an active brain and the courage to undertake new things, she had little of his sanguine temperament which blinds one to difficulties and possible failures. She had little confidence in the many schemes which had been about to lift her father out of all his embarrassments and into great wealth, ever since she was a child; as she grew older, she rather wondered that they were as prosperous as they seemed to be, and that they did not all go to smash amid so many brilliant projects. She was nothing but a woman, and did not know how much of the business prosperity of the world is only a bubble of credit and speculation, one scheme helping to float another which is no better than it, and the whole liable to come to naught and confusion as soon as the busy brain that conceived them ceases its power to devise, or when some accident produces a sudden panic.

"Perhaps, I shall be the stay of the family, yet," said Ruth, with an approach to gaiety. "When we move into a little house in town, will thee let me put a little sign on the door— DR. RUTH BOLTON? Mrs. Dr. Longstreet, thee knows, has a great income."

"Who will pay for the sign, Ruth?" asked Mr. Bolton.

A servant entered with the afternoon mail from the office. Mr. Bolton took his letters listlessly, dreading to open them. He knew well what they contained, new difficulties, more urgent demands for money.

"Oh, here is one from Philip. Poor fellow. I shall feel his disappointment as much as my own bad luck. It is hard to bear when one is young."

He opened the letter and read. As he read his face lightened, and he fetched such a sigh of relief, that Mrs. Bolton and Ruth both exclaimed.

"Read that," he cried, "Philip has found coal!"

The world was changed in a moment. One little sentence had done it. There was no more trouble. Philip had found coal. That meant relief. That meant fortune. A great weight was taken off, and the spirits of the whole household rose magically. Good Money! beautiful demon of Money, what an enchanter thou art! Ruth felt that she was of less consequence in the household, now that Philip had found coal, and perhaps she was not sorry to feel so.

Mr. Bolton was ten years younger the next morning. He went into the city, and showed his letter on change. It was the sort of news his friends were quite willing to listen to. They took a new interest in him. If it was confirmed, Bolton would come right up again. There would be no difficulty about his getting all the money he wanted. The money market did not seem to be half so tight as it was the day before. Mr. Bolton spent a very pleasant day in his office, and went home revolving some new plans, and the execution of some projects he had long been prevented from entering upon by the lack of money.

The day had been spent by Philip in no less excitement. By daylight, with Philip's letters to the mail, word had gone down to Ilium that coal had been found, and very early a crowd of eager spectators had come up to see for themselves.

The "prospecting" continued day and night for upwards of a week, and during the first four or five days the indications grew more and more promising, and the telegrams and letters kept Mr. Bolton duly posted. But at last a change came, and the promises began to fail with alarming rapidity. In the end it was demonstrated without the possibility of a doubt that the great "find" was nothing but a worthless seam.

Philip was cast down, all the more so because he had been so foolish as to send the news to Philadelphia before he knew what he was writing about. And now he must contradict it. "It turns out to be only a mere seam," he wrote, "but we look upon it as an indication of better further in."

Alas! Mr. Bolton's affairs could not wait for "indications." The future might have a great deal in store, but the present was black and hopeless. It was doubtful if any sacrifice could save him from ruin. Yet sacrifice he must make, and that instantly, in the hope of saving something from the wreck of his fortune.

His lovely country home must go. That would bring the most ready money. The house that he had built with loving thought for each one of his family, as he planned its luxurious apartments and adorned it; the grounds that he had laid out, with so much delight in following the tastes of his wife, with whom the country, the cultivation of rare trees and flowers, the care of garden and lawn and conservatories were a passion almost; this home, which he had hoped his children would enjoy long after he had done with it, must go.

The family bore the sacrifice better than he did. They declared in fact—women are such hypocrites—that they quite enjoyed the city (it was in August) after living so long in the country, that it was a thousand times more convenient in every respect; Mrs. Bolton said it was a relief from the worry of a large establishment, and Ruth reminded her father that she should have had to come to town anyway before long.

Mr. Bolton was relieved, exactly as a water-logged ship is lightened by throwing overboard the most valuable portion of the cargo—but the leak was not stopped. Indeed his credit was injured instead of helped by the prudent step he had taken. It was regarded as a sure evidence of his embarrassment, and it was much more difficult for him to obtain help than if he had, instead of retrenching, launched into some new speculation.

Philip was greatly troubled, and exaggerated his own share in the bringing about of the calamity.

"You must not look at it so!" Mr. Bolton wrote him. "You have neither helped nor hindered—but you know you may help by and by. It would have all happened just so, if we had never begun to dig that hole. That is only a drop. Work away. I still have hope that something will occur to relieve me. At any rate we must not give up the mine, so long as we have any show."

Alas! the relief did not come. New misfortunes came instead. When the extent of the Bigler swindle was disclosed there was no more hope that Mr. Bolton could extricate himself, and he had, as an honest man, no resource except to surrender all his property for the benefit of his creditors.

The Autumn came and found Philip working with diminished force but still with hope. He had again and again been encouraged by good "indications," but he had again and again been disappointed. He could not go on much longer, and almost everybody except himself had thought it was useless to go on as long as he had been doing.

When the news came of Mr. Bolton's failure, of course the work stopped. The men were discharged, the tools were housed, the hopeful noise of pickman and driver ceased, and the mining camp had that desolate and mournful aspect which always hovers over a frustrated enterprise.

Philip sat down amid the ruins, and almost wished he were buried in them. How distant Ruth was now from him, now, when she might need him most. How changed was all the Philadelphia world, which had hitherto stood for the exemplification of happiness and prosperity.

He still had faith that there was coal in that mountain. He made a picture of himself living there a hermit in a shanty by the tunnel, digging away with solitary pick and wheelbarrow, day after day and year after year, until he grew gray and aged, and was known in all that region as the old man of the mountain. Perhaps some day—he felt it must be so some day—he should strike coal. But what if he did? Who would be alive to care for it then? What would he care for it then? No, a man wants riches in his youth, when the world is fresh to him. He wondered why Providence could not have reversed the usual process, and let the majority of men begin with wealth and gradually spend it, and die poor when they no longer needed it.

Harry went back to the city. It was evident that his services were no longer needed. Indeed, he had letters from his uncle, which he did not read to Philip, desiring him to go to San Francisco to look after some government contracts in the harbor there.

Philip had to look about him for something to do; he was like Adam; the world was all before him where to choose. He made, before he went elsewhere, a somewhat painful visit to Philadelphia, painful but yet not without its sweetnesses. The family had never shown him so much affection before; they all seemed to think his disappointment of more importance than their own misfortune. And there was that in Ruth's manner—in what she gave him and what she withheld—that would have made a hero of a very much less promising character than Philip Sterling.

Among the assets of the Bolton property, the Ilium tract was sold, and Philip bought it in at the vendue, for a song, for no one cared to even undertake the mortgage on it except himself. He went away the owner of it, and had ample time before he reached home in November, to calculate how much poorer he was by possessing it.

Chapter L

þá eymdir striða á sorgfullt sinn,
og svipur mótgángs um vánga, ríða,
    og bakivendir þér veröldin,
og vellyst brosir að þínum qvíða;
þeink allt er knöttótt, og hverfast lætr,
    sá hló í dag er á morgun grætr;
        Alt jafnar sig!

Sigurd Peterson.

I T IS IMPOSSIBLE for the historian, with even the best intentions, to control events or compel the persons of his
narrative to act wisely or to be successful. It is easy to see how
things might have been better managed; a very little change
here and there would have made a very different history of
this one now in hand.

If Philip had adopted some regular profession, even some
trade, he might now be a prosperous editor or a conscientious
plumber, or an honest lawyer, and have borrowed money at
the saving's bank and built a cottage, and be now furnishing
it for the occupancy of Ruth and himself. Instead of this, with
only a smattering of civil engineering, he is at his mother's
house, fretting and fuming over his ill-luck, and the hardness
and dishonesty of men, and thinking of nothing but how to
get the coal out of the Ilium hills.

If Senator Dilworthy had not made that visit to Hawkeye,
the Hawkins family and Col. Sellers would not now be dancing attendance upon Congress, and endeavoring to tempt
that immaculate body into one of those appropriations, for
the benefit of its members, which the members find it so difficult to explain to their constituents; and Laura would not be
lying in the Tombs, awaiting her trial for murder, and doing
her best, by the help of able counsel, to corrupt the pure
fountain of criminal procedure in New York.

If Henry Brierly had been blown up on the first Mississippi
steamboat he set foot on, as the chances were that he would
be, he and Col. Sellers never would have gone into the
Columbus Navigation scheme, and probably never into the
East Tennessee Land scheme, and he would not now be de-

tained in New York from very important business operations on the Pacific coast, for the sole purpose of giving evidence to convict of murder the only woman he ever loved half as much as he loves himself.

If Mr. Bolton had said the little word "no" to Mr. Bigler, Alice Montague might now be spending the winter in Philadelphia, and Philip also (waiting to resume his mining operations in the spring); and Ruth would not be an assistant in a Philadelphia hospital, taxing her strength with arduous routine duties, day by day, in order to lighten a little the burdens that weigh upon her unfortunate family.

It is altogether a bad business. An honest historian who had progressed thus far, and traced everything to such a condition of disaster and suspension, might well be justified in ending his narrative and writing—"after this the deluge." His only consolation would be in the reflection that he was not responsible for either characters or events.

And the most annoying thought is that a little money, judiciously applied, would relieve the burdens and anxieties of most of these people; but affairs seem to be so arranged that money is most difficult to get when people need it most.

A little of what Mr. Bolton has weakly given to unworthy people would now establish his family in a sort of comfort, and relieve Ruth of the excessive toil for which she inherited no adequate physical vigor. A little money would make a prince of Col. Sellers; and a little more would calm the anxiety of Washington Hawkins about Laura, for however the trial ended, he could feel sure of extricating her in the end. And if Philip had a little money he could unlock the stone door in the mountain whence would issue a stream of shining riches. It needs a golden wand to strike that rock. If the Knobs University bill could only go through, what a change would be wrought in the condition of most of the persons in this history. Even Philip himself would feel the good effects of it; for Harry would have something and Col. Sellers would have something; and have not both these cautious people expressed a determination to take an interest in the Ilium mine when they catch their larks?

Philip could not resist the inclination to pay a visit to Fallkill. He had not been at the Montagues' since the time he saw

Ruth there, and he wanted to consult the Squire about an occupation. He was determined now to waste no more time in
waiting on Providence, but to go to work at something, if it
were nothing better than teaching in the Fallkill Seminary, or
digging clams on Hingham beach. Perhaps he could read law
in Squire Montague's office while earning his bread as a
teacher in the Seminary.

It was not altogether Philip's fault, let us own, that he was
in this position. There are many young men like him in American society, of his age, opportunities, education and abilities,
who have really been educated for nothing and have let themselves drift, in the hope that they will find somehow, and by
some sudden turn of good luck, the golden road to fortune.
He was not idle or lazy, he had energy and a disposition to
carve his own way. But he was born into a time when all
young men of his age caught the fever of speculation, and expected to get on in the world by the omission of some of the
regular processes which have been appointed from of old.
And examples were not wanting to encourage him. He saw
people, all around him, poor yesterday, rich to-day, who had
come into sudden opulence by some means which they could
not have classified among any of the regular occupations of
life. A war would give such a fellow a career and very likely
fame. He might have been a "rail-road man," or a politician,
or a land speculator, or one of those mysterious people who
travel free on all rail roads and steamboats, and are continually crossing and re-crossing the Atlantic, driven day and
night about nobody knows what, and make a great deal of
money by so doing. Probably, at last, he sometimes thought
with a whimsical smile, he should end by being an insurance
agent, and asking people to insure their lives for his benefit.

Possibly Philip did not think how much the attractions of
Fallkill were increased by the presence of Alice there. He had
known her so long, she had somehow grown into his life by
habit, that he would expect the pleasure of her society without thinking much about it. Latterly he never thought of her
without thinking of Ruth, and if he gave the subject any attention, it was probably in an undefined consciousness that he
had her sympathy in his love, and that she was always willing
to hear him talk about it. If he ever wondered that Alice her-

self was not in love and never spoke of the possibility of her own marriage, it was a transient thought—for love did not seem necessary, exactly, to one so calm and evenly balanced and with so many resources in her herself.

Whatever her thoughts may have been they were unknown to Philip, as they are to these historians; if she was seeming to be what she was not, and carrying a burden heavier than any one else carried, because she had to bear it alone, she was only doing what thousands of women do, with a self-renunciation and heroism of which men, impatient and complaining, have no conception. Have not these big babies with beards filled all literature with their outcries, their griefs and their lamentations? It is always the gentle sex which is hard and cruel and fickle and implacable.

"Do you think you would be contented to live in Fallkill, and attend the county Court?" asked Alice, when Philip had opened the budget of his new programme.

"Perhaps not always," said Philip, "I might go and practice in Boston maybe, or go to Chicago."

"Or you might get elected to Congress."

Philip looked at Alice to see if she was in earnest and not chaffing him. Her face was quite sober. Alice was one of those patriotic women in the rural districts, who think men are still selected for Congress on account of qualifications for the office.

"No," said Philip, "the chances are that a man cannot get into congress now without resorting to arts and means that should render him unfit to go there; of course there are exceptions; but do you know that I could not go into politics if I were a lawyer, without losing standing somewhat in my profession, and without raising at least a suspicion of my intentions and unselfishness? Why, it is telegraphed all over the country and commented on as something wonderful if a congressman votes honestly and unselfishly and refuses to take advantage of his position to steal from the government."

"But," insisted Alice, "I should think it a noble ambition to go to congress, if it is so bad, and help reform it. I don't believe it is as corrupt as the English parliament used to be, if there is any truth in the novels, and I suppose that is reformed."

"I'm sure I don't know where the reform is to begin. I've seen a perfectly capable, honest man, time and again, run against an illiterate trickster, and get beaten. I suppose if the people wanted decent members of congress they would elect them. Perhaps," continued Philip with a smile, "the women will have to vote."

"Well, I should be willing to, if it were a necessity, just as I would go to war and do what I could, if the country couldn't be saved otherwise," said Alice, with a spirit that surprised Philip, well as he thought he knew her. "If I were a young gentleman in these times—"

Philip laughed outright. "It's just what Ruth used to say, 'if she were a man.' I wonder if all the young ladies are contemplating a change of sex."

"No, only a changed sex," retorted Alice; "we comtemplate for the most part young men who don't care for anything they ought to care for."

"Well," said Philip, looking humble, "I care for some things, you and Ruth for instance; perhaps I ought not to. Perhaps I ought to care for Congress and that sort of thing."

"Don't be a goose, Philip. I heard from Ruth yesterday."

"Can I see her letter?"

"No, indeed. But I am afraid her hard work is telling on her, together with her anxiety about her father."

"Do you think, Alice," asked Philip with one of those selfish thoughts that are not seldom mixed with real love, "that Ruth prefers her profession to—to marriage?"

"Philip," exclaimed Alice, rising to quit the room, and speaking hurriedly as if the words were forced from her, "you are as blind as a bat; Ruth would cut off her right hand for you this minute."

Philip never noticed that Alice's face was flushed and that her voice was unsteady; he only thought of the delicious words he had heard. And the poor girl, loyal to Ruth, loyal to Philip, went straight to her room, locked the door, threw herself on the bed and sobbed as if her heart would break. And then she prayed that her Father in Heaven would give her strength. And after a time she was calm again, and went to her bureau drawer and took from a hiding place a little piece of paper, yellow with age. Upon it was pinned a four-leaved clover, dry and yellow also. She looked long at this foolish memento. Under the clover leaf was written in a school-girl's hand—"*Philip, June, 186–.*"

Squire Montague thought very well of Philip's proposal. It would have been better if he had begun the study of the law as soon as he left college, but it was not too late now, and besides he had gathered some knowledge of the world.

"But," asked the Squire, "do you mean to abandon your land in Pennsylvania?" This track of land seemed an immense possible fortune to this New England lawyer-farmer. "Hasn't it good timber, and doesn't the railroad almost touch it?"

"I can't do anything with it now. Perhaps I can sometime."

"What is your reason for supposing that there is coal there?"

"The opinion of the best geologist I could consult, my own observation of the country, and the little veins of it we found. I feel certain it is there. I shall find it some day. I know it. If I can only keep the land till I make money enough to try again."

Philip took from his pocket a map of the anthracite coal region, and pointed out the position of the Ilium mountain which he had begun to tunnel.

"Doesn't it look like it?"

"It certainly does," said the Squire, very much interested. It is not unusual for a quiet country gentleman to be more taken with such a venture than a speculator who has had more experience in its uncertainty. It was astonishing how many New England clergymen, in the time of the petroleum excitement, took chances in oil. The Wall street brokers are said to do a good deal of small business for country clergymen, who are moved no doubt with the laudable desire of purifying the New York stock board.

"I don't see that there is much risk," said the Squire, at length. "The timber is worth more than the mortgage; and if that coal seam does run there, it's a magnificent fortune. Would you like to try it again in the spring, Phil?"

Like to try it! If he could have a little help, he would work himself, with pick and barrow, and live on a crust. Only give him one more chance.

And this is how it came about that the cautious old Squire Montague was drawn into this young fellow's speculation, and began to have his serene old age disturbed by anxieties and by the hope of a great stroke of luck.

"To be sure, I only care about it for the boy," he said. The Squire was like everybody else; sooner or later he must "take a chance."

It is probably on account of the lack of enterprise in women that they are not so fond of stock speculations and mine ventures as men. It is only when woman becomes demoralized that she takes to any sort of gambling. Neither Alice nor Ruth were much elated with the prospect of Philip's renewal of his mining enterprise.

But Philip was exultant. He wrote to Ruth as if his fortune were already made, and as if the clouds that lowered over the house of Bolton were already in the deep bosom of a coal mine buried. Towards spring he went to Philadelphia with his plans all matured for a new campaign. His enthusiasm was irresistible.

"Philip has come, Philip has come," cried the children, as if some great good had again come into the household; and the refrain even sang itself over in Ruth's heart as she went the weary hospital rounds. Mr. Bolton felt more courage than he had had in months, at the sight of his manly face and the sound of his cheery voice.

Ruth's course was vindicated now, and it certainly did not become Philip, who had nothing to offer but a future chance against the visible result of her determination and industry, to open an argument with her. Ruth was never more certain that she was right and that she was sufficient unto herself. She, may be, did not much heed the still small voice that sang in her maiden heart as she went about her work, and which lightened it and made it easy, "Philip has come."

"I am glad for father's sake," she said to Philip, "that thee has come. I can see that he depends greatly upon what thee can do. He thinks women won't hold out long," added Ruth with the smile that Philip never exactly understood.

"And aren't you tired sometimes of the struggle?"

"Tired? Yes, everybody is tired I suppose. But it is a glorious profession. And would you want me to be dependent, Philip?"

"Well, yes, a little," said Philip, feeling his way towards what he wanted to say.

"On what, for instance, just now?" asked Ruth, a little maliciously Philip thought.

"Why, on—" he couldn't quite say it, for it occurred to him that he was a poor stick for any body to lean on in the present state of his fortune, and that the woman before him was at least as independent as he was.

"I don't mean depend," he began again. "But I love you, that's all. Am I nothing to you?" And Philip looked a little defiant, and as if he had said something that ought to brush away all the sophistries of obligation on either side, between man and woman.

Perhaps Ruth saw this. Perhaps she saw that her own theories of a certain equality of power, which ought to precede a union of two hearts, might be pushed too far. Perhaps she had felt sometimes her own weakness and the need after all of so dear a sympathy and so tender an interest confessed, as that which Philip could give. Whatever moved her—the riddle is as old as creation—she simply looked up to Philip and said in a low voice,

"Everything."

And Philip clasping both her hands in his, and looking down into her eyes, which drank in all his tenderness with the thirst of a true woman's nature—

"Oh! Philip, come out here," shouted young Eli, throwing the door wide open.

And Ruth escaped away to her room, her heart singing again, and now as if it would burst for joy, "Philip has come."

That night Philip received a dispatch from Harry—"The trial begins to-morrow."

Chapter LI

Mpethie ou sagar lou nga thia gawantou kone yoboul goube.
Wolof Proverb.

"Mitsoda eb volna a' te szolgád, hogy illyen nagy dolgot tselekednek?"

Királyok II. K. 8. 13.

D ECEMBER, 18—, found Washington Hawkins and Col. Sellers once more at the capitol of the nation, standing guard over the University bill. The former gentleman was despondent, the latter hopeful. Washington's distress of mind was chiefly on Laura's account. The court would soon sit to try her case, he said, and consequently a great deal of ready money would be needed in the engineering of it. The University bill was sure to pass, this time, and that would make money plenty, but might not the help come too late? Congress had only just assembled, and delays were to be feared.

"Well," said the Colonel, "I don't know but you are more or less right, there. Now let's figure up a little on the preliminaries. I think Congress always tries to do as near right as it can, according to its lights. A man can't ask any fairer than that. The first preliminary it always starts out on, is to clean itself, so to speak. It will arraign two or three dozen of its members, or maybe four or five dozen, for taking bribes to vote for this and that and the other bill last winter."

"It goes up into the dozens, does it?"

"Well, yes; in a free country like ours, where any man can run for Congress and anybody can vote for him, you can't expect immortal purity all the time—it ain't in nature.—Sixty or eighty or a hundred and fifty people are bound to get in who are not angels in disguise, as young Hicks the correspondent says; but still it is a very good average; very good indeed. As long as it averages as well as that, I think we can feel very well satisfied. Even in these days, when people growl so much and the newspapers are so out of patience, there is still a very respectable minority of honest men in Congress."

"Why a respectable *minority* of honest men can't do any good, Colonel."

"Oh, yes it can, too."

"Why, how?"

"Oh, in many ways, many ways."

"But what *are* the ways?"

"Well—I don't know—it is a question that requires time; a body can't answer every question right off-hand. But it *does* do good. I am satisfied of that."

"All right, then; grant that it does good; go on with the preliminaries."

"That is what I am coming to. First, as I said, they will try a lot of members for taking money for votes. That will take four weeks."

"Yes, that's like last year; and it is a sheer waste of the time for which the nation pays those men to *work*—that is what that is. And it pinches when a body's got a bill waiting."

"A waste of time, to purify the fountain of public law? Well, I never heard anybody express an idea like that before. But if it were, it would still be the fault of the minority, for the majority don't institute these proceedings. *There* is where that minority becomes an obstruction—but still one can't say it is on the wrong side.—Well, after they have finished the bribery cases, they will take up cases of members who have bought their seats with money. That will take another four weeks."

"Very good; go on. You have accounted for two-thirds of the session."

"Next they will try each other for various smaller irregularities, like the sale of appointments to West Point cadetships, and that sort of thing—mere trifling pocket-money enterprises that might better be passed over in silence, perhaps, but then one of our Congresses can never rest easy till it has thoroughly purified itself of all blemishes—and that is a thing to be applauded."

"How long does it take to disinfect itself of these minor impurities?"

"Well, about two weeks, generally."

"So Congress always lies helpless in quarantine ten weeks of a session. That's encouraging. Colonel, poor Laura will never get any benefit from our bill. Her trial will be over before Congress has half purified itself.—And doesn't it occur to you that by the time it has expelled all its impure members there may not be enough members left to do business legally?"

"Why I did not say Congress would expel anybody."

"Well *won't* it expel anybody?"

"Not necessarily. Did it last year? It never does. That would not be regular."

"Then why waste all the session in that tomfoolery of trying members?"

"It is usual; it is customary; the country requires it."

"Then the country is a fool, *I* think."

"Oh, no. The country *thinks* somebody is going to be expelled."

"Well, when nobody *is* expelled, what does the country think then?"

"By that time, the thing has strung out so long that the country is sick and tired of it and glad to have a change on any terms. But all that inquiry is not lost. It has a good moral effect."

"Who does it have a good moral effect on?"

"Well—I don't know. On foreign countries, I think. We have always been under the gaze of foreign countries. There is no country in the world, sir, that pursues corruption as inveterately as we do. There is no country in the world whose representatives try each other as much as ours do, or stick to it as long on a stretch. I think there is something great in being a model for the whole civilized world, Washington."

"You don't mean a model; you mean an example."

"Well, it's all the same; it's just the same thing. It shows that a man can't be corrupt in this country without sweating for it, I can tell you that."

"Hang it, Colonel, you just said we never punish anybody for villainous practices."

"But good God we *try* them, don't we! Is it nothing to show a disposition to sift things and bring people to a strict account? I tell you it has its effect."

"Oh, bother the effect!—What is it they *do* do? How do they proceed? You know perfectly well—and it is all bosh, too. Come, now, how do they proceed?"

"Why they proceed right and regular—and it ain't bosh, Washington, it ain't bosh. They appoint a committee to investigate, and that committee hears evidence three weeks, and all the witnesses on one side swear that the accused took money or stock or something for his vote. Then the accused stands up and testifies that he *may* have done it, but he was receiving and handling a good deal of money at the time and he doesn't remember this particular circumstance—at least with sufficient distinctness to enable him to grasp it tangibly. So of course the thing is not proven—and that is what they say in the verdict. They don't acquit, they don't condemn. They just say, 'Charge not proven.' It leaves the accused in a kind of a shaky condition before the country, it purifies Congress, it satisfies everybody, and it doesn't seriously hurt anybody. It has taken a long time to perfect our system, but it is the most admirable in the world, now."

"So one of those long stupid investigations always turns out in that lame silly way. Yes, you are correct. I thought maybe you viewed the matter differently from other people. Do you think a Congress of ours could convict the devil of anything if he were a member?"

"My dear boy, don't let these damaging delays prejudice you against Congress. Don't use such strong language; you talk like a newspaper. Congress has inflicted frightful punishments on its members—now you know that. When they tried Mr. Fairoaks, and a cloud of witnesses proved him to be— well, you know what they proved him to be—and his own testimony and his own confessions gave him the same character, what did Congress do then?—come!"

"Well, what *did* Congress do?"

"You know what Congress did, Washington. Congress intimated plainly enough, that they considered him almost a stain upon their body; and without waiting ten days, hardly, to think the thing over, they rose up and hurled at him a resolution declaring that they disapproved of his conduct! Now *you* know that, Washington."

"It *was* a terrific thing—there is no denying that. If he had been proven guilty of theft, arson, licentiousness, infanticide, and defiling graves, I believe they would have suspended him for two days."

"You can depend on it, Washington. Congress is vindictive, Congress is savage, sir, when it gets waked up once. It will go to any length to vindicate its honor at such a time."

"Ah well, we have talked the morning through, just as usual in these tiresome days of waiting, and we have reached the same old result; that is to say, we are no better off than when we began. The land bill is just as far away as ever, and the trial is closer at hand. Let's give up everything and die."

"Die and leave the Duchess to fight it out all alone? Oh, no, that won't do. Come, now, don't talk so. It is all going to come out right. Now you'll see.'

"It never will, Colonel, never in the world. Something tells me that. I get more tired and more despondent every day. I don't see any hope; life is only just a trouble. I am so miserable these days!"

The Colonel made Washington get up and walk the floor with him, arm in arm. The good old speculator wanted to comfort him, but he hardly knew how to go about it. He made many attempts, but they were lame; they lacked spirit; the words were encouraging, but they were only words—he could not get any heart into them. He could not always warm up, now, with the old Hawkeye fervor. By and by his lips trembled and his voice got unsteady. He said:

"Don't give up the ship, my boy—don't do it. The wind's bound to fetch around and set in our favor. I *know* it."

And the prospect was so cheerful that he wept. Then he blew a trumpet-blast that started the meshes of his handkerchief, and said in almost his breezy old-time way:

"Lord bless us, this is all nonsense! Night doesn't last always; day has got to break some time or other. Every silver lining has a cloud behind it, as the poet says; and that remark has always cheered me, though I never could see any meaning to it. Everybody uses it, though, and everybody gets comfort out of it. I wish they would start something fresh. Come, now, let's cheer up; there's been as good fish in the sea as there are now. It shall never be said that Eschol Sellers—. Come in?"

It was the telegraph boy. The Colonel reached for the message and devoured its contents.

"I said it! Never give up the ship! The trial's postponed till February, and we'll save the child yet. Bless my life, what lawyers they have in New York! Give them money to fight with, and the ghost of an excuse, and they would manage to postpone anything in this world, unless it might be the millennium or something like that. Now for work again, my boy. The trial will last to the middle of March, sure; Congress ends the fourth of March. Within three days of the end of the session they will be done putting through the preliminaries, and then they will be ready for national business. Our bill will go through in forty-eight hours, then, and we'll telegraph a million dollars to the jury—to the lawyers, I mean—and the verdict of the jury will be 'Accidental murder resulting from justifiable insanity'—or something to that effect, something to that effect. Everything is dead sure, now. Come, what is the matter? What are you wilting down like that, for? You mustn't be a girl, you know."

"Oh, Colonel, I am become so used to troubles, so used to failures, disappointments, hard luck of all kinds, that a little good news breaks me right down. Everything has been so hopeless that now I can't stand good news at all. It is too good to be true, anyway. Don't you see how our bad luck has worked on me? My hair is getting gray, and many nights I don't sleep at all. I wish it was all over and we could rest. I wish we could lie down and just forget everything, and let it all be just a dream that is done and can't come back to trouble us any more. I am so tired."

"Ah, poor child, don't talk like that—cheer up—there's daylight ahead. Don't give up. You'll have Laura again, and Louise, and your mother, and oceans and oceans of money—and then you can go away, ever so far away somewhere, if you want to, and forget all about this infernal place. And by George I'll go with you! I'll go with you—now there's my word on it. Cheer up. I'll run out and tell the friends the news."

And he wrung Washington's hand and was about to hurry away when his companion, in a burst of grateful admiration said:

"I think you are the best soul and the noblest I ever knew, Colonel Sellers! and if the people only knew you as I do, you would not be tagging around here a nameless man—you would be in Congress."

The gladness died out of the Colonel's face, and he laid his hand upon Washington's shoulder and said gravely:

"I have always been a friend of your family, Washington, and I think I have always tried to do right as between man and man, according to my lights. Now I don't think there has ever been anything in my conduct that should make you feel justified in saying a thing like that."

He turned, then, and walked slowly out, leaving Washington abashed and somewhat bewildered. When Washington had presently got his thoughts into line again, he said to himself, "Why, honestly, I only meant to compliment him—indeed I would not have hurt him for the world."

Chapter LII

Aucune chose au monde et plus noble et plus belle
Que la sainte ferveur d'un véritable zèle.
Le Tartuffe, a. i, sc. 6.

With faire discourse the evening so they pas;
For that olde man of pleasing wordes had store,
And well could file his tongue, as smooth as glas—
Faerie Queene.

——Il prit un air bénin et tendre,
D'un *Laudate Deum* leur prêta le bon jour,
Puis convia le monde au fraternal amour!
Roman du Renard (*Prologue*).

THE WEEKS drifted by monotonously enough, now. The "preliminaries" continued to drag along in Congress, and life was a dull suspense to Sellers and Washington, a weary waiting which might have broken their hearts, maybe, but for the relieving change which they got out of an occasional visit to New York to see Laura. Standing guard in Washington or anywhere else is not an exciting business in time of peace, but standing guard was all that the two friends had to do; all that was needed of them was that they should be on hand and ready for any emergency that might come up. There was no work to do; that was all finished; this was but the second session of the last winter's Congress, and its action on the bill could have but one result—its passage. The House must do its work over again, of course, but the same membership was there to see that it did it.—The Senate was secure—Senator Dilworthy was able to put all doubts to rest on that head. Indeed it was no secret in Washington that a two-thirds vote in the Senate was ready and waiting to be cast for the University bill as soon as it should come before that body.

Washington did not take part in the gaieties of "the season," as he had done the previous winter. He had lost his interest in such things; he was oppressed with cares, now. Senator Dilworthy said to Washington that an humble deportment, under punishment, was best, and that there was but one way in which the troubled heart might find perfect repose and peace. The suggestion found a response in Washington's breast, and the Senator saw the sign of it in his face.

From that moment one could find the youth with the Senator even oftener than with Col. Sellers. When the statesman presided at great temperance meetings, he placed Washington in the front rank of impressive dignitaries that gave tone to the occasion and pomp to the platform. His bald headed surroundings made the youth the more conspicuous. When the statesman made remarks in these meetings, he not infrequently alluded with effect to the encouraging spectacle of one of the wealthiest and most brilliant young favorites of society forsaking the light vanities of that butterfly existence to nobly and self-sacrificingly devote his talents and his riches to the cause of saving his hapless fellow creatures from shame and misery here and eternal regret hereafter. At the prayer meetings the Senator always brought Washington up the aisle on his arm and seated him prominently; in his prayers he referred to him in the cant terms which the Senator employed, perhaps unconsciously, and mistook, maybe, for religion, and in other ways brought him into notice. He had him out at gatherings for the benefit of the negro, gatherings for the benefit of the Indian, gatherings for the benefit of the heathen in distant lands. He had him out time and again, before Sunday Schools, as an example for emulation. Upon all these occasions the Senator made casual references to many benevolent enterprises which his ardent young friend was planning against the day when the passage of the University bill should make his ample means available for the amelioration of the condition of the unfortunate among his fellow men of all nations and all climes. Thus as the weeks rolled on Washington grew up into an imposing lion once more, but a lion that roamed the peaceful fields of religion and temperance, and revisited the glittering domain of fashion no more. A great moral influence was thus brought to bear in favor of the bill; the weightiest of friends flocked to its standard; its most energetic enemies said it was useless to fight longer; they had tacitly surrendered while as yet the day of battle was not come.

Chapter LIII

—He seekes, of all his drifte the aymed end:
Thereto his subtile engins he does bend,
His practick witt and his fayre fyled tongue,
With thousand other sleightes; for well he kend
His credit now in doubtful ballaunce hong:
For hardly could bee hurt, who was already stong.

Faerie Queene.

Selons divers besoins, il est une science
D'étendre les liens de notre conscience,
Et de rectifier le mal de l'action
Avec la pureté de notre intention.

Le Tartuffe, a. 4, sc. 5.

THE SESSION was drawing toward its close. Senator Dilworthy thought he would run out west and shake hands with his constituents and let them look at him. The legislature whose duty it would be to re-elect him to the United States Senate, was already in session. Mr. Dilworthy considered his re-election certain, but he was a careful, painstaking man, and if, by visiting his State he could find the opportunity to persuade a few more legislators to vote for him, he held the journey to be well worth taking. The University bill was safe, now; he could leave it without fear; it needed his presence and his watching no longer. But there was a person in his State legislature who did need watching—a person who, Senator Dilworthy said, was a narrow, grumbling, uncomfortable malcontent—a person who was stolidly opposed to reform, and progress and *him*,—a person who, he feared, had been bought with money to combat him, and through him the commonwealth's welfare and its political purity.

"If this person Noble," said Mr. Dilworthy, in a little speech at a dinner party given him by some of his admirers, "merely desired to sacrifice *me*, I would willingly offer up my political life on the altar of my dear State's weal, I would be glad and grateful to do it; but when he makes of me but a cloak to hide his deeper designs, when he proposes to strike *through* me at the heart of my beloved State, all the lion in me

378

is roused—and I say, Here I stand, solitary and alone, but un-flinching, unquailing, thrice armed with my sacred trust; and whoso passes, to do evil to this fair domain that looks to me for protection, must do so over my dead body."

He further said that if this Noble were a pure man, and merely misguided, he could bear it, but that he should suc-ceed in his wicked designs through a base use of money would leave a blot upon his State which would work untold evil to the morals of the people, and *that* he would not suffer; the public morals must not be contaminated. He would seek this man Noble; he would argue, he would persuade, he would appeal to his honor.

When he arrived on the ground he found his friends unter-rified; they were standing firmly by him and were full of courage. Noble was working hard, too, but matters were against him, he was not making much progress. Mr. Dilwor-thy took an early opportunity to send for Mr. Noble; he had a midnight interview with him, and urged him to forsake his evil ways; he begged him to come again and again, which he did. He finally sent the man away at 3 o'clock one morning; and when he was gone, Mr. Dilworthy said to himself,

"I feel a good deal relieved, now, a great deal relieved."

The Senator now turned his attention to matters touching the souls of his people. He appeared in church; he took a leading part in prayer meetings; he met and encouraged the temperance societies; he graced the sewing circles of the ladies with his presence, and even took a needle now and then and made a stitch or two upon a calico shirt for some poor Bible-less pagan of the South Seas, and this act enchanted the ladies, who regarded the garments thus honored as in a man-ner sanctified. The Senator wrought in Bible classes, and nothing could keep him away from the Sunday Schools—nei-ther sickness nor storms nor weariness. He even traveled a te-dious thirty miles in a poor little rickety stagecoach to comply with the desire of the miserable hamlet of Cattleville that he would let its Sunday School look upon him.

All the town was assembled at the stage office when he ar-rived, two bonfires were burning, and a battery of anvils was popping exultant broadsides; for a United States Senator was a sort of god in the understanding of these people who never had seen any creature mightier than a county judge. To them a United States Senator was a vast, vague colossus, an awe inspiring unreality.

Next day everybody was at the village church a full half hour before time for Sunday School to open; ranchmen and farmers had come with their families from five miles around, all eager to get a glimpse of the great man—the man who had been to Washington; the man who had seen the President of the United States, and had even talked with him; the man who had seen the actual Washington Monument—perhaps touched it with his hands.

When the Senator arrived the Church was crowded, the windows were full, the aisles were packed, so was the vestibule, and so indeed was the yard in front of the building. As he worked his way through to the pulpit on the arm of the minister and followed by the envied officials of the village, every neck was stretched and every eye twisted around intervening obstructions to get a glimpse. Elderly people directed each other's attention and said, "There! that's him, with the grand, noble forehead!" Boys nudged each other and said, "Hi, Johnny, here he is! There, that's him, with the peeled head!"

The Senator took his seat in the pulpit, with the minister on one side of him and the Superintendent of the Sunday School on the other. The town dignitaries sat in an impressive row within the altar railings below. The Sunday School children occupied ten of the front benches, dressed in their best and most uncomfortable clothes, and with hair combed and faces too clean to feel natural. So awed were they by the presence of a living United States Senator, that during three minutes not a "spit-ball" was thrown. After that they began to come to themselves by degrees, and presently the spell was wholly gone and they were reciting verses and pulling hair.

The usual Sunday School exercises were hurried through, and then the minister got up and bored the house with a speech built on the customary Sunday School plan; then the Superintendent put in his oar; then the town dignitaries had their say. They all made complimentary reference to "their friend the Senator," and told what a great and illustrious man he was and what he had done for his country and for religion and temperance, and exhorted the little boys to be good and diligent and try to become like him some day. The speakers won the deathless hatred of the house by these delays, but at last there was an end and hope revived; inspiration was about to find utterance.

Senator Dilworthy rose and beamed upon the assemblage for a full minute in silence. Then he smiled with an access of sweetness upon the children and began:

"My little friends—for I hope that all these bright-faced little people are my friends and will let me be their friend—my little friends, I have traveled much, I have been in many cities and many States, everywhere in our great and noble country, and by the blessing of Providence I have been permitted to see many gatherings like this—but I am proud, I am truly proud to say that I never have looked upon so much intelligence, so much grace, such sweetness of disposition as I see in the charming young countenances I see before me at this moment. I have been asking myself as I sat here, Where am I? Am I in some far-off monarchy, looking upon little princes and princesses? No. Am I in some populous centre of my own country, where the choicest children of the land have been selected and brought together as at a fair for a prize? No. Am I in some strange foreign clime where the children are marvels that we know not of? No. Then where am I? Yes—where am I? I am in a simple, remote, unpretending settlement of my own dear State, and these are the children of the noble and virtuous men who have made me what I am! My soul is lost in wonder at the thought! And I humbly thank Him to whom we are but as worms of the dust, that He has been pleased to call me to serve such men! Earth has no higher, no grander position for me. Let kings and emperors keep their tinsel crowns, I want them not; my heart is here!

"Again I thought, Is this a theatre? No. Is it a concert or a gilded opera? No. Is it some other vain, brilliant, beautiful temple of soul-staining amusement and hilarity? No. Then what is it? What did my consciousness reply? I ask you, my little friends, What did my consciousness reply? It replied, It is the temple of the Lord! Ah, think of that, now. I could hardly keep the tears back, I was so grateful. Oh, how beautiful it is to see these ranks of sunny little faces assembled here to learn the way of life; to learn to be good; to learn to be useful; to learn to be pious; to learn to be great and glorious men and women; to learn to be props and pillars of the State and shining lights in the councils and the households of the nation; to be bearers of the banner and soldiers of the cross in the rude campaigns of life, and ransomed souls in the happy fields of Paradise hereafter.

"Children, honor your parents and be grateful to them for providing for you the precious privileges of a Sunday School.

"Now my dear little friends, sit up straight and pretty—there, that's it—and give me your attention and let me tell you about a poor little Sunday School scholar I once knew.—He lived in the far west, and his parents were poor. They could not give him a costly education, but they were good and wise and they sent him to the Sunday School. He loved the Sunday School. I hope you love your Sunday School—ah, I see by your faces that you do! That is right.

"Well, this poor little boy was always in his place when the bell rang, and he always knew his lesson; for his teachers wanted him to learn and he loved his teachers dearly. Always love your teachers, my children, for they love you more than you can know, now. He would not let bad boys persuade him to go to play on Sunday. There was one little bad boy who was always trying to persuade him, but he never could.

"So this poor little boy grew up to be a man, and had to go out in the world, far from home and friends to earn his living. Temptations lay all about him, and sometimes he was about to yield, but he would think of some precious lesson he learned in his Sunday School a long time ago, and that would save him. By and by he was elected to the legislature. Then he did everything he could for Sunday Schools. He got laws passed for them; he got Sunday Schools established wherever he could.

"And by and by the people made him governor—and he said it was all owing to the Sunday School.

"After a while the people elected him a Representative to the Congress of the United States, and he grew very famous.—Now temptations assailed him on every hand. People tried to get him to drink wine, to dance, to go to theatres; they even tried to buy his vote; but no, the memory of his

Sunday School saved him from all harm; he remembered the fate of the bad little boy who used to try to get him to play on Sunday, and who grew up and became a drunkard and was hanged. He remembered that, and was glad he never yielded and played on Sunday.

"Well, at last, what do you think happened? Why the people gave him a towering, illustrious position, a grand, imposing position. And what do you think it was? What should you say it was, children? It was Senator of the United States! That poor little boy that loved his Sunday School became that man. *That man stands before you!* All that he is, he owes to the Sunday School.

"My precious children, love your parents, love your teachers, love your Sunday School, be pious, be obedient, be honest, be diligent, and then you will succeed in life and be honored of all men. Above all things, my children, be honest. Above all things be pure-minded as the snow. Let us join in prayer."

When Senator Dilworthy departed from Cattleville, he left three dozen boys behind him arranging a campaign of life whose objective point was the United States Senate.

When he arrived at the State capital at midnight Mr. Noble came and held a three-hours' conference with him, and then as he was about leaving said:

"I've worked hard, and I've got them at last. Six of them haven't got quite back-bone enough to slew around and come right out for you on the first ballot to-morrow, but they're going to vote against you on the first for the sake of appearances, and then come out for you all in a body on the second—I've fixed all that! By supper time to-morrow you'll be re-elected. You can go to bed and sleep easy on that."

After Mr. Noble was gone, the Senator said:

"Well, to bring about a complexion of things like this was worth coming West for."

Chapter LIV

भेदस्तमसो ऽष्टाविधो मोहस्य च दशाविधो महामोहः
तामिस्रो ऽष्टादशधा तया भवत्यन्धतामिस्रः

Sánkhya Kárika, xlvii.

Ny byd ynat nep yr dysc; yr adysco dyn byth ny byd ynat ony byd doethineb yny callon; yr doethet uyth uo dyn ny byd ynat ony byd dysc gyt ar doethinab.

Cyvreithiau Cymru.

T HE CASE of the State of New York against Laura Hawkins was finally set down for trial on the 15th day of February, less than a year after the shooting of George Selby.

If the public had almost forgotten the existence of Laura and her crime, they were reminded of all the details of the murder by the newspapers, which for some days had been announcing the approaching trial. But they had not forgotten. The sex, the age, the beauty of the prisoner; her high social position in Washington, the unparalled calmness with which the crime was committed had all conspired to fix the event in the public mind, although nearly three hundred and sixty-five subsequent murders had occurred to vary the monotony of metropolitan life.

No, the public read from time to time of the lovely prisoner, languishing in the city prison, the tortured victim of the law's delay; and as the months went by it was natural that the horror of her crime should become a little indistinct in memory, while the heroine of it should be invested with a sort of sentimental interest. Perhaps her counsel had calculated on this. Perhaps it was by their advice that Laura had interested herself in the unfortunate criminals who shared her prison confinement, and had done not a little to relieve, from her own purse, the necessities of some of the poor creatures. That she had done this, the public read in the journals of the day, and the simple announcement cast a softening light upon her character.

The court room was crowded at an early hour, before the arrival of judges, lawyers and prisoner. There is no enjoyment so keen to certain minds as that of looking upon the slow torture of a human being on trial for life, except it be an execution; there is no display of human ingenuity, wit and power so fascinating as that made by trained lawyers in the trial of an important case, nowhere else is exhibited such subtlety, acumen, address, eloquence.

All the conditions of intense excitement meet in a murder trial. The awful issue at stake gives significance to the lightest word or look. How the quick eyes of the spectators rove from the stolid jury to the keen lawyers, the impassive judge, the anxious prisoner. Nothing is lost of the sharp wrangle of the counsel on points of law, the measured decisions of the bench, the duels between the attorneys and the witnesses. The crowd sways with the rise and fall of the shifting testimony, in sympathetic interest, and hangs upon the dicta of the judge in breathless silence. It speedily takes sides for or against the accused, and recognizes as quickly its favorites among the lawyers. Nothing delights it more than the sharp retort of a witness and the discomfiture of an obnoxious attorney. A joke, even if it be a lame one, is no where so keenly relished or quickly applauded as in a murder trial.

Within the bar the young lawyers and the privileged hangers-on filled all the chairs except those reserved at the table for those engaged in the case. Without, the throng occupied all the seats, the window ledges and the standing room. The atmosphere was already something horrible. It was the peculiar odor of a criminal court, as if it were tainted by the presence, in different persons, of all the crimes that men and women can commit.

There was a little stir when the Prosecuting Attorney, with two assistants, made his way in, seated himself at the table, and spread his papers before him. There was more stir when the counsel of the defense appeared. They were Mr. Braham, the senior, and Mr. Quiggle and Mr. O'Keefe, the juniors.

Everybody in the court room knew Mr. Braham, the great criminal lawyer, and he was not unaware that he was the object of all eyes as he moved to his place, bowing to his friends in the bar. A large but rather spare man, with broad shoulders and a massive head, covered with chestnut curls which fell down upon his coat collar and which he had a habit of shaking as a lion is supposed to shake his mane. His face was clean shaven, and he had a wide mouth and rather small dark eyes, set quite too near together. Mr. Braham wore a brown frock coat buttoned across his breast, with a rose-bud in the the upper button-hole, and light pantaloons. A diamond stud was seen to flash from his bosom, and as he seated himself and drew off his gloves a heavy seal ring was displayed upon his white left hand. Mr. Braham having seated himself, deliberately surveyed the entire house, made a remark to one of his assistants, and then taking an ivory-handled knife from his pocket began to pare his finger nails, rocking his chair backwards and forwards slowly.

A moment later Judge O'Shaunnessy entered at the rear door and took his seat in one of the chairs behind the bench; a gentleman in black broadcloth, with sandy hair, inclined to curl, a round, reddish and rather jovial face, sharp rather than intellectual, and with a self-sufficient air. His career had nothing remarkable in it. He was descended from a long line of Irish Kings, and he was the first one of them who had ever come into his kingdom—the kingdom of such being the city of New York. He had, in fact, descended so far and so low that he found himself, when a boy, a sort of street Arab in that city; but he had ambition and native shrewdness, and he speedily took to boot-polishing, and newspaper hawking, became the office and errand boy of a law firm, picked up knowledge enough to get some employment in police courts, was admitted to the bar, became a rising young politician, went to the legislature, and was finally elected to the bench which he now honored. In this democatic country he was obliged to conceal his royalty under a plebeian aspect. Judge O'Shaunnessy never had a lucrative practice nor a large salary, but he had prudently laid away money—believing that a dependant judge can never be impartial—and he had lands and houses to the value of three or four hundred thousand dollars. Had he not helped to build and furnish this very Court House? Did he not know that the very "spittoon" which his judgeship used cost the city the sum of one thousand dollars?

As soon as the judge was seated, the court was opened, with the "oi yis, oi yis" of the officer in his native language, the case called, and the sheriff was directed to bring in the prisoner. In the midst of a profound hush Laura entered, leaning on the arm of the officer, and was conducted to a seat by her counsel. She was followed by her mother and by Washington Hawkins, who were given seats near her.

Laura was very pale, but this pallor heightened the lustre of her large eyes and gave a touching sadness to her expressive face. She was dressed in simple black, with exquisite taste, and without an ornament. The thin lace vail which partially covered her face did not so much conceal as heighten her beauty. She would not have entered a drawing room with more self-poise, nor a church with more haughty humility. There was in her manner or face neither shame nor boldness, and when she took her seat in full view of half the spectators, her eyes were downcast. A murmur of admiration ran through the room. The newspaper reporters made their pencils fly. Mr. Braham again swept his eyes over the house as if in approval. When Laura at length raised her eyes a little, she saw Philip and Harry within the bar, but she gave no token of recognition.

The clerk then read the indictment, which was in the usual form. It charged Laura Hawkins, in effect, with the premeditated murder of George Selby, by shooting him with a pistol, with a revolver, shot-gun, rifle, repeater, breech-loader, cannon, six-shooter, with a gun, or some other weapon; with killing him with a slung-shot, a bludgeon, carving knife, bowie knife, pen knife, rolling pin, car hook, dagger, hair pin, with a hammer, with a screw-driver, with a nail, and with all other weapons and utensils whatsoever, at the Southern hotel and in all other hotels and places wheresoever, on the thirteenth day of March and all other days of the christian era whensoever.

Laura stood while the long indictment was read, and at the end, in response to the inquiry of the judge, she said in a clear, low voice, "Not guilty." She sat down and the court proceeded to impannel a jury.

The first man called was Michael Lanigan, saloon keeper.

"Have you formed or expressed any opinion on this case, and do you know any of the parties?"

"Not any," said Mr. Lanigan.

"Have you any conscientious objections to capital punishment?"

"No, sir, not to my knowledge."

"Have you read anything about this case?"

"To be sure, I read the papers, y'r Honor."

Objected to by Mr. Braham, for cause, and discharged.

Patrick Coughlin.

"What is your business?"

"Well—I haven't got any particular business."

"Haven't any particular business, eh? Well, what's your general business? What do you do for a living?"

"I own some terriers, sir."

"Own some terriers, eh? Keep a rat pit?"

"Gentlemen comes there to have a little sport. *I* never fit 'em, sir."

"Oh, I see—you are probably the amusement committee of the city council. Have you ever heard of this case?"

"Not till this morning, sir."

"Can you read?"

"Not fine print, y'r Honor."

The man was about to be sworn, when Mr. Braham asked, "Could your father read?"

"The old gentleman was mighty handy at that, sir."

Mr. Braham submitted that the man was disqualified. Judge thought not. Point argued. Challenged peremptorily, and set aside.

Ethan Dobb, cart-driver.

"Can you read?"

"Yes, but haven't a habit of it."

"Have you heard of this case?"

"I think so—but it might be another. I have no opinion about it."

Dist. A. "Tha—tha—there! Hold on a bit? Did anybody tell you to say you had no opinion about it?"

"N-n-o, sir."

"Take care now, take care. Then what suggested it to you to volunteer that remark?"

"They've always asked that, when I was on juries."

"All right, then. Have you any conscientious scruples about capital punishment?"

"Any which?"

"Would you object to finding a person guilty of murder on evidence?"

"I might, sir, if I thought he wan't guilty."

The district attorney thought he saw a point.

"Would this feeling rather incline you against a capital conviction?"

The juror said he hadn't any feeling, and didn't know any of the parties. Accepted and sworn.

Dennis Laflin, laborer. Have neither formed nor expressed an opinion. Never had heard of the case. Believed in hangin' for them that deserved it. Could read if it was necessary.

Mr. Braham objected. The man was evidently bloody minded. Challenged peremptorily.

Larry O'Toole, contractor. A showily dressed man of the style known as "vulgar genteel," had a sharp eye and a ready tongue. Had read the newspaper reports of the case, but they made no impression on him. Should be governed by the evidence. Knew no reason why he could not be an impartial juror.

Question by District Attorney.

"How is it that the reports made no impression on you?"

"Never believe anything I see in the newspapers." (Laughter from the crowd, approving smiles from his Honor and Mr. Braham.) Juror sworn in. Mr. Braham whispered to O'Keefe, "that's the man."

Avery Hicks, pea-nut peddler. Did he ever hear of this case? The man shook his head.

"Can you read?"

"No."

"Any scruples about capital punishment?"

"No."

He was about to be sworn, when the district attorney turning to him carelessly, remarked,

"Understand the nature of an oath?"

"Outside," said the man, pointing to the door.

"I say, do you know what an oath is?"

"Five cents," explained the man.

"Do you mean to insult me?" roared the prosecuting officer. "Are you an idiot?"

"Fresh baked. I'm deefe. I don't hear a word you say."

The man was discharged. "He wouldn't have made a bad juror, though," whispered Braham. "I saw him looking at the prisoner sympathizingly. That's a point you want to watch for."

The result of the whole day's work was the selection of only two jurors. These however were satisfactory to Mr. Braham. He had kept off all those he did not know. No one knew better than this great criminal lawyer that the battle was fought on the selection of the jury. The subsequent examination of witnesses, the eloquence expended on the jury are all for effect outside. At least that is the theory of Mr. Braham. But human nature is a queer thing, he admits; sometimes jurors are unaccountably swayed, be as careful as you can in choosing them.

It was four weary days before this jury was made up, but when it was finally complete, it did great credit to the counsel for the defence. So far as Mr. Braham knew, only two could read, one of whom was the foreman, Mr. Braham's friend, the showy contractor. Low foreheads and heavy faces they all had; some had a look of animal cunning, while the most were only stupid. The entire pannel formed that boasted heritage commonly described as the "bulwark of our liberties."

The District Attorney, Mr. McFlinn, opened the case for the state. He spoke with only the slightest accent, one that had been inherited but not cultivated. He contented himself with a brief statement of the case. The state would prove that Laura Hawkins, the prisoner at the bar, a fiend in the form of a beautiful woman, shot dead George Selby, a Southern gentleman, at the time and place described. That the murder was in cold blood, deliberate and without provocation; that it had been long premeditated and threatened; that she had followed the deceased from Washington to commit it. All this would be proved by unimpeachable witnesses. The attorney added that the duty of the jury, however painful it might be, would be plain and simple. They were citizens, husbands, perhaps fathers. They knew how insecure life had become in the metropolis. To-morrow their own wives might be widows,

their own children orphans, like the bereaved family in yonder hotel, deprived of husband and father by the jealous hand
of some murderous female. The attorney sat down, and the
clerk called,

"Henry Brierly."

Chapter LV

"Dyden i Midten," sagde Fanden, han sad imellem to Procutorer.

Eur breûtaer brâz eo! Ha klevet hoc'h eûz-hu hé vreût?

HENRY BRIERLY took the stand. Requested by the District Attorney to tell the jury all he knew about the killing, he narrated the circumstances substantially as the reader already knows them.

He accompanied Miss Hawkins to New York at her request, supposing she was coming in relation to a bill then pending in Congress, to secure the attendance of absent members. Her note to him was here shown. She appeared to be very much excited at the Washington station. After she had asked the conductor several questions, he heard her say, "He can't escape." Witness asked her "Who?" and she replied "Nobody." Did not see her during the night. They traveled in a sleeping car. In the morning she appeared not to have slept, said she had a headache. In crossing the ferry she asked him about the shipping in sight; he pointed out where the Cunarders lay when in port. They took a cup of coffee that morning at a restaurant. She said she was anxious to reach the Southern Hotel where Mr. Simons, one of the absent members, was staying, before he went out. She was entirely self-possessed, and beyond unusual excitement did not act unnaturally. After she had fired twice at Col. Selby, she turned the pistol towards her own breast, and witness snatched it from her. She had been a great deal with Selby in Washington, appeared to be infatuated with him.

(Cross-examined by Mr. Braham.) "Mist-er . . . . er Brierly!" (Mr. Braham had in perfection this lawyer's trick of annoying a witness, by drawling out the "Mister," as if unable to recall the name, until the witness is sufficiently aggravated, and then suddenly, with a rising inflection, flinging his name at him with startling unexpectedness.) "Mist-er . . . . er Brierly! What is your occupation?"

"Civil Engineer, sir."

"Ah, *civil* engineer, (with a glance at the jury). Following that occupation with Miss Hawkins?" (Smiles by the jury).

"No, sir," said Harry, reddening.

"How long have you known the prisoner?"

"Two years, sir. I made her acquaintance in Hawkeye, Missouri."

"'M . . . m . . m. Mist-er . . . . . er Brierly! Were you not a lover of Miss Hawkins?"

Objected to. "I submit, your Honor, that I have the right to establish the relation of this unwilling witness to the prisoner." Admitted.

"Well, sir," said Harry hesitatingly, "we were friends."

"You act like a friend!" (sarcastically.) The jury were beginning to hate this neatly dressed young sprig. "Mist-er . . . . . er Brierly! Didn't Miss Hawkins refuse you?"

Harry blushed and stammered and looked at the judge. "You must answer, sir," said His Honor.

"She—she—didn't accept me."

"No. I should think not. Brierly! do you dare tell the jury that you had not an interest in the removal of your rival, Col. Selby?" roared Mr. Braham in a voice of thunder.

"Nothing like this, sir, nothing like this," protested the witness.

"That's all, sir," said Mr. Braham severely.

"One word," said the District Attorney. "Had you the least suspicion of the prisoner's intention, up to the moment of the shooting?"

"Not the least," answered Harry earnestly.

"Of course not, of course not," nodded Mr. Braham to the jury.

The prosecution then put upon the stand the other witnesses of the shooting at the hotel, and the clerk and the attending physicians. The fact of the homicide was clearly established. Nothing new was elicited, except from the clerk, in reply to a question by Mr. Braham, the fact that when the prisoner enquired for Col. Selby she appeared excited and there was a wild look in her eyes.

The dying deposition of Col. Selby was then produced. It set forth Laura's threats, but there was a significant addition to it, which the newspaper report did not have. It seemed that after the deposition was taken as reported, the Colonel was told for the first time by his physicians that his wounds were mortal. He appeared to be in great mental agony and fear, and said he had not finished his deposition. He added, with great difficulty and long pauses these words. "I—have—not—told—all. I must tell—put—it—down—I—wronged—her. Years—ago—I—can't—see—O—God—I—deserved—" That was all. He fainted and did not revive again.

The Washington railway conductor testified that the prisoner had asked him if a gentleman and his family went out on the evening train, describing the persons he had since learned were Col. Selby and family.

Susan Cullum, colored servant at Senator Dilworthy's, was sworn. Knew Col. Selby. Had seen him come to the house often, and be alone in the parlor with Miss Hawkins. He came the day but one before he was shot. She let him in. He appeared flustered like. She heard talking in the parlor, 'peared like it was quarrelin'. Was afeared sumfin' was wrong. Just put her ear to the keyhole of the back parlor door. Heard a man's voice, "I can't, I can't, Good God," quite beggin' like. Heard young Miss' voice, "Take your choice, then. If you 'bandon me, you knows what to 'spect." Then he rushes outen the house. I goes in and I says, "Missis did you ring?" She was a standin', like a tiger, her eyes flashin'. I come right out.

This was the substance of Susan's testimony, which was not shaken in the least by a severe cross-examination. In reply to Mr. Braham's question, if the prisoner did not look insane, Susan said, "Lord, no, sir, just mad as a hawnet."

Washington Hawkins was sworn. The pistol, identified by the officer as the one used in the homicide, was produced. Washington admitted that it was his. She had asked him for it one morning, saying she thought she had heard burglars the night before. Admitted that he never had heard burglars in the house. Had anything unusual happened just before that? Nothing that he remembered. Did he accompany her to a reception at Mrs. Shoonmaker's a day or two before? Yes. What occurred? Little by little it was dragged out of the witness that Laura had behaved strangely there, appeared to be sick, and he had taken her home. Upon being pushed he admitted that she had afterwards confessed that she saw Selby there. And

Washington volunteered the statement that Selby was a black-hearted villain.

The District Attorney said, with some annoyance, "There—there! That will do."

The defence declined to examine Mr. Hawkins at present. The case for the prosecution was closed. Of the murder there could not be the least doubt, or that the prisoner followed the deceased to New York with a murderous intent. On the evidence the jury must convict, and might do so without leaving their seats. This was the condition of the case two days after the jury had been selected. A week had passed since the trial opened, and a Sunday had intervened. The public who read the reports of the evidence saw no chance for the prisoner's escape. The crowd of spectators who had watched the trial were moved with the most profound sympathy for Laura.

Mr. Braham opened the case for the defence. His manner was subdued, and he spoke in so low a voice that it was only by reason of perfect silence in the court room that he could be heard. He spoke very distinctly, however, and if his nationality could be discovered in his speech it was only in a certain richness and breadth of tone.

He began by saying that he trembled at the responsibility he had undertaken; and he should altogether despair, if he did not see before him a jury of twelve men of rare intelligence, whose acute minds would unravel all the sophistries of the prosecution, men with a sense of honor, which would revolt at the remorseless persecution of this hunted woman by the state, men with hearts to feel for the wrongs of which she was the victim. Far be it from him to cast any suspicion upon the motives of the able, eloquent and ingenious lawyers of the state; they act officially; their business is to convict. It is our business, gentlemen, to see that justice is done.

"It is my duty, gentlemen, to unfold to you one of the most affecting dramas in all the history of misfortune. I shall have to show you a life, the sport of fate and circumstances, hurried along through shifting storm and sun, bright with trusting innocence and anon black with heartless villainy, a career which moves on in love and desertion and anguish, always hovered over by the dark spectre of INSANITY,—an insanity hereditary and induced by mental torture,—until it ends, if end it must in your verdict, by one of those fearful accidents which are inscrutable to men and of which God alone knows the secret.

"Gentlemen, I shall ask you to go with me away from this court room and its minions of the law, away from the scene of this tragedy, to a distant, I wish I could say a happier day. The story I have to tell is of a lovely little girl, with sunny hair and laughing eyes, traveling with her parents, evidently people of wealth and refinement, upon a Mississippi steamboat. There is an explosion, one of those terrible catastrophes which leave the imprint of an unsettled mind upon the survivors. Hundreds of mangled remains are sent into eternity. When the wreck is cleared away this sweet little girl is found among the panic stricken survivors, in the midst of a scene of horror enough to turn the steadiest brain. Her parents have disappeared. Search even for their bodies is in vain. The bewildered, stricken child—who can say what changes the fearful event wrought in her tender brain?—clings to the first person who shows her sympathy. It is Mrs. Hawkins, this good lady who is still her loving friend. Laura is adopted into the Hawkins family. Perhaps she forgets in time that she is not their child. She is an orphan. No, gentlemen, I will not deceive you, she is *not* an orphan. Worse than that. There comes another day of agony. She knows that her father lives. But who is he, where is he? Alas, I cannot tell you. Through the scenes of this painful history he flits here and there, a lunatic! If he seeks his daughter, it is the purposeless search of a lunatic, as one who wanders bereft of reason, crying, where is my child? Laura seeks her father. In vain! Just as she is about to find him, again and again he disappears, he is gone, he vanishes.

"But this is only the prologue to the tragedy. Bear with with me while I relate it. (Mr. Braham takes out his handkerchief, unfolds it slowly, crushes it in his nervous hand, and throws it on the table). Laura grew up in her humble southern home, a beautiful creature, the joy of the house, the pride of the neighborhood, the loveliest flower in all the sunny south. She might yet have been happy; she was happy. But the destroyer came into this paradise. He plucked the sweetest bud that grew there, and having enjoyed its odor, trampled it in the mire beneath his feet. George Selby, the deceased, a handsome, accomplished Confederate Colonel, was this human fiend. He deceived her with a mock marriage; after some months he brutally abandoned her, and spurned her as if she were a contemptible thing; all the time he had a wife in New Orleans. Laura was crushed. For weeks, as I shall show you by the testimony of her adopted mother and brother, she hovered over death in delirium. Gentlemen, did she ever emerge from this delirium? I shall show you that when she recovered her health, her mind was changed, she was not what she had been. You can judge yourselves whether the tottering reason ever recovered its throne.

"Years pass. She is in Washington, apparently the happy favorite of a brilliant society. Her family have become enormously rich by one of those sudden turns in fortune that the inhabitants of America are familiar with—the discovery of immense mineral wealth in some wild lands owned by them. She is engaged in a vast philanthropic scheme for the benefit of the poor, by the use of this wealth. But, alas, even here and now, the same relentless fate pursued her. The villain Selby appears again upon the scene, as if on purpose to complete the ruin of her life. He appeared to taunt her with her dishonor, he threatened exposure if she did not become again the mistress of his passion. Gentlemen, do you wonder if this woman, thus pursued, lost her reason, was beside herself with fear, and that her wrongs preyed upon her mind until she was no longer responsible for her acts? I turn away my head as one who would not willingly look even upon the just vengeance of Heaven. (Mr. Braham paused as if overcome by his emotions. Mrs. Hawkins and Washington were in tears, as were many of the spectators also. The jury looked scared.)

"Gentlemen, in this condition of affairs it needed but a spark—I do not say a suggestion, I do not say a hint—from this butterfly Brierly, this rejected rival, to cause the explosion. I make no charges, but if this woman was in her right mind when she fled from Washington and reached this city in company with Brierly, then I do not know what insanity is."

When Mr. Braham sat down, he felt that he had the jury with him. A burst of applause followed, which the officer promptly suppressed. Laura, with tears in her eyes, turned a grateful look upon her counsel. All the women among the spectators saw the tears and wept also. They thought as they also looked at Mr. Braham, how handsome he is!

Mrs. Hawkins took the stand. She was somewhat confused to be the target of so many eyes, but her honest and good face at once told in Laura's favor.

"Mrs. Hawkins," said Mr. Braham, "will you be kind enough to state the circumstances of your finding Laura?"

"I object," said Mr. McFlinn, rising to his feet. "This has nothing whatever to do with the case, your honor. I am surprised at it, even after the extraordinary speech of my learned friend."

"How do you propose to connect it, Mr. Braham?" asked the judge.

"If it please the court," said Mr. Braham, rising impressively, "your Honor has permitted the prosecution, and I have submitted without a word, to go into the most extraordinary testimony to establish a motive. Are we to be shut out from showing that the motive attributed to us could not by reason of certain mental conditions exist? I purpose, may it please your Honor, to show the cause and the origin of an aberration of mind, to follow it up with other like evidence, connecting it with the very moment of the homicide, showing a condition of the intellect of the prisoner that precludes responsibility."

"The State must insist upon its objections," said the District Attorney. "The purpose evidently is to open the door to a mass of irrelevant testimony, the object of which is to produce an effect upon the jury your Honor well understands."

"Perhaps," suggested the judge, "the court ought to hear the testimony, and exclude it afterwards, if it is irrelevant."

"Will your honor hear argument on that?"

"Certainly."

And argument his honor did hear, or pretend to, for two whole days, from all the counsel in turn, in the course of which the lawyers read contradictory decisions enough to perfectly establish both sides, from volume after volume, whole libraries in fact, until no mortal man could say what the rules were. The question of insanity in all its legal aspects was of course drawn into the discussion, and its application affirmed and denied. The case was felt to turn upon the admission or rejection of this evidence. It was a sort of test trial of strength between the lawyers. At the end the judge decided to admit the testimony, as the judge usually does in such cases, after a sufficient waste of time in what are called arguments.

Mrs. Hawkins was allowed to go on.

Chapter LVI

—Voyre mais (demandoit Trinquamelle) mon amy, comment procedez vous en action criminelle, la partie coupable prinse *flagrante crimine?*—Comme vous aultres Messieurs (respondit Bridoye)—

"Hag eunn drâ-bennâg hoc'h eûz-hu da lavaroud évid hé wennidigez?"

MRS. HAWKINS slowly and conscientiously, as if every detail of her family history was important, told the story of the steamboat explosion, of the finding and adoption of Laura. Silas, that is Mr. Hawkins, and she always loved Laura as if she had been their own child.

She then narrated the circumstances of Laura's supposed marriage, her abandonment and long illness, in a manner that touched all hearts. Laura had been a different woman since then.

Cross-examined. At the time of first finding Laura on the steamboat, did she notice that Laura's mind was at all deranged? She couldn't say that she did. After the recovery of Laura from her long illness, did Mrs. Hawkins think there were any signs of insanity about her? Witness confessed that she did not think of it *then*.

Re-Direct examination. "But she was different after that?"

"O, yes, sir."

Washington Hawkins corroborated his mother's testimony as to Laura's connection with Col. Selby. He was at Harding during the time of her living there with him. After Col. Selby's desertion she was almost dead, never appeared to know anything rightly for weeks. He added that he never saw such a scoundrel as Selby. (Checked by District attorney.) Had he noticed any change in Laura after her illness? Oh, yes. Whenever any allusion was made that might recall Selby to mind, she looked awful—as if she could kill him.

"You mean," said Mr. Braham, "that there was an unnatural, insane gleam in her eyes?"

"Yes, certainly," said Washington in confusion.

All this was objected to by the district attorney, but it was got before the jury, and Mr. Braham did not care how much it was ruled out after that.

Eschol Sellers was the next witness called. The Colonel made his way to the stand with majestic, yet bland deliberation. Having taken the oath and kissed the Bible with a smack intended to show his great respect for that book, he bowed to his Honor with dignity, to the jury with familiarity, and then turned to the lawyers and stood in an attitude of superior attention.

"Mr. Sellers, I believe?" began Mr. Braham.

"Eschol Sellers, Missouri," was the courteous acknowledgement that the lawyer was correct.

"Mr. Sellers, you know the parties here, you are a friend of the family?"

"Know them all, from infancy, sir. It was me, sir, that induced Silas Hawkins, Judge Hawkins, to come to Missouri, and make his fortune. It was by my advice and in company with me, sir, that he went into the operation of—"

"Yes, yes. Mr. Sellers, did you know a Major Lackland?"

"Knew him well, sir, knew him and honored him, sir. He was one of the most remarkable men of our country, sir. A member of congress. He was often at my mansion sir, for weeks. He used to say to me, 'Col. Sellers, if you would go into politics, if I had you for a colleague, we should show Calhoun and Webster that the brain of the country didn't lie east of the Alleganies'. But I said—"

"Yes, yes. I believe Major Lackland is not living, Colonel?"

There was an almost imperceptible sense of pleasure betrayed in the Colonel's face at this prompt acknowledgment of his title.

"Bless you, no. Died years ago, a miserable death, sir, a ruined man, a poor sot. He was suspected of selling his vote in Congress, and probably he did; the disgrace killed him, he was an outcast, sir, loathed by himself and by his constituents. And I think, sir—"

The Judge. "You will confine yourself, Col. Sellers, to the questions of the counsel."

"Of course, your honor. This," continued the Colonel in confidential explanation, "was twenty years ago. I shouldn't have thought of referring to such a trifling circumstance *now*. If I remember rightly, sir"—

A bundle of letters was here handed to the witness.

"Do you recognize that hand-writing?"

"As if it was my own, sir. It's Major Lackland's. I was knowing to these letters when Judge Hawkins received them. [The Colonel's memory was a little at fault here. Mr. Hawkins had never gone into details with him on this subject.] He used to show them to me, and say, 'Col, Sellers you've a mind to untangle this sort of thing.' Lord, how everything comes back to me. Laura was a little thing then. The Judge and I were just laying our plans to buy the Pilot Knob, and—"

"Colonel, one moment. Your Honor, we put these letters in evidence."

The letters were a portion of the correspondence of Major Lackland with Silas Hawkins; parts of them were missing and important letters were referred to that were not here. They related, as the reader knows, to Laura's father. Lackland had come upon the track of a man who was searching for a lost child in a Mississippi steamboat explosion years before. The man was lame in one leg, and appeared to be flitting from place to place. It seemed that Major Lackland got so close track of him that he was able to describe his personal appearance and learn his name. But the letter containing these particulars was lost. Once he heard of him at a hotel in Washington; but the man departed, leaving an empty trunk, the day before the major went there. There was something very mysterious in all his movements.

Col. Sellers, continuing his testimony, said that he saw this lost letter, but could not now recall the name. Search for the supposed father had been continued by Lackland, Hawkins and himself for several years, but Laura was not informed of it till after the death of Hawkins, for fear of raising false hopes in her mind.

Here the District Attorney arose and said,

"Your Honor, I must positively object to letting the witness wander off into all these irrelevant details."

Mr. Braham. "I submit, your Honor, that we cannot be interrupted in this manner. We have suffered the state to have full swing. Now here is a witness, who has known the prisoner from infancy, and is competent to testify upon the one point vital to her safety. Evidently he is a gentleman of character, and his knowledge of the case cannot be shut out without increasing the aspect of persecution which the State's attitude towards the prisoner already has assumed."

The wrangle continued, waxing hotter and hotter. The Colonel seeing the attention of the counsel and Court entirely withdrawn from him, thought he perceived here his opportunity. Turning and beaming upon the jury, he began simply to talk, but as the grandeur of his position grew upon him—his talk broadened unconsciously into an oratorial vein.

"You see how she was situated, gentlemen; poor child, it might have broken her heart to let her mind get to running on such a thing as that. You see, from what we could make out her father was lame in the left leg and had a deep scar on his left forehead. And so ever since the day she found out she *had* another father, she never could run across a lame stranger without being taken all over with a shiver, and almost fainting where she stood. And the next minute she would go right after that man. Once she stumbled on a stranger with a game leg, and she was the most grateful thing in this world—but it was the wrong leg, and it was days and days before she could leave her bed. Once she found a man with a scar on his forehead, and she was just going to throw herself into his arms, but he stepped out just then, and there wasn't anything the matter with his legs. Time and time again, gentlemen of the jury, has this poor suffering orphan flung herself on her knees with all her heart's gratitude in her eyes before some scarred and crippled veteran, but always, always to be disappointed, always to be plunged into new despair—if his legs were right his scar was wrong, if his scar was right his legs were wrong. Never could find a man that would fill the bill. Gentlemen of the jury, you have hearts, you have feelings, you have warm human sympathies, you can feel for this poor suffering child. Gentlemen of the jury, if I had time, if I had the opportunity, if I might be permitted to go on and tell you the thousands and thousands and thousands of mutilated strangers this poor girl has started out of cover, and hunted from city to city, from state to state, from continent to continent, till she has run them down and found they wan't the ones, I know your hearts—"

By this time the Colonel had become so warmed up, that his voice, had reached a pitch above that of the contending counsel; the lawyers suddenly stopped, and they and the Judge turned towards the Colonel and remained for several seconds too surprised at this novel exhibition to speak. In this interval of silence, an appreciation of the situation gradually stole over the audience, and an explosion of laughter followed, in which even the Court and the bar could hardly keep from joining.

Sheriff. "Order in the Court."

The Judge. "The witness will confine his remarks to answers to questions."

The Colonel turned courteously to the Judge and said,

"Certainly, your Honor, certainly. I am not well acquainted with the forms of procedure in the courts of New York, but in the West, sir, in the West—"

The Judge. "There, there, that will do, that will do."

"You see, your Honor, there were no questions asked me, and *I* thought I would take advantage of the lull in the proceedings to explain to the jury a very significant train of—"

The Judge. "That will *do*, sir! Proceed Mr. Braham."

"Col. Sellers, have you any reason to suppose that this man is still living?"

"Every reason, sir, every reason."

"State why."

"I have never heard of his death, sir. It has never come to my knowledge. In fact, sir, as I once said to Governor—"

"Will you state to the jury what has been the effect of the knowledge of this wandering and evidently unsettled being, supposed to be her father, upon the mind of Miss Hawkins for so many years?"

Question objected to. Question ruled out.

Cross-examined. "Major Sellers, what is your occupation?"

The Colonel looked about him loftily, as if casting in his mind what would be the proper occupation of a person of such multifarious interests, and then said with dignity.

"A gentleman, sir. My father used to always say, sir"—

"Capt. Sellers, did you ever see this man, this supposed father?"

"No, sir. But upon one occasion, old Senator Thompson said to me, it's my opinion, Colonel Sellers"—

"Did you ever see any body who *had* seen him?"

"No, sir. It was reported around at one time, that"—

"That is all."

The defense then spent a day in the examination of medical experts in insanity, who testified, on the evidence heard, that sufficient causes had occurred to produce an insane mind in the prisoner. Numerous cases were cited to sustain this opinion. There was such a thing as momentary insanity, in which the person, otherwise rational to all appearances, was for the time actually bereft of reason, and not responsible for his acts. The causes of this momentary possession could often be found in the person's life. [It afterwards came out that the chief expert for the defense, was paid a thousand dollars for looking into the case.]

The prosecution consumed another day in the examination of experts refuting the notion of insanity. These causes might have produced insanity, but there was no evidence that they have produced it in this case, or that the prisoner was not at the time of the commission of the crime in full possession of her ordinary faculties.

The trial had now lasted two weeks. It required four days now for the lawyers to "sum up." These arguments of the counsel were very important to their friends, and greatly enhanced their reputation at the bar; but they have small interest to us. Mr. Braham in his closing speech surpassed himself; his effort is still remembered as the greatest in the criminal annals of New York.

Mr. Braham re-drew for the jury the picture of Laura's early life; he dwelt long upon that painful episode of the pretended marriage and the desertion. Col. Selby, he said, belonged, gentlemen, to what is called the "upper classes." It is the privilege of the "upper classes" to prey upon the sons and daughters of the people. The Hawkins family, though allied to the best blood of the South, were at the time in humble circumstances. He commented upon her parentage. Perhaps her agonized father, in his intervals of sanity, was still searching for his lost daughter. Would he one day hear that she had died a felon's death? Society had pursued her, fate had pursued her, and in a moment of delirium she had turned and defied fate and society. He dwelt upon the admission of base wrong in Col. Selby's dying statement. He drew a vivid picture of the villain at last overtaken by the vengeance of Heaven. Would the jury say that this retributive justice, inflicted by an outraged, a deluded woman, rendered irrational by the most cruel wrongs, was in the nature of a foul, premeditated murder? "Gentlemen, it is enough for me to look upon the life of this most beautiful and accomplished of her sex, blasted by the heartless villainy of man, without seeing, at the end of it, the horrible spectacle of a gibbet. Gentlemen, we are all human, we have all sinned, we all have need of mercy. But I do not ask mercy of you who are the guardians of society and of the poor waifs, its sometimes wronged victims; I ask only that justice which you and I shall need in that last dreadful hour, when death will be robbed of half its terrors if we can reflect that we have never wronged a human being. Gentlemen, the life of this lovely and once happy girl, this now stricken woman, is in your hands."

The jury were visibly affected. Half the court room was in tears. If a vote of both spectators and jury could have been taken *then*, the verdict would have been, "let her go, she has suffered enough."

But the district attorney had the closing argument. Calmly and without malice or excitement he reviewed the testimony. As the cold facts were unrolled, fear settled upon the listeners. There was no escape from the murder or its premeditation. Laura's character as a lobbyist in Washington, which had been made to appear incidentally in the evidence, was also against her. The whole body of the testimony of the defense was shown to be irrelevant, introduced only to excite sympathy, and not giving a color of probability to the absurd supposition of insanity. The attorney then dwelt upon the insecurity of life in the city, and the growing immunity with which women committed murders. Mr. McFlinn made a very able speech, convincing the reason without touching the feelings.

The Judge in his charge reviewed the testimony with great show of impartiality. He ended by saying that the verdict must be acquital or murder in the first degree. If you find that the prisoner committed a homicide, in possession of her reason and with premeditation, your verdict will be accordingly. If you find she was not in her right mind, that she was the victim of insanity, hereditary or momentary, as it has been explained, your verdict will take that into account.

As the Judge finished his charge, the spectators anxiously watched the faces of the jury. It was not a remunerative study. In the court room the general feeling was in favor of Laura, but whether this feeling extended to the jury, their stolid faces did not reveal. The public outside hoped for a conviction, as it always does; it wanted an example; the newspapers trusted the jury would have the courage to do its duty. When Laura was convicted, then the public would turn around and abuse the governor if he did not pardon her.

The jury went out. Mr. Braham preserved his serene confidence, but Laura's friends were dispirited. Washington and Col. Sellers had been obliged to go to Washington, and they had departed under the unspoken fear that the verdict would be unfavorable,—a disagreement was the best they could hope for, and money was needed. The necessity of the passage of the University bill was now imperative.

The Court waited for some time, but the jury gave no signs of coming in. Mr. Braham said it was extraordinary. The Court then took a recess for a couple of hours. Upon again coming in, word was brought that the jury had not yet agreed.

But the jury had a question. The point upon which they wanted instruction was this:—They wanted to know if Col. Sellers was related to the Hawkins family. The court then adjourned till morning.

Mr. Braham, who was in something of a pet, remarked to Mr. O'Toole that they must have been deceived—that juryman with the broken nose could read!

Chapter LVII

"Wegotogwen ga-ijiwebadogwen; gonima ta-matchi-inakamigad."

THE momentous day was at hand—a day that promised to make or mar the fortunes of the Hawkins family for all time. Washington Hawkins and Col. Sellers were both up early, for neither of them could sleep. Congress was expiring, and was passing bill after bill as if they were gasps and each likely to be its last. The University was on file for its third reading this day, and to-morrow Washington would be a millionaire and Sellers no longer impecunious; but this day, also, or at farthest the next, the jury in Laura's case would come to a decision of some kind or other—they would find her guilty, Washington secretly feared, and then the care and the trouble would all come back again and there would be wearing months of besieging judges for new trials; on this day, also, the re-election of Mr. Dilworthy to the Senate would take place. So Washington's mind was in a state of turmoil; there were more interests at stake than it could handle with serenity. He exulted when he thought of his millions; he was filled with dread when he thought of Laura. But Sellers was excited and happy. He said:

"Everything is going right, everything's going perfectly right. Pretty soon the telegrams will begin to rattle in, and then you'll see, my boy. Let the jury do what they please; what difference is it going to make? To-morrow we can send a million to New York and set the lawyers at work on the judges; bless your heart they will go before judge after judge and exhort and beseech and pray and shed tears. They always do; and they always win, too. And they will win this time. They will get a writ of habeas corpus, and a stay of proceedings, and a supersedeas, and a new trial and a nolle prosequi, and there you are! That's the routine, and it's no trick at all to a New York lawyer. That's the regular routine—everything's red tape and routine in the law, you see; it's all Greek to you, of course, but to a man who is acquainted with those things it's mere—I'll explain it to you sometime. Everything's going to glide right along easy and comfortable now. You'll see, Washington, you'll see how it will be. And then, let me think . . . . . Dilworthy will be elected to-day, and by day after to-morrow night he will be in New York ready to put in *his* shovel—and you haven't lived in Washington all this time not to know that the people who walk right by a Senator whose term is up without hardly seeing him will be down at the deepo to say 'Welcome back and God bless you, Senator, I'm glad to see you, sir!' when he comes along back re-elected, you know. Well, you see, his influence was naturally running low when he left here, but now he has got a new six-years' start, and his suggestions will simply just weigh a couple of tons a-piece day after to-morrow. Lord bless you he could rattle through that habeas corpus and supersedeas and all those things for Laura all by himself if he wanted to, when he gets back."

"I hadn't thought of that," said Washington, brightening, "but it is so. A newly-elected Senator *is* a power, I know that."

"Yes indeed he is.—Why it is just human nature. Look at me. When we first came here, I was *Mr.* Sellers, and *Major* Sellers, and *Captain* Sellers, but nobody could ever get it right, somehow; but the minute our bill went through the House, I was *Colonel* Sellers every time. And nobody could do enough for me; and whatever I said was wonderful, Sir, it was always wonderful; I never seemed to say any flat things at all. It was Colonel won't you come and dine with us; and Colonel why *don't* we ever see you at our house; and the Colonel says this; and the Colonel says that; and we know such-and-such is so-and-so, because husband heard Col. Sellers *say* so. Don't you see? Well, the Senate adjourned and left our bill high and dry, and I'll be hanged if I warn't *Old Sellers* from that day till our bill passed the House again last week. Now I'm the *Colonel* again; and if I were to eat all the dinners I am invited to, I reckon I'd wear my teeth down level with my gums in a couple of weeks."

"Well I do wonder what you will be to-morrow, Colonel, after the President signs the bill?"

"*General*, sir!—General, without a doubt. Yes, sir, to-morrow it will be General, let me congratulate you, sir; General, you've done a great work, sir;—you've done a great

work for the niggro; Gentlemen, allow me the honor to introduce my friend General Sellers, the humane friend of the
niggro. Lord bless me, you'll see the newspapers say, General
Sellers and servants arrived in the city last night and is stopping at the Fifth Avenue; and General Sellers has accepted a
reception and banquet by the Cosmopolitan Club; you'll see
the General's opinions quoted, too—and what the General
has to say about the propriety of a new trial and a habeas corpus for the unfortunate Miss Hawkins will not be without
weight in influential quarters, I can tell you."

"And I want to be the first to shake your faithful old hand
and salute you with your new honors, and I want to do it
now—General!" said Washington, suiting the action to the
word, and accompanying it with all the meaning that a cordial
grasp and eloquent eyes could give it.

The Colonel was touched; he was pleased and proud, too;
his face answered for that.

Not very long after breakfast the telegrams began to arrive.
The first was from Braham, and ran thus:

> "We feel certain that the verdict will be rendered to-
> day. Be it good or bad, let it find us ready to make the
> next move instantly, whatever it may be."

"That's the right talk," said Sellers. "That Braham's a wonderful man. He was the only man there that really understood
me; he told me so himself, afterwards."

The next telegram was from Mr. Dilworthy:

> "I have not only brought over the Great Invincible,
> but through him a dozen more of the opposition. Shall
> be re-elected to-day by an overwhelming majority."

"Good again!" said the Colonel. "That man's talent for organization is something marvelous. He wanted me to go out
there and engineer that thing, but I said, No, Dilworthy, I
must be on hand here, both on Laura's account and the
bill's—but you've no trifling genius for organization yourself,
said I—and I was right. You go ahead, said I—you can fix it—
and so he has. But I claim no credit for that—if I stiffened up
his back-bone a little, I simply put him in the way to make his

fight—didn't make it myself. He has captured Noble—I consider that a splendid piece of diplomacy—Splendid, sir!"

By and by came another dispatch from New York:

"Jury still out. Laura calm and firm as a statue. The report that the jury have brought her in guilty is false and premature."

"Premature!" gasped Washington, turning white. "Then they all expect that sort of a verdict, when it comes."

And so did he; but he had not had courage enough to put it into words. He had been preparing himself for the worst, but after all his preparation the bare suggestion of the possibility of such a verdict struck him cold as death.

The friends grew impatient, now; the telegrams did not come fast enough; even the lightning could not keep up with their anxieties. They walked the floor talking disjointedly and listening for the door-bell. Telegram after telegram came. Still no result. By and by there was one which contained a single line:

"Court now coming in after brief recess to hear verdict. Jury ready."

"Oh, I wish they would finish!" said Washington. "This suspense is killing me by inches!"

Then came another telegram:

"Another hitch somewhere. Jury want a little more time and further instructions."

"Well, well, well, this *is* trying," said the Colonel. And after a pause, "No dispatch from Dilworthy for two hours, now. Even a dispatch from him would be better than nothing, just to vary this thing."

They waited twenty minutes. It seemed twenty hours.

"Come!" said Washington. "I can't wait for the telegraph boy to come all the way up here. Let's go down to Newspaper Row—meet him on the way."

While they were passing along the Avenue, they saw some one putting up a great display-sheet on the bulletin board of a newspaper office, and an eager crowd of men was collecting about the place. Washington and the Colonel ran to the spot and read this:

> "Tremendous Sensation! Startling news from Saint's Rest! On first ballot for U.S. Senator, when voting was about to begin, Mr. Noble rose in his place and drew forth a package, walked forward and laid it on the Speaker's desk, saying, 'This contains $7,000 in bank bills and was given me by Senator Dilworthy in his bed-chamber at midnight last night to buy my vote for him—I wish the Speaker to count the money and retain it to pay the expense of prosecuting this infamous traitor for bribery.' The whole legislature was stricken speechless with dismay and astonishment. Noble further said that there were fifty members present with money in their pockets, placed there by Dilworthy to buy their votes. Amidst unparalleled excitement the ballot was now taken, and J. W. Smith elected U.S. Senator; Dilworthy receiving not one vote! *Noble promises damaging exposures concerning Dilworthy and certain measures of his now pending in Congress.*

"Good heavens and earth!" exclaimed the Colonel.

"To the Capitol!" said Washington. "Fly!"

And they did fly. Long before they got there the newsboys were running ahead of them with Extras, hot from the press, announcing the astounding news.

Arrived in the gallery of the Senate, the friends saw a curious spectacle—every Senator held an Extra in his hand and looked as interested as if it contained news of the destruction of the earth. Not a single member was paying the least attention to the business of the hour.

The Secretary, in a loud voice, was just beginning to read the title of a bill:

"House-Bill-No.-4,231,-An-Act-to-Found-and-Incorporate-the-Knobs-Industrial-University!-Read-first-and-second-time—considered-in-committee-of-the-whole-ordered-engrossed-and-passed-to-third-reading-and-final-passage!"

The President—"Third reading of the *bill!*"

The two friends shook in their shoes. Senators threw down their extras and snatched a word or two with each other in whispers. Then the gavel rapped to command silence while the names were called on the ayes and nays. Washington grew paler and paler, weaker and weaker while the lagging list progressed; and when it was finished, his head fell helplessly forward on his arms. The fight was fought, the long struggle was over, and he was a pauper. Not a man had voted for the bill!

Col. Sellers was bewildered and well nigh paralyzed, himself. But no man could long consider his own troubles in the presence of such suffering as Washington's. He got him up and supported him—almost carried him indeed—out of the building and into a carriage. All the way home Washington lay with his face against the Colonel's shoulder and merely groaned and wept. The Colonel tried as well as he could under the dreary circumstances to hearten him a little, but it was of no use. Washington was past all hope of cheer, now. He only said:

"Oh, it is all over—it is all over for good, Colonel. We must beg our bread, now. We never can get up again. It was our last chance, and it is gone. They will hang Laura! My God they will hang her! Nothing can save the poor girl now. Oh, I wish with all my soul they would hang me instead!"

Arrived at home, Washington fell into a chair and buried his face in his hands and gave full way to his misery. The Colonel did not know where to turn nor what to do. The servant maid knocked at the door and passed in a telegram, saying it had come while they were gone.

The Colonel tore it open and read with the voice of a man-of-war's broadside:

"VERDICT OF JURY, NOT GUILTY AND LAURA IS FREE!"

Chapter LVIII

分 不 白 皂

Papel y tinta y poco justicia.

THE COURT ROOM was packed on the morning on which the verdict of the jury was expected, as it had been every day of the trial, and by the same spectators, who had followed its progress with such intense interest.

There is a delicious moment of excitement which the frequenter of trials well knows, and which he would not miss for the world. It is that instant when the foreman of the jury stands up to give the verdict, and before he has opened his fateful lips.

The court assembled and waited. It was an obstinate jury. It even had another question—this intelligent jury—to ask the judge this morning.

The question was this:—"Were the doctors clear that the deceased had no disease which might soon have carried him off, if he had not been shot?" There was evidently one juryman who didn't want to waste life, and was willing to strike a general average, as the jury always does in a civil case, deciding not according to the evidence but reaching the verdict by some occult mental process.

During the delay the spectators exhibited unexampled patience, finding amusement and relief in the slightest movements of the court, the prisoner and the lawyers. Mr. Braham divided with Laura the attention of the house. Bets were made by the sheriff's deputies on the verdict, with large odds in favor of a disagreement.

It was afternoon when it was announced that the jury was coming in. The reporters took their places and were all attention; the judge and lawyers were in their seats; the crowd swayed and pushed in eager expectancy, as the jury walked in and stood up in silence.

Judge. "Gentlemen, have you agreed upon your verdict?"
Foreman. "We have."
Judge. "What is it?"

Foreman. "NOT GUILTY."

A shout went up from the entire room and a tumult of cheering which the court in vain attempted to quell. For a few moments all order was lost. The spectators crowded within the bar and surrounded Laura who, calmer than anyone else, was supporting her aged mother, who had almost fainted from excess of joy.

And now occurred one of those beautiful incidents which no fiction-writer would dare to imagine, a scene of touching pathos, creditable to our fallen humanity. In the eyes of the women of the audience Mr. Braham was the hero of the occasion; he had saved the life of the prisoner; and besides he was such a handsome man. The women could not restrain their long pent-up emotions. They threw themselves upon Mr. Braham in a transport of gratitude; they kissed him again and again, the young as well as the advanced in years, the married as well as the ardent single women; they improved the opportunity with a touching self-sacrifice; in the words of a newspaper of the day they "lavished him with kisses." It was something sweet to do; and it would be sweet for a woman to remember in after years, that she had kissed Braham! Mr. Braham himself received these fond assaults with the gallantry of his nation, enduring the ugly, and heartily paying back beauty in its own coin.

This beautiful scene is still known in New York as "the kissing of Braham."

When the tumult of congratulation had a little spent itself, and order was restored, Judge O'Shaunnessy said that it now became his duty to provide for the proper custody and treatment of the acquitted. The verdict of the jury having left no doubt that the woman was of an unsound mind, with a kind of insanity dangerous to the safety of the community, she could not be permitted to go at large. "In accordance with the directions of the law in such cases," said the Judge, "and in obedience to the dictates of a wise humanity, I hereby commit Laura Hawkins to the care of the Superintendent of the State Hospital for Insane Criminals, to be held in confinement until the State Commissioners on Insanity shall order her discharge. Mr. Sheriff, you will attend at once to the execution of this decree."

Laura was overwhelmed and terror-stricken. She had expected to walk forth in freedom in a few moments. The revulsion was terrible. Her mother appeared like one shaken with an ague fit. Laura insane! And about to be locked up with madmen! She had never contemplated this. Mr. Braham said he should move at once for a writ of *habeas corpus*.

But the judge could not do less than his duty, the law must have its way. As in the stupor of a sudden calamity, and not fully comprehending it, Mrs. Hawkins saw Laura led away by the officer.

With little space for thought she was rapidly driven to the railway station, and conveyed to the Hospital for Lunatic-Criminals. It was only when she was within this vast and grim abode of madness that she realized the horror of her situation. It was only when she was received by the kind physician and read pity in his eyes, and saw his look of hopeless incredulity when she attempted to tell him that she was not insane; it was only when she passed through the ward to which she was consigned and saw the horrible creatures, the victims of a double calamity, whose dreadful faces she was hereafter to see daily, and was locked into the small, bare room that was to be her home, that all her fortitude forsook her. She sank upon the bed, as soon as she was left alone—she had been searched by the matron—and tried to think. But her brain was in a whirl. She recalled Braham's speech, she recalled the testimony regarding her lunacy. She wondered if she *were* not mad; she felt that she soon should be among these loathsome creatures. Better almost to have died, than to slowly go mad in this confinement.

—We beg the reader's pardon. This is not history, which has just been written. It is really what would have occurred if this were a novel. If this were a work of fiction, we should not dare to dispose of Laura otherwise. True art and any attention to dramatic proprieties required it. The novelist who would turn loose upon society an insane murderess could not escape condemnation. Besides, the safety of society, the decencies of criminal procedure, what we call our modern civilization, all would demand that Laura should be disposed of in the manner we have described. Foreigners, who read this sad story, will be unable to understand any other termination of it.

But this is history and not fiction. There is no such law or custom as that to which his Honor is supposed to have referred; Judge O'Shaunnessy would not probably pay any attention to it if there were. There is no Hospital for Insane Criminals; there is no State commission of lunacy. What actually occurred when the tumult in the court room had subsided the sagacious reader will now learn.

Laura left the court room, accompanied by her mother and other friends, amid the congratulations of those assembled, and was cheered as she entered a carriage, and drove away. How sweet was the sunlight, how exhilarating the sense of freedom! Were not these following cheers the expression of popular approval and affection? Was she not the heroine of the hour?

It was with a feeling of triumph that Laura reached her hotel, a scornful feeling of victory over society with its own weapons.

Mrs. Hawkins shared not at all in this feeling; she was broken with the disgrace and the long anxiety.

"Thank God, Laura," she said, "it is over. Now we will go away from this hateful city. Let us go home at once."

"Mother," replied Laura, speaking with some tenderness, "I cannot go with you. There, don't cry, I cannot go back to that life."

Mrs. Hawkins was sobbing. This was more cruel than anything else, for she had a dim notion of what it would be to leave Laura to herself.

"No, mother, you have been everything to me. You know how dearly I love you. But I cannot go back."

A boy brought in a telegraphic despatch. Laura took it and read:

"The bill is lost. Dilworthy is ruined.
                              (Signed)   WASHINGTON."

For a moment the words swam before her eyes. The next her eyes flashed fire as she handed the dispatch to her mother and bitterly said,

"The world is against me. Well, let it be, let it. I am against it."

"This is a cruel disappointment," said Mrs. Hawkins, to

whom one grief more or less did not much matter now, "to you and Washington; but we must humbly bear it."

"Bear it," replied Laura scornfully, "I've all my life borne it, and fate has thwarted me at every step."

A servant came to the door to say that there was a gentleman below who wished to speak with Miss Hawkins. "J. Adolphe Griller" was the name Laura read on the card. "I do not know such a person. He probably comes from Washington. Send him up."

Mr. Griller entered. He was a small man, slovenly in dress, his tone confidential, his manner wholly void of animation, all his features below the forehead protruding—particularly the apple of his throat—hair without a kink in it, a hand with no grip, a meek, hang-dog countenance. He was a falsehood done in flesh and blood; for while every visible sign about him proclaimed him a poor, witless, useless weakling, the truth was that he had the brains to plan great enterprises and the pluck to carry them through. That was his reputation, and it was a deserved one.

He softly said:

"I called to see you on business, Miss Hawkins. You have my card?"

Laura bowed.

Mr. Griller continued to purr, as softly as before:

"I will proceed to business. I am a business man. I am a lecture-agent, Miss Hawkins, and as soon as I saw that you were acquitted, it occurred to me that an early interview would be mutually beneficial."

"I don't understand you, sir," said Laura coldly.

"No? You see, Miss Hawkins, this is your opportunity. If you will enter the lecture field under good auspices, you will carry everything before you."

"But, sir, I never lectured, I haven't any lecture, I don't know anything about it."

"Ah, madam, that makes no difference—no real difference. It is not necessary to be able to lecture in order to go into the lecture field. If one's name is celebrated all over the land, especially, and if she is also beautiful, she is certain to draw large audiences."

"But what should I lecture about?" asked Laura, beginning in spite of herself to be a little interested as well as amused.

"Oh, why, woman—something about woman, I should say; the marriage relation, woman's fate, anything of that sort. Call it The Revelations of a Woman's Life; now, there's a good title. I wouldn't want any better title than that. I'm prepared to make you an offer, Miss Hawkins, a liberal offer,— twelve thousand dollars for thirty nights."

Laura thought. She hesitated. Why not? It would give her employment, money. She must do something:

"I will think of it, and let you know soon. But still, there is very little likelihood that I—however, we will not discuss it further now."

"Remember, that the sooner we get to work the better, Miss Hawkins, public curiosity is so fickle. Good day, madam."

The close of the trial released Mr. Harry Brierly and left him free to depart upon his long talked of Pacific-coast mission. He was very mysterious about it, even to Philip.

"It's confidential, old boy," he said, "a little scheme we have hatched up. I don't mind telling you that it's a good deal bigger thing than that in Missouri, and a sure thing. I wouldn't take a half a million just for my share. And it will open something for you, Phil. You will hear from me."

Philip did hear from Harry a few months afterward. Everything promised splendidly, but there was a little delay. Could Phil let him have a hundred, say for ninety days?

Philip himself hastened to Philadelphia, and, as soon as the spring opened, to the mine at Ilium, and began transforming the loan he had received from 'Squire Montague into laborers' wages. He was haunted with many anxieties; in the first place, Ruth was overtaxing her strength in her hospital labors, and Philip felt as if he must move heaven and earth to save her from such toil and suffering. His increased pecuniary obligation oppressed him. It seemed to him also that he had been one cause of the misfortune to the Bolton family, and that he was dragging into loss and ruin everybody who associated with him. He worked on day after day and week after week, with a feverish anxiety.

It would be wicked, thought Philip, and impious, to pray for luck; he felt that perhaps he ought not to ask a blessing upon the sort of labor that was only a venture; but yet in that daily petition, which this very faulty and not very consistent young Christian gentleman put up, he prayed earnestly enough for Ruth and for the Boltons and for those whom he loved and who trusted in him, and that his life might not be a misfortune to them and a failure to himself.

Since this young fellow went out into the world from his New England home, he had done some things that he would rather his mother should not know, things maybe that he would shrink from telling Ruth. At a certain green age young gentlemen are sometimes afraid of being called milksops, and Philip's associates had not always been the most select, such as these historians would have chosen for him, or whom at a later period he would have chosen for himself. It seemed inexplicable, for instance, that his life should have been thrown so much with his college acquaintance, Henry Brierly.

Yet, this was true of Philip, that in whatever company he had been he had never been ashamed to stand up for the principles he learned from his mother, and neither raillery nor looks of wonder turned him from that daily habit he learned at his mother's knees. Even flippant Harry respected this, and perhaps it was one of the reasons why Harry and all who knew Philip trusted him implicitly. And yet it must be confessed that Philip did not convey the impression to the world of a very serious young man, or of a man who might not rather easily fall into temptation. One looking for a real hero would have to go elsewhere.

The parting between Laura and her mother was exceedingly painful to both. It was as if two friends parted on a wide plain, the one to journey towards the setting and the other towards the rising sun, each comprehending that every step henceforth must separate their lives wider and wider.

Chapter LIX

Ebok imana ebok ofut idibi.
Epik Proverb.

‘Ο καρκίνος ὧδ εφα
Χαλ ᾷ τὸν ὄφιν λαβών·
Εὐθὺν χρὴ τον ἑταῖρον ἔμμεν,
Καὶ μὴ σκολιὰ φρονεῖν.

Mishittœnaeog nœwaog
ayeuuhkone neen,
Nashpe nuskesukqunnonut
ho, ho, nunnaumunun.

WHEN Mr. Noble's bombshell fell in Senator Dilworthy's camp, the statesman was disconcerted for a moment.— For a moment; that was all. The next moment he was calmly up and doing. From the centre of our country to its circumference, nothing was talked of but Mr. Noble's terrible revelation, and the people were furious. Mind, they were not furious because bribery was uncommon in our public life, but merely because here was *another* case. Perhaps it did not occur to the nation of good and worthy people that while they continued to sit comfortably at home and leave the true source of our political power (the "primaries,") in the hands of saloon-keepers, dog-fanciers and hod-carriers, they could go on expecting "another" case of this kind, and even dozens and hundreds of them, and never be disappointed. However, they may have thought that to sit at home and grumble would some day right the evil.

Yes, the nation was excited, but Senator Dilworthy was calm—what was left of him after the explosion of the shell. Calm, and up and doing. What did he do first? What would you do first, after you had tomahawked your mother at the breakfast table for putting too much sugar in your coffee? You would "ask for a suspension of public opinion." That is what Senator Dilworthy did. It is the custom. He got the usual amount of suspension. Far and wide he was called a thief, a briber, a promoter of steamship subsidies, railway swindles,

robberies of the government in all possible forms and fashions. Newspapers and everybody else called him a pious
hypocrite, a sleek, oily fraud, a reptile who manipulated temperance movements, prayer meetings, Sunday schools, public
charities, missionary enterprises, all for his private benefit.
And as these charges were backed up by what seemed to be
good and sufficient evidence, they were believed with national
unanimity.

Then Mr. Dilworthy made another move. He moved instantly to Washington and "demanded an investigation."
Even this could not pass without comment. Many papers used
language to this effect:

"Senator Dilworthy's remains have demanded an investigation.
This sounds fine and bold and innocent; but when we reflect that
they demand it at the hands of the Senate of the United States, it
simply becomes matter for derision. One might as well set the
gentlemen detained in the public prisons to trying each other.
This investigation is likely to be like all other Senatorial 'investigations'—amusing but not useful. Query. Why does the Senate still
stick to this pompous word, 'Investigation?' One does not blindfold
one's self in order to investigate an object."

Mr. Dilworthy appeared in his place in the Senate and offered a resolution appointing a committee to investigate his
case. It carried, of course, and the committee was appointed.
Straightway the newspapers said:

"Under the guise of appointing a committee to investigate the late
Mr. Dilworthy, the Senate yesterday appointed a committee to *investigate his accuser, Mr. Noble*. This is the exact spirit and meaning of the
resolution, and the committee cannot try anybody but Mr. Noble
without overstepping its authority. That Mr. Dilworthy had the ef-
frontery to offer such a resolution will surprise no one; and that the
Senate could entertain it without blushing and pass it without shame
will surprise no one. We are now reminded of a note which we have
received from the notorious burglar Murphy, in which he finds fault
with a statement of ours to the effect that he had served one term in
the penitentiary and also one in the U.S. Senate. He says, 'The latter
statement is untrue and does me great injustice.' After an unconscious
sarcasm like that, further comment is unnecessary."

And yet the Senate was roused by the Dilworthy trouble.
Many speeches were made. One Senator (who was accused in

the public prints of selling his chances of re-election to his opponent for $50,000 and had not yet denied the charge) said
that, "the presence in the Capital of such a creature as this
man Noble, to testify against a brother member of their body,
was an insult to the Senate."

Another Senator said, "Let the investigation go on; and let
it make an example of this man Noble; let it teach him and
men like him that they could not attack the reputation of a
United States Senator with impunity."

Another said he was glad the investigation was to be had,
"for it was high time that the Senate should crush some cur
like this man Noble, and thus show his kind that it was able
and resolved to uphold its ancient dignity."

A by-stander laughed, at this finely delivered peroration,
and said,

"Why, this is the Senator who franked his baggage home
through the mails last week—registered, at that. However,
perhaps he was merely engaged in 'upholding the ancient dignity of the Senate,' then."

"No, the modern dignity of it," said another by-stander.
"It don't resemble its ancient dignity, but it fits its modern
style like a glove."

There being no law against making offensive remarks about
U.S. Senators, this conversation, and others like it, continued
without let or hindrance. But our business is with the investi-
gating committee.

Mr. Noble appeared before the Committee of the Senate,
and testified to the following effect:

He said that he was a member of the State legislature of the
Happy-Land-of-Canaan; that on the —— day of —— he assembled himself together at the city of Saint's Rest, the capital of the State, along with his brother legislators; that he was
known to be a political enemy of Mr. Dilworthy and bitterly
opposed to his re-election; that Mr. Dilworthy came to Saint's
Rest and was reported to be buying pledges of votes with
money; that the said Dilworthy sent for him to come to his
room in the hotel at night, and he went; was introduced to
Mr. Dilworthy; called two or three times afterward at Dilworthy's request—usually after midnight; Mr. Dilworthy
urged him to vote for him; Noble declined; Dilworthy argued;

said he was bound to be elected, and could then ruin him (Noble) if he voted no; said he had every railway and every public office and stronghold of political power in the State under his thumb, and could set up or pull down any man he chose; gave instances showing where and how he had used this power; if Noble would vote for him he would make him a Representative in Congress; Noble still declined to vote, and said he did not believe Dilworthy was going to be elected; Dilworthy showed a list of men who would vote for him—a majority of the legislature; gave further proofs of his power by telling Noble everything the opposing party had done or said in secret caucus; claimed that his spies reported everything to him, and that——

Here a member of the Committee objected that this evidence was irrelevant and also in opposition to the spirit of the Committee's instructions, because if these things reflected upon any one it was upon Mr. Dilworthy. The chairman said, let the person proceed with his statement—the Committee could exclude evidence that did not bear upon the case.

Mr. Noble continued. He said that his party would cast him out if he voted for Mr. Dilworthy; Dilworthy said that that would inure to his benefit because he would then be a recognized friend of his (Dilworthy's) and he could consistently exalt him politically and make his fortune; Noble said he was poor, and it was hard to tempt him so; Dilworthy said he would fix that; he said, Tell me what you want, and say you will vote for me;" Noble could not say; Dilworthy said "I will give you $5,000—"

A Committee man said, impatiently, that this stuff was all outside the case, and valuable time was being wasted; this was all a plain reflection upon a brother Senator. The Chairman said it was the quickest way to proceed, and the evidence need have no weight.

Mr. Noble continued. He said he told Dilworthy that $5,000 was not much to pay for a man's honor, character and everything that was worth having; Dilworthy said he was surprised; he considered $5,000 a fortune for some men; asked what Noble's figure was; Noble said he could not think $10,000 too little; Dilworthy said it was a great deal too much; he would not do it for any other man, but he had conceived a liking for Noble, and where he liked a man his heart yearned to help him; he was aware that Noble was poor, and had a family to support, and that he bore an unblemished reputation at home; for such a man and such a man's influence he could do much, and feel that to help such a man would be an act that would have its reward; the struggles of the poor always touched him; he believed that Noble would make a good use of this money and that it would cheer many a sad heart and needy home; he would give the $10,000; all he desired in return was that when the balloting began, Noble should cast his vote for him and should explain to the legislature that upon looking into the charges against Mr. Dilworthy of bribery, corruption, and forwarding stealing measures in Congress he had found them to be base calumnies upon a man whose motives were pure and whose character was stainless; he then took from his pocket $2,000 in bank bills and handed them to Noble, and got another package containing $5,000 out of his trunk and gave to him also. He—

A Committee man jumped up, and said:

"*At last*, Mr. Chairman, this shameless person has arrived at the point. This is sufficient and conclusive. By his own confession he has received a bribe, and did it deliberately. This is a grave offense, and cannot be passed over in silence, sir. By the terms of our instructions we can now proceed to mete out to him such punishment as is meet for one who has maliciously brought disrespect upon a Senator of the United States. We have no need to hear the rest of his evidence."

The Chairman said it would be better and more regular to proceed with the investigation according to the usual forms. A note would be made of Mr. Noble's admission.

Mr. Noble continued. He said that it was now far past midnight; that he took his leave and went straight to certain legislators, told them everything, made them count the money, and also told them of the exposure he would make in joint convention; he made that exposure, as all the world knew. The rest of the $10,000 was to be paid the day after Dilworthy was elected.

Senator Dilworthy was now asked to take the stand and tell what he knew about the man Noble. The Senator wiped his mouth with his handkerchief, adjusted his white cravat, and said that but for the fact that public morality required an example, for the warning of future Nobles, he would beg that in Christian charity this poor misguided creature might be forgiven and set free. He said that it was but too evident that this person had approached him in the hope of obtaining a bribe; he had intruded himself time and again, and always with moving stories of his poverty. Mr. Dilworthy said that his heart had bled for him—insomuch that he had several times been on the point of trying to get some one to do something for him. Some instinct had told him from the beginning that this was a bad man, an evil-minded man, but his inexperience of such had blinded him to his real motives, and hence he had never dreamed that his object was to undermine the purity of a United States Senator. He regretted that it was plain, now, that such was the man's object and that punishment could not with safety to the Senate's honor be withheld. He grieved to say that one of those mysterious dispensations of an inscrutable Providence which are decreed from time to time by His wisdom and for His righteous purposes, had given this conspirator's tale a color of plausibility,—but this would soon disappear under the clear light of truth which would now be thrown upon the case.

It so happened, (said the Senator,) that about the time in question, a poor young friend of mine, living in a distant town of my State, wished to establish a bank; he asked me to lend him the necessary money; I said I had no money just then, but would try to borrow it. The day before the election a friend said to me that my election expenses must be very large—especially my hotel bills,—and offered to lend me some money. Remembering my young friend, I said I would like a few thousands now, and a few more by and by; whereupon he gave me two packages of bills said to contain $2,000 and $5,000 respectively; I did not open the packages or count the money; I did not give any note or receipt for the same; I made no memorandum of the transaction, and neither did my friend. That night this evil man Noble came troubling me again. I could not rid myself of him, though my time was very precious. He mentioned my young friend and said he was very anxious to have $7,000 now to begin his banking operations with, and could wait a while for the rest. Noble wished to get the money and take it to him. I finally gave him the two packages of bills; I took no note or receipt from him, and made no memorandum of the matter. I no more look for duplicity and deception in another man than I would look for it in myself. I never thought of this man again until I was overwhelmed the next day by learning what a shameful use he had made of the confidence I had reposed in him and the money I had entrusted to his care. This is all, gentlemen. To the absolute truth of every detail of my statement I solemnly swear, and I call Him to witness who is the Truth and the loving Father of all whose lips abhor false speaking; I pledge my honor as a Senator, that I have spoken but the truth. May God forgive this wicked man—as I do.

Mr. Noble—"Senator Dilworthy, your bank account shows that up to that day, and even on that very day, you conducted all your financial business through the medium of checks instead of bills, and so kept careful record of every moneyed transaction. Why did you deal in bank bills on this particular occasion?"

The Chairman—"The gentleman will please to remember that the Committee is conducting this investigation."

Mr. Noble—"Then will the Committee ask the question?"

The Chairman—"The Committee will—when it desires to know."

Mr. Noble—"Which will not be during this century perhaps."

The Chairman—"Another remark like that, sir, will procure you the attentions of the Sergeant-at-arms."

Mr. Noble—"D——n the Sergeant-at-arms, and the Committee too!"

Several Committeemen—"Mr. Chairman, this is contempt!"

Mr. Noble—"Contempt of whom?"

"Of the Committee! Of the Senate of the United States!"

Mr. Noble—"Then I am become the acknowledged representative of a nation. You know as well as I do that the whole nation hold as much as three-fifths of the United States Senate in entire contempt.—Three-fifths of you are Dilworthys."

The Sergeant-at-arms very soon put a quietus upon the observations of the representative of the nation, and convinced him that he was not in the over-free atmosphere of his Happy-Land-of-Canaan.

The statement of Senator Dilworthy naturally carried conviction to the minds of the committee.—It was close, logical, unanswerable; it bore many internal evidences of its truth.— For instance, it is customary in all countries for business men to loan large sums of money in bank bills instead of checks. It is customary for the lender to make no memorandum of the transaction. It is customary for the borrower to receive the money without making a memorandum of it, or giving a note or a receipt for it—because the borrower is not likely to die or forget about it. It is customary to lend nearly anybody money to start a bank with, especially if you have not the money to lend him and have to borrow it for the purpose. It is customary to carry large sums of money in bank bills about your person or in your trunk. It is customary to hand a large sum in bank bills to a man you have just been introduced to (if he asks you to do it,) to be conveyed to a distant town and delivered to another party. It is not customary to make a memorandum of this transaction; it is not customary for the conveyor to give a note or a receipt for the money; it is not customary to require that he shall get a note or a receipt from the man he is to convey it to in the distant town. It would be at least singular in you to say to the proposed conveyor, "You might be robbed; I will deposit the money in bank and send a check for it to my friend through the mail."

Very well. It being plain that Senator Dilworthy's statement was rigidly true, and this fact being strengthened by his adding to it the support of "his honor as a Senator," the Committee rendered a verdict of "Not proven that a bribe had been offered and accepted." This in a manner exonerated Noble and let him escape.

The Committee made its report to the Senate, and that body proceeded to consider its acceptance. One Senator—indeed, several Senators—objected that the Committee had failed of its duty; they had proved this man Noble guilty of nothing, they had meted out no punishment to him; if the report were accepted, he would go forth free and scathless, glorying in his crime, and it would be a tacit admission that any blackguard could insult the Senate of the United States and conspire against the sacred reputation of its members with impunity; the Senate owed it to the upholding of its ancient dignity to make an example of this man Noble—he should be crushed.

An elderly Senator got up and took another view of the case. This was a Senator of the worn-out and obsolete pattern; a man still lingering among the cobwebs of the past, and behind the spirit of the age. He said that there seemed to be a curious misunderstanding of the case. Gentlemen seemed exceedingly anxious to preserve and maintain the honor and dignity of the Senate.

Was this to be done by trying an obscure adventurer for attempting to trap a Senator into bribing him? Or would not the truer way be to find out whether the Senator was capable of *being* entrapped into so shameless an act, and then try *him*? Why, of course. *Now* the whole idea of the Senate seemed to be to shield the Senator and turn inquiry away from him. The true way to uphold the honor of the Senate was to have none but honorable men in its body. If this Senator had yielded to temptation and had offered a bribe, he was a soiled man and ought to be instantly expelled; therefore he wanted the Senator tried, and not in the usual namby-pamby way, but in good earnest. He wanted to know the truth of this matter. For himself, he believed that the guilt of Senator Dilworthy was established beyond the shadow of a doubt; and he considered that in trifling with his case and shirking it the Senate was doing a shameful and cowardly thing—a thing which suggested that in its willingness to sit longer in the company of such a man, it was acknowledging that it was itself of a kind with him and was therefore not dishonored by his presence. He desired that a rigid examination be made into Senator Dilworthy's case, and that it be continued clear into the approaching extra session if need be. There was no dodging this thing with the lame excuse of want of time.

In reply, an honorable Senator said that he thought it would be as well to drop the matter and accept the Committee's report. He said with some jocularity that the more one agitated this thing, the worse it was for the agitator. He was not able to deny that he believed Senator Dilworthy to be guilty—but what then? Was it such an extraordinary case? For his part, even allowing the Senator to be guilty, he did not think his continued presence during the few remaining days of the Session would contaminate the Senate to a dreadful degree. [This humorous sally was received with smiling admiration—notwithstanding it was not wholly new, having originated with the Massachusetts General in the House a day or two before, upon the occasion of the proposed expulsion of a member for selling his vote for money.]

The Senate recognized the fact that it could not be contaminated by sitting a few days longer with Senator Dilworthy, and so it accepted the committee's report and dropped the unimportant matter.

Mr. Dilworthy occupied his seat to the last hour of the session. He said that his people had reposed a trust in him, and it was not for him to desert them. He would remain at his post till he perished, if need be.

His voice was lifted up and his vote cast for the last time, in support of an ingenious measure contrived by the General from Massachusetts whereby the President's salary was proposed to be doubled and every Congressman paid several thousand dollars extra for work previously done, under an accepted contract, and already paid for once and receipted for.

Senator Dilworthy was offered a grand ovation by his friends at home, who said that their affection for him and their confidence in him were in no wise impaired by the persecutions that had pursued him, and that he was still good enough for them.*

*The $7,000 left by Mr. Noble with his state legislature was placed in safe keeping to await the claim of the legitimate owner. Senator Dilworthy made one little effort through his protégé the embryo banker to recover it, but there being no notes of hand or other memoranda to support the claim, it failed. The moral of which is, that when one loans money to start a bank with, one ought to take the party's written acknowledgment of the fact.

Chapter LX

ᨾᨷᨵᩣᩣ᩶ ᩓᩮᨸᩥᨾᩣᨾᩥ

"Ow holan whath ythew prowte
kynthoma ogas marowe"—

F OR some days Laura had been a free woman once more. During this time, she had experienced—first, two or three days of triumph, excitement, congratulations, a sort of sunburst of gladness, after a long night of gloom and anxiety; then two or three days of calming down, by degrees—a receding of tides, a quieting of the storm-wash to a murmurous surf-beat, a diminishing of devastating winds to a refrain that bore the spirit of a truce—days given to solitude, rest, self-communion, and the reasoning of herself into a realization of the fact that she was actually done with bolts and bars, prison horrors and impending death; then came a day whose hours filed slowly by her, each laden with some remnant, some remaining fragment of the dreadful time so lately ended—a day which, closing at last, left the past a fading shore behind her and turned her eyes toward the broad sea of the future. So speedily do we put the dead away and come back to our place in the ranks to march in the pilgrimage of life again!

And now the sun rose once more and ushered in the first day of what Laura comprehended and accepted as a new life.

The past had sunk below the horizon, and existed no more for her; she was done with it for all time. She was gazing out over the trackless expanses of the future, now, with troubled eyes. Life must be begun again—at eight and twenty years of age. And where to begin? The page was blank, and waiting for its first record; so this was indeed a momentous day.

Her thoughts drifted back, stage by stage, over her career. As far as the long highway receded over the plain of her life, it was lined with the gilded and pillared splendors of her ambition all crumbled to ruin and ivy-grown; every milestone marked a disaster; there was no green spot remaining anywhere in memory of a hope that had found its fruition; the unresponsive earth had uttered no voice of flowers in testimony that one who was blest had gone that road.

Her life had been a failure. That was plain, she said. No more of that. She would now look the future in the face; she would mark her course upon the chart of life, and follow it; follow it without swerving, through rocks and shoals, through storm and calm, to a haven of rest and peace—or, shipwreck. Let the end be what it might, she would mark her course now—to-day—and follow it.

On her table lay six or seven notes. They were from lovers; from some of the prominent names in the land; men whose devotion had survived even the grisly revealments of her character which the courts had uncurtained; men who knew her now, just as she was, and yet pleaded as for their lives for the dear privilege of calling the murderess wife.

As she read these passionate, these worshiping, these supplicating missives, the woman in her nature confessed itself; a strong yearning came upon her to lay her head upon a loyal breast and find rest from the conflict of life, solace for her griefs, the healing of love for her bruised heart.

With her forehead resting upon her hand, she sat thinking, thinking, while the unheeded moments winged their flight. It was one of those mornings in early spring when nature seems just stirring to a half consciousness out of a long, exhausting lethargy; when the first faint balmy airs go wandering about, whispering the secret of the coming change; when the abused brown grass, newly relieved of snow, seems considering whether it can be worth the trouble and worry of contriving its green raiment again only to fight the inevitable fight with the implacable winter and be vanquished and buried once more; when the sun shines out and a few birds venture forth and lift up a forgotten song; when a strange stillness and suspense pervades the waiting air. It is a time when one's spirit is subdued and sad, one knows not why; when the past seems a storm-swept desolation, life a vanity and a burden, and the future but a way to death. It is a time when one is filled with vague longings; when one dreams of flight to peaceful islands in the remote solitudes of the sea, or folds his hands and says, What is the use of struggling, and toiling and worrying any more? let us give it all up.

It was into such a mood as this that Laura had drifted from the musings which the letters of her lovers had called up. Now she lifted her head and noted with surprise how the day had wasted. She thrust the letters aside, rose up and went and stood at the window. But she was soon thinking again, and was only gazing into vacancy.

By and by she turned; her countenance had cleared; the dreamy look was gone out of her face, all indecision had vanished; the poise of her head and the firm set of her lips told that her resolution was formed. She moved toward the table with all the old dignity in her carriage, and all the old pride in her mien. She took up each letter in its turn, touched a match to it and watched it slowly consume to ashes. Then she said:

"I have landed upon a foreign shore, and burned my ships behind me. These letters were the last thing that held me in sympathy with any remnant or belonging of the old life. Henceforth that life and all that appertains to it are as dead to me and as far removed from me as if I were become a denizen of another world."

She said that love was not for her—the time that it could have satisfied her heart was gone by and could not return; the opportunity was lost, nothing could restore it. She said there could be no love without respect, and she would only despise a man who could content himself with a thing like her. Love, she said, was a woman's first necessity: love being forfeited, there was but one thing left that could give a passing zest to a wasted life, and that was fame, admiration, the applause of the multitude.

And so her resolution was taken. She would turn to that final resort of the disappointed of her sex, the lecture platform. She would array herself in fine attire, she would adorn herself with jewels, and stand in her isolated magnificence before massed audiences and enchant them with her eloquence and amaze them with her unapproachable beauty. She would move from city to city like a queen of romance, leaving marveling multitudes behind her and impatient multitudes awaiting her coming. Her life, during one hour of each day, upon the platform, would be a rapturous intoxication—and when the curtain fell, and the lights were out, and the people gone, to nestle in their homes and forget her, she would find in

sleep oblivion of her homelessness, if she could, if not she
would brave out the night in solitude and wait for the next
day's hour of ecstasy.

So, to take up life and begin again was no great evil. She
saw her way. She would be brave and strong; she would make
the best of what was left for her among the possibilities.

She sent for the lecture agent, and matters were soon
arranged.

Straightway all the papers were filled with her name, and all
the dead walls flamed with it. The papers called down impre-
cations upon her head; they reviled her without stint; they
wondered if all sense of decency was dead in this shameless
murderess, this brazen lobbyist, this heartless seducer of the
affections of weak and misguided men; they implored the
people, for the sake of their pure wives, their sinless daughters, for the sake of decency, for the sake of public morals, to
give this wretched creature such a rebuke as should be an all-
sufficient evidence to her and to such as her, that there was a
limit where the flaunting of their foul acts and opinions before the world must stop; certain of them, with a higher art,
and to her a finer cruelty, a sharper torture, uttered no abuse,
but always spoke of her in terms of mocking eulogy and iron-
ical admiration. Everybody talked about the new wonder,
canvassed the theme of her proposed discourse, and marveled
how she would handle it.

Laura's few friends wrote to her or came and talked with
her, and pleaded with her to retire while it was yet time, and
not attempt to face the gathering storm. But it was fruitless.
She was stung to the quick by the comments of the newspapers; her spirit was roused, her ambition was towering, now.
She was more determined than ever. She would show these
people what a hunted and persecuted woman could do.

The eventful night came. Laura arrived before the great lecture hall in a close carriage within five minutes of the time set
for the lecture to begin. When she stepped out of the vehicle
her heart beat fast and her eyes flashed with exultation: the
whole street was packed with people, and she could hardly
force her way to the hall! She reached the ante-room, threw
off her wraps and placed herself before the dressing-glass. She
turned herself this way and that—everything was satisfactory,

her attire was perfect. She smoothed her hair, re-arranged a jewel here and there, and all the while her heart sang within her, and her face was radiant. She had not been so happy for ages and ages, it seemed to her. Oh, no, she had never been so overwhelmingly grateful and happy in her whole life before. The lecture agent appeared at the door. She waved him away and said:

"Do not disturb me. I want no introduction. And do not fear for me; the moment the hands point to eight I will step upon the platform."

He disappeared. She held her watch before her. She was so impatient that the second-hand seemed whole tedious minutes dragging its way around the circle. At last the supreme moment came, and with head erect and the bearing of an empress she swept through the door and stood upon the stage. Her eyes fell upon—

Only a vast, brilliant emptiness—there were not forty people in the house! There were only a handful of coarse men and ten or twelve still coarser women, lolling upon the benches and scattered about singly and in couples.

Her pulses stood still, her limbs quaked, the gladness went out of her face. There was a moment of silence, and then a brutal laugh and an explosion of cat-calls and hisses saluted her from the audience. The clamor grew stronger and louder, and insulting speeches were shouted at her. A half-intoxicated man rose up and threw something, which missed her but bespattered a chair at her side, and this evoked an outburst of laughter and boisterous admiration. She was bewildered, her strength was forsaking her. She reeled away from the platform, reached the ante-room, and dropped helpless upon a sofa. The lecture agent ran in, with a hurried question upon his lips; but she put forth her hands, and with the tears raining from her eyes, said:

"Oh, do not speak! Take me away—please take me away, out of this dreadful place! Oh, this is like all my life—failure, disappointment, misery—always misery, always failure. What have I done, to be so pursued! Take me away, I beg of you, I implore you!"

Upon the pavement she was hustled by the mob, the surging masses roared her name and accompanied it with every species of insulting epithet; they thronged after the carriage, hooting, jeering, cursing, and even assailing the vehicle with missiles. A stone crushed through a blind, wounding Laura's forehead, and so stunning her that she hardly knew what further transpired during her flight.

It was long before her faculties were wholly restored, and then she found herself lying on the floor by a sofa in her own sitting-room, and alone. So she supposed she must have sat down upon the sofa and afterward fallen. She raised herself up, with difficulty, for the air was chilly and her limbs were stiff. She turned up the gas and sought the glass. She hardly knew herself, so worn and old she looked, and so marred with blood were her features. The night was far spent, and a dead stillness reigned. She sat down by her table, leaned her elbows upon it and put her face in her hands.

Her thoughts wandered back over her old life again and her tears flowed unrestrained.—Her pride was humbled, her spirit was broken. Her memory found but one resting place; it lingered about her young girlhood with a caressing regret; it dwelt upon it as the one brief interval in her life that bore no curse. She saw herself again in the budding grace of her twelve years, decked in her dainty pride of ribbons, consorting with the bees and the butterflies, believing in fairies, holding confidential converse with the flowers, busying herself all day long with airy trifles that were as weighty to her as the affairs that tax the brains of diplomats and emperors. She was without sin, then, and unacquainted with grief; the world was full of sunshine and her heart was full of music. From that— to this!

"If I could only die!" she said. "If I could only go back, and be as I was then, for one hour—and hold my father's hand in mine again, and see all the household about me, as in that old innocent time—and then die! My God, I am humbled, my pride is all gone, my stubborn heart repents—have pity!"

When the spring morning dawned, the form still sat there, the elbows resting upon the table and the face upon the hands. All day long the figure sat there, the sunshine enriching its costly raiment and flashing from its jewels; twilight came, and presently the stars, but still the figure remained;

the moon found it there still, and framed the picture with the shadow of the window sash, and flooded it with mellow light; by and by the darkness swallowed it up, and later the gray dawn revealed it again; the new day grew toward its prime, and still the forlorn presence was undisturbed.

But now the keepers of the house had become uneasy; their periodical knockings still finding no response, they burst open the door.

The jury of inquest found that death had resulted from heart disease, and was instant and painless. That was all. Merely heart disease.

Chapter LXI

Han ager ikke ilde som veed at vende.

Wanna unyanpi kta. Niye de kta he?
Iapi Oaye, vol. i., no. 7.

C LAY HAWKINS, years gone by, had yielded, after many a
struggle, to the migratory and speculative instinct of our
age and our people, and had wandered further and further
westward upon trading ventures. Settling finally in Melbourne, Australia, he ceased to roam, became a steady-going
substantial merchant, and prospered greatly. His life lay beyond the theatre of this tale.

His remittances had supported the Hawkins family, entirely,
from the time of his father's death until latterly when Laura
by her efforts in Washington had been able to assist in this
work. Clay was away on a long absence in some of the eastward islands when Laura's troubles began, trying (and almost
in vain,) to arrange certain interests which had become disordered through a dishonest agent, and consequently he knew
nothing of the murder till he returned and read his letters and
papers. His natural impulse was to hurry to the States and
save his sister if possible, for he loved her with a deep and
abiding affection.—His business was so crippled now, and so
deranged, that to leave it would be ruin; therefore he sold out
at a sacrifice that left him considerably reduced in worldly
possessions, and began his voyage to San Francisco. Arrived
there, he perceived by the newspapers that the trial was near
its close. At Salt Lake later telegrams told him of the acquittal, and his gratitude was boundless—so boundless, indeed,
that sleep was driven from his eyes by the pleasurable excitement almost as effectually as preceding weeks of anxiety had
done it. He shaped his course straight for Hawkeye, now, and
his meeting with his mother and the rest of the household
was joyful—albeit he had been away so long that he seemed
almost a stranger in his own home.

But the greetings and congratulations were hardly finished
when all the journals in the land clamored the news of Laura's

miserable death. Mrs. Hawkins was prostrated by this last blow, and it was well that Clay was at her side to stay her with comforting words and take upon himself the ordering of the household with its burden of labors and cares.

Washington Hawkins had scarcely more than entered upon that decade which carries one to the full blossom of manhood which we term the beginning of middle age, and yet a brief sojourn at the capital of the nation had made him old. His hair was already turning gray when the late session of Congress began its sittings; it grew grayer still, and rapidly, after the memorable day that saw Laura proclaimed a murderess; it waxed grayer and still grayer during the lagging suspense that succeeded it and after the crash which ruined his last hope—the failure of his bill in the Senate and the destruction of its champion, Dilworthy. A few days later, when he stood uncovered while the last prayer was pronounced over Laura's grave, his hair was whiter and his face hardly less old than the venerable minister's whose words were sounding in his ears.

A week after this, he was sitting in a double-bedded room in a cheap boarding house in Washington, with Col. Sellers. The two had been living together lately, and this mutual cavern of theirs the Colonel sometimes referred to as their "premises" and sometimes as their "apartments"—more particularly when conversing with persons outside. A canvas-covered modern trunk, marked "G.W.H." stood on end by the door, strapped and ready for a journey; on it lay a small morocco satchel, also marked "G.W.H." There was another trunk close by—a worn, and scarred, and ancient hair relic, with "E.S." wrought in brass nails on its top; on it lay a pair of saddle-bags that probably knew more about the last century than they could tell. Washington got up and walked the floor a while in a restless sort of way, and finally was about to sit down on the hair trunk.

"Stop, don't sit down on that!" exclaimed the Colonel. "There, now—that's all right—the chair's better. I couldn't get another trunk like that—not another like it in America, I reckon."

"I am afraid not," said Washington, with a faint attempt at a smile.

"No indeed; the man is dead that made that trunk and that saddle-bags."

"Are his great-grand-children still living?" said Washington, with levity only in the words, not in the tone.

"Well, I don't know—I hadn't thought of that—but anyway they can't make trunks and saddle-bags like that, if they are—no man can," said the Colonel with honest simplicity. "Wife didn't like to see me going off with that trunk—she said it was nearly certain to be stolen."

"Why?"

"Why? Why, aren't trunks always being stolen?"

"Well, yes—some kinds of trunks are."

"Very well, then; this is some kind of a trunk—and an almighty rare kind, too."

"Yes, I believe it is."

"Well, then, why shouldn't a man want to steal it if he got a chance?"

"Indeed I don't know.—Why should he?"

"Washington, I never heard anybody talk like you. Suppose you were a thief, and that trunk was lying around and nobody watching—wouldn't you steal it? Come, now, answer fair—wouldn't you steal it?"

"Well, now, since you corner me, I don't know but I would *take* it,—but I wouldn't consider it stealing."

"You wouldn't! Well, that beats me. Now what would you call stealing?"

"Why, taking property is stealing."

"Property! Now what a way to talk that is. What do you suppose that trunk is worth?"

"Is it in good repair?"

"Perfect. Hair rubbed off a little, but the main structure is perfectly sound."

"Does it leak anywhere?"

"Leak? Do you want to carry water in it? What do you mean by does it leak?"

"Why—a—do the clothes fall out of it when it is—when it is stationary?"

"Confound it, Washington, you are trying to make fun of me. I don't know what has got into you to-day; you act mighty curious. What *is* the matter with you?"

"Well, I'll tell you, old friend. I am almost happy. I am, indeed. It wasn't Clay's telegram that hurried me up so and got me ready to start with you. It was a letter from Louise."

"Good! What is it? What does she say?"

"She says come home—her father has consented, at last."

"My boy, I want to congratulate you; I want to shake you by the hand! It's a long turn that has no lane at the end of it, as the proverb says, or somehow that way. You'll be happy yet, and Eschol Sellers will be there to see, thank God!"

"I believe it. General Boswell is pretty nearly a poor man, now. The railroad that was going to build up Hawkeye made short work of him, along with the rest. He isn't so opposed to a son-in-law without a fortune, now."

"Without a fortune, indeed! Why that Tennessee Land—"

"Never mind the Tennessee Land, Colonel. I am done with that, forever and forever—"

"Why no! You can't mean to say—"

"My father, away back yonder, years ago, bought it for a blessing for his children, and—"

"Indeed he did! Si Hawkins said to me—"

"It proved a curse to him as long as he lived, and never a curse like it was inflicted upon any man's heirs—"

"I'm bound to say there's more or less truth—"

"It began to curse me when I was a baby, and it has cursed every hour of my life to this day—"

"Lord, lord, but it's so! Time and again my wife—"

"I depended on it all through my boyhood and never tried to do an honest stroke of work for my living—"

"Right again—but then you—"

"I have chased it years and years as children chase butterflies. We might all have been prosperous, now; we might all have been happy, all these heart-breaking years, if we had accepted our poverty at first and gone contentedly to work and built up our own weal by our own toil and sweat—"

"It's so, it's so; bless my soul, how often I've told Si Hawkins—"

"Instead of that, we have suffered more than the damned themselves suffer! I loved my father, and I honor his memory and recognize his good intentions; but I grieve for his mistaken ideas of conferring happiness upon his children. I am going to begin my life over again, and begin it and end it with good solid work! I'll leave *my* children no Tennessee Land!"

"Spoken like a man, sir, spoken like a man! Your hand, again my boy! And always remember that when a word of advice from Eschol Sellers can help, it is at your service. I'm going to begin again, too!"

"Indeed!"

"Yes, sir. I've seen enough to show me where my mistake was. The law is what I was born for. I shall begin the study of the law. Heavens and earth, but that Braham's a wonderful man—a wonderful man sir! Such a head! And such a way with him! But I could see that he was jealous of me. The little licks I got in in the course of my argument before the jury—"

"Your argument! Why, you were a witness."

"Oh, yes, to the popular eye, to the popular eye—but *I* knew when I was dropping information and when I was letting drive at the court with an insidious argument. But the court knew it, bless you, and weakened every time! And Braham knew it. I just reminded him of it in a quiet way, and its final result, and he said in a whisper, 'You did it, Colonel, you did it, sir—but keep it mum for *my* sake; and I'll tell you what *you* do,' says he, 'you go into the law, Col. Sellers—go into the law, sir; that's *your* native element!' And into the law the subscriber is going. There's worlds of money in it!—whole worlds of money! Practice first in Hawkeye, then in Jefferson, then in St. Louis, then in New York! In the metropolis of the western world! Climb, and climb, and climb—and wind up on the *Su*preme bench. Eschol Sellers, Chief Justice of the *Su*preme Court of the United States, sir! A made man for all time and eternity! That's the way *I* block it out, sir—and it's as clear as day—clear as the rosy morn!"

Washington had heard little of this. The first reference to Laura's trial had brought the old dejection to his face again, and he stood gazing out of the window at nothing, lost in reverie.

There was a knock—the postman handed in a letter. It was from Obedstown, East Tennessee, and was for Washington. He opened it. There was a note saying that enclosed he would please find a bill for the current year's taxes on the 75,000 acres of Tennessee Land belonging to the estate of

Silas Hawkins, deceased, and added that the money must be paid within sixty days or the land would be sold at public auction for the taxes, as provided by law. The bill was for $180— something more than twice the market value of the land, perhaps.

Washington hesitated. Doubts flitted through his mind. The old instinct came upon him to cling to the land just a little longer and give it one more chance. He walked the floor feverishly, his mind tortured by indecision. Presently he stopped, took out his pocket book and counted his money. Two hundred and thirty dollars—it was all he had in the world.

"One hundred and eighty . . . . from two hundred and thirty," he said to himself. "Fifty left . . . . It is enough to get me home . . . . Shall I do it, or shall I not? . . . . I wish I had somebody to decide for me."

The pocket book lay open in his hand, with Louise's small letter in view. His eye fell upon that, and it decided him.

"It shall go for taxes," he said, "and never tempt me or mine any more!"

He opened the window and stood there tearing the tax bill to bits and watching the breeze waft them away, till all were gone.

"The spell is broken, the life-long curse is ended!" he said. "Let us go."

The baggage wagon had arrived; five minutes later the two friends were mounted upon their luggage in it, and rattling off toward the station, the Colonel endeavoring to sing "Homeward Bound," a song whose words he knew, but whose tune, as he rendered it, was a trial to auditors.

Chapter LXII

Gedi kanadiben tsannawa.

—La xalog, la xamaih mi-x-ul nu qiza u quïal gih, u quïal agab?
Rabinal-Achi.

Philip Sterling's circumstances were becoming straightened. The prospect was gloomy. His long siege of unproductive labor was beginning to tell upon his spirits; but what told still more upon them was the undeniable fact that the promise of ultimate success diminished every day, now. That is to say, the tunnel had reached a point in the hill which was considerably beyond where the coal vein should pass (according to all his calculations) if there were a coal vein there; and so, every foot that the tunnel now progressed seemed to carry it further away from the object of the search.

Sometimes he ventured to hope that he had made a mistake in estimating the direction which the vein should naturally take after crossing the valley and entering the hill. Upon such occasions he would go into the nearest mine on the vein he was hunting for, and once more get the bearings of the deposit and mark out its probable course; but the result was the same every time; his tunnel had manifestly pierced beyond the natural point of junction; and then his spirits fell a little lower. His men had already lost faith, and he often overheard them saying it was perfectly plain that there was no coal in the hill.

Foremen and laborers from neighboring mines, and no end of experienced loafers from the village, visited the tunnel from time to time, and their verdicts were always the same and always disheartening—"No coal in that hill." Now and then Philip would sit down and think it all over and wonder what the mystery meant; then he would go into the tunnel and ask the men if there were no signs yet? None—always "none." He would bring out a piece of rock and examine it, and say to himself, "It is limestone—it has crinoids and corals in it—the rock is right." Then he would throw it down with a sigh, and say, "But that is nothing; where coal is, limestone with these fossils in it is pretty certain to lie against its foot casing; but it does not necessarily follow that where this peculiar rock is, coal must lie above it or beyond it; this sign is not sufficient."

The thought usually followed:—"There *is* one infallible sign—if I could only strike *that*!"

Three or four times in as many weeks he said to himself, "Am I a visionary? I *must* be a visionary; everybody is in these days; everybody chases butterflies: everybody seeks sudden fortune and will not lay one up by slow toil. This is not right, I will discharge the men and go at some honest work. There is no coal here. What a fool I have been; I will give it up."

But he never could do it. A half hour of profound thinking always followed; and at the end of it he was sure to get up and straighten himself and say: "There *is* coal there; I will *not* give it up; and coal or no coal I will drive the tunnel clear through the hill; I will not surrender while I am alive."

He never thought of asking Mr. Montague for more money. He said there was now but one chance of finding coal against nine hundred and ninety nine that he would not find it, and so it would be wrong in him to make the request and foolish in Mr. Montague to grant it.

He had been working three shifts of men. Finally, the settling of a weekly account exhausted his means. He could not afford to run in debt, and therefore he gave the men their discharge. They came into his cabin presently, where he sat with his elbows on his knees and his chin in his hands, the picture of discouragement and their spokesman said:

"Mr. Sterling, when Tim was down a week with his fall you kept him on half wages and it was a mighty help to his family; whenever any of us was in trouble you've done what you could to help us out; you've acted fair and square with us every time, and I reckon we are men and know a man when we see him. We haven't got any faith in that hill, but we have a respect for a man that's got the pluck that you've showed; you've fought a good fight, with everybody agin you and if we had grub to go on, I'm d—d if we wouldn't stand by you till the cows come home! That is what the boys say. Now we want to put in one parting blast for luck. We want to work three days more; if we don't find anything, we won't bring in no bill against you. That is what we've come to say."

Philip was touched. If he had had money enough to buy three days' "grub" he would have accepted the generous offer, but as it was, he could not consent to be less magnanimous than the men, and so he declined in a manly speech, shook hands all around and resumed his solitary communings. The men went back to the tunnel and "put in a parting blast for luck" anyhow. They did a full day's work and then took their leave. They called at his cabin and gave him good-bye, but were not able to tell him their day's effort had given things a more promising look.

The next day Philip sold all the tools but two or three sets; he also sold one of the now deserted cabins as old lumber, together with its domestic wares, and made up his mind that he would buy provisions with the trifle of money thus gained and continue his work alone. About the middle of the afternoon he put on his roughest clothes and went to the tunnel. He lit a candle and groped his way in. Presently he heard the sound of a pick or a drill, and wondered what it meant. A spark of light now appeared in the far end of the tunnel, and when he arrived there he found the man Tim at work. Tim said:

"I'm to have a job in the Golden Brier mine by and by—in a week or ten days—and I'm going to work here till then. A man might as well be at some thing, and besides I consider that I owe you what you paid me when I was laid up."

Philip said, Oh, no, he didn't owe anything; but Tim persisted, and then Philip said he had a little provision, now, and would share. So for several days Philip held the drill and Tim did the striking. At first Philip was impatient to see the result of every blast, and was always back and peering among the smoke the moment after the explosion. But there was never any encouraging result; and therefore he finally lost almost all interest, and hardly troubled himself to inspect results at all. He simply labored on, stubbornly and with little hope.

Tim staid with him till the last moment, and then took up his job at the Golden Brier, apparently as depressed by the continued barrenness of their mutual labors as Philip was himself. After that, Philip fought his battle alone, day after day, and slow work it was; he could scarcely see that he made any progress.

Late one afternoon he finished drilling a hole which he had been at work at for more than two hours; he swabbed it out, and poured in the powder and inserted the fuse; then filled up the rest of the hole with dirt and small fragments of stone; tamped it down firmly, touched his candle to the fuse, and ran. By and by the dull report came, and he was about to walk back mechanically and see what was accomplished; but he halted; presently turned on his heel and thought, rather than said:

"No, this is useless, this is absurd. If I found anything it would only be one of those little aggravating seams of coal which doesn't mean anything, and—."

By this time he was walking out of the tunnel. His thought ran on:

"I am conquered. . . . . . I am out of provisions, out of money. . . . . I have got to give it up. . . . . . All this hard work lost! But I am *not* conquered! I will go and work for money, and come back and have another fight with fate. Ah me, it may be years, it may be years."

Arrived at the mouth of the tunnel, he threw his coat upon the ground, sat down on a stone, and his eye sought the westering sun and dwelt upon the charming landscape which stretched its woody ridges, wave upon wave, to the golden horizon.

Something was taking place at his feet which did not attract his attention.

His reverie continued, and its burden grew more and more gloomy. Presently he rose up and cast a look far away toward the valley, and his thoughts took a new direction:

"There it is! How good it looks! But down there is not up here. Well, I will go home and pack up—there is nothing else to do."

He moved off moodily toward his cabin. He had gone some distance before he thought of his coat; then he was about to turn back, but he smiled at the thought, and continued his journey—such a coat as that could be of little use in a civilized land. A little further on, he remembered that there were some papers of value in one of the pockets of the relic, and then with a petulant ejaculation he turned back, picked up the coat and put it on.

He made a dozen steps, and then stopped very suddenly. He stood still a moment, as one who is trying to believe something and cannot. He put a hand up over his shoulder and felt his back, and a great thrill shot through him. He grasped the skirt of the coat impulsively and another thrill followed. He snatched the coat from his back, glanced at it, threw it from him and flew back to the tunnel. He sought the spot where the coat had lain—he had to look close, for the light was waning—then to make sure, he put his hand to the ground and a little stream of water swept against his fingers:

"Thank God, I've struck it at last!"

He lit a candle and ran into the tunnel; he picked up a piece of rubbish cast out by the last blast, and said:

"This clayey stuff is what I've longed for—I know what is behind it."

He swung his pick with hearty good will till long after the darkness had gathered upon the earth, and when he trudged home at length he knew he had a coal vein and that it was seven feet thick from wall to wall.

He found a yellow envelop lying on his rickety table, and recognized that it was of a family sacred to the transmission of telegrams.

He opened it, read it, crushed it in his hand and threw it down. It simply said:

"Ruth is very ill."

Chapter LXIII

Alaila pomaikai kaua, ola na iwi iloka o ko kaua mau la elemakule.

Laieikawai, 9.

ܘܪܟܘ ܡܟܢܢܘ ܟܘܟܟܚܝ ܂ ܘܡܗܘܡܗܢܢ ܟܡܪܝܢܪܚܝ ܂
ܕܘܟܗܝ ܀ ܦ ܀ ܢܘܗܟܝ

IT WAS EVENING when Philip took the cars at the Ilium station. The news of his success had preceded him, and while he waited for the train, he was the center of a group of eager questioners, who asked him a hundred things about the mine, and magnified his good fortune. There was no mistake this time.

Philip, in luck, had become suddenly a person of consideration, whose speech was freighted with meaning, whose looks were all significant. The words of the proprietor of a rich coal mine have a golden sound, and his common sayings are repeated as if they were solid wisdom.

Philip wished to be alone; his good fortune at this moment seemed an empty mockery, one of those sarcasms of fate, such as that which spreads a dainty banquet for the man who has no appetite. He had longed for success principally for Ruth's sake; and perhaps now, at this very moment of his triumph, she was dying.

"Shust what I said, Mister Sderling," the landlord of the Ilium hotel kept repeating. "I dold Jake Schmidt he find him dere shust so sure as noting."

"You ought to have taken a share, Mr. Dusenheimer," said Philip.

"Yaas, I know. But d'old woman, she say 'You sticks to your pisiness. So I sticks to 'em. Und I makes noting. Dat Mister Prierly, he don't never come back here no more, ain't it?"

"Why?" asked Philip.

"Vell, dere is so many peers, und so many oder dhrinks, I got 'em all set down, ven he coomes back."

It was a long night for Philip, and a restless one. At any other time the swing of the cars would have lulled him to sleep, and the rattle and clank of wheels and rails, the roar of the whirling iron would have only been cheerful reminders of swift and safe travel. Now they were voices of warning and taunting; and instead of going rapidly the train seemed to crawl at a snail's pace. And it not only crawled, but it frequently stopped; and when it stopped it stood dead still, and there was an ominous silence. Was anything the matter, he wondered. Only a station probably. Perhaps, he thought, a telegraphic station. And then he listened eagerly. Would the conductor open the door and ask for Philip Sterling, and hand him a fatal dispatch?

How long they seemed to wait. And then slowly beginning to move, they were off again, shaking, pounding, screaming through the night. He drew his curtain from time to time and looked out. There was the lurid sky line of the wooded range along the base of which they were crawling. There was the Susquehannah, gleaming in the moon-light. There was a stretch of level valley with silent farm houses, the occupants all at rest, without trouble, without anxiety. There was a church, a graveyard, a mill, a village; and now, without pause or fear, the train had mounted a trestle-work high in air and was creeping along the top of it while a swift torrent foamed a hundred feet below.

What would the morning bring? Even while he was flying to her, her gentle spirit might have gone on another flight, whither he could not follow her. He was full of foreboding. He fell at length into a restless doze. There was a noise in his ears as of a rushing torrent when a stream is swollen by a freshet in the spring. It was like the breaking up of life; he was struggling in the consciousness of coming death: when Ruth stood by his side, clothed in white, with a face like that of an angel, radiant, smiling, pointing to the sky, and saying, "Come." He awoke with a cry—the train was roaring through a bridge, and it shot out into daylight.

When morning came the train was industriously toiling along through the fat lands of Lancaster, with its broad farms of corn and wheat, its mean houses of stone, its vast barns and granaries, built as if for storing the riches of Heliogabalus. Then came the smiling fields of Chester, with their English green, and soon the county of Philadelphia itself, and the increasing signs of the approach to a great city. Long trains of coal cars, laden and unladen, stood upon sidings; the tracks of other roads were crossed; the smoke of other locomotives was seen on parallel lines; factories multiplied; streets appeared; the noise of a busy city began to fill the air; and with a slower and slower clank on the connecting rails and interlacing switches the train rolled into the station and stood still.

It was a hot August morning. The broad streets glowed in the sun, and the white-shuttered houses stared at the hot thoroughfares like closed bakers'-ovens set along the highway. Philip was oppressed with the heavy air; the sweltering city lay as in a swoon. Taking a street car, he rode away to the northern part of the city, the newer portion, formerly the district of Spring Garden, for in this the Boltons now lived, in a small brick house, befitting their altered fortunes.

He could scarcely restrain his impatience when he came in sight of the house. The window shutters were not "bowed"; thank God, for that. Ruth was still living, then. He ran up the steps and rang. Mrs. Bolton met him at the door.

"Thee is very welcome, Philip."

"And Ruth?"

"She is very ill, but quieter than she has been, and the fever is a little abating. The most dangerous time will be when the fever leaves her. The doctor fears she will not have strength enough to rally from it. Yes, thee can see her."

Mrs. Bolton led the way to the little chamber where Ruth lay. "Oh," said her mother, "if she were only in her cool and spacious room in our old home. She says that seems like heaven."

Mr. Bolton sat by Ruth's bedside, and he rose and silently pressed Philip's hand. The room had but one window; that was wide open to admit the air, but the air that came in was hot and lifeless. Upon the table stood a vase of flowers. Ruth's eyes were closed; her cheeks were flushed with fever, and she moved her head restlessly as if in pain.

"Ruth," said her mother, bending over her, "Philip is here."

Ruth's eyes unclosed, there was a gleam of recognition in them, there was an attempt at a smile upon her face, and she tried to raise her thin hand, as Philip touched her forehead with his lips; and he heard her murmur,

"Dear Phil."

There was nothing to be done but to watch and wait for the cruel fever to burn itself out. Dr. Longstreet told Philip that the fever had undoubtedly been contracted in the hospital, but it was not malignant, and would be little dangerous if Ruth were not so worn down with work, or if she had a less delicate constitution.

"It is only her indomitable will that has kept her up for weeks. And if that should leave her now, there will be no hope. You can do more for her now, sir, than I can."

"How?" asked Philip eagerly.

"Your presence, more than anything else, will inspire her with the desire to live."

When the fever turned, Ruth was in a very critical condition. For two days her life was like the fluttering of a lighted candle in the wind. Philip was constantly by her side, and she seemed to be conscious of his presence, and to cling to him, as one borne away by a swift stream clings to a stretched-out hand from the shore. If he was absent a moment her restless eyes sought something they were disappointed not to find.

Philip so yearned to bring her back to life, he willed it so strongly and passionately, that his will appeared to affect hers and she seemed slowly to draw life from his.

After two days of this struggle with the grasping enemy, it was evident to Dr. Longstreet that Ruth's will was beginning to issue its orders to her body with some force, and that strength was slowly coming back. In another day there was a decided improvement. As Philip sat holding her weak hand and watching the least sign of resolution in her face, Ruth was able to whisper,

"I so want to live, for you, Phil!"

"You will, darling, you must," said Philip in a tone of faith and courage that carried a thrill of determination—of command—along all her nerves.

Slowly Philip drew her back to life. Slowly she came back, as one willing but well nigh helpless. It was new for Ruth to feel this dependence on another's nature, to consciously draw strength of will from the will of another. It was a new but a dear joy, to be lifted up and carried back into the happy world, which was now all aglow with the light of love; to be lifted and carried by the one she loved more than her own life.

"Sweetheart," she said to Philip, "I would not have cared to come back but for thy love."

"Not for thy profession?"

"Oh, thee may be glad enough of that some day, when thy coal bed is dug out and thee and father are in the air again."

When Ruth was able to ride she was taken into the country, for the pure air was necessary to her speedy recovery. The family went with her. Philip could not be spared from her side, and Mr. Bolton had gone up to Ilium to look into that wonderful coal mine and to make arrangements for developing it, and bringing its wealth to market. Philip had insisted on re-conveying the Ilium property to Mr. Bolton, retaining only the share originally contemplated for himself, and Mr. Bolton, therefore, once more found himself engaged in business and a person of some consequence in Third street. The mine turned out even better than was at first hoped, and would, if judiciously managed, be a fortune to them all. This also seemed to be the opinion of Mr. Bigler, who heard of it as soon as anybody, and, with the impudence of his class called upon Mr. Bolton for a little aid in a patent car-wheel he had bought an interest in. That rascal, Small, he said, had swindled him out of all he had.

Mr. Bolton told him he was very sorry, and recommended him to sue Small.

Mr. Small also came with a similar story about Mr. Bigler; and Mr. Bolton had the grace to give him like advice. And he added, "If you and Bigler will procure the indictment of each other, you may have the satisfaction of putting each other in the penitentiary for the forgery of my acceptances."

Bigler and Small did not quarrel however. They both attacked Mr. Bolton behind his back as a swindler, and circulated the story that he had made a fortune by failing.

In the pure air of the highlands, amid the golden glories of ripening September, Ruth rapidly came back to health. How beautiful the world is to an invalid, whose senses are all clarified, who has been so near the world of spirits that she is sensitive to the finest influences, and whose frame responds with a thrill to the subtlest ministrations of soothing nature. Mere life is a luxury, and the color of the grass, of the flowers, of the sky, the wind in the trees, the out-lines of the horizon, the forms of clouds, all give a pleasure as exquisite as the sweetest music to the ear famishing for it. The world was all new and fresh to Ruth, as if it had just been created for her, and love filled it, till her heart was overflowing with happiness.

It was golden September also at Fallkill. And Alice sat by the open window in her room at home, looking out upon the meadows where the laborers were cutting the second crop of clover. The fragrance of it floated to her nostrils. Perhaps she did not mind it. She was thinking. She had just been writing to Ruth, and on the table before her was a yellow piece of paper with a faded four-leaved clover pinned on it—only a memory now. In her letter to Ruth she had poured out her heartiest blessings upon them both, with her dear love forever and forever.

"Thank God," she said, "they will never know."

They never would know. And the world never knows how many women there are like Alice, whose sweet but lonely lives of self-sacrifice, gentle, faithful, loving souls, bless it continually.

"She is a dear girl," said Philip, when Ruth showed him the letter.

"Yes, Phil, and we can spare a great deal of love for her, our own lives are so full."

טוב אחרית דבר מראשיתו

APPENDIX.

Perhaps some apology to the reader is necessary in view of our failure to find Laura's father. We supposed, from the ease with which lost persons are found in novels, that it would not be difficult. But it was; indeed, it was impossible; and therefore the portions of the narrative containing the record of the search have been stricken out. Not because they were not interesting—for they were; but inasmuch as the man was not found, after all, it did not seem wise to harass and excite the reader to no purpose.

THE AUTHORS.

THE AMERICAN CLAIMANT

EXPLANATORY

THE Colonel Mulberry Sellers here re-introduced to the public is the same person who appeared as *Eschol* Sellers in the first edition of the tale entitled "The Gilded Age," years ago, and as *Beriah* Sellers in the subsequent editions of the same book, and finally as *Mulberry* Sellers in the drama played afterward by John T. Raymond.

The name was changed from Eschol to Beriah to accommodate an Eschol Sellers who rose up out of the vasty deeps of uncharted space and preferred his request—backed by threat of a libel suit—then went his way appeased, and came no more. In the play Beriah had to be dropped to satisfy another member of the race, and Mulberry was substituted in the hope that the objectors would be tired by that time and let it pass unchallenged. So far it has occupied the field in peace; therefore we chance it again, feeling reasonably safe, this time, under shelter of the statute of limitations.

MARK TWAIN.

Hartford, 1891.

THE WEATHER IN THIS BOOK

No weather will be found in this book. This is an attempt to pull a book through without weather. It being the first attempt of the kind in fictitious literature, it may prove a failure, but it seemed worth the while of some dare-devil person to try it, and the author was in just the mood.

Many a reader who wanted to read a tale through was not able to do it because of delays on account of the weather. Nothing breaks up an author's progress like having to stop every few pages to fuss-up the weather. Thus it is plain that persistent intrusions of weather are bad for both reader and author.

Of course weather is necessary to a narrative of human experience. That is conceded. But it ought to be put where it will not be in the way; where it will not interrupt the flow of the narrative. And it ought to be the ablest weather that can be had, not ignorant, poor-quality, amateur weather. Weather is a literary specialty, and no untrained hand can turn out a good article of it. The present author can do only a few trifling ordinary kinds of weather, and he cannot do those very good. So it has seemed wisest to borrow such weather as is necessary for the book from qualified and recognized experts—giving credit, of course. This weather will be found over in the back part of the book, out of the way. *See Appendix*. The reader is requested to turn over and help himself from time to time as he goes along.

CONTENTS

CHAPTER XXIII.

CHAPTER XXIV.

CHAPTER XXV.

APPENDIX.

Chapter I

IT IS a matchless morning in rural England. On a fair hill we
see a majestic pile, the ivied walls and towers of Cholmondeley Castle, huge relic and witness of the baronial
grandeurs of the Middle Ages. This is one of the seats of the
Earl of Rossmore, K.G., G.C.B., K.C.M.G., etc., etc., etc.,
etc., etc., who possesses twenty-two thousand acres of English
land, owns a parish in London with two thousand houses on
its lease-roll, and struggles comfortably along on an income
of two hundred thousand pounds a year. The father and
founder of this proud old line was William the Conqueror his
very self; the mother of it was not inventoried in history by
name, she being merely a random episode and inconsequential, like the tanner's daughter of Falaise.

In a breakfast room of the castle on this breezy fine morning there are two persons and the cooling remains of a deserted meal. One of these persons is the old lord, tall, erect,
square-shouldered, white-haired, stern-browed, a man who
shows character in every feature, attitude, and movement, and
carries his seventy years as easily as most men carry fifty. The
other person is his only son and heir, a dreamy-eyed young
fellow, who looks about twenty-six but is nearer thirty. Candor, kindliness, honesty, sincerity, simplicity, modesty—it is
easy to see that these are cardinal traits of his character; and
so when you have clothed him in the formidable components
of his name, you somehow seem to be contemplating a lamb
in armor: his name and style being the Honourable Kirkcudbright Llanover Marjoribanks Sellers Viscount Berkeley, of
Cholmondeley Castle, Warwickshire. (Pronounced K'koobry
Thlanover Marshbanks Sellers Vycount Barkly, of Chumly
Castle, Warrikshr.) He is standing by a great window, in an attitude suggestive of respectful attention to what his father is
saying and equally respectful dissent from the positions and
arguments offered. The father walks the floor as he talks, and
his talk shows that his temper is away up toward summer
heat.

"Soft-spirited as you are, Berkeley, I am quite aware that
when you have once made up your mind to do a thing which

your ideas of honor and justice require you to do, argument and reason are (for the time being,) wasted upon you—yes, and ridicule, persuasion, supplication, and command as well. To my mind—"

"Father, if you will look at it without prejudice, without passion, you must concede that I am not doing a rash thing, a thoughtless, wilful thing, with nothing substantial behind it to justify it. *I* did not create the American claimant to the earldom of Rossmore; I did not hunt for him, did not find him, did not obtrude him upon your notice. He found himself, he injected himself into our lives—"

"And has made mine a purgatory for ten years with his tiresome letters, his wordy reasonings, his acres of tedious evidence,—"

"Which you would never read, would never consent to read. Yet in common fairness he was entitled to a hearing. That hearing would either prove he was the rightful earl—in which case our course would be plain—or it would prove that he wasn't—in which case our course would be equally plain. I have read his evidences, my lord. I have conned them well, studied them patiently and thoroughly. The chain seems to be complete, no important link wanting. I believe he is the rightful earl."

"And I a usurper—a nameless pauper, a tramp! Consider what you are saying, sir."

"Father, *if* he is the rightful earl, would you, could you—that fact being established—consent to keep his titles and his properties from him a day, an hour, a minute?"

"You are talking nonsense—nonsense—lurid idiotcy! Now, listen to me. I will make a confession—if you wish to call it by that name. I did not read those evidences because I had no occasion to—I was made familiar with them in the time of this claimant's father and of my own father forty years ago. This fellow's predecessors have kept mine more or less familiar with them for close upon a hundred and fifty years. The truth is, the rightful heir did go to America, with the Fairfax heir or about the same time—but disappeared somewhere in the wilds of Virginia, got married, and began to breed savages for the Claimant market; wrote no letters home; was supposed to be dead; his younger brother softly took possession;

presently the American did die, and straightway his eldest product put in his claim—by letter—letter still in existence—and died before the uncle in possession found time—or maybe inclination—to answer. The infant son of that eldest product grew up—long interval, you see—and *he* took to writing letters and furnishing evidences. Well, successor after successor has done the same, down to the present idiot. It was a succession of paupers; not one of them was ever able to pay his passage to England or institute suit. The Fairfaxes kept their lordship alive, and so they have never lost it to this day, although they live in Maryland; their friend lost his by his own neglect. You perceive now, that the facts in this case bring us to precisely this result: morally the American tramp *is* rightful earl of Rossmore; legally he has no more right than his dog. There now—are you satisfied?"

There was a pause, then the son glanced at the crest carved in the great oaken mantel and said, with a regretful note in his voice:

"Since the introduction of heraldic symbols, the motto of this house has been *Suum cuique*—to every man his own. By your own intrepidly frank confession, my lord, it is become a sarcasm. If Simon Lathers—"

"Keep that exasperating name to yourself! For ten years it has pestered my eye and tortured my ear; till at last my very footfalls time themselves to the brain-racking rhythm of *Simon Lathers!—Simon Lathers!—Simon Lathers!* And now, to make its presence in my soul eternal, immortal, imperishable, you have resolved to—to—what is it you have resolved to do?"

"To go to Simon Lathers, in America, and change places with him."

"What? Deliver the reversion of the earldom into his hands?"

"That is my purpose."

"Make this tremendous surrender without even trying the fantastic case in the Lords?"

"Ye—s—" with hesitation and some embarrassment.

"By all that is amazing, I believe you are insane, my son. See here—have you been training with that ass again—that radical, if you prefer the term, though the words are synonymous—Lord Tanzy, of Tollmache?"

The son did not reply, and the old lord continued:

"Yes, you confess. That puppy, that shame to his birth and caste, who holds all hereditary lordships and privilege to be usurpation, all nobility a tinsel sham, all aristocratic institutions a fraud, all inequalities in rank a legalized crime and an infamy, and no bread honest bread that a man doesn't earn by his own work—*work*, pah!"—and the old patrician brushed imaginary labor-dirt from his white hands. "You have come to hold just those opinions yourself, I suppose," he added with a sneer.

A faint flush in the younger man's cheek told that the shot had hit and hurt, but he answered with dignity—

"I have. I say it without shame—I feel none. And now my reason for resolving to renounce my heirship without resistance is explained. I wish to retire from what to me is a false existence, a false position, and begin my life over again—begin it right—begin it on the level of mere manhood, unassisted by factitious aids, and succeed or fail by pure merit or the want of it. I will go to America, where all men are equal and all have an equal chance; I will live or die, sink or swim, win or lose as just a man—that alone, and not a single helping gaud or fiction back of it."

"Hear, hear!" The two men looked each other steadily in the eye a moment or two, then the elder one added, musingly, "Ab-so-lutely cra-zy—ab-so-lutely!" After another silence, he said, as one who, long troubled by clouds, detects a ray of sunshine, "Well, there will be one satisfaction—Simon Lathers will come here to enter into his own, and I will drown him in the horsepond. That poor devil—always so humble in his letters, so pitiful, so deferential; so steeped in reverence for our great line and lofty station; so anxious to placate us, so prayerful for recognition as a relative, a bearer in his veins of our sacred blood—and withal so poor, so needy, so threadbare and pauper-shod as to raiment, so despised, so laughed at for his silly claimantship by the lewd American scum around him—ach, the vulgar, crawling, insufferable tramp! To read one of his cringing, nauseating letters—well?"

This to a splendid flunkey, all in inflamed plush and buttons and knee-breeches as to his trunk, and a glinting white frost-work of ground-glass paste as to his head, who stood with his heels together and the upper half of him bent forward, a salver in his hands:

"The letters, my lord."

My lord took them, and the servant disappeared.

"Among the rest, an American letter. From the tramp, of course. Jove, but here's a change! No brown paper envelop this time, filched from a shop and carrying the shop's advertisement in the corner. Oh, no, a proper enough envelop—with a most ostentatiously broad mourning border—for his cat, perhaps, since he was a bachelor—and fastened with red wax—a batch of it as big as a half-crown—and—and—our crest for a seal!—motto and all. And the ignorant, sprawling hand is gone; he sports a secretary, evidently—a secretary with a most confident swing and flourish to his pen. Oh indeed, our fortunes are improving over there—our meek tramp has undergone a metamorphosis."

"Read it, my lord, please."

"Yes, this time I will. For the sake of the cat:

14,042 SIXTEENTH STREET,
WASHINGTON, May 2.

My Lord—

It is my painful duty to announce to you that the head of our illustrious house is no more—The Right Honourable, The Most Noble, The Most Puissant Simon Lathers Lord Rossmore having departed this life ("Gone at last—this is unspeakably precious news, my son,") at his seat in the environs of the hamlet of Duffy's Corners in the grand old State of Arkansas,—and his twin brother with him, both being crushed by a log at a smoke-house-raising, owing to carelessness on the part of all present, referable to over-confidence and gaiety induced by over-plus of sour-mash—("Extolled be sour-mash, whatever that may be, eh Berkeley?") five days ago, with no scion of our ancient race present to close his eyes and inter him with the honors due his historic name and lofty rank—in fact, he is on the ice yet, him and his brother—friends took up a collection for it. But I shall take immediate occasion to have their noble remains shipped to you ("Great heavens!") for interment, with due ceremonies and solemnities, in the family vault or mausoleum of our house. Meantime I shall put up a pair of hatchments on my house-front, and you will of course do the same at your several seats.

I have also to remind you that by this sad disaster I as sole heir, inherit and become seized of all the titles, honors, lands, and goods of our lamented relative, and must of necessity, painful as the duty is, shortly require at the bar of the Lords restitution of these dignities and properties, now illegally enjoyed by your titular lordship.

With assurance of my distinguished consideration and warm cousinly regard, I remain

Your titular lordship's
Most obedient servant,
Mulberry Sellers Earl Rossmore.

"Im-mense! Come, this one's interesting. Why, Berkeley, his breezy impudence is—is—why, it's colossal, it's sublime."

"No, this one doesn't seem to cringe much."

"Cringe—why, he doesn't know the meaning of the word. Hatchments! To commemorate that sniveling tramp and his fraternal duplicate. And he is going to send me the remains. The late Claimant was a fool, but plainly this new one's a maniac. What a name! *Mulberry* Sellers—there's music for you. Simon Lathers—Mulberry Sellers—Mulberry Sellers—Simon Lathers. Sounds like machinery working and churning. Simon Lathers, Mulberry Sel— Are you going?"

"If I have your leave, father."

The old gentleman stood musing some time, after his son was gone. This was his thought:

"He is a good boy, and lovable. Let him take his own course—as it would profit nothing to oppose him—make things worse, in fact. My arguments and his aunt's persuasions have failed; let us see what America can do for us. Let us see what equality and hardtimes can effect for the mental health of a brain-sick young British lord. Going to renounce his lordship and be a man! Yas!"

Chapter II

COLONEL MULBERRY SELLERS—this was some days before he wrote his letter to Lord Rossmore—was seated
in his "library," which was also his "drawing-room" and was
also his "picture gallery" and likewise his "work-shop."
Sometimes he called it by one of these names, sometimes by
another, according to occasion and circumstance. He was
constructing what seemed to be some kind of a frail mechanical toy, and was apparently very much interested in his work.
He was a white-headed man, now, but otherwise he was as
young, alert, buoyant, visionary and enterprising as ever. His
loving old wife sat near by, contentedly knitting and thinking,
with a cat asleep in her lap. The room was large, light, and
had a comfortable look, in fact a home-like look, though the
furniture was of a humble sort and not over abundant, and
the knick-knacks and things that go to adorn a living-room
not plenty and not costly. But there were natural flowers, and
there was an abstract and unclassifiable something about the
place which betrayed the presence in the house of somebody
with a happy taste and an effective touch.

Even the deadly chromos on the walls were somehow without offence; in fact they seemed to belong there and to add
an attraction to the room—a fascination, anyway; for whoever
got his eye on one of them was like to gaze and suffer till he
died—you have seen that kind of pictures. Some of these terrors were landscapes, some libeled the sea, some were ostensible portraits, all were crimes. All the portraits were
recognizable as dead Americans of distinction, and yet,
through labeling added by a daring hand, they were all doing
duty here as "Earls of Rossmore." The newest one had left
the works as Andrew Jackson, but was doing its best now, as
"Simon Lathers Lord Rossmore, Present Earl." On one wall
was a cheap old railroad map of Warwickshire. This had been
newly labeled "The Rossmore Estates." On the opposite wall
was another map, and this was the most imposing decoration
of the establishment and the first to catch a stranger's attention, because of its great size. It had once borne simply the title SIBERIA; but now the word "FUTURE" had been written

in front of that word. There were other additions, in red ink—many cities, with great populations set down, scattered over the vast country at points where neither cities nor populations exist to-day. One of these cities, with population placed at 1,500,000, bore the name "Libertyorloffskoizalinski," and there was a still more populous one, centrally located and marked "Capital," which bore the name "Freedomolovnaivanovich."

The "mansion"—the Colonel's usual name for the house—was a rickety old two-story frame of considerable size, which had been painted, some time or other, but had nearly forgotten it. It was away out in the ragged edge of Washington and had once been somebody's country place. It had a neglected yard around it, with a paling fence that needed straightening up, in places, and a gate that would stay shut. By the door-post were several modest tin signs. "Col. Mulberry Sellers, Attorney at Law and Claim Agent," was the principal one. One learned from the others that the Colonel was a Materializer, a Hypnotizer, a Mind-Cure dabbler, and so on. For he was a man who could always find things to do.

A white-headed negro man, with spectacles and damaged white cotton gloves appeared in the presence, made a stately obeisance and announced—

"Marse Washington Hawkins, suh."

"Great Scott! Show him in, Dan'l, show him in."

The Colonel and his wife were on their feet in a moment, and the next moment were joyfully wringing the hands of a stoutish, discouraged-looking man whose general aspect suggested that he was fifty years old, but whose hair swore to a hundred.

"Well, well, well, Washington, my boy, it *is* good to look at you again. Sit down, sit down, and make yourself at home. There, now—why, you look perfectly natural; aging a little, just a little, but you'd have known him anywhere, wouldn't you, Polly?"

"Oh, yes, Berry, he's *just* like his pa would have looked if he'd lived. Dear, dear, where have you dropped from? Let me see, how long is it since—"

"I should say it's all of fifteen years, Mrs. Sellers."

"Well, well, how time does get away with us. Yes, and oh, the changes that—"

There was a sudden catch of her voice and a trembling of the lip, the men waiting reverently for her to get command of herself and go on; but after a little struggle she turned away, with her apron to her eyes, and softly disappeared.

"Seeing you made her think of the children, poor thing— dear, dear, they're all dead but the youngest. But banish care, it's no time for it now—on with the dance, let joy be uncon- fined is my motto, whether there's any dance to dance, or any joy to unconfine—you'll be the healthier for it every time,— every time, Washington—it's my experience, and I've seen a good deal of this world. Come—where have you disappeared to all these years, and are you from there, now, or where are you from?"

"I don't quite think you would ever guess, Colonel. Chero- kee Strip."

"My land!"

"Sure as you live."

"You can't mean it. Actually *living* out there?"

"Well, yes, if a body may call it that; though it's a pretty strong term for 'dobies and jackass rabbits, boiled beans and slapjacks, depression, withered hopes, poverty in all its vari- eties—"

"Louise out there?"

"Yes, and the children."

"Out there now?"

"Yes, I couldn't afford to bring them with me."

"Oh, I see,—you had to come—claim against the govern- ment. Make yourself perfectly easy—I'll take care of that."

"But it isn't a claim against the government."

"No? Want to be postmaster? *That's* all right. Leave it to me. I'll fix it."

"But it isn't postmaster—you're all astray yet."

"Well, good gracious, Washington, why don't you come out and tell me what it is? What do you want to be so re- served and distrustful with an old friend like me, for? Don't you reckon I can keep a se—"

"There's no secret about it—you merely don't give me a chance to—"

"Now look here, old friend; I know the human race; and I know that when a man comes to Washington, I don't care if it's from heaven, let alone Cherokee Strip, it's because he *wants* something. And I know that as a rule he's not going to get it; that he'll stay and try for another thing and won't get that; the same luck with the next and the next and the next; and keeps on till he strikes bottom, and is too poor and ashamed to go back, even to Cherokee Strip; and at last his heart breaks and they take up a collection and bury him. There—don't interrupt me, I know what I'm talking about. Happy and prosperous in the Far West wasn't I? *You* know that. Principal citizen of Hawkeye, looked up to by everybody, kind of an autocrat, actually a kind of an autocrat, Washington. Well, nothing would do but I must go Minister to St. James, the Governor and everybody insisting, you know, and so at last I consented—no getting out of it, *had* to do it, so here I came. *A day too late*, Washington. Think of that—what little things change the world's history—yes, sir, the place had been filled. Well, there I was, you see. I offered to compromise and go to Paris. The President was very sorry and all that, but *that* place, you see, didn't belong to the West, so there I was again. There was no help for it, so I had to stoop a little—we all reach the day some time or other when we've got to do that, Washington, and it's not a bad thing for us, either, take it by and large and all around— I had to stoop a little and offer to take Constantinople. Washington, consider this—for it's perfectly true—within a month I *asked* for China; within another month I *begged* for Japan; one year later I was away down, down, down, supplicating with tears and anguish for the bottom office in the gift of the government of the United States—Flint-Picker in the cellars of the War Department. And by George I didn't get it."

"Flint-Picker?"

"Yes. Office established in the time of the Revolution, last century. The musket-flints for the military posts were supplied from the capitol. They do it yet; for although the flint-arm has gone out and the forts have tumbled down, the decree hasn't been repealed—been overlooked and forgotten, you see—and so the vacancies where old Ticonderoga and others used to stand, still get their six quarts of gun-flints a year just the same."

Washington said musingly after a pause:

"How strange it seems—to start for Minister to England at twenty thousand a year and fail for flint-picker at—"

"Three dollars a week. It's human life, Washington—just an epitome of human ambition, and struggle, and the outcome: you aim for the palace and get drowned in the sewer."

There was another meditative silence. Then Washington said, with earnest compassion in his voice—

"And so, after coming here, against your inclination, to satisfy your sense of patriotic duty and appease a selfish public clamor, you get absolutely nothing for it."

"Nothing?" The Colonel had to get up and stand, to get room for his amazement to expand. "*Nothing*, Washington? I ask you this: to be a Perpetual Member and the *only* Perpetual Member of a Diplomatic Body accredited to the greatest country on earth—do you call that nothing?"

It was Washington's turn to be amazed. He was stricken dumb; but the wide-eyed wonder, the reverent admiration expressed in his face were more eloquent than any words could have been. The Colonel's wounded spirit was healed and he resumed his seat pleased and content. He leaned forward and said impressively:

"What was due to a man who had become forever conspicuous by an experience without precedent in the history of the world?—a man made permanently and diplomatically sacred, so to speak, by having been connected, temporarily, through solicitation, with every single diplomatic post in the roster of this government, from Envoy Extraordinary and Minister Plenipotentiary to the Court of St. James all the way down to Consul to a guano rock in the Straits of Sunda—salary payable in guano—which disappeared by volcanic convulsion the day before they got down to my name in the list of applicants. Certainly something august enough to be answerable to the size of this unique and memorable experience was my due, and I got it. By the common voice of this community, by acclamation of the people, that mighty utterance which brushes aside laws and legislation, and from whose decrees there is no appeal, I was named Perpetual Member of the

Diplomatic Body representing the multifarious sovereignties and civilizations of the globe near the republican court of the United States of America. And they brought me home with a torchlight procession."

"It is wonderful, Colonel, simply wonderful."

"It's the loftiest official position in the whole earth."

"I should think so—and the most commanding."

"You have named the word. Think of it. I frown, and there is war; I smile, and contending nations lay down their arms."

"It is awful. The responsibility, I mean."

"It is nothing. Responsibility is no burden to me; I am used to it; have always been used to it."

"And the work—the work! Do you have to attend all the sittings?"

"Who, I? Does the Emperor of Russia attend the conclaves of the governors of the provinces? He sits at home, and indicates his pleasure."

Washington was silent a moment, then a deep sigh escaped him.

"How proud I was an hour ago; how paltry seems my little promotion now! Colonel, the reason I came to Washington is,—I am Congressional Delegate from Cherokee Strip!"

The Colonel sprang to his feet and broke out with prodigious enthusiasm:

"Give me your hand, my boy—this is immense news! I congratulate you with all my heart. My prophecies stand confirmed. I always said it was in you. I always said you were born for high distinction and would achieve it. You ask Polly if I didn't."

Washington was dazed by this most unexpected demonstration.

"Why, Colonel, there's nothing *to* it. That little narrow, desolate, unpeopled, oblong streak of grass and gravel, lost in the remote wastes of the vast continent—why, it's like representing a billiard table—a discarded one."

"Tut-tut, it's a great, it's a staving preferment, and just opulent with influence here."

"Shucks, Colonel, I haven't even a vote."

"That's nothing; you can make speeches."

"No, I can't. The population's only two hundred—"

"That's all right, that's all right—"

"And they hadn't any right to elect me; we're not even a territory, there's no Organic Act, the government hasn't any official knowledge of us whatever."

"Never mind about that; I'll fix that. I'll rush the thing through, I'll get you organized in no time."

"*Will* you, Colonel?—it's *too* good of you; but it's just your old sterling self, the same old ever-faithful friend," and the grateful tears welled up in Washington's eyes.

"It's just as good as done, my boy, just as good as done. Shake hands. We'll hitch teams together, you and I, and we'll make things hum!"

Chapter III

MRS. SELLERS returned, now, with her composure restored, and began to ask after Hawkins's wife, and about his children, and the number of them, and so on, and her examination of the witness resulted in a circumstantial history of the family's ups and downs and driftings to and fro in the far West during the previous fifteen years. There was a message, now, from out back, and Colonel Sellers went out there in answer to it. Hawkins took this opportunity to ask how the world had been using the Colonel during the past half-generation.

"Oh, it's been using him just the same; it couldn't change its way of using him if it wanted to, for he wouldn't let it."

"I can easily believe that, Mrs. Sellers."

"Yes, you see, he doesn't change, himself—not the least little bit in the world—he's always Mulberry Sellers."

"I can see *that* plain enough."

"Just the same old scheming, generous, good-hearted, moonshiny, hopeful, no-account failure he always was, and still everybody likes him just as well as if he was the shiningest success."

"They always did: and it was natural, because he was so obliging and accommodating, and had something about him that made it kind of easy to ask help of him, or favors—you didn't feel shy, you know, or have that wish-you-didn't-have-to-try feeling that you have with other people."

"It's just so, yet; and a body wonders at it, too, because he's been shamefully treated, many times, by people that had used him for a ladder to climb up by, and then kicked him down when they didn't need him any more. For a time you can see he's hurt, his pride's wounded, because he shrinks away from that thing and don't want to talk about it—and so I used to think *now* he's learned something and he'll be more careful hereafter—but laws! in a couple of weeks he's forgotten all about it, and any selfish tramp out of nobody knows where can come and put up a poor mouth and walk right into his heart with his boots on."

"It must try your patience pretty sharply sometimes."

"Oh, no, I'm used to it; and I'd rather have him so than the other way. When I call him a failure, I mean to the world he's a failure; he isn't to me. I don't know as I want him different—much different, anyway. I have to scold him some, snarl at him, you might even call it, but I reckon I'd do that just the same, if he was different—it's my make. But I'm a good deal less snarly and more contented when he's a failure than I am when he isn't."

"Then he isn't always a failure," said Hawkins, brightening.

"Him? Oh, bless you, no. He makes a strike, as he calls it, from time to time. Then's my time to fret and fuss. For the money just flies—first come first served. Straight off, he loads up the house with cripples and idiots and stray cats and all the different kinds of poor wrecks that other people don't want and he *does*, and then when the poverty comes again I've *got* to clear the most of them out or we'd starve; and that distresses him, and me the same, of course. Here's old Dan'l and old Jinny, that the sheriff sold south one of the times that we got bankrupted before the war—they came wandering back after the peace, worn out and used up on the cotton plantations, helpless, and not another lick of work left in their old hides for the rest of this earthly pilgrimage—and we so pinched, *oh* so pinched for the very crumbs to keep life in us, and he just flung the door wide, and the way he received them you'd have thought they had come straight down from heaven in answer to prayer. I took him one side and said, 'Mulberry we can't have them—we've nothing for ourselves—we can't feed them.' He looked at me kind of hurt, and said, 'Turn them out?—and they've come to me just as confident and trusting as—as—why Polly, I must have *bought* that confidence sometime or other a long time ago, and given my note, so to speak—you don't get such things as a *gift*—and how am I going to go back on a debt like that? And you see, they're so poor, and old, and friendless, and—' But I was ashamed by that time, and shut him off, and somehow felt a new courage in me, and so I said, softly, 'We'll keep them—the Lord will provide.' He was glad, and started to blurt out one of those over-confident speeches of his, but checked himself in time, and said humbly, '*I* will, anyway.' It was years and years and years ago. Well, you see those old wrecks are here yet."

"But don't they do your housework?"

"Laws! The idea. They would if they could, poor old things, and perhaps they think they *do* do some of it. But it's a superstition. Dan'l waits on the front door, and sometimes goes on an errand; and sometimes you'll see one or both of them letting on to dust around in here—but that's because there's something they want to hear about and mix their gabble into. And they're always around at meals, for the same reason. But the fact is, we have to keep a young negro girl just to take care of *them*, and a negro woman to do the housework and *help* take care of them."

"Well, they ought to be tolerably happy, I should think."

"It's no name for it. They quarrel together pretty much all the time—most always about religion, because Dan'l's a Dunker Baptist and Jinny's a shouting Methodist, and Jinny believes in special Providences and Dan'l don't, because he thinks he's a kind of a free-thinker—and they play and sing plantation hymns together, and talk and chatter just eternally and forever, and are sincerely fond of each other and think the world of Mulberry, and he puts up patiently with all their spoiled ways and foolishness, and so—ah, well, they're happy enough if it comes to that. And I don't mind—I've got used to it. I can get used to anything, with Mulberry to help; and the fact is, I don't much care what happens, so long as he's spared to me."

"Well, here's to him, and hoping he'll make another strike soon."

"And rake in the lame, the halt and the blind, and turn the house into a hospital again? It's what he would do. I've seen a plenty of that and more. No, Washington, I want his strikes to be mighty moderate ones the rest of the way down the vale."

"Well, then, big strike or little strike, or no strike at all, here's hoping he'll never lack for friends—and I don't reckon he ever will while there's people around who know enough to—"

"Him lack for friends!" and she tilted her head up with a frank pride—"why, Washington, you can't name a man that's anybody that isn't fond of him. I'll tell you privately, that I've had Satan's own time to keep them from appointing him to some office or other. They knew he'd no business with an office, just as well as I did, but he's the hardest man to refuse anything to, a body ever saw. Mulberry Sellers with an office! laws goodness, you know what that would be like. Why, they'd come from the ends of the earth to see a circus like that. I'd just as lieves be married to Niagara Falls, and done with it." After a reflective pause she added—having wandered back, in the interval, to the remark that had been her text: "Friends?—oh, indeed, no man ever had more; and *such* friends: Grant, Sherman, Sheridan, Johnston, Longstreet, Lee—many's the time they've sat in that chair you're sitting in—" Hawkins was out of it instantly, and contemplating it with a reverential surprise, and with the awed sense of having trodden shod upon holy ground—

"*They!*" he said.

"Oh, indeed, yes, a many and a many a time."

He continued to gaze at the chair fascinated, magnetized; and for once in his life that continental stretch of dry prairie which stood for his imagination was afire, and across it was marching a slanting flame-front that joined its wide horizons together and smothered the skies with smoke. He was experiencing what one or another drowsing, geographically-ignorant alien experiences every day in the year when he turns a dull and indifferent eye out of the car window and it falls upon a certain station-sign which reads "Stratford-on-Avon!" Mrs. Sellers went gossiping comfortably along:

"Oh, they like to hear him talk, especially if their load is getting rather heavy on one shoulder and they want to shift it. He's all air, you know,—breeze, you may say—and he freshens them up; it's a trip to the country, they say. Many a time he's made General Grant laugh—and that's a tidy job, I can tell you, and as for Sheridan, his eye lights up and he listens to Mulberry Sellers the same as if he was artillery. You see, the charm about Mulberry is, he is so catholic and unprejudiced that he fits in anywhere and everywhere. It makes him powerful good company and as popular as scandal. You go to the White House when the President's holding a general reception—sometime when Mulberry's there. Why, dear me, *you* can't tell which of them it is that's holding that reception."

"Well, he certainly is a remarkable man—and he always was. Is he religious?"

"Clear to his marrow—does more thinking and reading on that subject than any other except Russia and Siberia: thrashes around over the whole field, too; nothing bigoted about him."

"What is his religion?"

"He—" She stopped, and was lost for a moment or two in thinking, then she said, with simplicity, "I think he was a Mohammedan or something last week."

Washington started down town, now, to bring his trunk, for the hospitable Sellerses would listen to no excuses; their house must be his home during the session. The Colonel returned presently and resumed work upon his plaything. It was finished when Washington got back.

"There it is," said the Colonel, "all finished."

"What is it for, Colonel?"

"Oh, it's just a trifle. Toy to amuse the children."

Washington examined it.

"It seems to be a puzzle."

"Yes, that's what it is. I call it Pigs in the Clover. Put them in—see if you can put them in the pen."

After many failures Washington succeeded, and was as pleased as a child.

"It's wonderfully ingenious, Colonel, it's ever so clever. And interesting—why, I could play with it all day. What are you going to do with it?"

"Oh, nothing. Patent it and throw it aside."

"Don't you do anything of the kind. There's money in that thing."

A compassionate look traveled over the Colonel's countenance, and he said:

"Money—yes; pin money: a couple of hundred thousand, perhaps. Not more."

Washington's eyes blazed.

"A couple of hundred thousand dollars! do you call that pin money?"

The colonel rose and tip-toed his way across the room, closed a door that was slightly ajar, tip-toed his way to his seat again, and said, under his breath—

"You can keep a secret?"

Washington nodded his affirmative, he was too awed to speak.

"You have heard of materialization—materialization of departed spirits?"

Washington had heard of it.

"And probably didn't believe in it; and quite right, too. The thing as practised by ignorant charlatans is unworthy of attention or respect—where there's a dim light and a dark cabinet, and a parcel of sentimental gulls gathered together, with their faith and their shudders and their tears all ready, and one and the same fatty degeneration of protoplasm and humbug comes out and materializes himself into anybody you want, grandmother, grandchild, brother-in-law, Witch of Endor, John Milton, Siamese twins, Peter the Great, and all such frantic nonsense—no, that is all foolish and pitiful. But when a man that is competent brings the vast powers of *science* to bear, it's a different matter, a totally different matter, you see. The spectre that answers *that* call has come to stay. Do you note the commercial value of that detail?"

"Well, I—the—the truth is, that I don't quite know that I do. Do you mean that such, being permanent, not transitory, would give more general satisfaction, and so enhance the price of tickets to the show—"

"Show? Folly—listen to me; and get a good grip on your breath, for you are going to need it. Within three days I shall have completed my method, and then—let the world stand aghast, for it shall see marvels. Washington, within three days—ten at the outside—you shall see me call the dead of any century, and they will arise and walk. Walk?—they shall walk forever, and never die again. Walk with all the muscle and spring of their pristine vigor."

"Colonel! Indeed it does take one's breath away."

"*Now* do you see the money that's in it?"

"I'm—well, I'm—not really sure that I do."

"Great Scott, look here. I shall have a monopoly; they'll all belong to me, won't they? Two thousand policemen in the city of New York. Wages, four dollars a day. I'll replace them with dead ones at half the money."

"Oh, prodigious! I never thought of that. F-o-u-r thousand dollars a day. Now I do begin to see! But will dead policemen answer?"

"Haven't they—up to this time?"

"Well, if you put it that way—"

"Put it any way you want to. Modify it to suit yourself, and my lads shall still be superior. They won't eat, they won't drink—don't need those things; they won't wink for cash at gambling dens and unlicensed rum-holes, they won't spark the scullery maids; and moreover the bands of toughs that ambuscade them on lonely beats, and cowardly shoot and knife them will only damage the uniforms and not live long enough to get more than a momentary satisfaction out of that."

"Why, Colonel, if you can furnish policemen, then of course—"

"Certainly—I can furnish any line of goods that's wanted. Take the army, for instance—now twenty-five thousand men; expense, twenty-two millions a year. I will dig up the Romans, I will resurrect the Greeks, I will furnish the government, for ten millions a year, ten thousand veterans drawn from the victorious legions of all the ages—soldiers that will chase Indians year in and year out on materialized horses, and cost never a cent for rations or repairs. The armies of Europe cost two billions a year now—I will replace them all for a billion. I will dig up the trained statesmen of all ages and all climes, and furnish this country with a Congress that knows enough to come in out of the rain—a thing that's never happened yet, since the Declaration of Independence, and never will happen till these practically dead people are replaced with the genuine article. I will re-stock the thrones of Europe with the best brains and the best morals that all the royal sepulchres of all the centuries can furnish—which isn't promising very much—and I'll divide the wages and the civil list, fair and square, merely taking my half and—"

"Colonel, if the half of this is true, there's millions in it—millions."

"Billions in it—billions; that's what you mean. Why, look here; the thing is so close at hand, so imminent, so absolutely immediate, that if a man were to come to me now and say,

Colonel, I am a little short, and if you could lend me a couple of billion dollars for—come in!"

This in answer to a knock. An energetic looking man bustled in with a big pocket-book in his hand, took a paper from it and presented it, with the curt remark—

"Seventeenth and last call—you want to out with that three dollars and forty cents this time without fail, Colonel Mulberry Sellers."

The Colonel began to slap this pocket and that one, and feel here and there and everywhere, muttering—

"What *have* I done with that wallet?—let me see—um—not here, not there—Oh, I must have left it in the kitchen; I'll just run and—"

"No you won't—you'll stay right where you are. And you're going to disgorge, too—this time."

Washington innocently offered to go and look. When he was gone the Colonel said—

"The fact is, I've got to throw myself on your indulgence just this once more, Suggs; you see the remittances I was expecting—"

"Hang the remittances—it's too stale—it won't answer. Come!"

The Colonel glanced about him in despair. Then his face lighted; he ran to the wall and began to dust off a peculiarly atrocious chromo with his handkerchief. Then he brought it reverently, offered it to the collector, averted his face and said—

"Take it, but don't let me see it go. It's the sole remaining Rembrandt that—"

"Rembrandt be damned, it's a chromo."

"Oh, don't speak of it so, I beg you. It's the only really great original, the only supreme example of that mighty school of art which—"

"Art! It's the sickest looking thing I—"

The colonel was already bringing another horror and tenderly dusting it.

"Take this one too—the gem of my collection—the only genuine Fra Angelico that—"

"Illuminated liver-pad, that's what it is. Give it here—good day—people will think I've robbed a nigger barber-shop."

As he slammed the door behind him the Colonel shouted with an anguished accent—

"Do please cover them up—don't let the damp get at them. The delicate tints in the Angelico—"

But the man was gone.

Washington re-appeared and said he had looked everywhere, and so had Mrs. Sellers and the servants, but in vain; and went on to say he wished he could get his eye on a certain man about this time—no need to hunt up that pocketbook then. The Colonel's interest was awake at once.

"What man?"

"One-armed Pete they call him out there—out in the Cherokee country I mean. Robbed the bank in Tahlequah."

"Do they have banks in Tahlequah?"

"Yes—a bank, anyway. He was suspected of robbing it. Whoever did it got away with more than twenty thousand dollars. They offered a reward of five thousand. I believe I saw that very man, on my way east."

"No—is that so?"

"I certainly saw a man on the train, the first day I struck the railroad, that answered the description pretty exactly—at least as to clothes and a lacking arm."

"Why didn't you get him arrested and claim the reward?"

"I couldn't. I had to get a requisition, of course. But I meant to stay by him till I got my chance."

"Well?"

"Well, he left the train during the night some time."

"Oh, hang it, that's too bad."

"Not so very bad, either."

"Why?"

"Because he came down to Baltimore in the very train I was in, though I didn't know it in time. As we moved out of the station I saw him going toward the iron gate with a satchel in his hand."

"Good; we'll catch him. Let's lay a plan."

"Send description to the Baltimore police?"

"Why, what are you talking about? No. Do you want them to get the reward?"

"What shall we do, then?"

The Colonel reflected.

"I'll tell you. Put a personal in the Baltimore *Sun*. Word it like this:

A.   DROP ME A LINE, PETE—

—"Hold on. Which arm has he lost?"
"The right."
"Good. Now then—

A.   DROP ME A LINE, PETE, EVEN IF YOU HAVE
   to write with your left hand. Address X. Y. Z., General
   Postoffice, Washington. From YOU KNOW WHO.

"There—that'll fetch him."
"But he *won't* know who—will he?"
"No, but he'll want to know, won't he?"
"Why, certainly—I didn't think of that. What made you think of it?"
"Knowledge of human curiosity. Strong trait, very strong trait."
"Now I'll go to my room and write it out and enclose a dollar and tell them to print it to the worth of that."

Chapter IV

THE DAY wore itself out. After dinner the two friends put in a long and harassing evening trying to decide what to do with the five thousand dollars reward which they were going to get when they should find One-Armed Pete, and catch him, and prove him to be the right person, and extradite him, and ship him to Tahlequah in the Indian Territory. But there were so many dazzling openings for ready cash that they found it impossible to make up their minds and keep them made up. Finally, Mrs. Sellers grew very weary of it all, and said:

"What is the sense in cooking a rabbit before it's caught?"

Then the matter was dropped, for the time being, and all went to bed. Next morning, being persuaded by Hawkins, the colonel made drawings and specifications and went down and applied for a patent for his toy puzzle, and Hawkins took the toy itself and started out to see what chance there might be to do something with it commercially. He did not have to go far. In a small old wooden shanty which had once been occupied as a dwelling by some humble negro family he found a keen-eyed Yankee engaged in repairing cheap chairs and other second-hand furniture. This man examined the toy indifferently; attempted to do the puzzle; found it not so easy as he had expected; grew more interested, and finally emphatically so; achieved a success at last, and asked—

"Is it patented?"

"Patent applied for."

"That will answer. What do you want for it?"

"What will it retail for?"

"Well, twenty-five cents, I should think."

"What will you give for the exclusive right?"

"I couldn't give twenty dollars, if I had to pay cash down; but I'll tell you what I'll do. I'll make it and market it, and pay you five cents royalty on each one."

Washington sighed. Another dream disappeared; no money in the thing. So he said—

"All right, take it at that. Draw me a paper."

He went his way with the paper, and dropped the matter out of his mind—dropped it out to make room for further attempts to think out the most promising way to invest his half of the reward, in case a partnership investment satisfactory to both beneficiaries could not be hit upon.

He had not been very long at home when Sellers arrived sodden with grief and booming with glad excitement—working both these emotions successfully, sometimes separately, sometimes together. He fell on Hawkins's neck sobbing, and said—

"Oh, mourn with me my friend, mourn for my desolate house: death has smitten my last kinsman and I am Earl of Rossmore—congratulate me!"

He turned to his wife, who had entered while this was going on, put his arms about her and said—"You will bear up, for my sake, my lady—it had to happen, it was decreed."

She bore up very well, and said—

"It's no great loss. Simon Lathers was a poor well-meaning useless thing and no account, and his brother never was worth shucks."

The rightful earl continued—

"I am too much prostrated by these conflicting griefs and joys to be able to concentrate my mind upon affairs; I will ask our good friend here to break the news by wire or post to the Lady Gwendolen and instruct her to—"

"*What* Lady Gwendolen?"

"Our poor daughter, who, alas!—"

"Sally Sellers? Mulberry Sellers, are you losing your mind?"

"There—please do not forget who you are, and who I am; remember your own dignity, be considerate also of mine. It were best to cease from using my family name, now, Lady Rossmore."

"Goodness gracious, well, I never! What *am* I to call you then?"

"In private, the ordinary terms of endearment will still be admissible, to some degree; but in public it will be more becoming if your ladyship will speak *to* me as my lord, or your lordship, and *of* me as Rossmore, or the Earl, or his Lordship, and—"

"Oh, scat! I can't ever do it, Berry."

"But indeed you must, my love—we must live up to our altered position and submit with what grace we may to its requirements."

"Well, all right, have it your own way; I've never set my wishes against your commands yet, Mul—my lord, and it's late to begin now, though to my mind it's the rottenest foolishness that ever was."

"Spoken like my own true wife! There, kiss and be friends again."

"But—Gwendolen! I don't know how I am ever going to stand that name. Why, a body wouldn't *know* Sally Sellers in it. It's too large for her; kind of like a cherub in an ulster, and it's a most outlandish sort of a name, anyway, to my mind."

"You'll not hear her find fault with it, my lady."

"That's a true word. She takes to any kind of romantic rubbish like she was born to it. She never got it from me, that's sure. And sending her to that silly college hasn't helped the matter any—just the other way."

"Now hear her, Hawkins! Rowena-Ivanhoe College is the selectest and most aristocratic seat of learning for young ladies in our country. Under no circumstances can a girl get in there unless she is either very rich and fashionable or can prove four generations of what may be called American nobility. Castellated college-buildings—towers and turrets and an imitation moat—and everything about the place named out of Sir Walter Scott's books and redolent of royalty and state and style; and all the richest girls keep phaetons, and coachmen in livery, and riding-horses, with English grooms in plug hats and tight-buttoned coats, and top-boots, and a whip-handle without any whip to it, to ride sixty-three feet behind them—"

"And they don't learn a blessed thing, Washington Hawkins, not a single blessed thing but showy rubbish and unamerican pretentiousness. But send for the Lady Gwendolen—do; for I reckon the peerage regulations require that she must come home and let on to go into seclusion and mourn for those Arkansas blatherskites she's lost."

"My darling! Blatherskites? Remember—*noblesse oblige.*"

"There, there—talk to me in your own tongue, Ross—you don't know any other, and you only botch it when you try. Oh, don't stare—it was a slip, and no crime; customs of a lifetime can't be dropped in a second. Ross*more*—there, now, be appeased, and go along with you and attend to Gwendolen. Are you going to write, Washington?—or telegraph?"

"He will telegraph, dear."

"I thought as much," my lady muttered, as she left the room. "Wants it so the address will have to appear on the envelop. It will just make a fool of that child. She'll get it, of course, for if there are any other Sellerses there they'll not be able to claim it. And just leave her alone to show it around and make the most of it.——Well, maybe she's forgivable for that. She's so poor and they're so rich, of course she's had her share of snubs from the livery-flunkey sort, and I reckon it's only human to want to get even."

Uncle Dan'l was sent with the telegram; for although a conspicuous object in a corner of the drawing-room was a telephone hanging on a transmitter, Washington found all attempts to raise the central office vain. The Colonel grumbled something about its being "*always* out of order when you've got particular and especial use for it," but he didn't explain that one of the reasons for this was that the thing was only a dummy and hadn't any wire attached to it. And yet the Colonel often used it—when visitors were present—and seemed to get messages through it. Mourning paper and a seal were ordered, then the friends took a rest.

Next afternoon, while Hawkins, by request, draped Andrew Jackson's portrait with crape, the rightful earl wrote off the family bereavement to the usurper in England—a letter which we have already read. He also, by letter to the village authorities at Duffy's Corners, Arkansas, gave order that the remains of the late twins be embalmed by some St. Louis expert and shipped at once to the usurper—with bill. Then he drafted out the Rossmore arms and motto on a great sheet of brown paper, and he and Hawkins took it to Hawkins's Yankee furniture-mender and at the end of an hour came back with a couple of stunning hatchments, which they nailed up on the front of the house—attractions calculated to draw, and they did; for it was mainly an idle and shiftless negro neighborhood, with plenty of ragged children and indolent dogs to spare for a point of interest like that, and keep on sparing them for it, days and days together.

The new earl found—without surprise—this society item in the evening paper, and cut it out and scrap-booked it:

By a recent bereavement our esteemed fellow citizen, Colonel Mulberry Sellers, Perpetual Member-at-large of the Diplomatic Body, succeeds, as rightful lord, to the great earldom of Rossmore, third by order of precedence in the earldoms of Great Britain, and will take early measures, by suit in the House of Lords, to wrest the title and estates from the present usurping holder of them. Until the season of mourning is past, the usual Thursday evening receptions at Rossmore Towers will be discontinued.

Lady Rossmore's comment—to herself:

"Receptions! People who don't rightly know him may think he is commonplace, but to my mind he is one of the most unusual men I ever saw. As for suddenness and capacity in imagining things, his beat don't exist, I reckon. As like as not it wouldn't have occurred to anybody else to name this poor old rat-trap Rossmore Towers, but it just comes natural to him. Well, no doubt it's a blessed thing to have an imagination that can always make you satisfied, no matter how you are fixed. Uncle Dave Hopkins used to always say, 'Turn me into John Calvin, and I want to know which place I'm going to; turn me into Mulberry Sellers and I don't care.' "

The rightful earl's comment—to himself:

"It's a beautiful name, beautiful. Pity I didn't think of it before I wrote the usurper. But I'll be ready for him when he answers."

Chapter V

NO ANSWER to that telegram; no arriving daughter. Yet nobody showed any uneasiness or seemed surprised; that is, nobody but Washington. After three days of waiting, he asked Lady Rossmore what she supposed the trouble was. She answered, tranquilly;

"Oh, it's some notion of hers, you never can tell. She's a Sellers, all through—at least in some of her ways; and a Sellers can't tell you beforehand what he's going to do, because he don't know himself till he's done it. *She's* all right; no occasion to worry about *her*. When she's ready she'll come or she'll write, and you can't tell which, till it's happened."

It turned out to be a letter. It was handed in at that moment, and was received by the mother without trembling hands or feverish eagerness, or any other of the manifestations common in the case of long delayed answers to imperative telegrams. She polished her glasses with tranquility and thoroughness, pleasantly gossiping along, the while, then opened the letter and began to read aloud:

KENILWORTH KEEP, REDGAUNTLET HALL,
ROWENA-IVANHOE COLLEGE, THURSDAY.

DEAR PRECIOUS MAMMA ROSSMORE:

Oh, the joy of it!—you can't think. They had always turned up their noses at our pretentions, you know; and I had fought back as well as I could by turning up mine at theirs. They always said it might be something great and fine to be rightful Shadow of an earldom, but to merely be shadow *of* a shadow, and two or three times removed at that—pooh-pooh! And I always retorted that not to be able to show four generations of American-Colonial-Dutch-Peddler-and-Salt-Cod-McAllister-Nobility might be endurable, but to *have* to confess such an origin—pfew-few! Well, the telegram, it was just a cyclone! The messenger came right into the great Rob Roy Hall of Audience, as excited as he could be, singing out, "Dispatch for Lady Gwendolen Sellers!" and you ought to have seen that simpering chattering assemblage of pinchbeck aristocrats turn to stone! I was off in the corner, of course, by myself—it's where Cinderella belongs. I took the telegram and read it, and tried to faint—and I could have done it if I had had any preparation, but it was all so sudden, you know—but no matter, I did the next best thing: I put my handkerchief to my eyes and fled sobbing to my room, dropping the telegram as I started. I released one corner of my eye a moment—just enough to see the herd swarm for the telegram—and then continued my broken-hearted flight just as happy as a bird.

Then the visits of condolence began, and I had to accept the loan of Miss Augusta-Templeton-Ashmore Hamilton's quarters because the press was so great and there isn't room for three and a cat in mine. And I've been holding a Lodge of Sorrow ever since and defending myself against people's attempts to claim kin. And do you know, the very first girl to fetch her tears and sympathy to my market was that foolish Skimperton girl who has always snubbed me so shamefully and claimed lordship and precedence of the whole college because some ancestor of hers, some time or other, was a McAllister. Why it was like the bottom bird in the menagerie putting on airs because its head ancestor was a pterodactyl.

But the ger-reatest triumph of all was—guess. But you'll never. This is it. That little fool and two others have always been fussing and fretting over which was entitled to precedence—by rank, you know. They've nearly starved themselves at it; for each claimed the right to take precedence of all the college in leaving the table, and so neither of them ever finished her dinner, but broke off in the middle and tried to get out ahead of the others. Well, after my first day's grief and seclusion—I was fixing up a mourning dress you see—I appeared at the public table again, and then—what do you think? Those three fluffy goslings sat there contentedly, and squared up the long famine—lapped and lapped, munched and munched, ate and ate, till the gravy appeared in their eyes—humbly waiting for the Lady Gwendolen to take precedence and move out first, you see!

Oh, yes, I've been having a darling good time. And do you know, not one of these collegians has had the cruelty to ask me how I came by my new name. With some, this is due to charity, but with the others it isn't. They refrain, not from native kindness but from educated discretion. I educated them.

Well, as soon as I shall have settled up what's left of the old scores and snuffed up a few more of those pleasantly intoxicating clouds of incense, I shall pack and depart homeward. Tell papa I am as fond of him as I am of my new name. I couldn't put it stronger than that. What an inspiration it was! But inspirations come easy to him.

These, from your loving daughter,
GWENDOLEN.

Hawkins reached for the letter and glanced over it.

"Good hand," he said, "and full of confidence and animation, and goes racing right along. She's bright—that's plain."

"Oh, they're all bright—the Sellerses. Anyway, they would be, if there were any. Even those poor Latherses would have been bright if they had been Sellerses; I mean full blood. Of course they had a Sellers strain in them—a big strain of it, too—but being a Bland dollar don't make it a *dollar* just the same."

The seventh day after the date of the telegram Washington came dreaming down to breakfast and was set wide awake by an electrical spasm of pleasure. Here was the most beautiful young creature he had ever seen in his life. It was Sally Sellers Lady Gwendolen; she had come in the night. And it seemed to him that her clothes were the prettiest and the daintiest he had ever looked upon, and the most exquisitely contrived and fashioned and combined, as to decorative trimmings, and fixings, and melting harmonies of color. It was only a morning dress, and inexpensive, but he confessed to himself, in the English common to Cherokee Strip, that it was a "corker." And now, as he perceived, the reason why the Sellers household poverties and sterilities had been made to blossom like the rose, and charm the eye and satisfy the spirit, stood explained; here was the magician; here in the midst of her works, and furnishing in her own person the proper accent and climaxing finish of the whole.

"My daughter, Major Hawkins—come home to mourn; flown home at the call of affliction to help the authors of her being bear the burden of bereavement. She was very fond of the late earl—idolized him, sir, idolized him—"

"Why, father, I've never seen him."

"True—she's right, I was thinking of another—er—of her mother—"

"*I* idolized that smoked haddock?—that sentimental, spiritless—"

"I was thinking of myself! Poor noble fellow, we were inseparable com—"

"Hear the man! Mulberry Sel—Mul—Rossmore!—hang the troublesome name I can never—if I've heard you say once, I've heard you say a thousand times that if that poor sheep—"

"I was thinking of—of—I don't know who I was thinking of, and it doesn't make any difference anyway; *some*body idolized him, I recollect it as if it were yesterday; and—"

"Father, I am going to shake hands with Major Hawkins, and let the introduction work along and catch up at its leisure. I remember you very well indeed, Major Hawkins, although I was a little child when I saw you last; and I am very, very glad indeed to see you again and have you in our house as one of us;" and beaming in his face she finished her cordial shake with the hope that he had not forgotten her.

He was prodigiously pleased by her outspoken heartiness, and wanted to repay her by assuring her that he remembered her, and not only that but better even than he remembered his own children, but the facts would not quite warrant this; still, he stumbled through a tangled sentence which answered just as well, since the purport of it was an awkward and unintentional confession that her extraordinary beauty had so stupefied him that he hadn't got back to his bearings, yet, and therefore couldn't be certain as to whether he remembered her at all or not. The speech made him her friend; it couldn't well help it.

In truth the beauty of this fair creature was of a rare type, and may well excuse a moment of our time spent in its consideration. It did not consist in the *fact* that she had eyes, nose, mouth, chin, hair, ears, it consisted in their arrangement. In true beauty, more depends upon right location and judicious distribution of feature than upon multiplicity of them. So also as regards color. The very combination of colors which in a volcanic irruption would add beauty to a landscape might detach it from a girl. Such was Gwendolen Sellers.

The family circle being completed by Gwendolen's arrival, it was decreed that the official mourning should now begin; that it should begin at six o'clock every evening, (the dinner hour,) and end with the dinner.

"It's a grand old line, major, a sublime old line, and deserves to be mourned for, almost royally; almost imperially, I may say. Er—Lady Gwendolen—but she's gone; never mind; I wanted my Peerage; I'll fetch it myself, presently, and show you a thing or two that will give you a realizing idea of what our house is. I've been glancing through Burke, and I find that of William the Conqueror's sixty-four natural ch—my dear, would you mind getting me that book? It's on the escritoire in our boudoir. Yes, as I was saying, there's only St. Albans, Buccleugh and Grafton ahead of us on the list—all the rest of the British nobility are in procession behind us. Ah, thanks, my lady. Now then, we turn to William, and we find—letter for XYZ? Oh, splendid—when'd you get it?"

"Last night; but I was asleep before you came, you were out so late; and when I came to breakfast Miss Gwendolen—well, she knocked everything out of me, you know—"

"Wonderful girl, wonderful; her great origin is detectable in her step, her carriage, her features—but what does he *say*? Come, this is exciting."

"I haven't read it—er—Rossm—Mr. Rossm—er—"

"M'lord! Just cut it short like that. It's the English way. I'll open it. Ah, now let's see."

A. TO YOU KNOW WHO. Think I know you. Wait ten days. Coming to Washington.

The excitement died out of both men's faces. There was a brooding silence for a while, then the younger one said with a sigh:

"Why, *we* can't wait ten days for the money."

"No—the man's unreasonable; we are down to the bed rock, financially speaking."

"If we could explain to him in some way, that we are so situated that time is of the utmost importance to us—"

"Yes-yes, that's it—and so if it would be as convenient for him to come at once it would be a great accommodation to us, and one which we—which we—"

—"which we—wh—"

—"well, which we should sincerely appreciate—"

"That's it—and most gladly reciprocate—"

"Certainly—that'll fetch him. Worded right, if he's a *man*—got any of the *feelings* of a man, *sympathies* and all that, he'll be here inside of twenty-four hours. Pen and paper—come, we'll get right at it."

Between them they framed twenty-two different advertisements, but none was satisfactory. A main fault in all of them was urgency. That feature was very troublesome: if made prominent, it was calculated to excite Pete's suspicion; if modified below the suspicion-point it was flat and meaning-less. Finally the Colonel resigned, and said—

"I have noticed, in such literary experiences as I have had, that one of the most taking things to do is to conceal your meaning when you are *trying* to conceal it. Whereas, if you go at literature with a free conscience and nothing to conceal, you can turn out a book, every time, that the very elect can't understand. They all do."

Then Hawkins resigned also, and the two agreed that they must manage to wait the ten days some how or other. Next, they caught a ray of cheer: since they had something definite to go upon, now, they could probably borrow money on the reward—enough, at any rate, to tide them over till they got it; and meantime the materializing recipe would be perfected, and then good bye to trouble for good and all.

The next day, May the tenth, a couple of things happened—among others. The remains of the noble Arkansas twins left our shores for England, consigned to Lord Ross-more, and Lord Rossmore's son, Kirkcudbright Llanover Marjoribanks Sellers Viscount Berkeley, sailed from Liverpool for America to place the reversion of the earldom in the hands of the rightful peer, Mulberry Sellers, of Rossmore Towers in the District of Columbia, U.S.A.

These two impressive shipments would meet and part in mid-Atlantic, five days later, and give no sign.

Chapter VI

I N THE COURSE of time the twins arrived and were delivered to their great kinsman. To try to describe the rage of that old man would profit nothing, the attempt would fall so far short of the purpose. However when he had worn himself out and got quiet again, he looked the matter over and decided that the twins had some moral rights, although they had no legal ones; they were of his blood, and it could not be decorous to treat them as common clay. So he laid them with their majestic kin in the Cholmondeley church, with imposing state and ceremony, and added the supreme touch by officiating as chief mourner himself. But he drew the line at hatchments.

Our friends in Washington watched the weary days go by, while they waited for Pete and covered his name with reproaches because of his calamitous procrastinations. Meantime, Sally Sellers, who was as practical and democratic as the Lady Gwendolen Sellers was romantic and aristocratic, was leading a life of intense interest and activity and getting the most she could out of her double personality. All day long in the privacy of her work-room, Sally Sellers earned bread for the Sellers family; and all the evening Lady Gwendolen Sellers supported the Rossmore dignity. All day she was American, practically, and proud of the work of her head and hands and its commercial result; all the evening she took holiday and dwelt in a rich shadow-land peopled with titled and coroneted fictions. By day, to her, the place was a plain, unaffected, ramshackle old trap—just that, and nothing more; by night it was Rossmore Towers. At college she had learned a trade without knowing it. The girls had found out that she was the designer of her own gowns. She had no idle moments after that, and wanted none; for the exercise of an extraordinary gift is the supremest pleasure in life, and it was manifest that Sally Sellers possessed a gift of that sort in the matter of costume-designing. Within three days after reaching home she had hunted up some work; before Pete was yet due in Washington, and before the twins were fairly asleep in English soil, she was already nearly swamped with work, and the sacrificing of the family chromos for debt had got an effective check.

"She's a brick," said Rossmore to the Major; "just her father all over: prompt to labor with head or hands, and not ashamed of it; capable, always capable, let the enterprise be what it may; successful by nature—don't know what defeat is; thus, intensely and practically American by inhaled nationalism, and at the same time intensely and aristocratically European by inherited nobility of blood. Just me, exactly: Mulberry Sellers in matter of finance and invention; after office hours, what do you find? The same clothes, yes, but what's in them? Rossmore of the peerage."

The two friends had haunted the general post-office daily. At last they had their reward. Toward evening the 20th of May, they got a letter for XYZ. It bore the Washington postmark; the note itself was not dated. It said:

> "Ash barrel back of lamp post Black horse Alley. If you are playing square go and set on it to-morrow morning 21st 10.22 not sooner not later wait till I come."

The friends cogitated over the note profoundly. Presently the earl said:

"Don't you reckon he's afraid we are a sheriff with a requisition?"

"Why, m'lord?"

"Because that's no place for a séance. Nothing friendly, nothing sociable about it. And at the same time, a body that wanted to know who was roosting on that ash-barrel without exposing himself by going near it, or seeming to be interested in it, could just stand on the street corner and take a glance down the alley and satisfy himself, don't you see?"

"Yes, his idea is plain, now. He seems to be a man that can't *be* candid and straightforward. He acts as if he thought we—shucks, I wish he had come out like a man and told us what hotel he—"

"Now you've struck it! you've struck it sure, Washington; he has told us."

"Has he?"

"Yes, he has; but he didn't mean to. That alley is a lone-some little pocket that runs along one side of the New Gadsby. That's his hotel."

"What makes you think that?"

"Why, I just know it. He's got a room that's just across from that lamp post. He's going to sit there perfectly comfortable behind his shutters at 10.22 to-morrow, and when he sees us sitting on the ash-barrel, he'll say to himself, 'I saw *one* of those fellows on the train'—and then he'll pack his satchel in half a minute and ship for the ends of the earth."

Hawkins turned sick with disappointment:

"Oh, dear, it's all up, Colonel—it's exactly what he'll do."

"Indeed he won't!"

"Won't he? Why?"

"Because *you* won't be holding the ash barrel down, it'll be me. You'll be coming in with an officer and a requisition in plain clothes—the officer, I mean—the minute you see him arrive and open up a talk with me."

"Well, what a head you have got, Colonel Sellers! I never should have thought of that in the world."

"Neither would any earl of Rossmore, betwixt William's contribution and Mulberry—*as* earl; but it's office hours, now, you see, and the earl in me sleeps. Come—I'll show you his very room."

They reached the neighborhood of the New Gadsby about nine in the evening, and passed down the alley to the lamp post.

"There you are," said the colonel, triumphantly, with a wave of his hand which took in the whole side of the hotel. "There it is—what did I tell you?"

"Well, but—why, Colonel, it's six stories high. I don't quite make out which window you—"

"All the windows, all of them. Let him have his choice—I'm indifferent, now that I have located him. You go and stand on the corner and wait; I'll prospect the hotel."

The earl drifted here and there through the swarming lobby, and finally took a waiting position in the neighborhood of the elevator. During an hour crowds went up and crowds came down; and all complete as to limbs; but at last the watcher got a glimpse of a figure that was satisfactory—got a glimpse of the back of it, though he had missed his chance at the face through waning alertness. The glimpse revealed a cowboy hat, and below it a plaided sack of rather loud pattern, and an empty sleeve pinned up to the shoulder. Then the elevator snatched the vision aloft and the watcher fled away in joyful excitement, and rejoined the fellow-conspirator.

"We've got him, Major—got him sure! I've seen him—seen him good; and I don't care where or when that man approaches me backwards, I'll recognize him everytime. We're all right. Now for the requisition."

They got it, after the delays usual in such cases. By half past eleven they were at home and happy, and went to bed full of dreams of the morrow's great promise.

Among the elevator load which had the suspect for fellow-passenger was a young kinsman of Mulberry Sellers, but Mulberry was not aware of it and didn't see him. It was Viscount Berkeley.

Chapter VII

A RRIVED in his room Lord Berkeley made preparations for that first and last and all-the-time duty of the visiting Englishman—the jotting down in his diary of his "impressions" to date. His preparations consisted in ransacking his "box" for a pen. There was a plenty of steel pens on his table with the ink bottle, but he was English. The English people manufacture steel pens for nineteen-twentieths of the globe, but they never use any themselves. They use exclusively the pre-historic quill. My lord not only found a quill pen, but the best one he had seen in several years—and after writing diligently for some time, closed with the following entry:

But in one thing I have made an immense mistake. I ought to have sunk my title and changed my name before I started.

He sat admiring that pen a while, and then went on:

"All attempts to mingle with the common people and become permanently one of them are going to fail, unless I can get rid of it, disappear from it, and re-appear with the solid protection of a new name. I am astonished and pained to see how eager the most of these Americans are to get acquainted with a lord, and how diligent they are in pushing attentions upon him. They lack English servility, it is true—but they could acquire it, with practice. My quality travels ahead of me in the most mysterious way. I write my family name without additions, on the register of this hotel, and imagine that I am going to pass for an obscure and unknown wanderer, but the clerk promptly calls out, 'Front! show his lordship to four-eighty-two!' and before I can get to the lift there is a reporter trying to interview me, as they call it. This sort of thing shall cease at once. I will hunt up the American Claimant the first thing in the morning, accomplish my mission, then change my lodging and vanish from scrutiny under a fictitious name."

He left his diary on the table, where it would be handy in case any new "impressions" should wake him up in the night, then he went to bed and presently fell asleep. An hour or two passed, and then he came slowly to consciousness with a confusion of mysterious and augmenting sounds hammering at the gates of his brain for admission; the next moment he was sharply awake, and those sounds burst with the rush and roar and boom of an undammed freshet into his ears. Banging and slamming of shutters; smashing of windows and the ringing clash of falling glass; clatter of flying feet along the halls; shrieks, supplications, dumb moanings of despair, within, hoarse shouts of command outside; cracklings and snappings, and the windy roar of victorious flames!

Bang, bang, bang! on the door, and a cry—

"Turn out—the house is on fire!"

The cry passed on, and the banging. Lord Berkeley sprang out of bed and moved with all possible speed toward the clothes-press in the darkness and the gathering smoke, but fell over a chair and lost his bearings. He groped desperately about on his hands, and presently struck his head against the table and was deeply grateful, for it gave him his bearings again, since it stood close by the door. He seized his most precious possession, his journaled Impressions of America, and darted from the room.

He ran down the deserted hall toward the red lamp which he knew indicated the place of a fire-escape. The door of the room beside it was open. In the room the gas was burning full head; on a chair was a pile of clothing. He ran to the window, could not get it up, but smashed it with a chair, and stepped out on the landing of the fire-escape; below him was a crowd of men, with a sprinkling of women and youth, massed in a ruddy light. Must he go down in his spectral night dress? No—this side of the house was not yet on fire except at the further end; he would snatch on those clothes.

Which he did. They fitted well enough, though a trifle loosely, and they were just a shade loud as to pattern. Also as to hat—which was of a new breed to him, Buffalo Bill not having been to England yet. One side of the coat went on, but the other side refused; one of its sleeves was turned up and stitched to the shoulder. He started down without waiting to get it loose, made the trip successfully, and was promptly hustled outside the limit-rope by the police.

The cowboy hat and the coat but half on made him too much of a centre of attraction for comfort, although nothing could be more profoundly respectful, not to say deferential, than was the manner of the crowd toward him. In his mind he framed a discouraged remark for early entry in his diary: "It is of no use; they know a lord through any disguise, and show awe of him—even something very like fear, indeed."

Presently one of the gaping and adoring half-circle of boys ventured a timid question. My lord answered it. The boys glanced wonderingly at each other and from somewhere fell the comment—

"*English* cowboy! Well, if that ain't curious."

Another mental note to be preserved for the diary: "Cowboy. Now what might a cowboy be? Perhaps—" But the viscount perceived that some more questions were about to be asked; so he worked his way out of the crowd, released the sleeve, put on the coat and wandered away to seek a humble and obscure lodging. He found it and went to bed and was soon asleep.

In the morning, he examined his clothes. They were rather assertive, it seemed to him, but they were new and clean, at any rate. There was considerable property in the pockets. Item, five one-hundred dollar bills. Item, near fifty dollars in small bills and silver. Plug of tobacco. Hymn-book, which refuses to open; found to contain whiskey. Memorandum book bearing no name. Scattering entries in it, recording in a sprawling, ignorant hand, appointments, bets, horse-trades, and so on, with people of strange, hyphenated name—Six-Fingered Jake, Young-Man-afraid-of-his-Shadow, and the like. No letters, no documents.

The young man muses—maps out his course. His letter of credit is burned; he will borrow the small bills and the silver in these pockets, apply part of it to advertising for the owner, and use the rest for sustenance while he seeks work. He sends out for the morning paper, next, and proceeds to read about the fire. The biggest line in the display-head announces his own death! The body of the account furnishes all the particulars; and tells how, with the inherited heroism of his caste, he went on saving women and children until escape for himself was impossible; then with the eyes of weeping multitudes upon him, he stood with folded arms and sternly awaited the approach of the devouring fiend; "and so standing, amid a tossing sea of flame and on-rushing billows of smoke, the noble young heir of the great house of Rossmore was caught up in a whirlwind of fiery glory, and disappeared forever from the vision of men."

The thing was so fine and generous and knightly that it brought the moisture to his eyes. Presently he said to himself: "What to do is as plain as day, now. My Lord Berkeley is dead—let him stay so. Died creditably, too; that will make the calamity the easier for my father. And I don't have to report to the American Claimant, now. Yes, nothing could be better than the way matters have turned out. I have only to furnish myself with a new name, and take my new start in life totally untrammeled. Now I breathe my first breath of real freedom; and how fresh and breezy and inspiring it is! At last I am a man! a man on equal terms with my neighbor; and by my manhood, and by it alone, I shall rise and be seen of the world, or I shall sink from sight and deserve it. This *is* the gladdest day, and the proudest, that ever poured its sun upon my head!"

Chapter VIII

"GOD BLESS my soul, Hawkins!"

The morning paper dropped from the Colonel's nerveless grasp.

"What is it?"

"He's gone!—the bright, the young, the gifted, the noblest of his illustrious race—gone! gone up in flames and unimaginable glory!"

"Who?"

"My precious, precious young kinsman—Kirkcudbright Llanover Marjoribanks Sellers Viscount Berkeley, son and heir of usurping Rossmore."

"No!"

"It's true—too true."

"When?"

"Last night."

"Where?"

"Right here in Washington, where he arrived from England last night, the papers say."

"You don't say!"

"Hotel burned down."

"What hotel?"

"The New Gadsby!"

"Oh, my goodness! And have we lost *both* of them?"

"Both *who*?"

"One-Arm Pete."

"Oh, great guns, I forgot all about him. Oh, I hope not."

"Hope! Well, I should say! Oh, we *can't* spare *him*! We can better afford to lose a million viscounts than our only support and stay."

They searched the paper diligently, and were appalled to find that a one-armed man had been seen flying along one of the halls of the hotel in his under-clothing and apparently out of his head with fright, and as he would listen to no one and persisted in making for a stairway which would carry him to certain death, his case was given over as a hopeless one.

"Poor fellow," sighed Hawkins; "and he had friends so near. I wish we hadn't come away from there—maybe we could have saved him."

The earl looked up and said calmly—

"His being dead doesn't matter. He was uncertain before. We've got him sure, this time."

"Got him? How?"

"I will materialize him."

"Rossmore, don't—don't trifle with me. Do you mean that? Can you do it?"

"I can do it, just as sure as you are sitting there. And I will."

"Give me your hand, and let me have the comfort of shaking it. I was perishing, and you have put new life into me. Get at it, oh, get at it right away."

"It will take a little time, Hawkins, but there's no hurry, none in the world—in the circumstances. And of course certain duties have devolved upon me now, which necessarily claim my first attention. This poor young nobleman—"

"Why, yes, I am sorry for my heartlessness, and you smitten with this new family affliction. Of course you must materialize him first—I quite understand that."

"I—I—well, I wasn't meaning just that, but,—why, what am I thinking of! Of course I must materialize him. Oh, Hawkins, selfishness is the bottom trait in human nature; I was only thinking that now, with the usurper's heir out of the way—— But you'll forgive that momentary weakness, and forget it. Don't ever remember it against me that Mulberry Sellers was once mean enough to think the thought that I was thinking. I'll materialize him—I will, on my honor—and I'd do it were he a thousand heirs jammed into one and stretching in a solid rank from here to the stolen estates of Rossmore, and barring the road forever to the rightful earl!

"There spoke the real Sellers—the other had a false ring, old friend."

"Hawkins, my boy, it just occurs to me—a thing I keep forgetting to mention—a matter that we've got to be mighty careful about."

"What is that?"

"We must keep absolutely still about these materializations. Mind, not a hint of them must escape—not a hint. To say nothing of how my wife and daughter—high-strung, sensitive organizations—might feel about them, the negroes wouldn't stay on the place a minute."

"That's true, they wouldn't. It's well you spoke, for I'm not naturally discreet with my tongue when I'm not warned."

Sellers reached out and touched a bell-button in the wall; set his eye upon the rear door and waited; touched it again and waited; and just as Hawkins was remarking admiringly that the Colonel was the most progressive and most alert man he had ever seen, in the matter of impressing into his service every modern convenience the moment it was invented, and always keeping breast to breast with the drum major in the great work of material civilization, he forsook the button (which hadn't any wire attached to it,) rang a vast dinner bell which stood on the table, and remarked that he had tried that new-fangled dry battery, now, to his entire satisfaction, and had got enough of it; and added—

"Nothing would do Graham Bell but I must try it; said the mere *fact* of my trying it would secure public confidence, and get it a chance to show what it could do. I *told* him that in theory a dry battery was just a curled darling and no mistake, but when it come to *practice*, sho!—and here's the result. Was I right? What should *you* say, Washington Hawkins? You've seen me try that button twice. Was I right?—that's the idea. Did I know what I was talking about, or didn't I?"

"Well, you know how I feel about you, Colonel Sellers, and always have felt. It seems to me that you always know everything about *every*thing. If that man had known you as I know you he would have taken your judgment at the start, and dropped his dry battery where it was."

"Did you ring, Marse Sellers?"

"No, Marse Sellers didn't."

"Den it was you, Marse Washington. I's heah, suh."

"No, it wasn't Marse Washington, either."

"De good lan'! who did ring her, den?"

"Lord Rossmore rang it!"

The old negro flung up his hands and exclaimed—

"Blame my skin if I hain't gone en forgit dat name agin! Come heah, Jinny—run heah, honey."

Jinny arrived.

"You take dish-yer order de lord gwine to give you. I's gwine down suller and study dat name tell I git it."

"I take de order! Who's yo' nigger las' year? De bell rung for *you*."

"Dat don't make no diffunce. When a bell ring for anybody, en old marster tell me to—"

"Clear out, and settle it in the kitchen!"

The noise of the quarreling presently sank to a murmur in the distance, and the earl added: "That's a trouble with old house servants that were your slaves once and have been your personal friends always."

"Yes, and members of the family."

"Members of the family is just what they become—*the* members of the family, in fact. And sometimes master and mistress of the household. These two are mighty good and loving and faithful and honest, but hang it, they do just about as they please, they chip into a conversation whenever they want to, and the plain fact is, they ought to be killed."

It was a random remark, but it gave him an idea—however, nothing could happen without that result.

"What I wanted, Hawkins, was to send for the family and break the news to them."

"O, never mind bothering with the servants, then. I will go and bring them down."

While he was gone, the earl worked his idea.

"Yes," he said to himself, "when I've got the materializing down to a certainty, I will get Hawkins to kill them, and after that they will be under better control. Without doubt a materialized negro could easily be hypnotized into a state resembling silence. And this could be made permanent—yes, and also modifiable, at will—sometimes *very* silent, sometimes turn on more talk, more action, more emotion, according to what you want. It's a prime good idea. Make it adjustable—with a screw or something."

The two ladies entered, now, with Hawkins, and the two negroes followed, uninvited, and fell to brushing and dusting around, for they perceived that there was matter of interest to the fore, and were willing to find out what it was.

Sellers broke the news with stateliness and ceremony, first warning the ladies, with gentle art, that a pang of peculiar sharpness was about to be inflicted upon their hearts—hearts still sore from a like hurt, still lamenting a like loss—then he took the paper, and with trembling lips and with tears in his voice he gave them that heroic death-picture.

The result was a very genuine outbreak of sorrow and sympathy from all the hearers. The elder lady cried, thinking how proud that great-hearted young hero's mother would be, if she were living, and how unappeasable her grief; and the two old servants cried with her, and spoke out their applauses and their pitying lamentations with the eloquent sincerity and simplicity native to their race. Gwendolen was touched, and the romantic side of her nature was strongly wrought upon. She said that such a nature as that young man's was rarely and truly noble, and nearly perfect; and that with nobility of birth added it was entirely perfect. For such a man she could endure all things, suffer all things, even to the sacrificing of her life. She wished she could have seen him; the slightest, the most momentary, contact with such a spirit would have ennobled her own character and made ignoble thoughts and ignoble acts thereafter impossible to her forever.

"Have they found the body, Rossmore?" asked the wife.

"Yes, that is, they've found several. It must be one of them, but none of them are recognizable."

"What are you going to do?"

"I am going down there and identify one of them and send it home to the stricken father."

"But papa, did you ever see the young man?"

"No, Gwendolen—why?"

"How will you identify it?"

"I—well, you know it says none of them are recognizable. I'll send his father one of them—there's probably no choice."

Gwendolen knew it was not worth while to argue the matter further, since her father's mind was made up and there was a chance for him to appear upon that sad scene down yonder in an authentic and official way. So she said no more—till he asked for a basket.

"A basket, papa? What for?"

"It might be ashes."

Chapter IX

THE EARL and Washington started on the sorrowful errand, talking as they walked.

"And as *usual!*"

"What, Colonel?"

"Seven of them in that hotel. Actresses. And all burnt out, of course."

"Any of them burnt *up?*"

"Oh, no they escaped; they always do; but there's never a one of them that knows enough to fetch out her jewelry with her."

"That's strange."

"Strange—it's the most unaccountable thing in the world. Experience teaches them nothing; they can't seem to learn anything except out of a book. In some cases there's manifestly a fatality about it. For instance, take What's-her-name, that plays those sensational thunder and lightning parts. She's got a perfectly immense reputation—draws like a dog-fight—and it all came from getting burnt out in hotels."

"Why, how could that give her a reputation as an actress?"

"It didn't—it only made her name familiar. People want to see her play because her name is familiar, but they don't know what made it familiar, because they don't remember. First, she was at the bottom of the ladder, and absolutely obscure—wages thirteen dollars a week and find her own pads."

"Pads?"

"Yes—things to fat up her spindles with so as to be plump and attractive. Well, she got burnt out in a hotel and lost $30,000 worth of diamonds——"

"She? Where'd she get them?"

"Goodness knows—given to her, no doubt, by spoony young flats and sappy old bald-heads in the front row. All the papers were full of it. She struck for higher pay and got it. Well, she got burnt out again and lost all her diamonds, and it gave her such a lift that she went starring."

"Well, if hotel fires are all she's got to depend on to keep up her name, it's a pretty precarious kind of a reputation I should think."

"Not with her. No, anything but that. Because she's so lucky; born lucky, I reckon. Every time there's a hotel fire she's in it. She's always there—and if she can't be there herself, her diamonds are. Now you can't make anything out of that but just sheer luck."

"I never heard of such a thing. She must have lost quarts of diamonds."

"Quarts, she's lost bushels of them. It's got so that the hotels are superstitious about her. They won't let her in. They think there will be a fire; and besides, if she's there it cancels the insurance. She's been waning a little lately, but this fire will set her up. She lost $60,000 worth last night."

"I think she's a fool. If I had $60,000 worth of diamonds I wouldn't trust them in a hotel."

"I wouldn't either; but you can't teach an actress that. This one's been burnt out thirty-five times. And yet if there's a hotel fire in San Francisco to-night she's got to bleed again, you mark my words. Perfect ass; they say she's got diamonds in every hotel in the country."

When they arrived at the scene of the fire the poor old earl took one glimpse at the melancholy morgue and turned away his face overcome by the spectacle. He said:

"It is too true, Hawkins—recognition is impossible, not one of the five could be identified by its nearest friend. You make the selection, I can't bear it."

"Which one had I better—"

"Oh, take any of them. Pick out the best one."

However, the officers assured the earl—for they knew him, everybody in Washington knew him—that the position in which these bodies were found made it impossible that any one of them could be that of his noble young kinsman. They pointed out the spot where, if the newspaper account was correct, he must have sunk down to destruction; and at a wide distance from this spot they showed him where the young man must have gone down in case he was suffocated in his room; and they showed him still a third place, quite remote, where he might possibly have found his death if perchance he tried to escape by the side exit toward the rear. The old Colonel brushed away a tear and said to Hawkins—

"As it turns out there was something prophetic in my fears. Yes, it's a matter of ashes. Will you kindly step to a grocery and fetch a couple more baskets?"

Reverently they got a basket of ashes from each of those now hallowed spots, and carried them home to consult as to the best manner of forwarding them to England, and also to give them an opportunity to "lie in state,"—a mark of respect which the colonel deemed obligatory, considering the high rank of the deceased.

They set the baskets on the table in what was formerly the library, drawingroom and workshop—now the Hall of Audience—and went up stairs to the lumber room to see if they could find a British flag to use as a part of the outfit proper to the lying in state. A moment later, Lady Rossmore came in from the street and caught sight of the baskets just as old Jinny crossed her field of vision. She quite lost her patience and said—

"Well, what will you do next? What in the world possessed you to clutter up the parlor table with these baskets of ashes?"

"Ashes?" And she came to look. She put up her hands in pathetic astonishment. "Well, I *never* see de like!"

"Didn't you do it?"

"Who, me? Clah to goodness it's de fust time I've sot eyes on 'em, Miss Polly. Dat's Dan'l. Dat ole moke is losin' his mine."

But it wasn't Dan'l, for he was called, and denied it.

"Dey ain't no way to 'splain dat. Wen hit's one er dese-yer common 'currences, a body kin reckon maybe de cat—"

"Oh!" and a shudder shook Lady Rossmore to her foundations. "I see it all. Keep away from them—they're *his.*"

"*His,* m' lady?"

"Yes—your young Marse Sellers from England that's burnt up."

She was alone with the ashes—alone before she could take half a breath. Then she went after Mulberry Sellers, purposing to make short work with his program, whatever it might be; "for," said she, "when his sentimentals are up, he's a numskull, and there's no knowing what extravagance he'll contrive, if you let him alone." She found him. He had found the flag and was bringing it. When she heard that his idea was to have the remains "lie in state, and invite the government and the public," she broke it up. She said—

"Your intentions are all right—they always are—you want to do honour to the remains, and surely nobody can find any fault with that, for he was your kin; but you are going the wrong way about it, and you will see it yourself if you stop and think. You can't file around a basket of ashes trying to look sorry for it and make a sight that is really solemn, because the solemner it is, the more it isn't—anybody can see that. It would be so with one basket; it would be three times so with three. Well, it stands to reason that if it wouldn't be solemn with one mourner, it wouldn't be with a procession—and there would be five thousand people here. I don't know but it would be pretty near ridiculous; I think it would. No, Mulberry, they can't lie in state—it would be a mistake. Give that up and think of something else."

So he gave it up; and not reluctantly, when he had thought it over and realized how right her instinct was. He concluded to merely sit up with the remains—just himself and Hawkins. Even this seemed a doubtful attention, to his wife, but she offered no objection, for it was plain that he had a quite honest and simple-hearted desire to do the friendly and honourable thing by these forlorn poor relics which could command no hospitality in this far off land of strangers but his. He draped the flag about the baskets, put some crape on the door-knob, and said with satisfaction—

"There—he is as comfortable, now, as we can make him in the circumstances. Except—yes, we must strain a point there—one must do as one would wish to be done by—he must have it."

"Have what, dear?"

"Hatchment."

The wife felt that the house-front was standing about all it could well stand, in that way; the prospect of another stunning decoration of that nature distressed her, and she wished the thing had not occurred to him. She said, hesitatingly—

"But I thought such an honour as that wasn't allowed to any but very *very* near relations, who—"

"Right, you are quite right, my lady, perfectly right; but there aren't any nearer relatives than relatives by usurpation.

We cannot avoid it; we are slaves of aristocratic custom and must submit."

The hatchments were unnecessarily generous, each being as large as a blanket, and they were unnecessarily volcanic, too, as to variety and violence of color, but they pleased the earl's barbaric eye, and they satisfied his taste for symmetry and completeness, too, for they left no waste room to speak of on the house-front.

Lady Rossmore and her daughter assisted at the sitting-up till near midnight, and helped the gentlemen to consider what ought to be done next with the remains. Rossmore thought they ought to be sent home—with a committee and resolutions,—at once. But the wife was doubtful. She said:

"Would you send all of the baskets?"

"Oh, yes, all."

"All at once?"

"To his father? Oh, no—by no means. Think of the shock. No—one at a time; break it to him by degrees."

"Would *that* have that effect, father?"

"Yes, my daughter. Remember, you are young and elastic, but he is old. To send him the whole at once might well be more than he could bear. But mitigated—one basket at a time, with restful intervals between, he would be used to it by the time he got all of him. And sending him in three ships is safer anyway. On account of wrecks and storms."

"I don't like the idea, father. If I were his father it would be dreadful to have him coming in that—in that—"

"On the installment plan," suggested Hawkins, gravely, and proud of being able to help.

"Yes—dreadful to have him coming in that incoherent way. There would be the strain of suspense upon me all the time. To have so depressing a thing as a funeral impending, delayed, waiting, unaccomplished—"

"Oh, no, my child," said the earl reassuringly, "there would be nothing of that kind; so old a gentleman could not endure a long-drawn suspense like that. There will be three funerals."

Lady Rossmore looked up surprised, and said—

"How is *that* going to make it easier for him? It's a total mistake, to my mind. He ought to be buried all at once; I'm sure of it."

"I should think so, too," said Hawkins.

"And certainly *I* should," said the daughter.

"You are all wrong," said the earl. "You will see it yourselves, if you think. Only one of these baskets has got him in it."

"Very well, then," said Lady Rossmore, "the thing is perfectly simple—bury *that* one."

"Certainly," said Lady Gwendolen.

"But it is *not* simple," said the earl, "because we do not know which basket he is in. We know he is in *one* of them, but that is all we *do* know. You see now, I reckon, that I was right; it takes three funerals, there is no other way."

"And three graves and three monuments and three inscriptions?" asked the daughter.

"Well—yes—to do it right. That is what I should do."

"It could not be done so, father. Each of the inscriptions would give the same name and the same facts and say he was under each and all of these monuments, and that would not answer at all."

The earl nestled uncomfortably in his chair.

"No," he said, "that *is* an objection. That is a serious objection. I see no way out."

There was a general silence for a while. Then Hawkins said—

"It seems to me that if we mixed the three ramifications together—"

The earl grasped him by the hand and shook it gratefully.

"It solves the whole problem," he said. "One ship, one funeral, one grave, one monument—it is admirably conceived. It does you honor, Major Hawkins, it has relieved me of a most painful embarrassment and distress, and it will save that poor stricken old father much suffering. Yes, he shall go over in one basket."

"When?" asked the wife.

"To-morrow—immediately, of course."

"I would wait, Mulberry."

"Wait? Why?"

"*You* don't want to break that childless old man's heart."

"God knows I don't!"

"Then wait till he sends for his son's remains. If you do that, you will never have to give him the last and sharpest pain a parent can know—I mean, the *certainty* that his son is dead. For he will never send."

"Why won't he?"

"Because to send—and find out the truth—would rob him of the one precious thing left him, the *uncertainty*, the dim hope that maybe, after all, his boy escaped, and he will see him again some day."

"Why Polly, he'll know by the *papers* that he was burnt up."

"He won't let himself *believe* the papers; he'll argue against anything and everything that proves his son is dead; and he will keep that up and live on it, and on nothing else till he dies. But if the *remains* should actually come, and be put before that poor old dim-hoping soul—"

"Oh, my God, they never shall! Polly, you've saved me from a crime, and I'll bless you for it always. *Now* we know what to do. We'll place them reverently away, and he shall never know."

Chapter X

THE YOUNG Lord Berkeley, with the fresh air of freedom in his nostrils, was feeling invincibly strong for his new career; and yet—and yet—if the fight should prove a very hard one at first, very discouraging, very taxing on untoughened moral sinews, he might in some weak moment want to retreat. Not likely, of course, but possibly that might happen. And so on the whole it might be pardonable caution to burn his bridges behind him. Oh, without doubt. He must not stop with advertising for the owner of that money, but must put it where he could not borrow from it himself, meantime, under stress of circumstances. So he went down town, and put in his advertisement, then went to a bank and handed in the $500 for deposit.

"What name?"

He hesitated and colored a little; he had forgotten to make a selection. He now brought out the first one that suggested itself—

"Howard Tracy."

When he was gone the clerks, marveling, said—

"The cowboy blushed."

The first step was accomplished. The money was still under his command and at his disposal, but the next step would dispose of that difficulty. He went to another bank and drew upon the first bank for the $500 by check. The money was collected and deposited a second time to the credit of Howard Tracy. He was asked to leave a few samples of his signature, which he did. Then he went away, once more proud and of perfect courage, saying—

"No help for me now, for henceforth I couldn't draw that money without identification, and that is become legally impossible. No resources to fall back on. It is work or starve from now to the end. I am ready—and not afraid!"

Then he sent this cablegram to his father:

> "Escaped unhurt from burning hotel. Have taken fictitious name. Goodbye."

During the evening, while he was wandering about in one

of the outlying districts of the city, he came across a small brick church, with a bill posted there with these words printed on it: "MECHANICS' CLUB DEBATE. ALL INVITED." He saw people, apparently mainly of the working class, entering the place, and he followed and took his seat. It was a humble little church, quite bare as to ornamentation. It had painted pews without cushions, and no pulpit, properly speaking, but it had a platform. On the platform sat the chairman, and by his side sat a man who held a manuscript in his hand and had the waiting look of one who is going to perform the principal part. The church was soon filled with a quiet and orderly congregation of decently dressed and modest people. This is what the chairman said:

"The essayist for this evening is an old member of our club whom you all know, Mr. Parker, assistant editor of the Daily Democrat. The subject of his essay is the American Press, and he will use as his text a couple of paragraphs taken from Mr. Matthew Arnold's new book. He asks me to read these texts for him. The first is as follows:

> " 'Goethe says somewhere that "the thrill of awe," that is to say, REVERENCE,' is the best thing humanity has."

"Mr. Arnold's other paragraph is as follows:

> " 'I should say that if one were searching for the best means to efface and kill in a whole nation the discipline of respect, one could not do better than take the American newspapers."

Mr. Parker rose and bowed, and was received with warm applause. He then began to read in a good round resonant voice, with clear enunciation and careful attention to his pauses and emphases. His points were received with approval as he went on.

The essayist took the position that the most important function of a public journal in any country was the propagating of national feeling and pride in the national name—the keeping the people "in love with *their* country and *its* institutions, and shielded from the allurements of alien and inimical systems." He sketched the manner in which the reverent

Turkish or Russian journalist fulfilled this function—the one assisted by the prevalent "discipline of respect" for the bastinado, the other for Siberia. Continuing, he said—

The chief function of an English journal is that of all other journals the world over: it must keep the public eye fixed admiringly upon certain things, and keep it diligently diverted from certain others. For instance, it must keep the public eye fixed admiringly upon the glories of England, a processional splendor stretching its receding line down the hazy vistas of time, with the mellowed lights of a thousand years glinting from its banners; and it must keep it diligently diverted from the fact that all these glories were for the enrichment and aggrandizement of the petted and privileged few, at cost of the blood and sweat and poverty of the unconsidered masses who achieved them but might not enter in and partake of them. It must keep the public eye fixed in loving and awful reverence upon the throne as a sacred thing, and diligently divert it from the fact that no throne was ever set up by the unhampered vote of a majority of any nation; and that hence no throne exists that has a right to exist, and no symbol of it, flying from any flagstaff, is righteously entitled to wear any device but the skull and crossbones of that kindred industry which differs from royalty only business-wise—merely as retail differs from wholesale. It must keep the citizen's eye fixed in reverent docility upon that curious invention of machine politics, an Established Church, and upon that bald contradiction of common justice, a hereditary nobility; and diligently divert it from the fact that the one damns him if he doesn't wear its collar, and robs him under the gentle name of taxation whether he wears it or not, and the other gets all the honors while he does all the work.

The essayist thought that Mr. Arnold, with his trained eye and intelligent observation, ought to have perceived that the very quality which he so regretfully missed from our press—respectfulness, reverence—was exactly the thing which would make our press useless to us if it had it—rob it of the very thing which differentiates it from all other journalism in the world and makes it distinctively and preciously American, its frank and cheerful irreverence being by all odds the most valuable of all its qualities. "For its mission—overlooked by Mr. Arnold—is to stand guard over a nation's liberties, not its humbugs and shams." He thought that if during fifty years the institutions of the old world could be exposed to the fire of a flouting and scoffing press like ours, "monarchy and its attendant crimes would disappear from Christendom." Monarchists might doubt this; then "why not persuade the Czar to give it a trial in Russia?" Concluding, he said—

Well, the charge is, that our press has but little of that old world quality, reverence. Let us be candidly grateful that it is so. With its limited reverence it at least reveres the things which this nation reveres, as a rule, and that is sufficient: what other people revere is fairly and properly matter of light importance to us. Our press does not reverence kings, it does not reverence so called nobilities, it does not reverence established ecclesiastical slaveries, it does not reverence laws which rob a younger son to fatten an elder one, it does not reverence any fraud or sham or infamy, howsoever old or rotten or holy, which sets one citizen above his neighbor by accident of birth: it does not reverence any law or custom, howsoever old or decayed or sacred, which shuts against the best man in the land the best place in the land and the divine right to prove property and go up and occupy it. In the sense of the poet Goethe—that meek idolater of provincial three carat royalty and nobility—our press is certainly bankrupt in the "thrill of awe"—otherwise reverence; reverence for nickel plate and brummagem. Let us sincerely hope that this fact will remain a fact forever: for to my mind a discriminating irreverence is the creator and protector of human liberty—even as the other thing is the creator, nurse, and steadfast protector of all forms of human slavery, bodily and mental.

Tracy said to himself, almost shouted to himself, "I'm glad I came to this country. I was right. I was right to seek out a land where such healthy principles and theories are in men's hearts and minds. Think of the innumerable slaveries imposed by misplaced reverence! How well he brought that out, and how true it is. There's manifestly prodigious force in reverence. If you can get a man to reverence your ideals, he's your slave. Oh, yes, in all the ages the peoples of Europe have been diligently taught to avoid reasoning about the shams of monarchy and nobility, been taught to avoid examining them, been taught to reverence them; and now, as a natural result, to reverence them is second nature. In order to shock them it is sufficient to inject a thought of the opposite kind into their dull minds. For ages, any expression of so-called irreverence from their lips has been sin and crime. The sham and swindle of all this is apparent the moment one reflects that he is himself the only legitimately qualified judge of what *is* entitled to reverence and what is not. Come, I hadn't thought of that before, but it is true, absolutely true. What right has Goethe, what right has Arnold, what right has any dictionary, to define the word Irreverence for me? What their ideals are is nothing to me. So long as I reverence my own ideals my whole duty is done, and I commit no profanation if I laugh at theirs. I may scoff at other people's ideals as much as I want to. It is my right and my privilege. No man has any right to deny it."

Tracy was expecting to hear the essay debated, but this did not happen. The chairman said, by way of explanation—

"I would say, for the information of the strangers present here, that in accordance with our custom the subject of this meeting will be debated at the next meeting of the club. This is in order to enable our members to prepare what they may wish to say upon the subject with pen and paper, for we are mainly mechanics and unaccustomed to speaking. We are obliged to write down what we desire to say."

Many brief papers were now read, and several off-hand speeches made in discussion of the essay read at the last meeting of the club, which had been a laudation, by some visiting professor, of college culture, and the grand results flowing from it to the nation. One of the papers was read by a man approaching middle age, who said he hadn't had a college education, that he had got his education in a printing office, and had graduated from there into the patent office, where he had been a clerk now for a great many years. Then he continued to this effect:

The essayist contrasted the America of to-day with the America of bygone times, and certainly the result is the exhibition of a mighty progress. But I think he a little overrated the college-culture share in the production of that result. It can no doubt be easily shown that the colleges have contributed the intellectual part of this progress, and that that part is vast; but that the material progress has been immeasurably vaster, I think you will concede. Now I have been looking over a list of inventors—the creators of this amazing material development—and I find that they were not college-bred men. Of course there are exceptions—like Professor Henry of Princeton, the inventor of Mr. Morse's system of telegraphy—but these exceptions are few. It is not overstatement to say that the imagination-stunning material development of this century, the only century worth living in since time itself was invented, is the creation of men not college-bred. We think we see what these inventors have done: no, we see only the visible vast frontage of their work; behind it is their far vaster work, and it is invisible to the careless glance. They have reconstructed this nation—made it over, that is—and metaphorically speaking, have multiplied its numbers almost beyond the power of figures to express. I will explain what I mean. What constitutes the population of a land? Merely the numberable packages of meat and bones in it called by courtesy men and women? Shall a million ounces of brass and a million ounces of gold be held to be of the same value? Take a truer standard: the measure of a man's contributing capacity to his time and his people—the work he can do—and then number the population of this country to-day, as multiplied by what a man can now do, more than his grandfather could do. By this standard of measurement, this nation, two or three generations ago, consisted of mere cripples, paralytics, dead men, as compared with the men of to-day. In 1840 our population was 17,000,000. By way of rude but striking illustration, let us consider, for argument's sake, that four of these millions consisted of aged people, little children, and other incapables, and that the remaining 13,000,000 were divided and employed as follows:

2,000,000 as ginners of cotton.
6,000,000 (women) as stocking-knitters.
2,000,000 (women) as thread-spinners.
500,000 as screw makers.
400,000 as reapers, binders, etc.
1,000,000 as corn shellers.
40,000 as weavers.
1,000 as stitchers of shoe soles.

Now the deductions which I am going to append to these figures may sound extravagant, but they are not. I take them from Miscellaneous Documents No. 50, second session 45th Congress, and they are official and trustworthy. To-day, the work of those 2,000,000 cotton-ginners is done by 2,000 men; that of the 6,000,000 stocking-knitters is done by 3,000 boys; that of the 2,000,000 thread-spinners is done by 1,000 girls; that of the 500,000 screw makers is done by 500 girls; that of the 400,000 reapers, binders, etc., is done by 4,000 boys; that of the 1,000,000 corn shellers is done by 7,500 men; that of the 40,000 weavers is done by 1,200 men; and that of the 1,000 stitchers of shoe soles is done by 6 men. To bunch the figures, 17,000 persons to-day do the above work, whereas fifty years ago it would have taken thirteen millions of persons to do it. Now then, how many of that ignorant race—our fathers and grandfathers—with their ignorant methods, would it take to do our work to-day? It would take forty thousand millions—a hundred times the swarming population of China—twenty times the present population of the globe. You look around you and you see a nation of sixty millions—apparently; but secreted in their hands and brains, and invisible to your eyes, is the true population of this Republic, and it numbers forty billions! It is the stupendous creation of those humble unlettered, un-college-bred inventors—all honor to their name.

"How grand that is!" said Tracy, as he wended homeward. "What a civilization it is, and what prodigious results these are! and brought about almost wholly by common men; not by Oxford-trained aristocrats, but men who stand shoulder to shoulder in the humble ranks of life and earn the bread that they eat. Again, I'm glad I came. I have found a country at last where one may start fair, and breast to breast with his fellow man, rise by his own efforts, and be something in the world and be proud of that something; not be something created by an ancestor three hundred years ago."

Chapter XI

DURING the first few days he kept the fact diligently before his mind that he was in a land where there was "work and bread for all." In fact, for convenience' sake he fitted it to a little tune and hummed it to himself; but as time wore on the fact itself began to take on a doubtful look, and next the tune got fatigued and presently ran down and stopped. His first effort was to get an upper clerkship in one of the departments, where his Oxford education could come into play and do him service. But he stood no chance whatever. There, competency was no recommendation; political backing, without competency, was worth six of it. He was glaringly English, and that was necessarily against him in the political centre of a nation where both parties prayed for the Irish cause on the house-top and blasphemed it in the cellar. By his dress he was a cowboy; that won him respect—when his back was not turned—but it couldn't get a clerkship for him. But he had said, in a rash moment, that he would wear those clothes till the owner or the owner's friends caught sight of them and asked for that money, and his conscience would not let him retire from that engagement now.

At the end of a week things were beginning to wear rather a startling look. He had hunted everywhere for work, descending gradually the scale of quality, until apparently he had sued for all the various kinds of work a man without a special calling might hope to be able to do, except ditching and the other coarse manual sorts—and had got neither work nor the promise of it.

He was mechanically turning over the leaves of his diary, meanwhile, and now his eye fell upon the first record made after he was burnt out:

"I myself did not doubt my stamina before, nobody could doubt it now, if they could see how I am housed, and realize that I feel absolutely no disgust with these quarters, but am as serenely content with them as any dog would be in a similar kennel. Terms, twenty-five dollars a week. I said I would start at the bottom. I have kept my word."

A shudder went quaking through him, and he exclaimed—

"What have I been thinking of! *This* the bottom! Mooning along a whole week, and these terrific expenses climbing and climbing all the time! I must end this folly straightway."

He settled up at once and went forth to find less sumptuous lodgings. He had to wander far and seek with diligence, but he succeeded. They made him pay in advance—four dollars and a half; this secured both bed and food for a week. The good-natured, hard-worked landlady took him up three flights of narrow, uncarpeted stairs and delivered him into his room. There were two double-bedsteads in it, and one single one. He would be allowed to sleep alone in one of the double beds until some new boarder should come, but he wouldn't be charged extra.

So he would presently be required to sleep with some stranger! The thought of it made him sick. Mrs. Marsh, the landlady, was very friendly and hoped he would like her house—they all liked it, she said.

"And they're a very nice set of boys. They carry on a good deal, but that's their fun. You see, this room opens right into this back one, and sometimes they're all in one and sometimes in the other; and hot nights they all sleep on the roof when it don't rain. They get out there the minute it's hot enough. The season's so early that they've already had a night or two up there. If you'd like to go up and pick out a place, you can. You'll find chalk in the side of the chimney where there's a brick wanting. You just take the chalk and—but of course you've done it before."

"Oh, no, I haven't."

"Why, of course you haven't—what am I thinking of? Plenty of room on the Plains without chalking, I'll be bound. Well, you just chalk out a place the size of a blanket anywhere on the tin that ain't already marked off, you know, and that's your property. You and your bed-mate take turn-about carrying up the blanket and pillows and fetching them down again; or one carries them up and the other fetches them down, you fix it the way you like, you know. You'll like the boys, they're everlasting sociable—except the printer. He's the one that sleeps in that single bed—the strangest creature; why, I don't believe you could get that man to sleep with another man, not if the house was afire. Mind you, I'm not just talking, I *know*. The boys tried him, to see. They took his bed out one night, and so when he got home about three in the morning—he was on a morning paper then, but he's on an evening one now—there wasn't any place for him but with the iron-moulder; and if you'll believe me, he just set up the rest of the night—he did, honest. They say he's cracked, but it ain't so, he's English—they're awful particular. You won't mind my saying that. You—you're English?"

"Yes."

"I thought so. I could tell it by the way you mispronounce the words that's got *a*'s in them, you know; such as saying loff when you mean laff—but you'll get over that. He's a right down good fellow, and a little sociable with the photographer's boy and the caulker and the blacksmith that work in the navy yard, but not so much with the others. The fact is, though it's private, and the others don't know it, he's a kind of an aristocrat, his father being a doctor, and *you* know what style *that* is—in England, I mean, because in this country a doctor ain't so *very* much, even if he's *that*. But over there of course it's different. So this chap had a falling out with his father, and was pretty high strung, and just cut for this country, and the first he knew he had to get to work or starve. Well, he'd been to college, you see, and so he judged *he* was all right—did you say anything?"

"No—I only sighed."

"And there's where he was mistaken. Why, he mighty near starved. And I reckon he would have starved sure enough, if some jour' printer or other hadn't took pity on him and got him a place as apprentice. So he learnt the trade, and then he was all right—but it was a close call. Once he thought he had *got* to haul in his pride and holler for his father and—why, you're sighing again. Is anything the matter with you?—does my clatter—"

"Oh, *dear*—no. Pray go on—I like it."

"Yes, you see, he's been over here ten years; he's twenty-eight, now, and he ain't pretty well satisfied in his mind, because he can't get reconciled to being a mechanic and associating with mechanics, he being, as he says to me, a *gentleman*, which is a pretty plain letting-on that the boys ain't, but of course I know enough not to let that cat out of the bag."

"Why—would there be any harm in it?"

"Harm in it? They'd lick him, wouldn't they? Wouldn't *you*? Of course you would. Don't you ever let a man say you ain't a gentleman in *this* country. But laws, what am I thinking about? I reckon a body would think twice before he said a cowboy wasn't a gentleman."

A trim, active, slender and very pretty girl of about eighteen walked into the room now, in the most satisfied and unembarrassed way. She was cheaply but smartly and gracefully dressed, and the mother's quick glance at the stranger's face as he rose, was of the kind which inquires what effect has been produced, and expects to find indications of surprise and admiration.

"This is my daughter Hattie—we call her Puss. It's the new boarder, Puss." This without rising.

The young Englishman made the awkward bow common to his nationality and time of life in circumstances of delicacy and difficulty, and these were of that sort; for, being taken by surprise, his natural, life-long self sprang to the front, and that self of course would not know just how to act when introduced to a chambermaid, or to the heiress of a mechanics' boarding house. His other self—the self which recognized the equality of all men—would have managed the thing better, if it hadn't been caught off guard and robbed of its chance. The young girl paid no attention to the bow, but put out her hand frankly and gave the stranger a friendly shake and said—

"How do you do?"

Then she marched to the one washstand in the room, tilted her head this way and that before the wreck of a cheap mirror that hung above it, dampened her fingers with her tongue, perfected the circle of a little lock of hair that was pasted against her forehead, then began to busy herself with the slops.

"Well, I must be going—it's getting towards supper time. Make yourself at home, Mr. Tracy, you'll hear the bell when it's ready."

The landlady took her tranquil departure, without commanding either of the young people to vacate the room. The young man wondered a little that a mother who seemed so honest and respectable should be so thoughtless, and was reaching for his hat, intending to disembarrass the girl of his presence; but she said—

"Where are you going?"

"Well—nowhere in particular, but as I am only in the way here—"

"Why, who said you were in the way? Sit down—I'll move you when you are in the way."

She was making the beds, now. He sat down and watched her deft and diligent performance.

"What gave you that notion? Do you reckon I need a whole room just to make up a bed or two in?"

"Well no, it wasn't that, exactly. We are away up here in an empty house, and your mother being gone—"

The girl interrupted him with an amused laugh, and said—

"Nobody to protect me? Bless you, I don't need it. I'm not afraid. I might be if I was alone, because I do hate ghosts, and I don't deny it. Not that I believe in them, for I don't. I'm only just afraid of them."

"How can you be afraid of them if you don't believe in them?"

"Oh, *I* don't know the *how* of it—that's too many for *me*; I only know it's *so*. It's the same with Maggie Lee."

"Who is that?"

"One of the boarders; young lady that works in the factry."

"She works in a factory?"

"Yes. Shoe factry."

"In a shoe factory; and you call her a young lady?"

"Why, she's only twenty-two; what should you call her?"

"I wasn't thinking of her age, I was thinking of the title. The fact is, I came away from England to get away from artificial forms—for artificial forms suit artificial people only—and here you've got them too. I'm sorry. I hoped you had only men and women; everybody equal; no differences in rank."

The girl stopped with a pillow in her teeth and the case spread open below it, contemplating him from under her brows with a slightly puzzled expression. She released the pillow and said—

"Why, they *are* all equal. Where's any difference in rank?"

"If you call a factory girl a young *lady*, what do you call the President's wife?"

"Call her an *old* one."

"Oh, you make age the only distinction?"

"There ain't any other to make as far as I can see."

"Then *all* women are ladies?"

"Certainly they are. All the respectable ones."

"Well, that puts a better face on it. Certainly there is no harm in a title when it is given to everybody. It is only an offense and a wrong when it is restricted to a favored few. But Miss—er—"

"Hattie."

"Miss Hattie, be frank; confess that that title *isn't* accorded by everybody to everybody. The rich American doesn't call her cook a lady—isn't that so?"

"Yes, it's so. What of it?"

He was surprised and a little disappointed, to see that his admirable shot had produced no perceptible effect.

"What *of* it?" he said. "Why this: equality is *not* conceded here, after all, and the Americans are no better off than the English. In fact there's no difference."

"Now *what* an idea. There's nothing in a title except what is *put* into it—you've said that yourself. Suppose the title is *clean*, instead of lady. You get that?"

"I believe so. Instead of speaking of a woman as a *lady*, you substitute clean and say she's a clean person."

"That's it. In England the swell folks don't speak of the working people as gentlemen and ladies?"

"Oh, no."

"And the working people don't call *themselves* gentlemen and ladies?"

"Certainly not."

"So if you used the other word there wouldn't be any change. The swell people wouldn't call anybody but themselves 'clean,' and those others would drop sort of meekly into their way of talking and *they* wouldn't call themselves clean. We don't do that way here. Everybody calls himself a lady or gentleman, and thinks he *is*, and don't care what anybody else thinks him, so long as he don't say it out loud. You think there's no difference. You *knuckle down* and we *don't.* Ain't that a difference?"

"It is a difference I hadn't thought of; I admit that. Still— *calling* one's self a lady doesn't—er—"

"I wouldn't go on if I were you."

Howard Tracy turned his head to see who it might be that had introduced this remark. It was a short man about forty years old, with sandy hair, no beard, and a pleasant face badly freckled but alive and intelligent, and he wore slop-shop clothing which was neat but showed wear. He had come from the front room beyond the hall, where he had left his hat, and he had a chipped and cracked white wash-bowl in his hand. The girl came and took the bowl.

"I'll get it for you. You go right ahead and *give* it to him, Mr. Barrow. He's the new boarder—Mr. Tracy—and I'd just got to where it was getting too deep for me."

"Much obliged if you will, Hattie. I was coming to borrow of the boys." He sat down at his ease on an old trunk, and said, "I've been listening and got interested; and as I was saying, I wouldn't go on, if I were you. You see where you are coming to, don't you? *Calling* yourself a lady doesn't elect you; that is what you were going to say; and you saw that if you said it you were going to run right up against another difference that you hadn't thought of: to-wit, Whose *right* is it to do the electing? Over there, twenty thousand people in a million elect themselves gentlemen and ladies, and the nine hundred and eighty thousand *accept* that decree and swallow the affront which it puts upon them. Why, if they didn't accept it, it wouldn't *be* an election, it would be a dead letter and have no force at all. Over here the twenty thousand would-be exclusives come up to the polls and vote themselves to be ladies and gentlemen. But the thing doesn't stop there. The nine hundred and eighty thousand come and vote themselves to be ladies and gentlemen *too*, and that elects the whole nation. Since the whole million vote themselves ladies and gentlemen, there is no question about that election. It *does* make absolute equality, and there is no fiction about it; while over yonder the *inequality*, (by decree of the infinitely feeble, and consent of the infinitely strong,) is also absolute— as real and absolute as our equality."

Tracy had shrunk promptly into his English shell when this speech began, notwithstanding he had now been in severe training several weeks for contact and intercourse with the common herd on the common herd's terms; but he lost no time in pulling himself out again, and so by the time the speech was finished his valves were open once more, and he was forcing himself to accept without resentment the common herd's frank fashion of dropping sociably into other people's conversations unembarrassed and uninvited. The process was not very difficult this time, for the man's smile and voice and manner were persuasive and winning. Tracy would even have liked him on the spot, but for the fact—fact which he was not really aware of—that the equality of men was not yet a reality to him, it was only a theory; the *mind* perceived, but the *man* failed to feel it. It was Hattie's ghost over again, merely turned around. Theoretically Barrow was his equal, but it was distinctly distasteful to see him exhibit it. He presently said:

"I hope in all sincerity that what you have said is true, as regards the Americans, for doubts have crept into my mind several times. It seemed that the equality must be ungenuine where the sign-names of castes were still in vogue; but those sign-names have certainly lost their offence and are wholly neutralized, nullified and harmless if they are the undisputed property of every individual in the nation. I think I realize that caste does not exist and cannot exist except by common consent of the masses outside of its limits. I thought caste created itself and perpetuated itself; but it seems quite true that it only creates itself, and is perpetuated by the people whom it despises, and who can dissolve it at any time by assuming its mere sign-names themselves."

"It's what I think. There isn't any power on earth that can prevent England's thirty millions from electing themselves dukes and duchesses to-morrow and calling themselves so. And within six months all the former dukes and duchesses would have retired from the business. I wish they'd try that. Royalty itself couldn't survive such a process. A handful of frowners against thirty million laughers in a state of irruption: Why, it's Herculaneum against Vesuvius; it would take another eighteen centuries to find that Herculaneum after the cataclysm. What's a Colonel in our South? He's a nobody; because they're all colonels down there. No, Tracy" (shudder from Tracy) "nobody in England would call you a gentleman and you wouldn't call yourself one; and I tell you it's a state of things that makes a man put himself into most unbecoming attitudes sometimes—the broad and general recognition and acceptance of caste *as* caste does, I mean. Makes him do it unconsciously—being bred in him, you see, and never thought over and reasoned out. You couldn't conceive of the Matterhorn being flattered by the notice of one of your comely little English hills, could you?"

"Why, no."

"Well, then, let a man in his right mind try to conceive of Darwin feeling flattered by the notice of a princess. It's so grotesque that it—well, it paralyzes the imagination. Yet that Memnon *was* flattered by the notice of that statuette; he *says* so—says so himself. The system that can make a god disown his godship and profane it—oh, well, it's all wrong, it's all wrong and ought to be abolished, I should say."

The mention of Darwin brought on a literary discussion, and this topic roused such enthusiasm in Barrow that he took off his coat and made himself the more free and comfortable for it, and detained him so long that he was still at it when the noisy proprietors of the room came shouting and skylarking in and began to romp, scuffle, wash, and otherwise entertain themselves. He lingered yet a little longer to offer the hospitalities of his room and his book shelf to Tracy and ask him a personal question or two:

"What is your trade?"

"They—well, they call me a cowboy, but that is a fancy; I'm not that. I haven't any trade."

"What do you work at for your living?"

"Oh, anything—I mean I *would* work at anything I could get to do, but thus far I haven't been able to find an occupation."

"Maybe I can help you; I'd like to try."

"I shall be very glad. I've tried, myself, to weariness."

"Well, of course where a man hasn't a regular trade he's pretty bad off in this world. What you needed, I reckon, was less book learning and more bread-and-butter learning. I don't know what your father could have been thinking of. You ought to have had a trade, you ought to have had a trade, by *all* means. But never mind about that; we'll stir up *something* to do, I guess. And don't you get homesick; that's a bad business. We'll talk the thing over and look around a little. You'll come out all right. Wait for me—I'll go down to supper with you."

By this time Tracy had achieved a very friendly feeling for Barrow and would have *called* him a friend, maybe, if not taken too suddenly on a straight-out requirement to realize on his theories. He was glad of his society, anyway, and was feeling lighter hearted than before. Also he was pretty curious to know what vocation it might be which had furnished Barrow such a large acquaintanceship with books and allowed him so much time to read.

Chapter XII

PRESENTLY the supper bell began to ring in the depths of the house, and the sound proceeded steadily upward, growing in intensity all the way up towards the upper floors. The higher it came the more maddening was the noise, until at last what it lacked of being absolutely deafening, was made up of the sudden crash and clatter of an avalanche of boarders down the uncarpeted stairway. The peerage did not go to meals in this fashion; Tracy's training had not fitted him to enjoy this hilarious zoölogical clamor and enthusiasm. He had to confess that there was something about this extraordinary outpouring of animal spirits which he would have to get inured to before he could accept it. No doubt in time he would prefer it; but he wished the process might be modified and made just a little more gradual, and not quite so pronounced and violent. Barrow and Tracy followed the avalanche down through an ever increasing and ever more and more aggressive stench of bygone cabbage and kindred smells; smells which are to be found nowhere but in a cheap private boarding house; smells which once encountered can never be forgotten; smells which encountered generations later are instantly recognizable, but never recognizable with pleasure. To Tracy these odors were suffocating, horrible, almost unendurable; but he held his peace and said nothing. Arrived in the basement, they entered a large dining-room where thirty-five or forty people sat at a long table. They took their places. The feast had already begun and the conversation was going on in the liveliest way from one end of the table to the other. The table cloth was of very coarse material and was liberally spotted with coffee stains and grease. The knives and forks were iron, with bone handles, the spoons appeared to be iron or sheet iron or something of the sort. The tea and coffee cups were of the commonest and heaviest and most durable stone ware. All the furniture of the table was of the commonest and cheapest sort. There was a single large thick slice of bread by each boarder's plate, and it was observable that he economized it as if he were not expecting it to be duplicated. Dishes of butter were distributed along the table within reach

of people's arms, if they had long ones, but there were no private butter plates. The butter was perhaps good enough, and
was quiet and well behaved; but it had more bouquet than
was necessary, though nobody commented upon that fact or
seemed in any way disturbed by it. The main feature of the
feast was a piping hot Irish stew made of the potatoes and
meat left over from a procession of previous meals. Everybody
was liberally supplied with this dish. On the table were a couple of great dishes of sliced ham, and there were some other
eatables of minor importance—preserves and New Orleans
molasses and such things. There was also plenty of tea and
coffee of an infernal sort, with brown sugar and condensed
milk, but the milk and sugar supply was not left at the discretion of the boarders, but was rationed out at headquarters—
one spoonful of sugar and one of condensed milk to each cup
and no more. The table was waited upon by two stalwart negro women who raced back and forth from the bases of supplies with splendid dash and clatter and energy. Their labors
were supplemented after a fashion by the young girl Puss. She
carried coffee and tea back and forth among the boarders, but
she made pleasure excursions rather than business ones in this
way, to speak strictly. She made jokes with various people. She
chaffed the young men pleasantly—and wittily, as she supposed, and as the rest also supposed, apparently, judging by
the applause and laughter which she got by her efforts. Manifestly she was a favorite with most of the young fellows and
sweetheart of the rest of them. Where she conferred notice
she conferred happiness, as was seen by the face of the recip-
ient; and at the same time she conferred unhappiness—one
could see it fall and dim the faces of the other young fellows
like a shadow. She never "Mistered" these friends of hers, but
called them "Billy," "Tom," "John," and they called her
"Puss" or "Hattie."

Mr. Marsh sat at the head of the table, his wife sat at the
foot. Marsh was a man of sixty, and was an American; but if
he had been born a month earlier he would have been a
Spaniard. He was plenty good enough Spaniard as it was; his
face was very dark, his hair very black, and his eyes were not
only exceedingly black but were very intense, and there was
something about them that indicated that they could burn

with passion upon occasion. He was stoop-shouldered and lean-faced, and the general aspect of him was disagreeable; he was evidently not a very companionable person. If looks went for anything, he was the very opposite of his wife, who was all motherliness and charity, good will and good nature. All the young men and the women called her Aunt Rachael, which was another sign. Tracy's wandering and interested eye presently fell upon one boarder who had been overlooked in the distribution of the stew. He was very pale and looked as if he had but lately come out of a sick bed, and also as if he ought to get back into it again as soon as possible. His face was very melancholy. The waves of laughter and conversation broke upon it without affecting it any more than if it had been a rock in the sea and the words and the laughter veritable waters. He held his head down and looked ashamed. Some of the women cast glances of pity toward him from time to time in a furtive and half afraid way, and some of the youngest of the men plainly had compassion on the young fellow—a compassion exhibited in their faces but not in any more active or compromising way. But the great majority of the people present showed entire indifference to the youth and his sorrows. Marsh sat with his head down, but one could catch the malicious gleam of his eyes through his shaggy brows. He was watching that young fellow with evident relish. He had not neglected him through carelessness, and apparently the table understood that fact. The spectacle was making Mrs. Marsh very uncomfortable. She had the look of one who hopes against hope that the impossible may happen. But as the impossible did not happen, she finally ventured to speak up and remind her husband that Nat Brady hadn't been helped to the Irish stew.

Marsh lifted his head and gasped out with mock courtliness, "Oh, he hasn't, hasn't he? What a pity that is. I don't know how I came to overlook him. Ah, he must pardon me. You must indeed Mr—er—Baxter—Barker, you must pardon me. I—er—my attention was directed to some other matter, I don't know what. The thing that grieves me mainly is, that it happens every meal now. But you must try to overlook these little things, Mr. Bunker, these little neglects on my part. They're always likely to happen with me in any case, and they are especially likely to happen where a person has—er—well, where a person is, say, about three weeks in arrears for his board. You get my meaning?—you get my idea? Here is your Irish stew, and—er—it gives me the greatest pleasure to send it to you, and I hope that you will enjoy the charity as much as I enjoy conferring it."

A blush rose in Brady's white cheeks and flowed slowly backward to his ears and upward toward his forehead, but he said nothing and began to eat his food under the embarrassment of a general silence and the sense that all eyes were fastened upon him. Barrow whispered to Tracy:

"The old man's been waiting for that. He wouldn't have missed that chance for anything."

"It's a brutal business," said Tracy. Then he said to himself, purposing to set the thought down in his diary later:

"Well, here in this very house is a republic where all are free and equal, if men are free and equal anywhere in the earth, therefore I have arrived at the place I started to find, and I am a man among men, and on the strictest equality possible to men, no doubt. Yet here on the threshold I find an inequality. There are people at this table who are looked up to for some reason or another, and here is a poor devil of a boy who is looked down upon, treated with indifference, and shamed by humiliations, when he has committed no crime but that common one of being poor. Equality ought to make men noble-minded. In fact I had supposed it did do that."

After supper, Barrow proposed a walk, and they started. Barrow had a purpose. He wanted Tracy to get rid of that cowboy hat. He didn't see his way to finding mechanical or manual employment for a person rigged in that fashion. Barrow presently said—

"As I understand it, you're not a cowboy."

"No, I'm not."

"Well, now if you will not think me too curious, how did you come to mount that hat? Where'd you get it?"

Tracy didn't know quite how to reply to this, but presently said,—

"Well, without going into particulars, I exchanged clothes with a stranger under stress of weather, and I would like to find him and re-exchange."

"Well, why don't you find him? Where is he?"

"I don't know. I supposed the best way to find him would be to continue to wear his clothes, which are conspicuous enough to attract his attention if I should meet him on the street."

"Oh, very well," said Barrow, "the rest of the outfit is well enough, and while it's not too conspicuous, it isn't quite like the clothes that anybody else wears. Suppress the hat. When you meet your man he'll recognize the rest of his suit. That's a mighty embarrassing hat, you know, in a centre of civilization like this. I don't believe an angel could get employment in Washington in a halo like that."

Tracy agreed to replace the hat with something of a modester form, and they stepped aboard a crowded car and stood with others on the rear platform. Presently, as the car moved swiftly along the rails, two men crossing the street caught sight of the backs of Barrow and Tracy, and both exclaimed at once, "There he is!" It was Sellers and Hawkins. Both were so paralyzed with joy that before they could pull themselves together and make an effort to stop the car, it was gone too far, and they decided to wait for the next one. They waited a while; then it occurred to Washington that there could be no use in chasing one horse-car with another, and he wanted to hunt up a hack. But the Colonel said:

"When you come to think of it, there's no occasion for that at all. Now that I've got him materialized, I can command his motions. I'll have him at the house by the time we get there."

Then they hurried off home in a state of great and joyful excitement.

The hat exchange accomplished, the two new friends started to walk back leisurely to the boarding house. Barrow's mind was full of curiosity about this young fellow. He said,—

"You've never been to the Rocky Mountains?"

"No."

"You've never been out on the plains?"

"No."

"How long have you been in this country?"

"Only a few days."

"You've never been in America before?"

"No."

Then Barrow communed with himself. "Now what odd shapes the notions of romantic people take. Here's a young fellow who's read in England about cowboys and adventures on the plains. He comes here and buys a cowboy's suit. Thinks he can play himself on folks for a cowboy, all inexperienced as he is. Now the minute he's caught in this poor little game, he's ashamed of it and ready to retire from it. It is that exchange that he has put up as an explanation. It's rather thin, too thin altogether. Well, he's young, never been anywhere, knows nothing about the world, sentimental, no doubt. Perhaps it was the natural thing for him to do, but it was a most singular choice, curious freak, altogether."

Both men were busy with their thoughts for a time, then Tracy heaved a sigh and said,—

"Mr. Barrow, the case of that young fellow troubles me."

"You mean Nat Brady?"

"Yes, Brady, or Baxter, or whatever it was. The old landlord called him by several different names."

"Oh, yes, he has been very liberal with names for Brady, since Brady fell into arrears for his board. Well, that's one of his sarcasms—the old man thinks he's great on sarcasm."

"Well, what is Brady's difficulty? What is Brady—who is he?"

"Brady is a tinner. He's a young journeyman tinner who was getting along all right till he fell sick and lost his job. He was very popular before he lost his job; everybody in the house liked Brady. The old man was rather especially fond of him, but you know that when a man loses his job and loses his ability to support himself and to pay his way as he goes, it makes a great difference in the way people look at him and feel about him."

"Is that so! *Is* it so?"

Barrow looked at Tracy in a puzzled way. "Why of course it's so. Wouldn't you know that, naturally. Don't you know that the wounded deer is always attacked and killed by its companions and friends?"

Tracy said to himself, while a chilly and boding discomfort spread itself through his system, "In a republic of deer and men where all are free and equal, misfortune is a crime, and the prosperous gore the unfortunate to death." Then he said aloud, "Here in the boarding house, if one would have friends and be popular instead of having the cold shoulder turned upon him, he must be prosperous."

"Yes," Barrow said, "that is so. It's their human nature. They do turn against Brady, now that he's unfortunate, and they don't like him as well as they did before; but it isn't because of any lack in Brady—he's just as he was before, has the same nature and the same impulses, but they—well, Brady is a thorn in their consciences, you see. They know they ought to help him and they're too stingy to do it, and they're ashamed of themselves for that, and they ought also to hate themselves on that account, but instead of that they hate Brady because he makes them ashamed of themselves. I say that's human nature; that occurs everywhere; this boarding house is merely the world in little, it's the case all over— they're all alike. In prosperity we are popular; popularity comes easy in that case, but when the other thing comes our friends are pretty likely to turn against us."

Tracy's noble theories and high purposes were beginning to feel pretty damp and clammy. He wondered if by any possibility he had made a mistake in throwing his own prosperity to the winds and taking up the cross of other people's unprosperity. But he wouldn't listen to that sort of thing; he cast it out of his mind and resolved to go ahead resolutely along the course he had mapped out for himself.

Extracts from his diary:

Have now spent several days in this singular hive. I don't know quite what to make out of these people. They have merits and virtues, but they have some other qualities, and some ways that are hard to get along with. I can't enjoy them. The moment I appeared in a hat of the period, I noticed a change. The respect which had been paid me before, passed suddenly away, and the people became friendly—more than that—they became familiar, and I'm not used to familiarity, and can't take to it right off; I find that out. These people's familiarity amounts to impudence, sometimes. I suppose it's all right; no doubt I can get used to it, but it's not a satisfactory process at all. I have accomplished my dearest wish, I am a man among men, on an equal footing with Tom, Dick and Harry, and yet it isn't just exactly what I thought it was going to be. I—I miss home. Am obliged to say I am homesick. Another thing—and this is a confession—a reluctant one, but I will make it: The thing I miss most and most severely, is the respect, the deference, with which I was treated all my life in England, and which seems to be somehow necessary to me. I get along very well without the luxury and the wealth and the sort of society I've been accustomed to, but I do miss the respect and can't seem to get reconciled to the absence of it. There is respect, there is deference here, but it doesn't fall to my share. It is lavished on two men. One of them is a portly man of middle age who is a retired plumber. Everybody is pleased to have that man's notice. He's full of pomp and circumstance and self complacency and bad grammar, and at table he is Sir Oracle and when he opens his mouth not any dog in the kennel barks. The other person is a policeman at the capitol-building. He represents the government. The deference paid to these two men is not so very far short of that which is paid to an earl in England, though the method of it differs. Not so much courtliness, but the deference is all there.

Yes, and there is obsequiousness, too.

It does rather look as if in a republic where all are free and equal, prosperity and position constitute *rank*.

Chapter XIII

THE DAYS drifted by, and they grew ever more dreary. For Barrow's efforts to find work for Tracy were unavailing. Always the first question asked was, "What Union do you belong to?"

Tracy was obliged to reply that he didn't belong to any trade-union.

"Very well, then, it's impossible to employ you. My men wouldn't stay with me if I should employ a 'scab,' or 'rat,' " or whatever the phrase was.

Finally, Tracy had a happy thought. He said, "Why the thing for me to do, of course, is to *join* a trade-union."

"Yes," Barrow said, "that is the thing for you to do—if you can."

"If I *can*? Is it difficult?"

"Well, yes," Barrow said, "it's sometimes difficult—in fact, very difficult. But you can try, and of course it will be best to try."

Therefore Tracy tried; but he did not succeed. He was refused admission with a good deal of promptness, and was advised to go back home, where he belonged, not come here taking honest men's bread out of their mouths. Tracy began to realize that the situation was desperate, and the thought made him cold to the marrow. He said to himself, "So there is an aristocracy of position here, and an aristocracy of prosperity, and apparently there is also an aristocracy of the ins as opposed to the outs, and I am with the outs. So the ranks grow daily, here. Plainly there are all kinds of castes here and only one that I belong to, the outcasts." But he couldn't even smile at his small joke, although he was obliged to confess that he had a rather good opinion of it. He was feeling so defeated and miserable by this time that he could no longer look with philosophical complacency on the horseplay of the young fellows in the upper rooms at night. At first it had been pleasant to see them unbend and have a good time after having so well earned it by the labors of the day, but now it all rasped upon his feelings and his dignity. He lost patience with the spectacle. When they were feeling good, they shouted, they scuffled, they sang songs, they romped about the place like cattle, and they generally wound up with a pillow fight, in which they banged each other over the head, and threw the pillows in all directions, and every now and then he got a buffet himself; and they were always inviting him to join in. They called him "Johnny Bull," and invited him with excessive familiarity to take a hand. At first he had endured all this with good nature, but latterly he had shown by his manner that it was distinctly distasteful to him, and very soon he saw a change in the manner of these young people toward him. They were souring on him as they would have expressed it in their language. He had never been what might be called popular. That was hardly the phrase for it; he had merely been liked, but now dislike for him was growing. His case was not helped by the fact that he was out of luck, couldn't get work, didn't belong to a union, and couldn't gain admission to one. He got a good many slights of that small ill-defined sort that you can't quite put your finger on, and it was manifest that there was only one thing which protected him from open insult, and that was his muscle. These young people had seen him exercising, mornings, after his cold sponge bath, and they had perceived by his performance and the build of his body, that he was athletic, and also versed in boxing. He felt pretty naked now, recognizing that he was shorn of all respect except respect for his fists. One night when he entered his room he found about a dozen of the young fellows there carrying on a very lively conversation punctuated with horse-laughter. The talking ceased instantly, and the frank affront of a dead silence followed. He said,

"Good evening gentlemen," and sat down.

There was no response. He flushed to the temples but forced himself to maintain silence. He sat there in this uncomfortable stillness some time, then got up and went out.

The moment he had disappeared he heard a prodigious shout of laughter break forth. He saw that their plain purpose had been to insult him. He ascended to the flat roof, hoping to be able to cool down his spirit there and get back his tranquility. He found the young tinner up there, alone and brooding, and entered into conversation with him. They were pretty fairly matched, now, in unpopularity and general ill-luck and misery, and they had no trouble in meeting upon this common ground with advantage and something of comfort to both. But Tracy's movements had been watched, and in a few minutes the tormentors came straggling one after another to the roof, where they began to stroll up and down in an apparently purposeless way. But presently they fell to dropping remarks that were evidently aimed at Tracy, and some of them at the tinner. The ringleader of this little mob was a short-haired bully and amateur prize-fighter named Allen, who was accustomed to lording it over the upper floor, and had more than once shown a disposition to make trouble with Tracy. Now there was an occasional cat-call, and hootings, and whistlings, and finally the diversion of an exchange of connected remarks was introduced:

"How many does it take to make a pair?"

"Well, two generally makes a pair, but sometimes there ain't stuff enough in them to make a whole pair." General laugh.

"What were you saying about the English a while ago?"

"Oh, nothing, the English are all right, only—I—"

"What was it you *said* about them?"

"Oh, I only said they swallow well."

"Swallow better than other people?"

"Oh, yes, the English swallow a good deal better than other people."

"What is it they swallow best?"

"Oh, insults." Another general laugh.

"Pretty hard to make 'em fight, ain't it?"

"No, tain't hard to make 'em fight."

"Ain't it, really?"

"No, tain't hard. It's impossible." Another laugh.

"This one's kind of spiritless, that's certain."

"*Couldn't* be the other way—in his case."

"Why?"

"Don't you know the secret of his birth?"

"No! has *he* got a secret of his birth?"

"You bet he has."

"What is it?"

"His father was a wax-figger."

Allen came strolling by where the pair were sitting; stopped, and said to the tinner;

"How are you off for friends, these days?"

"Well enough off."

"Got a good many?"

"Well, as many as I need."

"A friend is valuable, sometimes—as a protector, you know. What do you reckon would happen if I was to snatch your cap off and slap you in the face with it?"

"Please don't trouble me, Mr. Allen, I ain't doing anything to you."

"You answer me! What do you reckon would happen?"

"Well, I don't know."

Tracy spoke up with a good deal of deliberation and said,

"Don't trouble the young fellow, I can tell you what would happen."

"Oh, you can, can you? Boys, Johnny Bull can tell us what would happen if I was to snatch this chump's cap off and slap him in the face with it. Now you'll see."

He snatched the cap and struck the youth in the face, and before he could inquire what was going to happen, it had already happened, and he was warming the tin with the broad of his back. Instantly there was a rush, and shouts of "A ring, a ring, make a ring! Fair play all round! Johnny's grit; give him a chance."

The ring was quickly chalked on the tin, and Tracy found himself as eager to begin as he could have been if his antagonist had been a prince instead of a mechanic. At bottom he was a little surprised at this, because although his theories had been all in that direction for some time, he was not prepared to find himself actually eager to measure strength with quite so common a man as this ruffian. In a moment all the windows in the neighborhood were filled with people, and the roofs also. The men squared off, and the fight began. But Allen stood no chance whatever, against the young Englishman. Neither in muscle nor in science was he his equal. He measured his length on the tin time and again; in fact, as fast as he could get up he went down again, and the applause was kept up in liberal fashion from all the neighborhood around. Finally, Allen had to be helped up. Then Tracy declined to punish him further and the fight was at an end. Allen was carried off by some of his friends in a very much humbled condition, his face black and blue and bleeding, and Tracy was at once surrounded by the young fellows, who congratulated him, and told him that he had done the whole house a service, and that from this out Mr. Allen would be a little more particular about how he handed slights and insults and maltreatment around amongst the boarders.

Tracy was a hero now, and exceedingly popular. Perhaps nobody had ever been quite so popular on that upper floor before. But if being discountenanced by these young fellows had been hard to bear, their lavish commendations and approval and hero-worship was harder still to endure. He felt degraded, but he did not allow himself to analyze the reasons why, too closely. He was content to satisfy himself with the suggestion that he looked upon himself as degraded by the public spectacle which he had made of himself, fighting on a tin roof, for the delectation of everybody a block or two around. But he wasn't entirely satisfied with that explanation of it. Once he went a little too far and wrote in his diary that his case was worse than that of the prodigal son. He said the prodigal son merely fed swine, he didn't have to chum with them. But he struck that out, and said "All men are equal. I will not disown my principles. These men are as good as I am."

Tracy was become popular on the lower floors also. Everybody was grateful for Allen's reduction to the ranks, and for his transformation from a doer of outrages to a mere threatener of them. The young girls, of whom there were half a dozen, showed many attentions to Tracy, particularly that boarding house pet Hattie, the landlady's daughter. She said to him, very sweetly,—

"I think you're ever so nice." And when he said, "I'm glad you think so, Miss Hattie," she said, still more sweetly,—

"Don't call me Miss Hattie—call me Puss."

Ah, here was promotion! He had struck the summit. There were no higher heights to climb in that boarding house. His popularity was complete.

In the presence of people, Tracy showed a tranquil outside, but his heart was being eaten out of him by distress and despair.

In a little while he should be out of money, and then what should he do? He wished, now, that he had borrowed a little more liberally from that stranger's store. He found it impossible to sleep. A single torturing, terrifying thought went racking round and round in his head, wearing a groove in his brain: What should he do—What was to become of him? And along with it began to intrude a something presently which was very like a wish that he had not joined the great and noble ranks of martyrdom, but had stayed at home and been content to be merely an earl and nothing better, with nothing more to do in this world of a useful sort than an earl finds to do. But he smothered that part of his thought as well as he could; he made every effort to drive it away, and with fair success, but he couldn't keep it from intruding a little now and then, and when it intruded it came suddenly and nipped him like a bite, a sting, a burn. He recognized that thought by the peculiar sharpness of its pang. The others were painful enough, but that one cut to the quick when it came. Night after night he lay tossing to the music of the hideous snoring of the honest bread-winners until two and three o'clock in the morning, then got up and took refuge on the roof, where he sometimes got a nap and sometimes failed entirely. His appetite was leaving him and the zest of life was going along with it. Finally, one day, being near the imminent verge of total discouragement, he said to himself—and took occasion to blush privately when he said it, "If my father knew what my American name is,—he—well, my duty to my father rather *requires* that I furnish him my name. I have no right to make his days and nights unhappy, I can do enough unhappiness for the family all by myself. Really he ought to know what my American name is." He thought over it a while and framed a cablegram in his mind to this effect:

"My American name is Howard Tracy."

That wouldn't be suggesting anything. His father could understand that as he chose, and doubtless he would understand it as it was meant, as a dutiful and affectionate desire on the part of a son to make his old father happy for a moment. Continuing his train of thought, Tracy said to himself, "Ah, but if he should cable me to come home! I—I—couldn't do that—I *mustn't* do that. I've started out on a mission, and I mustn't turn my back on it in cowardice. No, no, I couldn't go home, at—at—least I shouldn't want to go home." After a reflective pause: "Well, maybe—perhaps—it would be my *duty* to go in the circumstances; he's very old and he does need me by him to stay his footsteps down the long hill that inclines westward toward the sunset of his life. Well, I'll think about that. Yes, of course it wouldn't be right to stay here. I—if I—well, perhaps I could just drop him a line and put it off a little while and satisfy him in that way. It would be—well, it would mar everything to have him require me to come instantly." Another reflective pause—then: "And yet if he should do that I don't know but—oh, dear me—*home!* how good it sounds! and a body is excusable for wanting to see his home again, now and then, anyway."

He went to one of the telegraph offices in the avenue and got the first end of what Barrow called the "usual Washington courtesy," where "they treat you as a tramp until they find out you're a congressman, and then they slobber all over you." There was a boy of seventeen on duty there, tying his shoe. He had his foot on a chair and his back turned towards the wicket. He glanced over his shoulder, took Tracy's measure, turned back, and went on tying his shoe. Tracy finished writing his telegram and waited, still waited, and still waited, for that performance to finish, but there didn't seem to be any finish to it; so finally Tracy said:

"Can't you take my telegram?"

The youth looked over his shoulder and said, by his manner, not his words:

"Don't you think you could wait a minute, if you tried?"

However, he got the shoe tied at last, and came and took the telegram, glanced over it, then looked up surprised, at Tracy. There was something in his look that bordered upon respect, almost reverence, it seemed to Tracy, although he had been so long without anything of this kind he was not sure that he knew the signs of it.

The boy read the address aloud, with pleased expression in face and voice.

"The Earl of Rossmore! Cracky! Do you know him?"

"Yes."

"Is that so! Does he know you?"

"Well—yes."

"Well, I swear! Will he answer you?"

"I think he will."

"Will he though? Where'll you have it sent?"

"Oh, nowhere. I'll call here and get it. When shall I call?"

"Oh, I don't know—I'll send it to you. Where shall I send it? Give me your address; I'll send it to you soon's it comes."

But Tracy didn't propose to do this. He had acquired the boy's admiration and deferential respect, and he wasn't willing to throw these precious things away, a result sure to follow if he should give the address of that boarding house. So he said again that he would call and get the telegram, and went his way.

He idled along, reflecting. He said to himself, "There *is* something pleasant about being respected. I have acquired the respect of Mr. Allen and some of those others, and almost the deference of some of them on pure merit, for having thrashed Allen. While their respect and their deference—if it is deference—is pleasant, a deference based upon a sham, a shadow, does really seem pleasanter still. It's no real merit to be in correspondence with an earl, and yet after all, that boy makes me feel as if there was."

The cablegram was actually gone home! The thought of it gave him an immense uplift. He walked with a lighter tread. His heart was full of happiness. He threw aside all hesitances and confessed to himself that he was glad through and through that he was going to give up this experiment and go back to his home again. His eagerness to get his father's answer began to grow, now, and it grew with marvelous celerity, after it began. He waited an hour, walking about, putting in his time as well as he could, but interested in nothing that came under his eye, and at last he presented himself at the office again and asked if any answer had come yet. The boy said,

"No, no answer yet," then glanced at the clock and added, "I don't think it's likely you'll get one to-day."

"Why not?"

"Well, you see it's getting pretty late. You can't always tell where 'bouts a man is when he's on the other side, and you can't always find him just the minute you want him, and you see it's getting about six o'clock now, and over there it's pretty late at night."

"Why yes," said Tracy, "I hadn't thought of that."

"Yes, pretty late, now, half past ten or eleven. Oh yes, you probably won't get any answer to-night."

Chapter XIV

So Tracy went home to supper. The odors in that supper room seemed more strenuous and more horrible than ever before, and he was happy in the thought that he was so soon to be free from them again. When the supper was over he hardly knew whether he had eaten any of it or not, and he certainly hadn't heard any of the conversation. His heart had been dancing all the time, his thoughts had been far away from these things, and in the visions of his mind the sumptuous appointments of his father's castle had risen before him without rebuke. Even the plushed flunkey, that walking symbol of a sham inequality, had not been unpleasant to his dreaming view. After the meal Barrow said,—

"Come with me. I'll give you a jolly evening."

"Very good. Where are you going?"

"To my club."

"What club is that?"

"Mechanics' Debating Club."

Tracy shuddered, slightly. He didn't say anything about having visited that place himself. Somehow he didn't quite relish the memory of that time. The sentiments which had made his former visit there so enjoyable, and filled him with such enthusiasm, had undergone a gradual change, and they had rotted away to such a degree that he couldn't contemplate another visit there with anything strongly resembling delight. In fact he was a little ashamed to go; he didn't want to go there and find out by the rude impact of the thought of those people upon his reorganized condition of mind, how sharp the change had been. He would have preferred to stay away. He expected that now he should hear nothing except sentiments which would be a reproach to him in his changed mental attitude, and he rather wished he might be excused. And yet he didn't quite want to say that, he didn't want to show how he did feel, or show any disinclination to go, and so he forced himself to go along with Barrow, privately purposing to take an early opportunity to get away.

After the essayist of the evening had read his paper, the chairman announced that the debate would now be upon the subject of the previous meeting, "The American Press." It saddened the back-sliding disciple to hear this announcement. It brought up too many reminiscences. He wished he had happened upon some other subject. But the debate began, and he sat still and listened.

In the course of the discussion one of the speakers—a blacksmith named Tompkins—arraigned all monarchs and all lords in the earth for their cold selfishness in retaining their unearned dignities. He said that no monarch and no son of a monarch, no lord and no son of a lord ought to be able to look his fellow man in the face without shame. Shame for consenting to keep his unearned titles, property, and privileges at the expense of other people; shame for consenting to remain, on any terms, in dishonourable possession of these things, which represented bygone robberies and wrongs inflicted upon the general people of the nation. He said, "if there were a lord or the son of a lord here, I would like to reason with him, and try to show him how unfair and how selfish his position is. I would try to persuade him to relinquish it, take his place among men on equal terms, earn the bread he eats, and hold of slight value all deference paid him because of artificial position, all reverence not the just due of his own personal merits."

Tracy seemed to be listening to utterances of his own made in talks with his radical friends in England. It was as if some eavesdropping phonograph had treasured up his words and brought them across the Atlantic to accuse him with them in the hour of his defection and retreat. Every word spoken by this stranger seemed to leave a blister on Tracy's conscience, and by the time the speech was finished he felt that he was all conscience and one blister. This man's deep compassion for the enslaved and oppressed millions in Europe who had to bear with the contempt of that small class above them, throned upon shining heights whose paths were shut against them, was the very thing he had often uttered himself. The pity in this man's voice and words was the very twin of the pity that used to reside in his own heart and come from his own lips when he thought of these oppressed peoples.

The homeward tramp was accomplished in brooding silence. It was a silence most grateful to Tracy's feelings. He wouldn't have broken it for anything; for he was ashamed of himself all the way through to his spine. He kept saying to himself:

"How unanswerable it all is—how absolutely unanswerable! It *is* basely, degradingly selfish to keep those unearned honors, and—and—oh, hang it, nobody but a cur—"

"What an idiotic damned speech that Tompkins made!"

This outburst was from Barrow. It flooded Tracy's demoralized soul with waters of refreshment. These were the darlingest words the poor vacillating young apostate had ever heard—for they whitewashed his shame for him, and that is a good service to have when you can't get the best of all verdicts, self-acquittal.

"Come up to my room and smoke a pipe, Tracy."

Tracy had been expecting this invitation, and had had his declination all ready: but he was glad enough to accept, now. Was it possible that a reasonable argument could be made against that man's desolating speech? He was burning to hear Barrow try it. He knew how to start him, and keep him going: it was to seem to combat his positions—a process effective with most people.

"What is it you object to in Tompkins's speech, Barrow?"

"Oh, the leaving out of the factor of human nature; requiring another man to do what you wouldn't do yourself."

"Do you mean—"

"Why here's what I mean; it's very simple. Tompkins is a blacksmith; has a family; works for wages; and hard, too—fooling around won't furnish the bread. Suppose it should turn out that by the death of somebody in England he is suddenly an earl—income, half a million dollars a year. What would he do?"

"Well, I—I suppose he would have to decline to—"

"Man, he would grab it in a second!"

"Do you really think he would?"

"Think?—I don't think anything about it, I know it."

"Why?"

"Why? Because he's not a fool."

"So you think that if he were a fool, he—"

"No, I don't. Fool or *no* fool, he would grab it. Anybody would. Anybody that's alive. And I've seen dead people that would get up and go for it. I would myself."

This was balm, this was healing, this was rest and peace and comfort.

"But I thought you were opposed to nobilities."

"Transmissible ones, yes. But that's nothing. I'm opposed to millionaires, but it would be dangerous to offer me the position."

"You'd take it?"

"I would leave the funeral of my dearest enemy to go and assume its burdens and responsibilities."

Tracy thought a while, then said—

"I don't know that I quite get the bearings of your position. You say you are opposed to hereditary nobilities, and yet if you had the chance you would—"

"Take one? In a minute I would. And there isn't a mechanic in that entire club that wouldn't. There isn't a lawyer, doctor, editor, author, tinker, loafer, railroad president, saint—land, there isn't a human *being* in the United States that wouldn't jump at the chance!"

"Except me," said Tracy softly.

"Except you!" Barrow could hardly get the words out, his scorn so choked him. And he couldn't get any further than that form of words; it seemed to dam his flow, utterly. He got up and came and glared upon Tracy in a kind of outraged and unappeasable way, and said again, "Except *you*!" He walked around him—inspecting him from one point of view and then another, and relieving his soul now and then by exploding that formula at him; "Except *you*!" Finally he slumped down into his chair with the air of one who gives it up, and said—

"He's straining his viscera and he's breaking his heart trying to get some low-down job that a good dog wouldn't have, and yet wants to let on that if he had a chance to scoop an earldom he wouldn't do it. Tracy, don't put this kind of a strain on me. Lately I'm not as strong as I was."

"Well, I wasn't meaning to put a strain on you, Barrow, I was only meaning to intimate that if an earldom ever does fall in my way—"

"There—I wouldn't give myself any worry about *that*, if I was you. And besides, I can settle what you would do. Are you any different from me?"

"Well—no."

"Are you any better than me?"

"O,—er—why, certainly not."

"Are you as *good*? Come!"

"Indeed, I—the fact is you take me so suddenly,—"

"Suddenly? What is there sudden about it? It isn't a difficult question is it? Or doubtful? Just measure us on the only fair lines—the lines of merit—and of course you'll admit that a journeyman chair-maker that earns his twenty dollars a week, and has had the good and genuine culture of contact with men, and care, and hardship, and failure, and success, and downs and ups and ups and downs, is just a trifle the superior of a young fellow like you, who doesn't know how to do anything that's valuable, can't earn his living in any secure and steady way, hasn't had any experience of life and its seriousness, hasn't any culture but the artificial culture of books, which adorns but doesn't really educate—come! if *I* wouldn't scorn an earldom, what the devil right have *you* to do it!"

Tracy dissembled his joy, though he wanted to thank the chair-maker for that last remark. Presently a thought struck him, and he spoke up briskly and said:

"But look here, I really can't quite get the hang of your notions—your principles, if they are principles. You are inconsistent. You are opposed to aristocracies, yet you'd take an earldom if you could. Am I to understand that you don't blame an earl for being and remaining an earl?"

"I certainly don't."

"And you wouldn't blame Tompkins, or yourself, or me, or anybody, for accepting an earldom if it was offered?"

"Indeed I wouldn't."

"Well, then, who *would* you blame?"

"The whole nation—any bulk and mass of population anywhere, in any country, that will put up with the infamy, the outrage, the insult of a hereditary aristocracy which *they* can't enter—and on absolutely free and equal terms."

"Come, aren't you beclouding yourself with distinctions that are not differences?"

"Indeed I am not. I am entirely clear-headed about this thing. If I could extirpate an aristocratic system by declining its honors, *then* I should be a rascal to accept them. And if enough of the mass would join me to make the extirpation possible, *then* I should be a rascal to do otherwise than help in the attempt."

"I believe I understand—yes, I think I get the idea. You have no blame for the lucky few who naturally decline to vacate the pleasant nest they were born into, you only despise the all-powerful and stupid mass of the nation for allowing the nest to exist."

"That's it, that's it! You *can* get a simple thing through your head if you work at it long enough."

"Thanks."

"Don't mention it. And I'll give you some sound advice: when you go back, if you find your nation up and ready to abolish that hoary affront, lend a hand; but if that isn't the state of things and you get a chance at an earldom, don't you be a fool—you take it."

Tracy responded with earnestness and enthusiasm—

"As I live, I'll do it!"

Barrow laughed.

"I never saw such a fellow. I begin to think you've got a good deal of imagination. With you, the idlest fancy freezes into a reality at a breath. Why, you looked, then, as if it wouldn't astonish you if you did tumble into an earldom." Tracy blushed. Barrow added: "Earldom! Oh, yes, take it, if it offers; but meantime we'll go on looking around, in a modest way, and if you get a chance to superintend a sausage-stuffer at six or eight dollars a week, you just trade off the earldom for a last year's almanac and stick to the sausage-stuffing."

Chapter XV

TRACY went to bed happy once more, at rest in his mind once more. He had started out on a high emprise—that was to his credit, he argued; he had fought the best fight he could, considering the odds against him—that was to his credit; he had been defeated—certainly there was nothing discreditable in that. Being defeated, he had a right to retire with the honors of war and go back without prejudice to the position in the world's society to which he had been born. Why not? even the rabid republican chair-maker would do that. Yes, his conscience was comfortable once more.

He woke refreshed, happy, and eager for his cablegram. He had been born an aristocrat, he had been a democrat for a time, he was now an aristocrat again. He marveled to find that this final change was not merely intellectual, it had invaded his feeling; and he also marveled to note that this feeling seemed a good deal less artificial than any he had entertained in his system for a long time. He could also have noted, if he had thought of it, that his bearing had stiffened, over night, and that his chin had lifted itself a shade. Arrived in the basement, he was about to enter the breakfast room when he saw old Marsh in the dim light of a corner of the hall, beckoning him with his finger to approach. The blood welled slowly up in Tracy's cheek, and he said with a grade of injured dignity almost ducal—

"Is that for me?"

"Yes."

"What is the purpose of it?"

"I want to speak to you—in private."

"This spot is private enough for me."

Marsh was surprised; and not particularly pleased. He approached and said—

"Oh, in public, then, if you prefer. Though it hasn't been my way."

The boarders gathered to the spot, interested.

"Speak out," said Tracy. "What is it you want?"

"Well, haven't you—er—forgot something?"

"I? I'm not aware of it."

"Oh, you're not? Now you stop and think, a minute."

"I refuse to stop and think. It doesn't interest me. If it interests you, speak out."

"Well, then," said Marsh, raising his voice to a slightly angry pitch, "You forgot to pay your board yesterday—if you're *bound* to have it public."

Oh, yes, this heir to an annual million or so had been dreaming and soaring, and had forgotten that pitiful three or four dollars. For penalty he must have it coarsely flung in his face in the presence of these people—people in whose countenances was already beginning to dawn an uncharitable enjoyment of the situation.

"Is *that* all! Take your money and give your terrors a rest."

Tracy's hand went down into his pocket with angry decision. But—it didn't come out. The color began to ebb out of his face. The countenances about him showed a growing interest; and some of them a heightened satisfaction. There was an uncomfortable pause—then he forced out, with difficulty, the words—

"I've—been robbed!"

Old Marsh's eyes flamed up with Spanish fire, and he exclaimed—

"Robbed, is it? *That's* your tune? It's too old—been played in this house too often; everybody plays it that can't get work when he wants it, and won't work when he can get it. Trot out Mr. Allen, somebody, and let *him* take a toot at it. It's *his* turn next, *he* forgot, too, last night. I'm laying for him."

One of the negro women came scrambling down stairs as pale as a sorrel horse with consternation and excitement:

"Misto Marsh, Misto Allen's skipped out!"

"What!"

"Yes-sah, and cleaned out his room *clean*; tuck bofe towels en de soap!"

"You lie, you hussy!"

"It's jes' so, jes' as I tells you—en Misto Sumner's socks is gone, en Misto Naylor's yuther shirt."

Mr. Marsh was at boiling point by this time. He turned upon Tracy—

"Answer up now—when are you going to settle?"

"To-day—since you seem to be in a hurry."

"*To-day* is it? Sunday—and you out of work? I like that. Come—where are you going to get the money?"

Tracy's spirit was rising again. He proposed to impress these people:

"I am expecting a cablegram from home."

Old Marsh was caught out, with the surprise of it. The idea was so immense, so extravagant, that he couldn't get his breath at first. When he did get it, it came rancid with sarcasm.

"A *cablegram*—think of it, ladies and gents, he's expecting a cablegram! *He's* expecting a cablegram—this duffer, this scrub, this bilk! From his father—eh? Yes—without a doubt. A dollar or two a word—oh, that's nothing—*they* don't mind a little thing like that—*this* kind's fathers don't. Now his father is—er—well, I reckon his father—"

"My father is an English earl!"

The crowd fell back aghast—aghast at the sublimity of the young loafer's "cheek." Then they burst into a laugh that made the windows rattle. Tracy was too angry to realize that he had done a foolish thing. He said—

"Stand aside, please. I—"

"Wait a minute, your lordship," said Marsh, bowing low, "where is your lordship going?"

"For the cablegram. Let me pass."

"Excuse me, your lordship, you'll stay right where you are."

"What do you mean by that?"

"I mean that I didn't begin to keep boarding-house yesterday. It means that I am not the kind that can be taken in by every hack-driver's son that comes loafing over here because he can't bum a living at home. It means that you can't skip out on any such—"

Tracy made a step toward the old man, but Mrs. Marsh sprang between, and said—

"Don't, Mr. Tracy, please." She turned to her husband and said, "*Do* bridle your tongue. What has he done to be treated so? Can't you *see* he has lost his mind, with trouble and distress? He's not responsible."

"Thank your kind heart, madam, but I've not lost my mind; and if I can have the mere privilege of stepping to the telegraph office—"

"Well, you can't," cried Marsh.

"—or sending—"

"Sending! That beats everything. If there's anybody that's fool enough to go on such a chuckleheaded errand—"

"Here comes Mr. Barrow—he will go for me. Barrow—"

A brisk fire of exclamations broke out—

"Say, Barrow, he's expecting a cablegram!"

"Cablegram from his father, you know!"

"Yes—cablegram from the wax-figger!"

"And say, Barrow, this fellow's an earl—take off your hat, pull down your vest!"

"Yes, he's come off and forgot his crown, that he wears Sundays. He's cabled over to his pappy to send it."

"You step out and get that cablegram, Barrow; his majesty's a little lame to-day."

"Oh stop," cried Barrow; "give the man a chance." He turned, and said with some severity, "Tracy, what's the matter with you? What kind of foolishness is this you've been talking. You ought to have more sense."

"I've not been talking foolishness; and if you'll go to the telegraph office—"

"Oh, don't talk so. I'm your friend in trouble and out of it, before your face and behind your back, for anything in *reason*; but you've lost your head, you see, and this moonshine about a cablegram—"

"*I'll* go there and ask for it!"

"Thank you from the bottom of my heart, Brady. Here, I'll give you a written order for it. Fly, now, and fetch it. We'll soon see!"

Brady flew. Immediately the sort of quiet began to steal over the crowd which means dawning doubt, misgiving; and might be translated into the words, "Maybe he *is* expecting a cablegram—maybe he *has* got a father somewhere—maybe we've been just a little too fresh, just a shade too 'previous'!" Loud talk ceased; then the mutterings and low murmurings and whisperings died out. The crowd began to crumble apart. By ones and twos the fragments drifted to the breakfast table. Barrow tried to bring Tracy in; but he said—

"Not yet, Barrow—presently."

Mrs. Marsh and Hattie tried, offering gentle and kindly persuasions; but he said;

"I would rather wait—till he comes."

Even old Marsh began to have suspicions that maybe he had been a trifle too "brash," as he called it in the privacy of his soul, and he pulled himself together and started toward Tracy with invitation in his eyes; but Tracy warned him off with a gesture which was quite positive and eloquent. Then followed the stillest quarter of an hour which had ever been known in that house at that time of day. It was so still, and so solemn withal, that when somebody's cup slipped from his fingers and landed in his plate the shock made people start, and the sharp sound seemed as indecorous there and as out of place as if a coffin and mourners were imminent and being waited for. And at last when Brady's feet came clattering down the stairs the sacrilege seemed unbearable. Everybody rose softly and turned toward the door, where stood Tracy; then with a common impulse, moved a step or two in that direction, and stopped. While they gazed, young Brady arrived, panting, and put into Tracy's hand,—sure enough—an envelope. Tracy fastened a bland victorious eye upon the gazers, and kept it there till one by one they dropped their eyes, vanquished and embarrassed. Then he tore open the telegram and glanced at its message. The yellow paper fell from his fingers and fluttered to the floor, and his face turned white. There was nothing there but one word—

"*Thanks.*"

The humorist of the house, the tall, raw-boned Billy Nash, caulker from the navy yard, was standing in the rear of the crowd. In the midst of the pathetic silence that was now brooding over the place and moving some few hearts there toward compassion, he began to whimper, then he put his handkerchief to his eyes and buried his face in the neck of the bashfulest young fellow in the company, a navy-yard blacksmith, shrieked "Oh, pappy, how *could* you!" and began to bawl like a teething baby, if one may imagine a baby with the energy and the devastating voice of a jackass.

So perfect was the imitation of a child's cry, and so vast the scale of it, and so ridiculous the aspect of the performer, that all gravity was swept from the place as if by a hurricane, and almost everybody there joined in the crash of laughter provoked by the exhibition. Then the small mob began to take its revenge—revenge for the discomfort and apprehension it had brought upon itself by its own too rash freshness of a little while before. It guyed its poor victim, baited him, worried him, as dogs do with a cornered cat. The victim answered back with defiances and challenges which included everybody, and which only gave the sport new spirit and variety; but when he changed his tactics and began to single out individuals and invite them by name, the fun lost its funniness and the interest of the show died out, along with the noise.

Finally Marsh was about to take an innings, but Barrow said—

"Never mind, now—leave him alone. You've no account with him but a money account. I'll take care of that myself."

The distressed and worried landlady gave Barrow a fervently grateful look for his championship of the abused stranger; and the pet of the house, a very prism in her cheap but ravishing Sunday rig, blew him a kiss from the tips of her fingers and said, with the darlingest smile and a sweet little toss of her head—

"You're the only man here, and I'm going to set my cap for you, you dear old thing!"

"For shame, Puss! How you talk! I *never* saw such a child!"

It took a good deal of argument and persuasion—that is to say, petting, under these disguises—to get Tracy to entertain the idea of breakfast. He at first said he would never eat again in that house; and added that he had enough firmness of character, he trusted, to enable him to starve like a man when the alternative was to eat insult with his bread.

When he had finished his breakfast, Barrow took him to his room, furnished him a pipe, and said cheerily—

"*Now*, old fellow, take in your battle-flag out of the wet, you're not in the hostile camp any more. You're a little upset by your troubles, and that's natural enough, but don't let your mind run on them any more than you can help; drag your thoughts away from your troubles—by the ears, by the heels, or any other way, so you manage it; it's the healthiest thing a body can do; dwelling on troubles is deadly, just deadly—and that's the softest name there is for it. You must keep your mind amused—you must, indeed."

"Oh, miserable me!"

"*Don't!* There's just pure heart-break in that tone. It's just as I say; you've got to get right down to it and amuse your mind, as if it was salvation."

"They're easy words to say, Barrow, but how am I going to amuse, entertain, divert a mind that finds itself suddenly assaulted and overwhelmed by disasters of a sort not dreamed of and not provided for? No-no, the bare idea of amusement is repulsive to my feelings. Let us talk of death and funerals."

"No—not yet. That would be giving up the ship. We'll not give up the ship yet. I'm going to amuse you; I sent Brady out for the wherewithal before you finished breakfast."

"You did? What is it?"

"Come, this is a good sign—curiosity. Oh, there's hope for you yet."

Chapter XVI

B RADY arrived with a box, and departed, after saying—
"They're finishing one up, but they'll be along as soon as it's done."

Barrow took a frameless oil portrait a foot square from the box, set it up in a good light, without comment, and reached for another, taking a furtive glance at Tracy, meantime. The stony solemnity in Tracy's face remained as it was, and gave out no sign of interest. Barrow placed the second portrait beside the first, and stole another glance while reaching for a third. The stone image softened, a shade. No. 3 forced the ghost of a smile, No. 4 swept indifference wholly away, and No. 5 started a laugh which was still in good and hearty condition when No. 14 took its place in the row.

"Oh, *you're* all right, yet," said Barrow. "You see you're not past amusement."

The pictures were fearful, as to color, and atrocious as to drawing and expression; but the feature which squelched animosity and made them funny was a feature which could not achieve its full force in a single picture, but required the wonder-working assistance of repetition. One loudly dressed mechanic in stately attitude, with his hand on a cannon, ashore, and a ship riding at anchor in the offing,—this is merely odd; but when one sees the same cannon and the same ship in fourteen pictures in a row, and a different mechanic standing watch in each, the thing gets to be funny.

"Explain—explain these aberrations," said Tracy.

"Well, they are not the achievement of a single intellect, a single talent—it takes two to do these miracles. They are collaborations; the one artist does the figure, the other the accessories. The figure-artist is a German shoemaker with an untaught passion for art, the other is a simple hearted old Yankee sailor-man whose possibilities are strictly limited to his ship, his cannon and his patch of petrified sea. They work these things up from twenty-five-cent tintypes; they get six dollars apiece for them, and they can grind out a couple a day when they strike what they call a boost—that is, an inspiration."

"People actually pay money for these calumnies?"

"They actually do—and quite willingly, too. And these abortionists could double their trade and work the women in, if Capt. Saltmarsh could whirl a horse in, or a piano, or a guitar, in place of his cannon. The fact is, he fatigues the market with that cannon. Even the male market, I mean. These fourteen in the procession are not all satisfied. One is an old "independent" fireman, and he wants an engine in place of the cannon; another is a mate of a tug, and wants a tug in place of the ship—and so on, and so on. But the captain can't make a tug that is deceptive, and a fire engine is many flights beyond his power."

"This *is* a most extraordinary form of robbery, I never have heard of anything like it. It's interesting."

"Yes, and so are the artists. They are perfectly honest men, and sincere. And the old sailor-man is full of sound religion, and is as devoted a student of the Bible and misquoter of it as you can find anywhere. I don't know a better man or kinder hearted old soul than Saltmarsh, although he does swear a little, sometimes."

"He seems to be perfect. I want to know him, Barrow."

"You'll have the chance. I guess I hear them coming, now. We'll draw them out on their art, if you like."

The artists arrived and shook hands with great heartiness. The German was forty and a little fleshy, with a shiny bald head and a kindly face and deferential manner. Capt. Saltmarsh was sixty, tall, erect, powerfully built, with coal-black hair and whiskers, and he had a well tanned complexion, and a gait and countenance that were full of command, confidence and decision. His horny hands and wrists were covered with tattoo-marks, and when his lips parted, his teeth showed up white and blemishless. His voice was the effortless deep bass of a church organ, and would disturb the tranquility of a gas flame fifty yards away.

"They're wonderful pictures," said Barrow. "We've been examining them."

"It is very bleasant dot you like dem," said Handel, the German, greatly pleased. "Und you, Herr Tracy, you haf peen bleased mit dem too, alretty?"

"I can honestly say I have never seen anything just like them before."

"Schön!" cried the German, delighted. "You hear, Gaptain? Here is a chentleman, yes, vot abbreciate unser aart."

The captain was charmed, and said:

"Well, sir, we're thankful for a compliment yet, though they're not as scarce now as they used to be before we made a reputation."

"Getting the reputation is the up-hill time in most things, captain."

"It's so. It ain't enough to know how to reef a gasket, you got to make the mate know you know it. That's reputation. The good word, said at the right time, that's the word that makes us; and evil be to him that evil thinks, as Isaiah says."

"It's very relevant, and hits the point exactly," said Tracy. "Where did you study art, Captain?"

"I haven't studied; it's a natural gift."

"He is born mit dose cannon in him. He tondt haf to do noding, his chenius do all de vork. Of he is asleep, und take a pencil in his hand, out come a cannon. Py crashus, of he could do a clavier, of he could do a guitar, of he could do a vashtub, it is a fortune, heiliger Yohanniss it is yoost a fortune!"

"Well, it is an immense pity that the business is hindered and limited in this unfortunate way."

The captain grew a trifle excited, himself, now—

"You've said it, Mr. Tracy! Hindered? well, I should say so. Why, look here. This fellow here, No. 11, he's a hackman,—a flourishing hackman, I may say. He wants his hack in this picture. Wants it where the cannon is. I got around that difficulty, by telling him the cannon's our trademark, so to speak—proves that the picture's our work, and I was afraid if we left it out people wouldn't know for certain if it *was* a Saltmarsh-Handel—now you wouldn't yourself—"

"What, Captain? You wrong yourself, indeed you do. Anyone who has once seen a genuine Saltmarsh-Handel is safe from imposture forever. Strip it, flay it, skin it out of every detail but the bare color and expression, and that man will still recognize it, still stop to worship—"

"Oh, how it makes me feel to hear dose oxpressions!—"

—"still say to himself again as he had said a hundred times before, the art of the Saltmarsh-Handel is an art apart, there is nothing in the heavens above or in the earth beneath that resembles it,—"

"Py chiminy, nur hören Sie einmal! In my lifeday haf I never heard so brecious worts."

"So I talked him out of the hack, Mr. Tracy, and he let up on that, and said put in a hearse, then—because he's chief mate of a hearse but don't own it—stands a watch for wages, you know. But I can't do a hearse any more than I can a hack; so here we are—becalmed, you see. And it's the same with women and such. They come and they want a little johnry picture—"

"It's the accessories that make it a *genre?*"

"Yes—cannon, or cat, or any little thing like that, that you heave in to whoop up the effect. We could do a prodigious trade with the women if we could foreground the things they like, but they don't give a damn for artillery. Mine's the lack," continued the captain with a sigh, "Andy's end of the business is all right—I tell you *he's* an artist from wayback!"

"Yoost hear dot old man! He always talk 'poud me like dot," purred the pleased German.

"Look at his work yourself! Fourteen portraits in a row. And no two of them alike."

"Now that you speak of it, it is true; I hadn't noticed it before. It is very remarkable. Unique, I suppose."

"I should say so. That's the very *thing* about Andy—he *discriminates*. Discrimination's the thief of time—forty-ninth Psalm; but that ain't any matter, it's the honest thing, and it pays in the end."

"Yes, he certainly is great in that feature, one is obliged to admit it; but—now mind, I'm not really criticising—don't you think he is just a trifle over-strong in technique?"

The captain's face was knocked expressionless by this remark. It remained quite vacant while he muttered to himself — "Technique — technique — poly-technique— pyro-technique; that's it, likely—fireworks—too much color." Then he spoke up with serenity and confidence, and said—

"Well, yes, he does pile it on pretty loud; but they all like it, you know—fact is, it's the life of the business. Take that No. 9, there, Evans the butcher. He drops into the stoodio as sober-colored as anything you ever see: *now* look at him. You can't tell him from scarlet fever. Well, it pleases that butcher to death. I'm making a study of a sausage-wreath to hang on the cannon, and I don't really reckon I can do it right, but if I can, we can break the butcher."

"Unquestionably your confederate—I mean your—your fellowcraftsman—is a great colorist—"

"Oh, danke schön!—"

—"in fact a quite extraordinary colorist; a colorist, I make bold to say, without imitator here or abroad—and with a most bold and effective touch, a touch like a battering ram; and a manner so peculiar and romantic, and extraneous, and ad libitum, and heart-searching, that—that—he—he is an impressionist, I presume?"

"No," said the captain simply, "he is a Presbyterian."

"It accounts for it all—all—there's something divine about his art,—soulful, unsatisfactory, yearning, dim-hearkening on the void horizon, vague-murmuring to the spirit out of ultramarine distances and far-sounding cataclysms of uncreated space—oh, if he—if he—has he ever tried distemper?"

The captain answered up with energy—

"Not if he knows himself! But his dog has, and—"

"Oh, no, it vas not *my* dog."

"Why, you *said* it was your dog."

"Oh, no, gaptain, I—"

"It was a white dog, wasn't it, with his tail docked, and one ear gone, and—"

"Dot's him, dot's him!—der fery dog. Wy, py Chorge, dot dog he vould eat baint yoost de same like—"

"Well, never mind that, now—'vast heaving—I never saw such a man. You start him on that dog and he'll dispute a year. Blamed if I haven't *seen* him keep it up a level two hours and a half."

"Why captain!" said Barrow. "I guess that must be hearsay."

"No, sir, no hearsay about it—he disputed with me."

"I don't see how you stood it."

"Oh, you've got to—if you run with Andy. But it's the only fault he's got."

"Ain't you afraid of acquiring it?"

"Oh, no," said the captain, tranquilly, "no danger of that, I reckon."

The artists presently took their leave. Then Barrow put his hands on Tracy's shoulders and said—

"Look me in the eye, my boy. Steady, steady. There—it's just as I thought—hoped, anyway; *you're* all right, thank goodness. Nothing the matter with your mind. But don't do that again—even for fun. It isn't wise. They wouldn't have believed you if you'd *been* an earl's son. Why, they *couldn't*— don't you know that? What ever possessed you to take such a freak? But never mind about that; let's not talk of it. It was a mistake; you see that yourself."

"Yes—it *was* a mistake."

"Well, just drop it out of your mind; it's no harm; we all make them. Pull your courage together, and don't brood, and don't give up. I'm at your back, and we'll pull through, don't you be afraid."

When he was gone, Barrow walked the floor a good while, uneasy in his mind. He said to himself, "I'm troubled about him. He never would have made a break like that if he hadn't been a little off his balance. But I know what being out of work and no prospect ahead can do for a man. First it knocks the pluck out of him and drags his pride in the dirt; worry does the rest, and his mind gets shaky. I must talk to these people. No—if there's any humanity in them—and there is, at bottom—they'll be easier on him if they think his troubles have disturbed his reason. But I've *got* to find him some work; work's the only medicine for his disease. Poor devil! away off here, and not a friend."

Chapter XVII

THE MOMENT Tracy was alone his spirits vanished away, and all the misery of his situation was manifest to him. To be moneyless and an object of the chair-maker's charity—this was bad enough, but his folly in proclaiming himself an earl's son to that scoffing and unbelieving crew, and, on top of that, the humiliating result—the recollection of these things was a sharper torture still. He made up his mind that he would never play earl's son again before a doubtful audience.

His father's answer was a blow he could not understand. At times he thought his father imagined he could get work to do in America without any trouble, and was minded to let him try it and cure himself of his radicalism by hard, cold, disenchanting experience. That seemed the most plausible theory, yet he could not content himself with it. A theory that pleased him better was, that this cablegram would be followed by another, of a gentler sort, requiring him to come home. Should he write and strike his flag, and ask for a ticket home? Oh, no, that he couldn't *ever* do. At least, not yet. That cablegram would come, it certainly would. So he went from one telegraph office to another every day for nearly a week, and asked if there was a cablegram for Howard Tracy. No, there wasn't any. So they answered him at first. Later, they said it before he had a chance to ask. Later still they merely shook their heads impatiently as soon as he came in sight. After that he was ashamed to go any more.

He was down in the lowest depths of despair, now; for the harder Barrow tried to find work for him the more hopeless the possibilities seemed to grow. At last he said to Barrow—

"Look here. I want to make a confession. I have got down, now, to where I am not only willing to acknowledge to myself that I am a shabby creature and full of false pride, but am willing to acknowledge it to you. Well, I've been allowing you to wear yourself out hunting for work for me when there's been a chance open to me all the time. Forgive my pride— what was left of it. It is all gone, now and I've come to confess that if those ghastly artists want another confederate, I'm their man—for at last I am dead to shame."

"No? Really, can you paint?"

"Not as badly as *they*. No, I don't claim that, for I am not a genius; in fact, I am a very indifferent amateur, a slouchy dabster, a mere artistic sarcasm; but drunk or asleep I can beat *those* buccaneers."

"Shake! I want to shout! Oh, I tell you, I am immensely delighted and relieved. Oh, just to work—that is life! No matter what the work is—that's of no consequence. Just work itself is bliss when a man's been starving for it. I've *been* there! Come right along, we'll hunt the old boys up. Don't you feel good? I tell you *I* do."

The freebooters were not at home. But their "works" were,—displayed in profusion all about the little ratty studio. Cannon to the right of them, cannon to the left of them, cannon in front—it was Balaclava come again.

"Here's the uncontented hackman, Tracy. Buckle to—deepen the sea-green to turf, turn the ship into a hearse. Let the boys have a taste of your quality."

The artists arrived just as the last touch was put on. They stood transfixed with admiration.

"My souls but she's a stunner, that hearse! The hackman will just go all to pieces when he sees that—won't he Andy?"

"Oh, it is sphlennid, sphlennid! Herr Tracy, why haf you not said you vas a so sublime aartist? Lob' Gott, of you had lif'd in Paris you would be a Pree de Rome, dot's vot's de matter!"

The arrangements were soon made. Tracy was taken into full and equal partnership, and he went straight to work, with dash and energy, to reconstructing gems of art whose accessories had failed to satisfy. Under his hand, on that and succeeding days, artillery disappeared and the emblems of peace and commerce took its place—cats, hacks, sausages, tugs, fire engines, pianos, guitars, rocks, gardens, flower-pots, landscapes—whatever was wanted, he flung it in; and the more out of place and absurd the required object was, the more joy he got out of fabricating it. The pirates were delighted, the customers applauded, the sex began to flock in, great was the prosperity of the firm. Tracy was obliged to confess to himself that there was something about work,—even such grotesque and humble work as this—which most pleasantly satisfied a something in his nature which had never been satisfied before, and also gave him a strange new dignity in his own private view of himself.

The Unqualified Member from Cherokee Strip was in a state of deep dejection. For a good while, now, he had been leading a sort of life which was calculated to kill; for it had consisted in regularly alternating days of brilliant hope and black disappointment. The brilliant hopes were created by the magician Sellers, and they always promised that *now* he had got the trick, sure, and would effectively influence that materialized cowboy to call at the Towers before night. The black disappointments consisted in the persistent and monotonous failure of these prophecies.

At the date which this history has now reached, Sellers was appalled to find that the usual remedy was inoperative, and that Hawkins's low spirits refused absolutely to lift. Something must be done, he reflected; it was heart-breaking, this woe, this smileless misery, this dull despair that looked out from his poor friend's face. Yes, he must be cheered up. He mused a while, then he saw his way. He said in his most conspicuously casual vein—

"Er-uh—by the way, Hawkins, we are feeling disappointed about this thing—the way the materializee is acting, I mean—we are disappointed; you concede that?"

"Concede it? Why, yes, if you like the term."

"Very well; so far, so good. Now for the *basis* of the feeling. It is not that your heart, your affections are concerned; that is to say, it is not that you *want* the materializee *Itself.* You concede that?"

"Yes, I concede that, too—cordially."

"Very well, again; we are making progress. To sum up: The feeling, it is conceded, is not engendered by the mere conduct of the materializee; it is conceded that it does not arise from any pang which the *personality* of the materializee could assuage. Now then," said the earl, with the light of triumph in his eye, "the inexorable logic of the situation narrows us down to this: our feeling has its source in the *money*-loss involved. Come—isn't that so?"

"Goodness knows I concede that, with all my heart."

"Very well. When you've found out the source of a disease, you've also found out what remedy is required—just as in this case. In this case money is required. And *only* money."

The old, old seduction was in that airy, confident tone and those significant words—usually called pregnant words in books. The old answering signs of faith and hope showed up in Hawkins's countenance, and he said—

"*Only* money? Do you mean that you know a way to—"

"Washington, have you the impression that I have no resources but those I allow the public and my intimate friends to know about?"

"Well, I—er—"

"Is it *likely*, do you think, that a man moved by nature and taught by experience to keep his affairs to himself and a cautious and reluctant tongue in his head, wouldn't be thoughtful enough to keep a few resources in reserve for a rainy day, when he's got as many as I have to select from?"

"Oh, you make me feel so much better already, Colonel!"

"Have you ever been in my laboratory?"

"Why, no."

"That's it. You see you didn't even know that I had one. Come along. I've got a little trick there that I want to show you. I've kept it perfectly quiet, not fifty people know anything about it. But that's my way, always been my way. Wait till you're *ready*, that's the idea; and *when* you're ready, *zzip!*—let her go!"

"Well, Colonel, I've never seen a man that I've had such unbounded confidence in as you. When you say a thing right out, I always feel as if that ends it; as if that is evidence, and proof, and everything else."

The old earl was profoundly pleased and touched.

"I'm glad *you* believe in me, Washington; not everybody is so just."

"I always have believed in you; and I always shall as long as I live."

"Thank you, my boy. You shan't repent it. And you *can't.*" Arrived in the "laboratory," the earl continued, "Now, cast your eye around this room—what do you see? *Apparently* a

junk-shop; *apparently* a hospital connected with a patent office—in *reality*, the mines of Golconda in disguise! Look at
that thing there. Now what would you take that thing to be?"

"I don't believe I could ever imagine."

"Of course you couldn't. It's my grand adaptation of the
phonograph to the marine service. You store up profanity in
it for use at sea. You know that sailors don't fly around worth
a cent unless you swear at them—so the mate that can do the
best job of swearing is the most valuable man. In great emergencies his talent saves the ship. But a ship is a large thing,
and he can't be everywhere at once; so there have been times
when one mate has lost a ship which could have been saved if
they had had a hundred. Prodigious storms, you know. Well,
a ship can't afford a hundred mates; but she can afford a
hundred Cursing Phonographs, and distribute them all over
the vessel—and there, you see, she's armed at every point.
Imagine a big storm, and a hundred of my machines all
cursing away at once—splendid spectacle, splendid!—you
couldn't hear yourself think. Ship goes through that storm
perfectly serene—she's just as safe as she'd be on shore."

"It's a wonderful idea. How do you prepare the thing?"

"Load it—simply load it."

"How?"

"Why you just stand over it and swear into it."

"That loads it, does it?"

"Yes—because every word it collars, it *keeps*—keeps it forever. Never wears out. Any time you turn the crank, out it'll
come. In times of great peril, you can reverse it, and it'll
swear backwards. *That* makes a sailor hump himself!"

"O, I see. Who loads them?—the mate?"

"Yes, if he chooses. Or I'll furnish them already loaded. I
can hire an expert for $75 a month who will load a hundred
and fifty phonographs in 150 hours, and do it *easy*. And an expert can furnish a stronger article, of course, than the mere
average uncultivated mate could. Then you see, all the ships
of the world will buy them ready loaded—for I shall have
them loaded in any language a customer wants. Hawkins, it
will work the grandest moral reform of the 19th century. Five
years from now, *all* the swearing will be done by machinery—
you won't ever hear a profane word come from human lips on

a ship. Millions of dollars have been spent by the churches, in the effort to abolish profanity in the commercial marine. Think of it—my name will live forever in the affections of good men as the man, who, solitary and alone, accomplished this noble and elevating reform."

"O, it *is* grand and beneficent and beautiful. How *did* you ever come to think of it? You have a wonderful mind. How did you say you loaded the machine?"

"O, it's no trouble—perfectly simple. If you want to load it up loud and strong, you stand right over it and shout. But if you leave it open and all set, it'll *eavesdrop*, so to speak—that is to say, it will load itself up with any sounds that are made within six feet of it. Now I'll show you how it works. I had an expert come and load this one up yesterday. Hello, it's been left open—it's too bad—still I reckon it hasn't had much chance to collect irrelevant stuff. All you do is to press this button in the floor—so."

The phonograph began to sing in a plaintive voice:

> There is a boarding-house, far far away,
> Where they have ham and eggs, 3 times a day.

"Hang it, *that* ain't it. Somebody's been singing around here."

The plaintive song began again, mingled with a low, gradually rising wail of cats slowly warming up toward a fight;

> O, *how* the boarders yell,
> When they hear that dinner bell—
> They give that landlord—

(momentary outburst of terrific catfight which drowns out one word.)

> Three times a day.

(Renewal of furious catfight for a moment. The plaintive voice on a high fierce key, "*Scat*, you devils"—and a racket as of flying missiles.)

"Well, never mind—let it go. I've got some sailor-profanity down in there somewhere, if I could get to it. But it isn't any matter; you see how the machine works."

Hawkins responded with enthusiasm—

"O, it works admirably! I know there's a hundred fortunes in it."

"And mind, the Hawkins family get their share, Washington."

"O, thanks, thanks; you are just as generous as ever. Ah, it's the grandest invention of the age!"

"Ah, well, we live in wonderful times. The elements are crowded *full* of beneficent forces—always *have* been—and ours is the first generation to turn them to account and make them work for us. Why Hawkins, *everything* is useful—*nothing* ought ever to be wasted. Now look at sewer gas, for instance. Sewer gas has always been wasted, heretofore; nobody tried to save up sewer-gas—you can't name me a man. Ain't that so? *you* know perfectly well it's so."

"Yes it is so—but I never—er—I don't quite see why a body—"

"Should *want* to save it up? Well, I'll tell you. Do you see this little invention here?—it's a decomposer—I call it a decomposer. I give you my word of honor that if you show me a house that produces a given quantity of sewer-gas in a day, I'll engage to set up my decomposer there and make that house produce a hundred times that quantity of sewer-gas in less than half an hour."

"Dear me, but why should you want to?"

"*Want* to? Listen, and you'll see. My boy, for illuminating purposes and economy combined, there's nothing in the world that begins with sewer-gas. And really, it don't cost a cent. You put in a good inferior article of plumbing,—such as you find everywhere—and add my decomposer, and there you are. Just use the ordinary gas pipes—and there your expense ends. Think of it. Why, Major, in five years from now you won't see a house lighted with anything but sewer-gas. Every physician I talk to, recommends it; and every plumber."

"But isn't it dangerous?"

"O, yes, more or less, but everything is—coal gas, candles, electricity—there isn't anything that ain't."

"It lights up well, does it?"

"O, magnificently."

"Have you given it a good trial?"

"Well, no, not a first rate one. Polly's prejudiced, and she won't let me put it in here; but I'm playing my cards to get it adopted in the President's house, and *then* it'll go—don't you doubt it. I shall not need this one for the present, Washington; you may take it down to some boarding-house and give it a trial if you like."

Chapter XVIII

WASHINGTON shuddered slightly at the suggestion, then his face took on a dreamy look and he dropped into a trance of thought. After a little, Sellers asked him what he was grinding in his mental mill.

"Well, this. Have you got some secret project in your head which requires a Bank of England back of it to make it succeed?"

The Colonel showed lively astonishment, and said—

"Why, Hawkins, are you a mind-reader?"

"I? I never thought of such a thing."

"Well, then how did you happen to drop onto that idea in this curious fashion? It's just mind-reading,—that's what it is, though you may not know it. Because I *have* got a private project that requires a Bank of England at its back. How could you divine that? What was the process? This is interesting."

"There wasn't any process. A thought like this happened to slip through my head by accident: How much would make you or me comfortable? A hundred thousand. Yet you are expecting two or three of these inventions of yours to turn out some billions of money—and you are *wanting* them to do that. If you wanted ten millions, I could understand that—it's inside the human limits. But billions! That's clear outside the limits. There must be a definite project back of that somewhere."

The earl's interest and surprise augmented with every word, and when Hawkins finished, he said with strong admiration—

"It's wonderfully reasoned out, Washington, it certainly is. It shows what I think is quite extraordinary penetration. For you've hit it; you've driven the centre, you've plugged the bulls-eye of my dream. Now I'll tell you the whole thing, and you'll understand it. I don't need to ask you to keep it to yourself, because you'll see that the project will prosper all the better for being kept in the background till the right time. Have you noticed how many pamphlets and books I've got lying around relating to Russia?"

580

"Yes, I think most anybody would notice that—anybody who wasn't dead."

"Well, I've been posting myself a good while. That's a great and splendid nation, and deserves to be set free." He paused, then added in a quite matter-of-fact way, "When I get this money I'm going to set it free."

"Great guns!"

"Why, what makes you jump like that?"

"Dear me, when you are going to drop a remark under a man's chair that is likely to blow him out through the roof, why don't you put some expression, some force, some noise into it that will prepare him? You shouldn't flip out such a gigantic thing as this in that colorless kind of a way. You do jolt a person up, so. Go on, now, I'm all right again. Tell me all about it. I'm all interest—yes, and sympathy, too."

"Well, I've looked the ground over, and concluded that the methods of the Russian patriots, while good enough considering the way the boys are hampered, are not the best; at least not the quickest. They are trying to revolutionize Russia from *within*; that's pretty slow, you know, and liable to interruption all the time, and is full of perils for the workers. Do you know how Peter the Great started his army? He didn't start it on the family premises under the noses of the Strelitzes; no, he started it away off yonder, privately,—only just one regiment, you know, and he built to *that*. The first thing the Strelitzes knew, the regiment was an *army*, their position was turned, and they had to take a walk. Just that little idea *made* the biggest and worst of all the despotisms the world has seen. The same idea can *un*make it. I'm going to prove it. I'm going to get out to one side and work my scheme the way Peter did."

"This is mighty interesting, Rossmore. What is it you are going to do?"

"I am going to buy Siberia and start a republic."

"There,—bang you go again, without giving any notice! Going to *buy* it?"

"Yes, as soon as I get the money. I don't care what the price is, I shall take it. I can afford it, and I will. Now then, consider this—and you've never thought of it, I'll warrant. Where is the place where there is twenty-five times more manhood, pluck, true heroism, unselfishness, devotion to high and noble ideals, adoration of liberty, wide education, and *brains*, per thousand of population, than any other domain in the whole world can show?"

"Siberia!"

"Right."

"It is true; it certainly is true, but I never thought of it before."

"Nobody ever thinks of it. But it's so, just the same. In those mines and prisons are gathered together the very finest and noblest and capablest multitude of human beings that God is able to create. Now if you had that kind of a population to sell, would you offer it to a despotism? No, the despotism has no use for it; you would lose money. A despotism has no use for anything but human cattle. But suppose you want to start a republic?"

"Yes, I see. It's just the material for it."

"Well, I should say so! There's Siberia with just the very finest and choicest material on the globe for a republic, and more coming—more coming all the time, don't you see! It is being daily, weekly, monthly recruited by the most perfectly devised system that has ever been invented, perhaps. By this system the whole of the hundred millions of Russia are being constantly and patiently sifted, sifted, sifted, by myriads of trained experts, spies appointed by the Emperor personally; and whenever they catch a man, woman or child that has got any brains or education or character, they ship that person straight to Siberia. It is admirable, it is wonderful. It is so searching and so effective that it keeps the general level of Russian intellect and education down to that of the Czar."

"Come, that sounds like exaggeration."

"Well, it's what they say anyway. But I think, myself, it's a lie. And it doesn't seem right to slander a whole nation that way, anyhow. Now, then, you see what the material is, there in Siberia, for a republic." He paused, and his breast began to heave and his eye to burn, under the impulse of strong emotion. Then his words began to stream forth, with constantly increasing energy and fire, and he rose to his feet as if to give himself larger freedom. "The minute I organize that republic, the light of liberty, intelligence, justice, humanity, bursting from it, flooding from it, flaming from it, will concentrate the gaze of the whole astonished world as upon the miracle of a new sun; Russia's countless multitudes of slaves will rise up and march, march!—eastward, with that great light transfiguring their faces as they come, and far back of them you will see—what will you see?—a vacant throne in an empty land! It can be done, and by God I will do it!"

He stood a moment bereft of earthy consciousness by his exaltation; then consciousness returned, bringing him a slight shock, and he said, with grave earnestness—

"I must ask you to pardon me, Major Hawkins. I have never used that expression before, and I beg you will forgive it this time."

Hawkins was quite willing.

"You see, Washington, it is an error which I am by nature not liable to. Only excitable people, impulsive people, are exposed to it. But the circumstances of the present case—I being a democrat by birth and preference, and an aristocrat by inheritance and relish—"

The earl stopped suddenly, his frame stiffened, and he began to stare speechless through the curtainless window. Then he pointed, and gasped out a single rapturous word—

"Look!"

"What *is* it, Colonel?"

"*It!*"

"No!"

"Sure as you're born. Keep perfectly still. I'll apply the influence—I'll turn on all my force. I've brought It thus far—I'll fetch It right into the house. You'll see."

He was making all sorts of passes in the air with his hands.

"There! Look at that. I've made It smile! See?"

Quite true. Tracy, out for an afternoon stroll, had come unexpectedly upon his family arms displayed upon this shabby house-front. The hatchments made him smile; which was nothing, they had made the neighborhood cats do that.

"Look, Hawkins, look! I'm drawing It over!"

"You're drawing it sure, Rossmore. If I ever had any doubts about materialization, they're gone, now, and gone for good. Oh, this is a joyful day!"

Tracy was sauntering over to read the door-plate. Before he

was half way over he was saying to himself, "Why, manifestly these are the American Claimant's quarters."

"It's coming—coming right along. I'll slide down and pull It in. You follow after me."

Sellers, pale and a good deal agitated, opened the door and confronted Tracy. The old man could not at once get his voice: then he pumped out a scattering and hardly coherent salutation, and followed it with—

"Walk in, walk right in, Mr.—er—"

"Tracy—Howard Tracy."

—"Tracy—thanks—walk right in, you're expected."

Tracy entered, considerably puzzled, and said—

"Expected? I think there must be some mistake."

"Oh, I judge not," said Sellers, who noticing that Hawkins had arrived, gave him a sidewise glance intended to call his close attention to a dramatic effect which he was proposing to produce by his next remark. Then he said, slowly and impressively—"I am—*You Know Who.*"

To the astonishment of both conspirators the remark produced no dramatic effect at all; for the new comer responded with a quite innocent and unembarrassed air—

"No, pardon me. I don't *know* who you are. I only suppose—but no doubt correctly—that you are the gentleman whose title is on the doorplate."

"Right, quite right—sit down, pray sit down." The earl was rattled, thrown off his bearings, his head was in a whirl. Then he noticed Hawkins standing apart and staring idiotically at what to him was the apparition of a defunct man, and a new idea was born to him. He said to Tracy briskly—

"But a thousand pardons, dear sir, I am forgetting courtesies due to a guest and stranger. Let me introduce my friend General Hawkins—General Hawkins, our new Senator—Senator from the latest and grandest addition to the radiant galaxy of sovereign States, Cherokee Strip"—(to himself, "that name will shrivel him up!"—but it didn't, in the least, and the Colonel resumed the introduction piteously disheartened and amazed),—"Senator Hawkins, Mr. Howard Tracy, of—er—"

"England."

"England!—Why that's im—"

"England, yes, native of England."

"Recently from there?"

"Yes, quite recently."

Said the Colonel to himself, "This phantom lies like an expert. Purifying this kind by fire don't work. I'll sound him a little further, give him another chance or two to work his gift." Then aloud—with deep irony—

"Visiting our great country for recreation and amusement, no doubt. I suppose you find that traveling in the majestic expanses of our Far West is—"

"I haven't been West, and haven't been devoting myself to amusement with any sort of exclusiveness, I assure you. In fact, to merely live, an artist has got to work, not play."

"Artist!" said Hawkins to himself, thinking of the rifled bank; "that *is* a name for it!"

"Are *you* an artist?" asked the colonel; and added to himself, "*now* I'm going to catch him."

"In a humble way, yes."

"What line?" pursued the sly veteran.

"Oils."

"I've got him!" said Sellers to himself. Then aloud, "This is fortunate. Could I engage you to restore some of my paintings that need that attention?"

"I shall be very glad. Pray let me see them."

No shuffling, no evasion, no embarrassment, even under this crucial test. The Colonel was nonplussed. He led Tracy to a chromo which had suffered damage in a former owner's hands through being used as a lamp mat, and said, with a flourish of his hand toward the picture—

"This del Sarto—"

"Is *that* a del Sarto?"

The colonel bent a look of reproach upon Tracy, allowed it to sink home, then resumed as if there had been no interruption—

"This del Sarto is perhaps the only original of that sublime master in our country. You see, yourself, that the work is of such exceeding delicacy that the risk—could—er—would you mind giving me a little example of what you can do before we—"

"Cheerfully, cheerfully. I will copy one of these marvels."

Water-color materials—relics of Miss Sally's college life—were brought. Tracy said he was better in oils, but would take a chance with these. So he was left alone. He began his work, but the attractions of the place were too strong for him, and he got up and went drifting about, fascinated; also amazed.

Chapter XIX

MEANTIME the earl and Hawkins were holding a troubled and anxious private consultation. The earl said—

"The mystery that bothers me, is, where did It get its other arm?"

"Yes—it worries me, too. And another thing troubles me—the apparition is English. How do you account for that, Colonel?"

"Honestly, I don't know, Hawkins, I don't really know. It is very confusing and awful."

"Don't you think maybe we've waked up the wrong one?"

"The wrong one? How do you account for the clothes?"

"The clothes *are* right, there's no getting around it. What are we going to do? We can't collect, as I see. The reward is for a one-armed American. This is a two-armed Englishman."

"Well, it may be that that is not objectionable. You see it isn't *less* than is called for, it is *more*, and so,—"

But he saw that this argument was weak, and dropped it. The friends sat brooding over their perplexities some time in silence. Finally the earl's face began to glow with an inspiration, and he said, impressively:

"Hawkins, this materialization is a grander and nobler science than we have dreamed of. We have little imagined what a solemn and stupendous thing we have done. The whole secret is perfectly clear to me, now, clear as day. *Every man is made up of heredities*, long-descended atoms and particles of his ancestors. This present materialization is incomplete. We have only brought it down to perhaps the beginning of this century."

"What do you mean, Colonel!" cried Hawkins, filled with vague alarms by the old man's awe-compelling words and manner.

"This. We've materialized this burglar's ancestor!"

"Oh, don't—don't say that. It's hideous."

"But it's true, Hawkins, I *know* it. Look at the facts. This apparition is distinctly English—note that. It uses good grammar—note that. It is an Artist—note that. It has the manners and carriage of a gentleman—note that. Where's your cowboy? Answer me that."

"Rossmore, this is dreadful—it's too dreadful to think of!"

"Never resurrected a rag of that burglar but the clothes, not a solitary rag of him but the clothes."

"Colonel, do you really mean—"

The Colonel brought his fist down with emphasis and said—

"I mean exactly this. The materialization was immature, the burglar has evaded us, this is nothing but a damned ancestor!"

He rose and walked the floor in great excitement. Hawkins said plaintively—

"It's a bitter disappointment—bitter."

"I know it. I know it, Senator; I feel it as deeply as anybody could. But we've got to submit—on moral grounds. I need money, but God knows I am not poor enough or shabby enough to be an accessory to the punishing of a man's ancestor for crimes committed by that ancestor's posterity."

"But Colonel!" implored Hawkins; "stop and think; don't be rash; you know it's the *only* chance we've got to get the money; and besides, the Bible itself says posterity to the fourth generation shall be punished for the sins and crimes committed by ancestors four generations back that hadn't anything to do with them; and so it's only fair to turn the rule around and make it work both ways."

The Colonel was struck with the strong logic of this position. He strode up and down, and thought it painfully over. Finally he said:

"There's reason in it; yes, there's reason in it. And so, although it seems a piteous thing to sweat this poor ancient devil for a burglary he hadn't the least hand in, still if duty commands I suppose we must give him up to the authorities."

"*I* would," said Hawkins, cheered and relieved, "I'd give him up if he was a thousand ancestors compacted into one."

"Lord bless me, that's just what he is," said Sellers, with something like a groan, "it's exactly what he is; there's a contribution in him from every ancestor he ever had. In him there's atoms of priests, soldiers, crusaders, poets, and sweet and gracious women—all kinds and conditions of folk who trod this earth in old, old centuries, and vanished out of it ages ago, and now by act of ours they are summoned from their holy peace to answer for gutting a one-horse bank away out on the borders of Cherokee Strip, and it's just a howling outrage!"

"Oh, don't talk like that, Colonel; it takes the heart all out of me, and makes me ashamed of the part I am proposing to—"

"Wait—I've got it!"

"A saving hope? Shout it out, I am perishing."

"It's perfectly simple; a child would have thought of it. He is all right, not a flaw in him, as far as I have carried the work. If I've been able to bring him as far as the beginning of this century, what's to stop me now? I'll go on and materialize him down to date."

"Land, I never thought of that!" said Hawkins all ablaze with joy again. "It's the very thing. What a brain you have got! And will he shed the superfluous arm?"

"He will."

"And lose his English accent?"

"It will wholly disappear. He will speak Cherokee Strip—and other forms of profanity."

"Colonel, maybe he'll confess!"

"Confess? Merely that bank robbery?"

"Merely? Yes, but why 'merely'?"

The Colonel said in his most impressive manner:

"Hawkins, he will be wholly under my command. I will make him confess every crime he ever committed. There must be a thousand. Do you get the idea?"

"Well—not quite."

"The rewards will come to us."

"Prodigious conception! I *never* saw such a head for seeing with a lightning glance all the outlying ramifications and possibilities of a central idea."

"It is nothing; it comes natural to me. When his time is out in one jail he goes to the next and the next, and we shall have nothing to do but collect the rewards as he goes along. It is a perfectly steady income as long as we live, Hawkins. And much better than other kinds of investments, because he is indestructible."

"It looks—it really does look the way you say; it does indeed."

"Look?—why it *is*. It will not be denied that I have had a pretty wide and comprehensive financial experience, and I do not hesitate to say that I consider this one of the most valuable properties I have ever controlled."

"Do you really think so?"

"I do, indeed."

"O, Colonel, the wasting grind and grief of poverty! If we could realize immediately. I don't mean sell it all, but sell part—enough, you know, to—"

"See how you tremble with excitement. That comes of lack of experience. My boy, when you have been familiar with vast operations as long as I have, you'll be different. Look at me; is my eye dilated? do you notice a quiver anywhere? Feel my pulse: plunk—plunk—plunk—same as if I were asleep And yet, what is passing through my calm cold mind? A procession of figures which would make a financial novice drunk—just the sight of them. Now it is by keeping cool, and looking at a thing all around, that a man sees what's really in it, and saves himself from the novice's unfailing mistake—the one you've just suggested—eagerness to *realize*. Listen to me. Your idea is to sell a part of him for ready cash. Now mine is—guess."

"I haven't an idea. What is it?"

"Stock him—of course."

"Well, I should never have thought of that."

"Because you are not a financier. Say he has committed a thousand crimes. Certainly that's a low estimate. By the look of him, even in his unfinished condition, he has committed all of a million. But call it only a thousand to be perfectly safe; five thousand reward, multiplied by a thousand, gives us a dead sure cash basis of—what? Five million dollars!"

"Wait—let me get my breath."

"And the property indestructible. Perpetually fruitful—perpetually; for a property with his disposition will go on committing crimes and winning rewards."

"You daze me, you make my head whirl!"

"Let it whirl, it won't do it any harm. Now that matter is all fixed—leave it alone. I'll get up the company and issue the stock, all in good time. Just leave it in my hands. I judge you don't doubt my ability to work it up for all it is worth."

"Indeed I don't. I can say that with truth."

"All right, then. That's disposed of. Everything in its turn.

We old operators go by order and system—no helter-skelter business with us. What's the next thing on the docket? The carrying on of the materialization—the bringing it down to date. I will begin on that at once. I think—"

"Look here, Rossmore. You didn't lock It in. A hundred to one it has escaped!"

"Calm yourself, as to that; don't give yourself any uneasiness."

"But why shouldn't it escape?"

"Let it, if it wants to! What of it?"

"Well, *I* should consider it a pretty serious calamity."

"Why, my dear boy, once in my power, always in my power. It may go and come freely. I can produce it here whenever I want it, just by the exercise of my will."

"Well, I am truly glad to hear that, I do assure you."

"Yes, I shall give it all the painting it wants to do, and we and the family will make it as comfortable and contented as we can. No occasion to restrain its movements. I hope to persuade it to remain pretty quiet, though, because a materialization which is in a state of arrested development must of necessity be pretty soft and flabby and substanceless, and—er—by the way, I wonder where It comes from?"

"How? What do you mean?"

The earl pointed significantly—and interrogatively—toward the sky. Hawkins started; then settled into deep reflection; finally shook his head sorrowfully and pointed downwards.

"What makes you think so, Washington?"

"Well, I hardly know, but really you can see, yourself, that he doesn't seem to be pining for his last place."

"It's well thought! Soundly deduced. We've done that Thing a favor. But I believe I will pump it a little, in a quiet way, and find out if we are right."

"How long is it going to take to finish him off and fetch him down to date, Colonel?"

"I wish I knew, but I don't. I am clear knocked out by this new detail—this unforeseen necessity of working a subject down gradually from his condition of ancestor to his ultimate result as posterity. But I'll make him hump himself, anyway."

"Rossmore!"

"Yes, dear. We're in the laboratory. Come—Hawkins is here. Mind, now Hawkins—he's a sound, living, *human being* to all the family—don't forget that. Here she comes."

"Keep your seats, I'm not coming in. I just wanted to ask, who is it that's painting down there?"

"That? Oh, that's a young artist; young Englishman, named Tracy; very promising—favorite pupil of Hans Christian Andersen or one of the other old masters—Andersen I'm pretty sure it is; he's going to half-sole some of our old Italian masterpieces. Been talking to him?"

"Well, only a word. I stumbled right in on him without expecting anybody was there. I tried to be polite to him; offered him a snack"—(Sellers delivered a large wink to Hawkins from behind his hand), "but he declined, and said he wasn't hungry" (another sarcastic wink); "so I brought some apples" (double wink), "and he ate a couple of—"

"What!" and the colonel sprang some yards toward the ceiling and came down quaking with astonishment.

Lady Rossmore was smitten dumb with amazement. She gazed at the sheepish relic of Cherokee Strip, then at her husband, and then at the guest again. Finally she said—

"What is the matter with you, Mulberry?"

He did not answer immediately. His back was turned; he was bending over his chair, feeling the seat of it. But he answered next moment, and said—

"Ah, there it is; it was a tack."

The lady contemplated him doubtfully a moment, then said, pretty snappishly—

"All that for a tack! Praise goodness it wasn't a shingle nail, it would have landed you in the Milky Way. I do hate to have my nerves shook up so." And she turned on her heel and went her way.

As soon as she was safely out, the Colonel said, in a suppressed voice—

"Come—we must see for ourselves. It *must* be a mistake."

They hurried softly down and peeped in. Sellers whispered, in a sort of despair—

"It *is* eating! What a grisly spectacle! Hawkins it's horrible! Take me away—I can't stand it."

They tottered back to the laboratory.

Chapter XX

TRACY made slow progress with his work, for his mind wandered a good deal. Many things were puzzling him. Finally a light burst upon him all of a sudden—seemed to, at any rate—and he said to himself, "I've got the clew at last— this man's mind is off its balance; I don't know how much, but it's off a point or two, sure; off enough to explain this mess of perplexities, anyway. These dreadful chromos—which he takes for old masters; these villainous portraits—which to his frantic mind represent Rossmores; the hatchments; the pompous name of this ramshackle old crib—Rossmore Towers; and that odd assertion of his, that I was expected. How could I be expected? that is, Lord Berkeley. He knows by the papers that that person was burned up in the New Gadsby. Why, hang it, he really doesn't know *who* he was expecting; for his talk showed that he was not expecting an Englishman, or yet an artist, yet I answer his requirements notwithstanding. He seems sufficiently satisfied with me. Yes, he is a little off; in fact I am afraid he is a good deal off, poor old gentleman. But he's interesting—all people in about his condition are, I suppose. I hope he'll like my work; I would like to come every day and study him. And when I write my father— ah, that hurts! I mustn't get on that subject; it isn't good for my spirits. Somebody coming—I must get to work. It's the old gentleman again. He looks bothered. Maybe my clothes are suspicious; and they are—for an artist. If my conscience would allow me to make a change,—but that is out of the question. I wonder what he's making those passes in the air for, with his hands. I seem to be the object of them. Can he be trying to mesmerize me? I don't quite like it. There's something uncanny about it."

The colonel muttered to himself, "It has an effect on him, I can see it myself. That's enough for one time, I reckon. He's not very solid, yet, I suppose, and I might disintegrate him. I'll just put a sly question or two at him, now, and see if I can find out what his condition is, and where he's from."

He approached and said affably—

"Don't let me disturb you, Mr. Tracy; I only want to take

a little glimpse of your work. Ah, that's fine—that's very fine indeed. You are doing it elegantly. My daughter will be charmed with this. May I sit down by you?"

"Oh, do; I shall be glad."

"It won't disturb you? I mean, won't dissipate your inspirations?"

Tracy laughed and said they were not ethereal enough to be very easily discommoded.

The colonel asked a number of cautious and well-considered questions—questions which seemed pretty odd and flighty to Tracy—but the answers conveyed the information desired, apparently, for the colonel said to himself, with mixed pride and gratification—

"It's a good job as far as I've got with it. He's solid. Solid and going to last; solid as the real thing. It's wonderful—wonderful. I believe I could petrify him."

After a little he asked, warily:

"Do you prefer being here, or—or there?"

"There? Where?"

"Why—er—where you've been?"

Tracy's thought flew to his boarding-house, and he answered with decision—

"Oh, *here*, much!"

The colonel was startled, and said to himself, "There's no uncertain ring about that. It indicates where *he's* been to, poor fellow. Well, I am satisfied, now. I'm glad I got him out."

He sat thinking, and thinking, and watching the brush go. At length he said to himself, "Yes, it certainly seems to account for the failure of my endeavors in poor Berkeley's case. *He* went in the other direction. Well, it's all right. He's better off."

Sally Sellers entered from the street, now, looking her divinest, and the artist was introduced to her. It was a violent case of mutual love at first sight, though neither party was entirely aware of the fact, perhaps. The Englishman made this irrelevant remark to himself, "Perhaps he is not insane, after all." Sally sat down, and showed an interest in Tracy's work which greatly pleased him, and a benevolent forgiveness of it which convinced him that the girl's nature was cast in a large mould. Sellers was anxious to report his discoveries to Hawkins; so he took his leave, saying that if the two "young devotees of the colored Muse" thought they could manage without him, he would go and look after his affairs. The artist said to himself, "I think he *is* a little eccentric, perhaps, but that is all." He reproached himself for having injuriously judged a man without giving him any fair chance to show what he really was.

Of course the stranger was very soon at his ease and chatting along comfortably. The average American girl possesses the valuable qualities of naturalness, honesty, and inoffensive straightforwardness; she is nearly barren of troublesome conventions and artificialities, consequently her presence and her ways are unembarrassing, and one is acquainted with her and on the pleasantest terms with her before he knows how it came about. This new acquaintanceship—friendship, indeed—progressed swiftly; and the unusual swiftness of it, and the thoroughness of it are sufficiently evidenced and established by one noteworthy fact—that within the first half hour both parties had ceased to be conscious of Tracy's clothes. Later this consciousness was re-awakened; it was then apparent to Gwendolen that she was almost reconciled to them, and it was apparent to Tracy that he wasn't. The re-awakening was brought about by Gwendolen's inviting the artist to stay to dinner. He had to decline, because he wanted to live, now—that is, now that there was something to live for—and he could not survive in those clothes at a gentleman's table. He thought he knew that. But he went away happy, for he saw that Gwendolen was disappointed.

And whither did he go? He went straight to a slop-shop and bought as neat and reasonably well-fitting a suit of clothes as an Englishman could be persuaded to wear. He said—*to* himself, but *at* his conscience—"I know it's wrong; but it would be wrong *not* to do it; and two wrongs do not make a right."

This satisfied him, and made his heart light. Perhaps it will also satisfy the reader—if he can make out what it means.

The old people were troubled about Gwendolen at dinner, because she was so distraught and silent. If they had noticed, they would have found that she was sufficiently alert and interested whenever the talk stumbled upon the artist and his work; but they didn't notice, and so the chat would swap around to some other subject, and then somebody would presently be privately worrying about Gwendolen again, and wondering if she were not well, or if something had gone wrong in the millinery line. Her mother offered her various reputable patent medicines, and tonics with iron and other hardware in them, and her father even proposed to send out for wine, relentless prohibitionist and head of the order in the District of Columbia as he was, but these kindnesses were all declined—thankfully, but with decision. At bedtime, when the family were breaking up for the night, she privately looted one of the brushes, saying to herself, "It's the one he has used the most."

The next morning Tracy went forth wearing his new suit, and equipped with a pink in his button-hole—a daily attention from Puss. His whole soul was full of Gwendolen Sellers, and this condition was an inspiration, art-wise. All the morning his brush pawed nimbly away at the canvases, almost without his awarity—awarity, in this sense being the sense of being aware, though disputed by some authorities—turning out marvel upon marvel, in the way of decorative accessories to the portraits, with a felicity and celerity which amazed the veterans of the firm and fetched out of them continuous explosions of applause.

Meantime Gwendolen was losing her morning, and many dollars. She supposed Tracy was coming in the forenoon—a conclusion which she had jumped to without outside help. So she tripped down stairs every little while from her work-parlor to arrange the brushes and things over again, and see if he had arrived. And when she was in her work-parlor it was not profitable, but just the other way—as she found out to her sorrow. She had put in her idle moments during the last little while back, in designing a particularly rare and capable gown for herself, and this morning she set about making it up; but she was absent minded, and made an irremediable botch of it. When she saw what she had done, she knew the reason of it and the meaning of it; and she put her work away from her and said she would accept the sign. And from that time forth she came no more away from the Audience Chamber, but remained there and waited. After luncheon she waited again. A whole hour. Then a great joy welled up in her heart, for she saw him coming. So she flew back up stairs thankful, and could hardly wait for him to miss the principal brush, which she had mislaid down there, but knew where she had mislaid it. However, all in good time the others were called in and couldn't find the brush, and then she was sent for, and she couldn't find it herself for some little time; but then she found it when the others had gone away to hunt in the kitchen and down cellar and in the woodshed, and all those other places where people look for things whose ways they are not familiar with. So she gave him the brush, and remarked that she ought to have seen that everything was ready for him, but it hadn't seemed necessary, because it was so early that she wasn't expecting—but she stopped there, surprised at herself for what she was saying; and he felt caught and ashamed, and said to himself, "I knew my impatience would drag me here before I was expected, and betray me, and that is just what it has done; she sees straight through me—and is laughing at me, inside, of course."

Gwendolen was very much pleased, on one account, and a little the other way in another; pleased with the new clothes and the improvement which they had achieved; less pleased by the pink in the buttonhole. Yesterday's pink had hardly interested her; this one was just like it, but somehow it had got her immediate attention, and kept it. She wished she could think of some way of getting at its history in a properly colorless and indifferent way. Presently she made a venture. She said—

"Whatever a man's age may be, he can reduce it several years by putting a bright-colored flower in his button-hole. I have often noticed that. Is that your sex's reason for wearing a boutonnière?"

"I fancy not, but certainly that reason would be a sufficient one. I've never heard of the idea before."

"You seem to prefer pinks. Is it on account of the color, or the form?"

"Oh no," he said, simply, "they are given to me. I don't think I have any preference."

"They are given to him," she said to herself, and she felt a coldness toward that pink. "I wonder who it is, and what she is like." The flower began to take up a good deal of room; it obtruded itself everywhere, it intercepted all views, and marred them; it was becoming exceedingly annoying and conspicuous for a little thing. "I wonder if he cares for her." That thought gave her a quite definite pain.

Chapter XXI

S HE HAD made everything comfortable for the artist; there was no further pretext for staying. So she said she would go, now, and asked him to summon the servants in case he should need anything. She went away unhappy; and she left unhappiness behind her; for she carried away all the sunshine. The time dragged heavily for both, now. He couldn't paint for thinking of her; she couldn't design or millinerize with any heart, for thinking of him. Never before had painting seemed so empty to him, never before had millinerizing seemed so void of interest to her. She had gone without repeating that dinner-invitation—an almost unendurable disappointment to him. On her part—well, she was suffering, too; for she had found she *couldn't* invite him. It was not hard yesterday, but it was impossible to-day. A thousand innocent privileges seemed to have been filched from her unawares in the past twenty-four hours. To-day she felt strangely hampered, restrained of her liberty. To-day she couldn't propose to herself to do anything or say anything concerning this young man without being instantly paralyzed into non-action by the fear that he might "suspect." Invite him to dinner *to-day*? It made her shiver to think of it.

And so her afternoon was one long fret. Broken at intervals. Three times she had to go down stairs on errands—that is, she thought she had to go down stairs on errands. Thus, going and coming, she had six glimpses of him, in the aggregate, without seeming to look in his direction; and she tried to endure these electric ecstasies without showing any sign, but they fluttered her up a good deal, and she felt that the naturalness she was putting on was overdone and quite too frantically sober and hysterically calm to deceive.

The painter had his share of the rapture; he had his six glimpses, and they smote him with waves of pleasure that assaulted him, beat upon him, washed over him deliciously, and drowned out all consciousness of what he was doing with his brush. So there were six places in his canvas which had to be done over again.

At last Gwendolen got some peace of mind by sending word to the Thompsons, in the neighborhood, that she was coming there to dinner. She wouldn't be reminded, at *that* table, that there was an absentee who ought to be a presentee—a word which she meant to look out in the dictionary at a calmer time.

About this time the old earl dropped in for a chat with the artist, and invited him to stay to dinner. Tracy cramped down his joy and gratitude by a sudden and powerful exercise of all his forces; and he felt that now that he was going to be close to Gwendolen, and hear her voice and watch her face during several precious hours, earth had nothing valuable to add to his life for the present.

The earl said to himself, "This spectre can eat apples, apparently. We shall find out, now, if that is a specialty. I think, myself, it's a specialty. Apples, without doubt, constitute the spectral limit. It was the case with our first parents. No, I am wrong—at least only partly right. The line *was* drawn at apples, just as in the present case, but it was from the other direction." The new clothes gave him a thrill of pleasure and pride. He said to himself, "I've got part of him down to date, anyway."

Sellers said he was pleased with Tracy's work; and he went on and engaged him to restore his old masters, and said he should also want him to paint his portrait and his wife's and possibly his daughter's. The tide of the artist's happiness was at flood, now. The chat flowed pleasantly along while Tracy painted and Sellers carefully unpacked a picture which he had brought with him. It was a chromo; a new one, just out. It was the smirking, self-satisfied portrait of a man who was inundating the Union with advertisements inviting everybody to buy his specialty, which was a three-dollar shoe or a dress-suit or something of that kind. The old gentleman rested the chromo flat upon his lap and gazed down tenderly upon it, and became silent and meditative. Presently Tracy noticed that he was dripping tears on it. This touched the young fellow's sympathetic nature, and at the same time gave him the painful sense of being an intruder upon a sacred privacy, an observer of emotions which a stranger ought not to witness. But his pity rose superior to other considerations, and compelled him to try to comfort the old mourner with kindly words and a show of friendly interest. He said—

"I am very sorry—is it a friend whom—"

"Ah, more than that, far more than that—a relative, the dearest I had on earth, although I was never permitted to see him. Yes, it is young Lord Berkeley, who perished so heroically in the awful confla—why, what is the matter?"

"Oh, nothing, nothing. It was a little startling to be so suddenly brought face to face, so to speak, with a person one has heard so much talk about. Is it a good likeness?"

"Without doubt, yes. I never saw him, but you can easily see the resemblance to his father," said Sellers, holding up the chromo and glancing from it to the chromo misrepresenting the Usurping Earl and back again with an approving eye.

"Well, no—I am not sure that I make out the likeness. It is plain that the Usurping Earl there has a great deal of character and a long face like a horse's, whereas his heir here is smirky, moon-faced and characterless."

"We are all that way in the beginning—all the line," said Sellers, undisturbed. "We all start as moon-faced fools, then later we tadpole along into horse-faced marvels of intellect and character. It is by that sign and by that fact that I detect the resemblance here and know this portrait to be genuine and perfect. Yes, all our family are fools at first."

"This young man seems to meet the hereditary requirement, certainly."

"Yes, yes, he was a fool, without any doubt. Examine the face, the shape of the head, the expression. It's all fool, fool, fool, straight through."

"Thanks," said Tracy, involuntarily.

"Thanks?"

"I mean for explaining it to me. Go on, please."

"As I was saying, fool is printed all over the face. A body can even read the *de*tails."

"What do they say?"

"Well, added up, he is a wobbler."

"A which?"

"Wobbler. A person that's always taking a firm stand about something or other—kind of a Gibraltar stand, *he* thinks, for unshakable fidelity and everlastingness—and then, inside of a little while, he begins to wobble; no more Gibraltar there; no, sir, a mighty ordinary commonplace weakling wobbling around on stilts. That's Lord Berkeley to a dot, you can *see* it—*look* at that sheep! But,—why are you blushing like sunset! Dear sir, have I unwittingly offended in some way?"

"Oh, no indeed, no indeed. Far from it. But it always makes me blush to hear a man revile his own blood." He said to himself, "How strangely his vagrant and unguided fancies have hit upon the truth. By accident, he has described me. I am that contemptible thing. When I left England I thought I knew myself; I thought I was a very Frederick the Great for resolution and staying capacity; whereas in truth I am just a Wobbler, simply a Wobbler. Well—after all, it is at least creditable to *have* high ideals and give birth to lofty resolutions; I will allow myself that comfort." Then he said, aloud, "Could this sheep, as you call him, breed a great and self-sacrificing idea in his head, do you think? Could he meditate such a thing, for instance, as the renunciation of the earldom and its wealth and its glories, and voluntary retirement to the ranks of the commonalty, there to rise by his own merit or remain forever poor and obscure?"

"*Could* he? Why, look at him—look at this simpering self-righteous mug! There is your answer. It's the very thing he would think of. And he would start in to do it, too."

"And then?"

"He'd wobble."

"And back down?"

"Every time."

"Is that to happen with *all* my—I mean would that happen to *all* his high resolutions?"

"Oh certainly—certainly. It's the Rossmore of it."

"Then this creature was fortunate to die! Suppose, for argument's sake, that I was a Rossmore, and—"

"It can't be done."

"Why?"

"Because it's not a supposable case. To be a Rossmore at your age, you'd have to be a fool, and you're not a fool. And you'd have to be a Wobbler, whereas anybody that is an expert in reading character can see at a glance that when you set your foot down once, it's there to stay; an earthquake can't wobble it." He added to himself, "That's enough to say to him, but it isn't half strong enough for the facts. The more I observe him, now, the more remarkable I find him. It is the strongest face I have ever examined. There is almost superhuman firmness here, immovable purpose, iron steadfastness of will. A most extraordinary young man."

He presently said, aloud—

"Some time I want to ask your advice about a little matter, Mr. Tracy. You see, I've got that young lord's remains—my goodness, how you jump!"

"Oh, it's nothing, pray go on. You've got his remains?"

"Yes."

"Are you sure they are his, and not somebody else's?"

"Oh, perfectly sure. Samples, I mean. Not all of him."

"Samples?"

"Yes—in baskets. Some time you will be going home; and if you wouldn't mind taking them along—"

"Who? I?"

"Yes—certainly. I don't mean *now*; but after a while; after—but look here, would you like to see them?"

"No! Most certainly not. I don't want to see them."

"O, very well. I only thought—heyo, where are you going, dear?"

"Out to dinner, papa."

Tracy was aghast. The colonel said, in a disappointed voice—

"Well, I'm sorry. Sho, I didn't know she was going out, Mr. Tracy." Gwendolen's face began to take on a sort of apprehensive What-have-I-done expression. "Three old people to one young one—well, it *isn't* a good team, that's a fact." Gwendolen's face betrayed a dawning hopefulness and she said—with a tone of reluctance which hadn't the hall-mark on it—

"If you prefer, I will send word to the Thompsons that I—"

"Oh, is it the Thompsons? That simplifies it—sets everything right. We can fix it without spoiling your arrangements, my child. You've got your heart set on—"

"But papa, I'd *just* as soon go there some other—"

"No—I won't have it. You are a good hard-working darling child, and your father is not the man to disappoint you when you—"

"But papa, I—"

"Go along, I won't hear a word. We'll get along, dear."

Gwendolen was ready to cry with vexation. But there was nothing to do but start; which she was about to do when her father hit upon an idea which filled him with delight because it so deftly covered all the difficulties of the situation and made things smooth and satisfactory:

"I've got it, my love, so that you won't be robbed of your holiday and at the same time we'll be pretty satisfactorily fixed for a good time here. You send Belle Thompson here—perfectly beautiful creature, Tracy, per-fectly beautiful; I want you to see that girl; why, you'll just go mad; you'll go mad inside of a minute; yes, you send her right along, Gwendolen, and tell her—why, she's gone!" He turned—she was already passing out at the gate. He muttered, "I wonder what's the matter; I don't know what her mouth's doing, but I think her shoulders are swearing. Well," said Sellers blithely to Tracy, "I shall miss her—parents always miss the children as soon as they're out of sight, it's only a natural and wisely ordained partiality—but you'll be all right, because Miss Belle will supply the youthful element for you and to your entire content; and we old people will do our best, too. We shall have a good enough time. And you'll have a chance to get better acquainted with Admiral Hawkins. That's a rare character, Mr. Tracy—one of the rarest and most engaging characters the world has produced. You'll find him worth studying. I've studied him ever since he was a child and have always found him developing. I really consider that one of the main things that has enabled me to master the difficult science of character-reading was the livid interest I always felt in that boy and the baffling inscrutabilities of his ways and inspirations."

Tracy was not hearing a word. His spirits were gone, he was desolate.

"Yes, a most wonderful character. Concealment—that's the basis of it. Always the first thing you want to do is to find the keystone a man's character is built on—then you've got it. No misleading and apparently inconsistent peculiarities can fool you then. What do you read on the Senator's surface? Simplicity; a kind of rank and protuberant simplicity; whereas, in fact, that's one of the deepest minds in the world. A perfectly honest man—an absolutely honest and honorable man—and yet without doubt the profoundest master of dissimulation the world has ever seen."

"O, it's devilish!" This was wrung from the unlistening Tracy by the anguished thought of what might have been if only the dinner arrangements hadn't got mixed.

"No, I shouldn't call it that," said Sellers, who was now placidly walking up and down the room with his hands under his coat-tails and listening to himself talk. "One could quite properly call it devilish in another man, but not in the Senator. Your *term* is right—perfectly right—I grant that—but the application is wrong. It makes a great difference. Yes, he is a marvelous character. I do not suppose that any other statesman ever had such a colossal sense of humor, combined with the ability to totally conceal it. I may except George Washington and Cromwell, and perhaps Robespierre, but I draw the line there. A person not an expert might be in Judge Hawkins's company a lifetime and never find out he had any more sense of humor than a cemetery."

A deep-drawn yard-long sigh from the distraught and dreaming artist, followed by a murmured "Miserable, oh, miserable!"

"Well, no, I shouldn't say *that* about it, quite. On the contrary, I admire his ability to conceal his humor even more if possible than I admire the gift itself, stupendous as it is. Another thing—General Hawkins is a thinker; a keen, logical, exhaustive, analytical thinker—perhaps the ablest of modern times. That is, of course, upon themes suited to his size, like the glacial period, and the correlation of forces, and the evolution of the Christian from the caterpillar—any of those things; give him a subject according to his size, and just stand back and watch him think! Why you can see the place rock! Ah, yes, you must know him; you must get on the inside of him. Perhaps the most extraordinary mind since Aristotle."

Dinner was kept waiting for a while for Miss Thompson, but as Gwendolen had not delivered the invitation to her the waiting did no good, and the household presently went to the meal without her. Poor old Sellers tried everything his hospitable soul could devise to make the occasion an enjoyable one for the guest, and the guest tried his honest best to be cheery and chatty and happy for the old gentleman's sake; in fact all hands worked hard in the interest of a mutual good time, but the thing was a failure from the start; Tracy's heart was lead in his bosom, there seemed to be only one prominent feature in the landscape and that was a vacant chair, he couldn't drag his mind away from Gwendolen and his hard luck; consequently his distractions allowed deadly pauses to slip in every now and then when it was his turn to say something, and of course this disease spread to the rest of the conversation—wherefore, instead of having a breezy sail in sunny waters, as anticipated, everybody was bailing out and praying for land. What *could* the matter be? Tracy alone could have told, the others couldn't even invent a theory.

Meanwhile they were having a similarly dismal time at the Thompson house; in fact a twin experience. Gwendolen was ashamed of herself for allowing her disappointment to so depress her spirits and make her so strangely and profoundly miserable; but feeling ashamed of herself didn't improve the matter any; it only seemed to aggravate the suffering. She explained that she was not feeling very well, and everybody could see that this was true; so she got sincere sympathy and commiseration; but that didn't help the case. Nothing helps that kind of a case. It is best to just stand off and let it fester. The moment the dinner was over the girl excused herself, and she hurried home feeling unspeakably grateful to get away from that house and that intolerable capitivity and suffering.

Will he be gone? The thought arose in her brain, but took effect in her heels. She slipped into the house, threw off her things and made straight for the dining room. She stopped and listened. Her father's voice—with no life in it; presently her mother's—no life in that; a considerable vacancy, then a sterile remark from Washington Hawkins. Another silence; then, not Tracy's but her father's voice again.

"He's gone," she said to herself despairingly, and listlessly opened the door and stepped within.

"Why, my child," cried the mother, "how white you are! Are you—has anything—"

"White?" exclaimed Sellers. "It's gone like a flash; 'twasn't serious. Already she's as red as the soul of a watermelon! Sit down, dear, sit down—goodness knows you're welcome. Did you have a good time? We've had great times here—immense. Why didn't Miss Belle come? Mr. Tracy is not feeling well, and she'd have made him forget it."

She was content now; and out from her happy eyes there went a light that told a secret to another pair of eyes there and got a secret in return. In just that infinitely small fraction of a second those two great confessions were made, received, and perfectly understood. All anxiety, apprehension, uncertainty, vanished out of these young people's hearts and left them filled with a great peace.

Sellers had had the most confident faith that with the new reinforcement victory would be at this last moment snatched from the jaws of defeat, but it was an error. The talk was as stubbornly disjointed as ever. He was proud of Gwendolen, and liked to show her off, even against Miss Belle Thompson, and here had been a great opportunity, and what had she made of it? He felt a good deal put out. It vexed him to think that this Englishman, with the traveling Briton's everlasting disposition to generalize whole mountain ranges from single sample-grains of sand, would jump to the conclusion that American girls were as dumb as himself—generalizing the whole tribe from this single sample and she at her poorest, there being nothing at that table to inspire her, give her a start, keep her from going to sleep. He made up his mind that for the honor of the country he would bring these two together again over the social board before long. There would be a different result another time, he judged. He said to himself, with a deep sense of injury, "He'll put in his diary—they all keep diaries—he'll put in his diary that she was miraculously uninteresting—dear, dear, but *wasn't* she!—I never saw the like—and yet looking as beautiful as Satan, too—and couldn't seem to do anything but paw bread crumbs, and pick flowers to pieces, and look fidgety. And it isn't any better here in the Hall of Audience. I've had enough; I'll haul down my flag; the others may fight it out if they want to."

He shook hands all around and went off to do some work which he said was pressing. The idolaters were the width of the room apart, and apparently unconscious of each other's presence. The distance got shortened a little, now. Very soon the mother withdrew. The distance narrowed again. Tracy stood before a chromo of some Ohio politician which had been retouched and chain-mailed for a crusading Rossmore, and Gwendolen was sitting on the sofa not far from his elbow artificially absorbed in examining a photograph album that hadn't any photographs in it.

The "Senator" still lingered. He was sorry for the young people; it had been a dull evening for them. In the goodness of his heart he tried to make it pleasant for them now; tried to remove the ill impression necessarily left by the general defeat; tried to be chatty, even tried to be gay. But the responses were sickly, there was no starting any enthusiasm; he would give it up and quit—it was a day specially picked out and consecrated to failures.

But when Gwendolen rose up promptly and smiled a glad smile and said with thankfulness and blessing—"*Must* you go?" it seemed cruel to desert, and he sat down again.

He was about to begin a remark when—when he didn't. We have all been there. He didn't know how he knew his concluding to stay longer had been a mistake, he merely knew it; and knew it for dead certain, too. And so he bade goodnight, and went mooning out, wondering what he could have done that changed the atmosphere that way. As the door closed behind him those two were standing side by side, looking at that door—looking at it in a waiting, second-counting, but deeply grateful kind of way. And the instant it closed they flung their arms about each other's necks, and there, heart to heart and lip to lip—

"Oh, my God, she's kissing it!"

Nobody heard this remark, because Hawkins, who bred it, only thought it, he didn't utter it. He had turned, the moment he had closed the door, and had pushed it open a little, intending to re-enter and ask what ill-advised thing he had done or said, and apologize for it. But he didn't re-enter; he staggered off stunned, terrified, distressed.

Chapter XXII

FIVE MINUTES later he was sitting in his room, with his head bowed within the circle of his arms, on the table— final attitude of grief and despair. His tears were flowing fast, and now and then a sob broke upon the stillness. Presently he said—

"I knew her when she was a little child and used to climb about my knees; I love her as I love my own, and now—oh, poor thing, poor thing, I cannot bear it!—she's gone and lost her heart to this mangy materializee! Why *didn't* we see that that might happen? But how could we? Nobody could; nobody could ever have dreamed of such a thing. You couldn't expect a person would fall in love with a wax-work. And this one doesn't even amount to that."

He went on grieving to himself, and now and then giving voice to his lamentations.

"It's done, oh, it's done, and there's no help for it, no undoing the miserable business. If I had the nerve, I would kill it. But that wouldn't do any good. *She* loves it; she thinks it's genuine and authentic. If she lost it she would grieve for it just as she would for a real person. And who's to break it to the family! Not I—I'll die first. Sellers is the best human being I ever knew and I wouldn't any more think of—oh, dear, why it'll break his heart when he finds it out. And Polly's too. *This* comes of meddling with such infernal matters! But for this, the creature would still be roasting in Sheol where it belongs. How is it that these people don't smell the brimstone? Sometimes I can't come into the same room with him without nearly suffocating."

After a while he broke out again:

"Well, there's *one* thing, sure. The materializing has got to stop right where it is. If she's got to marry a spectre, let her marry a decent one out of the Middle Ages, like this one— not a cowboy and a thief such as this protoplasmic tadpole's going to turn into if Sellers keeps on fussing at it. It costs five thousand dollars cash and shuts down on the incorporated company to stop the works at this point, but Sally Sellers's happiness is worth more than that."

He heard Sellers coming, and got himself to rights. Sellers took a seat, and said—

"Well, I've got to confess I'm a good deal puzzled. It did certainly eat, there's no getting around it. Not eat, exactly, either, but it nibbled; nibbled in an appetiteless way, but still it nibbled; and that's just a marvel. Now the question is, what does it do with those nibblings? That's it—what does it do with them? My idea is that we don't begin to know all there is to this stupendous discovery yet. But time will show—time and science—give us a chance, and don't get impatient."

But he couldn't get Hawkins interested; couldn't make him talk to amount to anything; couldn't drag him out of his depression. But at last he took a turn that arrested Hawkins's attention.

"I'm coming to like him, Hawkins. He is a person of stupendous character—absolutely gigantic. Under that placid exterior is concealed the most dare-devil spirit that was ever put into a man—he's just a Clive over again. Yes, I'm all admiration for him, on account of his character, and liking naturally follows admiration, you know. I'm coming to like him immensely. Do you know, I haven't the heart to degrade such a character as that down to the burglar estate for money or for anything else; and I've come to ask if you are willing to let the reward go, and leave this poor fellow—"

"Where he is?"

"Yes—not bring him down to date."

"Oh, there's my hand; and my heart's in it, too!"

"I'll never forget you for this, Hawkins," said the old gentleman in a voice which he found it hard to control. "You are making a great sacrifice for me, and one which you can ill afford, but I'll never forget your generosity, and if I live you shall not suffer for it, be sure of that."

Sally Sellers immediately and vividly realized that she was become a new being; a being of a far higher and worthier sort than she had been such a little while before; an earnest being, in place of a dreamer; and supplied with a reason for her presence in the world, where merely a wistful and troubled curiosity about it had existed before. So great and so comprehensive was the change which had been wrought, that she seemed to herself to be a real person who had lately been a shadow; a something which had lately been a nothing; a purpose, which had lately been a fancy; a finished temple, with the altar-fires lit and the voice of worship ascending, where before had been but an architect's confusion of arid working plans, unintelligible to the passing eye and prophesying nothing.

"Lady" Gwendolen! The pleasantness of that sound was all gone; it was an offense to her ear now. She said—

"There—that sham belongs to the past; I will not be called by it any more."

"I may call you simply Gwendolen? You will allow me to drop the formalities straightway and name you by your dear first name without additions?"

She was dethroning the pink and replacing it with a rosebud.

"There—that is better. I hate pinks—some pinks. Indeed yes, you are to call me by my first name without additions—that is,—well, I don't mean without additions *entirely*, but—"

It was as far as she could get. There was a pause; his intellect was struggling to comprehend; presently it did manage to catch the idea in time to save embarrassment all around, and he said gratefully—

"*Dear* Gwendolen! I may say that?"

"Yes—part of it. But—don't kiss me when I am talking, it makes me forget what I was going to say. You can call me by part of that form, but not the last part. Gwendolen is not my name."

"Not your name?" This in a tone of wonder and surprise.

The girl's soul was suddenly invaded by a creepy apprehension, a quite definite sense of suspicion and alarm. She put his arms away from her, looked him searchingly in the eye, and said—

"Answer me truly, on your honor. You are not seeking to marry me on account of my *rank?*"

The shot almost knocked him through the wall, he was so little prepared for it. There was something so finely grotesque about the question and its parent suspicion, that he stopped to wonder and admire, and thus was he saved from laughing. Then, without wasting precious time, he set about the task of convincing her that he had been lured by herself alone, and had fallen in love with her only, not her title and position; that he loved her with all his heart, and could not love her more if she were a duchess, or less if she were without home, name or family. She watched his face wistfully, eagerly, hopefully, translating his words by its expression; and when he had finished there was gladness in her heart—a tumultuous gladness, indeed, though outwardly she was calm, tranquil, even judicially austere. She prepared a surprise for him, now, calculated to put a heavy strain upon those disinterested protestations of his; and thus she delivered it, burning it away word by word as the fuse burns down to a bombshell, and watching to see how far the explosion would lift him:

"Listen—and do not doubt me, for I shall speak the exact truth. Howard Tracy, I am no more an earl's child than you are!"

To her joy—and secret surprise, also—it never phased him. He was ready, this time, and saw his chance. He cried out with enthusiasm, "Thank heaven for that!" and gathered her to his arms.

To express her happiness was almost beyond her gift of speech.

"You make me the proudest girl in all the earth," she said, with her head pillowed on his shoulder. "I thought it only natural that you should be dazzled by the title—maybe even unconsciously, you being English—and that you might be deceiving yourself in thinking you loved only me, and find you didn't love me when the deception was swept away; so it makes me proud that the revelation stands for nothing and that you *do* love just me, only me—oh, prouder than any words can tell!"

"It is only you, sweetheart, I never gave one envying glance toward your father's earldom. That is utterly true, dear Gwendolen."

"There—you mustn't call me that. I hate that false name. I told you it wasn't mine. My name is Sally Sellers—or Sarah, if you like. From this time I banish dreams, visions, imaginings, and will no more of them. I am going to be myself—my genuine self, my honest self, my natural self, clear and clean of sham and folly and fraud, and worthy of you. There is no grain of social inequality between us; I, like you, am poor; I, like you, am without position or distinction; you are a struggling artist, I am that, too, in my humbler way. Our bread is honest bread, we work for our living. Hand in hand we will walk hence to the grave, helping each other in all ways, living for each other, being and remaining one in heart and purpose, one in hope and aspiration, inseparable to the end. And though our place is low, judged by the world's eye, we will make it as high as the highest in the great essentials of honest work for what we eat and wear, and conduct above reproach. We live in a land, let us be thankful, where this is all-sufficient, and no man is better than his neighbor by the grace of God, but only by his own merit."

Tracy tried to break in, but she stopped him and kept the floor herself.

"I am not through, yet. I am going to purge myself of the last vestiges of artificiality and pretence, and then start fair on your own honest level and be worthy mate to you thenceforth. My father honestly thinks he is an earl. Well, leave him his dream, it pleases him and does no one any harm. It was the dream of his ancestors before him. It has made fools of the house of Sellers for generations, and it made something of a fool of me, but took no deep root. I am done with it now, and for good. Forty-eight hours ago I was privately proud of being the daughter of a pinchbeck earl, and thought the proper mate for me must be a man of like degree; but to-day—oh, how grateful I am for your love which has healed my sick brain and restored my sanity!—I could make oath that no earl's son in all the world—"

"Oh,—well, but—but—"

"Why, you look like a person in a panic. What is it? What is the matter?"

"Matter? Oh, nothing—nothing. I was only going to say"—but in his flurry nothing occurred to him to say, for a moment; then by a lucky inspiration he thought of something entirely sufficient for the occasion, and brought it out with eloquent force: "Oh, how beautiful you are! You take my breath away when you look like that."

It was well conceived, well timed, and cordially delivered—and it got its reward.

"Let me see. Where was I? Yes, my father's earldom is pure moonshine. Look at those dreadful things on the wall. You have of course supposed them to be portraits of his ancestors, earls of Rossmore. Well, they are not. They are chromos of distinguished Americans—all moderns; but he has carried them back a thousand years by re-labeling them. Andrew Jackson there, is doing what he can to be the late American earl; and the newest treasure in the collection is supposed to be the young English heir—I mean the idiot with the crape; but in truth it's a shoemaker, and not Lord Berkeley at all."

"Are you sure?"

"Why of course I am. He wouldn't look like that."

"Why?"

"Because his conduct in his last moments, when the fire was sweeping around him shows that he was a man. It shows that he was a fine, high-souled young creature."

Tracy was strongly moved by these compliments, and it seemed to him that the girl's lovely lips took on a new loveliness when they were delivering them. He said, softly—

"It is a pity he could not know what a gracious impression his behavior was going to leave with the dearest and sweetest stranger in the land of—"

"Oh, I almost loved him! Why, I think of him every day. He is always floating about in my mind."

Tracy felt that this was a little more than was necessary. He was conscious of the sting of jealousy. He said—

"It is quite right to think of him—at least now and then—that is, at intervals—in perhaps an admiring way—but it seems to me that—"

"Howard Tracy, are you jealous of that dead man?"

He was ashamed—and at the same time not ashamed. He was jealous—and at the same time he was not jealous. In a sense the dead man was himself; in that case compliments and affection lavished upon that corpse went into his own till and were clear profit. But in another sense the dead man was not himself; and in that case all compliments and affection lavished there were wasted, and a sufficient basis for jealousy. A tiff was the result of the dispute between the two. Then they made it up, and were more loving than ever. As an affectionate clincher of the reconciliation, Sally declared that she had now banished Lord Berkeley from her mind; and added, "And in order to make sure that he shall never make trouble between us again, I will teach myself to detest that name and all that have ever borne it or ever shall bear it."

This inflicted another pang, and Tracy was minded to ask her to modify that a little—just on general principles, and as practice in not overdoing a good thing—perhaps he might better leave things as they were and not risk bringing on another tiff. He got away from that particular, and sought less tender ground for conversation.

"I suppose you disapprove wholly of aristocracies and nobilities, now that you have renounced your title and your father's earldom."

"*Real* ones? Oh, dear no—but I've thrown aside our sham one for good."

This answer fell just at the right time and just in the right place, to save the poor unstable young man from changing his political complexion once more. He had been on the point of beginning to totter again, but this prop shored him up and kept him from floundering back into democracy and re-renouncing aristocracy. So he went home glad that he had asked the fortunate question. The girl would accept a little thing like a genuine earldom, she was merely prejudiced against the brummagem article. Yes, he could have his girl and have his earldom, too: that question was a fortunate stroke.

Sally went to bed happy, too; and remained happy, deliriously happy, for nearly two hours; but at last, just as she was sinking into a contented and luxurious unconsciousness, the shady devil who lives and lurks and hides and watches inside of human beings and is always waiting for a chance to do the proprietor a malicious damage, whispered to her soul and said, "That question had a harmless look, but what was *back* of it?—what was the secret motive of it?—what suggested it?"

The shady devil had knifed her, and could retire, now, and take a rest; the wound would attend to business for him. And it did.

Why should Howard Tracy ask that question? If he was not trying to marry her for the sake of her rank, what should suggest that question to him? Didn't he plainly look gratified when she said her objections to aristocracy had their limitations? Ah, he is after that earldom, that gilded sham—it isn't poor me he wants.

So she argued, in anguish and tears. Then she argued the opposite theory, but made a weak, poor business of it, and lost the case. She kept the arguing up, one side and then the other, the rest of the night, and at last fell asleep at dawn; fell in the fire at dawn, one may say; for that kind of sleep resembles fire, and one comes out of it with his brain baked and his physical forces fried out of him.

Chapter XXIII

TRACY wrote his father before he sought his bed. He wrote a letter which he believed would get better treatment than his cablegram received, for it contained what ought to be welcome news; namely, that he had tried equality and working for a living; had made a fight which he could find no reason to be ashamed of, and in the matter of earning a living had proved that he was able to do it; but that on the whole he had arrived at the conclusion that he could not reform the world single-handed, and was willing to retire from the conflict with the fair degree of honor which he had gained, and was also willing to return home and resume his position and be content with it and thankful for it for the future, leaving further experiment of a missionary sort to other young people needing the chastening and quelling persuasions of experience, the only logic sure to convince a diseased imagination and restore it to rugged health. Then he approached the subject of marriage with the daughter of the American Claimant with a good deal of caution and much painstaking art. He said praiseful and appreciative things about the girl, but didn't dwell upon that detail or make it prominent. The thing which he made prominent was the opportunity now so happily afforded, to reconcile York and Lancaster, graft the warring roses upon one stem, and end forever a crying injustice which had already lasted far too long. One could infer that he had thought this thing all out and chosen this way of making all things fair and right because it was sufficiently fair and considerably wiser than the renunciation-scheme which he had brought with him from England. One could infer that, but he didn't say it. In fact the more he read his letter over, the more he got to inferring it himself.

When the old earl received that letter, the first part of it filled him with a grim and snarly satisfaction; but the rest of it brought a snort or two out of him that could be translated differently. He wasted no ink in this emergency, either in cablegrams or letters; he promptly took ship for America to look into the matter himself. He had staunchly held his grip all this long time, and given no sign of the hunger at his heart to see his son; hoping for the cure of his insane dream, and resolute that the process should go through all the necessary stages without assuaging telegrams or other nonsense from home, and here was victory at last. Victory, but stupidly marred by this idiotic marriage project. Yes, he would step over and take a hand in this matter himself.

During the first ten days following the mailing of the letter Tracy's spirits had no idle time; they were always climbing up into the clouds or sliding down into the earth as deep as the law of gravitation reached. He was intensely happy or intensely miserable by turns, according to Miss Sally's moods. He never could tell when the mood was going to change, and when it changed he couldn't tell what it was that had changed it. Sometimes she was so in love with him that her love was tropical, torrid, and she could find no language fervent enough for its expression; then suddenly, and without warning or any apparent reason, the weather would change, and the victim would find himself adrift among the icebergs and feeling as lonesome and friendless as the north pole. It sometimes seemed to him that a man might better be dead than exposed to these devastating varieties of climate.

The case was simple. Sally *wanted* to believe that Tracy's preference was disinterested; so she was always applying little tests of one sort or another, hoping and expecting that they would bring out evidence which would confirm or fortify her belief. Poor Tracy did not know that these experiments were being made upon him, consequently he walked promptly into all the traps the girl set for him. These traps consisted in apparently casual references to social distinction, aristocratic title and privilege, and such things. Often Tracy responded to these references heedlessly and not much caring what he said provided it kept the talk going and prolonged the séance. He didn't suspect that the girl was watching his face and listening for his words as one who watches the judge's face and listens for the words which will restore him to home and friends and freedom or shut him away from the sun and human companionship forever. He didn't suspect that his careless words were being weighed, and so he often delivered sentence of death when it would have been just as handy and all the same to him to pronounce acquittal. Daily he broke the girl's heart, nightly he sent her to the rack for sleep. He couldn't understand it.

Some people would have put this and that together and perceived that the weather never changed until one particular subject was introduced, and that then it *always* changed. And they would have looked further, and perceived that that subject was always introduced by the one party, never the other. They would have argued, then, that this was done for a purpose. If they could not find out what that purpose was in any simpler or easier way, they would *ask*.

But Tracy was not deep enough or suspicious enough to think of these things. He noticed only one particular; that the weather was always sunny when a visit *began*. No matter how much it might cloud up later, it always began with a clear sky. He couldn't explain this curious fact to himself, he merely knew it to be a fact. The truth of the matter was, that by the time Tracy had been out of Sally's sight six hours she was so famishing for a sight of him that her doubts and suspicions were all consumed away in the fire of that longing, and so always she came into his presence as surprisingly radiant and joyous as she wasn't when she went out of it.

In circumstances like these a growing portrait runs a good many risks. The portrait of Sellers, by Tracy, was fighting along, day by day, through this mixed weather, and daily adding to itself ineradicable signs of the checkered life it was leading. It was the happiest portrait, in spots, that was ever seen; but in other spots a damned soul looked out from it; a soul that was suffering all the different kinds of distress there are, from stomach ache to rabies. But Sellers liked it. He said it was just himself all over—a portrait that sweated moods from every pore, and no two moods alike. He said he had as many different kinds of emotions in him as a jug.

It was a kind of a deadly work of art, maybe, but it was a starchy picture for show; for it was life size, full length, and represented the American earl in a peer's scarlet robe, with the three ermine bars indicative of an earl's rank, and on the gray head an earl's coronet, tilted just a wee bit to one side in a most gallus and winsome way. When Sally's weather was sunny the portrait made Tracy chuckle, but when her weather was overcast it disordered his mind and stopped the circulation of his blood.

Late one night when the sweethearts had been having a flawless visit together, Sally's interior devil began to work his specialty, and soon the conversation was drifting toward the customary rock. Presently, in the midst of Tracy's serene flow of talk, he felt a shudder which he knew was not his shudder, but exterior to his breast although immediately against it. After the shudder came sobs; Sally was crying.

"Oh, my darling, what have I done—what have I said? It has happened again! What *have* I done to wound you?"

She disengaged herself from his arms and gave him a look of deep reproach.

"What have you done? I will tell you what you have done. You have unwittingly revealed—oh, for the twentieth time, though I *could* not believe it, *would* not believe it!—that it is not me you love, but that foolish sham my father's imitation earldom; and you have broken my heart!"

"Oh, my child, what are you saying! I never dreamed of such a thing."

"Oh, Howard, Howard, the things you have uttered when you were forgetting to guard your tongue, have betrayed you."

"Things I have uttered when I was *forgetting* to guard my tongue? These are hard words. When have I *remembered* to guard it? Never in one instance. It has no office but to speak the truth. It needs no guarding for that."

"Howard, I have noted your words and weighed them, when you were not thinking of their significance—and they have told me more than you meant they should."

"Do you mean to say you have answered the trust I had in you by using it as an ambuscade from which you could set snares for my unsuspecting tongue and be safe from detection while you did it? You have not done this—surely you have not done this thing. Oh, one's enemy could not do it."

This was an aspect of the girl's conduct which she had not clearly perceived before. Was it treachery? Had she abused a trust? The thought crimsoned her cheeks with shame and remorse.

"Oh, forgive me," she said, "I did not know what I was

doing. I have been so tortured—you *will* forgive me, you *must*; I have suffered so much, and I am so sorry and so humble; you *do* forgive me, *don't* you?—don't turn away, don't refuse me; it is only my love that is at fault, and you *know* I love you, love you with all my heart; I couldn't bear to—oh, dear, dear, I am so miserable, and I *never* meant any harm, and I didn't see where this insanity was carrying me, and how it was wronging and abusing the dearest heart in all the world to me—and—and—oh, take me in your arms again, I have no other refuge, no other home and hope!"

There was reconciliation again—immediate, perfect, all-embracing—and with it utter happiness. This would have been a good time to adjourn. But no, now that the cloud-breeder was revealed at last; now that it was manifest that all the sour weather had come from this girl's dread that Tracy was lured by her rank and not herself, he resolved to lay that ghost immediately and permanently by furnishing the best possible proof that he *couldn't* have had back of him at any time the suspected motive. So he said—

"Let me whisper a little secret in your ear—a secret which I have kept shut up in my breast all this time. Your rank *couldn't* ever have been an enticement. I am son and heir to an English earl!"

The girl stared at him—one, two, three moments, maybe a dozen—then her lips parted—

"You?" she said, and moved away from him, still gazing at him in a kind of blank amazement.

"Why—why, certainly I am. Why do you act like this? What have I done *now*?"

"What have you done? You have certainly made a most strange statement. You must see that yourself."

"Well," with a timid little laugh, "it may be a strange enough statement; but of what consequence is that, if it is true?"

"*If* it is true. You are already retiring from it."

"Oh, not for a moment! You should not say that. I have not deserved it. I have spoken the truth; why do you doubt it?"

Her reply was prompt.

"Simply because you didn't speak it earlier!"

"Oh!" It wasn't a groan, exactly, but it was an intelligible enough expression of the fact that he saw the point and recognized that there was reason in it.

"You have seemed to conceal nothing from me that I ought to know concerning yourself, and you were not privileged to keep back such a thing as this from me a moment after—after—well, after you had determined to pay your court to me."

"It's true, it's true, I know it! But there were circumstances—in—in the way—circumstances which—"

She waved the circumstances aside.

"Well, you see," he said, pleadingly, "you seemed so bent on our traveling the proud path of honest labor and honorable poverty, that I was terrified—that is, I was afraid—of—of—well, *you* know how you talked."

"Yes, I know how I talked. And I also know that before the talk was finished you inquired how I stood as regards aristocracies, and my answer was calculated to relieve your fears."

He was silent a while. Then he said, in a discouraged way—

"I don't see any way out of it. It was a mistake. That is in truth all it was, just a mistake. No harm was meant, no harm in the world. I didn't see how it might some time look. It is my way. I don't seem to see far."

The girl was almost disarmed, for a moment. Then she flared up again.

"An Earl's son! Do earls' sons go about working in lowly callings for their bread and butter?"

"God knows they don't! I have wished they did."

"Do earls' sons sink their degree in a country like this, and come sober and decent to sue for the hand of a born child of poverty when they can go drunk, profane, and steeped in dishonorable debt and buy the pick and choice of the millionaires' daughters of America? *You* an earl's son! Show me the signs."

"I thank God I am not able—if those are the signs. But yet I am an earl's son and heir. It is all I can say. I wish you would believe me, but you will not. I know no way to persuade you."

She was about to soften again, but his closing remark made her bring her foot down with smart vexation, and she cried out—

"Oh, you drive all patience out of me! Would you have one believe that you haven't your proofs at hand, and yet are what you say you are? You do not put your hand in your pocket *now*—for you have nothing there. You make a claim like this, and then venture to travel without credentials. These are simply incredibilities. Don't you see that, yourself?"

He cast about in his mind for a defence of some kind or other—hesitated a little, and then said, with difficulty and diffidence—

"I will tell you just the truth, foolish as it will seem to you—to anybody, I suppose—but it *is* the truth. I had an ideal—call it a dream, a folly, if you will—but I wanted to renounce the privileges and unfair advantages enjoyed by the nobility and wrung from the nation by force and fraud, and purge myself of my share of those crimes against right and reason, by thenceforth comrading with the poor and humble on equal terms, earning with my own hands the bread I ate, and rising by my own merit if I rose at all."

The young girl scanned his face narrowly while he spoke; and there was something about his simplicity of manner and statement which touched her—touched her almost to the danger point; but she set her grip on the yielding spirit and choked it to quiescence; it could not be wise to surrender to compassion or any kind of sentiment, yet; she must ask one or two more questions. Tracy was reading her face; and what he read there lifted his drooping hopes a little.

"An earl's son to do that! Why, he were a man! A man to love!—oh, more, a man to worship!"

"Why, I—"

"But he never lived! He is not born, he will not be born. The self-abnegation that could do that—even in utter folly, and hopeless of conveying benefit to any, beyond the mere example—could be mistaken for greatness; why, it would *be* greatness in this cold age of sordid ideals! A moment—wait—let me finish; I have one question more. Your father is earl of what?"

"Rossmore—and I am Viscount Berkeley!"

The fat was in the fire again. The girl felt so outraged that it was difficult for her to speak.

"How *can* you venture such a brazen thing! You know that he is dead, and you know that I know it. Oh, to rob the living of name and honors for a selfish and temporary advantage is crime enough, but to rob the defenceless dead—why it is more than crime, it *degrades* crime!"

"Oh, listen to me—just a word—don't turn away like that. Don't go—don't leave me, so—stay one moment. On my honor—"

"Oh, on your honor!"

"On my honor I am what I say! And I will prove it, and you will believe, I know you will. I will bring you a message—a cablegram—"

"When?"

"To-morrow—next day—"

"Signed 'Rossmore'?"

"Yes—signed Rossmore."

"What will that prove?"

"What will it prove? What *should* it prove?"

"If you force me to say it—possibly the presence of a confederate somewhere."

This was a hard blow, and staggered him. He said, dejectedly—

"It is true. I did not think of it. Oh, my God, I do not know any way to do; I do everything wrong. You are going? —and you won't say even good-night—or good-bye? Ah, we have not parted like this before."

"Oh, I *want* to run and—no, go, now." A pause—then she said, "You may bring the message when it comes."

"Oh, may I? God bless you."

He was gone; and none too soon; her lips were already quivering, and now she broke down. Through her sobbings her words broke from time to time.

"Oh, he is gone. I have lost him, I shall never see him any more. And he didn't kiss me good-bye; never even offered to force a kiss from me, and he *knowing* it was the very, very last, and I expecting he would, and never *dreaming* he would treat me so after all we have been to each other. Oh, oh, oh, oh, what shall I do, what *shall* I do! He is a dear, poor, miserable, good-hearted, transparent liar and humbug, but oh, I *do* love him so!" After a little she broke into speech again. "How dear he is! and I shall miss him so, I shall miss him so! Why *won't* he ever think to *forge* a message and fetch it?—but no, he never will, he never thinks of anything; he's so honest and simple it wouldn't ever occur to him. Oh, what *did* possess him to think he could succeed as a fraud—and he hasn't the first requisite except duplicity that I can see. Oh, dear, I'll go to bed and give it all up. Oh, I *wish* I had told him to come and tell me whenever he didn't get any telegram—and now it's all my own fault if I never see him again. How my eyes must look!"

Chapter XXIV

NEXT DAY, sure enough, the cablegram didn't come. This was an immense disaster; for Tracy couldn't go into the presence without that ticket, although it wasn't going to possess any value as evidence. But if the failure of the cablegram on that first day may be called an immense disaster, where is the dictionary that can turn out a phrase sizeable enough to describe the tenth day's failure? Of course every day that the cablegram didn't come made Tracy all of twenty-four hours' more ashamed of himself than he was the day before, and made Sally fully twenty-four hours more certain than ever that he not only hadn't any father anywhere, but hadn't even a confederate—and so it followed that he was a double-dyed humbug and couldn't be otherwise.

These were hard days for Barrow and the art firm. All these had their hands full, trying to comfort Tracy. Barrow's task was particularly hard, because he was made a confidant in full, and therefore had to humor Tracy's delusion that he had a father, and that the father was an earl, and that he was going to send a cablegram. Barrow early gave up the idea of trying to convince Tracy that he hadn't any father, because this had such a bad effect on the patient, and worked up his temper to such an alarming degree. He had tried, as an experiment, letting Tracy think he had a father; the result was so good that he went further, with proper caution, and tried letting him think his father was an earl; this wrought so well, that he grew bold, and tried letting him think he had two fathers, if he wanted to, but he didn't want to, so Barrow withdrew one of them and substituted letting him think he was going to get a cablegram—which Barrow judged he wouldn't, and was right; but Barrow worked the cablegram daily for all it was worth, and it was the one thing that kept Tracy alive; that was Barrow's opinion.

And these were bitter hard days for poor Sally, and mainly delivered up to private crying. She kept her furniture pretty damp, and so caught cold, and the dampness and the cold and the sorrow together undermined her appetite, and she was a pitiful enough object, poor thing. Her state was bad enough, as per statement of it above quoted; but all the forces of nature and circumstance seemed conspiring to make it worse—and succeeding. For instance, the morning after her dismissal of Tracy, Hawkins and Sellers read in the associated press dispatches that a toy puzzle called Pigs in the Clover, had come into sudden favor within the past few weeks, and that from the Atlantic to the Pacific all the populations of all the States had knocked off work to play with it, and that the business of the country had now come to a standstill by consequence; that judges, lawyers, burglars, parsons, thieves, merchants, mechanics, murderers, women, children, babies—everybody, indeed, could be seen from morning till midnight, absorbed in one deep project and purpose, and only one—to pen those pigs, work out that puzzle successfully; that all gayety, all cheerfulness had departed from the nation, and in its place care, preoccupation and anxiety sat upon every countenance, and all faces were drawn, distressed, and furrowed with the signs of age and trouble, and marked with the still sadder signs of mental decay and incipient madness; that factories were at work night and day in eight cities, and yet to supply the demand for the puzzle was thus far impossible. Hawkins was wild with joy, but Sellers was calm. Small matters could not disturb his serenity. He said—

"That's just the way things go. A man invents a thing which could revolutionize the arts, produce mountains of money, and bless the earth, and who will bother with it or show any interest in it?—and so you are just as poor as you were before. But you invent some worthless thing to amuse yourself with, and would throw it away if let alone, and all of a sudden the whole world makes a snatch for it and out crops a fortune. Hunt up that Yankee and collect, Hawkins—half is yours, you know. Leave me to potter at my lecture."

This was a temperance lecture. Sellers was head chief in the Temperance camp, and had lectured, now and then in that interest, but had been dissatisfied with his efforts; wherefore he was now about to try a new plan. After much thought he had concluded that a main reason why his lectures lacked fire or something, was, that they were too transparently amateurish; that is to say, it was probably too plainly perceptible that the lecturer was trying to tell people about the horrid effects of liquor when he didn't really know anything about those effects except from hearsay, since he had hardly ever tasted an intoxicant in his life. His scheme, now, was to prepare himself to speak from bitter experience. Hawkins was to stand by with the bottle, calculate the doses, watch the effects, make notes of results, and otherwise assist in the preparation. Time was short, for the ladies would be along about noon—that is to say, the temperance organization called the Daughters of Siloam—and Sellers must be ready to head the procession.

The time kept slipping along—Hawkins did not return—Sellers could not venture to wait longer; so he attacked the bottle himself, and proceeded to note the effects. Hawkins got back at last; took one comprehensive glance at the lecturer, and went down and headed off the procession. The ladies were grieved to hear that the champion had been taken suddenly ill and violently so, but glad to hear that it was hoped he would be out again in a few days.

As it turned out, the old gentleman didn't turn over or show any signs of life worth speaking of for twenty-four hours. Then he asked after the procession, and learned what had happened about it. He was sorry; said he had been "fixed" for it. He remained abed several days, and his wife and daughter took turns in sitting with him and ministering to his wants. Often he patted Sally's head and tried to comfort her.

"Don't cry, my child, don't cry so; *you* know your old father did it by mistake and didn't mean a bit of harm; you know he wouldn't intentionally do anything to make you ashamed for the world; you know he was trying to do good and only made the mistake through ignorance, not knowing the right doses and Washingington not there to help. Don't cry so, dear, it breaks my old heart to see you, and think I've brought this humiliation on you and you so dear to me and so good. I won't ever do it again, indeed I won't; now be comforted, honey, that's a good child."

But when she wasn't on duty at the bedside the crying went on just the same; then the mother would try to comfort her, and say—

"Don't cry, dear, *he* never meant any harm; it was all one of those happens that you can't guard against when you are trying experiments, that way. You see *I* don't cry. It's because I know him so well. I could never look anybody in the face again if he had got into such an amazing condition as that a-purpose; but bless you his intention was pure and high, and that makes the *act* pure, though it was higher than was necessary. We're not humiliated, dear, he did it under a noble impulse and we don't need to be ashamed. There, don't cry any more, honey."

Thus, the old gentleman was useful to Sally, during several days, as an explanation of her tearfulness. She felt thankful to him for the shelter he was affording her, but often said to herself, "It's a shame to let him see in my cryings a reproach—as if he could ever do anything that could make me reproach him! But I can't confess; I've got to go on using him for a pretext, he's the only one I've got in the world, and I do need one so much."

As soon as Sellers was out again, and found that stacks of money had been placed in bank for him and Hawkins by the Yankee, he said, "*Now* we'll soon see who's the Claimant and who's the Authentic. I'll just go over there and warm up that House of Lords." During the next few days he and his wife were so busy with preparations for the voyage that Sally had all the privacy she needed, and all the chance to cry that was good for her. Then the old pair left for New York—and England.

Sally had also had a chance to do another thing. That was, to make up her mind that life was not worth living upon the present terms. If she *must* give up her impostor and die, doubtless she must submit; but might she not lay her whole case before some disinterested person, first, and see if there wasn't perhaps some saving way out of the matter? She turned this idea over in her mind a good deal. In her first visit with Hawkins after her parents were gone, the talk fell upon Tracy, and she was impelled to set her case before the statesman and take his counsel. So she poured out her heart, and he listened with painful solicitude. She concluded, pleadingly, with—

"*Don't* tell me he is an impostor. I suppose he is, but doesn't it look to you as if he isn't? You are cool, you know, and outside; and so, maybe it can look to you as if he isn't one, when it can't to me. *Doesn't* it look to you as if he isn't?

Couldn't you—*can't* it look to you that way—for—for my sake?"

The poor man was troubled, but he felt obliged to keep in the neighborhood of the truth. He fought around the present detail a little while, then gave it up and said he couldn't really see his way to clearing Tracy.

"No," he said, "the truth is, he's an impostor."

"That is, you—you feel a little certain, but not entirely—oh, not *entirely*, Mr. Hawkins!"

"It's a pity to have to say it—I do hate to say it,—but I don't think anything about it, I *know* he's an impostor."

"Oh, now, Mr. Hawkins, you *can't* go that far. A body *can't* really know it, you know. It isn't *proved* that he's not what he says he is."

Should he come out and make a clean breast of the whole wretched business? Yes—at least the most of it—it ought to be done. So he set his teeth and went at the matter with determination, but purposing to spare the girl one pain—that of knowing that Tracy was a criminal.

"Now I am going to tell you a plain tale; one not pleasant for me to tell or for you to hear, but we've got to stand it. I know all about that fellow; and I *know* he is no earl's son."

The girl's eyes flashed, and she said:

"I don't care a snap for that—go on!"

This was so wholly unexpected that it at once obstructed the narrative; Hawkins was not even sure that he had heard aright. He said—

"I don't know that I quite understand. Do you mean to say that if he was all right and proper otherwise you'd be indifferent about the earl part of the business?"

"Absolutely."

"You'd be entirely satisfied with him and wouldn't *care* for his not being an earl's son,—that *being* an earl's son wouldn't add any value to him?"

"Not the least value that I would care for. Why, Mr. Hawkins, I've gotten over all that day-dreaming about earldoms and aristocracies and all such nonsense and am become just a plain ordinary nobody and content with it; and it is to *him* I owe my cure. And as to anything being able to add a value to him, nothing can do that. He is the whole world to me, just as he is; he comprehends *all* the values there are—then how can you *add* one?"

"She's pretty far gone." He said that to himself. He continued, still to himself, "I must change my plan again; I can't seem to strike one that will stand the requirements of this most variegated emergency five minutes on a stretch. Without making this fellow a criminal, I believe I will invent a name and a character for him calculated to disenchant her. If it fails to do it, then I'll know that the next rightest thing to do will be to help her to her fate, poor thing, not hinder her." Then he said aloud:

"Well, Gwendolen—"

"I want to be called Sally."

"I'm glad of it; I like it better, myself. Well, then, I'll tell you about this man Snodgrass."

"Snodgrass! Is *that* his name?"

"Yes—Snodgrass. The other's his nom de plume."

"It's hideous!"

"I know it is, but we can't help our names."

"And that is truly his real name—and not Howard Tracy?"

Hawkins answered, regretfully—

"Yes, it seems a pity."

The girl sampled the name musingly, once or twice—

"Snodgrass. Snodgrass. No, I could not endure that. I could not get used to it. No, I should call him by his first name. What is his first name?"

"His—er—his initials are S. M."

"His initials? I don't care anything about his initials. I can't call him by his initials. What do they *stand* for?"

"Well, you see, his father was a physician, and he—he—well he was an idolater of his profession, and he—well, he was a very eccentric man, and—"

"What do they *stand* for! What are you shuffling about?"

"They—well they stand for Spinal Meningitis. His father being a phy—"

"I never heard such an infamous name! Nobody can ever call a person *that*—a person they love. I wouldn't call an enemy by such a name. It sounds like an epithet." After a moment, she added with a kind of consternation, "Why, it would be *my* name! Letters would come with it on."

"Yes—Mrs. Spinal Meningitis Snodgrass."

"Don't repeat it—don't; I can't bear it. Was the father a lunatic?"

"No, that is not charged."

"I am glad of that, because that is transmissible. What do you think *was* the matter with him, then?"

"Well, I don't really know. The family used to run a good deal to idiots, and so, maybe—"

"Oh, there isn't any maybe about it. This one was an idiot."

"Well, yes—he could have been. He was suspected."

"Suspected!" said Sally, with irritation. "Would one *suspect* there was going to be a dark time if he saw the constellations fall out of the sky? But that is enough about the idiot, I don't take any interest in idiots; tell me about the son."

"Very well, then, this one was the eldest, but not the favorite. His brother, Zylobalsamum—"

"Wait—give me a chance to realize that. It is perfectly stupefying. Zylo—what did you call it?"

"Zylobalsamum."

"I never heard such a name. It sounds like a disease. Is it a disease?"

"No, I don't think it's a disease. It's either Scriptural or—"

"Well, it's not Scriptural."

"Then it's anatomical. I knew it was one or the other. Yes, I remember, now, it *is* anatomical. It's a ganglion—a nerve centre—it is what is called the zylobalsamum process."

"Well, go on; and if you come to any more of them, omit the names; they make one feel so uncomfortable."

"Very well, then. As I said, this one was not a favorite in the family, and so he was neglected in every way, never sent to school, always allowed to associate with the worst and coarsest characters, and so of course he has grown up a rude, vulgar, ignorant, dissipated ruffian, and—"

"He? It's no such thing! You ought to be more generous than to make such a statement as that about a poor young stranger who—who—why, he is the very opposite of that! He is considerate, courteous, obliging, modest, gentle, refined, cultivated—*oh*, for shame! how can you say such things about him?"

"I don't blame you, Sally—indeed I haven't a word of blame for you for being blinded by your affection—blinded to these minor defects which are so manifest to others who—"

"Minor defects? Do you call these minor defects? What are murder and arson, pray?"

"It is a difficult question to answer straight off—and of course estimates of such things vary with environment. With us, out our way, they would not necessarily attract as much attention as with you, yet they are often regarded with disapproval—"

"Murder and arson are regarded with disapproval?"

"Oh, frequently."

"With disapproval. Who *are* those Puritans you are talking about? But wait—how did you come to know so much about this family? Where did you get all this hearsay evidence?"

"Sally, it isn't hearsay evidence. That is the serious part of it. I *knew* that family—personally."

This was a surprise.

"You? You actually knew them?"

"Knew Zylo, as we used to call him, and knew his father, Dr. Snodgrass. I didn't know your own Snodgrass, but have had glimpses of him from time to time, and I heard about him all the time. He was the common talk, you see, on account of his—"

"On account of his not being a house-burner or an assassin, I suppose. That would have made him commonplace. Where did you know these people?"

"In Cherokee Strip."

"Oh, how preposterous! There are not enough people in Cherokee Strip to *give* anybody a reputation, good or bad. There isn't a quorum. Why the whole population consists of a couple of wagon loads of horse thieves."

Hawkins answered placidly—

"Our friend was one of those wagon loads."

Sally's eyes burned and her breath came quick and fast, but she kept a fairly good grip on her anger and did not let it get the advantage of her tongue. The statesman sat still and waited for developments. He was content with his work. It was as handsome a piece of diplomatic art as he had ever turned out, he thought; and now, let the girl make her own choice. He judged she would let her spectre go; he hadn't a doubt of it in fact; but anyway, let the choice be made, and he was ready to ratify it and offer no further hindrance.

Meantime Sally had thought her case out and made up her mind. To the major's disappointment the verdict was against him. Sally said:

"He has no friend but me, and I will not desert him now. I will not marry him if his moral character is bad; but if he can prove that it isn't, I will—and he shall have the chance. To me he seems utterly good and dear; I've never seen anything about him that looked otherwise—except, of course, his calling himself an earl's son. Maybe that is only vanity, and no real harm, when you get to the bottom of it. I do *not* believe he is any such person as you have painted him. I want to see him. I want you to find him and send him to me. I will implore him to be honest with me, and tell me the whole truth, and not be afraid."

"Very well; if that is your decision I will do it. But Sally, you know, he's poor, and—"

"Oh, *I* don't care anything about that. That's neither here nor there. Will you bring him to me?"

"I'll do it. When?"

"Oh, dear, it's getting toward dark, now, and so you'll have to put it off till morning. But you *will* find him in the morning, *won't* you? Promise."

"I'll have him here by daylight."

"Oh, *now* you're your own old self again—and lovelier than ever!"

"I couldn't ask fairer than that. Good-bye, dear."

Sally mused a moment alone, then said earnestly, "I love him in *spite* of his name!" and went about her affairs with a light heart.

Chapter XXV

Hawkins went straight to the telegraph office and disburdened his conscience. He said to himself, "She's not going to give this galvanized cadaver up, that's plain. Wild horses can't pull her away from him. I've done my share; it's for Sellers to take an innings, now." So he sent this message to New York:

"Come back. Hire special train. She's going to marry the materializee."

Meantime a note came to Rossmore Towers to say that the Earl of Rossmore had just arrived from England, and would do himself the pleasure of calling in the evening. Sally said to herself, "It is a pity he didn't stop in New York; but it's no matter; he can go up to-morrow and see my father. He has come over here to tomahawk papa, very likely—or buy out his claim. This thing would have excited me, a while back; but it has only one interest for me now, and only one value. I can say to—to—Spine, Spiny, Spinal—I don't like any *form* of that name!—I can say to him to-morrow, '*Don't* try to keep it up any more, or I shall have to tell you whom I have been talking with last night, and then you will be embarrassed.'"

Tracy couldn't know he was to be invited for the morrow, or he might have waited. As it was, he was too miserable to wait any longer; for his last hope—a letter—had failed him. It was fully due to-day; it had not come. Had his father really flung him away? It looked so. It was not like his father, but it surely looked so. His father was a rather tough nut, in truth, but had never been so with his son—still, this implacable silence had a calamitous look. Anyway, Tracy would go to the Towers and—then what? He didn't know; his head was tired out with thinking—he wouldn't think about what he must do or say—let it all take care of itself. So that he saw Sally once more, he would be satisfied, happen what might; he wouldn't care.

He hardly knew how he got to the Towers, or when. He knew and cared for only one thing—he was alone with Sally. She was kind, she was gentle, there was moisture in her eyes, and a yearning something in her face and manner which she could not wholly hide—but she kept her distance. They talked. Bye and bye she said—watching his downcast countenance out of the corner of her eye—

"It's so lonesome—with papa and mamma gone. I try to read, but I can't seem to get interested in any book. I try the newspapers, but they do put such rubbish in them. You take up a paper and start to read something you think's interesting, and it goes on and on and on about how somebody—well, Dr. Snodgrass, for instance—"

Not a movement from Tracy, not the quiver of a muscle. Sally was amazed—what command of himself he must have! Being disconcerted, she paused so long that Tracy presently looked up wearily and said—

"Well?"

"Oh, I thought you were not listening. Yes, it goes on and on about this Doctor Snodgrass, till you are *so* tired, and then about his younger son—*the favorite son*—Zylobalsamum Snodgrass—"

Not a sign from Tracy, whose head was drooping again. What supernatural self-possession! Sally fixed her eye on him and began again, resolved to blast him out of his serenity this time if she knew how to apply the dynamite that is concealed in certain forms of words when those words are properly loaded with unexpected meanings.

"And next it goes on and on and on about the eldest son—*not* the favorite, this one—and how he is neglected in his poor barren boyhood, and allowed to grow up unschooled, ignorant, coarse, vulgar, the comrade of the community's scum, and become in his completed manhood a rude, profane, dissipated ruffian—"

That head still drooped! Sally rose, moved softly and solemnly a step or two, and stood before Tracy—his head came slowly up, his meek eyes met her intense ones—then she finished with deep impressiveness—

"—named Spinal Meningitis Snodgrass!"

Tracy merely exhibited signs of increased fatigue. The girl was outraged by this iron indifference and callousness, and cried out—

"What *are* you made of?"

"I? Why?"

"Haven't you *any* sensitiveness? Don't these things touch any poor *remnant* of delicate feeling in you?"

"N-no," he said wonderingly, "they don't seem to. Why should they?"

"O, dear me, *how* can you look so innocent, and foolish, and good, and empty, and gentle, and all that, right in the hearing of such things as those! Look me in the eye—straight in the eye. There, now then, answer me without a flinch. Isn't Doctor Snodgrass your father, and isn't Zylobalsamum your brother," [here Hawkins was about to enter the room, but changed his mind upon hearing these words, and elected for a walk down town, and so glided swiftly away], "and isn't your name Spinal Meningitis, and isn't your father a doctor and an idiot, like all the family for generations, and doesn't he name all his children after poisons and pestilences and abnormal anatomical eccentricities of the human body? Answer me, some way or somehow—and quick. *Why* do you sit there looking like an envelope without any address on it and see me going mad before your face with suspense!"

"Oh, I wish I could do—do—I wish I could do something, *anything* that would give you peace again and make you happy; but I know of nothing—I know of no way. I have never heard of these awful people before."

"What? Say it again!"

"I have never—never in my life till now."

"Oh, you *do* look so honest when you say that! It *must* be true—surely you *couldn't* look that way, you *wouldn't* look that way if it were not true—*would* you?"

"I couldn't and wouldn't. It *is* true. Oh, let us end this suffering—take me back into your heart and confidence—"

"Wait—one more thing. Tell me you told that falsehood out of mere vanity and are sorry for it; that you're *not* expecting to ever wear the coronet of an earl—"

"Truly I am cured—cured this very day—I am *not* expecting it!"

"O, now you *are* mine! I've got you back in the beauty and glory of your unsmirched poverty and your honorable obscurity, and nobody shall ever take you from me again but the grave! And if—"

"De earl of Rossmore, fum Englan'!"

"My father!" The young man released the girl and hung his head.

The old gentleman stood surveying the couple—the one with a strongly complimentary right eye, the other with a mixed expression done with the left. This is difficult, and not often resorted to. Presently his face relaxed into a kind of constructive gentleness, and he said to his son—

"Don't you think you could embrace me, too?"

The young man did it with alacrity.

"Then you *are* the son of an earl, after all," said Sally, reproachfully.

"Yes, I—"

"Then I won't have you!"

"O, but you know—"

"No, I will not. You've told me another fib."

"She's right. Go away and leave us. I want to talk with her."

Berkeley was obliged to go. But he did not go far. He remained on the premises. At midnight the conference between the old gentleman and the young girl was still going blithely on, but it presently drew to a close, and the former said—

"I came all the way over here to inspect you, my dear, with the general idea of breaking off this match if there were *two* fools of you, but as there's only one, you can have him if you'll take him."

"Indeed I will, then! May I kiss you?"

"You may. Thank you. Now you shall have that privilege whenever you are good."

Meantime Hawkins had long ago returned and slipped up into the laboratory. He was rather disconcerted to find his late invention, Snodgrass, there. The news was told him: that the English Rossmore was come, "and I'm his son, Viscount Berkeley, not Howard Tracy any more."

Hawkins was aghast. He said—

"Good gracious, then you're dead!"

"Dead?"

"Yes, you are—we've got your ashes."

"Hang those ashes, I'm tired of them; I'll give them to my father."

Slowly and painfully the statesman worked the truth into his head that this was really a flesh and blood young man, and not the insubstantial resurrection he and Sellers had so long supposed him to be. Then he said with feeling—

"I'm so glad; so glad on Sally's account, poor thing. We took you for a departed materialized bank thief from Tahlequah. This will be a heavy blow to Sellers." Then he explained the whole matter to Berkeley, who said—

"Well, the Claimant must manage to stand the blow, severe as it is. But he'll get over the disappointment."

"Who—the colonel? He'll get over it the minute he invents a new miracle to take its place. And he's already at it by this time. But look here—what do you suppose became of the man you've been *representing* all this time?"

"I don't know. I saved his clothes—it was all I could do. I am afraid he lost his life."

"Well, you must have found twenty or thirty thousand dollars in those clothes, in money or certificates of deposit."

"No, I found only five hundred and a trifle. I borrowed the trifle and banked the five hundred."

"What'll we do about it?"

"Return it to the owner."

"It's easy said, but not easy to manage. Let's leave it alone till we get Sellers's advice. And that reminds me. I've got to run and meet Sellers and explain who you are *not* and who you *are*, or he'll come thundering in here to stop his daughter from marrying a phantom. But—suppose your father came over here to break off the match?"

"Well, isn't he down stairs getting acquainted with Sally? That's all safe."

So Hawkins departed to meet and prepare the Sellerses.

Rossmore Towers saw great times and late hours during the succeeding week. The two earls were such opposites in nature that they fraternized at once. Sellers said privately that Rossmore was the most extraordinary character he had ever met— a man just made out of the condensed milk of human kindness, yet with the ability to totally hide the fact from any but the most practised character-reader; a man whose whole being was sweetness, patience and charity, yet with a cunning so profound, an ability so marvelous in the acting of a double part, that many a person of considerable intelligence might live with him for centuries and never suspect the presence in him of these characteristics.

Finally there was a quiet wedding at the Towers, instead of a big one at the British embassy, with the militia and the fire brigades and the temperance organizations on hand in torch-light procession, as at first proposed by one of the earls. The art-firm and Barrow were present at the wedding, and the tin-ner and Puss had been invited, but the tinner was ill and Puss was nursing him—for they were engaged.

The Sellerses were to go to England with their new allies for a brief visit, but when it was time to take the train from Washington, the colonel was missing. Hawkins was going as far as New York with the party, and said he would explain the matter on the road. The explanation was in a letter left by the colonel in Hawkins's hands. In it he promised to join Mrs. Sellers later, in England, and then went on to say:

The truth is, my dear Hawkins, a mighty idea has been born to me within the hour, and I must not even stop to say good-bye to my dear ones. A man's highest duty takes precedence of all minor ones, and must be attended to with his best promptness and energy, at whatso-ever cost to his affections or his convenience. And first of all a man's du-ties is his duty to his own honor—he must keep that spotless. Mine is threatened. When I was feeling sure of my imminent future solidity, I forwarded to the Czar of Russia—perhaps prematurely—an offer for the purchase of Siberia, naming a vast sum. Since then an episode has warned me that the method by which I was expecting to acquire this money—materialization upon a scale of limitless magnitude—is marred by a taint of temporary uncertainty. His imperial majesty may accept my offer at any moment. If this should occur now, I should find myself painfully embarrassed, in fact financially inadequate. I could not take Siberia. This would become known, and my credit would suffer.

Recently my private hours have been dark indeed, but the sun shines again, now; I see my way; I shall be able to meet my obliga-tion, and without having to ask an extension of the stipulated time, I think. This grand new idea of mine—the sublimest I have ever con-ceived, will save me whole, I am sure. I am leaving for San Francisco this moment, to test it, by the help of the great Lick telescope. Like all of my more notable discoveries and inventions, it is based upon hard, practical scientific laws; all other bases are unsound and hence untrustworthy.

In brief, then, I have conceived the stupendous idea of reorganizing the climates of the earth according to the desire of the populations interested. That is to say, I will furnish climates to order, for cash or negotiable paper, taking the old climates in part payment, of course, at a fair discount, where they are in condition to be repaired at small cost and let out for hire to poor and remote communities not able to afford a good climate and not caring for an expensive one for mere display. My studies have convinced me that the regulation of climates and the breeding of new varieties at will from the old stock is a feasible thing. Indeed I am convinced that it has been done before: done in prehistoric times by now forgotten and unrecorded civilizations. Everywhere I find hoary evidences of artificial manipulation of climates in bygone times. Take the glacial period. Was that produced by accident? Not at all; it was done for money. I have a thousand proofs of it, and will some day reveal them.

I will confide to you an outline of my idea. It is to utilize the spots on the sun—get control of them, you understand, and apply the stupendous energies which they wield to beneficent purposes in the reorganizing of our climates. At present they merely make trouble and do harm in the evoking of cyclones and other kinds of electric storms; but once under humane and intelligent control this will cease and they will become a boon to man.

I have my plan all mapped out, whereby I hope and expect to acquire complete and perfect control of the sun-spots, also details of the method whereby I shall employ the same commercially; but I will not venture to go into particulars before the patents shall have been issued. I shall hope and expect to sell shop-rights to the minor countries at a reasonable figure and supply a good business article of climate to the great empires at special rates, together with fancy brands for coronations, battles and other great and particular occasions. There are billions of money in this enterprise, no expensive plant is required, and I shall begin to realize in a few days—in a few weeks at furthest. I shall stand ready to pay cash for Siberia the moment it is delivered, and thus save my honor and my credit. I am confident of this.

I would like you to provide a proper outfit and start north as soon as I telegraph you, be it night or be it day. I wish you to take up all the country stretching away from the north pole on all sides for many degrees south, and buy Greenland and Iceland at the best figure you can get now while they are cheap. It is my intention to move one of the tropics up there and transfer the frigid zone to the equator. I will have the entire Arctic Circle in the market as a summer resort next year, and will use the surplusage of the old climate, over and above what can be utilized on the equator, to reduce the temperature of opposition resorts. But I have said enough to give you an idea of the prodigious nature of my scheme and the feasible and enormously profitable character of it. I shall join all you happy people in England as soon as I shall have sold out some of my principal climates and arranged with the Czar about Siberia.

Meantime, watch for a sign from me. Eight days from now, we shall be wide asunder; for I shall be on the border of the Pacific, and you far out on the Atlantic, approaching England. That day, if I am alive and my sublime discovery is proved and established, I will send you greeting, and my messenger shall deliver it where you are, in the solitudes of the sea; for I will waft a vast sun-spot across the disk like drifting smoke, and you will know it for my love-sign, and will say "Mulberry Sellers throws us a kiss across the universe."

APPENDIX

Selected from the Best Authorities.

A brief though violent thunderstorm which had raged over the city was passing away; but still, though the rain had ceased more than an hour before, wild piles of dark and coppery clouds, in which a fierce and rayless glow was laboring, gigantically overhung the grotesque and huddled vista of dwarf houses, while in the distance, sheeting high over the low, misty confusion of gables and chimneys, spread a pall of dead, leprous blue, suffused with blotches of dull, glistening yellow, and with black plague-spots of vapor floating and faint lightnings crinkling on its surface. Thunder, still muttering in the close and sultry air, kept the scared dwellers in the street within, behind their closed shutters; and all deserted, cowed, dejected, squalid, like poor, stupid, top-heavy things that had felt the wrath of the summer tempest, stood the drenched structures on either side of the narrow and crooked way, ghastly and picturesque under the giant canopy. Rain dripped wretchedly in slow drops of melancholy sound from their projecting eaves upon the broken flagging, lay there in pools or trickled into the swollen drains, where the fallen torrent sullenly gurgled on its way to the river.—*"The Brazen Android."*—*W. D. O'Connor.*

> The fiery mid-March sun a moment hung
> Above the bleak Judean wilderness;
> Then darkness swept upon us, and 't was night.
> —*"Easter-Eve at Kerak-Moab."*—*Clinton Scollard.*

The quick-coming winter twilight was already at hand. Snow was again falling, sifting delicately down, incidentally as it were —*"Felicia."*—*Fanny N. D. Murfree.*

Merciful heavens! The whole west, from right to left, blazes up with a fierce light, and next instant the earth reels and quivers with the awful shock of ten thousand batteries of artillery. It is the signal for the Fury to spring—for a thousand demons to scream and shriek—for innumerable serpents of fire to writhe and light up the blackness.

Now the rain falls—now the wind is let loose with a terrible shriek—now the lightning is so constant that the eyes burn, and the thunder-claps merge into an awful roar, as did the 800 cannon at Gettysburg. Crash! Crash! Crash! It is the cottonwood trees falling to earth. Shriek! Shriek! Shriek! It is the Demon racing along the plain and uprooting even the blades of grass. Shock! Shock! Shock! It is the Fury flinging his fiery bolts into the bosom of the earth. —*"The Demon and the Fury."—M. Quad.*

Away up the gorge all diurnal fancies trooped into the wide liberties of endless luminous vistas of azure sunlit mountains beneath the shining azure heavens. The sky, looking down in deep blue placidities, only here and there smote the water to azure emulations of its tint.—*"In the Stranger's Country."—Charles Egbert Craddock.*

There was every indication of a dust-storm, though the sun still shone brilliantly. The hot wind had become wild and rampant. It was whipping up the sandy coating of the plain in every direction. High in the air were seen whirling spires and cones of sand—a curious effect against the deep-blue sky. Below, puffs of sand were breaking out of the plain in every direction, as though the plain were alive with invisible horsemen. These sandy cloudlets were instantly dissipated by the wind; it was the larger clouds that were lifted whole into the air, and the larger clouds of sand were becoming more and more the rule.

Alfred's eye, quickly scanning the horizon, descried the roof of the boundary-rider's hut still gleaming in the sunlight. He remembered the hut well. It could not be farther than four miles, if as much as that, from this point of the track. He also knew these dust-storms of old; Bindarra was notorious for them. Without thinking twice, Alfred put spurs to his horse and headed for the hut. Before he had ridden half the distance the detached clouds of sand banded together in one dense whirlwind, and it was only owing to his horse's instinct that he did not ride wide of the hut altogether; for during the last half-mile he never saw the hut, until its outline loomed suddenly over his horse's ears; and by then the sun was invisible.—*"A Bride from the Bush."*

It rained forty days and forty nights.—*Genesis.*

TOM SAWYER ABROAD

By Huck Finn

Edited by Mark Twain

CONTENTS

Chapter 1

D O YOU RECKON Tom Sawyer was satisfied after all them
adventures? I mean the adventures we had down the
river the time we set the nigger Jim free and Tom got shot in
the leg. No, he wasn't. It only just pisoned him for more.
That was all the effects it had. You see, when we three come
back up the river in glory, as you may say, from that long
travel, and the village received us with a torchlight procession
and speeches, and everybody hurrah'd and shouted, and some
got drunk, it made us heroes, and that was what Tom Sawyer
had always been hankerin' to be.

For a while he *was* satisfied. Everybody made much of him,
and he tilted up his nose and stepped around the town like he
owned it. Some called him Tom Sawyer the Traveler, and that
just swelled him up fit to bust. You see he laid over me and
Jim considerable, because we only went down the river on a
raft and come back by the steamboat, but Tom went by the
steamboat both ways. The boys envied me and Jim a good
deal, but land! they just knuckled to the dirt before Tom.

Well, I don't know; maybe he might have been satisfied if it
hadn't been for old Nat Parsons, which was postmaster, and
powerful long and slim, and kind of good-hearted and silly
and baldheaded, on accounts of his age, and most about the
talkiest old animal I ever see. For as much as thirty years he'd
been the only man in the village that had a ruputation—I
mean, a ruputation for being a traveler, and of course he was
mortal proud of it, and it was reckoned that in the course of
that thirty years he had told about that journey over a million
times and enjoyed it every time, and now comes along a boy
not quite fifteen and sets everybody gawking and admiring
over *his* travels, and it just give the poor old thing the jim-
jams. It made him sick to listen to Tom and hear the people
say "My land!" "Did you ever!" "My goodness sakes alive!"
and all them sorts of things, but he couldn't pull away from
it, any more than a fly that's got its hind leg fast in the
molasses. And always when Tom come to a rest, the poor old
cretur would chip in on *his* same old travels and work them

for all they was worth, but they was pretty faded and didn't go for much, and it was pitiful to see. And then Tom would take another innings, and then the old man again—and so on, and so on, for an hour and more, each trying to sweat out the other.

You see, Parsons's travels happened like this. When he first got to be postmaster and was green in the business, there was a letter come for somebody he didn't know, and there wasn't any such person in the village. Well, he didn't know what to do nor how to act, and there the letter stayed and stayed, week in and week out, till the bare sight of it give him the dry gripes. The postage wasn't paid on it, and that was another thing to worry about. There wasn't any way to collect that ten cents, and he reckoned the Gov'ment would hold him responsible for it and maybe turn him out besides, when they found he hadn't collected it. Well at last he couldn't stand it any longer. He couldn't sleep nights, he couldn't eat, he was thinned down to a shadder, yet he dasn't ask anybody's advice, for the very person he asked for the advice might go back on him and let the Gov'ment know about that letter. He had the letter buried under the floor, but that didn't do no good; if he happened to see a person standing over the place it give him the cold shivers and loaded him up with suspicions, and he would set up that night till the town was still and dark and then he would sneak there and get it out and bury it in another place. Of course people got to avoiding him, and shaking their heads and whispering, because, the way he was looking and acting, they judged he had killed somebody or done something they didn't know what, and if he had been a stranger they would a lynched him.

Well, as I was saying, it got so he couldn't stand it any longer; so he made up his mind to pull out for Washington and just go to the President of the United States and make a clean breast of the whole thing, not keeping back an atom, and then fetch the letter out and lay her down before the whole Gov'ment and say, "Now, there she is, do with me what you're a mind to, though as heaven is my judge I am an innocent man and not deserving of the full penalties of the law, and leaving behind me a family which must starve and yet ain't had a thing to do with it, which is the truth and I can swear to it."

So he done it. He had a little wee bit of steamboating, and some stage-coaching, but all the rest of the way was horse-back, and took him three weeks to get to Washington. He saw lots of land, and lots of villages, and four cities. He was gone most eight weeks, and there never was such a proud man in the village as when he got back. His travels made him the greatest man in all that region, and the most talked about; and people come from as much as thirty miles back in the country, and from over in the Illinois bottoms, too, just to look at him—and there they'd stand and gawk, and he'd gab-ble. You never see anything like it.

Well, there wasn't any way, now, to settle which was the greatest traveler; some said it was Nat, some said it was Tom. Everybody allowed that Nat had seen the most longitude, but they had to give in that whatever Tom was short in longitude he had made up in latitude and climate. It was about a stand-off; so both of them had to whoop-up their dangersome ad-ventures, and try to get ahead that way. That bullet-wound in Tom's leg was a tough thing for Nat Parsons to buck against, but he done the best he could; done it at a disadvantage, too, for Tom didn't set still, as he'd orter done, to be fair, but al-ways got up and santered around and worked his limp whilst Nat was painting up the adventure that he had one day in Washington; for Tom he never let go that limp after his leg got well, but practiced it nights at home, and kept it as good as new, right along.

Nat's adventure was like this; and I will say this for him, that he *did* know how to tell it. He could make anybody's flesh crawl and turn pale and hold his breath when he told it, and sometimes women and girls got so faint they couldn't stick it out. Well, it was this way, as near as I remember:

He come a-loping into Washington and put up his horse and shoved out to the President's house with his letter, and they told him the President was up to the Capitol and just going to start for Philadelphia—not a minute to lose if he wanted to catch him. Nat most dropped, it made him so sick. His horse was put up, and he didn't know what *to* do. But just then along comes a nigger driving an old ramshackly hack, and he see his chance. He rushes out and shouts—

"A half a dollar if you git me to the capitol in a half an hour, and a quarter extra if you do it in twenty minutes!"

"Done!" says the nigger.

Nat he jumped in and slammed the door and away they went, a-ripping and a-tearing and a-bumping and a-bouncing over the roughest road a body ever see, and the racket of it was something awful. Nat passed his arms through the loops and hung on for life and death, but pretty soon the hack hit a rock and flew up in the air and the bottom fell out, and when it come down Nat's feet was on the ground, and he see he was in the most desperate danger if he couldn't keep up with the hack. He was horrible scared, but he laid into his work for all he was worth, and hung tight to the arm-loops and made his legs fairly fly. He yelled and shouted to the driver to stop, and so did the crowds along the street, for they could see his legs a-spinning along under the coach and his head and shoulders bobbing inside, through the windows, and knowed he was in awful danger; but the more they all shouted the more the nigger whooped and yelled and lashed the horses and said, "Don't you fret, I's gwyne to git you dah in time, boss, I's gwyne to do it sho'!" for you see *he* thought they was all hurrying him up, and of course he couldn't hear anything for the racket he was making. And so they went ripping along, and everybody just petrified and cold to see it; and when they got to the Capitol at last it was the quickest trip that ever was made, and everybody said so. The horses laid down, and Nat dropped, all tuckered out; and then they hauled him out and he was all dust and rags and barefooted; but he was in time, and just in time, and caught the President and give him the letter and everything was all right and the President give him a free pardon on the spot, and Nat give the nigger two extra quarters instead of one, because he could see that if he hadn't had the hack he wouldn't a got there in time, nor anywhere near it.

It *was* a powerful good adventure, and Tom Sawyer had to work his bullet-wound mighty lively to hold his own and keep his end up against it.

Well, by and by Tom's glory got to paling down graduly,

on accounts of other things turning up for the people to talk about, first a horse-race, and on top of that a house afire, and on top of that the circus, and on top of that a big auction of niggers, and on top of that the eclipse, and that started a revival, same as it always does, and by that time there warn't no more talk about Tom to speak of, and you never see a person so sick and disgusted. Pretty soon he got to worrying and fretting right along, day in and day out, and when I asked him what *was* he in such a state about, he said it most broke his heart to think how time was slipping away, and him getting older and older, and no wars breaking out and no way of making a name for himself that he could see. Now that is the way boys is always thinking, but he was the first one I ever heard come out and say it.

So then he set to work to get up a plan to make him celebrated, and pretty soon he struck it, and offered to take me and Jim in. Tom Sawyer was always free and generous that way. There's plenty of boys that's mighty good and friendly when *you've* got a good thing, but when a good thing happens to come their way they don't say a word to you and try to hog it all. That warn't ever Tom Sawyer's style, I can say that for him. There's plenty of boys that will come hankering and gruvveling around when you've got an apple and beg the core off of you, but when *they've* got one and you beg for the core and remind them how you give them a core one time, they make a mouth at you and say thank you most to death but there ain't a-going to *be* no core. But I notice they always git come up with; all you got to do is to wait. Jake Hooker always done that way, and it warn't two years till he got drownded.

Well, we went out in the woods on the hill, and Tom told us what it was. It was a Crusade.

"What's a crusade?" I says.

He looked scornful, the way he always done when he was ashamed of a person, and says—

"Huck Finn, do you mean to tell me you don't know what a crusade is?"

"No," says I, "I don't. And I don't care, nuther. I've lived till now and done without it, and had my health, too. But as soon as you tell me, I'll know, and that's soon enough. I don't see no use in finding out things and clogging my head up with them when I mayn't ever have any occasion for them. There was Lance Williams, he learnt how to talk Choctaw, and there warn't ever a Choctaw here till one come along and dug his grave for him. Now, then, what's a Crusade? But I can tell you one thing before you begin; if it's a patent right, there ain't no money in it. Bill Thompson, he—"

"Patent right!" he says. "I never see such an idiot. Why, a crusade is a kind of a war."

I thought he must be losing his mind. But no, he was in real earnest, and went right on, perfectly cam:

"A crusade is a war to recover the Holy Land from the paynim."

"Which Holy Land?"

"Why, *the* Holy Land—there ain't but one."

"What do *we* want of it?"

"Why, can't you understand? It's in the hands of the paynim, and it's our duty to take it away from them."

"How did we come to let them git holt of it?"

"We didn't come to let them git hold of it. They always had it."

"Why, Tom, then it must belong to them, don't it?"

"Why of course it does. Who said it didn't?"

I studied over it, but couldn't seem to git at the rights of it no way. I says—

"It's too many for me, Tom Sawyer. If I had a farm, and it was mine, and another person wanted it, would it be right for him to—"

"Oh, shucks! you don't know enough to come in when it rains, Huck Finn. It ain't a farm, it's entirely different. You see, it's like this. They own the land, just the mere land, and that's all they *do* own; but it was our folks, our Jews and Christians, that made it holy, and so they haven't any business to be there defiling it. It's a shame, and we oughtn't to stand it a minute. We ought to march against them and take it away from them."

"Why, it does seem to me it's the most mixed-up thing I ever see. Now if I had a farm, and another person—"

"Don't I tell you it hasn't got anything to *do* with farming? Farming is business; just common low-down worldly business, that's all it is, it's all you can say for it; but this is higher, this is religious, and totally different."

"Religious to go and take the land away from the people that owns it?"

"Certainly; it's always been considered so."

Jim he shook his head and says—

"Mars Tom, I reckon dey's a mistake 'bout it somers—dey mos' sholy is. I's religious mysef; en I knows plenty religious people, but I hain't run acrost none dat acts like dat."

It made Tom hot, and he says—

"Well, it's enough to make a body sick, such mullet-headed ignorance. If either of you knowed anything about history, you'd know that Richard Cur de Lyon, and the Pope, and Godfrey de Bulloyn, and lots more of the most noble-hearted and pious people in the world hacked and hammered at the paynims for more than two hundred years trying to take their land away from them and swum neck deep in blood the whole time—and yet here's a couple of sap-headed country yahoos out in the backwoods of Missouri setting themselves up to know more about the rights and the wrongs of it than they did! Talk about cheek!"

Well, of course that put a more different light on it, and me and Jim felt pretty cheap and ignorant, and wished we hadn't been quite so chipper. I couldn't say nothing, and Jim he couldn't for a while; then he says—

"Well, den, I reckon it's all right, becaze ef *dey* didn't know, dey ain' no use for po' ignorant folks like us to be tryin' to know; en so ef it's our duty we got to go en tackle it en do de bes' we kin. Same time, I feel as sorry for dem paynims as—Mars Tom, de hard part gwyne to be to kill folks dat a body hain't 'quainted wid and hain't done him no harm. Dat's it, you see. Ef we uz to go 'mongst 'em, jist us three, and say we's hungry, en ast 'em for a bite to eat, why maybe dey's jist like yuther people en niggers, don't you reckon dey is? Why, *dey'd* give it, I know dey would; en den—"

"Then what?"

"Well, Mars Tom, my idea is like dis. It ain't no use, we *can't* kill dem po' strangers dat ain't doin' us no harm, till we've had practice—I knows it perfectly well, Mars Tom, 'deed I knows it perfectly well. But ef we takes a axe or two, jist you en me en Huck, en slips acrost de river to-night arter de moon's gone down, en kills dat sick fambly dat's over on de Sny, en burns dey house down, en—"

"Oh, shut your head! you make me tired. I don't want to argue no more with people like you and Huck Finn, that's always wandering from the subject and ain't got any more sense than to try to reason out a thing that's pure theology by the laws that protects real estate."

Now that's just where Tom Sawyer warn't fair. Jim didn't mean no harm, and I didn't mean no harm. We knowed well enough that he was right and we was wrong, and all we was after was to get at the *how* of it, that was all; and the only reason he couldn't explain it so we could understand it was because we was ignorant—yes, and pretty dull, too, I ain't denying that; but land! that ain't no crime, I should think.

But he wouldn't hear no more about it; just said if we had tackled the thing in a proper spirit he would a raised a couple of thousand knights, and put them up in steel armor from head to heel and made me a lieutenant and Jim a sutler, and took the command himself and brushed the whole paynim outfit into the sea like flies and come back across the world in a glory like sunset. But he said we didn't know enough to take the chance when we had it, and he wouldn't ever offer it again. And he didn't. When he once got set, you couldn't budge him.

But I didn't care much. I am peaceable, and don't get up no rows with people that ain't doing nothing to me. I allowed if the paynims was satisfied I was, and we would let it stand at that.

Now Tom he got all that wild notion out of Walter Scott's books, which he was always reading. And it *was* a wild notion, because in my opinion he never could a raised the men, and if he did, as like as not he would a got licked. I took the books and read all about it, and as near as I could make out, most of the folks that shook farming to go crusading had a mighty rocky time of it.

Chapter 2

WELL Tom got up one thing after another, but they all
had sore places in them somewheres and he had to
shove them aside. So at last he was most about in despair.
Then the St. Louis papers begun to talk a good deal about
the balloon that was going to sail to Europe, and Tom sort of
thought he wanted to go down and see what it looked like,
but couldn't make up his mind. But the papers went on talking, and so he allowed that maybe if he didn't go he mightn't
ever have another chance to see a balloon; and next, he found
out that Nat Parsons was going down to see it, and that decided him of course. He wasn't going to have Nat Parsons
coming back bragging about seeing the balloon and him having to listen to it and keep his head shut. So he wanted me
and Jim to go, too, and we went.

It was a noble big balloon, and had wings, and fans, and all
sorts of things, and wasn't like any balloon that is in the pictures. It was away out towards the edge of town in a vacant
lot corner of Twelfth street, and there was a big crowd
around it making fun of it and making fun of the man, which
was a lean, pale feller with that soft kind of moonlight in his
eyes, you know, and they kept saying it wouldn't go. It made
him hot to hear them, and he would turn on them and shake
his fist and say they was animals and blind, but some day they
would find they'd stood face to face with one of the men that
lifts up nations and makes civilizations, and was too dull to
know it, and right here on this spot their own children and
grandchildren would build a monument to him that would
last a thousand years but his name would outlast the monument; and then the crowd would bust out in a laugh again
and yell at him and ask him what was his name before he was
married, and what he would take to don't, and what was his
sister's cat's grandmother's name, and all them kinds of things
that a crowd says when they've got hold of a feller they see
they can plague. Well, the things they said *was* funny, yes, and
mighty witty too, I ain't denying that, but all the same it
warn't fair nor brave, all them people pitching on one, and

657

they so glib and sharp, and him without any gift of talk to answer back with. But good land! what did he *want* to sass back
for? You see it couldn't do him no good, and it was just nuts
for them. They *had* him, you know. But that was his way; I
reckon he couldn't help it; he was made so, I judge. He was
a good enough sort of a cretur, and hadn't no harm in him,
and was just a genius, as the papers said, which wasn't his
fault, we can't all be sound, we've got to be the way we are
made. As near as I can make out, geniuses think they know it
all, and so they won't take people's advice, but always go their
own way, which makes everybody forsake them and despise
them, and that is perfectly natural. If they was humbler, and
listened and tried to learn, it would be better for them.

The part the Professor was in was like a boat, and was big
and roomy and had water-tight lockers around the inside to
keep all sorts of things in, and a body could set on them and
make beds on them, too. We went aboard, and there was
twenty people there, snooping around and examining, and
old Nat Parsons was there, too. The Professor kept fussing
around getting ready, and the people went ashore, drifting
out one at a time, and old Nat he was the last. Of course it
wouldn't do to let him go out behind *us*. We mustn't budge
till he was gone, so we could be last ourselves.

But he was gone, now, so it was time for us to follow. I
heard a big shout, and turned around—the city was dropping
from under us like a shot! It made me sick all through, I was
so scared. Jim turned gray, and couldn't say a word, and Tom
didn't say nothing, but looked excited. The city went on
dropping, down, and down, and down, but we didn't seem to
do nothing but hang in the air and stand still. The houses got
smaller and smaller, and the city pulled itself together closer
and closer, and the men and wagons got to looking like ants
and bugs crawling around, and the streets was like cracks and
threads; and then it all kind of melted together and there
wasn't any city any more, it was only a big scab on the earth,
and it seemed to me a body could see up the river and down
the river about a thousand miles, though of course it wasn't
so much. By and by the earth was a ball—just a round ball, of
a dull color, with shiny stripes wriggling and winding around
over it which was rivers. And the weather was getting pretty

chilly. The widder Douglas always told me the world was round like a ball, but I never took no stock in a lot of them superstitions o' hern, and of course I never paid no attention to that one, because I could see, myself, that the world was the shape of a plate, and flat. I used to go up on the hill and take a look all around and prove it for myself, because I reckon the best way to get a sure thing on a fact is to go and examine for yourself and not take it on anybody's say-so. But I had to give in, now, that the widder was right. That is, she was right as to the rest of the world, but she warn't right about the part our village is in: that part is the shape of a plate, and flat, I take my oath.

The Professor was standing still all this time like he was asleep, but he broke loose, now, and he was mighty bitter. He says something like this:

"Idiots! they said it wouldn't go. And they wanted to examine it and spy around and get the secret of it out of me. But I beat them. Nobody knows the secret but me. Nobody knows what makes it move but me—and it's a new power! A new power, and a thousand times the strongest in the earth. Steam's foolishness to it. They said I couldn't go to Europe. To Europe! why, there's power aboard to last five years, and food for three months; they are fools, what do *they* know about it? Yes, and they said my air-ship was flimsy—why, she's good for fifty years. I can sail the skies all my life if I want to, and steer where I please, though they laughed at that, and said I couldn't. Couldn't steer! Come here, boy; we'll see. You press these buttons as I tell you."

He made Tom steer the ship all about and every which way, and learnt him the whole thing in nearly no time, and Tom said it was perfectly easy. He made him fetch the ship down most to the earth, and had him spin her along so close to the Illinois prairies that a body could talk to the farmers and hear everything they said, perfectly plain; and he flung out printed bills to them that told about the balloon and said it was going to Europe. Tom got so he could steer straight for a tree till he got nearly to it and then dart up and skin right along over the top of it. Yes, and he learnt Tom how to land her; and he done it first rate, too, and set her down in the prairie as soft as wool; but the minute we started to skip out, the

Professor says, "No you don't!" and shot her up into the air again. It was awful. I begun to beg, and so did Jim; but it only give his temper a rise, and he begun to rage around and look wild out of his eyes, and I was scared of him.

Well, then he got onto his troubles again, and mourned and grumbled about the way he was treated, and couldn't seem to git over it, and especially people's saying his ship was flimsy. He scoffed at that, and at their saying she warn't simple and would be always getting out of order. Get out of order—that graveled him; he said she couldn't any more get out of order than the solar sister. He got worse and worse, and I never see a person take on so. It give me the cold shivers to see him, and so it did Jim. By and by he got to yelling and screaming, and then he swore the world shouldn't ever have his secret at all, now, it had treated him so mean. He said he would sail his balloon around the globe just to show what it could do, and then he would sink it in the sea, and sink us all along with it, too. Well, it was the awfulest fix to be in—and here was night coming on.

He give us something to eat, and made us go to the other end of the boat, and laid down on a locker where he could boss all the works, and put his old pepper-box revolver under his head and said anybody that come fooling around there trying to land her, he would kill him.

We set scrunched up together, and thought considerable, but didn't say nothing, only just a word once in a while when a body had to say something or bust, we was *so* scared and worried. The night dragged along slow and lonesome. We was pretty low down, and the moonshine made everything soft and pretty, and the farm houses looked snug and homeful, and we could hear the farm sounds, and wished we could be down there, but laws! we just slipped along over them like a ghost, and never left a track.

Away in the night, when all the sounds was late sounds, and the air had a late feel, too, and a late smell—about a two o'clock feel, as near as I could make out,—Tom said the Professor was so quiet this long time he must be asleep, and we better—

"Better what?" I says, in a whisper, and feeling sick all over, because I knowed what he was thinking about.

"Better slip back there and tie him and land the ship," he says.

I says—

"No, sir! Don't you budge, Tom Sawyer."

And Jim—well, Jim was kind of gasping, he was so scared. He says—

"Oh, Mars Tom, *don't*! Ef you tetches him we's gone— we's gone, sho'! *I* ain't gwyne anear him, not for nothin' in dis worl'. Mars Tom, he's plum crazy."

Tom whispers and says—

"That's *why* we've got to do something. If he wasn't crazy I wouldn't give shucks to be anywhere but here; you couldn't hire me to get out, now that I've got used to this balloon and over the scare of being cut loose from the solid ground, if he was in his right mind; but it's no good politics sailing around like this with a person that's out of his head and says he's going around the world and then drown us all. We've got to do something, I tell you, and do it before he wakes up, too, or we mayn't ever get another chance. Come!"

But it made us turn cold and creepy just to think of it, and we said we wouldn't budge. So Tom was for slipping back there by himself to see if he couldn't get at the steering gear and land the ship. We begged and begged him not to, but it warn't no use; so he got down on his hands and knees and begun to crawl an inch at a time, we a-holding our breath and watching. After he got to the middle of the boat he crept slower than ever, and it did seem like years to me. But at last we see him get to the Professor's head and sort of raise up soft and look a good spell in his face and listen. Then we see him begin to inch along again towards the Professor's feet where the steering-buttons was. Well, he got there all safe, and was reaching slow and steady towards the buttons, but he knocked down something that made a noise, and we see him slump flat and soft in the bottom and lay still. The Professor stirred, and says "What's that?" But everybody kept dead still and quiet, and he begun to mutter and mumble and nestle, like a person that's going to wake up, and I thought I was going to die I was so worried and scared.

Then a cloud come over the moon, and I most cried, I was so glad. She buried herself deeper and deeper in the cloud, and it got so dark we couldn't see Tom no more. Then it begun to sprinkle rain, and we could hear the Professor fussing at his ropes and things and abusing the weather. We was afraid every minute he would touch Tom, and then we would be goners and no help, but Tom was already on his way home, and when we felt his hands on our knees my breath stopped sudden and my heart fell down amongst my other works, because I couldn't tell in the dark but it might be the Professor, which I thought it *was*.

Dear! I was so glad to have him back that I was just as near happy as a person could be that was up in the air that way with a deranged man. You can't land a balloon in the dark, and so I hoped it would keep on raining, for I didn't want Tom to go meddling any more and make us so awful uncomfortable. Well, I got my wish. It drizzled and drizzled along the rest of the night, which wasn't long, though it did seem so; and at daybreak it cleared, and the world looked mighty soft and gray and pretty, and the forests and fields so good to see again, and the horses and cattle standing sober and thinking. Next, the sun come a-blazing up gay and splendid, and then we begun to feel rusty and stretchy, and first we knowed we was all asleep.

Chapter 3

W E WENT to sleep about four o'clock and woke up about eight. The Professor was setting back there at his end looking glum. He pitched us some breakfast, but he told us not to come abaft the midship compass. That was about the middle of the boat. Well, when you are sharp set, and you eat and satisfy yourself, everything looks pretty different from what it done before. It makes a body feel pretty near comfortable, even when he is up in a balloon with a genius. We got to talking together.

There was one thing that kept bothering me, and by and by I says—

"Tom, didn't we start east?"

"Yes."

"How fast have we been going?"

"Well, you heard what the Professor said when he was raging around; sometimes, he said, we was making fifty miles an hour, sometimes ninety, sometimes a hundred—said that with a gale to help he could make three hundred any time, and said if he wanted the gale, and wanted it blowing the right direction, he only had to go up higher or down lower and find it."

"Well, then, it's just as I reckoned. The Professor lied."

"Why?"

"Because if we was going so fast we ought to be past Illinois, oughtn't we?"

"Certainly."

"Well, we ain't."

"What's the reason we ain't?"

"I know by the color. We're right over Illinois yet. And you can see for yourself that Indiana ain't in sight."

"I wonder what's the matter with you, Huck. You know by the *color*?"

"Yes—of course I do."

"What's the color got to do with it?"

"It's got everything to do with it. Illinois is green, Indiana is pink. You show me any pink down here if you can. No, sir, it's green."

"Indiana *pink*? Why, what a lie!"

"It ain't no lie; I've seen it on the map, and it's pink."

You never see a person so aggravated and disgusted. He says—

"Well, if I was such a numskull as you, Huck Finn, I would jump over. Seen it on the map! Huck Finn, did you reckon the States was the same color out doors that they are on the map?"

"Tom Sawyer, what's a map for? Ain't it to learn you facts?"

"Of course."

"Well, then, how is it going to do that if it tells lies?—that's what I want to know."

"Shucks, you muggins, it *don't* tell lies."

"It don't, don't it?"

"No, it don't."

"All right, then; if it don't, there ain't no two States the same color. You git around *that*, if you can, Tom Sawyer."

He see I *had* him, and Jim see it, too, and I tell you I felt pretty good, for Tom Sawyer was always a hard person to git ahead of. Jim slapped his leg and says—

"I tell *you*! dat's smart, dat's right down smart! Ain't no use, Mars Tom, he got you *dis* time, he done got you dis time, sho'!" He slapped his leg again, and says, "My *lan'* but it was a smart one!"

I never felt so good in my life; and yet *I* didn't know I was saying anything much till it was out. I was just mooning along, perfectly careless, and not expecting anything was going to happen, and never *thinking* of such a thing at all, when all of a sudden out it come. Why, it was just as much a surprise to me as it was to any of them. It was just the same way it is when a person is munching along on a hunk of corn pone and not thinking about anything, and all of a sudden bites onto a di'mond. Now all that *he* knows, first-off, is, that it's some kind of gravel he's bit onto, but he don't find out it's a di'mond till he gits it out and brushes off the sand and crumbs and one thing or another and has a look at it, and then he's surprised and glad. Yes, and proud, too; though when you come to look the thing straight in the eye he ain't entitled to as much credit as he would a been if he'd been *hunting* di'monds. You can see the difference easy, if you think it over. You see, an accident, that way, ain't fairly as big a thing as a thing that's done a purpose. Anybody could find that di'mond in that corn-pone; but mind you, it's got to be somebody that's got *that kind of corn-pone.* That's where that feller's credit comes in, you see; and that's where mine comes in. I don't claim no great things, I don't reckon I could a done it again, but I done it that time, that's all I claim. And I hadn't no more idea I could do such a thing and warn't any more thinking about it or trying to, than you be, this minute. Why, I was just as cam, a body couldn't be any cammer, and yet all of a sudden out it come. I've often thought of that time, and I can remember just the way everything looked, same as if it was only last week. I can see it all; beautiful rolling country with woods and fields and lakes for hundreds and hundreds of miles all around, and towns and villages scattered everywheres under us, here and there and yonder, and the Professor mooning over a chart on his little table, and Tom's cap flopping in the rigging where it was hung up to dry, and one thing in particular was a bird right alongside, not ten foot off, going our way and trying to keep up, but losing ground all the time, and a railroad train doing the same, down there, sliding along amongst the trees and farms, and pouring out a long cloud of black smoke and now and then a little puff of white; and when the white was gone so long you had most forgot it, you would hear a little faint toot, and that was the whistle; and we left the bird and the train both behind, way behind, and done it easy, too.

But Tom he was huffy, and said me and Jim was a couple of ignorant blatherskites, and then he says—

"Suppose there's a brown calf and a big brown dog, and an artist is making a picture of them. What is the *main* thing that that artist has got to do? He has got to paint them so you can tell 'em apart the minute you look at them, hain't he? Of course. Well, then, do you want him to go and paint *both* of them brown? Certainly you don't. He paints one of them blue, and then you can't make no mistake. It's just the same with the maps. That's why they make every State a different color; it ain't to deceive you, it's to keep you from deceiving yourself."

But I couldn't see no argument about that, and neither could Jim. Jim shook his head, and says—

"Why, Mars Tom, ef you knowed what chuckleheads dem painters is, you'd wait a long time befo' you'd fetch one er *dem* in to back up a fac'. I's gwyne to tell you—den you kin see for youseff. I see one er 'em a-paintin' away, one day, down in old Hank Wilson's back lot, en I went down to see, en he was paintin' dat ole brindle cow wid de near horn gone—you knows de one I means. En I ast him what's he paintin' her for, en he say when he git her painted de picture's wuth a hunderd dollars. Mars Tom, he could a got de *cow* fer fifteen, en I *tole* him so. Well, sah, ef you'll b'lieve me, he jes' shuck his head en went on a-dobbin'. Bless you, Mars Tom, *dey* don't know nothin'."

Tom he lost his temper; I notice a person most always does, that's got laid out in an argument. He told us to shut up and don't stir the slush in our skulls any more, hold still and let it cake, and maybe we'd feel better. Then he see a town clock away off down yonder, and he took up the glass and looked at it, and then looked at his silver turnip, and then at the clock, and then at the turnip again, and says—

"That's funny—that clock's near about an hour fast."

So he put up his turnip. Then he see another clock, and took a look, and it was an hour fast, too. That puzzled him.

"That's a mighty curious thing," he says; "I don't understand that."

Then he took the glass and hunted up another clock, and sure enough it was an hour fast, too. Then his eyes begun to spread and his breath to come out kind of gaspy like, and he says—

"Ger-reat Scott, it's the *longitude!*"

I says, considerable scared—

"Well, what's been and gone and happened now?"

"Why, the thing that's happened is, that this old bladder has slid over Illinois and Indiana and Ohio like nothing, and this is the east end of Pennsylvania or New York, or somewheres around there."

"Tom Sawyer, you don't mean it!"

"Yes, I do, and it's so, dead sure. We've covered about fifteen degrees of longitude since we left St. Louis yesterday afternoon, and them clocks are *right*. We've come close onto eight hundred mile."

I didn't believe it, but it made the cold streaks trickle down my back just the same. In my experience I knowed it wouldn't take much short of two weeks to do it down the Mississippi on a raft.

Jim was working his mind, and studying. Pretty soon he says—

"Mars Tom, did you say dem clocks uz right?"

"Yes, they're right."

"Ain't yo' watch right, too?"

"She's right for St. Louis, but she's an hour wrong for here."

"Mars Tom, is you tryin' to let on dat de time ain't de *same* everywheres?"

"No, it ain't the same everywheres, by a long shot."

Jim he looked distressed, and says—

"It grieve me to hear you talk like dat, Mars Tom; I's right down 'shamed to hear you talk like dat, arter de way you's been raised. Yassir, it'd break yo' aunt Polly's heart to hear you."

Tom was astonished. He looked Jim over, wondering, and didn't say nothing, and Jim he went on:

"Mars Tom, who put de people out yonder in St. Louis? De Lord done it. Who put de people here whah we is? De Lord done it. Ain' dey bofe His chillen? 'Cose dey is. *Well*, den! is He gwyne to *'scriminate* 'twix' 'em?"

"'Scrimminate! I never heard such ignorant rot. There ain't no discriminating about it. When He makes you and some more of His children black, and makes the rest of us white, what do you call that?"

Jim see the pint. He was stuck. He couldn't answer. Tom says—

"He does discriminate, you see, when He wants to—but this case *here* ain't no discrimination of His, it's man's. The Lord made the day, and He made the night; but He didn't invent the hours, and He didn't distribute them around—man done it."

"Mars Tom, is dat so? Man done it?"

"Certainly."

"Who tole him he could?"

"Nobody. He never asked."

Jim studied a minute, and says—

"Well, dat do beat me. I wouldn't a tuck no sich resk. But some people ain't scared o' nothin'. Dey bangs right ahead, *dey* don't care what happens. So den dey's allays an hour's diffunce everywhah, Mars Tom?"

"An hour? No! It's four minutes' difference for every degree—of longitude, you know. Fifteen of 'em's an hour, thirty of 'em's two hours, and so on. When it's one o'clock Tuesday morning in England, it's eight o'clock the night before, in New York."

Jim moved a little away along the locker, and you could see he was insulted. He kept shaking his head and muttering, and so I slid along to him and patted him on the leg and petted him up, and got him over the worst of his feelings, and then he says—

"Mars Tom talkin' sich talk as dat—Choosday in one place en Monday in t'other, bofe in de same day! Huck, dis ain' no place to joke—up here whah we is. Two days in one day! How you gwyne to git two days inter one day—can't git two hours inter one hour, kin you? can't git two niggers inter one nigger-skin, kin you? can't git two gallons o' whisky inter a one-gallon jug, kin you? No, sir, 'twould strain de jug. Yas, en even den you couldn't, *I* doan b'lieve. Why, looky here, Huck, sposen de Choosday was New Year's—*now* den! Is you gwyne to tell me it's dis year in one place en las' year in t'other, bofe in de identical same minute? It's de beatenest rubbage—I can't stan' it, I can't stan' to hear tell 'bout it." Then he begun to shiver and turn gray, and Tom says—

"*Now* what's the matter? What's the trouble?"

Jim could hardly speak, but he says—

"Mars Tom, you ain't jokin', en it's *so*?"

"No, I'm not, and it *is* so."

Jim shivered again, and says—

"Den dat Monday could be de Las' Day, en day wouldn't *be* no Las' Day in England en de dead wouldn't be called. We mustn't go over dah, Mars Tom, please git him to turn back; I wants to be whah—"

All of a sudden we see something, and all jumped up, and forgot everything and begun to gaze. Tom says—

"Ain't that the—" He catched his breath, then says: "It *is*, sure as you live—it's the ocean!"

That made me and Jim catch our breath, too. Then we all stood putrified but happy, for none of us had ever seen an ocean, or ever expected to. Tom kept muttering—

"Atlantic Ocean—Atlantic. Land, don't it sound great! . . . . . And *that's* it—and *we* are a-looking at it—we! My, it's just too splendid to believe!"

Then we see a big bank of black smoke; and when we got nearer, it was a city, and a monster she was, too, with a thick fringe of ships around one edge; and wondered if it was New York, and begun to jaw and dispute about it, and first we knowed, it slid from under us and went flying behind, and here we was, out over the very ocean itself, and going like a cyclone. Then we woke up, I tell you!

We made a break aft, and raised a wail, and begun to beg the Professor to take pity on us and turn back and land us and let us go back to our folks, which would be so grieved and anxious about us, and maybe die if anything happened to us, but he jerked out his pistol and motioned us back, and we went, but nobody will ever know how bad we felt.

The land was gone, all but a little streak, like a snake, away off on the edge of the water, and down under us was just ocean, ocean, ocean—millions of miles of it, heaving, and pitching and squirming, and white sprays blowing from the wave-tops, and only a few ships in sight, wallowing around and laying over, first on one side and then on t'other, and sticking their bows under and then their sterns; and before long there warn't no ships at all, and we had the sky and the whole ocean all to ourselves, and the roomiest place I ever see and the lonesomest.

Chapter 4

A ND IT got lonesomer and lonesomer. There was the big
sky up there, empty and awful deep, and the ocean
down there without a thing on it but just the waves. All
around us was a ring, a perfectly round ring, where the sky
and the water come together; yes, a monstrous big ring, it
was, and we right in the dead centre of it. Plum in the centre.
We was racing along like a prairie fire, but it never made any
difference, we couldn't seem to git past that centre no way; I
couldn't see that we ever gained an inch on that ring. It made
a body feel creepy, it was so curious and unaccountable.

Well, everything was so awful still that we got to talking in
a very low voice, and kept on getting creepier and lonesomer
and less and less talky, till at last the talk run dry altogether
and we just set there and "thunk," as Jim calls it, and never
said a word, the longest time.

The Professor never stirred till the sun was overhead, then
he stood up and put a kind of a triangle to his eye, and Tom
said it was a sextant and he was taking the sun, to see whereabouts the balloon was. Then he ciphered a little, and looked
in a book, and then he begun to carry on again. He said lots
of wild things, and amongst others he said he would keep up
this hundred-mile gait till the middle of to-morrow afternoon
and then he'd land in London.

We said we would be humbly thankful.

He was turning away, but he whirled around when we said
that, and give us a long look, of his blackest kind—one of the
maliciousest and suspiciousest looks I ever see. Then he
says—

"You want to leave me. Don't try to deny it."

We didn't know what to say, so we held in and didn't say
nothing at all.

He went aft and set down, but he couldn't seem to git that
thing out of his mind. Every now and then he would rip out
something about it, and try to make us answer him, but we
dasn't.

It got lonesomer and lonesomer right along, and it did seem

to me I couldn't stand it. It was still worse when night begun to come on. By and by Tom pinched me and whispers—

"Look!"

I took a glance aft and see the Professor taking a whet out of a bottle. I didn't like the looks of that. By and by he took another drink, and pretty soon he begun to sing. It was dark, now, and getting black and stormy. He went on singing, wilder and wilder, and the thunder begun to mutter and the wind to wheeze and moan amongst the ropes, and altogether it was awful. It got so black we couldn't see him any more, and wished we couldn't hear him, but we could. Then he got still; but he warn't still ten minutes till we got suspicious, and wished he would start up his noise again, so we could tell where he was. By and by there was a flash of lightning, and we see him start to get up, but he was drunk, and staggered and fell down. We heard him scream out in the dark—

"They don't want to go to England—all right, I'll change the course. They want to leave me. Well, they shall—and *now*!"

I most died when he said that. Then he was still again; still so long I couldn't bear it, and it did seem to me the lightning wouldn't *ever* come again. But at last there was a blessed flash, and there he was, on his hands and knees, crawling, and not four foot from us. My, but his eyes was terrible. He made a lunge for Tom and says, "Overboard *you* go!" but it was already pitch dark again, and I couldn't see whether he got him or not, and Tom didn't make a sound.

There was another long, horrible wait, then there was a flash and I see Tom's head sink down, outside the boat and disappear. He was on the rope ladder that dangled down in the air from the gunnel. The Professor let off a shout and jumped for him, and straight off it was pitch dark again, and Jim groaned out, "Po' Mars Tom, he's a goner!" and made a jump for the Professor, but the Professor warn't there.

Then we heard a couple of terrible screams—and then another, not so loud, and then another that was way below, and you could only *just* hear it, and I hear Jim say, "*Po'* Mars Tom!"

Then it was awful still, and I reckon a person could a counted four hundred thousand before the next flash come.

When it come I see Jim on his knees, with his arms on the locker and his face buried in them, and he was crying. Before I could look over the edge, it was all dark again, and I was kind of glad, because I didn't want to see. But when the next flash come I was watching, and down there I see somebody a-swinging in the wind on that ladder, and it was Tom!

"Come up!" I shouts, "Come up, Tom!"

His voice was so weak, and the wind roared so, I couldn't make out what he said, but I thought he asked was the Professor up there. I shouts,—

"No, he's down in the ocean! Come up! Can we help you?"

Of course, all this in the dark.

"Huck, who is you hollerin' at?"

"I'm hollering at Tom."

"Oh, Huck, how kin you act so, when you knows po' Mars Tom's"—then he let off an awful scream and flung his head and his arms back and let off another one; because there was a white glare just then, and he had raised up his face just in time to see Tom's, as white as snow, rise above the gunnel and look him right in the eye. He thought it was Tom's ghost, you see.

Tom clumb aboard, and when Jim found it *was* him and not his ghost, he hugged him and slobbered all over him, and called him all sorts of loving names, and carried on like he was gone crazy, he was so glad. Says I—

"What did you wait for, Tom? Why didn't you come up at first?"

"I dasn't, Huck. I knowed somebody plunged down past me, but I didn't know who it was, in the dark. It could a been you, it could a been Jim."

That was the way with Tom Sawyer—always sound. He warn't coming up till he knowed where the Professor was.

The storm let go, about this time, with all its might, and it was dreadful the way the thunder boomed and tore, and the lightning glared out, and the wind sung and screamed in the rigging and the rain come down. One second you couldn't see your hand before you, and the next you could count the threads in your coat sleeve, and see a whole wide desert of waves pitching and tossing, through a kind of veil of rain. A storm like that is the loveliest thing there is, but it ain't at its best when you are up in the sky and lost, and it's wet and lonesome and there's just been a death in the family.

We set there huddled up in the bow, and talked low about the poor Professor, and everybody was sorry for him, and sorry the world had made fun of him and treated him so harsh, when he was doing the best he could and hadn't a friend nor nobody to encourage him and keep him from brooding his mind away and going deranged. There was plenty of clothes and blankets and everything at the other end, but we thought we druther take the rain than go meddling back there; you see it would seem so crawly to be where it was warm yet, as you might say, from a dead man. Jim said he would soak till he was mush before he would go there and maybe run up against that ghost betwixt the flashes. He said it always made him sick to *see* a ghost, and he'd druther die than *feel* of one.

Chapter 5

WE TRIED to make some plans, but we couldn't come to no agreement. Me and Jim was for turning around and going back home, but Tom allowed that by the time daylight come, so we could see our way, we would be so far towards England that we might as well go there and come back in a ship and have the glory of saying we done it.

About midnight the storm quit and the moon come out and lit up the ocean, and then we begun to feel comfortable and drowsy; so we stretched out on the lockers and went to sleep, and never woke up again till sun-up. The sea was sparkling like di'monds, and it was nice weather, and pretty soon our things was all dry again.

We went aft to find some breakfast, and the first thing we noticed was that there was a dim light burning in a compass back there under a hood. Then Tom was disturbed. He says—

"You know what that means, easy enough. It means that somebody has got to stay on watch and steer this thing the same as he would a ship, or she'll wander around and go wherever the wind wants her to."

"Well," I says, "what's she been doing since—er—since we had the accident?"

"Wandering," he says, kind of troubled, "Wandering, without any doubt. She's in a wind, now, that's blowing her south of east. We don't know how long that's been going on, either."

So then he pinted her east, and said he would hold her there whilst we rousted out the breakfast. The Professor had laid in everything a body could want; he couldn't a been better fixed. There warn't no milk for the coffee, but there was water and everything else you could want, and a charcoal stove and the fixings for it, and pipes and cigars and matches; and wine and liquor, which warn't in our line; and books and maps and charts, and an accordion, and furs and blankets, and no end of rubbish, like glass beads and brass jewelry, which Tom said was a sure sign that he had an idea of visiting around amongst savages. There was money, too. Yes, the Professor was well enough fixed.

After breakfast Tom learned me and Jim how to steer, and divided all of us up into four-hour watches, turn and turn about; and when his watch was out I took his place, and he got out the Professor's paper and pens and wrote a letter home to his aunt Polly telling her everything that had happened to us, and dated it *"In the Welkin, approaching England,"* and folded it together and stuck it fast with a red wafer, and directed it, and wrote above the direction in big writing, *"From Tom Sawyer the Erronort,"* and said it would sweat old Nat Parsons the postmaster when it come along in the mail. I says—

"Tom Sawyer, this ain't no welkin, it's a balloon."

"Well, now, who *said* it was a welkin, smarty?"

"You've wrote it on the letter, anyway."

"What of it? That don't mean that the balloon's the welkin."

"Oh, I thought it did. Well, then, what *is* a welkin?"

I see in a minute he was stuck. He raked and scraped around in his mind, but he couldn't find nothing, so he had to say—

"*I* don't know, and nobody don't know. It's just a word. And it's a mighty good word, too. There ain't many that lays over it. I don't believe there's *any* that does."

"Shucks," I says, "but what does it *mean?*—that's the pint."

"*I* don't know what it means, I tell you. It's a word that people uses for—for—well, it's ornamental. They don't put ruffles on a shirt to help keep a person warm, do they?"

"'Course they don't."

"But they put them *on*, don't they?"

"Yes."

"All right, then; that letter I wrote is a shirt, and the welkin's the ruffle on it."

I judged that that would gravel Jim, and it did. He says—

"Now, Mars Tom, it ain't no use to talk like dat, en moreover it's sinful. *You* knows a letter ain't no shirt, en dey ain't no ruffles on it, nuther. Dey ain't no place to put 'em on, you can't put 'em on, en dey wouldn't stay on ef you did."

"Oh, *do* shut up, and wait till something's started that you know something about."

"Why, Mars Tom, sholy you don't mean to say I don't know about shirts, when goodness knows I's toted home de washin' ever sence—"

"I tell you this hasn't got anything to *do* with shirts. I only—"

"Why, Mars Tom! You said, yo' own self, dat a letter—"

"Do you want to drive me crazy? Keep still. I only used it as a metaphor."

That word kind of bricked us up for a minute. Then Jim says, ruther timid, because he see Tom was getting pretty tetchy—

"Mars Tom, what is a metaphor?"

"A metaphor's a—well, it's a—a metaphor's an illustration." He see that *that* didn't git home; so he tried again. "When I say birds of a feather flocks together, it's a metaphorical way of saying—"

"But dey *don't*, Mars Tom. No, sir, 'deed dey don't. Dey ain't no feathers dat's more alike den a bluebird's en a jaybird's, but ef you waits tell you catches *dem* birds a-flockin' together, you'll—"

"Oh, *give* us a rest. You can't get the simplest little thing through your thick skull. Now, don't bother me any more."

Jim was satisfied to stop. He was dreadful pleased with himself for catching Tom out. The minute Tom begun to talk about birds I judged he was a goner, because Jim knowed more about birds than both of us put together. You see, he had killed hundreds and hundreds of them, and that's the way to find out about birds. That's the way the people does that writes books about birds, and loves them so that they'll go hungry and tired and take any amount of trouble to find a new bird and kill it. Their name is ornithologers, and I could a been an ornithologer myself, because I always loved birds and creatures; and I started out to learn how to be one, and I see a bird setting on a dead limb of a high tree, singing, with his head tilted back and his mouth open, and before I thought I fired, and his song stopped and he fell straight down from the limb, all limp like a rag, and I run and picked him up, and he was dead, and his body was warm in my hand,

and his head rolled about, this way and that, like his neck was broke, and there was a white skin over his eyes, and one little drop of blood on the side of his head, and laws! I couldn't see nothing more for the tears; and I hain't ever murdered no creature since, that warn't doing me no harm, and I ain't going to.

But I was aggravated about that welkin. I wanted to know. I got the subject up again, and then Tom explained, the best he could. He said when a person made a big speech the newspapers said the shouts of the people made the welkin ring. He said they always said that, but none of them ever told what it was, so he allowed it just meant out-doors and up high. Well, that seemed sensible enough, so I was satisfied, and said so. That pleased Tom and put him in a good humor again, and he says—

"Well, it's all right, then, and we'll let bygones be bygones. I don't know for certain what a welkin is, but when we land in London we'll make it ring, anyway, and don't you forget it."

He said an Erronort was a person who sailed around in balloons; and said it was a mighty sight finer to be Tom Sawyer the Erronort than to be Tom Sawyer the Traveler, and would be heard of all around the world, if we pulled through all right, and so he wouldn't give shucks to be a Traveler, now.

Towards the middle of the afternoon we got everything ready to land, and we felt pretty good, too, and proud; and we kept watching with the glasses, like Clumbus discovering America. But we couldn't see nothing but ocean. The afternoon wasted out and the sun shut down, and still there warn't no land anywheres. We wondered what was the matter, but reckoned it would come out all right, so we went on steering east, but went up on a higher level so we wouldn't hit any steeples or mountains in the dark.

It was my watch till midnight, and then it was Jim's; but Tom stayed up, because he said ship captains done that when they was making the land, and didn't stand no regular watch.

Well, when daylight come, Jim give a shout, and we jumped up and looked over, and there was the land, sure enough; land all around, as far as you could see, and perfectly level and yaller. We didn't know how long we had been over it. There warn't no trees, nor hills, nor rocks, nor towns, and Tom and Jim had took it for the sea. They took it for the sea in a dead cam; but we was so high up, anyway, that if it had been the sea and rough, it would a looked smooth, all the same, in the night, that way.

We was all in a powerful excitement, now, and grabbed the glasses and hunted everywheres for London, but couldn't find hide nor hair of it, nor any other settlement. Nor any sign of a lake or a river, either. Tom was clean beat. He said it warn't his notion of England, he thought England looked like America, and always had that idea. So he said we better have breakfast, and then drop down and inquire the quickest way to London. We cut the breakfast pretty short, we was so impatient. As we slanted along down, the weather begun to moderate, and pretty soon we shed our furs. But it kept *on* moderating, and in a precious little while it was most too moderate. Why, the sweat begun to fairly bile out of us. We was close down, now, and just blistering!

We settled down to within thirty foot of the land. That is, it was land if sand is land; for this wasn't anything but pure sand. Tom and me clumb down the ladder and took a run to stretch our legs, and it felt amazing good; that is, the stretching did, but the sand scorched our feet like hot embers. Next, we see somebody coming, and started to meet him; but we heard Jim shout, and looked around, and he was fairly dancing, and making signs, and yelling. We couldn't make out what he said, but we was scared, anyway, and begun to heel it back to the balloon. When we got close enough, we understood the words, and they made me sick:

"Run! run fo' yo' life! hit's a lion, I kin see him thoo de glass! Run, boys, do please heel it de bes' you kin, he's busted outen de menagerie en dey ain't nobody to stop him!"

It made Tom fly, but it took the stiffening all out of my legs. I could only just gasp along the way you do in a dream when there's a ghost a-gaining on you.

Tom got to the ladder and shinned up it a piece and waited for me; and as soon as I got a footholt on it he shouted to Jim to soar away. But Jim had clean lost his head, and said he had forgot how. So Tom shinned along up and told me to follow, but the lion was arriving, fetching a most gashly roar with every lope, and my legs shook so I dasn't try to take one of them out of the rounds for fear the other one would give way under me.

But Tom was aboard by this time, and he started the balloon up, a little, and stopped it again as soon as the end of the ladder was ten or twelve foot above ground. And there was the lion, a-ripping around under me, and roaring, and springing up in the air at the ladder and only missing it about a quarter of an inch, it seemed to me. It was delicious to be out of his reach, perfectly delicious, and made me feel good and thankful all up one side; but I was hanging there helpless and couldn't climb, and that made me feel perfectly wretched and miserable all down the other. It is most seldom that a person feels so mixed, like that; and is not to be recommended, either.

Tom asked me what he better do, but I didn't know. He asked me if I could hold on whilst he sailed away to a safe place and left the lion behind. I said I could if he didn't go no higher than he was now, but if he went higher I would lose my head and fall, sure. So he said, "Take a good grip," and he started.

"Don't go so fast," I shouted, "it makes my head swim."

He had started like a lightning express. He slowed down, and we glided over the sand slower, but still in a kind of sickening way, for it *is* uncomfortable to see things gliding and sliding under you like that and not a sound.

But pretty soon there was plenty of sound, for the lion was catching up. His noise fetched others. You could see them coming on the lope from every direction, and pretty soon there was a couple of dozen of them under me skipping up at the ladder and snarling and snapping at each other; and so we went skimming along over the sand, and these fellers doing what they could to help us to not forgit the occasion; and then some tigers come, without an invite, and they started a regular riot down there.

We see this plan was a mistake. We couldn't ever git away from them at this gait, and I couldn't hold on forever. So Tom took a think and struck another idea. That was, to kill a lion with the pepper-box revolver and then sail away while the others stopped to fight over the carcase. So he stopped the balloon still, and done it, and then we sailed off while the fuss was going on, and come down a quarter of a mile off, and they helped me aboard; but by the time we was out of reach again, that gang was on hand once more. And when they see we was really gone and they couldn't get us, they set down on their hams and looked up at us so kind of disappointed that it was as much as a person could do not to see *their* side of the matter.

Chapter 6

I was so weak that the only thing I wanted was a chance to lay down, so I made straight for my locker-bunk and stretched myself out there. But a body couldn't git back his strength in no such oven as that, so Tom give the command to soar, and Jim started her aloft. And mind you, it was a considerable strain on that balloon to lift the fleas, and reminded Tom of Mary had a little lamb its fleas was white as snow, but these wasn't; these was the dark-complected kind, the kind that's always hungry and ain't particular, and will eat pie when they can't git Christian. Wherever there's sand, you are a-going to find that bird; and the more sand the bigger the flock. Here it was all sand, and the result was according. I never see such a turnout.

We had to go up a mile before we struck comfortable weather; and we had to go up another mile before we got rid of them creturs; but when they begun to freeze, they skipped overboard. Then we come down a mile again where it was breezy and pleasant and just right, and pretty soon I was all straight again. Tom had been setting quiet and thinking; but now he jumps up and says—

"I bet you a thousand to one *I* know where we are. We're in the Great Sahara, as sure as guns!"

He was so excited he couldn't hold still. But I wasn't; I says—

"Well, then, where's the Great Sahara? In England, or in Scotland?"

" 'Tain't in either, it's in Africa."

Jim's eyes bugged out, and he begun to stare down with no end of interest, because that was where his originals come from; but I didn't more than half believe it. I couldn't, you know; it seemed too awful far away for us to have traveled.

But Tom was full of his discovery, as he called it, and said the lions and the sand meant the Great Desert, sure. He said he could a found out, before we sighted land, that we was crowding the land somewheres, if he had thought of one thing; and when we asked him what, he said—

"These clocks. They're chronometers. You always read about them in sea-voyages. One of them is keeping Grinnage time, and the other one is keeping St. Louis time, like my watch. When we left St. Louis, it was four in the afternoon by my watch and this clock, and it was ten at night by this Grinnage clock. Well, at this time of the year the sun sets about seven o'clock. Now I noticed the time yesterday evening when the sun went down, and it was half past five o'clock by the Grinnage clock, and half past eleven, a.m., by my watch and the other clock. You see, the sun rose and set by my watch in St. Louis, and the Grinnage clock was six hours fast; but we've come so far east that it comes within less than an hour and a half of setting by the Grinnage clock, now, and I'm away out—more than four hours and a half out. You see, that meant that we was closing up on the longitude of Ireland, and would strike it before long if we was pinted right—which we wasn't. No, sir, we've been a-wandering—wandering way-down south of east, and it's my opinion we are in Africa. Look at this map. You see how the shoulder of Africa sticks out to the west. Think how fast we've traveled; if we had gone straight east we would be long past England by this time. You watch for noon, all of you, and we'll stand up, and when we can't cast a shadow we'll find that this Grinnage clock is coming mighty close to marking twelve. Yes, sir, *I* think we're in Africa; and it's just bully."

Jim was gazing down with the glass. He shook his head and says—

"Mars Tom, I reckon dey's a mistake somers, I hain't seen no niggers, yit."

"That's nothing; they don't live in the Desert. What is that, way off yonder? Gimme a glass."

He took a long look, and said it was like a black string stretched across the sand, but he couldn't guess what it was.

"Well," I says, "I reckon maybe you've got a chance, now, to find out whereabouts this balloon is, because as like as not that is one of these lines here, that's on the map, that you call meridians of longitude, and we can drop down and look at its number, and—"

"Oh, shucks, Huck Finn, I never see such a lunkhead as

you. Did you s'pose there's meridians of longitude on the *earth*?"

"Tom Sawyer, they're set down on the map, and you know it perfectly well, and here they are, and you can see for yourself."

"Of course they're on the map, but that's nothing; there ain't any on the *ground*."

"Tom, do you know that to be so?"

"Certainly I do."

"Well, then, that map's a liar again. I never see such a liar as that map."

He fired up at that, and I was ready for him, and Jim was warming up his opinion, too, and the next minute we'd a broke loose on another argument, if Tom hadn't dropped the glass and begun to clap his hands like a maniac and sing out—

"Camels!—camels!"

So I grabbed a glass, and Jim, too, and took a look, but I was disappointed, and says—

"Camels your granny, they're spiders."

"Spiders in a desert, you shad? Spiders walking in a procession? You don't ever reflect, Huck Finn, and I reckon you really haven't got anything to reflect *with*. Don't you know we're as much as a mile up in the air, and that that string of crawlers is two or three miles away? Spiders, good land! Spiders as big as a cow? P'raps you'd like to go down and milk one of 'em. But they're camels, just the same. It's a caravan, that's what it is, and it's a mile long."

"Well, then, le's go down and look at it. I don't believe in it, and ain't going to till I see it and know it."

"All right," he says, and give the command: "Lower away."

As we come slanting down into the hot weather, we could see that it was camels, sure enough, plodding along, an everlasting string of them, with bales strapped to them, and several hundred men, in long white robes, and a thing like a shawl bound over their heads and hanging down with tassels and fringes; and some of the men had long guns and some hadn't, and some was riding and some was walking. And the weather—well it was just roasting. And how slow they did creep along! We swooped down, now, all of a sudden, and stopped about a hundred yards over their heads.

The men all set up a yell, and some of them fell flat on their stomachs, some begun to fire their guns at us, and the rest broke and scampered every which way, and so did the camels.

We see that we was making trouble, so we went up again about a mile, to the cool weather, and watched them from there. It took them an hour to get together and form the procession again; then they started along, but we could see by the glasses that they wasn't paying much attention to anything but us. We poked along, looking down at them with the glasses, and by and by we see a big sand mound, and something like people the other side of it, and there was something like a man laying on top of the mound, that raised his head up every now and then, and seemed to be watching the caravan or us, we didn't know which. As the caravan got nearer, he sneaked down on the other side and rushed to the other men and horses—for that is what they was—and we see them mount in a hurry; and next, here they come, like a house afire, some with lances and some with long guns, and all of them yelling the best they could.

They come a-tearing down onto the caravan, and the next minute both sides crashed together and was all mixed up, and there was such another popping of guns as you never heard, and the air got so full of smoke you could only catch glimpses of them struggling together. There must a been six hundred men in that battle, and it was terrible to see. Then they broke up into gangs and groups, fighting, tooth and nail, and scurrying and scampering around, and laying into each other like everything; and whenever the smoke cleared a little you could see dead and wounded people and camels scattered far and wide and all about, and camels racing off in every direction.

At last the robbers see they couldn't win, so their chief sounded a signal, and all that was left of them broke away and went scampering across the plain. The last man to go snatched up a child and carried it off in front of him on his horse, and a woman run screaming and begging after him, and followed him away off across the plain till she was separated a long ways from her people; but it warn't no use, and she had to give it up, and we see her sink down on the sand and cover her face with her hands. Then Tom took the hellum, and started for that yahoo, and we come a-whizzing down and made a swoop, and knocked him out of the saddle, child and all; and he was jarred considerable, but the child wasn't hurt, but laid there working its hands and legs in the air like a tumble-bug that's on its back and can't turn over. The man went staggering off to overtake his horse, and didn't know what had hit him, for we was three or four hundred yards up in the air by this time.

We judged the woman would go and get the child, now, but she didn't. We could see her, through the glass, still setting there, with her head bowed down on her knees; so of course she hadn't seen the performance, and thought her child was clean gone with the man. She was nearly a half a mile from her people, so we thought we might go down to the child, which was about a quarter of a mile beyond her, and snake it to her before the caravan people could git to us to do us any harm; and besides, we reckoned they had enough business on their hands for one while, anyway, with the wounded. We thought we'd chance it, and we did. We swooped down and stopped, and Jim shinned down the ladder and fetched up the cub, which was a nice fat little thing, and in a noble good humor, too, considering it was just out of a battle and been tumbled off of a horse; and then we started for the mother, and stopped back of her and tolerable near by, and Jim slipped down and crept up easy, and when he was close back of her the child goo-goo'd, the way a child does, and she heard it, and whirled and fetched a shriek of joy, and made a jump for the kid and snatched it and hugged it, and dropped it and hugged Jim, and then snatched off a gold chain and hung it around Jim's neck, and hugged him again, and jerked up the child again and mashed it to her breast, a-sobbing and glorifying all the time, and Jim he shoved for the ladder and up it and in a minute we was back up in the sky and the woman was staring up, with the back of her head between her shoulders and the child with its arms locked around her neck. And there she stood, as long as we was in sight a-sailing away in the sky.

Chapter 7

Noon!" says Tom, and so it was. His shadder was just a blot around his feet. We looked, and the Grinnage clock was so close to twelve the difference didn't amount to nothing. So Tom said London was right north of us or right south of us, one or t'other, and he reckoned by the weather and the sand and the camels it was north; and a good many miles north, too; as many as from New York to the city of Mexico, he guessed.

Jim said he reckoned a balloon was a good deal the fastest thing in the world, unless it might be some kinds of birds—a wild pigeon, maybe, or a railroad.

But Tom said he had read about railroads in England going nearly a hundred miles an hour for a little ways, and there never was a bird in the world that could do that—except one, and that was a flea.

"A flea? Why, Mars Tom, in de fust place he ain't a bird, strickly speakin'—"

"He ain't a bird, ain't he? Well, then, what is he?"

"I don't rightly know, Mars Tom, but I speck he's only jist a animal. No, I reckon dat won't do, nuther, he ain't big enough for a animal. He mus' be a bug. Yassir, dat's what he is, he's a bug."

"I bet he ain't, but let it go. What's your second place?"

"Well, in de second place, birds is creturs dat goes a long ways, but a flea don't."

"He don't, don't he? Come, now, what *is* a long distance, if you know?"

"Why, it's miles, en lots of 'em—anybody knows dat."

"Can't a man walk miles?"

"Yassir, he kin."

"As many as a railroad?"

"Yassir, if you give him time."

"Can't a flea?"

"Well,—I s'pose so—ef you gives him heaps of time."

"Now you begin to see, don't you, that *distance* ain't the thing to judge by, at all; it's the time it takes to go the distance *in*, that *counts*, ain't it?"

686

"Well, hit do look sorter so, but I wouldn't a b'lieved it, Mars Tom."

"It's a matter of *proportion*, that's what it is; and when you come to gage a thing's speed by its size, where's your bird and your man and your railroad, alongside of a flea? The fastest man can't run more than about ten miles in an hour—not much over ten thousand times his own length. But all the books says any common ordinary third-class flea can jump a hundred and fifty times his own length; yes, and he can make five jumps a second, too,—seven hundred and fifty times his own length, in one little second—for he don't fool away any time stopping and starting—he does them both at the same time; you'll see, if you try to put your finger on him. Now that's a common ordinary third-class flea's gait; but you take an Eyetalian *first*-class, that's been the pet of the nobility all his life and hasn't ever knowed what want or sickness or exposure was, and he can jump more than three hundred times his own length, and keep it up all day, five such jumps every second, which is fifteen hundred times his own length. Well, suppose a man could go fifteen hundred times his own length in a second—say, a mile and a half? It's ninety miles a minute; it's considerable more than five thousand miles an hour. Where's your man, *now*?—yes, and your bird, and your railroad, and your balloon? Laws, they don't amount to shucks 'longside of a flea. A flea is just a comet biled down small."

Jim was a good deal astonished, and so was I. Jim said—

"Is dem figgers jist edjackly true, en no jokin' en no lies, Mars Tom?"

"Yes, they are; they're perfectly true."

"Well, den, honey, a body's got to respec' a flea. I ain't had no respec' for um befo', scasely, but dey ain' no gittin' roun' it, dey do deserve it, dat's certain."

"Well, I bet they do. They've got ever so much more sense, and brains, and brightness, in proportion to their size, than any other cretur in the world. A person can learn them most anything; and they learn it quicker than any other cretur, too. They've been learnt to haul little carriages in harness, and go this way and that way and t'other way according to orders; yes, and to march and drill like soldiers, doing it as exact, according to orders, as soldiers does it. They've been learnt to do all sorts of hard and troublesome things. S'pose you could cultivate a flea up to the size of a man, and keep his natural smartness a-growing and a-growing right along up, bigger and bigger, and keener and keener, in the same proportion—where'd the human race be, do you reckon? That flea would be President of the United States, and you couldn't any more prevent it than you can prevent lightning."

"My lan', Mars Tom, I never knowed dey was so much *to* de beas'. No, sir, I never had no idea of it, and dat's de fac'."

"There's more to him, by a long sight, than there is to any other cretur, man or beast, in proportion to size. He's the interestingest of them all. People have so much to say about an ant's strength, and an elephant's, and a locomotive's. Shucks, they don't begin with a flea. He can lift two or three hundred times his own weight. And none of them can come anywhere near it. And moreover, he has got notions of his own, and is very particular, and you can't fool him; his instinct, or his judgment, or whatever it is, is perfectly sound and clear, and don't ever make a mistake. People think all humans are alike to a flea. It ain't so. There's folks that he won't go anear, hungry or not hungry, and I'm one of them. I've never had one of them on me in my life."

"Mars Tom!"

"It's so; I ain't joking."

"Well, sah, I hain't ever heard de likes er dat, befo'."

Jim couldn't believe it, and I couldn't; so we had to drop down to the sand and git a supply, and see. Tom was right. They went for me and Jim by the thousand, but not a one of them lit on Tom. There warn't no explaining it, but there it was, and there warn't no getting around it. He said it had always been just so, and he'd just as soon be where there was a million of them as not, they'd never touch him nor bother him.

We went up to the cold weather for a freeze-out, and stayed a little spell, and then come back to the comfortable weather and went lazying along twenty or twenty-five mile an hour, the way we'd been doing for the last few hours. The reason was, that the longer we was in that solemn, peaceful Desert, the more the hurry and fuss got kind of soothed down in us, and the more happier and contented and satisfied we got to feeling, and the more we got to liking the Desert, and then loving it. So we had cramped the speed down, as I was saying, and was having a most noble good lazy time, sometimes watching through the glasses, sometimes stretched out on the lockers reading, sometimes taking a nap.

It didn't seem like we was the same lot that was in such a sweat to find land and git ashore, but it was. But we had got over that—clean over it. We was used to the balloon, now, and not afraid any more, and didn't want to be anywheres else. Why, it seemed just like home; it most seemed as if I had been born and raised in it, and Jim and Tom said the same. And always I had had hateful people around me, a-nagging at me, and pestering of me, and scolding, and finding fault, and fussing and bothering, and sticking to me, and keeping after me, and making me do this, and making me do that and t'other, and always selecting out the things I didn't want to do, and then giving me Sam Hill because I shirked and done something else, and just aggravating the life out of a body all the time; but up here in the sky it was so still, and sunshiny and lovely, and plenty to eat, and plenty of sleep, and strange things to see, and no nagging and pestering, and no good people, and just holiday all the time. Land, I warn't in no hurry to git out and buck at civilization again. Now, one of the worst things about civilization is, that anybody that gits a letter with trouble in it comes and tells you all about it and makes you feel bad, and the newspapers fetches you the troubles of everybody all over the world, and keeps you downhearted and dismal most all the time, and it's such a heavy load for a person. I hate them newspapers; and I hate letters; and if I had my way I wouldn't allow nobody to load his troubles onto other folks he ain't acquainted with, on t'other side of the world, that way. Well, up in a balloon there ain't any of that, and it's the darlingest place there is.

We had supper, and that night was one of the prettiest nights I ever see. The moon made it just like daylight, only a heap softer; and once we see a lion standing all alone by himself, just all alone in the earth, it seemed like, and his shadder laid on the sand by him like a puddle of ink. That's the kind of moonlight to have.

Mainly we laid on our backs and talked, we didn't want to go to sleep. Tom said we was right in the midst of the Arabian

Nights, now. He said it was right along here that one of the cutest things in that book happened; so we looked down and watched while he told about it, because there ain't anything that is so interesting to look at as a place that a book has talked about. It was a tale about a camel driver that had lost his camel, and he come along in the Desert and met a man, and says—

"Have you run across a stray camel to-day?"

And the man says—

"Was he blind in his left eye?"

"Yes."

"Had he lost an upper front tooth?"

"Yes."

"Was his off hind leg lame?"

"Yes."

"Was he loaded with millet seed on one side and honey on the other?"

"Yes, but you needn't go into no more details—that's the one, and I'm in a hurry. Where did you see him?"

"I hain't seen him at all," the man says.

"Hain't seen him at all? How can you describe him so close, then?"

"Because when a person knows how to use his eyes, everything he sees has got a meaning to it; but most people's eyes ain't any good to them. I knowed a camel had been along, because I seen his track. I knowed he was lame in his off hind leg because he had favored that foot and trod light on it and his track showed it. I knowed he was blind on his left side because he only nibbled the grass on the right side of the trail. I knowed he had lost an upper front tooth because where he bit into the sod his teeth-print showed it. The millet seed sifted out on one side—the ants told me that; the honey leaked out on the other—the flies told me that. I know all about your camel, but I hain't seen him."

Jim says—

"Go on, Mars Tom, hit's a mighty good tale, and powerful interestin'."

"That's all," Tom says.

"*All?*" says Jim, astonished. "What come o' de camel?"

"I don't know."

"Mars Tom, don't de tale say?"

"No."

Jim puzzled a minute, then he says—

"Well! ef dat ain't de beatenes' tale ever *I* struck. Jist gits to de place whah de intrust is gittin' red hot, en down she breaks. Why, Mars Tom, dey ain't no *sense* in a tale dat acts like dat. Hain't you got no *idea* whether de man got de camel back er not?"

"No, I haven't."

I see, myself, there warn't no sense in the tale, to chop square off, that way, before it come to anything, but I warn't going to say so, because I could see Tom was souring up pretty fast over the way it flatted out and the way Jim had popped onto the weak place in it, and I don't think it's fair for everybody to pile onto a feller when he's down. But Tom he whirls on me and says—

"What do *you* think of the tale?"

Of course, then, I had to come out and make a clean breast and say it did seem to me, too, same as it did to Jim, that as long as the tale stopped square in the middle and never got to no place, it really warn't worth the trouble of telling.

Tom's chin dropped on his breast, and 'stead of being mad, as I reckoned he'd be, to hear me scoff at his tale that way, he seemed to be only sad; and he says—

"Some people can see, and some can't—just as that man said. Let alone a camel, if a cyclone had gone by, *you* duffers wouldn't a noticed the track."

I don't know what he meant by that, and he didn't say; it was just one of his irrulevances, I reckon—he was full of them, sometimes, when he was in a close place and couldn't see no other way out—but I didn't mind. We'd spotted the soft place in that tale sharp enough, he couldn't git away from that little fact. It graveled him like the nation, too, I reckon, much as he tried not to let on.

Chapter 8

W E HAD an early breakfast in the morning, and set looking down on the Desert, and the weather was ever so bammy and lovely, although we warn't high up. You have to come down lower and lower after sundown, in the Desert, because it cools off so fast; and so, by the time it is getting towards dawn you are skimming along only a little ways above the sand.

We was watching the shadder of the balloon slide along the ground, and now and then gazing off across the Desert to see if anything was stirring, and then down at the shadder again, when all of a sudden almost right under us we see a lot of men and camels laying scattered about, perfectly quiet, like they was asleep.

We shut off the power, and backed up and stood over them, and then we see that they was all dead. It give us the cold shivers. And it made us hush down, too, and talk low, like people at a funeral. We dropped down slow, and stopped, and me and Tom clumb down and went amongst them. There was men, and women, and children. They was dried by the sun, and dark and shriveled and leathery, like the pictures of mummies you see in books. And yet they looked just as human, you wouldn't a believed it; just like they was asleep; some laying on their backs, with their arms spread on the sand, some on their sides, some on their faces, just as natural, though the teeth showed more than usual. Two or three was setting up. One was a woman, with her head bent over, and a child was laying across her lap. A man was setting with his hands locked around his knees, staring out of his dead eyes at a young girl that was stretched out before him. He looked so mournful, it was pitiful to see. And you never see a place so still as that was. He had straight black hair hanging down by his cheeks, and when a little faint breeze fanned it and made it wag, it made me shudder, because it seemed as if he was wagging his head.

Some of the people and animals was partly covered with sand, but most of them not, for the sand was thin there, and the bed was gravel, and hard. Most of the clothes had rotted away and left the bodies partly naked; and when you took hold of a rag, it tore with a touch, like spider-web. Tom reckoned they had been laying there for years.

Some of the men had rusty guns by them, some had swords on, and had shawl-belts with long silver-mounted pistols stuck in them. All the camels had their loads on, yet, but the packs had busted or rotted and spilt the freight out on the ground. We didn't reckon the swords was any good to the dead people any more, so we took one apiece, and some pistols. We took a small box, too, because it was so handsome and inlaid so fine; and then we wanted to bury the people; but there warn't no way to do it that we could think of, and nothing to do it with but sand, and that would blow away again, of course. We did start to cover up that poor girl, first laying some shawls from a busted bale on her; but when we was going to put sand on her, the man's hair wagged again and give us a shock, and we stopped, because it looked like he was trying to tell us he didn't want her covered up so he couldn't see her no more. I reckon she was dear to him, and he would a been so lonesome.

Then we mounted high and sailed away, and pretty soon that black spot on the sand was out of sight and we wouldn't ever see them poor people again in this world. We wondered, and reasoned, and tried to guess how they come to be there, and how it had all happened to them, but we couldn't make it out. First we thought maybe they got lost, and wandered around and about till their food and water give out and they starved to death; but Tom said no wild animals nor vultures hadn't meddled with them, and so that guess wouldn't do. So at last we give it up, and judged we wouldn't think about it no more, because it made us low spirited.

Then we opened the box, and it had gems and jewels in it, quite a pile, and some little veils of the kind the dead women had on, with fringes made out of curious gold money that we warn't acquainted with. We wondered if we better go and try to find them again and give it back; but Tom thought it over and said no, it was a country that was full of robbers, and they would come and steal it, and then the sin would be on us for putting the temptation in their way. So we went on; but I wished we had took all they had, so there wouldn't a been no temptation at all left.

We had had two hours of that blazing weather down there, and was dreadful thirsty when we got aboard again. We went straight for the water, but it was spoiled and bitter, besides being pretty near hot enough to scald your mouth. We couldn't drink it. It was Mississippi river water, the best in the world, and we stirred up the mud in it to see if that would help, but no, the mud wasn't any better than the water.

Well, we hadn't been so very, very thirsty before, whilst we was interested in the lost people, but we was, now, and as soon as we found we couldn't have a drink, we was more than thirty-five times as thirsty as we was a quarter of a minute before. Why, in a little while we wanted to hold our mouths open and pant like a dog.

Tom said keep a sharp lookout, all around, everywheres, because we'd got to find an oasis or there warn't no telling what would happen. So we done it. We kept the glasses gliding around all the time, till our arms got so tired we couldn't hold them any more. Two hours—three hours—just gazing and gazing, and nothing but sand, sand, *sand*, and you could see the quivery heat-shimmer playing over it. Dear, dear, a body don't know what real misery is till he is thirsty all the way through, and is certain he ain't ever going to come to any water any more. At last I couldn't stand it to look around on them baking plains; I laid down on the locker and give it up.

But by and by Tom raised a whoop, and there she was! A lake, wide and shiny, with pam trees leaning over it asleep, and their shadders in the water just as soft and delicate as ever you see. I never see anything look so good. It was a long ways off, but that warn't anything to us; we just slapped on a hundred-mile gait, and calculated to be there in seven minutes; but she stayed the same old distance away, all the time; we couldn't seem to gain on her; yes, sir, just as far, and shiny, and like a dream, but we couldn't get no nearer; and at last, all of a sudden, she was gone!

Tom's eyes took a spread, and he says—

"Boys, it was a *my*ridge!"

Said it like he was glad. I didn't see nothing to be glad about. I says—

"Maybe. I don't care nothing about its name, the thing I want to know is, what's become of it?"

Jim was trembling all over, and so scared he couldn't speak, but he wanted to ask that question himself if he could a done it. Tom says—

"What's *become* of it? Why, you see, yourself, it's gone."

"Yes, I know; but where's it gone *to*?"

He looked me over and says—

"Well, now, Huck Finn, where *would* it go to? Don't you know what a myridge is?"

"No, I don't. What is it?"

"It ain't anything but imagination. There ain't anything *to* it."

It warmed me up a little to hear him talk like that, and I says—

"What's the use you talking that kind of stuff, Tom Sawyer? Didn't I see the lake?"

"Yes—you think you did."

"I don't think nothing about it, I *did* see it."

"I tell you you *didn't* see it, either—because it warn't there to see."

It astonished Jim to hear him talk so, and he broke in and says, kind of pleading and distressed—

"Mars Tom, *please* don't say sich things in sich an awful time as dis. You ain't only reskin' yo' own self, but you's reskin' us—same way like Anna Nias en Suffira. De lake *wuz* dah—I seen it jis as plain as I sees you en Huck dis minute."

I says—

"Why, he seen it himself! He was the very one that seen it first. *Now*, then!"

"Yes, Mars Tom, hit's so—you can't deny it. We all seen it, en dat *prove* it was dah."

"Proves it! *How* does it prove it?"

"Same way it does in de courts en everywheres, Mars Tom. One pusson might be drunk or dreamy or suthin', en he could be mistaken; en two might, maybe; but I tell you, sah, when three sees a thing, drunk er sober, it's *so*. Dey ain't no gittin' aroun' dat, en you knows it, Mars Tom."

"I don't know nothing of the kind. There used to be forty thousand million people that seen the sun move from one side of the sky to the other every day. Did that prove that the sun *done* it?"

" 'Course it did. En besides, dey warn't no 'casion to prove it. A body 'at's got any sense ain't gwyne to doubt it. Dah she is, now—a-sailin' thoo de sky des like she allays done."

Tom turned on me, then, and says—

"What do *you* say—is the sun standing still?"

"Tom Sawyer, what's the use to ask such a jackass question? Anybody that ain't blind can see it don't stand still."

"Well," he says, "I'm lost in the sky with no company but a passel of low-down animals that don't know no more than the head boss of a university did three or four hundred years ago. Why, blame it, Huck Finn, there was Popes, in them days, that knowed as much as *you* do."

It warn't fair play, and I let him know it. I says—

"Throwin' mud ain't arguin', Tom Sawyer."

"Who's throwin' mud?"

"You done it."

"I never. It ain't no disgrace, I reckon, to compare a back-woods Missouri muggins like you to a Pope, even the orneri-est one that ever set on the throne. Why, it's an honor to you, you tadpole, the *Pope's* the one that's hit hard, not *you*, and you couldn't blame him for cussing about it, only they don't cuss. Not now they don't, I mean."

"Sho, Tom, did they ever?"

"In the Middle Ages? Why, it was their common diet."

"No! You don't really mean they cussed?"

That started his mill a-going and he ground out a regular speech, the way he done sometimes when he was feeling his oats, and I got him to write down some of the last half of it for me, because it was like book-talk and tough to remember, and had words in it that I warn't used to and is pretty tire-some to spell:

"Yes, they did. I don't mean that they went charging around the way Ben Miller does, and put the cuss-words just the same way *he* puts them. No, they used the same words, but they put them together different, because they'd been learnt by the very best masters, and they knowed *how*, which

Ben Miller don't, because he just picked it up, here and there and around, and hain't had no competent person to learn him. But *they* knowed. It warn't no frivolous random cussing, like Ben Miller's, that starts in anywheres and comes out nowheres, it was scientific cussing, and systematic; and it was stern, and solemn, and awful, not a thing for you to stand off and laugh at, the way people does when that poor ignorant Ben Miller gits a-going. Why, Ben Miller's kind can stand up and cuss a person a week, steady, and it wouldn't phaze him no more than a goose cackling, but it was a mighty different thing in them Middle Ages when a Pope, educated to cuss, got his cussing-things together and begun to lay into a king, or a kingdom, or a heretic, or a Jew, or anybody that was un-satisfactory and needed straightening out. He didn't go at it harum-scarum; no, he took that king or that other person, and begun at the top, and cussed him all the way down in de-tail. He cussed him in the hairs of his head, and in the bones of his skull, and in the hearing of his ears, and in the sight of his eyes, and in the breath of his nostrils, and in his vitals, and in his veins, and in his limbs and his feet and his hands, and the blood and flesh and bones of his whole body; and cussed him in the loves of his heart and in his friendships, and turned him out in the world, and cussed anybody that give him food to eat, or shelter and bed, or water to drink, or rags to cover him when he was freezing. Land, *that* was cussing worth talk-ing about; that was the only cussing worth shucks that's ever been done in this world—the man it fell on, or the country it fell on, would better a been dead, forty times over. Ben Miller! The idea of him thinking *he* can cuss! Why, the poor-est little one-horse back-country bishop in the Middle Ages could cuss all around him. *We* don't know nothing about cussing now-a-days."

"Well," I says, "you needn't cry about it, I reckon we can git along. Can a bishop cuss, now, the way they useter?"

"Yes, they learn it, because it's part of the polite learning that belongs to his lay-out—kind of bells letters, as you may say—and although he ain't got no more use for it than Mis-souri girls has for French, he's got to learn it, same as they do, because a Missouri girl that can't polly-voo and a bishop that can't cuss ain't got no business in society."

"Don't they ever cuss at all, now, Tom?"

"Not but very seldom. Praps they do in Peru, but amongst people that knows anything, it's played out, and they don't mind it no more than they do Ben Miller's kind. It's because they've got so far along that they know as much now as the grasshoppers did in the Middle Ages."

"The grasshoppers?"

"Yes. In the Middle Ages, in France, when the grasshoppers started in to eat up the crops, the bishop would go out in the fields and pull a solemn face and give them a most solid good cussing. Just the way they done with a Jew or a heretic or a king, as I was telling you."

"And what did the grasshoppers do, Tom?"

"Just laughed, and went on and et up the crop, same as they started *in* to do. The difference betwixt a man and a grasshopper, in the Middle Ages, was that the grasshopper warn't a fool."

"Oh, my goodness, oh, my goodness gracious, dah's de lake agin!" yelled Jim, just then. "*Now*, Mars Tom, what you gwyne to say?"

Yes, sir, there was the lake again, away yonder across the Desert, perfectly plain, trees and all, just the same as it was before. I says—

"I reckon you're satisfied now, Tom Sawyer."

But he says, perfectly cam—

"Yes, satisfied there ain't no lake there."

Jim says—

"*Don't* talk so, Mars Tom—it sk'yers me to hear you. It's so hot, en you's so thirsty, dat you ain't in yo' right mine, Mars Tom. Oh, but don't she look good! 'clah I doan' know how I's gwyne to wait tell we gits dah, I's *so* thirsty."

"Well, you'll have to wait; and it won't do you no good, either, because there ain't no lake there, I tell you."

I says—

"Jim, don't you take your eye off of it, and I won't, either."

"'Deed I won't; en bless you, honey, I couldn't ef I wanted to."

We went a-tearing along towards it, piling the miles behind us like nothing, but never gaining an inch on it—and all of a sudden it was gone again! Jim staggered, and most fell down. When he got his breath he says, gasping like a fish—

"Mars Tom, hit's a *ghos'*, dat's what it is, en I hopes to goodness we ain't gwyne to see it no mo'. Dey's *ben* a lake, en suthin's happened, en de lake's dead, en we's seen its ghos'; we's seen it twyste, and dat's proof. De Desert's ha'nted, it's ha'nted, sho'; oh, Mars Tom, le's git outen it, I druther die than have de night ketch us in it agin en de ghos' er dat lake come a-mournin' aroun' us en we asleep en doan' know de danger we's in."

"Ghost, you gander! it ain't anything but air and heat and thirstiness pasted together by a person's imagination. If I— gimme the glass!"

He grabbed it and begun to gaze, off to the right.

"It's a flock of birds," he says. "It's getting towards sundown, and they're making a bee line across our track for somewheres. They mean business—maybe they're going for food or water, or both. Let her go to starboard!—port your hellum! Hard down! There—ease up—steady, as you go."

We shut down some of the power, so as not to out-speed them, and took out after them. We went skimming along a quarter of a mile behind them, and when we had followed them an hour and a half and was getting pretty discouraged, and thirsty clean to unendurableness, Tom says—

"Take the glass, one of you, and see what that is, away ahead of the birds."

Jim got the first glimpse, and slumped down on a locker, sick. He was most crying, and says—

"She's dah agin, Mars Tom, she's dah agin, en I knows I's gwyne to die, 'caze when a body sees a ghos' de third time, dat's what it means. I wisht I'd never come in dis balloon, dat I does."

He wouldn't look no more, and what he said made me afraid, too, because I knowed it was true, for that has always been the way with ghosts; so then I wouldn't look any more, either. Both of us begged Tom to turn off and go some other way, but he wouldn't, and said we was ignorant superstitious blatherskites. Yes, and he'll git come up with, one of these days, I says to myself, insulting ghosts that way. They'll stand it for a while, maybe, but they won't stand it always, for anybody that knows about ghosts knows how easy they are hurt, and how revengeful they are.

So we was all quiet and still, Jim and me being scared, and Tom busy. By and by Tom fetched the balloon to a standstill, and says—

"*Now* get up and look, you sapheads."

We done it, and there was the sure-enough water right under us!—clear, and blue, and cool, and deep, and wavy with the breeze, the loveliest sight that ever was. And all about it was grassy banks, and flowers, and shady groves of big trees, looped together with vines, and all looking so peaceful and comfortable, enough to make a body cry, it was so beautiful.

Jim did *did* cry, and rip and dance and carry on, he was so thankful and out of his mind for joy. It was my watch, so I had to stay by the works, but Tom and Jim clumb down and drunk a barrel apiece, and fetched me up a lot, and I've tasted a many a good thing in my life, but nothing that ever begun with that water. Then they went down and had a swim, and then Tom come up and spelled me, and me and Jim had a swim, and then Jim spelled Tom, and me and Tom had a footrace and a boxing-mill, and I don't reckon I ever had such a good time in my life. It warn't so very hot, because it was close on to evening, and we hadn't any clothes on, anyway. Clothes is well enough in school, and in towns, and at balls, too, but there ain't no sense in them when there ain't no civilization nor other kinds of bothers and fussiness around.

"Lions a-comin'!—lions! Quick, Mars Tom, jump for yo' life, Huck!"

Oh, and didn't we! We never stopped for clothes, but waltzed up the ladder just so. Jim lost his head, straight off— he always done it whenever he got excited and scared; and so now, 'stead of just easing the ladder up from the ground a little, so the animals couldn't reach it, he turned on a raft of power, and we went whizzing up and was dangling in the sky before he got his wits together and seen what a foolish thing he was doing. Then he stopped her, but had clean forgot what to do next; so there we was, so high that the lions looked like pups, and we was drifting off on the wind.

But Tom he shinned up and went for the works and begun to slant her down, and back towards the lake, where the animals was gathering like a camp meeting, and I judged he had lost *his* head, too; for he knowed I was too scared to climb, and did he want to dump me amongst the tigers and things?

But no, his head was level, he knowed what he was about. He swooped down to within thirty or forty foot of the lake, and stopped right over the centre, and sung out—

"Leggo, and drop!"

I done it, and shot down, feet first, and seemed to go about a mile towards the bottom; and when I come up, he says—

"Now lay on your back and float till you're rested and got your pluck back, then I'll dip the ladder in the water and you can climb aboard."

I done it.

Now that was ever so smart in Tom, because if he had started off somewheres else to drop down on the sand, the menagerie would a come along, too, and might a kept us hunting a safe place till I got tuckered out and fell.

And all this time the lions and tigers was sorting out the clothes, and trying to divide them up so there would be some for all, but there was a misunderstanding about it somewheres, on accounts of some of them trying to hog more than their share; so there was another insurrection, and you never see anything like it in the world. There must a been fifty of them, all mixed up together, snorting and roaring and snapping and biting and tearing, legs and tails in the air and you couldn't tell which belonged to which, and the sand and fur a-flying. And when they got done, some was dead, and some was limping off crippled, and the rest was setting around on the battle field, some of them licking their sore places and the others looking up at us and seemed to be kind of inviting us to come down and have some fun, but which we didn't want any.

As for the clothes, there warn't any, any more. Every last rag of them was inside of the animals; and not agreeing with them very well, I don't reckon, for there was considerable many brass buttons on them, and there was knives in the pockets, too, and smoking tobacco, and nails and chalk and marbles and fishhooks and things. But I wasn't caring. All that was bothering me was, that all we had, now, was the Professor's clothes, a big enough assortment, but not suitable to go into company with, if we come across any, because the britches was as long as tunnels, and the coats and things according. Still, there was everything a tailor needed, and Jim was a kind of a jack-legged tailor, and he allowed he could soon trim a suit or two down for us that would answer.

Chapter 9

STILL, we thought we would drop down there a minute, but on another errand. Most of the Professor's cargo of food was put up in cans, in the new way that somebody had just invented, the rest was fresh. When you fetch Missouri beefsteak to the Great Sahara, you want to be particular and stay up in the coolish weather. Ours was all right till we stayed down so long amongst the dead people. That spoilt the water, and it ripened up the beefsteak to a degree that was just right for an Englishman, Tom said, but was most too gay for Americans; so we reckoned we would drop down into the lion market and see how we could make out there.

We hauled in the ladder and dropped down till we was just above the reach of the animals, then we let down a rope with a slip-knot in it and hauled up a dead lion, a small tender one, then yanked up a cub tiger. We had to keep the congregation off with the revolver, or they would a took a hand in the proceedings and helped.

We carved off a supply from both, and saved the skins, and hove the rest overboard. Then we baited some of the Professor's hooks with the fresh meat and went a-fishing. We stood over the lake just a convenient distance above the water, and catched a lot of the nicest fish you ever see. It was a most amazing good supper we had: lion steak, tiger steak, fried fish and hot corn pone. I don't want nothing better than that.

We had some fruit to finish off with. We got it out of the top of a monstrous tall tree. It was a very slim tree that hadn't a branch on it from the bottom plum to the top, and there it busted out like a feather-duster. It was a pam tree, of course; anybody knows a pam tree the minute he sees it, by the pictures. We went for coconuts in this one, but there warn't none. There was only big loose bunches of things like oversized grapes, and Tom allowed they was dates, because he said they answered the description in the Arabian Nights and the other books. Of course they mightn't be, and they might be pison; so we had to wait a spell, and watch and see if the birds et them. They done it; so we done it too, and they was most amazing good.

By this time monstrous big birds begun to come and settle on the dead animals. They was plucky creturs; they would tackle one end of a lion that was being gnawed at the other end by another lion. If the lion drove the bird away, it didn't do no good, he was back again the minute the lion was busy.

The big birds come out of every part of the sky—you could make them out with the glass whilst they was still so far away you couldn't see them with your naked eye. The dead meat was too fresh to have any smell—at least any that could reach to a bird that was five mile away; so Tom said the birds didn't find out the meat was there by the smell, they had to find it out by seeing it. Oh, but ain't that an eye for you! Tom said at the distance of five mile a patch of dead lions couldn't look any bigger than a person's finger nail, and he couldn't imagine how the birds could notice such a little thing so far off.

It was strange and unnatural to see lion eat lion, and we thought maybe they warn't kin. But Jim said that didn't make no difference. He said a hog was fond of her own children, and so was a spider, and he reckoned maybe a lion was pretty near as unprincipled though maybe not quite. He thought likely a lion wouldn't eat his own father, if he knowed which was him, but reckoned he would eat his brother-in-law if he was uncommon hungry, and eat his mother-in-law any time. But *reckoning* don't settle nothing. You can reckon till the cows comes home, but that don't fetch you no decision. So we give it up and let it drop.

Generly it was very still in the Desert, nights, but this time there was music. A lot of other animals come to dinner: sneaking yelpers that Tom allowed was jackals, and roach-backed ones that he said was hyenas; and all the whole biling of them kept up a racket all the time. They made a picture in the moonlight that was more different than any picture I ever see. We had a line out and made fast to the top of a tree, and didn't stand no watch, but all turned in and slept, but I was up two or three times to look down at the animals and hear the music. It was like having a front seat at a menagerie for nothing, which I hadn't ever had before, and so it seemed foolish to sleep and not make the most of it, I mightn't ever have such a chance again.

We went a-fishing again in the early dawn, and then lazied around all day in the deep shade on an island, taking turn about to watch and see that none of the animals come a-snooping around there after erronorts for dinner. We was going to leave next day, but couldn't, it was too lovely.

The day after, when we rose up towards the sky and sailed off eastward, we looked back and watched that place till it warn't nothing but just a speck in the Desert, and I tell you it was like saying good bye to a friend that you ain't ever going to see any more.

Jim was thinking to himself, and at last he says—

"Mars Tom, we's mos' to de end er de Desert now, I speck."

"Why?"

"Well, hit stan' to reason we is. You knows how long we's ben a-skimmin' over it. Mus' be mos' out o' san'. Hit's a wonder to me dat it's hilt out as long as it has."

"Shucks, there's plenty sand, you needn't worry."

"Oh, I ain't a-worryin', Mars Tom, only wonderin', dat's all. De Lord's got plenty san', I ain't doubtin' dat, but nemmine, He ain' gwyne to *was'e* it jist on dat account; en I allows dat dis Desert's plenty big enough now, jist de way she is, en you can't spread her out no mo' 'dout was'in' san'."

"Oh, go 'long! we ain't much more than fairly *started* across this Desert yet. The United States is a pretty big country, ain't it? Ain't it, Huck?"

"Yes," I says, "there ain't no bigger one, I don't reckon."

"Well," he says, "this Desert is about the shape of the United States, and if you was to lay it down on top of the United States, it would cover the land of the free out of sight like a blanket. There'd be a little corner sticking out, up at Maine, and away up north-west, and Florida sticking out like a turtle's tail, and that's all. We've took California away from the Mexicans two or three years ago, so that part of the Pacific coast is ours, now, and if you laid the Great Sahara down with her edge on the Pacific she would cover the United States and stick out past New York six hundred miles into the Atlantic ocean."

I says—

"Good land! have you got the documents for that, Tom Sawyer?"

"Yes, and they're right here, and I've been studying them. You can look for yourself. From New York to the Pacific is 2,600 miles. From one end of the Great Desert to the other is 3,200. The United States contains 3,600,000 square miles, the Desert contains 4,162,000. With the Desert's bulk you could cover up every last inch of the United States, and in under where the edges projected out, you could tuck England, Scotland, Ireland, France, Denmark, and all Germany. Yes, sir, you could hide the home of the brave and all of them countries clean out of sight under the Great Sahara, and you would still have 2,000 square miles of sand left."

"Well," I says, "it clean beats me. Why, Tom, it shows that the Lord took as much pains making this Desert as He did to make the United States and all them other countries. I reckon He must a been a-working at this Desert two or three days before He got it done."

Jim says—

"Huck, dat doan' stan' to reason. I reckon dis Desert wan't made, at all. Now you take en look at it like dis—you look at it, and see ef I's right. What's a desert good for? 'Tain't good for nuthin'. Dey ain't no way to make it pay. Hain't dat so, Huck?"

"Yes, I reckon."

"Hain't it so, Mars Tom?"

"I guess so. Go on."

"Ef a thing ain't no good, it's made in vain, ain't it?"

"Yes."

"*Now*, den! Do de Lord make anything in vain? You answer me dat."

"Well—no, He don't."

"Den how come He make a desert?"

"Well, go on. How *did* He come to make it?"

"Mars Tom, it's my opinion He never *made* it, at all; dat is, He didn't plan out no desert, never sot out to make one. Now I's gwyne to show you, den you kin see. *I* b'lieve it uz jes' like when you's buildin' a house; dey's allays a lot o' truck en rubbish lef' over. What does you do wid it? Doan' you take en k'yart it off en dump it onto a ole vacant back lot?

'Course. Now, den, it's my opinion hit was jes' like dat. When de Lord uz gwyne to buil' de worl', He tuck en made a lot o' rocks en put 'em in a pile, en made a lot o' yearth en put it in a pile handy to de rocks, den a lot o' san', en put dat in a pile, handy, too. Den He begin. He measure out some rocks en yearth en san', en stick 'em together en say 'Dat's Germany,' en pas'e a label on it en set it out to dry; en measure out some mo' rocks en yearth en san', en stick 'em together, en say, 'Dat's de United States,' en pas'e a label on it and set *it* out to dry—en so on, en so on, tell it come supper time Sataday, en He look roun' en see dey's all done, en a mighty good worl' for de time she took. Den He notice dat whilst He's cal'lated de yearth en de rocks jes' right, dey's a mos' turrible lot o' san' lef' over, which He can't 'member how it happened. So He look roun' to see if dey's any ole back lot anywheres dat's vacant, en see dis place, en is pow'ful glad, en tell de angels to take en dump de san' here. Now, den, dat's *my* idea 'bout it—dat de Great Sahara warn't *made* at all, she jes' *happen*'."

I said it was a real good argument, and I believed it was the best one Jim ever made. Tom he said the same, but said the trouble about arguments is, they ain't nothing but *theories*, after all, and theories don't prove nothing, they only give you a place to rest on, a spell, when you are tuckered out butting around and around trying to find out something there ain't no way *to* find out. And he says—

"There's another trouble about theories: there's always a hole in them somewheres, sure, if you look close enough. It's just so with this one of Jim's. Look what billions and billions of stars there is. How does it come that there was just exactly enough star-stuff, and none left over? How does it come there ain't no sand-pile up there?"

But Jim was fixed for him and says—

"What's de Milky Way?—dat's what *I* wants to know. What's de Milky Way? Answer me dat!"

In my opinion it was just a sockdologer. It's only an opinion, it's only *my* opinion, and others may think different; but I said it then and I stand to it now—it was a sockdologer. And moreover besides, it landed Tom Sawyer. He couldn't say a word. He had that stunned look of a person that's been shot

in the back with a kag of nails. All he said was, as for people
like me and Jim, he'd just as soon have intellectual intercourse
with a catfish. But anybody can say that—and I notice they always do, when somebody has fetched them a lifter. Tom
Sawyer was tired of that end of the subject.

So we got back to talking about the size of the Desert
again, and the more we compared it with this and that and
t'other thing, the more nobler and bigger and grander it got
to look, right along. And so, hunting amongst the figgers,
Tom found, by and by, that it was just the same size as the
Empire of China. Then he showed us the spread the Empire
of China made on the map and the room she took up in the
world. Well, it was wonderful to think of, and I says—

"Why, I've heard talk about this Desert plenty of times, but
I never knowed, before, how important she was."

Then Tom says—

"Important! Sahara important! That's just the way with
some people. If a thing's big, it's important. That's all the
sense they've got. All they can see is *size*. Why, look at England. It's the most important country in the world; and yet
you could put it in China's vest pocket; and not only that, but
you'd have the dickens's own time to find it again the next
time you wanted it. And look at Russia. It spreads all around
and everywheres, and yet ain't no more important in this
world than Rhode Island is, and hasn't got half as much in it
that's worth saving. My Uncle Abner, which was a Presbyterian preacher and the bluest they made, *he* always said that if
size was a right thing to judge importance by, where would
heaven be, alongside of the other place? He always said
heaven was the Rhode Island of the Hereafter."

Away off, now, we see a low hill, a-standing up just on the
edge of the world. Tom broke off his talk, and reached for a
glass very much excited, and took a look, and says—

"That's it—it's the one I've been looking for, sure. If I'm
right, it's the one the dervish took the man into and showed
him all the treasures of the world."

So we begun to gaze, and he begun to tell about it out of
the Arabian Nights.

Chapter 10

TOM SAID it happened like this.

A dervish was stumping it along through the Desert, on foot, one blazing hot day, and he had come a thousand miles and was pretty poor, and hungry, and ornery and tired, and along about where we are now, he run across a camel driver with a hundred camels, and asked him for some ams. But the camel driver he asked to be excused. The dervish says—

"Don't you own these camels?"

"Yes, they're mine."

"Are you in debt?"

"Who—me? No."

"Well, a man that owns a hundred camels and ain't in debt, is rich—and not only rich, but very rich. Ain't it so?"

The camel driver owned up that it was so. Then the dervish says—

"God has made you rich, and He has made me poor. He has His reasons, and they are wise, blessed be his Name! But He has willed that His rich shall help His poor, and you have turned away from me, your brother, in my need, and He will remember this, and you will lose by it."

That made the camel driver feel shaky, but all the same he was born hoggish after money and didn't like to let go a cent, so he begun to whine and explain, and said times was hard, and although he had took a full freight down to Balsora and got a fat rate for it, he couldn't git no return freight, and so he warn't making no great things out of his trip. So the dervish starts along again, and says—

"All right, if you want to take the risk, but I reckon you've made a mistake this time, and missed a chance."

Of course the camel driver wanted to know what kind of a chance he had missed, because maybe there was money in it; so he run after the dervish and begged him so hard and earnest to take pity on him and tell him, that at last the dervish give in, and says—

"Do you see that hill yonder? Well, in that hill is all the treasures of the earth, and I was looking around for a man with a particular good kind heart and a noble generous disposition, because if I could find just that man, I've got a kind of a salve I could put on his eyes and he could see the treasures and get them out."

So then the camel driver was in a sweat; and he cried, and begged, and took on, and went down on his knees, and said he was just that kind of a man, and said he could fetch a thousand people that would say he wasn't ever described so exact before.

"Well, then," says the dervish, "all right. If we load the hundred camels, can I have half of them?"

The driver was so glad he couldn't hardly hold in, and says—

"Now you're shouting."

So they shook hands on the bargain, and the dervish got out his box and rubbed the salve on the driver's right eye, and the hill opened and he went in, and there, sure enough, was piles and piles of gold and jewels sparkling like all the stars in heaven had fell down.

So him and the dervish laid into it and they loaded every camel till he couldn't carry no more, then they said good bye, and each of them started off with his fifty. But pretty soon the camel driver come a-running and overtook the dervish and says—

"You ain't in society, you know, and you don't really need all you've got. Won't you be good, and let me have ten of your camels?"

"Well," the dervish says, "I don't know but what you say is reasonable enough."

So he done it, and they separated and the dervish started off again with his forty. But pretty soon here comes the camel driver bawling after him again, and whines and slobbers around and begs another ten off of him, saying thirty camel loads of treasures was enough to see a dervish through, because they live very simple, you know, and don't keep house but board around and give their note.

But that warn't the end, yet. That ornery hound kept coming and coming till he had begged back all the camels and had the whole hundred. Then he was satisfied, and ever so grateful, and said he wouldn't ever forgit the dervish as long as he lived, and nobody hadn't ever been so good to him before, and liberal. So they shook hands good bye, and separated and started off again.

But do you know, it warn't ten minutes till the camel driver was unsatisfied again—he was the low-downest reptyle in seven counties—and he come a-running again. And this time the thing he wanted was to get the dervish to rub some of the salve on his other eye.

"Why?" says the dervish.

"Oh, you know," says the driver.

"Know what?" says the dervish.

"Well, you can't fool me," says the driver. "You're trying to keep back something from me, you know it mighty well. You know, I reckon, that if I had the salve on the other eye I could see a lot more things that's valuable. Come—please put it on."

The dervish says—

"I wasn't keeping anything back from you. I don't mind telling you what would happen if I put it on. You'd never see again. You'd be stone blind the rest of your days."

But do you know, that beat wouldn't believe him. No, he begged and begged, and whined and cried, till at last the dervish opened his box and told him to put it on, if he wanted to. So the man done it, and sure enough he was as blind as a bat, in a minute.

Then the dervish laughed at him and mocked at him and made fun of him, and says—

"Good-bye—a man that's blind hain't got no use for jewelry."

And he cleared out with the hundred camels, and left that man to wander around poor and miserable and friendless the rest of his days in the desert.

Jim said he'd bet it was a lesson to him.

"Yes," Tom says, "and like a considerable many lessons a body gets. They ain't no account, because the thing don't ever happen the same way again—and can't. The time Hen Scovil fell down the chimbly and crippled his back for life, everybody said it would be a lesson to him. What kind of a lesson? How was he going to use it? He couldn't climb chimblies no more, and he hadn't no more backs to break."

"All de same, Mars Tom, dey *is* sich a thing as learnin' by expe'ence. De Good Book say de burnt chile shun de fire."

"Well, I ain't denying that a thing's a lesson if it's a thing that can happen twice just the same way. There's lots of such things, and *they* educate a person, that's what uncle Abner always said; but there's forty *million* lots of the other kind—the kind that don't happen the same way twice—and they ain't no real use, they ain't no more instructive than the small pox. When you've got it, it ain't no good to find out you ought to been vaccinated, and it ain't no good to get vaccinated afterwards, because the small-pox don't come but once. But on the other hand Uncle Abner said that the person that had took a bull by the tail once had learnt sixty or seventy times as much as a person that hadn't; and said a person that started in to carry a cat home by the tail was gitting knowledge that was always going to be useful to him, and warn't ever going to grow dim or doubtful. But I can tell you, Jim, Uncle Abner was down on them people that's all the time trying to dig a lesson out of everything that happens, no matter whether—"

But Jim was asleep. Tom looked kind of ashamed, because you know a person always feels bad when he is talking uncommon fine, and thinks the other person is admiring, and that other person goes to sleep that way. Of course he oughtn't to go to sleep, because it's shabby, but the finer a person talks the certainer it is to make you sleepy, and so when you come to look at it it ain't nobody's fault in particular, both of them's to blame.

Jim begun to snore—soft and blubbery, at first, then a long rasp, then a stronger one, then a half a dozen horrible ones like the last water sucking down the plug-hole of a bath-tub, then the same with more power to it, and some big coughs and snorts flung in, the way a cow does that is choking to death; and when the person has got to that point he is at his level best, and can wake up a man that is in the next block with a dipper-full of loddanum in him, but can't wake himself up, although all that awful noise of his'n ain't but three inches from his own ears. And that is the curiosest thing in the world, seems to me. But you rake a match to light the candle, and that little bit of a noise will fetch him. I wish I knowed what was the reason of that, but there don't seem to be no way to find out. Now there was Jim alarming the whole Desert, and yanking the animals out, for miles and miles around, to see what in the nation was going on up there; there warn't nobody nor nothing that was as close to the noise as *he* was, and yet he was the only cretur that wasn't disturbed by it. We yelled at him and whooped at him, it never done no good, but the first time there come a little wee noise that wasn't of a usual kind it woke him up. No, sir, I've thought it all over, and so has Tom, and there ain't no way to find out why a snorer can't hear himself snore.

Jim said he hadn't been asleep, he just shut his eyes so he could listen better.

Tom said nobody warn't accusing him.

That made him look like he wished he hadn't said anything. And he wanted to git away from the subject, I reckon, because he begun to abuse the camel driver, just the way a person does when he has got catched in something and wants to take it out of somebody else. He let into the camel driver the hardest he knowed how, and I had to agree with him; and he praised up the dervish the highest he could, and I had to agree with him there, too. But Tom says—

"I ain't so sure. You call that dervish so dreadful liberal and good and unselfish, but I don't quite see it. He didn't hunt up another poor dervish, did he? No, he didn't. If he was so unselfish, why didn't he go in there himself and take a pocket full of jewels and go along and be satisfied? No, sir, the person he was hunting for was a man with a hundred camels. He wanted to get away with all the treasure he could."

"Why, Mars Tom, he was willin' to divide, fair and square; he only struck for fifty camels."

"Because he knowed how he was going to get all of them by and by."

"Mars Tom, he *tole* de man de truck would make him bline."

"Yes, because he knowed the man's character. It was just the kind of a man he was hunting for—a man that never believes in anybody's word or anybody's honorableness, because he ain't got none of his own. I reckon there's lots of people like that dervish. They swindle, right and left, but they always

make the other person *seem* to swindle himself. They keep inside of the letter of the law all the time, and there ain't no
way to git hold of them. *They* don't put the salve on—oh, no,
that would be sin; but they know how to fool *you* into putting
it on, then it's you that blinds yourself. I reckon the dervish
and the camel driver was just a pair—a fine, smart, brainy rascal, and a dull, coarse, ignorant one, but both of them rascals,
just the same."

"Mars Tom, does you reckon dey's any o' dat kind o' salve
in de worl' now?"

"Yes, uncle Abner says there is. He says they've got it in
New York, and they put it on country people's eyes and show
them all the railroads in the world, and they go in and git
them, and then when they rub the salve on the other eye, the
other man bids them good bye and goes off with their railroads. Here's the treasure-hill, now. Lower away!"

We landed, but it warn't as interesting as I thought it was
going to be, because we couldn't find the place where they
went in to git the treasure. Still, it was plenty interesting
enough, just to see the mere hill itself where such a wonderful thing happened. Jim said he wouldn't a missed it for three
dollars, and I felt the same way.

And to me and Jim, as wonderful a thing as any, was the
way Tom could come into a strange big country like this and
go straight and find a little hump like that and tell it in a
minute from a million other humps that was almost just like
it, and nothing to help him but only his own learning and his
own natural smartness. We talked and talked it over together,
but couldn't make out how he done it. He had the best head
on him I ever see; and all he lacked was age, to make a name
for himself equal to Captain Kidd or George Washington. I
bet you it would a crowded either of *them* to find that hill,
with all their gifts, but it warn't nothing to Tom Sawyer; he
went across Sahara and put his finger on it as easy as you
could pick a nigger out of a bunch of angels.

We found a pond of salt water close by and scraped up a
raft of salt around the edges and loaded up the lion's skin and
the tiger's so as they would keep till Jim could tan them.

Chapter II

WE WENT a-fooling along for a day or two, and then just as the full moon was touching the ground on the other side of the Desert, we see a string of little black figgers moving across its big silver face. You could see them as plain as if they was painted on the moon with ink. It was another caravan. We cooled down our speed and tagged along after it just to have company, though it warn't going our way. It was a rattler, that caravan, and a most bully sight to look at, next morning when the sun come a-streaming across the Desert and flung the long shadders of the camels on the gold sand like a thousand grand-daddy-longlegses marching in procession. We never went very near it, because we knowed better, now, than to act like that and scare people's camels and break up their caravans. It was the gayest outfit you ever see, for rich clothes and nobby style. Some of the chiefs rode on dromedaries, the first we ever see, and very tall, and they go plunging along like they was on stilts, and they rock the man that is on them pretty violent and churn up his dinner considerable, I bet you, but they make noble good time and a camel ain't nowheres with them for speed.

The caravan camped, during the middle part of the day, and then started again about the middle of the afternoon. Before long the sun begun to look very curious. First it kind of turned to brass, and then to copper, and after that it begun to look like a blood red ball, and the air got hot and close, and pretty soon all the sky in the west darkened up and looked thick and foggy, but fiery and dreadful like it looks through a piece of red glass, you know. We looked down and see a big confusion going on in the caravan and a rushing every which way like they was scared, and then they all flopped down flat in the sand and laid there perfectly still.

Pretty soon we see something coming that stood up like an amazing wide wall, and reached from the Desert up into the sky and hid the sun, and it was coming like the nation, too. Then a little faint breeze struck us, and then it come harder,

715

and grains of sand begun to sift against our faces and sting
like fire, and Tom sung out—

"It's a sand-storm—turn your backs to it!"

We done it, and in another minute it was blowing a gale
and the sand beat against us by the shovelfull and the air was
so thick with it we couldn't see a thing. In five minutes the
boat was level full and we was setting on the lockers buried up
to the chin in sand and only our heads out and could hardly
breathe.

Then the storm thinned, and we see that monstrous wall go
a-sailing off across the Desert, awful to look at, I tell you. We
dug ourselves out and looked down, and where the caravan
was before, there wasn't anything but just the sand ocean,
now and all still and quiet. All them people and camels was
smothered and dead and buried—buried under ten foot of
sand, we reckoned, and Tom allowed it might be years before
the wind uncovered them, and all that time their friends
wouldn't ever know what become of that caravan. Tom said—

"*Now* we know what it was that happened to the people we
got the swords and pistols from."

Yes, sir, that was just it. It was as plain as day, now. They
got buried in a sand-storm, and the wild animals couldn't get
at them, and the wind never uncovered them again till they
was dried to leather and warn't fit to eat. It seemed to me we
had felt as sorry for them poor people as a person could for
anybody, and as mournful, too, but we was mistaken; this last
caravan's death went harder with us, a good deal harder. You
see, the others was total strangers, and we never got to feeling acquainted with them at all, except, maybe, a little with
the man that was watching the girl, but it was different with
this last caravan. We was huvvering around them a whole
night and most a whole day, and had got to feeling real
friendly with them, and acquainted. I have found out that
there ain't no surer way to find out whether you like people
or hate them, than to travel with them. Just so with these. We
kind of liked them from the start, and traveling with them put
on the finisher. The longer we traveled with them, and the
more we got used to their ways, the better and better we liked
them and the gladder and gladder we was that we run across
them. We had come to know some of them so well that we

called them by name when we was talking about them, and soon got so familiar and sociable that we even dropped the Miss and the Mister and just used their plain names without any handle, and it did not seem unpolite, but just the right thing. Of course it wasn't their own names, but names we give them. There was Mr. Elexander Robinson and Miss Adaline Robinson, and Col. Jacob McDougal and Miss Harryet McDougal, and Judge Jeremiah Butler and young Bushrod Butler, and these was big chiefs, mostly, that wore splendid great turbans and simmeters, and dressed like the Grand Mogul, and their families. But as soon as we come to know them good, and like them very much, it warn't Mister, nor Judge, nor nothing, any more, but only Elleck, and Addy, and Jake, and Hattie, and Jerry and Buck, and so on.

And you know, the more you join in with people in their joys and their sorrows, the more nearer and dearer they come to be to you. Now we warn't cold and indifferent, the way most travelers is, we was right down friendly and sociable, and took a chance in everything that was going, and the caravan could depend on us to be on hand every time, it didn't make no difference what it was.

When they camped, we camped right over them, ten or twelve hundred foot up in the air. When they et a meal, we et ourn, and it made it ever so much homeliker to have their company. When they had a wedding, that night, and Buck and Addy got married, we got ourselves up in the very starchiest of the Professor's duds for the blow-out, and when they danced we joined in and shook a foot up there.

But it is sorrow and trouble that brings you the nearest, and it was a funeral that done it with us. It was next morning, just in the still dawn. We didn't know the diseased, and he warn't in our set, but that never made no difference, he belonged to the caravan, and that was enough, and there warn't no more sincerer tears shed over him than the ones we dripped on him from up there eleven hundred foot on high.

Yes, parting with this caravan was much more bitterer than it was to part with them others, which was comparative strangers, and been dead so long, anyway. We had knowed these in their lives, and was fond of them, too, and now to

have death snatch them from right before our faces whilst we
was looking, and leave us so lonesome and friendless in the
middle of that big Desert, it did hurt so, and we wished we
mightn't ever make any more friends on that voyage if we was
going to lose them again like that.

We couldn't keep from talking about them, and they was all
the time coming up in our memory, and looking just the way
they looked when we was all alive and happy together. We
could see the line marching, and the shiny spear-heads a-
winking in the sun, we could see the dromedaries lumbering
along, we could see the wedding and the funeral, and more
oftener than anything else we could see them praying, because they didn't allow nothing to prevent that; whenever the
call come, several times a day, they would stop right there,
and stand up and face to the east, and lift back their heads,
and spread out their arms and begin, and four or five times
they would go down on their knees, and then fall forwards
and touch their forehead to the ground.

Well, it warn't good to go on talking about them, lovely as
they was in their life, and dear to us in their life and death both,
because it didn't do no good, and made us too down-hearted.
Jim allowed he was going to live as good a life as he could, so
he could see them again in a better world; and Tom kept still
and didn't tell him they was only Mahometans, it warn't no use
to disappoint him, he was feeling bad enough just as it was.

When we woke up next morning we was feeling a little
cheerfuller, and had had a most powerful good sleep, because
sand is the comfortablest bed there is, and I don't see why
people that can afford it don't have it more. And it's terrible
good ballast, too; I never see the balloon so steady before.

Tom allowed we had twenty tons of it, and wondered what
we better do with it; it was good sand, and it didn't seem
good sense to throw it away. Jim says—

"Mars Tom, can't we tote it back home en sell it? How
long'll it take?"

"Depends on the way we go."

"Well, sah, she's wuth a quarter of a dollar a load, at home,
en I reckon we's got as much as twenty loads, hain't we? How
much would dat be?"

"Five dollars."

"By jings, Mars Tom, le's shove for home right on de spot! Hit's more'n a dollar en a half apiece, hain't it?"

"Yes."

"Well, ef dat ain't makin' money de easiest ever *I* struck! She jes' rained in—never cos' us a lick o' work. Le's mosey right along, Mars Tom."

But Tom was thinking and ciphering away so busy and excited he never heard him. Pretty soon he says—

"Five dollars—sho! Look here, this sand's worth—worth—why, it's worth no end of money."

"How is dat, Mars Tom? Go on, honey, go on!"

"Well, the minute people knows it's genuwyne sand from the genuwyne Desert of Sahara, they'll just be in a perfect state of mind to git hold of some of it to keep on the whatnot in a vial with a label on it for a curiosity. All we got to do, is, to put it up in vials and float around all over the United States and peddle them out at ten cents apiece. We've got all of ten thousand dollars' worth of sand in this boat."

Me and Jim went all to pieces with joy, and begun to shout whoopjamboreehoo, and Tom says—

"And we can keep on coming back and fetching sand, and coming back and fetching more sand, and just keep it a-going till we've carted this whole Desert over there and sold it out; and there ain't ever going to be any opposition, either, because we'll take out a patent."

"My goodness," I says, "we'll be as rich as Creoosote, won't we, Tom?"

"Yes—Creesus, you mean. Why, that dervish was hunting in that little hill for the treasures of the earth, and didn't know he was walking over the real ones for a thousand miles. He was blinder than he made the driver."

"Mars Tom, how much is we gwyne to be wuth?"

"Well, I don't know, yet. It's got to be ciphered, and it ain't the easiest job to do, either, because it's over four million square miles of sand at ten cents a vial."

Jim was awful excited, but this faded it out considerable, and he shook his head and says—

"Mars Tom, we can't 'ford all dem vials—a king couldn't. We better not try to take de whole Desert, Mars Tom, de vials gwyne to bust us, sho'."

Tom's excitement died out, too, now, and I reckoned it was on account of the vials, but it wasn't. He set there thinking, and got bluer and bluer, and at last he says—

"Boys, it won't work; we got to give it up."

"Why, Tom?"

"On account of the duties."

I couldn't make nothing out of that, neither could Jim. I says—

"What *is* our duty, Tom? Because if we can't git around it, why can't we just *do* it? People often has to."

But he says—

"Oh, it ain't that kind of duty. The kind I mean is a tax. Whenever you strike a frontier—that's the border of a country, you know—you find a custom house there, and the gov'ment officers comes and rummages amongst your things and charges a big tax, which they call a duty because it's their duty to bust you if they can, and if you don't pay the duty they'll hog your sand. They call it confiscating, but that don't deceive nobody, it's just hogging, and that's all it is. Now if we try to carry this sand home the way we're pointed now, we got to climb fences till we git tired—just frontier after frontier—Egypt, Arabia, Hindostan, and so on, and they'll all whack on a duty, and so you see, easy enough, we *can't* go *that* road."

"Why, Tom," I says, "we can sail right over their old frontiers; how are *they* going to stop us?"

He looked sorrowful at me, and says, very grave—

"Huck Finn, do you think that would be honest?"

I hate them kind of interruptions. I never said nothing, and he went on—

"Well, we're shut off the other way, too. If we go back the way we've come, there's the New York custom house, and that is worse than all of them others put together, on account of the kind of cargo we've got."

"Why?"

"Well, they can't raise Sahara sand in America, of course, and when they can't raise a thing there, the duty is fourteen hundred thousand per cent on it if you try to fetch it in from where they do raise it."

"There ain't no sense in that, Tom Sawyer."

"Who said there *was*? What do you talk to me like that, for, Huck Finn? You wait till I say a thing's got sense in it before you go to accusing me of saying it."

"All right, consider me crying about it, and sorry. Go on."

Jim says—

"Mars Tom, do dey jam dat duty onto everything we can't raise in America, en don't make no 'stinction twix' anything?"

"Yes, that's what they do."

"Mars Tom, ain't de blessin' o' de Lord de mos' valuable thing dey is?"

"Yes, it is."

"Don't de preacher stan' up in de pulpit en call it down on de people?"

"Yes."

"Whah do it come from?"

"From heaven."

"Yassir! You's jes' right, 'deed you is, honey—it come from heaven, en dat's a foreign country. *Now* den! do dey put a tax on dat blessin'?"

"No, they don't."

"'Course dey don't; en so it stan' to reason dat you's mistaken, Mars Tom. Dey wouldn't put de tax on po' truck like san', dat nobody ain't 'bleeged to have, en leave it off'n de bes' thing dey is, which nobody can't git along widout."

Tom Sawyer was stumped; he see Jim had got him where he couldn't budge. He tried to wiggle out by saying they had *forgot* to put on that tax, but they'd be sure to remember about it, next session of Congress, and then they'd put it on, but that was a poor lame come-off, and he knowed it. He said there warn't nothing foreign that warn't taxed but just that one, and so they couldn't be consistent without taxing it, and to be consistent was the first law of politics. So he stuck to it that they'd left it out unintentional and would be certain to do their best to fix it before they got caught and laughed at.

But I didn't feel no more interest in such things, as long as we couldn't git our sand through, and it made me low-spirited, and Jim the same. Tom he tried to cheer us up by saying he would think up another speculation for us that would be just as good as this one and better, but it didn't do no good, we didn't believe there was any as big as this. It was mighty hard; such a little while ago we was so rich, and could a bought a country and started a kingdom and been celebrated and happy, and now we was so poor and ornery again, and had our sand left on our hands. The sand was looking so lovely, before, just like gold and di'monds, and the feel of it was so soft and so silky and nice, but now I couldn't bear the sight of it, it made me sick to look at it, and I knowed I wouldn't ever feel comfortable again till we got shut of it, and didn't have it there no more to remind us of what we had been and what we had got degraded down to. The others was feeling the same way about it that I was. I knowed it, because they cheered up so, the minute I says le's throw this truck overboard.

Well, it was going to be work, you know, and pretty solid work, too; so Tom he divided it up according to fairness and strength. He said me and him would clear out a fifth apiece, of the sand, and Jim three fifths. Jim he didn't quite like that arrangement. He says—

"'Course I's de stronges', en I's willin' to do a share accordin', but by jings you's kinder pilin' it onto ole Jim, Mars Tom, hain't you?"

"Well, I didn't think so, Jim, but you try your hand at fixing it, and let's see."

So Jim he reckoned it wouldn't be no more than fair if me and Tom done a *tenth* apiece. Tom he turned his back to git room and be private, and then he smole a smile that spread around and covered the whole Sahara to the westard, back to the Atlantic edge of it where we come from. Then he turned around again and said it was a good enough arrangement, and we was satisfied if Jim was. Jim said he was.

So then Tom measured off our two tenths in the bow and left the rest for Jim, and it surprised Jim a good deal to see how much difference there was and what a raging lot of sand his share come to, and said he was powerful glad, now, that he had spoke up in time and got the first arrangement altered, for he said that even the way it was now, there was more sand than enjoyment in his end of the contract, he believed.

Then we laid into it. It was mighty hot work, and tough; so hot we had to move up into cooler weather or we couldn't a stood it. Me and Tom took turn about, and one worked while t'other rested, but there warn't nobody to spell poor old Jim, and he made all that part of Africa damp, he sweated so. We couldn't work good, we was so full of laugh, and Jim he kept fretting and wanting to know what tickled us so, and we had to keep making up things to account for it, and they was pretty poor inventions, but they done well enough, Jim didn't see through them. At last when we got done we was most dead, but not with work but with laughing. By and by Jim was most dead too, but it was with work; then we took turns and spelled him, and he was as thankful as he could be, and would set on the gunnel and swab the sweat, and heave and pant, and say how good we was to a poor old nigger, and he wouldn't ever forgit us. He was always the gratefulest nigger I ever see, for any little thing you done for him. He was only nigger outside; inside he was as white as you be.

Chapter 12

THE NEXT few meals was pretty sandy, but that don't make no difference when you are hungry, and when you ain't it ain't no satisfaction to eat, anyway, and so a little grit in the meat ain't no particular drawback, as far as I can see.

Then we struck the east end of the Desert at last, sailing on a north-east course. Away off on the edge of the sand, in a soft pinky light, we see three little sharp roofs like tents, and Tom says—

"It's the Pyramids of Egypt."

It made my heart fairly jump. You see, I had seen a many and a many a picture of them, and heard tell about them a hundred times, and yet to come on them all of a sudden, that way, and find they was *real*, 'stead of imaginations, most knocked the breath out of me with surprise. It's a curious thing, that the more you hear about a grand and big and bully thing or person, the more it kind of dreamies out, as you may say, and gets to be a big dim wavery figger made out of moonshine and nothing solid to it. It's just so with George Washington, and the same with them Pyramids.

And moreover besides, the things they always said about them seemed to me to be stretchers. There was a feller come to the Sunday school, once, and had a picture of them, and made a speech, and said the biggest Pyramid covered thirteen acres, and was most five hundred foot high, just a steep mountain, all built out of hunks of stone as big as a bureau, and laid up in perfectly regular layers, like stair-steps. Thirteen acres, you see, for just one building; it's a farm. If it hadn't been in Sunday school, I would a judged it was a lie; and outside I was certain of it. And he said there was a hole in the Pyramid, and you could go in there with candles, and go ever so far up a long slanting tunnel, and come to a large room in the stomach of that stone mountain, and there you would find a big stone chest with a king in it, four thousand years old. I said to myself, then, if that ain't a lie I will eat that king if they will fetch him, for even Methusalem warn't that old, and nobody claims it.

As we come a little nearer we see the yaller sand come to an end in a long straight edge like a blanket, and onto it was joined, edge to edge, a wide country of bright green, with a snaky stripe crooking through it, and Tom said it was the Nile. It made my heart jump again, for the Nile was another thing that wasn't real to me. Now I can tell you one thing which is dead certain: if you will fool along over three thousand miles of yaller sand, all glimmery with heat so that it makes your eyes water to look at it, and you've been a considerable part of a week doing it, the green country will look so like home and heaven to you that it will make your eyes water *again*. It was just so with me, and the same with Jim.

And when Jim got so he could believe it *was* the land of Egypt he was looking at, he wouldn't enter it standing up, but got down on his knees and took off his hat, because he said it wasn't fitten for a humble poor nigger to come any other way where such men had been as Moses and Joseph and Pharaoh and the other prophets. He was a Presbyterian, and had a most deep respect for Moses, which was a Presbyterian too, he said. He was all stirred up, and says—

"Hit's de lan' of Egypt, de lan' of Egypt, en I's 'lowed to look at it wid my own eyes! En dah's de river dat was turn' to blood, en I's lookin' at de very same groun' whah de plagues was, en de lice, en de frogs, en de locus', en de hail, en whah dey marked de door-pos', en de angel o' de Lord come by in de darkness o' de night en slew de fust-born in all de lan' of Egypt. Ole Jim ain't worthy to see dis day!"

And then he just broke down and cried, he was so thankful. So between him and Tom there was talk enough, Jim being excited because the land was so full of history—Joseph and his brethren, Moses in the bulrushers, Jacob coming down into Egypt to buy corn, the silver cup in the sack, and all them interesting things, and Tom just as excited too, because the land was so full of history that was in *his* line, about Noureddin, and Bedreddin, and such like monstrous giants, that made Jim's wool rise, and a raft of other Arabian Nights folks, which the half of them never done the things they let on they done, I don't believe.

Then we struck a disappointment, for one of them early-morning fogs started up, and it warn't no use to sail over the top of it, because we would go by Egypt, sure, so we judged it was best to set her by compass straight for the place where the Pyramids was gitting blurred and blotted out, and then drop low and skin along pretty close to the ground and keep a sharp lookout. Tom took the hellum, I stood by to let go the anchor, and Jim he straddled the bow to dig through the fog with his eyes and watch out for danger ahead. We went along a steady gait, but not very fast, and the fog got solider and solider, so solid that Jim looked dim and ragged and smoky through it. It was awful still, and we talked low and was anxious. Now and then Jim would say—

"Highst her a pint, Mars Tom, highst her!" and up she would skip, a foot or two, and we would slide right over a flat-roofed mud cabin, with people that had been asleep on it just beginning to turn out and gap and stretch; and once when a feller was clear up on his hind legs so he could gap and stretch better, we took him a blip in the back and knocked him off. By and by, after about an hour, and everything dead still and we a-straining our ears for sounds and holding our breath, the fog thinned a little, very sudden, and Jim sung out in an awful scare—

"Oh, for de lan's sake, set her back, Mars Tom, here's de biggest giant outen de 'Rabian Nights a-comin' for us!" and he went over backwards in the boat.

Tom slammed on the back-action, and as we slowed to a stand-still, a man's face as big as our house at home looked in over the gunnel, same as a house looks out of its windows, and I laid down and died. I must a been clear dead and gone for as much as a minute or more; then I come to, and Tom had hitched a boat-hook onto the lower lip of the giant and was holding the balloon steady with it whilst he canted his head back and got a good long look up at that awful face.

Jim was on his knees with his hands clasped, gazing up at the thing in a begging way, and working his lips but not getting anything out. I took only just a glimpse, and was fading out again, but Tom says—

"He ain't alive, you fools, it's the Sphinx!"

I never see Tom look so little and like a fly; but that was because the giant's head was so big and awful. Awful, yes, so it was, but not dreadful, any more, because you could see it was a noble face, and kind of sad, and not thinking about you, but about other things and larger. It was stone, reddish stone, and its nose and ears battered, and that give it an abused look, and you felt sorrier for it for that.

We stood off a piece, and sailed around it and over it, and it was just grand. It was a man's head, or maybe a woman's, on a tiger's body a hundred and twenty-five foot long, and there was a dear little temple between its front paws. All but the head used to be under the sand, for hundreds of years, maybe thousands, but they had just lately dug the sand away and found that little temple. It took a power of sand to bury that cretur; most as much as it would to bury a steamboat, I reckon.

We landed Jim on top of the head, with an American flag to protect him, it being a foreign land, then we sailed off to this and that and t'other distance, to git what Tom called effects and perspectives and proportions, and Jim he done the best he could, striking all the different kinds of attitudes and positions he could study up, but standing on his head and working his legs the way a frog does was the best. The further we got away, the littler Jim got, and the grander the Sphinx got, till at last it was only a clothes-pin on a dome, as you might say. That's the way perspective brings out the correct proportions, Tom said; he said Julus Cesar's niggers didn't know how big he was, they was too close to him.

Then we sailed off further and further, till we couldn't see Jim at all, any more, and then that great figger was at its noblest, a-gazing out over the Nile valley so still and solemn and lonesome, and all the little shabby huts and things that was scattered about it clean disappeared and gone, and nothing around it now but a soft wide spread of yaller velvet, which was the sand.

That was the right place to stop, and we done it. We set there a-looking and a-thinking for a half an hour, nobody a-saying anything, for it made us feel quiet and kind of solemn to remember it had been looking out over that valley just that same way, and thinking its awful thoughts all to itself for thousands of years, and nobody can't find out what they are to this day.

At last I took up the glass and see some little black things a-capering around on that velvet carpet, and some more a-climbing up the cretur's back, and then I see two or three little wee puffs of white smoke, and told Tom to look. He done it, and says—

"They're bugs. No—hold on; they—why, I believe they're men. Yes, it's men—men and horses, both. They're hauling a long ladder up onto the Sphinx's back—now ain't that odd? And now they're trying to lean it up a—there's some more puffs of smoke—it's guns! Huck, they're after Jim!"

We clapped on the power, and went for them a-biling. We was there in no time, and come a-whizzing down amongst them, and they broke and scattered every which way, and some that was climbing the ladder after Jim let go all holts and fell. We soared up and found him laying on top of the head panting and most tuckered out, partly from howling for help and partly from scare. He had been standing a siege a long time—a week, *he* said, but it warn't so, it only just seemed so to him because they was crowding him so. They had shot at him, and rained the bullets all around him, but he warn't hit, and when they found he wouldn't stand up and the bullets couldn't git at him when he was laying down, they went for the ladder, and then he knowed it was all up with him if we didn't come pretty quick. Tom was very indignant, and asked him why he didn't show the flag and command them to *git*, in the name of the United States. Jim said he done it, but they never paid no attention. Tom said he would have this thing looked into at Washington, and says—

"You'll see that they'll have to apologize for insulting the flag, and pay an indemnity, too, on top of it, even if they git off *that* easy."

Jim says—

"What's an indemnity, Mars Tom?"

"It's cash, that's what it is."

"Who gits it, Mars Tom?"

"Why, *we* do."

"En who gits de apology?"

"The United States. Or, we can take whichever we please. We can take the apology, if we want to, and let the gov'ment take the money."

"How much money will it be, Mars Tom?"

"Well, in an aggravated case like this one, it will be at least three dollars apiece, and I don't know but more."

"Well, den, we'll take de money, Mars Tom, blame de 'pology. Hain't dat yo' notion, too? En hain't it yourn, Huck?"

We talked it over a little and allowed that that was as good a way as any, so we agreed to take the money. It was a new business to me, and I asked Tom if countries always apologized when they had done wrong, and he says—

"Yes; the little ones does."

We was sailing around examining the Pyramids, you know, and now we soared up and roosted on the flat top of the biggest one, and found it was just like what the man said in the Sunday school. It was like four pairs of stairs that starts broad at the bottom and slants up and comes together in a point at the top, only these stair-steps couldn't be clumb the way you climb other stairs; no, for each step was as high as your chin, and you have to be boosted up from behind. The two other Pyramids warn't far away, and the people moving about on the sand between looked like bugs crawling, we was so high above them.

Tom he couldn't hold himself he was so worked up with gladness and astonishment to be in such a celebrated place, and he just dripped history from every pore, seemed to me. He said he couldn't scarcely believe he was standing on the very identical spot the prince flew from on the Bronze Horse. It was in the Arabian Night times, he said. Somebody give the prince a bronze horse with a peg in its shoulder, and he could git on him and fly through the air like a bird, and go all over the world, and steer it by turning the peg, and fly high or low and land wherever he wanted to.

When he got done telling it there was one of them uncomfortable silences that comes, you know, when a person has been telling a whopper and you feel sorry for him and wish you could think of some way to change the subject and let him down easy, but git stuck and don't see no way, and before you can pull your mind together and *do* something, that silence has got in and spread itself and done the business. I was embarrassed, Jim he was embarrassed, and neither of us couldn't say a word. Well, Tom he glowered at me a minute, and says—

"Come, out with it. What do you think?"

I says—

"Tom Sawyer, *you* don't believe that, yourself."

"What's the reason I don't? What's to hender me?"

"There's one thing to hender you: it couldn't happen, that's all."

"What's the reason it couldn't happen?"

"You tell me the reason it *could* happen."

"This balloon is a good enough reason it could happen, I should reckon."

" *Why* is it?"

" *Why* is it? I never saw such an idiot. Ain't this balloon and the bronze horse the same thing under different names?"

"No, they're not. One is a balloon and the other's a horse. It's very different. Next you'll be saying a house and a cow is the same thing."

"By Jackson, Huck's got him agin! Dey ain't no wigglin' outer dat!"

"Shut your head, Jim; you don't know what you're talking about. And Huck don't. Look here, Huck, I'll make it plain to you, so you can understand. You see, it ain't the mere *form* that's got anything to do with their being similar or unsimi-lar, it's the *principle* involved; and the principle is the same in both. Don't you see, now?"

I turned it over in my mind, and says—

"Tom, it ain't no use. Principles is all very well, but they don't git around that one big fact, that the thing that a bal-loon can do ain't no sort of proof of what a horse can do."

"Shucks, Huck, you don't get the idea at all. Now look here a minute—it's perfectly plain. Don't we fly through the air?"

"Yes."

"Very well. Don't we fly high or fly low, just as we please?"

"Yes."

"Don't we steer whichever way we want to?"

"Yes."

"And don't we land when and where we please?"

"Yes."

"How do we move the balloon and steer it?"

"By touching the buttons."

"*Now* I reckon the thing is clear to you at last. In the other case the moving and steering was done by turning a peg. We touch a button, the prince turned a peg. There ain't an atom of difference, you see. I knowed I could git it through your head if I stuck to it long enough."

He felt so happy he begun to whistle. But me and Jim was silent, so he broke off surprised, and says—

"Looky here, Huck Finn, don't you see it *yet*?"

I says—

"Tom Sawyer, I want to ask you some questions."

"Go ahead," he says, and I see Jim chirk up to listen.

"As I understand it, the whole thing is in the buttons and the peg—the rest ain't of no consequence. A button is one shape, a peg is another shape, but that ain't any matter?"

"No, that ain't any matter, as long as they've both got the same power."

"All right, then. What is the power that's in a candle and in a match?"

"It's the fire."

"It's the same in both, then?"

"Yes, just the same in both."

"All right. Suppose I set fire to a carpenter shop with a match, what will happen to that carpenter shop?"

"She'll burn up."

"And suppose I set fire to this Pyramid with a candle—will she burn up?"

"Of course she won't."

"All right. Now the fire's the same, both times. *Why* does the shop burn, and the Pyramid don't?"

"Because the Pyramid *can't* burn."

"Aha! and *a horse can't fly*!"

"My lan', ef Huck ain't got him agin! Huck's landed him high en dry dis time, *I* tell you! Hit's de smartes' trap I ever see a body walk inter—en ef I—"

But Jim was so full of laugh he got to strangling and couldn't go on, and Tom was that mad to see how neat I had floored him, and turned his own argument agin him and knocked him all to rags and flinders with it that all he could manage to say was that whenever he heard me and Jim try to argue it made him ashamed of the human race. I never said nothing, I was feeling pretty well satisfied. When I have got the best of a person that way, it ain't my way to go around crowing about it the way some people does, for I consider that if I was in his place I wouldn't wish him to crow over me. It's better to be generous, that's what I think.

Chapter 13

BY AND BY we left Jim to float around up there in the neighborhood of the Pyramids, and we clumb down to the hole where you go into the tunnel, and went in with some Arabs and candles, and away in there in the middle of the Pyramid we found a room and a big stone box in it where they used to keep that king, just as the man in the Sunday school said, but he was gone, now, somebody had got him. But I didn't take no interest in the place, because there could be ghosts there, of course; not fresh ones, but I don't like no kind.

So then we come out and got some little donkeys and rode a piece, and then went in a boat another piece, and then more donkeys, and got to Cairo; and all the way the road was as smooth and beautiful a road as ever I see, and had tall date pams on both sides, and naked children everywhere, and the men was as red as copper, and fine and strong and handsome. And the city was a curiosity. Such narrow streets—why, they were just lanes, and crowded with people with turbans, and women with veils, and everybody rigged out in blazing bright clothes and all sorts of colors, and you wondered how the camels and the people got by each other in such narrow little cracks, but they done it—a perfect jam, you see, and everybody noisy. The stores warn't big enough to turn around in, but you didn't have to go in; the storekeeper sat tailor fashion on his counter, smoking his snaky long pipe, and had his things where he could reach them to sell, and he was just as good as in the street, for the camel-loads brushed him as they went by.

Now and then a grand person flew by in a carriage with fancy dressed men running and yelling in front of it and whacking anybody with a long rod that didn't get out of the way. And by and by along comes the Sultan riding horseback at the head of a procession, and fairly took your breath away his clothes was so splendid; and everybody fell flat and laid on his stomach while he went by. I forgot, but a feller helped me remember. He was one that had a rod and run in front.

There was churches, but they don't know enough to keep

Sunday, they keep Friday and break the Sabbath. You have to take off your shoes when you go in. There was crowds of men and boys in the church, setting in groups on the stone floor and making no end of noise—getting their lessons by heart, Tom said, out of the Koran, which they think is a Bible, and people that knows better knows enough to not let on. I never see such a big church in my life before, and most awful high, it was; it made you dizzy to look up; our village church at home ain't a circumstance to it; if you was to put it in there, people would think it was a dry-goods box.

What I wanted to see was a dervish, because I was interested in dervishes on accounts of the one that played the trick on the camel driver. So we found a lot in a kind of a church, and they called themselves Whirling Dervishes; and they did whirl, too, I never see anything like it. They had tall sugar-loaf hats on, and linen petticoats; and they spun and spun and spun, round and round like tops, and the petticoats stood out on a slant, and it was the prettiest thing I ever see, and made me drunk to look at it. They was all Moslems, Tom said, and when I asked him what a Mostem was, he said it was a person that wasn't a Presbyterian. So there is plenty of them in Missouri, though I didn't know it before.

We didn't see half there was to see in Cairo, because Tom was in such a sweat to hunt out places that was celebrated in history. We had a most tiresome time to find the granary where Joseph stored up the grain before the famine, and when we found it it warn't worth much to look at, being such an old tumble-down wreck, but Tom was satisfied, and made more fuss over it than I would make if I stuck a nail in my foot. How he ever found that place was too many for me. We passed as much as forty just like it before we come to it, and any of them would a done for me, but none but just the right one would suit him; I never see anybody so particular as Tom Sawyer. The minute he struck the right one he recconized it as easy as I would reconnize my other shirt if I had one, but how he done it he couldn't any more tell than he could fly; he said so himself.

Then we hunted a long time for the house where the boy lived that learned the cadi how to try the case of the old olives and the new ones, and said it was out of the Arabian Nights and he would tell me and Jim about it when he got time. Well, we hunted and hunted till I was ready to drop, and I wanted Tom to give it up and come next day and git somebody that knowed the town and could talk Missourian and could go straight to the place; but no, he wanted to find it himself, and nothing else would answer. So on we went. Then at last the remarkablest thing happened I ever see. The house was gone—gone hundreds of years ago—every last rag of it gone but just one mud brick. Now a person wouldn't ever believe that a backwoods Missouri boy that hadn't ever been in that town before could go and hunt that place over and find that brick, but Tom Sawyer done it. I know he done it, because I see him do it. I was right by his very side at the time, and see him see the brick and see him reconnize it. Well, I says to myself, how *does* he do it? is it knowledge, or is it instink?

Now there's the facts, just as they happened: let everybody explain it their own way. I've ciphered over it a good deal, and it's my opinion that some of it is knowledge but the main bulk of it is instink. The reason is this. Tom put the brick in his pocket to give to a museum with his name on it and the facts when he went home, and I slipped it out and put another brick considerable like it in its place, and he didn't know the difference—but there was a difference, you see. I think that settles it—it's mostly instink, not knowledge. Instink tells him where the exact *place* is for the brick to be in, and so he reconnizes it by the place it's in, not by the look of the brick. If it was knowledge, not instink, he would know the brick again by the look of it the next time he seen it—which he didn't. So it shows that for all the brag you hear about knowledge being such a wonderful thing, instink is worth forty of it for real unerringness. Jim says the same.

When we got back Jim dropped down and took us in, and there was a young man there with a red skull cap and tassel on and a beautiful blue silk jacket and baggy trousers with a shawl around his waist and pistols in it that could talk English and wanted to hire to us as guide and take us to Mecca and Medina and Central Africa and everywheres for a half a dollar a day and his keep, and we hired him and left, and piled on the power, and by the time we was through dinner we was over the place where the Israelites crossed the Red Sea when

Pharaoh tried to overtake them and was caught by the waters. We stopped, then, and had a good look at the place, and it done Jim good to see it. He said he could see it all, now, just the way it happened; he could see the Israelites walking along between the walls of water, and the Egyptians coming, from away off yonder, hurrying all they could, and see them start in as the Israelites went out, and then, when they was all in, see the walls tumble together and drown the last man of them. Then we piled on the power again and rushed away and huvvered over Mount Sinai, and saw the place where Moses broke the tables of stone, and where the children of Israel camped in the plain and worshiped the golden calf, and it was all just as interesting as could be, and the guide knowed every place as well as I know the village at home.

But we had an accident, now, and it fetched all the plans to a standstill. Tom's old ornery corn-cob pipe had got so old and swelled and warped that she couldn't hold together any longer, notwithstanding the strings and bandages, but caved in and went to pieces. Tom he didn't know *what* to do. The Professor's pipe wouldn't answer, it warn't anything but a mershum, and a person that's got used to a cob pipe knows it lays a long ways over all the other pipes in this world, and you can't git him to smoke any other. He wouldn't take mine, I couldn't persuade him. So there he was.

He thought it over, and said we must scour around and see if we could roust out one in Egypt or Arabia or around in some of these countries, but the guide said no, it warn't no use, they didn't have them. So Tom was pretty glum for a little while, then he chirked up and said he'd got the idea and knowed what to do. He says—

"I've got another corn-cob pipe, and it's a prime one, too, and nearly new. It's laying on the rafter that's right over the kitchen stove at home in the village. Jim, you and the guide will go and get it, and me and Huck will camp here on Mount Sinai till you come back."

"But Mars Tom, we couldn't ever find de village. I could find de pipe, 'caze I knows de kitchen, but my lan', *we* can't ever find de village, nur Sent Louis, nur none o' dem places. We don't know de way, Mars Tom."

That was a fact, and it stumped Tom for a minute. Then he said—

"Looky here, it can be done, sure; and I'll tell you how. You set your compass and sail west as straight as a dart, till you find the United States. It ain't any trouble, because it's the first land you'll strike, the other side of the Atlantic. If it's daytime when you strike it, bulge right on, straight west from the upper part of the Florida coast, and in an hour and three quarters you'll hit the mouth of the Mississippi—at the speed that I'm going to send you. You'll be so high up in the air that the earth will be curved considerable—sorter like a washbowl turned upside down—and you'll see a raft of rivers crawling around every which way, long before you get there, and you can pick out the Mississippi without any trouble. Then you can follow the river north nearly an hour and three quarters, till you see the Ohio come in; then you want to look sharp, because you're getting near. Away up to your left you'll see another thread coming in—that's the Missouri and is a little above St. Louis. You'll come down low, then, so as you can examine the villages as you spin along. You'll pass about twenty-five in the next fifteen minutes, and you'll reconnize ours when you see it—and if you don't, you can yell down and ask."

"Ef it's dat easy, Mars Tom, I reckon we kin do it—yassir, I knows we kin."

The guide was sure of it, too, and thought that he could learn to stand his watch in a little while.

"Jim can learn you the whole thing in a half an hour," Tom said. "This balloon's as easy to manage as a canoe."

Tom got out the chart and marked out the course and measured it, and says—

"To go back west is the shortest way, you see. It's only about seven thousand miles. If you went east, and so on around, it's over twice as far." Then he says to the guide, "I want you both to watch the tell-tale all through the watches, and whenever it don't mark three hundred miles an hour, you go higher or drop lower till you find a storm-current that's going your way. There's a hundred miles an hour in this old thing without any wind to help. There's two-hundred-mile gales to be found, any time you want to hunt for them."

"We'll hunt for them, sir."

"See that you do. Sometimes you may have to go up a couple of miles, and it'll be pison cold, but most of the time you'll find your storm a good deal lower. If you can only strike a cyclone—that's the ticket for you! You'll see by the Professor's books that they travel west in these latitudes; and they travel low, too."

Then he ciphered on the time and says—

"Seven thousand miles, three hundred miles an hour—you can make the trip in a day—twenty-four hours. This is Thursday; you'll be back here Saturday afternoon. Come, now, hustle out some blankets and food and books and things for me and Huck, and you can start right along. There ain't no occasion to fool around—I want a smoke, and the quicker you fetch that pipe the better."

All hands jumped for the things, and in eight minutes our things was out and the balloon was ready for America. So we shook hands good-bye, and Tom give his last orders:

"It's 10 minutes to 2 p.m., now, Mount Sinai time. In 24 hours you'll be home, and it'll be 6 to-morrow morning, village time. When you strike the village, land a little back of the top of the hill, in the woods, out of sight; then you rush down, Jim, and shove these letters in the post office, and if you see anybody stirring, pull your slouch down over your face so they won't know you. Then you go and slip in the back way, to the kitchen and git the pipe, and lay this piece of paper on the kitchen table and put something on it to hold it, and then slide out and git away and don't let Aunt Polly catch a sight of you, nor nobody else. Then you jump for the balloon and shove for Mount Sinai three hundred miles an hour. You won't have lost more than an hour. You'll start back at 7 or 8 a.m., village time, and be here in 24 hours, arriving at 2 or 3 p.m., Mount Sinai time."

Tom he read the piece of paper to us. He had wrote on it—

"THURSDAY AFTERNOON. Tom Sawyer the Erronort sends his love to Aunt Polly from MOUNT SINAI where the Ark was, and so does Huck Finn and she will get it to-morrow morning half past six.*

"TOM SAWYER THE ERRONORT."

*This misplacing of the Ark is probably Huck's error, not Tom's.—M.T.

"That'll make her eyes bug out and the tears come," he says. Then he says—

"Stand by! One—two—three—away you go!"

And away she *did* go! Why, she seemed to whiz out of sight in a second.

Then we found a most comfortable cave that looked out over that whole big plain, and there we camped to wait for the pipe.

The balloon come back all right, and brung the pipe; but Aunt Polly had catched Jim when he was getting it, and anybody can guess what happened: she sent for Tom. So Jim he says—

"Mars Tom, she's out on de porch wid her eye sot on de sky a-layin' for you, en she say she ain't gwyne to budge from dah tell she gits hold of you. Dey's gwyne to be trouble, Mars Tom, 'deed dey is."

So then we shoved for home, and not feeling very gay, neither.

TOM SAWYER, DETECTIVE

AS TOLD BY HUCK FINN

Chapter 1

WELL, it was the next spring after me and Tom Sawyer set our old nigger Jim free the time he was chained up for a runaway slave down there on Tom's uncle Silas's farm in Arkansaw. The frost was working out of the ground and out of the air, too, and it was getting closer and closer onto barefoot time every day; and next it would be marble time, and next mumbletypeg, and next tops and hoops, and next kites, and then right away it would be summer and going in a-swimming. It just makes a boy homesick to look ahead like that and see how far off summer is. Yes, and it sets him to sighing and saddening around, and there's something the matter with him, he don't know what. But anyway, he gets out by himself and mopes and thinks; and mostly he hunts for a lonesome place high up on the hill in the edge of the woods and sets there and looks away off on the big Mississippi down there a-reaching miles and miles around the points where the timber looks smoky and dim it's so far off and still, and everything's so solemn it seems like everybody you've loved is dead and gone and you most wish you was dead and gone too, and done with it all.

Don't you know what that is? It's spring fever. That is what the name of it is. And when you've got it, you want—oh, you don't quite know what it is you *do* want, but it just fairly makes your heart ache, you want it so! It seems to you that mainly what you want is, to get away; get away from the same old tedious things you're so used to seeing and so tired of, and see something new. That is the idea; you want to go and be a wanderer; you want to go wandering far away to strange countries where everything is mysterious and wonderful and romantic. And if you can't do that, you'll put up with considerable less; you'll go anywhere you *can* go, just so as to get away, and be thankful of the chance, too.

Well, me and Tom Sawyer had the spring fever, and had it bad, too; but it warn't any use to think about Tom trying to get away, because, as he said, his aunt Polly wouldn't let him quit school and go traipsing off somers wasting time; so we was pretty blue. We was setting on the front steps one day about sundown talking this way, when out comes his aunt Polly with a letter in her hand and says—

"Tom, I reckon you've got to pack up and go down to Arkansaw—your aunt Sally wants you."

I most jumped out of my skin for joy. I reckoned Tom would fly at his aunt and hug her head off; but if you will believe me he set there like a rock, and never said a word. It made me fit to cry to see him act so foolish, with such a noble chance as this opening up. Why, we might lose it if he didn't speak up and show he was thankful and grateful. But he set there and studied and studied till I was that distressed I didn't know what to do; then he says, very ca'm—and I could a shot him for it:

"Well," he says, "I'm right down sorry, aunt Polly, but I reckon I got to be excused—for the present."

His aunt Polly was knocked so stupid and so mad at the cold impudence of it, that she couldn't say a word for as much as a half a minute, and this give me a chance to nudge Tom and whisper:

"Ain't you got any sense? Sp'iling such a noble chance as this and throwing it away?"

But he warn't disturbed. He mumbled back:

"Huck Finn, do you want me to let her *see* how bad I want to go? Why, she'd begin to doubt, right away, and imagine a lot of sicknesses and dangers and objections, and first you know she'd take it all back. You lemme alone; I reckon I know how to work her."

Now I never would a thought of that. But he was right. Tom Sawyer was always right—the levelest head I ever see, and always *at* himself and ready for anything you might spring on him. By this time his aunt Polly was all straight again, and she left fly. She says:

"You'll be excused! *You* will! Well, I never heard the like of it in all my days! The idea of you talking like that to *me*! Now take yourself off and pack your traps; and if I hear another word out of you about what you'll be excused from and what you won't, I lay *I'll* excuse you—with a hickory!"

She hit his head a thump with her thimble as we dodged by, and he let on to be whimpering as we struck for the stairs.

Up in his room he hugged me, he was so out of his head for gladness because we was going traveling. And he says:

"Before we get away she'll wish she hadn't let me go, but she won't know any way to get around it, now. After what she's said, her pride won't let her take it back."

Tom was packed in ten minutes, all except what his aunt and Mary would finish up for him; then we waited ten more for her to get cooled down and sweet and gentle again; for Tom said it took her ten minutes to unruffle in times when half of her feathers was up, but twenty when they was all up, and this was one of the times when they was all up. Then we went down, being in a sweat to know what the letter said.

She was setting there in a brown study, with it laying in her lap. We set down, and she says:

"They're in considerable trouble down there, and they think you and Huck'll be a kind of a diversion for them—'comfort,' they say. Much of that they'll get out of you and Huck Finn, I reckon. There's a neighbor named Brace Dunlap that's been wanting to marry their Benny for three months, and at last they told him pine blank and once for all, he *couldn't*; so he has soured on them and they're worried about it. I reckon he's somebody they think they better be on the good side of, for they've tried to please him by hiring his no-account brother to help on the farm when they can't hardly afford it and don't want him around anyhow. Who are the Dunlaps?"

"They live about a mile from uncle Silas's place, aunt Polly,—all the farmers live about a mile apart, down there—and Brace Dunlap is a long sight richer than any of the others, and owns a whole grist of niggers. He's a widower thirty-six years old, without any children, and is proud of his money and overbearing, and everybody is a little afraid of him, and knuckles down to him and tries to keep on the good side of him. I judge he thought he could have any girl he wanted, just for the asking, and it must have set him back a good deal when he found he couldn't get Benny. Why, Benny's only half as old as he is, and just as sweet and lovely as—well, you've seen her. Poor old uncle Silas—why, it's pitiful, him trying to curry favor that way—so hard pushed and poor, and yet hiring that useless Jubiter Dunlap to please his ornery brother."

"What a name—Jubiter! Where'd he get it?"

"It's only just a nickname. I reckon they've forgot his real name long before this. He's twenty-seven, now, and has had it ever since the first time he ever went in swimming. The school teacher seen a round brown mole the size of a dime on his left leg above his knee and four little bits of moles around it, when he was naked, and he said it minded him of Jubiter and his moons; and the children thought it was funny, and so they got to calling him Jubiter, and he's Jubiter yet. He's tall, and lazy, and sly, and sneaky, and ruther cowardly, too, but kind of good natured, and wears long brown hair and no beard, and hasn't got a cent, and Brace boards him for nothing, and gives him his old clothes to wear, and despises him. Jubiter is a twin."

"What's t'other twin like?"

"Just exactly like Jubiter—so they say; used to was, anyway, but he hain't been seen for seven years. He got to robbing, when he was nineteen or twenty, and they jailed him; but he broke jail and got away—up North here, somers. They used to hear about him robbing and burglaring now and then, but that was years ago. He's dead, now. At least that's what they say. They don't hear about him any more."

"What was his name?"

"Jake."

There wasn't anything more said for a considerable while; the old lady was thinking. At last she says:

"The thing that is mostly worrying your aunt Sally is the tempers that that man Jubiter gets your uncle into."

Tom was astonished, and so was I. Tom says:

"Tempers? Uncle Silas? Land, you must be joking! I didn't know he *had* any temper."

"Works him up into perfect rages, your aunt Sally says; says he acts as if he would really hit the man, sometimes."

"Aunt Polly, it beats anything I ever heard of. Why, he's just as gentle as mush."

"Well, she's worried, anyway. Says your uncle Silas is like a changed man, on account of all this quarreling. And the neighbors talk about it, and lay all the blame on your uncle, of course, because he's a preacher and hain't got any business to quarrel. Your aunt Sally says he hates to go into the pulpit he's so ashamed; and the people have begun to get cool towards him, and he ain't as popular now as he used to was."

"Well, ain't it strange? Why, aunt Polly, he was always so good and kind and moony and absent-minded and chuckle-headed and lovable—why, he was just an angel! What *can* be the matter of him, do you reckon?"

Chapter 2

W E HAD powerful good luck; because we got a chance in a sternwheeler from away North which was bound for one of them bayous or one-horse rivers away down Louisiana-way, and so we could go all the way down the Upper Mississippi and all the way down the Lower Mississippi to that farm in Arkansaw without having to change steamboats at St. Louis: not so very much short of a thousand miles at one pull.

A pretty lonesome boat; there warn't but few passengers, and all old folks, that set around, wide apart, dozing, and was very quiet. We was four days getting out of the "upper river," because we got aground so much. But it warn't dull—couldn't be for boys that was traveling, of course.

From the very start me and Tom allowed that there was somebody sick in the stateroom next to ourn, because the meals was always toted in there by the waiters. By and by we asked about it—Tom did—and the waiter said it was a man, but he didn't look sick.

"Well, but *ain't* he sick?"

"I don't know; maybe he is, but 'pears to me he's jest letting on."

"What makes you think that?"

"Because if he was sick he would pull his clothes off *some* time or other, don't you reckon he would? Well, this one don't. At least he don't ever pull off his boots, anyway."

"The mischief he don't! Not even when he goes to bed?"

"No."

It was always nuts for Tom Sawyer—a mystery was. If you'd lay out a mystery and a pie before me and him, you wouldn't have to say take your choice, it was a thing that would regulate itself. Because in my nature I have always run to pie, whilst in his nature he has always run to mystery. People are made different. And it is the best way. Tom says to the waiter:

"What's the man's name?"

"Phillips."

"Where'd he come aboard?"

"I think he got aboard at Elexandria, up on the Iowa line."

"What do you reckon he's a-playing?"

"I hain't any notion—I never thought of it."

I says to myself, here's another one that runs to pie.

"Anything peculiar about him?—the way he acts or talks?"

"No—nothing, except he seems so scary, and keeps his doors locked night and day both, and when you knock he won't let you in till he opens the door a crack and sees who it is."

"By jimminy, it's intresting! I'd like to get a look at him. Say—the next time you're going in there, don't you reckon you could spread the door and—"

"No indeedy! He's always behind it. He would block that game."

Tom studied over it, and then he says:

"Looky-here. You lend me your apern and let me take him his breakfast in the morning. I'll give you a quarter."

The boy was plenty willing enough, if the head steward wouldn't mind. Tom says that's all right, he reckoned he could fix it with the head steward; and he done it. He fixed it so as we could both go in with aperns on and toting vittles.

He didn't sleep much, he was in such a sweat to get in there and find out the mystery about Phillips; and moreover he done a lot of guessing about it all night, which warn't no use, for if you are going to find out the facts of a thing, what's the sense in guessing out what ain't the facts and wasting ammunition? I didn't lose no sleep. I wouldn't give a dern to know what's the matter of Phillips, I says to myself.

Well, in the morning we put on the aperns and got a couple of trays of truck, and Tom he knocked on the door. The man opened it a crack, and then he let us in and shut it quick. By Jackson, when we got a sight of him we most dropped the trays! and Tom says:

"Why, Jubiter Dunlap, where'd *you* come from!"

Well, the man was astonished, of course; and first-off he looked like he didn't know whether to be scared, or glad, or both, or which, but finally he settled down to being glad; and then his color come back, though at first his face had turned pretty white. So we got to talking together while he et his breakfast. And he says:

"But I ain't Jubiter Dunlap. I'd just as soon tell you who I am, though, if you'll swear to keep mum, for I ain't no Phillips, either."

Tom says:

"We'll keep mum, but there ain't any need to tell who you are if you ain't Jubiter Dunlap."

"Why?"

"Because if you ain't him you're t'other twin, Jake. You're the spit'n image of Jubiter."

"Well, I *am* Jake. But looky-here, how do you come to know us Dunlaps?"

Tom told about the adventures we'd had down there at his uncle Silas's last summer; and when he see that there warn't anything about his folks,—or him either, for that matter— that we didn't know, he opened out and talked perfectly free and candid. He never made any bones about his own case; said he'd been a hard lot, was a hard lot yet, and reckoned he'd *be* a hard lot plum to the end. He said of course it was a dangersome life, and—

He give a kind of a gasp, and set his head like a person that's listening. We didn't say anything, and so it was very still for a second or so and there warn't no sounds but the screaking of the woodwork and the chug-chugging of the machinery down below.

Then we got him comfortable again, telling him about his people, and how Brace's wife had been dead three years, and Brace wanted to marry Benny and she shook him, and Jubiter was working for uncle Silas, and him and uncle Silas quarreling all the time—and then he let go and laughed.

"Land!" he says, "it's like old times to hear all this tittle-tattle, and does me good. It's been seven years and more since I heard any. How do they talk about me these days?"

"Who?"

"The farmers—and the family."

"Why, they don't talk about you at all—at least only just a mention, once in a long time."

"The nation!" he says, surprised, "why is that?"

"Because they think you are dead long ago."

"No! Are you speaking true?—honor bright, now." He jumped up, excited.

"Honor bright. There ain't anybody thinks you are alive."

"Then I'm saved—I'm saved, sure! I'll go home. They'll hide me and save my life. You keep mum. Swear you'll keep mum—swear you'll never, never tell on me. Oh, boys, be good to a poor devil that's being hunted day and night, and dasn't show his face! I've never done you any harm—I'll never do you any, as God is in the heavens—swear you'll be good to me and help me save my life!"

We'd a swore it if he'd been a dog; and so we done it. Well, he couldn't love us enough for it or be grateful enough, poor cuss; it was all he could do to keep from hugging us.

We talked along, and he got out a little handbag and begun to open it, and told us to turn our backs. We done it, and when he told us to turn again he was perfectly different to what he was before. He had on blue goggles and the naturalest-looking long brown whiskers and mustashers you ever see. His own mother wouldn't a knowed him. He asked us if he looked like his brother Jubiter, now.

"No," Tom said, "there ain't anything left that's like him except the long hair."

"All right, I'll get that cropped close to my head before I get there; then him and Brace will keep my secret, and I'll live with them as being a stranger and the neighbors won't ever guess me out. What do you think?"

Tom he studied a while, then he says:

"Well, of course me and Huck are going to keep mum there, but if you don't keep mum yourself there's going to be a little bit of a risk—it ain't much, maybe, but it's a little. I mean, if you talk won't people notice that your voice is just like Jubiter's, and mightn't it make them think of the twin they reckoned was dead but maybe after all was hid all this time under another name?"

"By George," he says, "you're a sharp one! You're perfectly right. I've got to play deef and dumb when there's a neighbor around. If I'd struck for home and forgot that little detail— However, I wasn't striking for home. I was breaking for any place where I could get away from these fellows that are after me; then I was going to put on this disguise and get some different clothes and—"

He jumped for the outside door and laid his ear against

it and listened, pale and kind of panting. Presently he whispers—

"Sounded like cocking a gun! Lord what a life to lead!"

Then he sunk down in a chair all limp and sick-like, and wiped the sweat off of his face.

Chapter 3

FROM THAT time out, we was with him most all the time, and one or t'other of us slept in his upper berth. He said he had been so lonesome, and it was such a comfort to him to have company, and somebody to talk to in his troubles. We was in a sweat to find out what his secret was, but Tom said the best way was not to seem anxious, then likely he would drop into it himself in one of his talks, but if we got to asking questions he would get suspicious and shet up his shell. It turned out just so. It warn't no trouble to see that he *wanted* to talk about it, but always along at first he would scare away from it when he got on the very edge of it, and go to talking about something else. At last he come out with it, though. The way it come about, was this. He got to asking us, kind of indifferent-like, about the passengers down on deck. We told him about them. But he warn't satisfied; we warn't particular enough. He told us to describe them better. Tom done it. At last, when Tom was describing one of the roughest and raggedest ones, he give a shiver and a gasp and says:

"Oh, lordy, that's one of them! They're aboard sure—I just knowed it. I sort of hoped I had got away, but I never believed it. Go on."

Presently when Tom was describing another mangy rough deck passenger, he give that shiver again and says—

"That's him!—that's the other one. If it would only come a good black stormy night and I could get ashore! You see, they've got spies on me. They've got a right to come up and buy drinks at the bar yonder forrard, and they take that chance to bribe somebody to keep watch on me—porter or boots or somebody. If I was to slip ashore without anybody seeing me they would know it inside of an hour."

So then he got to wandering along and pretty soon, sure enough, he was telling! He was poking along through his ups and downs, and when he come to that place he went right along. He says:

"It was a confidence-game. We played it on a julery shop in St. Louis. What we was after was a couple of noble big di'-

monds as big as hazelnuts, which everybody was running to see. We was dressed up fine, and we played it on them in broad daylight. We ordered the di'monds sent to the hotel for us to see if we wanted to buy, and when we was examining them we had paste counterfeits all ready, and *them* was the things that went back to the shop when we said the water wasn't quite fine enough for twelve thousand dollars."

"Twelve—thousand—dollars!" Tom says. "Was they really worth all that money, do you reckon?"

"Every cent of it."

"And you fellows got away with them?"

"As easy as nothing. I don't reckon the julery people know they've been robbed, yet. But it wouldn't be good sense to stay around St. Louis, of course, so we considered where we'd go. One was for going one way, one another; so we throwed up heads or tails and the upper Mississippi won. We done up the di'monds in a paper and put our names on it and put it in the keep of the hotel clerk and told him not to ever let either of us have it again without the others was on hand to see it done; then we went down town, each by his own self—because I reckon maybe we all had the same notion. I don't know for certain, but I reckon maybe we had."

"What notion?" Tom says.

"To rob the others."

"What—one take everything, after all of you had helped to get it?"

"Cert'nly."

It disgusted Tom Sawyer, and he said it was the orneriest low-downest thing he ever heard of. But Jake Dunlap said it warn't unusual in the profession. Said when a person was in that line of business he'd got to look out for his own intrust, there warn't nobody else going to do it for him. And then he went on. He says:

"You see, the trouble was, you couldn't divide up two di'-monds amongst three. If there'd been three—but never mind about that, there *warn't* three. I loafed along the back streets studying and studying. And I says to myself, I'll hog them di'-monds the first chance I get, and I'll have a disguise all ready, and I'll give the boys the slip, and when I'm safe away I'll put it on, and then let them find me if they can. So I got the false whiskers and the goggles and this countrified suit of clothes, and fetched them along back in a hand-bag; and when I was passing a shop where they sell all sorts of things, I got a glimpse of one of my pals through the window. It was Bud Dixon. I was glad, you bet. I says to myself, I'll see what he buys. So I kept shady, and watched. Now what do you reckon it was he bought?"

"Whiskers?" says I.

"No."

"Goggles?"

"No."

"Oh, keep still, Huck Finn, can't you, you're only just hendering all you can. What *was* it he bought, Jake?"

"You'd never guess in the world. It was only just a screwdriver—just a wee little bit of a screw-driver."

"Well, I declare! What did he want with that?"

"That's what *I* thought. It was curious. It clean stumped me. I says to myself, what can he want with that thing? Well, when he come out I stood back out of sight and then tracked him to a second-hand slop-shop and see him buy a red flannel shirt and some old ragged clothes—just the ones he's got on now, as you've described. Then I went down to the wharf and hid my things aboard the up-river boat that we had picked out, and then started back and had another streak of luck. I seen our other pal lay in *his* stock of old rusty secondhanders. We got the di'monds and went aboard the boat.

"But now we was up a stump, for we couldn't go to bed. We had to set up and watch one another. Pity, that was; pity to put that kind of a strain on us, because there was bad blood between us from a couple of weeks back, and we was only friends in the way of business. Bad anyway, seeing there was only two di'monds betwixt three men. First we had supper, and then tramped up and down the deck together smoking till most midnight, then we went and set down in my stateroom and locked the doors and looked in the piece of paper to see if the di'monds was all right, then laid it on the lower berth right in full sight; and there we set, and set, and by and by it got to be dreadful hard to keep awake. At last Bud Dixon he dropped off. As soon as he was snoring a good regular gait that was likely to last, and had his chin on his breast and looked permanent, Hal Clayton nodded towards the di'monds and then towards the outside door, and I understood. I reached and got the paper, and then we stood up and waited perfectly still; Bud never stirred; I turned the key of the outside door very soft and slow, then turned the knob the same way and we went tip-toeing out onto the guard and shut the door very soft and gentle.

"There warn't nobody stirring, anywhere, and the boat was slipping along, swift and steady, through the big water in the smoky moonlight. We never said a word, but went straight up onto the hurricane deck and plum back aft and set down on the end of the skylight. Both of us knowed what that meant, without having to explain to one another. Bud Dixon would wake up and miss the swag, and would come straight for us, for he ain't afeard of anything or anybody, that man ain't. He would come, and we would heave him overboard, or get killed trying. It made me shiver, because I ain't as brave as some people, but if I showed the white feather—well, I knowed better than do that. I kind of hoped the boat would land somers and we could skip ashore and not have to run the risk of this row, I was so scared of Bud Dixon, but she was an upper-river tub and there warn't no real chance of that.

"Well, the time strung along and along, and that feller never come! Why, it strung along till dawn begun to break, and still he never come. 'Thunder,' I says, 'what do you make out of this?—ain't it suspicious?' 'Land!' Hal says, 'do you reckon he's playing us?—open the paper!' I done it, and by gracious there warn't anything in it but a couple of little pieces of loaf sugar! *That's* the reason he could set there and snooze all night so comfortable. Smart? Well, I reckon! He had had them two papers all fixed and ready, and he had put one of them in place of t'other right under our noses.

"We felt pretty cheap. But the thing to do, straight off, was to make a plan; and we done it. We would do up the paper again, just as it was, and slip in, very elaborate and soft, and lay it on the bunk again and let on *we* didn't know about any trick and hadn't any idea he was a-laughing at us behind them bogus snores of his'n; and we would stick by him, and the first night we was ashore we would get him drunk and search him, and get the di'monds; and *do* for him, too, if it warn't too risky. If we got the swag, we'd *got* to do for him, or he would hunt us down and do for us, sure. But I didn't have no real hope. I knowed we could get him drunk,—he was always ready for that—but what's the good of it? You might search him a year and never find—

"Well, right there I catched my breath and broke off my thought! For an idea went ripping through my head that tore my brains to rags—and land, but I felt gay and good! You see, I had had my boots off, to unswell my feet, and just then I took up one of them to put it on, and I catched a glimpse of the heel-bottom, and it just took my breath away. You re-member about that puzzlesome little screw-driver?"

"You bet I do," says Tom, all excited.

"Well, when I catched that glimpse of that boot-heel, the idea that went smashing through my head was, *I* know where he's hid the di'monds! You look at this boot-heel, now. See, it's bottomed with a steel plate, and the plate is fastened on with little screws. Now there wasn't a screw about that feller anywhere but in his boot-heels; so, if he needed a screw-driver I reckoned I knowed why."

"Huck, ain't it bully!" says Tom.

"Well, I got my boots on and we went down and slipped in and laid the paper of sugar on the berth and set down soft and sheepish and went to listening to Bud Dixon snore. Hal Clayton dropped off pretty soon, but I didn't; I wasn't ever so wide awake in my life. I was spying out from under the shade of my hat brim, searching the floor for leather. It took me a long time, and I begun to think maybe my guess was wrong, but at last I struck it. It laid over by the bulkhead, and was nearly the color of the carpet. It was a little round plug about as thick as the end of your little finger, and I says to myself there's a di'mond in the nest you've come from. Be-fore long I spied out the plug's mate.

"Think of the smartness and the coolness of that blather-skite! He put up that scheme on us and reasoned out what we would do, and we went ahead and done it perfectly exact, like a couple of pudd'nheads. He set there and took his own time to unscrew his heel-plates and cut out his plugs and stick in the di'monds and screw on his plates again. He allowed we would steal the bogus swag and wait all night for him to come up and get drownded, and by George it's just what we done! *I* think it was powerful smart."

"You bet your life it was!" says Tom, just full of admiration.

Chapter 4

WELL, all day we went through the humbug of watching one another, and it was pretty sickly business for two of us and hard to act out, I can tell you. About night we landed at one of them little Missouri towns high up towards Iowa, and had supper at the tavern, and got a room up stairs with a cot and a double bed in it, but I dumped my bag under a deal table in the dark hall whilst we was moving along it to bed, single file, me last, and the landlord in the lead with a tallow candle. We had up a lot of whisky and went to playing high-low-jack for dimes, and as soon as the whisky begun to take hold of Bud we stopped drinking but we didn't let him stop. We loaded him till he fell out of his chair and laid there snoring.

"We was ready for business, now. I said we better pull our boots off, and his'n too, and not make any noise, then we could pull him and haul him around and ransack him without any trouble. So we done it. I set my boots and Bud's side by side, where they'd be handy. Then we stripped him and searched his seams and his pockets and his socks and the inside of his boots, and everything, and searched his bundle. Never found any di'monds. We found the screw-driver, and Hal says, 'What do you reckon he wanted with that?' I said I didn't know; but when he wasn't looking I hooked it. At last Hal he looked beat and discouraged and said we'd got to give it up. That was what I was waiting for. I says:

" 'There's one place we hain't searched.'

" 'What place is that?' he says.

" 'His stomach.'

" 'By gracious, I never thought of that! *Now* we're on the home stretch, to a dead moral certainty. How'll we manage?'

" 'Well,' I says, 'just stay by him till I turn out and hunt up a drug store and I reckon I'll fetch something that'll make them di'monds tired of the company they're keeping.'

"He said that's the ticket, and with him looking straight at me I slid myself into Bud's boots instead of my own, and he never noticed. They was just a shade large for me, but that was considerable better than being too small. I got my bag as I went a-groping through the hall, and in about a minute I was out the back way and stretching up the river road at a five-mile gait.

"And not feeling so very bad, neither—walking on di'-monds don't have no such effect. When I had gone fifteen minutes I says to myself there's more'n a mile behind me and everything quiet. Another five minutes and I says there's considerable more land behind me now, and there's a man back there that's begun to wonder what's the trouble. Another five and I says to myself he's getting real uneasy—he's walking the floor, now. Another five, and I says to myself, there's two mile and a half behind me, and he's *awful* uneasy—beginning to cuss, I reckon. Pretty soon I says to myself, forty minutes gone—he *knows* there's something up! Fifty minutes—the truth's a-busting on him, now! he is reckoning I found the di'monds whilst we was searching, and shoved them in my pocket and never let on—yes, and he's starting out to hunt for me. He'll hunt for new tracks in the dust, and they'll as likely send him down the river as up.

"Just then I see a man coming down on a mule, and before I thought I jumped into the bush. It was stupid! When he got abreast he stopped and waited a little for me to come out; then he rode on again. But I didn't feel gay any more. I says to myself I've botched my chances by that; I surely have, if he meets up with Hal Clayton.

"Well, about three in the morning I fetched Elexandria and see this sternwheeler laying there and was very glad, because I felt perfectly safe, now, you know. It was just daybreak. I went aboard and got this stateroom and put on these clothes and went up in the pilot house—to watch, though I didn't reckon there was any need of it. I set there and played with my di'monds and waited and waited for the boat to start, but she didn't. You see, they was mending her machinery, but I didn't know anything about it, not being very much used to steamboats.

"Well, to cut the tale short, we never left there till plum noon; and long before that I was hid in this stateroom; for before breakfast I see a man coming, away off, that had a gait like Hal Clayton's, and it made me just sick. I says to myself, it's him, sure. If he finds out I'm aboard this boat, he's got me like a rat in a trap. All he's got to do is to have me watched, and wait—wait till I slip ashore, thinking he is a thousand miles away, then slip after me and dog me to a good place and make me give up the di'monds, and then he'll—oh, *I* know what he'll do! Ain't it awful—awful! And now to think the *other* one's aboard, too! Oh, ain't it hard luck, boys—ain't it hard! But you'll help save me, *won't* you?—oh, boys, be good to a poor devil that's being hunted to death, and save me—I'll worship the very ground you walk on!"

We turned in and soothed him down and told him we would plan for him and help him and he needn't be so afeard; and so, by and by he got to feeling kind of comfortable again, and unscrewed his heel-plates and held up his di'monds this way and that admiring them and loving them; and when the light struck into them they *was* beautiful, sure; why they seemed to kind of bust, and snap fire out all around. But all the same I judged he was a fool. If I had been him I would 'a' handed the di'monds to them pals and got them to go ashore and leave me alone. But he was made different. He said it was a whole fortune and he couldn't bear the idea.

Twice we stopped to fix the machinery and laid a good while, once in the night; but it wasn't dark enough and he was afeard to skip. But the third time we had to fix it there was a better chance. We laid up at a country woodyard about forty mile above uncle Silas's place a little after one at night, and it was thickening up and going to storm. So Jake he laid for a chance to slide. We begun to take in wood. Pretty soon the rain come a-drenching down, and the wind blowed hard. Of course every boat-hand fixed a gunny sack and put it on like a bonnet the way they do when they are toting wood and we got one for Jake and he slipped down aft with his hand-bag and come tramping forrard in the rank of men, and he looked just like the rest, and walked ashore with them and when we see him pass out of the light of the torch-basket and get swallowed up in the dark we got our breath again and just felt grateful and splendid. But it wasn't for long. Somebody told, I reckon; for in about eight or ten minutes them two pals come tearing forrard as tight as they could jump, and darted ashore and was gone. We waited plum till dawn for them to come back, and kept hoping they would, but they never did. We was awful sorry and low spirited. All the hope we had was, that Jake had got such a start that they couldn't get on his track and he would get to his brother's and hide there and be safe.

He was going to take the river road, and told us to find out if Brace and Jubiter was to home and no strangers there, and then slip out about sundown and tell him. Said he would wait for us in a little bunch of sycamores right back of Tom's uncle Silas's tobacker field, on the river road, a lonesome place.

We set and talked a long time about his chances, and Tom said he was all right if the pals struck up the river instead of down, but it wasn't likely, because maybe they knowed where he was from; more likely they would go right, and dog him all day, him not suspecting, and kill him when it come dark and take the boots. So we was pretty sorrowful.

Chapter 5

WE DIDN'T get done tinkering the machinery till away late in the afternoon, and so it was so close to sundown when we got home that we never stopped on our road but made a break for the sycamores as tight as we could go, to tell Jake what the delay was, and have him wait till we could go to Brace's and find out how things was, there. It was getting pretty dim by the time we turned the corner of the woods, sweating and panting with that long run, and see the sycamores thirty yards ahead of us; and just then we see a couple of men run into the bunch and heard two or three terrible screams for help. "Poor Jake is killed, sure," we says. We was scared through and through, and broke for the tobacker field and hid there, trembling so our clothes would hardly stay on; and just as we skipped in there a couple of men went tearing by, and into the bunch they went, and in a second out jumps four men and took out up the road as tight as they could go, two chasing two.

We laid down, kind of weak and sick, and listened for more sounds, but didn't hear none, for a good while, but just our hearts. We was thinking of that awful thing laying yonder in the sycamores, and it seemed like being that close to a ghost, and it give me the cold shudders. The moon come a-swelling up out of the ground, now, powerful big and round and bright, behind a comb of trees, like a face looking through prison bars, and the black shadders and white places begun to creep around and it was miserable quiet and still and night-breezy and grave-yardy and scary. All of a sudden Tom whispers:

"Look!—what's that?"

"Don't!" I says. "Don't take a person by surprise that way. I'm most ready to die, anyway, without you doing that."

"Look, I tell you. It's something coming out of the sycamores."

"*Don't*, Tom!"

"It's terrible tall!"

"Oh, lordy-lordy! let's—"

"Keep still—it's a-coming this way."

He was so excited he could hardly get breath enough to whisper. I had to look, I couldn't help it. So now we was both on our knees with our chins on a fence-rail and gazing—Yes, and gasping, too. It was coming down the road—coming in the shadder of the trees, and you couldn't see it good; not till it was pretty close to us; then it stepped into a bright splotch of moonlight and we sunk right down in our tracks—it was Jake Dunlap's ghost! That was what we said to ourselves.

We couldn't stir for a minute or two; then it was gone. We talked about it in low voices. Tom says:

"They're mostly dim and smoky, or like they're made out of fog, but this one wasn't."

"No," I says, "I seen the goggles and the whiskers perfectly plain."

"Yes, and the very colors in them loud countrified Sunday clothes—plaid breeches, green and black—"

"Cotton-velvet westcot, fire-red and yaller squares—"

"Leather straps to the bottoms of the breeches-legs and one of them hanging unbuttoned—"

"Yes, and that hat—"

"What a hat for a ghost to wear!"

You see it was the first season anybody wore that kind—a black stiff-brim stove-pipe, very high, and not smooth, with a round top—just like a sugar-loaf.

"Did you notice if its hair was the same, Huck?"

"No—seems to me I did, then again it seems to me I didn't."

"I didn't either, but it had its bag along, I noticed that."

"So did I. How can there be a ghost-bag, Tom?"

"Sho! I wouldn't be as ignorant as that if I was you, Huck Finn. Whatever a ghost has, turns to ghost-stuff. They've got to have their things, like anybody else. You see, yourself, that its clothes was turned to ghost-stuff. Well, then, what's to hender its bag from turning, too? Of course it done it."

That was reasonable. I couldn't find no fault with it. Bill Withers and his brother Jack come along by, talking, and Jack says:

"What do you reckon it was he was toting?"

"I dunno; but it was pretty heavy."

"Yes, all he could lug. Nigger stealing corn from old parson Silas, I judged."

"So did I. And so I allowed I wouldn't let on to see him."

"That's me, too!"

Then they both laughed, and went on out of hearing. It showed how unpopular old uncle Silas had got to be, now. They wouldn't 'a' let a nigger steal anybody else's corn and never done anything to him.

We heard some more voices mumbling along towards us and getting louder, and sometimes a cackle of a laugh. It was Lem Beebe and Jim Lane. Jim Lane says:

"Who?—Jubiter Dunlap?"

"Yes."

"Oh, I don't know. I reckon so. I seen him spading up some ground along about an hour ago, just before sun-down—him and the parson. Said he guessed he wouldn't go to-night, but we could have his dog if we wanted him."

"Too tired, I reckon."

"Yes—works so hard!"

"Oh, you bet!"

They cackled at that, and went on by. Tom said we better jump out and tag along after them, because they was going our way and it wouldn't be comfortable to run across the ghost all by ourselves. So we done it, and got home all right.

That night was the second of September—a Saturday. I shan't ever forget it. You'll see why, pretty soon.

Chapter 6

W E TRAMPED along behind Jim and Lem till we come to the back stile where old Jim's cabin was that he was captivated in, the time we set him free, and here come the dogs piling around us to say howdy, and there was the lights of the house, too; so we warn't afeard, any more, and was going to climb over, but Tom says:

"Hold on; set down here a minute. By George!"

"What's the matter?" says I.

"Matter enough!" he says. "Wasn't you expecting we would be the first to tell the family who it is that's been killed yonder in the sycamores, and all about them rapscallions that done it, and about the di'monds they've smouched off of the corpse, and paint it up fine and have the glory of being the ones that knows a lot more about it than anybody else?"

"Why, of course. It wouldn't be you, Tom Sawyer, if you was to let such a chance go by. I reckon it ain't going to suffer none for lack of paint," I says, "when you start in to scollop the facts."

"Well, now," he says, perfectly ca'm, "what would you say if I was to tell you I ain't going to start in at all?"

I was astonished to hear him talk so. I says:

"I'd say it's a lie. You ain't in earnest, Tom Sawyer."

"You'll soon see. Was the ghost barefooted?"

"No it wasn't. What of it?"

"You wait—I'll show you what. Did it have its boots on?"

"Yes. I seen them plain."

"Swear it?"

"Yes, I swear it."

"So do I. Now do you know what that means?"

"No. What does it mean?"

"Means that them thieves *didn't get the di'monds!*"

"Jimminy! What makes you think that?"

"I don't only think it, I know it. Didn't the breeches and goggles and whiskers and hand-bag and every blessed thing turn to ghost-stuff? Everything it had on turned, didn't it? It shows that the reason its boots turned, too, was because it still had them on after it started to go ha'nting around, and if that ain't proof that them blatherskites didn't get the boots I'd like to know what you'd *call* proof."

Think of that, now. I never see such a head as that boy had. Why *I* had eyes and I could see things, but they never meant nothing to me. But Tom Sawyer was different. When Tom Sawyer seen a thing it just got up on its hind legs and *talked* to him—told him everything it knowed. *I* never see such a head.

"Tom Sawyer," I says, "I'll say it again as I've said it a many a time before: I ain't fitten to black your boots. But that's all right—that's neither here nor there. God Amighty made us all, and some He gives eyes that's blind, and some He gives eyes that can see, and I reckon it ain't none of our lookout what He done it for; it's all right, or He'd a fixed it some other way. Go on—I see plenty plain enough, now, that them thieves didn't get away with the di'monds. Why didn't they, do you reckon?"

"Because they got chased away by them other two men before they could pull the boots off of the corpse."

"*That's* so! I see it now. But looky here, Tom, why ain't we to go and tell about it?"

"Oh, shucks, Huck Finn, can't you see? Look at it. What's a-going to happen? There's going to be an inquest in the morning. Them two men will tell how they heard the yells and rushed there just in time to not save the stranger. Then the jury'll twaddle and twaddle and twaddle, and finally they'll fetch in a verdict that he got shot or stuck or busted over the head with something, and come to his death by the inspiration of God. And after they've buried him they'll auction off his things for to pay the expenses, and then's *our* chance."

"How, Tom?"

"Buy the boots for two dollars!"

Well, it most took my breath.

"My land! Why Tom, *we'll* get the di'monds!"

"You bet. Some day there'll be a big reward offered for them—a thousand dollars, sure. That's our money! Now we'll trot in and see the folks. And mind you we don't know anything about any murder, or any di'monds, or any thieves—don't you forget that."

I had to sigh a little over the way he had got it fixed. I'd a *sold* them di'monds—yes, sir, for twelve thousand dollars; but I didn't say anything. It wouldn't done any good. I says:

"But what are we going to tell your aunt Sally has made us so long getting down here from the village, Tom?"

"Oh, I'll leave that to you," he says. "I reckon you can explain it somehow."

He was always just that strict and delicate. He never would tell a lie himself.

We struck across the big yard, noticing this, that and t'other thing that was so familiar, and we so glad to see it again; and when we got to the roofed big passageway betwixt the double log house and the kitchen part, there was everything hanging on the wall just as it used to was, even to uncle Silas's old faded green baize working-gown with the hood to it and the raggedy white patch between the shoulders that always looked like somebody had hit him with a snowball; and then we lifted the latch and walked in. Aunt Sally she was just a-ripping and a-tearing around, and the children was huddled in one corner and the old man he was huddled in the other and praying for help in time of need. She jumped for us with joy and tears running down her face and give us a whacking box on the ear, and then hugged us and kissed us and boxed us again, and just couldn't seem to get enough of it she was so glad to see us; and she says:

"Where *have* ye been a-loafing to, you good-for-nothing trash! I've been that worried about ye I didn't know what to do. Your traps has been here *ever* so long, and I've had supper cooked fresh about four times so as to have it hot and good when you come, till at last my patience is just plum wore out, and I declare I—I—why I could skin you alive! You must be starving, poor things!—set down, set down, everybody, don't lose no more time."

It was mighty good to be there again behind all that noble corn pone and spare-ribs and everything that you could ever want in this world. Old uncle Silas he peeled off one of his bulliest old-time blessings, with as many layers to it as an onion, and whilst the angels was hauling in the slack of it I was trying to study up what to say about what kept us so long. When our plates was all loadened and we'd got a-going, she asked me and I says:

"Well, you see,—er—Mizzes—"

"Huck Finn! Since when am I Mizzes to you? Have I ever been stingy of cuffs or kisses for you since the day you stood in this room and I took you for Tom Sawyer and blessed God for sending you to me, though you told me four thousand lies and I believed every one of them like a simpleton? Call me aunt Sally—like you always done."

So I done it. And I says:

"Well, me and Tom allowed we would come along afoot and take a smell of the woods, and we run across Lem Beebe and Jim Lane and they asked us to go with them blackberrying to-night, and said they could borrow Jubiter Dunlap's dog, because he had told them just that minute—"

"Where did they see him?" says the old man; and when I looked up to see how *he* come to take an intrust in a little thing like that, his eyes was just burning into me he was that eager. It surprised me so it kind of throwed me off, but I pulled myself together again and says:

"It was when he was spading up some ground along with you, towards sundown or along there."

He only just said "Um," in a kind of a disappointed way, and didn't take no more intrust. So I went on. I says:

"Well then, as I was a-saying—"

"That'll do, you needn't go no furder." It was aunt Sally. She was boring right into me with her eyes, and very indignant. "Huck Finn," she says, "how'd them men come to talk about going a-blackberrying in September—in *this* region?"

I see I had slipped up, and I couldn't say a word. She waited, still a-gazing at me, then she says:

"And how'd they come to strike that idiot idea of going a-blackberrying in the night?"

"Well m'm, they—er—they told us they had a lantern, and—"

"Oh, *shet* up—do! Looky-here; what was they going to do with a dog?—hunt blackberries with it?"

"I think, m'm, they—."

"Now, Tom Sawyer, what kind of a lie are you fixing *your* mouth to contrib to this mess of rubbage? Speak out—and

I warn you before you begin, that I don't believe a word of it. You and Huck's been up to something you no business to—*I* know it perfectly well; *I* know you, *both* of you. Now you explain that dog, and them blackberries, and the lantern, and the rest of that rot—and mind you talk as straight as a string—do you hear?"

Tom he looked considerable hurt, and says, very dignified:

"It is a pity if Huck is to be talked to thataway, just for making a little bit of a mistake that anybody could make."

"What mistake has he made?"

"Why, only the mistake of saying blackberries when of course he meant strawberries."

"Tom Sawyer, I lay if you aggravate me a little more, I'll—"

"Aunt Sally, without knowing it—and of course without intending it—you are in the wrong. If you'd 'a' studied natural history the way you ought, you would know that all over the world except just here in Arkansaw they *always* hunt strawberries with a dog—and a lantern—"

But she busted in on him there and just piled into him and snowed him under. She was so mad she couldn't get the words out fast enough, and she gushed them out in one everlasting freshet. That was what Tom Sawyer was after. He allowed to work her up and get her started and then leave her alone and let her burn herself out. Then she would be so aggravated with that subject that she wouldn't say another word about it nor let anybody else. Well, it happened just so. When she was tuckered out and had to hold up, he says, quite ca'm:

"And yet, all the same, aunt Sally—"

"Shet up!" she says, "I don't want to hear another word out of you."

So we was perfectly safe, then, and didn't have no more trouble about that delay. Tom done it elegant.

Chapter 7

BENNY she was looking pretty sober, and she sighed some, now and then; but pretty soon she got to asking about Mary, and Sid, and Tom's aunt Polly, and then aunt Sally's clouds cleared off and she got in a good humor and joined in on the questions and was her lovingest best self, and so the rest of the supper went along gay and pleasant. But the old man he didn't take any hand hardly, and was absent-minded and restless, and done a considerable amount of sighing; and it was kind of heart-breaking to see him so sad and troubled and worried.

By and by, a spell after supper, come a nigger and knocked on the door and put his head in with his old straw hat in his hand bowing and scraping, and said his Marse Brace was out at the stile and wanted his brother, and was getting tired waiting supper for him, and would Marse Silas please tell him where he was? I never see uncle Silas speak up so sharp and fractious before. He says:

"Am *I* his brother's keeper?" And then he kind of wilted together, and looked like he wished he hadn't spoke so, and then he says, very gentle: "But you needn't say that, Billy; I was took sudden and irritable, and I ain't very well these days, and not hardly responsible. Tell him he ain't here."

And when the nigger was gone he got up and walked the floor, backwards and forrards and backwards and forrards, mumbling and muttering to himself and plowing his hands through his hair. It was real pitiful to see him. Aunt Sally she whispered to us and told us not to take notice of him, it embarrassed him. She said he was always thinking and thinking, since these troubles come on, and she allowed he didn't more'n about half know what he was about when the thinking spells was on him; and she said he walked in his sleep considerable more now than he used to, and sometimes wandered around over the house and even out doors in his sleep, and if we catched him at it we must let him alone and not disturb him. She said she reckoned it didn't do him no harm, and maybe it done him good. She said Benny was the only one that was much help to him these days. Said Benny appeared to know just when to try to soothe him and when to leave him alone.

So he kept on tramping up and down the floor and muttering, till by and by he begun to look pretty tired; then Benny she went and snuggled up to his side and put one hand in his and one arm around his waist and walked with him; and he smiled down on her, and reached down and kissed her; and so, little by little the trouble went out of his face and she persuaded him off to his room. They had very pretty petting ways together, and it was uncommon pretty to see.

Aunt Sally she was busy getting the children ready for bed; so by and by it got dull and tedious, and me and Tom took a turn in the moonlight, and fetched up in the watermelon patch and et one, and had a good deal of talk. And Tom said he'd bet the quarreling was all Jubiter's fault, and he was going to be on hand the first time he got a chance, and see; and if it was so, he was going to do his level best to get uncle Silas to turn him off.

And so we talked and smoked and stuffed watermelon as much as two hours, and then it was pretty late, and when we got back the house was quiet and dark and everybody gone to bed.

Tom he always seen everything, and now he see that the old green baize work-gown was gone, and said it wasn't gone when we went out; and so we allowed it was curious, and then we went up to bed.

We could hear Benny stirring around in her room, which was next to ourn, and judged she was worried a good deal about her father and couldn't sleep. We found we couldn't, neither. So we set up a long time and smoked and talked in a low voice, and felt pretty dull and down-hearted. We talked the murder and the ghost over and over again, and got so creepy and crawly we couldn't get sleepy no how and no way.

By and by, when it was away late in the night and all the sounds was late sounds and solemn, Tom nudged me and whispers to me to look, and I done it, and there we see a man poking around in the yard like he didn't know just what he wanted to do, but it was pretty dim and we couldn't see him good. Then he started for the stile, and as he went over it the moon come out strong and he had a long-handled shovel over his shoulder and we see the white patch on the old work-gown. So Tom says:

"He's a-walking in his sleep. I wish we was allowed to fol-low him and see where he's going to. There, he's turned down by the tobacker field. Out of sight, now. It's a dreadful pity he can't rest no better."

We waited a long time, but he didn't come back any more, or if he did he come around the other way; so at last we was tuckered out and went to sleep and had nightmares, a million of them. But before dawn we was awake again, because mean-time a storm had come up and been raging, and the thunder and lightning was awful and the wind was a-thrashing the trees around and the rain was driving down in slanting sheets, and the gullies was running rivers. Tom says:

"Looky-here, Huck, I'll tell you one thing that's mighty curious. Up to the time we went out, last night, the family hadn't heard about Jake Dunlap being murdered. Now the men that chased Hal Clayton and Bud Dixon away would spread the thing around in a half an hour, and every neighbor that heard it would shin out and fly around from one farm to t'other and try to be the first to tell the news. Land, they don't have such a big thing as that to tell twice in thirty year! Huck, it's mighty strange; I don't understand it."

So then he was in a fidget for the rain to let up, so we could turn out and run across some of the people and see if they would say anything about it to us. And he said if they did we must be horribly surprised and shocked.

We was out and gone the minute the rain stopped. It was just broad day, then. We loafed along up the road, and now and then met a person and stopped and said howdy, and told them when we come, and how we left the folks at home, and how long we was going to stay, and all that, but none of them said a word about that thing—which was just astonishing, and no mistake. Tom said he believed if we went to the sycamores we would find that body laying there solitary and alone and not a soul around. Said he believed the men chased the thieves so far into the woods that the thieves prob'ly seen a good chance and turned on them at last, and maybe they all killed each other and so there wasn't anybody left to tell.

First we knowed, gabbling along thataway, we was right at the sycamores. The cold chills trickled down my back and I wouldn't budge another step, for all Tom's persuading. But he couldn't hold in; he'd *got* to see if the boots was safe on that body yet. So he crope in—and the next minute out he come again with his eyes bulging he was so excited, and says:

"Huck, it's gone!"

I *was* astonished! I says:

"Tom, you don't mean it."

"It's gone, sure. There ain't a sign of it. The ground is trompled some, but if there was any blood it's all washed away by the storm, for it's all puddles and slush in there."

At last I give in, and went and took a look myself; and it was just as Tom said—there wasn't a sign of a corpse.

"Dern it," I says, "the di'monds is gone. Don't you reckon the thieves slunk back and lugged him off, Tom?"

"Looks like it. It just does. Now where'd they hide him, do you reckon?"

"I don't know," I says, disgusted, "and what's more I don't care. They've got the boots, and that's all *I* cared about. He'll lay around these woods a long time before *I* hunt him up."

Tom didn't feel no more intrust in him neither, only curiosity to know what come of him; but he said we'd lay low and keep dark and it wouldn't be long till the dogs or somebody rousted him out.

We went back home to breakfast ever so bothered and put out and disappointed and swindled. I warn't ever so down on a corpse before.

Chapter 8

I T WARN'T very cheerful at breakfast. Aunt Sally she looked old and tired and let the children snarl and fuss at one another and didn't seem to notice it was going on, which wasn't her usual style; me and Tom had a plenty to think about without talking; Benny she looked like she hadn't had much sleep, and whenever she'd lift her head a little and steal a look towards her father you could see there was tears in her eyes; and as for the old man his things stayed on his plate and got cold without him knowing they was there, I reckon, for he was thinking and thinking all the time, and never said a word and never et a bite.

By and by when it was stillest, that nigger's head was poked in at the door again, and he said his Marse Brace was getting powerful uneasy about Marse Jubiter, which hadn't come home yet, and would Marse Silas please—

He was looking at uncle Silas, and he stopped there, like the rest of his words was froze; for uncle Silas he rose up shaky and steadied himself leaning his fingers on the table, and he was panting, and his eyes was set on the nigger, and he kept swallowing, and put his other hand up to his throat a couple of times, and at last he got his words started, and says:

"Does he—does he—think—*what* does he think! Tell him—tell him—" Then he sunk down in his chair limp and weak, and says, so as you could hardly hear him: "Go away—go away!"

The nigger looked scared, and cleared out, and we all felt—well I don't know how we felt, but it was awful, with the old man panting there, and his eyes set and looking like a person that was dying. None of us could budge; but Benny she slid around soft, with her tears running down, and stood by his side, and nestled his old gray head up against her and begun to stroke it and pet it with her hands, and nodded to us to go away, and we done it, going out very quiet, like the dead was there.

Me and Tom struck out for the woods mighty solemn, and saying how different it was now to what it was last summer when we was here and everything was so peaceful and happy and everybody thought so much of uncle Silas, and he was so cheerful and simple-hearted and pudd'nheaded and good—and now look at him. If he hadn't lost his mind he wasn't much short of it. That was what we allowed.

It was a most lovely day, now, and bright and sunshiny; and the further and further we went over the hill towards the prairie the lovelier and lovelier the trees and flowers got to be and the more it seemed strange and somehow wrong that there had to be trouble in such a world as this. And then all of a sudden I catched my breath and grabbed Tom's arm, and all my livers and lungs and things fell down into my legs.

"There it is!" I says. We jumped back behind a bush shivering, and Tom says:

"Sh!—don't make a noise."

It was setting on a log right in the edge of the little prairie, thinking. I tried to get Tom to come away, but he wouldn't, and I dasn't budge by myself. He said we mightn't ever get another chance to see one, and he was going to look his fill at this one if he died for it. So I looked too, though it give me the fan-tods to do it. Tom he *had* to talk, but he talked low. He says:

"Poor Jakey, it's got all its things on, just as he said he would. *Now* you see what we wasn't certain about—its hair. It's not long, now, the way it was; it's got it cropped close to its head, the way he said he would. Huck, I never see anything look any more naturaler than what It does."

"Nor I neither," I says; "I'd reconnize it anywheres."

"So would I. It looks perfectly solid and genuwyne, just the way it done before it died."

So we kept a-gazing. Pretty soon Tom says:

"Huck, there's something mighty curious about this one; don't you know that? *It* oughtn't to be going around in the daytime."

"That's so, Tom—I never heard the like of it before."

"No, sir, they don't ever come out only at night—and then not till after twelve. There's something wrong about this one, now you mark my words. I don't believe it's got any right to be around in the daytime. But don't it look natural! Jake said he was going to play deef and dumb here, so the neighbors wouldn't know his voice. Do you reckon it would do that if we was to holler at it?"

"Lordy, Tom, don't talk so! If you was to holler at it I'd die in my tracks."

"Don't you worry, I ain't going to holler at it. Look, Huck, it's a-scratching its head—don't you see?"

"Well, what of it?"

"Why, this. What's the sense of it scratching its head? There ain't anything there to itch; its head is made out of fog or something like that, and *can't* itch. A fog can't itch; any fool knows that."

"Well, then, if it don't itch and can't itch, what in the nation is it scratching it for? Ain't it just habit, don't you reckon?"

"No, sir, I don't. I ain't a bit satisfied about the way this one acts. I've a blame good notion it's a bogus one—I have, as sure as I'm a-setting here. Because, if it—Huck!"

"Well, what's the matter now?"

"You can't see the bushes through it!"

"Why, Tom, it's so, sure! It's as solid as a cow. I sort of begin to think—"

"Huck, it's biting off a chaw of tobacker! By George *they* don't chaw—they hain't got anything to chaw *with*. Huck!"

"I'm a-listening."

"It ain't a ghost at all. It's Jake Dunlap his own self!"

"Oh, your granny!" I says.

"Huck Finn, did we find any corpse in the sycamores?"

"No."

"Or any sign of one?"

"No."

"Mighty good reason. Hadn't ever been any corpse there."

"Why Tom, you know we heard—"

"Yes, we did—heard a howl or two. Does that prove anybody was killed? Course it don't. And we seen four men run, then this one come walking out and we took it for a ghost. No more ghost than you are. It was Jake Dunlap his own self, and it's Jake Dunlap now. He's been and got his hair cropped, the way he said he would, and he's playing himself for a stranger, just the same as he said he would. Ghost! Him?—he's as sound as a nut."

Then I see it all, and how we had took too much for granted. I was powerful glad he didn't get killed, and so was Tom, and we wondered which he would like the best—for us to never let on to know him, or how? Tom reckoned the best way would be to go and ask him. So he started; but I kept a little behind, because I didn't know but it might be a ghost, after all. When Tom got to where he was, he says:

"Me and Huck's mighty glad to see you again, and you needn't be afeard we'll tell. And if you think it'll be safer for you if we don't ever let on to know you when we run across you, say the word and you'll see you can depend on us and would ruther cut our hands off than get you into the least little bit of danger."

First-off he looked surprised to see us, and not very glad, either; but as Tom went on he looked pleasanter, and when he was done he smiled, and nodded his head several times, and made signs with his hands, and says:

"Goo-goo,—goo-goo," the way deef and dummies does.

Just then we see some of Steve Nickerson's people coming that lived t'other side of the prairie, so Tom says:

"You do it elegant; I never see anybody do it better. You're right: play it on us, too; play it on us same as the others; it'll keep you in practice and prevent you making blunders. We'll keep away from you and let on we don't know you, but any time we can be any help, you just let us know."

Then we loafed along past the Nickersons, and of course they asked if that was the new stranger yonder, and where'd he come from, and what was his name, and which communion was he, Babtis or Methodis, and which politics, whig or democrat, and how long is he staying, and all them other questions that humans always asks when a stranger comes, and dogs does too. But Tom said he warn't able to make anything out of deef and dumb signs, and the same with goo-gooing. Then we watched them go and bullyrag Jake; because we was pretty uneasy for him. Tom said it would take him days to get so he wouldn't forget he was a deef and dummy sometimes, and speak out before he thought. When we had watched long enough to see that Jake was getting along all right and working his signs very good, we loafed along again, allowing to strike the school-house about recess time, which was a three-mile tramp.

I was so disappointed not to hear Jake tell about the row in the sycamores and how near he come to getting killed, that I couldn't seem to get over it; and Tom he felt the same, but said if we was in Jake's fix we would want to go careful and keep still and not take any chances.

The boys and girls was all glad to see us again, and we had a real good time all through recess. Coming to school the Henderson boys had come across the new deef and dummy and told the rest; so all the scholars was chuck full of him and couldn't talk about anything else, and was in a sweat to get a sight of him because they hadn't ever seen a deef and dummy in their lives, and it made a powerful excitement.

Tom said it was tough to have to keep mum now; said we would be heroes if we could come out and tell all we knowed; but after all it was still more heroic to keep mum, there warn't two boys in a million could do it. That was Tom Sawyer's idea about it, and I reckoned there warn't anybody could better it.

Chapter 9

IN THE NEXT two or three days Dummy he got to be powerful popular. He went associating around with the neighbors, and they made much of him and was proud to have such a rattling curiosity amongst them. They had him to breakfast, they had him to dinner, they had him to supper; they kept him loaded up with hog and hominy, and warn't ever tired staring at him and wondering over him, and wishing they knowed more about him he was so uncommon and romantic. His signs warn't no good; people couldn't understand them and he prob'ly couldn't himself, but he done a sight of goo-gooing, and so everybody was satisfied, and admired to hear him go it. He toted a piece of slate around, and a pencil; and people wrote questions on it and he wrote answers; but there warn't anybody could read his writing but Brace Dunlap. Brace said he couldn't read it very good, but he could manage to dig out the meaning most of the time. He said Dummy said he belonged away off somers, and used to be well off but got busted by swindlers which he had trusted, and was poor now, and hadn't any way to make a living.

Everybody praised Brace Dunlap for being so good to that stranger. He let him have a little log-cabin all to himself, and had his niggers take care of it and fetch him all the vittles he wanted.

Dummy was at our house some, because old uncle Silas was so afflicted himself, these days, that anybody else that was afflicted was a comfort to him. Me and Tom didn't let on that we had knowed him before, and he didn't let on that he had knowed us before. The family talked their troubles out before him the same as if he wasn't there, but we reckoned it wasn't any harm for him to hear what they said. Generly he didn't seem to notice, but sometimes he did.

Well, two or three days went along, and everybody got to getting uneasy about Jubiter Dunlap. Everybody was asking everybody if they had any idea what had become of him. No, they hadn't, they said; and they shook their heads and said there was something powerful strange about it. Another and another day went by; then there was a report got around that praps he was murdered. You bet it made a big stir! Everybody's tongue was clacking away after that. Saturday two or three gangs turned out and hunted the woods to see if they could run across his remainders. Me and Tom helped, and it was noble good times and exciting. Tom he was so brim full of it he couldn't eat nor rest. He said if we could find that corpse we would be celebrated, and more talked about than if we got drownded.

The others got tired and give it up; but not Tom Sawyer— that warn't his style. Saturday night he didn't sleep any, hardly, trying to think up a plan; and towards daylight in the morning he struck it. He snaked me out of bed and was all excited, and says—

"Quick, Huck, snatch on your clothes—I've got it! Bloodhound!"

In two minutes we was tearing up the river road in the dark towards the village. Old Jeff Hooker had a bloodhound and Tom was going to borrow him. I says—

"The trail's too old, Tom—and besides, it's rained, you know."

"It don't make any difference, Huck. If the body's hid in the woods anywhere around, the hound will find it. If he's been murdered and buried, they wouldn't bury him deep, it ain't likely, and if the dog goes over the spot he'll scent him, sure. Huck, we're going to be celebrated, sure as you're born!"

He was just a-blazing; and whenever he got afire he was most likely to get afire all over. That was the way this time. In two minutes he had got it all ciphered out, and wasn't only just going to find the corpse—no, he was going to get on the track of that murderer and hunt *him* down, too; and not only that, but he was going to stick to him till—

"Well," I says, "you better find the corpse first; I reckon that's a plenty for to-day. For all we know, there *ain't* any corpse and nobody hain't been murdered. That cuss could 'a' gone off somers and not been killed at all."

That graveled him and he says—

"Huck Finn, I never see such a person as you to want to

spoil everything. As long as *you* can't see anything hopeful in
a thing, you won't let anybody else. What good can it do you
to throw cold water on that corpse and get up that selfish theory that there hain't been any murder? None in the world. I
don't see how you can act so. I wouldn't treat you like that,
and you know it. Here we've got a noble good opportunity
to make a reputation, and—"

"Oh, go ahead," I says, "I'm sorry, and I take it all back. I
didn't mean nothing. Fix it any way you want it. *He* ain't any
consequence to me. If he's killed, I'm as glad of it as you are;
and if he—"

"I never said anything about being glad; I only—"

"Well, then, I'm as *sorry* as you are. Any way you druther
have it, that is the way *I* druther have it. He—"

"There ain't any druthers *about* it, Huck Finn; nobody said
anything about druthers. And as for—"

He forgot he was talking, and went tramping along, studying. He begun to get excited again, and pretty soon he says—

"Huck, it'll be the bulliest thing that ever happened if we
find the body after everybody else has quit looking, and then
go ahead and hunt up the murderer. It won't only be an
honor to us, but it'll be an honor to uncle Silas because it was
us that done it. It'll set him up again, you see if it don't."

But old Jeff Hooker he throwed cold water on the whole
business when we got to his blacksmith shop and told him
what we come for.

"You can take the dog," he says, "but you ain't a-going to
find any corpse, because there ain't any corpse to find. Everybody's quit looking, and they're right. Soon as they come to
think, they knowed there warn't no corpse. And I'll tell you
for why. What does a person kill another person *for*, Tom
Sawyer?—answer me that."

"Why, he—er—"

"Answer up! You ain't no fool. What does he kill him *for*?"

"Well, sometimes it's for revenge, and—"

"Wait. One thing at a time. Revenge, says you; and right
you are. Now who ever had anything agin that poor trifling
no-account? Who do you reckon would want to kill *him*?—
that rabbit!"

Tom was stuck. I reckon he hadn't thought of a person

having to have a reason for killing a person before, and now he see it warn't likely anybody would have that much of a grudge against a lamb like Jubiter Dunlap. The blacksmith says, by and by—

"The revenge idea won't work, you see. Well then, what's next? Robbery? B'gosh that must 'a' been it, Tom! Yes, sir-ree, I reckon we've struck it this time. Some feller wanted his gallus-buckles, and so he—"

But it was so funny he busted out laughing, and just went *on* laughing and laughing and laughing till he was most dead, and Tom looked so put out and cheap that I knowed he was ashamed he had come, and wished he hadn't. But old Hooker never let up on him. He raked up everything a person ever could want to kill another person about; and any fool could see they didn't any of them fit this case, and he just made no end of fun of the whole business and of the people that had been hunting the body; and he said—

"If they'd had any sense they'd 'a' knowed the lazy cuss slid out because he wanted a loafing spell after all this work. He'll come pottering back in a couple of weeks, and then how'll you fellers feel? But laws bless you, take the dog and go and hunt up his remainders. Do, Tom."

Then he busted out and had another of them forty-rod laughs of his'n. Tom couldn't back down after all this, so he said "All right, unchain him," and the blacksmith done it and we started home and left that old man laughing yet.

It was a lovely dog. There ain't any dog that's got a love-lier disposition than a bloodhound, and this one knowed us and liked us. He capered and raced around, ever so friendly and powerful glad to be free and have a holiday; but Tom was so cut up he couldn't take any intrust in him and said he wished he'd stopped and thought a minute before he ever started on such a fool errand. He said old Jeff Hooker would tell everybody, and we'd never hear the last of it.

So we loafed along home down the back lanes, feeling pretty glum and not talking. When we was passing the far cor-ner of our tobacker field we heard the dog set up a long howl in there, and we went to the place and he was scratching the ground with all his might and every now and then canting up his head sideways and fetching another howl.

It was a long square the shape of a grave; the rain had made it sink down and show the shape. The minute we come and stood there we looked at one another and never said a word. When the dog had dug down only a few inches he grabbed something and pulled it up and it was an arm and a sleeve. Tom kind of gasped out and says—

"Come away, Huck—it's found."

I just felt awful. We struck for the road and fetched the first men that come along. They got a spade at the crib and dug out the body, and you never see such an excitement. You couldn't make anything out of the face, but you didn't need to. Everybody said—

"Poor Jubiter; it's his clothes, to the last rag!"

Some rushed off to spread the news and tell the justice of the peace and have an inquest, and me and Tom lit out for the house. Tom was all afire and most out of breath when we came tearing in where uncle Silas and aunt Sally and Benny was. Tom sung out—

"Me and Huck's found Jubiter Dunlap's corpse all by ourselves with a bloodhound after everybody else had quit hunting and given it up; and if it hadn't a been for us it never *would* 'a' been found; and he *was* murdered, too—they done it with a club or something like that; and I'm going to start in and find the murderer, next, and I bet I'll do it!"

Aunt Sally and Benny sprung up pale and astonished, but uncle Silas fell right forrard out of his chair onto the floor and groans out—

"Oh, my God, you've found him *now*!"

Chapter 10

THEM AWFUL WORDS froze us solid. We couldn't move hand or foot for as much as a half a minute. Then we kind of come to, and lifted the old man up and got him into his chair, and Benny petted him and kissed him and tried to comfort him, and poor old aunt Sally she done the same; but poor things they was so broke up and scared and knocked out of their right minds that they didn't hardly know what they was about. With Tom it was awful; it most petrified him to think maybe he had got his uncle into a thousand times more trouble than ever, and maybe it wouldn't ever happened if he hadn't been so ambitious to get celebrated, and let the corpse alone the way the others done. But pretty soon he sort of come to himself again and says—

"Uncle Silas, don't you say another word like that. It's dangerous, and there ain't a shadder of truth in it."

Aunt Sally and Benny was thankful to hear him say that, and they said the same; but the old man he wagged his head sorrowful and hopeless, and the tears run down his face and he says—

"No—I done it; poor Jubiter, I done it!"

It was dreadful to hear him say it. Then he went on and told about it; and said it happened the day me and Tom come—along about sundown. He said Jubiter pestered him and aggravated him till he was so mad he just sort of lost his mind and grabbed up a stick and hit him over the head with all his might, and Jubiter dropped in his tracks. Then he was scared and sorry, and got down on his knees and lifted his head up, and begged him to speak and say he wasn't dead; and before long he come to, and when he see who it was holding his head, he jumped like he was most scared to death, and cleared the fence and tore into the woods, and was gone. So he hoped he wasn't hurt bad.

"But laws," he says, "it was only just fear that give him that last little spurt of strength, and of course it soon played out and he laid down in the bush and there wasn't anybody to help him, and he died."

Then the old man cried and grieved, and said he was a murderer and the mark of Cain was on him, and he had disgraced his family and was going to be found out and hung. But Tom said—

"No, you ain't going to be found out. You *didn't* kill him. *One* lick wouldn't kill him. Somebody else done it."

"Oh, yes," he says, "I done it—nobody else. Who else had anything against him? Who else *could* have anything against him?"

He looked up kind of like he hoped some of us could mention somebody that could have a grudge against that harmless no-account, but of course it warn't no use—he *had* us; we couldn't say a word. He noticed that, and he saddened down again and I never see a face so miserable and so pitiful to see. Tom had a sudden idea and says—

"But hold on!—somebody *buried* him. Now who—"

He shut off sudden. I knowed the reason. It give me the cold shudders when he said them words, because right away I remembered about us seeing uncle Silas prowling around with a long-handled shovel away in the night that night. And I knowed Benny seen him, too, because she was talking about it one day. The minute Tom shut off he changed the subject and went to begging uncle Silas to keep mum, and the rest of us done the same, and said he *must*, and said it wasn't his business to tell on himself, and if he kept mum nobody would ever know, but if it was found out and any harm come to him it would break the family's hearts and kill them, and yet never do anybody any good. So at last he promised. We was all of us more comfortable, then, and went to work to cheer up the old man. We told him all he'd got to do was to keep still and it wouldn't be long till the whole thing would blow over and be forgot. We all said there wouldn't anybody ever suspect uncle Silas, nor ever dream of such a thing, he being so good and kind and having such a good character; and Tom says, cordial and hearty, he says—

"Why, just look at it a minute; just consider. Here is uncle Silas, all these years a preacher—at his own expense; all these years doing good with all his might and every way he can think of—at his own expense, all the time; always been loved by everybody, and respected; always been peaceable and minding his own business, the very last man in this whole deestrict to touch a person, and everybody knows it. Suspect *him*? Why, it ain't any more possible than—"

"By authority of the State of Arkansaw—I arrest you for the murder of Jubiter Dunlap!" shouts the sheriff at the door.

It was awful. Aunt Sally and Benny flung themselves at uncle Silas, screaming and crying, and hugged him and hung to him, and aunt Sally said go away, she wouldn't ever give him up, they shouldn't have him, and the niggers they come crowding and crying to the door and—well, I couldn't stand it; it was enough to break a person's heart; so I got out.

They took him up to the little one-horse jail in the village, and we all went along to tell him good-bye, and Tom was feeling elegant, and says to me, "We'll have a most noble good time and heaps of danger some dark night, getting him out of there, Huck, and it'll be talked about everywheres and we will be celebrated;" but the old man busted that scheme up the minute he whispered to him about it. He said no, it was his duty to stand whatever the law done to him, and he would stick to the jail plum through to the end, even if there warn't no door to it. It disappointed Tom, and graveled him a good deal, but he had to put up with it.

But he felt responsible and bound to get his uncle Silas free; and he told aunt Sally, the last thing, not to worry, because he was going to turn in and work night and day and beat this game and fetch uncle Silas out innocent; and she was very loving to him and thanked him and said she knowed he would do his very best. And she told us to help Benny take care of the house and the children, and then we had a good-bye cry all around and went back to the farm, and left her there to live with the jailer's wife a month till the trial in October.

Chapter II

WELL, that was a hard month on us all. Poor Benny, she kept up the best she could, and me and Tom tried to keep things cheerful there at the house, but it kind of went for nothing, as you may say. It was the same up at the jail. We went up every day to see the old people, but it was awful dreary, because the old man warn't sleeping much, and was walking in his sleep considerable, and so he got to looking fagged and miserable, and his mind got shaky, and we all got afraid his troubles would break him down and kill him. And whenever we tried to persuade him to feel cheerfuler, he only shook his head and said if we only knowed what it was to carry around a murderer's load on your heart we wouldn't talk that way. Tom and all of us kept telling him it *wasn't* murder, but just accidental killing, but it never made any difference—it was murder, and he wouldn't have it any other way. He actu'ly begun to come out plain and square towards trial-time and acknowledge that he *tried* to kill the man. Why, that was awful, you know. It made things seem fifty times as dreadful, and there warn't no more comfort for aunt Sally and Benny. But he promised he wouldn't say a word about his murder when others was around, and we was glad of that.

Tom Sawyer racked the head off of himself all that month trying to plan some way out for uncle Silas, and many's the night he kept me up most all night with this kind of tiresome work, but he couldn't seem to get on the right track no way. As for me, I reckoned a body might as well give it up, it all looked so blue and I was so down-hearted; but he wouldn't. He stuck to the business right along, and went on planning and thinking and ransacking his head.

So at last the trial come on, towards the middle of October, and we was all in the court. The place was jammed of course. Poor old uncle Silas, he looked more like a dead person than a live one, his eyes was so hollow and he looked so thin and so mournful. Benny she set on one side of him and aunt Sally on the other, and they had veils on, and was full of trouble. But Tom he set by our lawyer, and had his finger in everywheres, of course. The lawyer let him, and the judge let him. He most took the business out of the lawyer's hands sometimes; which was well enough, because that was only a mudturtle of a back-settlement lawyer and didn't know enough to come in when it rains, as the saying is.

They swore in the jury, and then the lawyer for the prostitution got up and begun. He made a terrible speech against the old man, that made him moan and groan, and made Benny and aunt Sally cry. The way *he* told about the murder kind of knocked us all stupid it was so different from the old man's tale. He said he was going to prove that uncle Silas was *seen* to kill Jubiter Dunlap by two good witnesses, and done it deliberate, and *said* he was going to kill him the very minute he hit him with the club; and they seen him hide Jubiter in the bushes, and they seen that Jubiter was stone-dead. And said uncle Silas come later and lugged Jubiter down into the tobacker field, and two men seen him do it. And said uncle Silas turned out, away in the night, and buried Jubiter, and a man seen him at it.

I says to myself, poor old uncle Silas has been lying about it because he reckoned nobody seen him and he couldn't bear to break aunt Sally's heart and Benny's; and right he was: as for me, I would 'a' lied the same way, and so would anybody that had any feeling, to save them such misery and sorrow which *they* warn't no ways responsible for. Well, it made our lawyer look pretty sick; and it knocked Tom silly, too, for a little spell, but then he braced up and let on that he warn't worried—but I knowed he *was*, all the same. And the people —my, but it made a stir amongst them!

And when that lawyer was done telling the jury what he was going to prove, he set down and begun to work his witnesses.

First, he called a lot of them to show that there was bad blood betwixt uncle Silas and the diseased; and they told how they had heard uncle Silas threaten the diseased, at one time and another, and how it got worse and worse and everybody was talking about it, and how diseased got afraid of his life, and told two or three of them he was certain uncle Silas would up and kill him some time or another.

Tom and our lawyer asked them some questions; but it warn't no use, they stuck to what they said.

Next, they called up Lem Beebe, and he took the stand. It come into my mind, then, how Lem and Jim Lane had come along talking, that time, about borrowing a dog or something from Jubiter Dunlap; and that brought up the blackberries and the lantern; and that brought up Bill and Jack Withers, and how *they* passed by, talking about a nigger stealing uncle Silas's corn; and that fetched up our old ghost that come along about the same time and scared us so—and here *he* was too, and a privileged character, on accounts of his being deef and dumb and a stranger, and they had fixed him a chair inside the railing, where he could cross his legs and be comfortable, whilst the other people was all in a jam so they couldn't hardly breathe. So it all come back to me just the way it was that day; and it made me mournful to think how pleasant it was up to then, and how miserable ever since.

Lem Beebe, sworn, said: "I was a-coming along, that day, second of September, and Jim Lane was with me, and it was towards sundown, and we heard loud talk, like quarreling, and we was very close, only the hazel bushes between (that's along the fence); and we heard a voice say, 'I've told you more'n once I'd kill you,' and knowed it was this prisoner's voice; and then we see a club come up above the bushes and down out of sight again, and heard a smashing thump and then a groan or two; and then we crope soft to where we could see, and there laid Jubiter Dunlap dead, and this prisoner standing over him with the club; and the next he hauled the dead man into a clump of bushes and hid him, and then we stooped low, to be out of sight, and got away."

Well, it was awful. It kind of froze everybody's blood to hear it, and the house was most as still whilst he was telling it as if there warn't nobody in it. And when he was done, you could hear them gasp and sigh, all over the house, and look at one another the same as to say, "Ain't it perfectly terrible—ain't it awful!"

Now happened a thing that astonished me. All the time the first witnesses was proving the bad blood and the threats and all that, Tom Sawyer was alive and laying for them; and the minute they was through, he went for them, and done his level best to catch them in lies and spile their testimony. But now, how different! When Lem first begun to talk, and never said anything about speaking to Jubiter or trying to borrow a dog off of him, he was all alive and laying for Lem, and you could see he was getting ready to cross-question him to death pretty soon, and then I judged him and me would go on the stand by and by and tell what we heard him and Jim Lane say. But the next time I looked at Tom I got the cold shivers. Why, he was in the brownest study you ever see—miles and miles away. He warn't hearing a word Lem Beebe was saying; and when he got through he was still in that brown study, just the same. Our lawyer joggled him, and then he looked up startled, and says, "Take the witness if you want him. Lemme alone—I want to think."

Well, that beat me. I couldn't understand it. And Benny and her mother—oh, they looked sick, they was so troubled. They shoved their veils to one side and tried to get his eye, but it warn't any use, and I couldn't get his eye either. So the mud-turtle he tackled the witness, but it didn't amount to nothing; and he made a mess of it.

Then they called up Jim Lane, and he told the very same story over again, exact. Tom never listened to this one at all, but set there thinking and thinking, miles and miles away. So the mud-turtle went in alone again and come out just as flat as he done before. The lawyer for the prostitution looked very comfortable, but the judge looked disgusted. You see, Tom was just the same as a regular lawyer, nearly, because it was Arkansaw law for a prisoner to choose anybody he wanted to help his lawyer, and Tom had had uncle Silas shove him into the case, and now he was botching it and you could see the judge didn't like it much.

All that the mud-turtle got out of Lem and Jim was this: he asked them—

"Why didn't you go and tell what you saw?"

"We was afraid we would get mixed up in it ourselves. And we was just starting down the river a-hunting for all the week besides; but as soon as we come back we found out they'd been searching for the body, so then we went and told Brace Dunlap all about it."

"When was that?"

"Saturday night, September 9th."

The judge he spoke up and says—

"Mr. Sheriff, arrest these two witnesses on suspicions of being accessionary after the fact to the murder."

The lawyer for the prostitution jumps up all excited, and says—

"Your Honor! I protest against this extraordi—"

"Set down!" says the judge, pulling his bowie and laying it on his pulpit. "I beg you to respect the Court."

So he done it. Then he called Bill Withers.

Bill Withers, sworn, said: "I was coming along about sundown, Saturday, September 2d, by the prisoner's field, and my brother Jack was with me, and we seen a man toting off something heavy on his back and allowed it was a nigger stealing corn; we couldn't see distinct; next we made out that it was one man carrying another; and the way it hung, so kind of limp, we judged it was somebody that was drunk; and by the man's walk we said it was parson Silas, and we judged he had found Sam Cooper drunk in the road, which he was always trying to reform him, and was toting him out of danger."

It made the people shiver to think of poor old uncle Silas toting off the diseased down to the place in his tobacker field where the dog dug up the body, but there warn't much sympathy around amongst the faces, and I heard one cuss say, "'Tis the coldest-blooded work I ever struck, lugging a murdered man around like that, and going to bury him like a animal, and him a preacher at that."

Tom he went on thinking, and never took no notice; so our lawyer took the witness and done the best he could, and it was plenty poor enough.

Then Jack Withers he come on the stand and told the same tale, just like Bill done.

And after him comes Brace Dunlap, and he was looking very mournful, and most crying; and there was a rustle and a stir all around, and everybody got ready to listen, and lots of the women folks said, "Poor cretur, poor cretur," and you could see a many of them wiping their eyes.

Brace Dunlap, sworn, said: "I was in considerable trouble a long time about my poor brother, but I reckoned things warn't near so bad as he made out, and I couldn't make myself believe anybody would have the heart to hurt a poor harmless cretur like that"—[by jings, I was sure I seen Tom give a kind of a faint little start, and then look disappointed again]—"and you know I *couldn't* think a preacher would hurt him—it warn't natural to think such an onlikely thing—so I never paid much attention, and now I sha'n't ever, ever forgive myself; for if I had a done different, my poor brother would be with me this day, and not laying yonder murdered, and him so harmless." He kind of broke down there and choked up, and waited to get his voice; and people all around said the most pitiful things, and women cried; and it was very still in there, and solemn, and old uncle Silas, poor thing, he give a groan right out so everybody heard him. Then Brace he went on, "Saturday, September 2d, he didn't come home to supper. By and by I got a little uneasy, and one of my niggers went over to this prisoner's place, but come back and said he warn't there. So I got uneasier and uneasier, and couldn't rest. I went to bed, but I couldn't sleep; and turned out, away late in the night, and went wandering over to this prisoner's place and all around about there a good while, hoping I would run across my poor brother, and never knowing he was out of his troubles and gone to a better shore—" So he broke down and choked up again, and most all the women was crying now. Pretty soon he got another start and says: "But it warn't no use; so at last I went home and tried to get some sleep, but couldn't. Well, in a day or two everybody was uneasy, and they got to talking about this prisoner's threats, and took to the idea, which I didn't take no stock in, that my brother was murdered; so they hunted around and tried to find his body, but couldn't and give it up. And so I reckoned he was gone off somers to have a little peace, and would come back to us when his troubles was kind of healed. But late Saturday night, the 9th, Lem Beebe and Jim Lane come to my house and told me all—told me the whole awful 'sassination, and my heart was broke. And *then* I remembered something that hadn't took no hold of me at the time, because reports said this prisoner had took to walking in his sleep and doing all kind of things of no consequence, not knowing what he was about. I will tell you what that thing was that come back into my memory. Away late that awful Saturday night when I was wandering around about this prisoner's place, grieving and troubled, I was down by the corner of the tobacker field and I heard a sound like digging in a gritty soil; and I crope nearer and peeped through the vines that hung on the rail fence and seen this prisoner *shoveling*—shoveling with a long-handled shovel—heaving earth into a big hole that was most filled up; his back was to me, but it was bright moonlight and I knowed him by his old green baize work-gown with a splattery white patch in the middle of the back like somebody had hit him with a snowball. *He was burying the man he'd murdered!*"

And he slumped down in his chair crying and sobbing, and most everybody in the house busted out wailing, and crying, and saying, "Oh, it's awful—awful—horrible!" and there was a most tremenduous excitement, and you couldn't hear yourself think; and right in the midst of it up jumps old uncle Silas, white as a sheet, and sings out—

"It's true, every word—I murdered him in cold blood!"

By Jackson, it petrified them! People rose up wild all over the house, straining and staring for a better look at him, and the judge was hammering with his mallet and the sheriff yelling "Order—order in the court—order!"

And all the while the old man stood there a-quaking and his eyes a-burning, and not looking at his wife and daughter, which was clinging to him and begging him to keep still, but pawing them off with his hands and saying he *would* clear his black soul from crime, he *would* heave off this load that was more than he could bear, and he *wouldn't* bear it another hour! And then he raged right along with his awful tale, everybody a-staring and gasping, judge, jury, lawyers, and everybody, and Benny and aunt Sally crying their hearts out. And by George, Tom Sawyer never looked at him once! Never once—just set there gazing with all his eyes at something else, I couldn't tell what. And so the old man raged right along, pouring his words out like a stream of fire:

"I killed him! I am guilty! But I never had the notion in my life to hurt him or harm him, spite of all them lies about my threatening him, till the very minute I raised the club—then my heart went cold!—then the pity all went out of it, and I struck to kill! In that one moment all my wrongs come into my mind; all the insults that that man and the scoundrel his brother, there, had put upon me, and how they had laid in together to ruin me with the people, and take away my good name, and *drive* me to some deed that would destroy me and my family that hadn't ever done *them* no harm, so help me God! And they done it in a mean revenge—for why? Because my innocent pure girl here at my side wouldn't marry that rich, insolent, ignorant coward, Brace Dunlap, who's been sniveling here over a brother he never cared a brass farthing for"—[I see Tom give a jump and look glad *this* time, to a dead certainty]—"and in that moment I've told you about, I

forgot my God and remembered only my heart's bitterness—
God forgive me!—and I struck to kill. In one second I was
miserably sorry—oh, filled with remorse; but I thought of my
poor family, and I *must* hide what I'd done for their sakes;
and I did hide that corpse in the bushes; and presently I carried it to the tobacker field; and in the deep night I went with
my shovel and buried it where—"

Up jumps Tom and shouts—

"*Now*, I've got it!" and waves his hand, oh, ever so fine and
starchy, towards the old man, and says—

"Set down! A murder *was* done, but you never had no
hand in it!"

Well, sir, you could a heard a pin drop. And the old man he
sunk down kind of bewildered in his seat and aunt Sally and
Benny didn't know it, because they was so astonished and
staring at Tom with their mouths open and not knowing what
they was about. And the whole house the same. *I* never seen
people look so helpless and tangled up, and I hain't ever seen
eyes bug out and gaze without a blink the way theirn did.
Tom says, perfectly ca'm—

"Your Honor, may I speak?"

"For God's sake, yes—go on!" says the judge, so astonished and mixed up he didn't know what he was about hardly.

Then Tom he stood there and waited a second or two—
that was for to work up an "effect," as he calls it—then he
started in just as ca'm as ever, and says:

"For about two weeks, now, there's been a little bill sticking on the front of this court-house offering two thousand
dollars reward for a couple of big di'monds—stole at St.
Louis. Them di'monds is worth twelve thousand dollars. But
never mind about that till I get to it. Now about this murder.
I will tell you all about it—how it happened—who done it—
every *de*tail."

You could see everybody nestle, now, and begin to listen
for all they was worth.

"This man here, Brace Dunlap, that's been sniveling so
about his dead brother that *you* know he never cared a straw
for, wanted to marry that young girl there, and she wouldn't
have him. So he told uncle Silas he would make him sorry.
Uncle Silas knowed how powerful he was, and how little

chance he had against such a man, and he was scared and worried, and done everything he could think of to smooth him over and get him to be good to him: he even took his no-account brother Jubiter on the farm and give him wages and stinted his own family to pay them; and Jubiter done everything his brother could contrive to insult uncle Silas, and fret and worry him, and try to drive uncle Silas into doing him a hurt, so as to injure uncle Silas with the people. And it done it. Everybody turned against him and said the meanest kind of things about him, and it graduly broke his heart—yes, and he was so worried and distressed that often he warn't hardly in his right mind.

"Well, on that Saturday that we've had so much trouble about, two of these witnesses here, Lem Beebe and Jim Lane, come along by where uncle Silas and Jubiter Dunlap was at work—and that much of what they've said is true, the rest is lies. They didn't hear uncle Silas say he would kill Jubiter; they didn't hear no blow struck; they didn't see no dead man, and they didn't see uncle Silas hide anything in the bushes. Look at them now—how they set there, wishing they hadn't been so handy with their tongues; anyway, they'll wish it before I get done.

"That same Saturday evening Bill and Jack Withers *did* see one man lugging off another one. That much of what they said is true, and the rest is lies. First off they thought it was a nigger stealing uncle Silas's corn—you notice it makes them look silly, now, to find out somebody overheard them say that. That's because they found out by and by who it was that was doing the lugging, and *they* know best why they swore here that they took it for uncle Silas by the gait—which it *wasn't,* and they knowed it when they swore to that lie.

"A man out in the moonlight *did* see a murdered person put under ground in the tobacker field—but it wasn't uncle Silas that done the burying. He was in his bed at that very time.

"Now, then, before I go on, I want to ask you if you've ever noticed this: that people, when they're thinking deep, or when they're worried, are most always doing something with their hands, and they don't know it, and don't notice what it is their hands are doing. Some stroke their chins; some stroke their noses; some stroke up *under* their chin with their hand; some twirl a chain, some fumble a button, then there's some that draws a figure or a letter with their finger on their cheek, or under their chin or on their under lip. That's *my* way. When I'm restless, or worried, or thinking hard, I draw capital V's on my cheek or on my under lip or under my chin, and never anything *but* capital V's—and half the time I don't notice it and don't know I'm doing it."

That was odd. That is just what I do; only I make an O. And I could see people nodding to one another, same as they do when they mean "*that's* so."

"Now then, I'll go on. That same Saturday—no, it was the night before—there was a steamboat laying at Flagler's Landing, forty miles above here, and it was raining and storming like the nation. And there was a thief aboard, and he had them two big di'monds that's advertised out here on this court-house door; and he slipped ashore with his hand-bag and struck out into the dark and the storm, and he was a-hoping he could get to this town all right and be safe. But he had two pals aboard the boat, hiding, and he knowed they was going to kill him the first chance they got and take the di'monds; because all three stole them, and then this fellow he got hold of them and skipped.

"Well, he hadn't been gone more'n ten minutes before his pals found it out, and they jumped ashore and lit out after him. Prob'ly they burnt matches and found his tracks. Anyway, they dogged along after him all day Saturday and kept out of his sight; and towards sundown he come to the bunch of sycamores down by uncle Silas's field, and he went in there to get a disguise out of his hand-bag and put it on before he showed himself here in the town—and mind you he done that just a little after the time that uncle Silas was hitting Jubiter Dunlap over the head with a club—for he *did* hit him.

"But the minute the pals see that thief slide into the bunch of sycamores, they jumped out of the bushes and slid in after him.

"They fell on him and clubbed him to death.

"Yes, for all he screamed and howled so, they never had no mercy on him, but clubbed him to death. And two men that was running along the road heard him yelling that way, and they made a rush into the sycamore bunch—which was where they was bound for, anyway—and when the pals saw them they lit out and the two new men after them a-chasing them as tight as they could go. But only a minute or two—then these two new men slipped back very quiet into the sycamores.

"*Then* what did they do? I will tell you what they done. They found where the thief had got his disguise out of his carpet-sack to put on; so one of them strips and puts on that disguise."

Tom waited a little here, for some more "effect"—then he says, very deliberate—

"The man that put on that dead man's disguise was— *Jubiter Dunlap!*"

"Great Scott!" everybody shouted, all over the house, and old uncle Silas he looked perfectly astonished.

"Yes, it was Jubiter Dunlap. Not dead, you see. Then they pulled off the dead man's boots and put Jubiter Dunlap's old ragged shoes on the corpse and put the corpse's boots on Jubiter Dunlap. Then Jubiter Dunlap stayed where he was, and the other man lugged the dead body off in the twilight; and after midnight he went to uncle Silas's house, and took his old green work-robe off of the peg where it always hangs in the passage betwixt the house and the kitchen and put it on, and stole the long-handled shovel and went off down into the tobacker field and buried the murdered man."

He stopped, and stood a half a minute. Then—

"And who do you reckon the murdered man *was*? It was— *Jake* Dunlap, the long-lost burglar!"

"Great Scott!"

"And the man that buried him was—*Brace* Dunlap, his brother!"

"Great Scott!"

"And who do you reckon is this mowing idiot here that's letting on all these weeks to be a deef and dumb stranger? It's—*Jubiter* Dunlap!"

My land, they all busted out in a howl, and you never see the like of that excitement since the day you was born. And Tom he made a jump for Jubiter and snaked off his goggles and his false whiskers, and there was the murdered man, sure enough, just as alive as anybody! And aunt Sally and Benny they went to hugging and crying and kissing and smothering old uncle Silas to that degree he was more muddled and confused and mushed up in his mind than he ever was before, and that is saying considerable. And next, people begun to yell—

"Tom Sawyer! Tom Sawyer! Shut up everybody, and let him go on! Go on, Tom Sawyer!"

Which made him feel uncommon bully, for it was nuts for Tom Sawyer to be a public character thataway, and a hero, as he calls it. So when it was all quiet, he says—

"There ain't much left, only this. When that man there, Brace Dunlap, had most worried the life and sense out of uncle Silas till at last he plum lost his mind and hit this other blatherskite his brother with a club, I reckon he seen his chance. Jubiter broke for the woods to hide, and I reckon the game was for him to slide out, in the night, and leave the country. Then Brace would make everybody believe uncle Silas killed him and hid his body somers; and that would ruin uncle Silas and drive *him* out of the country—hang him, maybe; I dunno. But when they found their dead brother in the sycamores without knowing him, because he was so battered up, they see they had a better thing; disguise *both* and bury Jake and dig him up presently all dressed up in Jubiter's clothes, and hire Jim Lane and Bill Withers and the others to swear to some handy lies—which they done. And there they set, now, and I told them they would be looking sick before I got done, and that is the way they're looking now.

"Well, me and Huck Finn here, we come down on the boat with the thieves, and the dead one told us all about the di'-monds, and said the others would murder him if they got the chance; and we was going to help him all we could. We was bound for the sycamores when we heard them killing him in there; but we was in there in the early morning after the storm and allowed nobody hadn't been killed, after all. And when we see Jubiter Dunlap here spreading around in the very same disguise Jake told us *he* was going to wear, we thought it was Jake his own self—and he was goo-gooing deef and dumb, and *that* was according to agreement.

"Well, me and Huck went on hunting for the corpse after

the others quit, and we found it. And was proud, too; but uncle Silas he knocked us crazy by telling us *he* killed the man. So we was mighty sorry we found the body, and was bound to save uncle Silas's neck if we could; and it was going to be tough work, too, because he wouldn't let us break him out of prison the way we done with our old nigger Jim, you remember.

"I done everything I could the whole month to think up some way to save uncle Silas, but I couldn't strike a thing. So when we come into court to-day I come empty, and couldn't see no chance anywheres. But by and by I had a glimpse of something that set me thinking—just a little wee glimpse—only that, and not enough to make sure; but it set me thinking hard—and *watching*, when I was only letting on to think; and by and by, sure enough, when uncle Silas was piling out that stuff about *him* killing Jubiter Dunlap, I catched that glimpse again, and this time I jumped up and shut down the proceedings, because I *knowed* Jubiter Dunlap was a-setting here before me. I knowed him by a thing which I seen him do—and I remembered it. I'd seen him do it when I was here a year ago."

He stopped then, and studied a minute—laying for an "effect"—I knowed it perfectly well. Then he turned off like he was going to leave the platform, and says, kind of lazy and indifferent—

"Well, I believe that is all."

Why, you never heard such a howl!—and it come from the whole house:

"What *was* it you seen him do? Stay where you are, you little devil! You think you are going to work a body up till his mouth's a-watering and stop there? What *was* it he done?"

That was it, you see—he just done it to get an "effect;" you couldn't 'a' pulled him off of that platform with a yoke of oxen.

"Oh, it wasn't anything much," he says. "I seen him looking a little excited when he found uncle Silas was actuly fixing to hang himself for a murder that warn't ever done; and he got more and more nervous and worried, I a-watching him sharp but not seeming to look at him—and all of a sudden his hands begun to work and fidget, and pretty soon his left crept up and *his finger drawed a cross on his cheek*, and then I *had* him!"

Well, then they ripped and howled and stomped and clapped their hands till Tom Sawyer was that proud and happy he didn't know what to do with himself. And then the judge he looked down over his pulpit and says—

"My boy, did you *see* all the various details of this strange conspiracy and tragedy that you've been describing?"

"No, your Honor, I didn't see any of them."

"Didn't see any of them! Why, you've told the whole history straight through, just the same as if you'd seen it with your eyes. How did you manage that?"

Tom says, kind of easy and comfortable—

"Oh, just noticing the evidence and piecing this and that together, your Honor; just an ordinary little bit of detective work; anybody could 'a' done it."

"Nothing of the kind! Not two in a million could 'a' done it. You are a very remarkable boy."

Then they let go and give Tom another smashing round, and he—well, he wouldn't 'a' sold out for a silver mine. Then the judge says—

"But are you certain you've got this curious history straight?"

"Perfectly, your Honor. Here is Brace Dunlap—let him deny his share of it if he wants to take the chance; I'll engage to make him wish he hadn't said anything. . . . Well, you see *he's* pretty quiet. And his brother's pretty quiet, and them four witnesses that lied so and got paid for it, they're pretty quiet. And as for uncle Silas, it ain't any use for him to put in his oar, I wouldn't believe him under oath!"

Well, sir, that fairly made them shout; and even the judge he let go and laughed. Tom he was just feeling like a rainbow. When they was done laughing he looks up at the judge and says—

"Your Honor, there's a thief in this house."

"A thief?"

"Yes, sir. And he's got them twelve-thousand-dollar di'-monds on him."

By gracious, but it made a stir! Everybody went to shouting—

"Which is him? which is him? p'int him out!"

And the judge says—

"Point him out, my lad. Sheriff, you will arrest him. Which one is it?"

Tom says—

"This late dead man here—Jubiter Dunlap."

Then there was another thundering let-go of astonishment and excitement; but Jubiter, which was astonished enough before, was just fairly putrefied with astonishment this time. And he spoke up, about half crying, and says—

"Now *that's* a lie! Your Honor, it ain't fair; I'm plenty bad enough without that. I done the other things—Brace he put me up to it, and persuaded me, and promised he'd make me rich, some day, and I done it, and I'm sorry I done it, and I wisht I hadn't; but I hain't stole no di'monds, and I hain't *got* no di'monds; I wisht I may never stir if it ain't so. The sheriff can search me and see."

Tom says—

"Your Honor, it wasn't right to call him a thief, and I'll let up on that a little. He did steal the di'monds, but he didn't know it. He stole them from his brother Jake when he was laying dead, after Jake had stole them from the other thieves; but Jubiter didn't know he was stealing them; and he's been swelling around here with them a month; yes, sir, twelve thousand dollars' worth of di'monds on him—all that riches, and going around here every day just like a poor man. Yes, your Honor, he's got them on him now."

The judge spoke up and says—

"Search him, sheriff."

Well, sir, the sheriff he ransacked him high and low, and everywhere: searched his hat, socks, seams, boots, everything—and Tom he stood there quiet, laying for another of them effects of his'n. Finally the sheriff he give it up, and everybody looked disappointed, and Jubiter says—

"There, now! what'd I tell you?"

And the judge says—

"It appears you were mistaken this time, my boy."

Then Tom he took an attitude and let on to be studying with all his might, and scratching his head. Then all of a sudden he glanced up chipper, and says—

"Oh, now I've got it! I'd forgot."

Which was a lie, and I knowed it. Then he says—

"Will somebody be good enough to lend me a little small screw-driver? There was one in your brother's hand-bag that you smouched, Jubiter, but I reckon you didn't fetch it with you."

"No, I didn't. I didn't want it, and I give it away."

"That was because you didn't know what it was for."

Jubiter had his boots on again, by now, and when the thing Tom wanted was passed over the people's heads till it got to him, he says to Jubiter—

"Put up your foot on this chair." And he kneeled down and begun to unscrew the heel-plate, everybody watching; and when he got that big di'mond out of that boot-heel and held it up and let it flash and blaze and squirt sunlight everwhich-away, it just took everybody's breath; and Jubiter he looked so sick and sorry you never see the like of it. And when Tom held up the other di'mond he looked sorrier than ever. Land! he was thinking how he would 'a' skipped out and been rich and independent in a foreign land if he'd only had the luck to guess what the screw-driver was in the carpet-bag for.

Well, it was a most exciting time, take it all around, and Tom got cords of glory. The judge took the di'monds, and stood up in his pulpit, and cleared his throat, and shoved his spectacles back on his head, and says—

"I'll keep them and notify the owners; and when they send for them it will be a real pleasure to me to hand you the two thousand dollars, for you've earned the money—yes, and you've earned the deepest and most sincerest thanks of this community besides, for lifting a wronged and innocent family out of ruin and shame, and saving a good and honorable man from a felon's death, and for exposing to infamy and the punishment of the law a cruel and odious scoundrel and his miserable creatures!"

Well, sir, if there'd been a brass band to bust out some music, then, it would 'a' been just the perfectest thing I ever see, and Tom Sawyer he said the same.

Then the sheriff he nabbed Brace Dunlap and his crowd, and by and by next month the judge had them up for trial and jailed the whole lot. And everybody crowded back to uncle Silas's little old church, and was ever so loving and kind to him and the family and couldn't do enough for them; and uncle Silas he preached them the blamedest jumbledest idiotic sermons you ever struck, and would tangle you up so you couldn't find your way home in daylight; but the people never let on but what they thought it was the clearest and brightest and elegantest sermons that ever was; and they would set there and cry, for love and pity; but, by George, they give me the jim-jams and the fan-tods and caked up what brains I had, and turned them solid; but by and by they loved the old man's intellects back into him again and he was as sound in his skull as ever he was, which ain't no flattery, I reckon. And so the whole family was as happy as birds, and nobody could be gratefuler and lovinger than what they was to Tom Sawyer; and the same to me, though I hadn't done nothing. And when the two thousand dollars come, Tom give half of it to me, and never told anybody so, which didn't surprise me, because I knowed him.

NO. 44,
THE MYSTERIOUS STRANGER

BEING AN ANCIENT TALE FOUND IN A JUG,
AND FREELY TRANSLATED FROM THE JUG

Chapter 1

IT WAS in 1490—winter. Austria was far away from the world, and asleep; it was still the Middle Ages in Austria, and promised to remain so forever. Some even set it away back centuries upon centuries and said that by the mental and spiritual clock it was still the Age of Faith in Austria. But they meant it as a compliment, not a slur, and it was so taken, and we were all proud of it. I remember it well, although I was only a boy; and I remember, too, the pleasure it gave me.

Yes, Austria was far from the world, and asleep, and our village was in the middle of that sleep, being in the middle of Austria. It drowsed in peace in the deep privacy of a hilly and woodsy solitude where news from the world hardly ever came to disturb its dreams, and was infinitely content. At its front flowed the tranquil river, its surface painted with cloud-forms and the reflections of drifting arks and stone-boats; behind it rose the woody steeps to the base of the lofty precipice; from the top of the precipice frowned the vast castle of Rosenfeld, its long stretch of towers and bastions mailed in vines; beyond the river, a league to the left, was a tumbled expanse of forest-clothed hills cloven by winding gorges where the sun never penetrated; and to the right, a precipice overlooked the river, and between it and the hills just spoken of lay a far-reaching plain dotted with little homesteads nested among orchards and shade-trees.

The whole region for leagues around was the hereditary property of prince Rosenfeld, whose servants kept the castle always in perfect condition for occupancy, but neither he nor his family came there oftener than once in five years. When they came it was as if the lord of the world had arrived, and had brought all the glories of its kingdoms along; and when they went they left a calm behind which was like the deep sleep which follows an orgy.

Eseldorf was a paradise for us boys. We were not overmuch pestered with schooling. Mainly we were trained to be good Catholics; to revere the Virgin, the Church and the saints above everything; to hold the Monarch in awful reverence, speak of him with bated breath, uncover before his picture, regard him as the gracious provider of our daily bread and of all our earthly blessings, and ourselves as being sent into the world with the one only mission, to labor for him, bleed for him, die for him, when necessary. Beyond these matters we were not required to know much; and in fact, not allowed to. The priests said that knowledge was not good for the common people, and could make them discontented with the lot which God had appointed for them, and God would not endure discontentment with His plans. This was true, for the priests got it of the Bishop.

It was discontentment that came so near to being the ruin of Gretel Marx the dairyman's widow, who had two horses and a cart, and carried milk to the market town. A Hussite woman named Adler came to Eseldorf and went slyly about, and began to persuade some of the ignorant and foolish to come privately by night to her house and hear "God's *real* message," as she called it. She was a cunning woman, and sought out only those few who could read—flattering them by saying it showed their intelligence, and that only the intelligent could understand her doctrine. She gradually got ten together, and these she poisoned nightly with her heresies in her house. And she gave them Hussite sermons, all written out, to keep for their own, and persuaded them that it was no sin to read them.

One day Father Adolf came along and found the widow sitting in the shade of the horse-chestnut that stood by her house, reading these iniquities. He was a very loud and zealous and strenuous priest, and was always working to get more reputation, hoping to be a Bishop some day; and he was always spying around and keeping a sharp lookout on other people's flocks as well as his own; and he was dissolute and profane and malicious, but otherwise a good enough man, it was generally thought. And he certainly had talent; he was a most fluent and chirpy speaker, and could say the cuttingest things and the wittiest, though a little coarse, maybe—however it was only his enemies who said that, and it really wasn't any truer of him than of others; but he belonged to the village council, and lorded it there, and played smart dodges that carried his projects through, and of course that nettled the others; and in their resentment they gave him nicknames privately, and called him the "Town Bull," and "Hell's Delight," and all sorts of things; which was natural, for when you are in politics you are in the wasp's nest with a short shirt-tail, as the saying is.

He was rolling along down the road, pretty full and feeling good, and braying "We'll sing the wine-cup and the lass" in his thundering bass, when he caught sight of the widow reading her book. He came to a stop before her and stood swaying there, leering down at her with his fishy eyes, and his purple fat face working and grimacing, and said—

"What is it you've got there, Frau Marx? What are you reading?"

She let him see. He bent down and took one glance, then he knocked the writings out of her hand and said angrily—

"Burn them, burn them, you fool! Don't you know it's a sin to read them? Do you want to damn your soul? Where did you get them?"

She told him, and he said—

"By God I expected it. I will attend to that woman; I will make this place sultry for her. You go to her meetings, do you? What does she teach you—to worship the Virgin?"

"No—only God."

"I thought it. You are on your road to hell. The Virgin will punish you for this—you mark my words." Frau Marx was getting frightened; and was going to try to excuse herself for her conduct, but Father Adolf shut her up and went on storming at her and telling her what the Virgin would do with her, until she was ready to swoon with fear. She went on her knees and begged him to tell her what to do to appease the Virgin. He put a heavy penance on her, scolded her some more, then took up his song where he had left off, and went rolling and zigzagging away.

But Frau Marx fell again, within the week, and went back to Frau Adler's meeting one night. Just four days afterward both of her horses died! She flew to Father Adolf, full of repentance and despair, and cried and sobbed, and said she was ruined and must starve; for how could she market her milk now? What *must* she do? tell her what to do. He said—

"I told you the Virgin would punish you—didn't I tell you

that? Hell's bells! did you think I was lying? You'll pay attention next time, I reckon."

Then he told her what to do. She must have a picture of
the horses painted, and walk on pilgrimage to the Church of
Our Lady of the Dumb Creatures, and hang it up there, and
make her offerings; then go home and sell the skins of her
horses and buy a lottery ticket bearing the number of the date
of their death, and then wait in patience for the Virgin's answer. In a week it came, when Frau Marx was almost perishing with despair—her ticket drew fifteen hundred ducats!

That is the way the Virgin rewards a real repentance. Frau
Marx did not fall again. In her gratitude she went to those
other women and told them her experience and showed them
how sinful and foolish they were and how dangerously they
were acting; and they all burned their sermons and returned
repentant to the bosom of the Church, and Frau Adler had to
carry her poisons to some other market. It was the best lesson
and the wholesomest our village ever had. It never allowed
another Hussite to come there; and for reward the Virgin
watched over it and took care of it personally, and made it
fortunate and prosperous always.

It was in conducting funerals that Father Adolf was at his
best, if he hadn't too much of a load on, but only about
enough to make him properly appreciate the sacredness of his
office. It was fine to see him march his procession through
the village, between the kneeling ranks, keeping one eye on
the candles blinking yellow in the sun to see that the acolytes
walked stiff and held them straight, and the other watching
out for any dull oaf that might forget himself and stand staring and covered when the Host was carried past. He would
snatch that oaf's broad hat from his head, hit him a staggering whack in the face with it and growl out in a low snarl—

"Where's your manners, you beast?—and the Lord God
passing by!"

Whenever there was a suicide he was active. He was on
hand to see that the government did its duty and turned the
family out into the road, and confiscated its small belongings
and didn't smouch any of the Church's share; and he was on
hand again at midnight when the corpse was buried at the
cross-roads—not to do any religious office, for of course that

was not allowable—but to see, for himself, that the stake was driven through the body in a right and permanent and workmanlike way.

It was grand to see him make procession through the village in plague-time, with our saint's relics in their jeweled casket, and trade prayers and candles to the Virgin for her help in abolishing the pest.

And he was always on hand at the bridge-head on the 9th of December, at the Assuaging of the Devil. Ours was a beautiful and massive stone bridge of five arches, and was seven hundred years old. It was built by the Devil in a single night. The prior of the monastery hired him to do it, and had trouble to persuade him, for the Devil said he had built bridges for priests all over Europe, and had always got cheated out of his wages; and this was the last time he would trust a Christian if he got cheated now. Always before, when he built a bridge, he was to have for his pay the first passenger that crossed it—everybody knowing he meant a Christian, of course. But no matter, he didn't *say* it, so they always sent a jackass or a chicken or some other undamnable passenger across first, and so got the best of him. This time he *said* Christian, and wrote it in the bond himself, so there couldn't be any misunderstanding. And that isn't tradition, it is history, for I have seen that bond myself, many a time; it is always brought out on Assuaging Day, and goes to the bridge-head with the procession; and anybody who pays ten groschen can see it and get remission of thirty-three sins besides, times being easier for every one then than they are now, and sins much cheaper; so much cheaper that all except the very poorest could afford them. Those were good days, but they are gone and will not come any more, so every one says.

Yes, he put it in the bond, and the prior said he didn't want the bridge built yet, but would soon appoint a day—perhaps in about a week. There was an old monk wavering along between life and death, and the prior told the watchers to keep a sharp eye out and let him know as soon as they saw that the monk was actually dying. Towards midnight the 9th of December the watchers brought him word, and he summoned the Devil and the bridge was begun. All the rest of the night the prior and the Brotherhood sat up and prayed that the dying one might be given strength to rise up and walk across the bridge at dawn—strength enough, but not too much. The prayer was heard, and it made great excitement in heaven; insomuch that all the heavenly host got up before dawn and came down to see; and there they were, clouds and clouds of angels filling all the air above the bridge; and the dying monk tottered across, and just had strength to get over; then he fell dead just as the Devil was reaching for him, and as his soul escaped the angels swooped down and caught it and flew up to heaven with it, laughing and jeering, and Satan found he hadn't anything but a useless carcase.

He was very angry, and charged the prior with cheating him, and said "*this* isn't a Christian," but the prior said "Yes it is, it's a *dead* one." Then the prior and all the monks went through with a great lot of mock ceremonies, pretending it was to assuage the Devil and reconcile him, but really it was only to make fun of him and stir up his bile more than ever. So at last he gave them all a solid good cursing, they laughing at him all the time. Then he raised a black storm of thunder and lightning and wind and flew away in it; and as he went the spike on the end of his tail caught on a capstone and tore it away; and there it always lay, throughout the centuries, as proof of what he had done. I have seen it myself, a thousand times. Such things speak louder than written records; for written records can lie, unless they are set down by a priest. The mock Assuaging is repeated every 9th of December, to this day, in memory of that holy thought of the prior's which rescued an imperiled Christian soul from the odious Enemy of mankind.

There have been better priests, in some ways, than Father Adolf, for he had his failings, but there was never one in our commune who was held in more solemn and awful respect. This was because he had absolutely no fear of the Devil. He was the only Christian I have ever known of whom that could be truly said. People stood in deep dread of him, on that account; for they thought there must be something supernatural about him, else he could not be so bold and so confident. All men speak in bitter disapproval of the Devil, but they do it reverently, not flippantly; but Father Adolf's way was very different; he called him by every vile and putrid name he could lay his tongue to, and it made every one shudder that heard him; and often he would even speak of him scornfully and scoffingly; then the people crossed themselves and went quickly out of his presence, fearing that something fearful might happen; and this was natural, for after all is said and done Satan is a sacred character, being mentioned in the Bible, and it cannot be proper to utter lightly the sacred names, lest heaven itself should resent it.

Father Adolf had actually met Satan face to face, more than once, and defied him. This was known to be so. Father Adolf said it himself. He never made any secret of it, but spoke it right out. And that he was speaking true, there was proof, in at least one instance; for on that occasion he quarreled with the Enemy, and intrepidly threw his bottle at him, and there, upon the wall of his study was the ruddy splotch where it struck and broke.

The priest that we all loved best and were sorriest for, was Father Peter. But the Bishop suspended him for talking around in conversation that God was all goodness and would find a way to save *all* his poor human children. It was a horrible thing to say, but there was never any absolute proof that Father Peter said it; and it was out of character for him to say it, too, for he was always good and gentle and truthful, and a good Catholic, and always teaching in the pulpit just what the Church required, and nothing else. But there it was, you see: he wasn't charged with saying it in the pulpit, where all the congregation could hear and testify, but only outside, in talk; and it is easy for enemies to manufacture *that*. Father Peter denied it; but no matter, Father Adolf wanted his place, and he told the Bishop, and swore to it, that he overheard Father Peter say it; heard Father Peter say it to his niece, when Father Adolf was behind the door listening—for he was suspicious of Father Peter's soundness, he said, and the interests of religion required that he be watched.

The niece, Gretchen, denied it, and implored the Bishop to believe her and spare her old uncle from poverty and disgrace; but Father Adolf had been poisoning the Bishop against the old man a long time privately, and he wouldn't listen; for he had a deep admiration of Father Adolf's bravery toward the Devil, and an awe of him on account of his having met the

Devil face to face; and so he was a slave to Father Adolf's influence. He suspended Father Peter, indefinitely, though he wouldn't go so far as to excommunicate him on the evidence of only one witness; and now Father Peter had been out a couple of years, and Father Adolf had his flock.

Those had been hard years for the old priest and Gretchen. They had been favorites, but of course that changed when they came under the shadow of the Bishop's frown. Many of their friends fell away entirely, and the rest became cool and distant. Gretchen was a lovely girl of eighteen, when the trouble came, and she had the best head in the village, and the most in it. She taught the harp, and earned all her clothes and pocket money by her own industry. But her scholars fell off one by one, now; she was forgotten when there were dances and parties among the youth of the village; the young fellows stopped coming to the house, all except Wilhelm Meidling—and he could have been spared; she and her uncle were sad and forlorn in their neglect and disgrace, and the sunshine was gone out of their lives. Matters went worse and worse, all through the two years. Clothes were wearing out, bread was harder and harder to get. And now at last, the very end was come. Solomon Isaacs had lent all the money he was willing to put on the house, and gave notice that to-morrow he should foreclose.

Chapter 2

I HAD BEEN familiar with that village life, but now for as much as a year I had been out of it, and was busy learning a trade. I was more curiously than pleasantly situated. I have spoken of Castle Rosenfeld; I have also mentioned a precipice which overlooked the river. Well, along this precipice stretched the towered and battlemented mass of a similar castle—prodigious, vine-clad, stately and beautiful, but mouldering to ruin. The great line that had possessed it and made it their chief home during four or five centuries was extinct, and no scion of it had lived in it now for a hundred years. It was a stanch old pile, and the greater part of it was still habitable.

Inside, the ravages of time and neglect were less evident than they were outside. As a rule the spacious chambers and the vast corridors, ballrooms, banqueting halls and rooms of state were bare and melancholy and cobwebbed, it is true, but the walls and floors were in tolerable condition, and they could have been lived in. In some of the rooms the decayed and ancient furniture still remained, but if the empty ones were pathetic to the view, these were sadder still.

This old castle was not wholly destitute of life. By grace of the Prince over the river, who owned it, my master, with his little household, had for many years been occupying a small portion of it, near the centre of the mass. The castle could have housed a thousand persons; consequently, as you may say, this handful was lost in it, like a swallow's nest in a cliff.

My master was a printer. His was a new art, being only thirty or forty years old, and almost unknown in Austria. Very few persons in our secluded region had ever seen a printed page, few had any very clear idea about the art of printing, and perhaps still fewer had any curiosity concerning it or felt any interest in it. Yet we had to conduct our business with some degree of privacy, on account of the Church. The Church was opposed to the cheapening of books and the indiscriminate dissemination of knowledge. Our villagers did not trouble themselves about our work, and had no commerce in it; we published nothing there, and printed nothing that they could have read, they being ignorant of abstruse sciences and the dead languages.

We were a mixed family. My master, Heinrich Stein, was portly, and of a grave and dignified carriage, with a large and benevolent face and calm deep eyes—a patient man whose temper could stand much before it broke. His head was bald, with a valance of silky white hair hanging around it, his face was clean shaven, his raiment was good and fine, but not rich. He was a scholar, and a dreamer or a thinker, and loved learning and study, and would have submerged his mind all the days and nights in his books and been pleasantly and peacefully unconscious of his surroundings, if God had been willing. His complexion was younger than his hair; he was four or five years short of sixty.

A large part of his surroundings consisted of his wife. She

was well along in life, and was long and lean and flat-breasted, and had an active and vicious tongue and a diligent and dev-ilish spirit, and more religion than was good for her, consid-ering the quality of it. She hungered for money, and believed there was a treasure hid in the black deeps of the castle some-where; and between fretting and sweating about that and try-ing to bring sinners nearer to God when any fell in her way she was able to fill up her time and save her life from getting uninteresting and her soul from getting mouldy. There was old tradition for the treasure, and the word of Balthasar Hoff-man thereto. He had come from a long way off, and had brought a great reputation with him, which he concealed in our family the best he could, for he had no more ambition to be burnt by the Church than another. He lived with us on light salary and board, and worked the constellations for the treasure. He had an easy berth and was not likely to lose his job if the constellations held out, for it was Frau Stein that hired him; and her faith in him, as in all things she had at heart, was of the staying kind. Inside the walls, where was safety, he clothed himself as Egyptians and magicians should, and moved stately, robed in black velvet starred and mooned and cometed and sun'd with the symbols of his trade done in silver, and on his head a conical tower with like symbols glint-ing from it. When he at intervals went outside he left his busi-ness suit behind, with good discretion, and went dressed like anybody else and looking the Christian with such cunning art that St. Peter would have let him in quite as a matter of course, and probably asked him to take something. Very nat-urally we were all afraid of him—abjectly so, I suppose I may say—though Ernest Wasserman professed that he wasn't. Not that he did it publicly; no, he didn't; for, with all his talk, Ernest Wasserman had a judgment in choosing the right place for it that never forsook him. He wasn't even afraid of ghosts, if you let him tell it; and not only that but didn't believe in them. That is to say, he *said* he didn't believe in them. The truth is, he would say any foolish thing that he thought would make him conspicuous.

To return to Frau Stein. This masterly devil was the mas-ter's second wife, and before that she had been the widow Vogel. She had brought into the family a young thing by her first marriage, and this girl was now seventeen and a blister, so to speak; for she was a second edition of her mother—just plain galley-proof, neither revised nor corrected, full of turned letters, wrong fonts, outs and doubles, as we say in the printing-shop—in a word, *pi*, if you want to put it remorselessly strong and yet not strain the facts. Yet if it ever would be fair to strain facts it would be fair in her case, for she was not loath to strain them herself when so minded. Moses Haas said that whenever she took up an en-quad fact, just watch her and you would see her try to cram it in where there wasn't breathing-room for a 4-m space; and she'd do it, too, if she had to take the sheep-foot to it. Isn't it neat! Doesn't it describe it to a dot? Well, he could say such things, Moses could—as malicious a devil as we had on the place, but as bright as a lightning-bug and as sudden, when he was in the humor. He had a talent for getting himself hated, and always had it out at usury. That daughter kept the name she was born to—Maria Vogel; it was her mother's preference and her own. Both were proud of it, without any reason, except reasons which they invented, themselves, from time to time, as a market offered. Some of the Vogels may have been distinguished, by not getting hanged, Moses thought, but no one attached much importance to what the mother and daughter claimed for them. Maria had plenty of energy and vivacity and tongue, and was shapely enough but not pretty, barring her eyes, which had all kinds of fire in them, according to the mood of the moment—opal-fire, fox-fire, hell-fire, and the rest. She hadn't any fear, broadly speaking. Perhaps she had none at all, except for Satan, and ghosts, and witches and the priest and the magician, and a sort of fear of God in the dark, and of the lightning when she had been blaspheming and hadn't time to get in *aves* enough to square up and cash-in. She despised Marget Regen, the master's niece, along with Marget's mother, Frau Regen, who was the master's sister and a dependent and bedridden widow. She loved Gustav Fischer, the big and blonde and handsome and good-hearted journeyman, and detested the rest of the tribe impartially, I think. Gustav did not reciprocate.

Marget Regen was Maria's age—seventeen. She was lithe and graceful and trim-built as a fish, and she was a blue-eyed blonde, and soft and sweet and innocent and shrinking and winning and gentle and beautiful; just a vision for the eyes, worshipful, adorable, enchanting; but that wasn't the hive for her. She was a kitten in a menagerie.

She was a second edition of what her mother had been at her age; but struck from the standing forms and needing no revising, as one says in the printing-shop. That poor meek mother! yonder she had lain, partially paralysed, ever since her brother my master had brought her eagerly there a dear and lovely young widow with her little child fifteen years before; the pair had been welcome, and had forgotten their poverty and poor-relation estate and been happy during three whole years. Then came the new wife with her five-year brat, and a change began. The new wife was never able to root out the master's love for his sister, nor to drive sister and child from under the roof, but she accomplished the rest: as soon as she had gotten her lord properly trained to harness, she shortened his visits to his sister and made them infrequent. But she made up for this by going frequently herself and roasting the widow, as the saying is.

Next was old Katrina. She was cook and housekeeper; her forbears had served the master's people and none else for three or four generations; she was sixty, and had served the master all his life, from the time when she was a little girl and he was a swaddled baby. She was erect, straight, six feet high, with the port and stride of a soldier; she was independent and masterful, and her fears were limited to the supernatural. She believed she could whip anybody on the place, and would have considered an invitation a favor. As far as her allegiance stretched, she paid it with affection and reverence, but it did not extend beyond "her family"—the master, his sister, and Marget. She regarded Frau Vogel and Maria as aliens and intruders, and was frank about saying so.

She had under her two strapping young wenches—Sara and Duffles (a nickname), and a manservant, Jacob, and a porter, Fritz.

Next, we have the printing force.

Adam Binks, sixty years old, learnèd bachelor, proof-reader, poor, disappointed, surly.

Hans Katzenyammer, 36, printer, huge, strong, freckled,

red-headed, rough. When drunk, quarrelsome. Drunk when opportunity offered.

Moses Haas, 28, printer; a looker-out for himself; liable to say acid things about people and to people; take him all around, not a pleasant character.

Barty Langbein, 15; cripple; general-utility lad; sunny spirit; affectionate; could play the fiddle.

Ernest Wasserman, 17, apprentice; braggart, malicious, hateful, coward, liar, cruel, underhanded, treacherous. He and Moses had a sort of half fondness for each other, which was natural, they having one or more traits in common, down among the lower grades of traits.

Gustav Fischer, 27, printer; large, well built, shapely and muscular; quiet, brave, kindly, a good disposition, just and fair; a slow temper to ignite, but a reliable burner when well going. He was about as much out of place as was Marget. He was the best man of them all, and deserved to be in better company.

Last of all comes August Feldner, 16, 'prentice. This is myself.

Chapter 3

OF several conveniences there was no lack; among them, fire-wood and room. There was no end of room, we had it to waste. Big or little chambers for all—suit yourself, and change when you liked. For a kitchen we used a spacious room which was high up over the massive and frowning gateway of the castle and looked down the woody steeps and southward over the receding plain.

It opened into a great room with the same outlook, and this we used as dining room, drinking room, quarreling room—in a word, family room. Above its vast fire-place, which was flanked with fluted columns, rose the wide granite mantel, heavily carved, to the high ceiling. With a cart-load of logs blazing here within and a snow-tempest howling and whirling outside, it was a heaven of a place for comfort and contentment and cosiness, and the exchange of injurious personalities. Especially after supper, with the lamps going and the day's work done. It was not the tribe's custom to hurry to bed.

The apartments occupied by the Steins were beyond this room to the east, on the same front; those occupied by Frau Regen and Marget were on the same front also, but to the west, beyond the kitchen. The rooms of the rest of the herd were on the same floor, but on the other side of the principal great interior court—away over in the north front, which rose high in air above precipice and river.

The printing-shop was remote, and hidden in an upper section of a round tower. Visitors were not wanted there; and if they had tried to hunt their way to it without a guide they would have concluded to give it up and call another time before they got through.

One cold day, when the noon meal was about finished, a most forlorn looking youth, apparently sixteen or seventeen years old, appeared in the door, and stopped there, timid and humble, venturing no further. His clothes were coarse and old, ragged, and lightly powdered with snow, and for shoes he had nothing but some old serge remnants wrapped about his feet and ancles and tied with strings. The war of talk stopped at once and all eyes were turned upon the apparition; those of the master, and Marget, and Gustav Fischer, and Barty Langbein, in pity and kindness, those of Frau Stein and the rest in varying shades of contempt and hostility.

"What do you want here?" said the Frau, sharply.

The youth seemed to wince under that. He did not raise his head, but with eyes still bent upon the floor and shyly fumbling his ruin of a cap which he had removed from his head, answered meekly—

"I am friendless, gracious lady, and am so—*so* hungry!"

"*So* hungry, are you?"—mimicking him. "Who invited you? How did you get in? Take yourself out of this!"

She half rose, as if minded to help him out with her hands. Marget started to rise at the same moment, with her plate in her hands and an appeal on her lips: "May I, madam?"

"No! Sit down!" commanded the Frau. The master, his face all pity, had opened his lips—no doubt to say the kind word—but he closed them now, discouraged. Old Katrina emerged from the kitchen, and stood towering in the door. She took in the situation, and just as the boy was turning sorrowfully away, she hailed him:

"Come back, child, there's room in my kitchen, and plenty to eat, too!"

"Shut your mouth you hussy, and mind your own affairs and keep to your own place!" screamed the Frau, rising and turning toward Katrina, who, seeing that the boy was afraid to move, was coming to fetch him. Katrina, answering no word, came striding on. "Command her, Heinrich Stein! will you allow your own wife to be defied by a servant?"

The master said "It isn't the first time," and did not seem ungratified.

Katrina came on, undisturbed; she swung unheeding past her mistress, took the boy by the hand, and led him back to her fortress, saying, as she crossed its threshold,

"If any of you wants this boy, you come and get him, that's all!"

Apparently no one wanted him at that expense, so no one followed. The talk opened up briskly, straightway. Frau Stein wanted the boy turned out as soon as might be; she was willing he should be fed, if he was so hungry as he had said he was, which was probably a lie, for he had the look of a liar, she said, but shelter he could have none, for in her opinion he had the look of a murderer and a thief; and she asked Maria if it wasn't so. Maria confirmed it, and then the Frau asked for the general table's judgment. Opinions came freely: negatives from the master and from Marget and Fischer, affirmatives from the rest; and then war broke out. Presently, as one could easily see, the master was beginning to lose patience. He was likely to assert himself when that sign appeared. He suddenly broke in upon the wrangle, and said,

"Stop! This is a great to-do about nothing. The boy is not necessarily *bad* because he is unfortunate. And if he *is* bad, what of it? A bad person can be as hungry as a good one, and hunger is always respectable. And so is weariness. The boy is worn and tired, any one can see it. If he wants rest and shelter, *that* is no crime; let him say it and have it, be he bad or good—there's room enough."

That settled it. Frau Stein was opening her mouth to try

and unsettle it again when Katrina brought the boy in and stood him before the master and said, encouragingly,

"Don't be afraid, the master's a just man. Master, he's a plenty good enough boy, for all he looks such a singed cat. He's out of luck, there's nothing else the matter with him. Look at his face, look at his eye. He's not a beggar for love of it. He wants work."

"*Work!*" scoffed Frau Stein; "that tramp?" And "work!" sneered this and that and the other one. But the master looked interested, and not unpleased. He said,

"Work, is it? What kind of work are you willing to do, lad?"

"He's willing to do any kind, sir," interrupted Katrina, eagerly, "and he don't want any pay."

"What, no pay?"

"No sir, nothing but food to eat and shelter for his head, poor lad."

"Not even clothes?"

"He shan't go naked, sir, if you'll keep him, my wage is bail for that."

There was an affectionate light in the boy's eye as he glanced gratefully up at his majestic new friend—a light which the master noted.

"Do you think you could do rough work—rough, hard drudgery?"

"Yes, sir, I could, if you will try me; I am strong."

"Carry fire-logs up these long stairways?"

"Yes, sir."

"And scrub, like the maids; and build fires in the rooms; and carry up water to the chambers; and split wood; and help in the laundry and the kitchen; and take care of the dog?"

"Yes, sir, all those things, if you will let me try."

"All for food and shelter? Well, I don't see how a body is going to refu—"

"Heinrich Stein, wait! If you think you are going to nest this vermin in this place without ever so much as a by-your-leave to me, I can tell you you are very much mis—"

"Be quiet!" said the husband, sternly. "Now, then, you have all expressed your opinions about this boy, but there is one vote which you have not counted. I value that one above some of the others—above any of the others, in fact. On that vote by itself I would give him a trial. That is my decision. You can discuss some other subject, now—this one is finished. Take him along, Katrina, and give him a room and let him get some rest."

Katrina stiffened with pride and satisfaction in her triumph. The boy's eyes looked his gratitude, and he said,

"I would like to go to work *now*, if I may, sir."

Before an answer could come, Frau Stein interrupted:

"I want to *know*. Whose vote was it that wasn't counted? I'm not hard of hearing, and I don't know of any."

"The dog's."

Everybody showed surprise. But there it was: the dog hadn't made a motion when the boy came in. Nobody but the master had noticed it, but it was the fact. It was the first time that that demon had ever treated a stranger with civil indifference. He was chained in the corner, and had a bone between his paws and was gnawing it; and not even growling, which was not his usual way. Frau Stein's eyes beamed with a vicious pleasure, and she called out,

"You want work, do you? Well, there it is, cut out for you. Take the dog out and give him an airing!"

Even some of the hardest hearts there felt the cruelty of it, and their horror showed in their faces when the boy stepped innocently forward to obey.

"Stop!" shouted the master, and Katrina, flushing with anger, sprang after the youth and halted him.

"Shame!" she said; and the master turned his indignation loose and gave his wife a dressing down that astonished her. Then he said to the stranger,

"You are free to rest, lad, if you like, but if you would rather work, Katrina will see what she can find for you. What is your name?"

The boy answered, quietly,

"Number 44, New Series 864,962."

Everybody's eyes came open in a stare. Of course. The master thought perhaps he hadn't heard aright; so he asked again, and the boy answered the same as before,

"Number 44, New Series 864,962."

"What a hell of a name!" ejaculated Hans Katzenyammer, piously.

"Jail-number, likely," suggested Moses Haas, searchingly examining the boy with his rat eyes, and unconsciously twisting and stroking his silky and scanty moustache with his fingers, a way he had when his cogitations were concentrated upon a thing.

"It's a strange name," said the master, with a barely noticeable touch of suspicion in his tone, "where did you get it?"

"I don't know, sir," said No. 44, tranquilly, "I've always had it."

The master forbore to pursue the matter further, probably fearing that the ice was thin, but Maria Vogel chirped up and asked,

"Have you ever been in jail?"

The master burst in with—

"There, that's enough of that! You needn't answer, my boy, unless you want to." He paused—hopeful, maybe—but 44 did not seize the opportunity to testify for himself. He stood still and said nothing. Satirical smiles flitted here and there, down the table, and the master looked annoyed and disappointed, though he tried to conceal it. "Take him along, Katrina." He said it as kindly as he could, but there was just a trifle of a chill in his manner, and it delighted those creatures.

Katrina marched out with 44.

Out of a wise respect for the temper the master was in, there was no outspoken comment, but a low buzz skimmed along down the table, whose burden was, "That silence was a confession—the chap's a Jail-Bird."

It was a bad start for 44. Everybody recognized it. Marget was troubled, and asked Gustav Fischer if he believed the boy was what these people were calling him. Fischer replied, with regret in his tone,

"Well, you know, Fräulein, he could have denied it, and he didn't do it."

"Yes, I know, but think what a good face he has. And pure, too; and beautiful."

"True, quite true. And it's astonishing. But there it is, you see—he didn't deny it. In fact he didn't even seem greatly interested in the matter."

"I know it. It is unaccountable. What do you make out of it?"

"The fact that he didn't see the gravity of the situation marks him for a fool. But it isn't the face of a fool. That he could be silent at such a time is constructive evidence that he is a Jail-Bird—with that face! which is impossible. I can't solve you that riddle, Fräulein—it's beyond my depth."

Forty-Four entered, straining under a heavy load of logs, which he dumped into a great locker and went briskly out again. He was quickly back with a similar load; and another, and still another.

"There," said the master, rising and starting away, "that will do; you are not required to kill yourself."

"One more—just one more," said the boy, as if asking a favor.

"Very well, but let that be the last," said the master, as if granting one; and he left the room.

Forty-Four brought the final load, then stood, apparently waiting for orders. None coming, he asked for them. It was Frau Stein's chance. She gave him a joyfully malicious glance out of her yellow eyes, and snapped out—

"Take the dog for an airing!"

Outraged, friend and foe alike rose at her! They surged forward to save the boy, but they were too late; he was already on his knees loosing the chain, his face and the dog's almost in contact. And now the people surged back to save themselves; but the boy rose and went, with the chain in his hand, and the dog trotted after him happy and content.

Chapter 4

DID it make a stir? Oh, on your life! For nearly two minutes the herd were speechless; and if I may judge by myself, they quaked, and felt pale; then they all broke out at once, and discussed it with animation and most of them said what an astonishing thing it was—and unbelievable, too, if they hadn't seen it with their own eyes. With Marget and Fischer and Barty the note was admiration. With Frau Stein, Maria, Katzenyammer and Binks it was wonder, but wonder mixed with maledictions—maledictions upon the devil that

possessed the Jail-Bird—they averring that no stranger unpro-
tected by a familiar spirit could touch that dog and come
away but in fragments; and so, in their opinion the house was
in a much more serious plight, now, than it was before when
it only had a thief in it. Then there were three silent ones:
Ernest and Moses indicated by their cynical manner and
mocking smiles that they had but a small opinion of the exploit, it wasn't a matter to make such a fuss about; the other
silent one—the magician—was so massively silent, so weight-
ily silent, that it presently attracted attention. Then a light began to dawn upon some of the tribe; they turned reverent and
marveling eyes upon the great man, and Maria Vogel said
with the happy exultation of a discoverer—

"There he stands, and let him deny it if he can! He put
power upon that boy with his magic. I just suspected it, and
now I know it! Ah, you are caught, you can't escape—own
up, you wonder of the ages!"

The magician smiled a simpering smile, a detected and convicted smile, and several cried out—

"There, he *is* caught—he's trying to deny it, and he can't!
Come, be fair, be good, confess!" and Frau Stein and Maria
took hold of his great sleeves, peering worshipingly up in his
face and tried to detain him; but he gently disengaged himself
and fled from the room, apparently vastly embarrassed. So
that settled the matter. It was such a manifest confession that
not a doubter was left, every individual was convinced; and
the praises that that man got would have gone far to satisfy a
god. He was great before, he was held in awe before, but that
was as nothing to the towering repute to which he had soared
now. Frau Stein was in the clouds. She said that this was the
most astonishing exhibition of magic power Europe had ever
seen, and that the person who could doubt, after this, that he
could work any miracle he wanted to would justly take rank
as a fool. They all agreed that that was so, none denying it or
doubting; and Frau Stein, taking her departure with the other
ladies, declared that hereafter the magician should occupy her
end of the table and she would move to a humbler place at his
right, where she belonged.

All this was gall and vinegar to that jealous reptile Ernest
Wasserman, who could not endure to hear anybody praised,

and he began to cast about to turn the subject. Just then Fischer opened the way by remarking upon the Jail-Bird's strength, as shown in the wood-carrying. He said he judged that the Jail-Bird would be an ugly customer in a rough stand-up fight with a youth of his own age.

"*Him!*" scoffed Ernest, "I'm of his age, and I'll bet I'd make him sorry if he was to tackle me!"

This was Moses's chance. He said, with mock solicitude,

"Don't. Think of your mother. Don't make trouble with him, he might hurt you badly."

"Never you mind worrying about me, Moses Haas. Let him look out for himself if he meddles with me, that's all."

"Oh," said Moses, apparently relieved, "I was afraid you were going to meddle with *him.* I see he is not in any danger." After a pause, "Nor you," he added carelessly.

The taunt had the intended effect.

"Do you think I'm afraid to meddle with him? I'm not afraid of fifty of him. *I'll* show him!"

Forty-Four entered with the dog, and while he was chaining him Ernest began to edge toward the door.

"Oh," simpered Moses, "good-bye, ta-ta, I thought you were going to meddle with the Jail-Bird."

"What, to-day—and him all tired out and not at his best? I'd be ashamed of myself."

"Haw-haw-haw!" guffawed that lumbering ox, Hans Katzenyammer, "hear the noble-hearted poltroon!"

A whirlwind of derisive laughter and sarcastic remarks followed, and Ernest, stung to the quick, threw discretion to the winds and marched upon the Jail-Bird, and planted himself in front of him, crying out,

"Square off! Stand up like a man, and defend yourself."

"Defend myself?" said the boy, seeming not to understand. "From what?"

"From me—do you hear?"

"From you? I have not injured you; why should you wish to hurt me?"

The spectators were disgusted—and disappointed. Ernest's courage came up with a bound. He said fiercely,

"Haven't you any sense? Don't you know anything? You've got to fight me—do you understand that?"

"But I cannot fight you; I have nothing against you."

Ernest, mocking: "Afraid of *hurting* me, I suppose."

The Jail-Bird answered quite simply,

"No, there is no danger of that. I have nothing to hurt you for, and I shall not hurt you."

"Oh, thanks—how kind. Take that!"

But the blow did not arrive. The stranger caught both of Ernest's wrists and held them fast. Our apprentice tugged and struggled and perspired and swore, while the men stood around in a ring and laughed, and shouted, and made fun of Ernest and called him all sorts of outrageous pet names; and still the stranger held him in that grip, and did it quite easily and without puffing or blowing, whereas Ernest was gasping like a fish; and at last, when he was worn out and couldn't struggle any more, he snarled out,

"I give in—let go!" and 44 let go and said gently, "if you will let me I will stroke your arms for you and get the stiffness and the pain out;" but Ernest said "You go to hell," and went grumbling away and shaking his head and saying what he would do to the Jail-Bird one of these days, he needn't think it's over yet, he'd better look out or he'll find he's been fooling with the wrong customer; and so flourished out of the place and left the men jeering and yelling, and the Jail-Bird standing there looking as if it was all a puzzle to him and he couldn't make it out.

Chapter 5

THINGS were against that poor waif. He had maintained silence when he had had an opportunity to deny that he was a Jail-Bird, and that was bad for him. It got him that name, and he was likely to keep it. The men considered him a milksop because he spared Ernest Wasserman when it was evident that he could have whipped him. Privately my heart bled for the boy, and I wanted to be his friend, and longed to tell him so, but I had not the courage, for I was made as most people are made, and was afraid to follow my own instincts when they ran counter to other people's. The best of us would rather be popular than right. I found that out a good while ago. Katrina remained the boy's fearless friend, but she was alone in this. The master used him kindly, and protected him when he saw him ill treated, but further than this it was not in his nature to go except when he was roused, the current being so strong against him.

As to the clothes, Katrina kept her word. She sat up late, that very first night, and made him a coarse and cheap, but neat and serviceable doublet and hose with her own old hands; and she properly shod him, too. And she had her reward, for he was a graceful and beautiful creature, with the most wonderful eyes, and these facts all showed up, now, and filled her with pride. Daily he grew in her favor. Her old hungry heart was fed, she was a mother at last, with a child to love,—a child who returned her love in full measure, and to whom she was the salt of the earth.

As the days went along, everybody talked about 44, everybody observed him, everybody puzzled over him and his ways; but it was not discoverable that he ever concerned himself in the least degree about this or was in any way interested in what people thought of him or said about him. This indifference irritated the herd, but the boy did not seem aware of it.

The most ingenious and promising attempts to ruffle his temper and break up his calm went for nothing. Things flung at him struck him on the head or the back, and fell at his feet unnoticed; now and then a leg was shoved out and he tripped over it and went heavily down amid delighted laughter, but he picked himself up and went on without remark; often when he had brought a couple of twenty-pound cans of water up two long flights of stairs from the well in the court, they were seized and their winter-cold contents poured over him, but he went back unmurmuring for more; more than once, when the master was not present, Frau Stein made him share the dog's dinner in the corner, but he was content and offered no protest. The most of these persecutions were devised by Moses and Katzenyammer, but as a rule were carried out by that shabby poor coward, Ernest.

You see, now, how I was situated. I should have been despised if I had befriended him; and I should have been treated as he was, too. It is not everybody that can be as brave as Katrina was. More than once she caught Moses devising those tricks and Ernest carrying them out, and gave both of them an awful hiding; and once when Hans Katzenyammer interfered she beat that big ruffian till he went on his knees and begged.

What a devil to work the boy was! The earliest person up found him at it by lantern-light, the latest person up found him still at it long past midnight. It was the heaviest manual labor, but if he was ever tired it was not perceptible. He always moved with energy, and seemed to find a high joy in putting forth his strange and enduring strength.

He made reputation for the magician right along; no matter what unusual thing he did, the magician got the credit of it; at first the magician was cautious, when accused, and contented himself with silences which rather confessed than denied the soft impeachment, but he soon felt safe to throw that policy aside and frankly take the credit, and he did it. One day 44 unchained the dog and said "Now behave yourself, Felix, and don't hurt any one," and turned him loose, to the consternation of the herd, but the magician sweetly smiled and said,

"Do not fear. It is a little caprice of mine. My spirit is upon him, he cannot hurt you."

They were filled with adoring wonder and admiration, those people. They kissed the hem of the magician's robe, and beamed unutterable things upon him. Then the boy said to the dog,

"Go and thank your master for this great favor which he has granted you."

Well, it was an astonishing thing that happened, then. That ignorant and malignant vast animal, which had never been taught language or manners or religion or any other valuable thing, and could not be expected to understand a dandy speech like that, went and stood straight up on its hind feet before the magician, with its nose on a level with his face, and curved its paws and ducked its head piously, and said

"Yap-yap!—yap-yap!—yap-yap!" most reverently, and just as a Christian might at prayers.

Then it got down on all fours, and the boy said,

"Salute the master, and retire as from the presence of royalty."

The dog bowed very solemnly, then backed away stern-first to his corner—not with grace it is true, but well enough for a dog that hadn't had any practice of that kind and had never heard of royalty before nor its customs and etiquettes.

Did that episode take those people's breath away? You will not doubt it. They actually went on their knees to the magician, Frau Stein leading, the rest following. I know, for I was there and saw it. I was amazed at such degraded idolatry and hypocrisy—at least servility—but I knelt, too, to avert remark.

Life was become very interesting. Every few days there was a fresh novelty, some strange new thing done by the boy, something to wonder at; and so the magician's reputation was augmenting all the time. To be envied is the secret longing of pretty much all human beings—let us say *all;* to be envied makes them happy. The magician was happy, for never was a man so envied; he lived in the clouds.

I passionately longed to know 44, now. The truth is, he was being envied himself! Spite of all his shames and insults and persecutions. For, there is no denying it, it was an enviable conspicuousness and glory to be the instrument of such a dreaded and extraordinary magician as that and have people staring at you and holding their breath with awe while you did the miracles he devised. It is not for me to deny that I was one of 44's enviers. If I hadn't been, I should have been no natural boy. But I *was* a natural boy, and I longed to be conspicuous, and wondered at and talked about. Of course the case was the same with Ernest and Barty, though they did as I did—concealed it. I was always throwing myself in the magician's way whenever I could, in the hope that he would do miracles through me, too, but I could not get his attention. He never seemed to see me when he was preparing a prodigy.

At last I thought of a plan that I hoped might work. I would seek 44 privately and tell him how I was feeling and see if he would help me attain my desire. So I hunted up his room, and slipped up there clandestinely one night after the herd were in bed, and waited. After midnight an hour or two he came, and when the light of his lantern fell upon me he set it quickly down, and took me by both of my hands and beamed his gladness from his eyes, and there was no need to say a word.

Chapter 6

H E closed the door, and we sat down and began to talk, and he said it was good and generous of me to come and see him, and he hoped I would be his friend, for he was lonely and so wanted companionship. His words made me ashamed—so ashamed, and I felt so shabby and mean, that I almost had courage enough to come out and tell him how ignoble my errand was and how selfish. He smiled most kindly and winningly, and put out his hand and patted me on the knee, and said,

"Don't mind it."

I did not know what he was referring to, but the remark puzzled me, and so, in order not to let on, I thought I would throw out an observation—anything that came into my head; but nothing came but the weather, so I was dumb. He said,

"Do you care for it?"

"Care for what?"

"The weather."

I was puzzled again; in fact astonished; and said to myself "This is uncanny; I'm afraid of him."

He said cheerfully,

"Oh, you needn't be. Don't you be uneasy on my account."

I got up trembling, and said,

"I—I am not feeling well, and if you don't mind, I think I will excuse myself, and—"

"Oh, don't," he said, appealingly, "don't go. Stay with me a little. Let me do something to relieve you—I shall be so glad."

"You are so kind, so good," I said, "and I wish I could stay, but I will come another time. I—well, I—you see, it is cold, and I seem to have caught a little chill, and I think it will soon pass if I go down and cover up warm in bed—"

"Oh, a hot drink is a hundred times better, a hundred times!—that is what you really want. Now isn't it so?"

"Why yes; but in the circumstances—"

"Name it!" he said, all eager to help me. "Mulled claret, blazing hot—isn't that it?"

"Yes, indeed; but as we haven't any way to—"

"Here—take it as hot as you can bear it. You'll soon be all right."

He was holding a tumbler to me—fine, heavy cut-glass, and the steam was rising from it. I took it, and dropped into my chair again, for I was faint with fright, and the glass trembled in my hand. I drank. It was delicious; yes, and a surprise to my ignorant palate.

"Drink!" he said. "Go on—drain it. It will set you right, never fear. But this is unsociable; I'll drink with you."

A smoking glass was in his hand; I was not quick enough to see where it came from. Before my glass was empty he gave me a full one in its place and said heartily,

"Go right on, it will do you good. You are feeling better already, now aren't you?"

"Better?" said I to myself; "as to temperature, yes, but I'm scared to rags."

He laughed a pleasant little laugh and said,

"Oh, I give you my word there's no occasion for that. You couldn't be safer in my good old Mother Katrina's protection. Come, drink another."

I couldn't resist; it was nectar. I indulged myself. But I was miserably frightened and uneasy, and I couldn't stay; I didn't know what might happen next. So I said I must go. He wanted me to sleep in his bed, and said he didn't need it, he should be going to work pretty soon; but I shuddered at the idea, and got out of it by saying I should rest better in my own, because I was accustomed to it. So then he stepped outside the door with me, earnestly thanking me over and over again for coming to see him, and generously forbearing to notice how pale I was and how I was quaking; and he made me promise to come again the next night, I saying to myself that I should break that promise if I died for it. Then he said good-bye, with a most cordial shake of the hand, and I stepped feebly into the black gloom—and found myself in my own bed, with my door closed, my candle blinking on the table, and a welcome great fire flaming up the throat of the chimney!

It made me gasp! But no matter, I presently sank deliciously off to sleep, with that noble wine weltering in my head, and my last expiring effort at cerebration hit me with a cold shock:

"Did he *overhear* that thought when it passed through my mind—when I said I would break that promise if I died for it?"

Chapter 7

To my astonishment I got up thoroughly refreshed when called at sunrise. There was not a suggestion of wine or its effects in my head.

"It was all a dream," I said, gratefully. "I can get along without the mate to it."

By and by, on a stairway I met 44 coming up with a great load of wood, and he said, beseechingly,

"You *will* come again to-night, won't you?"

"Lord! I thought it was a dream," I said, startled.

"Oh, no, it was not a dream. I should be sorry, for it was a pleasant night for me, and I was *so* grateful."

There was something so pathetic in his way of saying it that a great pity rose up in me and I said impulsively,

"I'll come if I die for it!"

He looked as pleased as a child, and said,

"It's the same phrase, but I like it better this time." Then he said, with delicate consideration for me, "Treat me just as usual when others are around; it would injure you to befriend me in public, and I shall understand and not feel hurt."

"You are just lovely!" I said, "and I honor you, and would brave them all if I had been born with any spirit—which I wasn't."

He opened his big wondering eyes upon me and said,

"Why do you reproach yourself? You did not make yourself; how then are you to blame?"

How perfectly sane and sensible that was—yet I had never

thought of it before, nor had ever heard even the wisest of the professionally wise people say it—nor anything half so intelligent and unassailable, for that matter. It seemed an odd thing to get it from a boy, and he a vagabond landstreicher at that. At this juncture a proposition framed itself in my head, but I suppressed it, judging that there could be no impropriety in my acting upon it without permission if I chose. He gave me a bright glance and said,

"Ah, you couldn't if you tried!"

"Couldn't what?"

"Tell what happened last night."

"Couldn't I?"

"No. Because I don't wish it. What I don't wish, doesn't happen. I'm going to tell you various secrets by and by, one of these days. You'll keep them."

"I'm sure I'll try to."

"Oh, tell them if you think you *can*! Mind, I don't say you shan't, I only say you can't."

"Well, then, I shan't try."

Then Ernest came whistling gaily along, and when he saw 44 he cried out,

"Come, hump yourself with that wood, you lazy beggar!"

I opened my mouth to call him the hardest name in my stock, but nothing would come. I said to myself, jokingly, "Maybe it's because 44 disapproves."

Forty-Four looked back at me over his shoulder and said,

"Yes, that is it."

These things were dreadfully uncanny, but interesting. I went musing away, saying to myself, "he must have read my thoughts when I was minded to ask him if I might tell what happened last night." He called back from far up the stairs,

"I did!"

Breakfast was nearing a finish. The master had been silent all through it. There was something on his mind; all could see it. When he looked like that, it meant that he was putting the sections of an important and perhaps risky resolution together, and bracing up to pull it off and stand by it. Conversation had died out; everybody was curious, everybody was waiting for the outcome.

Forty-Four was putting a log on the fire. The master called him. The general curiosity rose higher still, now. The boy came and stood respectfully before the master, who said,

"Forty-Four, I have noticed—Forty-Four is correct, I believe?—"

The boy inclined his head and added gravely,

"New Series 864,962."

"We will not go into that," said the master with delicacy, "that is your affair and I conceive that into it charity forbids us to pry. I have noticed, as I was saying, that you are diligent and willing, and have borne a hard lot these several weeks with exemplary patience. There is much to your credit, nothing to your discredit."

The boy bent his head respectfully, the master glanced down the table, noted the displeasure along the line, then went on.

"You have earned friends, and it is not your fault that you haven't them. You haven't one in the castle, except Katrina. It is not fair. I am going to be your friend myself."

The boy's eyes glowed with happiness, Maria and her mother tossed their heads and sniffed, but there was no other applause. The master continued.

"You deserve promotion, and you shall have it. Here and now I raise you to the honorable rank of apprentice to the printer's art, which is the noblest and the most puissant of all arts, and destined in the ages to come to promote the others and preserve them."

And he rose and solemnly laid his hand upon the lad's shoulder like a king delivering the accolade. Every man jumped to his feet excited and affronted, to protest against this outrage, this admission of a pauper and tramp without name or family to the gate leading to the proud privileges and distinctions and immunities of their great order; but the master's temper was up, and he said he would turn adrift any man that opened his mouth; and he commanded them to sit down, and they obeyed, grumbling, and pretty nearly strangled with wrath. Then the master sat down himself, and began to question the new dignitary.

"This is one of the learned professions. Have you studied the Latin, Forty-Four?"

"No, sir."

Everybody laughed, but not aloud.

"The Greek?"

"No, sir."

Another clandestine laugh; and this same attention greeted all the answers, one after the other. But the boy did not blush, nor look confused or embarrassed; on the contrary he looked provokingly contented and happy and innocent. I was ashamed of him, and felt for him; and that showed me that I was liking him very deeply.

"The Hebrew?"

"No, sir."

"Any of the sciences?—the mathematics? astrology? astronomy? chemistry? medicine? geography?"

As each in turn was mentioned, the youth shook his untroubled head and answered "No, sir," and at the end said,

"None of them, sir."

The amusement of the herd was almost irrepressible by this time; and on his side the master's annoyance had risen very nearly to the bursting point. He put in a moment or two crowding it down, then asked,

"Have you ever studied *anything?*"

"No, sir," replied the boy, as innocently and idiotically as ever.

The master's project stood defeated all along the line! It was a critical moment. Everybody's mouth flew open to let go a triumphant shout; but the master, choking with rage, rose to the emergency, and it was his voice that got the innings:

"By the splendor of God I'll teach you myself!"

It was just grand! But it was a mistake. It was all I could do to keep from raising a hurrah for the generous old chief. But I held in. From the apprentices' table in the corner I could see every face, and I knew the master had made a mistake. I knew those men. They could stand a good deal, but the master had played the limit, as the saying is, and I knew it. He had struck at their order, the apple of their eye, their pride, the darling of their hearts, their dearest possession, their nobility—as they ranked it and regarded it—and had degraded it. They would not forgive that. They would seek revenge, and find it. This thing that we had witnessed, and which had

had the form and aspect of a comedy, was a tragedy. It was a turning point. There would be consequences. In ordinary cases where there was matter for contention and dispute, there had always been chatter and noise and jaw, and a general row; but now the faces were black and ugly, and not a word was said. It was an omen.

We three humble ones sat at our small table staring; and thinking thoughts. Barty looked pale and sick. Ernest searched my face with his evil eyes, and said,

"I caught you talking with the Jail-Bird on the stairs. You needn't try to lie out of it, I saw you."

All the blood seemed to sink out of my veins, and a cold terror crept through me. In my heart I cursed the luck that had brought upon me that exposure. What should I do? What could I do? What could I say in my defence? I could think of nothing; I had no words, I was dumb—and that creature's merciless eyes still boring into me. He said,

"Say—you are that animal's *friend*. Now deny it if you can."

I was in a bad scrape. He would tell the men, and I should be an outcast, and they would make my life a misery to me. I was afraid enough of the men, and wished there was a way out, but I saw there was none, and that if I did not want to complete my disaster I must pluck up some heart and not let this brute put me under his feet. I wasn't afraid of *him*, at any rate; even *my* timidity had its limitations. So I pulled myself together and said,

"It's a lie. I did talk with him, and I'll do it again if I want to, but that's no proof that I'm his friend."

"Oho, so you don't deny it! That's enough. I wouldn't be in your shoes for a good deal. When the men find it out you'll catch it, I can tell you that."

That distressed Barty, and he begged Ernest not to tell on me, and tried his best to persuade him; but it was of no use. He said he would tell if he died for it.

"Well, then," I said, "go ahead and do it; it's just like your sort, anyway. Who cares?"

"Oh, you don't care, don't you? Well, we'll see if you won't. And I'll tell them you're his friend, too."

If that should happen! The terror of it roused me up, and I said,

"Take that back, or I'll stick this dirk into you!"

He was badly scared, but pretended he wasn't, and laughed a sickly laugh and said he was only funning. That ended the discussion, for just then the master rose to go, and we had to rise, too, and look to our etiquette. I was sufficiently depressed and unhappy, for I knew there was sorrow in store for me. Still, there was one comfort: I should not be charged with being poor 44's friend, I hoped and believed; so matters were not quite so calamitous for me as they might have been.

We filed up to the printing rooms in the usual order of precedence, I following after the last man, Ernest following after me, and Barty after him. Then came 44.

Forty-Four would have to do his studying after hours. During hours he would now fill Barty's former place and put in a good deal of his time in drudgery and dirty work; and snatch such chances as he could, in the intervals, to learn the first steps of the divine art—composition, distribution and the like.

Certain ceremonies were Forty-Four's due when as an accredited apprentice he crossed the printing-shop's threshold for the first time. He should have been invested with a dagger, for he was now privileged to bear minor arms—foretaste and reminder of the future still prouder day when as a journeyman he would take the rank of a gentleman and be entitled to wear a sword. And a red chevron should have been placed upon his left sleeve to certify to the world his honorable new dignity of printer's apprentice. These courtesies were denied him, and omitted. He entered unaccosted and unwelcomed.

The youngest apprentice should now have taken him in charge and begun to instruct him in the rudimentary duties of his position. Honest little Barty was commencing this service, but Katzenyammer the foreman stopped him, and said roughly,

"Get to your case!"

So 44 was left standing alone in the middle of the place. He

looked about him wistfully, mutely appealing to all faces but
mine, but no one noticed him, no one glanced in his direction, or seemed aware that he was there. In the corner old
Binks was bowed over a proof-slip; Katzenyammer was bending over the imposing-stone making up a form; Ernest, with
ink-ball and coarse brush was proving a galley; I was overrun-
ning a page of Haas's to correct an out; Fischer, with paste-
pot and brown linen, was new-covering the tympan; Moses
was setting type, pulling down his guide for every line, weav-
ing right and left, bobbing over his case with every type he
picked up, fetching the box-partition a wipe with it as he
brought it away, making two false motions before he put it in
the stick and a third one with a click on his rule, justifying like
a rail fence, spacing like an old witch's teeth—hair-spaces and
m-quads turn about—just a living allegory of falseness and pretence from his green silk eye-shade down to his lifting and
sinking heels, making show and bustle enough for 3,000 an
hour, yet never good for 600 on a fat take and double-leaded
at that. It was inscrutable that God would endure a comp like
that, and lightning so cheap.

It was pitiful to see that friendless boy standing there forlorn in that hostile stillness. I did wish somebody would re-
lent and say a kind word and tell him something to do. But it
could not happen; they were all waiting to see trouble come
to him, all expecting it, all tremulously alert for it, all knowing it was preparing for him, and wondering whence it would
come, and in what form, and who would invent the occasion.
Presently they knew. Katzenyammer had placed his pages,
separated them with reglets, removed the strings from around
them, arranged his bearers; the chase was on, the sheep-foot
was in his hand, he was ready to lock up. He slowly turned his
head and fixed an inquiring scowl upon the boy. He stood so,
several seconds, then he stormed out,

"Well, are you going to fetch me some quoins, or *not?*"

Cruel! How could *he* know what the strange word meant?
He begged for the needed information with his eloquent
eyes—the men were watching and exulting—Katzenyammer
began to move toward him with his big hand spread for cuffing—ah, my God, I mustn't venture to speak, was there no
way to save him? Then I had a lightning thought; would he

gather it from my brain?—*"Forty-Four, that's the quoin-box, under the stone table!"*

In an instant he had it out and on the imposing-stone! He was saved. Katzenyammer and everybody looked amazed. And deeply disappointed.

For a while Katzenyammer seemed to be puzzling over it and trying to understand it; then he turned slowly to his work and selected some quoins and drove them home. The form was ready. He set that inquiring gaze upon the boy again. Forty-Four was watching with all his eyes, but it wasn't any use; how was he to guess what was wanted of him? Katzenyammer's face began to work, and he spat dry a couple of times, spitefully; then he shouted,

"Am *I* to do it—or *who?*"

I was ready this time. I said to myself, "Forty-Four, raise it carefully on its edge, get it under your right arm, carry it to that machine yonder, which is the press, and lay it gently down flat on that stone, which is called the bed of the press."

He went tranquilly to work, and did the whole thing as right as nails—did it like an old hand! It was just astonishing. There wasn't another untaught and unpractised person in all Europe who could have carried that great and delicate feat half-way through without piing the form. I was so carried away that I wanted to shout. But I held in.

Of course the thing happened, now, that was to be expected. The men took Forty-Four for an old apprentice, a refugee flying from a hard master. They could not ask him, as to that, custom prohibiting it; but they could ask him other questions which could be awkward. They could be depended upon to do that. The men all left their work and gathered around him, and their ugly looks promised trouble. They looked him over silently—arranging their game, no doubt— he standing in the midst, waiting, with his eyes cast down. I was dreadfully sorry for him. I knew what was coming, and I saw no possibility of his getting out of the hole he was in. The very first question would be unanswerable, and quite out of range of help from me. Presently that sneering Moses Haas asked it:

"So you are an experienced apprentice to this art, and yet don't know the Latin!"

There it was! I knew it. But—oh, well, the boy was just an ever-fresh and competent mystery! He raised his innocent eyes and placidly replied,

"Who—I? Why yes, I know it."

They gazed at him puzzled—stupefied, as you might say. Then Katzenyammer said,

"Then what did you tell the master that lie for?"

"I? I didn't know I told him a lie; I didn't mean to."

"Didn't mean to? Idiot! he asked you if you knew the Latin, and you said no."

"Oh, no," said the youth, earnestly, "it was quite different. He asked me if I had *studied* it—meaning in a school or with a teacher, as I judged. Of course I said no, for I had only picked it up—from books—by myself."

"Well, upon my soul, you *are* a purist, when it comes to cast-iron exactness of statement," said Katzenyammer, exasperated. "Nobody knows how to take you or what to make of you; every time a person puts his finger on you you're not there. Can't you do *anything* but the unexpected? If you belonged to me, damned if I wouldn't drown you."

"Look here, my boy," said Fischer, not unkindly, "do you know—as required—the rudiments of all those things the master asked you about?"

"Yes, sir."

"Picked them up?"

"Yes, sir."

I wished he hadn't made that confession. Moses saw a chance straightway:

"Honest people don't get into this profession on picked-up culture; they don't get in on odds and ends, they have to *know* the initial stages of the sciences and things. You sneaked in without an examination, but you'll pass one now, or out you go."

It was a lucky idea, and they all applauded. I felt more comfortable, now, for if he could take the answers from my head I could send him through safe. Adam Binks was appointed inquisitor, but I soon saw that 44 had no use for me. He was away up. I would have shown off if I had been in his place and equipped as he was. But he didn't. In knowledge Binks was a child to him—that was soon apparent. He wasn't competent to examine 44; 44 took him out of his depth on every language and art and science, and if erudition had been water he would have been drowned. The men had to laugh, they couldn't help it; and if they had been manly men they would have softened toward their prey, but they weren't and they didn't. Their laughter made Binks ridiculous, and he lost his temper; but instead of venting it on the laughters he let drive at the boy, the shameless creature, and would have felled him if Fischer hadn't caught his arm. Fischer got no thanks for that, and the men would have resented his interference, only it was not quite safe and they didn't want to drive him from their clique, anyway. They could see that he was at best only lukewarm on their side, and they didn't want to cool his temperature any more.

The examination-scheme was a bad failure—a regular collapse, in fact,—and the men hated the boy for being the cause of it, whereas they had brought it upon themselves. That is just like human beings. The foreman spoke up sharply, now, and told them to get to work; and said that if they fooled away any more of the shop's time he would dock them. Then he ordered 44 to stop idling around and get about his business. No one watched 44 now; they all thought he knew his duties, and where to begin. But it was plain to me that he didn't; so I prompted him out of my mind, and couldn't keep my attention on my work, it was so interesting and so wonderful to see him perform.

Under my unspoken instructions he picked up all the good type and broken type from about the men's feet and put the one sort in the pi pile and the other in the hell-box; turpentined the inking-balls and cleaned them; started up the lye-hopper; washed a form in the sink, and did it well; removed last week's stiff black towel from the roller and put a clean one in its place; made paste; dusted out several cases with a bellows; made glue for the bindery; oiled the platen-springs and the countersunk rails of the press; put on a paper apron and inked the form while Katzenyammer worked off a token of signature 16 of a Latin Bible, and came out of the job as black as a chimney-sweep from hair to heels; set up pi; struck galley-proofs; tied up dead matter like an artist, and set it away on the standing galley without an accident; brought the quads when the men jeff'd for takes, and restored them whence they came when the lucky comps were done chuckling over their fat and the others done damning their lean; and would have gone innocently to the village saddler's after strap-oil and *got* it—on his rear—if it had occurred to the men to start him on the errand—a thing they didn't think of, they supposing he knew that sell by memorable experience; and so they lost the best chance they had in the whole day to expose him as an impostor who had never seen a printing-outfit before.

A marvelous creature; and he went through without a break; but by consequence of my having to watch over him so persistently I set a proof that had the smallpox, and the foreman made me distribute his case for him after hours as a "lesson" to me. He was not a stingy man with that kind of tuition.

I had saved 44, unsuspected and without damage or danger to myself, and it made me lean toward him more than ever. That was natural.

Then, when the day was finished, and the men were washing up and I was feeling good and fine and proud, Ernest Wasserman came out and told on me!

Chapter 8

I SLIPPED out and fled. It was wise, for in this way I escaped the first heat of their passion, or I should have gotten not merely insults but kicks and cuffs added. I hid deep down and far away, in an unvisited part of the castle among a maze of dark passages and corridors. Of course I had no thought of keeping my promise to visit 44; but in the circumstances he would not expect it—I knew that. I had to lose my supper, and that was hard lines for a growing lad. And I was like to freeze, too, in that damp and frosty place. Of sleep little was to be had, because of the cold and the rats and the ghosts. Not that I saw any ghosts, but I was expecting them all the time, and quite naturally, too, for that historic old ruin was lousy with them, so to speak, for it had had a tough career through all the centuries of its youth and manhood—a career filled with romance and sodden with crime—and it is my experience that between the misery of watching and listening for ghosts and the fright of seeing them there is not much choice. In truth I was not sorry sleep was chary, for I did not wish to sleep. I was in trouble, and more was preparing for me, and I wanted to pray for help, for therein lay my best hope and my surest. I had moments of sleep now and then, being a young creature and full of warm blood, but in the long intervals I prayed persistently and fervently and sincerely. But I knew I needed more powerful prayers than my own— prayers of the pure and the holy—prayers of the consecrated—prayers certain to be heard, whereas mine might not be. I wanted the prayers of the Sisters of Perpetual Adoration. They could be had for 50 silver groschen. In time of threatened and imminent trouble, trouble which promised to be continuous, one valued their championship far above that of any priest, for his prayers would ascend at regularly appointed times only, with nothing to protect you in the exposed intervals between, but theirs were perpetual—hence their name— there were no intervals, night or day: when two of the Sisters rose from before the altar two others knelt at once in their place and the supplications went on unbroken. Their convent was on the other side of the river, beyond the village, but Katrina would get the money to them for me. They would take special pains for any of us in the castle, too, for our Prince had been doing them a valuable favor lately, to appease God on account of a murder he had done on an elder brother of his, a great Prince in Bohemia and head of the house. He had repaired and renovated and sumptuously fitted up the ancient chapel of our castle, to be used by them while their convent, which had been struck by lightning again and much damaged, was undergoing reparations. They would be coming over for Sunday, and the usual service would be greatly augmented, in fact doubled: the Sacred Host would be exposed in the monstrance, and four Sisters instead of two would hold the hours of adoration; yet if you sent your 50 groschen in time you would be entitled to the advantage of this, which is getting in on the ground floor, as the saying is.

Our Prince not only did for them what I have mentioned,

but was paying for one-third of those repairs on their convent besides. Hence we were in great favor. That dear and honest old Father Peter would conduct the service for them. Father Adolf was not willing, for there was no money in it for the priest, the money all going to the support of a little house of homeless orphans whom the good Sisters took care of.

At last the rats stopped scampering over me, and I knew the long night was about at an end; so I groped my way out of my refuge. When I reached Katrina's kitchen she was at work by candle-light, and when she heard my tale she was full of pity for me and maledictions for Ernest, and promised him a piece of her mind, with foot-notes and illustrations; and she bustled around and hurried up a hot breakfast for me, and sat down and talked and gossiped, and enjoyed my voracity, as a good cook naturally would, and indeed I was fairly famished. And it was good to hear her rage at those rascals for perse-cuting her boy, and scoff at them for that they couldn't pro-duce one individual manly enough to stand up for him and the master. And she burst out and said she wished to God Doangivadam was here, and I just jumped up and flung my arms around her old neck and hugged her for the thought! Then she went gently down on her knees before the little shrine of the Blessed Virgin, I doing the same of course, and she prayed for help for us all out of her fervent and faithful heart, and rose up refreshed and strengthened and gave our enemies as red-hot and competent a damning as ever came by natural gift from uncultured lips in my experience.

The dawn was breaking, now, and I told her my project concerning the Sisters of the Perpetual Adoration, and she praised me and blest me for my piety and right-heartedness, and said she would send the money for me and have it arranged. I had to ask would she lend me two groschen, for my savings lacked that much of being fifty, and she said promptly—

"Will I? and you in this trouble for being good to my boy? That I will; and I'd do it if it was five you wanted!"

And the tears came in her eyes and she gave me a hug; then I hasted to my room and shut the door and locked it, and fished my hoard out of its hiding-place and counted the coins, and there were *fifty*. I couldn't understand it. I counted them again—twice; but there was no error, there were two there that didn't belong. So I didn't have to go into debt, after all. I gave the money to Katrina and told her the marvel, and she counted it herself and was astonished, and couldn't understand it any more than I could. Then came sudden comprehension! and she sank down on her knees before the shrine and poured out her thanks to the Blessed Virgin for this swift and miraculous answer.

She rose up the proudest woman in all that region; and she was justified in feeling so. She said—and tried to say it humbly—

"To think She would do it for me, a poor lowly servant, dust of the earth: There's crowned monarchs She wouldn't do it for!" and her eyes blazed up in spite of her.

It was all over the castle in an hour, and wheresoever she went, there they made reverence and gave her honor as she passed by.

It was a bad day that had dawned for 44 and me, this wretched Tuesday. The men were sour and ugly. They snarled at me whenever they could find so much as half an occasion, they sneered at me and made jokes about me; and when Katzenyammer wittily called me by an unprintable name they shouted with laughter, and sawed their boxes with their composing-rules, which is a comp's way of expressing sarcastic applause. The laughter was praise of the foreman's wit, the sarcasm was for me. You must choose your man when you saw your box; not every man will put up with it. It is the most capable and eloquent expression of derision that human beings have ever invented. It is an urgent and strenuous and hideous sound, and when an expert makes it it shrieks out like the braying of a jackass. I have seen a comp draw his sword for that. As for that name the foreman gave me, it stung me and embittered me more than any of the other hurts and humiliations that were put upon me; and I was girl-boy enough to cry about it, which delighted the men beyond belief, and they rubbed their hands and shrieked with delight. Yet there was no point in that name when applied to a person of my shape, therefore it was entirely witless. It was the slang name (imported from England), used by printers to describe a certain kind of type. All types taper slightly, and are narrower at the letter than at the base of the shank; but in some fonts this spread is so pronounced that you can almost detect it with the eye, loose and exaggerative talkers asserting that it was exactly the taper of a leather bottle. Hence that odious name: and now they had fastened it upon me. If I knew anything about printers, it would stick. Within the hour they had added it to my slug! Think of that. Added it to my number, by initials, and there you could read it in the list above the take-file: "*Slug 4, B.-A.*" It may seem a small thing; but I can tell you that not all seemingly small things are small to a boy. That one shamed me as few things have done since.

The men were persistently hard on poor unmurmuring 44. Every time he had to turn his back and cross the room they rained quoins and 3-m quads after him, which struck his head and bounded off in a kind of fountain-shower. Whenever he was bending down at any kind of work that required that attitude, the nearest man would hit him a blistering whack on his southern elevation with the flat of a galley, and then apologise and say,

"Oh, was it you? I'm sorry; I thought it was the master."

Then they would all shriek again.

And so on and so on. They insulted and afflicted him in every way they could think of—and did it far more for the master's sake than for his own. It was their purpose to provoke a retort out of 44, then they would thrash him. But they failed, and considered the day lost.

Wednesday they came loaded with new inventions, and expected to have better luck. They crept behind him and slipped cakes of ice down his back; they started a fire under the sink, and when he discovered it and ran to put it out they swarmed there in artificial excitement with buckets of water and emptied them on him instead of on the fire, and abused him for getting in the way and defeating their efforts; while he was inking for Katzenyammer, this creature continually tried to catch him on the head with the frisket before he could get out of the way, and at last fetched it down so prematurely that it failed to get home, but struck the bearers and got itself bent like a bow—and he got a cursing for it, as if it had been his fault.

They led him a dog's life all the forenoon—but they failed

again. In the afternoon they gave him a Latin Bible-take that took him till evening to set up; and after he had proved it and was carrying away the galley, Moses tripped him and he fell sprawling, galley and all. The foreman raged and fumed over his clumsiness, putting all the blame on him and none on Moses, and finished with a peculiarly mean piece of cruelty: ordering him to come back after supper and set up the take again, by candle-light, if it took him all night.

This was a little too much for Fischer's stomach, and he began to remonstrate; but Katzenyammer told him to mind his own business; and the others moved up with threatenings in their eyes, and so Fischer had to stand down and close his mouth. He had occasion to be sorry he had tried to do the boy a kindness, for it gave the foreman an excuse to double-up the punishment. He turned on Fischer and said,

"You think you've got some influence here, don't you? I'll give you a little lesson that'll teach you that the best way for you to get this Jail-Bird into trouble is to come meddling around here trying to get him out of it."

Then he told 44 he must set up the pi'd matter and distribute it before he began on the take!

An all-night job!—and that poor friendless creature hadn't done a thing to deserve it. Did the master know of these outrages? Yes, and was privately boiling over them; but he had to swallow his wrath, and not let on. The men had him in their power, and knew it. He was under heavy bonds to finish a formidable piece of work for the University of Prague—it was almost done, a few days more would finish it, to fall short of completion would mean ruin. He must see nothing, hear nothing, of these wickednesses: if his men should strike—and they only wanted an excuse and were playing for it—where would he get others? Venice? Frankfort? Paris? London? Why, these places were weeks away!

The men went to bed exultant that Wednesday night, and I sore-hearted.

But lord, how premature we were: the boy's little job was all right in the morning! Ah, he *was* the most astonishing creature!

Then the disaster fell: the men gave it up and struck! The poor master, when he heard the news, staggered to his bed, worn out with worry and wounded pride and despair, to toss there in fever and delirium and gabble distressful incoherencies to his grieving nurses, Marget and Katrina. The men struck in the forenoon of Thursday, and sent the master word. Then they discussed and discussed—trying to frame their grounds. Finally the document was ready, and they sent it to the master. He was in no condition to read it, and Marget laid it away. It was very simple and direct. It said that the Jail-Bird was a trial to them, and an unendurable aggravation; and that they would not go back to work again until he was sent away.

They knew the master couldn't send the lad away. It would break his sword and degrade him from his guild, for he could prove no offence against the apprentice. If he did not send 44 away work would stand still, he would fail to complete his costly printing-contract and be ruined.

So the men were happy; the master was their meat, as they expressed it, no matter which move he made, and he had but the two.

Chapter 9

IT was a black and mournful time, that Friday morning that the works stood idle for the first time in their history. There was no hope. As usual the men went over to early mass in the village, like the rest of us, but they did not come back for breakfast—naturally. They came an hour later, and idled about and put in the dull time the best they could, with dreary chat, and gossip, and prophecies, and cards. They were holding the fort, you see; a quite unnecessary service, since there was none to take it. It would not have been safe for any one to set a type there.

No, there was no hope. By and by Katrina was passing by a group of the strikers, when Moses, observing the sadness in her face, could not forbear a gibe:

"I wouldn't look so disconsolate, Katrina, prayer can pull off anything, you know. Toss up a hint to your friend the Virgin."

You would have thought, by the sudden and happy change

in her aspect, that he had uttered something very much pleasanter than a coarse blasphemy. She retorted,

"Thanky, dog, for the idea. I'll do it!" and she picked up
her feet and moved off briskly.

I followed her, for that remark had given me an idea, too.
It was this: to cheer up, on our side, and stop despairing and
get down to work—bring to our help every supernatural force
that could be had for love or money: the Blessed Mother,
Balthasar the magician, and the Sisters of the Perpetual Adoration. It was a splendid inspiration, and she was astonished at
my smartness in thinking of it. She was electrified with hope
and she praised me till I blushed; and indeed I was worthy of
some praise, on another count: for I told her to withdraw my
former "intention," (you have to name your desire—called
"intention"—when you apply to the P. A.,) and tell the Sisters
not to pray for my relief, but leave me quite out and throw all
their strength into praying that Doangivadam might come to
the master's rescue—an exhibition of self-sacrifice on my part
which Katrina said was noble and beautiful and God would
remember it and requite it to me; and indeed I had thought
of that already, for it would be but right and customary.

At my suggestion she said she would get 44 to implore his
overlord the magician to exert his dread powers in the master's favor. So now our spirits had a great uplift; our clouds
began to pass, and the sun to shine for us again. Nothing
could be more judicious than the arrangement we had arrived at; by it we were pooling our stock, not scattering it;
by it we had our money on three cards instead of one, and
stood to win on one turn or another. Katrina said she would
have all these great forces at work within the hour, and keep
them at it without intermission until the winner's flag went
up.

I went from Katrina's presence walking on air, as the saying
is. Privately I was afraid we had one card that was doubtful—
the magician. I was entirely certain that he could bring victory to our flag if he chose, but would he choose? He
probably would if Maria and her mother asked him, but who
was to ask them to ask him? Katrina? They would not want
the master ruined, since that would be their own ruin; but
they were in the dark, by persuasion of the strikers, who had

made them believe that no one's ruin was really going to result except 44's. As for 44 having any influence with his mighty master, I did not take much stock in that; one might as well expect a poor lackey to have the ear and favor of a sovereign.

I expected a good deal of Katrina's card, and as to my own I hadn't the least doubt. It would fetch Doangivadam, let him be where he might; of that I felt quite sure. What he might be able to accomplish when he arrived—well, that was another matter. One thing could be depended upon, anyway—he would take the side of the under dog in the fight, be that dog in the right or in the wrong, and what man could do he would do—and up to the limit, too.

He was a wandering comp. Nobody knew his name, it had long ago sunk into oblivion under that nickname, which described him to a dot. Hamper him as you might, obstruct him as you might, make things as desperate for him as you pleased, he didn't give a damn, and said so. He was always gay and breezy and cheerful, always kind and good and generous and friendly and careless and wasteful, and couldn't keep a copper, and never tried. But let his fortune be up or down you never could catch him other than handsomely dressed, for he was a dandy from the cradle, and a flirt. He was a beauty, trim and graceful as Satan, and was a born masher and knew it. He was not afraid of anything or anybody, and was a fighter by instinct and partiality. All printers were pretty good swordsmen, but he was a past master in the art, and as agile as a cat and as quick. He was very learned, and could have occupied with credit the sanctum sanctorum, as the den of a book-editor was called, in the irreverent slang of the profession. He had a baritone voice of great power and richness, he had a scientific knowledge of music, was a capable player upon instruments, was possessed of a wide knowledge of the arts in general, and could swear in nine languages. He was a good son of the Church, faithful to his religious duties, and the most pleasant and companionable friend and comrade a person could have.

But you never could get him to stay in a place, he was always wandering, always drifting about Europe. If ever there was a perpetual sub, he was the one. He could have had a case anywhere for the asking, but if he had ever had one, the fact had passed from the memory of man. He was sure to turn up with us several times a year, and the same in Frankfort, Venice, Paris, London, and so on, but he was as sure to flit again after a week or two or three—that is to say, as soon as he had earned enough to give the boys a rouse and have enough left over to carry him to the next front-stoop on his milk-route, as the saying is.

Here we were, standing still, and so much to do! So much to do, and so little time to do it in: it must be finished by next Monday; those commissioners from Prague would arrive then, and demand their two hundred Bibles—the sheets, that is, we were not to bind them. Half of our force had been drudging away on that great job for eight months; 30,000 ems would finish the composition; but for our trouble, we could turn on our whole strength and do it in a day of 14 hours, then print the final couple of signatures in a couple of hours more and be far within contract-time—and here we were, idle, and ruin coming on!

All Friday and Saturday I stumped nervously back and forth between the Owl Tower and the kitchen—watching from the one, in hope of seeing Doangivadam come climbing up the winding road; seeking Katrina in the other for consultation and news. But when night shut down, Saturday, nothing definite had happened, uncertainty was still our portion, and we did not know where we were at, as the saying is. The magician had treated 44 to an exceedingly prompt snub and closed out his usefulness as an ambassador; then Katrina had scared Maria and her mother into a realization of their danger and they had tried *their* hands with Balthasar. He was very gracious, very sympathetic, quite willing to oblige, but pretty non-committal. He said that these printers were not the originators of this trouble, and were acting in opposition to their own volition; they were only unwitting tools—tools of three of the most malignant and powerful demons in hell, demons whom he named, and whom he had battled with once before, overcoming them, but at cost of his life almost. They were not conspiring against the master, that was only a blind—he, the magician, was the prey they were after, and he could not as yet foresee how the struggle would come out; but he was consulting the stars, and should do his best. He believed that three other strong demons were in the conspiracy, and he was working spells to find out as to this; if it should turn out to be so, he should have to command the presence and aid of the very Prince of Darkness himself! The result would necessarily be terrible, for many innocent persons would be frightened to death by his thunders and lightnings and his awful aspect; still, if the ladies desired it—

But the ladies didn't! nor any one else, for that matter. So there it stood. If the three extra fiends didn't join the game, we might expect Balthasar to go in and win it and make everything comfortable again for the master; but if they joined, the game was blocked, of course, since no one was willing to have Lucifer go to the bat. It was a momentous uncertainty; there was nothing for it but to wait and see what those extras would elect to do.

Meantime Balthasar was doing his possible—we could see that. He was working his incantations right along, and sprinkling powders, and lizards, and newts, and human fat, and all sorts of puissant things into his caldron, and enveloping himself in clouds of smoke and raising a composite stink that made the castle next to unendurable, and could be smelt in heaven.

I clung to my hope, and stuck to the Owl Tower till night closed down and veiled the road and the valley in a silvery mist of moonlight, but Doangivadam did not come, and my heart was very heavy.

But in the morrow was promise; the service in our chapel would have double strength, because four Sisters would be on duty before the altar, whereas two was the custom. That thought lifted my hope again.

Apparently all times are meet for love, sad ones as well as bright and cheerful ones. Down on the castle roof I could see two couples doing overtime—Fischer and Marget, and Moses and Maria. I did not care for Maria, but if I had been older, and Fischer had wanted to put on a sub—but it was long ago, long ago, and such things do not interest me now. She was a beautiful girl, Marget.

Chapter 10

I T was a lovely Sunday, calm and peaceful and holy, and bright with sunshine. It seemed strange that there could be jarrings and enmities in so beautiful a world. As the forenoon advanced the household began to appear, one after another, and all in their best; the women in their comeliest gowns, the men in velvets and laces, with snug-fitting hose that gave the tendons and muscles of their legs a chance to show their quality. The master and his sister were brought to the chapel on couches, that they might have the benefit of the prayers—he pale and drowsing and not yet really at himself; then the rest of us (except 44 and the magician) followed and took our places. It was not a proper place for sorcerers and their tools. The villagers had come over, and the seats were full.

The chapel was fine and sumptuous in its new paint and gilding; and there was the organ, in full view, an invention of recent date, and hardly any in the congregation had ever seen one before. Presently it began to softly rumble and moan, and the people held their breath for wonder at the adorable sounds, and their faces were alight with ecstasy. And I—I had never heard anything so plaintive, so sweet, so charged with the deep and consoling spirit of religion. And oh, so dreamily it moaned, and wept, and sighed and sang, on and on, gently rising, gently falling, fading and fainting, retreating to dim distances and reviving and returning, healing our hurts, soothing our griefs, steeping us deeper and deeper in its un-utterable peace—then suddenly it burst into breath-taking rich thunders of triumph and rejoicing, and the consecrated ones came filing in! You will believe that all worldly thoughts, all ungentle thoughts, were gone from that place, now; you will believe that these uplifted and yearning souls were as a garden thirsting for the fructifying dew of truth, and prepared to receive it and hold it precious and give it husbandry.

Father Peter's face seemed to deliver hope and blessing and grace upon us just by the benignity and love that was in it and beaming from it. It was good to look at him, that true man. He described to us the origin of the Perpetual Adoration, which was a seed planted in the heart of the Blessed Margaret

Alacoque by Our Lord himself, that time he complained to her of the neglect of his worship by the people, after all he had done for men. And Father Peter said,

"The aim of the Perpetual Adoration is to give joy to Our Lord, and to make at least some compensation by its atonement for the ingratitude of mankind. It keeps guard day and night before the Most Holy, to render to the forgotten and unknown Eucharistic God acts of praise and thanksgiving, of adoration and reparation. It is not deterred by the summer's heat nor the winter's cold. It knows no rest, no ceasing, night or day. What a sublime vocation! After the sacerdotal dignity, one more sublime can hardly be imagined. A priestly virgin should the adorer be, who raises her spotless hands and pure heart in supplication toward heaven imploring mercy, who continually prays for the welfare of her fellow creatures, and in particular for those who have recommended themselves to her prayers."

Father Peter spoke of the blessings both material and spiritual that would descend upon all who gave of their substance toward the repairing of the convent of the Sisters of the Adoration and its new chapel, and said,

"In our new chapel the Blessed Sacrament will be solemnly exposed for adoration during the greater part of the year. It is our hearts' desire to erect for Our Lord and Savior a beautiful altar, to place Him on a magnificent throne, to surround Him with splendor and a sea of light; for," continued he, "Our Lord said again to his servant Margaret Alacoque: 'I have a burning thirst to be honored by men, in the Blessed Sacrament—I wish to be treated as king in a royal palace.' You have therefore His own warrant and word: it is Our Lord's desire to dwell in a royal palace and to be treated as a king."

Many among us, recognizing the reasonableness of this ambition, rose and went forward and contributed money, and I would have done likewise, and gladly, but I had already given all I possessed. Continuing, Father Peter said, referring to testimonies of the supernatural origin and manifold endorsements of the Adoration,

"Miracles not contained in Holy Scripture are not articles of faith, and are only to be believed when proved by trustworthy witnesses."

"But," he added, "God permits such miracles from time to time, in order to strengthen our faith or to convert sinners." Then most earnestly he warned us to be on our guard against accepting miracles, or what seemed to be miracles, upon our own judgment and without the educated and penetrating help of a priest or a bishop. He said that an occurrence could be extraordinary without necessarily being miraculous; that indeed a true miracle was usually not merely extraordinary, it was also a thing likely to happen. Likely, for the reason that it happened in circumstances where it manifestly had a service to perform—circumstances which showed that it was not idly sent, but for a solemn and sufficient purpose. He illustrated this with several most interesting instances where both the likelihood of the events and their unusual nature were strikingly perceptible; and not to cultured perceptions alone perhaps, but possibly to even untrained intelligences. One of these he called "The miracle of Turin," and this he told in these words:

"In the year 1453 a church in Isiglo was robbed and among other things a precious monstrance was stolen which still contained the Sacred Host. The monstrance was put in a large sack and a beast of burden carried the booty of the robbers. On the 6th of June the thieves were passing through the streets of Turin with their spoil, when suddenly the animal became furious and no matter how much it was beaten could not be forced from the spot. At once the cords with which the burden was fastened to the ass's back broke, the sack opened of itself, the monstrance appeared, rose on high, and miraculously remained standing in the air to the astonishment of the many spectators. The news of this wonderful event was quickly spread through the city. Bishop Louis appeared with the chapter of his cathedral and the clergy of the city. But behold, a new prodigy! The Sacred Host leaves the case in which it was enclosed, the monstrance lowers itself to the ground, but the Sacred Host remains immovable and majestic in the air, shining like the sun and sending forth in all directions rays of dazzling splendor. The astonished multitude loudly expressed its joy and admiration, and prostrated itself weeping and adoring before the divine Savior, who displayed His glory here in such a visible manner. The bishop too on his knees implored our Lord to descend into the chalice which he raised up to Him. Thereupon the Sacred Host slowly descended and was carried to the church of St. John amid the inexpressible exultation of the people. The city of Turin had a grand basilica built on the spot where the miracle took place."

He observed that here we had two unchallengeable testimonies to the genuineness of the miracle: that of the bishop, who would not deceive, and that of the ass, who could not. Many in the congregation who had thitherto been able to restrain themselves, now went forward and contributed. Continuing, Father Peter said,

"But now let us hear how our dear Lord, in order to call His people to repentance, once showed something of His majesty in the city of Marseilles, in France. It was A.D. 1218 that the Blessed Sacrament was exposed for adoration in the convent church of the Cordeliers for the forty hours devotion. Many devout persons were assisting at the divine service, when suddenly the sacramental species disappeared and the people beheld the King of Glory in person. His countenance shone with brightness, His look was at once severe and mild, so that no one could bear His gaze. The faithful were motionless with fear, for they soon comprehended what this august apparition meant. Bishop Belsune had more than sixty persons witness to this fact, upon oath."

Yet notwithstanding this the people continued in sin, and had to be again admonished. As Father Peter pointed out:

"At the same time it was revealed to two saintly persons that our Lord would soon visit the city with a terrible punishment if it would not be converted. After two years a pestilence really came and carried off a great part of the inhabitants."

Father Peter told how, two centuries before, in France, Beelzebub and another devil had occupied a woman, and refused to come forth at the command of the bishop, but fled from her, blaspheming, when the Sacred Host was exposed, "this being witnessed by more than 150,000 persons;" he also told how a picture of the Sacred Host, being painted in the great window of a church that was habitually being struck by lightning, protected it afterward; then he used that opportunity to explain that churches are not struck by lightning by accident, but for a worthy and intelligent purpose:

"Four times our chapel has been struck by lightning. Now some might ask: why did God not turn away the lightning? God has in all things his most wise design, and we are not permitted to search into it. But certain it is, that if our chapel had not been visited in this way, we would not have called on the kindness and charity of the devout lovers of the Holy Eucharist. We would have remained hidden and would have been happy in our obscurity. Perhaps just *this* was His loving design."

Some who had never contributed since the chapel was first struck, on account of not understanding the idea of it before, went forward cheerfully, now, and gave money; but others, like the brewer Hummel, ever hard-headed and without sentiment, said it was an extravagant way to advertise, and God the Father would do well to leave such things to persons in the business, practical persons who had had experience; so Hummel and his like gave nothing. Father Peter told one more miracle, and all were sorry it was the last, for we could have listened hours, with profit, to these moving and convincing wonders:

"On the afternoon of February 3d, 1322, the following incident took place in the Loretto Chapel at Bordeaux. The learned priest, Dr. Delort, professor of theology in Bordeaux, exposed the Blessed Sacrament for adoration. After the Pange lingua had been chanted the sacristan suddenly arises, taps the priest on the shoulder and says: 'God appears in the Sacred Host.' Dr. Delort raises his eyes, looks at the Sacred Host and perceives the apparition. Thinking it might be a mere effect of the light he changes his position in order to be able to see better. He now sees that the Sacred Host had, so to say, separated into two parts, in order to make room in the middle for the form of a young man of wondrous beauty. The breast of Jesus projected beyond the circle of the monstrance, and He graciously moved His head whilst with His right hand He blessed the assembly. His left hand rested on His heart. The sacristan, several children, and many adults saw the apparition, which lasted during the entire time of the exposition. With superhuman strength the priest then took the monstrance—and constantly gazing at the divine countenance—he gave the final benediction. The commemoration of this apparition is celebrated every year in this convent."

There was not a dry eye in the house.

At this moment the lightning struck the chapel once more and emptied it in a moment, everybody fleeing from it in a frenzy of terror.

This was clearly another miracle, for there was not a cloud in the sky. Proof being afterward collected and avouched by Father Peter, it was accepted and consecrated at Rome, and our chapel became celebrated by reason of it, and a resort for pilgrims.

Chapter II

To Katrina and me the miracle meant that my card had turned up, and we were full of joy and confidence. Doangivadam was coming, we were sure of it. I hurried to the Owl Tower and resumed my watch.

But it was another disappointment. The day wasted away, hour by hour, the night closed down, the moon rose, and still he did not come. At eleven I gave it up and came down heavy-hearted and stiff with the cold. We could not understand it. We talked it over, we turned it this way and that, it was of no use, the thing was incomprehensible. At last Katrina had a thought that seemed to throw light, and she uttered it, saying,

"Sometimes such things are delayed, for a wise purpose, a purpose hidden from us, and which it is not meet for us to inquire into: to punish Marseilles and convert it, the cholera was promised, by a revelation—but it did not come for two years."

"Ah, dear, that is it," I said, "I see it now. He will come in two years, but then it will be too late. The poor master! nothing can save him, he is lost. Before sunset to-morrow the strikers will have triumphed, and he will be a ruined man. I will go to bed; I wish I might never wake again."

About nine the next morning, Doangivadam arrived! Ah, if he could only have come a few short days before! I was all girl-boy again, I couldn't keep the tears back. At his leisure he had strolled over from the village inn, and he marched in among us, gay and jovial, plumed and gorgeous, and took everybody by surprise. Here he was in the midst, scattering salutations all around. He chucked old Frau Stein under the chin and said,

"Beautiful as ever, symbol of perpetual youth!" And he called Katrina his heart's desire and snatched a kiss; and fell into raptures over Maria, and said she was just dazzling and lit up the mouldy castle like the sun; then he came flourishing in where the men were at their early beer and their rascal plans, now at the threshold of success; and he started to burst out with some more cordialities there, but not a man rose nor gave him a look of welcome, for they knew him, and that as soon as he found out how things stood he would side with the under dog in the fight, from nature and habit. He glanced about him, and his face sobered. He backed against an unoccupied table, and half-sitting upon its edge, crossed his ancles, and continued his examination of the faces. Presently he said, gravely,

"There's something the matter, here; what is it?"

The men sat glum and ugly, and no one answered. He looked toward me, and said,

"Tell me about it, lad."

I was proud of his notice, and it so lifted my poor courage that although I dreaded the men and was trembling inside, I actually opened my mouth to begin; but before I could say anything 44 interposed and said, meekly,

"If you please, sir, it would get him into trouble with the men, and he is not the cause of the difficulty, but only I. If I may be allowed to explain it—"

Everybody was astonished to see poor 44 making so hardy a venture, but Katzenyammer glanced at him contemptuously and cut him short:

"Shut your mouth, if you please, and look to it that you don't open it again."

"Suppose *I* ask him to open it," said Doangivadam; "what will you do about it?"

"*Close* it for him—that's what."

A steely light began to play in Doangivadam's eyes, and he called 44 to his side and said,

"Stand there. I'll take care of you. Now go on."

The men stirred in their chairs and straightened up, their faces hardening—a sort of suggestion of preparation, of clearing for action, so to speak. There was a moment's pause, then the boy said in a level and colorless voice, like one who is not aware of the weight of his words,

"I am the new apprentice. Out of unmerited disapproval of me, and for no other or honorable reason, these cowardly men conspired to ruin the master."

The astonished men, their indignant eyes fixed upon the boy, began slowly to rise; said Doangivadam,

"They did, did they?"

"Yes," said the boy.

"The—*sons* of bitches!" and every sword was out of its sheath in an instant, and the men on their feet.

"Come on!" shouted Doangivadam, fetching his long rapier up with a whiz and falling into position.

But the men hesitated, wavered, gave back, and that was the friend of the under dog's opportunity—he was on them like a cat. They recovered, and braced up for a moment, but they could not stand against the man's impetuous assault, and had to give way before it and fall back, one sword after another parting from their hands with a wrench and flying, till only two of the enemy remained armed—Katzenyammer and Binks—then the champion slipped and fell, and they jumped for him to impale him, and I turned sick at the sight; but 44 sprang forward and gripped their necks with his small hands and they sank to the floor limp and gasping. Doangivadam was up and on guard in a moment, but the battle was over. The men formally surrendered—except the two that lay there. It was as much as ten minutes before they recovered; then they sat up, looking weak and dazed and uncertain, and maybe thinking the lightning had struck again; but the fight was all out of them and they did not need to surrender; they only felt of their necks and reflected.

We victors stood looking down upon them, the prisoners of war stood grouped apart and sullen.

"How was that done?" said Doangivadam, wondering; "what was it done with?"

"He did it with his hands," I said.

"With his hands? Let me see them, lad . . . . Why, they are soft and plump—just a girl's. Come, there's no strength in these paddies; what is the secret of this thing?"

So I explained:

"It isn't his own strength, sir; his master gives it him by magic—Balthasar the enchanter."

So then he understood it.

He noticed that the men had fallen apart and were picking up their swords, and he ordered 44 to take the swords away from them and bring them to him. And he chuckled at the thought of what the boy had done, and said,

"If they resist, try those persuaders of yours again."

But they did not resist. When 44 brought him the swords he piled them on the table and said,

"Boy, you were not in the conspiracy; with that talent of yours, why didn't you make a stand?"

"There was no one to back me, sir."

"There's something in that. But I'm here, now. It's backing enough, isn't it? You'll enlist for the war?"

"Yes, sir."

"That settles it. I'll be the right wing of the army, and you'll be the left. We will concentrate on the conspiracy here and now. What is your name?"

The boy replied with his customary simplicity,

"No. 44, New Series 864,962."

Doangivadam, who was inserting the point of his rapier into its sheath, suspended the operation where it was, and after a moment asked,

"What did I understand you to say?"

"No. 44, New Series 864,962."

"Is—is that your *name*?"

"Yes, sir."

"My—word, but it's a daisy! In the hurry of going to press, let's dock it to Forty-Four and put the rest on the standing-galley and let it go for left-over at half rates. Will that do?"

"Yes, sir."

"Come, now—range up, men, and plant yourselves! Forty-Four is going to resume his account of the conspiracy. Now go on, 44, and speak as frankly as you please."

Forty-Four told the story, and was not interrupted. When

it was finished Doangivadam was looking sober enough, for he recognized that the situation was of a seriousness beyond anything he had guessed—in fact it had a clearly hopeless look, so far as he could at the moment see. The men had the game in their hands; how could he, or any other, save the master from the ruin they had planned? That was his thought. The men read it in his face, and they looked the taunts which they judged it injudicious to put into words while their weapons were out of their reach. Doangivadam noted the looks and felt the sting of them as he sat trying to think out a course. He finished his thinkings, then spoke:

"The case stands like this. If the master dismisses 44—but he can't lawfully do it; that way out is blocked. If 44 remains, you refuse to work, and the master cannot fulfill his contract. That is ruin for him. You hold all the cards, that is evident."

Having conceded this, he began to reason upon the matter, and to plead for the master, the just master, the kind and blameless master, the generous master, now so sorely bested, a master who had never wronged any one, a master who would be compassionate if he were in their place and they in his . . . . .

It was time to interrupt him, lest his speech begin to produce effects, presently; and Katzenyammer did it.

"That's enough of that taffy—shut it off!" he said. "We stand solid; the man that weakens—let him look to himself!"

The war-light began to rise in Doangivadam's eyes, and he said—

"You refuse to work. Very well, I can't make you, and I can't persuade you—but starvation can! I'll lock you into the shop, and put guards over you, and the man that breaks out shall have his reward."

The men realized that the tables had been turned; they knew their man—he would keep his word; he had their swords, he was master of the situation. Even Katzenyammer's face went blank with the suddenness of the checkmate, and his handy tongue found nothing at the moment to say. By order the men moved by in single file and took up their march for the shop, followed by 44 and Doangivadam, who carried swords and maintained peace and order. Presently—

"Halt!" cried the commander. "There's a man missing. Where is Ernest Wasserman?"

It was found that he had slipped out while 44 was telling his story. But all right, he was heard coming, now. He came swaying and tottering in, sank into a chair, looking snow white, and said, "O, Lord!"

Everybody forgot the march, and crowded around him, eager to find out what dreadful thing had happened. But he couldn't answer questions, he could only moan and shiver and say—

"Don't ask *me*! I've been to the shop! O, *lordy*-lord, oh, *lordy*-lord!"

They couldn't get a thing out of him but that, he was that used up and gone to pieces. Then there was a break for the shop, Doangivadam in the lead, and the rest clattering after him through the dim and musty corridors. When we arrived we saw a sight to turn a person to stone: there before our eyes the press was whirling out printed sheets faster than a person could count them—just *snowing* them onto the pile, as you may say—yet *there wasn't a human creature in sight anywhere!*

And that wasn't all, nor the half. All the *other* printing-shop work was going briskly on—yet nobody there, not a living thing to be seen! You would see a sponge get up and dip itself in a basin of water; see it sail along through the air; see it halt an inch above a galley of dead matter and squeeze itself and drench the galley, then toss itself aside; then an invisible expert would flirt the leads out of that matter so fast they fairly seemed to rain onto the imposing-stone, and you would see the matter contract and shrink together under the process; next you would see as much as five inches of that matter separate itself from the mass and rise in the air and stand upright; see it settle itself upon that invisible expert's ring-finger as upon a seat; see it move across the room and pause above a case and go to scattering itself like lightning into the boxes— raining again? yes, it was like that. And in half or three-quarters of no time you would see that five inches of matter scatter itself out and another five come and take its place; and in another minute or two there would be a mountain of wet type in every box and the job finished.

At other cases you would see "sticks" hovering in the air above the space-box; see a line set, spaced, justified and the rule slipped over in the time it takes a person to snap his fingers; next minute the stick is full! next moment it is emptied into the galley! and in ten minutes the *galley's* full and the case empty! It made you dizzy to see these incredible things, these impossible things.

Yes, all the different kinds of work were racing along like Sam Hill—*and all in a sepulchral stillness.* The way the press was carrying on, you would think it was making noise enough for an insurrection, but in a minute you would find it was only your fancy, it wasn't producing a sound—then you would have that sick and chilly feeling a person always has when he recognizes that he is in the presence of creatures and forces not of this world. The invisibles were making up forms, locking up forms, unlocking forms, carrying new signatures to the press and removing the old: abundance of movement, you see, plenty of tramping to and fro, yet you couldn't hear a footfall; there wasn't a spoken word, there wasn't a whisper, there wasn't a sigh—oh, the saddest, uncanniest silence that ever was.

But at last I noticed that there really was one industry lacking—a couple of them: no proofs were taken, no proofs were read! Oh, these *were* experts, sure enough! When *they* did a thing, they did it right, apparently, and it hadn't any occasion to be corrected.

Frightened? We were paralyzed; we couldn't move a limb to get away, we couldn't even cross ourselves, we were so nerveless. And we couldn't look away, the spectacle of those familiar objects drifting about in the air unsupported, and doing their complex and beautiful work without visible help, was so terrifyingly fascinating that we had to look and keep on looking, we couldn't help it.

At the end of half an hour the distribution stopped, and the composing. In turn, one industry after another ceased. Last of all, the churning and fluttering press's tremendous energies came to a stand-still; invisible hands removed the form and washed it, invisible hands scraped the bed and oiled it, invisible hands hung the frisket on its hook. Not anywhere in the place was any motion, any movement, now; there was nothing there but a soundless emptiness, a ghostly hush. This lasted during a few clammy moments, then came a sound from the furthest case—soft, subdued, but harsh, gritty, mocking, sarcastic: the scraping of a rule on a box-partition! and with it came half a dozen dim and muffled spectral chuckles, the dry and crackly laughter of the dead, as it seemed to me.

In about a minute something cold passed by. Not wind, just cold. I felt it on my cheek. It was one of those ghosts; I did not need any one to tell me that; it had that damp, tomby feel which you do not get from any live person. We all shrank together, so as not to obstruct the others. They straggled along by at their leisure, and we counted the frosts as they passed: eight.

Chapter 12

WE arrived back to our beer-and-chess room troubled and miserable. Our adventure went the rounds of the castle, and soon the ladies and the servants came, pale and frightened, and when they heard the facts it knocked them dumb for one while, which was not a bad thing.

But the men were not dumb. They boldly proposed to denounce the magician to the Church and get him burnt, for this thing was a little *too* much, they said. And just then the magician appeared, and when he heard those awful words, fire and the Church, he was that scared he couldn't stand; the bones fairly melted in his legs and he squshed down in a chair alongside of Frau Stein and Maria, and began to beg and beseech. His airy pride and self-sufficiency had all gone out of him, and he pretended with all his might that he hadn't brought those spectres and hadn't had anything to do with it. He seemed so earnest that a body could hardly keep from believing him, and so distressed that I had to pity him though I had no love for him, but only admiration.

But Katzenyammer pressed him hard, and so did Binks and Moses Haas, and when Maria and her mother tried to put in a word for him they convinced nobody and did him no good.

Doangivadam put the climax to the poor man's trouble and hit the nail on the head with a remark which everybody recognized as the wisest and tellingest thing that had been said yet. He said—

"Balthasar Hoffman, such things don't happen by accident—you know that very well, and we all do. You are the only person in the castle that has the power to do a miracle like that. Now then—firstly, it *happened*; secondly, it didn't happen by itself; thirdly, *you are here*. What would anybody but a fool conclude?"

Several shouted—

"He's *got* him! got him where he can't budge!"

Another shouted—

"He doesn't answer, and he can't—the stake's the place for him!"

The poor old thing began to cry. The men rose against him in a fury; they were going to seize him and hale him before the authorities, but Doangivadam interposed some more wisdom, good and sound. He said—

"Wait. It isn't the best way. He will leave the enchantment on, for revenge. We want it taken off, don't we?"

Everybody agreed, by acclamation. Doangivadam certainly had a wonderful head, and full of talent.

"Very well, then. Now Balthasar Hoffman, you've got a chance for your life. It has suited you to deny, in the most barefaced way, that you put that enchantment on—let that pass, it doesn't signify. What we want to know now, is, if we let you alone, do you promise it shan't happen again?"

It brought up his spirits like raising the dead, he was so glad and grateful.

"I do, I do!" he said; "on my honor it shan't happen again."

It made the greatest change. Everybody was pleased, and the awful shadow of that fear vanished from all faces, and they were as doomed men that had been saved. Doangivadam made the magician give his honor that he would not try to leave the castle, but would stand by, and be a safeguard; and went on to say—

"That enchantment had malice back of it. It is my opinion that those invisible creatures have been setting up and printing mere rubbish, in order to use up the paper-supply and defeat the master's contract and ruin him. I want somebody to go and see. Who will volunteer?"

There was a large silence; enough of it to spread a foot deep over four acres. It spread further and further, and got thicker and thicker. Finally Moses Haas said, in his mean way—

"Why don't *you* go?"

They all had to smile at that, for it was a good hit. Doangivadam managed to work up a smile, too, but you could see it didn't taste good; then he said—

"I'll be frank about it. I don't go because I am afraid to. Who is the bravest person here?"

Nearly everybody nominated Ernest Wasserman, and laughed, and Doangivadam ordered him to go and see, but he spoke out with disgust and indignation and said—

"See you in hell, first, and *then* I wouldn't!"

Then old Katrina spoke up proud and high, and said—

"There's my boy, there. I lay he's not afraid. Go 'long and look, child."

They thought 44 wouldn't, but I thought he would, and I was right, for he started right along, and Doangivadam patted him on the head and praised his pluck as he went by. It annoyed Ernest Wasserman and made him jealous, and he pursed up his lips and said—

"I wasn't *afraid* to go, but I'm no slave and I wasn't going to do it on any random unclassified Tom-Dick-and-Harry's orders."

Not a person laughed or said a word, but every man got out his composing rule and scraped wood, and the noise of it was like a concert of jackasses. That is a thing that will take the stiffening out of the conceitedest donkey you can start, and it squelched Ernest Wasserman, and he didn't pipe up any more. Forty-Four came back with an astonisher. He said—

"The invisibles have finished the job, and it's perfect. The contract is saved."

"Carry that news to the master!" shouted Doangivadam, and Marget got right up and started on that mission; and when she delivered it and her uncle saw he was saved in purse and honor and everything, it was medicine for him, and he was a well man again or next to it before he was an hour older.

Well, the men looked that disgusted, you can't think—at least those that had gotten up the strike. It was a good deal of a pill, and Katzenyammer said so; and said—

"We've got to take it—but there'll be sugar on it. We've lost the game, but I'll not call off the strike nor let a man go to work till we've been paid *waiting*-wages."

The men applauded.

"What's waiting-wages?" inquired Doangivadam.

"Full wages for the time we've lost during the strike."

"M-y—word! Well, if that isn't cheek! You're to be paid for time lost in trying to ruin the master! Meantime, where does *he* come in? Who pays him *his* waiting-time?"

The leaders tossed their heads contemptuously, and Binks said he wasn't interested in irrelevances.

So there we were, you see—at a stand-still. There was plenty of work on hand, and the "takes" were on the hooks in the shop, but the men stood out; they said they wouldn't go near the place till their waiting-wages had been paid and the shop spiritually disinfected by the priest. The master was as firm; he said he would never submit to that extortion.

It seemed to be a sort of drawn battle, after all. The master had won the biggest end of the game, but the rest of it re-mained in the men's hands. This was exasperating and humil-iating, but it was a fact just the same, and the men did a proper amount of crowing over it.

About this time Katzenyammer had a thought which per-haps had occurred to others, but he was the first to utter it. He said, with a sneer—

"A lot is being taken for granted—on not even respectable *evidence*, let alone proof. How do *we* know the contract has been completed and saved?"

It certainly was a hit, everybody recognized that; in fact you could call it a sockdolajer, and not be any out of the way. The prejudice against 44 was pretty strong, you know. Doan-givadam was jostled—you could see it. He didn't know what to say—you could see that, too. Everybody had an expression on his face, now—a very exultant one on the rebel side, a very uncomfortable one on the other—with two exceptions: Katrina and 44; 44 hadn't any expression at all—his face was wood; but Katrina's eyes were snapping. She said—

"*I* know what you mean, you ornery beer-jug, you Katzenyammer; you mean he's a liar. Well, then, why don't you go and see for yourself? Answer me that—why *don't* you?"

"I don't *need* to, if you want to know. It's nothing to me—*I* don't care what becomes of the contract."

"Well, then, keep your mouth shut and mind your own business. You *dasn't* go, and you know it. Why, you great big mean coward, to call a poor friendless boy a liar, and then ain't man enough to go and prove it!"

"Look here, woman, if you—"

"Don't you call *me* woman, you scum of the earth!" and she strode to him and stood over him; "say it again and I'll tear you to rags!"

The bully murmured—

"I take it back," which made many laugh.

Katrina faced about and challenged the house to go and see. There was a visible shrinkage all around. No answer. Katrina looked at Doangivadam. He slowly shook his head, and said—

"I'll not deny it—I lack the grit."

Then Katrina stretched herself away up in the air and said—

"I'm under the protection of the Queen of Heaven, and I'll go myself! Come along, 44."

They were gone a considerable time. When they returned Katrina said—

"He showed me everything and explained it all, and it's just exactly as he told you." She searched the house, face by face, with her eyes, then settled them upon Katzenyammer and finished: "Is there any polecat here that's got the sand to doubt it *now?*"

Nobody showed up. Several of our side laughed, and Doangivadam he laughed too, and fetched his fist down with a bang on the table like the Lord Chief Justice delivering an opinion, and said—

"That settles it!"

Chapter 13

NEXT day was pretty dreary. The men wouldn't go to work, but loafed around moody and sour and uncomfortable. There was not much talk; what there was was mumbled, in the main, by pairs. There was no general conversation. At meals silence was the rule. At night there was no jollity, and before ten all had disappeared to their rooms and the castle was a dim and grim solitude.

The day after, the same. Wherever 44 came he got ugly looks, threatening looks, and I was afraid for him and wanted to show sympathy but was too timid. I tried to think I avoided him for his own good, but did not succeed to my satisfaction. As usual, he did not seem to know he was being so scowled at and hated. He certainly could be inconceivably stupid at times, for all he was so capable at others. Marget pitied him and said kind things to him, and Doangivadam was cordial and handsome to him, and whenever Doangivadam saw one of those scowls he insulted the man that exhibited it and invited him to exhibit it again, which he didn't. Of course Katrina was 44's friend right along. But the friendliness was confined to those three, at least as far as any open show of it went.

So things drifted along, till the contract-gentlemen came for the goods. They brought a freight wagon along, and it waited in the great court. There was an embarrassment, now. Who would box-up the goods? Our men? Indeed, no. They refused, and said they wouldn't allow any outsider to do it, either. And Katzenyammer said to Doangivadam, while he was pleading—

"Save your breath—the contract has failed, after all!"

It made Doangivadam mad, and he said—

"It hasn't failed, either. I'll box the things myself, and Katrina and I will load them into the wagon. Rather than see you people win, I'll chance death by ghost and fright. I reckon Katrina's Virgin can protect the two of us. Perhaps you boys will interfere. I have my doubts."

The men chuckled, furtively. They knew he had spoken rashly. They knew he had not taken into account the size and weight of those boxes.

He hurried away and had a private word with the master, saying—

"It's all arranged, sir. Now if you—"

"Excellent! and most unexpected. Are the men—"

"No, but no matter, it's arranged. If you can feed and wine and otherwise sumptuously and satisfactorily entertain your guests three hours, I'll have the goods in the wagon then."

"Oh, many, many thanks—I'll make them stay all night."

Doangivadam came to the kitchen, then, and told Katrina and 44 all this, and I was there just at that time and heard it; and Katrina said all right, she would protect him to the shop, now, and leave him in the care of the Virgin while he did the packing, and in two hours and a half dinner would be down to the wine and nuts and then she would come and help carry the boxes. Then he left with her, but I stayed, for no striker would be likely to venture into the kitchen, therefore I could be in 44's company without danger. When Katrina got back, she said—

"That Doangivadam's a gem of the ocean—he's a *man*, that's what he is, not a waxwork, like that Katzenyammer. I wasn't going to discourage him, but *we* can't carry the boxes. There's five, and each of them a barrow-load; and besides, there has to be four carriers to the barrow. And then—"

Forty-Four interrupted:

"There's two of you, and I'll be the other two. You two will carry one end, and I'll carry the other. I am plenty strong enough."

"Child, you'll just stay out of sight, that's what you'll do. Do you want to provoke the men every way you can think of, you foolish little numskull? Ain't they down on you a plenty, just the way it is?"

"But you see, you two *can't* carry the boxes, and if you'll only let me help—"

"You'll not budge a step—do you hear me?" She stood stern and resolute, with her knuckles in her hips. The boy looked disappointed and grieved, and that touched her. She dropped on her knees where he sat, and took his face between her hands, and said, "Kiss your old mother, and forgive"— which he did, and the tears came into her eyes, which a moment before were so stormy. "Ain't you all I've got in the world? and don't I love the ground you walk on, and can I bear to see you getting into more and more danger all the time, and no need of it? Here, bless your heart," and she jumped up and brought a pie, "You and August sample *that*, and be good. It ain't the kind you get outside of this kitchen, that you can't tell from plate-mail when you bite it in the dark."

We began on the pie with relish, and of course conversation failed for a time. By and by 44 said, softly—

"Mother, he gave his word, you know."

Katrina was hit. She had to suspend work and think that over. She seated herself against the kitchen table, with her legs aslant and braced, and her arms folded and her chin down, and muttered several times, "Yes, that's so, he did." Finally she unlimbered and reached for the butcher-knife, which she fell to sharpening with energy on a brick. Then she lightly tested its edge with the ball of her thumb, and said—

"I know it—we've got to have two more. Doangivadam will force one, and I bet I'll persuade the other."

"*Now* I'm content," said 44, fervently, which made Katrina beam with pleasure.

We stayed there in the comfortable kitchen and chatted and played checkers, intending to be asked by Katrina to take our dinner with her, for she was the friendliest and best table-company *we* had. As time drew on, it became jolly in the master's private dining-room where it was his custom to feed guests of honor and distinction, and whenever a waiter came in or went out we could hear the distant bursts of merriment, and by and by bursts of song, also, showing that the heavy part of the feeding had been accomplished. Then we had our dinner with Katrina, and about the time we had finished, Doangivadam arrived hungry and pretty well tired out and said he had packed every box; but he wouldn't take a bite, he said, until his job was finished up and the wagon loaded. So Katrina told him her plan for securing extra help by compulsion and persuasion, and he liked it and they started. Doangivadam said he hadn't seen any of the men in sight, therefore he judged they must be lying in wait somewhere about the great court so as to interrupt any scheme of bribing the two porters of the freight wagon to help carry the boxes; so it was his idea to go there and see.

Katrina ordered us to stay behind, which we didn't do, after they were out of sight. We went down by secret passages and reached the court ahead of them, and hid. We were near the wagon. The driver and porters had been given their supper, and had been to the stalls to feed and water the horses, and now they were walking up and down chatting and waiting to receive the freight. Our two friends arrived now, and in low voices began to ask these men if they had seen any men of the castle around about there, but before they could answer, something happened: we saw some dim big bulks emerge from our side of the court about fifty yards away and come in procession in our direction. Swiftly they grew more and more distinct under the stars and by the dim lamps, and they turned out to be men, and each of them was drooping under one of our big freight boxes. The idea—carrying it all alone! And another surprising thing was, that when the first man passed us it turned out to be Katzenyammer! Doangivadam was delighted out of his senses, almost, and said some splendid words of praise about his change of heart, but Katzenyammer could only grunt and growl, he was strained so by his burden.

And the next man was Binks! and there was more praise and more grunts. And next came Moses Haas—think of it! And then Gustav Fischer! And after him, the end of the procession—Ernest Wasserman! Why, Doangivadam could hardly believe it, and said he *didn't* believe it, and *couldn't*; and said "*Is* it you, Ernest?" and Ernest told him to go to hell, and then Doangivadam was satisfied and said "that settles it."

For that was Ernest's common word, and you could know him by it in the dark.

Katrina couldn't say a word, she just stood there dazed. She saw the boxes stowed in the wagon, she saw the gang file back and disappear, and still she couldn't get her voice till then; and even then all she could say, was—

"Well, it beats the band!"

Doangivadam followed them a little way, and wanted to have a supper and a night of it, but they answered him roughly and he had to give it up.

Chapter 14

THE freight wagon left at dawn; the honored guests had a late breakfast, paid down the money on the contract, then after a good-bye bottle they departed in their carriage. About ten the master, full of happiness and forgiveness and benevolent feeling, had the men assembled in the beer-and-chess room, and began a speech that was full of praises of the generous way they had thrown ill-will to the winds at the last moment and loaded the wagon last night and saved the honor and the life of his house—and went on and on, like that, with the water in his eyes and his voice trembling; and there the men sat and stared at one another, and at the master, with their mouths open and their breath standing still; till at last Katzenyammer burst out with—

"What in the nation *are* you mooning about? Have you lost your mind? *We've* saved you nothing; *we've* carried no boxes"—here he rose excited and banged the table—"and what's more, we've arranged that nobody *else* shall carry a box or load that wagon till our waiting-time's paid!"

Well, think of it! The master was so astonished that for a moment or two he couldn't pull his language; then he turned sadly and uncertainly to Doangivadam and said—

"I could not have dreamed it. Surely you told me that they—"

"Certainly I did. I told you they brought down the boxes—"

"*Listen* at him!" cried Binks, springing to his feet.

"—those five *there*—Katzenyammer at the head, Wasserman at the tail—"

"As sure as my name's Was—"

"—each with a box on his shoulders—"

All were on their feet, now, and they drowned out the speaker with a perfect deluge of derisive laughter, out of the midst of which burst Katzenyammer's bull-voice shouting—

"Oh, listen to the maniac! *Each* carrying a box weighing *five—hundred—pounds!*"

Everybody took up that telling refrain and screamed it and yelled it with all his might. Doangivadam saw the killing force of the argument, and began to look very foolish—which the men saw, and they roared at him, challenging him to get up and purge his soul and trim his imagination. He was caught in a difficult place, and he did not try to let on that he was in easy circumstances. He got up and said, quietly, and almost humbly—

"I don't understand it, I can't explain it. I realize that no man here could carry one of those boxes; and yet as sure as I am alive I saw it done, just as I have said. Katrina saw it too. We were awake, and not dreaming. I spoke to every one of the five. I saw them load the boxes into the wagon. I—"

Moses Haas interrupted:

"Excuse me, nobody loaded any boxes into the wagon. It wouldn't have been allowed. We've kept the wagon under watch." Then he said, ironically, "Next, the gentleman will work his imagination up to saying the wagon is gone and the master paid."

It was good sarcasm, and they all laughed; but the master said, gravely, "Yes, I have been paid," and Doangivadam said, "Certainly the wagon is gone."

"Oh, come!" said Moses, leaving his seat, "this is going a little *too* far; it's a trifle *too* brazen; come out and say it to the wagon's face. If you've got the cheek to do it, follow me."

He moved ahead, and everybody swarmed after him, eager to see what would happen. I was getting worried; nearly half convinced, too; so it was a relief to me when I saw that the court was empty. Moses said—

"Now then, what do you call *that*? Is it the wagon, or isn't it?"

Doangivadam's face took on the light of a restored confidence and a great satisfaction, and he said—

"I see no wagon."

"What!" in a general chorus.

"No—I don't see any wagon."

"Oh, great guns! perhaps the master will say *he* doesn't see a wagon."

"Indeed I see none," said the master.

"Wel-l, well, *well!"* said Moses, and was plumb nonplussed. Then he had an idea, and said, "Come, Doangivadam, you seem to be near-sighted—please to follow me and *touch* the wagon, and see if you'll have the hardihood to go on with this cheap comedy."

They walked briskly out a piece, then Moses turned pale and stopped.

"By God, it's gone!" he said.

There was more than one startled face in the crowd. They crept out, silent and looking scared; then they stopped, and sort of moaned—

"It *is* gone; it was a ghost-wagon."

Then they walked right over the place where it had been, and crossed themselves and muttered prayers. Next they broke into a fury, and went storming back to the chess-room, and sent for the magician, and charged him with breaking his pledge, and swore the Church should have him now; and the more he begged the more they scared him, till at last they grabbed him to carry him off—then he broke down, and said that if they would spare his life he would confess. They told him to go ahead, and said if his confession was not satisfactory it would be the worse for him. He said—

"I hate to say it—I wish I could be spared it—oh, the shame of it, the ingratitude of it! But—pity me, pity me!—I have been nourishing a viper in my bosom. That boy, that pupil whom I have so loved—in my foolish fondness I taught him several of my enchantments, and now he is using them for your hurt and my ruin!"

It turned me sick and faint, the way the men plunged at 44, crying "Kill him, kill him!" but the master and Doangivadam jumped in and stood them off and saved him. Then Doangivadam talked some wisdom and reasonableness into the gang which had good effect. He said—

"What is the use to kill the boy? He isn't the *source*; whatever power he has, he gets from his master, this magician here. Don't you believe that if the magician wants to, he can put a spell on the boy that will abolish his power and make him harmless?"

Of course that was so, and everybody saw it and said so. So then Doangivadam worked some more wisdom: instead of letting on to know it all himself, he gave the others a chance to seem to know a little of what was left. He asked them to assist him in this difficult case and suggest some wise and practical way to meet this emergency. It flattered them, and they unloaded the suggestion that the magician be put under bond to shut off the boy's enchantments, on pain of being delivered to the Church if anything happened again.

Doangivadam said it was the very thing; and praised the idea, and let on to think it was wonderfully intelligent, whereas it was only what he had suggested himself, and what anybody would have thought of and suggested, including the cat, there being no other way with any sense in it.

So they bonded the magician, and he didn't lose any time in furnishing the pledge and getting a new lease on his hide. Then he turned on the boy and reproached him for his ingratitude, and then he fired up on his subject and turned his tongue and his temper loose, and most certainly he did give him down the banks and roll Jordan roll! I never felt so sorry for a person, and I think others were sorry for him, too, though they would have said that as long as he deserved it he couldn't expect to be treated any gentler, and it would be a valuable lesson to him anyway, and save him future trouble, and worse. The way the magician finished, was awful; it made your blood run cold. He walked majestically across the room with his solemn professional stride, which meant that something was going to happen. He stopped in the door and faced around, everybody holding their breath, and said, slow and distinct, and pointing his long finger—

"Look at him, there where he sits—and remember my words, and the doom they are laden with. I have put him under my spells; if he thinks he can dissolve them and do you further harm, let him try. But I make this pledge and compact: on the day that he succeeds I will put an enchantment upon him, here in this room, which shall slowly consume him to ashes before your eyes!"

Then he departed. Dear me, but it was a startled crowd! Their faces were that white—and they couldn't seem to say a word. But there was one good thing to see—there was pity in every face of them! That was human nature, wasn't it—when your enemy is in awful trouble, to be sorry for him, even when your pride won't let you go and say it to him before company? But the master and Doangivadam went and comforted him and begged him to be careful and work no spells and run no risks; and even Gustav Fischer ventured to go by, and heave out a kindly word in passing; and pretty soon the news had gone about the castle, and Marget and Katrina came; *they* begged him, too, and both got to crying, and that made him so conspicuous and heroic, that Ernest Wasserman was bursting with jealousy, and you could see he wished *he* was advertised for roasting, too, if this was what you get for it.

Katrina had sassed the magician more than once and had not seemed to be afraid of him, but this time her heart was concerned and her pluck was all gone. She went to him, with the crowd at her heels, and went on her knees and begged him to be good to her boy, and stay his hand from practising enchantments, and be his guardian and protector and save him from the fire. Everybody was moved. Except the boy. It was one of his times to be an ass and a wooden-head. He certainly could choose them with the worst judgment I ever saw. Katrina was alarmed; she was afraid his seeming lack of interest would have a bad effect with the magician, so she did his manners for him and conveyed his homage and his pledges of good behavior, and hurried him out of the presence.

Well, to my mind there is nothing that makes a person interesting like his being about to get burnt up. We had to take 44 to the sick lady's room and let her gaze at him, and shudder, and shrivel, and wonder how he would look when he was done; she hadn't had such a stirring up for years, and it acted on her kidneys and her spine and her livers and all those things and her other works, and started up her flywheel and her circulation, and she said, herself, it had done her more good than any bucketful of medicine she had taken that week. And begged him to come again, and he promised he would if he could. Also said if he couldn't he would send her some of the ashes; for he certainly was a good boy at bottom, and thoughtful.

They all wanted to see him, even people that had taken hardly any interest in him before—like Sara and Duffles and the other maids, and Fritz and Jacob and the other menservants. And they were all tender toward him, and ever so gentle and kind, and gave him little things out of their poverty, and were ever so sorry, and showed it by the tears in their eyes. But not a tear out of *him*, you might have squeezed him in the hydraulic press and you wouldn't have got dampness enough to cloud a razor, it being one of his blamed wooden times, you know.

Why, even Frau Stein and Maria were full of interest in him, and gazed at him, and asked him how it felt—in prospect, you know—and said a lot of things to him that came nearer being kind, than anything they were used to saying, by a good deal. It was surprising how popular he was, all of a sudden, now that he was in such awful danger if he didn't behave himself. And although I was around with him I never got a sour look from the men, and so I hadn't a twinge of fear the whole time. And then the supper we had that night in the kitchen!— Katrina laid out her whole strength on it, and cried all over it, and it was wonderfully good and salty.

Katrina told us to go and pray all night that God would not lead 44 into temptation, and she would do the same. I was ready and anxious to begin, and we went to my room.

Chapter 15

BUT when we got there I saw that 44 was not minded to pray, but was full of other and temporal interests. I was shocked, and deeply concerned; for I felt rising in me with urgency a suspicion which had troubled me several times before, but which I had ungently put from me each time—that he was indifferent to religion. I questioned him—he confessed it! I leave my distress and consternation to be imagined, I cannot describe them.

In that paralysing moment my life changed, and I was a different being; I resolved to devote my life, with all the affections and forces and talents which God had given me to the rescuing of this endangered soul. Then all my spirit was invaded and suffused with a blessed feeling, a divine sensation, which I recognized as the approval of God. I knew by that sign, as surely as if He had spoken to me, that I was His appointed instrument for this great work. I knew that He would help me in it; I knew that whenever I should need light and leading I could seek it in prayer, and have it; I knew—

"I get the idea," said 44, breaking lightly in upon my thought, "it will be a Firm, with its headquarters up there and its hindquarters down here. There's a duplicate of it in every congregation—in every family, in fact. Wherever you find a warty little devotee who isn't in partnership with God—as *he* thinks—on a speculation to save some little warty soul that's no more worth saving than his own, stuff him and put him in the museum, it is where he belongs."

"Oh, don't say such things, I beseech you! They are so shocking, and so awful. And so unjust; for in the sight of God all souls are precious, there is no soul that is not worth saving."

But the words had no effect. He was in one of his frivolous moods, and when these were upon him one could not interest him in serious things. For all answer to what I had been saying, he said in a kindly but quite unconcerned way that we would discuss this trifle at another time, but not now. That was the very word he used; and plainly he used it without any sense of its gross impropriety. Then he added this strange remark—

"For the moment, I am not living in the present century, but in one which interests me more, for the time being. *You* pray, if you like—never mind me, I will amuse myself with a curious toy if it won't disturb you."

He got a little steel thing out of his pocket and set it between his teeth, remarking "it's a jew's-harp—the niggers use it"—and began to buffet out of it a most urgent and strenuous and vibrant and exceedingly gay and inspiriting kind of music, and at the same time he went violently springing and capering and swooping and swirling all up and down the room in a way to banish prayer and make a person dizzy to look at him; and now and then he would utter the excess of his joy in a wild whoop, and at other times he would leap into the air and spin there head over heels for as much as a minute like a wheel, and so frightfully fast that he was all webbed together and you could hear him buzz. And he kept perfect time to his music all the while. It was a most extravagant and stirring and heathen performance.

Instead of being fatigued by it he was only refreshed. He came and sat down by me and rested his hand on my knee in his winning way, and smiled his beautiful smile, and asked me how I liked it. It was so evident that he was expecting a compliment, that I was obliged to furnish it. I had not the heart to hurt him, and he so innocently proud of his insane exhibition. I could not expose to him how undignified it was, and how degrading, and how difficult it had been for me to stand it through; I forced myself to say it was "ideal—*more* than ideal;" which was of course a perfectly meaningless phrase, but he was just hungry enough for a compliment to make him think this was one, and also make him overlook what was going on in my mind; so his face was fairly radiant with thanks and happiness, and he impulsively hugged me and said—

"It's lovely of you to like it so. I'll do it again!"

And at it he went, God assoil him, like a tempest. I couldn't say anything, it was my own fault. Yet I was not really to blame, for I could not foresee that he would take that uninflamed compliment for an invitation to do the fiendish orgy over again. He kept it up and kept it up until my heart was broken and all my body and spirit so worn and tired and desperate that I could not hold in any longer, I *had* to speak out and beg him to stop, and not tire himself so. It was another mistake; damnation, he thought I was suffering on *his* account! so he piped out cheerily, as he whizzed by—

"Don't worry about *me*; sit right where you are and enjoy it, I can do it all night."

I thought I would go out and find a good place to die, and was starting, when he called out in a grieved and disappointed tone—

"Ah, you are not going, are you?"

"Yes."

"What for? Don't go—please don't."

"Are you going to keep still? Because I am not going to stay here and see you tire yourself to death."

"Oh, it doesn't tire me in the least, I give you my word. *Do* stay."

Of course I wanted to stay, but not unless he would sit down and act civilized, and give me a rest. For a time he could *not* seem to get the situation through his head—for he certainly could be the dullest animal that ever was, at times—

but at last he looked up with a wounded expression in his big soft eyes, and said—

"August, I believe you do not *want* any more."

Of course that broke me all down and made me ashamed of myself, and in my anxiety to heal the hurt I had given and see him happy again I came within a hair's breadth of throwing all judgment and discretion to the winds and saying I *did* want more. But I did not do it; the dread and terror of what would certainly follow, tied my tongue and saved my life. I adroitly avoided a direct answer to what he had said, by suddenly crying "ouch!" and grabbing at an imaginary spider inside my collar, whereupon he forgot his troubles at once in his concern for me. He plunged his hand in and raked it around my neck and fetched out three spiders—real ones, whereas I had supposed there was none there but imaginary ones. It was quite unusual for any but imaginary ones to be around at that time of the year, which was February.

We had a pleasant time together, but no religious conversation, for whenever I began to frame a remark of that color he saw it in my mind and squelched it with that curious power of his whereby he barred from utterance any thought of mine it happened to suit him to bar. It was an interesting time, of course, for it was the nature of 44 to be interesting. Pretty soon I noticed that we were not in my room, but in his. The change had taken place without my knowing when it happened. It was beautiful magic, but it made me feel uneasy. Forty-Four said—

"It is because you think I am traveling toward temptation."

"I am sure you are, 44. Indeed you are already arrived there, for you are doing things of a sort which the magician has prohibited."

"Oh, that's nothing! I don't obey him except when it suits me. I mean to use his enchantments whenever I can get any entertainment out of them, and whenever I can annoy him. I know every trick he knows, and some that he doesn't know. Tricks of my own—for I bought them; bought them from a bigger expert than he is. When I play my own, he is a puzzled man, for he thinks I do it by his inspiration and command, and inasmuch as he can't remember furnishing either the order or the inspiration, he is puzzled and bothered, and thinks there is something the matter with his head. He has to father everything I do, because he has begun it and can't get out of it now, and so between working his magic and my own I mean to build him up a reputation that will leave all other second-class magicians in the shade."

"It's a curious idea. Why don't you build it up for yourself?"

"I don't want it. At home we don't care for a small vanity like that, and I shouldn't value it here."

"Where is your ho—"

It got barred before I could finish. I wished in my heart *I* could have that gorgeous reputation which he so despised! But he paid no attention to the thought; so I sighed, and did not pursue it. Presently I got to worrying again, and said—

"Forty-Four, I foresee that before you get far with the magician's reputation you will bring a tragedy upon yourself. And you are so unprepared. You ought to prepare, 44, you ought indeed; every moment is precious. I do wish you would become a Christian; won't you try?"

He shook his head, and said—

"I should be too lonesome."

"Lonesome? How?"

"I should be the only one."

I thought it an ill jest, and said so. But he said it was not a jest—some time he would go into the matter and prove that he had spoken the truth; at present he was busy with a thing of "importance"—and added, placidly, "I must jack-up the magician's reputation, first." Then he said in his kindest manner—

"You have a quality which I do not possess—fear. You are afraid of Katzenyammer and his pals, and it keeps you from being with me as much as you would like and as I would like. That can be remedied, in a quite simple way. I will teach you how to become invisible, whenever you please. I will give you a magic word. Utter it in your mind, for you can't do it with your tongue, though I can. Say it when you wish to disappear, and say it again when you wish to be visible again."

He uttered the word, and vanished. I was so startled and so pleased and so grateful that I did not know where I was, for a moment, nor which end of me was up; then I perceived that

I was sitting by the fire in my own room, but I did not know how I got there.

Being a boy, I did what another boy would have done: as long as I could keep awake I did nothing but appear and disappear, and enjoy myself. I was very proud, and considered myself the superior of any boy in the land; and that was foolish, for I did not invent the art, it was a gift, and no merit to me that I could exercise it. Another boy with the same luck would be just as superior as I was. But these were not my thoughts, I got them later, and at second hand—where all thoughts are acquired, 44 used to say. Finally I disappeared and went to sleep happy and content, without saying one prayer for 44, and he in such danger. I never thought of it.

Chapter 16

FORTY-FOUR, by grace of his right to wear a sword, was legally a gentleman. It suited his whim, now, to come out dressed as one. He was clever, but ill balanced; and whenever he saw a particularly good chance to be a fool, pie couldn't persuade him to let it go by; he had to sample it, he couldn't seem to help it. He was as unpopular as he could be, but the hostile feeling, the intense bitterness, had been softening little by little for twenty-four hours, on account of the awful danger his life was in, so of course he must go and choose *this* time of all times, to flaunt in the faces of the comps the offensive fact that he was their social equal. And not only did he appear in the dress of a gentleman, but the quality and splendor of it surpassed even Doangivadam's best, and as for the others they were mere lilies of the valley to his Solomon. Embroidered buskins, with red heels; pink silk tights; pale blue satin trunks; cloth of gold doublet; short satin cape, of a blinding red; lace collar fit for a queen; the cunningest little blue velvet cap, with a slender long feather standing up out of a fastening of clustered diamonds; dress sword in a gold sheath, jeweled hilt. That was his outfit; and he carried himself like a princeling "doing a cake-walk," as he described it. He was as beautiful as a picture, and as satisfied with himself as if he owned the earth. He had a lace handkerchief in his hand, and now and then he would give his nose a dainty little dab or two with it, the way a duchess does. It was evident that he thought he was going to be admired, and it was pitiful to see his disappointment when the men broke out on him with insults and ridicule and called him offensive names, and asked him where he had stolen his clothes.

He defended himself the best he could, but he was so near to crying that he could hardly control his voice. He said he had come by the clothes honestly, through the generosity of his teacher the good magician, who created them instantly out of nothing just by uttering a single magic word; and said the magician was a far mightier enchanter than they supposed; that he hadn't shown the world the half of the wonders he could do, and he wished he was here now, he would not like it to have his humble servant abused so when he wasn't doing any harm; said he believed if he was here he would do Katzenyammer a hurt for calling his servant a thief and threatening to slap his face.

"He would, would he? Well, there he comes—let's *see* if he loves his poor dear servant so much," said Katzenyammer, and gave the boy a cruel slap that you could have heard a hundred yards.

The slap spun Forty-Four around, and as soon as he saw the magician he cried out eagerly and supplicatingly—

"Oh, noble master, oh greatest and sublimest of magicians, I read your command in your eyes, and I must obey if it is your will, but I pray you, I beseech you spare me the office, do it yourself with your own just hand!"

The magician stood still and looked steadily and mutely at Forty-Four as much as half a minute, we waiting and gazing and holding our breath; then at last 44 made a reverent bow, saying, "You are master, your will is law, and I obey," and turned to Katzenyammer and said—

"In not very many hours you will discover what you have brought upon yourself and the others. You will see that it is not well to offend the master."

You have seen a cloud-shadow sweep along and sober a sunlit field; just so, that darkling vague threat was a cloud-shadow to those faces there. There is nothing that is more depressing and demoralizing than the promise of an indefinite calamity when one is dealing with a powerful and malicious necromancer. It starts large, plenty large enough, but it does not stop there, the imagination goes on spreading it, till at last it covers all the space you've got, and takes away your appetite, and fills you with dreads and miseries, and you start at every noise and are afraid of your own shadow.

Old Katrina was sent by the women to beg 44 to tell what was going to happen so that they could get relieved of a part of the crushing burden of suspense, but she could not find him, nor the magician either. Neither of them was seen, the rest of the day. At supper there was but little talk, and no mention of *the* subject. In the chess-room after supper there was some private and unsociable drinking, and much deep sighing, and much getting up and walking the floor unconsciously and nervously a little while, then sitting down again unconsciously; and now and then a tortured ejaculation broke out involuntarily. At ten o'clock nobody moved to go to bed; apparently each troubled spirit found a sort of help and solace in the near presence of its kind, and dreaded to separate itself from companionship. At half past ten no one had stirred. At eleven the same. It was most melancholy to be there like this, in the dim light of unquiet and flickering candles and in a stillness that was broken by but few sounds and was all the more impressive because of the moaning of the wintry wind about the towers and battlements.

It was at half past eleven that it happened. Everybody was sitting steeped in musings, absorbed in thought, listening to that dirge the wind was chanting—Katzenyammer like the rest. A heavy step was heard, all glanced up nervously, and yonder in the door appeared a *duplicate Katzenyammer!* There was one general gasping intake of breath that nearly sucked the candles out, then the house sat paralyzed and gazing. This creature was in shop-costume, and had a "take" in its hand. It was the exact reproduction of the other Katzenyammer to the last shade and detail, a mirror couldn't have told them apart. It came marching up the room with the only gait that could be proper to it—aggressive, decided, insolent—and held out the "take" to its twin and said—

"Here! how do you want that set, leaded, or solid?"

For about a moment the original Katzenyammer was surprised out of himself; but the next moment he was all there, and jumped up shouting—

"You bastard of black magic, I'll"—he finished with his fist, delivering a blow on the twin's jaw that would have broken anybody else's, but this jaw stood it uncrushed; then the pair danced about the place hammering, banging, ramming each other like battering machines, everybody looking on with wonder and awe and admiration, and hoping neither of them would survive. They fought half an hour, then sat down panting, exhausted, and streaming with blood—they hadn't strength to go on.

The pair sat glaring at each other a while, then the original said—

"Look here, my man, who *are* you, anyway? Answer up!"

"I'm Katzenyammer, foreman of the shop. That's who I am, if you want to know."

"It's a lie. Have you been setting type in there?"

"Yes, I have."

"The hell you have! who told you you could?"

"I told myself. That's sufficient."

"Not on your life! Do you belong to the union?"

"No, I don't."

"Then you're a scab. Boys, up and at him!"

Which they did, with a will, fuming and cursing and swearing in a way which it was an education to listen to. In another minute there would not have been anything left of that Duplicate, I reckon, but he promptly set up a ringing shout of "Help, boys, help!" and in the same moment perfect Duplicates of all the *rest* of us came swarming in and plunged into the battle!

But it was another draw. It had to be, for each Duplicate fought his own mate and was his exact match, and neither could whip the other. Then they tried the issue with swords, but it was a draw once more. The parties drew apart, now, and acrimoniously discussed the situation. The Duplicates refused to join the union, neither would they throw up their job; they were stubbornly deaf to both threats and persuasion. So there it was—just a deadlock! If the Duplicates remained, the Originals were without a living—why, they couldn't even collect their waiting-time, now! Their impregnable position, which they had been so proud of and so arrogant about had turned to air and vacancy. These were very grave and serious facts, cold and clammy ones; and the deeper they sank down into the consciousness of the ousted men the colder and clammier they became.

It was a hard situation, and pitiful. A person may say that the men had only gotten what they deserved, but when that is said is all said? I think not. They were only human beings, they had been foolish, they deserved some punishment, but to take their very bread was surely a punishment beyond the measure of their fault. But there it was—the disaster was come, the calamity had fallen, and no man could see a way out of the difficulty. The more one examined it the more perplexing and baffling and irremediable it seemed. And all so unjust, so unfair; for in the talk it came out that the Duplicates did not need to eat or drink or sleep, so long as the Originals did those things—there was enough for both; but when a *Duplicate* did them, by George, his Original got no benefit out of it! Then look at that other thing: the Originals were out of work and wageless, yet they would be supporting these intruding scabs, out of *their* food and drink, and by gracious not even a thank-you for it! It came out that the scabs got no pay for their work in the shop, and didn't care for it and wouldn't ask for it. Doangivadam finally hit upon a fair and honorable compromise, as he thought, and the boys came up a little out of their droop to listen. Doangivadam's idea was, for the Duplicates to do the work, and for the Originals to take the pay, and fairly and honorably eat and sleep enough for both. It looked bright and hopeful for a moment, but then the clouds settled down again: the plan wouldn't answer; it would not be lawful for unions and scabs to have dealings together. So that idea had to be given up, and everybody was gloomier than ever. Meantime Katzenyammer had been drinking hard, to drown his exasperations, but it was not effective, he couldn't seem to hold enough, and yet he was full. He was only half drunk; the trouble was, that his Duplicate had gotten the other half of the dividend, and was just as drunk, and as insufficiently drunk, as *he* was. When he realized this he was deeply hurt, and said reproachfully to his Duplicate, who sat there blinking and suffused with a divine contentment—

"Nobody *asked* you to partake; such conduct is grossly ill-bred; no gentleman would do such a thing."

Some were sorry for the Duplicate, for he was not to blame, but several of the Originals were evidently not sorry for him, but offended at him and ashamed of him. But the Duplicate was not affected, he did not say anything, but just blinked and looked drowsy and grateful, the same as before.

The talk went on, but it arrived nowhere, of course. The situation remained despairingly incurable and desperate. Then the talk turned upon the magician and 44, and quickly became bitter and vengeful. When it was at its sharpest, the magician came mooning in; and when he saw all those Duplicates he was either thunderstruck with amazement or he played it well. The men were vexed to see him act so, and they said, indignantly—

"It's your own fiendish work and you needn't be pretending surprise."

He was frightened at their looks and their manner, and hastened to deny, with energy and apparent earnestness, that *this* was any work of his; he said he had given a quite different command, and he only wished 44 were here, he would keep his word and burn him to ashes for misusing his enchantments; he said he would go and find him; and was starting away, but they jumped in front of him and barred his way, and Katzenyammer-original was furious, and said—

"You are trying to escape, but you'll not! You don't have to stir out of your tracks to produce that limb of perdition, and you know it and we know it. Summon him—summon him and destroy him, or I give my honor I will denounce you to the Holy Office!"

That was a plenty. The poor old man got white and shaky, and put up his hand and mumbled some strange words, and in an instant, *bang!* went a thunderclap, and there stood 44 in the midst, dainty and gay in his butterfly clothes!

All sprang up with horror in their faces to protest, for at bottom no one really wanted the boy destroyed, they only *believed* they did; there was a scream, and Katrina came flying, with her gray hair streaming behind her; for one moment a blot of black darkness fell upon the place and extinguished us all; the next moment in our midst stood that slender figure transformed to a core of dazzling white fire; in the succeeding moment it crumbled to ashes and we were blotted out in the black darkness again. Out of it rose an adoring cry—broken in the middle by a pause and a sob—

"The Lord gave, the Lord hath taken away . . . . blessed be the name of the Lord!"

It was Katrina; it was the faithful Christian parting with its all, yet still adoring the smiting hand.

Chapter 17

I WENT invisible the most of the next day, for I had no heart to talk about common matters, and had rather a shrinking from talking about the matter which was uppermost in all minds. I was full of sorrow, and also of remorse, which is the way with us in the first days of a bereavement, and at such times we wish to be alone with our trouble and our bitter recallings of failings of loyalty or love toward the comrade who is gone. There were more of these sins to my charge than I could have believed; they rose up and accused me at every turn, and kept me saying with heart-wearing iteration, "Oh, if he were only back again, how true I would be, and how differently I would act." I remembered so many times when I could perhaps have led him toward the life eternal, and had let the chance go by; and now he was lost and I to blame, and where was I to find comfort?

I always came back to that, I could not long persuade myself to other and less torturing thoughts—such, for instance, as wonderings over his yielding to the temptation to overstep the bounds of the magician's prohibition when he knew so well that it could cost him his life. Over that, of a surety, I might and did wonder in vain, quite in vain; there was no understanding it. He was volatile, and lacking in prudence, I knew that; but I had not dreamed that he was *entirely* destitute of prudence, I had not dreamed that he could actually risk his life to gratify a whim. Well, and what was I trying to get out of these reasonings? This—and I had to confess it: I was trying to excuse myself for my desertion of him in his sore need; when my promised prayers, which might have saved him, were withheld, and neglected, and even forgotten. I turned here and there and yonder for solace, but in every path stood an accusing spirit and barred the way; solace for me there was none.

No one of the household was indifferent to Katrina's grief, and the most of them went to her and tried to comfort her. I was not of these, I could not have borne it if she had asked me if I had prayed as I had said I would, or if she had thanked me for my prayers, taking for granted that I had kept my word. But I sat invisible while the others offered their comforting words; and every sob that came from her broken heart was another reproach and gave me a guilty pang. But her misery could not be abated. She moaned and wept, saying over and over again that if the magician had only shown a little mercy, which could have cost him nothing, and had granted time for a priest to come and give her boy absolution, all would have been well, and now he would be happy in heaven and she in the earth—but no! he had cruelly sent the lad unassoiled to judgment and the eternal fires of hell, and so had doomed her also to the pains of hell forevermore, for in heaven she should feel them all the days of eternity, looking down upon him suffering there and she powerless to assuage his thirst with one poor drop of water!

There was another thing which wrung her heart, and she could not speak of it without new floods of tears: her boy had died unreconciled to the Church, and his ashes could not be buried in holy ground; no priest could be present, no prayer uttered above them by consecrated lips, they were as the ashes of the beasts that perish, and fit only to lie in a dishonored grave.

And now and then, with a new outburst of love and grief she would paint the graces of his form, and the beauty of his young face, and his tenderness for her, and tell this and that and the other little thing that he had done or said, so dear and fond, so prized at the time, so sacred now forevermore!

I could not endure it; and I floated from the place upon the unrevealing air, and went wandering here and there disconsolate and finding everywhere reminders of him, and a new heartbreak with each.

By reason of the strange and uncanny tragedy, all the household were in a subdued and timorous state, and full of vague and formless and depressing apprehensions and boding terrors, and they went wandering about, aimless, comfortless and forlorn; and such talking together as there was, was of the disjointed and rambling sort that indicates preoccupation. However, if the Duplicates were properly of the household, what I have just been saying does not include them. They were not affected, they did not seem interested. They stuck industriously to their work, and one met them going to it or coming from it, but they did not speak except when spoken to. They did not go to the table, nor to the chess-room; they did not seem to avoid us, they took no pains about that, they merely did not seek us. But we avoided them, which was natural. Every time I met myself unexpectedly I got a shock and caught my breath, and was as irritated for being startled as a person is when he runs up against himself in a mirror which he didn't know was there.

Of course the destruction of a youth by supernatural flames summoned unlawfully from hell was not an event that could be hidden. The news of it went quickly all about and made a great and terrifying excitement in the village and the region, and at once a summons came for the magician to appear before a commission of the Holy Office. He could not be found. Then a second summons was posted, admonishing him to appear within twenty-four hours or remain subject to the pains and penalties attaching to contumacy. It did not seem to us likely that he would accept either of these invitations, if he could get out of it.

All day long, things went as I have described—a dreary time. Next day it was the same, with the added gloom of the preparations for the burial. This took place at midnight, in accordance with the law in such cases, and was attended by all the occupants of the castle except the sick lady and the Duplicates. We buried the ashes in waste ground half a mile from the castle, without prayer or blessing, unless the tears of Katrina and our sorrow were in some sense a blessing. It was a gusty night, with flurries of snow, and a black sky with ragged cloud-rack driving across it. We came on foot, bearing flaring and unsteady torches; and when all was over, we inverted the torches and thrust them into the soft mould of the grave and so left them, sole and perishable memorial and remembrancer of him who was gone.

Home again, it was with a burdened and desolate weight at my heart that I entered my room. There sat the corpse!

Chapter 18

MY senses forsook me and I should have fallen, but it put up its hand and flipped its fingers toward me and this brought an influence of some kind which banished my faint and restored me; yes, more than that, for I was fresher and finer now than I had been before the fatigues of the funeral. I started away at once and with such haste as I could command, for I had never seen the day that I was not afraid of a ghost or would stay where one was if there was another place convenient. But I was stopped by a word, in a voice which I knew and which was music to my ears—

"Come back! I am alive again, it is not a ghost."

I returned, but I was not comfortable, for I could not at once realize that he was really and solidly alive again, although I knew he was, for the fact was plain enough, the cat could have recognized it. As indeed the cat did; he came loafing in, waving his tail in greeting and satisfaction, and when he saw 44 he roached his back and inflated his tail and dropped a pious word and started away on urgent business; but 44 laughed, and called him back and explained to him in the cat language, and stroked him and petted him and sent him away to the other animals with the news; and in a minute here they came, padding and pattering from all directions, and they piled themselves all over him in their joy, nearly hiding him from sight, and all talking at once, each in his own tongue, and 44 answering in the language of each; and finally he fed them liberally with all sorts of palatable things from my cupboard (where there hadn't been a thing before), and sent them away convinced and happy.

By this time my tremors were gone and I was at rest, there was nothing in my mind or heart but thankfulness to have him back again, except wonder as to how it could be, and whether he had really been dead or had only seemed to perish in a magic-show and illusion; but he answered the thought while fetching a hot supper from my empty cupboard, saying—

"It wasn't an illusion, I died;" and added indifferently, "it is nothing, I have done it many a time!"

It was a hardy statement, and I did not strain myself with trying to believe it, but of course I did not say so. His supper was beyond praise for toothsomeness, but I was not acquainted with any of the dishes. He said they were all foreign, from various corners of the globe. An amazing thing, I thought, yet it seemed to me it must be true. There was a very rare-done bird that was peculiarly heavenly; it seemed to be a kind of duck.

"Canvas-back," he said, "hot from America!"

"What is America?"

"It's a country."

"A country?"

"Yes."

"Where?"

"Oh, away off. It hasn't been discovered yet. Not quite. Next fall."

"Have you—"

"Been there? Yes; in the past, in the present, in the future. You should see it four or five centuries from now! This duck is of that period. How do you like the Duplicates?"

It was his common way, the way of a boy, and most provoking: careless, capricious, unstable, never sticking to a subject, forever flitting and sampling here and there and yonder, like a bee; always, just as he was on the point of becoming interesting, he changed the subject. I was annoyed, but concealed it as well as I could, and answered—

"Oh, well, they are well enough, but they are not popular. They won't join the union, they work for nothing, the men resent their intrusion. There you have the situation: the men dislike them, and they are bitter upon the magician for sending them."

It seemed to give 44 an evil delight. He rubbed his hands vigorously together, and said—

"They were a good idea, the Duplicates; judiciously handled, they will make a lot of trouble! Do you know, those creatures are not uninteresting, all things considered, for they are not *real* persons."

"Heavens, what are they, then!"

"I will explain. Move up to the fire."

We left the table and its savory wreckage, and took comfortable seats, each at his own customary side of the fire, which blazed up briskly now, as if in a voluntary welcome of us. Then 44 reached up and took from the mantelpiece some things which I had not noticed there before: a slender reed stem with a small red-clay cup at the end of it, and a dry and dark-colored leaf, of a breed unknown to me. Chatting along,—I watching curiously—he crushed the crisp leaf in his palm, and filled that little cup with it; then he put the stem in his mouth and touched the cup with his finger, which instantly set fire to the vegetable matter and sent up a column of smoke and I dived under the bed, thinking something might happen. But nothing did, and so upon persuasion I returned to my chair but moved it a little further, for 44 was tilting his head far back and shooting ring after ring of blue smoke toward the ceiling—delicate gauzy revolving circlets, beautiful to see; and always each new ring took enlargement and 44 fired the next one through it with a good aim and happy art, and he *did* seem to enjoy it so; but not I, for I believed his entrails were on fire, and could perhaps explode and hurt some one, and most likely the wrong person, just as happens at riots and such things.

But nothing occurred, and I grew partially reconciled to the conditions, although the odor of the smoke was nauseating and a little difficult to stand. It seemed strange that he could endure it, and stranger still that he should seem to enjoy it. I turned the mystery over in my mind and concluded it was most likely a pagan religious service, and therefore I took my cap off, not in reverence but as a matter of discretion. But he said—

"No, it is only a vice, merely a vice, but not a religious one. It originated in Mexico."

"What is Mexico?"

"It's a country."

"A country?"

"Yes."

"Where is it?"

"Away off. It hasn't been discovered yet."

"Have you ever—"

"Been there? Yes, many times. In the past, in the present, and in the future. No, the Duplicates are not real, they are fictions. I will explain about them."

I sighed, but said nothing. He was always disappointing; I wanted to hear about Mexico.

"The way of it is this," he said. "You know, of course, that you are not one person, but two. One is your Workaday-Self, and 'tends to business, the other is your Dream-Self, and has no responsibilities, and cares only for romance and excursions and adventure. It sleeps when your other self is awake; when your other self sleeps, your Dream-Self has full control, and does as it pleases. It has far more imagination than has the Workaday-Self, therefore its pains and pleasures are far more real and intense than are those of the other self, and its adventures correspondingly picturesque and extraordinary. As a rule, when a party of Dream-Selves—whether comrades or strangers—get together and flit abroad in the globe, they have a tremendous time. But you understand, they have no substance, they are only spirits. The Workaday-Self has a harder lot and a duller time; it can't get away from the flesh, and is clogged and hindered by it; and also by the low grade of its own imagination."

"But 44, these Duplicates are solid enough!"

"So they are, apparently, but it is only fictitious flesh and bone, put upon them by the magician and me. We pulled them out of the Originals and gave them this independent life."

"Why, 44, they fight and bleed, like anybody!"

"Yes, and they *feel*, too. It is not a bad job, in the solidifying line, I've never seen better flesh put together by enchantment; but no matter, it is a pretty airy fabric, and if we should remove the spell they would vanish like blowing out a candle. Ah, they are a capable lot, with their measureless imaginations! If they imagine there is a mystic clog upon them and it takes them a couple of hours to set a couple of lines, that is what happens; but on the contrary, if they imagine it takes them but half a second to set a whole galleyful of matter, *that* is what happens! A dandy lot is that handful of Duplicates, and the easy match of a thousand real printers! Handled judiciously, they'll make plenty of trouble."

"But why should you *want* them to make trouble, 44?"

"Oh, merely to build up the magician's reputation. If they once get their imaginations started . . . . . oh, the consuming intensity and effectiveness of it!" He pondered a while, then said, indolently, "Those Originals are in love with these women and are not making any headway; now then, if we arrange it so that the Duplicates . . . . . lad, it's getting late—for you; time does not exist, for me. August, that is a nice table-service—you may have it. Good-night!" and he vanished.

It was heavy silver, and ornate, and on one great piece was engraved "America Cup;" on the others were chased these words, which had no meaning for me: "New York Yacht Club, 1903."

I sighed, and said to myself, "It may be that he is not honest." After some days I obliterated the words and dates, and sold the service at a good price.

Chapter 19

D AY after day went by, and Father Adolf was a busy man, for he was the head of the Commission charged with trying and punishing the magician; but he had no luck, he could come upon no trace of the necromancer. He was disappointed and exasperated, and he swore hard and drank hard, but nothing came of it, he made no progress in his hunt. So, as a vent for his wrath he turned upon the poor Duplicates, declaring them to be evil spirits, wandering devils, and condemned them to the stake on his own arbitrary authority, but 44 told me he (44,) wouldn't allow them to be hurt, they being useful in the building up of the magician's reputation.

Whether 44 was really their protector or not, no matter, they certainly had protection, for every time Father Adolf chained them to the stake they vanished and left the stake empty before the fire could be applied, and straightway they would be found at work in the shop and not in any way frightened or disturbed. After several failures Father Adolf gave it up in a rage, for he was becoming ridiculous and a butt for everybody's private laughter. To cover his chagrin he pretended that he had not really tried to burn them, he only wanted to scare them; and said he was only postponing the roasting, and that it would take place presently, when he should find that the right time had come. But not many believed him, and Doangivadam, to show how little he cared for Adolf's pretensions, took out a fire insurance policy upon his Duplicate. It was an impudent thing to do, and most irreverent, and made Father Adolf very angry, but he pretended that he did not mind it.

As 44 had expected, the Duplicates fell to making love to the young women, and in such strenuous fashion that they soon cut out the Originals and left them out in the cold; which made bad blood, and constant quarrels and fights resulted. Soon the castle was no better than a lunatic asylum. It was a cat-and-dog's life all around, but there was no helping it. The master loved peace, and he tried his best to reconcile the parties and make them friendly to each other, but it was not possible, the brawling and fighting went on in spite of all he could do. Forty-Four and I went about, visible to each other but to no one else, and we witnessed these affrays, and 44 enjoyed them and was perfectly charmed with them. Well, he had his own tastes. I was not always invisible, of course, for that would have caused remark; I showed up often enough to prevent that.

Whenever I thought I saw a good opportunity I tried to interest 44 in the life eternal, but the innate frivolity of his nature continually defeated my efforts, he could not seem to care for anything but building up the magician's reputation. He said he was interested in that, and in one other thing, *the human race*. He had nettled me more than once by seeming to speak slightingly of the human race. Finally, one day, being annoyed once more by some such remark, I said, acidly—

"You don't seem to think much of the human race; it's a pity you have to belong to it."

He looked a moment or two upon me, apparently in gentle wonder, then answered—

"What makes you think I belong to it?"

The bland audacity of it so mixed my emotions that it was a question which would get first expression, anger or mirth; but mirth got precedence, and I laughed. Expecting him to laugh, too, in response; but he did not. He looked a little hurt at my levity, and said, as in mild reproach—

"I think the human race is well enough, in its way, all things considered, but surely, August, I have never intimated that I belonged to it. Reflect. Now have I?"

It was difficult to know what to say; I seemed to be a little stunned. Presently I said, wonderingly—

"It makes me dizzy; I don't quite know where I am; it is as if I had had a knock on the head. I have had no such confusing and bewildering and catastrophical experience as this before. It is a new and strange and fearful idea: a person who is a person and yet *not a human being*. I cannot grasp it, I do not know how it can be, I have never dreamed of so tremendous a thing, so amazing a thing! Since you are not a human being, what *are* you?"

"Ah," he said, "now we have arrived at a point where words are useless; words cannot even convey *human* thought capably, and they can do nothing at all with thoughts whose realm and orbit are outside the human solar system, so to speak. I will use the language of my country, where words are not known. During half a moment my spirit shall speak to yours and tell you something about me. Not much, for it is not much of me that you would be able to understand, with your limited human mentality."

While he was speaking, my head was illuminated by a single sudden flash as of lightning, and I recognised that it had conveyed to me some knowledge of him; enough to fill me with awe. Envy, too—I do not mind confessing it. He continued—

"Now then, things which have puzzled you heretofore are not a mystery to you any more, for you are now aware that there is nothing I cannot do—and lay it on the magician and increase his reputation; and you are also now aware that the difference between a human being and me is as the difference between a drop of water and the sea, a rushlight and the sun, the difference between the infinitely trivial and the infinitely sublime! I say—we'll be comrades, and have scandalous good times!" and he slapped me on the shoulder, and his face was all alight with good-fellowship.

I said I was in awe of him, and was more moved to pay him reverence than to—

"Reverence!" he mocked; "put it away; the sun doesn't care for the rushlight's reverence, put it away. Come, we'll be boys together and comrades! Is it agreed?"

I said I was too much wounded, just now, to have any heart in levities, I must wait a little and get somewhat over this hurt; that I would rather beseech and persuade him to put all light things aside for a season and seriously and thoughtfully study my unjustly disesteemed race, whereby I was sure he would presently come to estimate it at its right and true value, and worthy of the sublime rank it had always held, undisputed, as the noblest work of God.

He was evidently touched, and said he was willing, and would do according to my desire, putting light things aside and taking up this small study in all heartiness and candor.

I was deeply pleased; so pleased that I would not allow his thoughtless characterization of it as a "small" study to greatly mar my pleasure; and to this end admonishing myself to remember that he was speaking a foreign language and must not be expected to perceive nice distinctions in the values of words. He sat musing a little while, then he said in his kindest and thoughtfulest manner—

"I am sure I can say with truth that I have no prejudices against the human race or other bugs, and no aversions, no malignities. I have known the race a long time, and out of my heart I can say that I have always felt more sorry for it than ashamed of it."

He said it with the gratified look of a person who has uttered a graceful and flattering thing. By God, I think he expected thanks! He did not get them; I said not a word. That made a pause, and was a little awkward for him for the moment; then he went on—

"I have often visited this world—often. It shows that I felt an interest in this race; it is proof, proof absolute, that I felt an interest in it." He paused, then looked up with one of those inane self-approving smiles on his face that are so trying, and added, "there is nothing just like it in any other world, it is a race by itself, and in many ways amusing."

He evidently thought he had said another handsome thing; he had the satisfied look of a person who thought he was oozing compliments at every pore. I retorted, with bitter sarcasm—I couldn't help it—

"As 'amusing' as a basket of monkeys, no doubt!"

It clean failed! He didn't know it was sarcasm.

"Yes," he said, serenely, "as amusing as those—and even more so, it may be claimed; for monkeys, in their mental and moral freaks show not so great variety, and therefore are the less entertaining."

This was too much. I asked, coldly—

But he was gone.

Chapter 20

A WEEK passed.
    Meantime, where was he? what was become of him? I had gone often to his room, but had always found it vacant. I was missing him sorely. Ah, he was so interesting! there was none that could approach him for that. And there could not be a more engaging mystery than he. He was always doing and saying strange and curious things, and then leaving them but half explained or not explained at all. Who was he? what was he? where was he from? I wished I knew. Could he be converted? could he be saved? Ah, if only this could happen, and I be in some humble way a helper toward it!

While I was thus cogitating about him, he appeared—gay, of course, and even more gaily clad than he was that day that the magician burnt him. He said he had been "home." I pricked up my ears hopefully, but was disappointed: with that mere touch he left the subject, just as if because it had no interest for him it couldn't have any for others. A chuckleheaded idea, certainly. He was handy about disparaging other people's reasoning powers, but it never seemed to occur to him to look nearer home. He smacked me on the thigh and said,

"Come, you need an outing, you've been shut up here quite long enough. I'll do the handsome thing by you, now— I'll show you something creditable to your race."

That pleased me, and I said so; and said it was very kind and courteous of him to find *something* to its credit, and be good enough to mention it.

"Oh, yes," he said, lightly, and paying no attention to my sarcasm, "I'll show you a really creditable thing. At the same time I'll have to show you something discreditable, too, but that's nothing—that's merely human, you know. Make yourself invisible."

I did so, and he did the like. We were presently floating away, high in the air, over the frosty fields and hills.

"We shall go to a small town fifty miles removed," he said. "Thirty years ago Father Adolf was priest there, and was thirty years old. Johann Brinker, twenty years old, resided there, with his widowed mother and his four sisters—three younger than himself, and one a couple of years older, and marriageable. He was a rising young artist. Indeed one might say that he had already risen, for he had exhibited a picture in Vienna which had brought him great praise, and made him at once a celebrity. The family had been very poor, but now his pictures were wanted, and he sold all of his little stock at fine prices, and took orders for as many more as he could paint in two or three years. It was a happy family! and was suddenly become courted, caressed and—envied, of course, for that is human. To be envied is the human being's chiefest joy.

"Then a thing happened. On a winter's morning Johann was skating, when he heard a choking cry for help, and saw that a man had broken through the ice and was struggling; he flew to the spot, and recognised Father Adolf, who was becoming exhausted by the cold and by his unwise strugglings, for he was not a swimmer. There was but one way to do, in the circumstances, and that was, to plunge in and keep the priest's head up until further help should come—which was on the way. Both men were quickly rescued by the people.

Within the hour Father Adolf was as good as new, but it was not so with Johann. He had been perspiring freely, from energetic skating, and the icy water had consequences for him. Here is his small house, we will go in and see him."

We stood in the bedroom and looked about us. An elderly woman with a profoundly melancholy face sat at the fireside with her hands folded in her lap, and her head bowed, as with age-long weariness—that pathetic attitude which says so much! Without audible words the spirit of 44 explained to me—

"The marriageable sister. There was no marriage."

On a bed, half reclining and propped with pillows and swathed in wraps was a grizzled man of apparently great age, with hollow cheeks, and with features drawn by immemorial pains; and now and then he stirred a little, and softly moaned—whereat a faint spasm flitted across the sister's face, and it was as if that moan had carried a pain to her heart. The spirit of 44 breathed upon me again:

"Since that day it has been like this—thirty years!—"

"My God!"

"It is true. Thirty years. He has his wits—the worse for him—the cruelty of it! He cannot speak, he cannot hear, he cannot see, he is wholly helpless, the half of him is paralysed, the other half is but a house of entertainment for bodily miseries. At risk of his life he saved a fellow-being. It has cost him ten thousand deaths!"

Another sad-faced woman entered. She brought a bowl of gruel with her, and she fed it to the man with a spoon, the other woman helping.

"August, the four sisters have stood watches over this bed day and night for thirty years, ministering to this poor wreck. Marriage, and homes and families of their own was not for them; they gave up all their hopeful young dreams and suffered the ruin of their lives, in order to ameliorate as well as they might the miseries of their brother. They laid him upon this bed in the bright morning of his youth and in the golden glory of his new-born fame—and look at him now! His mother's heart broke, and she went mad. Add up the sum: one broken heart, five blighted and blasted young lives. All this it costs to save a priest for a life-long career of vice and all forms of shameless rascality! Come, come, let us go, before these enticing rewards for well-doing unbalance my judgment and persuade me to become a human being myself!"

In our flight homeward I was depressed and silent, there was a heavy weight upon my spirit; then presently came a slight uplift and a glimmer of cheer, and I said—

"Those poor people will be richly requited for all they have sacrificed and suffered."

"Oh, perhaps," he said, indifferently.

"It is my belief," I retorted. "And certainly a large mercy has been shown the poor mother, in granting her a blessed mental oblivion and thus emancipating her from miseries which the others, being younger, were better able to bear."

"The madness was a mercy, you think?"

"With the broken heart, yes; for without doubt death resulted quickly and she was at rest from her troubles."

A faint spiritual cackle fell upon my ear. After a moment 44 said—

"At dawn in the morning I will show you something."

Chapter 21

I SPENT a wearying and troubled night, for in my dreams I was a member of that ruined family and suffering with it through a dragging long stretch of years; and the infamous priest whose life had been saved at cost of these pains and sorrows seemed always present and drunk and mocking. At last I woke. In the dimmest of cold gray dawns I made out a figure sitting by my bed—an old and white-headed man in the coarse dress of a peasant.

"Ah," I said, "who are you, good man?"

It was 44. He said, in a wheezy old voice, that he was merely showing himself to me so that I would recognize him when I saw him later. Then he disappeared, and I did the same, by his order. Soon we were sailing over the village in the frosty air, and presently we came to earth in an open space behind the monastery. It was a solitude, except that a thinly and rustily clad old woman was there, sitting on the frozen ground and fastened to a post by a chain around her waist. She could hardly hold her head up for drowsiness and the chill in her bones. A pitiful spectacle she was, in the vague dawn and the stillness, with the faint winds whispering around her and the powdery snow-whorls frisking and playing and chasing each other over the black ground. Forty-Four made himself visible, and stood by, looking down upon her. She raised her old head wearily, and when she saw that it was a kindly face that was before her she said appealingly—

"Have pity on me—I am *so* tired and so cold, and the night has been so long, so long! light the fire and put me out of my misery!"

"Ah, poor soul, I am not the executioner, but tell me if I can serve you, and I will."

She pointed to a pile of fagots, and said,

"They are for me, a few can be spared to warm me, they will not be missed, there will be enough left to burn me with, oh, much more than enough, for this old body is sapless and dry. Be good to me!"

"You shall have your wish," said 44, and placed a fagot before her and lit it with a touch of his finger.

The flame flashed crackling up, and the woman stretched her lean hands over it, and out of her eyes she looked the gratitude that was too deep for words. It was weird and pathetic to see her getting comfort and happiness out of that fuel that had been provided to inflict upon her an awful death! Presently she looked up wistfully and said—

"You are good to me, you are very good to me, and I have no friends. I am not bad—you must not think I am bad, I am only poor and old, and smitten in my wits these many many years. They think I am a witch; it is the priest, Adolf, that caught me, and it is he that has condemned me. But I am not that—no, God forbid! You do not believe I am a witch?—say you do not believe that of me."

"Indeed I do not."

"Thank you for that kind word! . . . . . How long it is that I have wandered homeless—oh, many years, many! . . . . Once I had a home—I do not know where it was; and four sweet girls and a son—how dear they were! The name . . . . . the name . . . . . but I have forgotten the name. All dead,

now, poor things, these many years . . . . . . If you could
have seen my son! ah, so good he was, and a painter . . . .
oh, such pictures he painted! . . . . Once he saved a man's
life . . . . . or it could have been a woman's . . . . . . a person drowning in the ice—"

She lost her way in a tangle of vague memories, and fell to
nodding her head and mumbling and muttering to herself,
and I whispered anxiously in the ear of 44—

"You will save her? You will get the word to the priest, and
when he knows who she is he will set her free and we will restore her to her family, God be praised!"

"No," answered 44.

"No? Why?"

"She was appointed from the beginning of time to die at
the stake this day."

"How do *you* know?"

He made no reply. I waited a moment, in growing distress,
then said—

"At least *I* will speak! I will tell her story. I will make myself visible, and I—"

"It is not so written," he said; "that which is not foreor-
dained will not happen."

He was bringing a fresh fagot. A burly man suddenly appeared, from the monastery, and ran toward him and struck
the fagot from his hand, saying roughly—

"You meddling old fool, mind what you are about! Pick it
up and carry it back."

"And if I don't—what then?"

In his fury at being so addressed by so mean and humble a
person the man struck a blow at 44's jaw with his formidable
fist, but 44 caught the fist in his hand and crushed it; it was
sickening to hear the bones crunch. The man staggered away,
groaning and cursing, and 44 picked up the fagot and renewed the old woman's fire with it. I whispered—

"Quick—disappear, and let us get away from here; that
man will soon—"

"Yes, I know," said 44, "he is summoning his underlings;
they will arrest me."

"Then come—come along!"

"What good would it do? It is written. What is written

must happen. But it is of no consequence, nothing will come of it."

They came running—half a dozen—and seized him and dragged him away, cuffing him with fists and beating him with sticks till he was red with his own blood. I followed, of course, but I was merely a substanceless spirit, and there was nothing that I could do in his defence. They chained him in a dim chamber under the monastery and locked the doors and departed, promising him further attentions when they should be through with burning the witch. I was troubled beyond measure, but he was not. He said he would use this opportunity to increase the magician's reputation: he would spread the report that the aged hand-crusher was the magician in disguise.

"They will find nothing here but the prisoner's clothes when they come," he said, "then they will believe."

He vanished out of the clothes, and they slumped down in a pile. He could certainly do some wonderful things, feather-headed and frivolous as he was! There was no way of accounting for 44. We soared out through the thick walls as if they had been made of air, and followed a procession of chanting monks to the place of the burning. People were gathering, and soon they came flocking in crowds, men, women, youths, maidens; and there were even children in arms.

There was a half hour of preparation: a rope ring was widely drawn around the stake to keep the crowd at a distance; within this a platform was placed for the use of the preacher—Adolf. When all was ready he came, imposingly attended, and was escorted with proper solemnity and ceremony to this pulpit. He began his sermon at once and with business-like energy. He was very bitter upon witches, "familiars of the Fiend, enemies of God, abandoned of the angels, foredoomed to hell;" and in closing he denounced this present one unsparingly, and forbade any to pity her.

It was all lost upon the prisoner; she was warm, she was comfortable, she was worn out with fatigue and sorrow and privation, her gray head was bowed upon her breast, she was asleep. The executioners moved forward and raised her upon her feet and drew her chains tight, around her breast. She looked drowsily around upon the people while the fagots were being piled, then her head drooped again, and again she slept.

The fire was applied and the executioners stepped aside, their mission accomplished. A hush spread everywhere: there was no movement, there was not a sound, the massed people gazed, with lips apart and hardly breathing, their faces petrified in a common expression, partly of pity, mainly of horror. During more than a minute that strange and impressive absence of motion and movement continued, then it was broken in a way to make any being with a heart in his breast shudder—a man lifted his little child and sat her upon his shoulder, that she might see the better!

The blue smoke curled up about the slumberer and trailed away upon the chilly air; a red glow began to show at the base of the fagots; this increased in size and intensity and a sharp crackling sound broke upon the stillness; suddenly a sheet of flame burst upward and swept the face of the sleeper, setting her hair on fire, she uttered an agonizing shriek which was answered by a horrified groan from the crowd, then she cried out "Thou art merciful and good to Thy sinful servant, blessed be Thy holy Name—sweet Jesus receive my spirit!"

Then the flames swallowed her up and hid her from sight. Adolf stood sternly gazing upon his work. There was now a sudden movement upon the outskirts of the crowd, and a monk came plowing his way through and delivered a message to the priest—evidently a pleasant one to the receiver of it, if signs go for anything. Adolf cried out—

"Remain, everybody! It is reported to me that that arch malignant the magician, that son of Satan, is caught, and lies a chained prisoner under the monastery, disguised as an aged peasant. He is already condemned to the flames, no preliminaries are needed, his time is come. Cast the witch's ashes to the winds, clear the stake! Go—you, and you, and you—bring the sorcerer!"

The crowd woke up! this was a show to their taste. Five minutes passed—ten. What might the matter be? Adolf was growing fiercely impatient. Then the messengers returned, crestfallen. They said the magician was gone—gone, through the bolted doors and the massive walls; nothing was left of him but his peasant clothes! And they held them up for all to see.

The crowd stood amazed, wondering, speechless—and disappointed. Adolf began to storm and curse. Forty-Four whispered—

"The opportunity is come. I will personate the magician and make some more reputation for him. Oh, just watch me raise the limit!"

So the next moment there was a commotion in the midst of the crowd, which fell apart in terror exposing to view the supposed magician in his glittering oriental robes; and his face was white with fright, and he was trying to escape. But there was no escape for him, for there was one there whose boast it was that he feared neither Satan nor his servants—this being Adolf the admired. Others fell back cowed, but not he; he plunged after the sorcerer, he chased him, gained upon him, shouted, "Yield—in His Name I command!"

An awful summons! Under the blasting might of it the spurious magician reeled and fell as if he had been smitten by a bolt from the sky. I grieved for him with all my heart and in the deepest sincerity, and yet I rejoiced for that at last he had learned the power of that Name at which he had so often and so recklessly scoffed. And all too late, too late, forever and ever too late—ah, why had he not listened to me!

There were no cowards there, now! Everybody was brave, everybody was eager to help drag the victim to the stake, they swarmed about him like raging wolves; they jerked him this way and that, they beat him and reviled him, they cuffed him and kicked him, he wailing, sobbing, begging for pity, the conquering priest exulting, scoffing, boasting, laughing. Briskly they bound him to the stake and piled the fagots around him and applied the fire; and there the forlorn creature stood weeping and sniffling and pleading in his fantastic robes, a sorry contrast to that poor humble Christian who but a little while before had faced death there so bravely. Adolf lifted his hand and pronounced with impressive solemnity the words—

"Depart, damned soul, to the regions of eternal woe!"

Whereat the weeping magician laughed sardonically in his face and vanished away, leaving his robes empty and hanging collapsed in the chains! There was a whisper at my ear—

"Come, August, let us to breakfast and leave these animals to gape and stare while Adolf explains to them the unexplainable—a job just in his line. By the time I have finished with the sorcerer he will have a dandy reputation—don't you think?"

So all his pretence of being struck down by the Name was a blasphemous jest. And I had taken it so seriously, so confidingly, innocently, exultantly. I was ashamed. Ashamed of him, ashamed of myself. Oh, manifestly nothing was serious to him, levity was the blood and marrow of him, death was a joke; his ghastly fright, his moving tears, his frenzied supplications—by God, it was all just coarse and vulgar horseplay! The only thing he was capable of being interested in, was his damned magician's reputation! I was too disgusted to talk, I answered him nothing, but left him to chatter over his degraded performance unobstructed, and rehearse it and chuckle over it and glorify it up to his taste.

Chapter 22

IT was in my room. He brought it—the breakfast—dish after dish, smoking hot, from my empty cupboard, and briskly set the table, talking all the while—ah, yes, and pleasantly, fascinatingly, winningly; and not about that so-recent episode, but about these fragrant refreshments and the far countries he had summoned them from—Cathay, India, and everywhere; and as I was famishing, this talk was pleasing, indeed captivating, and under its influence my sour mood presently passed from me. Yes, and it was healing to my bruised spirit to look upon the rich and costly table-service—quaint of shape and pattern, delicate, ornate, exquisite, beautiful!—and presently quite likely to be mine, you see.

"Hot corn-pone from Arkansas—split it, butter it, close your eyes and enjoy! Fried spring chicken—milk-and-flour gravy—from Alabama. Try it, and grieve for the angels, for they have it not! Cream-smothered strawberries, with the prairie-dew still on them—let them melt in your mouth, and don't try to say what you feel! Coffee from Vienna—fluffed cream—two pellets of saccharin—drink, and have compassion for the Olympian gods that know only nectar!"

I ate, I drank, I reveled in these alien wonders; truly I was in Paradise!

"It is intoxication," I said, "it is delirium!"

"It's a jag!" he responded.

I inquired about some of the refreshments that had outlandish names. Again that weird detail: they were non-existent as yet, they were products of the unborn *future!* Understand it? How could I? Nobody could. The mere *trying* muddled the head. And yet it was a pleasure to turn those curious names over on the tongue and taste them: Corn-pone! Arkansas! Alabama! Prairie! Coffee! Saccharin! Forty-Four answered my thought with a stingy word of explanation—

"Corn-pone is made from maize. Maize is known only in America. America is not discovered yet. Arkansas and Alabama will be States, and will get their names two or three centuries hence. Prairie—a future French-American term for a meadow like an ocean. Coffee: they have it in the Orient, they will have it here in Austria two centuries from now. Saccharin—concentrated sugar, 500 to 1; as it were, the sweetness of five hundred pretty maids concentrated in a young fellow's sweetheart. Saccharin is not due yet for nearly four hundred years; I am furnishing you several advance-privileges, you see."

"Tell me a little, *little* more, 44—please! You starve me so! and I am so hungry to know how you find out these strange marvels, these impossible things."

He reflected a while, then he said he was in a mood to enlighten me, and would like to do it, but did not know how to go about it, because of my mental limitations and the general meanness and poverty of my construction and qualities. He said this in a most casual and taken-for-granted way, just as an archbishop might say it to a cat, never suspecting that the cat could have any feelings about it or take a different view of the matter. My face flushed, and I said with dignity and a touch of heat—

"I must remind you that I am made in the image of God."

"Yes," he said carelessly, but did not seem greatly impressed

by it, certainly not crushed, not overpowered. I was more indignant than ever, but remained mute, coldly rebuking him
by my silence. But it was wasted on him; he did not see it, he
was thinking. Presently he said—

"It is difficult. Perhaps impossible, unless I should make
you over again." He glanced up with a yearningly explanatory
and apologetic look in his eyes, and added, "For you are an
animal, you see—you understand that?"

I could have slapped him for it, but I austerely held my
peace, and answered with cutting indifference—

"Quite so. It happens to happen that all of us are that."

Of course I was including him, but it was only another
waste—he didn't perceive the inclusion. He said, as one
might whose way has been cleared of an embarrassing obstruction—

"Yes, that is just the trouble! It makes it ever so difficult.
With my race it is different; we have no limits of any kind, we
comprehend all things. You see, for your race there is such a
thing as *time*—you cut it up and measure it; to your race
there is a past, a present and a future—out of one and the
same thing you make *three*; and to your race there is also
such a thing as *distance*—and hang it, you measure *that*, too!
. . . . . Let me see: if I could only . . . . if I . . . . oh, no,
it is of no use—there is no such thing as enlightening that
kind of a mind!" He turned upon me despairingly, pathetically, adding, "If it only had *some* capacity, some depth, or
breadth, or—or—but you see it doesn't *hold* anything; one
cannot pour the starred and shoreless expanses of the universe
into a jug!"

I made no reply; I sat in frozen and insulted silence; I
would not have said a word to save his life. But again he was
not aware of what was happening—he was thinking. Presently
he said—

"Well, it is *so* difficult! If I only had a starting-point, a basis
to proceed from—but I can't find any. If—look here: *can't*
you extinguish time? *can't* you comprehend eternity? can't
you conceive of a thing like that—a thing with *no* beginning—a thing that *always* was? Try it!"

"Don't! I've tried it a hundred times," I said. "It makes my
brain whirl just to think of it!"

He was in despair again.

"Dear me—to think that there can be an ostensible Mind that cannot conceive of so simple a trifle as that! . . . . Look here, August: there are really no divisions of time—none at all. The past is always present when I want it—the *real* past, not an image of it; I can summon it, and there it *is*. The same with the future: I can summon it out of the unborn ages, and there it is, before my eyes, alive and real, not a fancy, an image, a creation of the imagination. Ah, these troublesome limitations of yours!—they hamper me. Your race cannot even conceive of something being made out of nothing—I am aware of it, your learned men and philosophers are always confessing it. They say there had to be *something* to start with—meaning a solid, a substance—to build the world out of. Man, it is perfectly simple—it was built out of *thought*. Can't you comprehend that?"

"No, I can't! *Thought!* There is no substance to thought; then how is a material thing going to be constructed out of it?"

"But August, I don't mean *your* kind of thought, I mean my kind, and the kind that the gods exercise."

"Come, what is the difference? Isn't thought just *thought*, and all said?"

"No. A man *originates* nothing in his head, he merely observes exterior things, and *combines* them in his head—puts several observed things together and draws a conclusion. His mind is merely a machine, that is all—an *automatic* one, and he has no control over it; it cannot conceive of a *new* thing, an original thing, it can only gather material from the outside and combine it into new *forms* and patterns. But it always has to have the *materials* from the *outside*, for it can't make them itself. That is to say, a man's mind cannot *create*—a god's can, and my race can. That is the difference. *We* need no contributed materials, we *create* them—out of thought. All things that exist were made out of thought—and out of nothing else."

It seemed to me charitable, also polite, to take him at his word and not require proof, and I said so. He was not offended. He only said—

"Your automatic mind has performed its function—its sole

function—and without help from you. That is to say, it has
listened, it has observed, it has put this and that together, and
drawn a conclusion—the conclusion that my statement was a
doubtful one. It is now privately beginning to wish for a test.
Is that true?"

"Well, yes," I said, "I won't deny it, though for courtesy's
sake I would have concealed it if I could have had my way."

"Your mind is automatically suggesting that I offer a specific proof—that I create a dozen gold coins out of nothing;
that is to say, out of *thought*. Open your hand—they are
there."

And so they were! I wondered; and yet I was not very
greatly astonished, for in my private heart I judged—and not
for the first time—that he was using magic learned from the
magician, and that he had no gifts in this line that did not
come from that source. But was this so? I dearly wanted to
ask this question, and I started to do it. But the words refused
to leave my tongue, and I realized that he had applied that
mysterious check which had so often shut off a question
which I wanted to ask. He seemed to be musing. Presently he
ejaculated—

"That poor old soul!"

It gave me a pang, and brought back the stake, the flames
and the death-cry; and I said—

"It was a shame and a pity that she wasn't rescued."

"Why a pity?"

"*Why?* How can you ask, 44?"

"What would she have gained?"

"An extension of life, for instance; is that nothing?"

"Oh, there spoke the human! He is always pretending that
the eternal bliss of heaven is such a priceless boon! Yes, and
always keeping out of heaven just as long as he can! At bottom, you see, he is far from being certain about heaven."

I was annoyed at my carelessness in giving him that chance.
But I allowed it to stand at that, and said nothing; it could
not help the matter to go into it further. Then, to get away
from it I observed that there was at least one gain that the
woman could have had if she had been saved: she might have
entered heaven by a less cruel death.

"She isn't going there," said 44, placidly.

It gave me a shock, and also it angered me, and I said with some heat—

"You seem to know a good deal about it—*how* do you know?"

He was not affected by my warmth, neither did he trouble to answer my question; he only said—

"The woman could have gained nothing worth considering—certainly nothing worth measuring by your curious methods. What are ten years, subtracted from ten billion years? It is the ten-thousandth part of a second—that is to say, it is nothing at all. Very well, she is in hell now, she will remain there forever. Ten years subtracted from it wouldn't count. Her bodily pain at the stake lasted six minutes—to save her from *that* would not have been worthwhile. That poor creature is in hell; see for yourself!"

Before I could beg him to spare me, the red billows were sweeping by, and she was there among the lost.

The next moment the crimson sea was gone, with its evoker, and I was alone.

Chapter 23

YOUNG as I was—I was barely seventeen—my days were now sodden with depressions, there was little or no rebound. My interest in the affairs of the castle and of its occupants faded out and disappeared; I kept to myself and took little or no note of the daily happenings; my Duplicate performed all my duties, and I had nothing to do but wander aimlessly about and be unhappy.

Thus the days wore heavily by, and meantime I was missing something; missing something, and growing more and more conscious of it. I hardly had the daring to acknowledge to myself what it was. It was the master's niece—Marget! I was a secret worshipper; I had been that a long time; I had worshipped her face and her form with my eyes, but to go further would have been quite beyond my courage. It was not for me to aspire so high; not yet, certainly; not in my timid and callow youth. Every time she had blessed me with a passing remark, the thrill of it, the bliss of it had tingled through me and swept along every nerve and fibre of me with a sort of celestial ecstasy and given me a wakeful night which was better than sleep. These casual and unconsidered remarks, unvalued by her were treasures to me, and I hoarded them in my memory, and knew when it was that she had uttered each of them, and the occasion and the circumstance that had produced each one, and the tone of her voice and the look of her face and the light in her eye; and there was not a night that I did not pass them through my mind caressingly, and turn them over and pet them and play with them, just as a poor girl possessed of half a dozen cheap seed-pearls might do with her small hoard. But that Marget should ever give me an actual thought—any word or notice above what she might give the cat—ah, I never dreamed of it! As a rule she had never been conscious of my presence at all; as a rule she gave me merely a glance of recognition and nothing more when she passed me by in hall or corridor.

As I was saying, I had been missing her, a number of days. It was because her mother's malady was grown a trifle worse and Marget was spending all her time in the sick room. I recognized, now, that I was famishing to see her, and be near that gracious presence once more. Suddenly, not twenty steps away, she rose upon my sight—a fairy vision! That sweet young face, that dainty figure, that subtle exquisite something that makes seventeen the perfect year and its bloom the perfect bloom—oh, there it all was, and I stood transfixed and adoring! She was coming toward me, walking slowly, musing, dreaming, heeding nothing, absorbed, unconscious. As she drew near I stepped directly in her way; and as she passed through me the contact invaded my blood as with a delicious fire! She stopped, with a startled look, the rich blood rose in her face, her breath came quick and short through her parted lips, and she gazed wonderingly about her, saying twice, in a voice hardly above a whisper—

"What could it have been?"

I stood devouring her with my eyes, she remained as she was, without moving, as much as a minute, perhaps more; then she said in that same low soliloquising voice, "I was surely asleep—it was a dream—it must have been that—why did I wake?" and saying this, she moved slowly away, down the great corridor.

Nothing can describe my joy. I believed she loved me, and had been keeping her secret, as maidens will; but now I would persuade it out of her; I would be bold, brave, and speak! I made myself visible, and in a minute had overtaken her and was at her side. Excited, happy, confident, I touched her arm, and the warm words began to leap from my mouth—

"Dear Marget! oh, my own, my dar—"

She turned upon me a look of gentle but most chilly and dignified rebuke, allowed it a proper time to freeze where it struck, then moved on, without a word, and left me there. I did not feel inspired to follow.

No, I could not follow, I was petrified with astonishment. Why should she act like that? Why should she be glad to dream of me and not glad to meet me awake? It was a mystery; there was something very strange about this; I could make nothing out of it. I went on puzzling and puzzling over the enigma for a little while, still gazing after her and half crying for shame that I had been so fresh and had gotten such a blistering lesson for it, when I saw her stop. Dear me, she might turn back! I was invisible in half an instant—I wouldn't have faced her again for a province.

Sure enough, she did turn back. I stepped to the wall, and gave her the road. I wanted to fly, but I had no power to do that, the sight of her was a spell that I could not resist; I had to stay, and gaze, and worship. She came slowly along in that same absorbed and dreamy way, again; and just as she was passing by me she stopped, and stood quite still a moment—two or three moments, in fact—then moving on, she said, with a sigh, "I was mistaken, but I thought I faintly felt it again."

Was she sorry it was a mistake? It certainly sounded like that. It put me in a sort of ecstasy of hope, it filled me with a burning desire to test the hope, and I could hardly refrain from stepping out and barring her way again, to see what would happen; but that rebuff was too recent, its smart was still too fresh, and I hadn't the pluck to do it.

But I could feast my eyes upon her loveliness, at any rate,

and in safety, and I would not deny myself that delight. I followed her at a distance, I followed all her wanderings; and when at last she entered her apartment and closed the door, I went to my own place and to my solitude, desolate. But the fever born of that marvelous first contact came back upon me and there was no rest for me. Hour after hour I fought it, but still it prevailed. Night came, and dragged along, there was no abatement. At ten the castle was asleep and still, but I could not sleep. I left my room and went wandering here and there, and presently I was floating through the great corridor again. In the vague light I saw a figure standing motionless in that memorable spot. I recognized it—even less light would have answered for that. I could not help approaching it, it drew me like a magnet. I came eagerly on; but when I was within two or three steps of it I remembered, with a chill, who I was, and stopped. No matter: To be so near to Marget was happiness enough, riches enough! With a quick movement she lifted her head and poised it in the attitude of one who listens—listens with a tense and wistful and breathless interest; it was a happy and longing face that I saw in the dim light; and out of it, as through a veil, looked darkling and humid the eyes I loved so well. I caught a whisper: "I cannot hear anything—no, there is no sound—but it is near, I know it is near, and the dream is come again!" My passion rose and overpowered me and I floated to her like a breath and put my arms about her and drew her to my breast and put my lips to hers, unrebuked, and drew intoxication from them! She closed her eyes, and with a sigh which seemed born of measureless content, she said dreamily, "I love you so—and have so longed for you!"

Her body trembled with each kiss received and repaid, and by the power and volume of the emotions that surged through me I realized that the sensations I knew in my fleshly estate were cold and weak by contrast with those which a spirit feels.

I was invisible, impalpable, substanceless, I was as transparent as the air, and yet I seemed to support the girl's weight and bear it up. No, it was more than seeming, it was an actuality. This was new; I had not been aware that my spirit possessed this force. I must exploit this valuable power, I must examine it, test it, make experiments. I said—

"When I press your hand, dear, do you feel it?"

"Why, of course."

"And when I kiss you?"

"Indeed yes!" and she laughed.

"And do you *feel* my arms about you when I clasp you in them?"

"Why, certainly. What strange questions!"

"Oh, well, it's only to make talk, so that I can hear your voice. It is such music to me, Marget, that I—"

"Marget? Marget? Why do you call me that?"

"Oh, you little stickler for the conventions and proprieties! Have I got to call you Miss Regen? Dear me, I thought we were further along than that!"

She seemed puzzled, and said—

"But why should you call me *that*?"

It was my turn to be puzzled.

"Why should I? I don't know any really good reason, except that it's your name, dear."

"My name, indeed!" and she gave her comely head a toss. "I've never heard it before!"

I took her face between my hands and looked into her eyes to see if she were jesting, but there was nothing there but sweet sincerity. I did not quite know what to say, so at a venture I said—

"Any name that will be satisfactory to you will be lovely to me, you unspeakably adorable creature! Mention it! What shall I call you?"

"Oh, what a time you do have, to make talk, as you call it! What shall you *call* me? Why, call me by my own name—my *first* name—and don't put any Miss to it!"

I was still in the fog, but that was no matter—the longer it might take to work out of it the pleasanter and the better. So I made a start:

"Your first name . . . . your first name . . . . . how annoying, I've forgotten it! What is it, dear?"

The music of her laugh broke out rich and clear, like a birdsong, and she gave me a light box on the ear, and said—

"Forgotten it?—oh, no, that won't do! You are playing some kind of a game—I don't know what it is, but you are not going to catch me. You want me to say it, and then—

then—why then you are going to spring a trap or a joke or
something and make me feel foolish. Is that it? What *is* it you
are going to do if I say it, dearheart?"

"*I'll* tell you," I said, sternly, "I am going to bend your
head back and cradle your neck in the hollow of my left
arm,—so—and squeeze you close—so—and the moment you
say it I am going to kiss you on the mouth."

She gazed up from the cradling arm with the proper play-
acting humility and resignation, and whispered—

"Lisabet!" and took her punishment without a protest.

"You have been a very good girl," I said, and patted her
cheek approvingly. "There wasn't any trap, Lisabet—at least
none but this: I pretended that forgetfulness because when
the sweetest of all names comes from the sweetest of all lips it
is sweeter then than ever, and I wanted to hear you say it."

"Oh, you dear thing! I'll say the rest of it at the same
price!"

"Done!"

"Elisabeth von Arnim!"

"One—two—three: a kiss for each component!"

I was out of the fog, I had the name. It was a triumph of
diplomacy, and I was proud of it. I repeated the name several
times, partly for the pleasure of hearing it and partly to nail it
in my memory, then I said I wished we had some more things
to trade between us on the same delicious basis. She caught
at that, and said—

"We can do *your* name, Martin."

Martin! It made me jump. Whence had she gathered this
batch of thitherto unheard-of names? What was the secret of
this mystery, the how of it, the why of it, the explanation of
it? It was too deep for me, much too deep. However, this was
no time to be puzzling over it, I ought to be resuming trade
and finding out the rest of my name; so I said—

"Martin is a poor name, except when you say it. Say it
again, sweetheart."

"Martin. Pay me!"

Which I did.

"Go on, Betty dear; more music—say the rest of it."

"Martin von Giesbach. I wish there was more of it. Pay!"

I did, and added interest.

Boom-m-m-m! from the solemn great bell in the main tower.

"Half-past eleven—oh, what will mother say! I did not dream it was so late, did you Martin?"

"No, it seemed only fifteen minutes."

"Come, let us hurry," she said, and we hurried—at least after a sort of fashion—with my left arm around her waist and the hollow of her right hand cupped upon my left shoulder by way of having a support. Several times she murmured dreamily, "How happy I am, how happy, happy, happy!" and seemed to lose herself in that thought and be conscious of nothing else. By and by I had a rare start—my Duplicate stepped suddenly out from a bunch of shadows, just as we were passing by! He said, reproachfully—

"Ah, Marget, I waited so long by your door, and you broke your promise! Is this kind of you? is it affectionate?"

Oh, jealousy—I felt the pang of it for the first time.

To my surprise—and joy—the girl took no more notice of him than if he had not been there. She walked right on, she did not seem to see him nor hear him. He was astonished, and stopped still and turned, following her with his eyes. He muttered something, then in a more definite voice he said—

"What a queer attitude—to be holding her hand up in the air like that! . . . . . Why, she's walking in her sleep!"

He began to follow, a few steps behind us. Arrived at Marget's door, I took her—no, Lisbet's!—peachy face between my hands and kissed the eyes and the lips, her delicate hands resting upon my shoulders the while; then she said "Goodnight—good-night and blessed dreams," and passed within. I turned toward my Duplicate. He was standing near by, staring at the vacancy where the girl had been. For a time he did only that. Then he spoke up and said joyfully—

"I've been a jealous fool! That was a kiss—and it was for me! She was dreaming of me. I understand it all, now. And that loving good-night—it was for me, too. Ah, it makes all the difference!" He went to the door and knelt down and kissed the place where she had stood.

I could not endure it. I flew at him and with all my spirit-strength I fetched him an open-handed slat on the jaw that sent him lumbering and spinning and floundering over and over along the stone floor till the wall stopped him. He was greatly surprised. He got up rubbing his bruises and looking admiringly about him for a minute or two, then went limping away, saying—

"I wonder what in hell *that* was!"

Chapter 24

I FLOATED off to my room through the unresisting air, and stirred up my fire and sat down to enjoy my happiness and study over the enigma of those names. By ferreting out of my memory certain scraps and shreds of information garnered from 44's talks I presently untangled the matter, and arrived at an explanation—which was this: the presence of my flesh-and-blood personality was not a circumstance of any interest to Marget Regen, but my presence as a spirit acted upon her hypnotically—as 44 termed it—and plunged her into the somnambulic sleep. This removed her Day-Self from command and from consciousness, and gave the command to her Dream-Self for the time being. Her Dream-Self was a quite definite and independent personality, and for reasons of its own it had chosen to name itself Elisabeth von Arnim. It was entirely unacquainted with Marget Regen, did not even know she existed, and had no knowledge of her affairs, her feelings, her opinions, her religion, her history, nor of any other matter concerning her. On the other hand, Marget was entirely unacquainted with Elisabeth and wholly ignorant of her existence and of all other matters concerning her, including her name.

Marget knew me as August Feldner, her Dream-Self knew me as Martin von Giesbach—*why*, was a matter beyond guessing. Awake, the girl cared nothing for me; steeped in the hypnotic sleep, I was the idol of her heart.

There was another thing which I had learned from 44, and that was this: each human being contains not merely two independent entities, but three—the Waking-Self, the Dream-Self, and the Soul. This last is immortal, the others are functioned by the brain and the nerves, and are physical and mortal; they are not functionable when the brain and nerves are paralysed by a temporary hurt or stupefied by narcotics; and when the man dies *they* die, since their life, their energy and their existence depend solely upon physical sustenance, and they cannot get that from dead nerves and a dead brain. When I was invisible the whole of my physical make-up was gone, nothing connected with it or depending upon it was left. My soul—my immortal spirit—alone remained. Freed from the encumbering flesh, it was able to exhibit forces, passions and emotions of a quite tremendously effective character.

It seemed to me that I had now ciphered the matter out correctly, and unpuzzled the puzzle. I was right, as I found out afterward.

And now a sorrowful thought came to me: all three of my Selves were in love with the one girl, and how could we all be happy? It made me miserable to think of it, the situation was so involved in difficulties, perplexities and unavoidable heart-burnings and resentments.

Always before, I had been tranquilly unconcerned about my Duplicate. To me he was merely a stranger, no more no less; to him I was a stranger; in all our lives we had never chanced to meet until 44 had put flesh upon him; we could not have met if we had wanted to, because whenever one of us was awake and in command of our common brain and nerves the other was of necessity asleep and unconscious. All our lives we had been what 44 called Box and Cox lodgers in the one chamber: aware of each other's existence but not interested in each other's affairs, and never encountering each other save for a dim and hazy and sleepy half-moment on the threshold, when one was coming in and the other going out, and never in any case halting to make a bow or pass a greeting.

And so it was not until my Dream-Self's fleshing that he and I met and spoke. There was no heartiness; we began as mere acquaintances, and so remained. Although we had been born together, at the same moment and of the same womb, there was no spiritual kinship between us; spiritually we were a couple of distinctly independent and unrelated individuals, with equal rights in a common fleshly property, and we cared no more for each other than we cared for any other stranger. My fleshed Duplicate did not even bear my name, but called himself Emil Schwarz.

I was always courteous to my Duplicate, but I avoided him. This was natural, perhaps, for he was my superior. My imagination, compared with his splendid dream-equipment, was as a lightning bug to the lightning; in matters of our trade he could do more with his hands in five minutes than I could do in a day; he did all my work in the shop, and found it but a trifle; in the arts and graces of beguilement and persuasion I was a pauper and he a Croesus; in passion, feeling, emotion, sensation—whether of pain or pleasure—I was phosphorus, he was fire. In a word he had all the intensities one suffers or enjoys in a dream!

This was the creature that had chosen to make love to Marget! In my coarse dull human form, what chance was there for me? Oh, none in the world, none! I knew it, I realized it, and the heartbreak of it was unbearable.

But my Soul, stripped of its vulgar flesh—what was my Duplicate in competition with *that?* Nothing, and less than nothing. The conditions were reversed, as regarded passions, emotions, sensations, and the arts and graces of persuasion. Lisbet was mine, and I could hold her against the world—but only when she was Lisbet, only when her Dream-Self was in command of her person! when she was Marget she was her Waking-Self, and the slave of that reptile! Ah, there could be no help for this, no way out of this fiendish complication. I could have only half of her; the other half, no less dear to me, must remain the possession of another. She was mine, she was his, turn-about.

These desolating thoughts kept racing and chasing and scorching and blistering through my brain without rest or halt, and I could find no peace, no comfort, no healing for the tortures they brought. Lisbet's love, so limitlessly dear and precious to me, was almost lost sight of because I couldn't have Marget's too. By this sign I perceived that I was still a human being; that is to say, a person who wants the earth, and cannot be satisfied unless he can have the whole of it. Well, we are made so; even the humblest of us has the voracity of an emperor.

At early mass the next morning my happiness came back to me, for Marget was there, and the sight of her cured all my sorrows. For a time! She took no notice of me, and I was not expecting she would, therefore I was not troubled about that, and was content to look at her, and breathe the same air with her, and note and admire everything she did and everything she didn't do, and bless myself in these privileges; but when I found she had over-many occasions to glance casually and fleetingly around to her left I was moved to glance around, myself, and see if there was anything particular there. Sure enough there was. It was Emil Schwarz. He was already become a revolting object to me, and I now so detested him that I could hardly look at anything else during the rest of the service; except, of course, Marget.

When the service was over, I lingered outside, and made myself invisible, purposing to follow Marget and resume the wooing. But she did not come. Everybody came out but two,—*those* two. After a little, Marget put her head out and looked around to see if any one was in sight, then she glanced back, with a slight nod, and moved swiftly away. That saddened me, for I interpreted it to mean that the other wooing was to have first place. Next came Schwarz, and him I followed—upward, always upward, by dim and narrow stairways seldom used; and so, to a lofty apartment in the south tower, the luxurious quarters of the departed magician. He entered, and closed the door, but I followed straight through the heavy panels, without waiting, and halted just on the inside. There was a great fire of logs at the other end of the room, and Marget was there! She came briskly to meet this odious Dream-stuff, and flung herself into his arms, and kissed him—and he her, and she him again, and he her again, and so on, and so on, and so on, till it was most unpleasant to look at. But I bore it, for I wanted to know all my misfortune, the full magnitude of it and the particulars. Next, they went arm-in-arm and sat down and cuddled up together on a sofa, and did that all over again—over and over and over and over—the most offensive spectacle I had ever seen, as it seemed to me. Then Schwarz tilted up that beautiful face, using his profane forefinger as a fulcrum under the chin that should have been sacred to me, and looked down into the luminous eyes which should have been wholly mine by rights, and said, archly—

"Little traitor!"

"Traitor? I? How, Emil?"

"You didn't keep your tryst last night."

"Why, Emil, I did!"

"Oh, not you! Come—what did we do? where did we go? For a ducat you can't tell!"

Marget looked surprised—then nonplussed—then a little frightened.

"It is very strange," she said, "very strange . . . . . unaccountable. I seem to have forgotten everything. But I know I was out; I was out till near midnight; I know it because my mother chided me, and tried her best to make me confess what had kept me out so late; and she was very uneasy, and I was cruelly afraid she would suspect the truth. I remember nothing at all of what happened before. Isn't it strange!"

Then the devil Schwarz laughed gaily and said that for a kiss he would unriddle the riddle. So he told her how he had encountered her, and how she was walking in her sleep, and how she was dreaming of him, and how happy it made him to see her kiss the air, imagining she was kissing him. And then they both laughed at the odd incident, and dropped the trifle out of their minds, and fell to trading caresses and endearments again, and thought no more about it.

They talked of the "happy day!"—a phrase that scorched me like a coal. They would win over the mother and the uncle presently—yes, they were quite sure of it. Then they built their future—built it out of sunshine and rainbows and rapture; and went on adding and adding to its golden ecstasies until they were so intoxicated with the prospect that words were no longer adequate to express what they were foreseeing and pre-enjoying, and so died upon their lips and gave place to love's true and richer language, wordless soul-communion: the heaving breast, the deep sigh, the unrelaxing embrace, the shoulder-pillowed head, the bliss-dimmed eyes, the lingering kiss . . . .

By God, my reason was leaving me! I swept forward and enveloped them as with a viewless cloud! In an instant Marget was Lisbet again; and as she sprang to her feet divinely aflame with passion for me I stepped back, and back, and back, she following, then I stopped and she fell panting in my arms, murmuring—

"Oh, my own, my idol, how wearily the time has dragged—do not leave me again!"

That Dream-mush rose astonished, and stared stupidly, his mouth working, but fetching out no words. Then he thought he understood, and started toward us, saying—

"Walking in her sleep again—how suddenly it takes her! . . . . . I wonder how she can lean over like that without falling?"

He arrived and put his arms through me and around her to support her, saying tenderly—

"Wake, dearheart, shake it off, I cannot bear to see you so!"

Lisbet freed herself from his arms and bent a stare of astonishment and wounded dignity upon him, accompanied by words to match—

"Mr. Schwarz, you forget yourself!"

It knocked the reptile stupid for a moment; then he got his bearings and said—

"Oh, please come to yourself, dear, it is so hard to see you like this. But if you can't wake, do come to the divan and sleep it off, and I will so lovingly watch over you, my darling, and protect you from intrusion and discovery. Come, Marget—do!"

"Marget!" Lisbet's eyes kindled, as at a new affront. "*What* Marget, please? Whom do you take me for? And why do you venture these familiarities?" She softened a little then, seeing how dazed and how pitiably distressed he looked, and added, "I have always treated you with courtesy, Mr. Schwarz, and it is very unkind of you to insult me in this wanton way."

In his miserable confusion he did not know what to say, and so he said the wrong thing—

"Oh, my poor afflicted child, shake it off, be your sweet self again, and let us steep our souls once more in dreams of our happy marriage day and—"

It was too much. She would not let him finish, but broke wrathfully into the midst of his sentence.

"Go away!" she said; "your mind is disordered, you have

been drinking. Go—go at once! I cannot bear the sight of you!"

He crept humbly away and out at the door, mopping his eyes with his handkerchief and muttering "Poor afflicted thing, it breaks my heart to see her so!"

Dear Lisbet, she was just a girl—alternate sunshine and shower, peremptory soldier one minute, crying the next. Sobbing, she took refuge on my breast, saying—

"Love me, oh my precious one, give me peace, heal my hurts, charm away the memory of the shame this odious creature has put upon me!"

During half an hour we re-enacted that sofa-scene where it had so lately been played before, detail by detail, kiss for kiss, dream for dream, and the bliss of it was beyond words. But with an important difference: in Marget's case there was a mamma to be pacified and persuaded, but Lisbet von Arnim had no such incumbrances; if she had a relative in the world she was not aware of it; she was free and independent, she could marry whom she pleased and when she pleased. And so, with the dearest and sweetest naivety she suggested that to-day and now was as good a time as any! The suddenness of it, the unexpectedness of it, would have taken my breath if I had had any. As it was, it swept through me like a delicious wind and set my whole fabric waving and fluttering. For a moment I was gravely embarrassed. Would it be right, would it be honorable, would it not be treason to let this confiding young creature marry herself to a viewless detail of the atmosphere? I knew how to accomplish it, and was burning to do it, but would it be fair? Ought I not to at least tell her my condition, and let her decide for herself? Ah . . . . . She might decide the wrong way!

No, I couldn't bring myself to it, I couldn't run the risk. I must think—think—think. I must hunt out a good and righteous reason for the marriage without the revelation. That is the way we are made; when we badly want a thing, we go to hunting for good and righteous reasons for it; we give it that fine name to comfort our consciences, whereas we privately know we are only hunting for plausible ones.

I seemed to find what I was seeking, and I urgently pretended to myself that it hadn't a defect in it. Forty-Four was

my friend; no doubt I could persuade him to return my
Dream-Self into my body and lock it up there for good.
Schwarz being thus put out of the way, wouldn't my wife's
Waking-Self presently lose interest in him and cease from loving him? That looked plausible. Next, by throwing *my* Waking-Self in the way of *her* Waking-Self a good deal and using
tact and art, would not a time come when . . . . . oh, it was
all as clear as a bell! Certainly. It wouldn't be long, it could-
n't be long, before I could retire my Soul into my body, then
both Lisbet and Marget being widows and longing for solace
and tender companionship, would yield to the faithful be-
seechings and supplications of my poor inferior Waking-Self
and marry *him*. Oh, the scheme was perfect, it was flawless,
and my enthusiasm over it was without measure or limit. Lisbet caught that enthusiasm from my face and cried out—

"I know what it is! It is going to be *now*!"

I began to volley the necessary "suggestions" into her head
as fast as I could load and fire—for by "suggestion," as 44
had told me, you make the hypnotised subject see and do and
feel whatever you please: see people and things that are not
there, hear words that are not spoken, eat salt for sugar, drink
vinegar for wine, find the rose's sweetness in a stench, carry
out all suggested acts—and forget the whole of it when he
wakes, and remember the whole of it again whenever the hypnotic sleep returns!

In obedience to suggestion, Lisbet clothed herself as a
bride; by suggestion she made obeisance to imaginary altar
and priest, and smiled upon imaginary wedding-guests; made
the solemn responses; received the ring, bent her dear little
head to the benediction, put up her lips for the marriage kiss,
and blushed as a new-made wife should before people!

Then, by suggestion altar and priest and friends passed
away and we were alone—alone, immeasurably content, the
happiest pair in the Duchy of Austria!

Ah . . . . . footsteps! some one coming! I fled to the middle of the room, to emancipate Lisbet from the embarrassment of the hypnotic sleep and be Marget again and ready for
emergencies. She began to gaze around and about, surprised,
wondering, also a little frightened, I thought.

"Why, where is Emil?" she said. "How strange; I did not

see him go. How could he go and I not see him? . . . . Emil!
. . . . No answer! Surely this magician's den is bewitched.
But we've been here many times, and nothing happened."

At that moment Emil slipped in, closed the door, and said,
apologetically and in a tone and manner charged with the
most respectful formality—

"Forgive me, Miss Regen, but I was afraid for you and have
stood guard—it would not do for you to be found in this
place, and asleep. Your mother is fretting about your absence—her nurse is looking for you everywhere—I have mis-
directed her . . . . . pardon, what is the matter?"

Marget was gazing at him in a sort of stupefaction, with the
tears beginning to trickle down her face. She began to sob in
her hands, and said—

"If I have been asleep it was cruel of you to leave me. Oh,
Emil, how could you desert me at such a time, if you love
me?"

The astonished and happy bullfrog had her in his arms in a
minute and was blistering her with kisses, which she paid back
as fast as she could register them, and she not cold yet from
her marriage-oath! A man—and such a man as that—hugging
my wife before my eyes, and she getting a gross and voracious
satisfaction out of it!—I could not endure the shameful sight.
I rose and winged my way thence, intending to kick a couple
of his teeth out as I passed over, but his mouth was employed
and I could not get at it.

Chapter 25

THAT night I had a terrible misfortune. The way it came
about was this. I was so unutterably happy and so unspeakably unhappy that my life was become an enchanted ecstasy and a crushing burden. I did not know what to do, and
took to drink. Merely for that evening. It was by Doangivadam's suggestion that I did this. He did not know what the
matter was, and I did not tell him; but he could see that
something *was* the matter and wanted regulating, and in his
judgment it would be well to try drink, for it might do good

and couldn't do harm. He was ready to do any kindness for
me, because I had been 44's friend; and he loved to have
me talk about 44, and mourn with him over his burning. I
couldn't tell him 44 was alive again, for the mysterious check
fell upon my tongue whenever I tried to. Very well; we were
drinking and mourning together, and I took a shade too
much and it biased my judgment. I was not what one could
call at all far gone, but I had reached the heedless stage, the
unwatchful stage, when we parted, and I forgot to make myself invisible! And so, eager and unafraid, I entered the
boudoir of my bride confident of the glad welcome which
would of course have been mine if I had come as Martin von
Giesbach, whom she loved, instead of as August Feldner,
whom she cared nothing about. The boudoir was dark, but
the bedroom door was standing open, and through it I saw
an enchanting picture and stopped to contemplate it and enjoy it. It was Marget. She was sitting before a pier glass, snow-
ily arrayed in her dainty nightie, with her left side toward me;
and upon her delicate profile and her shining cataract of dark
red hair streaming unvexed to the floor a strong light was
falling. Her maid was busily grooming her with brush and
comb, and gossiping, and now and then Marget smiled up at
her and she smiled back, and I smiled at both in sympathy
and good-fellowship out of the dusk, and altogether it was a
gracious and contenting condition of things, and my heart
sang with happiness. But the picture was not quite complete,
not wholly perfect—there was a pair of lovely blue eyes that
persistently failed to turn my way. I thought I would go
nearer and correct that defect. Supposing that I was invisible
I tranquilly stepped just within the room and stood there; at
the same moment Marget's mother appeared in the further
door; and also at the same moment the three indignant
women discovered me and began to shriek and scream in the
one breath!

I fled the place. I went to my quarters, resumed my flesh,
and sat mournfully down to wait for trouble. It was not long
coming. I expected the master to call, and was not disappointed. He came in anger—which was natural,—but to my
relief and surprise I soon found that his denunciations were
not for me! What an uplift it was! No, they were all for my

Duplicate—all that the master wanted from me was a denial that I was the person who had profaned the sanctity of his niece's bedchamber. When he said *that* . . . . well, it took the most of the buoyancy out of the uplift. If he had stopped there and challenged me to testify, I—but he didn't. He went right on recounting and re-recounting the details of the exasperating episode, never suspecting that they were not news to me, and all the while he freely lashed the Duplicate and took quite for granted that he was the criminal and that my character placed me above suspicion. This was all so pleasant to my ear that I was glad to let him continue: indeed the more he abused Schwarz the better I liked it, and soon I was feeling grateful that he had neglected to ask for my testimony. He was very bitter, and when I perceived that he was minded to handle my detestable rival with severity I rejoiced exceedingly in my secret heart. Also I became evilly eager to keep him in that mind, and hoped for chances to that end.

It appeared that both the mother and the maid were positive that the Duplicate was the offender. The master kept dwelling upon that, and never referring to Marget as a witness, a thing that seemed so strange to me that at last I ventured to call his attention to the omission.

"Oh, her unsupported opinion is of no consequence!" he said, indifferently. "She says it was you—which is nonsense, in the face of the other evidence and your denial. She is only a child—how can *she* know one of you from the other? To satisfy her I said I would bring your denial; as for Emil Schwarz's testimony I don't want it and shouldn't value it. These Duplicates are ready to say anything that comes into their dreamy heads. This one is a good enough fellow, there's no deliberate harm in him, but—oh, as a witness he is not to be considered. He has made a blunder—in another person it would have been a crime—and by consequence my niece is compromised, for sure, for the maid can't keep the secret; poor thing, she's like all her kind—a secret, in a lady's-maid, is water in a basket. Oh, yes, it's true that this Duplicate has merely committed a blunder, but all the same my mind is made up as to one thing . . . . . the bell is tolling midnight, it marks a change for him . . . . . when I am through with him to-day, let him blunder as much as he likes he'll not compromise my niece again!"

I suppose it was wicked to feel such joy as I felt, but I couldn't help it. To have that hated rival put summarily out of my way and my road left free—the thought was intoxicating! The master asked me—as a formality—to deny that I was the person who had invaded Marget's chamber.

I promptly furnished the denial. It had always cost me shame to tell an injurious lie before, but I told this one without a pang, so eager was I to ruin the creature that stood between me and my worshipped little wife. The master took his leave, then, saying—

"It is sufficient. It is all I wanted. He shall marry the girl before the sun sets!"

Good heavens! in trying to ruin the Duplicate, I had only ruined myself.

Chapter 26

I WAS so miserable! A whole endless hour dragged along. Oh, why didn't he come, *why* didn't he come! wouldn't he *ever* come, and I so in need of his help and comfort!

It was awfully still and solemn and midnighty, and this made me feel creepy and shivery and afraid of ghosts; and that was natural, for the place was foggy with them, as Ernest Wasserman said, who was the most unexact person in his language in the whole castle, foggy being a noun of multitude and not applicable to ghosts, for they seldom appear in large companies, but mostly by ones and twos, and then—oh, then, when they go flitting by in the gloom like forms made of delicate smoke, and you see the furniture through them—

My, what is that! . . . . I heard it again! . . . . I was quaking like a jelly, and my heart was *so* cold and scared! Such a dry, bony noise, such a kl—lackety klackclack, kl—lackety klackclack!—dull, muffled, far away down the distant caverns and corridors—but approaching! oh, dear, approaching! It shriveled me up like a spider in a candle-flame, and I sat scrunched together and quivering, the way the spider does in his death-agony, and I said to myself, "skeletons a-coming, oh, what *shall* I do!"

Do? Shut my door, of course! if I had the strength to get to it—which I wouldn't have, on my legs, I knew it well; but I collapsed to the floor and crawled to the door, and panted there and listened, to see if the noise was certainly coming my way—which it was!—and I took a look; and away down the murky hall a long square of moonlight lay across the floor, and a tall figure was capering across it, with both hands held aloft and violently agitated and clacking out that clatter—and next moment the figure was across and blotted out in the darkness, but not the racket, which was getting loud and sharp, now—then I pushed the door to, and crept back a piece and lay exhausted and gasping.

It came, and came,—that dreadful noise—straight to my door, then that figure capered in and slammed the door to, and went on capering gaily all around me and everywhere about the room; and it was not a skeleton; no, it was a tall man, clothed in the loudest and most clownish and out-landish costume, with a vast white collar that stood above its ears, and a battered hat like a bucket, tipped gallusly to one side, and betwixt the fingers of the violent hands were curved fragments of dry bone which smote together and made that terrible clacking; and the man's mouth reached clear across his face and was unnaturally red, and had extraordinarily thick lips, and the teeth showed intensely white between them, and the face was as black as midnight. It was a terrible and fero-cious spectre, and would bound as high as the ceiling, and crack its heels together, and yah-yah-yah! like a fiend, and keep the bones going, and soon it broke into a song in a sort of bastard English,

> "Buffalo gals can't you come out to-night,
>   Can't you come out to-night,
>   Can't you come out to-night,
>   O, Buffalo gals can't you come out to-night—
>   A-n-d *dance* by de light er de moon!"

And then it burst out with a tremendous clatter of laughter, and flung itself furiously over and over in the air like the wings of a windmill in a gale, and landed with a whack! on its feet alongside of me and looked down at me and shouted most cheerfully—

"*Now* den, Misto' Johnsing, how does yo' corporsosity seem to segashuate!"

I gasped out—

"Oh, dread being, have pity, oh—if—if—"

"Bress yo' soul, honey, *I* ain' no dread being, I's Cunnel Bludso's nigger fum Souf C'yarlina, en I's heah th'ee hund'd en fifty year ahead o' time, caze you's down in de mouf en I got to 'muse you wid de banjo en make you feel all right en comfy agin. So you jist lay whah you is, boss, en listen to de music; I gwineter sing to you, honey, de way de po' slave-niggers sings when dey's sol' away fum dey home en is home-sick en down in de mouf."

Then out of nowhere he got that thing that he called a banjo, and sat down and propped his left ancle on his right knee, and canted his bucket-hat a little further and more gal-lusly over his ear, and rested the banjo in his lap, and set the grip of his left fingers on the neck of it high up, and fetched a brisk and most thrilling rake across the strings low down, giving his head a toss of satisfaction, as much as to say "I reckon *that* gets in to where you live, oh I guess not!" Then he canted his head affectionately toward the strings, and twisted the pegs at the top and tuned the thing up with a mu-sical plunkety-plunk or so; then he re-settled himself in his chair and lifted up his black face toward the ceiling, grave, far-away, kind of pathetic, and began to strum soft and low—and then! Why then his voice began to tremble out and float away toward heaven—such a sweet voice, such a divine voice, and so touching—

> "Way down upon de Swanee river,
>   Far, far away,
>   Dah's whah my heart is turnin' ever,
>   Dah's whah de ole folks stay."

And so on, verse after verse, sketching his humble lost home, and the joys of his childhood, and the black faces that had been dear to him, and which he would look upon no more—and there he sat lost in it, with his face lifted up that way, and there was never anything so beautiful, never anything so heart-breaking, oh, never any music like it below the skies! and by the magic of it that uncouth figure lost its uncouthness and became lovely like the song, because it so fitted the song, so belonged to it, and was such a part *of* it, so helped to body forth the feeling of it and make it visible, as it were, whereas a silken dress and a white face and white graces would have profaned it, and cheapened its noble pathos.

I closed my eyes, to try if I could picture to myself that lost home; and when the last notes were dying away, and apparently receding into the distance, I opened them again: the singer was gone, my room was gone, but afar off the home was there, a cabin of logs nestling under spreading trees, a soft vision steeped in a mellow summer twilight—and steeped in that music, too, which was dying, dying, fading, fading; and with it faded the vision, like a dream, and passed away; and as it faded and passed, my room and my furniture began to dimly reappear—spectrally, with the perishing home showing vaguely, through it, as through a veil; and when the transformation was accomplished my room was its old self again, my lights were burning, and in the black man's place sat Forty-Four beaming a self-complimenting smile. He said—

"Your eyes are wet; it's the right applause. But it's nothing, I could fetch that effect if they were glass. Glass? I could do it if they were knot-holes. Get up, and let's feed."

I *was* so glad to see him again! The very sight of him was enough to drive away my terrors and despairs and make me forget my deplorable situation. And then there was that mysterious soul-refreshment, too, that always charged the atmosphere as with wine and set one's spirits a-buzzing whenever he came about, and made you perceive that he was come, whether he was visible or not.

***When we had finished feeding, he lit his smoke-factory and we drew up to the fire to discuss my unfortunate situation and see what could be done about it. We examined it all around, and I said it seemed to me that the first and most urgent thing to be done was to stop the lady's-maid's gossiping mouth and keep her from compromising Marget; I said the master hadn't a doubt that she would spread the fact of the unpleasant incident of an hour or two ago. Next, I thought

we ought to stop that marriage, if possible. I concluded
with—

"Now, 44, the case is full of intolerable difficulties, as you
see, but do try and think of some way out of them, won't
you?"

To my grief I soon saw that he was settling down into one
of his leather-headed moods. Ah, how often they came upon
him when there was a crisis and his very brightest intelligence
was needed!

He said he saw no particular difficulties in the situation if I
was right about it: the first and main necessity was to silence
the maid and stop Schwarz from proceeding with his marriage—and then blandly proposed that we *kill* both of them!

It almost made me jump out of my clothes. I said it was a
perfectly insane idea, and if he was actually in earnest—

He stopped me there, and the argument-lust rose in his
dull eye. It always made me feel depressed to see that look,
because he loved to get a chance to show off how he could
argue, and it was so dreary to listen to him—dreary and irritating, for when he was in one of his muddy-minded moods
he couldn't argue any more than a clam. He said, big-eyed
and asinine—

"What makes you think it insane, August?"

What a hopeless question! what could a person answer to
such a foolishness as that?

"Oh, dear, me," I said, "can't you *see* that it's insane?"

He looked surprised, puzzled, pathetically mystified for a
little while, then said—

"Why, *I* don't see how you make it out, August. We don't
need those people, you know. No one needs them, so far as I
can see. There's a plenty of them around, you can get as many
as you want. Why, August, you don't seem to have any practical ideas—business ideas. You stay shut up here, and you
don't know about these things. There's dozens and dozens of
those people. I can turn out and in a couple of hours I can
fetch a whole swarm of—"

"Oh, wait, 44! Dear me, is supplying their places the whole
thing? is it the important thing? Don't you suppose *they*
would like to have something to say about it?"

That simple aspect of it did seem to work its way into his

head—after boring and tugging a moment or two—and he said, as one who had received light—

"Oh, I didn't think of that. Yes—yes, I see now." Then he brightened, and said, "but you know, they've got to die anyway, and so the *when* isn't any matter. Human beings aren't of any particular consequence; there's plenty more, plenty. Now then, after we've got them killed—"

"Damnation, we are not *going* to kill them!—now don't say another word about it; it's a perfectly atrocious idea; I should think you would be ashamed of it; and ashamed to hang to it and stick to it the way you do, and be so reluctant to give it up. Why, you act as if it was a child, and the first one you ever had."

He was crushed, and looked it. It hurt me to see him look cowed, that way; it made me feel mean, and as if I had struck a dumb animal that had been doing the best it knew how, and not meaning any harm; and at bottom I was vexed at myself for being so rough with him at such a time; for *I* know at a glance when he has a leather-headed mood on, and that he is not responsible when his brains have gone mushy; but I just *couldn't* pull myself together right off and say the gentle word and pet away the hurt I had given. I had to take time to it and work down to it gradually. But I managed it, and by and by his smiles came back, and his cheer, and then he was all right again, and as grateful as a child to see me friends with him once more.

Then he went zealously to work on the problem again, and soon evolved another scheme. The idea this time was to turn the maid into a cat, and make some *more* Schwarzes, then Marget would not be able to tell t'other from which, and couldn't choose the right one, and it wouldn't be lawful for her to marry the whole harem. That would postpone the wedding, he thought.

It certainly had the look of it! Any blind person could see that. So I gave praise, and was glad of the chance to do it and make up for bygones. He was as pleased as could be. In about ten minutes or so we heard a plaintive sound of meyow-yowing wandering around and about, away off somewhere, and 44 rubbed his hands joyfully and said—

"There she is, now!"

"Who?"

"The lady's-maid."

"No! Have you already transmuted her?"

"Yes. She was sitting up waiting for her room-mate to come, so she could tell her. Waiting for her mate to come from larking with the porter's new yunker. In a minute or two it would have been too late. Set the door ajar; she'll come when she sees the light, and we'll see what she has to say about the matter. She mustn't recognize me; I'll change to the magician. It will give him some more reputation. Would you like me to make you able to understand what she says?"

"Oh, *do*, 44, do, please!"

"All right. Here she is."

It was the magician's voice, exactly counterfeited; and there he stood, the magician's duplicate, official robes and all. I went invisible; I did not want to be seen in the condemned enchanter's company, even by a cat.

She came sauntering sadly in, a very pretty cat. But when she saw the necromancer her tail spread and her back went up and she let fly a spit or two and would have scurried away, but I flew over her head and shut the door in time. She backed into the corner and fixed her glassy eyes on 44, and said—

"It was you who did this, and it was mean of you. I never did you any harm."

"No matter, you brought it on yourself."

"How did I bring it on myself?"

"You were going to tell about Schwarz; you would have compromised your young mistress."

"It's not so; I wish I may never die if—"

"Nonsense! Don't talk so. You were waiting up to tell. I know all about it."

The cat looked convicted. She concluded not to argue the case. After thinking a moment or two she said, with a kind of sigh—

"Will they treat me well, do you think?"

"Yes."

"Do you know they will?"

"Yes, I know it."

After a pause and another sigh—

"I would rather be a cat than a servant—a slave, that has to smile, and look cheerful, and pretend to be happy, when you are scolded for every little thing, the way Frau Stein and her daughter do, and be sneered at and insulted, and they haven't any right to, *they* didn't pay my wage, I wasn't *their* slave—a hateful life, an odious life! I'd rather be a cat. Yes, I would. Will everybody treat me well?"

"Yes, everybody."

"Frau Stein, too, and the daughter?"

"Yes."

"Will *you* see that they do?"

"I will. It's a promise."

"Then I thank you. They are all afraid of you, and the most of them hate you. And it was the same with me—but not now. You seem different to me now. You have the same voice and the same clothes, but you seem different. You seem kind; I don't know why, but you do; you seem kind and good, and I trust you; I think you will protect me."

"I will keep my promise."

"I believe it. And keep me as I am. It was a bitter life. You would think those Steins would not have been harsh with me, seeing I was a poor girl, with not a friend, nor anybody that was mine, and I never did them any harm. I *was* going to tell. Yes, I was. To get revenge. Because the family said I was bribed to let Schwarz in there—and it was a lie! Even Miss Marget believed that lie—I could see it, and she—well, she tried to defend me, but she let them convince her. Yes, I was going to tell. I was hot to tell. I was angry. But I am glad I didn't get the chance, for I am not angry any more; cats do not carry anger, I see. Don't change me back, leave me as I am. Christians go—I know where they go; some to the one place some to the other; but I think cats—where do *you* think cats go?"

"Nowhere. After they die."

"Leave me as I am, then; don't change me back. Could I have these leavings?"

"And welcome—yes."

"Our supper was there, in our room, but the other maid was frightened of me because I was a strange cat, and drove me out, and I didn't get any. This is wonderful food, I wonder how it got to this room? there's never been anything like it in this castle before. Is it enchanted food?"

"Yes."

"I just guessed it was. Safe?"

"Perfectly."

"Do you have it here a good deal?"

"Always—day and night."

"How gaudy! But this isn't your room?"

"No, but I'm here a great deal, and the food is here all the time. Would you like to do your feeding here?"

"Too good to be true!"

"Well, you can. Come whenever you like, and speak at the door."

"How dear and lovely! I've had a narrow escape—I can see it now."

"From what?"

"From not getting to be a cat. It was just an accident that that idiot came blundering in there drunk; if I hadn't been there—but I *was*, and never shall I get done being thankful. This is amazing good food; there's never been anything like it in this castle before—not in my time, I can tell you. I am thankful I may come here when I'm hungry."

"Come whenever you like."

"I'll do what I can for pay. I've never caught a mouse, but I feel it in me that I could do it, and I will keep a lookout here. I'm not so sad, now; no, things look very different; but I was pretty sad when I came. Could I room here, do you think? Would you mind?"

"Not at all. Make yourself quite at home. There'll be a special bed for you. I'll see to it."

"What larks! I never knew what nuts it was to be a cat before."

"It has its advantages."

"Oh, I should smile! I'll step out, now, and browse around a little, and see if there's anything doing in my line. Au revoir, and many many thanks for all you have done for me. I'll be back before long."

And so she went out, waving her tail, which meant satisfaction.

"There, now," said 44, "that part of the plan has come out all right, and no harm done."

"No, indeed," I said, resuming my visible form, "we've done her a favor. And in her place I should feel about it just as she does. Forty-Four, it was beautiful to hear that strange language and understand it—I understood every word. Could I learn to speak it, do you think?"

"You won't have to learn it, I'll put it *into* you."

"Good. When?"

"Now. You've already got it. Try! Speak out—do The Boy Stood on the Burning Deck—in catapult, or cataplasm, or whatever one might call that tongue."

"The Boy—what was it you said?"

"It's a poem. It hasn't been written yet, but it's very pretty and stirring. It's English. But I'll empty it into you, where you stand, in cataplasm. Now you've got it. Go ahead—recite."

I did it, and never missed a wail. It was certainly beautiful in that tongue, and quaint and touching; 44 said if it was done on a back fence, by moonlight, it would make people cry—especially a quartette would. I was proud; he was not always so complimentary. I said I was glad to have the cat, particularly now that I could talk to her; and she would be happy with me, didn't he think? Yes, he said, she would. I said—

"It's a good night's work we've done for that poor little blonde-haired lady's-maid, and I believe, as you do, that quite soon she is going to be contented and happy."

"As soon as she has kittens," he said, "and it won't be long."

Then we began to think out a name for her, but he said—

"Leave that, for the present, you'd better have a nap."

He gave a wave of his hand, and that was sufficient; before the wave was completed I was asleep.

Chapter 27

I WOKE UP fresh and fine and vigorous, and found I had been asleep a little more than six minutes. The sleeps which he furnished had no dependence upon time, no connection with it, no relation to it; sometimes they did their work in one interval, sometimes in another, sometimes in half a second, sometimes in half a day, according to whether there was an interruption or wasn't; but let the interval be long or short, the result was the same: that is to say, the reinvigoration was perfect, the physical and mental refreshment complete.

There had been an interruption, a voice had spoken. I glanced up, and saw myself standing there, within the half-open door. That is to say, I saw Emil Schwarz, my Duplicate. My conscience gave me a little prod, for his face was sad. Had he found out what had been happening at midnight, and had he come at three in the morning to reproach me?

Reproach me? What for? For getting him falsely saddled with a vulgar indiscretion? What of it? Who was the loser by it? Plainly, I, myself—I had lost the girl. And who was the gainer? He himself, and none other—he had acquired her. Ah, very well, then—let him reproach me; if he was dissatisfied, let him trade places: he wouldn't find me objecting. Having reached solid ground by these logical reasonings, I advised my conscience to go take a tonic, and leave me to deal with this situation as a healthy person should.

Meantime, during these few seconds, I was looking at myself, standing there—and for once, I was admiring. Just because I had been doing a very handsome thing by this Duplicate, I was softening toward him, my prejudices were losing strength. I hadn't intended to do the handsome thing, but no matter, it had happened, and it was natural for me to take the credit of it and feel a little proud of it, for I was human. Being human accounts for a good many insanities, according to 44—upwards of a thousand a day was his estimate.

It is actually the truth that I had never looked this Duplicate over before. I never could bear the sight of him. I wouldn't look at him when I could help it; and until this moment I *couldn't* look at him dispassionately and with fairness. But now I could, for I had done him a great and creditable kindness, and it quite changed his aspects.

In those days there were several things which I didn't know. For instance I didn't know that my voice was not the same voice to me that it was to others; but when 44 made me talk into the thing which he brought in, one day, when he had arrived home from one of his plundering-raids among the unborn centuries, and then reversed the machine and allowed me to listen to my voice as other people were used to hearing it, I recognized that it had so little resemblance to the voice *I* was accustomed to hearing that I should have said it was not my voice at all if the proof had not been present that it was.

Also, I had been used to supposing that the person I saw in the mirror was the person others saw when they looked at me—whereas that was not the case. For once, when 44 had come back from robbing the future he brought a camera and made some photographs of me—those were the names which he gave the things, names which he invented out of his head for the occasion, no doubt, for that was his habit, on account of his not having any principles—and *always* the pictures which were like me as I saw myself in the glass he pronounced poor, and those which I thought exceedingly bad, he pronounced almost supernaturally good.

And here it was again. In the figure standing by the door I was now seeing myself as others saw me, but the resemblance to the self which I was familiar with in the glass was *merely* a resemblance, nothing more; not approaching the common resemblance of brother to brother, but reaching only as far as the resemblance which a person usually bears to his brother-in-law. Often one does not notice that, at all, until it is pointed out; and sometimes, even then, the resemblance owes as much to imagination as to fact. It's like a cloud which resembles a horse after some one has pointed out the resemblance. You perceive it, then, though I have often seen a cloud that didn't. Clouds often have nothing more than a brother-in-law resemblance. I wouldn't say this to everybody, but I believe it to be true, nevertheless. For I myself have seen clouds which looked like a brother-in-law, whereas I knew very well they didn't. Nearly all such are hallucinations, in my opinion.

Well, there he stood, with the strong white electric light flooding him, (more plunder,) and he hardly even reached the brother-in-law standard. I realized that I had never really seen this youth before. Of course I could recognize the general pattern, I don't deny it, but that was only because I knew who the creature was; but if I had met him in another country, the most that could have happened would have been this: that I would turn and look after him and say "I wonder if I have seen him somewhere before?" and then I would drop the matter out of my mind, as being only a fancy.

Well, there he was; that is to say, there *I* was. And I was interested; interested at last. He was distinctly handsome, distinctly trim and shapely, and his attitude was easy, and well-bred and graceful. Complexion—what it should be at seventeen, with a blonde ancestry: peachy, bloomy, fresh, wholesome. Clothes—precisely like mine, to a button—or the lack of it.

I was well satisfied with this front view. I had never seen my back; I was curious to see it. I said, very courteously—

"Would you please turn around for a moment?—only a moment? . . . Thank you."

Well, well, how little we know what our backs are like! This one was all right, I hadn't a fault to find with it, but it was all new to me, it was the back of a stranger—hair-aspects and all. If I had seen it walking up the street in front of me it would not have occurred to me that I could be in any personal way interested in it.

"Turn again, please, if you will be so good . . . . Thank you kindly."

I was to inspect the final detail, now—mentality. I had put it last, for I was reluctant, afraid, doubtful. Of course one glance was enough—I was expecting that. It saddened me: he was of a loftier world than I, he moved in regions where I could not tread, with my earth-shod feet. I wished I had left that detail alone.

"Come and sit down," I said, "and tell me what it is. You wish to speak with me about something?"

"Yes," he said, seating himself, "if you will kindly listen."

I gave a moment's thought to my defence, as regards the impending reproach, and was ready. He began, in a voice and manner which were in accord with the sadness which sat upon his young face—

"The master has been to me and has charged me with profaning the sanctity of his niece's chamber."

It was a strange place to stop, but there he stopped, and looked wistfully at me, just as a person might stop in a dream, and wait for another person to take up the matter there, without any definite text to talk to. I had to say something, and so for lack of anything better to offer, I said—

"I am truly sorry, and I hope you will be able to convince him that he is mistaken. You can, can't you?"

"Convince him?" he answered, looking at me quite vacantly, "Why should I wish to convince him?"

I felt pretty vacant myself, now. It was a most unlooked-for question. If I had guessed a week I should not have hit upon that one. I said—and it was the only thing a body would ever think of saying—

"But you do, don't you?"

The look he gave me was a look of compassion, if I know the signs. It seemed to say, gently, kindly, but clearly, "alas, this poor creature doesn't know anything." Then he uttered his answer—

"Wh-y, no, I do not see that I have that wish. It—why, you see, it isn't any matter."

"Good heavens! It isn't any matter whether you stand disgraced or not?"

He shook his head, and said quite simply—

"No, it isn't any matter, it is of no consequence."

It was difficult to believe my ears. I said—

"Well, then, if disgrace is nothing to you, consider *this* point. If the report gets around, it can mean disgrace for the young *lady*."

It had no effect that I could see! He said—

"Can it?" just as an idiot child might have said it.

"*Can* it? Why of course it can! You wouldn't want *that* to happen, would you?"

"We-ll," (reflectively), "I don't know. I don't see the bearing of it."

"Oh, great guns, this infantile stu—this—this—why, it's perfectly disheartening! You love her, and yet you don't care whether her good name is ruined or not?"

"Love her?" and he had the discouraged aspect of a person who is trying to look through a fog and is not succeeding, "why, *I* don't love her; what makes you think I do?"

"Well, I must say! Well, certainly this is too many for *me*. Why, hang it, *I* know you've been courting her."

"Yes—oh, yes, that is true."

"Oh, it is, is it! Very well, then, how is it that you were courting her and yet didn't love her?"

"No, it isn't that way. No, I loved her."

"Oh—go on, I'll take a breath or two—I don't know where I am, I'm all at sea."

He said, placidly—

"Yes, I remember about that. I loved her. It had escaped me. No—it hadn't escaped me; it was not important, and I was thinking of something else."

"Tell me," I said, "is *anything* important to you?"

"Oh, yes!" he responded, with animation and a brightening face; then the animation and the brightness passed, and he added, wearily, "but not these things."

Somehow, it touched me; it was like the moan of an exile. We were silent a while, thinking, ruminating, then I said—

"Schwarz, I'm not able to make it out. It is a sweet young girl, you certainly did love her, and—"

"Yes," he said, tranquilly, "it is quite true. I believe it was yesterday . . . . yes, I think it was yesterday."

"Oh, you *think* it was! But of course it's not important. Dear me, why should it be?—a little thing like that. Now then, something has changed it. What was it? What has happened?"

"Happened? Nothing, I think. Nothing that I know of."

"Well, then, why the devil . . . . oh, great Scott, I'll never get my wits back again! Why, look here, Schwarz, you wanted to *marry* her!"

"Yes. Quite true. I think . . . . yesterday? Yes, I think it was yesterday. I am to marry her to-day. I think it's to-day; anyway, it is pretty soon. The master requires it. He has told me so."

"Well . . . . upon my word!"

"What is the matter?"

"Why, you are as indifferent about this as you are about everything else. You show no feeling whatever, you don't even show interest. Come! surely you've got a heart hidden away somewhere; open it up; give it air; show at least some little corner of it. Land, I wish I were in your place! Don't you *care* whether you marry her or not?"

"Care? Why, *no,* of course I don't. You do ask the *strangest* questions! I wander, wander, wander! I try to make you out, I try to understand you, but it's all fog, fog, fog—you're just a riddle, nobody *can* understand you!"

Oh, the idea! the impudence of it! this to *me*!—from this frantic chaos of unimaginable incomprehensibilities, who couldn't by any chance utter so much as half a sentence that Satan himself could make head or tail of!

"Oh, I like *that*!" I cried, flying out at him. "*You* can't understand *me*! Oh, but that *is* good! It's immortal! Why, look here, when you came, I thought I knew what you came for— I thought I knew all about it—I would have said you were coming to reproach me for—for—"

I found it difficult to get it out, and so I left it in, and after a pause, added—

"Why, Schwarz, you certainly had something on your mind when you came—I could see it in your face—but if ever you've got to it I've not discovered it—oh, not even a sign of it! You *haven't* got to it, *have* you?"

"*Oh*, no!" he answered, with an outburst of very real energy. "These things were of no sort of consequence. *May* I tell it now? Oh, *will* you be good and hear me? I shall be so grateful, if you will!"

"Why, certainly, and glad to! Come, *now* you're waking up, at last! You've got a heart in you, sure enough, and plenty of feeling—why, it burns in your eye like a star! Go ahead—I'm all interest, all sympathy."

Oh, well, he was a different creature, now. All the fogs and puzzlings and perplexities were gone from his face, and had left it clear and full of life. He said—

"It was no idle errand that brought me. No, far from it! I came with my heart in my mouth, I came to beg, to plead, to pray—to beseech you, to implore you, to have mercy upon me!"

"Mercy—upon *you*?"

"Yes, mercy. Have mercy, oh, be merciful, and set me free!"

"Why, I—I—Schwarz, I don't understand. You say, yourself, that if they want you to marry, you are quite indif—"

"Oh, not *that*! I care nothing for that—it is these bonds" —stretching his arms aloft—"oh, free me from *them*; these bonds of flesh—this decaying vile matter, this foul weight, and clog, and burden, this loathsome sack of corruption in which my spirit is imprisoned, her white wings bruised and soiled—oh, be merciful and set her free! Plead for me with that malicious magic-monger—he has been here—I saw him issue from this door—he will come again—say you will be my friend, as well as brother! for brothers indeed we are; the same womb was mother to us both, I live by you, I perish when you die—brother, be my friend! plead with him to take away this rotting flesh and set my spirit free! Oh, this human life, this earthy life, this weary life! It is so groveling, and so mean; its ambitions are so paltry, its prides so trivial, its vanities so childish; and the glories that it values and applauds—lord, how empty! Oh, here I am a servant!—I who never served before; here I am a slave—slave among little mean kings and emperors made of clothes, the kings and emperors slaves themselves, to mud-built carrion that are *their* slaves!

"To think you should think I came here concerned about those other things—those inconsequentials! Why should they concern me, a spirit of air, habitant of the august Empire of Dreams? *We* have no morals; the angels have none; morals are for the impure; we have no principles, those chains are for men. We love the lovely whom we meet in dreams, we forget them the next day, and meet and love their like. They are dream-creatures—no others are real. Disgrace? We care nothing for disgrace, we do not know what it is. Crime? we commit it every night, while you sleep; it is nothing to us. We have no character, no *one* character, we have *all* characters; we are honest in one dream, dishonest in the next; we fight in one battle and flee from the next. We wear no chains, we cannot abide them; we have no home, no prison, the universe is our province; we do not know time, we do not know space— we live, and love, and labor, and enjoy, fifty years in an hour, while you are sleeping, snoring, repairing your crazy tissues; we circumnavigate your little globe while you wink; we are not tied within horizons, like a dog with cattle to mind, an emperor with human sheep to watch—we visit hell, we roam in heaven, our playgrounds are the constellations and the Milky Way. Oh, help, help! be my friend and brother in my need—beseech the magician, beg him, plead with him; he will listen, he will be moved, he will release me from this odious flesh!"

I was powerfully stirred—so moved, indeed, that in my pity for him I brushed aside unheeded or but half-heeded the scoffs and slurs which he had flung at my despised race, and jumped up and seized him by both hands and wrung them passionately, declaring that with all my heart and soul I would plead for him with the magician, and would not rest from these labors until my prayers should succeed or their continuance be peremptorily forbidden.

Chapter 28

H E could not speak, for emotion; for the same cause my voice forsook me; and so, in silence we grasped hands again; and that grip, strong and warm, said for us what our tongues could not utter. At that moment the cat entered, and stood looking at us. Under her grave gaze a shame-faced discomfort, a sense of embarrassment, began to steal over me, just as would have been the case if she had been a human being who had caught me in that gushy and sentimental situation, and I felt myself blushing. Was it because I was aware that she had lately been that kind of a being? It annoyed me to see that my brother was not similarly affected. And yet, why mind it? didn't I already know that no human intelligence could guess what occurrence would affect *him* and what event would leave him cold? With an uncomfortable feeling of being critically watched by the cat, I pressed him with clumsy courtesy into his seat again, and slumped into my own.

The cat sat down. Still looking at us in that disconcerting way, she tilted her head first to one side and then the other, inquiringly and cogitatively, the way a cat does when she has struck the unexpected and can't quite make out what she had better do about it. Next she washed one side of her face, making such an awkward and unscientific job of it that almost anybody would have seen that she was either out of practice or didn't know how. She stopped with the one side, and looked bored, and as if she had only been doing it to put in the time, and wished she could think of something else to do to put in some more time. She sat a while, blinking drowsily, then she hit an idea, and looked as if she wondered she hadn't thought of it earlier. She got up and went visiting around among the furniture and belongings, sniffing at each and every article, and elaborately examining it. If it was a chair, she examined it all around, then jumped up in it and sniffed all over its seat and its back; if it was any other thing she could examine all around, she examined it all around; if it was a chest and there was room for her between it and the wall, she crowded herself in behind there and gave it a thorough over-hauling; if it was a tall thing, like a washstand, she would stand on her hind toes and stretch up as high as she could, and reach across and paw at the toilet things and try to rake them to where she could smell them; if it was the cupboard, she stood on her toes and reached up and pawed the knob; if it was the table she would squat, and measure the distance, and make a leap, and land in the wrong place, owing to new-ness to the business; and, part of her going too far and slid-ing over the edge, she would scramble, and claw at things desperately, and save herself and make good; then she would smell everything on the table, and archly and daintily paw everything around that was movable, and finally paw some-thing off, and skip cheerfully down and paw it some more, throwing herself into the prettiest attitudes, rising on her hind feet and curving her front paws and flirting her head this way and that and glancing down cunningly at the object, then pouncing on it and spatting it half the length of the room, and chasing it up and spatting it again, and again, and racing after it and fetching it another smack—and so on and so on; and suddenly she would tire of it and try to find some way to get to the top of the cupboard or the wardrobe, and if she couldn't she would look troubled and disappointed; and to-ward the last, when you could see she was getting her bear-ings well lodged in her head and was satisfied with the place and the arrangements, she relaxed her intensities, and got to purring a little to herself, and praisefully waving her tail be-tween inspections—and at last she was done—done, and everything satisfactory and to her taste.

Being fond of cats, and acquainted with their ways, if I had been a stranger and a person had told me that this cat had spent half an hour in that room before, but hadn't happened to think to examine it until now, I should have been able to say with conviction, "Keep an eye on her, that's no orthodox cat, she's an imitation, there's a flaw in her make-up, you'll find she's born out of wedlock or some other arrested-development accident has happened, she's no true Christian cat, if *I* know the signs."

She couldn't think of anything further to do, now, so she thought she would wash the other side of her face, but she couldn't remember which one it was, so she gave it up, and sat down and went to nodding and blinking; and between nods she would jerk herself together and make remarks. I heard her say—

"One of them's the Duplicate, the other's the Original, but I can't tell t'other from which, and I don't suppose *they* can. I am sure I couldn't if I were them. The missuses said it was the Duplicate that broke in there last night, and I voted with the majority for policy's sake, which is a servant's only protection from trouble, but I would like to know how *they* knew. *I* don't believe they could tell them apart if they were stripped. Now my idea is—"

I interrupted, and intoned musingly, as if to myself,—

"The boy stood on the burning deck,
    Whence all but him had fled—"

and stopped there, and seemed to sink into a reverie.

It gave her a start! She muttered—

"*That's* the Duplicate. Duplicates know languages—everything, sometimes, and then again they don't know anything at all. That is what Fischer says, though of course it could have been his Duplicate that said it, there's never any telling, in this bewitched place, whether you are talking to a person himself, or only to his heathen image. And Fischer says they haven't any morals nor any principles—though of course it could have been his Duplicate that said it—one never knows. Half the time when you say to a person *he* said so-and-so, he says he didn't—so then you recognize it was the other one. As between living in such a place as this and being crazy, you don't know *which* it is, the most of the time. I would rather be a cat and not have any Duplicate, then I always know which one I am. Otherwise, not. If they haven't any principles, it was this Duplicate that broke in there, though of course, being drunk he wouldn't know which one he was, and so it could be the other without him suspecting it, which leaves the matter where it was before—not certain enough to be certain, and just uncertain enough to be *un*certain. So I don't see that anything's decided. In fact I know it isn't. Still, I think this one that wailed is the Duplicate, because sometimes they know all languages a minute, and next minute they don't know their own, if they've got one, whereas a *man* doesn't. Doesn't, and can't even *learn* it—can't learn cat-language, anyway. It's what Fischer says—Fischer or his Duplicate. So this is the one—*that's* decided. He couldn't talk cataract, nor ever learn it, either, if it was the Christian one . . . . . I'm awful tired!"

I didn't let on, but pretended to be dozing; my brother was a little further along than that—he was softly snoring. I wanted to wait and see, if I could, what was troubling the cat, for it seemed plain to me that she had something on her mind, she certainly was not at her ease. By and by she cleared her throat, and I stirred up and looked at her, as much as to say, "well, I'm listening—proceed." Then she said, with studied politeness—

"It is very late. I am sorry to disturb you gentlemen, but I am very tired, and would like to go to bed."

"Oh, dear me," I said, "don't wait up on our account I beg of you. Turn right in!"

She looked astonished.

"With you present?" she said.

So then I was astonished myself, but did not reveal it.

"Do you mind it?" I asked.

"Do I *mind* it! You will grant, I make no doubt, that so extraordinary a question is hardly entitled to the courtesy of an answer from one of my sex. You are offensive, sir; I beg that you will relieve me of your company at once, and take your friend with you."

"Remove him? I could not do that. He is my guest, and it is his place to make the first move. This is my room."

I said it with a submerged chuckle, as knowing quite well,

that soft-spoken as it was, it would knock some of the starch out of her. As indeed it did.

"*Your* room! Oh, I beg a thousand pardons, I am ashamed of my rude conduct, and will go at once. I assure you sir, I was the innocent victim of a mistake: I thought it was my room."

"And so it is. There has been no mistake. Don't you see?—there is your bed."

She looked whither I was pointing, and said with surprise—

"How strange that is! it wasn't there five seconds ago. Oh, *isn't* it a love!"

She made a spring for it—cat-like, forgetting the old interest in the new one; and feminine-like, eager to feast her native appetite for pretty things upon its elegancies and daintinesses. And really it *was* a daisy! It was a canopied four-poster, of rare wood, richly carved, with bed twenty inches wide and thirty long, sumptuously bepillowed and belaced and beruffled and besatined and all that; and when she had petted it and patted it and searched it and sniffed it all over, she cried out in an agony of delight and longing—

"Oh, I would just *love* to stretch out on that!"

The enthusiasm of it melted me, and I said heartily—

"Turn right in, Mary Florence Fortescue Baker G. Nightingale, and make yourself at home—that is the magician's own present to you, and it shows you he's no imitation-friend, but the true thing!"

"Oh, what a pretty name!" she cried; "is it mine for sure enough, and may I keep it? Where *did* you get it?"

"I don't know—the magician hooked it from somewhere, he is always at that, and it just happened to come into my mind at the psychological moment, and I'm glad it did, for your sake, for it's a dandy! Turn in, now, Baker G., and make yourself entirely at home."

"You are *so* good, dear Duplicate, and I am just as grateful as I can be, but—but—well, you see how it is. I have never roomed with any person not of my own sex, and—"

"You will be perfectly safe here, Mary, I assure you, and—"

"I should be an ingrate to doubt it, and I do not doubt it, be sure of that; but at this particular time—at this time of all others—er—well, you know, for a smaller matter than this,

Miss Marget is already compromised beyond repair, I fear, and if I—"

"Say no more, Mary Florence, you are perfectly right, perfectly. My dressing-room is large and comfortable, I can get along quite well without it, and I will carry your bed in there. Come along . . . Now then, there you are! Snug and nice and all right, isn't it? Contemplate that! Satisfactory?—yes?"

She cordially confessed that it was. So I sat down and chatted along while she went around and examined *that* place all over, and pawed everything and sampled the smell of each separate detail, like an old hand, for she was getting the hang of her trade by now; then she made a final and special examination of the button on our communicating-door, and stretched herself up on her hind-toes and fingered it till she got the trick of buttoning-out inquisitives and undesirables down fine and ship-shape, then she thanked me handsomely for fetching the bed and taking so much trouble; and gave me good-night, and when I asked if it would disturb her if I talked a while with my guest, she said no, talk as much as we pleased, she was tired enough to sleep through thunderstorms and earthquakes. So I said, right cordially—

"Good-night, Mary G., und schlafen Sie wohl!" and passed out and left her to her slumbers. As delicate-minded a cat as ever I've struck, and I've known a many of them.

Chapter 29

I STIRRED my brother up, and we talked the time away while waiting for the magician to come. I said his coming was a most uncertain thing, for he was irregular, and not at all likely to come when wanted, but Schwarz was anxious to stay and take the chances; so we did as I have said—talked and waited. He told me a great deal about his life and ways as a dream-sprite, and did it in a skipping and disconnected fashion proper to his species. He would side-track a subject right in the middle of a sentence if another subject attracted him, and he did this without apology or explanation—well, just as a dream would, you know. His talk was scatteringly seasoned with strange words and phrases, picked up in a thousand worlds, for he had been everywhere. Sometimes he could tell me their meaning and where he got them, but not always; in fact not very often, the dream-memory being pretty capricious, he said—sometimes good, oftener bad, and always flighty. "Side-track," for instance. He was not able to remember where he had picked that up, but thought it was in a star in the belt of Orion where he had spent a summer one night with some excursionists from Sirius whom he had met in space. That was as far as he could remember with anything like certainty; as to *when* it was, that was a blank with him; perhaps it was in the past, maybe it was in the future, he couldn't tell which it was, and probably didn't know, at the time it happened. *Couldn't* know, in fact, for Past and Future were human terms and not comprehendable by him, past and future being all one thing to a dream-sprite, and not distinguishable the one from the other. "And not important, anyway." How natural that sounded, coming from him! His notions of the important were just simply elementary, as you may say.

He often dropped phrases which had clear meanings to him, but which he labored in vain to make comprehensible by me. It was because they came from countries where none of the conditions resembled the conditions I had been used to; some from comets where nothing was solid, and nobody had legs; some from our sun, where nobody was comfortable except when white-hot, and where you needn't talk to people about cold and darkness, for you would not be able to explain the words so that they could understand what you were talking about; some from invisible black planets swimming in eternal midnight and thick-armored in perpetual ice, where the people have no eyes, nor any use for them, and where you might wear yourself out trying to make them understand what you meant by such words as warmth and light, you wouldn't ever succeed; and some from *general space*—that sea of ether which has no shores, and stretches on, and on, and arrives nowhere; which is a waste of black gloom and thick darkness through which you may rush forever at thought-speed, encountering at weary long intervals spirit-cheering archipelagoes of suns which rise sparkling far in front of you, and swiftly grow and swell, and burst into blinding glories of light, apparently measureless in extent, but you plunge through and in a moment they are far behind, a twinkling archipelago again, and in another moment they are blotted out in darkness; constellations, these? yes; and the earliest of them the property of your own solar system; the rest of that unending flight is through solar systems not known to men.

And he said that in that flight one came across *such* interesting dream-sprites! coming from a billion worlds, bound for a billion others; always friendly, always glad to meet up with you, always full of where they'd been and what they'd seen, and dying to tell you about it; doing it in a million foreign languages, which sometimes you understood and sometimes you didn't, and the tongue you understood to-day you forgot to-morrow, there being *nothing* permanent about a dream-sprite's character, constitution, beliefs, opinions, intentions, likes, dislikes, or anything else; all he cares for is to travel, and talk, and see wonderful things and have a good time. Schwarz said dream-sprites are well-disposed toward their fleshly brothers, and did what they could to make them partakers of the wonders of their travels, but it couldn't be managed except on a poor and not-worth-while scale, because they had to communicate through the flesh-brothers' Waking-Self imagination, and *that* medium—oh, well, it was like "emptying rainbows down a rat-hole."

His tone was not offensive. I think his tone was never that, and was never meant to be that; *it* was all right enough, but his phrasing was often hurtful, on account of the ideal frankness of it. He said he was once out on an excursion to Jupiter with some fellows about a million years ago, when—

I stopped him there, and said—

"I am only seventeen, and you said you were born with me."

"Yes," he said, "I've been with you only about two million years, I believe—counting as you count; *we* don't measure time at all. Many a time I've been abroad five or ten or twenty thousand years in a single night; I'm always abroad when you are asleep; I always leave, the moment you fall asleep, and I never return until you wake up. You are dreaming all the time I am gone, but you get little or nothing of what I see—never more than some cheap odds and ends, such as your groping Mortal Mind is competent to perceive—and sometimes there's nothing for you at all, in a whole night's adventures, covering many centuries; it's all above your dull Mortal Mind's reach."

Then he dropped into his "chances." That is to say, he went to discussing my health—as coldly as if I had been a piece of mere property that he was commercially interested in, and which ought to be thoughtfully and prudently taken care of for *his* sake. And he even went into particulars, by gracious! advising me to be very careful about my diet, and to take a good deal of exercise, and keep regular hours, and avoid dissipation and religion, and not get married, because a family brought love, and distributed it among many objects, and intensified it, and this engendered wearing cares and anxieties, and when the objects suffered or died the miseries and anxieties multiplied and broke the heart and shortened life; whereas if I took good care of myself and avoided these indiscretions, there was no reason why he should not live ten million years and be hap—

I broke in and changed the subject, so as to keep from getting inhospitable and saying language; for really I was a good deal tried. I started him on the heavens, for he had been to a good many of them and liked ours the best, on account of there not being any Sunday there. They kept Saturday, and it was very pleasant: plenty of rest for the tired, and plenty of innocent good times for the others. But no Sunday, he said; the Sunday-Sabbath was a commercial invention and quite local, having been devised by Constantine to equalize prosperities in this world between the Jews and the Christians. The government statistics of that period showed that a Jew could make as much money in five days as a Christian could in six; and so Constantine saw that at this rate the Jews would by and by have all the wealth and the Christians all the poverty. There was nothing fair nor right about this, a righteous government should have equal laws for all, and take just as much care of the incompetent as of the competent—more, if anything. So he added the Sunday-Sabbath, and it worked just right, because it equalized the prosperities. After that, the Jew had to lie idle 104 days in the year, the Christian only 52, and this enabled the Christian to catch up. But my brother said there was now talk among Constantine and other early Christians up there, of some more equalizing; because, in looking forward a few centuries they could notice that along in the twentieth century somewhere it was going to be necessary to furnish the Jews another Sabbath to keep, so as to save what might be left of Christian property at that time. Schwarz said he had been down into the first quarter of the twentieth century lately, and it looked so to him.

Then he "side-tracked" in his abrupt way, and looked avidly at my head and said he did wish he was back in my skull, he would sail out the first time I fell asleep and have a scandalous good time!—wasn't that magician *ever* coming back?

"And oh," he said, "what wouldn't I see! wonders, spectacles, splendors which your fleshly eyes couldn't endure; and what wouldn't I hear! the music of the spheres—no mortal could live through five minutes of *that* ecstasy! If he would only come! If he . . . ." He stopped, with his lips parted and his eyes fixed, like one rapt. After a moment he whispered, *"do you feel that?"*

I recognized it; it was that life-giving, refreshing, mysterious something which invaded the air when 44 was around. But I dissembled, and said—

"What is it?"

"It's the magician; he's coming. He doesn't always let that influence go out from him, and so we dream-sprites took him for an ordinary necromancer for a while; but when he burnt 44 we were all there and close by, and he let it out then, and in an instant we knew what he was! We knew he was a . . . we knew he was a . . . . a . . . a . . . how curious!—my tongue won't *say* it!"

Yes, you see, 44 wouldn't let him say it—and I so near to getting that secret at last! It was a sorrowful disappointment.

Forty-Four entered, still in the disguise of the magician, and Schwarz flung himself on his knees and began to beg passionately for release, and I put in my voice and helped. Schwarz said—

"Oh, mighty one, you imprisoned me, you can set me free, and no other can. You have the power; you possess *all* the powers, all the forces that defy Nature, nothing is impossible to you, for you are a . . . a . . ."

So there it was again—he couldn't say it. I was that close to it a second time, you see; 44 wouldn't let him say that word, and I would have given anything in the world to hear it. It's the way we are made, you know: if we can get a thing, we don't want it, but if we can't get it, why—well, it changes the whole aspect of it, you see.

Forty-Four was very good about it. He said he would let this one go—Schwarz was hugging him around the knees and lifting up the hem of his robe and kissing it and kissing it before he could get any further with his remark—yes, he would let this one go, and make some fresh ones for the wedding, the family could get along very well that way. So he told Schwarz to stand up and melt. Schwarz did it, and it was very pretty. First, his clothes thinned out so you could see him through them, then they floated off like shreds of vapor, leaving him naked, then the cat looked in, but scrambled out again; next, the flesh fell to thinning, and you could see the skeleton through it, very neat and trim, a good skeleton; next the bones disappeared and nothing was left but the empty form—just a statue, perfect and beautiful, made out of the delicatest soap-bubble stuff, with rainbow-hues dreaming around over it and the furniture showing through it the same as it would through a bubble; then—poof! and it was gone!

Chapter 30

THE CAT walked in, waving her tail, then gathered it up in her right arm, as she might a train, and minced her way to the middle of the room, where she faced the magician and rose up and bent low and spread her hands wide apart, as if it was a gown she was spreading, then sank her body grandly rearward—certainly the neatest thing you ever saw, considering the limitedness of the materials. I think a curtsy is the very prettiest thing a woman ever does, and I think a lady's-maid's curtsy is prettier than any one else's; which is because they get more practice than the others, on account of being at it all the time when there's nobody looking. When she had finished her work of art she smiled quite Cheshirely (my dream-brother's word, he knew it was foreign and thought it was future, he couldn't be sure), and said, very engagingly—

"Do you think I could have a bite now, without waiting for the second table, there'll be *such* goings-on this morning, and I would just give a whole basket of rats to be in it! and if I—"

At that moment the wee-wee'est little bright-eyed mousie you ever saw went scrabbling across the floor, and Baker G. gave a skip and let out a scream and landed in the highest chair in the room and gathered up her imaginary skirts and stood there trembling. Also at that moment her breakfast came floating out of the cupboard on a silver tray, and she asked that it come to the chair, which it did, and she took a hurried bite or two to stay her stomach, then rushed away to get her share of the excitements, saying she would like the rest of her breakfast to be kept for her till she got back.

"Now then, draw up to the table," said 44. "We'll have Vienna coffee of two centuries hence—it is the best in the world—buckwheat cakes from Missouri, vintage of 1845, French eggs of last century, and deviled breakfast-whale of the post-pliocene, when he was whitebait size, and just *too* delicious!"

By now I was used to these alien meals, raked up from countries I had never heard of and out of seasons a million years apart, and was getting indifferent about their age and nationalities, seeing that they always turned out to be fresh and good. At first I couldn't stand eggs a hundred years old and canned manna of Moses's time, but that effect came from habit and prejudiced imagination, and I soon got by it, and enjoyed what came, asking few or no questions. At first I would not have touched whale, the very thought of it would have turned my stomach, but now I ate a hundred and sixty of them and never turned a hair. As we chatted along during breakfast, 44 talked reminiscently of dream-sprites, and said they used to be important in the carrying of messages where secrecy and dispatch were a desideratum. He said they took a pride in doing their work well, in old times; that they conveyed messages with perfect verbal accuracy, and that in the

matter of celerity they were up to the telephone and away beyond the telegraph. He instanced the Joseph-dreams, and
gave it as his opinion that if they had gone per Western Union
the lean kine would all have starved to death before the
telegrams arrived. He said the business went to pot in Roman
times, but that was the fault of the interpreters, not of the
dream-sprites, and remarked—

"You can easily see that accurate interpreting was as necessary as accurate wording. For instance, suppose the Founder
sends a telegram in the Christian Silence dialect, what are you
going to do? Why, there's nothing to do but *guess* the best
you can, and take the chances, because there isn't anybody in
heaven or earth that can understand *both* ends of it, and so,
there you are, you see! Up a stump."

"Up a which?"

"Stump. American phrase. Not discovered yet. It means defeated. You are bound to misinterpret the end you do not understand, and so the matter which was to have been
accomplished by the message miscarries, fails, and vast damage is done. Take a specific example, then you will get my
meaning. Here is a telegram from the Founder to her disciples. Date, June 27, four hundred and thirteen years hence;
it's in the paper—Boston paper—I fetched it this morning."

"What is a Boston paper?"

"It can't be described in just a mouthful of words—pictures, scare-heads and all. You wait, I'll tell you all about it
another time; I want to read the telegram, now."

"Hear, O Israel, the Lord God is one Lord.

"I now request that the members of my Church cease
special prayer for the peace of nations, and cease in full
faith that God does not hear our prayers only because of
oft speaking; but that He will bless all the inhabitants of
the earth, and 'none can stay His hand nor say unto
Him what doest thou.' Out of His allness He must bless
all with His own truth and love.

"MARY BAKER G. EDDY."

"Pleasant View, Concord, N.H., June 27, 1905."

"You see? Down to the word 'nations' anybody can understand it. There's been a prodigious war going on for about

seventeen months, with destruction of whole fleets and armies, and in seventeen words she indicates certain things, to-wit: I believed we could squelch the war with prayer, therefore I ordered it; it was an error of Mortal Mind, whereas I had supposed it was an inspiration; I now order you to cease from praying for peace and take hold of something nearer our size, such as strikes and insurrections. The rest seems to mean—seems to mean . . . . Let me study it a minute. It seems to mean that He does not listen to our prayers any more because we pester Him too much. This carries us to the phrase 'oft-speaking.' At that point the fog shuts down, black and impenetrable, it solidifies into uninterpretable irrelevancies. Now then, you add up, and get these results: the praying must be stopped—which is clear and definite; the reason for the stoppage is—well, uncertain. Don't you know that the incomprehensible and uninterpretable remaining half of the message may be of *actual* importance? we may be even sure of it, I think, because the first half wasn't; then what are we confronted with? what is the world confronted with? Why, possible disaster—isn't it so? Possible disaster, absolutely impossible to avoid; and all because one cannot get at the meaning of the words intended to describe it and tell how to prevent it. You now understand how important is the interpreter's share in these matters. If you put part of the message in school-girl and the rest in Choctaw, the interpreter is going to be defeated, and colossal harm can come of it."

"I am sure it is true. What is His allness?"

"I pass."

"You which?"

"Pass. Theological expression. It probably means that she entered the game because she thought only His halfness was in it and would need help; then perceiving that His allness was there and playing on the other side, she considered it best to cash-in and draw out. I think that that must be it; it looks reasonable, you see, because in seventeen months she hadn't put up a single chip and got it back again, and so in the circumstances it would be natural for her to want to go out and see a friend. In Roman times the business went to pot through bad interpreting, as I told you before. Here in Suetonius is an instance. He is speaking of Atia, the mother of Augustus Caesar:

"'Before her delivery she dreamed that her bowels stretched to the stars, and expanded through the whole circuit of heaven and earth.'

"Now how would you interpret that, August?"

"Who—me? I do not think I could interpret it at all, but I do wish I could have seen it, it must have been magnificent."

"Oh, yes, like enough; but doesn't it suggest anything to you?"

"Why, n-no, I can't see that it does. What would *you* think—that there had been an accident?"

"Of course not! It wasn't real, it was only a dream. It was sent to inform her that she was going to be delivered of something remarkable. What should you think it was?"

"I—why, I don't know."

"Guess."

"Do you think—well, would it be a slaughter-house?"

"Sho, you've no talent for interpretation. But that is a striking instance of what the interpreter had to deal with, in that day. The dream-messages had become loose and rickety and indefinite, like the Founder's telegram, and soon the natural thing happened: the interpreters became loose and careless and discouraged, and got to guessing instead of interpreting, and the business went to ruin. Rome had to give up dream-messages, and the Romans took to entrails for prophetic information."

"Why, then, these ones must have come good, 44, don't you think?"

"I mean *bird* entrails—entrails of chickens."

"I would stake my money on the others; what does a chicken know about the future?"

"Sho, you don't get the idea, August. It isn't what the chicken knows; a chicken doesn't know anything, but by examining the condition of its entrails when it was slaughtered, the augurs could find out a good deal about what was going to happen to emperors, that being the way the Roman gods had invented to communicate with them when dream-transportation went out and Western Union hadn't come in yet. It was a good idea, too, because often a chicken's entrails knew more than a Roman god did, if he was drunk, and he generally was."

"Forty-Four, aren't you afraid to speak like that about a god?"

"No. Why?"

"Because it's irreverent."

"No, it isn't."

"Why isn't it? What do you *call* irreverence?"

"Irreverence is *another person's* disrespect to *your* god; there isn't any word that tells what your disrespect to *his* god is."

I studied it over and saw that it was the truth, but I hadn't ever happened to look at it in that way before.

"Now then, August, to come back to Atia's dream. It beat every soothsayer. None of them got it right. The real meaning of it was—"

The cat dashed in, excited, and said, "I heard Katzenyammer say there's hell to pay down below!" and out she dashed again. I jumped up, but 44 said—

"Sit down. Keep your head. There's no hurry. Things are working; I think we can have a good time. I have shut down the prophecy-works and prepared for it."

"The prophecy-works?"

"Yes. Where I come from, we—"

"*Where* do you co—"

It was as far as I could get. My jaw caught, there, and he gave me a look and went on as if nothing had happened:

"Where I come from we have a gift which we get tired of, now and then. We foresee everything that is going to happen, and so when it happens there's nothing *to* it, don't you see? we don't get any surprises. We can't shut down the prophecy-works there, but we can here. That is one of the main reasons that I come here so much. I do love surprises! I'm only a youth, and it's natural. I love shows and spectacles, and stunning dramatics, and I love to astonish people, and show off, and be and do all the gaudy things a boy loves to be and do; and whenever I'm here and have got matters worked up to where there is a good prospect to the fore, I shut down the works and have a time! I've shut them down now, two hours ago, and I don't know a thing that's ahead, any more than you do. That's all—now we'll go. I wanted to tell you that. I had plans, but I've thrown them aside. I haven't any now. I will let things go their own way, and act as circumstances suggest. Then there will be surprises. They may be small ones, and nothing to you, because you are used to them; but even the littlest ones are grand to me!"

The cat came racing in, greatly excited, and said—

"Oh, I'm so glad I'm in time! Shut the door—there's people everywhere—don't let them see in. Dear magician, get a disguise, you are in greater danger now than ever before. You have been seen, and everybody knows it, everybody is watching for you, it was most imprudent in you to show yourself. Do put on a disguise and come with me, I know a place in the castle where they'll never find you. Oh, please, please hurry! don't you hear the distant noises? they're hunting for you—do *please* hurry!"

Forty-Four was that gratified, you can't think! He said—

"There it is, you see! I hadn't any idea of it, any more than you! And there'll be more—I just feel it."

"Oh, please don't stop to talk, but get the disguise! you don't know what may happen any moment. Everybody is searching for me, and for you, too, Duplicate, and for your Original; they've been at it some time, and are coming to think all three of us is murdered—"

"*Now* I know what I'll do!" cried 44; "oh but we'll have the gayest time! go on with your news!"

"—and Katrina is wild to get a chance at you because you burnt up 44, which was the idol of her heart, and she's got a carving knife three times as long as my tail, and is ambushed behind a marble column in the great hall, and it's awful to see how savagely she rakes it and whets it up and down that column and makes the sparks fly, and darts her head out, with her eyes glaring, to see if she can see you—oh, *do* get the disguise and come with me, quick! and laws bless me, there's a conspiracy, and—"

"Oh, it's grand, August, it's just grand! and I didn't know a thing about it, any more than you. *What* conspiracy are you talking about, pussy?"

"It's the strikers, going to kill the Duplicates—I sat in Fischer's lap and heard them talk the whole thing in whispers; and they've got signs and grips and passwords and all that,

so't they can tell which is themselves and which is other people, though I hope to goodness if *I* can, not if I had a thousand such; *do* get the disguise and come, I'm just ready to
cry!"

"Oh, bother the disguise, I'm going just so, and if they offer to do anything to me I will give them a piece of my
mind."

And so he opened the door and started away, Mary following him, with the tears running down, and saying—

"Oh, *they* won't care for your piece of mind—why *will* you
be so imprudent and throw your life away, and you *know*
they'll abuse me and bang me when you are gone!"

I became invisible and joined them.

Chapter 31

I T was a dark, sour, gloomy morning, and bleak and cold,
with a slanting veil of powdery snow driving along, and a
clamorous hollow wind bellowing down the chimneys and
rumbling around the battlements and towers—just the right
weather for the occasion, 44 said, nothing could improve it
but an eclipse. That gave him an idea, and he said he would
do an eclipse; not a real one, but an artificial one that nobody
but Simon Newcomb could tell from the original Jacobs—so
he started it at once, and it certainly did make those yawning
old stone tunnels pretty dim and sepulchral, and also of
course it furnished an additional uncanniness and muffledness
to way-off footfalls, taking the harshness out of them and the
edge off their echoes, because when you walk on that kind of
eclipsy gloominess on a stone floor it squshes under the foot
and makes that dull effect which is so shuddery and uncomfortable in these crumbly old castles where there has been
such ages of cruelty and captivity and murder and mystery.
And to-night would be Ghost-Night besides, and 44 did not
forget to remember that, and said he wished eclipses weren't
so much trouble after sundown, hanged if he wouldn't run
this one all night, because it could be a great help, and a lot
of ghastly effects could be gotten out of it, because all the

castle ghosts turn out then, on account of its coming only every ten years, which makes it kind of select and distinguished, and still more so every Hundredth Year—which this one was—because the best ghosts from many other castles come by invitation, then, and take a hand at the great ball and banquet at midnight, a good spectacle and full of interest, insomuch that 44 had come more than once on the Hundredth Night to see it, he said, and it was very pathetic and interesting to meet up with shadowy friends that way that you haven't seen for one or two centuries and hear them tell the same mouldy things over again that they've told you several times before; because they don't have anything fresh, the way they are situated, poor things. And besides, he was going to make this the swellest Hundredth Night that had been celebrated in this castle in twelve centuries, and said he was inviting A 1 ghosts from everywhere in the world and from all the ages, past and future, and each could bring a friend if he liked—any friend, character no object, just so he is dead—and if I wanted to invite some I could, he hoped to accumulate a thousand or two, and make this *the* Hundredth Night of Hundredth Nights, and discourage competition for a thousand years.

We didn't see a soul, all the murky way from my door to the central grand staircase and half way down it—then we began to see plenty of people, our own and men from the village—and they were armed, and stood in two ranks, waiting, a double fence across the spacious hall—for the magician to pass between, if it might please him to try it; and Katrina was there, between the fences, grim and towering and soldierly, and she was watching and waiting, with her knife. I glanced back, by chance, and there was also a living fence *behind!* dim forms, men who had been keeping watch in ambush, and had silently closed in upon the magician's tracks as he passed along. Mary G. had apparently had enough of this grisly journey—she was gone.

When the people below saw that their plans had succeeded, and that their quarry was in the trap they had set, they set up a loud cheer of exultation, but it didn't seem to me to ring true; there was a doubtful note in it, and I thought likely those folks were not as glad they had caught their bird as they

were letting on to be; and they kept crossing themselves industriously; I took that for a sign, too.

Forty-Four moved steadily down. When he was on the last
step there was turmoil down the hall, and a volley of shout-
ings, with cries of "make way—Father Adolf is come!" then
he burst panting through one of the ranks and threw himself
in the way, just as Katrina was plunging for the disguised 44,
and stormed out—

"Stop her, everybody! Donkeys, would you let her butcher
him, and cheat the Church's fires!"

They jumped for Katrina, and in a moment she was struggling in the jumble of swaying forms, with nothing visible
above it but her head and her long arm with the knife in it;
and her strong voice was pouring out her feelings with energy, and easily making itself heard above the general din and
the priest's commands:

"Let me at him—he burnt my child, my darling!" . . . .
"Keep her off, men, keep her off!" . . . . "He is *not* the
Church's, his blood is *mine* by rights—out of my way! I *will*
have it!" . . . . *"Back! woman, back, I tell you—force her back,
men, have you no strength? are you nothing but boys?"* . . . . "A
hundred of you shan't stay me, woman though I be!"

And sure enough, with one massy surge she wrenched herself free, and flourished her knife, and bent her head and body
forward like a foot-racer and came charging down the living
lane through the gathering darkness—

Then suddenly there was a great light! she lifted her head
and caught it full in her swarthy face, which it transfigured
with its white glory, as it did also all that place, and its marble pillars, and the frightened people, and Katrina dropped
her knife and fell to her knees, with her hands clasped, everybody doing the same; and so there they were, all kneeling,
like that, with hands thrust forward or clasped, and they and
the stately columns all awash in that unearthly splendor; and
there where the magician had stood, stood 44 now, in his su-
pernal beauty and his gracious youth; and it was from him
that that flooding light came, for all his form was clothed in
that immortal fire, and flashing like the sun; and Katrina crept
on her knees to him, and bent down her old head and kissed
his feet, and he bent down and patted her softly on the shoul-

der and touched his lips to the gray hair—*and was gone!*—and for two or three minutes you were so blinded you couldn't see your next neighbor in that submerging black darkness. Then after that it was better, and you could make out the murky forms, some still kneeling, some lying prone in a swoon, some staggering about, here and there, with their hands pressed over their eyes, as if that light had hurt them and they were in pain. Katrina was wandering off, on unsteady feet, and her knife was lying there in the midst.

It was good he thought of the eclipse, it helped out ever so much; the effects would have been fine and great in any case, but the eclipse made them grand and stunning—just letter-perfect, as it seemed to me; and he said himself it beat Barnum and Bailey hands down, and was by as much as several shades too good for the provinces—which was all Sanscrit to me, and hadn't any meaning even in Sanscrit I reckon, but was invented for the occasion, because it had a learned sound, and he liked sound better than sense as a rule. There's been others like that, but he was the worst.

I judged it would take those people several hours to get over that, and accumulate their wits again and get their bearings, for it had knocked the whole bunch dizzy; meantime there wouldn't be anything doing. I must put in the time some way until they should be in a condition to resume business at the old stand. I went to my room and put on my flesh and stretched myself out on a lounge before the fire with a book, first setting the door ajar, so that the cat could fetch news if she got hold of any, which I wished she might; but in a little while I was asleep. I did not stir again until ten at night. I woke then, and found the cat finishing her supper, and my own ready on the table and hot; and very welcome, for I hadn't eaten anything since breakfast. Mary came and occupied a chair at my board, and washed herself and delivered her news while I ate. She had witnessed the great transformation scene, and had been so astonished by it and so interested in it that she did not wait to see the end, but went up a chimney and stayed there half an hour freezing, until somebody started a fire under her, and then she was thankful and very comfortable. But it got too comfortable, and she climbed out and came down a skylight stairway and went visiting around, and a little while ago she caught a rat, and did it as easy as nothing, and would teach me how, sometime, if I cared for such things; but she didn't eat it, it wasn't a fresh rat, or was out of season or something, but it reminded her that she was hungry, so she came home. Then she said—

"If you like to be astonished, I can astonish you. The magician isn't dead!"

I threw my hands up and did the astonishment-act like an old expert, crying out—

"Mary Florence Fortescue, what *can* you mean!"

She was delighted, and exclaimed—

"There, it's just as I said! I *told* him you wouldn't ever believe it; but I can lay my paw on my heart, just so, and I wish I may never stir if I haven't *seen* him!—*seen* him, you hear?— and he's just as alive as ever he was since the day he was born!"

"Oh, go 'long, you're deceiving me!"

She was almost beside herself with joy over the success of her astonisher, and said—

"Oh, it's lovely, it's too lovely, and just as I *said* it would be—I *told* him you wouldn't, and it's come out just so!"

In her triumph and delight she tried to clap her hands, but it was a failure, they wouldn't clap any more than mushrooms. Then she said—

"Duplicate, would you believe he is alive if I should prove it?"

"Sho," I said, "come off!—what are you giving me?—as he used to say. You're talking nonsense, Mary. When a person is dead, *known* to be dead, permanently dead, demonstrably dead, you *can't* prove him alive, there isn't any *way*. Come, don't you know that?"

Well, she was just beaming, by now, and she could hardly hold her system together, she was that near to bursting with the victory she was going to spring on me. She skipped to the floor and flirted something to my foot with her paw; I picked it up, and she jumped into her chair again and said—

"There, now, he said you would know what that is; what is it?"

"It's a thing he calls a paper—Boston paper."

"That's right, that's what he said. And he said it is future

English and you know present English and can read it. Did he say right?"

"The *fact* is right, but he didn't say it, because he's dead."

"You wait—that's all. He said look at the date."

"Very well. He didn't say it, because he's dead, and of course wouldn't think of it; but here it is, all the same—June 28, 1905."

"That's right, it's what he said. Then he said ask you what was the Founder's message to her disciples, that was in the other Boston paper. What was it?"

"Well, he told me there was an immense war going on, and she got tired having her people pray for peace and never take a trick for seventeen months, so she ordered them to quit, and put their battery out of commission. And he said nobody could understand the rest of the message, and like enough that very ignorance would bring on an immense disaster."

"Aha! well, it *did*! He says the very minute she was stopping the praying, the two fleets were meeting, and the uncivilized one utterly annihilated the civilized one, and it wouldn't have happened if she had let the praying go on. Now then, you didn't know *that*, did you!"

"No, and I don't know it yet."

"Well, you soon will. The message was June 27, wasn't it?"

"Yes."

"Well, the disaster was *that very day*—right after the praying was stopped—and you'll find the news of it in the very next day's paper, which you've got in your hand—date, *June 28*."

I took a glance at the big headings, and said—

"M-y word! why it's absolutely *so*! Baker G., don't you know this is the most astounding thing that ever happened? It proves he *is* alive—nobody else could bring this paper. He certainly is alive, and back with us, after that tremendous abolishment and extinction which we witnessed; yes, he's alive, Mary, alive, and glad am I, oh, grateful beyond words!"

"Oh!" she cried, in a rapture, "it's just splendid, oh, just too lovely! I knew I could prove it; I knew it just as well! I thought he was gone, when he blazed up and went out, that way, and I *was* so scared and grieved—and isn't he a wonder! Duplicate, there isn't another necromancer in the business that can begin with him, now *is* there?"

"You can stake your tale and your ears on it, Mary, and don't you forget it—as he used to say. In my opinion he can give the whole trade ninety-nine in the hundred and go out every time, cross-eyed and left-handed."

"But he isn't, Duplicate."

"Isn't what?"

"Cross-eyed and left-handed."

"Who said he was, you little fool?"

"Why, you did."

"I never said anything of the kind; I said he could if he *was*. That isn't *saying* he was; it was a supposititious case, and literary; it was a figure, a metaphor, and its function was to augment the force of the—"

"Well, he *isn't*, anyway; because I've noticed, and—"

"Oh, shut up! don't I tell you it was only a *figure*, and I never meant—"

"I don't care, you'll never make *me* believe he's cross-eyed and left-handed, because the time he—"

"Baker G., if you open your mouth again I'll jam the boot-jack down it! you're as random and irrelevant and incoherent and mentally impenetrable as the afflicted Founder herself."

But she was under the bed by that time; and reflecting, probably, if she had the machinery for it.

Chapter 32

FORTY-FOUR, still playing Balthasar Hoffman the magician, entered briskly now, and threw himself in a chair. The cat emerged with confidence, spread herself, purring, in his lap, and said—

"This Duplicate wouldn't believe me when I told him, and when I proved it he tried to cram a boot-jack down my throat, thinking to scare me, which he didn't, *didn't* you, Duplicate?"

"Didn't I *what*?"

"Why, what I just *said*."

"*I* don't know what you just said; it was Christian Silence and untranslatable; but I'll say yes to the whole of it if that will quiet you. Now then, keep still, and let the master tell what is on his mind."

"Well, this is on my mind, August. Some of the most distinguished people can't come. Flora McFlimsey—nothing to wear; Eve, ditto; Adam, previous engagement, and so on and so on; Nero and ever so many others find the notice too short, and are urgent to have more time. Very well, we've got to accommodate them."

"But how can we do it? The show is due to begin in an hour. Listen!"

Boom-m-m—boom-m-m—boom-m-m!—

It was the great bell of the castle tolling the hour. Our American clock on the wall struck in, and simultaneously the clock of the village—faint and far, and half of the notes overtaken in their flight and strangled by the gusty wind. We sat silent and counted, to the end.

"You see?" said I.

"Yes, I see. Eleven. Now there are two ways to manage. One is, to have time stand still—which has been done before, a lot of times; and the other one is, to turn time backward for a day or two, which is comparatively new, and offers the best effects, besides.

> " 'Backward, turn backward, O Time, in thy flight—
> Make me a child again, just for to-night!'—

"—'Beautiful Snow,' you see; it hasn't been written yet. *I* vote to reverse—and that is what we will do, presently. We will make the hands of the clocks travel around in the other direction."

"But will they?"

"Sure. It will attract attention—make yourself easy, as to that. But the stunning effect is going to be the sun."

"How?"

"Well, when they see him come rising up out of the west, about half a dozen hours from now, it will secure the interest of the entire world."

"I should think as much."

"Oh, yes, depend upon it. There is going to be more early rising than the human race has seen before. In my opinion it'll be a record."

"I believe you are right about it. I mean to get up and see it myself. Or stay up."

"I think it will be a good idea to have it rise in the south-west, instead of the west. More striking, you see; and hasn't been done before."

"Master, it will be wonderful! It will be the very greatest marvel the world has ever seen. It will be talked about and written about as long as the human race endures. And there'll not be any disputing over it, because every human being that's alive will get up to look at it, and there won't be one single person to say it's a lie."

"It's so. It will be the only perfectly authenticated event in all human history. All the other happenings, big and little, have got to depend on minority-testimony, and very little of that—but not so, this time, dontcherknow. And this one's patented. There aren't going to be any encores."

"How long shall we go backwards, Balthasar?"

"Two or three days or a week; long enough to accommodate Robert Bruce, and Henry I and such, who have hearts and things scattered around here and there and yonder, and have to get a basket and go around and collect; so we will let the sun and the clocks go backwards a while, then start them ahead in time to fetch up all right at midnight to-night—then the shades will begin to arrive according to schedule."

"It grows on me! It's going to be the most prodigious thing that ever happened, and—"

"Yes," he burst out, in a rapture of eloquence, "and will round out and perfect the reputation I've been building for Balthasar Hoffman, and make him the most glorious magician that ever lived, and get him burnt, to a dead moral certainty. You know I've taken a lot of pains with that reputation; I've taken more interest in it than anything I've planned out in centuries; I've spared neither labor nor thought, and I feel a pride in it and a sense of satisfaction such as I have hardly ever felt in a mere labor of love before; and when I get it completed, now, in this magnificent way, and get him burnt, or pulverized, or something showy and picturesque, like that, I shan't mind the trouble I've had, in the least; not in the least, I give you my word."

Boom-m-m—boom-m-m—boom-m-m—

"There she goes! striking eleven again."

"Is it really?"

"Count—you'll see."

It woke the cat, and she stretched herself out about a yard and a half, and asked if time was starting back—which showed that she had heard the first part of the talk. And understood it of course, because it was in German. She was informed that time was about to start back; so she arranged herself for another nap, and said that when we got back to ten she would turn out and catch that rat again.

I was counting the clock-strokes—counting aloud—

"*Eight . . . . nine . . . . ten . . . . eleven*—"

Forty-Four shouted—

"Backward! turn backward! O Time in thy flight! Look at the clock-hands! Listen!"

Instantly I found myself counting the strokes again, aloud—

"Eleven . . . ten . . . . nine . . . eight . . . . seven . . . six . . . . five . . . . four . . . two . . . one!"

At once the cat woke and repeated her remark about recatching the rat—saying it backwards!

Then Forty-Four said—

"see you'll—Count."

Whereupon I said—

"really? it Is"

And he remarked—the booming of the great castle clock mixing with his words—

"again. eleven striking goes! she There word (here his voice began to become impressive, then to nobly rise, and swell, and grow in eloquent feeling and majestic expression), my you give I least, the in not least; the in had, I've trouble the mind shan't I that, like picturesque, and showy something or pulverized, or burnt, him get and way, magnificent this in now, completed, it get I when and before; love of labor mere a in felt ever hardly have I as such satisfaction of sense a and it in pride (here his voice was near to breaking, so deeply were his feelings stirred) a feel I and thought, nor labor neither spared I've centuries; in out planned I've anything than it in interest more taken I've reputation; that with pains of lot a taken I've know You (here his winged eloquence reached its loftiest flight, and in his deep organ-tones he thundered forth his sublime words) certainty. moral dead a to burnt, him get and lived, ever that magician glorious most the him make and Hoffman, Balthasar for building been I've reputation the perfect and out round will and Yes,"—

My brain was spinning, it was audibly whizzing, I rose reeling, and was falling lifeless to the floor, when 44 caught me. His touch restored me, and he said—

"I see it is too much for you, you cannot endure it, you would go mad. Therefore I relieve you of your share in this grand event. You shall look on and enjoy, taking no personal part in the backward flight of time, nor in its return, until it reaches the present hour again and resumes its normal march forward. Go and come as you please, amuse yourself as you choose."

Those were blessed words! I could not tell him how thankful I was.

A considerable blank followed—a silent one, for it represented the unrepeated conversation which he and I had had about the turning back of time and the sun.

Then another silent blank followed; it represented the interval occupied by my dispute with the cat as to whether the magician was come alive again or not.

I filled in these intervals not wearily nor drearily—oh, no indeed, just the reverse; for my gaze was glued to that American clock—watching its hands creeping backward around its face, an uncanny spectacle!

Then I fell asleep, and when I woke again the clock had gone back seven hours, and it was mid-afternoon. Being privileged to go and come as I pleased, I threw off my flesh and went down to see the grand transformation-spectacle repeated backwards.

It was as impressive and as magnificent as ever. In the darkness some of the people lay prone, some were kneeling, some were wandering and tottering about with their hands over their eyes, Katrina was walking backwards on unsteady feet; she backed further and further, then knelt and bowed her head—then that white glory burst upon the darkness and 44 stood clothed as with the sun; and he bent and kissed the old head—and so on and so on, the scene repeated itself backwards, detail by detail, clear to the beginning; then the magician, the cat and I walked backward up the stairs and through the gathering eclipse to my room.

After that, as time drifted rearward, I skipped some things and took in others, according to my humor. I watched my Duplicate turn from nothing into a lovely soap-bubble statue with delicate rainbow-hues playing over it; watched its skeleton gather form and solidity; watched it put on flesh and clothes, and all that; but I skipped the interviews with the cat; I also skipped the interview with the master; and when the clock had gone back twenty-three hours and I was due to appear drunk in Marget's chamber, I took the pledge and stayed away.

Then, for amusement and to note effects, 44 and I—invisible—appeared in China, where it was noonday. The sun was just ready to turn downward on his new north-eastern track, and millions of yellow people were gazing at him, dazed and stupid, while other millions lay stretched upon the ground everywhere, exhausted with the terrors and confusions they had been through, and now blessedly unconscious. We loafed along behind the sun around the globe, tarrying in all the great cities on the route, and observing and admiring the effects. Everywhere weary people were re-chattering previous conversations backwards and not understanding each other, and oh, they did look so tuckered out and tired of it all! and always there were groups gazing miserably at the town-clocks; in every city funerals were being held again that had already been held once, and the hearses and the processions were marching solemnly backwards; where there was war, yesterday's battles were being refought, wrong-end-first; the previously killed were getting killed again, the previously wounded were getting hit again in the same place and complaining about it; there were blood-stirring and tremendous charges of masses of steel-clad knights across the field—backwards; and on the oceans the ships, with full-bellied sails were speeding backwards over the same water they had traversed the day before, and some of each crew were scared and praying, some were gazing in mute anguish at the crazy sun, and the rest were doing profanity beyond imagination.

At Rouen we saw Henry I gathering together his split skull and his other things.

Chapter 33

SURELY Forty-Four was the flightiest creature that ever was! Nothing interested him long at a time. He would contrive the most elaborate projects, and put his whole mind and heart into them, then he would suddenly drop them, in the midst of their fulfilment, and start something fresh. It was just so with his Assembly of the Dead. He summoned those forlorn wrecks from all the world and from all the epochs and ages, and then, when everything was ready for the exhibition, he wanted to flit back to Moses's time and see the Egyptians floundering around in the Dead Sea, and take me along with him. He said he had seen it twice, and it was one of the handsomest and most exciting incidents a body ever saw. It was all I could do to persuade him to wait a while.

To me the Procession was very good indeed, and most impressive. First, there was an awful darkness. All visible things gloomed down gradually, losing their outlines little by little, then disappeared utterly. The thickest and solidest and blackest darkness followed, and a silence which was so still it was as if the world was holding its breath. That deep stillness continued, and continued, minute after minute, and got to be so oppressive that presently I was holding *my* breath—that is, only half-breathing. Then a wave of cold air came drifting along, damp, searching, and smelling of the grave, and was shivery and dreadful. After about ten minutes I heard a faint clicking sound coming as from a great distance. It came slowly nearer and nearer, and a little louder and a little louder, and increasing steadily in mass and volume, till all the place was filled with a dry sharp clacking and was right abreast of us and passing by! Then a vague twilight suffused the place and through it and drowned in it we made out the spidery dim forms of thousands of skeletons marching! It made me catch my breath. It was that grewsome and grisly and horrible, you can't think.

Soon the light paled to a half dawn, and we could distinguish details fairly well. Forty-Four had enlarged the great hall of the castle, so as to get effects. It was a vast and lofty corridor, now, and stretched away for miles and miles, and the Procession drifted solemnly down it sorrowfully clacking, losing definiteness gradually, and finally fading out in the far distances, and melting from sight.

Forty-Four named no end of those poor skeletons, as they passed by, and he said the most of them had been distinguished, in their day and had cut a figure in the world. Some of the names were familiar to me, but the most of them were not. Which was natural, for they belonged to nations that perished from the earth ten, and twenty, and fifty, and a hundred, and three hundred, and six hundred thousand years ago, and so of course I had never heard of them.

By force of 44's magic each skeleton had a tab on him giving his name and date, and telling all about him, in brief. It was a good idea, and saved asking questions. Pharaoh was there, and David and Goliath and several other of the sacred characters; and Adam and Eve, and some of the Caesars, and Cleopatra, and Charlemagne, and Dagobert, and kings, and kings and kings till you couldn't count them—the most of them from away back thousands and thousands of centuries before Adam's time. Some of them fetched their crowns along, and had a rotten velvet rag or two dangling about their bones, a kind of pathetic spectacle.

And there were skeletons whom I had known, myself, and been at their funerals, only three or four years before—men and women, boys and girls; and they put out their poor bony hands and shook with me, and looked so sad. Some of the skeletons dragged the rotting ruins of their coffins after them by a string, and seemed pitifully anxious that that poor property shouldn't come to harm.

But to think how long the pathos of a thing can last, and still carry its touching effect, the same as if it was new and happened yesterday! There was a slim skeleton of a young woman, and it went by with its head bowed and its bony hands to its eyes, crying, apparently. Well, it was a young mother whose little child disappeared one day and was never heard of again, and so her heart was broken, and she cried her life away. It brought the tears to my eyes and made my heart ache to see that poor thing's sorrow. When I looked at her tab I saw it had happened five hundred thousand years ago! It seemed strange that it should still affect me, but I suppose such things never grow old, but remain always new.

King Arthur came along, by and by, with all his knights. That interested me, because we had just been printing his history, copying it from Caxton. They rode upon bony crates that had once been horses, and they looked very stately in their ancient armor, though it was rusty and lacked a piece here and there, and through those gaps you could see the bones inside. They talked together, skeletons as they were, and you could see their jawbones go up and down through the slits in their helmets. By grace of Forty-Four's magic I could understand them. They talked about Arthur's last battle, and seemed to think it happened yesterday, which shows that a thousand years in the grave is merely a night's sleep, to the dead, and counts for nothing.

It was the same with Noah and his sons and their wives. Evidently they had forgotten that they had ever left the Ark, and could not understand how they came to be wandering around on land. They talked about the weather; they did not seem to be interested in anything else.

The skeletons of Adam's predecessors outnumbered the later representatives of our race by myriads, and they rode upon undreamt-of monsters of the most extraordinary bulk and aspect. They marched ten thousand abreast, our walls receding and melting away and disappearing, to give them room, and the earth was packed with them as far as the eye could reach. Among them was the Missing Link. That is what 44 called him. He was an undersized skeleton, and he was perched on the back of a long-tailed and long-necked creature ninety feet long and thirty-three feet high; a creature that had been dead eight million years, 44 said.

For hours and hours the dead passed by in continental masses, and the bone-clacking was so deafening you could hardly hear yourself think. Then, all of a sudden 44 waved his hand and we stood in an empty and soundless world.

Chapter 34

A ND you are going away, and will not come back any
more."

"Yes," he said. "We have comraded long together, and it
has been pleasant—pleasant for both; but I must go now, and
we shall not see each other any more."

"In this life, 44, but in another? We shall meet in another,
surely, 44?"

Then all tranquilly and soberly he made the strange answer—
"There is no other."

A subtle influence blew upon my spirit from his, bringing
with it a vague, dim, but blessed and hopeful feeling that the
incredible words might be true—even *must* be true.

"Have you never suspected this, August?"

"No—how could I? But if it can only be true—"

"It is true."

A gush of thankfulness rose in my breast, but a doubt
checked it before it could issue in words, and I said—

"But—but—we have *seen* that future life—seen it in its actuality, and so—"

"It was a vision—it had no existence."

I could hardly breathe for the great hope that was struggling in me—

"A vision?—a vi—"

"Life itself is only a vision, a dream."

It was electrical. By God I had had that very thought a
thousand times in my musings!

"*Nothing* exists; all is a dream. God—man—the world,—
the sun, the moon, the wilderness of stars: a dream, all a
dream, they have no existence. *Nothing exists save empty
space—and you!*"

"I!"

"And you are not you—you have no body, no blood, no
bones, you are but a *thought*. I myself have no existence, I am
but a dream—your dream, creature of your imagination. In a
moment you will have realized this, then you will banish me
from your visions and I shall dissolve into the nothingness out
of which you made me . . . . ."

"I am perishing already—I am failing, I am passing away. In a little while you will be alone in shoreless space, to wander its limitless solitudes without friend or comrade forever—for you will remain a *Thought*, the only existent Thought, and by your nature inextinguishable, indestructible. But I your poor servant have revealed you to yourself and set you free. Dream other dreams, and better! . . . .

"Strange! that you should not have suspected, years ago, centuries, ages, aeons ago! for you have existed, companionless, through all the eternities. Strange, indeed, that you should not have suspected that your universe and its contents were only dreams, visions, fictions! Strange, because they are so frankly and hysterically insane—like all dreams: a God who could make good children as easily as bad, yet preferred to make bad ones; who could have made every one of them happy, yet never made a single happy one; who made them prize their bitter life, yet stingily cut it short; who gave his angels eternal happiness unearned, yet required his other children to earn it; who gave his angels painless lives, yet cursed his other children with biting miseries and maladies of mind and body; who mouths justice, and invented hell—mouths mercy, and invented hell—mouths Golden Rules, and foregiveness multiplied by seventy times seven, and invented hell; who mouths morals to other people, and has none himself; who frowns upon crimes, yet commits them all; who created man without invitation, then tries to shuffle the responsibility for man's acts upon man, instead of honorably placing it where it belongs, upon himself; and finally, with altogether divine obtuseness, invites this poor abused slave to worship him! . . . .

"You perceive, *now*, that these things are all impossible, except in a dream. You perceive that they are pure and puerile insanities, the silly creations of an imagination that is not conscious of its freaks—in a word, that they are a dream, and you the maker of it. The dream-marks are all present—you should have recognized them earlier . . . . .

"It is true, that which I have revealed to you: there is no God, no universe, no human race, no earthly life, no heaven, no hell. It is all a Dream, a grotesque and foolish dream. Nothing exists but You. And You are but a *Thought*—a vagrant Thought, a useless Thought, a homeless Thought, wandering forlorn among the empty eternities!"

He vanished, and left me appalled; for I knew, and realized, that all he had said was true.

THE END

CHRONOLOGY

NOTE ON THE TEXTS

NOTES

Chronology

1835   Samuel Langhorne Clemens born on November 30 in
        Florida, Missouri, fifth surviving child of John Marshall
        Clemens (b. 1798) and Jane Lampton Clemens (b. 1803).
        Siblings are brother Orion (b. 1825), sisters Pamela (b.
        1827) and Margaret (b. 1830), and brother Benjamin (b.
        1832). At time of birth Halley's Comet is still visible in
        the sky (Clemens will often mention this later in life).
        Father runs store with John Adams Quarles, husband
        of Jane Lampton Clemens' sister, Martha Ann "Patsy"
        Quarles. (Grandparents Samuel and Pamelia Clemens
        were slave-owning farmers in Campbell County, Virginia,
        before moving family to Mason County, Virginia—now
        West Virginia—in 1803 or 1804. Grandmother, widowed
        in 1805, moved with her five children to Adair County,
        Kentucky. Father and siblings settled their father's estate
        in 1821; John Clemens' share included three slaves. He
        then studied law in Columbia, Kentucky, received his li-
        cense to practice in 1822, and in 1823 married Jane Lamp-
        ton; the daughter of Benjamin and Margaret Casey
        Lampton, she was born in Columbia and was descended
        from early English and Irish settlers of Kentucky. They
        moved to Gainesborough, Tennessee, then Jamestown,
        Tennessee, where John Clemens built a large house,
        practiced law, opened a store, and bought 75,000 acres of
        uncleared land before moving to nearby Three Forks of
        Wolf River. In 1835 the family moved to Florida, Mis-
        souri, on the Salt River, where John and Martha Ann
        Quarles were already established and where grandfather
        Benjamin Lampton and other members of mother's fam-
        ily also lived. After their arrival in June father acquired
        120 acres of government land and a small homesite.)

1836   Clemens is frequently sick and mother is unsure if he
        will live. Family buys house in town from grandfather
        Lampton.

1837   Grandfather dies. Father dissolves partnership with
        Quarles and sets up his own store; heads committees to
        improve Salt River navigation, develop railroads, and start
        an academy. Father becomes Monroe County judge.

1838   Family moves into new house built by father. Brother
            Henry born July 13.

1839   Sister Margaret dies August 17. Father earns $5,000 from
            land sales and then purchases $7,000 worth of property in
            Hannibal, Missouri, a rapidly growing village of a thou-
            sand inhabitants on the Mississippi, 30 miles from Florida
            and about 130 miles north of St. Louis. Family moves to
            Hannibal in November; other Florida residents move as
            well. Father opens store and family lives in the Virginia
            House, former hotel that is part of purchased property.

1840   Clemens enters school taught by Elizabeth Horr and
            Mary Ann Newcomb (will attend three other schools in
            Hannibal).

1841   Mother and sister Pamela join Presbyterian church in
            February. Father sells house in Florida to uncle John
            Quarles in August and transfers title to Virginia House to
            creditor in October.

1842   Brother Benjamin dies May 12. Orion moves to St. Louis
            to work as printer. Clemens continues to be sickly. Family
            sells slave Jenny.

1843   Clemens enjoys visits to the Quarles' family farm in
            Florida (will spend two or three months a year with them
            for several years). Takes with him his trained cat (will have
            lifelong love of cats). Attends country summer school
            with cousins and enjoys playing with the slaves on the
            farm. Becomes especially appreciative of the friendship
            and counsel of Daniel, a slave in his late thirties (emanci-
            pated by Quarles in 1855). Father auctions off much of his
            Hannibal property to pay debts. James C. Clemens, a dis-
            tant cousin, buys one lot on Hill Street and leases it to
            father to build house.

1844   During epidemic in spring, Clemens deliberately catches
            measles from Will Bowen, his best friend, and nearly dies
            as a result. Father helps found Hannibal Library Institute
            (will later head civic committees promoting railroad con-
            struction and higher education) and is elected justice of
            the peace. Clemens is horrified when he finds a corpse in
            his father's office.

1845   Group of friends includes Will Bowen and his brother Sam, John Briggs, Ed Stevens, John Garth, Laura Hawkins, and Tom Blankenship. Health improves, and enjoys swimming, fishing, and playing Robin Hood, pirates, and Crusaders. Attends school taught by Samuel Cross.

1846   Mother takes in paying guests for meals. Family sells furniture to help pay debts and moves in with pharmacist Orville Grant; mother supplies him with meals in exchange for rent. In November father announces candidacy for clerk of the circuit court. Clemens and friends enjoy watching local volunteer infantry drill for service in Mexican War.

1847   Father dies of pneumonia on March 24. Clemens watches postmortem examination through keyhole. Family moves back to house on Hill Street. Orion, working as printer in St. Louis, provides main family support, while Pamela gives music lessons, mother continues to take in paying guests for meals, and Clemens works at odd jobs, including clerking in a grocery store, a pharmacy, and a bookstore. Begins attending John D. Dawson's school. Witnesses drowning of friend Clint Levering while swimming in the Mississippi in August. While fishing a few days later, Clemens and several friends discover the body of a drowned fugitive slave, whom Bence Blankenship (Tom's older brother) had been secretly supplying with food. Gets job in fall delivering papers for printer Henry La Cossitt at the Hannibal *Gazette*.

1848   Still attending Dawson's school, begins working in late spring in the office of Joseph P. Ament's *Missouri Courier* as errand boy and printer's devil. Lives meagerly in Ament's house as an apprentice. Goes skating late in the year on the Mississippi with friend Tom Nash; when the ice breaks, Clemens manages to get to shore safely, but Nash falls through, eventually leaving him deaf.

1849   Gold rush emigrants pass through Hannibal en route to California, and many Hannibal residents join them, including John Dawson and Samuel Cross. Enjoys company of fellow apprentices Wales McCormick and T. P. "Pet" McMurry. Reads Cooper, Marryat, Dickens, Byron,

Scott, and anything else he can find that features knights, pirates, or Crusaders.

1850   Joins Cadets of Temperance, briefly gives up smoking and chewing tobacco, and marches in parades with friends. In May witnesses a poor widow shoot and kill the leader of a group of strangers forcing their way into her house. Orion returns from St. Louis and begins publishing weekly newspaper, the *Western Union.*

1851   Clemens leaves the *Missouri Courier* and, with Henry, goes to work for Orion as typesetter and editorial assistant; although Orion promises Clemens wages, no money is ever available. Likes apprentice Jim Wolf, who boards with Clemens family. Publishes first known sketch, "A Gallant Fireman," in the *Western Union* January 16. Orion buys Hannibal *Journal* in September. Sister Pamela marries William A. Moffett on September 20 and moves to St. Louis.

1852   Fire destroys *Journal* office, and Orion rents new space. Clemens writes humorous sketches for the Hannibal *Journal.* "The Dandy Frightening the Squatter" appears in the Boston *Carpet-Bag* and "Hannibal, Missouri" in the Philadelphia *American Courier* in May. During Orion's absence on business trips, Clemens becomes responsible for getting paper out. On September 9 signs sketch "W. Epaminondas Adrastus Perkins," his first known pseudonym.

1853   In January Clemens and Will Bowen give matches to a drunk in the town jail, who later that night sets fire to his cell and burns to death. (Clemens will often recall this incident.) Leaves Hannibal in June and works as a typesetter in St. Louis. Goes to New York City in late August. Visits Crystal Palace, center of New York exposition. Works for low pay in John A. Gray's large print shop. Takes pride in his typesetting skill, attends theater, and spends evenings reading in the printers' free library. Has two letters from New York printed in Hannibal *Journal* before Orion sells paper in September and moves with mother and brother Henry to Muscatine, Iowa, where Orion becomes co-editor of the Muscatine *Journal.* Clemens moves to Philadelphia in October. Works as typesetter, writes letters for the Muscatine *Journal*, and enjoys visiting sites connected with Benjamin Franklin and the Revolution.

1854   Briefly visits Washington, D.C., in February and records his impressions in letter for the Muscatine *Journal*. Returns to Philadelphia for a few weeks, then goes to New York where he finds high unemployment among printers due to fires that destroyed Harpers publishing house. Goes to Muscatine in spring and works for the *Journal*. Moves to St. Louis in summer and resumes work at the *Evening News*, boarding and lodging with the Paveys from Hannibal. Mother moves in with Pamela and William Moffett in St. Louis. Orion marries Mary Eleanor (Mollie) Stotts of Keokuk, Iowa, on December 19.

1855   Writes four letters for the Muscatine *Journal* before Orion sells paper in June and moves to Keokuk where he sets up a printing shop. Clemens joins him in mid-June, working for pay and board before becoming a partner in the business. Travels to Hannibal in July to arrange for sale of Hill Street house, then goes on to Florida, Missouri, to settle mother's inheritance from grandfather Benjamin Lampton. Visits with uncle John Quarles.

1856   Sees mother and Pamela in St. Louis in October, and writes his first "Thomas Jefferson Snodgrass" letter for the Keokuk *Post*. Moves to Cincinnati where he works as a typesetter and writes two more Snodgrass letters for the *Post*.

1857   Leaves Cincinnati in April by steamboat for New Orleans, intending to seek his fortune in South America, but instead becomes apprentice riverboat pilot under Horace Bixby. Works on several boats and learns Mississippi River between New Orleans and St. Louis. Orion sells print shop and goes to Jamestown, Tennessee, where family owns land, to study law and try to sell the property (is unsuccessful and returns to Keokuk in 1858 to practice law).

1858   Clemens serves on the *Pennsylvania* under pilot William Brown, whom he considers a tyrant. Arranges job as purser's assistant for brother Henry on the boat. Falls in love with Laura Wright, the daughter of a Missouri judge (her family does not approve and intercepts letters). Hits Brown after the pilot strikes Henry, then leaves the *Pennsylvania*. Henry remains and is badly injured in a boiler explosion below Memphis on June 13. Clemens is with Henry when he dies on June 21. Feels crazed with grief and guilt. Clemens resumes apprenticeship and steers for two pilot friends from Hannibal, Bart and Sam Bowen.

1859–60   Receives his pilot's license in April 1859. Becomes steadily employed and well paid for his work. Continues his self-education. In May 1859 publishes lampoon of senior pilot Isaiah Sellers (from whom Clemens later claimed he appropriated the pen name "Mark Twain") and writes several other sketches.

1861   Clemens becomes member of a St. Louis Masonic lodge (maintains contact until formally resigning in October 1869). Takes mother on private steamboat excursion from St. Louis to New Orleans and back. Is much impressed by Frederick Church's painting *Heart of the Andes*, on exhibit in St. Louis. Through the influence of Edward Bates, attorney general in the Lincoln administration, Orion is appointed secretary of new Nevada Territory in March. By May outbreak of the Civil War has severely disrupted river traffic. Fearful of being impressed as gunboat pilot by Union forces, Clemens goes to Hannibal in June and helps form the Marion Rangers, group of Confederate volunteers composed of old Hannibal schoolmates. After two weeks of camping and retreating across countryside, half the group decides to disband. Clemens leaves with Orion for Nevada on July 18. Travels up the Missouri to St. Joseph, then goes by stagecoach through Fort Kearny, Scotts Bluff, South Pass, Fort Bridger, and Salt Lake City, arriving in Carson City, Nevada, on August 14. Travels to Aurora, Nevada, in the Esmeralda mining district in September, where he shares claims with Horatio G. Phillips. Takes trips with John D. Kinney to establish timber claims near Lake Bigler (later Tahoe), and accidentally starts forest fire. Speculates in silver- and gold-mining stocks and serves as Orion's secretary during fall session of the territorial legislature. Meets Clement T. Rice, who will become journalistic collaborator. Goes on prospecting trip to Humboldt County with Keokuk friend William H. Clagett in December.

1862 Returns to Carson City in January, then to Aurora in April. Continues prospecting with Phillips without much success and writes occasional letters for the Keokuk *Gate City* and Carson City *Silver Age*; begins sending letters to the Virginia City, Nevada, *Territorial Enterprise* in late April, using pen name "Josh." In July feels restless and wants to move on. Becomes partner in potentially lucrative mining claim and shares cabin with Calvin H. Higbie (will later dedicate *Roughing It* to him). "Josh" letters to the *Territorial Enterprise* attract attention of business manager William H. Barstow and editor Joseph T. Goodman; they offer Clemens a salaried job as reporter in July. Takes walking trip through the White Mountains along the Nevada-California border for pleasure. Moves to Virginia City to work as local reporter for the *Territorial Enterprise* in September; duties include covering fall legislative session in Carson City. Writes "The Petrified Man," a hoax made up to "worry" Judge G. T. Sewall of Humboldt County. Begins lasting friendships with editor Goodman and Dan De Quille (William Wright), fellow reporter and humorist. Becomes responsible for local reporting when De Quille leaves at end of year.

1863 Continues to trade in mining stocks, sometimes receiving free shares in return for favorable mention in *Enterprise*. Clemens goes to Carson City and sends letters to the *Enterprise*, published February 3, 5, and 8, signing them "Mark Twain," his first known use of the name. Continues mock feud in print with fellow reporter Clement Rice. Leaves Virginia City with Rice early in May to visit San Francisco, where he sees Neil Moss, former classmate from Hannibal, who has been prospecting without success, and Bill Briggs (brother of Hannibal friend John Briggs), who is running a successful gambling establishment. Enjoys San Francisco; makes money selling and trading stocks. Arranges to become Nevada correspondent for the San Francisco *Morning Call*. Returns to Virginia City in July and moves into new White House hotel; it burns down on July 26 and Clemens loses all his possessions, including his mine stocks. Sick with a severe cold and bronchitis, goes to Lake Bigler with journalist friend Adair Wilson, and then to Steamboat Springs to try its hot mineral water. When Dan De Quille returns to Virginia City and resumes duties as local editor for the

Enterprise, Clemens goes to San Francisco for a month. Writes "How to Cure a Cold," his first piece for *Golden Era*, a San Francisco literary weekly. Writes hoax about a man killing his family, "A Bloody Massacre Near Carson"; when it is uncovered other papers that had reported it as a true story are furious and refuse to reprint news stories from the *Enterprise*. Clemens offers to resign, but Goodman and De Quille assure him that the anger will diminish and the story will be remembered. Goes to Carson City to cover convention drafting first state constitution, then returns to Virginia City to meet humorist Artemus Ward (Charles Farrar Browne), who encourages him to write for the New York *Mercury*.

1864   Reports on rejection by the voters of proposed state constitution (clause proposing tax on undeveloped mines is unpopular). Publishes two articles in the New York *Mercury*, "Doings in Nevada" (February 7) and "Those Blasted Children" (February 21). Sees Reuel Gridley, friend from Hannibal, in May when he tours Nevada raising funds for the United States Sanitary Commission in St. Louis (commission aids sick and wounded Union soldiers). Joins Gridley in repeatedly auctioning off flour sack in Storey County (county eventually contributes $22,000). Writes two controversial pieces for the *Enterprise* in May; one repeats rumor that Carson City women were diverting funds intended for the Sanitary Commission to a freedman's society; the other alleges that the Virginia City *Union* has not fulfilled its bid in the flour-sack auction. When reply in the *Union* calls him "an unmitigated *liar, a poltroon and a puppy*," Clemens challenges its editor, James L. Laird, to a duel, while apologizing to Carson City women. Leaves with Stephen E. Gillis, news editor at the *Enterprise*, and Goodman for San Francisco at end of May. Becomes reporter for the San Francisco *Morning Call* and continues to contribute pieces to the *Golden Era*. Finds long hours at the *Call* tedious and makes arrangement to work only during daylight hours. Contracts to write four articles for newly established literary magazine, the *Californian*, which is owned by Charles Henry Webb and edited by Bret Harte. Resigns from the *Call* in October at the suggestion of one of the proprietors. Writes several articles for the *Enterprise* criticizing San Francisco police for corruption, incompetence, and mistreatment of Chinese immigrants. When Gillis is charged for his part in a barroom brawl, they decide in December to go to Jackass Hill in Tuolumne County, California, where Jim and William Gillis, Stephen's brothers, have pocket-mine claims. Remains in camp after Stephen Gillis returns to Virginia City.

1865   In January goes with Jim Gillis to Angel's Camp in Calaveras County and stays there four weeks, listening to stories told by prospectors, one of which is about a jumping frog. Goes to San Francisco in February. Writes articles for the *Californian*, and pieces for the *Golden Era* and the *Enterprise*. Befriends Charles Warren Stoddard, another contributor to the *Californian*. Articles reprinted in New York begin to bring recognition (the New York *Round Table* calls him "the foremost among the merry gentlemen of the California press"). After repeated requests from Artemus Ward for a sketch to include in a collection of humorous works, sends "Jim Smiley and His Jumping Frog" to him, but the text arrives too late for inclusion in the book and is published in Henry Clapp's *Saturday Press*. The story is widely reprinted all over the country.

1866   Stops writing for the *Californian* (both it and the *Golden Era* will reprint articles published in the *Enterprise*). Begins to think of writing a book about the Mississippi, and also reviews his articles, saving some and destroying others. Sails for the Sandwich Islands (Hawaii) as roving correspondent for the Sacramento *Union*. Arrives in Honolulu on March 18. Explores Oahu on horseback and meets King Kamehameha V. Goes to Maui and the island of Hawaii where he sees the volcano Kilauea erupting. Returns to Oahu June 16. Meets Anson Burlingame, American minister to China. Takes notes while Burlingame interviews survivors of the shipwrecked *Hornet* and writes report for the *Union* that scoops all other papers. Sails for San Francisco July 19. Sees Orion and his wife, Mollie, who are in the city before sailing for the East Coast. Writes articles for the *Union* and the New York *Weekly Review*, and covers California State Agricultural Society Fair in Sacramento. Delivers first lecture on October 2, speaking on the Sandwich Islands to a large, appreciative audience at Maguire's Academy of Music in San Francisco. Goes on tour, lecturing in Sacramento, Marysville, Grass Valley, Nevada City, Red Dog, and You Bet in California, and then in Virginia City, Carson City, Dayton, Silver City, Washoe City, and Gold City in Nevada. Returns to California and appears in San Francisco, San Jose, Petaluma, and Oakland, concluding tour with a special appearance in San Francisco on December 10 at the request of Frederick F. Low, governor of California, and Henry G. Blasdel, governor of Nevada. Becomes traveling correspondent for the San Francisco *Alta California* and leaves San Francisco December 15 aboard ship captained by Edgar Wakeman. Enjoys company of Wakeman and writes down some of his stories.

1867   Clemens arrives in New York January 12 and takes rooms at the Metropolitan Hotel (establishment frequented by westerners). Sees old California friends Frank Fuller (who will later manage a series of lectures for him) and Charles Henry Webb, who offers to help him put together a book of sketches (Webb will publish it himself after other publishers turn it down). Through Webb meets Edward House of the New York *Tribune*, Henry Clapp, and John Hay. Sends letters to the *Alta* and makes arrangements to contribute articles to the New York *Sunday Mercury*, the *Evening Express,* and the New York *Weekly.* Has no success finding a publisher for the Sandwich Islands letters. Reserves cabin on the *Quaker City* for the first American transatlantic excursion, then goes to St. Louis to visit family. Publishes three satirical articles on woman suffrage in the *Missouri Democrat.* Lectures successfully in St. Louis, Hannibal, Keokuk, and Quincy, Illinois, and sees old friends. *The Celebrated Jumping Frog of Calaveras County, and Other Sketches* published by Webb on April 30 (Clemens is unhappy with Webb's editing and sales are poor). Gives successful lectures in New York and Brooklyn in May. Accepts assignments to write for the New York *Tribune*, the New York *Herald* (unsigned articles), and the *Alta.* After two days anchored off Brooklyn because of bad weather, the *Quaker City* sails on June 10 for Europe and the Holy Land. Finds most of the passengers too pious and staid, but makes friends with Daniel Slote, his cabin mate, Moses Sperry Beach, editor of the New York *Sun*, Beach's daughter Emma, John A. Van Nostrand,

Julius Moulton, Dr. Abraham Reeves Jackson, Julia Newell, Solon Long Severance and his wife, Emily, Mary Mason Fairbanks ("Mother Fairbanks"), who becomes one of his closest friends and advisers, and Charles Jervis Langdon, from Elmira, New York, who shows Clemens a picture of his sister Olivia. Travels to North Africa, Spain, France, Italy, Greece, Russia, Turkey, the Holy Land, and Egypt. Returns to New York on November 19. Goes to Washington, D.C., where he serves for a few weeks as private secretary to William M. Stewart, senator from Nevada. Acts as Washington correspondent for the *Territorial Enterprise*, the *Alta California*, and the New York *Tribune*. Receives several offers from book publishers; prefers one from the American Publishing Company, a subscription firm in Hartford, Connecticut. Returns to New York and is invited by Charles Langdon to dine with his family at the St. Nicholas Hotel; meets Olivia Louise (Livy) Langdon (b. Nov. 27, 1845). Goes with the Langdons to hear Charles Dickens read.

1868   Spends New Year's Day visiting with Livy and her friend Alice Hooker. Attends services given by Henry Ward Beecher as guest of *Quaker City* friends Moses and Emma Beach. Has dinner at Beecher's home and meets his sister, Harriet Beecher Stowe. Returns to Washington and delivers lecture "The Frozen Truth," an account of the cruise, and gives a successful toast to "Woman" at the Washington Newspaper Correspondents' Club. Tries unsuccessfully to obtain Patent Office clerkship for Orion. Makes agreement in Hartford with Elisha Bliss to have his book on the excursion published by the American Publishing Company. Returns to Washington and works on book. Sails for California in March to arrange republication rights for his *Alta* letters from the excursion, which the newspaper had copyrighted. Lectures in San Francisco and Sacramento, then travels to Virginia City. Lectures there and in Carson City. Returns to San Francisco. Reaches agreement with the *Alta* regarding *Quaker City* material. Works intensively on book, revising, arranging, and cutting letters and adding new passages. In June asks Bret Harte to read the manuscript and make suggestions. In New York in August where he sees Anson Burlingame; writes, with his help, "The Treaty with China," article that is published on the front page of the New York *Tribune*.

Goes to Hartford and stays with the Blisses while he works
on the book. Visits the Langdon family in Elmira. (The
Langdons prospered in the lumber business and then became wealthy in the coal trade. When Livy was 16 years
old, a fall on the ice invalided her for two years, and for
the remainder of her life she is unable to walk very far.)
Clemens falls in love with Livy and proposes to her in
early September, but is refused. Leaves with Charles Langdon to visit Mary and Abel Fairbanks at their home in
Cleveland. Courts Livy with letters. Visits her again in late
September, and then goes to Hartford to work on book.
Meets the Reverend Joseph H. Twichell, a Congrega-
tional minister who will become one of his closest friends.
Returns to New York in October and gives lecture, "The
American Vandal Abroad." Proposes to Livy again and she
confesses that she loves him. Promises to reform himself,
to become religious, and to stop drinking. Jervis Langdon
makes inquiries about Clemens' past. Resumes lectures in
December, appearing in New Jersey, New York, Pennsylvania, Michigan, Indiana, and Illinois.

1869   Continues lecture tour through Ohio, Illinois, Michigan,
Iowa, Wisconsin, Pennsylvania, and New Jersey. Writes
long letters to Livy, and marks up books for her to read,
in particular Oliver Wendell Holmes' *The Autocrat of the
Breakfast Table* (they call it their "courting-book"); she
sends him marked copies of Henry Ward Beecher's sermons. Clemens learns that some Californians have responded unfavorably to Jervis Langdon's inquiries about
his character; he tells Langdon that he is no longer the
same person he was then. Engagement is formally announced February 4. Concerned about earning steady
income, investigates buying share in either the Cleveland
Herald, partly owned by Abel Fairbanks, or the Hartford
Courant, published in a city where he and Livy have
many friends. Hears Petroleum V. Nasby (David Ross
Locke) lecture in Hartford. Goes to Boston where Nasby
introduces him to Holmes. Returns to Elmira to read
proofs, with Livy's assistance (she will continue to help
edit his work). Leaves Elmira with Charles Langdon in
early May and goes to New York and Hartford where he
continues work on book. Engages James Redpath as his
lecture agent. Writes articles, including "Personal Habits
of the Siamese Twins." Finishes reading proofs and goes

with Langdon family to Hartford where they attend the June wedding of Alice Hooker and John Day. Meets Charles Dudley Warner, part-owner of the Hartford *Courant*; he will become a close friend. Unable to buy a share in the Hartford *Courant*, and feeling the price of investing in the Cleveland *Herald* is too high, on the advice of Jervis Langdon buys one-third interest in the Buffalo *Express* (Clemens puts in $2,500 and Langdon lends him $12,500; the remainder is to be paid in installments). Moves to Buffalo. Changes the typographical look of the *Express*, using smaller type for headlines and saving larger type for important news. Works closely with part-owner and editor-in-chief Josephus Nelson Larned. *The Innocents Abroad*, account of the *Quaker City* excursion, is published by American Publishing Company on August 15; it receives good reviews and sells well. Visits Elmira whenever possible. Prepares lecture "Our Fellow Savages of the Sandwich Islands" and begins fall tour in Pittsburgh on November 1. Continues lecturing in Massachusetts, Rhode Island, Maine, Connecticut, New York, and Washington, D.C. Meets other lyceum lecturers, including humorist Josh Billings (Henry Wheeler Shaw). Begins long, close friendship with William Dean Howells, who had enthusiastically reviewed *The Innocents Abroad*. Returns briefly to Hartford to pick up royalty check and learns that the Hartford *Courant* is now eager to have him, but is unable to accept because of his commitment to the *Express*. Meets Frederick Douglass in Boston and is impressed by him.

1870   No longer drinks, and cuts down on smoking. Sees Joseph Goodman when he comes to New York. Elated by sales of book. Continues lecturing in New York until January 21. Marries Livy in Elmira on February 2, with Thomas Beecher (half-brother of Henry Ward Beecher and uncle of Alice Hooker) and Twichell performing the service. Goes by private train to Buffalo with Livy and a small party of guests on February 3. Clemens expects to be moving into a boarding house and is surprised by generous gift from Jervis Langdon of furnished house at 472 Delaware Street, with three servants, stable, and carriage. House guests include sister Pamela and niece Annie Moffett, the Twichells, and Petroleum V. Nasby. Clemens goes to the *Express* offices only twice a week. Signs contract in March with *Galaxy* to supply a monthly humorous column, reserving all republication rights to himself (first column appears in May). Continues writing for the *Express*, but feels that *Galaxy* allows him more freedom. Livy begins to address him as "Youth" (will do so for the rest of her life). Mother comes to visit in April (her first meeting with Livy), while sister prepares to move to Fredonia, New York. Jervis Langdon's health deteriorates, and Clemenses go to Elmira for two weeks to help nurse him. Goes to Washington, D.C., in early July to lobby for passage of bill to divide Tennessee into two judicial districts (measure would benefit Jervis Langdon's lumber business and Orion's plans to sell family land). Meets President Ulysses S. Grant. Returns to Elmira and signs contract with Bliss for book on the West. Jervis Langdon dies August 6 of stomach cancer. Emma Nye, Livy's old classmate, comes to visit in Buffalo late in August. Nye falls ill with typhoid; Livy cares for her with help of hired nurse. Clemens continues to write *Galaxy* articles and works on western book. Writes Orion expressing his exasperation over Orion's schemes for selling Tennessee land. Visits mother, sister, nephew, and niece in Fredonia. Susan Langdon Crane (Livy's foster sister) comes to take care of Livy, who is pregnant and exhausted. Clemens gets Orion a job in Hartford as editor of Bliss's new magazine, *American Publisher*. Son Langdon born prematurely on November 7. Mary Fairbanks comes to help nurse Livy. Clemens goes to New York to meet Webb about obtaining rights to *The Celebrated Jumping Frog of Calaveras County*. Contracts with Bliss for *Sketches New & Old*. Son's health continues to be poor.

1871   Livy falls dangerously ill with typhoid in February. Clemens hires nurses and doctors, including Dr. Rachel Brooks Gleason, to care for her and stays up nights watching over her. Susan Crane and Livy's friend Clara Spaulding assist in nursing. Decides to stop writing for *Galaxy* in order to work more on books. Has come to "loathe Buffalo" and puts house and interest in the *Express* up for sale, hoping to move to Hartford. When Livy's health improves slightly, takes her to Elmira on March 18. Chagrined by unfavorable reception of pamphlet *Mark Twain's (Burlesque) Autobiography and First Romance*, published by Isaac E. Sheldon, the same firm that published *Galaxy*. Works hard on *Roughing It*, his western book, writing at Quarry Farm, located on a hill outside Elmira and owned by Susan and Theodore Crane. Pleased when Goodman visits in April and works with him on the manuscript. Sells interest in the *Express* at a big loss. Pamela and her son Samuel Erasmus Moffett stay at Quarry Farm in June. Livy's and baby's health improve. Arranges another lecture tour with Redpath, but asks that he be paid at least as much as his friend Nasby receives. Clemens writes lecture "Reminiscences of Some Un-Commonplace Characters I Have Chanced to Meet." Goes to Hartford in August to complete *Roughing It*. Sees mother and Annie, who have come to visit Orion and Mollie in Hartford, and brings them with him to visit Elmira. Baby is very sick again. Clemens goes to Washington in September to secure patent on "elastic strap" (granted patent for "Improvement in Adjustable and De-tachable Straps for Garments"). Leases John and Isabella Beecher Hooker's house in "Nook Farm" area of Hart-ford. Returns to Buffalo to pack, and moves to Hartford in October. Lectures in Pennsylvania, Washington, D.C., Massachusetts, Vermont, New Hampshire, Maine, and New York. Sees Howells and Bret Harte. Dislikes his pre-pared lectures and writes one about Artemus Ward, then writes another based on *Roughing It*. Goes on to Chicago and is struck by the extent of damage caused by the great fire.

1872   Lectures in Indiana, Ohio, West Virginia, Pennsylvania, and New York, where he attends birthday celebration for Horace Greeley, editor of the New York *Tribune*, on Feb-ruary 3. *Roughing It* is published in February and sells well. Orion quits as editor of Bliss's *American Publisher* and tells Clemens that Bliss is cheating him on produc-tion costs of *Roughing It*. Clemens questions figures but does not break with Bliss. Returns to Elmira in early March. Daughter Olivia Susan (Susy) born March 19. Vis-its Fairbanks in Cleveland with Livy in early May. Son Langdon dies June 2 of diptheria. In July family goes to stay in Saybrook, Connecticut, to escape summer heat. Prepares preface and makes revisions for English edition of *The Innocents Abroad*, published by Routledge & Sons. Devises idea for "Mark Twain's Self-Pasting Scrap-Book" (it is successfully marketed by his friend Dan Slote). Sails for Liverpool on August 21 intending to write a book on England. Speaks at the Whitefriars, a London literary club, and is made honorary member. Tours Warwickshire with American publisher James R. Osgood. Meets actor Henry Irving, clergyman Moncure Conway, and sees Henry Morton Stanley, whom he had met in St. Louis in 1867. Writes letter to the *Spectator* protesting John Camden Hotten's printing of books attributed to him that include articles he did not write. Speaks at the Savage Club, a literary and arts club. Overwhelmed by social activities, invitations to private houses, and ceremonial functions and is amazed and flattered by his fame in England. Sails for America on November 12. Begins work on novel *The Gilded Age* with friend and neighbor, Charles Dudley Warner.

1873   Buys large lot in "Nook Farm" area of Hartford, planning to build house on it. Lectures in Hartford to raise money for charity, and in New York and Brooklyn in February on the Sandwich Islands. Made a member of the Lotos Club in New York City. Becomes a director of the American Publishing Company. Clemens and Warner finish *The Gilded Age*. Family, accompanied by Clara Spaulding, sails for England on May 17. Intrigued by trial for perjury of claimant to the Tichborne title. Sees poet Joaquin Miller whom he had met in California. Arranges for Routledge to bring out *The Gilded Age* in England. Begins writing letters for the *Herald* on the activities of the shah of Persia during his visit to England and Europe. Meets Thomas Hughes, Herbert Spencer, Anthony Trollope, Robert Browning, and Wilkie Collins, among others. Moncure Conway takes Clemens and Livy to Stratford-on-Avon, where they are guests of the mayor. Goes to Edinburgh, Scotland, and meets Dr. John Brown, who is called in to treat Livy who is exhausted after the hectic London season; the doctor becomes a lifelong friend. Visits Belfast and Dublin, then returns to London. Clemenses go to Paris in September to buy household items. Having spent more money than expected, Clemens has George Dolby, Dickens' agent, arrange for him to lecture in London in October. Family sails for America on October 21, arriving in New York November 2. Clemens sails again for England on November 8 to obtain copyright for *The Gilded Age* and to give further lectures. Lectures in December on the Sandwich Islands, then changes to "Roughing It on the Silver Frontier." Writes out after-dinner speeches because he is often called on to give them. *The Gilded Age* published simultaneously in England and America on December 23. Spends Christmas holiday at Salisbury and visits Stonehenge.

1874   Lectures in Leicester and Liverpool. Sails for Boston on January 13. Introduces lecture by English writer Charles Kingsley at the Essex Institute in Salem, Massachusetts, and lectures in Boston. Mary Fairbanks and her children visit Hartford. Sales of *The Gilded Age* are very good. Buys Orion a chicken farm outside Keokuk (will begin sending regular payments to Orion, who considers them loans, though he will be unable to repay more than nominal amounts of interest). Goes to Quarry Farm in May, where Susan Crane has built a free-standing octagonal study for him. Daughter Clara Langdon born June 8. Works on five-act play *Colonel Sellers*, dramatization of *The Gilded Age*, and *Tom Sawyer*. Pleased when "A True Story" is accepted by Howells for the *Atlantic* (published November 1874), his first piece to appear there. Stops in New York to help with rehearsals for *Colonel Sellers*; play opens September 16, starring John T. Raymond. Returns to Hartford September 19 and moves into still unfinished house designed by architect Edward T. Potter. With Howells' encouragement, begins writing articles about the Mississippi ("Old Times on the Mississippi," begins to appear in January 1875 *Atlantic*). Buys a typewriter and writes to Howells on it (later boasts to friends that he was the first writer to use one). Attends *Atlantic* contributors' dinner in Boston on December 15.

1875   Enjoys new home, spending hours playing billiards in room at top of house; close neighbors are the Warners and Stowes. Describes his taste in reading: "I like history, biography, travels, curious facts & strange happenings, & science. And I detest novels, poetry & theology." Reminiscences of life as a pilot on the Mississippi appear in the *Atlantic* until August. Pleased with royalties received from *Colonel Sellers*, which successfully tours the country. Goes to New York to attend Henry Ward Beecher's trial for adultery. Decides not to go to Quarry Farm for the summer. Resumes work on *Tom Sawyer*. Invites Dan De Quille to Hartford and helps him get his book *The Big Bonanza* published by Bliss. Clemens and Howells frequently visit each other in Hartford and Cambridge. Hires George Griffin as butler; he becomes a family favorite (household includes about seven servants, among them nurses for the children). Finishes *Tom Sawyer* in July. Goes to Newport, Rhode Island, at the end of month and stays through August. *Sketches New & Old* published September 25 by Bliss. Moncure Conway visits the Clemenses in Hartford.

1876   Clemens is ill for several weeks. Employs private secretary to take dictation and answer letters. Makes revisions in *Tom Sawyer* based on Howells' suggestions. Gives talk, "The Facts Concerning the Recent Carnival of Crime in Connecticut," to the Monday Evening Club, Hartford literary group. Mother and sister visit. Clemens goes to Quarry Farm for summer. *The Adventures of Tom Sawyer* published in England by Chatto & Windus. Begins work on *Huckleberry Finn*. Attends centennial celebration in Philadelphia with other authors. Angered by widespread sales in the United States of pirated Canadian editions of *Tom Sawyer*. Works on scatological tale [*Date, 1601.*] *Conversation, as it Was by the Social Fireside, in the Time of the Tudors* (published privately 1880), and reads it to friends Twichell, Howells, and Hay. Collaborates with Harte on play, *Ah Sin,* Harte staying at the Clemenses' house for two weeks. Frank Millet comes to Hartford to paint Clemens' portrait. American edition of *Tom Sawyer*, published December 8 by the American Publishing Company, sells moderately well.

1877   Continues work on play with Harte until late February. Relations with Harte become strained over their financial and publishing ties, and then break off completely when Clemens receives an angry letter from him. Oversees rehearsals of *Ah Sin* in Baltimore in April (play opens in Washington on May 7). Travels with Twichell to Bermuda for short holiday, then goes with family to Elmira in June. Writes "Some Rambling Notes of an Idle Excursion" about Bermuda trip for the *Atlantic*. Attends New York rehearsals for *Ah Sin* in July (produced by Augustin Daly, the play opens July 31 and runs for five weeks). Tries to persuade cartoonist Thomas Nast to go on a lecture tour with him. At banquet in Boston on December 17 delivers the "Whittier Birthday Speech," a burlesque of three tramps who pass themselves off as Longfellow, Emerson, and Holmes. Many listeners, including Howells, are shocked, and some newspapers are severely critical. Chagrined, sends letters of apology to the three writers.

1878   Works on *The Prince and the Pauper*. Signs contract with Elisha Bliss for book about Europe. Visits Elmira and Fredonia (niece Annie is now married to Charles Webster). Sails for Europe April 11 with family and Clara Spaulding. Family stops in Hamburg and then travels slowly through Germany to Heidelberg, arriving May 6. Clemens takes excursions into the countryside, then they leave on July 23 for Baden-Baden. Twichell arrives August 1. Clemens and Twichell take "walking tour," traveling by rail, carriage, boat, and foot through the Black Forest and the Swiss Alps. Family travels through Italy, staying in Venice, Florence, and Rome until November, then settles in Munich for three months.

1879   Family goes to Paris at the end of February. Clemens is ill with rheumatism and dysentery. Feels better in April and works on *A Tramp Abroad*. Dislikes Paris, but meets artists and literary men who belong to the Stomach Club, including Edwin Austin Abbey and Augustus Saint-Gaudens, and attends wedding of Frank Millet. Has two meetings with Ivan Turgenev, a writer he admires. Family leaves Paris in July and travels through Belgium and the Netherlands, then spends a month in England. Renews old acquaintances and meets Charles Darwin in the Lake District. Family sails to New York on August 23, then goes to Quarry Farm. Clemens visits his family in Fredonia. Returns to Hartford in late October. Installs telephone in his home. Attends reunion banquet of Army of the Tennessee, held in Chicago on November 13 with Ulysses S. Grant as the guest of honor. Responds to toast with speech "The Babies." Becomes friends with orator Robert G. Ingersoll. Attends *Atlantic* breakfast in honor of Oliver Wendell Holmes and gives well-received speech.

1880   Goes to Elmira with Livy, who is exhausted from redecorating house and installing furniture bought in Europe.

Works for a short time on *Huckleberry Finn*, then sets it aside. Visits mother, who is not well, in Fredonia. Buys four-fifths interest in Dan Slote's patent on Kaola-type, a chalk-plate process for engraving illustrations, and forms company with himself as president. *A Tramp Abroad* published in March by the American Publishing Company. It sells well. Increases payments to Orion, telling him that the money is for his role in making him more aware of the need to obtain better terms from publishers. Works happily on *The Prince and the Pauper* and encourages Orion to write autobiography (Orion will write several chapters, but never finishes). Daughter Jane Lampton (Jean) born July 26. Death of Elisha Bliss causes Clemens to seek new publisher. Clemens accompanies Grant to Hartford and delivers welcoming speech. Actively supports James A. Garfield, the Republican presidential nominee.

1881   Writes letter to president-elect Garfield describing Frederick Douglass as a personal friend and asking that he be retained in the office of marshal of the District of Columbia (Garfield makes Douglass recorder of deeds for the District). Buys additional land next to house to keep neighbor from building and begins renovations of house and grounds. Hires Charles Webster, niece Annie's husband, to be his business agent. Enjoys reading out loud works of Joel Chandler Harris. Spends early summer in Branford, Connecticut, before going to Elmira. By now has made numerous investments in various speculative ventures, including Paige typesetter (will eventually invest at least $190,000 trying to get machine perfected). Howells reads proofs and suggests revisions of *The Prince and the Pauper*. Clemens and James R. Osgood travel to Canada to issue an edition of the book there (their presence in the country is needed to secure Canadian copyright). *The Prince and the Pauper* is published by Osgood in the United States in late December.

1882   Visits the aged Emerson with Howells, and is pleased when Emerson recognizes him. In preparation for expanding 1875 *Atlantic* articles about the Mississippi into a book, Clemens travels with Osgood and shorthand secretary Roswell Phelps to St. Louis, then goes by steamboat to New Orleans, where he meets Joel Chandler Harris, George Washington Cable, and old friend Horace Bixby.

Travels up the Mississippi with Bixby in pilothouse, stopping in Hannibal. *The Stolen White Elephant*, collection of short pieces, published by Osgood. Trip to Quarry Farm delayed when Jean, Susy, and Clemens get scarlet fever and house is quarantined. Struggles over writing *Life on the Mississippi*. Has doubts about Osgood's ability to sell books by subscription; makes Webster his subscription agent for the New York area.

1883   Finishes book. Livy is sick with diphtheria for over a month. Goes again to Canada to safeguard copyright. *Life on the Mississippi* published in May by Osgood. Resumes work on *Huckleberry Finn* and enjoys the writing. Collaborates with Howells on play *Colonel Sellers as Scientist*. Begins work on dramatizations of *Tom Sawyer* and *The Prince and the Pauper*. Becomes dissatisfied with sales of books under Osgood's direction. Meets Matthew Arnold in Hartford during his American lecture tour.

1884   Cable visits in January and gets the mumps. Clemens tries unsuccessfully to get plays produced. Howells reads typescript of *Huckleberry Finn* and suggests revisions. Clemens has attack of gout. Founds his own publishing firm, Charles L. Webster & Co. Learns to ride a bicycle. Reads proofs of *Huckleberry Finn* from June through August, with help from Howells. Karl Gerhardt makes bust of Clemens. Needing more money, contracts with Major J. B. Pond to do four-month lecture tour with Cable. Joins other Republican "mugwumps," who consider Republican presidential candidate James G. Blaine to be dishonest, in voting for Democrat Grover Cleveland. Lecture tour begins November 5 in New Haven. Learns from Richard Watson Gilder, editor of *Century Magazine*, that General Grant is writing his memoirs. Visits Grant in New York, tells him that terms offered by Century Company are inadequate, and urges him not to sign any contract until Webster & Co. can make an offer. In December visits president-elect Cleveland in Albany at his invitation. *Century* publishes first of three excerpts from *Huckleberry Finn*.

1885   Continues lecture tour, which includes Hannibal and Keokuk, where mother is now living with Orion. *Adventures of Huckleberry Finn* published in the United States by Webster & Co. on February 16; Clemens again goes to Canada to protect copyright. Webster & Co. buys rights to books published by Osgood. Clemens visits Grant in New York on February 21 and learns that he is dying from throat cancer; urges him to accept Webster & Co. offer. Grant signs contract on February 27. Canvassing for the memoirs begins immediately. Lecture tour is very successful financially, and Clemens likes Cable, but is irritated by his strict observance of the Sabbath. Clemens makes Charles Webster a partner in Webster & Co. and gives him more money. When Concord, Massachusetts, library bans *Huckleberry Finn*, tells Webster that they will sell an extra 20,000 books as a result. Concerned that Grant may not live to complete the memoirs, Clemens helps in any way he can, reading proofs as pages are set and praising the writing. By May more than 60,000 two-volume sets have been ordered. Clemens is pleased when Susy begins writing biography of his life. Writes account of the Marion Rangers, "The Private History of a Campaign that Failed," and shows it to Grant, who enjoys it immensely (published in *Century Magazine* in December as part of its series on the Civil War). Works on sequel to *Huckleberry Finn*, "Tom and Huck among the Indians" (never finished). Grant dies in July, only a few days after finishing his memoirs. Clemens is involved in many ventures, including patents for a historical game, a perpetual calendar, and a "bed-clasp" for keeping babies' blankets in place; his major investment is the Paige typesetter. Touched when Oliver Wendell Holmes, Charles Dudley Warner, and others write tributes in the *Critic* for his fiftieth birthday. In December 325,000 copies of first volume of *Personal Memoirs of U. S. Grant* are bound and shipped (second volume appears in March 1886). Clemens begins paying board of Warner T. McGuinn, one of the first black students at the Yale Law School, whom he had met during a speaking engagement at Yale. (Later supports study of Charles Ethan Porter, a black sculptor, and pays tuition of a black undergraduate at Lincoln University.)

1886   Continues to entertain lavishly. Howells comes with his daughter Mildred to see staging of *The Prince and the Pauper* dramatized by Livy and performed by the Clemens children and their friends. Clemens frequently goes to New York on publishing business. Grant family eventually receives between $420,000 and $450,000 from sales of *Personal Memoirs*. Clemens makes Frederick J. Hall third partner in Webster & Co. Webster & Co. signs contract with Bernard O'Reilly, authorized biographer of Pope Leo XIII; Clemens expects that the papal biography will be more successful than Grant's memoirs (is disappointed by sales when book is published in 1887). Reads from his works at U.S. Military Academy at West Point. Resumes work with Howells on play *Colonel Sellers as Scientist* and makes arrangements to have it produced, but at the last moment Howells backs out. In July takes family to visit mother, Orion, and Mollie in Keokuk. Hires Frank G. Whitmore as business agent to supervise construction of the Paige typesetting machine at the Pratt & Whitney works in Hartford. Begins work on *A Connecticut Yankee in King Arthur's Court.*

1887   Attends benefit on March 31 for the Longfellow Memorial Fund in Boston and reads from "English as She Is Taught," after being introduced by Charles Eliot Norton, who tells anecdote about Darwin keeping Clemens' works on his bedside table. Defends General Grant's grammar against criticism by Matthew Arnold in speech in Hartford on April 27. Clemens financially backs production of *Colonel Sellers as Scientist*, retitled *The American Claimant* and credited solely to Mark Twain, that has a brief run starring A. P. Burbank. With Livy and several Hartford friends, visits artist Frederick Church in Hudson, New York. At Quarry Farm continues to work with pleasure on *A Connecticut Yankee in King Arthur's Court. Mark Twain's Library of Humor* (collaboration by Howells, Clemens, and Charles H. Clark) published in December by Webster & Co.

1888   Frederick Hall takes over Charles Webster's responsibilities. In April Clemens spends afternoon with Robert Louis Stevenson in New York's Washington Square Park. Visits Thomas Edison at his laboratory in West Orange, New Jersey, in June. Awarded honorary Master of Arts degree by Yale. Theodore Crane has partially paralyzing stroke and is nursed by Susan and Livy in Hartford in December. Hall buys Webster's interest in firm.

1889   Success of prototype Paige typesetter thrills Clemens, al-
             though technical problems again develop. Writes letter of
             tribute to Whitman for publication in *Camden's Compli-
             ment to Walt Whitman* (Clemens had joined others in fi-
             nancially assisting Whitman in 1885 and 1887). Theodore
             Crane dies at Quarry Farm in July. Clemens is charmed
             by Rudyard Kipling who visits him in Elmira. Works on
             revisions of *A Connecticut Yankee in King Arthur's
             Court*. Hoping to live on profits from Paige machine,
             calls the novel his "swan-song" and his "retirement from
             literature" in letter to Howells. Unable to read manu-
             script because of eye trouble, Livy asks Clemens to have
             Howells read proofs because she trusts Howells to keep
             Clemens from offending good taste. Certain that Paige
             typesetter will soon be ready for production, invites
             Joseph Goodman to come east and help find investors for
             machine. Anticipating that Chatto & Windus, his English
             publisher, will make changes in *A Connecticut Yankee* to
             avoid offending English sensibilities, writes letter to them
             refusing to alter text and saying that the book was "writ-
             ten for England." *A Connecticut Yankee in King Arthur's
             Court*, published in America December 10 by Webster &
             Co., sells moderately well. Dramatization of *The Prince
             and the Pauper* by Abby Sage Richardson opens in
             Philadelphia and is fairly successful.

1890   Financial problems become acute from continued cost of
             Paige machine and lack of profits from Webster & Co.
             (unsold books, subscription costs, and expense of pro-
             ducing and distributing 11-volume *Library of American
             Literature*, an anthology edited by Edmund C. Stedman,
             create constant cash-flow problems that drain away his
             book royalties). Edward House brings suit against drama-
             tization of *The Prince and the Pauper* by Richardson,
             claiming he had been given the rights long ago. Litiga-
             tion prevents Clemens from receiving royalties from play.
             Family goes for the summer to Onteora Park, artists' and
             writers' colony in the Catskills near Tannersville, New
             York. With Goodman's help Clemens travels frequently in
             search of investors for Paige machine. Goes to Keokuk
             in August when mother has stroke. Susy enters Bryn
             Mawr College in October. Clara takes piano lessons in
             New York City twice a week. Mother dies in Keokuk Oc-
             tober 27, and Clemens attends funeral in Hannibal. Goes

to Elmira where Livy's mother dies November 28. Clemens rushes back to Hartford because Jean is ill.

1891   Webster & Co. goes deeper into debt. Attempts at raising capital for Paige machine are unsuccessful, and Clemens stops his monthly payments in support of project. Suffering from rheumatism in right arm, finds writing difficult. Works on novel *The American Claimant.* Experiments with dictating into phonograph, but soon gives up. Susy leaves Bryn Mawr in April, too homesick to continue. Charles Webster dies in April. Clemens signs contract with *McClure's Magazine* to serialize *The American Claimant* in America and abroad and to write letters from Europe. No longer able to afford the maintenance of the Hartford home, decides to go to Europe, hoping that baths will help Livy's health (she is developing heart trouble) and relieve rheumatism in his arm. They close the house and find new positions for their servants. Family sails with Susan Crane on June 6. They stop in Paris before going to take baths at Aix-les-Bains. Susy and Clara attend boarding school in Geneva. Clemens hears Wagner operas at Bayreuth in August. Tries other baths at Marienbad. Settles family in Ouchy, Switzerland, in September, then takes trip down the Rhône. Family goes to Berlin for the winter.

1892   Clemens develops pneumonia. Doctors recommend that Livy and he go south. Has private dinner with Kaiser William II in February. Leaves daughters at school in Berlin and goes with Livy in March to Mentone, France, for three weeks and then to Italy, spending several weeks in Rome and Venice before returning to Berlin. Collection *Merry Tales* published in April and *The American Claimant* published in May, both by Webster & Co.; sales are poor. Many Americans visit, including Sarah Orne Jewett and Annie Fields. Family moves to Bad Nauheim for the summer. Clemens goes to New York in June to check on publishing business and to Chicago where factory has been set up to manufacture Paige typesetter. Returns to Europe in July. Works on "Those Extraordinary Twins" and then turns to *Tom Sawyer Abroad* (published serially in *St. Nicholas,* November 1893–April 1894, and as a book by Webster & Co. in 1894). Twichells visit in August, and Clemens and Twichell go to Bad

Homburg. In September the family goes to Florence, traveling slowly because of Livy's health and stopping in Frankfurt am Main and Lucerne on the way. Moves into the Villa Viviani, Settignano. Family enjoys living there, and Clemens concentrates on writing. Clara returns to Berlin to study music. Livy's health continues to be poor. Reworks "Those Extraordinary Twins" into *Pudd'nhead Wilson*.

1893   Works on *Personal Recollections of Joan of Arc*. Sails to New York for business reasons on March 22. Sees Howells and goes with Hall to Chicago, where he checks progress of Paige machine and attends the World's Columbian Exposition. Financial panic in America makes problems at Webster & Co. more severe. Disheartened, leaves for Europe on May 13. Tries to find buyer for his interest in Webster & Co. In June family goes to Munich and to spas. Clemens resumes work on *Pudd'nhead Wilson*. Feels depressed and distraught about financial circumstances. Borrows money and seeks financial advice from Charles Langdon. Sails with Clara to New York on August 29. Sells "The Esquimau Maiden's Romance" to *Cosmopolitan* and *Pudd'nhead Wilson* to *Century* (appears December 1893–June 1894). Tries to borrow money to meet pressing debts of Webster & Co. from friends in Hartford and Wall Street brokers and bankers, but panic has made money tight. Meets Henry Huttleston Rogers, vice-president of the Standard Oil Company, who begins examining the problems of the Paige typesetter company. Rogers arranges for his son-in-law, William E. Benjamin, to buy the *Library of American Literature* from Webster & Co. Clemens sees old friends, is often called upon for after-dinner speeches, and is touched by warmth of his reception in New York. Richard Watson Gilder and Howells arrange dinner in his honor at the Lotos Club on November 11. Clara returns to Europe to study music. Clemens travels with Rogers to Chicago to inspect Paige machine.

1894   Goes to Boston to participate in "Author's Reading and Music for the Poor," and has dinner with Sarah Orne Jewett and Oliver Wendell Holmes. Sees Mary Fairbanks in New York in February. Gives readings with James Whitcomb Riley. Becomes closer to Rogers and his family.

Gives Rogers power of attorney over all his affairs on March 6. Sails the next day and arrives in Paris where family is now living. Rogers assigns Clemens' property, including his copyrights and share in Paige machine, to Livy. Clemens returns to New York in April. On advice from Rogers, declares the failure of Webster & Co. on April 18 and assumes his share of its debts, causing his personal bankruptcy, which is widely and sympathetically reported in newspapers. Returns to Paris in May. Howells spends a week with him in June. For sake of Susy's health, family goes to La Bourboule-les-Bains. Clemens returns to New York in July and remains until August, then rejoins family at Étretat in Normandy. Susy is still ill, with persistent high fever. *Pudd'nhead Wilson* published in November as subscription book by the American Publishing Company (publisher includes earlier version of story as a separate work). Family returns to Paris, where Clemens is confined to bed with attack of gout. Devastated by news in December that Paige typesetter has failed a test because of broken type.

1895   Works on several short pieces and writes *Tom Sawyer, Detective* (published by Harper & Brothers in November 1896). Finishes *Personal Recollections of Joan of Arc* and sails from Southampton. Arrives in New York in early March; serial publication of *Personal Recollections of Joan of Arc* in *Harper's Magazine* begins in April. In hopes of having the work taken more seriously, asks that installments appear anonymously (his authorship soon becomes known, and book edition, published by Harper & Brothers in May 1896, is credited to Mark Twain). Moved by visit to family home in Hartford, now leased to friends John and Alice Hooker Day. Arranges with Major Pond for cross-country lecture tour. Clemens returns to France in March. Brings family to New York on May 18, then goes to Quarry Farm. Agrees to contract, signed on May 23, with Harpers that gives them rights to Mark Twain books published by Webster & Co. (negotiates with American Publishing Company for similar agreement; Clemens hopes that Harpers will bring out a uniform edition of his works). Suffers painful carbuncle on leg, and is forced to stay in bed for over six weeks, unable to stand or put on clothes. Leaving Susy and Jean to stay with Susan Crane at Quarry Farm, Clemens, Livy, and Clara leave on July 14 for first lecture in Cleveland. Tells reporters in Vancouver that he intends eventually to repay every creditor in full. Sails for Australia on August 23 with Livy and Clara, beginning around-the-world lecture tour arranged by R. S. Smythe. Visits Fiji and arrives in Sydney on September 16. Continues to suffer from carbuncles. Appears in Sydney, Melbourne, Adelaide, and other Australian towns before large, responsive audiences, reading from his books and telling stories. Sails for New Zealand on October 30, first stopping in Tasmania. Lectures in Dunedin, Christchurch, Wellington, Auckland, and other towns.

1896   Sails for India on January 4. Enjoys emptiness and calm of Indian Ocean. Stops briefly in Colombo, Ceylon, and arrives in Bombay on January 18. Suffers from persistent bronchial cough. Finds India fascinating and is warmly received by Indian princes and British officials. Takes train from Bombay to Allahabad and Benares. Lectures to packed audiences in Calcutta, February 10–13, then goes to Darjeeling in the foothills of the Himalayas. Exhilarated by trip to Darjeeling, 35 miles in open railway car. Returns to Calcutta and then visits Lucknow, Kanpur, Agra, Delhi, Lahore, Rawalpindi, and Jaipur. Sails from Calcutta for South Africa at the end of March. Stops in Madras, visits Mauritius, and lands May 6 at Durban in British colony of Natal. Livy and Clara stay in Durban while Clemens gives readings across South Africa. Goes to Pietermaritzburg, Johannesburg, and Pretoria, in the Boer Transvaal republic. Visits those imprisoned for their alleged complicity in 1895 Jameson Raid, an aborted invasion intended to bring the Transvaal under British rule. After leaving prison, Clemens makes humorous remark to reporter that is misinterpreted as implying that prisoners are being treated leniently. When their confinement is made harsher, Clemens goes to see President Kruger to explain the joke (prisoners are soon released). Goes to Bloemfontein, in Orange Free State, and Queenstown and East London in the British Cape Colony. Sails for England from Cape Town with Livy and Clara July 15 and arrives in Southampton on July 31. Takes a house in Guildford, Surrey, for a month. Rogers arranges contract with American Publishing Company to issue subscription volumes as well as a uniform subscription edition of the complete works, while Harpers will sell individual books and a less-inclusive uniform edition to the trade. Learns that Susy is ill. Livy and Clara leave for America August 15, Clemens remains in England. Susy dies on August 18 of spinal meningitis. Clemens learns of her death by telegram. Livy returns to England with Clara and Jean, whose health problems have recently been diagnosed as epilepsy. Rents house at 23 Tedworth Square, Chelsea, London, where they seclude themselves (family will not celebrate birthdays, Thanksgiving, Christmas, or other holidays for several years afterward). Begins writing travel book, *Following the Equator.*

1897   Clemens works long hours on book. In February writes Howells, who has published review praising the first five volumes in Harpers' "Uniform Edition," that he feels "indifferent to nearly everything but work." Finishes *Following the Equator* in May. In July family goes to the Villa Bühlegg on Lake Lucerne in Switzerland. Is deeply moved when he hears Fisk Jubilee Singers perform in village in August and entertains them at home after their concert. Family moves to Vienna in late September. Clemens suffers from gout. Interviewers from many newspapers come to the hotel. Works for many hours a day, but does not intend to publish much of what he writes. *Following the Equator* published in November. Clemens and Clara go out in society and attend operas. Clara is accepted as student of famed piano teacher Theodor Leschetizky. Begins work on "The Man That Corrupted Hadleyburg" (published in *Harper's Magazine*, December 1899). Orion dies in Keokuk on December 11.

1898   Pianist Ossip Gabrilowitsch comes to dinner. Clemens works for eight or nine hours at a time, trying to write for the stage again. Continues to follow Dreyfus case in France and admires Zola for his championing of Dreyfus' cause. Creditors are paid in full, and newspapers compare him to Walter Scott (who had also redeemed himself from bankruptcy). Because of Clara's study of music, meets many prominent musicians and concerts. Sends articles directly to magazine editors; if they reject them, has Rogers try to place them with other publications. Commands high prices for his work. When Spanish-American War begins in April, believes that freeing Cuba from

Spanish domination is a worthy cause. Livy's health does not improve. Writes article about the assassination of Elizabeth, Empress of Austria, and watches her funeral. Begins work on early version of *The Mysterious Stranger*. Writes autobiographical passages in November and considers publishing an autobiography. Feels more relaxed about financial matters, and is delighted with Rogers' investment of his money.

1899   Takes family to Budapest for a week when he delivers lecture there. Tells Howells in a letter that "it is a luxury! an intellectual drunk" to write material not intended for publication. Goes with family to London in May, then to Sweden in July, where they are treated at sanitarium run by Henrik Kellgren (Clemens hopes that Kellgren's methods will be beneficial to Jean, who has been having frequent seizures). Writes "Christian Science and the Book of Mrs. Eddy," published October in *Cosmopolitan*. Returns to London in October. Blames outbreak of Boer War on Cecil Rhodes and British colonial secretary Joseph Chamberlain.

1900   Becomes disillusioned with American policy in the Philippines, and has divided sympathies concerning the Boer War. Has portrait painted by James McNeill Whistler. In March enthusiastically invests in Plasmon, food supplement made from milk by-products, and becomes director of syndicate. Spends summer at Dollis Hill House on northwest outskirts of London. Sympathizes with Chinese in the Boxer Rebellion. Decides to return to America, having learned that osteopathy, now widely practiced in the United States, is similar to Kellgren's methods. Family sails to New York on October 6. Receives warm welcome from public, press, and friends. Goes to Hartford to attend funeral of Charles Dudley Warner. Rents house at 14 West 10th Street, New York City. Journalists constantly seek interviews. Introduces Winston S. Churchill to large New York audience on December 12. Writes "To the Person Sitting in Darkness," denunciation of imperialism, and is encouraged to publish it by Livy and Howells (article appears in *North American Review*, February 1901).

1901   Enjoys company of Howells, who now lives in New York and shares his anti-imperialist views. Clemens attacks missionary propaganda in China, and Tammany machine politics. Frequently invited to make speeches, presides over the Lincoln birthday celebration in Carnegie Hall. Troubled by attacks of gout. Family spends summer at Saranac Lake in the Adirondacks. Sails for two weeks with Rogers on his yacht to New Brunswick and Nova Scotia. Family finds sad memories make it impossible to live in Hartford, and they decide to sell the house there and rent a mansion overlooking the Hudson in Riverdale, New York. Receives honorary Doctor of Letters from Yale in October. Livy's health deteriorates. Rogers expresses concern to Clemens about fairness of Ida Tarbell's forthcoming investigative series in *McClure's Magazine* on Standard Oil.

1902   Clemens tells *McClure's* that they should have Tarbell speak with Rogers before running articles (Rogers agrees to interview; Tarbell will describe him as "candid" in her series). Jean has seizures. Clemens goes on yachting excursions with Rogers to Bahamas, Cuba, and Florida. Clara leaves for Paris in April to continue her studies. Clemens receives honorary Doctor of Laws from University of Missouri in June. Visits Hannibal and St. Louis for the last time. Takes trip on Mississippi with Bixby. Family goes to York Harbor, Maine, for the summer. Clemens is upset as he witnesses more of Jean's epileptic seizures (had previously seen only three of her attacks, though Livy had been present for many more). Clemens works on "Was It Heaven? Or Hell?" (published in *Harper's Magazine*, December 1902). In August Livy is violently ill, can barely breathe, and has severe heart palpitations; family fears she is dying. Clara comes from Europe and Susan Crane joins them. Jean's health improves. Livy continues to suffer from attacks and in October returns to Riverdale. Clemens is not allowed to go into her room. Attends large dinner in honor of his 67th birthday, given by George Harvey of Harper & Brothers at the Metropolitan Club in New York. Clara takes charge of house. Isabel Lyon, hired as Livy's secretary, now acts as Clemens' secretary. On December 30 Clemens is allowed to see Livy for five minutes.

1903   Sees Livy for five minutes on days when she is feeling better. Rarely goes into city. Livy's health improves during the spring months. Clemens is forced to stay in bed for a month by attacks of bronchitis, gout, and rheumatism. Sells Hartford house. Doctors tell Livy she should go to Europe to recover. Family leaves Riverdale in early July, going down the Hudson River on Rogers' yacht to Hoboken, where they take train to Elmira. At Quarry Farm Livy improves and resumes household responsibilities. Clemens works in octagonal study. Goes to New York in October to see publishers and signs contract giving Harpers rights to all his books, receiving guaranteed yearly payments. Family sails for Italy on October 24. Goes to Florence and rents the Villa di Quarto, a large house near the city. Trip is tiring for Livy, but she improves temporarily.

1904   Livy's condition worsens and she is confined to bed. Clemens writes magazine articles, then turns to autobiography, dictating to Lyon every day. Learns that sister-in-law Mollie Clemens died in Keokuk (does not tell Livy). Family dislikes landlady and searches for another villa (search proves beneficial to family's spirits because it encourages them to hope that Livy will live long enough for them to move). Clara sings on concert stage and Clemens is impressed by her professionalism. Livy dies on June 5. Clara breaks down. Jean has first seizure in 13 months, but soon recovers and plans family's return to America. They sail June 28. Charles Langdon, his daughter Julia Langdon Loomis, and her husband meet them at the pier and accompany them to Elmira. Funeral services are held in the Langdon house conducted by Twichell. Clemens takes cottage in July at Richard Watson Gilder's summer home in the Berkshires near Lee, Massachusetts. Clara, still suffering from shock, enters a rest-cure establishment in New York City. Jean is hit by a trolley while horseback riding; horse is killed, and she is knocked unconscious and suffers torn ankle tendon. Clemens goes to New York in August, finds Clara still ill, and is not allowed to see her. Searches for house to live in. Signs three-year lease for house at 21 Fifth Avenue. Stays in hotel while furnishings for new house are brought from Hartford. Jean remains in the Berkshires with Isabel Lyon. Spends a few days in late August as guest of George Harvey at Deal, New Jersey, where he sees Henry James, who is also visiting Harvey. Sister Pamela dies in Greenwich, Connecticut, in

September. Visits Elmira with Jean. Moves in December into Fifth Avenue house, where Jean joins him. Seldom goes out, but is visited by Rogers, Andrew Carnegie, and other old friends.

1905   Plays cards with Lyon and listens to music on player organ. Goes with Rogers to Fairhaven, Massachusetts, in May, then takes house for summer in Dublin, New Hampshire, with Jean. Writes "Eve's Diary" (published in *Harper's Magazine* in December), revises "Adam's Diary," and works on other manuscripts, including "3,000 Years Among the Microbes," and a new version of *The Mysterious Stranger*. Clara goes to Norfolk, Connecticut, to continue rest cure. Clemens is troubled by gout, dyspepsia, bronchitis, and the summer heat. Visits Clara in August (their first meeting in a year) and finds her well. Returns to Dublin and is forced by gout to stay in bed. Goes to New York in November after visit to Boston. Clara comes to live with him. Sees much of Rogers and his extended family. Attends gala 70th birthday party given in his honor by Harvey at Delmonico's on December 5 (172 guests attend). Relies on Lyon to manage household, financial, and literary matters.

1906   In January Albert Bigelow Paine, midwestern writer and editor, asks permission to write Clemens' biography. Clemens gives Paine a room in his house to work in and access to manuscripts and some letters and allows him to listen as he dictates sections of autobiography to stenographer and typist Josephine Hobby. At request of Booker T. Washington, gives talk at Carnegie Hall on the 25th anniversary of the founding of Tuskegee Institute. Continues to give speeches and readings, but no longer accepts money for them. Reluctantly withdraws support for Maxim Gorky, who is raising funds for the Russian Social Democratic party, after Gorky is discovered to be traveling with his mistress. Writes essay "William Dean Howells," praising his "perfect English" (appears in July *Harper's Magazine*). Goes to Dublin in May again to spend summer. Continues autobiographical dictations. Goes to New York in June on publishing business. Returns to Dublin in time for Jean's birthday. Harvey comes to Dublin to edit autobiography for publication (25 installments appear in *North American Review*,

September 1906–December 1907). Takes yachting trip in August with Rogers. Commissions John Howells to design and supervise building of house in Redding, Connecticut. *What Is Man?* published anonymously in limited edition by DeVinne Press in August. Goes yachting again in October. Delighted with gift of billiard table from Rogers' wife, Emilie. Plays billiards with Paine, Harvey, and Finley Peter Dunne ("Mr. Dooley"), and feels health improves as a result. Jean, who had suffered a number of seizures during the summer, is sent to a sanitarium in Katonah, New York. Clara takes rest cure before beginning concert tour. Clemens goes with Paine to Washington in December to lobby, with others, for new copyright bill; wears white suit to Capitol.

1907   Often feels lonely and dislikes Fifth Avenue house. Attends club dinners frequently. Spends week in Bermuda with Twichell. *Christian Science*, critical treatment of Mary Baker Eddy, published by Harpers in February. Summers in Tuxedo Park, New York. Goes to England to receive honorary Doctor of Literature from Oxford University. Sails from New York June 8. Plunges into social life in London, going to garden party at Windsor Castle, Lord Mayor's banquet, the Savage Club, and a party given in his honor by the proprietors of *Punch*. Lunches with George Bernard Shaw, who has called him the greatest American author and one of the great masters of the English language. Attends Oxford ceremony on June 26. Arrives in New York July 22 and goes to Tuxedo Park. Visits Fairhaven (Rogers had just suffered a stroke). Returns to New York in October. "Extract from Captain Stormfield's Visit to Heaven" appears in *Harper's Magazine* December 1907–January 1908.

1908   Goes to Bermuda with Ralph W. Ashcroft for two weeks, then returns there in late February with Rogers, who is in poor health, and Lyon (Emilie Rogers joins them in mid-March). Clemens makes friends with several schoolgirls, all between 10 and 16 years old and the daughters of friends and acquaintances. Calls them "angelfish," and conceives idea of forming a club called the "Aquarium." Returns to New York on April 11. House at Redding is completed; Clemens sees it for the first time on June 18, is very pleased, and moves in immediately. Names it "Innocence at Home" (at Clara's insistence, changes name to "Stormfield"). Enjoys receiving guests, including "angelfish," who stay two to eight days. Establishes free library in Redding, donating books from his collection, and starts fund to construct new library building. Goes to New York in August to attend funeral of nephew Samuel Moffett, who had drowned, and suffers from heatstroke and fatigue. Clara returns from European concert tour in September. House is burglarized in September. Although thieves are caught after a brief gunfight, household staff quits and new servants hired. Installs burglar alarm. Clemens accompanies Jean to New York, where she sails for Europe to consult specialist in Berlin. Clara moves to New York, making frequent visits to Redding. Forms The Mark Twain Company, corporation designed to keep royalties within the family even after copyrights expire, with himself as president, Ashcroft as secretary and treasurer, and Clara, Jean, and Lyon as directors (later replaces Lyon and Ashcroft with Paine).

1909   Enjoys listening to pianists Ossip Gabrilowitsch and Ethel Newcomb, who visit as Clara's guests. Gratified to learn that Congress has passed new copyright bill, extending holders' ownership for an additional 14 years. Attends celebration in New York of Rogers' 69th birthday (continues to see Rogers in the city, but turns down most invitations to New York events). Howells visits for the first time in late March. Clara begins to arouse his suspicions that Lyon and Ashcroft are mishandling his business affairs. Attends Clara's vocal recital in New York on April 13. Dismisses Lyon and Ashcroft in mid-April and writes lengthy, bitter denunciation of them. Jean comes to live at Stormfield on April 26 and takes over household management, including secretarial duties for Clemens, who is impressed by the quality of her mind. *Is Shakespeare Dead?*, supporting Francis Bacon's authorship of the plays, published by Harpers. Attends funeral services for Rogers in New York City on May 20. Travels to Baltimore to give promised talk at graduation of "angelfish" Frances Nunnally. Finds trip tiring and develops symptoms of heart disease, diagnosed as angina pectoris in July. Clara marries Ossip Gabrilowitsch at Stormfield on October 6. Twichell performs ceremony and Clemens wears Oxford gown for the occasion. Troubled by chest pains, goes with Paine to Bermuda in November for several weeks. Clara and Ossip leave for Europe in early December. Writes little for publication, but continues to work on "Letters from the Earth." Writes "The Turning Point of My Life" (published in *Harper's Bazar,* February 1910). Returns to Stormfield for the Christmas holidays. Jean dies on the morning of December 24, apparently having suffered heart failure during a seizure in her bathtub. Clemens is too distraught to attend services or to go to Elmira for her burial. Writes "The Death of Jean." Tells Paine: "It is the end of my autobiography. I shall never write any more." Paine and his family move into Stormfield.

1910   Goes to Bermuda on January 5, accompanied by his butler. Plays golf with Woodrow Wilson, then president of Princeton University. Howells' daughter Mildred is also in Bermuda for her health and visits him often. Chest pains grow more frequent and severe. Paine comes to help care for him. Clemens notices that Halley's Comet is again visible in the sky. Leaves Bermuda on April 12 in great pain. Dies at Stormfield on April 21. Funeral service is held at the Brick Presbyterian Church in New York City. Twichell delivers an emotional prayer. Buried in Elmira, April 24, in family plot with Langdon, Susy, Livy, and Jean.

Note on the Texts

This volume contains five novels by Mark Twain: *The Gilded Age* (written with Charles Dudley Warner), first published in 1873; its sequel, *The American Claimant* (written by Twain alone), first published in 1892; *Tom Sawyer Abroad* and *Tom Sawyer, Detective*, shorter works that first appeared in 1894 and 1896 respectively; and *No. 44, The Mysterious Stranger*, written between 1902 and 1905 and last revised in 1908 but not published during Twain's lifetime. The texts of *The Gilded Age* and *The American Claimant* presented here are those of the first American editions; *Tom Sawyer Abroad*, *Tom Sawyer, Detective*, and *No. 44, The Mysterious Stranger* have been printed from unmodernized critical editions prepared by the Mark Twain Project at the University of California and published by the University of California Press.

The Gilded Age, Twain's first novel, was conceived during the winter of 1872–73 while Sam and Livy Clemens were entertaining their neighbors Charles Dudley Warner and his wife, Susan. The men complained about the current state of American fiction; their wives challenged them to write a novel that would meet their high standards. Twain had already considered writing a fictional work based on the entrepreneurial and political activities of his mother's cousin, James Lampton, and began immediately, soon finishing the first 11 chapters. Warner, an associate editor at the *Hartford Courant* and the author of popular urbane essays and book reviews, then took up his portion of the novel, and by mid-April their collaboration was complete. In subsequent letters Twain accounted for the ways in which authorship had been divided, claiming for himself chapters 1–11, 24–25, 27–28, 30, 32–34, 36–37, 42–43, 45, 51–53, 57, and 59–62; for Warner chapters 12–23, 26, 29, 31, 38–41, 44, 46–48, 50, 54–55, 58, and 63; and joint responsibility for chapters 35, 49, and 56. The arcane chapter mottoes were provided by J. Hammond Trumbull, chief librarian at Trinity College in Hartford. Trumbull later supplied translations of the mottoes—included in the Notes to the present volume—for the Uniform Edition of the Writings of Mark Twain published by Harper & Brothers in 1899.

The Gilded Age, A Tale of To-Day was published in late December 1873 by the American Publishing Company of Hartford (Twain's publisher for *The Innocents Abroad* and *Roughing It*) and simultaneously in England by Routledge & Sons, under the title *The Gilded*

Age, A Novel. It was sold in the United States by subscription only. Soon after the book was released, George Escol Sellers, a western speculator whose name Twain had used (on Warner's suggestion) for his character Colonel Eschol Sellers, threatened a lawsuit against the authors and the publisher, Elisha Bliss. As a result, and with Twain's acquiescence, the American Publishing Company's printing plates were altered to read "Beriah" instead of "Eschol." This volume prints the text of the earlier printing of the first American edition of *The Gilded Age*, with the original "Eschol" throughout. Twain did not revise the novel after the first edition was published.

Twain returned to the Colonel Sellers character on several occasions: *Colonel Sellers*, a play, successfully toured the country in the mid-1870s, and another play, *The American Claimant*, originally begun in collaboration with William Dean Howells under the sometime working title "Colonel Sellers as Scientist," had a brief run in 1887. In February 1891, Twain started a novel loosely based on the 1887 play and also called *The American Claimant*, in which the Colonel, renamed Mulberry Sellers, pursues a claim to an English title of nobility. Twain seems to have enjoyed working on the novel ("I wake up in the night laughing at its ridiculous situations," he wrote his brother Orion), but worsening rheumatism forced him to dictate parts of it into a phonograph; about 6,000 to 8,000 words, from chapter 12 onward, were later transcribed for him by a typist. Twain finished the book on May 2, 1891, just 71 days after beginning it; it ran in serial form in American newspapers from January through March 1892. Unable to read proofs before the novel was published, Twain wrote to Fred J. Hall, the manager of Charles J. Webster & Company (Twain's own publishing firm), asking that "some competent and conscientious person" prepare the copy for the press and read proofs for him. The present volume prints the text of the first American edition of the novel, published by Charles L. Webster & Company in early May 1892. An English edition was published simultaneously by Chatto & Windus, and a second American edition—in the Uniform Edition of the Writings of Mark Twain—was published in 1899 by Harper & Brothers; but Twain did not revise the novel after its first appearance in book form.

Tom Sawyer Abroad, originally planned as one of a series of books (not ultimately written) in which the celebrated characters of *The Adventures of Tom Sawyer* (1874) would travel to different parts of the world, was begun in August 1892 and finished by early September. Twain sent a corrected typescript to Charles L. Webster & Company in two parts, the second by mid-October. The novel was first published in six installments in *St. Nicholas Magazine* November

1893–April 1894; the editor of *St. Nicholas*, Mary Mapes Dodge, extensively revised Twain's prose to eliminate what she perceived to be inappropriate references to religion, race, and drunkenness, among other topics. The first nine chapters of the first American edition of the novel, published by Charles L. Webster & Company in April 1894, were typeset from the bowdlerized *St. Nicholas* copy; chapters 10–13, and the entirety of the simultaneously published first English edition (London: Chatto & Windus, 1894), were set from Twain's typescript, not now known to be extant. This volume prints the text presented in *The Adventures of Tom Sawyer; Tom Sawyer Abroad; Tom Sawyer, Detective*, edited by John C. Gerber, Paul Baender, and Terry Firkins (Berkeley: University of California Press, 1980). The California edition is based on Twain's holograph manuscript in the Berg Collection at the New York Public Library, judged to resemble Twain's lost typescript more closely than the printed versions of the novel. The editors emended the manuscript text, however, where an examination of the *St. Nicolas* text and the American and English first editions suggested that Twain made revisions in the text of the typescript.

In the fall of 1893 Twain reported progress on "Tom Sawyer's Mystery"—his working title for *Tom Sawyer, Detective*, another sequel to *The Adventures of Tom Sawyer*—but in 1894, the year his publishing firm failed and he declared personal bankruptcy, he set the novel aside. In early January 1895, at a reception in Paris, Twain heard the story of a 17th-century Danish murder case and decided to adapt it for "Tom Sawyer's Mystery." By the beginning of February he had completed *Tom Sawyer, Detective*. Serialized in *Harper's New Monthly Magazine* August–September 1896, the novel was first published in book form by Harper & Brothers in November 1896 in *Tom Sawyer Abroad, Tom Sawyer, Detective, and Other Stories*. An English edition, published by Chatto & Windus and entitled *Tom Sawyer Detective as Told by Huck Finn and Other Tales*, was published in December. This volume prints the text presented in *The Adventures of Tom Sawyer; Tom Sawyer Abroad; Tom Sawyer, Detective* (Berkeley: University of California Press, 1980). The California edition prints chapters 1–10 of the novel from Twain's holograph manuscript (of which only chapters 1–10 are known to be extant) in the Mark Twain Papers at the University of California at Berkeley, and chapter 11 from the first American edition, with occasional emendations where an examination of the first serial printing, the first English edition, and Twain's holograph corrections to a typescript of chapters 1–10 at Kansas University suggested subsequent authorial revision.

No. 44, The Mysterious Stranger is the last, longest, and most complete of three independent but closely related manuscript narratives left unfinished at the time of Twain's death in 1910. Written between 1902 and 1905 and last revised by Twain in 1908, *No. 44* remained unpublished as such until 1969, when it appeared—along with "The Chronicle of Young Satan," written between 1897 and 1900, and "Schoolhouse Hill," written in 1898—in *Mark Twain's Mysterious Stranger Manuscripts* (Berkeley: University of California Press, 1969), edited by William M. Gibson. Before 1969, Twain's manuscript narratives had been published (and often reprinted) as *The Mysterious Stranger, A Romance* (New York: Harper & Brothers, 1916), edited by Albert Bigelow Paine, Twain's literary executor and biographer, and Frederick A. Duneka, an editor at Harper & Brothers, with prior serialization in *Harper's Monthly Magazine* (May–November 1916). Advertised as Twain's "final and complete work," the editors of the 1916 *Mysterious Stranger* in fact thoroughly and freely revised his manuscript texts: among other changes, they grafted the final chapter of "No. 44" onto the end of the first three-quarters of "The Chronicle of Young Satan" and altered character names to fit, added new material to join the two narratives together, excised passages throughout that were thought to be potentially offensive, and created a new character, an astrologer, out of the magician of "No. 44." This volume prints the text of *No. 44, The Mysterious Stranger* from the first paperback printing of Twain's narrative published by the University of California Press in 1982; the paperback text differs from the original 1969 University of California Press printing only in its adoption of the full title and subtitle preserved in Twain's manuscript.

The standards for American English continue to fluctuate and in some ways were different in earlier periods from what they are now. In 19th-century writings, for example, a word might be spelled in more than one way, even in the same work. Commas could be used expressively to suggest the movements of voice, and capitals sometimes gave significances to a word beyond those it might have in its lower-case form. Since modernization would remove these effects, this volume has preserved the spelling, punctuation, capitalization, and wording of the editions printed here.

The present edition is concerned only with presenting the texts of these editions; it does not attempt to reproduce features of their typographic design, such as the display capitalization of chapter openings. Typographical errors have been corrected, and the following is a list of those errors, cited by page and line number: 16.3, its; 87.24, its; 93.35, its; 94.31, its; 95.9, its; 105.34, sweet.; 105.35, himself; 127.2, —"We; 129.31, it's; 161.18, Ruth you; 167.2, it's; 207.16, it's; 209.10, lets; 234.35, its; 234.35, its; 245.6, its; 256.1, spare and; 259.29, *me*!; 311.6, and and; 325.16, labratories; 350.18, like—'; 357.3, embarass-ments; 362.40, Montague's; 366.3, —*Philip*; 388.24, disqualified Judge; 394.17–18, 'peared . . . quarrelin.'; 404.19, do.!'; 405.4, its; 412.34, the Knobs; 423.38, after ward; 425.18, containg; 441.12, is'nt; 445.35, youv'e; 452.10, can?"; 506.28, it's; 525.19, acestor; 548.5, han-dled; 551.24, the; 561.22, bowing ing; 591.10, to?; 717.24, every; 843.30–31, ley-hopper; 856.1, what; 864.15, evident.; 914.39, said,.

Notes

In the notes below, the reference numbers denote page and line of the present volume (the line count includes chapter headings). No note is made for material included in standard desk-reference books such as Webster's *Collegiate*, *Biographical*, and *Geographical* dictionaries. Biblical references are keyed to the King James Version. Quotations from Shakespeare have been keyed to *The Riverside Shakespeare* (Boston: Houghton Mifflin, 1974), edited by G. Blakemore Evans. Footnotes in the texts are Mark Twain's own. For more detailed notes and references to other studies, see Bryant Morey French, *Mark Twain and* The Gilded Age (Dallas: Southern Methodist University Press, 1965); The Works of Mark Twain: *The Adventures of Tom Sawyer; Tom Sawyer Abroad; Tom Sawyer, Detective*, ed. John C. Gerber, Paul Baender, and Terry Firkins (Berkeley: University of California Press, 1980); The Mark Twain Papers: *Mark Twain's Mysterious Stranger Manuscripts*, ed. William M. Gibson (Berkeley: University of California Press, 1969).

For further biographical background than is provided in the Chronology, see *Mark Twain's Letters*, ed. Albert Bigelow Paine, 2 vols. (New York: Harper & Brothers, 1917); *The Love Letters of Mark Twain*, ed. Dixon Wecter (New York: Harper & Brothers, 1949); *Mark Twain to Mrs. Fairbanks*, ed. Dixon Wecter (San Marino, Calif.: Huntington Library, 1949); *Mark Twain–Howells Letters*, ed. Henry Nash Smith and William M. Gibson, 2 vols. (Cambridge: Harvard University Press, 1960); *Mark Twain's Letters to His Publishers, 1867–1894*, ed. Hamlin Hill (Berkeley: University of California Press, 1967); *Mark Twain's Correspondence with Henry Huttleston Rogers, 1893–1909*, ed. Lewis Leary (Berkeley: University of California Press, 1969); *Mark Twain's Letters* (Berkeley: University of California Press, 1988–1997): vol. 1, 1853–1866, ed. Edgar Marquess Branch, Michael B. Frank, and Kenneth M. Sanderson, vol. 2, 1867–1868, ed. Harriet Elinor Smith and Richard Bucci, vol. 3, 1869, ed. Victor Fischer, Michael B. Frank, and Dahlia Armon, vol. 4, 1870–1871, ed. Victor Fischer, Michael B. Frank, and Lin Salamo, vol. 5, 1872–1873, ed. Lin Salamo and Harriet Elinor Smith; *Mark Twain's Aquarium: The Samuel Clemens–Angelfish Correspondence, 1905–1910*, ed. John Cooley (Athens: University of Georgia Press, 1991); *Mark Twain's Notebook*, ed. Albert Bigelow Paine (New York: Harper & Brothers, 1935); *Mark Twain's Notebooks & Journals* (Berkeley: University of

California Press, 1975–1979): vol. 1, 1855–1873, ed. Frederick Anderson, Michael B. Frank, and Kenneth M. Sanderson, vol. 2, 1877–1883, ed. Frederick Anderson, Lin Salamo, and Bernard L. Stein, vol. 3, 1883–1891, ed. Robert Pack Browning, Michael B. Frank, and Lin Salamo; *Mark Twain's Autobiography*, ed. Albert Bigelow Paine (New York: Harper & Brothers, 1924); *Mark Twain in Eruption*, ed. Bernard DeVoto (New York: Harper & Brothers, 1940).

THE GILDED AGE

The epigraph, chapter mottoes, and final motto were provided by the eminent philologist J. Hammond Trumbull for the 1873 first American edition published by the American Publishing Company. Trumbull also provided translations and the sources of the mottoes for the Harper & Brothers 1899 Uniform Edition of the Writings of Mark Twain, in part to extend the novel's copyright. Trumbull's translations are reprinted here as they appeared in the 1899 edition except for page numbers, which are keyed to this volume.

TRANSLATIONS

OF

CHAPTER-HEAD MOTTOES

BY

J. HAMMOND TRUMBULL, LL.D., L.H.D

TITLE, page 2.

Chinese: Hīe li shán ching yǔ: tung sin ní pien kin. *Literally,* By combined strength, a mountain becomes gems: by united hearts, mud turns to gold.

[A maxim often painted on the door-posts of a Chinese firm—which may be freely translated—Two heads, working together, out of commonplace materials, bring THE GILDED AGE.]

CHAPTER I, page 11.

Chippeway: "He owns much land."—*Baraga.*

CHAPTER II, page 20.

Ethiopic: "It behoveth Christian people who have not children, to take up the children of the departed, whether youths or virgins, and to make them as their own children," etc.

The Didascalia (translated by T. Platt), 121.

CHAPTER III, page 24.

Old French: [Pantagruel and Panurge, on their voyage to the Oracle of Bacbuc, are frightened by seeing afar off, "a huge monstrous physeter." "Poor Panurge began to cry and howl worse than ever:] Babillebabou, said he, [shrugging up his shoulders, quivering with fear, there will be the devil upon dun.] This will be a worse business than that the other day. Let us fly, let us fly! Old Nick take me, if it is not Leviathan, described by the noble prophet Moses, in the life of patient Job. It will swallow us all like a dose of pills. . . . Look, look, it is upon us. Oh! how horrible and abominable thou art! . . Oh, oh! Devil, Sathanas, Leviathan! I cannot bear to look upon thee, thou art so abominably ugly."—Motteux's Translation.

CHAPTER V, page 38.

Sindhi: "Having removed the little daughter, and placed her in their own house, they instructed her."—*Life of Abdul-Latif,* 46 (cited in Trumpp's Sindhi grammar, p. 356).

French Proverb: He would dry snow in the oven, to sell it for table salt.—Quitard, 193.

CHAPTER VI, page 46.

Chinese: [*Shap neen tseen sze, ke fan sun.*] The affairs of ten years past, how often have they been new.

Chippeway.

> "So blooms the human face divine,
>   When youth its pride of beauty shows:
> Fairer than Spring the colors shine,
>   And sweeter than the virgin rose."

Ojibwa Hymns. (Am. Tract Society), p. 78.

CHAPTER IX, page 71.

Italian: When I saw thee for the first time, it seemed to me that paradise was opened, and that the angels were coming, one by one, all to rest on thy lovely face, all to rest on thy beautiful head; Thou bindest me in chains, and I cannot loose myself.

J. Caselli, *Chants popul de l'Italie,* 21.

Choctaw: "Now therefore divide this land for an inheritance."—*Joshua,* xiii. 7.

Eskimo (Greenland), from Fabricius's translation of Genesis:—"And when he had made an end of commanding his sons, he gathered up his feet into the bed, and yielded up the ghost, and was gathered into his people."

First Book of Moses, xlix. 32.

CHAPTER X, page 77.

Eskimo:—"And said, 'Whose daughter art thou? tell me, I pray thee.' "—*Gen.* xxiv. 23.

Massachusetts Indian (Eliot's version of Psalm xlv. 10): "Harken, O daughter, and consider, and incline thine ear; forget also thine own people, and thy father's house."

Italian:—"Jeannette answered: 'Madame, you have taken me from my father and brought me up as your own child, and for this I ought to do all in my power to please you."

CHAPTER XI, page 85.

Japan: Though he eats, he knows not the taste of what he eats.

CHAPTER XII, page 90.

Egyptian (from the Book of the Dead, or Funereal Ritual, edited by Lepsius from the Turin papyrus; translated by Birch). "The Preparation in the West. The Roads of the West."

CHAPTER XIV, page 105.

From Thomas Makin's *Description of Pennsylvania* (Descriptio Pennsyl-
vaniæ) 1729. Translated [?] by Robert Proud:

> "Fair Philadelphia next is rising seen,
> Between two rivers plac'd, two miles between,
> The Delaware and Sculkil, new to fame,
> Both ancient streams, yet of a modern name.
> The city, form'd upon a beauteous plan,
> Has many houses built, tho' late began;
> Rectangular the streets, direct and fair;
> And rectilinear all the ranges are."

Italian (translated by Wiffen—from Tasso):

> "Of generous thoughts and principles sublime,
> Amongst them in the city lived a maid,
> The flower of virgins, in her ripest prime,
> Supremely beautiful! but that she made
> Never her care, or beauty only weighed
> In worth with virtue."

Jerusalem Delivered, c. ii., st. 14.

CHAPTER XV, page 111.

Latin: [Celsus] I think the healing art ought to be based on reason to
be sure, and too that it should be founded on unmistakable evidences, all
uncertainties being rejected, not from the serious attention of a physician,
but from the very profession itself.

CHAPTER XVI, page 119.

Egyptian (from the Book of the Dead), in Birch's translation: "I have
come." "*Make Road* expresses what I am" (i. e., is my name).

CHAPTER XVIII, page 134.

Tamachekh (Touareg): From an improvisation by a native poet, at Al-
giers; printed by Hanoteau, *Essai de Grammaise de Langeu Tamachek,*
p. 207.

—If she should come to our country (the plains), there is not a man
who would not run to see her.

Romance:

> —"Enough! she cries, henceforth thou art
> The friend and master of my heart.
> No other covenant I require
> Than this: 'I take thee for my wife.'
> That done, enjoy thy heart's desire,
> Of me and mine the lord for life."

A. Bruce Whyte's paraphrase.

CHAPTER XIX, page 142.

German: from the "Book of Songs" (Angelique, 4) of Heine.

> "O how rapidly develop
> From mere fugitive sensations

Passions that are fierce and boundless,
Tenderest associations!
Tow'rds this lady grows the bias
Of my heart on each occasion,
And that I'm enamoured of her
Has become my firm persuasion."

CHAPTER XX, page 150.

Old Irish: from the *Annals of the Four Masters* (vol. vi., p. 2298). O'Donovan translates:

—"A sweet-sounding trumpet; endowed with the gift of eloquence and address, of sense and counsel, and with the look of amiability in his countenance, which captivated every one who beheld him."

CHAPTER XXI, page 157.

[Let each one know how to follow his own path.]

CHAPTER XXII, page 164.

"Is there on earth such a transport as this,
When the look of the loved one avows her bliss?
Can life an equal joy impart
To the bliss that lives in a lover's heart?
O! he, be assured, hath never proved
Life's holiest joys who hath never loved!
Yet the joys of love, so heavenly fair,
Can exist but when honor and virtue are there."

Translated by Richardson.

Hawaiian: Love is that which excels in attractiveness (is much better than) the dish of *poi* and the *fish-bowl* (the favorite dishes of the Islanders).

CHAPTER XXIV, page 176.

Sioux-Dakota (from Riggs's translation of Bunyan's *Pilgrim's Progress*).

"*Christian.* This town of Fair-Speech—I have heard of it; and as I remember, they say it's a wealthy place.

By-Ends. Yes, I assure you that it is; and I have very many rich kindred there."

CHAPTER XXV, page 184.

Assyrian:—"A place very difficult."

Smith's Assurbanipal, p. 269 (l. 90).

CHAPTER XXVI, page 189.

Tamul: Money is very scarce.

CHAPTER XXVII, page 197.

Egyptian: "Things prepare I. I prepare a road."

Book of the Dead, xliv. 117. 1, 2.

Greek (post-classical):

"And when he saw his eyes were out,
With all his might and main,
He jumped into *another* bush,
And scratched them in again."

CHAPTER XXVIII, page 202.

Danish proverb: "He who would buy sausage of a dog, must give him bacon in exchange."

German: "Thrasyllus, with his unaided intellect, would not have succeeded; but such worthies can always find rogues who for money will lend brains, which is just as well as to have brains of their own."

CHAPTER XXIX, page 212.

Choctaw translation of Joshua xviii. 9: "And the men went and passed through the land, and described it [by cities, into seven parts] in a book."

CHAPTER XXX, page 220.

Italian: in Wiffen's translation:

> "I nurse a mighty project: the design
> But needs thy gentle guidance to commend
> My hopes to sure success; the thread I twine;
> Weave thou the web, the lively colors blend;
> What cautious Age begins, let Dauntless Beauty end."

Provençal: "Fair lady, your help is needful to me, if you please."

CHAPTER XXXI, page 223.

Italian: from the *Jerusalem Delivered,* c. vi. st. 76:

> "It would be some humanity to stand
> His dutiful physician! what delight
> Would it not be to lay thy healing hand
> Upon the young man's breast!"

Wiffen.

CHAPTER XXXIII, page 237.

Sioux (Dakota) translation of the *Pilgrim's Progress.* By-Ends names his distinguished friends, in the City of Fair-Speech:

—"My Lord Turn-about, my Lord Time-server, my Lord Fair-speech, from whose ancestors the town first took its name; also Mr. Smooth-man, Mr. Facing-both-ways, Mr. Anything," etc.

Semi-Saxon:

> "The richest women all—that were in the land,
> And the higher men's daughters—
> There was many a rich garment—on the fair folk,
> There was mickle envy—from [all parts of the country],
> For each weened to be—better than others."

CHAPTER XXXIV, page 252.

Danish proverb: One hair of a maiden's head pulls stronger than ten yoke of oxen.

CHAPTER XXXV, page 257.

Quiché (Guatemalan), from a native drama, published by Brasseur de Bourbourg:

"I have snared and caught him, I have taken and bound him, with my brilliant snares, with my white noose, with my bracelets of chiseled gold, with my rings, and with my enchantments."

Old French proverb: Every one has the palms of his hands turned *toward himself.*

CHAPTER XXXVI, page 263.

Chippeway: "My books are many and they are all good." "Although his books are good, he does not much look into them."

Tamul: "Books."

CHAPTER XXXVII, page 268.

Assyrian (from Smith's Assurbanipal): "Ni-ni-id [dag]-ga ra a-ha-mis," "We will (help) each other."

[Note. The fourth group varies in different copies of the cuneiform record. Mr. Smith puts *dag*, marking it as a variant, and translates by "help." Others may prefer to read *gul*, "to cheat." As philological criticism would have been out of place in *The Gilded Age*, and as the passage is a familiar one, it seemed best to *omit* the questionable group—leaving it to the reader to fill the blank as in his better judgment he might determine.]

Italian, from the *Jerusalem Delivered*, c. iv., st. 78:

> "All arts the enchantress practised to beguile
> Some new admirer in her well-spread snare;
> Nor used with all, nor always, the same wile,
> But shaped to every taste her grace and air."

CHAPTER XXXIX, page 279.

Provençal: Dear friend, return, for pity's sake, to me, at once.

Basque (*Souletin* dialect); from a popular song, published by Vallaberry: "You gave me your word—not once only, twice—that you would be mine. I am the same as in other times; I have not changed, for I took it to my heart, and I loved you."—*Chants populaires du pays Basque*, pp. 6, 7.

CHAPTER XLI, page 290.

Arabic:

> "And her denying increased his devotion in love:
> For lovely, as a thing, to man, is that which is denied him."

From an Arabic poet quoted in the *Táj el-'Aroos* (of the Seyyid Murtada), which, as everybody knows, is a commentary on the *Kámoos*—the Arabic "Webster's Unabridged."

Basque. From the *Poésies Basques* of Bernard d'Echeparre (Bordeaux, 1545), edited by G. Brunet, 1847:

"Was there ever any one so unfortunate as I am?

She whom I adore does not love me at all, and yet I cannot renounce her."

CHAPTER XLII, page 297.

Efik (or *Old Calabar*) proverb: "The rat enters the trap, the trap catches him; if he did not go into the trap, the trap would not do so." From R. F. Burton's *Wit and Wisdom of West Africa*, p. 367.

CHAPTER XLIII, page 311.

Arrawak version of Acts xix. 23: "And the same time there arose no small stir (Gr. τάραχος οὐκ ὀλίγος) about that way."

CHAPTER XLIV, page 316.

Latin (Seneca): "In an evil career a reckless downward course is inevitably taken."

Latin (Cicero): "For men are subject to their own impulses as soon as they have once parted company with reason; and their very weakness gives way to itself, incautiously sails into deep water and finds no place of anchorage."

CHAPTER XLV, page 322.

Quiché (Guatemalan), from the *Popol Vuh*, or Sacred Book, edited by Brasseur de Bourbourg, p. 222:

—" 'What will you give us, then, if we will take pity on you?' they said. 'Ah, well we will give you silver,' responded the associate [petitioners]."

CHAPTER XLVI, page 332.

Italian proverb: "Strong is the vinegar of sweet wine."

Anglo-Saxon:

> "Such is no feminine usage
> for a women to practise,
> although she be beautiful,—
> that a peace-weaver
> machinate to deprive of life,
> after burning anger,
> a man beloved."

—Thorpe's Translation, 3885–91.

CHAPTER XLVII, page 340.

Quiché (from a native drama): "My bravery and my power have availed me nothing! Alas, let heaven and earth hear me! Is it true that I must die, that I must die here, between earth and sky?"

CHAPTER XLVIII, page 347.

"A poison-toothed serpent *(moonihoawa)* is debt."

CHAPTER XLIX, page 354.

Russian: "The sun began to shine, but not for a long time; it shone for a moment and disappeared."

Yoruba proverb: "I *almost* killed the bird." "Nobody can make a stew of *almost*" (or "*Almost* never made a stew").—*Crowther's* Yoruba Proverbs, in Grammar, p. 229.

CHAPTER L, page 361.

Icelandic, from a modern poem:

> "When anguish wars in thy heavy breast,
> and adverse scourges lash thy cheeks,
> and the world turns her back on thee,
> and pleasure mocketh at thy pain:
> Think *all is round* and easily turns;
> he weeps to-morrow who laughs to-day;
> Time makes all good."

CHAPTER LI, page 369.

Wolof (Senegambian) proverb: "If you go to the sparrows' ball, take with you some ears of corn for them." R. F. Burton, from Dard's *Grammaire Wolofe*.

Hungarian, from 2 Kings, viii. 13:

—"Is thy servant a dog, that he should do this great thing?"

Chapter LII, page 376.

   French of Molière:

> "Nothing in the world is more noble and more beautiful
> Than the holy fervor of true zeal."—*Molière.*

   French: [The Fox] "assumed a benign and tender expression,
He bade them good day with a *Laudate Deum,*
And invited the whole world to share his brotherly love."

Chapter LIII, page 378.

   French of Molière: Tartufe, the hypocrite, is speaking:

> "According to differing emergencies, there is a science
> Of stretching the limitations of our conscience,
> And of compensating the evil of our acts
> By the purity of our motives."

Chapter LIV, page 384.

   Sanskrit: "The distinctions of obscurity are eightfold, as are also those of illusion; extreme illusion is tenfold; gloom is eighteenfold, and so is utter darkness."

   [This description of a New York jury is from Memorial Verses on the Sankya philosophy, translated by Colebrooke.]

   Old Welsh: "Nobody is a judge through learning; although a person may always learn he will not be a judge unless there be wisdom in his heart; however wise a person may be, he will not be a judge unless there be learning with the wisdom."—*Ancient Laws of Wales*, ii. 207.

Chapter LV, page 392.

   Danish proverb: "Virtue in the middle," said the Devil, when he sat down between two lawyers.

   Breton: "This is a great pleader! Have you heard him plead?"—*Legonidec's Descrip. de Braham.*

Chapter LVI, page 400.

   Old French: " 'Yea, but,' asked Trinquamelle, 'how do you proceed, my friend, in criminal causes, the culpable and guilty party being taken and seized upon *flagrante crimine*?' 'Even as your other worships use to do,' answered (Judge) Bridlegoose."—*Rabelais, Pantagruel,* b. ii., ch. 137.

   Breton: "Have you anything to say for her justification?"—*Legonidec.*

Chapter LVII, page 408.

   Chippeway: "I don't know what may have happened; perhaps we shall hear bad news!"—*Baraga.*

Chapter LVIII, page 414.

   Chinese (Canton dialect, *Tsow pak păt fun*): "Black and white not distinguished," i.e., Right and wrong not perceived.

   Spanish proverb (of a court of law): Paper and ink and little justice.

Chapter LIX, page 421.—

   Efik (Old Calabar) proverb: "One monkey does not like to see another get his belly full."—*Burton's W. African Proverbs.*

   Grecian. From the *Greek Anthology.* "When the Crab caught with his claw the Snake, he reproved him for his indirect course." [An old version of what the Pot said to the Kettle.]

Massachusetts Indian, from Eliot's translation of Psalm xxxv. 21: "Yea, they opened their mouth wide against me, and said, Aha, aha, our eye hath seen it!"

CHAPTER LX, page 431.

Javanese: "Alas!"

Cornish: "My heart yet is proud
     Though I am nearly dead."—*The Creation.*

CHAPTER LXI, page 438.

Danish proverb: "He is a good driver who knows how to *turn.*"

Sioux (Dakota): "Let us go now. Will you go?" [The *Iapi Oaye* is a Dakota newspaper published monthly in the Dakota language.]

CHAPTER LXII, page 444.

Kanuri (Borneo): "At the bottom of patience there is heaven."—*R. F. Burton's West African Proverbs.*

Quiché: "Is it in vain, is it without profit, that I am come here to lose so many days, so many nights?"

CHAPTER LXIII, page 449.

Hawaiian: "Then we two shall be happy, our offspring shall live in the days of our old age."

Syriac (from the Old Testament; the blessing on Naomi transferred to Ruth): "And he shall be unto thee a restorer of thy life [*consolator animæ,* as Walton translates from the Syriac version,] and a nourisher of thine old age." Ruth iv. 15.

TAIL-PIECE, page 454.

Hebrew: "The end of a thing is better than the beginning." Eccles. vii. 8.

11.8   Squire Hawkins]   Based on Samuel Clemens' father, John Marshall Clemens, who was proud of his Virginia ancestry, a frequent business failure, and eventually justice of the peace after the family settled in Hannibal, Missouri.

11.11   Obedstown, East Tennessee]   John Marshall Clemens, his wife, Jane Lampton Clemens, and their son Orion settled in the remote village of Jamestown in Fentress County, Tennessee.

12.17   "jeans,"]   Originally trousers made of strong twilled cotton cloth, in solid colors or stripes; the name derives from the French word for Genoa (Gênes). Blue jeans, or denin, were first made from "serge de Nîmes."

13.26–27   Talks 'bout goin' to Mozouri]   The Clemens family moved to Missouri in 1835 and settled in the village of Florida on the Salt River.

14.20–22   a slovenly urchin . . . own contriving;]   Washington Hawkins is based on Clemens' older brother Orion.

15.2–3   Seventy-five Thousand Acres . . . in this county]   John Marshall

Clemens owned about 70,000 acres of land in Fentress County, Tennessee, which he left to his family.

17.8   Eschol Sellers]   Based on Jane Lampton Clemens' cousin, James Lampton. In his autobiography Twain wrote: "I merely put him on paper as he was; he was not a person who could be exaggerated."

20.8   A boy about ten years old]   There is no biographical basis for the character of Clay Hawkins; it has been suggested that he is a version of Samuel Clemens himself.

22.11–12   "It's bread . . . many days,"]   Cf. Ecclesiastes 11:1: "Cast thy bread upon the waters: for thou shalt find it after many days."

24.22   "Uncle Dan'l"]   Based on a slave named Daniel who was owned by John Quarles, brother-in-law of Jane Lampton Clemens. Samuel Clemens would have known the real Uncle Daniel well during his many visits to the Quarles farm in Florida, Missouri. In his autobiography Twain described him as "a faithful and affectionate good friend, ally, and adviser."

27.5–6   Dah's de Hebrew chil'en dat went frough de fiah;]   Cf. Daniel 3:1–30.

33.6   "By the mark twain!"]   Two fathoms, or 12 feet.

35.22–24   And then . . . helplessly away!]   The explosion of the steamboat *Pennsylvania* and the death of the Clemens' younger brother, Henry, is described in chapter 20 of *Life on the Mississippi* (1883).

38.25   the child's name Laura.]   The young Laura Hawkins is based on Clemens' childhood sweetheart Laura Hawkins, who was also the model for Becky Thatcher in *The Adventures of Tom Sawyer*.

41.8–10   By the muddy roadside . . . some old.]   Based on Florida, Missouri, where John and Martha Ann Quarles had already established a farm. Samuel Clemens was born in Florida in November 1835, a few months after his father brought the family there.

42.14–16   there ain't . . . proverb says.]   Cf. Matthew 13:2: "A prophet is not without honor, save in his own country."

44.28   Godey's Lady's Book]   A highly popular women's magazine with colored plates of the latest fashions.

54.29–30   "Keep yourself . . . Clay."]   Samuel Clemens frequently provided financial support for his unsuccessful older brother Orion.

57.21   port-monnaie]   Purse.

60.29   Old-School Baptist]   General Baptists, founded in 1611, believed that Christ's atonement was not limited to the elect. The stricter Calvinist views of Particular Baptists, established in 1633, were more popular on the American frontier.

66.2   lucifer matches]   Friction matches.

69.36   outline maps]   Base maps, used for presenting specialized information.

86.3   Roderick Dhu]   Rebel Highland chief in Walter Scott's poem "The Lady of the Lake" (1810).

86.31–32   Baron Poniatowski]   Prince Jozef Michal Poniatowski (1816–73) lived in Paris and composed several operas.

90.8   Astor Library]   John Jacob Astor bequeathed money in the 1830s to establish a free public noncirculating library in New York City. In 1853 a building was constructed on Lafayette Street; in 1895 the library merged with other collections to form the New York Public Library.

90.34–91.1   old Chambers' Street box . . . pagan crew]   William Evans Burton (1804–60), American actor and producer; his small playhouse on Chambers Street was the most popular theater in New York City during the early 1850s.

91.33   Lt. Strain or Dr. Kane.]   Isaac Strain (1821–57), naval officer who explored Brazil, Argentina, and Panama; Elisha Kane (1820–57), medical officer who explored the Arctic.

94.40   Trautwine]   John Cresson Trautwine (1810–83), American civil engineer. In the early 1850s he surveyed a railroad route across Panama as part of a potential ship canal.

97.8   Duff Brown]   Based on John Duff, a director of the Union Pacific Railroad.

97.16–17   Rodney Schaick]   Based on Sidney Dillon (1812–92), builder and later chairman of the board of the Union Pacific Railroad.

101.6–7   There's millions in the job.]   Unregulated speculation in railroads and land—deemed essential to the opening of the West for settlement and markets—eventually contributed to the Panic of 1873 and the severe economic depression that followed.

105.30–31   Americans . . . without having seen.]   "See Naples and die," an old Italian proverb.

107.33–34   Was there . . . Girard College,]   Girard College was founded in 1848 as a free home and preparatory school for boys from Pennsylvania. Its main building, Founder's Hall, was designed by Thomas Walter in Greek revival style.

112.18   Mr. Bigler]   Based on William Bigler (1814–80), governor of Pennsylvania and United States senator, who was involved in the rivalry between the Pennsylvania Railroad and the Baltimore and Ohio Railroad for a charter of incorporation from the state.

114.7–8   the price . . . now,]   United States senators were elected by state legislatures prior to the ratification of the Seventeenth Amendment (1916), which established direct popular election.

115.16   First Days]   Sundays.

121.13–14   Jeff Thompson]   Railroad surveyor who had worked on the Hannibal and St. Joseph Railroad.

123.10   Odd Fellows]   The Independent Order of Odd Fellows, a social and benevolent organization that began in Britain in the 1700s.

123.16–17   Senator Atchison . . . United States,]   David Rice Atchison (1807–86), United States senator from Missouri, was president pro tem of the Senate in 1850 when President Zachary Taylor died in office and Vice-President Millard Fillmore became president. Under a law passed by Congress in 1792 the order of succession to the presidency after the vice-president was first the president pro tem of the Senate and then the speaker of the House of Representatives.

123.25   wide-awake]   A wide-brimmed hat made of soft felt.

125.25   juba]   A dance of African origin, with complex rhythms made by drums and sticks as well as hand clapping and the slapping of thighs and knees.

128.13   "refusal"]   The right to accept or reject a deal before it is offered to others.

135.24–25   as in most other Missouri towns,]   A slave-owning border state, Missouri remained in the Union during the Civil War despite a strong and active pro-Confederacy faction.

137.19   "Millions . . . tribute."]   Spoken by Charles Cotesworth Pinckney in 1796 in response to a French suggestion on how war could be avoided.

141.6   Beatrice Cenci]   Renaissance noblewoman (1577–99) who, with her brother and stepmother, procured the murder of her abusive and tyrannical father. The conspirators were all condemned to death. Her portrait, by Guido Reni, is in the Barberini Palace in Rome.

147.37   Senator Dilworthy]   Based on Samuel C. Pomeroy (1816–91), United States senator from Kansas. His reelection for a second term in 1867 was investigated by the state legislature on charges of bribery. He sought a third term but a leading legislator announced that Pomeroy had tried to buy his vote for $8,000.

178.31   a squat yellow temple]   The mansion and estate, originally the property of Confederate general Robert E. Lee, were confiscated by the federal government for back taxes; it is now Arlington National Cemetery.

178.35–36   the Monument to the Father of his Country]   Construction of the Washington Monument (designed by Robert Mills in 1833) began in 1848 with private funding, but the project was interrupted by political arguments, the Civil War, and, finally, lack of money. In 1876 Congress appropriated funds for the monument's completion; it was dedicated in 1885 and opened to the public three years later.

179.15–17   the Treasury building . . . in any capital.] Designed by Robert Mills and built in 1836.

179.19–21   a fine large white barn . . . lives there.] Designed by James Hoban, construction began on the President's House in 1792. It was officially named the White House when President Theodore Roosevelt had the name engraved on his stationery.

182.3   the President] This part of the narrative begins in 1868, the year Ulysses S. Grant was elected president.

217.27–28   "*Ilium fuit* . . . Anchises?"] In Virgil's account of the fall of Troy (Ilium) in book 2 of the *Aeneid*, Aeneas remarks (line 325): "Fuimus Troes, fuit Ilium"—"We used to be Trojans, Troy is no more." Anchises is Aeneas' father.

218.13–15   the iron horse . . . and others.] Near the end of their ten-year siege of Troy, the Greeks appeared to depart, leaving a large wooden horse. After the Trojans took the horse into the walled city, Greek warriors hidden inside it opened the city gates and began slaughtering Trojans.

218.28   witch-hazel] A common eastern North American shrub; its branches were often made into dowsers, or divining rods, for locating water or ore deposits.

223.29–30   Balaam] Senator Balaam is based on James Harlan (1820–99), secretary of the interior and United States senator from Iowa. He was accused of corruption regarding Indian lands.

227.6   play the bones] Hitting together thin pieces of bone or wood between the fingers for percussive or rhythmic effects.

227.27–28   Wasn't it . . . useful?"] Cf. Periander of Corinth, one of the seven sages of ancient Greece: "The useful and the beautiful are never separated."

229.14   the Barber;] Gioacchino Rossini's comic opera *The Barber of Seville* (1816).

229.15–16   "Oh, Summer Night;"] From *Don Pasquale* (1843), comic opera by Gaetano Donizetti.

229.16   "Batti, Batti,"] Zerlina's aria from act I of Wolfgang Amadeus Mozart's opera *Don Giovanni* (1787).

229.22   "Comin' thro' the Rye"] Traditional Scottish melody with lyrics (1796) by Robert Burns.

229.24   the Black Swan] Elizabeth Taylor Greenfield (1817?–76), popular African-American singer who performed in the United States and Britain in the 1850s; she was famous for her rich, resonant voice and her 27-note range.

230.9   "Yankee Doodle"] Traditional melody with lyrics composed in 1758 by British army doctor Richard Schuckburgh.

242.23   Hon. Patrique Oreillé] Patrick O'Riley is based on New York City politician Thomas Murphy, an unscrupulous contractor during the Civil War and business associate of William Tweed.

243.24   Wm. M. Weed] William Marcy Tweed (1823–78), New York City politician and leader of Tammany Hall. Boss Tweed and others swindled millions of dollars from the city treasury; convicted in 1873, Tweed eventually died in prison.

243.33–34   the new Court House] The actual courthouse was supposed to cost about $250,000 but finally cost over $8 million. The Tweed Ring, which included Mayor A. Oakey Hall, charged $470 apiece for chairs and $7,500 for thermometers.

257.22   Hopperson] Based on Congressman Benjamin H. Epperson of Texas.

259.4   Mr. Buckstone] Based on Congressman Charles W. Buckley of Alabama or Congressman Ralph P. Buckland of Ohio.

259.10   Senator Balloon] Based on James W. Nye (1814–76), governor of Nevada Territory and later United States senator from Nevada, an old friend of Samuel Clemens.

263.12   Taine's England] *Histoire de la littérature anglaise* (1863–64, translated into English 1871–72) by French critic Hippolyte-Adolphe Taine (1828–93). Taine used the scientific method in his analyses of literature and history.

263.19   George Francis Train] American merchant, entrepreneur, and author (1829–1904), involved in railroads, presidential campaigns, and the 1870 Paris Commune.

264.7–8   the Autocrat of the Breakfast Table] Book of literary sketches (1858) by Oliver Wendell Holmes (1809–94).

264.22   "Venetian Life"] Travel book (1866) by William Dean Howells (1837–1920).

266.26–27   Tupper . . . T. S. Arthur] Martin Farquhar Tupper (1810–89), English writer of didactic verse; Timothy Shay Arthur (1809–85), American temperance advocate, author of the highly popular *Ten Nights in a Barroom and What I Saw There* (1854).

274.26   Alabama business] The Confederate cruisers *Alabama*, *Florida*, and *Shenandoah*, built by the British during the Civil War, successfully attacked Union merchant ships. The United States government made claims against Britain for damages. In 1872 an international tribunal awarded the United States over $15 million for direct losses.

274.27   Gen. Sutler]   Based on Benjamin Butler (1818–93), Civil War general, radical Republican in the House of Representatives, and presidential candidate in 1884 for the Anti-Monopoly and Greenback parties.

274.34   patriots of Cuba]   Cubans waged war against Spanish colonial rule from 1868 to 1878, when a truce was established. Spain promised reforms and greater involvement by Cubans in governing the country. Most Cuban revolutionary leaders were in exile in the United States at that time.

279.23–24   the Square opposite the President's house.]   Jackson Square, with its statue of Andrew Jackson, victorious general of the battle of New Orleans (1815).

285.11   Willard's]   Washington hotel, founded in 1850. President Grant, escaping official duties at the nearby White House, would meet informally with politicians and power brokers in the Willard lobby.

286.3–5   Boutwell's . . . six months.]   George S. Boutwell (1818–1905), secretary of the treasury during the Grant administration, allowed greenbacks issued during the Civil War to remain in circulation.

286.24   Alabama Treaty]   Treaty of Washington (1871) by which the United States and Britain agreed to arbitration of the *Alabama* claims.

302.21–22   National Internal Improvement Directors' Relief Measure]   The Crédit Mobilier was established in 1867 as a construction company with contracts to build the Union Pacific Railroad. But the company existed in name only. An investigation of the financial scandal in 1872 revealed questionable involvement by a number of members of Congress. Two representatives were censured but there were no prosecutions.

317.3   Vanity Fair]   The town fair set up by Beelzebub in John Bunyan's allegory *The Pilgrim's Progress* (1678).

318.30–33   What we want . . . one product.]   In 1869 Treasury Secretary Boutwell released government gold to counter the Black Friday conspiracy to corner the gold market by unscrupulous financial speculators Jay Gould, James Fisk, and others.

339.28   Tombs]   The Manhattan Men's House of Detention on Centre Street (designed by John Haviland in Egyptian revival style) was constructed in 1838; it was replaced by another prison on the site in 1902.

372.26   Mr. Fairoaks]   Based on Oakes Ames (1804–73), congressman from Massachusetts and leader of the Crédit Mobilier. Ames was censured by Congress for his involvement in the scandal.

379.39–380.3   for a United States Senator . . . unreality.]   In chapter 22 of *The Adventures of Tom Sawyer* (1876) Mark Twain wrote: "the greatest man in the world (as Tom supposed) Mr. Benton, an actual United States Senator, proved an overwhelming disappointment—for he was not twenty-five feet high, nor even anywhere in the neighborhood of it."

386.35–38   Had he not . . . dollars?]   See note 243.33–34.

401.25–26   Calhoun and Webster]   John C. Calhoun (1782–1850), senator from South Carolina; Daniel Webster (1782–1852), senator from Massachusetts.

418.6–7   "J. Adolphe Griller"]   Mark Twain wrote in the margin of his own copy of *The Gilded Age*: "This is the late Mr. Brelsford," of the American Literary Bureau. Twain's regular agent was T. B. Pugh, of the Philadelphia-based Star Course of Lectures and Concerts.

441.7–8   It's a long turn . . . that way.]   "It's a long lane that knows no turnings," from Robert Browning's "The Flight of the Duchess" (1845).

443.29   "Homeward Bound,"]   Most likely from the anonymous sea chantey "Good-Bye, Fare You Well": "We're homeward bound for New York town, / Hurrah, my boys, we're homeward bound!"

455.1   APPENDIX.]   In the 1899 Harper & Brothers Uniform Edition of the Writings of Mark Twain, a quotation attributed to Herodotus is inserted: "Nothing gives such weight and dignity to a book as an Appendix."

THE AMERICAN CLAIMANT

458.6   the drama played afterward by John T. Raymond.]   Despite initial good sales *The Gilded Age* was not a financial success, due in part to the Panic of 1873. Twain recovered most of his losses by converting his portion of the narrative into a popular play, entitled *Colonel Sellers*, that toured the country in the mid-1870s with John T. Raymond (1836–87) in the title role.

465.10–14   The father . . . Falaise.]   William the Conqueror was the illegitimate son of Duke Robert of Normandy and a tanner's daughter named Arlette whom he saw washing clothes at Falaise.

471.21   chromos]   Chromolithographs, inexpensive color prints of historical subjects and contemporary scenes, made by firms such as Currier & Ives.

473.16–17   Cherokee Strip]   The western extension of Indian Territory along the southern border of Kansas. Owned by the Cherokees, the tract was sold to the federal government in 1892 and opened to white settlement the following year as part of Oklahoma Territory.

474.14–15   Minister to St. James,]   Ambassador to Great Britain. Diplomats present their credentials at St. James's Palace, the official residence of the sovereign.

474.40   Ticonderoga] A colonial fortification in upstate New York.

479.17–18   Old Dan'l and old Jinny,] See note 24.22. Jenny was the name of the slave brought to Missouri by the Clemens family in 1835; she was sold in 1842.

494.13   McAllister] Ward McAllister (1827–95) coined the phrase "the Four Hundred," a reference to the number of people who made up New York society.

495.5   Bland dollar] Richard Parks Bland (1835–99), congressman from Missouri, was a leader in the free silver movement. The Bland-Allison Act (1878) authorized significant coinage of silver.

505.3–4   Buffalo Bill not having been to England yet.] William F. Cody ("Buffalo Bill") (1846–1917) brought his Wild West Show to England for the first time in 1887 for Queen Victoria's Golden Jubilee.

520.17–18   Mr. Matthew Arnold's new book.] *Civilization in the United States* (1888). In the book Arnold also laments America's "addiction to 'the funny man,' who is a national misfortune there"—referring to Mark Twain.

520.20–22   " 'Goethe says . . . humanity has."] *Faust*, part II (1832): "chill of awe is man's best quality" (trans. Bayard Taylor).

534.16   Memnon] Mythical Ethiopian king who fought on the Trojan side and was killed by Achilles.

545.6   "Johnny Bull,"] Typical Englishman; derived from John Bull, the title character in John Arbuthnot's 1712 satirical political pamphlets.

554.26   phonograph] Originally an instrument for recording sound. Because of rheumatism Twain dictated this part of *The American Claimant* to a phonograph.

568.1   "Schön!"] Beautiful.

569.3   nur hören Sie einmal!] Listen just once.

570.19   distemper] Pigment mixed with an emulsion of egg yolk, as opposed to tempera, in which the albumin of the egg is used.

573.14–15   Cannon . . . Balaclava come again.] From Alfred Tennyson's poem about the Crimean War battle of Balaclava, "The Charge of the Light Brigade" (1854).

581.21–27   Do you know . . . take a walk.] Peter the Great (czar from 1682–1725) secretly studied Western military organization and tactics and eventually overthrew the semi-military units known as the *streltsi*.

627.5   toy puzzle called Pigs in the Clover,] Pigs in Clover, a hand-held maze puzzle made of wood, cardboard, and a glass cover, appeared in 1889.

It became a national obsession. Members of Congress played it during debates and President Benjamin Harrison reportedly was hooked on it.

631.17   "Yes—Snodgrass. The other's his nom de plume."] In 1856–57 Samuel Clemens wrote three comic travel letters to the Keokuk *Post* and signed them "Thomas Jefferson Snodgrass."

639.36–37   condensed milk of human kindness,] Cf. Lady Macbeth's doubt of her husband's determination—"Yet do I fear thy nature, / It is too full o' th' milk of human kindness / To catch the nearest way"—in Shakespeare's *Macbeth*, I.v.16–18.

640.38   Lick telescope] A few years before his death California millionaire James Lick (1796–1876) set aside funds for astronomical research. Lick Observatory (on Mt. Hamilton east of San Jose) with the world's most powerful telescope was completed in 1888.

643.21–22   *"The Brazen Android."—W. D. O'Connor.*] William Douglas O'Connor's story appeared in *The Atlantic Monthly* in May 1891.

643.26   *"Easter-Eve at Kerak-Moab."—Clinton Scollard.*] Scollard's poem appeared in *The Atlantic Monthly* in April 1891.

643.28–29   *"Felicia."—Fanny N. D. Murfree.*] Murfree's narrative appeared in *The Atlantic Monthly* July 1890–March 1891.

644.13   *"In the Stranger's Country."—Charles Egbert Craddock.*] Charles Egbert Craddock was the pen name of Mary Noailles Murfree. Her novel *In the "Stranger Peoples'" Country* was published in 1891.

644.35   *"A Bride from the Bush."*] Ernest William Hornung's novel was published in 1890.

644.36   *Genesis.*] Genesis 7:1: "And the rain was upon the earth forty days and forty nights."

TOM SAWYER ABROAD

649.3–5   the adventures . . . in the leg] See the last 11 chapters of *Adventures of Huckleberry Finn* (1884).

651.6   four cities] St. Louis, Columbus, Wheeling, and Baltimore. The latter three were connected by the National Road.

653.4   eclipse,] Solar eclipses visible in the United States occurred on July 28, 1842, and July 8, 1851.

654.12–13   "A crusade . . . the paynim."] The nine European Crusades to seize the Holy Land lasted from 1095 to 1272. Paynim is an archaic version of pagan, usually referring to a Muslim.

655.13–14   Richard . . . Bulloyn,]   Richard I (Coeur de Lion, or Lion-Heart) (1157–99), king of England from 1189 to 1199, was imprisoned for two years on his way home from the Third Crusade; Urban II (pope from 1088 to 1099) preached the First Crusade and Gregory VIII (pope in 1187) preached the Third Crusade; Godfrey of Bouillon (c. 1058–1100), duke of Lower Lorraine, was involved in the First Crusade, becoming the ruler of Jerusalem.

656.4   de Sny]   A regional expression in the Mississippi River valley referring to a narrow passage between the shore and an island.

656.32–33   Walter Scott's books,]   Scottish author (1771–1832) whose novels about the Crusades include *Ivanhoe* (1819), *The Betrothed* (1825), and *The Talisman* (1825).

657.6   balloon . . . to Europe,]   In 1859 John Wise sailed in a balloon from St. Louis, Missouri, to Henderson, New York. Twain was also familiar with L. Marion's *Wonderful Balloon Ascensions* (1871) and Jules Verne's *Five Weeks in a Balloon* (1863) and *The Tour of the World in Eighty Days* (1874).

659.1   widder Douglas]   In *Huckleberry Finn* the Widow Douglas adopts Huck and tries to civilize him.

666.20   silver turnip]   A thick watch in a silver case.

675.8   *the Welkin,*]   Archaic term meaning the vault of heaven, or the sky.

689.7–10   We was used . . . the same.]   Cf. the end of chapter 18 of *Huckleberry Finn*: "We said there warn't no home like a raft, after all. Other places do seem so cramped up and smothery, but a raft don't. You feel mighty free and easy and comfortable on a raft."

690.5   tale about a camel driver]   "The Anecdote of an Impudent Camel Driver" from *The Arabian Nights.*

695.28   Anna Nias en Suffira]   Ananias and his wife Sapphira fell down and died when they were accused of lying by Peter (Acts 5:1–11).

703.4   put up in cans,]   Tin cans began to replace glass jars as storage containers in the late 1830s.

705.34–36   We've took California . . . is ours, now,]   According to the terms of the Treaty of Guadalupe Hidalgo which ended the Mexican War (1846–48), California was ceded to the United States along with most of the present-day Southwest.

707.36   sockdologer]   Early 19th-century American slang—combining "sock" as punch with "doxology," words frequently at the end of a religious service—meaning knockout blow.

708.35–36   the one . . . treasures of the world."]   "The Story of the Blind Baba-Abdalla" from *The Arabian Nights.*

720.6   "On account of the duties."]   In the presidential election of 1892
Twain backed Grover Cleveland, the Democratic candidate, because of his
stand against protective tariffs.

724.10   "It's the Pyramids of Egypt."]   Twain described the Pyramids at
length in chapter 58 of *The Innocents Abroad* (1869).

725.34–35   about Noureddin, and Bedreddin.]   Noureddin appears in the
Arabian Nights story "Noureddin and the Fair Princess"; he is not a giant.
Bedreddin is a pun.

726.37   it's the Sphinx!"]   In chapter 58 of *The Innocents Abroad* Twain
wrote of the Sphinx: "And there is that in the overshadowing majesty of this
eternal figure of stone, with its accusing memory of the deeds of all ages,
which reveals to one something of what he shall feel when he shall stand at
last in the awful presence of God."

727.10–11   they had just lately dug . . . little temple.]   In 1852–53 the
French archaeologist Auguste Mariette excavated the area around the base of
the Sphinx.

729.25   the Bronze Horse.]   The story called "The Magic Horse" from
The Arabian Nights; the events do not take place in Egypt.

734.11   dervish]   An Islamic monk. Dervishes do not take final vows nor
are they cloistered; some orders engage in mystical practices that include
howling and whirling.

734.38–40   the house . . . new ones,]   "The Story of Ali Cogia" from *The
Arabian Nights*. A cadi is a judge who interprets and administers Islamic law.

735.40–736.2   the place . . . by the waters.]   Exodus 14:9–31.

736.10   Mount Sinai . . . the golden calf,]   Exodus 24:12–18, 32:1–6.

TOM SAWYER, DETECTIVE

743.2–5   it was . . . in Arkansaw.]   See note 649.3–5.

746.7–8   Jubiter and his moons;]   The planet Jupiter was thought to have
four moons in the early 19th century; a fifth moon was discovered in 1892 just
before Twain began writing *Tom Sawyer, Detective*.

748.5–6   the Upper Mississippi . . . the Lower Mississippi]   Geographi-
cally the mouth of the Missouri River marks the division between the upper
and lower sections of the Mississippi. On a pilot's license the midpoint is St.
Louis.

751.15–17   He had on . . . you ever see.]   The standard disguise of de-
tectives and villains in contemporary popular crime novels and stage pre-
sentations.

753.23–24   another mangy rough deck passenger,] Deck passage on a steamboat was the lowest fare. There were no beds, sanitary facilities, or food service. A special bar was available on an upper deck for the purchase of alcoholic drinks.

753.30   boots] The servant who cleaned and shined shoes and boots.

755.20   slop-shop] A store that sold cheap ready-made clothing.

757.35–36   blatherskite] A boaster or swaggerer.

757.38   pudd'nheads] Muddled or slow-witted individuals.

766.18–19   scollop] To embellish; originally a dressmaking term referring to scallop shell arcs on the edge of a piece of cloth.

768.11   We struck across the big yard,] As in *Huckleberry Finn* the Phelps farm is based on that of Clemens' uncle, John Quarles, in Florida, Missouri.

770.5–6   straight as a string] Referring to the string of a fiddle.

771.19   "Am *I* his brother's keeper?"] Cf. Genesis 4:9.

778.29–30   whig or democrat,] The leading American political parties of the early 19th century. The Whig party was founded in 1834; in the election of 1852 it was split by sectional interests, with many followers shifting to the newly formed Republican party. The Democratic party, the descendant of Jefferson's Democratic Republicans, was officially established in 1828. In the 1840s and 1850s the Whigs tended to favor a powerful legislative branch whereas the Democrats believed in a strong president.

783.23–24   forty-rod laughs] An indirect reference to forty-rod whiskey, which was liquor so powerful it could kill at forty rods or on sight.

786.2   mark of Cain] Genesis 4:15.

798.34   mowing] Mocking or grimacing.

800.5–6   break him . . . Jim,] In chapters 34–40 of *Huckleberry Finn*.

NO. 44, THE MYSTERIOUS STRANGER

817.9–11   en-quad fact . . . 4-m space;] Eight en-quads fit into a 4-em space. A quad is the basic unit of measure in printing.

817.12   sheep-foot] Iron claw hammer used to tighten and lock up forms in printing.

818.6   standing forms] A form stored to use in subsequent impressions of a text.

835.4   vagabond landstreicher] Hobo.

839.20   distribution] Refilling the case with washed type.

840.6   proving a galley]   Making a proof-sheet from a galley.

840.18   take]   Compositor's portion of copy when several compositors work on a single assignment. A "fat take" refers to an easily completed job—such as poetry or generously leaded prose. Compositors would sometimes play a game of chance with em-quads ("jeff for takes") to determine who received first choice of takes.

840.18   double-leaded]   Set with twice the usual space between lines of type.

840.19   comp]   Compositor.

840.30   bearers]   Strips placed in the form to allow smooth running of the ink-rollers during printing.

843.29   hell-box]   A box for damaged metal type.

843.30–31   lye-hopper]   A device for making a wood-ash lye solution used to clean type.

843.34   platen-springs]   Springs that lift the platen off of the impression.

843.35   countersunk rails of the press]   Rails for adjusting the type bed under the platen.

843.36   token]   One half-ream of paper.

843.39   dead matter]   Set type no longer required for printing.

844.1   jeff'd for takes,]   See note 840.18.

844.5   strap-oil]   Nonexistent printing material; new apprentices were hazed when they failed to find it.

859.25–26   Pange lingua]   A Gregorian chant.

885.18–23   I do wish . . . the only one."]   In notebook entries during 1897 and 1898 Twain recorded maxims on a similar theme: "If Christ were here now, there is one thing he would *not* be—a Christian" and "There has been only one Christian. They caught Him and crucified Him early."

892.7–8   "The Lord gave . . . of the Lord!"]   Cf. Job 1:21.

925.27   Box and Cox lodgers]   In John Maddison Morton's farce *Box and Cox* (1847), the printer Box works at night and the hatter Cox is employed during the day; their landlord rents the same room to both men and collects double rent.

936.19–20   it was a tall man,]   A composite of Banjo and Mr. Bones, characters who performed at the end of Negro minstrel shows.

936.33–37   "Buffalo gals . . . de moon"]   Song (1844) with music and lyrics by Cool White (John Hodges).

937.32–35   "Way down . . . ole folks stay."]   "Old Folks at Home" (1851) by Stephen Collins Foster (1826–64).

941.5   yunker]   Young man.

944.6–7   The Boy Stood on the Burning Deck]   "Casabianca," popular poem by Felicia Dorothea Hemans (1793–1835).

957.22   und schlafen Sie wohl!"]   And sleep tight.

964.39   prodigious war]   Russo-Japanese War (1905).

969.22   Simon Newcomb]   American astronomer (1835–1909), authority on solar eclipses.

974.18   two fleets were meeting,]   On May 27 and 28, 1905 (a month earlier than the date cited by Twain), the Japanese navy devastated the Russian fleet near Tsushima.

976.4   Flora McFlimsey]   Satirical character in "Nothing to Wear" (1857), popular poem by William Allen Butler (1825–1902).

976.23–24   " 'Backward . . . just for to-night!']   Opening lines of "Rock Me to Sleep," by Florence Percy, pen name of Elizabeth Akers Allen (1832–1911). Set to music by Ernest Leslie, it became one of the hit songs of a year also marked by the appearance of "Dixie" and "Old Black Joe." Alexander M. W. Ball and others writers falsely claimed authorship of the lyrics.

Library of Congress Cataloging-in-Publication Data

Twain, Mark, 1835–1910.
  [Novels. Selections]
  The gilded age and later novels / Mark Twain.
     p. cm. — (The Library of America ; 130)
  Contents: The gilded age — The American claimant — Tom Sawyer
  abroad — Tom Sawyer, detective — No. 44, the mysterious stranger.
  Includes bibliographical references (p.).
  ISBN 1–931082–10–3 (alk. paper)
  I. Title. II. Series.
PS1302 2002
813′.4—dc21   2001038053

THE LIBRARY OF AMERICA SERIES

The Library of America fosters appreciation and pride in America's literary heritage by publishing, and keeping permanently in print, authoritative editions of its best and most significant writing. An independent nonprofit organization, it was founded in 1979 with seed money from the National Endowment for the Humanities and the Ford Foundation.

This book is set in 10 point Linotron Galliard,
a face designed for photocomposition by Matthew Carter
and based on the sixteenth-century face Granjon. The paper is
acid-free Ecusta Nyalite and meets the requirements for permanence
of the American National Standards Institute. The binding
material is Brillianta, a woven rayon cloth made by
Van Heek-Scholco Textielfabrieken, Holland.
The composition is by The Clarinda
Company. Printing and binding by
R.R.Donnelley & Sons Company.
Designed by Bruce Campbell.

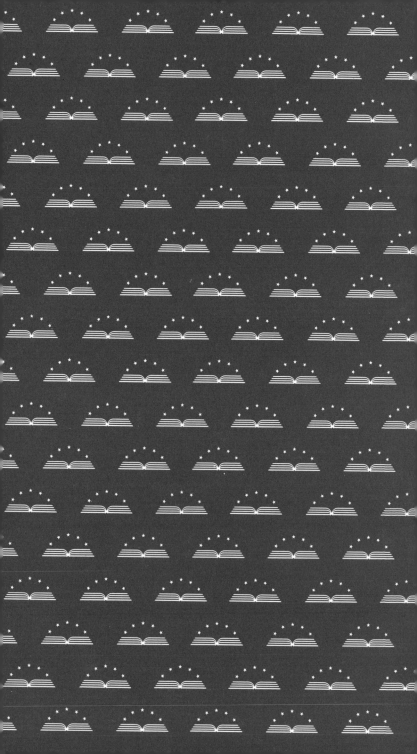